T

David Nobbs was born in Orpington, the only son of a schoolmaster. He has written many successful novels, including *The Fall and Rise of Reginald Perrin*, *A Bit of a Do*, *The Life and Times of Henry Pratt* and *Going Gently*. He has also written the television series *Rich Tea and Sympathy*, *The Glamour Girls* and *Fairly Secret Army*, and the television plays *Cupid's Darts*, *Our Young Mr Wignall* and *Stalag Luft*. His autobiography, *I Didn't Get Where I Am Today . . .*, was published to great acclaim in 2003. He lives in North Yorkshire.

The Complete Pratt:

Containing:

Second From Last in the Sack Race
Pratt of the Argus
The Cucumber Man

David Nobbs

arrow books

This omnibus edition first published in the United Kingdom
in 1998 by Arrow Books

3 5 7 9 10 8 6 4

Second From Last in the Sack Race first published in the
United Kingdom in 1983 by Methuen London

Pratt of the Argus first published in the
United Kingdom in 1988 by Methuen London

The Cucumber Man first published in the
United Kingdom in 1994 by Methuen London

Arrow Books
The Random House Group Ltd
20 Vauxhall Bridge Road, London SW1V 2SA

Random House Australia (Pty) Limited
20 Alfred Street, Milsons Point, Sydney,
New South Wales 2061, Australia

Random House New Zealand Limited
18 Poland Road, Glenfield, Auckland 10, New Zealand

Random House (Pty) Limited
Endulini, 5a Jubilee Road, Parktown 2193, South Africa

The Random House Group Limited Reg. No. 954009

www.randomhouse.co.uk

A CIP catalogue record for this book
is available from the British Library

Papers used by Random House are natural, recyclable
products made from wood grown in sustainable forests.
The manufacturing processes conform to the environmental
regulations of the country of origin

Printed and bound in Great Britain by
Cox & Wyman Ltd, Reading, Berkshire

ISBN 0 7493 2526 7

Second From Last in the Sack Race

The first Henry Pratt novel

For Dave, Chris and Kim

Contents

1 Death of a Parrot

Upstairs, in the tiny back bedroom, Ada's pains began. Ezra heard her first sharp cry at twenty-five to seven in the evening.

He shuddered and tried to bury himself in that morning's *Sheffield Telegraph*. 'Do women want careers or husbands?' he read without interest. 'County valuation officer dead,' he noted without pleasure or regret.

The parrot listened and watched, unaware of its impending doom.

Silence reigned briefly in Number 23 Paradise Lane, Thurmarsh, on that night of Wednesday March 13th, 1935.

Ezra sat in front of the lead-polished range, in the rocking chair. On the floor, in front of the range, was a rag rug. It had black edges, and a red diamond in the middle. Ada had made it, out of old coats and frocks.

A burst of molten light came from the open-hearth furnaces of the great steelworks of Crapp, Hawser and Kettlewell, which lay on the other side of the main road, dwarfing the dingy, back-to-back terraces, and a dun-coloured Thurmarsh Corporation tram clanked noisily down the main road.

'Bugger off,' said the parrot.

Ezra examined the bird sadly. It had been a bad buy. Henderson had assured Ada that it was a master of Yorkshire dialect, and would amaze her visitors with comments like 'Where there's muck, there's brass,' 'Ee, he's a right laddie-lass. He's neither nowt nor summat,' and 'Don't thee *tha* me; *tha* thee them that *tha's* thee.' Ada had spent long hours rehearsing it. All it ever said was 'Bugger off.' Admitted, it said it in a south Yorkshire accent, but that was scant consolation to its disappointed owner.

Ezra lit a Gold Flake. It had never occurred to him to ask to be present at the birth. Such a thing would have been unnatural. He had carried his obligations quite far enough by announcing his unavailability for the dominoes match at the Navigation Inn. Sid Lowson was substituting. (Don't bother to remember the name

Sid Lowson. Substituting for Ezra at the dominoes is the nearest he will come to the centre of our stage. He will acquit himself with credit, incidentally, sixing it up with aplomb at a vital moment.)

Cousin Hilda popped her head round the door.

'She's started,' she said.

'Aye, I've heard,' said Ezra.

'Bugger off,' said the parrot

Cousin Hilda sniffed. Her nose looked as if it disapproved of her mouth, and her mouth looked as if it disapproved of her nose, and probably they both did, since Cousin Hilda was known to disapprove of orifices of every kind.

'I don't blame t' parrot,' she said. 'It doesn't know owt different. I blame Henderson. That sort of thing comes from t' top. Look at Germany. Pet shop? Sodom and Gomorrah more like. Every animal from that shop's the same. Foul-mouthed.'

'They can't all talk,' protested Ezra. 'Fair dos, our Hilda. Tha's not suggesting Archie Halliday's goldfish swears, is tha?'

'It would if it could,' said Cousin Hilda, with another sniff. 'Have you seen the look in its eye? Foul-mouthed. I don't know why you didn't complain. Your Ada spends good money on a parrot guaranteed to be an expert in the Yorkshire dialect, and what does she get?'

'Bugger off,' said the parrot.

'Exactly,' said Cousin Hilda. 'That's modern shops for you. Craftsmanship? They don't know the meaning of the word. Any road, she's doing just fine, so don't worry yoursen.'

Cousin Hilda returned upstairs. Ada cried out. Sid Lowson played a crafty domino (the double five). A tram screeched furiously round the corner by Saxton's the newsagent. The parrot, perhaps mistaking it for a mating call, shrieked back. And Ezra worried.

He tried to concentrate on the paper. 'Air service opened – Doncaster to Croydon in 95 minutes', 'Razor Affray on Ship'.

'In your garden,' read Ezra, who had no garden, not even a back yard. 'When overhauling mowing machines it should be noted. . .'

Ada gave another, louder, sharper cry.

'Begonias must not be over-watered,' read Ezra desperately.

'Venizelos flees to Italian island. Greek rebel fleet surrenders.'

'Come on. Come on, Ada,' he implored. 'Get it over with.'

He went to the sink in the corner of the room, filled the kettle, and put it on the hob.

Big Ben began to strike nine on the wireless at number 21. They only had the wireless on once a day, for the news, so as not to wear it out, but they made up for it by having it on very loud, so that all the neighbours could hear.

The ninth stroke died away, and then came a tenth, a shriek of shocking physical agony that tore into Ezra's heart. He sank into his chair, stunned. His hands shook.

The parrot cocked its head to one side, listening intently.

There was another shriek from Ada. Ezra looked up at the ceiling, and shook his head slowly, as if reproving his maker for not coming up with a better way of bringing people into the world.

There was silence. He made the tea. Another tram clanked past.

'There's nowt so queer as folk,' said the parrot.

Ezra stared at the bright green bird in amazement. It twinkled maliciously in its cage above the sideboard.

He longed for Ada's agony to be over, so that he could bring her the glad tidings about her pet, so that she would know that the long hours of tuition had not been entirely in vain.

'Fifty-four years ago a postcard addressed to a Norwich firm was posted in London,' he read. 'It was delivered this week.'

'Please God,' he prayed. 'Let our child be delivered quicker than that.'

Ezra Pratt was twenty-nine years old, a thin man, a frail man, a shy man.

Her Mother came downstairs next, a big woman, a strong woman, not a shy woman.

'It's a right difficult one,' she said encouragingly. 'Our firsts allus are on our side. I had t' devil's own job wi' our Arnold.'

He closed his eyes. Arnold had been killed at Mons. He couldn't be doing with it just then.

'Was it worth it,' she said, 'in view of what happened?'

She went outside, to the lavatory, which was two doors away, in the yard.

He turned to the *Thurmarsh Evening Argus*. 'Youths Daub House with Treacle', 'Speed Limit of Thirty Miles an Hour in Built-up Areas from Monday', 'Headless Corpse could be Missing Thurmarsh Draper'.

Her Mother returned, shaking her sad, carved head.

'She hasn't scoured it out or owt,' she said.

They shared the lavatory with number 25, and they were supposed to take turns at cleaning it. It was a constant bone of contention.

He longed for her to go upstairs. He wanted to be alone with his tension.

Ada cried out again.

'Tha wouldn't think it'd be such a to-do,' said Her Mother. 'She's big enough.'

She managed to make it sound like a criticism of his smallness.

'We haven't heard owt from our Doris, then,' she said.

Ada's sister Doris was a social climber. She had married another social climber. Roped together, they were taking on the North Face of Life. They had, as yet, no children. Her Mother probed, hinted, joked that pregnancy was catching. 'Tha wants to be careful, Doris,' she'd said. 'It's smittling, tha knows.' It seemed that Doris had been careful.

She gave Ezra an assessing look. Was it just his imagination, or was it one of surprise that he had managed to sire the infant who was so reluctant to enter this world?

'It wouldn't surprise me if it's not born while Friday,' she said, and with this encouraging shot she was gone, and he was alone again with the parrot and his thoughts.

The Navigation Inn closed its doors. The peripheral Sid Lowson went home and out of this tale. The trams grew fewer, and Ada's screams more frequent. They were the shamed, reluctant screams of a dour woman who had been brought up never to make a fuss. The parrot listened intently. A thick film spread over Ezra's forgotten third cup of strong sweet tea.

On Wednesday, March 13th, 1935 Hitler had announced air parity with Britain, Golden Miller had won the Cheltenham Gold Cup for the fourth time and the Duke of Norfolk had shot a rhino. Now, at last, at three and a half minutes before midnight, Ezra heard the healthy protest of outraged young lungs, asking; 'What is this? Am I to be constantly ejected from warm, dark places into cold, light ones? Is this what life is?'

He leapt from his chair.

'Hey up, our parrot,' he said. 'I'm a father.'

'Bugger off,' said the parrot.

Ezra Pratt stared down at the pink, podgy, wrinkled infant. Everything seemed normal, blue eyes, wet mouth, snotty little nose, bald pate, chubby arms, wet podgy hands, fingers and thumbs like tiny sausages, little red stomach distended as a wind-sock in a gale, then a portion discreetly veiled from the world in a nappy. Below the nappy, there were two plump little legs with puffy knees. The legs ended in hideous but apparently normal feet, and ten absurd, angular toes.

'It's a boy,' said the midwife.

Ezra was aware that speech was expected of him, but no speech came.

He clutched Ada's arm.

'Ee, Ada,' he said at last.

She smiled wearily, proudly.

'Ee, Ada,' he repeated.

He glanced at Cousin Hilda, his eyes asking her to come downstairs.

She came downstairs, and stood by the door while he sought reassurance from the rhythmic movement of the rocking chair.

'Under t' nappy,' he began, and stopped.

'Well?' said Cousin Hilda, who had never helped a man in her life, and was too old to start now.

'I didn't like to ask in front of Her Mother and t' midwife,' said Ezra.

'Get on with it, man,' said Cousin Hilda, investing the last word with a goodly measure of disgust.

'Well. . .I could see t' nipper were all right as regards what I could see. Features, like. Extremities, like. What I could see,' said Ezra.

'So?' said Cousin Hilda.

'Under t' nappy,' said Ezra awkwardly. 'There's nowt wrong wi' 'im under t' nappy, like, is there?'

Cousin Hilda sniffed.

'It's all there,' she said, as if blaming the father for the presence of genitalia in the offspring.

'Aye,' said Ezra, clenching his fingers round his long-forgotten mug of cold tea. 'Aye. . .but. . .I mean. . .is it all normal?'

'I didn't examine it in close detail,' said Cousin Hilda. 'Such things don't interest me.'

'Aye,' said Ezra, 'but I mean. . .'

'I wouldn't have owt to compare it with, would I?' said Cousin Hilda.

'Aye. . .but. . .' persisted Ezra, 'is that safety pin all right?'

Cousin Hilda stared at him blankly.

'T' safety pin. On t' nappy. Is it correctly positioned?'

'Ask the midwife. She did it,' said Cousin Hilda, hand on the sneck of the door, eager for escape.

'Aye,' said Ezra, 'that's all very well, but I wouldn't like his little willie to get scratched.'

Cousin Hilda uttered a hoarse cry and then, with one last sniff, she was gone.

At eight minutes past five, on the morning of Thursday March 14th, shortly after the first tram had rolled down the deserted road towards Thurmarsh, there came a shriek of shocking physical agony which made Ezra sit bolt upright in bed, and sent the sweat streaming from his every pore. Poor Ada was having another baby.

Such a thing couldn't be. So why had she cried out? He reached over and gently patted the amplitude of her buttocks. She was asleep.

He swung out of the bed, fumbled for his shoes with his feet, tightened the cord of his thick, striped pyjamas, faintly clammy with sweat, and lit the candle at his bedside.

Another cry of agony rent the air, longer and rising to a crescendo. It was Ada, yet it could not be, for she still slept. She stirred, moaned tensely, but did not wake. The baby in his simple cot gave a cry that was half-gurgle, half-alarm, half-human, half-animal.

A hob-nailed boot rang out on the main road.

He peeped into the tiny front room, where Her Mother slept, snoring loudly, but certainly not shrieking in agony.

Another cry shattered the night. It came from downstairs, and the truth dawned on Ezra.

He hurried to the top of the stairs, the candle protesting at his speed. He crept down the bare, narrow staircase. A startled rat scampered off. The seventh stair creaked. The ninth groaned. The house smelt of soot and damp.

He entered the little room which served as kitchen, dining room, living room, bathroom and parrot house. It was warm from the heat of the range. The walls sweated gently with condensation.

He lit the gas mantle. The parrot's eyes shone wickedly. His cup of cold tea still lay on the dresser.

The parrot's eyes challenged the world. It screamed. It was Ada to a tee, and Ezra realised that the bird intended to reproduce faithfully the whole of her agony, scream by scream.

He grabbed the bird by the throat. It gave a dreadful scream which began as Ada's agony, became a brief squawk of outrage, then a choking almost-human gurgle, and finally a parrot's death rattle. Then silence.

He continued to strangle the parrot long after it was dead.

Grey, unshaven dawn found a still tableau in a terrace house in south Yorkshire. A polished range. A thin man with a grey face, rocking slowly in a chair. In his hands, a dead parrot.

Her Mother found him there. At first she thought that they were both dead.

Later, when he had dressed, Ezra wrapped the dead bird in the women's page of the *Thurmarsh Evening Argus* – headline: 'Cami-Knickers – Are They Here to Stay?' He took it along the road and up the alley into the yard, and tossed it into the midden.

Later still, he tried to talk to Ada about it.

He tried to say: 'I love thee, Ada. No creature has the right to mock thy suffering and live. I killed the parrot for love of thee, my darling.'

What he actually said was: 'It were a dead loss, Ada. All it ever said were "Bugger off".'

He hadn't the heart to tell her that it had also said: 'There's nowt so queer as folk.'

2 Brawn and Brain

Three days after Henry was born, Hitler introduced conscription. Twenty-five days after Henry was born, his Auntie Doris bought a genuine crocodile handbag for a pound at Cockayne's Hand Bag Event in Sheffield. Eighty-six days after Henry was born, Baldwin became Prime Minister. Slowly the shadows of war grew darker. Slowly Britain rearmed. Henry remembered none of this.

Away to the south-west lay Sheffield and cutlery country. To the east was pit country. The road north led to textiles country. Thurmarsh and its immediate environs were steel country.

Many of the men in Paradise Lane were steelworkers at the giant works of Crapp, Hawser and Kettlewell, across the road. Some of them worked on the Thurmarsh trams. Others were in the army of the unemployed. Ezra Pratt made penknives. He wasn't strong enough for the steelworks. Penknives were more his mark. Her Mother infuriated him by referring to them as pocket knives. 'I don't make pocket-knives, Norah,' he'd say. 'I make penknives. I'm a two-ended man. I wouldn't lower mesen to pocket-knives.' In the end he decided that she called them pocket-knives deliberately, and so he denied her the pleasure of seeing that it annoyed him. 'I won't give her t' satisfaction, mother,' he told Ada. He called his wife 'mother' and he called Her Mother 'Norah'.

Ezra Pratt was paid fifty bob a week, and after Christmas he was usually laid off for two or three days a week until trade picked up again in March. Ada became a dab hand at making things go a long way. She baked her own bread, and her brawn was legendary. Once a month they had roast beef for Sunday dinner, preceded by Yorkshire pudding served separately with gravy so that you weren't too hungry when you came to the joint. Ada Pratt added herbs to her Yorkshire pudding, and it was grand. Her Mother made the gravy. Nobody could touch Norah Higginbottom when it came to gravy, and so it came to gravy fairly often.

Every Sunday, after dinner, Her Mother took little Henry out.

Sometimes they went over to Thurmarsh Lane Bottom, to see her son Leonard. She'd had three sons. The eldest, Arnold, had been killed at Mons. Leonard was unemployed. Walter lived in Durban, and had never invited her over 'because of Jenny's nerves'. Dead, unemployed, and living in Durban with a nervous wife. She did not feel that she had been lucky in the matter of sons. Of daughters she had but two. Ada and Doris. One Sunday she took Henry to Sheffield to see Doris, but by the time they got there it was time to come back again, and Henry cried.

She was never sure whether these Sunday outings achieved their object. Certainly, no little brother or sister for Henry came along. Babies abounded in Paradise Lane and adjoining cul-de-sacs, but Ezra and Ada Pratt only ever had the one. 'And what's tha been up to?' she'd say on her return, but Ezra could make a clam seem talkative when he'd a mind to it.

'That parrot hasn't come between you, has it?' she enquired once, to no avail.

'Oh, well, it's none of my business, any road,' she said when she received no reply. 'Tha knows what tha's doing.'

'Or not doing,' she noisily refrained from adding.

Henry remembered none of this.

Many years later, when Henry was thirteen, and living with Uncle Teddy and Auntie Doris, Uncle Teddy showed him some photographs of his childhood. There weren't many, because Uncle Teddy and Auntie Doris were the only relations with a camera, and they rarely came to Paradise Lane. 'What's to do, Teddy?' Her Mother had said, noting Teddy's unease on one of these brief visits. 'Does tha think poverty s smittling or summat?' Uncle Teddy had flushed, because she had touched a nerve, and Ezra had flushed too, at the thought that he represented poverty.

In 1936, George V and Rudyard Kipling died. Edward VIII came, saw and abdicated. Her Mother, who considered herself a student of politics, announced: 'There's one good thing about t' abdication. It's shown up that Churchill for what he is. We've seen the last of 'im. Hitler invaded the Rhineland, Italy over-ran Abyssinia, the people of Jarrow marched to London, and the Spanish Civil War broke out. Henry's life during that momentous year was recalled only by two photos, taken in Uncle Teddy's garden. He'd just begun to walk. In one snapshot he stood between his highly self-conscious, stiffly-posed parents. On his left Ezra, small, ill-at-ease in his serge suit, dwarfed by his flat cap. On his right, Ada, large, shapeless, defiant, challenging the camera not to explode. The other shot, taken by Ezra, showed him with Uncle Teddy and Auntie Doris. Auntie Doris was wearing a well-cut suit and a Tyrolean-style hat with feathers. She looked very sunburnt. Probably Uncle Teddy looked very sunburnt too, but it was impossible to tell as his head was missing. They had just returned from a cruise on the *City of Nagpur*, calling at Oporto, Tunis, Palermo, Kotor, Dubrovnik, Venice, Split, Corfu and Malaga. It had cost them twenty-five guineas each. Uncle Teddy had gone on about it, and Auntie Doris, who always made things worse by protesting about them, had said: 'Give over, Teddy. Don't rub it in to them that hasn't got.'

1937 was a year of slow continuation. The world continued to advance slowly towards war. The factories continued to turn slowly to munitions. The dole queues continued to grow slowly shorter as the nation slowly discovered that it had a use for its manpower. Baldwin shrewdly retired, Ezra bought a wireless set, and there were two more photos of Henry in Uncle Teddy's scrapbook. They were taken on the beach at Bridlington. In one of them he was howling at being made to paddle. In the other he was with Auntie Doris, who was wearing one of the new two-piece bathing costumes. Henry had a bucket and spade, but didn't seem to know what to do with them. He'd been sick all over Uncle Teddy, just beyond Driffield. Uncle Teddy had been upset, but Auntie Doris had been very understanding, and had said that it had been Uncle Teddy's fault for driving too fast. On the way home Uncle Teddy had driven with exaggerated care, and Henry had been sick all over Auntie Doris, just beyond Goole.

That day, in his fourteenth summer, as Henry sat on Uncle Teddy's settee, facing the open French windows, looking at his unremembered youth, Uncle Teddy said: 'Now then, Henry. Doesn't my Doris look a picture in that two-piece bathing suit?'

'She certainly does, Uncle Teddy,' said Henry, who could

never think of anything interesting to say in Uncle Teddy's presence.

'Interested in girls yet, Henry?' said Uncle Teddy.

'Give over, Teddy,' said Auntie Doris.

'I'll tell you one thing,' said Uncle Teddy, stabbing at the old snapshot with a nicotined finger. 'Look at that bust. You don't get many of those to the pound.'

'Teddy!' said Auntie Doris.

Henry blushed, partly out of embarrassment and partly out of confusion at being seen to be blushing.

'It's part of his education, looking at a fine pair of Bristols,' persisted Uncle Teddy.

Henry felt the blood rushing to his face. He felt humiliatingly crimson. He wished he was two again, at Bridlington.

'Teddy!' hissed Auntie Doris, who always made things worse by protesting about them. 'Bristol was where it happened.'

'Oh Lord,' said Uncle Teddy, reddening in his turn. 'Oh Lordy Lord.'

Henry rushed through the French windows, hurtled across the lawn, tripped over the tortoiseshell cat, and fell into the goldfish pond. It wasn't the last pond that he would fall into, but it was infinitely the most humiliating

1938 was represented by a picture of Henry with Cousin Hilda, by the river at Bakewell. He was clinging to her hand, and she was looking down at him, her face radiant with affection, all sniffing forgotten.

Later still, when he was sixteen, and living with Cousin Hilda, he showed her this photo. She gave a stifled sob and rushed from the room. It was years later still before he realised why.

She was looking at herself as she might have been, if she had been born into a different time.

But I anticipate.

All the pictures of young Henry Pratt showed a distinctly podgy child. Since he was of a lively and nervy disposition, everyone knew that he would soon grow out of his podginess. But everyone was wrong. He never did.

When he looked at these pictures, Henry tried to fill in the gaps. He could summon up the old living room without too much trouble. The flagstone floor was covered with a brown carpet square, and lino edges. The rag rug stood in front of the leaded range, with oven, coal fire and hob. In one corner, behind a faded curtain, there was a sink with a square Ascot geyser. The window was over the oak dresser, and the street door led straight into the room. An army blanket hung over this door, to keep out the draught. Another door led down into the cellar. A tin bath with a handle at each end hung on this door. There was a battered mahogany sideboard, and an anonymous table. Over the mantelpiece there fitted an over-mantel. It was decorated with oak leaves and acorns. There were cracks in the walls and loose plaster hung threateningly from the ceiling. Condensation and rats were frequent visitors.

He could summon up Paradise Lane, the uneven cobbles, the two rows of brick terraces, wine-red, grimy. The cul-de-sac ended in a brick wall, beyond which was the canal. Between numbers 25 and 27, a narrow alley led to the yard, which was surrounded by blackened brick walls. At each side of the yard there were two lavatories, with a midden between them. Two houses shared each lavatory. You poured your rubbish in the midden, and when the midden men came they stood in the midden and scooped the rubbish out. The yard smelt of refuse, and the rats liked it.

He could summon it all up, but he couldn't be sure that these were genuine memories of his early childhood. After all, he had known that same world many years later, after the war, for Paradise Lane survived the Thurmarsh Blitz, and the Baedeker raids didn't touch it.

1938 brought his first genuine memory, dim and confused though it was. It involved the aforementioned wireless set, an argument, a sporting record and a dismembered insect. The date, had he known it, was Wednesday, August 24th.

Binks and Madeley Ltd were on holiday. Ezra had a whole week without making penknives. He didn't go for a cruise on the City of Nagpur. He didn't even go to Bridlington. He couldn't afford it, because he'd bought the wireless. His parents had come over for the day. His father had been a miner, and he coughed a lot, and spat into his handkerchief. His mother was small and steely. They had another son in Sheffield, but they lived with their daughter, who had married one of Penistone's foremost coal merchants.

Ada, Her Mother and Ezra's mother were out shopping. They would soon return with the ingredients for the making of brawn, and a fish and chip dinner from the Paradise Chippy. Ezra and his father had been ordered to keep an eye on Henry and lay the table. They had done neither, being too engrossed in the wireless.

Len Hutton was approaching Don Bradman's record of 334, the highest score ever made in a Test Match. Don Bradman himself was captaining the Australians. The tension in south Yorkshire was palpable.

Henry sat in the road, unwatched. A large, black beetle crawled over the warm, uneven cobbles towards him. He grabbed it, and began to pull its legs off. Quite soon it was dead.

He rushed excitedly into the house. His father and grandfather were crowded round the wireless, staring at it as if worshipping it, because they were afraid that they wouldn't be able to hear it if they didn't sit close to it and stare at it.

His grandfather smelt of moustache, blue cheese, tobacco and old age.

Fleetwood-Smith was beginning a new over, at the exact moment when Henry announced, proudly, 'I killed a inseck.'

'That's right. Now 'ush,' said Ezra.

'I deaded 'im a lot,' said Henry, producing a handful of limbs and organs to prove that this was no idle boast.

'Grand. Shut up now,' said Ezra.

'Dad, Dad. Look, Dad, dead,' said Henry, thrusting the evidence in front of his father's face.

'Bugger off, will yer?' shouted his father, as a great roar came from the wireless. 'Bloody hell. I missed it.'

'He cut Fleetwood-Smith for four,' said his grandfather, choking and getting out his handkerchief. 'He's got record.'

Henry wailed, hurled bits of beetle onto the floor, and began stamping them into the carpet, screaming.

The three women returned with their purchases, chatting happily, ignorant of the mayhem inside the house.

'There's nowt Cousin Hilda doesn't disapprove of,' said Her

Mother. 'I don't like that.'

'Betty Crabtree's another one,' said Ada.

'Tha what?' said Ezra's mother.

'Betty Crabtree,' said Ada, 'She never has owt good to say about folk. She's a right misery, is Betty Crabtree.'

'She gets it from her mother,' said Her Mother.

'That's Henry screaming,' said Ezra's mother.

They hurried into the house. Henry was still screaming. On the wireless the crowd was cheering and singing 'For He's a Jolly Good Fellow'.

'Shut that thing off,' shouted Ada. 'I can't hear mesen talk.'

'Tha what?' shouted Ezra.

Ada switched the wireless off.

'Ada!' said Ezra.

'That was cricket on there,' said Ezra's father.

Henry's cries grew quieter now that they had no competition.

'What's t' mess on t' floor?' said Ada.

'Henry's been stamping on an insect,' said Ezra.

Ada slapped Henry, and he began to scream again.

'Nay, mother, give over,' said Ezra. 'It weren't his fault.'

'Weren't his fault?' said Ada. 'Weren't his fault? Well whose fault was it? Neville Chamberlain's, was it? Or was it Lord Halifax? Did Lord Halifax pop in and show our Henry how to trample insects into t' floor?'

'I told him to bugger off,' said Ezra in a small voice.

'Lord Halifax?' said Ezra's father, and immediately wished he hadn't.

Her Mother began to clean the carpet with a great show of virtue.

'I'm keeping out of this,' she said, sweeping the beetle remains into the dustpan.

Henry howled.

'Tha told thy son to bugger off?' said Ada.

'Aye, but there were extenuating circumstances, Mother,' said Ezra.

'Extenuating circumstances?' said Ada. 'There'd better be and all. He's not content to strangle parrots now. He's got to swear at his own son. Animal.'

Ada put her arms round Henry, and made sure that her huge frame was between Henry and his father. Henry's sobs subsided slowly.

'Can I put t' wireless back on?' said Ezra's father, and immediately wished he hadn't.

Ezra's mother glared at her husband.

'Well, they were having drinks,' said Ezra's father.

'I thought it was cricket,' said Ezra's mother.

'It was cricket,' said Ezra's father. 'Then it was drinks.'

'He wants to listen to people having drinks now,' said Ezra's mother.

'Don't look at me,' said Her Mother.

'It weren't drinks as drinks,' said Ezra's father. 'It were drinks as a celebration of a Pudsey lad getting highest ever score in test cricket.'

Ada glared resolutely at Ezra. She seemed to swell, and he to shrink.

'Let's get this right,' said Ada. 'Tha told our Henry to bugger off because of cricket?'

'Aye. . .well. . .' said Ezra. 'It were the exact moment, does tha see? Fleetwood-Smith dropped one short.'

'Hutton, coolest man on t' ground, cut it to t' fence,' said Ezra's father, and immediately wished he hadn't.

'I'll drop thee both one short before I'm through,' said Ada. 'I'll give thee both Fleetwood-Smith.'

'I'm saying nowt,' said Her Mother.

'Shut up, Mother,' said Ada. 'Tha's getting on me nerves.'

'I haven't said owt,' said Her Mother.

Henry's sobs were merely exhausted remnants now.

'This is what happens when men are left to look after things,' said Ezra's mother.

'It's sport,' said Ada. 'They're sport mad, men. I'd abolish sport, if it was me.'

'Aye, but be fair, mother,' said Ezra. 'It was the greatest moment in English cricket history, ruined.'

'Good,' said Ada.

The fish and chips were getting cold, so they ate them straight from the newspapers. It was a subdued meal.

As he reached the end of his fish and chips, Ezra's father began to read the newspaper in which his had been wrapped.

'United have signed a new winger,' he said, and immediately wished he hadn't.

Ezra promised treats. But it takes a lot of atonement to make up to a child for one hurtful moment. The hurting is spontaneous, the atonement calculated. Henry sensed the difference, and never felt quite the same about his father again.

The first of Ezra's treats was not a success. It consisted of a visit to Blonk Lane to watch Thurmarsh United versus New Brighton in the Third Division North.

Henry enjoyed the tram ride, past the long, black corrugated-iron sheds of the great steelworks, up out of the Rundle Valley, and down the long hill into Thurmarsh Town Centre. A second, noisier, smokier tram, a football special, took them past the soot-black Gothic town hall, ringed by sandbags. The fear of war was everywhere. Men were digging a slit trench beside the old men's shelter in the Alderman Chandler Memorial Park.

There was a lingering smell of sweet baking and golden roasting around the biscuit factory. Then they were in the low, bleak eastern suburbs. They walked up Blonk Lane towards the stadium, in a tide of cheery, beery, flat-capped men. Newspaper vendors and hard-faced men with spare season tickets shouted, and Henry was frightened. When he had to leave his father to go through the turnstile of the juveniles' entrance, he screamed, and his father took him away. A great roar announced a Thurmarsh goal as they waited for the tram back. When they got home, the clothes horse was in front of the range, and the house was filled with the nourishing smell of steaming pants and singlets. There was brawn for tea, and Ada rebuked her husband, saying, 'He's nobbut three. Tha should have had more sense, tha great lummock.'

'I'm saying nowt,' said Her Mother.

Sunday dawned bright, if breezy.

'There'll be a hundred thousand gassed in t' streets on first day of hostilities,' said Her Mother cheerfully.

Ezra took Henry into Derbyshire, for a treat, to help him

recover from his treat. Ada did not accompany them, on account of her legs being a liability, and Her Mother was not invited.

A Sheffield Corporation tram, with dark blue and cream livery, took them to Sheffield. Even on Sunday, the industrial mist hung, dimming the sun.

'A mucky picture, set in a golden frame,' said Ezra proudly.

A gleaming cream bus took them out of the mucky picture and up into the golden frame. Hikers and cyclists abounded. The atmosphere was cautiously frenzied. They didn't know how many more summers there would be, and this one was almost over.

Henry sat rapt with wonder, wrapped in excitement, as the womb-bus rose warmly through the leafy, stone suburbs and out into the high country. There were stone walls and fields and then miles of lifeless swaying grass. Groups of hikers descended outside square stone pubs, and briefly a cold wind blew into the bus.

Soon came the moment that Henry had begun to dread. Out of the womb into a wide and empty world.

They walked for a few minutes, and then came to a place where the land fell away abruptly, and the view over the valleys and hills of the Peak District was splendid, but too large for a child's eye.

'Right, then,' said Ezra. 'We've got us brawn to contend with.'

Far below, a toy train came out of a tunnel, and its white smoke filled Henry with longings – to be on that train, to be that smoke, to be other than he was.

They sat in a hollow with their backs against a rock, and ate their brawn butties.

'I hate brawn,' said Ezra. 'I hate gravy, too. I like me food dry. It's more than me life's worth to tell her that. In life, Henry, tha has to eat a lot of gravy that tha doesn't want. There's going to be a war. That's what Reg Hammond reckons, any road. The world is changing. Think on, though, our Henry, before tha blames us for bringing thee into t' world. Remember this. Tha's English. Tha's Yorkshire. Tha could have been born Nepalese or Belgian or owt. Thank me for that, at least.'

Henry was puzzled. His father had never talked to him like that before. And he was a sensitive child, aware of the fear and unease around him, although he knew nothing about Hitler, and cared even less about the Sudetenland than all the hikers and cyclists.

'It's not going to be easy, lad,' said his father. 'But tha'll frame. Thy little mind's never still. Tha's got brains.'

Ezra handed Henry a last corner of brawn sandwich.

'Brains and brawn,' he said. 'Tha'll do. Tha'll do.'

They walked on, away from that hollow, which could have become a womb, given half a chance.

They walked along a track, across a featureless expanse of sheep-cropped, wind-stunted coarse grass. And Henry, sensitive, brainy young Henry, believed that he understood. His father was abandoning him, to fend for himself in the world. His father had encouraged him, told him that he could do it. His father, who had so recently told him to bugger off, was going home without him.

He clung to his father. He screamed. He yelled. His father had to pick him up and carry him, frail father struggling with podgy prodigy.

'Nay, lad. Nay,' said his father, disappointed that this day too was going to end in tears, totally unaware of what was going on in the little boy's brain. 'Ee, Henry, tha's not nesh, is tha? Does tha know what "nesh" means? "Nesh" means feeling t' cold, like cissy. We don't want t' lads at school calling us nesh, do we?'

He put Henry down, and they walked towards the road, hand in hand. Henry clutched his father's hand and whimpered. He was still whimpering when the bus arrived, and Ezra had to sit him on his knee throughout the journey home.

He didn't take Henry on any more treats.

The following Friday the headline in the *Daily Express* read 'Peace'. In smaller print were the words: 'The *Daily Express* declares that Britain will not be involved in a European war this year, or next year either.' Neville Chamberlain flew back from Munich and said: 'You may sleep quietly – it is peace for our time.' Her Mother said: 'I knew there'd be no war. All that worriting about nowt. It just goes to show. Tha can't believe all tha reads in t' papers. It were just a scare to take folks' minds off unemployment. Hitler? All it needed were a strong man to stand up to him. He's shot his bolt, he has.'

Henry's world began to expand. It was a world of parallel, cobbled, back-to-back cul-de-sacs called Paradise Yard, Back Paradise

Yard, Paradise Lane, Back Paradise Lane, Paradise Hill, Back Paradise Hill, Paradise Court, Back Paradise Court, Paradise Green and Back Paradise Green. All these cul-de-sacs rose gently from the main road to end in a brick wall, beyond which lay the stagnant, smelly waters of the Rundle and Gadd Navigation.

A narrow footpath, with posts to prevent cycling, ran between the cul-de-sacs and the brick wall. A gate in the brick wall led onto the towpath, which crossed to the other side of the canal on a bridge behind Paradise Court. Beyond the canal, and below it, were the less stagnant but equally smelly waters of the River Rundle, even in those days a Mecca for lovers of the polluted. Beyond the river was the railway, and beyond that, marching in rows all over the hills, were the semi-detached houses that had been built between the wars.

The canal and the river were out-of-bounds to Henry, for safety reasons, and he went there whenever he could.

It was a lively world, Henry's little womb-world to the south of the Thurmarsh-to-Rawlaston road. The cul-de-sacs were full of children. Barges and narrow boats chugged frequently along the canal. Trains roared regularly along the railway line. Dogs from the semis cavorted on the waste ground between the river and the canal. Thirty years later, when Henry came back, the trams were gone, the main road was clogged, the canal barely used, the railway derelict, whole streets razed to the ground and empty. But in his youth, before the planners got to work, it was all busy and bustling.

One Sunday morning, in 1939 – it was September 3rd, as it chanced – Henry slipped off along the cul-de-sac, through the gate onto the towpath, across the Rundle and Gadd Navigation, over the waste ground, and onto the wide footbridge over the Rundle.

Four boys were standing on the bridge, four boys near to his own age, four boys from Paradise Lane, four boys who often played together, four boys with whom Henry had often longed to play, four boys by whom Henry had never been accepted. Tommy Marsden, Martin Hammond, Billy Erpingham and Chalky White, who was the only West Indian for miles around in those days.

Henry approached them diffidently, trying to pluck up his

courage, a timid, brainy little boy. His podgy white knees stood out like headlights between his long, thick socks and his drooping, baggy shorts, proclaiming their owner's lack of physical strength and presence.

'Can I play?' he asked pathetically, although pathos had no power to touch the hearts of the four-year-old gang of four. Only Tommy Marsden could answer his question, because Tommy Marsden, black-haired, gaps in his teeth, dirt on his cheeks, rips in his shorts, paint on his jersey, scabs on his knees, was their leader. Tommy Marsden watched him like a hungry crow. Whim, not compassion, would decide his answer.

If Tommy Marsden was a crow, Martin Hammond was an owl. A solemn, intense, little old man with yellowing shorts. Chalky White smiled his gleaming, beaming, more-the-merrier smile. I forget what Billy Erpingham did.

'Can I play?' repeated Henry.

'All right,' said Tommy Marsden, generous only in order to prove that generosity was his to give.

Many years later, Martin Hammond wrote: 'I don't think there was a single one of us, however small, however deplorably apolitical the home environment that helped to shape us, who was not aware that an event of cataclysmic importance was casting its shadow over our little world and over the great world beyond our little world. I remember we played some kind of game on that fateful morning. I forget the rules. They don't matter. What matters is that we felt a compulsion to play a game, a clean game, a game with rules, because we knew, with the untainted instincts of youth, that the world was embarking on an adventure which was definitely not a game, and that for many years to come there would be no rules,' which was pitching it a bit strong, because Martin had been four at the time, and the clean game of his recollection consisted of racing dried-up dog turds along the sulphurous river.

If those scruffy youths had ever heard of Christopher Robin and Poohsticks, they might have called their game Pooh-Dried-Up-Dog-Jobs. But they hadn't. So they didn't.

Why did they use dog turds? Because it was exciting: some sink, others disintegrate, the element of chance is high. Because human beings are disgusting until lucky enough, in some cases, to be taught not to be. Because there were no trees in their environment, and therefore no sticks. Because, ultimately, as always, they were there.

The line up on the footbridge was Martin Hammond (Labrador), Tommy Marsden (Alsatian), Billy Erpingham (I forget), Chalky White (Cocker Spaniel) and Henry Pratt (Whippet).

Tommy Marsden lowered his left arm. Five tiny turds fell through the air. Henry's dropped into a dark corner under the bridge. He leant over to watch its early progress. Maybe he leant too far in his excitement. Maybe Tommy Marsden pushed him. He followed the dog turds into the filthy water.

He went into the Rundle head first. It was not the last river into which he would fall, but it was definitely the least prepossessing.

The foul waters met over his head. He took a great gulp of untreated sewage and chemical waste. He was choking, bursting, dying. Tommy Marsden's frail craft brushed his cheek. He struggled upwards, broke surface for a second, then sank again.

Then hands were underneath him, he was being lifted out of the water.

He was on the bank, upside down, gasping, heaving, retching, too concerned with survival yet to wail.

Slowly he recovered. The other four children had disappeared, as children will, given the slightest opportunity.

His two rescuers took him home. They were Fred Shilton, the lock-keeper, and Sid Lowson, that adequate domino substitute, suddenly proving less peripheral than expected.

His mouth tasted foul, his left knee was bleeding, his clothes were dripping, he was filthy and soaking and cold, he was crying from delayed shock, but he was alive.

The two men led him across the waste ground, over the canal, along the towpath, through the gate, and down the footpath until they came to Paradise Lane.

Neville Chamberlain's voice could be heard from the proliferating wirelesses: '. . . no such undertaking has been received. . .cannot believe there is anything more or anything different I could have. . .no chance of expecting that this man will ever give up. . .know that you will all play your part with calmness and courage.'

Fred Shilton knocked on the door of number 23.

'Now, may God bless you all. May He defend the right. It is the evil things that we shall be fighting against. . . .'

The door opened. Her Mother stood before them.

'There's been a bit of a to-do,' said Fred Shilton.

'Aye. I know,' said Her Mother. 'Hitler has not responded to our ultimatum. We're at war with Nazi Germany.'

'No,' said Sid Lowson. 'Your Henry's fallen in the Rundle.'

3 War

'I've decided to volunteer,' said Ezra.

'Volunteer?' said Ada.

'Volunteer,' said Ezra.

'Don't look at me,' said Her Mother.

Henry sat on the floor and looked from one face to another, forgetting his game, in which an empty tin of Parkinson's Old-Fashioned Humbugs, brought by Uncle Teddy and Auntie Doris on a rare visit, had represented a Thurmarsh Corporation tram. He sensed that this was important.

'Volunteer?' repeated Ada incredulously.

'Aye. . .well. . .' said Ezra. 'Let's face it, mother. It isn't a reserved occupation, isn't penknives.'

The month was May, the year 1940. Hitler had not invaded Thurmarsh. The Paradise cul-de-sacs had suffered only two casualties during the Phoney War. They were Archie Halliday and his goldfish. Archie Halliday had been knocked down by a car which hadn't seen him in the blackout. His goldfish had frozen to death during the long, hard winter.

'I've got to serve my country,' said Ezra. 'We all have. Think on, mother. What would tha reckon to me if I let t' others do all t' fighting?'

'There's ways to serve thy country baht volunteering,' said Ada.

'I know. I've tried 'em,' said Ezra

'I'm saying nowt,' said Her Mother.

Henry's life had hardly been affected by the war. He had his Mickey Mouse gas-mask, which he liked. A white circle had been painted on the wall of number 1 Paradise Lane. Ezra had explained that the letters inside the circle were an S and a P. They indicated that number 1 Paradise Lane, had the stirrup pump for the street.

'Look at him,' said Ada, pursing her lips. 'Is he fighting material? If Hitler's crack Panzer divisions see a scranny feller like him coming towards them, will they panic?'

'All right,' said Ezra. 'They may fail me, but I can try.'

'Pigs may fly,' said Ada.

The Phoney War was coming to an end. Hitler had invaded the Low Countries. Holland had fallen. Belgium was fighting for her life.

'I thought tha liked being an air raid warden,' said Ada. 'Tha looks just grand wi' t' helmet and navy blue pullover wi' yellow stripe.'

'Navy blue suits him,' said Her Mother. 'I've allus said that.'

Ezra stood up, drew himself up to his full five foot three, and glared down at the two large women in his life. Henry clutched his empty tin of Parkinson's Old-Fashioned Humbugs tightly. A railway engine whistled furiously, and a dog barked.

'I'm talking about resisting t' evil territorial demands of t' fascist dictator, not helmets,' said Ezra. 'I'm talking about survival of human freedom, not navy blue pullovers wi' yellow stripes. They don't want us part-timers any more any road, now they've got their paid officials. They complain we can't work eight-hour shifts because of us jobs. They say it upsets their rostering. Thus is the common man's idealistic spirit constantly thwarted by petty officialdom. That's what Reg Hammond says, any road.'

'Reg Hammond!' said Ada, as if that explained everything. 'Reg Hammond! He's allus got plenty to say for hisself. Is he volunteering?'

'He can't,' said Ezra. 'He's in a reserved occupation.'

'Nobody can make thy mind up for thee,' said Her Mother. 'That's what my Herbert used to say, any road.'

Henry couldn't sleep. Sleep was funny. There wasn't any way of making yourself fall asleep, so when you couldn't sleep you couldn't understand how you ever could.

It was a hot night in August. The Battle of Britain was in full cry. Germany had occupied the Channel Isles. The invasion of mainland Britain was expected at any moment. Her Mother said parachutists had landed at Rotherham. In the morning, Ezra would join the war. They hadn't failed him. They had failed Sid Lowson, who looked twice as fit as Ezra, but they hadn't failed Ezra. This surprised Ada, but not Henry. It was common knowledge that his father had strangled a parrot. Henry was still rather vague about the war, but he knew that the object of it was to kill Germans, and supposed that his father must be going to take a pretty exalted role in the strangling section of the British army.

Henry was frightened of his father, but he didn't want him to go off to the war. For one thing, his mother didn't want him to, and Henry loved his mother. For another thing, all change frightened him.

For many weeks the atmosphere in the terrace house had been tense. Production of brawn, that local barometer of stress, had increased dramatically. Now the moment had come. The night was stifling. Her Mother had gone to bed early, making a point of leaving Ezra and Ada alone together on their last night, displaying her tact so coyly that it became tactlessness. Henry could hear her snores from the front bedroom. He slept in his parents' room. There was barely room for the two beds. Normally he slept soundly, and didn't hear them come to bed.

That night it seemed to him that they would never come to bed. He couldn't bear it alone any longer. He would go downstairs, and tell them that he couldn't sleep.

As he got to the top of the stairs, he could hear their low voices, the hum of grown-up night-talk, from which he was always excluded. He knew straight away that they were talking about him, and he decided that he must hear what they were saying.

He crept carefully down the bare, narrow staircase. His legs were still too little to miss out a step. He trod softly on the seventh stair, which creaked, and on the ninth, which groaned.

Their voices continued. They hadn't heard him.

He pressed himself against the wall and listened.

'Take him to Kate's,' his father was saying. 'Get him away from here.'

'Become evacuees, does tha mean?'

'Not evacuees, mother. It's not evacuees, isn't staying wi' relations. I want to know he's safe, mother. In front line, fighting Jerry, I want to know our kid's safe.'

Conflicting emotions gripped Henry. It was nice to know that you were talked about when you weren't there. It provided reassuring evidence that you existed. It provided reassuring evidence that you were important to folk. But it was disturbing to hear your destination being discussed as if you were a parcel. It brought home to you how powerless you were. And it was worrying to learn of the prospect of massive change.

'We won't be any safer up there if there's an invasion,' she said.

'Course you would,' said Ezra. 'And there won't be one, any road.'

'Mother reckons it's imminent.'

'That's what I say. There won't be one. There'll be bombing, though.'

'They won't bomb civilians.'

'We won't. We've said we won't. They will. They're ruthless killers. Look at London.'

'London's London. They won't bomb us.'

'They'll bomb steelworks, mother. They'll bomb t' canal and railway. They'll try and cripple t' munitions industry and t' lines of communication. That's what Reg Hammond reckons, any road. There'll be stray bombs, Ada. There's forced to be. It isn't pin-point accuracy, isn't aerial bombardment.'

'Reg Hammond!' she said. 'Tha doesn't want to believe all he says. Him at chippy reckons he's a fifth columnist.'

'Him at chippy! Portions he serves, I reckon he's the fifth columnist. Go, Ada. It's best.'

'Will she want us?'

'Course she will. She likes having folk around her.'

'What about him?'

'He's all right.'

'What about t' house?'

'Evacuees can live here.'

'Evacuees?'

'Evacuees.'

'Why should evacuees want to live here?'

'Because it's safer.'

'So why are we going?'

'Evacuees come from London and Liverpool and Channel Isles and that, because it's safer here. We go to Kate's because it's safer still there. That's t' principle of evacuation, mother. That's how it works.'

34

Henry was in a quandary. He wasn't interested in the finer points of evacuation. His mind was whirling with the terrible possibility that he was going into the unknown, to Kates, wherever that was. He wanted to rush in and ask them about it, to beg them not to go. But that would reveal that he had been spying. He had done that once, and punishment had resulted.

'Ada?'

His father's tone of voice was different, softer.

'I've gorra headache.'

'Headache? It's me last night. I may never come back.'

'Ezra! Don't say that.'

'It's a possibility, mother. It's got to be faced.'

'I'm not making excuses, father. I have gorra headache.'

Henry decided to go back to bed. This business about headaches was boring.

'Is it a bad headache?'

'It's not that bad.'

'It's me last night, mother.'

'Go on up. I'll just make t' door.'

Up? His father was coming upstairs? Henry had begun to creep carefully up the stairs. Now he increased his pace. The stair which groaned groaned. The stair which creaked creaked. He prayed that the bedroom door wouldn't squeak. It didn't.

He snuggled down into the dark, warm womb of his bed. He pulled the bed-clothes over his head. The bed smelt pleasantly of himself. It was dark, warm and wonderful down there. If only he could stay there for ever.

He heard his father come upstairs. He heard the groan and the creak of the two errant steps. He pretended to be asleep. It was hard work pretending to be asleep, especially when your head was whirring with thoughts and worries. Perhaps if he pretended to be asleep hard enough he would find that he was asleep, except that you couldn't find that you were asleep, because when you were asleep you were always asleep, so you never knew you were asleep.

He heard his mother's heavier tread. The errant steps protested loudly. The house shook. He breathed deeply, rhythmically. He heard them getting into bed. He essayed a light snore. Their bed-springs were creaking. His father was grunting. His mother

35

was groaning. What on earth was going on?

His father was strangling his mother!

He leapt bravely from his womb and rushed over to the writhing, twisting couple. His mother was putting up brave resistance, but his father's strength belied his size, and she was definitely going under.

He grabbed his father with his frantic, podgy arms.

'Stop it! Stop it, dad! Give over!' he screamed. 'Don't do that to mam.'

'Hell's bells,' said his father. 'Hell's bells, Henry.'

They saw his father off at Thurmarsh (Midland Road) Station. The platform was crowded. Henry was frightened when the train roared in. It was packed. There were many soldiers. Ezra couldn't find a seat.

Henry wasn't so frightened as the train chugged out. All along the train, men with fixed smiles leant out of the windows and waved. On the platform, little groups of relations clutched each other helplessly. His dad waved until he was just a speck among many specks waving, and then the last carriage disappeared round the corner of the carriage sheds, and they walked away through the cruel August sunlight. Ada walked in the middle, with Her Mother on her left and Henry on her right. It was the first time that Henry had ever been exposed on one of life's flanks, the first time he had been required to give support, not receive it. He was tiny, and solemn, and frightened, as they waited for the tram home.

When they got home, Ada cried very briefly, and then busied herself mightily about her tasks. She gave him an extra portion of brawn as a treat. He asked the question that he could not contain within himself.

'Where's Kates?' he said.

'Kate's?'

'Aye. Where's Kates?'

'I've never heard of it,' she said.

'There's no such place,' said Her Mother.

'Only Kate's I know is your Great Aunt Kate's,' said Ada. Her mouth dropped open. 'Was tha listening last night?'

36

'No,' he said. Too late he added, 'What to?'

'Kate's our Ezra's father's sister,' said Ada. 'She married a farmer. They live on a lovely farm with cows and sheep and green hills all around. It's a grand life there. Come on, get thesen agate of that brawn. Was tha standing there, on t' stairs?'

Henry nodded miserably.

Ada raised her cup of tea to her lips, then lowered it without drinking.

'Happen it's best out,' she said. 'Ezra made me promise.'

'Promise what?' said Her Mother. 'Promise what, Ada?'

Ada's eyes avoided Her Mother's.

'To take Henry to Kate's.'

'To take Henry to Kate's? For how long?'

'Just for t' duration.'

'Just for t' duration?'

'I reckon I've got me parrot back again.'

'I don't want to go to Kate's,' said Henry. 'I 'ate Kate.'

'What about me?' said Her Mother. 'Did tha forget about me, or what?'

'Tha'll come wi' us,' said Ada. 'Tha lives wi' us, doesn't tha?'

'I'm not going there,' said Her Mother. 'I've lived all me life in Thurmarsh. I can't be doing wi' countryside, me.'

'It's a right nice place, mother. There's lovely hills and that.'

'Hills? They're nobbut lumps of muck. I'll go to our Leonard's. Now he's working.'

'Mother!'

'I'm not upset,' said Her Mother. 'I'm not hurt. T' lad comes first, and that's as it should be. I've had my life.' She sighed, thinking about it. 'It wouldn't matter if a bomb fell on my napper tomorrow. Nobody'd care. I wouldn't blame them. It's natural when tha's getting old.'

'Mother!'

'If Hitler doesn't oblige, I'll go and live wi' Leonard. It's all settled.'

'I feel awful now,' said Ada.

'Nay, luv, don't take on,' said Her Mother. 'I don't want to upset thee, not when tha's so upset. Countryside's safest for youngsters. I don't like t' countryside. Our Leonard's my son, and it's about time I lived wi' 'im. Let's leave it at that.'

'Well what about our Doris? She's got more room than Leonard.'

'I wouldn't impose on her.'

'If anyone has thee, it should be Doris.'

'I'd never axe our Doris for owt. I wouldn't demean mesen.'

Ada took a sip of tea.

'I don't like to see Doris getting away wi' it,' she said.

'Not doing her stint at putting up wi' me, does tha mean?' said Her Mother. 'Tha makes me sound like an air raid, not her mother.'

'I didn't mean that,' said Ada. 'I just meant Doris allus wriggles out of doing her bit.'

'I'm her bit now, am I? I'm summat unpleasant has to be undergone in line of duty, for t' war effort.'

'I don't want to go to Kate's,' said Henry. 'I 'ate Kate.'

'Mother!' said Ada, almost sobbing. 'I just know what Doris'll do. She'll wait till tha's settled wi' Leonard, then say, "You should have asked to come to us. We'd have been happy to have you, wouldn't we, Teddy?" '

Henry wondered if he had become invisible and inaudible at the same time. He made another plea for attention.

'I won't go,' he said. 'I won't go.'

'It's all settled. I'm not going to Doris,' said Her Mother. She took a piece of bread, and spread an ostentatiously thin scraping of margarine on it. She managed to make the gesture into a criticism of Teddy and Doris's whole lifestyle. This is my final word on the subject, said her eloquent knife.

Henry tried to be good, and reconcile himself to going to Kate's. He tried to support his mother, helping her scour the steps with the donkey stone, trying to carry the aspidistra out when it rained and everybody took their aspidistras out to stand on the causer edge. He went with her to the corner shop, holding her hand to reassure her. Her at the corner shop refused to take a slurpy halfpenny, because she couldn't see Britannia. Ada said, 'Some folk don't know there's a war on,' and almost cried, and Henry squeezed her hand.

They grew used to life without Ezra. For a week, Ada couldn't bring herself to mention him to Henry, for fear that she'd break down. Then she broached the subject that could not be avoided.

'Come here, Henry,' she said gently.

It was afternoon. Four pairs of stockings were drying on the clothes-horse in front of the range. Three of the stockings were laddered. Her Mother was over at Leonard's, discussing her room.

'That night, our Ezra's last night, upstairs,' she said. 'He wasn't trying to strangle me.'

She had to tell him that much, in fairness to Ezra.

'What *were* he doing, mam?'

She sighed. She'd known he'd ask it, of course. Why not describe the act in detail? He'd be as bored as he was bemused. He'd think it ridiculous. He'd have a point. But no, she couldn't tell him.

'Summat men do to women when they're grown up. Summat that happen tha'll do thysen one day.'

'What?'

'That's enough now. I just wanted tha to know that thy dad's a good man. He's gone to fight t' war so we can be safe.'

'What'll I do one day, mam?'

'We'll see.'

When Her Mother returned, she was well pleased with the room she had been allotted. 'It faces north, but it's got a nice outlook,' she said. 'I said to our Leonard, "It'll do, but tha can get shut of yon alablaster bust." He said, "That's Lord Hawke." I said, "I don't care if it's Lord Muck. It's going." He said, "Aye, but Lord Hawke were doyen of Yorkshire cricket." I said, "Aye, and he'll be doyen of bloody dustbin an' all in a minute. Get shut of him or I will."'

German bombers blitzed London and the Midlands. Allied bombers carried out night raids on German towns. There were fierce dog-fights in the skies over south-east England. The railings in front of the Georgian town houses behind the Alderman Chandler Memorial Park were ripped down and sent to join the war. Her Mother went to live with Leonard. 'It's a bit of a squeeze,' she said, 'but they can cope. She's quite nice when tha gets to know her. Me room faces north, but how much sun do we have any road? It'll be nice to have an inside toilet for a change, even if it has got an alablaster bust of Lord Hawke in it. So don't feel badly about it, Ada. It's my choice. I don't feel unwanted. I don't feel neglected.'

Their belongings were all packed and standing by the door of the little house. Uncle Teddy and Auntie Doris had insisted that everything be ready by the time they arrived.

'They said they'd be here early doors,' said Ada. 'Some folk have a funny idea of early doors.'

Soon there would be evacuees in the house. Moving had proved no problem. Him at corner shop didn't mind where his rent came from, provided it came.

Henry wanted to cry, but he was determined not to.

Uncle Teddy and Auntie Doris arrived at last.

'Cup of tea?' enquired Ada.

'No, no,' said Uncle Teddy hastily, and then he tried to soften the refusal with explanation. 'We've a long way to go, and there's the blackout.'

'I wish mother'd asked to come to us,' said Auntie Doris. 'We'd have been happy to have her, wouldn't we, Teddy?'

'Is this all there is?' said Uncle Teddy, surveying their meagre baggage.

'Teddy!' said Auntie Doris.

'Well there's not much, to say they're going for the duration,' said Uncle Teddy.

'Tact,' mouthed Auntie Doris.

'Tact?' said Uncle Teddy.

'Don't rub it in that some folk haven't got as much as others,' hissed Auntie Doris, who always made things worse by protesting about them.

'Oh. Right,' said Uncle Teddy. 'Travelling light, eh? That's the ticket. The rest'll be quite safe here.'

There was ample room for their luggage in the boot of the Armstrong-Siddeley 'Twelve Plus' Four-Light Saloon De Luxe.

And then Henry knew that he couldn't go.

'Don't want to go,' he whimpered.

Uncle Teddy gave Ada a sharp glance.

'It's nice there, Henry,' said Ada.

'I 'ate Kate,' said Henry.

'Don't be silly. Tha's never met her,' said Ada.

Henry began to scream.

'We'll be in the car,' said Uncle Teddy grimly. 'Come on, Doris.'

Henry screamed and screamed and screamed. At first he screamed because he was terrified of leaving this cobbled, terraced, canal-side womb. Then he screamed because he was upset with himself for giving way to his fear. Then he screamed because he was angry with life because he was a helpless thing about which other people made decisions, and he had no choice about being put into positions where he had to scream. Then he was empty of fear and anger and shame, and he screamed because he couldn't think of a way of stopping screaming without looking ridiculous.

In the end he stopped out of sheer exhaustion.

Ada closed the door for the last time, and led Henry to the waiting car. The top half of the headlights had been blacked out.

'I thought it best if we were out of the road,' said Uncle Teddy. 'I thought it might get it over with quicker if the performance was mainly for our benefit.'

'It wasn't a performance,' said Ada.

'Now you've not forgotten anything, have you?' said Uncle Teddy. 'We're late. We've been delayed. I'm not turning back.'

'He never turns back,' said Auntie Doris, whose perfume filled the car.

'I've not forgotten owt,' said Ada.

Uncle Teddy handed Ada a paper bag.

'In case he's car-sick,' he explained.

'You didn't have to say what it's for. It's obvious. You could just have handed it to her. You've made things worse,' said Auntie Doris, who always made things worse by protesting about them. 'You've put the idea of being car-sick into his head.'

'You won't be car-sick, will you, Henry?' said Uncle Teddy.

'No, Uncle Teddy,' said Henry in little more than a whisper.

'Let's gerron wi' it,' said Ada.

'He has to have his little argument,' said Auntie Doris.

'I do not have to have my little argument,' said Uncle Teddy. 'I do not have to have my little argument, Doris.'

'Don't clench your teeth at me,' said Auntie Doris.

'Tha can go now,' said Ada. 'T' whole street's seen her fur wrap.'

'I'll put that down to tension and ignore it,' said Uncle Teddy, crashing angrily into first gear and setting off with a jerk.

Henry Pratt had lived at number 23 Paradise Lane for five years and almost six months. Never, in the rest of his life, would he remain in one home for so long.

The nearest that he would come to it would be at Low Farm, near the village of Rowth Bridge, in the spectacular landscape of Upper Mitherdale.

But I anticipate. They weren't there yet. There were problems on the long journey from womb-cobble to world-hill.

The first problem was petrol. Or rather, the lack of it. 'He always leaves it too late,' said Auntie Doris, as Uncle Teddy trudged back into the distance with his can, towards the garage at which he had declined to stop because he 'didn't like the cut of its jib'.

The second problem was the signposts. Or rather, the lack of them. Most of them had been taken down, and the others had been pointed in the wrong direction, to confuse the Germans. It confused Uncle Teddy.

'It's lucky I know my county,' he said. 'I might get lost otherwise.'

The third problem was Uncle Teddy's war effort. Or rather, the lack of it. It came to the surface just after they had found themselves lost for the third time.

'Who are we supposed to be fighting, the Germans or ourselves?' said Uncle Teddy.

'Nobody, in your case,' said Ada.

Uncle Teddy slammed the brakes on. The car slewed to a halt across the road, almost catapulting Auntie Doris through the windscreen.

'I have flat feet,' said Uncle Teddy. 'I have very flat feet. I have fallen arches. I have very fallen arches. My worst enemy couldn't say that I am a man not to face the music when the chips are down. I want to do my bit. With my feet, I've no chance. No chance.'

'I'm sorry,' said Ada.

'We'll forget it,' said Uncle Teddy. 'We'll attribute it to tension, and wipe it from the minutes.'

They had left the big towns and the factories behind long ago. The hills were growing higher, the dale narrower. The little towns and villages were all of stone, plain, square, unadorned, and handsome. They crossed the river twice, catching glimpses of it slipping placidly over the rocks.

They came to another small town. There was no place-name to greet the Teutonic invader.

'If it's Troutwick, we turn right,' said Uncle Teddy.

He pulled up in a pleasant, jumbled square, and asked two elderly men, 'Is this Troutwick?'

The elderly men stared at him in amazement.

'Well of course it is,' said one. They had lived there all their lives, and they couldn't see how there could possibly be any doubt on the matter.

'How do I get to Rowth Bridge?' said Uncle Teddy, speaking more loudly and slowly than usual, as if to foreigners.

'Tha turns right,' said the second elderly man.

'Yes, but where?' said Uncle Teddy.

'Does tha see t' lane along o' t' Trustee Savings Bank?' said the first elderly man.

'Yes,' said Uncle Teddy.

'Not there,' said the first elderly man.

'Carry on along t' road,' said the second elderly man, 'till tha comes to an old inn, t' Three Magpies, that were demolished ten years ago.'

'More like twelve,' said the first elderly man. 'Our Annie were carrying our Albert.'

'Mebbe,' said the second elderly man. 'Tha turns right there, any road.'

Somehow they managed to find the turning. Soon they were in a narrower, steeper dale, with a smaller, livelier river. The road was slow and winding, the houses further apart, the villages

43

hamlets. Dry-stone walls criss-crossed the fields and hills, and at regular intervals in the walls there were stone field barns, like wayside chapels.

Some of the land was under the plough. Some was pasture for cattle. Most of it was a huge sheep run.

They crossed the old stone hump-bridge that gave Rowth Bridge its name. The river Mither was little more than a rocky beck up here.

They twisted through the village, a tight-packed cluster of low stone buildings, huddled together for warmth, for protection, and out of kinship.

Beyond the village the road ran on to the head of the dale, which was bounded by high fells to the north, with the impressive bulk of Mickleborough dominating the scene. The infant Mither tumbled joyously down from these hills, chuckling delightedly over its miniature gorge.

All this was unfamiliar and terrifying to Henry. He could see nothing good in this spectacular place. It was impossible to believe that life here could have anything in common with life in Paradise Lane.

There, tucked under the hills on their left, was Low Farm. It was a very long, low, seventeenth-century stone building, a typical long house of the Yorkshire Dales, with the cow barn built into the end of the house, as if it were part of it. Anywhere else it would have been a row of cottages.

A bumpy track led up to the farmhouse. Uncle Teddy negotiated it slowly, in pained silence, veering from side to side to avoid the worst potholes and cowpats. Sheep watched him, and protested.

'We'd have suggested you came and lived with us,' said Auntie Doris. 'But we're almost as likely to get bombed as you were.'

The track took them round the side of the house. There, at the back of the house, at the kitchen door, stood Ezra's Auntie Kate and her husband Frank.

Frank, five foot nine of solid rock, gazed at them with his expression of amiable gentleness which verged on a smile without ever quite breaking into it. Kate, five foot one of bouncing energy, beamed from ear to ear.

Their expressions did not say, 'We are prepared to have you here.' Their expressions said, 'We are grateful to you for coming.' Suddenly, Henry knew that it was going to be all right.

4 Peace and War

Ada and Kate stood at the landing window, watching little Henry marching sturdily up the hill in his Wellington boots. They were putting up paper-chains for Christmas. The paper-chains were sober and tasteful, in pastel colours.

It was Tuesday, December 17th. The Battle of Britain had been won. Churchill had said that never in the field of human conflict was so much owed by so many to so few. Dowding, whose planes had won the battle, had been relieved of his command. The war cabinet had agreed that the civilian population around the German target areas must be made to feel the weight of the war.

On Sunday night, Sheffield had been blitzed. Henry Hall and his band had been forced to leave the city without their instruments, and there were more than five hundred homeless. Uncle Teddy and Auntie Doris were not among them. On Monday night it had been Thurmarsh's turn. 173 houses had been struck, and there had been a direct hit on the biscuit factory, with an attendant loss of custard creams on a large scale. Paradise Lane had not been affected. Nor had Her Mother, Leonard and his family, or the alabaster bust of Lord Hawke. Cousin Hilda survived unscathed as well, although a bomb demolished the house three doors away.

Henry's right hand was firmly clasped in the left hand of the farm hand Billy, who wasn't quite all there. Beside them trotted Sam, the sheepdog.

Ada sighed.

'Is summat wrong, Ada?' said Kate.

'I don't like Henry being so friendly wi' animals,' said Ada.

'What does tha think he'll catch, Ada?' said Kate. 'Milk fever? Mastitis? Hard pad?'

Ada flushed, and Kate felt sorry that she had been so tart She had been a town person herself once. She had been the only person not to be surprised that they had arrived without Wellington boots.

'I'm not o'er pleased that he's such friends wi' Billy,' said Ada.

46

'Billy's safe enough,' said Kate. 'Manpower's short. There's a war on.'

Kate flushed now, and her hand went to her throat in distress. Ada knew more about the war than she did. She was on her own, in a strange place, without the support of her husband.

'I'm sorry,' said Kate. 'I'm sorry, Ada.'

'It doesn't matter,' said Ada. She felt tears coming into her eyes. A hot flush drenched her body in the illusion of sweat. Her legs, which she knew to be huge and horrible, were on fire. She stumbled towards the bedroom she shared with Henry.

The bedroom was the only thing she shared with Henry. She had lost him. Her husband had been taken by the army. Henry had been taken by Kate, by Frank, by Billy the half-wit, by Jackie the land-girl, by Sam the sheepdog, by the River Mither and the age-old hills.

By the time Henry got home, she had recovered.

'Well, what's tha been up to?' she asked him.

'Picking earth,' he said smugly.

'Picking earth?'

'Aye.'

He led his mother downstairs to the kitchen, and pointed to the flagged floor. Lumps of dark, wet, thick, winter earth lay on the beautiful bluish Horton flags.

Ada struck him violently, a big blow across the right ear.

'Clear it up,' she ordered, and rushed from the room.

Henry fell to the ground, his ear ringing with pain which exploded inside his head.

Tears filled his eyes, but he wouldn't cry. Wouldn't wouldn't wouldn't. Nearly did. Didn't.

His Great-Aunt Kate came in with a handful of turnips, and found him sitting there, lips puckering, a lone tear drying on his cheek, on the flagged floor, beneath the hanging hams, in front of the huge, leaded range, among the earth that he had dumped or the floor.

'What's to do?' she said.

'Mam hit me.'

'Why?'

'I picked lots of earth.

'Why did tha pick lots of earth, Henry?'

'I'm nobbut a lad. I have to be naughty sometimes.'

He hurried from the room, before he could be hit again.

Frank came in before Kate could clear the earth from her beautiful floor.

'Problem,' said Kate.

'Aye,' said Frank. 'I can see. Henry.'

'No,' said Kate. 'Ada.'

'Ada?'

'Ada.'

Frank sat in the big, wide-backed wooden chair which looked huge until he sat in it. He stretched his weary legs.

'Ada spilt earth on t' floor?'

'No. Henry,' said Kate.

'I don't know what she's on about half the time,' said Frank.

'Ada?' said Kate.

'No. Thee,' said Frank. 'I were just confiding in t' Lord.'

It had been a great sorrow to Uncle Frank – he refused to be known as Great-Uncle Frank: it made him sound so old, and he was only just the wrong side of sixty – that he had had no sons. The three Turnbull daughters had been famous throughout the district for their vitality and beauty. Their ephemeral charm and grace had contrasted exquisitely with the stark timelessness of the gritstone landscape of Upper Mitherdale. They could have had anybody, and for two worrying years it had seemed that Fiona had. Now they were gone, married (and who were Uncle Frank and Auntie Kate to say that their husbands were unworthy of them, just because everyone else said so?). Uncle Frank had been proud and amazed that he could have helped to produce three such lovely creatures, but he was a farmer, and he wanted sons.

Now Auntie Kate – she refused to be known as Great-Aunt Kate: it made her sound so old, and she was still the right side of sixty, if only just – saw Ada worrying about Ezra, and gave thanks to God that she had no sons. In war-time sons get killed.

She began to keep Ada busy. She tried to encourage her to talk about her worries, while they made bread and havercake and Christmas cake and Christmas pudding and stuffing for the goose and all the other things which Auntie Kate could have made in half the time if she hadn't been trying to get Ada to talk about her worries without appearing to do so.

The kitchen was large, but warm and cosy. A huge dresser occupied the wall opposite the range. The scrubbed deal table was covered in the preparations for a feast. Ada relaxed enough to explain the reasons why she found it impossible to relax.

These were 1 Ezra. (a) Was he sleeping well? He needed his sleep. He always had. (b) Was he getting enough food? He was a right gannet, despite his size. He'd be missing his brawn. She'd heard that the Red Cross sent parcels, but would they include brawn, or would it all be soft, southern stuff? (c) Would his food, even if adequate, be too dry? Ezra needed gravy to help him digest. (d) Would he be killed? 2 Self. (a) Was she a sour old hag, although only thirty-four years of age? (b) Were her legs getting bigger still? (c) She was still. . .tha knows. . .so why was she getting hot flushes? 3 Henry. (a) Why was he getting naughty? (b) Why was she jealous of him? (See 2 (a).) (c) Would he get mastoids because she'd struck his ear?

Auntie Kate felt that her responses were inadequate. They were 1 (a) Like a log, undoubtedly. (b) Definitely. An army marches on its stomach. Temporary brawn starvation might be a good thing. Absence makes the. . .etcetera. (c) Armies are great places for gravy. They're known for it. Hence the expression, the gravy train. (d) I don't know. 2 (a) No. (b) No. (c) God moves in a mysterious way. 3 (a) Because he feels more secure. (b) Because you're a mother. (c) Unlikely.

'That were t' best Christmas I've ever 'ad.'

Auntie Kate looked at Henry sadly, gladly. She was torn in two. A casual observer might have thought her possessive. She needed people. She needed to be useful to people. But she did not want to impinge upon their close family attachments. She had no wish to cross the demarcation lines of emotion. She was not vying with a mother's love. There had been hopes that Ezra might get leave before he went abroad, but he had not. Auntie Kate had been disappointed that Henry hadn't seemed disappointed. How could she make his life here secure and rich without leading him to compare it unfavourably with what Ada and Ezra had been able to offer him?

'It were t' best Christmas I've ever 'ad ever,' he repeated.

Jackie, the land-girl, had gone home for the holiday. Fiona, their youngest, had come over from Skipton with her husband, who was an assistant bank manager and had an artificial leg. They had married in October last year. The bride had looked charming in Burgundy marocain, with hat and shoes to tone. She had worn a spray of pink and white carnations, and carried her gas-mask. She had dark, deep eyes which were full of fun. Henry had liked her, but not her husband, who was right dull, in his opinion. Laura, their eldest, had come over from Nelson on Boxing Day with her husband and their three aggressive children. Laura was putting on weight. What her husband gained by being not quite as dull as Fiona's, he lost by being a Lancastrian. Norma's husband, who was duller than Laura's, but less dull than Fiona's, suffered from a far graver character defect than being a Lancastrian. He was German. They lived near Nuremberg. It had added insult to injury that Norma's husband was fit enough to fight for Germany, but neither Fiona's husband nor Laura's husband were fit enough to fight for Britain. People were right when they said that the lovely Turnbull girls could all have done better for themselves.

On Christmas morning they had gone to church. Henry had stared at the people from the big house, in their family pew, as at creatures from another planet. Except for Belinda Boyce-Uppingham, aged six. He had stared at her as at perfection. She had looked right through him. Ada had hoped that nobody would notice that she didn't know when to stand and when to kneel and when to sit. All the Boyce-Uppinghams had noticed. After church, people had lingered in the little churchyard and outside in the lane beside the aptly-named Mither. They had wished each other a happy Christmas. Humble villagers had touched vocal forelocks to the Turnbulls. The Turnbulls had touched vocal forelocks to the Boyce-Uppinghams. Old Percy Boyce-Uppingham had tapped Henry with his walking stick, as if he were a barometer, but instead of saying, 'Looks like rain,' he had said, 'So you're our new little town boy, then. Well done,' and had given him sixpence, and Auntie Kate had nudged Henry, and

Henry had said, 'Thank you very much, sir. Happy Christmas,' and then they had gone home and had roast goose with all the trimmings, and on Boxing Day they had had home-cured ham. And there had been a Christmas tree, and Henry had had a stocking, in which there was an orange, a Mars bar, an apple, a comb, a box of coloured pencils and a little woollen camel which squeaked. Round the Christmas tree there were other presents, which included a Dinky toy (a London bus), a book with stories and pictures, another book with pictures that you coloured and a humming top.

Now it was over, and Henry sat at the scrubbed deal table in the spacious kitchen, and managed to read a few words from his book out loud in a solemn, slow, artificial voice. It had been Auntie Kate's idea that Ada should teach him to read before he went to school in January.

'This is my best home ever,' he said.

Auntie Kate turned grave eyes upon him.

'This isn't your real home, Henry,' she said. 'Always remember that. You like it because it's new, and there are animals. It can be right lonely and cruel sometimes, specially in winter, and there's not many folk thy own age here, and that's why it can never be your real home.'

She hoped that this had made an impression on him, but what he said next was, 'I were right put out at first about eating t' goose, cos I knew him. He were my friend. Bur I et 'im. He were right tasty too.'

The words came slowly, solemnly, articulated with exaggerated care. Auntie Kate wanted to laugh at the grown-up sound of 'I were right put out' coming from the five-year-old boy, whose podgy legs were swinging above the flagstones as he sat in his kitchen chair.

'There were two things I didn't reckon much to,' said Henry.

Auntie Kate waited.

'Doesn't tha want to know what they were?' said Henry.

'Aye. Oh aye. I do. What didn't tha reckon much to, Henry?' said Auntie Kate.

'Children's party and Auntie Laura's bairns. I hate kids.'

Perhaps it was a mistake, holding him back from school till he'd settled down, thought Auntie Kate. Certainly Henry had not distinguished himself at the children's Christmas party in the Parish Hall. Local ladies had given entertainments comprising charades, sketches and musical items. A Mr Elland from Troutwick had made interesting shapes out of newspapers – all of which, he emphasised, would later be sent for salvage. Patrick Eckington and one or two other children had given turns. Father Christmas had put in an appearance, and there had been a gift of savings stamps for each child. They had played games including musical chairs. The evacuee children had been rowdy. So had the Luggs. Lorna Arrow had been sick. Henry had been paralysed with shyness and had just stared at everybody and reverted to sucking his thumb.

He didn't tell Auntie Kate the thing that he had hated most, which was being tapped by old Percy Boyce-Uppingham as if he were a barometer. He didn't tell her because he had fallen in love with Belinda Boyce-Uppingham, and everything to do with the Boyce-Uppinghams was therefore too private to be talked about. Old Percy Boyce-Uppingham's stick had made a deep impression on him. Its effect was seminal, he later decided, wondering at his youthful ability to feel to the full the horrors of being patronised many years before he even knew of the existence of the word 'patronising'.

'Auntie Kate?'

His solemnity was comical. He spoke with the air of someone who has thought long and hard about a subject of deep importance, as indeed he had. But she had herself under control. She wouldn't laugh at him now.

'Aye. What is it?'

'I saw me dad on top of me mam doing summat that weren't strangling, and I don't know what it were, and when I asked me mam she were right cagey about it. Does tha know what they were doing, Auntie Kate?'

Auntie Kate didn't reply. She was leaning on the window-sill and shaking.

'Only I thought tha might know what it were cos I thought happen Uncle Frank might have tried it with thee,' said Henry.

Auntie Kate threw back her head and roared with laughter. She went bright red with mirth.

Henry went red too. The shame of being laughed at and by Auntie Kate of all people was too much. The terrible hot shame of it.

Auntie Kate stopped laughing.

'I'm sorry,' she said.

And then, the unexpected happened. Henry Pratt, frightened of being laughed at, frightened of his own father, frightened of falling into water, frightened of railway engines, frightened of children, and frightened of being ejected from wombs, discovered that he had a fighting spirit.

'It's not fair to laugh at me because I don't know things,' he said. 'I can't know everything. I'm only little.'

'Oh dear. We've made a puddle, haven't we?'

It was Henry's first day at school. The exciting world of education was about to open up before him. He'd made a puddle.

His mother had walked with him down the lane to the village. The school was through the village, over the hump-bridge, on the right, beyond the Parish Hall. It was a square, stone building with high, Gothic windows and solid triangular gables. There was a large bell over the porch. He had his sandwiches in Fiona's old, stained satchel. He'd begun to want to go before he'd even crossed the playground.

Miss Forrest, the headmistress, tall and efficient, had pointed him in the direction of the junior classroom, and there he had met Miss Candy for the first time.

Miss Candy was fifty-three years old, and rode to school from Troutwick on a motor bike. She had three chins, and skin like leather. Her nose was large, her eyes were too close together. Her body had no definable shape. Her grey hair was pinned up into elaborate curls and rolls. A tuft of darker hair sprouted from the middle of her middle chin. Those who said that her moustache resembled the Fuehrer's were exaggerating.

There were children's paintings all round the walls of the classroom. Some of the paintings were just about recognisable as crude impressions of various local scenes. Others were less good. Pale winter sun streamed in through the high Gothic windows. The little desks were arranged in five groups for pupils of different ages. There were three small portable blackboards on easels. In front of the large, fixed blackboard there hung a blind covered with a picturesque representation of a farmyard. Yet it remained a classroom, filled with twenty-five strange children and presided over by a teacher of fearsome aspect. The pressure on his bladder grew rapidly, and he was far too shy to be able to ask to be permitted to relieve it.

Miss Candy sat him in a group with five of the youngest children, and asked him his name.

'Henry,' he mumbled.

'Oh dear. That's a little unfortunate, Henry, because we already have a Henry, don't we, Henry?'

'Aye, miss,' said a fair-haired boy in Henry's group.

'We can't have two Henrys in the same group, can we, Henry?' said Miss Candy.

'No, miss,' said the fair-haired boy, whose name was Henry Dinsdale.

'Have you got another name, Henry?' said Miss Candy.

'Aye,' said Henry.

'Well what is it?' said Miss Candy.

'Pratt,' said Henry, and a boy in the group giggled.

'Hush, Jane, there's nothing funny about names,' said Miss Candy to this boy, who was actually a girl. This was Jane Lugg, who came from a regrettably long line of Luggs.

'Haven't you got another Christian name?' said Miss Candy.

Henry nodded miserably.

'Well what is it?'

'Ezra,' he mumbled, hot with shame, wild with fury.

'Ezra,' said Miss Candy. 'Well, I'm glad to say we don't have any other Ezras here, so we'll be able to call you Ezra, won't we, Ezra?'

'Aye,' mumbled Henry, glaring at Henry Dinsdale, who had forced him to become an Ezra and inherit the curse of being a parrot-strangler.

It was lucky that Henry didn't know that Henry Dinsdale's real name was Cyril, but he'd had to be called Henry because there was already a Cyril. He had only just got over the problems associated with this change, and Miss Candy judged that to call him by a third name might provoke a severe identity crisis. So, Cyril remained Henry and Henry became Ezra.

The remaining members of Henry's group were Simon Eckington, the younger of the two Eckington boys from the Post Office, Cyril Orris, whose father was a farmer, and Pam Yardley, an evacuee.

There was no sign of Belinda Boyce-Uppingham. Henry was glad of that as he made his puddle.

'You'll have to go to the utility room, Ezra,' said Miss Candy. 'Take your trousers and pants off, wash them in the sink, and hang them on the pipes to dry. Show him the way, Henry, and bring me the bucket, the mop and the disinfectant.'

Cyril/Henry led Henry/Ezra to the utility room/locker room/boiler room, and there he spent his first morning at school.

In one corner there was a large sink. In another corner was the boiler. Hot pipes ran round the dark-green walls. There were many pegs on which hung satchels and coats, and all round the floor there were lockers. There was a window of frosted glass. There was nowhere to sit.

Henry took off his trousers and pants and washed them with a bar of green carbolic. He had never washed clothes before. The soap didn't produce lather, just a greeny-white slime. The world of rinsing was also an unexplored continent to him, and despite his best efforts, much of the soap proved impossible to remove. He gave up, and put the long, baggy shorts and thick yellowing pants on the pipes to dry. Time passes slowly when you're five years old and have nothing to do except stand and watch your clothes drying. That morning was an eternity of misery to Henry, standing with his fat legs bare, and his shirt not even covering his cowering little willie, in the hot little room with the noisy boiler and the frosted-glass window. His legs ached. There was a sudden eruption of children's voices and screams. It must be dinner-time, but nobody came into the utility room, and eventually the noise died down again. There was a distant slamming of doors, and silence reigned, save for the roaring and gurgling of the boiler.

Please, God, he said, as he stood beside his steaming clothes, I'm sorry I never came to see thee in Thurmarsh, but I didn't really know about thee, but now I do, so I will come in future. Please, God, kill Henry Dinsdale so I don't have to be an Ezra. Amen, and lots of love. Henry.

He began to wonder if everybody had gone home and left him. Perhaps he was locked in. Several times he felt that he would cry, but he fought against it.

Suddenly children were pouring into the utility room and looking at him and giggling as they collected their coats if they were going home to dinner or their sandwiches if they weren't. One older boy said, 'Look at his little willie,' and Patrick Eckington said, 'I can't. I forgot me magnifying glass,' and there was laughter, and then Miss Candy was there, saying, 'Your clothes are dry. Why haven't you put them on?' and he mumbled, 'Didn't tell me to,' and Miss Candy, who had a bottomless supply of minatory saws of her own invention, said, 'Mr Mumble shouted "fire" and nobody heard,' and he put his pants and shorts on with difficulty because the soap had caked hard, and the afternoon was a blur, and that was his first day at school, and it was to be the first of many, and they would all be like that, and life was awful.

There was still no sign of Belinda Boyce-Uppingham.

The snows came. Huge drifts swept up to the dry-stone walls. The ash woods were a magical tracery of white. Henry rushed into the kitchen with a snowball, and hurled it wildly in his excitement. It knocked a plate of best Worcester porcelain off the dresser. The plate smashed. Uncle Frank, who was never angry, strode abruptly from the room.

'Snow isn't funny here, Henry,' explained Auntie Kate. 'Uncle Frank's been out for hours, making sure his sheep are all right.'

Henry felt that awful hot shaming feeling all over.

Uncle Frank was out for hours again, with Billy and Jackie, taking fodder to any sheep they could find, but there were many more cut off in the huge drifts.

'Won't they die?' Henry asked Uncle Frank that evening.

'Grown up sheep are very tough,' explained Uncle Frank. 'We don't mind early snows so much. It's when we get snows in t' lambing season that we're in trouble.'

Henry was very thoughtful. If the sheep could survive out there, he thought, he wouldn't make any more fuss about going to schoo'

That Saturday afternoon, after the snows had stopped, and the sun was shining crisply, there was tobogganing down the lower slopes of Mickle Fell. Uncle Frank asked him if he'd like to use the girls' old toboggan. He tried to get out of it, on the grounds that it was unfair to sheep to enjoy the snow, but really because he was frightened. But Uncle Frank insisted, and suddenly it was important not to seem a coward in front of Uncle Frank.

The children of Rowth Bridge hurtled down the white slopes with apparent fearlessness on that ice-blue Saturday afternoon in war-time. Some had toboggans, some wooden boards, some tea-trays. The older children set off from quite high up. Some of them were fighter pilots, dive-bombing the vicious Hun.

Henry trudged up the slope somewhat fearfully. Patrick Eckington hurtled past. Surely this was high enough? And then he saw her. Belinda Boyce-Uppingham. Ravishing. High above him.

He couldn't start from below her, so he trudged on. Between him and Belinda a sturdy young man was carrying a tea-tray.

At last Belinda stopped and turned. The sturdy young man stopped beside her. They stood and waited for him.

He approached them, wheezing breathlessly. The sturdy young man turned out to be Jane Lugg. He wanted to speak to Belinda, but no words would come.

They began their descent. As his wooden toboggan gathered speed, Henry grew terrified. Faster and faster he went. Jane Lugg on her tea-tray was outclassed. Belinda Boyce-Uppingham, streamlined on her superb metal bobsleigh, was narrowly ahead of him.

Their speed increased. The field below was full of tiny figures.

Belinda Boyce-Uppingham was heading for the side of the field, where a slight incline slowed the toboggans and enabled you to stop quite gracefully. But Henry's toboggan was heading down to the bottom of the field, and there was nothing he could do to stop it.

Belinda dismounted from her bobsleigh gracefully. Jane Lugg landed underneath her tray in a clumsy, laughing heap. Henry's toboggan breasted the snows piled against the wall. It soared over the top, hurtled towards the thinner snow of the lower field, and landed with a bruising crunch. It gathered speed again. Wide-eyed and petrified he saw the trees at the edge of the ash wood rushing towards him.

He missed the trees by inches, and shot straight into the icy waters of the infant Mither. It was not the last river that Henry Pratt would fall into, but it was easily the smallest.

After that, things were better at school, and he began to settle in. Not quickly. Not easily. But steadily.

Within a week he had received two overtures of friendship. One he accepted, one he rejected.

The overture that he accepted was from Simon Eckington. Like him, Simon was shy. And Simon's father was also away at the war. His mother had her hands full running the Post Office and General Store, and his elder brother Patrick bullied him unmercifully. He was glad to find a good friend.

The overture that he didn't accept was from Pam Yardley. She was an evacuee, from Leeds. She had been taken in by the Wallingtons. Jim Wallington was the bus driver. Pam Yardley made the mistake of appealing for friendship on the grounds that they were both evacuees. Henry denied this angrily. He didn't add the clincher which prevented any possibility of friendship. Pam Yardley was a girl. Girls were useless, with one glorious exception. That exception was Belinda Boyce-Uppingham. Pam Yardley was not Belinda Boyce-Uppingham. Therefore she was useless.

The great strength of Belinda Boyce-Uppingham was that she was a beautiful and wonderful human being, despite her family.

The great weakness of Belinda Boyce-Uppingham was that she didn't go to the village school. Henry plucked up courage and, blushing, asked Auntie Kate why this was.

'The Boyce-Uppinghams send their children to private schools when they are young and then to public schools,' explained Auntie Kate.

It sounded to Henry as if the Boyce-Uppinghams were somewhat confused people, who had no cause to go around smugly tapping people as if they were barometers.

The school day started with a hymn and a prayer. Then they did painting and drawing. Henry's paintings were beautiful in his mind, but ghastly messes by the time they reached the paper. The younger children moulded plasticine and the older ones carved wood. Sometimes they would dance and even sing, quietly, so as not to disturb Miss Forrest's class. Sometimes they would dress up and perform little plays. Most of the class liked this part of the day, but Henry was doubtful.

There followed a bad time. This was the break. The playground was divided sexually by a tall wire fence. Miss Candy had argued against this. 'Put them in cages and they'll behave like animals,' she had said. 'Put them together and they'll behave like animals,' her superior had retorted. Henry didn't like the break because it exposed him to the bullying of *his* superiors. His tobogganing had not transformed him into a hero overnight. It had to be weighed against the puddle. It wasn't certain yet whether he was to be counted as an evacuee or not. More evidence was needed before judgement was passed on him.

After the break there came the best part of Henry's day – the lessons. They learnt reading and writing, and the basics of arithmetic, and he proved good at these things.

Dinner came next. The risk of bullying was less great than in the break, because many of the children went home. On the wall of the playground, however, a goal had been marked in chalk, and here football was often played. Henry had nothing against football, except that he couldn't play and always got hurt. There were also three stumps chalked against the wall, and when the summer came Henry would learn that his lack of talent extended to cricket also. These perils, when added to the lingering threat of brawn, made dinner a dangerous time.

In the afternoon, they applied their arithmetic, and their reading and writing, to various practical ends, like running a shop, or planning the farming year, or holding auctions, or even, as they got older, writing a local children's newspaper.

We have seen Miss Candy from the outside, a shapeless, greying motor-cyclist with an excess of chins, hair in unfortunate places, and a distant hint of the porcine in her features. Come with me now on a journey into the interior.

Miss Candy had always known that she would be a teacher. She had believed that she would be a good, perhaps even a great teacher. She was steeped in educational theory. She identified with those two alliterative lady educationalists, Maria Montessori and Margaret McMillan.

It was because of the influence of Maria Montessori that there was no rivalry in Miss Candy's class. Each child went at his or her own pace. There were no rewards. Punishment was reserved for naughtiness and breaches of communal discipline, and was never used as a weapon against the slow-witted. The communal discipline included tidying up the classroom before going home. Miss Candy believed that Maria Montessori, the great Italian, would approve, if only she could ever see Miss Candy's class of five- to ten-year-olds at Rowth Bridge Village School.

Being herself from Bradford, it was natural that Miss Candy associated herself even more closely with Margaret McMillan, who did much of her best work in that city between 1893 and 1902. Margaret McMillan believed that many schoolchildren went through school life using only a minimum of their powers and expressing only a fraction of their personalities. She believed in the importance of nursery schooling, where children could be given adventure, movement, dancing, music, talking, food and rest within the school environment. Extracts from her writings hung on the wall of Miss Candy's bedroom. 'You may ask why we give all this to the children? Because this is nurture, and without it they can never really have education. For education must grow out of nurture and the flower from its root, since nurture is organic. . . . Much of the money we spend on education is wasted, because we have not laid any real foundation for our educational system. . . .'

Nobody would ever read the educational theories of Miss Florence Candy. Her wise saws would hang on no one's bedroom wall. No international seminars of educationalists would ever hang breathless on her words. She looked ridiculous. She lived in a world which judges men partially and women almost entirely by appearance. The junior classroom at Rowth Bridge Village School was therefore her pinnacle. Her satisfaction was that she was achieving as much as could possibly be achieved by a woman of her appearance, in a classroom split up into five different groups of children who had not been to nursery schools, in a tiny village school with holes in the ground for lavatories, under a head teacher who disapproved of her, insisted that the children marched into school in lines, and would try to get rid of her as soon as the war was over.

It is time to reveal another of Miss Candy's secrets. She had always believed that one day one of the human seeds that she had helped to nurture would grow into a plant that would make her life worthwhile. One day she would have a pupil through whose reflected glory her work would live on.

She had a hope, just a faint hope, that she had found that pupil at last.

On Sunday mornings, as Henry got ready for church, cleaning shoes, brushing hair, he listened to the repeat of Tommy Handley in 'It's That Man Again' on the kitchen wireless. He didn't understand it very well but the grown-ups laughed a lot, and he was determined not to be left out.

This Sunday he didn't laugh. Henry Dinsdale, né Cyril Dinsdale, had not been to school for three days. Ezra Pratt, né Henry Pratt, remembered a prayer made in a utility room. Please, God, kill Henry Dinsdale, so I don't have to be an Ezra.

He was terrified that God had answered his prayer.

When they all knelt, in the little, squat-towered church beside the Mither, he prayed fervently.

Please, God, he prayed, it's me again. Tha knows I axed thee to kill Henry Dinsdale. I didn't really mean it. Bring him back to life, will tha, like tha did thy kid?

He had the utmost difficulty in eating his dinner that day.

After dinner, they listened to the gardening advice given by Roy Hay. Uncle Frank kept up a running commentary. 'I disagree!. . .Not up here, tha won't!. . .Never wi' our soil!'

The day dragged endlessly. Henry didn't sleep that night.

In the morning, Henry Dinsdale still wasn't at school. God had failed him.

He toyed listlessly with his plasticine.

'What's up, Ezra?' Miss Candy asked.

'Nowt, miss.'

In the break he longed to ask Miss Candy about Henry Dinsdale but he didn't dare. Patrick Eckington punched him in the tummy for no reason, and he didn't care.

His turn came to read out loud. Usually he liked that. Not

today. The words danced in front of his eyes. 'The young blind is not only hedgehog born, but deaf.'

He didn't even bother to scratch Pam Yardley's hand when she put it on his knee under his desk.

When dinner-time came, Miss Candy asked him to stay behind.

'What's wrong, Ezra?' she said.

'Nowt, miss.'

'You must tell me, Ezra.'

'I prayed to God to kill Henry Dinsdale, cos I didn't like being called Ezra, and now he's dead, miss.'

'Henry Dinsdale has measles, Ezra,' said Miss Candy.

Henry Pratt's measles came on the Wednesday. He lay, feverish and aching, in a darkened room, listening to the snow dripping off the roof. Outside, the country sounds were unusually sharp. Sam barking. A cow mooing. Billy the half-wit laughing. Jackie the land-girl sneezing. Henry pretended that Belinda Boyce-Uppingham was in the bed, having measles with him.

As a treat, while he recuperated, they bought him the *Beano* and the *Dandy*. He couldn't read them very well yet, especially the stories, but he managed to make sense of most of the cartoons. He liked Big Eggo, the ostrich, and Korky the Cat, and Freddy the Fearless Fly, but Keyhole Kate was horrid. He read out the words to himself with difficulty. Pansy Potter, the strong man's something.

Fiona came to visit, with her dull husband, and she came upstairs to see him. 'It's daughter,' she explained. ' "Pansy Potter, the strong man's daughter. Pansy's teeth are cracked and bent, eating a cake made from cement." '

'That's Jane Lugg,' said Henry. 'And Pam Yardley's Keyhole Kate.'

'My husband's Hungry Horace,' said Fiona.

Henry couldn't imagine her dull husband eating a lot, but he made no comment.

'Read me a story,' he said.

Fiona read a story about Derek, the wild boy of the woods, an outlaw branded as a traitor by Bagshot, Head of the Secret Service. Derek alone knew that Bagshot was a Nazi spy, and he foiled Bagshot with the aid of Kuru, his eagle pal. At the end of the story, the real British officer congratulated him. ' "If it hadn't been for you," he grinned,' read Fiona, ' "this 'U' boat would have got away with the secret plans of our new battleships. We owe everything to you and the wonderful eagle you have trained so well." '

Henry sighed ecstatically. He would be the wild boy of the woods when he was better.

'How did he grin all that?' he asked.

' "Grinned" means "said with a grin",' explained Fiona. 'In comics you never say "said". You say "suggested", "grunted", "snorted", "breathed", but not "said".'

'Why?' queried Henry.

'I don't know,' chuckled Fiona. 'I suppose that's their style, to make it more exciting.'

'Read me another one,' demanded Henry, the Boy with the Magic Measle, whose Every Wish was Granted.

That afternoon made a great impression on Henry, with dark-haired, brown-eyed, flashing Fiona, who smelt so nice, reading stories in her sparkling voice, glad to be free of her evil, greedy husband, whose Artificial Leg Contained Secret Plans of British Battleships.

When she had gone, Henry decided to learn to read better, to get better quickly, and to rescue Belinda Boyce-Uppingham from her Wicked Family, who were Nazi Spies.

Pssst!!!! Someone was coming. Who would it be? The foul Bagshot? Pansy Potter, the strong man's daughter? Or Keyhole Kate, eavesdropping again?

It was another Kate. Auntie Kate.

'Who's a lucky boy, then?' said Auntie Kate. 'Who's got pilchards for tea?'

They gave Henry the option of not going to church on Sunday, as he'd been ill. To their surprise, he chose to attend.

How he loved her! Who was the man sitting beside her in army uniform?

'That's Major Boyce-Uppingham, Belinda's father,' said Auntie Kate after the service.

'And a Nazi Spy!' breathed Henry to himself.

People stood around and discussed the weather, the losses in the Atlantic, the rationing, and their arthritis, but not God. They'd done that part.

Kit Orris, father of Cyril, approached.

'Now then, Frank,' he said.

'Now then, Kit,' said Uncle Frank. 'It's right thin and parky, i'n't it?'

'How's young Ezra, then?' said Kit Orris.

'I'm Henry,' said Henry. He wasn't going to start being called Ezra out of school. He began to suspect that Kit Orris was Another Nazi Spy.

'How's t' blackout, then, Kit?' said Uncle Frank.

'Well, I didn't know,' said Kit Orris, sheep-farmer, sheepishly. The story had swept the village. Jim Wallington, who was air-raid warden as well as bus driver, had called out, 'Put out them lights.' 'Lights?' Kit Orris had said. 'All t' lights at back of t' house.' 'Oh. Does tha have to black out t' back and all?'

Very suspicious, thought our hero. It sounded to him like a Beacon for Messerschmitts.

The Nazi Spy Boyce-Uppingham was approaching with his beautiful daughter. The Nazi Spy Kit Orris raised his eyes to heaven and hurried off as if he didn't want to meet him. That ruse did not fool Henry!

Major Andrew Boyce-Uppingham, to do him justice, did not tap Henry as if he were a barometer. He prodded him as if he were a potato. But instead of saying, 'Nearly done. Just needs another minute,' he said, 'A little bird tells me that somebody we know isn't exactly short of grey matter. Well done!'

Henry smiled at Belinda Boyce-Uppingham.

She looked straight through him.

'Play it that way if tha wants to. Keep us love secret,' thought the Wild Boy of the Woods.

Spring came late and fragile to Upper Mitherdale, and ripened uncertainly into summer. 'It's That Man Again' came from the seaside now, and was known briefly as 'It's That Sand Again'. Germany invaded Russia. In the Middle East, Wavell failed to dislodge Rommel. The losses in the Atlantic continued. The war was becoming long and grim, not exciting and heroic. The nation seemed to have survived so far through a chaotic mixture of luck and genius. Now luck had run out, and genius wouldn't do on its own any longer. The war was being rationalised. The planners were coming into their own, thus ensuring, did Henry but know it, that the nation would win the war and lose the peace that followed.

There was a heavily censored letter from Ezra, who was somewhere doing something, and was well. Clothes, jam and tinned food joined the list of rationed goods, and Henry enjoyed his first summer in the country.

He enjoyed collecting the hens' eggs with Billy, from the huts in the hen coop, which smelt of sweet, hot, healthy decay. He liked to go over to the new shippon, across the thick-mudded, glistening, treacly yard, to watch Jackie milking the red, white and roan cattle with her gnarled, agile fingers. The old shippon, built onto the house, was used for hay and crops now.

On her evenings off, Jackie looked an awesome sight, striding off to the Three Horseshoes in her baggy corduroy riding breeches, in search of men. Now, at work, she was jolly and friendly. She explained that the cattle were shorthorns, dual-purpose cattle, bred for milk and beef. The future belonged with the specialists even among cows. Uncle Frank was a bit old-fashioned. He hankered after the olden days.

Uncle Frank took him round in the cart, which was pulled by a Dales pony. A few of the better-off farmers had tractors, but most still used horses.

The sheep were Swaledales, with black heads and small, curved horns. The little lambs looked as if they had black socks. They all talked in individual voices. Some sounded like human babies, some like gruff old men.

War regulations had compelled Uncle Frank to put twenty-five per cent of his land under the plough. The land wasn't suited, and his two small fields of oats were indifferent in quality and quantity.

Henry's reading and writing were improving apace. Miss Candy attributed it to her nurturing, but it was because he wanted to be able to read his comics.

When he went out for walks with Simon Eckington, they were

65

two shy lads who sat and chatted, threw stones into the Mither and discovered the quiet pleasures of friendship. They were also naturalists. Simon taught Henry to recognise dippers, and pied wagtails, and how to tell yellow and grey wagtails apart. Once, a kingfisher flashed turquoise along the river. They watched common and palmated newts in the farm pond. They kept tadpoles in jars, which got knocked over. Simon kept budgerigars, but Henry rarely went to Simon's home, because Patrick was a rotter, who was not above tearing up a chap's cigarette cards.

They were also in part explorers, known as Sir Simon Eckington of that Ilkley, and Lord Pratt of Thurmarsh, surveying the millstone grit moorland around Mickleborough. High above the valley the two little boys trudged through the cotton-grass and heather in their Wellington boots and baggy shorts. Curlews were albatrosses. Buzzards were vultures. Redshank were Eckington's Cranes, named after Sir Simon Eckington of that Ilkley, who first discovered them.

They were also in part adventurers, the Wild Boy of the Woods and the Kid with the Magic Wellies. It couldn't have been mere coincidence that only one Hun was seen in Upper Mitherdale throughout the whole of 1941.

Some of the evacuees were fish out of water, tadpoles in knocked-over jars. Henry discovered that he was a country lad at heart. It was as if Paradise Lane, Thurmarsh, had never existed.

On the Sunday before the hay harvest began, Henry was determined to speak to Belinda Boyce-Uppingham.

They stood by the churchyard, after the service. Uncle Frank was talking to Kit Orris.

'Now then, Frank.'

'Now then, Kit. It's a right dowly day.'

There she was, with her mother and grandmother and older brother. Please look this way, Belinda.

'How's t' oats?'

'Rubbish. Regulations! Land's not suited. Those Whitehall willies wouldn't recognise a field of oats if they fell over it.'

She was coming this way!

'I'd like to see them come up here.'

'So would I. I'd set t' bull on 'em.'

He walked up to her.

'Belinda?' he said.

'I don't talk to evacuees,' she said, and walked on, her exquisite little nose pointing straight up to heaven.

This time he couldn't pretend that it was part of a game.

The hay harvest was below average, but store lambs fetched good prices.

One day, Jane Lugg followed Henry and Simon as they set off on one of their walks.

'There's a funny smell around here,' said Simon. 'Is it a dead hedgehog?'

'No. It's Jane Lugg,' said Henry.

But she persisted. 'Can I come too?' she kept saying.

The two six-year-old boys went into a huddle.

'She's a girl,' pointed out Simon.

'Aye, but be fair, she doesn't look like a girl,' said Henry.

They decided to admit Jane Lugg to their friendship as an honorary boy. She proved all right, for a Lugg. Where other people grew marrow and cabbage, the Luggs put their garden down to prams and rusty bikes. In 1909, in a brawl after a dance at the Troutwick Jubilee Hall, five Luggs had fought six Pitheys from Troutwick, and a Pithey had died. The Luggs bred like rabbits, and kept rabbits, which bred like Luggs. But Jane Lugg proved a keen naturalist, a resourceful explorer, and a doughty fighter against the only Hun seen in Upper Mitherdale that year. The fiendish Hun had a Magic Body, and could Disguise Himself as Anybody. That day he was disguised as Pam Yardley. He ran away, but Jane Lugg, alias Pansy Potter, the strong man's daughter, caught him and settled him. It was a long while before Pam Yardley dared go out on her own again.

Both boys would have got a lathering if they dared go to the Lugg abode, and the Post Office and General Store was dangerous also on account of Patrick, so the three often congregated at Low Farm. Henry wasn't banned from seeing Jane Lugg, but he was discouraged. Sometimes she would be sent home. Simon was sent home as well, to make it fair, but when Simon was there without

67

Jane he was never sent home. Henry defended Jane stoutly, and vowed to marry her when he grew up. He wouldn't have been heart-broken if news of his intention had reached the shapely little ears of Belinda Boyce-Uppingham.

The brief Dales summer slipped all too quickly into autumn. It began to look as if the Russians might hold out against the Germans till the winter. In Upper Mitherdale, the sickly oats were stooked. School began again. Maria Montessori did not visit Miss Candy's classroom, but the nit lady did. It was widely known that the evacuees were not clean, and it would be no surprise to find that they had nits.

None of the evacuee children had nits. Jane Lugg did. Henry's ardour cooled, and autumn slipped imperceptibly into winter. The oats were threshed communally, since there was only one machine.

Belinda Boyce-Uppingham rode past Henry on her pony, and he decided that he must ride. One Satuday, in late October, his riding career began. Fifty-three seconds later, his riding career ended.

It was the age of the wireless. It was on almost all day, in the dark, cosy kitchen of Low Farm. News bulletins were eagerly awaited, and a tense silence fell during them. Then the music began again. Charles Ernesco and his Sextet. Falkman and his Apache Band. Troise and his Banjoliers. And always, wafting faintly over the darkening, misty dale, one Reginald or another at the theatre organ. There was 'Music While You Work' twice a day, and Ensa concerts with Richard Tauber. And comedy. Slowly Henry was beginning to grasp the concept of humour. Apart from ITMA, there was 'Breakfast with the Murgatroyds', 'The Happidrome', with stars like Izzy Bonn and Suzette Tarri, who sang 'Red sails in the Sunset', 'Varie-tea' at tea-time, 'Workers' Playtime' and 'Works' Wonders', and it was all a wonder that it worked, that the bright, far-away world came flooding into the quiet, gas-lit farm kitchen beneath the stark, silent hills. For the children there was 'Children's Hour'. Henry liked the animal programmes, with David Seth-Smith, the Zoo Man, and 'Out with Romany', but 'Children's Hour' was of an improving nature, on the whole, and Henry didn't want to be improved, on the whole, and so, on the whole, he preferred the alternative programme, which was called 'Ack-ack, beer-beer' and came from the canteens of balloon barrage centres and anti-aircraft units.

The Japanese attacked Pearl Harbour, and the United States entered the war. In the school nativity play, Henry played a passer-by. He had one line, 'Look at them three funny men.' He forgot it, but he did remember to pass by. Jane Lugg, shorn and humiliated, was given the part of an angel by Miss Candy, for psychological reasons, and much against the wishes of Miss Forrest. As Henry passed by, an angel belted him round the ear-hole.

Christmas was quiet, but enjoyable. Henry's presents included an apple, an orange, a Mars bar, two Dinky toys (a Packard and a Lagonda) and a kaleidoscope. 'I'm right set up wi' me prezzies,' he said with satisfaction.

There was a letter from Ezra. He was in. . .they were hoping to advance to. . .before. . .and he loved them both very much.

Summer sunshine streamed into the kitchen. Reginald Foort at the theatre organ streamed out into the fields. Auntie Kate was bottling soft fruit. Ada was humming cheerfully. Henry was buried in his *Beano*. After the sad business with Jane Lugg, he was less sure about Pansy Potter, the strong man's daughter – 'Pansy laughs, the cheeky elf – she makes a 'U' Boat shoot itself' – and he could never quite forgive the Boy with the Whistling Scythe for replacing the Wild Boy of the Woods. His favourite was Lord Snooty and his Pals, who were Rosie, Hairpin Huggins, Skinny Lizzie, Scrapper Smith, Happy Hutton, Snitchy and Snatchy, and Gertie the Goat. They had some hard battles with the dreadful Gasworks Gang. He quite liked Cocky Dick – he's smart and slick – and Musso the Wop – he's a big-a-da flop. He liked it best when people bopped Huns. The Huns went 'Der Wow!' and 'Der Ouch!' and serve them right. Henry hated them. That was why, on this, his first day of the summer holidays, Simon and he were going to open up a second front. They owed it to the nation.

His dinner was in his satchel. A ham sandwich, an egg sandwich, a cake made by Auntie Kate out of cornflakes coated with chocolate, and an apple. A dinner fit for a man going to battle. Especially when supplemented by a Mars bar out of your own pocket-money. His pocket-money was threepence a week. This bought him the *Beano* and the *Dandy* on alternate weeks. If he had enough coupons he would spend the rest on sweets. In those days of rationing, sweets were luxuries to be savoured. At his peak, he could make a Mars bar last an hour.

The first seven months of 1942 had passed quite smoothly. One of Simon's budgerigars had won second prize in the cobalt or mauve cock or hen class at the Barnoldswick Fur and Feather Society. Henry's progress at school had been steady. The nation fought germs almost as keenly as Germans in this era of food shortages and rationing. The newspaper adverts aimed at the authority of military commands. 'Fortify those kidneys!' 'Yes, sir.' 'Stop that terrible itching.' 'Sorry, sir.' 'Wake up your liver bile.' 'Righto, sir.' Even in Upper Mitherdale, where ways of circumventing rationing were not difficult to find when you kept your own pigs, Henry was made to consume cod liver oil and Californian syrup of figs with the utmost regularity. There had been a big nationwide competition to see which area could collect the most waste-paper. Henry's *Beano* was full of poems exhorting him to save paper:

Waste littler, paste Hitler.

and:

Come on girls! Come on chaps!
Dot Hitler on the napper.
Save up all your little scraps,
And be a 'paper scrapper'.

and again:

Bop the Wop, Slap the Jap,
Stun the Hun, with paper scrap.

Dutifully Henry had added his old *Beanos* and *Dandies* to the Rowth Bridge pile much as he longed to keep them. Uncle Frank and Auntie Kate had rewarded his patriotic efforts by taking him and Ada to Skipton to see the opening of the Skipton and District Warship Week. The week was opened by Viscountess Snowden, and there were loud cheers as she moved the indicator to show that £109,557 had already been collected. The indicator had been made by members of the Skipton College of Art. There was a march past by the Skipton Home Guard, the Skipton A.T.C., the St John's Ambulance Brigade, the Civil Nursing Reserve, the Civil Defence workers, the Women's Land Army, which included Jackie, who looked very solemn, the Boy Scouts, the Wolf Cubs and the Girl Guides. Many of the stores featured attractive window displays with a naval theme. Henry wished that he was taking part in the march, although he knew that if he had been he would have wished that he wasn't.

In the war there had been losses on all sides and victories for nobody. The British had bombed Lübeck and Rostock. The old wooden houses had burnt well. The Germans had responded with the 'so-called' Baedeker raids, on historic British cities. Once or twice, Henry had heard Ada crying in the night. This morning, a letter had come from Ezra. He was safe. The battle of. . .had been a right. . .they were now dug in at. . .and likely to be there for some time. The food was very. . .but he was well, and he loved them both very much.

So Ada was smiling, the sun was shining, Reginald Foort was playing, Auntie Kate, was bottling soft fruit and it was good to be alive.

Henry and Simon climbed the hill on the east side of the dale, past the remains of the old smelt mill. It was a clear morning, with just a few puffy clouds forming above Mickleborough. They disturbed an oystercatcher, and above them lapwings tossed themselves around joyfully.

They lay in the cotton-grass, commanding a view of the dale from Mickle Head to Troutwick, and kept their eyes skinned for Huns while they ate their Mars bars slowly.

Their conversation was an attempt at the style of the comics.

'Gasp!' said Henry. 'Is that a Hun over there, Eckers?'

'A Hun? Ho ho, you silly twerp! It's a horse.'

Henry pointed excitedly.

'I think that's a Hun,' he said.

'Let's go and bag the blighter,' said Simon.

They crawled along the ground towards the unsuspecting enemy, which was actually Pam Yardley again. It was the first time the Leeds girl had dared brave the fells since she had last been taken for a Hun. She was collecting sphagnum moss to hand over to the Red Cross for use as padding in splints.

They got to within twenty yards of the Hun without his suspecting them. Then they charged. He ran off. They chased him. Henry brought the fiend crashing to the ground. It was the only successful rugby tackle he would ever make in his life, wasted on a lonely evacuee girl who didn't even know that she was supposed to be a Hun.

'Give over,' said the Hun, picking himself up and trying not to cry.

'Tha's a Hun. We've just captured thee,' explained Henry.

'Oh. Right,' said Pam Yardley, a little more resourceful than on her last capture. 'Hang on a sec.' She worked herself up into being a captured German. 'Der wow!' she cried. 'Der ouch! Der Gott in Himmel! Der lemme go, Britisher swine!'

The Deadly Duo discovered that capturing German prisoners was a mixed blessing. You had to share your dinner with them. They did think of starving her, but had to admit that she had been a pretty sporting blighter, for a rotter.

They saw no more Germans, and fairly soon grew bored. As they returned to Low Farm, they could hear the music of Reginald New at the theatre organ.

Henry volunteered to escort the prisoner home, but as soon as Simon had gone home, he abandoned the pretence that she was a Hun, and told her that he liked her. She kissed him quickly, and skipped off into the Wallington home, clutching her puny collection of sphagnum moss in her hot little hand.

Stay-at-home holiday activities were laid on in the towns that summer, and Skipton was no exception. Ada was to take Henry in the bus. He was so excited that he got up at half-past six. If he hadn't, he wouldn't have seen the Real Live Hun!

Uncle Frank had gone out early, to examine some sick sheep, whose complaint he was unable to diagnose.

Henry wandered up the field towards his great-uncle. The dew was heavy, and cloud hung over the top of Mickleborough.

Suddenly there was a great roar, and an aeroplane with a swastika on its side came rushing up the dale towards Mickle Head. A long trail of dark smoke was pouring from its tail. The pilot had a faulty compass, and was trying to get home after being the only man ever to make a Baedeker raid on Burnley.

Henry and Uncle Frank stared open-mouthed. The plane tried vainly to gather height. The pilot ejected, tumbled headlong for a hundred feet, then his parachute opened. The plane crashed into the side of Mickleborough and a great flame spurted into the air. Silence fell, save for the bleating of the surprised Swaledale sheep in the next field, as the Hun fiend landed gently among them.

Henry's flesh came out in goose-pimples as they approached the Terrible Teuton.

The pilot gathered up his parachute and walked towards them nervously. To Henry's surprise, he looked young, bewildered and frightened and really quite nice, not like a fiendish killer with bared teeth and a snarl.

The German youth looked at Uncle Frank nervously, but Uncle Frank seemed quite calm.

'Now then, lad,' said Uncle Frank. 'Does't tha know owt about sheep?'

It was a long day for Ada. There was the bus ride, on two buses, changing at Troutwick, down winding roads bordered by stone walls and grass verges flecked with meadow cranesbill. An advert on the village bus showed a drawing of a conductress. The caption was 'Give her a big hand – with (if possible) the correct fare in it!' On the village bus the conductor was the driver, Jim Wallington. He gave out brightly coloured tickets from his clip board. On the outskirts of Skipton, in the second bus, they passed a static water tank. They watched a display of blitz cookery by a team of Girl Guide camp advisors in the Friendly Society's yard. The girls demonstrated the use of the sawdust cooker, the haybox cooker, the camp cooker and the W.V.S. blackout cooker. They lunched in style on Australian minced-meat loaf at the café in the bus station. They joined a large crowd on the rugby field. The crowd were amazed at the speed with which the Home Guard put up barbed wire entanglements. She took him to the cinema for the very first time. They saw 'The Wizard of Oz' at the Plaza. It was his best film ever, so far. It was quite a day, and by the end of it Ada's ankles, large at the best of times, were swollen horribly. You couldn't have said that Henry hadn't enjoyed his day, but Ada felt that much of her thunder had been stolen by the real-life German prisoner.

Back at Rowth Bridge, Germans and outings over, the summer continued placidly, and Henry wrestled with his secrets.

His secrets were that he liked girls and evacuees! He liked the two in one! He liked Pam Yardley! He couldn't think why boys thought girls were soppy. Pam had a nice, square, honest face, and chubby, smooth legs, covered in bites and scratches. It gave him a warm feeling in his body to be near her. He went to the Wallingtons' house and listened to 'Children's Hour' with her. They sat with pencil and paper and tried to do puzzles, questions and catches set by P. Caton Baddeley. They listened to 'Mr Noah's Holiday', a Toytown story by S. G. Hulme-Beaman. They laughed together at an evacuee boy from the south who didn't know that 'laiking at taws on t' causer edge' meant playing marbles on the pavement. Pam Yardley showed Henry her marbles. They exceeded expectations. She came to Low Farm and they watched the harvest and listened to the faint strains of Reginald Dixon at the theatre organ wafting over the fields. Always there was music at Low Farm, exotic names from a magic world outside. Nat Gonella and his Georgians. Don Felipe and the Cuban Caballeros. The Winter Garden Orchestra under the direction of Tom Jenkins. They laughed together at Stainless Stephen, Jeanne de Casalis as 'Mrs Feather', Revnell and West, and Gillie Potter speaking to them in English from Hogsnorton, although they barely understood a quarter of it all.

Henry invited her to church one Sunday, and outside afterwards he held her hand and waited for Belinda Boyce-Uppingham to notice them and realise what she had missed.

Uncle Frank was chatting to Kit Orris.

'How's t' lambs, Frank?'

'Nobbut middling, Kit.'

There she was. If only she'd turn and see them.

'Tha's only got feed for six months. Tha feeds 'em up. They come on grand. Then they deteriorate. It's a bad do.'

Belinda Boyce-Uppingham turned and looked straight at them. Henry squeezed Pam's hand. Belinda Boyce-Uppingham turned away, her sang-froid apparently undisturbed, but Henry fancied that the thrust had gone home.

Pam came for Sunday dinner. Afterwards, they listened to the gardening advice of C. H. Middleton. 'Not at this latitude,' commented Uncle Frank. 'April! Tha'll be lucky. . .Six inches apart! Give over!' The young love-birds slipped out and wandered down by the river.

Simon Eckington was approaching. When he saw them he veered away.

'Simon!' shouted Henry.

He watched his best friend walk away without looking back.

'Forget him,' said Pam Yardley. 'Good riddance to bad rubbish.'

She put her arm round Henry. He blushed. He hoped nobody would see them, especially Simon.

'Give over,' he said, shaking himself free. 'Gerroff.' Then, so as not to seem unfriendly, he said, 'Race thee to t' top.' They ran up the slope, away from the river. The sheep, just about over the shock of the German airman, retreated before them in panic.

Pam Yardley beat him by about forty-five yards.

She flopped on her back and waited for him to arrive.

'What a weed,' she said. 'I couldn't marry a weed.'

'Marry,' he gasped.

Pam Yardley put her hand on his private parts.

'What's tha doing?' he said.

'Don't know,' she admitted, 'but I saw Debbie Carrington do it to Stanley Lugg, and he liked it.'

'Aye, well, he's a Lugg,' said Henry.

Pam Yardley squeezed.

'Give over. Tha's not doing it right, wherever it is,' he yelped.

Luckily, Pam Yardley gave over.

'Are we to get married when we're grown up then?' she said.

He considered the question seriously.

'I think we're a bit young to decide,' he said.

A cool evening breeze sprang up, and they ran helter-skelter down the hill, and tumbled breathlessly back into the farm fields.

They could hear the music of Reginald Porter-Brown at the theatre organ.

In the morning, Henry asked Auntie Kate if there was anything he could get at the Post Office and General Store. He needed an excuse to see Simon.

He stood in the cool interior of the shop, gazing longingly at the almost empty bottles of sweets. He'd used up his ration. He wanted two stamps, a packet of snap vacuum jar closers, some Eiffel Tower lemonade crystals, Gibbs Dentifrice (No Black Out for Teeth with Gibbs Dentifrice) and he could try for Reckitt's Blue.

Mrs Eckington served him and he asked for Simon. Simon came into the shop and hissed, 'Come outside.'

They went outside.

'What's up?' said Henry.

'I don't go around wi' evacuees,' said Simon.

'I'm not an evacuee,' shouted Henry.

'It's Patrick,' whispered Simon, and disappeared back into the shop.

School began again. The nit lady came. Pam Yardley had nits. Her brown hair was shorn and she was sent to Coventry and Henry didn't dare speak to her and Simon came up to him in the playground, and Henry knew that Simon was only pretending not to be his friend because he was frightened of Patrick, so he thought everything might be all right now he wasn't seeing Pam Yardley any more, but suddenly Simon's face was twisted into hatred, and he shouted, 'Pam Yardley's got nits. Pam Yardley's got nits.'

On account of his divided loyalties, Henry had ended up without a friend in the school. His little group of six had changed slightly. They had left Cyril Orris behind, and caught up with Lorna Arrow. Jane Lugg, Pam Yardley and Simon refused to speak to him at all. Henry Dinsdale was distant. Lorna Arrow, fair, tall, thin and toothy, tried to be friendly once on the way home, but he spurned her offer. 'It's nowt personal,' he said kindly, 'but girls are more bother than they're worth.'

Montgomery defeated Rommel at El Alamein. There was no news of Ezra. His son, Henry, buried himself in his studies and his reading. He listened to his good friend, the wireless. He heard an all-star concert with Naughton and Gold, and Rawicz and Landauer, Music Hall with Elsie and Doris Waters, Randolph Sutton and Magda Kun. On 'Children's Hour' there was 'Stuff and Nonsense', fun fare on the air concocted by Muriel Levy, with

Doris Gambell, Violet Carson, Wilfred Pickles, Muriel Levy and Nan. But, without friends, there was no fun in his heart any more.

Christmas drew near. One day, as he reached the end of the village on his way home, he found his path blocked by Simon and Patrick Eckington, Freddie Carter and Colin Lugg. They took him to Freddie Carter's.

Colin Lugg and Patrick Eckington grabbed him, and twisted his arms. Colin Lugg's breath smelt of sick and Patrick Eckington's breath smelt of freckles. They forced him to the lavatory, and thrust his head deep into the bowl, which was the creation of Cobbold and Sons, of Etruria. But Cobbold and Sons could not help him now.

The bowl was dark and smelt vaguely fetid. They held his head there until each boy had flushed the cistern, which took a long time to fill.

They let him go then, without a word. Simon Eckington couldn't look him in the eye.

At the Christmas carol service, Belinda Boyce-Uppingham sang a solo of 'Gloria in Excelsis Deo' quite exquisitely. Henry fancied that she was inspired by the desire to humiliate him.

He refused to go to the children's party in the Parish Hall. By all accounts he missed a treat. Coon songs were given by Mr Ballard, who also proved his ability with the banjo.

In April, news came that Ezra had been injured. He was on a troop ship, which would dock at Plymouth.

Ada set off to meet him. Henry wanted to accompany her, but was told that this was a crisis, not a treat. Nobody could be sure how badly Ezra had been injured.

On Troutwick Station, windswept among the high hills, Ada said, 'Now tha'll be a good, brave lad, won't tha?'

'Oh aye,' he said. 'How many wheels does tha think t' engine will have?'

The engine roared in and shuddered gasping to an exhausted halt.

'It's got ten wheels,' he told her. 'Two little 'uns and three big 'uns on each side.'

'Oh aye?' said Ada. 'Now think on. Be a good lad.'

The train started with such a display of skidding and coughing from the engine that Henry felt sorry for the iron monster.

Some chickens which had arrived from Carlisle in a wicker basket protested volubly.

Ada waved until she was just a speck.

'It had ten wheels,' said Henry on the way home. 'Two little 'uns and three big 'uns on each side.'

'Oh aye?' said Auntie Kate, who was determined not to give him too good a time, so that he would miss his mother. 'Now remember what our Ada said. Be a good boy.'

The summer term began. Miss Candy asked them about their experiences in the holidays.

'My dad's been injured in t' war,' he said proudly.

'My grandad was hurt in t' Dardanelles,' announced Henry Dinsdale.

'Does anybody know where the Dardanelles are?' said Miss Candy, ever the improviser.

'Just above the knackers,' said Jane Lugg. Everybody giggled.

'That's a bit silly, Jane,' said Miss Candy. 'And it's not the sort of thing we laugh at.'

Miss Forrest entered the classroom without knocking, which irritated Miss Candy, because if she had ever entered Miss Forrest's classroom without knocking there would have been ructions.

'Your great-uncle's here to see you, Ezra,' said Miss Forrest.

Uncle Frank stood in the corridor, in his battered green tweed jacket with leather elbow patches. He was twisting his hat in his hands. His face was as old as the hills and as dry as a stone wall. He put his hand on Henry's shoulder and led him out into the playground. It surprised Henry that the sun was shining.

So his father had died! He couldn't really feel much. He had almost forgotten his father.

Uncle Frank led him towards his car. Pleasure motoring was forbidden now, but this journey had not been for pleasure.

His father got out of the car with difficulty, and hobbled to meet him. His left leg was in plaster. He looked gaunt and old.

'She stepped straight in front of a bus,' he said. 'She never knew what hit her.'

•

His father's injuries had healed. He was going back to the war. Henry was glad, although he knew that he must never say so.

They sat beside the infant Mither. It worried away at its stones. Three months of its ceaseless efforts had passed since Henry had learnt of his mother's death.

They had so little to say to each other, father and son. It was nearly harvest time, and the sky promised rain again. There was to be bad weather for the harvest of 1943, although the hay crop had been good, and prices for sheep and calving cows had been good all year.

Henry dived off the top board of the pool of silence that separated them.

'Why does God kill people?' he asked.

Ezra had longed for, yet dreaded, some question such as this.

He would never tell Henry about the funeral. She'd gone to Bristol, on her way to Plymouth, to visit his sister, who had married a bus driver, and to arrange for them to break their journey there on the way back. She'd gone shopping. Perhaps she'd been dreaming of his return. The driver hadn't stood a chance.

His sister and her husband had gone to Plymouth to meet him. Her husband had said, 'I'm only glad it wasn't my bus.' They hadn't been church-goers, and there had only been three mourners at the funeral. Ezra, his sister and her husband. The harassed vicar had referred to Ada as 'our dear departed brother'. They hadn't told anybody at Rowth Bridge, because they might have felt obliged to come, and there was no point, and it was best that Henry should be told by his father.

'He doesn't kill people,' said Ezra at last. 'He lets them get on wi' things, and if they happen to get theirselves killed, well, that's it. He looks at them, and if they've been good, he takes them to a better place.'

'Was my mam good?'

'Aye. Very good.'

'Has she gone to a better place?'

'Oh aye. Happen.'

'Where is it?'

'Up there. In heaven.'

Henry looked up at the scudding clouds. Sometimes the sky was blue and you could see that it was empty. He found it difficult to believe that his mother could be up there.

He felt a spot of rain.

'Is rain t' people up there crying?' he said.

'I don't reckon so,' said Ezra. 'They're happy up there.'

'Doesn't she miss us?'

'Oh aye. She misses us. But she hopes she'll see us one day. That's why it's so important for thee to be good.'

Ezra was quite proud of that, and also a little ashamed.

'Tha's a lucky lad to be wi' Uncle Frank and Auntie Kate,' said Ezra. 'I doubt this war'll go on while next Christmas or more. Owt can happen to me, tha knows. Look at it this road. Uncle Frank and Auntie Kate, they're thy parents now.'

'I don't reckon there is a God,' said Henry. 'If there was, he wouldn't have killed me mam.'

Henry exchanged a big mother and a small father for a small mother and a big father, and life went on. At first, the nights were the worst times. His bed, which had been a womb, had become a prison. Perhaps, when your mother had died, you could no longer go back to wombs.

One day, not long after it had happened, he saw Simon and Patrick Eckington waiting for him, on his road home from school, and his blood ran cold.

Patrick Eckington's freckled face was blazing. He thrust a brown paper parcel into Henry's hands.

'Peace offering,' he mumbled.

Henry took it as if he had been handed a bomb. He opened it cautiously. It was a book about birds and animals. On the fly-leaf, there was written, 'To Henry, from his friends Simon and Patrick.'

'Thanks,' said Henry.

'Are we friends again, then?' said Simon.

'Happen,' said Henry.

One day, Henry and Simon climbed Mickleborough. On the way up, they saw a peregrine falcon. At the top they knighted each other. First Henry knighted Sir Simon Eckington of that Ilk (they knew now it wasn't Ilkley). Then Sir Simon knighted Lord

Pratt of Mitherdale (Thurmarsh was forgotten) and explained that he had never wanted to be beastly to his chum, but had been forced to, owing to the threats of his elder brother, Sir Freckle de Fish-face, who had regarded Lord Pratt of Mitherdale as a filthy swot, and a silly twerp to boot. Sir Simon apologised. Lord Pratt accepted. They became friends again, a little awkwardly at first perhaps, never quite the same again perhaps, but friends.

Miss Candy gave Henry special attention without the other children realising it. Even Jane Lugg and Pam Yardley declared an unspoken, uneasy truce. Lorna Arrow made passes at him. (Can it be that our podgy hero is going to turn out to be attractive to women? Women are strange in these matters. We have seen on what dross the lovely Turnbull sisters threw themselves away.) Uncle Frank and Auntie Kate no longer felt that they had to hold back to avoid stealing a mother's love. Not that they spoilt him. Food wasn't too short up here. You had your own pig, and you used every bit bar t' squeak. But thrift was still the order of the day. Auntie Kate put a bottle of borax by the wash-basin to add to the water in order to use less soap (even if at the cost of using more borax, a perfectionist might complain). She washed plum and prune stones, cracked them and retrieved the kernels. She made buttons out of small circles of calico. She encouraged still greater effort in the saving of scrap metal and waste paper. (Luckily she never knew that Jackie kept all her love letters *and* bound them with elastic bands.) Nevertheless, they treated Henry now as if he was the son they had never had. Love and attention were not spared. And the welcoming wireless thundered on. Gwen Catley singing. Sandy Macpherson at the theatre organ. Felix Mendelssohn and his Hawaiian Serenaders. 'Hi, Gang' with Bebe Daniels, Vic Oliver and Ben Lyon. 'The Happidrome' returned with Ramsbottom, Enoch and Mr Lovejoy, and guests with magical names like Flotsam and Jetsam and Two Ton Tessie O' Shea. He loved them all, utterly without discrimination. He had loved his mother, but he was eight years old, and gradually it became like trying to commemorate a drowned woman by preserving a hollow in the ocean where she had plunged. Life closed slowly over Ada's head.

The United States were leading the allies' effort now. In the *Dandy* and the *Beano*, more stories had American settings. Big Eggo was as likely to catch a Jap as a Hun, and Musso the Wop had long since been put on-a-da scrapheap, his propaganda value exhausted. The allies' shipping losses were plummeting as the battle against the 'U' boats took a 'U' turn. It was permissible to talk about eventual victory. Men's minds turned to thoughts of the kind of world that victory would bring. Sir William Beveridge was planning for universal social security. Poverty and mass unemployment were to be things of the past. R. A. Butler was preparing his plans for equal opportunity of education for all. Was it too much to hope that this time men would get it right after the war?

' "I feel a bit of a frost, Mr Barrett – always catching colds and letting the office down," ' read Henry. He had developed the habit of reading aloud from the newspapers, to prove how proficient he had become. Today it was the turn of the adverts. 'What's "a bit of a frost", Auntie Kate?'

'Somebody who lets the side down,' said Auntie Kate. 'Like tha'll be if tha doesn't go to Leeds with Miss Candy.'

Miss Candy wanted to take Henry to Leeds on Saturday. He didn't want to go. It wasn't what schoolteachers did. There was bound to be a catch in it.

'Why does she want to take me to Leeds?' he asked.

'Happen she reckons thee,' said Auntie Kate.

He agreed to go. He could hardly refuse after they'd said he could go to Troutwick on Jim Wallington's bus *on his own*.

He loved every minute of the bus ride, on that morning of Saturday, November 14th 1943. Mist clung to the hillsides. A black-market pig squealed under the back seat.

Miss Candy met him off the bus. She was wearing a brand-new utility skirt and jacket. Her grey hair was piled up on top of her head in a fearsome Victory Roll.

The train was late. On the platform opposite, the adverts stated 'Dr Carrot, your winter protector', and 'The navigator swears. By Kolynos, of course.' Henry read them out loud. He read everything out loud.

He'd never been on a train before. He'd only watched them disappearing into the distance, while he waved at vanishing parents.

The smoke from the engine poured past the window. Sheep ran away across the sodden fields, as if this was the first train they had ever seen. People got on at every station, many of them in uniform. By the time they reached Leeds, the train was jam-packed. Miss Candy chatted easily about the things they saw, and he completely forgot that he hadn't wanted to come.

They went to the British Restaurant and had Woolton Pie. Then they caught a bus to Elland Road, to see Leeds play Bradford, in the Wartime League North. There was only a small crowd in the large, windswept stadium.

Henry enjoyed the game, which was the first football match he had ever seen. Miss Candy was rooting for her native Bradford. 'Other way!' she shouted angrily at the ref, and flat-capped men turned to look. There weren't many women present, and certainly none with booming, posh voices, three chins and a moustache. Henry wished Miss Candy wouldn't draw attention to herself.

Leeds took a well-deserved lead through HENRY and HINDLE. Miss Candy was a picture of dejection, and Henry, who had begun by wanting Leeds to win, because they had a player called Henry, who, to Henry's delight, scored, found himself switching his allegiance after Leeds had gone 2–0 up.

'Where's your white stick, ref?' shouted Miss Candy.

In the last twenty minutes, Bradford equalised through STABB and FARRELL, who netted from the penalty spot. In fact Bradford might have snatched victory, had Butterworth not kicked off the line with the goalkeeper beaten.

They went back into the City in a state of physical well-being. Henry was particularly thrilled, because although it had been a two-all draw, the team he had been supporting at the time had scored all four goals.

The train to Skipton was crowded, and slow, and there was nothing to look at. The blinds were drawn. A dim bulb gave a light too faint for reading.

At Skipton they caught a local train. The only other person in their compartment was an airman, who was fast asleep.

Henry had felt sure that there would be a catch. There was. It came now, on the rattling, blacked-out little local train.

'Henry?' said Miss Candy. 'I want you to tell me what people say about me."

'Tha what?' said Henry.

'The children say things about me. I must know what they say,' said Miss Candy.

Miss Candy had given him a nice day. She didn't tell him that she had delivered her part of an unspoken bargain, and now it was his turn. She didn't need to.

'I won't be upset,' she said. 'And I won't be angry. But I must know.'

'They say tha used to ride in a circus,' said Henry. 'They say tha loved a Yank, and he went home and left thee broken-hearted. They say. . .'

He hesitated.

'Go on,' breathed Miss Candy.

If only the airman would wake up. But he snored deeply, as if to reassure them that it was safe to continue.

'They say tha drinks a bottle of a gin a day,' said Henry. 'They say tha has a pet wolf. They say. . .' He hesitated.

'Go on,' breathed Miss Candy.

'They say tha's got a special tube so tha never has to go to t' lav.'

'Go on,' breathed Miss Candy.

'They say tha used to be a stripper in a club in Wakefield,' said Henry.

'Really?' said Miss Candy, amazed. 'It must have been the masochists' club.'

'Tha what?'

'Never mind. Go on.'

'They say. . .'

'Go on. I won't be cross.'

'They say tha has great tufts of hair hanging down from thy nipples.'

There was silence. The train rattled on. The airman groaned and his head lolled.

'What an amazing woman I must be,' said Miss Candy.

Christmas came and went. Strikes were frequent. The British and Americans landed at Anzio. In the Far East the war was fierce.

The Rowth Bridge knitting circle knitted its two thousandth woollen garment. Every Sunday evening, Henry listened to 'Variety Band Box'. Then Albert Sandler and the Palm Court Orchestra played 'a programme of the kind of music heard in the Palm Court of your favourite hotel in the days before the war' and Henry, who had never been in the Palm Court of any hotel before the war, listened, because it was there.

One day, towards the end of May, 1944, he received a letter from his father, who was now in. . .and hoping that by Christmas he would be in. . .he was well, and he loved Henry very much. And Henry realised, with a shock, that the letter had come as a shock. He was happy here. Uncle Frank and Auntie Kate were his parents now. There wasn't any room for his father. And then he felt guilty about that, because he knew that you were supposed to love your father. That afternoon, after school, he saw one of the five-year-old boys crying. His name was Sidney Mold. He came from Five Houses, which was a tiny hamlet of six houses on the Troutwick road. He had to walk three miles on his own, and the previous day Simon Eckington had offered to escort him, but half-way home, Simon Eckington had dug his nails into him viciously. Henry sympathised. In fact he was shocked that his friend Simon could have done that. He offered to escort Sidney Mold home in good faith, but half-way to Five Houses he dug his nails into him viciously and made him cry.

In school the next day, Henry wondered if Miss Candy could see what he had done, and he felt guilty. He looked at Simon and felt shocked by Simon's cruelty more than by his own, and he wondered if Simon was thinking the same. He wandered home slowly. The weather was humid. He felt tired and nasty.

It is easier to cope with the shame of yesterday than with the shame of years past. Henry suddenly recalled the last time he had ever seen his mother. The last words he had ever said to her were, 'It's got ten wheels. Two little 'uns and three big 'uns on each side.' He could cope with the guilt of knowing that he had dug his nails into Sidney Mold and probably would again, much as he didn't want to. He couldn't cope with the guilt of his neglect of his mother.

He trudged towards the head of the valley, nine years and two months old, his chubby white legs still in short trousers, his shoes scuffed, his shirt grubby and hanging outside his trousers, a tiny, leaden figure in the great, natural bowl of Upper Mitherdale, and he vowed that from now on his heart would be a shrine for his mother, and he would be a loving son to his father, for his mother's sake.

Then he remembered that Uncle Frank and Auntie Kate regarded him as their son now. They wanted him to stay with them. He wanted to stay with them. He wanted to take over Low Farm, when Uncle Frank retired. He wanted to keep the shorthorn cattle, the Dales pony, Billy the half-wit, and other endangered species.

Where did that leave his father?

Had Henry not been in such a state, he might have made a better show of resisting Lorna Arrow. She was sitting on the dry-stone wall, swinging her long, thin legs, smiling her toothy smile.

She led him to one of the field barns, on Kit Orris's farm, at the back of the village. It was full of animal fodder. It smelt steamy and warm.

One of the best-known facts of human life was that girls were useless and soppy, yet Henry liked being with Lorna Arrow. He liked her husky voice, with the slight lisp. It made him tingle strangely. Why? He knew that grown-ups liked women. He knew that he was advanced at all his school subjects. Who could blame him, during the Lorna Arrow summer, if he deduced that the explanation was that he was advanced for his years?

The allies landed in northern France. The weather was wet, and Uncle Frank had great difficulty in gathering his hay. In the school sports Henry came second from last in the Sack Race, thus exceeding his achievements in the Hundred Yards, the Four-Forty, the Egg and Spoon Race, the High Jump, the Three-legged Race and the Potato Race. Yet Lorna Arrow did not desert him. He kept her apart from Simon. Some days were Simon days. Others were Lorna days. On Lorna days, they sometimes went to the field barn and he read her the comics. She didn't like reading. It made him feel good to read them, because he read well. Her favourites were Desperate Dan, Our Gang and Merry Marvo and his Magic Cigar. She laid her fair, toothy head against his chest, and he tingled as he read the exploits of Zogg, who turned Nick

86

Turner into the Headmaster of his Old School!, and of Wun Tun Joe, whose bones were so heavy that he weighed a ton. ' "Come here, Chink," snapped the bully,' he read. ' "No savvy," chirped Wun Ton Joe.'

'Let's be "Our Gang",' lisped Lorna.

'Not now,' sighed Henry.

'Do the Nigs,' commanded Lorna.

'I can't. I'm fair jiggered up,' protested Henry.

Lorna loved to enact the adventures of 'Our Gang'. She particularly liked Henry's accent when he portrayed Buckwheat and Billy, the darkies.

'Which does tha prefer – greengages or eggs?' queried Lorna.

'Both,' he responded.

'Tha can have a fried greengage for breakfast, then,' she exclaimed.

Once she brought him two Woodbines and insisted that he pretend to be Merry Marvo and his Magic Cigar, but he turned out to be Puking Pratt and his Soggy Ciggy.

When they ran out of comics, she made him read the All-Bran adverts. They were in comic strip form, featuring characters like Obstinate Oliver and Mary, Mary Not Contrary.

'Which would tha prefer? Seven hundred thousand tons of All-Bran, or a castle with six gold doors?' she said.

'Which would tha prefer? A smack in t' gob or a kick up t' arse-end?' said Henry.

She went home crying. It was all for the best. The boys were right. Girls were useless. So why did he apologise and take her out again?

'Which does tha prefer?' she said. 'Pencils or the Walls of Jericho?'

'Pencils,' he said at random. 'I don't rate t' Walls of Jericho, me.'

'Which would tha prefer?' she said. 'Come home to tea or a yacht?'

'A yacht,' he said.

Lorna's father came in late, and they started tea without him.

'Ee, I'm right twined,' he said grumpily, when he came in. 'I'm as twined as me arse.'

'Wash thy mouth out with soap and water,' said Lorna's mother.

'Which would tha prefer?' said Lorna. 'Two hundred bars of soap or a chest of sunken treasure?'

'Don't be silly, Lorna,' said Lorna's mother.

She *was* silly. Henry wished he wasn't there. But the next day, when he was with Simon, who was sensible, he longed to hear Lorna's husky, toothy lisp.

The summer slipped past. Paris was liberated. Henry wasn't. The weather was wet. Uncle Frank had the greatest difficulty in cutting his oats.

Fiona came over with her husband and his artificial leg. There was an element of the artificial about her legs, too. She had responded to the unavailability of silk stockings by using sun-tan lotion to give her legs the appearance of being stockinged, and had added the seams with eyebrow pencil. This was considered outrageously fast in Skipton banking circles, but then Fiona Brassingthwaite, née Turnbull, was known to be a law unto herself.

School resumed. Miss Candy rustled a lot. Her knickers were made of defective parachute silk. There was a war on. Miss Candy sometimes gave Henry glinting, conspiratorial looks. They embarrassed him less than he expected. The nit lady came. Lorna Arrow had nits. Henry vowed never again ever to have anything more to do with girls again ever.

The very next Sunday he ran across Belinda Boyce-Uppingham. She was riding, picking her way daintily through the little ash wood by the river. Henry was running home, to listen to a spelling bee between Post Office Workers and Red Cross Workers. He frightened her pony. The pony reared. Belinda Boyce-Uppingham, the great love of his life, because of whom all other loves were undergone, was deposited on the soggy, soggy ground.

He rushed forward to help her.

'Art tha all right?' he said.

She picked herself up and tested her limbs. Her face was scarlet with fury

'No thanks to you, you. . .you bloody oik,' she said.

The wet weather continued. Uncle Frank's oats lay sodden in the fields, till well into November. The newspaper adverts began to look forward to a time of returning plenty. 'After victory, our familiar packages will re-appear in all parts of the country,' said Parkinsons' Old-Fashioned Humbugs. 'When they have finished their vital war service, Dagenite and Perdrix batteries will again be available to all,' promised Dagenite and Perdrix batteries. 'It's in the shops again! Reckitt's Blue!' thundered Reckitt's Blue.

If Reckitt's Blue was back, could peace be far behind?

But first there was the bombing of Dresden. Twenty-five thousand people were killed in one night, in a war that had already been virtually won.

Tuesday, May 9th and Wednesday, May 10th, 1945, were declared public holidays. Hitler was dead. Germany had surrendered. Union Jacks fluttered from big house and humble cottage alike. There was a victory peal on the bells of Rowth Bridge Church.

In Skipton there was dancing in the streets, to music relayed by loudspeakers. In Rowth Bridge Parish Hall, a dance was hastily laid on. It was widely agreed that a new piano was one of the first priorities of peace.

The children lit many bonfires. Henry ran around uselessly in great excitement.

Forty people, many of them from as far away as Troutwick, climbed Mickleborough and lit a victory beacon.

Uncle Frank danced with Auntie Kate. Jackie, the land-girl, danced with anybody and everybody. Even Jane Lugg, Pam Yardley and Lorna Arrow bore no grudges that night.

Pools of light. Tinkling of a bad piano. Chunter of assembled Luggs in the Three Horseshoes. Bonfires on all sides, and a ghostly beacon roaring in the wind among the Mickleborough clouds. It was not entirely unrestrained. There was still war in the Far East. People had seen the end of a war to end all wars before. People were tired. But it was victory, and Rowth Bridge did its best. The little village celebrated with pools of light and noise in the dark, silent dale.

Uncle Frank died peacefully in his sleep. It was a dreadful shock for Auntie Kate, of course, but everyone said what a wonderful way it was for Uncle Frank to go. At peace, in victory.

5 What About the Crispy Bacon We Used to Get Before the War?

Auntie Kate insisted on coming with him, although she had problems enough in keeping the farm going until the sale went through.

A Labour government had been elected. The Cold War had begun. Britain had given her blessing to the dropping of atomic bombs on Hiroshima and Nagasaki. Henry was going back to Thurmarsh.

'I want to stay here, Auntie Kate,' he'd said.

'It's not possible, Henry,' she'd told him. 'The farm's sold. I'm going to live wi' Fiona in Skipton. It's not possible.'

He'd done most of his crying at night.

Simon Eckington came on the bus with them. Mrs Eckington and Patrick were there to wave goodbye. So was Billy, the half-wit, who waved furiously, exaggeratedly. Henry said, 'I hope there's lots of eggs tomorrow, Billy,' and Billy said, 'Nay, t' hens know tha's going. T' hens like thee.'

As Henry clattered out of the village, three girls sat on the hump-backed bridge. They were Jane Lugg, Lorna Arrow and Pam Yardley, whose father had not yet been demobbed. Henry waved. They stuck their tongues out.

And so Henry Pratt, liked by hens, hated by girls, rode out of hill-womb and began the long journey back to world-cobble. His heart was heavy. They rattled through Five Houses. He was glad there was no sign of Sidney Mold.

Miss Candy was at Troutwick Station to see him off. She was fifty-eight now, and even the tuft on her middle chin had gone grey. Miss Forrest had decided to put up with her till she was sixty, for the sake of her feelings.

'What's Miss Candy doing here?' Simon said.

'I don't know,' said Henry. 'She's probably meeting a friend.'

'Miss Candy hasn't got friends,' said Simon.

The engine screeched to a halt. Henry didn't care how many wheels it had.

He hated farewells, and there seemed to be so many of them. He leant out of the window, smiling inanely.

Henry and Simon, loquacious explorers, vivacious naturalists, enthusiastic pursuers of Huns, were unable to think of a single thing to say to each other.

Miss Candy came to the rescue.

'Clemmie and Winnie send their love,' she said.

'Clemmie and Winnie?' said Henry.

'My seals,' said Miss Candy. 'I train them for circuses, you know.'

They waved until they were so far away that he couldn't see Miss Candy's moustache.

On the train, he closed his eyes and willed it that when he opened them it would be a nightmare and he'd still be in Rowth Bridge. He opened them to see telegraph poles flashing by on a wet July day, traffic on a main road, and the last cows and sheep he would see for many a moon.

They changed trains at Leeds. As the train slipped out of City Station, Auntie Kate said, 'Tha's all he's got now. He's had five years of fighting. He'll miss our Ada so it hurts.'

'Does tha miss Uncle Frank so it hurts?' he said, as they passed a wet, forlorn Elland Road.

'Happen I do,' said Auntie Kate.

'That's Elland Road,' said Henry. 'Miss Candy took me there. She shouted at t' ref.'

'Miss Candy is a strange woman,' said Auntie Kate.

'Does tha think Uncle Frank's up in heaven?' said Henry.

'If any man deserves it, he does,' said Auntie Kate with a sigh.

'He might meet me mam.'

He didn't tell her his private theory. There was no God. There was a heaven and there was a hell, but they were on this earth. Heaven was Low Farm, Rowth Bridge, Upper Mitherdale. Hell was number 23 Paradise Lane, Thurmarsh.

His dad was at the station to meet them. They hadn't expected

91

him to look so gaunt and ill, his demob suit hanging off him like wool on a dying sheep. They hadn't realised that his swift demob had been on medical grounds. They hadn't expected that he would only have one eye.

'Grand snoek, this.'

'I don't like snoek, Dad.'

'Well tha'll have to lump it. There's a war on.'

'There isn't, Dad. It's over.'

'Tha wouldn't think so, would tha? No food. No clothes. No nowt. I mean, did we win or am I deluded?'

'We won, Dad.'

'I'm just slipping out to t' Navigation for a bevvy,' said Ezra. 'Will tha be all right?'

'Course I will. I'm norra kid. I'm ten.'

'I'll not be long.'

Please be long, because you don't belong and I don't belong, so be long, thought Henry. He had a lot of thoughts nowadays that nobody knew about. It was one of the best things about being a human being.

When his dad was in, Henry often went out. He'd enjoyed wandering around in Upper Mitherdale, in fact it had been a way of life. It was different here. The River Rundle was a sewer, compared to the Mither. The Rundle and Gadd Navigation was only marginally better. The little cobbled streets were mean and nasty. He hated the shared lav in the yard. He hated wiping his backside on squared-off bits of *Reynolds News*. He only liked two things in this environment – the trains and the trams. It was nice to stand on the footbridge, immediately over the trains, so that the smoke roared up behind you and then suddenly it stopped, and a moment later it roared up in front of you.

The best thing about the trams was that they led into Thurmarsh Town Centre, and there was a public library there. Auntie Kate had told him about the libraries they had in the towns, full of proper books, not comics. Just before he left Rowth Bridge, he'd read a Sexton Blake book which was ninety pages long! Everyone had been amazed.

Ezra gave him fourpence a week pocket-money. He spent it all on tram fares, to get books. The library was the only thing in Thurmarsh that was better than the worst thing in Rowth Bridge, which was its girls. There were girls in Thurmarsh too, but you ignored them.

His reading was wide and various. He read *Biggles Flies North*, *Biggles Flies South*, *Biggles Flies East*, *Biggles Flies West*, *Biggles Flies In*, *Biggles Flies Out* and *Biggles Sweeps The Desert*. They were written by Captain W. E. Johns, whose main virtue was that he was the greatest writer who ever lived. He had created four magnificent characters, Biggles, Algy, Ginger and Bertie, who defeated cruel Germans, wily orientals, unshaven dagoes and pock-marked mulattos in burning deserts, icy mountains, crocodile-infested swamps and spider-infested jungles, and never a woman in sight. But he read other books as well. He read *Gimlet Flies North*, *Gimlet Flies South*, *Gimlet Flies East* and *Gimlet Flies West*. Gimlet books were also written by Captain W. E. Johns and were better than everything in the world except Biggles books. Once he brought home a book called *Hamlet – A Shortened Version*, thinking it was Gimlet. It was rubbish, probably because it wasn't written by Captain W. E. Johns.

That evening, he found it difficult to concentrate. In the morning, he was starting at Brunswick Road Elementary School. Eager anticipation was not coursing through his veins. Even the works of Captain W. E. Johns couldn't take him away from his worries. If only they had a wireless.

Ezra returned, a little unsteady on his feet.

'Sorry,' he said. 'I were detained.'

'Why haven't we gorra wireless?' said Henry.

'We had one before t' war,' said Ezra. 'It's disappeared into thin air.'

'Only I were thinking,' said Henry. 'I wouldn't be that worried if tha stayed a bit longer at t' Navigation, if we had a wireless.'

High walls noise jostle confusion shouting bleak corridor smell stale greens green paint where to go tidal wave big room hubbub who are you Henry Pratt Henry Pratt? Henry Pratt ah! new boy returning evacuee no! lived with relations same thing how old ten ah! must be Mr Gibbins' class over there come with me sit here hubbub yell silence shuffling feet cough cough silence sing hymn sit let us pray oh God we thank thee for another term like hell we do notices shortages breakages cough cough stand shuffle off corridor smell stale greens green paint classroom big high cold dark damp dank clatter boys sitting don't know where to go stand small shy forlorn who are you?

He walked forward slowly towards the teacher's desk. Mr Gibbins was six foot four and entirely bald. How old? Age didn't come into it. He was Mr Gibbins, a fixture, an ageless chrome-dome.

'Who are you?' he repeated.

'Henry,' said Henry, determined that there should be no Ezra nonsense here.

'Henry what?'

'Henry Pratt.'

There was some laughter.

'Henry Pratt what?'

'Just Henry Pratt.'

Thirty-three white boys and one black boy hung breathless on the exchange.

'Are you new to this school?'

'Aye.'

'At your last school, if your teacher had said to you, "What's your name?" what would you have said?'

'Ezra.'

It came out before he could stop it.

'What?????'

'Ezra.'

'I thought your name was Henry Pratt.'

'Aye, but there was another Henry there, and they couldn't have two Henrys, so they called me Ezra.'

'I see. Now, Pratt, when you addressed your teacher, did you use a little word as a mark of respect to the teacher?'

'Oh aye.'

'Well we believe in respect for authority here at Brunswick Road, Pratt, so I'd like you to use that same word to me. Do you understand?'

'Oh aye.'

'Oh aye *what?*'

Henry shrugged, then did what he was told.

'Oh aye, miss,' he said.

There was a roar of laughter. He *hated* it when people laughed at him.

That evening, when Henry got home, he found that Ezra had bought a wireless.

The nights drew in. The *Beano* exhorted, 'We still need salvage, ton by ton – even though the war is won,' but Henry didn't read the *Beano* any more.

The only thing there was plenty of was shortages. Even professional men went to work in odd trousers and jackets! Miners threatened to strike due to a shortage of cigarettes. Four tons of dried-fruit slab cake were sent from Capetown. A third of all street lights were switched off. Britain had pawned herself, and there would be hard bargaining before America allowed her to redeem the goods.

The premises of Binks and Madeley Ltd had been destroyed in the Sheffield blitz, and Ezra was forced to swallow his pride, and take work making pocket-knives. The job didn't last, and he was able to go to the Navigation at dinner time as well.

Uncle Teddy sent Ezra the occasional sum of conscience money, not knowing that Auntie Doris, not knowing that he was sending conscience money, was also sending conscience money. Cousin Hilda, not knowing that either Uncle Teddy or Auntie Doris were sending conscience money, was also sending conscience money, in lieu of taking a closer interest in what was going on. Her Mother, over at Leonard's, had gone a bit funny, and ignored them completely. Ezra's father was dying, and his mother had her hands full making sure that love and dignity were at the bedside. Ezra made sure that Henry had enough to eat and went to school looking no less presentable than the other children. Ezra told the customers at the Navigation that Cousin Hilda was looking after the boy. The neighbours at number 25 were old and deaf. At number 21 she was on the game. There was nobody to object. Nobody knew that Henry spent evening after evening on his own, except Henry and Ezra, and neither of them would tell.

One evening, returning from the pub a little earlier than usual, and finding his son still up, Ezra told him that he had applied for a job at the steelworks that day.

'They said, "Sorry. No vacancies." Them were their exact words. I said, "Listen. Think on this. I spent six years fighting against the perils of Hitler's Reich. I lost an eye. If I hadn't fought, it wouldn't be Crapp, Hawser and Kettlewell. It'd be Krupp, Kaiser and bloody Goebbels." He said, "That's as may be, but I can't sack lads as have worked for me throughout t' duration." He said, "Tha wouldn't be up to t' work. Tha's not suited. Tha's a cutler." I said, "Get me Crapp. Fetch me Hawser. I want to speak to Mr Kettlewell hisself." '

'Did he fetch them, dad?'

'Did he hell as like. He told me to piss off.'

One Saturday, Henry borrowed four books from the library and settled down for a momentous weekend's reading. The four books were, as it chanced, all by Captain W. E. Johns. They were called *Worrals Flies North*, *Worrals Flies South*, *Worrals Flies East* and *Worrals Flies West*. He had read the complete canon of Biggles and Gimlet. Now for Worrals. He didn't start the books on the tram. He wouldn't waste them. He would wait till after tea.

At last tea was finished, and Ezra popped down to the Navigation for 'a quick bevvy'.

He opened the front page of the first book. Now for a wallow.

The dreadful truth hit him almost immediately. Worrals was a girl. Captain W. E. Johns, the greatest writer in the history of the universe, wrote books about girls.

He turned to the wireless, that faithful friend who had never let him down.

There was a roar of traffic. An old cockney woman shouted, 'Violets. Lovely violets.' The traffic stopped, and the announcer said, 'Once again we stop the mighty roar of London's traffic, and from the great crowds we bring to the microphone some of the interesting people who are "In Town Tonight".'

He found none of them interesting. He bitterly resented their good humour, their idle metropolitan and transatlantic chatter.

Worrals was a girl, the weekend stretched before him like a desert, and still they prattled on.

He was alone. He had no friends. He was in a rat-infested back-to-back terrace which was steadily falling to pieces. It all swept over him. And the little voice which told him that he must fight piped up again. You always have to fight, it said. Stop for even five minutes and you'll go under.

By gow, he would fight.

He got out a notebook, and pencil, and settled at the table. He'd show the world. He'd show Captain W. E. Johns. There'd be no girls in his books.

'Chapter One,' he wrote.

Inspiration failed him at this point in his endeavours. He thought he knew why. He must plan his book.

He decided to start by writing down the titles of his books. Then he would decide which one to write first, and begin.

Half an hour later, when Cousin Hilda, alias the sniffer, found him, he had listed six titles in his notebook.

1. *Pratt Flies North.*
2. *Pratt Flies South.*
3. *Pratt Flies East.*
4. *Pratt Flies West.*
5. *Pratt Sweeps the Desert.*
6. *What Is Happiness?*

Cousin Hilda looked round the room and sniffed.

'Where's our Ezra?' she said. 'He's never gone down the pub and left you on your own!'

She poured a reservoir of disapproval into the word 'pub'.

'He's gone for a walk,' said Henry. 'He likes walking.'

'Does he often leave you alone?'

'Well, not for long.'

'Does he ever go to the pub and leave you alone?'

He sensed that a total denial might not carry conviction.

'He might go for a quick bevvy every now and then,' he said.

Cousin Hilda sniffed.

She sat at the table and leant forward to talk earnestly to Henry.

'Does he feed you all right?' she said.

'Oh aye,' said Henry. 'We had whale today. I like whale.'

'Is he. . .does he treat you all right?'

'Course he does. He's me dad.'

'Aye, I know, but. . .war's a terrible thing, Henry. It upsets people. It upsets their nerves. Sometimes, people go. . .well, a bit funny. It's not their fault, so if they did go a bit funny, there wouldn't be any cause not to tell anybody about it, would there?'

'No, Cousin Hilda.

'Is he happy?'

Henry considered the question. It wasn't the sort of thing you normally wondered about, in connection with your father.

'I don't think he likes not having a job,' he said.

'Does his having one eye upset you?' said Cousin Hilda.

'No. They've made a right good job of t' false one,' said Henry.

He hoped she wouldn't stay too long. His dad was often unsteady when he got home.

'It's right nice of thee to call,' he said, 'but I've gorrus homework to do.'

'Is that your homework?' said Cousin Hilda, taking the notebook before he could stop her.

She read his list of titles.

'Homework?' she said.

'We've gorra write a book,' he said. 'I'm planning me titles.'

'Daydreams,' said Cousin Hilda. 'Nay, lad.'

'Daydreams?' he said.

'They're all about you,' she said.

'That isn't me,' he said. 'That's me dad.'

It was easy, telling lies, once you got into the swing of it.

Cousin Hilda handed him the notebook.

'You don't loop your pees right,' she said. It was her way of telling him that all the other letters were perfectly formed, but if she said it straight out, it might spoil him.

'I'm going to set to,' she said. 'The whole place is in a right pickle. I don't reckon it's seen a duster since VJ day.'

Cousin Hilda took a square of old pyjamas from under the sink, examined it, sniffed, and went to the door to give it a good shake. Then she went upstairs.

Henry had to pretend to be continuing with his homework.

'Ezra Pratt, known to all his friends as Prattles, stood on the

98

steps of the Royal Aero Club,' he began.

Every now and then he could hear her exclaiming with disgust, as she found more dirt.

Ten minutes later Ezra returned, slamming the door.

'Cousin Hilda's upstairs,' said Henry hastily.

'What's she doing here?' said Ezra.

'Dusting.'

Ezra grimaced.

'Is that you, Ezra?' shouted Cousin Hilda.

'Aye.'

'I told her tha's been for a walk,' said Henry quickly.

'What? Oh. Oh aye.'

Ezra looked at his son in astonishment.

Cousin Hilda came downstairs, carrying the pyjama duster as if it were a maggoty rat.

'I just went for a spot of air,' said Ezra.

'Oh aye?' said Cousin Hilda. 'Three times round t' bar of t' Navigation?'

'Just o'er t' river,' said Ezra. 'Just round t' roads.'

He sat in the rocking chair. It was his place as of right.

'That rag rug's coming unravelled,' said Cousin Hilda. 'It's a pig-sty. I could write my name in t' dust on your wardrobe.'

Henry grinned, but only internally. His sudden talent for dissembling surprised him. He found it exhilarating.

What he was grinning at was the thought of Cousin Hilda writing in dust. He imagined her writing, 'I'm filthy. Clean me,' in the dirt on Uncle Teddy's car.

'Well done, lad,' Ezra said, when Cousin Hilda had gone. 'Well done. She'd have torn t' bollocks off me if she'd known I'd gone to t' Navigation.'

Only a few months ago, at Rowth Bridge, Henry would have been astonished to have been praised by an adult for telling a lie. But Rowth Bridge seemed centuries ago.

'It's lucky tha came back early,' he said.

His dad snorted, rocked slowly in his chair, and began the longest speech he ever made in his life. Henry sat at the table, his notebook open, his pencil poised, as if he was taking the minutes of the meeting, although in fact he wrote nothing down.

'Aye, well,' said Ezra. 'It seems I'm not welcome at t' Navigation any more. I knew it spelt trouble when I saw t' new name over t' door. Cecil E. Jenkinson. I never trusted that E. It's t' end of an era, I thought. Still, fair dos, give him a chance, I thought. So I did. I gave him a chance. He says to me tonight, he says, "I'm not banning thee. Come here from time to time, fair enough. But tha's here all night every night." Well, I were flambergasted. I said, "So what? Tha's open, i'n't tha? I'm entitled." "Tha's not entitled wi'out I say so," he said. "I'm entitled to refuse to serve anybody." "So what's tha saying, then, Cecil?" I said. "I can but I can't, is that it?" "It's me other patrons," he said. "They don't see eye to eye wi' thee." "Aye," I said, "I knew it were me eye. I lost that eye so they could be free to come into t' pub," I said. "Aye," he said, "I agree, bur it's nowt to do wi' t' eye." He looked embarrassed. I'll gi'e 'im that. "Patrons don't like tha going on about t' war," he said. "T' war's over." "Aye," I said, "because I bloody fought it. That's why it's over. Don't give me other patrons," I said. "It's thee. Tha's never liked me." That struck home, cos he hasn't. And I'll tell thee why. Cos I don't like what he's done to t' pub, and he knows it. Well, I didn't fight Hitler for five years so that he could put bright-green upholstery in t' snug. "Tha's never liked me," I said. "I go away for five years and what happens? My place in t' dominoes team gets taken. It's a bloody disgrace." "They couldn't play a man short for five years," he said. "Fair enough, Cecil," I said. "Point taken, Cecil," I said. "Bur I'm back now. Darts, fair enough. I'm a shadow of me former self wi' one eye. But not dominoes. I played Sid Lowson last night," I said. "I won six games end-away." "Aye," he said, "but I can't split up a winning combination." Sid Lowson, to his eternal credit, offered to stand down. I refused. "Thanks, Sid," I said. "Much appreciated, but no. I don't want to be the cause célèbre of a domino crisis. I couldn't never represent this establishment again. There's a clash of personalities, and that's all there is to it." But I never thought I'd be banned from t' pub. Because that's whar I am. Wharever he says. Banned. Well, I can't go in there and say, "It's all right, Cecil. I'm only staying twenty minutes and I won't mention t' war once." Can I? Course I can't.'

They sat in silence for a moment, a pale, emaciated embittered wreck with a glass eye and a pale, podgy, ten-year-old boy with a notebook and a pencil.

'Sorry,' said Ezra. 'I didn't mean to burden thee wi' my problems.'

They spent Christmas Day at Cousin Hilda's. Auntie Doris said, 'Next year you must come to us. We insist.'

Cousin Hilda lived at number 66 Park View Road, Thurmarsh. It was a stone, semi-detached Victorian house on the town side of the Alderman Chandler Memorial Park. It had a bay window on the ground floor. Cousin Hilda owned the house. She had been a paid companion to a rich, autocratic, invalid lady. The family had disapproved of her dancing to this lady's sour tune. The family disapproved even more when the lady died at Deauville and left Cousin Hilda several thousand pounds, a vast sum in those days, and not to be sniffed at even by Cousin Hilda.

Into her modest, but pleasantly situated house, Cousin Hilda crammed four paying guests. They paid one pound ten shillings a week for a bed-sitting room, breakfast, tea, supper and laundry. On Sundays they had dinner instead of tea. Cousin Hilda referred to them as 'my businessmen'. They kept her occupied and solvent.

One of Cousin Hilda's 'businessmen' was present that Christmas Day. He was Len Arrowsmith, a French polisher, and he believed in reincarnation. He had no family living, in recognisable form, although every holiday he went to see a giraffe in Chester Zoo. Also present was Cousin Hilda's friend.

Cousin Hilda's living quarters were in the basement, which received only a poor ration of daylight. They ate their Christmas dinner around a large, square table in a corner of the room, with bench seats along two sides. This was where the 'businessmen' ate. A little blue-tiled stove, with a front of four panes of blue glass, shone merrily. It was set in a blue-tiled fireplace. There were two armchairs, which sagged badly, and a dresser, on which there were several plates. All the plates were blue. Blue was Cousin Hilda's favourite colour, being the colour of God, in her opinion.

At the back of this room there was a small, crowded scullery where Cousin Hilda slaved all day, cooking, ironing, washing clothes in a huge tub, with liberal usage of Reckitt's Blue, and rinsing them through a formidable mangle.

Henry missed Rowth Bridge again that day. Not that Cousin Hilda didn't do her best. They had roast chicken with all the trimmings, and Christmas pudding to follow. Henry got the threepenny bit. In Henry's cracker there was a joke, which ran 'What kind of ant waits on people? An attend-ant.' Len Arrowsmith said that that was a good one. His dad was on his best behaviour. They listened to a programme that linked up English-speaking people right round the world. Then came the King's speech. They stood up for the national anthem. Len Arrowsmith hummed it tunelessly.

Cousin Hilda's friend's left stocking developed a ladder which grew slowly longer as the day darkened.

They went for a short walk in the Alderman Chandler Memorial Park. The slit trenches remained. Three or four hardy children were playing on the swings and roundabouts, but the little cluster of animal and bird cages was empty. The glass in the old men's shelter had been shattered in the Blitz, and had still not been replaced. They went back to Cousin Hilda's and had tea and Christmas cake and then they played a card game in which you started with the sevens and had to go up to as far as the kings and down as far as the aces. Cousin Hilda's friend couldn't quite get the hang of it, but Len Arrowsmith revealed an unsuspected ruthless streak. His father was on his best behaviour. When Cousin Hilda's friend reached up for her handkerchief, which she kept in her knickers, Henry looked up her thigh to see how far the ladder had got.

'All over till next year,' said Cousin Hilda as they left.

Thank goodness, thought Henry.

1946 began quietly. More footwear was promised soon for civilians. In the January clearance sales, boys' school shirts were offered at 2/1d by the Thurmarsh and Rawlaston Cooperative Society. Gents' merino vests and trunks were 2/- and half a coupon. There were plans to stamp children's footwear to prevent parents pawning it, and complaints from housewives about the illogicality of aprons being on coupons when floor mops weren't.

Henry spent the time quietly with his friends. He had many friends. He particularly liked the boy detectives, Norman and Henry Bones, on 'Children's Hour', and there was an exciting serial called 'The Gay Dolphin Adventure' by Malcolm Saville. 'Nature Parliament' had begun, with Derek McCullough, Peter Scott and L. Hugh Newman. He loved this, and 'A Visit to Cowleaze Farm', although they both opened up a vein of painful nostalgia. But he would listen to anything. When they heard that Ezra's father had died, Henry was in the middle of a talk on squash rackets, with recorded illustrations, by F. N. S. Creek. In the evenings he liked boxing, comedy and adventure. He listened spell-bound to Arthur Dancha of Bethnal Green v Omar Kouidri of Paris. He laughed at 'Merry-Go-Round' from Waterlogged Spa, Sinking-in-the-Ooze, at 'Music Hall' with Nat Mills and Bobbie, who said, 'Well let's get on with it' and everybody laughed. They all had their catch phrases. Leon Cortez said, 'There was this 'ere geyser Caesar,' and everybody laughed. It seemed a shame to Henry to laugh at Shakespeare, just because he was so much worse a writer than Captain W. E. Johns.

He thrilled to Paul Temple and to 'Appointment with Fear'. These were his friends. He had no real-life friends.

Then, one dark, dismal, dank outside as well as in, electric-lit morning in early February, an incident occurred in Mr Gibbins' class which was to have a profound effect on Henry's social life.

Although Brunswick Road Elementary School had become Brunswick Road Primary School, it remained a stone, Victorian fortress, with high Dutch-style gables, a steep-pitched roof and green guttering. The walls and windows were high. There were three doors, for boys, girls and mixed infants. Beyond the infant level, boys and girls were still totally segregated.

Mr Gibbins' classroom had bare walls with peeling plaster. There wasn't a lot of fungus. The desks were fixed to the floor by iron legs, and the seats were benches fixed to the desks by iron arms. Sharp corners abounded. On each desk there was an ink-well.

Absentees were Chadwick (cold), Erpingham (I forget), Lewis (flu), Barton (death of grandmother – genuine) and Pilling (death of grandmother – false – got idea from Barton).

Among those present were Mr Gibbins, Henry, Tommy
Marsden, Martin Hammond, Ian Lowson (son of the peripheral
Sid) and Chalky White, the West Indian.

They took a test each week, and changed places according to
their results, moving to the front if bad, and to the back if good.
Henry had risen rapidly to the back of the class.

Mr Gibbins caned them on the hand if they didn't get seven out
of ten for mental arithmetic, but the biggest bee in his bonnet was
English grammar.

'Today,' he announced, 'we'll deal with subjects and objects.
You might say that the subject of the lesson is subjects and
objects, and the object is to cram as much knowledge into your
thick skulls as possible.'

To be honest, the class did not look as if they would be very
likely to say that.

'Joking apart,' said Mr Gibbins, to their surprise, 'give me a
sentence, Marsden.'

'Six months,' said Tommy Marsden from the front row.

'Six months what, Marsden?'

'Six months for nicking lead off the church roof.'

'Come here, Marsden.'

'Yes, sir.'

Tommy Marsden went forward and held out his hand. Mr
Gibbins smacked it three times with the cane.

'Let that be a warning to you all,' said Mr Gibbins. 'Give me a
sentence, Cuffley.'

Norbert Cuffley, a goody but not a genius, adorned the second
row from the back.

'The teacher asked me to give him a sentence, sir,' he said.

'Excellent, Cuffley, if not wildly imaginative.' Mr Gibbins
scraped the sentence agonisingly onto the blackboard. 'Now,
what is the subject of the sentence, Pratt?'

'You asking Cuffley to give you a sentence, sir.'

'No. I mean, yes, that is the subject in the sense of what it's
about. I meant, "What is the subject in the grammatical sense?"
What word in the sentence fulfils the role that we call the subject?
Milner?'

'Me, sir?'

'Yes, you. That's why I said Milner, Milner.'

'No, sir. I meant "me". "The teacher asked me." That "me", sir.'

'Why do you say that, Milner?'

A loud fart rent the air. Everybody laughed, except Cuffley.

'Who did that?' said Mr Gibbins.

'Me, sir,' said Tommy Marsden. 'I'm sorry, sir. I've got wind.'

'I choose to believe you,' said Mr Gibbins. 'I cannot believe that any boy would deliberately waste time, in the most important year in his school life, by breaking wind deliberately.'

'Exactly, sir,' said Tommy Marsden.

'Why is this the most important year in your school life?' said Mr Gibbins. 'Because we now have, for the first time, true equality of opportunity in education. At the end of the year you will take the Eleven Plus examination to see which of you are clever enough to win this equality of opportunity. Some of you will go to the grammar school, and the chance of being somebody in life. Others won't. It's up to you.'

'If we all work hard, sir, will we all go to grammar school, sir?' asked Tommy Marsden.

'No, of course not. There isn't room. The best will go,' said Mr Gibbins.

'So whether we all work or all do nowt, t' same people will go, sir,' said Tommy Marsden.

'Don't be silly, Marsden,' said Mr Gibbins. A thin bead of sweat was glistening on his forehead. 'Right. Hilarious joke over. Back to education. Milner, why did you say that "me" was the subject of the sentence?'

'T' teacher's like t' king, sir. So t' pupils are his subjects.'

'Ah! Very ingenious, Milner. I'm glad to see you're thinking, at any rate. It makes a change. Keep at it. You may find you grow to like it. But you're wrong. Hammond?'

'Is the subject the noun, sir?'

'Very good, but which noun?'

'Teacher, sir.'

'Very good, Hammond. Why?'

'Because it comes first, sir.'

'Well, that's not really the. . .'

A loud fart rent the air. Everybody laughed, except Cuffley.

'Who did that?' said Mr Gibbins wearily.

'Me, sir,' said Booth.

'Come here, Booth.'

'I couldn't help it, sir.'

'Come here, Booth.'

'It's not fair, sir.'

Booth held out his hand. Mr Gibbins smacked it twice with the cane.

'Let that be a lesson to you all,' he said. 'The subject of a sentence, and we did deal with the subject of subjects last week, the subject of a sentence is the nominative, the element in the sentence about which something is predicated. The object is that which is governed by a transitive verb or preposition.' Mr Gibbins looked at their blank faces and wished he hadn't started on this. The sweat was beginning to run down into his eyes. 'In simple terms, the subject is the doer, the object is that which is done to.'

'What's a doer, sir?' said Cuffley.

'It's t' thing in t' hoil in t' wall to stop t' draught,' said Appleyard.

'Write out fifty times "I must not make silly remarks in class", Appleyard,' said Mr Gibbins.

'Can't I have t' cane, sir?'

Mr Gibbins took a deep breath.

'The subject of the sentence is therefore the teacher,' said Mr Gibbins.

A loud fart rent the air. Everybody laughed, except Cuffley.

'Would your tiny minds laugh however often that happened?' said Mr Gibbins. 'Would you still laugh if it happened a hundred times – don't try it!!!! Right. Who was it that time?'

'Me, sir,' said Martin Hammond.

'You're an intelligent boy, Hammond,' said Mr Gibbins. 'You could go far. Sometimes I wish you would. Why do you deliberately break wind and ally yourself with these miserable cretins?'

'The working class must stick together. That's what my dad says, any road,' said Martin Hammond.

Mr Gibbins stared at Martin Hammond wildly.

'I won't punish you this time, Hammond,' he said, 'because I believe you to be fundamentally sensible.'

'That's not fair,' muttered Tommy Marsden.

'I heard that,' said Mr Gibbins. 'Come here, Marsden.'

'It's not fair, sir,' said Tommy Marsden. 'He makes a loud noise and gets nowt. I whisper one word and get caned.'

'I didn't say you were going to be caned,' said Mr Gibbins, realising that Tommy Marsden had a point, and back-tracking hurriedly. 'Come here.'

Tommy Marsden walked forward and held out his hand.

'Point to the subject of the sentence on the board,' said Mr Gibbins, handing Tommy Marsden his pointer.

Tommy Marsden pointed to the word 'teacher'.

'Good,' said Mr Gibbins. 'It's the teacher, because it's the teacher who asked. So what's the object?'

'Him, sir,' said Chalky White.

'Me, sir,' said Henry Pratt.

'No, sir. Me! Me! said Norbert Cuffley.

'Me,' said Mr Gibbins. 'Precisely.'

'How can it be you, sir?' said Appleyard. 'You're the subject.'

'I didn't mean me as a person,' said Mr Gibbins. 'I meant "me" in the sentence.'

Something approximating to order was gradually restored. Mr Gibbins' class didn't want to overthrow the law and order of the classroom, because they wouldn't have known what to do after they'd done it. A total collapse of discipline would have frightened them. It was a war of attrition, fought on safe ground, renewable every day.

Henry liked it when order was restored. He wanted to learn. Judge then of his discomfiture when he began to feel a genuine need to break wind. He fought against it. He was frightened of the cane. He had no wish to do anything but sit quietly, learn things (if possible) and give the occasional right answer without being a disgraceful goody like Norbert Cuffley.

Desperately he pressed his buttocks against each other. In vain! There emerged a piercing whistle of gargantuan duration. It was so high-pitched that only dogs, bats, all twenty-nine boys and Mr

Gibbins could hear it.

Everybody laughed, even Cuffley.

Henry could feel his cheeks burning. Then he realised that everything would be all right so long as he pretended that he had done it deliberately.

He grinned.

Mr Gibbins brought the cane down four times on his outstretched hand, but he could hardly feel the pain through the glory.

Henry had been made an honorary member of the Paradise Lane Gang, on account of a single act, the slow emission of a phenomenal amount of wind in the form of a high-pitched scream unique in the anal annals of the West Riding. The gang had never heard of Le Pétomane, but, if they had, they would have believed that the distinguished Gallic farter had a worthy rival in South Yorkshire.

Henry relished the fame uneasily, for he knew he was living on borrowed time.

'Do it again!' was the constant command of his new chums.

'On my birthday,' he said, and they accepted that. An artist of such rare talent was entitled to choose the stage for his performance.

He had four whole weeks in the gang. There were six members. Tommy Marsden, Billy Erpingham, Chalky White, Martin Hammond, Ian Lowson and Henry. They got on trams without any money, knocked on people's doors and ran away, pretended to be blind and got helped across roads by kind old ladies, dialled 999 and ran away, painted spots on their faces and went on a trolley bus disguised as an epidemic of chicken pox, gave each other haircuts, bought a bathing cap and some glue, and constructed a wig which they put in Mr Gibbins' desk.

On Friday, March 8th, Henry listened to Jackie Paterson of Glasgow v Bunty Doran of Belfast.

On Wednesday, March 13th, he faced exposure.

The Paradise Lane Gang laid on a birthday party for him. He would give the cabaret. Dress was informal. The venue was the waste ground between the Rundle and Gadd Navigation and the

River Rundle. Tommy Marsden brought a quart of pale ale, stolen from his dad. Ian Lowson brought a packet of Park Drive, ditto. Chalky White brought chewing gum. Martin Hammond brought a packet of digestive biscuits and a jar of strawberry jam.

I forget what Billy Erpingham brought.

The sky was bleak, and the light was fading. The wind was cold. There were a few flakes of sleet.

There was no escape. It was his birthday. He had boasted that he liked beer and smoking.

He ate three digestive biscuits, spread with raspberry jam, washed down by swigs of the nauseous, flat, bitter beer. Gamely, he struggled through the third cigarette of his life. He ate three more digestive biscuits, spread with raspberry jam, washed down by swigs of the nauseous, flat, bitter beer. Gamely, he struggled through the fourth cigarette of his life.

He took another swig of the beer, hoping against hope that it would help to produce some wind. To no avail! And he was fair perished with cold. Exposure of two different kinds was at hand.

He rushed over to the canal and was prodigiously sick into its murky waters.

He set off home, his head thumping. There could be no question of any performance now. The day of reckoning was postponed, yet he didn't feel cheered by this. His life was passing him by. When he was twice his present age he would be twenty-two. When he was twice that he would be forty-four. When he was twice that he would be eighty-eight, and already an old man. When he was twice that he would be. . .his head thumped. . .a hundred and seventy-six, and people would come from far and wide to discover the secret of his long life. Unless he was dead. Dead! He shuddered.

He'd be late home for his tea, but it didn't matter.

He walked slowly along the footpath under the brick wall that separated the cul-de-sacs from the canal. He didn't turn right into Paradise Lane. He didn't want to go home yet.

It was almost dark now, and sleeting gently. The cold wind soothed his burning brow, and provided a suitable background for his mood.

He walked on past the ends of Back Paradise Lane, Paradise

Hill, Back Paradise Hill, Paradise Court, Back Paradise Court and Paradise Green. He walked down Back Paradise Green to the main road. In a sudden surge of anger against life he ran across the road in front of a tram. The driver yelled at him. He went on down the side of Crapp, Hawser and Kettlewell. On all sides there were great sheds, topped by rows of narrow chimneys. Nothing moved around these stranded liners, but from time to time huge flashes of molten flame lit up the sky, and occasionally, through a ventilation gap, he would see the glow from a furnace mouth. He went right round the huge works of Crapp, Hawser and Kettlewell, his head thumping as if in time with some vast industrial hammer. A tiny shunting engine took its freight slowly across the road in front of him, blocking his path.

On an impulse he plunged deeper into this nightmare industrial estate. He would walk west, over the Pennines, to Liverpool, and there he would stow away on a cargo ship and work his passage when he was discovered. He'd break ship on a tropical island where there was plenty of sunshine and fruit, and no school or girls, and he'd live happily ever after.

It would serve them right. Nobody cared about him. Except Simon Eckington and Auntie Kate and Miss Candy. Maybe he wouldn't go straight to the tropical island. He'd call in at Rowth Bridge first.

It was very cold, and his headache was no better. He decided to go home, and set off tomorrow after a good night's sleep. This would give him a chance to write a suicide note, and really worry them.

He struggled back to the main road, very tired now. The main road seemed endless. He hadn't realised how far he had come. His mouth tasted as if it had been coated with shrimp and dead grasshopper paste. He began to compose his suicide note.

His father, Uncle Teddy, Auntie Doris and Cousin Hilda were sitting by the not-so-efficiently leaded range. They tried to hide their relief and show only their anger.

On the table there were sandwiches, a cake with eleven candles, and – unheard of for many years – a wine-red Chivers jelly.

There were also three brown paper parcels.

He burst into tears.

Ezra's father had died. Twice they had made the trip to the home of Penistone's leading coal merchant to see him. Now they went to see Ezra's mother, who was quietly fading away from sorrow. These trips made Henry uneasy, even vaguely frightened. He didn't know how to cope, or what to say. There was nothing he could say. He didn't even like it when he was given a shilling before they left. It seemed like payment for services that he had failed to render.

Family deaths often come in clusters, and now Her Mother was dying as well. She had gone funny, and hadn't wanted to see them. Now, in the face of the grim reaper, she had relented.

Henry hated everything about the visit to the hospital. He hated the long walk from the gates, in the torrential rain, following the signs for Radcliffe Ward. The hospital appeared to have been designed by someone whose only previous experience had been the creation of mazes, but at last they found the ward. It was a kind of Nissen hut, with six beds on each side, and a Nurse Waddle, who did.

Her Mother was in the end bed on the left. They collected two chairs from a pile of chairs at the end of the room, and hung their sodden coats over the backs.

'How's tha doing, then, Ezra? And who's this?' said Her Mother.

'This is Henry.'

'Nay. Henry's nobbut a baby.'

'That was years ago, Norah. Before tha went to our Leonard's.'

'I've only been at our Leonard's for a fortnight,' said her mother. 'Just to help her wi' t' bairn.'

'Tha lives there, Norah,' said Ezra.

'With Leonard?'

'Aye.'

'How long have I been there?'

'Six years.'

'Oh heck. I forget. How's Henry, then?'

'All right, thank you, Grandma,' said Henry. He longed to add something amusing, or compassionate, or even just vaguely interesting. Nothing came. It never did in the presence of the old and ill.

Nurse Waddle waddled down the ward towards them.

'I'm sorry,' said Ezra. 'We're making puddles on t' floor.'

It was true. Why else should Ezra have said it? Quite sizeable puddles were forming beneath their coats.

'Never mind,' said Nurse Waddle. 'Worse things'll happen before t' day's done.'

Henry remembered another puddle on another floor. The shame rose off him like the steam off his drying coat. He felt himself blushing. He caught Nurse Waddle's eye, and believed that she had seen into his soul, and he blushed all the more. Nurse Waddle waddled off to get a sponge and a bucket and then she waddled back and cleared up the puddles before they spread.

'Tha shouldn't have come on such a wet night,' said Her Mother. 'I'm not feeling neglected.'

'Aye, but Leonard said this were t' best night for him not to come,' said Ezra.

'Who's that?' said Her Mother.

'That's our Henry,' said Ezra.

'It can't be. Henry's nobbut a baby,' said Her Mother.

'Tha's lived with Leonard for six years,' said Ezra.

'Six years?'

'Aye.'

'Oh heck. I forget.'

The woman in the bed opposite, who was very elderly and emaciated, began to get out of bed very slowly, with great difficulty. She began to sing 'Throw out the life-line' in a mumble as she did so.

'Press the bell,' said Her Mother scornfully. 'Get back into bed,' she shouted.

Henry pressed the bell, glad to be of use, yet frightened of pressing the bell, in case it was the wrong thing to do. He caught sight of the old woman's naked, creased body, and shuddered at the shocking thinness of it.

Nurse Waddle waddled briskly up the ward like a clockwork toy. 'Where do we think we're going, Mrs Purkiss?' she said briskly, and started putting the very old woman back into bed.

Any hope of Henry thinking of anything interesting to say was dashed when Uncle Teddy and Auntie Doris arrived.

Auntie Doris smelt like a perfume factory, and put a bunch of bananas in Her Mother's bed-side bowl.

Bananas! Henry stared at them in wonder. They were an unheard-of luxury. It was rumoured that there had been a few in the corner shop, and Billy Erpingham had thought they were yellow polony, but these were the first Henry had seen.

That was something he could say. He waited for a gap in the conversation, into which he would slip the bon mot 'Billy Erpingham saw a banana and thought it were yellow polony'. But, as luck would have it, there was no gap.

'Is it all right to have four visitors?' said Uncle Teddy. 'Only it says two at a time.'

'It doesn't matter,' said Her Mother.

'We could go out and come back when you go, if you like,' said Auntie Doris.

'Or you could go out now and wait for us. We can't stay long. I've got some business to discuss,' said Uncle Teddy.

'It doesn't matter,' said Her Mother. 'She's not too bad, this one. Not like t' other one.'

'Pity we all came on the same day,' said Uncle Teddy.

'We could have given you a lift if we'd known,' said Auntie Doris. 'Then you needn't have got soaked.'

'I'm saying nowt,' said Her Mother.

'You're looking grand, Mother,' said Auntie Doris.

'I'm dying, but I'm not complaining. I don't feel hard done by,' said Her Mother.

Henry thought that perhaps it was just as well not to do the banana polony gag. It might suggest that he was hinting that his grandmother offer him a banana, and, much as he longed for one, he knew that under these circumstances he wouldn't enjoy it.

It was stifling. The bananas were looking more cheerful by the minute.

Biggles wouldn't be stuck for something to say. Or would he? Henry had never actually come across Biggles doing hospital visiting.

'You've got to help us, Bigglesworth,' pronounced the Air

Commodore. 'You've proved yourself singularly adept at solving this kind of devilish mystery.'

Biggles' eyes narrowed shrewdly. 'I'm awfully sorry, sir,' he countered evenly. 'It's jolly decent of you to say so, although I fear you exaggerate my powers. I'd dearly love to have a crack at the caper, but I've got to visit my Gran in hospital.'

Suddenly Henry thought of something to say. It wasn't witty. It wasn't even interesting. But it was, without doubt, a remark, and as such it mustn't go to waste. It was, in fact, 'We had to wait twenty minutes for a tram.'

Imagine his dismay when he heard his father say, at that very moment, 'We had to wait twenty minutes for a tram,' condemning him to another ten minutes' silence.

'Who's that?' said Her Mother.

'That's our Henry,' said Auntie Doris. 'Isn't it, Henry?'

'Aye,' riposted Henry amusingly.

'Nay,' said Her Mother. 'Henry's not much more than a baby.'

'You haven't seen him for six years,' said Uncle Teddy.

'Six years?' said Her Mother.

'Tha's lived wi' Leonard for six years,' said Ezra.

'Oh heck,' said Her Mother. 'I get confused. Why did I go to our Leonard's?'

'Because Ada took Henry to the country,' said Auntie Doris.

'I didn't want to go,' said Her Mother. 'I don't like t' countryside. It's nobbut fields. They went to Kate's, didn't they? No, I were better suited at our Leonard's. I were right set up wi' it there, specially after he sent Lord Hawke off to be broken up for t' war effort. I want thee all to know, before I go, that I didn't feel I were being flung out like a used duster.'

'We'd better be going,' said Uncle Teddy.

'Have we time to give them a lift home?' said Auntie Doris.

'Not really. It's pushing it a bit. We said we'd see Geoffrey,' said Uncle Teddy.

'In connection with business,' said Auntie Doris.

'It's all right,' said Ezra. 'We're on t' tram route.'

'Are you sure?' said Uncle Teddy.

'I'm keeping out of this,' said Her Mother.

'Right, if you're quite sure, we'll be off,' said Uncle Teddy.

Uncle Teddy and Auntie Doris kissed Her Mother.

The emaciated old woman began to get out of bed.

Henry rang the bell.

Another bell rang, for the ending of visiting time.

'Take those bananas,' said Her Mother. 'Our Leonard brought them. I don't like them.'

They kissed her goodbye. Nurse Waddle waddled in and said, 'And where do we think we're going, Mrs Purkiss?'

As they left the ward, they found themselves side by side with the man who had been visiting the woman in the next bed.

'At least your one talks,' he said. 'I can't get owt out of my one at all.'

It had stopped raining, but an ambulance roared through a large puddle and drenched them from head to foot. They had to wait twenty minutes for a tram. By the time it came, Uncle Teddy was already discussing his business, which consisted of paying the barman at the Robin Hood in Sheffield for two large whiskies and a large gin and It.

At last they got home, and Henry had his first banana. The old master of the Mars bar made it last seven minutes. Life's pleasures were not taken lightly in those days.

Visits to hospitals and to the home of Penistone's leading coal merchant could not delay the moment of truth for ever. Today was to be Henry's day of reckoning with the Paradise Lane Gang. He was to meet them at the bridge over the Rundle and Gadd Navigation, to demonstrate on that brick edifice that his prowess at emitting wind was no fluke.

Uncle Teddy had done his bit at last. He had given Ezra a job, at his import/export business in Sheffield. His father didn't get home till half-past six, so Henry often got his own tea. On this particular day he chose a tin of baked beans on toast, followed by a tin of baked beans not on toast.

He walked up Paradise Lane, along the footpath, through the gate onto the towpath, and along the towpath towards the bridge. It was a clear evening, and there wasn't a breath of wind. He regarded this as a bad omen.

The bridge over the canal was attractive, with the shallow

curve of the towpath at either side perfectly proportioned. Only five things marred its simple, functional beauty. Tommy Marsden, Martin Hammond, Chalky White, Billy Erpingham and Ian Lowson. They stood in line on the top of the bridge. Immobile. Stern. Ruthless. The Paradise Lane Gang.

Henry climbed slowly up the towpath to the top of the bridge. He took up his position, slightly bent over. He strained. Come on, beans. Do thy stuff, he implored. He strained again. A tiny, barely audible, semi-asthmatic wheeze dribbled from his backside.

They threw him into the Rundle and Gadd Navigation. It wasn't the last canal into which he would fall, but it was undoubtedly the most bruising to his ego.

6 Pratt Goes West

Another September. Another beginning. Henry got off the Thurmarsh tram at the stop before the terminus. The grammar school was in Link Lane, next to the fire station.

Boys were converging on the school from all sides, in black blazers and black-and-yellow-striped ties. The new boys stood out among the scruffy stream like barristers in a public bar.

The school building was long, brick, many-windowed, uninspired but also unforbidding. He was looking for Martin Hammond, but found only Norbert Cuffley. Although he didn't want to be seen as an ally of such an outrageous goody, they clung together in that vast strangeness.

He caught sight of Martin Hammond in the school hall. The boys sat in rows, with the younger boys at the front. The masters filed in, and sat facing the boys. The hubbub subsided, and the headmaster, Mr E. F. Crowther, entered.

They stood and sang a hymn. They sat and the headmaster intoned a prayer. Henry also noticed Milner and Trellis from Brunswick Road. He was surprised to find that he was feeling quite excited.

Mr E. F. Crowther addressed the school. Mr Quell stifled a yawn.

'Welcome back, old boys. Welcome to Thurmarsh Grammar, new boys,' began Mr E. F. Crowther. 'You see before you our staff, as fine as body of men as can be found. . .in this building.'

Mr Crosby had heard this joke twenty times before, but he still laughed exaggeratedly at it.

'Thurmarsh. It is not perhaps a name that resounds throughout the educational world. It is not an Eton or a Harrow. But is it any the worse for that?' Mr E. F. Crowther paused, as if defying some miserable urchin to say 'yes'. Nobody did. Nobody ever had. 'I am proud to be headmaster of Thurmarsh Grammar,' he continued at last. 'Perhaps I am biased, because I am Thurmarsh born and Thurmarsh bred.'

'And Thurmarsh bread is very nice when it's fresh,' whispered Henry to Norbert Cuffley. He hadn't expected to say it. It just came to him. He was a budding humorist, an emerging character, and he felt exhilarated. Besides, it terrified Norbert Cuffley.

The headmaster paused, and looked in his direction. Careful, Henry.

'In the great war that has strained the civilised world almost to breaking point,' resumed Mr E. F. Crowther, 'Old Thurmarshians have been up there beside Old Etonians and Old Harrovians. I am sure that in the battle to rebuild our nation and take up once again our rightful place in the forefront of history, there will once again be Thurmarshians in the van.'

'The bread van,' whispered Henry.

The headmaster turned towards him.

'Did somebody speak?' he asked.

Oh, miserable and aptly-named Pratt.

'Who spoke?' thundered the headmaster.

The room resounded to the loud silence of six hundred boys. You could have heard an earwig breathe.

'The whole school will stay in for one hour, unless somebody owns up,' said Mr E. F. Crowther.

'It were me, sir,' said Henry in a small voice.

'Stand up,' commanded Mr E. F. Crowther.

Henry stood up.

'Who are you?' said Mr E. F. Crowther.

'Pratt, sir.'

There was laughter.

'Silence,' said Mr E. F. Crowther. 'There is nothing funny about a boy's name. People who find names funny are puerile. You're new, aren't you, Pratt?'

'Yes, sir.'

'You have passed your eleven plus, and are therefore considered fit to come here rather than fester away in a secondary modern school,' said Mr E. F. Crowther. 'Allow us to share the epigrammatical delight of your secret discourse, Pratt, and help us to judge whether we find you fit.'

'Sir?'

'What did you say?'

His mind was a blank. He could think of nothing except the truth.

'The bread van, sir.'

'The bread van, Pratt?'

'Yes, sir. Tha said tha hoped there'd be Thurmarshians in the van. I said "the bread van".'

'Are you related to Oscar Wilde, by any chance, Pratt?'

'No, sir.'

'I thought not. You're an imbecile, Pratt. What are you?'

'An imbecile, sir.'

'You will come and see me in my study after school.'

'Yes, sir.'

The headmaster resumed his address. Everyone would be sorry to hear that Mr Budge had suffered a stroke. Extensive repairs had been carried out in the boiler room. They could face the winter with more confidence.

At Brunswick Road, all Henry's lessons had been taken by Mr Gibbins. At Thurmarsh Grammar his development was entrusted to several teachers, and much of the first day was spent in finding their classrooms and taking part in roll-calls.

His first lesson was given by Mr Quell, his form master, who would teach him English. Mr Quell was five foot five tall, large-framed and barrel-chested, and he had an absolutely square-topped head. He gave the impression of being quite a tough man, yet he looked at Henry with something approaching awe.

The boys in Henry's class were Astbury, Blake, Burgess, Crane, Cuffley, Dakins, Elmhurst, Hammond, Harrison, Huntley, Ibbotson, Jones, Larkins, Longfellow, Milner, Norris, Oberath, Openshaw, Pratt, Przíborski, Quayle, Smith, Stoner, Taylor, Tunnicliffe, Turner, Weston, Wilkinson, Wool and Yarnold.

After the day's chaotic activities were over, and a relatively ordered basis for the future had been established, Henry made his way uneasily towards the headmaster's study.

'Good luck, bread van,' said a senior boy, whom he met in the corridor.

He knocked.

'Come in,' said Mr E. F. Crowther.

He entered.

Mr E. F. Crowther sat behind a large desk on which there were several piles of papers arranged on spikes. His study was airy. The walls were liberally festooned with rosters and graphs. The room stated, 'Things get done here. We are plain, practical men, concerned with achievement, not pretension.'

'Good afternoon, Pratt,' said Mr E. F. Crowther.

'Good afternoon, sir,' said Henry.

'Thought up any more little gems, Pratt?'

'No, sir.'

'A pity. I've had a hard day. I was looking forward to being entertained.'

Mr E. F. Crowther picked up his cane, then let it fall onto the top of his desk.

'Can you furnish me with any arguments that might persuade me not to cane you, Pratt' he enquired.

'Yes, sir.'

The headmaster raised his eyebrows in eloquent surprise.

'Then do so.'

'I were excited, sir.'

'It's "I was excited," Pratt. You'll have to learn to speak grammatically here. After all, it is the grammar school.'

'I *was* excited, sir.'

'Why?'

'Coming to Thurmarsh Grammar, sir.'

Mr E. F. Crowther gave Henry a searching glance. He prided himself on his searching glances. Sometimes, he was so keen on making sure that his glance was searching that he forgot to look for the thing for which he was searching.

'I must warn you that I have the sole franchise for all sarcasm uttered between these four walls,' he said.

'Please, sir?'

'Are you seriously telling me that you said "the bread van" because you were excited about coming to Thurmarsh Grammar?'

'Yes, sir.'

Mr E. F. Crowther leant back in his chair. Behind him, a hazy autumn sun shone. There was a beam of dust in the air.

'Explain,' he said.

'Well, sir, I didn't like it that much at Brunswick Road because it were. . .it *was* mainly Reading, Writing and Arithmetic, with just a bit of Geography and that. I were. . .I *was* looking forward to learning all the different subjects, like, like History and French and that, and with seeing all the older boys and everything, I thought about everything I was going to learn and how after I left school I might get on in t' world and be summat, and I felt like my life was just starting at last, and I gor over-excited, sir. I'm only eleven.'

The headmaster stared at Henry with his mouth slightly open.

'Try to stay excited,' he said, 'but try not to get so carried away with your enthusiasm that you say "the bread van" while I'm talking. Run along now.'

'Yes, sir. Thank you, sir.'

Martin Hammond was waiting for him outside. He was astounded when he heard that Henry hadn't had the cane.

'I never wanted to throw thee out of t' gang,' said Martin Hammond. 'It were Tommy and Billy and Chalky and Ian. There was nowt I could do, not on me own.'

The Rawlaston tram was only half full. Most of the children had gone home, and the evening rush-hour had not yet started.

The tram dropped into the Rundle Valley, and swung round to the right, running alongside the canal for about a hundred yards. Then the cul-de-sacs began and they saw them waiting at the bus stop. Tommy Marsden. Ian Lowson. Billy Erpingham. Chalky White. Four boys who had not passed the eleven plus. On another day, the results might have been different, and the tramp ships of their lives might have been sent to different ports. But they hadn't, and now they stood facing each other, two grammar-school boys and four secondary-school boys.

'Art tha coming out tonight?' said Tommy Marsden. 'Well, we're all still members of t' gang, aren't we? Tha's not turned snotty-nosed just cos tha's gone to grammar school, has tha?'

'Course not,' said Martin Hammond.

'I was never made a proper member any road,' said Henry.

'We'll make thee a full member on Saturday,' said Tommy Marsden.

'I can't,' said Henry. 'I'm going t' match.'

'At six o clock,' said Tommy Marsden. 'After t' match. On t' waste ground. Be there.'

The match was against Accrington Stanley, in the Third Division North. This time Henry was excited by the crowd of flat-capped men and boys pouring up Blonk Lane. He felt six inches taller as he went through the juveniles' entrance and rejoined Ezra inside the ground.

The boys were handed to the front row over the heads of the good-natured crowd.

There was a cheer from the sizeable contingent of Stanleyites when the visitors emerged, but it was nothing compared to the roar that greeted the Reds. Eleven giants in their red shirts and long white shorts. Rawlings: Thong, Ibbotson: Salter, Cedarwood, Smailes: Ellison, Bunce, Gravel, Thompson and Hatch.

The Reds attacked from the start. The Peel Park men, who were wearing yellow due to a clash of colours, were pinned into their own half for long periods. There were cries of 'Windy' when they made back passes. BUNCE put the Reds into the lead in the twenty-third minute following a sinuous dribble by Hatch. In the eighty-third minute, the ubiquitous SMAILES popped up by the far post, to head a second for the home team. Unfortunately, by that time the visitors had scored three times in breakaways.

It took a long while to get back to Thurmarsh, and by the time they got there the 'Green 'Un' had already been published. They read about the match they'd just seen. 'The visitors were lucky to be on level terms at the interval,' opined the writer. 'When the Reds took the lead through the medium of young BUNCE, the cheers could have been heard as far away as Rotherham. The 13,671 crowd enjoyed the fast and furious exchanges. There was no question of cotton wool and swaddling clothes for these boys.' 13,671, thought Henry. That included me. Without me it would have been 13,670. I'm mentioned in the paper. It cheered him up a little, but not much. They had lost, unfairly. They had been robbed. Life wasn't worth living. And he dreaded his initiation into the Paradise Lane Gang.

He wandered over to the waste ground in his scuffed shoes with soles flapping loose, socks full of holes, torn trousers, torn shirt, and heavily-stained pullover.

There, on the waste ground, stood Tommy Marsden, Chalky White, Billy Erpingham and Ian Lowson. For an awful moment, he thought that Martin, his one ally, was going to let him down. But then Martin came, slowly, owlishly, reluctantly.

The sun was a pale orb, still just visible through the returning mist.

Tommy Marsden got out a penknife, such as Henry's father might have made, in his palmier days. He flicked one of its two blades open. There were crinkles in his black hair, and when he smiled he showed long, irregular teeth.

Henry stood with the river on his left and the canal on his right, facing the other five, who all looked very solemn.

'Members of t' Paradise Lane Gang,' said Tommy Marsden. 'Be silent for t' president, me. Does anybody know owt why Henry Pratt should not be elected a member of the Paradise Lane Gang?'

Nobody spoke.

A train steamed past, invisible in the thickening mist.

'Hold out thy left hand,' commanded Tommy Marsden.

Henry held out his left hand.

Tommy Marsden advanced, holding out the knife in front of him.

Henry closed his eyes. Don't shake, hand. Don't faint, body. It's up to thee. There's nowt I can do.

'Full name?' said Tommy Marsden.

'Henry Ezra Pratt.'

'Age?'

'Eleven.'

'Say after me. I, Henry Ezra Pratt. . .'

'I, Henry Ezra Pratt. . .'

'Of this parish. . .'

'Of this parish. . .'

'Do agree. . .'

'Do agree. . .'

'To obey all t' rules of t' Paradise Lane Gang.'

'To obey all t' rules of t' Paradise Lane Gang.'

'I now make t' cross of t' Paradise Lane Gang on thy left hand,' said Tommy Marsden.

Henry felt a searing pain in his left hand. It seemed to shoot right up his arm.

Then the pain came again.

He felt unsteady. He opened his eyes. Blood was trickling down his hand from the two incisions. He felt faint. He willed himself not to faint.

'I, Thomas John Marsden, welcome thee,' said Tommy Marsden, shaking Henry's right hand.

'Thanks,' said Henry, holding his left hand out stiffly, with the palm turned up, so that the blood wouldn't flow.

Ian Lowson came forward.

'I, Ian Sidney Lowson, welcome thee,' he said, shaking Henry's hand.

Martin Hammond came forward.

'I, Martin Ronald Hammond, welcome thee,' he said.

Henry shook his hand.

In the distance, trucks were being shunted. The noise was resonant in the fog.

Chalky White came forward.

'I, Benjamin Disraeli Gladstone White, welcome thee,' he said, grinning sheepishly.

Billy Erpingham came forward.

'I, Billy Erpingham, welcome thee,' he said.

Henry had achieved what he had wanted for so long. He was a member of the Paradise Lane Gang.

He no longer wanted it.

He woke up at three o'clock the next morning. His hand was throbbing.

His father was screaming. He rushed into his father's room.

'Wake up, dad,' he shouted.

His father sat up with a start. His ill-fitting dentures were in a glass at the side of the bed. With his empty mouth he looked hollow and ill and far older than his forty years. Both Henry's grandmothers had died during June. It had added to his father's gathering gloom.

'What is it?' said Ezra.

'Tha were screaming,' said Henry.

Sweat was pouring off Ezra's face.

'I had a nightmare,' he said. 'I were dreaming about t' war.'

'Were they trying to kill thee?' said Henry.

'Nay,' said Ezra. 'It were all the ones what I killed, coming back to haunt me.'

'How many Germans did tha kill, dad?'

'I don't know. Tha never knows, tha knows. Leastways, not in t' artillery. Tha fires in t' general direction of 'em, like, and that's about it.'

Henry had to strain to hear what his father was saying, without his teeth in.

'It were their faces. It were their faces, Henry.'

Henry felt a tingle of horror. He didn't want to know what their faces were like, and yet he did.

'I didn't recognise them at first,' said Ezra. 'Then it came to me who they were.'

'Who were they, dad?'

'Rawlings: Thong, Ibbotson: Salter, Cedarwood, Smailes: Ellison, Bunce, Gravel, Thompson and Hatch.'

One never-to-be-forgotten evening, at the beginning of October, 1946, two events occurred. One of them marked the end of an era. The other, although Henry didn't recognise this at the time, marked the start of what was quite soon to become the beginning of an era.

The evening began with the end of an era, and ended with the start of the beginning of an era.

Henry and Martin had been leading a double life. By day, studious young citizens, beginning to unravel the mysteries of Latin, French, Geometry, Physics, Chemistry, Geography and History. By night, members of the Paradise Lane Gang.

Their activities were relatively innocent.

They went to the pictures, to see Gary Cooper and Franchot Tone in *The Lives of a Bengal Lancer*, and by means of those who had already gone in coming out and handing tickets to the others in the lav, they managed to get the six of them in on three tickets. The cinema was still a novel, exciting experience to Henry, and he wished that he could enjoy the film and forget about manking about.

125

They sat in different parts of a tram and all pretended to be Polish refugees who didn't understand English, thus driving the conductor into a frenzy.

They went to see Thurmarsh United play Gateshead. The Reds won 4–1, over-running the Redheugh Park side with goals by GRAVEL (2), BUNCE and HATCH. After the match, they locked themselves into the gents and waited there for over an hour, and then they went out and played on the pitch. Henry went in goal. He was actually between the posts, in the Blonk Lane stadium, with shots being rained at him from all angles. He even saved two (both from Martin). Then men came running after them and they scattered to all parts of the ground, shinning up walls and managing to get everybody out of the ground safely, except Henry. A phrase that he had read came to him in the nick of time and he said, 'We just wanted to play on t' sacred turf,' and the man let him go with just a gentle clip round the ear-hole.

Then came that October evening. The end of an era. The final act in the saga of the Paradise Lane Gang.

They met on the waste ground as usual. Tommy Marsden led them over the river, over the railway and into the rows of semi-detached houses that wound up and over the hills, as far as the eye could see. He led them to a small row of shops – a grocer's, a greengrocer's, a butcher's, a newsagent's and a little sub-post office. Opposite them was a trolley-bus terminus, and here there was a tiny public garden. It was almost completely dark, the garden was deserted, and there was no trolley-bus due for thirty-five minutes. Street lighting was dim. Tommy Marsden got out a catapult, and asked Martin Hammond to break one of the shop windows. Martin refused, unless Tommy Marsden did so first. Tommy Marsden promptly catapulted a stone and shattered the butcher's window, sending glass splintering all over the empty slab. They ran away by different routes, silently, with orders to meet up again on the waste ground. They did meet up on the waste ground. Tommy Marsden told Martin Hammond that it was his turn next. Martin Hammond refused.

'We never broke windows before,' he said.

'We were nobbut kids,' said Tommy Marsden.

'Knocking on doors and running away, fair enough,' said

126

Martin Hammond.

'Kids' stuff,' said Tommy Marsden. 'Even breaking windows is kids' stuff really.'

'What isn't kids' stuff?' said Henry.

'Stealing,' said Tommy Marsden.

There was a brief silence.

'I'm not stealing,' said Martin Hammond, chucking a stone into the canal in a gentle parabola.

'Bloody nesh grammar-school cissy,' said Tommy Marsden.

'That's right,' said Billy Erpingham.

'Bloody stuck-up, snotty-nosed snob,' said Chalky White.

'That's right,' said Billy Erpingham.

'Henry,' said Tommy Marsden. 'Tha's t' newest member. Thursday, bring us stolen bread, jam and apples for us tea. And I need a watch.'

'I'm not stealing either,' said Henry.

Tommy Marsden grabbed his arm and twisted it.

'Tha promised to obey,' he said.

'Give over, Tommy,' said Ian Lowson. 'Let him be.'

'Tha promised to obey,' said Tommy Marsden.

'So did everybody else,' said Henry.

'No, they didn't,' said Tommy Marsden. 'We never had no initiation ceremonies before.'

'It's just a put-up job,' said Henry. 'It's not our fault we've gone to t' grammar school.'

'That's right,' said Billy Erpingham.

Henry kicked Tommy Marsden, and suddenly it was all flying fists and boots. Henry and Martin had no chance. They were outnumbered two to one, even though they suspected that neither Ian Lowson nor Chalky White felt particularly vicious towards them, and Billy Erpingham only did what he did because he always did what Tommy Marsden did.

Henry flailed and pummelled and scratched. He received one tremendous blow on the nose, which started to bleed. He only got in one decent blow himself. Unfortunately, it was on Martin Hammond. Boots crashed against his knees and back. An elbow thudded into his private parts with squelching venom. His ears rang. He could hardly breathe. Blood was pouring from his nose.

'Give up?' said Tommy Marsden.

'No,' he shrieked, desperate to give up, but unable to.

All six of them were writhing in the mud. He was pinned beneath the heap, trapped, dying, getting smaller and smaller and falling, falling, falling into the arms of death. He heard Tommy Marsden, a million miles away, say 'Give up?', almost beseeching them to surrender, but he couldn't have said 'yes' if he'd wanted to.

Then the heap just rolled slowly over and lay panting all around him, and he slowly came back to life and managed to roll over onto his back so that his nose wouldn't bleed so much.

Chalky White was being sick into the canal, having been inadvertently punched in the stomach by Tommy Marsden. Martin was gasping for breath. Billy Erpingham and Ian Lowson sat calmly, waiting for their leader to speak.

'That's that,' said Tommy Marsden.

They limped to their various homes in the cul-de-sac. The Paradise Lane Gang had met for the last time. An era had ended.

The start of the beginning of an era (although he didn't recognise it as such at the time) occurred when he got home.

A man sat slumped at a kitchen table in a decaying back-to-back terrace in south Yorkshire. He had a quarter-full bottle of whisky in his hands. His speech was slurred. A boy entered the room and collapsed into the other chair at the table. His lips were puffed up, there were cuts on his face and arms and legs. His clothes hung in tatters. Bruises were breaking out all over him. He held a grubby, scarlet-speckled handkerchief to his nose. His face was deathly pale. Every now and then he gave a rasping cough and winced.

'Bastard,' said the man. 'Bastard. Bastard sacked me. Bastard. Own wife's sister's husband. Absenteeism. "I've been badly," I said. "Badly?" he said. "Hangovers more like." "That's a bloody lie," I said. Told me I can't handle heavy loads. "Nor would tha," I said. "Nor would tha if tha'd been marching through bloody desert day after day, fighting t' might of Rommel's army, instead of getting thisen rich on bloody black-market Australian minced loaf." Bastard.'

The man seemed to grow dimly aware that all was not well with the boy.

'Hast tha been drinking?' he said. 'Bloody hell. Have a drop o' this.'

The man pushed the bottle across the table towards the boy. The boy took it, as in a dream, and put it to his lips.

The boy thought his life had ended. He choked and gasped and spluttered and pushed the bottle back to the man.

'Bastard,' said the man. 'Bastard sacked me. Bastard.'

'I want to discuss your essay with you, Pratt,' said Mr Quell, who was Irish, and a lapsed priest. 'Come and see me afterwards.'

After the lesson, Henry went up to Mr Quell's desk. Mr Quell raised his glasses so that they rested on the top of his massive forehead, and looked at Henry quizzically.

'It's Henry, isn't it?'

'Yes, sir.'

'Let's go and sit down and look through your essay a bit,' said Mr Quell.

Mr Quell sat in Mick Tunnicliffe's desk. Henry sat in Stefan Prziborski's desk, and was tempted to pretend he was Prziborski. He envied Prziborski deeply. At first everyone had laughed at Prziborski, like they laughed at Oberath, because they had foreign names. Unlike Oberath, whose German name and sullen disposition condemned him to endless torment, Prziborski soon won popularity by his skill on the football field. It wasn't fair. Henry loved football, and went to every home game at Blonk Lane, but he was hopeless at it. He concealed the fact that this grieved him deeply, by laughing at himself before everyone laughed at him. 'I reckon I know what it is I lack,' he said. 'Skill, control, strength, accuracy and speed,' or 'At least I'm not one-footed like some folk. I'm no-footed.' All this flashed through his mind as he sat in the desk of the great Prziborski.

'You're a bit of a comedian, aren't you?' said Mr Quell. 'I hear glowing reports of the Welsh grocer.'

Henry blushed. It was quite true. He had blossomed at Thurmarsh Grammar into a budding little comic. Partly it was the good start that he had got off to with the bread van incident. Partly it was because he was enjoying school life more than home life since his father had been sacked by Uncle Teddy. Pupils at Rowth Bridge Village School or Brunswick Road Primary School would have been astounded to see him standing at his desk, if a master was slightly late, and entertaining his class-mates with his dazzling impressions of a grocer from Abergavenny. 'Biscuits indeed to goodness I do have, isn't it? I do have cream crackers, custard creams, digestives, assorted, broken assorted and dog indeed to goodness yes. Dog, is it, Mrs Jones, the wet fish? I didn't know you had a dog, isn't it? Oh, you don't. It's for Mr Jones, the wet fish.' Suddenly, the grocer from Abergavenny didn't seem the most hilarious thing in the world, now that he knew that Mr Quell knew of it.

' "The best day of my holidays," ' said Mr Quell. 'So many boys chose Christmas. You strove for more originality than that.'

'I didn't have a very good Christmas, sir.'

They had gone to Cousin Hilda's again. 'You must come to us next year. I insist,' Auntie Doris had said. It had been exactly the same as the previous Christmas, with the single, dramatic exception that neither of Cousin Hilda's friend's stockings had laddered. Once again, his father had been on his best behaviour. Cousin Hilda had taken Henry into the scullery and asked searching questions about life at home. He had lied in his teeth to save his father. Why? Why why why?

'You didn't choose New Year's Day either,' said Mr Quell.

Children in the mining villages had been given parties to celebrate the nationalisation of the mines. But Henry didn't live in a mining village. 1946 had seen the nationalisation of the mines, the Bank of England, Cable and Wireless and civil aviation. It had seen the passing of the National Insurance Act, the National Injuries Act and National Health Act. It had been the most momentous year in British domestic history. That was what Reg Hammond said, any road.

'Your day begins quite badly. You haven't slept well. Your father has had nightmares. You're tired. You break a plate getting breakfast,' said Mr Quell. 'So how is this to be "the best day of the holidays"? I am intrigued. I read on out of curiosity, not duty. That is rare, Henry.'

'Thank you, sir.'

'You seem to spend a great deal of the day reading.'

'I like reading, sir.'

'You don't have a wireless?'

'No, sir.'

Two momentous events had occurred concerning the wireless. 'Dick Barton, Special Agent' had begun, and had proved to be the best ever wireless programme ever in the history of the universe, and his father had sold the wireless.

'You read for three hours, pausing only to say "Oh. Goodbye." That is to your father?'

'Yes, sir.'

'Where was he going?'

'Don't know, sir.'

'The pub?'

'Don't know, sir.'

'All right. So you get the dinner. Your father comes back?'

'Yes, sir.'

'More reading ensues. You're having a simply rivetting day. You get the tea. You wash up. What about your father?'

'His nerves are bad. It's best if I do it.'

'Then you read again.'

Sometimes Henry went to Martin Hammond's and listened to Dick Barton there, but he hadn't put that in the essay.

'Yes, sir.'

'You go to bed. You hear your father come in. We may safely deduce then that he had gone out again?'

'Yes, sir.'

'Where to?'

'Don't know, sir.'

'The pub?'

'Don't know, sir.'

'You lie in bed. Your father comes upstairs, and tells you that he's been fighting a villainous plot to overthrow the government and kill the king. And your adventure begins. You go out with your father and help him save the nation and bring the villainous thugs to heel.'

'Yes, sir.'

'And this dream that you have, this fantasy that you have, in which your father is a hero, this is what makes this "the best day of the holidays"?'

'Yes, sir.'

'It's imaginative. It's different. It's good. Do you have any other relatives?'

Mr Quell took him to see Uncle Teddy and Auntie Doris. Henry couldn't remember the way, but Mr Quell looked up their address in the phone book.

Mr Quell showed Uncle Teddy and Auntie Doris the essay. Then he talked to Uncle Teddy, while Auntie Doris took Henry into the kitchen and made a pot of tea. Auntie Doris cried a bit. Henry wished she wouldn't, in case it made him cry, and quite soon she stopped.

Henry carried the tray in. Uncle Teddy opted for whisky, and attempted to prevail on Mr Quell to join him, but Mr Quell declined, expressing a preference for tea 'under the circumstances'.

'Is there anywhere else he can go?' said Mr Quell, looking round the well-appointed living room.

'We'll have him, won't we, Teddy?' said Auntie Doris. 'Of course we will.'

Uncle Teddy looked at Auntie Doris, then at Henry, then at Mr Quell, then at his whisky, then at Auntie Doris again. Henry found it impossible to tell what he was thinking.

'He obviously can't stay at home. That's the first thing,' said Uncle Teddy. 'And nobody could live with the sniffer.'

'You shouldn't call her the sniffer in front of the boy, and she hasn't got room anyway,' said Auntie Doris.

'Of course we'll have him,' said Uncle Teddy. 'There isn't anywhere else.'

'Don't make it sound like a last resort,' said Auntie Doris, who always made things worse by protesting about them. 'We'll have him because we want him.'

Henry wanted to cry. He didn't want to live with Uncle Teddy and Auntie Doris. Once again his destination was being discussed as if he were a parcel. It wasn't fair. Sometimes eleven seemed so grown-up, compared to all his past life. Then suddenly it was almost a babyish age, compared with all the growing up he still had to do.

Uncle Teddy drove them to Paradise Lane. They made a detour to pick up Cousin Hilda.

'If we don't involve her, there'll be ructions,' said Uncle Teddy.

'I can understand that,' said Mr Quell. 'I was born into a family myself.'

They drove through the centre of Sheffield. The cinema queues were hunched into their coats against the rising January wind.

Uncle Teddy drove under the Wicker Arches, and up out of the Don Valley on the long Thurmarsh road. He was weaving inside and outside the trams in expert fashion.

In the back, Auntie Doris put an arm round Henry until she realised that he didn't want it. She withdrew the arm a bit at a time, as if hoping that Henry wouldn't notice that she was being forced to do it.

They dropped down into the smoking, glowing heavy industry of the Rundle Valley. A left turn would have taken them to Rawlaston and the Barnsley road. A right turn would have taken them to Paradise Lane. But Uncle Teddy drove straight on up the hill towards Thurmarsh.

'Are you a reading man, sir?' asked Mr Quell.

'I like a good book,' said Uncle Teddy.

'The boy has the spark,' said Mr Quell. 'He definitely has the spark. Yes, sir. Henry Pratt is a young man who can make you feel proud of him. Do you think it will snow?'

Uncle Teddy went into number 66 Park View Road and emerged a few minutes later with Cousin Hilda. Her face was grave.

'Well well well,' she said, and sniffed. On this occasion her disapproval was for herself. 'I've been remiss. But my businessmen take up so much of my time.'

Uncle Teddy drove even faster, now that Cousin Hilda was in the car, because he knew it frightened her. She had once accompanied them, on an outing, when Henry was two. She had kept up a stream of propaganda, aimed at Uncle Teddy, in the guise of a running commentary, aimed at Henry. 'Uncle Teddy'll slow down in a minute, because of the corner.' 'Watch Uncle Teddy put on the brakes, in case that car pulls out.' She could hardly do that now.

The car was spacious. There was no squeeze, even with three of them in the back.

'You have a pleasant prospect overlooking the park,' Mr Quell told Cousin Hilda, turning his huge, square-topped head.

They all fell silent as they approached Paradise Lane. Uncle Teddy drove very slowly over the cobbles.

The little terrace house was empty. The fire in the range was low. Its heat made little impression on the icy air. Mr Quell went down into the cellar and fetched more coal.

'Where'll he be, Henry?' said Uncle Teddy.

'Don't know,' said Henry.

'In the pub?'

'Don't know.'

'Which pub does he use?'

'He uses t' Navigation a bit, but he doesn't stay long. He goes up t' hill mainly. There's t' Pineapple and two or three others. Try t' Tennants houses first.'

Mr Quell and Uncle Teddy set off in search of Ezra.

Cousin Hilda made a pot of tea. 'It's mashing,' she announced, and sighed and sniffed at the same time. 'I've failed you, Henry,' she said. 'I were satisfied with the answers you gave, because I wanted to be satisfied. I pretended everything were all right. And I call myself a Christian.'

'We had no idea anything like this was going on,' said Auntie Doris. 'The state of the place. Poor boy.'

'He were all right till Uncle Teddy sacked him,' said Henry.

'Uncle Teddy offered him a job out of the goodness of his heart,' said Auntie Doris. 'He had no need to. He kept him on as long as he possibly could. But he runs a business, not a charity. Your father didn't help himself either, the things he said about your Uncle Teddy's war effort.'

Cousin Hilda sniffed.

'What's that supposed to mean?' said Auntie Doris.

'What?' said Cousin Hilda.

'That sniff,' said Auntie Doris. 'I distinctly heard you sniff.'

'I were breathing,' said Cousin Hilda, flushing blotchily. 'I'll try not to do it in future, if it upsets you.'

'You were insinuating that Teddy wasn't ready to do his bit,' said Auntie Doris. 'You were insinuating that his flat feet were a fraud.'

'There's lots I could say,' said Cousin Hilda. 'I could make some comment about guilty consciences. But I won't. I'll hold my tongue. I've been un-Christian enough already.'

Mr Quell and Uncle Teddy returned empty-handed.

'I need the smallest room in the house,' said Uncle Teddy. 'Where is it?'

"Ti'n't in t' house for a kick-off,' said Henry, fetching the torch. 'Tha goes up t' entry two doors away into t' yard. Ours is t' second one on t' left, beyond t' midden.'

Uncle Teddy shook his head, as if amazed that people could choose to live like that, as if he really believed that they did choose it. Then he put on the overcoat which he had just taken off, and set off into the street.

'It's starting to snow,' said Mr Quell. 'Do you think it's the harbinger of prolonged severe weather?'

Cousin Hilda smiled at Henry.

'I'll come and build a snowman with you, if it is,' she said.

Uncle Teddy came back in, very slowly. His face was white. He forgot to switch the torch off.

'What's the matter, Teddy?' said Auntie Doris. 'You look as if you've seen a ghost.'

'Switch the torch off,' said Cousin Hilda. 'There's no point in wasting batteries.'

'I've found him,' said Uncle Teddy. 'He's in the toilet. He's dead.'

The snow began in earnest that night, and Henry began his life at Cap Ferrat, the home of Uncle Teddy and Auntie Doris, in Wharfedale Road, in the salubrious western suburbs of Sheffield, among the foothills of the Pennines.

It was a substantial stone house, built in 1930. It had charmingly irregular gables, and to the right of the porch there was a tall, narrow window, in pale imitation of the high windows of a baronial hall.

In the morning, waking up in a sizeable bedroom, he couldn't think where he was. Then it all came back to him. His father was dead. Life stretched bleakly ahead of him. There was no point in getting up.

School! He got out of bed automatically. It was nice to feel a fitted carpet beneath your feet. If life was going to be bleak and awful, it might just as well be bleak and awful with fitted carpets.

He pulled back the curtains and gazed open-mouthed at a wonderland of white. The branches of huge trees sagged with the snow. It lay piled on the roofs of the substantial houses that rose and fell with the pleasant white hills. It was impossible to tell where lawns ended and flower beds began, and there would certainly be no school that day.

How could he be excited? His father had died. His poor, sick father had collapsed and expired in the outside lavatory they shared with number 25. And he had betrayed his father in his essay. One week more, and there would have been no need to betray him.

He didn't want to live with Uncle Teddy and Auntie Doris. His brain seized up totally in their presence. But there was no point in pretending that he disliked their bathroom. Soaking in the luxurious, fitted bath, with his face flannel lying beside the pumice stone on the rack that fitted onto the bath, it was impossible not to feel that this was the life. Not one inside lavatory, but two. He resented Uncle Teddy and Auntie Doris, of course. It was outrageous that some people should have two inside lavatories, one upstairs and one downstairs, while others had none. That was what Reg Hammond said, any road. But if you happened to live in a house with them, why not use them? Henry used them alternately, because they were there.

They gave him a wireless of his very own! It was one thing to resent Uncle Teddy and Auntie Doris and their eccentric life-style – they had dinner in the evening, and a meal called lunch at one o'clock. But, if you were there, you might as well enjoy the good food, the fitted carpets, the comfortable armchairs and settee, the view over the snowy garden through the French windows, the steaming baths, the luxurious lavatories, the bedroom which made such a deeply satisfying womb. A womb with patterned curtains, in russet and olive-green, a darker green carpet, a wardrobe, a chest of drawers, a reproduction of 'The Hay Wain'. A womb with a view.

One night Henry had a dream, in which a naked Lorna Arrow – he couldn't remember her body, when he woke up, but he remembered she was naked – said, 'Which do you prefer – your father or ninety-three thousand miles of fitted carpet?' And he didn't know the answer! He woke up all clammy and disorientatedly uneasy and not quite fitting the inside of his head. It was true, even when awake. He didn't know the answer. He had tried to be loyal to his father, and, until just before the end, he had been. But he'd never really liked him. He'd always been frightened of him. He'd spent several formative years apart from him. It was very difficult to feel any grief. Normal children grieved for their father. He didn't. Therefore he wasn't normal. Q.E.D.

At first he didn't go to school because of the snows. It was a long way to Thurmarsh Grammar, and the country was almost paralysed by the snow. Then came his mumps. By the time he was better, it was close to the end of term, the nation was facing a severe fuel crisis, the boilers at Thurmarsh Grammar had finally packed up completely, and there was no point in going back that term.

He read books about children who went sailing, children who went camping, children who went riding, and they were all good eggs. He read books about otters that talked, foxes that talked and birds that talked. They were all pretty good eggs too. Henry wished that he was a good egg, but if you weren't a good egg, the next best thing was to read about good eggs.

And his wireless poured forth its magic. 'Much-Binding-In-The-Marsh', in which people said 'Was there something?' and 'Not a word to Bessie' and 'When I was in Sidi Barrani', and everybody laughed. Henry wished he had a catch phrase. There was 'Ignorance Is Bliss' with Harold Berens and Gladys Hay. He could follow Dick Barton at last. There was Michael Miles in 'Radio Forfeits'. International boxing brought him Jackie Paterson v Cliff Anderson and Freddie Mills v Willi Quentemeyer. F. N. S. Creek gave hints about lacrosse. They might come in handy one day, or they might not, what did it matter? There was a new serial called 'Bunkle Butts In' on 'Children's

Hour'. Who needed real-life friends?

Henry did. Soon the summer term would begin, and he would see Martin Hammond again, and Stefan Prziborski. The thaws came, and with them the floods. The floods eased, and it was spring, and he couldn't wait to go back to school.

7 Oiky

'Oi. Oiky,' yelled Tubman-Edwards.

Henry turned and thumped Tubman-Edwards on the side of the head.

Tubman-Edwards knocked him flat.

'I thought you oiks could fight,' said Tubman-Edwards, walking away, but Henry was unconscious and didn't hear him.

When Henry came round, he couldn't remember where he was. It seemed to be becoming a frequent experience. What were these playing fields among the pine woods and rhododendrons? What was that large, brooding, ivy-covered mansion?

It came back to him with a thud only marginally less sickening than that dealt out by Tubman-Edwards. He was lying on the playing fields of Brasenose College, a preparatory school for boys, so named by its palindromic headmaster, Mr A. B. Noon B.A., in the hope that some of the educational glitter of the Oxford College of the same name would adhere to his crumbling pile among the rhododendrons (rhododendra? Mr Noon was nothing if not a pedant).

Mr A. B. Noon B.A. was approaching now, accompanied by his equally palindromic twin daughters, Hannah and Eve, who ran a riding school in Bagshot.

'What are you doing lying on the ground, laddie?' said Mr Noon, peering down at Henry.

'Nothing, sir,' said Henry.

'Splendid,' said Mr Noon. 'You evaded my little trap.'

Henry struggled to his feet. He felt dizzy and his legs were rubbery. He had no idea what little trap he had evaded. Luckily, Mr Noon explained to his daughters.

'I didn't ask him why he was on the ground,' said Mr Noon. 'I asked him what he was doing on the ground. He understood my question and replied, "Nothing". I have every reason to believe that he was speaking the truth.'

'Is he all right?' asked Eve anxiously.

'What?' said Mr Noon, a little irritated at this interruption of his linguistic flow. 'Are you all right, boy?'

'Yes, sir,' said Henry.

Mr A. B. Noon B.A. was – and maybe still is – a tall, shambling man with a long nose and a slight stoop.

'I shall now ask you the question which a less alert boy would already have answered,' he said. 'Why were you lying on the ground?'

'Tubman-Edwards knocked me out, sir.'

'Gentlemen don't tell tales,' said Mr Noon reprovingly.

'I'm not really telling tales, sir,' said Henry. 'He only knocked me out cos I hit him first.'

'You're Pratt, the new boy, aren't you?'

'Yes, sir.'

'Why did you hit Tubman-Edwards, Pratt?'

'I can't tell you, sir.'

Mr Noon raised his eyebrows.

'Oh?' he said. 'Why not?'

'Gentlemen don't tell tales, sir.'

It was just about the first good moment that Henry had experienced since coming to Brasenose.

Eve Noon, a tall, shambling girl with a long nose and a slight stoop, actually smiled.

'*Touché*,' said Mr Noon. 'Well done, boy. However, I, your headmaster, am now enquiring into an incident that happened at my school, so you will no longer be telling tales, you will be helping the authorities to arrive at the truth, and that is a very different matter. Why did you hit Tubman-Edwards?'

'He called me "Oiky", sir,' said Henry.

'Boys can be very cruel,' said Mr Noon.

The three Noons walked away, and a high-pitched roar came as a wicket fell in a junior cricket match. Hannah and Eve Noon, known to the boys as Before and After, turned and looked back at Henry. Hannah, a tall, shambling girl with a long nose and a slight stoop, looked at him as if she thought he was an oik, but Eve winked.

That night, in the dorm, when everyone else was asleep, Henry allowed himself to cry a little. He had felt like crying every day since Uncle Teddy dropped his bombshell.

It had been early evening in the living room of Cap Ferrat. The sun had set over the yard-arm, and Uncle Teddy had been enjoying his first whisky.

'You aren't going back to Thurmarsh Grammar,' he had said casually.

Henry had felt as if he was in a collapsing, plunging lift.

'It's too far away for you to go there every day,' Uncle Teddy had explained.

'Where am I going?' Henry had said.

'Brasenose College.'

'Where's that?'

'In Surrey.'

Henry had stared at Uncle Teddy in astonishment.

'It's a boarding school,' Uncle Teddy had explained. 'You come home during the holidays.'

Henry had protested that he didn't want to go to Brasenose College in Surrey. Uncle Teddy had explained that he was paying, out of his own pocket, to give Henry the privilege of private education. Some people had no choice. Others were lucky enough to have made enough money to be able to give the youngsters in their care opportunites that otherwise they would not have had. Maybe the system was wrong. Uncle Teddy didn't know. He was a businessman, not an educationalist or a politician. But, while the system existed, it would be very unfair of him not to give Henry all the opportunities he could, within that system.

'I'm your father now,' Uncle Teddy had said, as he poured his second whisky. 'You're my son. I'm sending you to boarding school. You're a lucky lad.'

Henry didn't feel like a lucky lad, lying in the dorm, listening to the ivy tapping gently against the windows, and the gurgling of a pipe somewhere in the water system, and the breathing of eleven sleeping boys.

Correction. Ten sleeping boys. Lush was awake.

'Oiky?' whispered that young worthy.

'What is it?'

'Are you asleep?'

141

'How can I be if I answered you?'

'Were you casing?'

Casing was Brasenose for crying.

'Course I wasn't.'

'You don't like being called Oiky, do you?'

'Would you?'

'I can't call you Pratt.'

'How about Henry?'

'O.K. I'm Gerald. I'll tell your fortune tomorrow if you like.'

'Thanks.'

'Night, Henry.'

'Night, Gerald.'

The craze in the school at the time was for fortune-telling. The method of telling fortunes was fairly primitive. You wrote out an enormous list of occupations, with numbers, and you asked the person to give you a number, and you looked the number up on your list, and told him what he was going to be when he grew up. The reader can no doubt imagine the many humorous incidents that resulted, especially when some of the occupations listed were of a somewhat ribald nature! Nevertheless, the craze only lasted for about ten days. After that, it was the most boring thing in the world, and all the lists were thrown away.

The conversation between Henry and Gerald took place during the height of this brief craze. He went to sleep feeling happier than at any time since he had discovered that he wasn't going back to Thurmarsh.

He had written to Mr Quell, telling him that he had been sent away to school. He had also written to Martin Hammond. He had imagined Mr Quell marching up to Uncle Teddy's house, and saying to Uncle Teddy and Auntie Doris, 'This nonsense must stop. The boy has the spark. I want to teach him. Brasenose College is useless. Thurmarsh Grammar is in the van. The boys have handed me a petition. "Get Bread Van back." They all signed it. Even Oberath. They chant it during morning assembly. "We want Bread Van. We want Bread Van." You've got to help us. Let him come back, and save our school.' He had received a reply from Mr Quell ten days later. He wished him luck and was sure that he would do well. Martin Hammond wrote to say that

Mick Tunnicliffe had broken a leg, Oberath was believed to be a spy, and people of working-class origins who gave their children private education were traitors. That was what his dad said, any road.

The next day was Sunday, and Henry wondered if Gerald Lush had forgotten all about the fortune-telling, not realising its symbolic importance to Henry as the first act of unsolicited kindness he had received at Brasenose.

They went to church in a crocodile. How Henry loathed that. He kept imagining that Martin Hammond and Stefan Prziborski, or even Tommy Marsden and Chalky White and Ian Lowson, would emerge from behind the rhododendrons, doubled up with mirth.

After church, many of the boys were fetched by their doting parents. Not Henry. Nor, on this occasion, Gerald Lush. Just as they were going in to dinner he said, 'Read your fortune afterwards.'

They had unidentifiable meat, with watery carrots and roast potatoes that managed to be extremely greasy and as hard as bullets at the same time. There was spotted dick and custard to follow. A purist would not have had difficulty in finding fault with the consistency of the custard.

The thing was developing a ridiculous importance. It was only a silly craze. It was impossible that the predictions could have any real validity.

After dinner, on the gravel area outside the boys' entrance to the house, Gerald Lush told Henry's fortune.

Also present were Bullock and Tubman-Edwards.

'Choose any number between one and eight hundred and sixty-two,' said Gerald Lush.

'Six hundred and thirty-six,' said Henry, for no particular reason.

Gerald Lush hunted down his huge list. Henry fought against his irrational conviction that this moment was of vital importance.

'Engine driver,' said Gerald Lush.

'Just about right for an oik,' said Bullock.

Gerald Lush walked away. He was prepared to tell Henry's

fortune and call him Henry in the middle of the night, but he wasn't prepared to stand up for him in public.

During the next few days, before the expiry of the craze, people rushed to tell Henry's future. It was impossible for him to refuse. His fortune always came out as something like 'sewage worker', 'burglar', 'lavatory attendant' or 'schoolmaster'. He suspected that the results were being falsified, especially as nobody would ever let him see the lists. He grabbed at Harcourt's list once, and it tore, and Harcourt beat him up. Perhaps the best result of all, to judge from the mirth which it provoked, was from Webber's list.

'Cricketer,' said Webber, and everybody fell about.

Under Mr Mallet's coaching, Henry discovered that he had certain valuable cricketing assets. He had a perfect forward defensive shot, a sound back defensive shot, a classical cover drive, an elegant force off the back foot on both sides of the wicket, a delicate late cut, a savage hook. There was only one snag. He never made contact with the ball. Never ever. In the golden summer of 1947, when Compton and Edrich set the land ablaze with the magnificence of their batting, and Henry alone at Brasenose College worshipped Len Hutton, who let him down by being out of form, every boy at Brasenose College who wasn't a total weed kept detailed records of his achievements upon the pitch. Henry kept his scores as diligently as anybody. They were 0, 0, 0, 0, 0 not out, 0, did not bat, retired hurt 0, 0, 4, 0, 0, 0 not out, 0 and 0. The 4 occurred when both he and the wicket-keeper missed the ball completely, but Penfold failed to signal four byes, and the runs were credited to him. Despite this appalling record, at the end of the term he completed his final averages, like everyone else. Innings 16, not outs 4, runs 4, highest score 4, average 0.3333333333333333333 recurring. It is hard to imagine a worse predicament for a youngster at an English preparatory school shortly after the war than to be appalling at sport. Add the fact that the youngster in question loved cricket and football passionately, and you will begin to imagine the depth of his unhappiness. Add to this stew of misery the fact that the school was in Surrey and Henry spoke with the flat-capped tones of south Yorkshire. Flavour this casserole of despair with the fact that his surname was Pratt and his legs were short and plump. Season this unappetising ragout of mental anguish with the reflection that he enjoyed reading books *and* was good at lessons, and you have a picture that would surely melt the stoniest heart.

In his first term at Brasenose College, Henry was several times near to breaking point, but he held on. He endured earth in his bed, a dead song thrush ditto, three apple-pie beds and being on the losing end of innumerable fights. With these physical humiliations, he could cope. He was developing a passive courage, a stoicism which allowed his tormentors to see no hint of his agony, and thus deprived them of the ultimate pleasure of the bully. What he found much more difficult to endure was his nickname. Oiky. Oiky Pratt. Because he believed it to be true.

He'd been told it at Rowth Bridge, by no less an authority than Belinda Boyce-Uppingham. He'd half believed it then. Now he knew it was true. He just didn't know how to cope when Tubman-Edward said, 'I say, Oiky, does your old man prefer claret or burgundy?' His oikishness was vividly brought home to him in connection with the name of Uncle Teddy and Auntie Doris's house. Cap Ferrat. The boys in his dorm accused him of not knowing what it meant. He reacted angrily, for he really did believe he knew what it meant.

'O.K., know-all, what does it mean?' said Bullock.

'It's a kind of hat they use in Yorkshire when they go rabbiting with ferrets,' he said.

How they all hooted.

He *felt* oiky. His body was inelegant. His movements were clumsy. He felt that he was never quite clean, however much he washed.

Once again, Henry was happiest when buried in his lessons. Throughout his school career so far, many of his fellow pupils had thought he was a swot. Some of his teachers had sensed the presence of that rare quality, a real enthusiasm for learning, and above all for learning to think. It grieves me to have to say that they were deluded. Henry still hadn't really grasped what education was all about. He liked lessons because they were safe.

There was no pecking order of bullying in the classroom. He liked lessons because he was good at them. He did them diligently so that he would continue to be good at them. It was as simple as that.

He was taught Latin by Mr Belling, dry as dust, a human Pompeii, who went round and round the class anti-clockwise firing staccato questions. Wrong answers were marked down, and ten wrong answers meant extra work at weekends. Henry rarely got extra work at weekends.

The French teacher, Mr Massey, had wanted to be a doctor, but he had failed his finals. A simple question about medicine would guarantee at least a ten-minute diversion, in English, often with diagrams on the blackboard. Hooper and Price-Ansty would faint, in that order, at the more grisly of Mr Massey's revelations. There was an awkward moment when Mr Noon came into the classroom to find a large diagram of the human kidneys on the blackboard. Mr Massey had hurriedly asked the French for kidneys. Nobody had known.

Mr Lee-Archer, the Maths master, hurled books at boys who got things wrong. Mr Lee-Archer had once represented Great Britain, at the discus, in a three-way international athletics match against Belgium and Finland. A Maths text-book hurled at one's head from ten yards with fearsome accuracy is almost as good an incentive to a lazy boy as fostering an interest in the subject, and a lot easier.

Mr Trench, the History master, was on the verge of a nervous breakdown. Mr Trench liked facts – names, dates, venues for the signing of treaties. He disliked ideas, theories, causes, effects, parallels, motives, anything that might necessitate delving into the reasons behind the facts. But he was now beginning to lose his grasp on facts as well, and was calling on the boys to reiterate constantly the diminishing fund of facts that he could still remember – the dates of the Battle of Hastings, the signing of Magna Carta, the Battle of Agincourt, Wat Tyler's rebellion, the length of the Thirty Years War, and a few others, round and round, with the boys embarrassed and helpless, not knowing what to do.

The Geography master, Mr Hill, had no disabilities except his age. He had been pressed back into service during the war, and had stayed on. He was a good teacher, but snoozed a lot. The boys read their Geography books while he snoozed, and when he was awake he tested them. It was a system that worked well for all concerned, and nobody rocked the boat.

The English teacher, Mr Mallender, believed that hand-writing was next to godliness. His pupils might not have much to say, but at least they would say it legibly. Twice a week, for the first fifteen minutes of the lesson, they would copy out a section of Keats' 'Endymion', to be handed in for Mr Mallender's inspection. If the hand-writing fell below a certain standard, you did the same section again the next time. When you got to the end of the poem, you were excused hand-writing and were allowed to read during the first fifteen minutes of the relevant lessons. But Keats' 'Endymion' is a long poem, and some untidy boys hadn't finished it when they left Brasenose. Henry, a late starter, had no chance of ever finishing it.

One day, around the middle of June, Mr A. B. Noon B.A. entered Mr Mallender's classroom unexpectedly. All the boys stood, except Henry.

It had been a tiring day. Mr Hill hadn't fallen asleep once. Mr Lee-Archer had struck Henry a glancing blow with *Geometry for Beginners*. Mr Belling had fired irregular verbs at fearsome speed. Mr Massey had described a delicate eye operation in terms so specific that Henry had almost joined Hooper and Price-Ansty in unconsciousness, and Mr Trench's store of facts had diminished so much that Webber had calculated that the date of the Battle of Hastings was now coming round every three minutes and sixteen seconds. Henry was eleven pages into Keats' 'Endymion', with a hundred and twenty-three to go. After a good start, his writing had deteriorated under the strain, and there had been moments when he wondered if he would remain on page ten for ever. He kept making mistakes in the couplet:

Oh thou, for whose soul-soothing quiet, turtles
Passion their voices cooingly 'mong myrtles.

A jolly good couplet if you like that kind of thing, of course, even if not one of Keats' absolute humdingers. Nobody can be on top form all the time. Anyway, it did begin to pall on Henry after he'd copied it out six times. The first mistake he made was due to a lapse of concentration. The preceding lines are – well, you don't need me to tell you, especially if you're an Old Brasenosian:

By all the trembling mazes that she ran,
Hear us, great Pan!

Boys will be boys, and Henry's mind strayed to another pan, made by Cobbold and Sons of Etruria. A chance association can have the power to unlock memories of the past. Proust touched on this, and now it was happening to Henry. He was not concentrating, therefore, and "mong myrtles' is a killer if you aren't alert. On this day, Henry had at last got onto page eleven. He was writing the lines:

Their ripen'd fruitage; yellow-girted bees
Their golden honeycombs; our village leas
Their fairest blossom'd beans and poppied corn;
The chuckling linnet its five young unborn,
To sing for thee;. . .

Relieved to have got over the myrtle hurdle, Henry made the fatal mistake, as any copier will tell you, of concentrating on the meaning of the lines. The village came to life in his mind, and he was gripped by a severe melancholic nostalgia. Memories of Rowth Bridge flooded over him. He was miles away when Mr Noon entered the room and all the other boys leapt to their feet. He was up on the high fells with Simon Eckington when the clip on his ear-hole came.

'Stand up, boy,' said Mr Noon.

Henry stood up.

'Why didn't you stand up when I came in the room?'

'I was working so hard I didn't see you come in, sir,' said Henry, who no longer used 'thee' and 'tha', although there was nothing he could do about his accent.

'Nonsense, boy,' said the headmaster. 'You were dreaming. You were in a brown study, weren't you, Pratt?'

'Yes, sir.'

'You will come along to another brown study after school. My study.'

When the lessons were over, Henry went along the stone corridor, past the door to the dining room, which smelt of the morning's cabbage, past the door to the kitchen, which smelt of the evening's rissoles, past the stairs down to the changing rooms, which smelt of dungeons, past Mr Belling's classroom, which smelt of dust, through the green baize fire-door into a wider corridor, past the common room, which smelt of pipe smoke, and so to the door of the headmaster's study.

He knocked.

'Come.'

He entered.

The headmaster sat behind an even larger desk than that of Mr E. F. Crowther. His study was oak-panelled, with a bay window, and one wall was lined with bookcases, filled with learned books which came with the house, and many of which were still uncut. This study announced, 'We are men of culture here. We will teach your boy civilised values. You are not throwing good money down the drain.'

'You're new to our customs, Pratt,' said Mr Noon, 'New perhaps to concepts of discipline and team spirit, of pulling together. Are you new to the concept of pulling together, Pratt?'

'No, sir.'

'When I enter a room, and you all stand up, it is not because I suffer from megalomania. It is because I am the symbol of authority. You boys are being groomed so that one day you will take up positions of authority yourselves. You must therefore learn to respect authority as a force beyond individuality. That is why I must thrash you, Pratt. Do you understand?'

'Yes, sir.'

Henry caught a brief glimpse of Mr Trench running stark-naked among the pines. His nervous breakdown had begun. Should he tell Mr Noon? Would he be believed, or would it be taken as a frenzied attempt to evade his punishment? He decided to remain silent.

'When a boy is beaten at Brasenose,' said Mr Noon, 'it is not a punishment. It is a part of his education, and therefore he should be grateful. That is why I insist on boys thanking me after I have thrashed them. Do you understand that?'

'Yes, sir.'

'Bend over.'

Henry bent over.

'Put your hands behind your back and raise the flaps of your jacket well clear of your buttocks.'

Henry put his hands behind his back and raised the flaps of his jacket well clear of his buttocks.

Mr Noon made a practice swish with the cane.

Henry closed his eyes and gritted his teeth.

Thwack.

Not too bad.

Thwack.

Worse. Think of something nice.

Thwack.

Ouch! Think of the summer holidays.

Thwack.

Not quite such a bad one. I don't want to think of the summer holidays.

Thwack.

That did hurt. I'm dreading the summer holidays. I don't want to spend them with Uncle. . .

Thwack.

. . .Teddy and, oh God that was a bad one, Auntie Doris.

'Stand up. That's it.'

Henry stood up and turned to face Mr Noon. His backside was stinging and raw. The pain was spreading like a sunset.

'Thank you, sir,' he said.

One hot day in August, Henry woke early, in his spacious bedroom in the substantial detached house with the attractive irregular gables, in Haggersley Edge, a salubrious residential area situated between the mucky picture of Sheffield and the golden frame of the Peak District. He woke early, because he had plans. He was going back, to Paradise Lane, to see his old friend Martin Hammond. He had delayed too long. There was nothing to fear.

He pulled back the curtains, and gazed on another steamy summer morning. Already, the houses were shimmering in the haze. On the right, the high hills merged with the sky, green and blue mingling in the haze.

He washed himself thoroughly, twice. During the last few weeks of term he had ceased to be quite so spectacularly unpopular. You were never quite so unpopular once you'd had your first beating from Mr Noon. But he had still felt oiky, still had difficulty in persuading himself that he was clean.

He descended the wide, carpeted staircase of the vermin-free house.

They breakfasted on the patio. The Welgar shredded wheat, boiled egg, and toast and Oxford marmalade were a treat, even if he would have preferred Golden Shred.

Auntie Doris was wearing white shorts and a red shirt. Her legs were amazingly brown and smooth. Both she and Uncle Teddy had been very brown when he arrived back from school. (Not home from school. He couldn't quite think of it as home.) It wasn't surprising. They spent so much time on the patio during that wonderful summer. Auntie Doris's knees were varnished like stair-knobs. He caught himself wondering if she put furniture polish on them.

'You're the early bird,' she said.

'I'm going to Thurmarsh to see my old friends,' he said.

'Good idea,' she said.

She always said 'good idea'. She was glad to get him out from under her feet. He had the idea that if he said, 'I'm going to collect a pile of sheep shit and throw it at the Master Cutler,' she'd still have said 'Good idea'.

'I might be back late. I might go to the pictures,' he said.

'Good idea,' said Auntie Doris.

On Sunday, Uncle Teddy and Auntie Doris had taken him to a restaurant. They had met their friends, Geoffrey and Daphne Porringer. Geoffrey Porringer had blackheads on his nose. Daphne Porringer didn't. Geoffrey Porringer chose the wine. Daphne Porringer didn't. Geoffrey Porringer made Henry try it. 'The sooner you civilise the brats, the better,' he said. He described the wine as 'a thoughtful if slightly morose Burgundy'. Uncle Teddy laughed. Daphne Porringer didn't. Henry thought the wine was horrible, but then he was an oik.

Uncle Teddy came down to breakfast, and Henry's brain seized up.

'How's young Henry?' said Uncle Teddy, immaculate in his business suit.

'All right,' improvised Henry amusingly.

A wasp bore down upon the marmalade jar. Uncle Teddy crushed it with ease. Henry knew that if he'd tried it, it would have stung him. His body didn't feel like a part of himself. It was an enemy with which he constantly had to wrestle. He'd finished his breakfast, but he didn't dare get up until Uncle Teddy had gone, for fear of knocking the table over.

At last Uncle Teddy went, and Henry was free to go too. Auntie Doris gave him some sandwiches and a bit of extra pocket money. She was very good that way.

'Don't eat them too early,' she said.

'I won't,' he promised.

He said goodbye, hurried upstairs, and changed into scruffier clothes. He didn't want to look like a snazzy dresser in the environs of Paradise Lane. He crept out of the house in his filthy garb. Auntie Doris was on the telephone and didn't see him.

He walked down Wharfedale Road, past pleasant houses whose names suggested a conspiracy to pretend that the road was nothing to do with the city. Birchbrook. Beech Croft. Dane's Oak. Coppice View. Marshfields.

He caught a bus to the city centre, then walked through the oven of the city, from the bus station, through Fitzalan Square, and waited for the Thurmarsh tram down by the markets. The sunlight was filtering palely through the industrial smog.

He meant to change trams at Rawlaston Four Roads, but on impulse he decided to carry on into Thurmarsh and eat his sandwiches before seeing Martin. Otherwise he'd have to share them.

The tram terminus was in Mabberley Street, by the public library. He walked past the library, past the tripe butcher's, past the Thurmarsh branch of Arthur Davy and Sons, past Ted's Café, which gave out a hot whiff of potato and armpit pie, past the Maypole Dairy and the offices of the *Thurmarsh Chronicle and Argus*. The newspaper placards announced, 'Worse than darkest

1940 – Eden', and 'My night of shame – Thurmarsh Councillor'.

He sat on a wooden bench in the little gardens opposite the Town Hall. The clock on the Town Hall said 11.07. He might as well eat his sandwiches. Exhausted sooty sparrows and dishevelled starlings eyed him hopefully. The sun beat down on him. He opened the packet. She'd given him Gentleman's Relish again. What on earth had possessed him to pretend to like it when she had given it to him as a treat on the first day of the holidays? A fear of seeming unsophisticated, perhaps. An urge to shed his oikishness. Possibly, the reader will suspect, an hereditary streak of gastronomic masochism. His father, a dry meat man, had suffered his food to be drowned in gravy throughout his married life. For years all three of them had endured brawn together, each in the mistaken belief that the other two liked it. Now, a twelve-year-old boy with no relish for becoming a gentleman struggled through his Gentleman's Relish on a seat stained by starling droppings.

He finished his sandwiches at 11.16, flinging a token crumb towards the birds. Three sparrows fought for it. A starling pushed them out of the way and ate it. A small cloud, barely visible in the haze, briefly obscured the sun.

Would he talk to Martin about the strange teachers at Brasenose College, about Miss Prune, the matron, who had nailed her flag to the mast of clean underwear, about the boys all calling him Oiky? Would they discuss the amazing form of Compton and Edrich, and the fortunes of Yorkshire cricket?

He caught the Rawlaston tram. They clanked past the end of Link Lane. Four men were washing a fire engine, but there was no life around the grammar school. How small it looked. How tiny the houses were, as the tram moaned wearily up the hill. They breasted the rise, and looked down into the hazy valley of the Rundle. On the right, Brunswick Road Primary School, Devil's Island in a sea of brick. Their descent levelled out; the road swung right. On the left was the canal, smaller and weedier than in his memory. The canal swung away from the road, and the cul-de-sacs began. How minute they were. Everything was tiny except the vast, blank wall of Crapp, Hawser and Kettlewell. 'Paradise,' yelled the conductor. His legs wouldn't move. The tram stopped.

There was the corner shop. There was the chippy. How grimy it all was. He remained seated. A wave of relief swept over him as he realised that he wasn't going to get off, and then as soon as the tram was on its way once more, and the last of the cul-de-sacs was left behind, and the vast world of Crapp, Hawser and Kettlewell became past history also, the relief changed to regret. He should have got off. He hadn't. He wouldn't.

'I thought tha wanted Paradise,' said the conductor.

'I've changed me mind,' he said.

Steam escaped from the slender chimneys of the steelworks. Steam drifted out of gaps in the walls. Steam rose from innumerable shunting engines. A steam train roared along the line to Henry's left. The hills drifted steamily in the weak sun. Henry was adrift in a steamy world. These were the doldrums.

He got off the tram at Rawlaston, because it went no further. He was parched. He didn't know what language to use, even to himself. He was in a linguistic no man's land. 'Ee, I'm fair clammed,' had been left behind. 'Gosh, I'm absolutely Hairy Mac Thirsters,' had not yet arrived. He bought a bottle of Tizer, a newspaper, a packet of Nuttall's Mintoes, and a lucky bag.

He sat on a wall, behind which there would soon be a building site. He could smell a nearby chippy. He sipped his Tizer and examined the contents of his lucky bag. It contained sherbet, a little saying and a trick. The saying blew away in a sudden gust of hot wind, and the trick fell into the building site as he tried to rescue the saying.

He'd bought the paper to find out the cinema programmes. Fool that he was. It was a national paper. He skimmed through the headlines, for want of anything better to do. 'Attlee may sack five ministers.' 'Lords told "Rule or Quit Palestine".' 'Cannot call barrow boys crooks – Isaacs.' 'August heat above normal.' 'Julius napped at Haydock.' One of the adverts showed a man with a far-away look. The caption read, 'He's dreaming of the days when Vantella Shirts and Van Heusen Collars Are Easy to Get Again (with curve-woven semi-stiff collars and cuffs!)' Could anyone really dream of things like that? He crumpled the paper up and tossed it into the building site. A middle-aged woman said, 'Now then. Tha shouldn't throw litter, tha knows.' 'Why don't you drop dead, you fat cow?' he shouted. 'Young people today. I don't know,' said the woman, continuing on her way. He took a swig of lukewarm Tizer and dropped down off the wall. He deliberately barged into a woman shopper. 'Look where you're going,' she said. 'Oh go home and stew yourself in your knickers,' he riposted wittily. The mood passed. He finished his Tizer, caught a tram to Sheffield, and bought a copy of the *Star*.

Most of the films were 'A' or 'X'. He had used up all his bravado, and, in any case, there was no way he could pretend to be sixteen.

The only 'U' films were Elizabeth Taylor in *Courage of Lassie* at the Roscoe, Deanna Durbin in *I'll be Yours* at the Gaumont, Norman Evans, Nat Jackley and Dan Young in *Demobbed* at the Forum, Southey, *The Jolson Story* at the Lyric, Darnall, *Old Mother Riley Detective* at the Hillsboro' Kinema, Abbott and Costello in *The Time of Their Lives* at the Paragon, Firth Park, and *My Brother Talks to Horses* at the Rex, Intake. After ten minutes of agonised debate, he realised that he probably hadn't enough money to go to any cinema which involved an extra bus ride. He checked on the state of his finances.

All he could afford was the News Theatre in Fitzalan Square. He saw the news, a Laurel and Hardy comedy, two cartoons, one of which was a Donald Duck and the other of which wasn't, a semi-humorous feature on dogs, a film about ice sports, the news, a Laurel and Hardy comedy, two cartoons, one of which was a Donald Duck, and the other of which wasn't, a semi-humorous feature on dogs, a film about ice sports, the news, a Laurel and Hardy comedy, and two cartoons, one of which was a Donald Duck and the other of which wasn't. The best programme begins to lose its savour when you've seen it two and a half times, and he emerged blearily into the glaring, late-afternoon furnace that was Sheffield, city of steel.

It was still only twenty to five when he arrived back at Wharfedale Road. The tar in the road was tacky. His legs were stuck. The pavement was made of glue. He was walking, yet hardly moving, as in a dream. He would never reach Cap Ferrat.

He entered through the French windows, forgetting that he had secretly changed into scruffy clothes before leaving.

Geoffrey Porringer was sitting beside Auntie Doris on the

settee. They were drinking China tea.

'What sort of day have you had, young sir?' said Geoffrey Porringer.

'Very nice,' said Henry, but he didn't elaborate.

Quite soon Geoffrey Porringer stood up and said, 'Well. I'm sorry I missed Teddy,' and Auntie Doris said, 'What is it I'm to tell him?' and Geoffrey Porringer said, 'Tell him Bingley can't cope. We'll have to explore other avenues,' and then he nodded at Henry, said, 'Don't worry, Einstein, it may never happen,' and departed through the French windows.

Henry went upstairs and had a lukewarm bath and still didn't feel clean and lay on his bed, dressed only in his pants, as the evening slowly began to cool.

He dressed, and went down for dinner. He was a far cry from any boy who might have been in Rawlaston earlier that day saying, 'Why don't you drop dead, you fat cow?'

He was resolved to make more of a conversational show than he had managed heretofore.

An opening gambit lay ready to hand.

'Don't forget Geoffrey Porringer's message,' he reminded Auntie Doris.

'Geoffrey Porringer?' said Uncle Teddy. 'Has he been here?'

'He popped in this afternoon,' said Auntie Doris. 'With a message.'

'Why couldn't he ring me at the office?' said Uncle Teddy.

'I don't know,' said Auntie Doris. 'I'm not a mind reader.'

'Perhaps it was secret. It sounded pretty secret,' said Henry.

'What was this message?' said Uncle Teddy.

'I can't remember,' said Auntie Doris.

'He brings me a message so secret and important that he can't phone me at the office, and you forget it!' said Uncle Teddy.

'I remember it,' said Henry. 'He said, "Bingley can't cope. We'll have to explore other avenues." '

'I don't understand it,' said Uncle Teddy. 'What the hell does he mean? Bingley?'

'It's probably in code,' said Henry.

Uncle Teddy glared at Auntie Doris, then turned to Henry. 'That'll be it,' he said.

'Pretty useless code,' said Henry, 'if nobody knows what it means.'

Uncle Teddy and Auntie Doris said little after that, giving Henry a golden opportunity, over the bread and butter pudding, to raise a subject that had been worrying him.

'I think you've been done at Brasenose,' he said.

'Done?' said Uncle Teddy.

'Yes,' said Henry. 'You're paying lots of money, but the education's worse than at Thurmarsh, which is free.'

He hoped that Uncle Teddy would be so upset that he would remove him from Brasenose immediately. But it didn't work.

'It's what we call a preparatory school,' explained Uncle Teddy. 'You aren't there to be educated. You're there to be prepared.'

'What for?'

'Dalton.'

Henry looked at Uncle Teddy blankly.

'Dalton is one of the best public schools in the country,' said Auntie Doris.

'Where is it?' said Henry.

'In Somerset,' said Uncle Teddy. 'Rather a long way away. That's the only fly in the ointment.'

'I'm Labour,' Henry said.

There was a horrified silence in the dorm.

The financial crisis of 1947, even thought it was largely a result of the nation having bankrupted itself in order to win the war, was proof to all the boys of Brasenose College, except Henry, that Labour were unfit to run the country. 1947 saw the nationalisation of railways, canals, road haulage and electricity. It saw the school-leaving age raised to fifteen (not a good selling-point at Brasenose). It saw the final transfer of power in India to India. All this was regarded as unarguably awful by all the boys of Brasenose College, except Henry.

Why had he told them, thought Henry bitterly after lights-out in the bare-boarded, uncurtained, Spartan dorm, with its row of wash-basins down the middle? How could he establish any relationship with them? How could he ever talk to them about his past? What could he ever tell them about it? That he had lived in a rat-infested, back-to-back terrace with a one-eyed, retired parrot-strangler?

Yes. Yes, yes, yes, yes, yes. The answer was so simple that he couldn't believe that he had been too stupid to see it before. There was no need of any grocer from Abergavenny here. He had himself. He would mock himself before they did.

He began to call himself 'Oiky'. 'Shut up, Oiky,' he'd say, or 'Come on, our Oik.' One day, at dinner, he convulsed the table by gazing at his plate and saying, 'It's months since I 'ad rat.' For years he had envied comedians their catch-phrases. Now, he had one of his own. It was a good 'un and all. 'It's months since I 'ad rat.'

That term, Henry discovered that he was as bad at rugby football as he was at cricket. He never once managed to repeat the successful tackle he had made on Pam Yardley. When he kicked the ridiculously shaped ball, he never knew where it would go. He even managed to achieve the near impossible by slicing it over his own goal-posts. Everyone collapsed with laughter, even Mr Lee-Archer, the referee, who wasn't sure whether you could score an own dropped goal at rugby. Henry stood there, looking sheepish. As the laughter died down, he knew that it was time for him to use his catchphrase.

'It's months since I 'ad rat,' he said.

It went down like a plate of cold sick. Why? Why?

Because it was inappropriate! Brilliant though his catch-phrase was, the opportunities for its use were too limited.

He needed something of more general application.

A catch-phrase must be ordinary. You couldn't imagine Oscar Wilde touring the halls and producing loud laughter every time he said, 'Fox hunting is the unspeakable in pursuit of the uneatable.' A witticism constantly repeated becomes a stale witticism. A catch phrase is, 'I won't take me coat off. I'm not stopping,' or 'It's agony, Ivy.'

Henry's came out by accident after he'd put his foot on the edge of his porridge plate while clambering to his place over the top of the bench. The plate tilted, and his portion of porridge flew through the air, like a slightly soggy discus, into his face. When the laughter died down, he said, 'E, by gum, I am daft.' It fitted him. It was comfortable. It was his. It was appropriate on all occasions. He was Henry 'Ee, by gum, I am daft' Pratt.

In the Christmas holidays, Uncle Teddy and Auntie Doris gave him a model railway, and he began to sample the delights of regular cinema-going. In the Easter term he discovered that he was as bad at hockey as at cricket and football. Mr Trench returned, having made an amazing recovery. He was helped by the fact that the boys never mocked him. In their eyes, a schoolmaster who ran naked through the woods had a certain heroic quality about him. Henry was past page fifty of Keats' 'Endymion' now, and if his French was a trifle sketchy, he could no doubt have had a shot at a simple appendectomy, had the need ever arisen.

One day, while Mr Hill dozed, Henry tried not to meander while reading why rivers did. So effective was he in this effort that once again he didn't know that Mr Noon was in the room until he received his old chum, the clip round the ear-hole.

'Why didn't you stand up when I came in the room?' said Mr Noon.

'I didn't hear you, sir,' said Henry. 'I was concentrating on my work.'

'Nonsense, boy, you were in a brown study,' said Mr Noon.

'No, sir. I wasn't,' said Henry.

'Come and see me in another brown study at the beginning of break,' said the headmaster.

'That's not fair, sir,' said Henry.

'Tut tut! Tut tut!' said Mr A. B. Noon B.A. palindromically. 'Not fair, eh? We'll see about that.'

In the break, Henry made the long trek to the headmaster's study, past the burgeoning sweat of rissoles, through the green baize door, past the acrid common-room fug.

'I really didn't know you were there, sir, because I was working so hard,' said Henry.

'I don't accuse you of lying,' said the headmaster. 'I merely say this. If you are lying, you deserve to be thrashed. If you aren't, then your thrashing will be unfair, and that will be an excellent preparation for life, because life is unfair, and it would be unfair of me to give you the impression that it isn't, so I shall thrash you anyway.'

Mr Noon gave him six of the best.

'Thank you, sir,' he said.

Back in the dorm that night, a bit of a hero because of his unjust thrashing, having shown his weals to the admiring throng, Henry was asked by Bullock, 'You've turned out not to be too bad a chap at all, Oiky. Are you honestly Labour?'

'Yes,' said Henry.

'Why?' said Bullock.

Now this was a shrewd question. Being Conservative or Labour didn't really have anything to do with politics. It was simply what one was. One was either Oxford or Cambridge, and similarly one was either Conservative or Labour, except that one was never Labour. Henry had accused them of being Conservative because they were sheep. Was he himself any better?

'Come on, Oiky. Why?' said Price-Ansty.

'I just don't think it's fair that some people should have so much more than others,' he said. He thought it sounded pretty lame, but it was the best he could do.

'They've earned it,' said Bullock.

'Not always,' said Henry. 'They get left it.'

'Their people earned it,' said Gerald Lush. 'You Labour chaps want to take everything away. That's what my father says anyway.'

'Don't you think there are working-class people capable of earning it?' said Henry.

'Of course I do,' said Price-Ansty. 'My father said that some of the working-class chaps in his regiment were jolly intelligent. He was quite surprised.'

'We're not getting at you, Oiky,' said Gerald Lush. 'You're pretty clever.'

'For an oik,' said Bullock, and everybody laughed.

Henry grinned too. Not as much inside as outside, perhaps, but if you grinned externally at a thing often enough, you did find that the internal pain began to ease.

By the end of his life at Brasenose, it was really quite tolerable. Nobody really seemed to hate him any more, except Tubman-Edwards, and he hated everybody.

Uncle Teddy and Auntie Doris were as brown as berries when he got home. He went to see Yorkshire play cricket twice and saw the first home games of Sheffield Wednesday and Sheffield

United. They took Cousin Hilda to Bakewell for tea, and Henry discovered that the greatest author in the world wasn't Captain W. E. Johns after all. It was a woman! Her name was Agatha Christie. He went to the pictures twice a week. You could forget all your worries there. You could even forget that before long you were going to Dalton College, and the whole painful business of beginning again was going to begin all over again.

8 It Rears Its Ugly Head

There were sixteen wash-basins round the walls and eight more in the middle of the room. On the floor there were slatted wooden boards. Beyond the wash-basins there were four large, heavily stained baths. The showers were downstairs, beyond the changing rooms. Such were the washing arrangements in Orange House, in Dalton College, in Somerset, and washing was still very important to Henry in the autumn of 1948. So diligently, with what thoroughness and vigour, did he ablute himself that he suddenly realised that he was all alone in a deserted wash-room.

A prefect poked his head round the door and said, 'Get to bed, you. It's past lights-out.'

He went out into the long, bare corridor. It was very dimly lit by a night-light at the far end.

He entered the dormitory. It was pitch dark. He knew that his bed was the third on the left. He felt his way round the walls. He edged past the first bed, walking very slowly, his left hand stretched out in front of him, his right hand clutching his towel and washing bag. His left hand connected with the second bed.

'Is that you, Badger?' whispered a voice from the second bed.

'No. I'm Pratt,' whispered Henry.

'Are you good-looking? If so, hop in,' whispered the voice from the second bed.

Henry moved on as fast as he dared in the impenetrable dark.

'Shut up, you blokes up that end,' shouted Hertford-Jones, the dorm prefect. 'Some of us want to get some crud.'

Henry edged his way round the third bed, and got in as quietly as he could.

'Get out,' yelled the bed's occupant, as Henry snuggled up against him.

'Shut up, Perkins,' shouted Hertford-Jones.

'No, honestly, Hertford-Jones,' said the one who must be Perkins. 'A raging homo's just got into bed with me.'

'Send him over here,' said another voice, and there was

laughter.

The dormitory was flooded with light. Henry was edging away from Perkins's bed, crimson with shame.

'I thought that was my bed,' he said, looking round desperately. Every bed appeared to be full, except the end one, and that must be Hertford-Jones's.

'I know moral standards are declining, but honestly,' said Perkins.

'Which dorm are you in?' said Hertford-Jones.

'South Africa,' said Henry.

'This is New Zealand,' said Hertford-Jones. 'You're in the wrong bloody dorm, you cretin.'

Henry edged his way out.

'See you later,' whispered the boy in the bed next to Perkins.

Henry closed the door of New Zealand carefully and groped his way down the corridor, away from the night-light, towards South Africa.

It was pitch black in South Africa. He felt his way carefully past the first two beds, still clutching his towel and washing bag. He was sweating freely. He might as well not have bothered to wash at all.

He found the third bed. This time he explored it with his hands before getting in.

It seemed empty.

He clambered into bed.

His feet touched something soft.

He screamed.

South Africa dorm was filled with blinding light, and alive with protestation.

'What the hell's going on?' said Nattrass, the dorm prefect.

'There's something in my bed,' said Henry, pulling back his bedclothes, to reveal a dead thrush.

Nattrass came over and examined it.

'It's a dead thrush,' he said. 'Who did this? Bloody little savages. I suppose nobody will have the guts to own up.'

Nobody spoke.

'What's your name?' Nattrass asked Henry.

'Pratt,' said Henry, knowing that laughter would follow as

163

surely as birth follows womb.

'Chuck it out of the window,' said Nattrass, and Henry picked up the horrible, lifeless bird, trying not to show his revulsion, trying not to catch its dead eye. The dead thrush at Brasenose College had been a song thrush (*Turdus philomelos*). This was the substantially larger mistle thrush (*Turdus viscivorus*). He hurled it far into the mellow Somerset night.

'Sleep on top of your sheets, Pratt,' said Nattrass. 'I'll get matron to change them tomorrow. Right, lights out. The fun's over, you bloody savages. Let's get some crud.'

The room was plunged into darkness, and Henry was glad of it, for he was on the verge of tears.

He lay on top of his sheets, reflecting on his somewhat unfortunate first day at Dalton College. Seeing that he was getting nervous about arriving at yet another new school, Auntie Doris had decided that he should be driven there. Uncle Teddy being too busy, she had driven him herself. On both his trunk and tuck box she had put sticky labels, which said 'H. E. Pratt. Orange House. Dalton College. Dalton. Somerset.' Henry had objected, on the grounds that the luggage was unlikely to go astray in transit while in the boot of their own car.

It had been a long drive to Somerset, and Auntie Doris had got lost twice. Eventually they had reached an attractive little stone-built town, and there, unmistakably, was the school. Auntie Doris had driven up to the gates. Henry hadn't been able to lift his trunk out of the boot. Auntie Doris had asked a passing seventeen-year-old to help them, and Henry had felt mortified about the labels, which would surely strike the seventeen-year-old as ridiculously fussy.

'Dalton College?' the seventeen-year-old had said.

'Yes,' Henry had said.

'This is King's School, Bruton,' the seventeen-year-old had said, not without a hint of amusement.

Henry had put his tuck box back in the boot, and they had driven on. Auntie Doris had said, 'You see. It was lucky I labelled them. I might have dropped you at the wrong school and driven off.' He had got into a lather because they were going to be late. And when they had at last found Dalton College, it had been to learn that Orange House was not actually on the premises. It was a large, rambling, three-storied, purpose-built, late-Victorian mansion on the edge of the town. By the time they had found it, it had been seventeen minutes past seven. Forty-seven minutes late! He had found the greatest difficulty in restraining himself from bursting into tears.

The porter, Gorringe, had tottered out, gasping for breath, his arms long, his legs bent, deformed by long years of carrying the trunks of the young gentry. Gorringe had grasped one end of the trunk and Henry the other. It had been extremely heavy, containing as it did the large number of clothes demanded by the school. Cousin Hilda had insisted that she sewed on the Cash's name-tapes, announcing that each item was the property of 287 H. Pratt. She had sniffed as she sewed one onto his jockstrap.

Henry had returned for his tuck box, which was also quite heavy, containing, among other delights, twelve jars of Gentleman's Relish, one for each week of term.

Aunti Doris had clasped him in a perfumed embrace, and smacked a great kiss onto his cheek, and *she* had cried. He had waved as she drove off half-blinded by tears, and he had felt empty of emotion. Then he had picked up his tuck box and struggled into the bowels of Orange House, a plump, nervous boy with a south Yorkshire accent, who smelt like a perfume factory and had a large smear of lipstick on his right cheek.

Henry had found his junior study, which he would share with seven other boys, each having a partition which he could decorate as he wished, within the confines of decorum. Senior boys had a study between two. Junior boys fagged for senior boys for two years. The roster informed Henry that he was to fag for Davey and Pilkington-Brick.

'You'd better go straight along,' the fair-haired boy in the next partition had advised him.

And so he had presented himself, nervously, at the second study from the end on the left upstairs.

Davey, tall, slim, dark, with a long, sad face, only sixteen but looking immensely grown up to Henry, had said, 'You've got lipstick on your cheek.'

Pilkington-Brick, even taller, and massive, with a large

moon-shaped, cheerful face, also only sixteen, also looking immensely grown up to Henry, had said, 'You smell like a Turkish brothel.'

Davey had said, 'Have we a sex maniac for our fag, Tosser?'

Pilkington-Brick had said, 'It could be an interesting couple of years, Lampo.'

Davey had said, 'Henry Pratt. What a deliciously uncompromising name. How proudly banal.'

Pilkington-Brick had said, 'Don't you worry about a thing, young Pratt. You've got a plum position here.'

Davey had said, 'It's true. Tosser is good-natured to the point of terminal boredom, and I'm just a clapped-out old roué.'

Lampo Davey had smiled. His mouth was slightly twisted when he smiled. Henry had left the room clumsily, in total bewilderment, utterly out of his depth.

He had welcomed bed-time, not knowing what horrors it would bring. Now he lay on top of his sheets, taking stock. Dead birds, to date, three. Parrot. Song thrush. Mistle thrush. What more did life hold in store for him? A rotting blackbird in his desk? A headless cormorant stuffed down his trousers?

There was a symphony of deep breathing, grunting and near-snoring. The odd whistle of breath. An occasional roar from a lorry on the main road. Should he run away and hitch-hike back to Cap Ferrat? How thrilled Uncle Teddy and Auntie Doris would be!

At last, shortly before the clock of St Peter's Church struck four, Henry fell into a light, uneasy crud.

The next day, as he walked up the main road, away from the little stone-built market town, towards the school, Henry found himself beside Paul Hargreaves, the fair-haired boy from the next partition in his junior study. Paul Hargreaves told him that his father was a brain surgeon. Henry told Paul Hargreaves that his father was a test pilot.

The school was set in a valley, surrounded by lush, wooded hills. It was a real jumble, with the original stone Queen Anne mansion flanked on one side by a high-roofed Victorian chapel which cried out for a spire and on the other by a two-storey block in the Bauhaus style, designed by an old Daltonian who died when the avant-garde squash court that he had designed collapsed on him in 1934. Many people thought it just retribution for a man who had done more than anybody else to ruin the look of the school.

In the chapel the boys sat in long rows, facing each other across the central aisle. In the middle of the first prayer, fruitily intoned by the chaplain, the Reverend L. A. Carstairs (known to the boys as Holy C), Henry had a nasty shock. He caught sight of Tubman-Edwards, who winked at him.

Henry was in Form 1A, the form for the brightest of the new boys. So was Paul Hargreaves. Tubman-Edwards wasn't.

And so there began again the process of finding classrooms and going through endless roll-calls, which made the first day a relatively undemanding exercise, a breather before the rigours to come. When lessons proper began, and his Maths teacher (Loopy L) picked up a text-book, Henry instinctively ducked. He found that he was backward at Maths, but a star performer at Latin, thanks to Mr Belling. And all the time he felt a sense of security that had come to him rarely in his school life. Friendship, which had so often proved so difficult, was suddenly easy here. Henry and Paul kept finding themselves next to each other. They were both sensitive and shy. Already, by Friday evening, Paul Hargreaves was his best friend ever.

That Friday evening, after tea (sausage and lumpy mash, served by the wheezing Gorringe), Henry and Paul were beginning the decoration of their partitions in the junior study. Paul was favouring a kind of collage of works of art which had a significance for him. There were postcards of works by people Henry had never heard of, like Salvador Dali and Braque. His own display promised to be slightly less sophisticated, consisting as it did entirely of cuttings from the *Picturegoer*. Uncle Teddy and Auntie Doris had arranged for him to receive the *Picturegoer* every week, and his growing interest in films blossomed into an obsession at a time when it was impossible for him to go out and see any.

Suddenly a cry rent the air. 'All new-bugs to the shower room.'

The sixteen new-bugs in Orange House assembled slightly uneasily in the bleak, stone-walled shower room, with its ten showers.

They were met by Hertford-Jones.

'O.K., you blokes,' said Hertford-Jones. 'Line up against the wall.'

They lined up against the wall, their uneasiness growing. Nothing pleasant in life is preceded by being lined up against a wall.

'O.K. Drop your shonkers,' said Hertford-Jones.

They stared at him blankly.

'Shonkers are trousers,' said Hertford-Jones impatiently, as if everybody knew that.

They dropped their shonkers.

'Ready, doctor,' sang out Hertford-Jones.

A cold autumn wind whistled through the shower room, lifting their shirts like cat-flaps.

A young doctor entered, in a white coat. He carried a small torch and a notebook. He examined their genitalia and surrounds with his torch and said either 'yes' or 'no' to Hertford-Jones, who put either a tick or a cross against their names. Henry and Paul both got ticks. Feltstein, who was Jewish, got a cross.

'Right,' said the doctor. 'The following thirteen boys – Keynes, Wellard, Curtis-Brown, Pratt, Hargreaves, Mallet, Needham, Renwick, Pellet, Forbes-Robinson, Bickerstaff, Tidewell and Willoughby – will be circumcised tomorrow. Be at the bottom of house drive at seven-thirty. Bring an overnight bag, just in case.'

'Please, sir,' said Paul Hargreaves, going red. 'My father's a doctor. I don't think he'd like me to be circumcised without his permission.'

'We have parental permission,' said the doctor. 'We wouldn't dream of doing it without.'

The doctor and Hertford-Jones departed, and the new-bugs debated. Could it be a hoax?

'It sounds like a hoax to me,' said Paul. 'I'm going to see Mr Satchel.'

Paul walked straight through the library and into the housemaster's part of the building.

Quite soon he returned, a little abashed.

'It's genuine,' he said.

That night, in South Africa, Nattrass tried to ease Henry's worries.

'I've had it,' he said. 'Nothing to it. Snip snip, thank you very much. They use a local anaesthetic and you don't have to look.'

After lights-out, Fletcher whispered to Henry from the next bed.

'Pratt?'

'Yes?'

'Good luck tomorrow. There's nothing to worry about. Doctor Wallis at Taunton General is the second best circumcision man in England. Only old Thursby at Barts is better. He hasn't had *any* cock-ups.'

'Has Doctor Wallis had cock-ups, then?'

'Only the one.'

'What happened?'

'Let's just say it was a bit of a balls-up, and leave it at that.'

'What happened?'

'I don't think you ought to know. It might spoil your crud.'

But Henry's crud was already spoilt. So was Keynes's, Wellard's, Curtis-Brown's, Hargreaves's, Mallet's, Needham's, Renwick's, Pellet's. Forbes-Robinson's, Bickerstaff's, Tidewell's and Willoughby's.

In the morning, the tremulous thirteen set off down the drive with three bags each, one in their hands, and one under each eye.

Shortly after eight o'clock, they trudged back, sheepish and red-faced, but also relieved, to cheers from the faces at the dormitory windows. It turned out that the doctor was Hertford-Jones's older brother.

That night, in South Africa, Nattrass explained that the ritual of the thirteen circumcisees of Orange House went back over a hundred years. It was mildly unpleasant when it happened to you, perhaps, but a real hoot in the years to come.

'But even Mr Satchel pretended it was true,' said Henry, puzzled.

'It's a tradition,' explained Nattrass, but he wasn't sure that Henry understood.

In the next weeks, a chain of events occurred concerning Henry's parentage.

When Paul had said that his father was a brain surgeon, Henry had only half believed it. He had said that his father was a test pilot on impulse, half thinking that he was involved in a joke routine. But Paul's father *was* a brain surgeon. Henry hoped that Paul had forgotten that his father was supposed to be a test pilot.

The first link in the chain was forged during a French lesson, given by Mr Wrigley (Sweaty W). His classroom was light and airy, in the Bauhaus block.

'No, Mallender,' said Sweaty W. 'It's a *pris*. The perfect of *prendre* takes *avoir*, as in "*Le mecanicien a pris le livre tout de suite*".' Sweaty W wrote the sentence on the blackboard. 'What does that mean, Pratt?' he said.

Henry's heart sank.

'The mechanic. . .' he began.

'Yes?'

'The mechanic has put the hare all over the furniture.'

'Are you trying to be funny, Pratt?'

'No, sir.'

'Hargreaves?'

'The mechanic. . .has taken. . .the book. . .at once,' said Paul, pretending that he found it difficult, so as not to humiliate his friend.

'The mechanic took the book at once,' said Sweaty W. 'What did you learn in French at your prep school, Pratt?'

'How to take out tonsils and gall-stones, sir.'

'What???'

'He means he went to Brasenose College, sir,' said Mallender.

Sweaty W stared at Mallender.

'What?' he said.

'The French master at Brasenose is a failed doctor, sir. He spends most of his time telling the boys how to do operations, in English,' said Mallender. 'My father teaches English there.'

Henry stared at Mallender in surprise, and wondered if he'd ever had to copy out the whole of Keats' 'Endymion'.

Sweaty W believed in improvisation, to give a certain vitality and edge to his French lessons. Should a window-cleaner ever fall off his ladder and drop head-first past the window onto the asphalt, no boy would have been allowed to go to his assistance until the class had produced the French for ' a window-cleaner has just fallen off his ladder and dropped head-first past the window onto the asphalt'.

'In French, Mallender,' said Sweaty W now. 'In French. My father is an English teacher.'

'*Mon père est un professeur de l'Anglais.*'

'Yes, though perhaps *professeur*'s putting it a big high for Brasenose College, and the French don't use *un* before an occupation. It's "*Mon père est professeur*".'

They went briefly round the class then, saying what their fathers did. '*Mon père est fermier.*' '*Mon père est aussi fermier.*' ('No, he isn't, Fuller.' 'I know, sir, but I don't know the French for estate agent.') '*Mon père est. . .il. . .*he's a lawyer, sir.' ('*Votre père est avocat*, Tremlett.') '*Mon père a laissé mon mère pour cinq ans.*' ('It's *ma mère*, and *depuis cinq ans*, and I'm sorry, Bairstow.') '*Mon père. . .*' Henry hesitated. Did Paul remember that he'd said that his father was a test pilot? Whether Paul remembered or not, should he now tell the truth? How could he, since he didn't know the French for a cutler, or a maker of penknives? Wasn't it an academic point, since he didn't know the French for test pilot either? Wouldn't it be simpler just to say that his father was dead?

'*Il essaye les avions*,' said Paul. 'He's a test pilot, sir.'

'*Votre père est pilote d'essai*, Pratt,' said Sweaty W.

Fair enough, thought Henry.

The second link occurred in Dalton Town. Boys were allowed into the town at certain times, and one of Henry's duties as a fag was to shop for Lampo Davey and Tosser Pilkington-Brick. On this occasion, as it chanced, he required writing paper, envelopes, instant coffee, condensed milk, drinking chocolate, a loaf and a tin of sardines.

Two unpleasant incidents occurred on this particular day. As he trudged down Eastgate in the rain, he was drenched from head to foot when a Carter Patterson removal van ploughed through a huge puddle outside Boots.

The second unfortunate incident happened in the market place, outside Butcher's the draper's. A charming square, in those days, Dalton market place. A jumble of Tudor and Georgian stone buildings with the Georgian Town Hall at the east end and the cathedral-like early-English parish church at the west end. Those are still there, but the north side is now totally disfigured by the hideous new shopping precinct, built in the late-sixties balance-sheet style. On that day, in early October, 1948, the north side of the market place was disfigured by an equally unpleasant sight, a human portent of the institutionalised vandalism to come. Tubman-Edwards.

'I thought you were going to Eton,' said Henry.

'It fell through,' said Tubman-Edwards, colouring. 'What's it worth to shut me up?'

'I don't understand,' said Henry.

'It doesn't understand,' said Tubman-Edwards. 'Well it soon will. It's changed a bit since I first knew it. It's still a pretty oiky individual, but it has toned down its accent quite a lot. Not totally successfully, of course, but still, it stands a reasonable chance of avoiding the nickname "Oiky". Specially now its father turns out to be a test pilot. Amazing. When Fuller told me there was a chap from Brasenose in his class, and it was you, and your father was a test pilot, I said nothing. Quick thinking, eh, Oiky? The possibilities struck me immediately. What's it worth for me not to reveal the truth, Oiky?'

Tubman-Edwards smirked. It was not a pretty sight. The church clock struck two, and reverberated into silence. Henry wished he was stronger than Tubman-Edwards.

'Seven hundred boys calling you "Oiky". Seven hundred boys knowing you're a shitty little liar. How much is it worth to shut me up, Oiky?'

'Twelve jars of Gentleman's Relish,' said Henry.

Perhaps, if it hadn't been for those twelve jars, he would have told Tubman-Edwards to shove off. The truth would have been out, and after some initial unpleasantness the matter might eventually have been forgotten. But it seemed like a master-stroke, a golden opportunity to get rid of Tubman-Edwards and his Gentleman's Relish at the same time.

'I don't like Gentleman's Relish,' said Tubman-Edwards.

'It's marvellous stuff,' said Henry. 'Every sandwich a treat.

Every mouthful a poem.'

'Why are you so eager to get rid of it, then?' said Tubman-Edwards.

'I'm not,' said Henry. 'But I've got to give you something, and it's all I've got.'

'I can swop them, I suppose,' said Tubman-Edwards. 'All right, you've got yourself a deal.'

Henry's reading had just passed through its detective-story period and was just coming onto its John Buchan, A. E. W. Mason and Scarlet Pimpernel stage. He should have been familiar with the old adage that 'the blackmailer always comes back for more'.

The following week, when he handed over his twelve jars of Gentleman's Relish outside Baker's the butcher's (they're all multiple stores now, but in those days an additional charm of Dalton market place was its cluster of shops whose proprietors bore the names of other kinds of shop), Tubman-Edwards said, 'That'll do for the first week.'

When they met the following week, outside Draper's the chemist's, Henry found himself committed to giving Tubman-Edwards all his pocket money for the rest of the term.

It was too late for Henry to tell the truth now. Tubman-Edwards was busily spreading false information about his father. Henry learnt that his father was testing amazing new prototypes. He was involved in a secret space project which might eventually make him the first man on the moon. He didn't need to boast. Tubman-Edwards did it for him. It was out of his control.

The following week, Tubman-Edwards took the money that he had been given by Lampo Davey and Tosser Pilkington-Brick for the purchase of instant coffee, condensed milk, drinking chocolate, mayonnaise, eggs and a tin of anchovies.

Henry walked back to Orange House in utter dejection, mocked by the soft sunshine of late October. The one ray of light in the whole gloomy business had been that Tubman-Edwards was in Plantaganet House. Orange House had remained a safe haven. How safe would it be, when he returned to Lampo Davey and Tosser Pilkington-Brick empty-handed?

He knocked timidly on their study door.

Davey was on his own, Pilkington-Brick having gone to train for the first fifteen.

Henry stood by the door, irresolute, silent.

'What is it, Pratt?' said Lampo Davey irritably.

'I dropped all your money down a drain,' said Henry, and to his horror his eyes filled with tears.

'Well for God's sake don't blatt,' said Lampo Davey.

Henry blew his nose and managed not to blatt.

'Sit down and have a coffee,' said Lampo Davey, his voice a mixture of kindness and disgust.

Henry sat down, and Lampo made two mugs of coffee, thickened and sweetened by the condensed milk. Henry felt ill-at-ease, a fag being made coffee by the boy for whom he fagged.

'Tosser'll be livid,' said Lampo. 'Serve him right. He eats the chocolate in powder form, with a teaspoon. He's disgusting.'

Mr Satchel (Dopy S) didn't allow senior boys to choose their study mates. He believed that you learnt more by being thrown together. Lampo Davey and Tosser Pilkington-Brick might have existed to justify his system. Total opposites, they had formed a bond of scorn and affection which was to survive a life-time.

'I am the most sensitive and artistic and subtle boy in Orange House, which isn't saying much,' said Lampo Davey. 'Tosser is a thick ape. Because he's good at games, House worships him. I have far too much natural good taste to be envious. You're not playing rugger today, are you? Good. Let's go for a walk before evening school.'

They turned right by the Methodist Chapel. 'They mistrust pleasure so deeply that even their buildings have to be hideous,' said Lampo Davey. They took the narrow lane that climbed up behind the town, winding through apple orchards, where sheep grazed between the trees. The countryside was a luscious green after the autumn rains. Now, the soft Indian summer had come and the trees were beginning to turn.

'Winter. I welcome it with open arms,' said Lampo Davey.

'Really?' said Henry.

'Oh yes,' said Lampo Davey, as if it was obvious. 'Autumn colours in England are beautiful, if a bit much. The first pale greens of spring have a certain brief charm. But winter! Ploughed fields. Farm buildings. The magnificent outlines of trees. It's spare. It's strong. Summer in England is dreadful. The banality of all that bright green, which slowly fades into weariness. The grotesque excess of plant life. The English countryside in summer is a featureless confusion of weeds. Compare it with Tuscany, Pratt. Compare it with Umbria. The English summer, like so much of English life, is totally without taste. Give me Italy every time.'

'I prefer England,' said Henry. 'Italy's full of wops.'

'My father works in the Italian embassy in Rome. They're the most civilised people in Europe,' said Lampo Davey, with a touch of anger.

A grassy path ran along the edge of the woods, above the orchards. Lampo Davey flung himself onto the ground, beside the path. Henry sat down beside him, after testing the grass to see if it was dry. Lampo Davey laughed.

'Mr Sat On Wet Grass went rusty inside,' said Henry, and blushed.

'What?' said Lampo Davey.

'Miss Candy said things like that all the time,' said Henry. 'She was our teacher.'

'Priceless,' said Lampo Davey. 'Utterly priceless. Tell me more.'

'Mr Pick-Nose was carried off by the bogey man,' said Henry boldly.

'Priceless,' said Lampo Davey. 'When I first saw you, I thought, "Oh dear. Clueless clotto, I'm afraid." I didn't even think you were remotely pretty. A little fatty-legs, I thought. But I've decided that I rather like little fatty faggy-chops.'

Lampo Davey put his arm round Henry. Henry went red and wriggled free desperately.

'Don't be so shocked,' said Lampo Davey. 'We're in the nineteen forties, not the Middle Ages. Come on. Walkies. No further advances, I promise. I'm a connoisseur of sexual pleasure, not a child molester.'

They walked on into the woods, although Henry longed to go back, to the communal safety of Orange House. He felt shocked, surprised, even a little flattered, which shocked him also. He also felt a bit of a spoil-sport, which struck him as ridiculous.

An aeroplane zoomed loud and low over their heads, crossed the valley and disappeared low over the woods on the other side.

'Your father, perhaps,' said Lampo Davey.

'You what?' said Henry.

'Flying that plane.'

'Oh. Yes. Happen. I mean "maybe".'

'How could a father like yours have such a clueless clot as a son?' said Lampo Davey. 'You are a clueless clot, aren't you?'

Henry nodded. In the presence of this young man with the long, sad, slightly twisted face and the deep, sardonic eyes, he felt ignorant, innocent, ugly, unwordly, oiky and a liar. Yet Lampo fancied him.

'Oh, I'm all in favour of clueless clots,' said Lampo Davey, sensing that he'd hurt Henry more than he'd intended. 'Come on. Time to go home. Enough of Confuse-A-Fag.'

That evening, after school, when Henry was alone with Tosser Pilkington-Brick for the first time, Tosser grinned and said, 'Lampo's livid about your losing that money. He has the most affected eating habits. He would have hard-boiled two eggs, covered them in bottled mayonnaise and bits of anchovy, and pretended that he was sophisticated. He's pathetic. Don't worry, though. I'll defend you. He fancies you, you know.'

'Yes,' said Henry.

'You are actually rather more appealing than I thought at first,' said Tosser Pilkington-Brick. 'Any chance of a bit of "how's your father?"?'

'Sorry,' said Henry, feeling six inches taller because he wasn't blushing.

'No hard feelings,' said Tosser Pilkington-Brick. 'Getting any hard feelings yet? No? Late developer. Well, you will soon. If you do, promise me one thing. Don't get involved with Madame Lampo. She's devious. She's poison. She's a corrupter of youth. With me it would just be a bit of fun. Good, clean filth.'

The third link was added to the chain on the following Satuday. It was a raw, misty forerunner of winter. The venue was the Bald-Headed Angel, an ancient coaching house whose name constituted its only flirtation with originality. Henry was suffering from a minor ailment, made the mistake of ordering soup, and met an old flame in highly embarrassing circumstances. The minor ailment was a streaming code in the dose, the soup was oxtail, and the old flame was Belinda Boyce-Uppingham.

Henry had been invited to take luncheon with the parents of his best friend, Paul Hargreaves. Also present would be Paul's twin sister Diana, and Diana's school-friend, who was staying with the Hargreaves for half-term.

Paul and Henry were picked up at the school gates in the family Bentley after Saturday-morning school. Boys were streaming back to Orange House on foot and bike. All the pleasure of driving past them in a Bentley was destroyed by the presence in the car of Belinda Boyce-Uppingham. Even the fact that she had a brace on her teeth didn't cheer him up. The four young ones were squashed together in the back seat. Had Belinda recognised him? Had she ever known his name?

They drove through the market place, it charms ruined by its association with Tubman-Edwards. Dr Hargreaves steered the Bentley expertly under the narrow arch at the side of the Bald-Headed Angel, and parked in the long, narrow courtyard. They entered through a side door and made for the cocktail bar. The Hargreaves parents exuded elegance well-heeled enough to look as if it was attempting to hide how well-heeled it was. Dr James Hargreaves wore a sober, well-cut suit. Mrs Celia Hargreaves favoured the new Parisian 'tube look' in grey. When she took off her tight-fitting cloche hat, her hair was revealed in its daring, post-war shortness. Eating out was no longer a total mystery to Henry, thanks to Uncle Teddy and Auntie Doris, but he would have felt at his oikiest, in the world of brain surgeons and their elegant spouses, even if Belinda Boyce-Uppingham hadn't been there, and even if his nose hadn't begun to run, in the warmth of the cocktail bar.

The younger element had squashes, the grown-ups dry sherry. The head waiter gave them menus, and returned all too quickly to take their orders. Henry hadn't even begun to choose. How could he, when he was supposed to be the son of a famous test pilot, but was sitting next to a girl who might recognise him as the son of a private soldier who had made penknives in civvy street, and whom he had knocked off her horse, to which she had responded by calling him an oik, providing a foretaste of the unpleasant soubriquet by which a whole school was later to identify him, and when he wanted to blow his nose but didn't dare in this elegant company, and when the whole menu was in French, one of his worst subjects?

The head waiter was standing over him.

'Are you all right, Henry? We're waiting for you to order,' said Paul.

'Oh. Right. I'll. . .I'll have the same as Paul.'

'That's silly,' said Diana.

'Not if it's what he wants,' said Dr James Hargreaves.

'It isn't,' said Diana. 'He's just saying it cos he can't decide.'

'Don't I know you?' said Belinda Boyce-Uppingham.

Henry's heart sank. On its way down it passed his blood, which was rushing up towards his cheeks. He went into violent internal convulsions, pumping, throbbing, sinking, burning. He sneezed five times.

'What on earth's wrong?' said Dr James Hargreaves.

'What did you say your other name was? said Belinda Boyce-Uppingham.

Henry opened his mouth, but no sound came.

'Pratt,' said Paul.

'I knew I knew you,' said Belinda Boyce-Uppingham. 'You were an evacuee at Rowth Bridge.'

'I wasn't an evacuee,' said Henry, finding his voice. 'I was staying with relations.'

'Of course he was,' said Paul, defending his friend. 'His father was fighting the war.'

Belinda Boyce-Uppingham frowned slightly. Perhaps she had just remembered calling him an oik, thought Henry.

Paul Hargreaves frowned too. His friend wasn't putting up a good show.

It was the memory of anger, not guilt, that had caused Belinda Boyce-Uppingham to frown. 'You knocked me off my horse,' she said.

'You called me an oik,' said Henry.

Belinda Boyce-Uppingham flushed.

'Surely not?' she said. 'I mean. . .'

'It's frightening when you're thrown off a horse,' said Mrs Celia Hargreaves. 'Do you ride, Henry?'

'No,' said Henry. How he wished he could have said 'yes', but he wasn't going to tell any more lies. If he did say 'yes', he'd probably discover that a string of thoroughbreds had been laid on for their post-prandial delectation.

'I think it was pretty rotten of you to remind Blin that she called you an oik,' said Diana. 'I think that *was* a bit oiky.'

'Diana!' said Dr Hargreaves.

'I don't agree,' said Paul. 'I mean you might forgive somebody for calling somebody an oik, if they were an oik, but not when they called you an oik and your father's a famous test pilot, even if they did knock you off your stupid horse.'

'Paleface was not stupid,' said Belinda Boyce-Uppingham, tossing her head, perhaps in sympathetic imitation of her erstwhile mount.

'I don't agree,' said Diana. 'It doesn't matter if you call somebody an oik if they obviously aren't, but if they are it's unforgiveable. Henry obviously isn't, so Blin's forgiven.'

'I think this is becoming a rather silly conversation,' said Mrs Hargreaves. 'I think we're all a little bit over-excited.'

'I'd like to meet your father, Henry. I hear he's fearsomely distinguished,' said Dr Hargreaves, not without a trace of smugness, as if he knew that Henry's father would have the utmost difficulty in being as distinguished as he was.

'What is all this about your father?' said Belinda Boyce-Uppingham.

'He's a famous test pilot,' said Paul. 'He tests all the new prototypes.'

'Well who was that funny little man with the bandage?' said Belinda Boyce-Uppingham.

'He was not a funny little man. He was my father. And he's dead,' said Henry.

'Your table's ready,' said the head waiter.

Henry found himself walking into the restaurant with the others, although he longed to run from the hotel. But he'd ordered, and social conventions are strong. Paul flashed him a look of fury, Belinda of scorn, Diana of encouragement. Dr and Mrs Hargreaves avoided his eye, which was easy, as he was avoiding everybody's eye.

He found that he had ordered oxtail soup. Its heat made his nose stream. Paul sat glaring at him as he continually blew his nose. The noise was like an air-raid warning in this temple of starched white linen and watery food.

The soup was watery, the conversation formal and evasive, till Paul said, 'For God's sake stop blowing your nose.'

'Paul!' said Mrs Hargreaves, reproving Paul for not giving Henry an example of what gracious manners were.

'Sorry,' said Henry. 'My cold's come out.'

'I wish you hadn't,' said Paul.

'Paul!' said Dr Hargreaves.

'Well, honestly, he's made me feel such an ass,' said Paul. 'He told me his father was a test pilot.'

'Yes, well,' said Dr Hargreaves, meaning, 'You feel an ass? What about him?'

The waiter advanced slowly, like one bad smell approaching another. They remained totally silent while he cleared the plates, as if it was of vital importance that he should know nothing about the matter.

Henry screwed himself up to provide some sort of explanation.

'Everyone at Brasenose called me Oiky,' he said. 'I hated being called Oiky. It wasn't my fault.'

It was Belinda Boyce-Uppingham's turn to go scarlet.

'Isn't embarrassment embarrassing,' said Diana. 'This is the most embarrassing meal I've ever been to.'

'Shut up, Diana,' said Paul.

'It really was mean of you actually, Blin, to call Henry an oik, because he really isn't,' said Diana.

The waiter ambled over with food that might have been hot when it left the kitchens. Henry found that he had ordered *le pâté de la maisonette* (cottage pie) *avec les choux du Bruxelles* (watery) *et les carottes* (tasteless).

'Waiter!' summoned Dr Hargreaves, as the waiter wandered off.

'Sir?' said the waiter.

'Tell the chef he does some amazing things with water,' said Dr

Hargreaves.

'James!' said Mrs Hargreaves.

The waiter sauntered off, mystified, across the half-empty room.

There was nothing Henry could have done to make matters worse, except to parody a clumsy young man in a restaurant by losing the top of the salt cellar and pouring all its contents onto his food. And that is exactly what he did.

'Never mind,' said Diana. 'It's horribly underseasoned actually.'

Henry scooped off what salt he could, and ate his meal bravely, although it did cause him to suffer a severe coughing fit just as his nasal flood had finally come to an end.

After the meal, as they were leaving the hotel, Diana pulled Henry back in.

'I don't think you're an oik,' she said, 'Knocking Blin off her horse like that, and pretending your father was a test pilot. I think it's a hoot.'

In the morning, there was a fire practice at Orange House. They descended down a canvas chute from their dormitory windows. South Africa dorm was on the second floor, and it was quite a long way down to the gravel. Runciman and Cranston held the chute rather high off the ground, and Henry took a nasty, scraping fall on the gravel.

'Terribly sorry,' said Runciman and Cranston in unison.

Henry caught sight of Paul, standing among a group of boys who had made their descent, grinning broadly.

'I paid them to do that,' said Paul. 'Serve you right for yesterday.'

They wandered along the path that led to the extensive vegetable garden.

'I'm sorry about yesterday,' said Henry.

'I won't tell anyone,' said Paul. 'Everyone will think your father's a test pilot except me.'

'But. . .'

'I'm your friend, aren't I?'

But for how long, thought Henry. Maybe Paul really was such a smashing bloke that his feelings wouldn't be undermined by the power he had over Henry, but what about Henry? Would his feelings of friendship survive the guilt and gratitude that he would always feel in Paul's presence?

The answer was 'no'. The fourth and final link in the chain was therefore inevitable.

The opportunity arose the following day, when the English master, Mr Foden (Foggy F), set them an essay on the subject of 'A building that's important to me'. Seven long days later, the essays were handed back by Foggy F. He approached Henry, his slightly vacant face grave with disapproval.

'Not an inspired effort, I'm afraid,' he said. 'You look an imaginative enough boy, Mallender, but this is dead prose. Correct, organised, dead as a doornail.'

'But, sir. . .' Henry began.

'Don't argue, Mallender,' said Foggy F. 'You must be able to take criticism.'

'But, sir. . .'

'Silence. You haven't shown any finesse in your approach. Imagine me, the reader, approaching your work. You've held nothing back. Your first paragraph reveals all, making the rest of the essay almost redundant. You should tempt me. You should lead me up a figurative garden path.'

'But, sir. . .'

'There are no buts about it, Mallender. Now Pratt here. . .'

Foggy F turned towards Mallender.

'But, sir. . .' began Mallender.

'Don't argue,' said Foggy F. 'I'm about to praise you. You, Pratt, you may sit there looking about as imaginative as a pumice stone, but, inside that sponge-like edifice which passes for your brain, you are actually thinking.'

'Please, sir. . .' said Mallender.

'Silence, Pratt. You'll get nowhere if you're embarrassed by praise. You paint a picture of a world, a world of back-to-back terraces in industrial Yorkshire. The building you describe was jerry-built in the industrial revolution. It's infested with vermin. It's probably condemned by now. Do you live there? No. In your last paragraph you tell us why it's important. Not the first paragraph, Mallender. The last. That house is important to you because you do not live there, because it makes you appreciate the running water, the fitted carpets, the electric light of the house where you do live.'

'But, sir,' said Henry. 'I'm Pratt.'

'Mallender, for the last time. . .you're Pratt? Well, why didn't you tell me?'

'I tried, sir.'

'Well, anyway, Pratt, it's a fine piece of work. As for you, Mallender, sitting there accepting credit for work you didn't do, I hope you're ashamed. Now, I want everyone to read Pratt's essay. It's a thoroughly imaginative. . .'

'It isn't imagination, sir,' said Henry. 'I lived in that back-to-back terrace.'

'Are you sure?' said Foggy F. 'I understood your father was a brain surgeon.'

'No, sir. My father's a brain surgeon,' said Paul Hargreaves. 'His father's a test pilot.'

'Thank you, Fuller,' said Foggy F.

'My father isn't a test pilot,' said Henry. 'I made that up. My father made penknives, and he died sitting on the outside lats.'

The relief was intense. The truth was out at last. The future wouldn't be easy, but now his real life at Dalton College could begin.

The future wasn't easy. The news of his true origins swept Orange House. As an hors d'oeuvre, on Friday evening, he met an old chum, the noddle down the porcelain bowl. This bowl was made by Bollingtons of Tunstall, just up the road from Etruria. The incident linked the little village school at Rowth Bridge with the great public school of Dalton, and might have been said to be the only evidence Henry ever received of true equality of opportunity in education, had it not been for the fact that, due to the primitive toilet arrangements at Rowth Bridge school, even that had been an extra-mural activity.

The main course took place on Saturday evening. Cranston and Runciman grabbed him as he was collecting his clean pants, vest and socks from matron's cupboard under the stairs, with its overpowering smell of ironing. They led him out, through the back door, into the dark November night. A thin drizzle was falling, and there was a light wind from the east.

Waiting outside were Shelton, Holmes, Philpot A. E., Philpot W. F. N. and Perkins. Philpot A. E. and Shelton carried coils of rope. Henry was led into a small corner of the gardens. The gardener had complained that the gardens were too much for him, and Dopy S had agreed to make his task easier by leaving a section as a nature reserve. It was known as 'The Dell'. They tied Henry to a tree in 'The Dell' with one of the ropes, the one carried by Philpot A. E. Then each boy gave him eight strokes with the other rope, doubled up. It hardly seems necessary to tell you that this was the rope carried by Shelton.

Eight strokes each from Cranston, Runciman, Shelton, Holmes, Philpot A. E., Philpot W. F. N. and Perkins. Fifty-six strokes with a doubled-up rope. They thudded into his backside until pain was an irrelevant word. He made no movement. He made no noise. He would die before he gave them the satisfaction.

They untied him, and led him back into the changing room.

'Did you have anything on, under there, for protection? said Perkins.

Henry shook his head, not trusting himself to speak.

They made him take down his shonkers, and examined his backside. They seemed awed by what they saw.

'Pull them up,' said Holmes flatly.

They seemed curiously subdued, almost crestfallen.

Henry decided that he must trust himself to speak. He must take a leaf out of the Brasenose book.

'Thank you,' he said.

And for dessert? There was no dessert. The bullying of Henry ended as abruptly as it had begun.

Not everybody was nasty to Henry.

Nattrass wasn't.

Nattrass summoned him to his study the next day.

'I believe something happened last night,' he said.

'No,' said Henry.

'Sit down,' said Nattrass.

'I'd rather stand,' said Henry.

Nattrass grinned.

'You had your buttocks beaten to pulp by a group of savages,' said Nattrass. 'This house is a cess-pit. It hasn't been cock house at anything since 1937. I want to clean it up. I want to turn it into a civilised, compassionate place. I want those bastards sacked.'

'I'm sorry,' said Henry. 'I want to forget it.'

'Shove off, then,' said Nattrass irritably, and added, in a kinder voice, 'If you're ever in any more trouble, come to me.'

Lampo Davey wasn't nasty.

On Sundays the senior boys often had fry-ups, cooked for them by their fags on the little gas stove in the alcove between the changing room and the showers. There were three favourite meals. Sausage and egg with fried bread and beans. Bacon and egg with fried bread and beans. Sausage, bacon and egg with fried bread and beans. Lampo opted for bacon and egg with fried bread but without the beans. The absence of baked beans was his way of asserting his sophistication.

To Henry's intense relief, he didn't break the egg. Tosser would eat anything, but it grieved Lampo deeply if the egg was broken.

Lampo signalled to him to sit down.

'I'd rather stand,' he said.

'Get me a coffee, then,' said Lampo.

The last November light was fading from the Sunday sky. Tosser was out. It was cosy in the study, with its smell of warm pipes and fried bread.

'Excellent,' said Lampo Davey, picking his way daintily through his fry-up. 'You're quite a good cook.'

'I'm not surprised you sound surprised,' said Henry. He was surprised himself.

'Priceless, this business of you being a slum kid,' said Lampo.

'It wasn't a slum,' said Henry. 'It was sub-standard housing, that's all.'

'Priceless, anyway,' said Lampo. 'Much better than that dreary old test pilot. He really was a bore. I bet he had a handlebar moustache. I'm so relieved to see him go.'

'I'm not too sorry myself,' said Henry.

'You worship Tosser, don't you?'

185

'He's pretty good at rugger.'

'You think the sun shines out of his arse. Well just as long as that's your only interest in that part of his anatomy. Now I've shocked you again. I understand why now. The working class has always hated homosexuality. All right, thanks for a nice meal. Dismiss, little Henry.'

Lampo Davey smiled his slightly distant, slightly crooked smile, and to his surprise Henry smiled back.

Paul Hargreaves wasn't nasty.

Paul hadn't abandoned him. He hadn't wavered when sentiment against Henry was running at its strongest. It seemed that although dreary to most people, Henry did have something, somewhere, that was not utterly and irremediably unattractive and boring.

On the Monday, two days after the beating, Henry took care during the Latin lesson of Mr Braithwaite (Busy B) not to make a mistake. Busy B ruled his class with a gymshoe of iron. The slightest mistake was rewarded with a sharp thwack across the backside. (It seemed to Henry that the most concrete thing which parents got for all the money they spent on private education was the knowledge that their loved ones would be beaten on the backside instead of the hand.) Henry sat, that morning, wary, alert, his backside throbbing, hoping that Busy B wouldn't touch on his Achilles heel, the gerund and gerundive. All seemed to be going well until Paul was asked to provide the supine of *rego*. It is, of course, *rectum*. Never did the old music-hall gag surface with such painful results. It sent Henry into a panic, from which there was no chance of recovery. Busy B asked him the second person singular of the past perfect of *audio*. You had been heard. *Auditus eras*. Normally a doddle, thank you very much, sir, tickety boo. Totally beyond Henry in his sudden panic.

Thwack. The impact of the gymshoe, which normally produced only a moderately unpleasant stinging, seemed to implode inside his rear-end. He had an image of Tubman-Edwards, huge, grotesque, filling the window with his smirking. Then the hallucination was gone, and he struggled back to his desk, resolved to end the threat of Tubman-Edwards.

After dinner the following day (egg and bacon pie with carrots and boiled potatoes, followed by sponge pudding with chocolate sauce), Henry took Paul with him into the market place.

There, outside Ironmonger's the newsagent's, they confronted Tubman-Edwards.

'This is my friend Paul Hargreaves,' said Henry. 'This is my blackmailer, Tubman-Edwards. Paul, tell Tubman-Edwards about my father.'

'The whole school knows that Henry's father made pocket-knives and died in the outside lats,' said Paul. 'So there's really no reason for Henry to worry about Shant knowing that he used to be called Oiky, and if you don't give everything back we'll tell the whole school what an inflated sack of blackmailing yak turd you are,' said Paul.

'I can't give it all back,' said Tubman-Edwards, who'd gone the colour of putty. 'I've sold the Gentleman's Relish.'

'The equivalent in cash value, in agreed weekly instalments, will do,' said Henry.

'Weekly?' said Tubman-Edwards weakly.

'Weekly,' said Henry. 'Otherwise I'll get my hatchet-men onto you.'

Henry had a rare stroke of luck at that moment. Tosser Pilkington-Brick walked past on his way back from the Coach and Horses. He was in a genial mood, and smiled as he said, 'Hello, Pratt.'

Tubman-Edwards gazed at Tosser's large frame, and his face changed from putty to flour.

'That won't be necessary,' he croaked.

Every Tuesday for the rest of that term and the next term, Henry met Tubman-Edwards in the market place and received his instalment.

Christmas was quiet, especially as the Porringers had gone to Canada. Cousin Hilda gave Henry a stamp album. Uncle Teddy and Auntie Doris gave him a Meccano set and equipment for his railway—two trucks, a guards van, four straight rails, two curves, a set of points, a turntable, a box of assorted conifers for scenery, a station platform and six mixed passengers. Henry wasn't interested in hobbies. He thought they must be a middle-class habit which he'd never acquired. Basic politeness demanded that he construct the odd Meccano monstrosity, stick the occasional desultory stamp in his album, arrange a conifer or two beside the track, even run a train once in a while when Uncle Teddy grew bored. He found Uncle Teddy's enthusiasm for the railway surprising and endearing, and felt dreadfully guilty about not being able to respond more wholeheartedly. What Henry loved were his books, his wireless – there was Jimmy Jewel and Ben Warris now, in 'Up the Pole', with Claude Dampier and Jon Pertwee, but Paul Temple and the Curzon Gang was spoilt because he'd missed the beginning and he'd have to go back to school before the last episode – and, above all, his new craze, the films. He went whenever he could, seeing, among others, *Scott of the Antarctic*, *The Winslow Boy*, *The Road to Rio*, *Green Grass of Wyoming*, *My Brother Jonathan* and *The Small Back Room*. Auntie Doris even came with him once or twice, although she liked to miss the second feature, especially when it was Ma and Pa Kettle.

Although he still dreaded his return to school, Henry found that he was looking forward to seeing Paul, and, more surprisingly, to fagging for Lampo Davey and Tosser Pilkington-Brick.

Lessons proceeded smoothly enough. The sports facilities provided wonderful opportunities for a boy who hitherto had only discovered that he was bad at cricket, soccer, hockey and rugger. By the end of his first year at Dalton College, Henry was bad at squash, fives, tennis and swimming as well. In the holidays, he no longer watched much sport. It wasn't much fun without friends. At school, he watched everything, especially if Tosser Pilkington-Brick was playing. Once again, Orange House failed to be cock house at anything. Plantaganet took rugger. (Blast. One up for Tubman-Edwards.) Tudor took hockey and cricket.

'All this sports watching will do you no good,' said Lampo Davey one Sunday evening in early March as he picked his way elegantly through Henry's egg, bacon and fried bread. 'You'll go blind. Has the slumbering giant still not stirred?'

'No.'

'Pour me a glass of claret.'

Lampo Davey and Tosser Pilkington-Brick kept wine under their floorboards. Henry poured Lampo Davey a glass of claret.

Lampo put his hand on Henry's knee.

'I wish you wouldn't do that,' said Henry.

Lampo removed his hand.

'I do wish you'd be my bit of rough trade, little slum boy,' he said. He saw the look in Henry's eye. 'Sorry. Little sub-standard housing boy. Maybe you will, when the slumbering giant stirs. You're probably just a late developer. At least you aren't interested in girls.'

'I used to be,' said Henry.

'When?'

'Till I was nine.'

'My God. You were nine before your latent sexuality period began. You *are* a late developer.'

Henry tried to let it all wash over him. He tried not to show how much the homosexuality still shocked him. He tried not to show how hurt he was at the suggestion that even his apparent precocity at Rowth Bridge had been nothing more than retarded infantilism. He still suffered some fairly fierce mockery of his humble origins, but he had learnt to cope now. Henry 'Ee by gum, I am daft' was back in play. He even tried it on Lampo Davey and Tosser Pilkington-Brick when he dropped a glass of claret. Tosser gave a snort of laughter and spooned some more powdered drinking chocolate into his capacious mouth. Claret and powdered chocolate were a favoured snack. Lampo showed no signs of amusement, but said, 'Priceless. Absolutely priceless.'

The high point of Henry's week was the arrival of the *Picturegoer*. He read it from cover to cover, from 'Should Betty Grable wear tights?' to 'Open pores – do they mar your beauty?'

One day, just before the end of the Easter term, he sat in his partition in the junior study, gazing at his montage of cuttings from the *Picturegoer*. The pictures were mostly of the stars at social functions. They had captions like 'At the Mocambo Club. William Powell selects a cigarette for socialite Mrs H. Bockwitz', 'Gene Kelly and Deborah Kerr found themselves having quite a serious conversation', 'Katharine Hepburn, seen with Lena Horne, caused top sensation. She wore slacks' (the accompanying picture showed only the top halves of the two ladies!) and Somebody must have called "yoo-hoo!" to judge from the faces of James

Stewart and veteran Frank Morgan'. They triggered off a fantasy world which might feature such captions as 'To judge from the friendly waves, it looks as though ex-oik Henry Pratt has won the hearts of the crowd at Elia Kazan's birthday party' and 'At the Mocambo Club, former slum kid Henry Pratt proffers a canapé to thrice-married Jasper K. Bungholtz. To judge from Bungholtz's expression, the tasty morsel is not unwelcome.' As Henry sat there, dreaming his fantasies of non-sexual social conquest, Paul butted in to announce that he had just had his second wank of the day, in the lats. Even Paul, elegant, shy, avant-garde, Braque-loving, discriminating, fractionally fastidious Paul was doing it. Henry sighed. His display suddenly looked very dull. He wanted to start wanting to offer people more than canapés.

The Easter holidays brought Chips Rafferty in *Eureka Stockade* and similar delights. The railway acquired another engine, two carriages, a tunnel and a footbridge. The slumbering giant remained a lifeless dwarf.

Henry remodelled the decoration of his partition. Out went the social events. In came the scantily clad females. The captions now were 'Possessor of these shapely underpinnings, of course, is Jean Kent, in her latest picture *Trottie True*', 'This is something like a pin-up. Gloria de Haven is wearing a striking swim-suit, although we doubt if she's ever actually dived off the deep end in it' and 'If you were running before the wind, wouldn't you like a sea nymph like Janice Carter, in contrasted slip and top, as part of the crew!' In Henry's fantasy, there were captions like 'Top glamour photographer Henry Pratt must have been up very early to catch this delightful pose by lovely Adele Jurgens. Poor fellow – or is he?' But the fantasy refused to come to life. The giant slumbered on.

One day, in the middle of June, 1949, two fourteen-year-old friends were watching Orange House play Plantaganet House at cricket on Middle Boggle. The sports fields were behind the school and slightly above it. They were on two levels, Middle Boggle and Lower Boggle. There had never been an Upper Boggle. This was just one more of life's many mysteries.

Orange House were 92 for 9. Tosser was 55 not out. From their position on the bank beside the Pavvy, they could see Lower Boggle studded with junior games, and the mish-mash of indifferent brick and stone buildings tumbling out of the back of the Queen Anne mansion like architectural faeces. Right at the back was the solid, pseudo-classical frontage of School Hall.

They could see Tubman-Edwards approaching. When he saw them, he turned away.

Tosser hit a massive six. They cheered lustily.

Lampo Davey walked past, ostentatiously reading a book on renaissance art and taking no notice of the game. Mr Satchel (Dopy S) glared at him. No wonder Orange never became cock house at anything if certain subversive elements preferred renaissance art.

Tosser preferred hitting sixes. Another massive pull brought up the hundred. Next ball he was out for 67. 104 all out. Not enough.

'I think I'll have a wank tonight,' said Paul, to cheer himself up.

'So will I,' said Henry.

'I didn't think you'd started,' said Paul.

'I started last night,' said Henry.

'Congratulingles.' Paul thumped his friend in delight.

'Thanks.'

'Fantastic, isn't it?'

'Fantastic.'

'The most fantangles thingles in the univingles.'

'Absolutelingles.'

Henry closed his eyes in dismay. Not at the awful new language which swept Shant mercifully briefly that term. At the stupidity of his lie. How many long weeks of pretence would follow? What a thing to feel the need to boast about. You pulled a bit of your body, it got longer, and some stuff came out. Amazingly clever!

'I don't believe it does make you go blind,' said Paul.

'Well if it did, everybody'd be blind,' said Henry.

'Exactly,' said Paul. 'I wonder if it ever makes people deaf.'

'Pardon?' said Henry.

'Oh, I forgot,' said Paul. 'I had a letter from mother today. She says it's perfectly all right.'

'Wanking?'

'Ass. You coming to stay for the first week of the hols.'

Henry's heart sank. He never wanted to see Dr and Mrs Hargreaves again.

'They won't eat you,' said Paul. 'They liked you. They understood.'

I know, thought Henry. That's what makes it so bad. They can see into my shallow, lying, dirty, oiky little soul.

'They've been burgled,' said Paul. 'All the burglar took was a wireless, a ball of string and two pounds of tomatoes.'

'Sounds like a nutcase,' said Henry. 'Perhaps he's going to bury the tomatoes in the ground, in rows marked by string, and play "Music While You Work" to them in the hope they'll seed themselves.'

'You will come, won't you?' said Paul as the Orange team made its way onto the field, followed by the Plantaganet openers.

'If my people will let me,' said Henry, who still found it odd to refer to his surrogate parents as his people.

That night Henry wrote to Uncle Teddy and Auntie Doris. He wrote dutifully, and found it hard to inject any real life into his efforts.

Dear Uncle Teddy and Auntie Doris [he wrote],

It's quite hot here. I am well. How are you? House lost to Plantaganet by three wickets today. We made 104. Tosser Pilkington-Brick, the one I fag for, made 67. They made 107 for 7. Tosser Pilkington-Brick took 4 for 36. Yesterday I played for Orange 4 v Hanover 4. Hanover 4 made 26. I didn't bowl. We made 17. I made 0. Shant (that's what we call school, it rhymes with pant) lost to Bruton by 8 runs on Saturday. They made 137. A bloke called Porringer made 43. I wonder if he's related to Geoffrey Porringer. Tosser Pilkington-Brick took 3 for 41. We made 129. Tosser Pilkington-Brick made 33. The blokes I fag for are really quite nice, compared to some of the blokes.

I did quite well at Latin and History this week. We're doing the Tudors. I told Toady D I thought some of the kings were no better than bullies. In chemistry my litmus paper went a different colour to everybody else's. Art is good. We just look at slides and Arty K talks about things and we don't have to write anything down.

We had a film show on Saturday in School Hall (that's Shant Shed in Shant Rant. [That means school language.]) It was *Monsieur Verdoux*, with Charlie Chaplin. It was very good, but rather boring.

Paul Hargreaves, who is still my best friend, wants me to go
and stay with his people in Hampstead for the first week of the
hols. They're frightfully posh and everything. His father's a
brain surgeon. They live in Hampstead. Oh, I said that! Paul's
got a twin sister, Diana. She's not bad for a girl. If I go I can
have a brain operation. I need it. Joke. I hope. Seriously, I'm
not bothered about going and if it's inconvenient I'd be just as
happy to come straight home.

I finished the Gentleman's Relish yesterday. It was super.
With lots of love.
Henry.

Five days later he got a reply from Auntie Doris. Her replies came
quicker than they used to, and were longer.

Dear Henry [he read],

Thank you for your nice, long letter. We're always really
interested to read all your interesting news. Nothing much is
happening here, business as usual. Your uncle is pretty fed up
about the economy. He says the Labour government don't
understand business. He calls them the groundnuts government. He says they penalise people like him who've got up off
their backsides and done something with their lives. We were
very interested in all your cricket scores. What a pity you aren't
in very good form yourself this term. Uncle Teddy says
everybody has these 'bad trots' from time to time. Yes, I believe
I did hear that the Porringer brat is at Bruton. The Porringers
have the same idea as your uncle, that a boy should go a long
way away so as to learn to be self-reliant. We were very pleased
that you did well in Latin etcetera. Where do you get the brains
from? We were glad that the film you saw was very good, but
sorry it was rather boring. We think it's a very good idea for you
to go to stay with your friends. It's not that we don't want you
for all the holidays, because we miss you very much, but it
worries us that you don't have any friends your own age here.
Stay longer than a week if you want to. Don't worry about us.
Actually it fits in very well with our plans, as your uncle has
some kind of conference thing to go to, and it means we won't

have to rush back, which we would have been very happy to do, to be here when you got back. I enclose some more Gentleman's Relish, also eight Canadian stamps. Mum's the word.

With lots of love to our lovely boy, from Uncle Teddy and Auntie Doris XXXXXXXXXXXXXXXXXXXXXXXX (Wipe off that lipstick!)

They took a taxi from Paddington to Hampstead. Mrs Hargreaves stood smiling at the door of the narrow, four-storey, Georgian town house. She looked elegant in a short yellow dress with straight lines, and high-heeled black leather court shoes.

Henry hadn't dared ask Paul if Diana would be there.

'No cold this time?' said Mrs Hargreaves.

'No,' said Henry. 'I don't usually get colds.'

'I know,' said Mrs Hargreaves. 'Only at the most embarrassing times.'

There was a faint hint of expensive perfume about her which Henry couldn't help comparing with Auntie Doris. She gave him an approving glance. He knew that he looked his best. He had grown quite a bit taller in the past nine months, and had lost some of his podgy look. But although there had been approval in her glance, he felt it to be the sort of approval a would-be owner might give a promising horse.

They had afternoon tea in the drawing room, on the first floor. The wallpaper, lamp-shades and curtains had a faintly Chinese air, and there was China tea. 'Isn't Diana here?' said Paul.

'She's upstairs, pretending not to care about Henry's arrival,' said Mrs Hargreaves.

'Ass,' said Paul. 'Girls can be asses. That appalling Brace-Uppingham girl isn't with her, is she?'

'Boyce-Uppingham, dear. She had a brace in her teeth, poor dear. I hope you like China tea, Henry.'

'Very much,' lied Henry. He'd had it at Auntie Doris's. It tasted like burnt rubber.

'Are you a post-lactarian?' said Mrs Hargreaves.

'No,' said Henry. 'I'm C of E.'

'Post-lactarian means you like the milk in last,' said Paul. 'It's considered correct.'

'I like the milk in first,' said Henry.

Mrs Hargreaves poured the milk in first. Henry sensed that she was trying to prevent her eyes from showing amusement. He sensed that he was Paul's funny little Northern friend, to whom they would all be very kind. He was also aware that he tended to imagine this even when it wasn't true, and that he sometimes played up to it, so he couldn't grumble.

Diana entered, dressed in skirt and scruffy old shirt, with flat shoes. Her cheeks were slightly pink.

'Oh hello, Henry. You here?' she said casually. 'Tea, please.'

Henry was aware that he was also slightly pink, and that yet again he couldn't think of a single thing to say. He was also deeply disappointed by Diana's appearance. She looked lumpy, like bad porridge. Her legs looked quite thick, her knees were uncompromisingly knobbly. In his memory she had been a cross between Mrs Hargreaves, Patricia Roc and Gloria de Haven, all much younger, of course. He had even felt vague stirrings of the slumbering giant as he thought about meeting her again.

'Henry's a pre-lactarian,' said Mrs Hargreaves.

'Sounds disgusting,' said Diana.

Her cheeks couldn't be pink because of him. Yet she had spoken nicely to him at the Bald-Headed Angel. He hoped she hadn't got a horrid schoolgirl crush on him, however flattering that would be. He didn't want this sack of potatoes round his neck.

With Diana such a wash-out, and the house so stiflingly elegant, and the tea tasting of burnt rubber, albeit better burnt rubber than Auntie Doris's, Henry didn't think he could stand a week of it.

'Your school's broken up too, has it?' he said.

'No. I'm still there,' said Diana. 'I have this amazing gift where I can send my body to lots of different places at once.'

Diana went off to her room, and Paul showed Henry the garden. It was quite small, terraced, walled, secret as only town gardens bother to be. Every square inch was used, and every plant was lovely. Probably the weeds all died of shame. Paul explained about the publisher on one side, the famous author on the other side and the potty professor at the bottom.

'I'll save the tour of the pictures for tomorrow,' said Paul.

'They're all originals, of course.'

Of course, thought Henry.

He was amazed to discover that Paul had an older brother, Jeremy, who was expected home from school within two or three days.

'You never even mentioned him,' said Henry.

'We don't get on awfully well,' said Paul. 'He's a little bit arty-crafty. My father sent him to one of these progressive schools, because it was such a Hampstead thing to do. He hated it at first. The headmaster asked him why. He said, "I like rules and regulations." The headmaster said, "Well, you can't have any here." He said, "Why not?" The headmaster said, "Because I say so."'

Henry laughed.

He washed and changed for dinner. By the time he came downstairs, Dr Hargreaves was back. Dr Hargreaves asked him if he liked sherry. He said he did. It tasted like razor blades.

Diana had changed into an elegant, short, black dress. She had moderately high-heeled shoes, which flattered the luscious fleshiness of her legs. No sack of potatoes ever looked like this. Only the cheery knobbliness of her knees revealed that she was still only fourteen. Henry caught his breath and hoped he wasn't gawping like a love-sick cod.

'Sherry?' said Dr Hargreaves.

'No fear. Your sherry tastes like razor blades. Lemonade, please,' she said.

With their dinner, in the olive-green dining room on the ground floor, they had claret. Henry said that he loved it, although he knew he hated it.

The stew was nice, though.

Back at Low Farm, casual conversation was discouraged at table, and Henry had always wanted to chatter. Here, table talk was de rigueur, and his brain seemed to have had gum poured into it.

'This stew's nice,' he said.

'It's boeuf bourguignon, ass,' said Paul.

They discussed art exhibitions and museums that they might visit. Paul said that Henry was good at Latin, and his French was

196

coming along too.

'A great language,' said Dr Hargreaves. 'Are you familiar with Baudelaire at all, Henry?'

'I've never been to France,' said Henry.

Diana choked.

'Baudelaire isn't a place,' she said. 'It's a song.'

'It's no such thing,' said her mother. 'He was a great French poet.'

Henry couldn't be sure, in fact he would never know, but he suspected that Diana knew about Baudelaire and had diverted the correction onto herself to spare him. What a magnificent girl she was. How little taste he had. How could he ever have preferred the tight-knit, arrogant scrawniness of Belinda Brace-Toothingham? How could he have likened this magnificent creature to a sack of potatoes? How nice her breasts looked.

The slumbering giant stirred, yawned, stretched his legs. Not now! Not at the Hargreaves's dining table! Get down, ass!

He looked away from Diana hurriedly. He racked his brains for something even vaguely interesting to say. He recalled a story somebody had told him at school. Well, that would do.

'My people were burgled last week,' he said, 'Do you know what the thief took? A wireless, a ball of string and two pounds of tomatoes.'

Why was Paul glaring at him?

'That's incredible,' said Dr Hargreaves. 'We had a burglar too, and that's exactly what he took.'

Henry closed his eyes. The one good thing about it was that the awakened giant shrivelled up in embarrassment.

'It's obviously the same one,' said Diana.

'It could be two different ones,' said Paul.

'Oh yes. The country's awash with people stealing wirelesses, string and tomatoes,' said Diana.

'Where did this happen? said Mrs Hargreaves.

'Sheffield,' said Henry.

'We must let the police know,' said Dr Hargreaves. 'It could be a vital link.'

'No,' said Henry. 'My aunt's very nervous of the police.'

'We really ought to report it. It's our duty,' said Dr Hargreaves.

'I wouldn't like to do it without their knowing,' said Henry 'When I get back, I can tell them about your case and try and persuade them to report it.'

Dr Hargreaves agreed to that, but it had been a narrow escape. Henry suspected that they all knew that there had been no burglary, but he couldn't bring himself to admit it.

After dinner, he pleaded exhaustion.

'Ass,' said Paul, as they said goodnight. 'Cretinous ass.'

He washed himself from head to foot, in his determination not to sully the sheets.

It was a warm night. He got into bed without his pyjamas.

He stretched his legs. They ached with tension. He began to feel drowsy. He thought about Diana. She was a nice girl. He thought about her breasts. He pretended she was in bed with him, also naked. He pressed his body against hers and kissed her mouth. He put the sheet over his head and moved down to kiss her breasts.

'Diana, darling, I love you,' he whispered. 'Oh, Diana. Diana.'

The slumbering giant awoke, leapt up, and spat. It was brief, burning, terrifying, amazing, wonderful.

For ten seconds after it was over, he felt exhilarated. He wasn't a freak. He was a man.

Then he began to feel embarrassed about the Hargreaves's sheets.

9 The Day Pratt Broke Out

'I wouldn't go myself if I hadn't helped to organise it,' said Uncle Teddy. 'Rawlaston Working Men's Club isn't the Moulin Rouge, you know.'

It was pre-prandial drinks time in Cap Ferrat, on a wet evening in January, 1950.

'I've never been to a club,' said Henry.

'You're under age,' said Auntie Doris.

'I don't want to drink,' said Henry. 'I just want to see the cabaret. I've never seen a cabaret. They'll let me in if you're the organiser.'

'I don't like abusing positions of influence,' said Uncle Teddy.

'You never take me anywhere,' said Henry. 'I'm nearly fifteen. I can behave myself. Every summer holidays, when I come back, you're as bronzed as Greek gods. You think I don't realise that you've been on holiday, but I'm not as green as I'm cabbage-looking. That's why I never get any letters towards the end of the summer term.'

Uncle Teddy and Auntie Doris didn't look as bronzed as Greek gods at that moment. In fact they'd both gone deathly pale.

'You go to Cap Ferrat,' said Henry. 'It's your favourite place. You named your house after it. I used to think it was a hat for ferreting. I was naive. You've given me the chance to be sophisticated, and that means I can see through you.'

Auntie Doris burst into tears and left the room.

'Now look what you've done,' said Uncle Teddy.

'It's what you've done,' said Henry.

'You don't like us very much, do you?' said Uncle Teddy.

'I want to,' shouted Henry. 'I want to, but you won't let me into your lives.'

It was quite a large room, with thirty-two tables. Some of the tables were square, others oblong. They were arranged in straight lines. The men came in flat caps and many of them had square, rugged faces. They drank their pints from straight glasses. It was a world that had eschewed curves as the product of weakness. Henry loved it. It was also a dark room. The lights were low. The decor and furnishings were a tribute to the versatility of brown. All the men wore dark clothes. Many of the women looked as if they hoped they'd be mistaken for men. Here and there, there was a blaze of blonde hair, some real, more false. Occasionally, a woman in a colourful dress. One woman had a bright yellow drink. These were exceptions. Auntie Doris wore a low-cut, blue evening dress. Her figure was still excellent.

The room smelt of stale beer, fresh beer, cigarettes, cheap perfume, furniture polish, disinfectant and sweat. The atmosphere was smoky.

Also seated at their table was Jack Ibbotson, his wife Mabel and her friend Denise. It was because he employed Jack that Uncle Teddy had allowed himself, so untypically, to be roped in. He resented it.

'It's never been properly ventilated, hasn't this venue,' said Jack Ibbotson. 'Not within living memory, any road.'

There were three acts on the bill. The Amazing Illingworth (The Crown Prince of Prestidigitation), Talwyn Jones (The Celtic Droll) and Doreen Tibbs (The Tadcaster Thrush). The weak spots of the cabaret, if one wished to be hypercritical, were that the Crown Prince of Prestidigitation was so drunk that he was pushed to say magic, let alone prestidigitation, that the Celtic Droll had about as much comic personality as a tent pole and the Tadcaster Thrush had a shocking cold, with incipient laryngitis.

The concert secretary was none other than the peripheral Sid Lowson, who was to take no further part in this narrative after his performance as a domino substitute almost fifteen years ago.

'Good evening, ladies and gentlemen,' said Sid Lowson. 'All proceeds tonight go to that very fine footballer, Don Ibbotson, of Thurmarsh United, who's had to pack it in due to injury. He was a great servant of the club. If he'd had a bit of pace, who knows how far he'd have gone? Let's hear it for Don Ibbotson.'

Don Ibbotson stood up. The audience applauded. There were tears in Jack Ibbotson's eyes.

'Thank you,' said Sid Lowson. 'And now, without further ado, our special cabaret, who have all dispensed with their services tonight for nowt. Thank you, each. First, a legendary Tyke entertainer what I saw last week at Mexborough. I didn't rate him mysen, but then I don't like magic. Any road, let's hear it for the Amazing Illingworth.'

The Amazing Illingworth's act wasn't going terribly well even before the escape of the doves. They flew around the room, fluttering wildly, and it was only after a quarter of an hour, and the use of a ladder, that they were all recovered.

Sid Lowson returned to the stage and called for silence. Slowly, the hubbub died down.

'I have three messages,' said Sid Lowson. 'One. Will the bar please not serve the Amazing Illingworth? Thank you. Two. If anybody has a cleaning bill, we will honour them, though as this will come out of what we raise for Don, we hope there won't be. Three, and I should have said this at t' beginning, but in view of the Amazing Illingworth's condition I forgot. With great regret I have to announce the death of one of t' best-loved members of this club, Reg Oldfield. Reg passed away peacefully last night. He was a good 'un. We sent all our sympathies to Madge and the family, and we hope to have a bit of a do to raise summat for them later. T' funeral's on Tuesday. And now, comedy. Let's hear it for Talwyn Jones, the Celtic Droll.'

You're in trouble when you come on in a bright red suit, with a giant leek in your buttonhole, wearing a pith helmet and one roller skate, and nobody laughs.

'Good evening, ladies and gentlemen, and concert secretary,' said the Celtic Droll. 'My name is Taff the Laff. I just came over from by there to by 'ere. So where's the tapestry? By 'ere. Bayeux tapestry. Get it? Nor do I, much. So, you've never heard of the Bayeux tapestry. It's Plan B. Sex. You've heard of sex, have you? It's what the upper classes bring their coal home in.'

Uncle Teddy looked at Auntie Doris in something approaching panic, but excitement coursed through Henry's veins. Suddenly, without a shadow of a doubt, he knew what he was going to be when he grew up. A stand-up comedian.

'. . .Still, accidents will happen, won't they? Take my friend the undertaker. Jones the bones. No, I can't do that one.

Somebody just snuffed it. There were these two Welshmen, Paddy and Mick. Well, I can't do the Irish accent. Paddy says, "I'm walking to Pembroke Dock, isn't it, begorrah?" Mick says, "How long is it?" Paddy says, "I don't know, I haven't looked." Hasn't the rationing been terrible, though. Terrible, the rationing. Mind you, my wife's been rationing me for years. I'm talking about meat, madam. Rissoles to you too. . .'

Many people never find their vocation in life. Lucky is the lad who finds it at the tender age of fourteen. Henry was awash with an amazing exhilaration.

'You can take your gas-mask off, sir. The war's been over for. . .oh, sorry, you haven't got it on. Laugh? I thought you'd never start. Right. What else we got? Oh yes. Thurmarsh United. We slaughtered you last year nil all. I hear you've gone into the transfer market – bought a spectator from Liverpool. What about Stalin then, eh? He's a lad, isn't he?'

No matter that the comedian was bad. No matter that he was dying on his feet. Henry knew that *he* wouldn't die on his feet. It had all fallen into place. His search for a catch-phrase. The long hours listening to the wireless. His insistence on coming tonight. It had all clicked in his head.

'Music's great, though, isn't it? It's great, music. There's this Welsh tenor, see. . .on a string attached to a Welsh wallet. . .tenner, see?. . .What a state I'm in. Tennessee, state, get it? Nor do I, much. No, there's this Welsh tenor, see, from Welsh Wales, has to have this operation, on his throat, this tenor. Comes round, after the operation, doctor says, "How are you?" "Fine, doctor, but I couldn't half go a cup of tea." "All right, but you'll have to not take it through the mouth, you see, because of the operation, you'll have to take it through the. . ." The doctor paused, trying to be polite, like. "Rectum?" said the tenor. "Well, it didn't do them much good," said the doctor.'

No matter that the joke was in tatters. Henry felt like an old pro. He'd practically worked the rectum gag himself, with old Busy B.

'So they pours the old cup of tea in the old rectum, and the tenor screams. "What's wrong?" said the doctor. "Was it too hot?" "No," said the tenor. "You forgot to put any sugar in." Thank you very much, and goodnight, ladies and gentlemen.'

There was sporadic applause, but Henry clapped wildly, less in tribute than in gratitude for having had his eyes opened.

Much of the night passed in a dream for Henry. He hardly heard the raffle draw, which was won by Cecil E. Jenkinson. He was barely conscious of the Tadcaster Thrush, her low-cut dress revealing the massive cleft between her huge breasts, her cold giving her the red nose the comic should have had. Her nasal voice gave her songs the sexual ambiguity of a Berlin cabaret in the thirties. After her first song, 'You're breaking my heart', somebody called out, 'You're not doing much for mine.' Henry was up on stage throughout the song, dreaming of a vast audience in stitches at his patter. He returned to earth to hear her graceful apology for her condition. 'Sorry about t' voice,' she said. 'I've got this dreadful cold. I'm right bunged up.' She launched herself into 'Now that I need you'. Henry reflected on the content of his act, trying out the odd phrase in his head to see how it fitted. It could be the big come-back for 'It's months since I 'ad rat.' During 'Far away places' he was in Hampstead, wondering what Dr and Mrs Hargreaves would make of this, how they would react to the drunk magician, the terrible comic and the singer who sounded like a man imitating Marlene Dietrich badly. She was embarked now upon 'I didn't dow the gud was doaded'. Henry thought briefly about Sid Lowson. Should he go up to him and say, 'I used to be a friend of your son before divisive social elements pulled us apart. Give him my best wishes, will you?' Next, Doreen Tibbs attempted 'Confidentially'. At one point the voice went completely, and somebody shouted, 'There's no need to be that confidential, luv,' and there was laughter, but she ploughed resolutely through it, and the voice returned. Henry's thoughts turned to Cecil E. Jenkinson, landlord of the Navigation, winner of the raffle. Should he go up to him and say, 'You virtually banned my dad from your pub. Well, he's dead now. I hope that makes you very happy.' There wasn't any point. All that part of his life was dead. It all seemed so very far away. It was amusing to touch it so secretly, so tangentially, tonight, by being in the same room as these people without their knowing. For her final number, the ailing Thrush (*Turdus Tadcasterus*) chose, 'I don't see be id your eyes ady bore'. Henry embarked upon a reprise of his opening number, the fantasy of standing on the stage, holding the multitude in his grip. Doreen Tibbs received the best ovation of her career. Her false notes, usually so clearly the result of lack of talent, were assumed tonight to be an unfortunate side-effect of her cold. It was an award for gallantry, and she accepted it with surprise and a sudden vulnerable charm. In Henry's mind the applause was for him. He had to restrain himself in order to remain in his seat. How embarrassed Uncle Teddy and Auntie Doris would be if he stood up and took a bow.

He sat suspended between his past and his future, in that dimly-lit, fetid, smoky, noisy, beery room.

'And now,' said a voice that filled the room, although Henry alone could hear it. 'Now, the moment you've been waiting for, our star turn tonight. He's droll. He's daft. He's Henry. Let's hear it for Henry "Ee By Gum I am Daft" Pratt.'

Dreams sometimes come true.

Life at Dalton College, in the spring term of 1950, still had its unpleasantnesses. Getting up at seven fifteen, in the freezing dorm, long before the dawn. The Spartan diet. The pale orange night-light in the stifling san when half the school went down with gastric flu, and the male nurse with the twisted lip came round with his night-time tray of Ovaltine, Horlicks or Milo, all of which made Henry feel sick. Hockey on Lower Boggle in a hailstorm, and a huge boy from Tudor House tripping him deliberately and sending him nose-first into the thick Somerset mud. The agony of those six-mile runs along the Somerton Road, gasping for breath, frozen, red, chapped legs smeared with mud, and the disgusting smell of Broadlees Farm's silage. The sound of crashing feet bounding off the walls of the gym as he struggled to climb a rope, hands cold, arms so feeble, up, up so slowly, and far below the supple vaulting of some natural athlete over the horse, across which he would shortly stumble in knee-wrenching, skin-scraping horror. Being beaten at table tennis 21–8, 21–7 by Brownlow, 21–6, 21–4 by Paul and 21–1, 21–2 by Prince Mangkukubono of Jogjakarta. There was the ever-present absence of Diana Hargreaves, in whose presence his courage had failed.

There was the pervasiveness of homosexuality, whose dark vapours invaded dorm and changing room. He interrupted glances, smelt entanglements, heard about orgies, and felt both disgusted and neglected.

But there were pleasant things, too. The friendship with Paul. The semi-sexual sparring with Lampo. The memorable day when Orange became cock house at hockey, beating Stuart 3–1, with two goals from Tosser Pilkington-Brick. How they cheered on Middle Boggle! With what fervour they sang 'Jerusalem the Golden' in house prayers that night, with the windows slightly open so that farmers, corn chandlers, labourers and auctioneers could pause on street corners in the little market town, if they so wished, and hear the proud, patriotic lines that sent the pimples goosing across the flesh of Dopy S and every boy except Lampo Davey, who closed his eyes and thought of Tuscany. Then there were the joys of self-abuse, and the redecoration of his partition, which consisted now entirely of pictures of Patricia Roc.

But lessons still took up the bulk of the day. It is time to consider Henry's progress at his lessons.

Art. This subject was not considered important at Dalton College. He sat quietly and caused no trouble.

Chemistry. 'Give me a test tube and I will show you a disaster,' might have been Henry's cry. Poor Stinky G. In Henry's hands even simple tests like the solubility of potassium permanganate or the preparation of oxygen from hydrogen peroxide H_2O_2 became dangerous adventures. As for the acids, whether sulphuric, hydrochloric or nitric, the less said the better. But Henry Pratt, budding comic, didn't seem to mind his disasters any more. He would grin vacantly. 'Ee, by gum, I am daft,' that grin would seem to say. Usually he came about twenty-first out of the class of twenty-five.

English. Doing less well this year, because Mr Lennox (Droopy L) didn't take to his style. Droopy L didn't take to any style. He didn't like style. He looked like a bloodhound which has lost its zest for life, but this morose exterior was merely a blind for his stony heart. Droopy L shredded your essays. His sole criterion of merit was that there should be no unnecessary words at all. ' "We set off *along the road*." You amaze me, Pratt. I thought you would have set off *on top of the hedge*.' Under Droopy L, he usually came about fourteenth.

French. Improving all the time, partly due to a secret ambition to become a bi-lingual comedian. Henri 'Ah par gomme je suis stupide' Pratt. Fifth to seventh.

Geography. Henry shared the enthusiams of his teacher, Mr Tenderfoot, who was hairy, grizzled, six foot three and known as High T. (This was a joke about food, not anticyclones, despite High T's preference for the latter over the former.) Henry and High T loved the bits of Geography without people in them. River erosion, corrasion and attrition. Lateral and medial moraines. Deltas, archipelagoes and gorges. Weather. Rainfall figures were High T's pornography, sunshine records his Bible. Once, in chapel, in the middle of a sermon given by the Bishop of Bath and Wells, High T strode boldly out, to watch a particularly severe thunderstorm. Unfortunately, Geography exams were mainly about the bits with people in them. Reasons for population densities, nature of farming, reasons for the location of industries. Fifth or sixth.

History. Henry sympathised with Mr Trench and his nervous breakdown. A very demanding subject, with its mixture of facts and interpretation. There was a lot to remember and a lot to understand. The understanding was not helped by doing History in blocks, so that you had no idea what happened before or after. It was a bit like studying a bottle of milk in order to understand the evolution of the cow. Not a lot like that, but a bit. Toady D claimed that Henry saw things too simply, because of his background. To Henry all history was the exploitation of the weak by the strong. This was simplistic. Usually about ninth.

Latin. His favourite subject, now that Droopy L had ruined English. Lampo Davey mocked him for this. 'But those Romans were so dreary, so greedy. All marching and plumbing and vomiting, and no imagination. Not like the modern Italians.' Could it be that Lampo was right about modern Italians, and the *Beano* wrong? 'The only Roman who comes over to me like a human being is Catullus,' said Lampo. 'I wouldn't have minded a stroll in the woods with him. No, forget the Romans. Go on to the Greeks.' Next year, Henry would. In the meantime, he usually came second in Latin.

Maths. He was doing worse as he came upon more advanced concepts. Calculus in particular was a closed book, and geometry and algebra sometimes hurt so much that he seemed able to feel the cracks in his brain across which the connections couldn't leap, and that gave him a pain in his toes, of all places, and made him worry about being dependent on such a complicated system of life-support as the human body. Had been as high as third, usually about fourteenth now.

Physics. It certainly wasn't as bad as Chemistry. Henry had difficulty in remembering the difference between Torricelli's experiment and Pascal's experiment, between Boyle's Law and Charles's Law. He tended to make silly jokes about this subject. 'I'm dense about density and relatively dense about relative density.' 'I'll tell you about good and bad conductors. What? Oh yes. There was this tram. . .' or 'The only magnetic pole I knew was Stefan Prziborski.' Partly this was due to a natural element of facetiousness in his personality, partly to his ambition to be a stand-up comic, but that alone would not explain why this eruption occurred so much more in Physics than in other subjects. The truth of the matter was that the nature of matter didn't matter to Henry. More, he felt that he couldn't function in the physical world *unless* he took it for granted. It was hard enough wielding a cricket bat without knowing about its molecular structure. He usually came about thirteenth in Physics.

Scripture. This subject was not considered important at Dalton College. He sat quietly and caused no trouble.

Henry's progress would have seemed very disappointing to Miss Candy, but it seemed good enough to him. He had no idea that anybody had ever had any special hopes for him.

In March, 1950, two events occurred, one of which showed Henry in a very negative light, the other in a much more positive light.

He was shown in a negative light during the general election. Shant held a mock election, with political meetings in Shant Shed. Henry went to the meeting of the Labour candidate, E. J. G. Holmes-Hankinson, of Stuart House. It was sparsely attended.

Only about fifty boys sat in the huge, tiered, semi-circular hall.

'In 1945,' said E. J. G. Holmes-Hankinson, 'this nation voted for a government of the people.'

'My father didn't,' shouted somebody.

'The people of Britain had fought together, as one nation, to win the war. Every man and woman, however humble, played their part.'

'My father didn't,' shouted another boy, and there was laughter.

'Now, they wanted a part to play in the peace that followed. Was that too much to ask?' said E. J. G. Holmes-Hankinson.

There were several cries of 'yes', and more laughter.

'The British people can no longer be cast off like old socks, when they've been used up,' said E. J. G. Holmes-Hankinson.

'Pity,' came a cry.

There were cries of 'S'sssh!' at this.

'They have rights,' said E. J. G. Holmes-Hankinson. 'They have proper unemployment pay and health insurance. They have the finest health service in the world, given by the Labour government. It will last for ever.'

Henry found it difficult to concentrate. E. J. G. Holmes-Hankinson's words about the achievements of nationalisation passed over him. He was imagining himself up on that stage, holding the school in thrall with his comical capers.

'Groundnuts,' shouted somebody.

'Do you think a government which has achieved so much, in such difficult times, should be pilloried for one mistake?' said E. J. G. Holmes-Hankinson.

There were cries of 'yes' and more cries of 'groundnuts'.

'Over a million homes have been built.'

'On our land.'

'Would you deny people the right to live? The Labour government has been forced to apply rationing and severe austerity longer than it would have wished to. Is that its fault? The nation was bankrupted by war. How could it recover over-night? Labour has sown the seeds for. . .'

'. .more groundnuts.'

'. .a gradual return to prosperity. The Labour government has been criticised for allowing the breach with Russia to grow so wide. Did Labour invent the Cold War? It had been made inevitable before we came to power. The Labour government has behaved responsibly, moderately, some would say conservatively. It has expelled communists. It has begun the painful, but inevitable, process of decolonisation.'

There were roars of anger, and more cries of 'groundnuts'.

'Yes. Inevitable,' said E. J. G. Holmes-Hankinson. 'All you can find to say is "groundnuts". That proves how good the government's record is.'

A bag of flour exploded over E. J. G. Holmes-Hankinson.

'You fear the Labour government,' said E. J. G. Holmes-Hankinson, his hair streaked with flour, his shoulders white. 'Why? You're still here, aren't you?'

A few boys cheered and applauded E. J. G. Holmes-Hankinson. Others jeered. Henry remained silent. He simply didn't know enough to do otherwise.

At Westminster, Labour were returned to power, with a majority of six. At Dalton College, E. J. G. Holmes-Hankinson got eight votes. The Liberals got nine. The Conservatives got 657.

The event which saw Henry in a more positive light occurred two days before the end of term. He knocked on Lampo and Tosser's door, received no reply, and entered, to find Lampo rehearsing a mime.

'I didn't say "come in",' said Lampo.

'You didn't say "stay out",' said Henry.

'I couldn't say anything,' said Lampo. 'Mime is silent. In future, wait till you're told.'

'You like me to clean your study when you're out,' said Henry. 'If you're out, you can't say "come in" so if I have to wait for you to say "come in" I can never clean your study while you're out.'

'I'm sorry,' said Lampo. 'I was upset at being interrupted.'

'What were you doing?'

'I'm appearing in the end of summer term concert. I'm doing a satirical mime about Sir Stafford Cripps in Hell. I'm calling it "Austerity in the Underworld". It's a satire on the mean spirit of post-war Britain. It's going to be *a* sensation. A sensation. Tosser's appearing too.' Lampo Davey sighed. 'A ballet skit done by the rugger fifteen. I ask you, Henry. What is that but the hoary old anti-art gag in new clothes? I am trying to do something avant-garde. Tosser is about as avant-garde as a mangle.'

'My auntie had a mangle,' said Henry. 'I won't say she was ugly, but I talked to it for five minutes before I realised it wasn't her.'

Lampo Davey stared at him in astonishment.

'What?' he said.

'I'm practising for my act,' said Henry.

'What act?' said Lampo Davey.

'My act in the end of summer term concert,' said Henry.

Lampo Davey gawped at him. Henry would have gawped at himself, had it been physically possible.

He spent the Easter holidays researching for his act. Twice, he went to the first house at the Sheffield Empire. He went on the Tuesday. That way he could buy the *Star* and read the review of what he was going to see, and build up his anticipation.

To his astonishment, Uncle Teddy and Auntie Doris came with him. He would have preferred to be on his own, for professional reasons, but he couldn't say this. They had taken his January strictures to heart.

On April 4th, he saw the Five Smith Brothers, who sang with lots of energy. Second on the bill was Robb Wilton, a hero of his. He was upset because Robb Wilton wasn't top of the bill. Uncle Teddy explained that he was on the way down. Others on the bill were Kay 'On the Keys' Cavendish, Tony Fayne and David Evans, with amusing impressions of BBC performers, and Donald B. Stuart, more comic than conjuror.

On April 11th he saw the Mack Triplets, American close-harmony singers, sometimes saucy and always tuneful; Wee Georgie Wood, assisted by Dolly Harmer; Leslie Sarony; the Three Jokers, energetic knock-about comedians; Morecambe and Wise, amusing entertainers; Irene and Stanley Davis, clever dancers; Freda Wyn, who certainly knew the ropes; and Jackie, with extraordinary balancing feats.

Then there was Emile Littler's *Waltzes from America* for two weeks, so that was a dead loss, but he did persuade Uncle Teddy to go once to the Thurmarsh Empire, where the bill was headed by Confidentially, from Variety Bandbox, Reg Dixon. The Two Valettos provided an exotic touch with Eastern dancing, the Allen Brothers and June tumbled and glided in a sophisticated comedy routine, and the Two Harvards cut college capers with verve. Aimee Fontenay and her partner provided thrills on the trapeze. Margery Manners sang with an intimate microphone manner that was more than pleasing. Saucy Iris Sadler and ventriloquist Roger Carne provided plenty of laughs, and Victor Seaforth, the man with a hundred voices, gave an electrifying interpretation of Charles Laughton's *The Hunchback of Notre Dame*.

Henry loved it all. He had no idea that he was witnessing a dying art form, and that quite soon many of these theatres would be demolished for improvement schemes, and the rest would be given over to bingo.

He learnt a great deal. The successful comedians presented the audience with a false image of themselves. Not a true image of themselves, which might well be boring, or a false image without themselves, in which case there would be no contact. Contact was more important than the quality of the jokes.

But he still hadn't got his act. He needed something more, an external element.

It came in the shape of the headmaster, Mr Lichfield.

The shape of the headmaster, Mr Lichfield, was oblong, with a sphere on top. He had no waist, very square shoulders, and vitually no neck. He looked like a message hoisted for sailors, sphere above oblong, meaning 'easterly gales imminent' or some such thing.

After house prayers, in the panelled dining room of Orange House, with its list of house rugby captains since 1838 (1949 E. L. F. Pilkington-Brick, 1950 E. L. F. Pilkington-Brick, the first since 1857 to be house rugby captain for two years) Dopy S announced that the following day the headmaster would visit all the houses to talk to them individually on a matter of the greatest importance. They would assemble at 8.25. Dopy S was so concerned about this that he forgot his rubber cushion, which he was carrying on account of an excruciating attack of piles which all the boys except Lampo Davey found hilarious. 'The banal anal English,' said Lampo sadly.

The following day, House assembled round the bare wooden refectory tables. The headmaster entered with the housemaster. Mr Lichfield carried his mortarboard in his right hand. Mr Satchel carried his rubber cushion in his left hand.

House stood.

'Sit down, boys,' said Mr Satchel.

House sat down.

Mr Satchel arranged his cushion, and also sat down. The cushion sighed gently, perhaps for Mr Satchel's lost, unhaemorrhoidal youth.

Mr Lichfield remained standing, sphere over oblong. He looked very worried. He held his mortarboard in front of his private parts, as if he were naked.

He began to speak. He spoke slowly, slightly too loud, as if he had learnt the art of public speaking by numbers. He had a slight speech impediment, being unable to say a soft 's' without aspirating. He seemed to be drawn to his impediment like a moth to a flame.

'I want to shpeak to you today on a very sherioush shubject,' he said. 'Sheksh. In particular, the shin of homoshekshuality. Because it is a shin. Oh yesh.'

Henry stared fixedly at the table, through downcast eyes. This wasn't out of shame, for he agreed with the headmaster. It was out of the fear that, if he so much as caught the eye of another boy, he would begin to shake with helpless hysterical laughter. Was it his fancy that he could sense a barely suppressed communal quivering all round him?

The idea struck him like a swing door. Here was the very thing he had been seeking. And he wasn't even listening to it. He had missed a whole section of the headmaster's talk. He forced himself to concentrate on the peroration.

'At every boarding shchool there are isholated inshidents of thish short of shekshual mishbehaviour, which musht be dealt with on an individual bashish,' the headmaster was saying. 'But here, in thish corner of Shomershet, it has become an imposhible shituation. As I shee you shitting there, sho sholemn, sho shad, your expressions shuffused with shame, yesh, the shame shame that I myshelf onshe felt at my shchool, I confesh that my shpirits shag. I feel for you. The innoshent are at rishk from the guilty. However, I musht shay what has to be shaid. No shchool of which I am headmashter will be allowed to remain a shink of iniquity. Any boy found guilty of any kind of shekshual offenshe will be shacked.'

The headmaster's face had gone purple with embarrassment and honest feeling. The boys' faces had gone purple from their efforts not to laugh. Only the housemaster seemed unaffected. Mr Satchel's smooth face remained totally innocent throughout.

House stood, and they departed, the headmaster with his mortarboard, the housemaster with his rubber cushion, and Henry with his act.

It was the first day of the first test match at Old Trafford. Debuts: England – R. Berry, G. H. G. Doggart; West Indies – S. Ramadhin, A. L. Valentine; Dalton College auditions for end of summer term concert – H. Pratt.

The auditions were held in a small, bare room at the back of the stage in Shant Shed. It had mustard-washed brick walls. Kington, the producer, sat back-to-front on a kitchen chair, his chin resting on top of the back of the chair.

If Henry felt nervous, he didn't show it. Here at last was an area of life in which he was confident.

Kington watched his rough-hewn act, intently still, poker-faced, wanting to see how Henry reacted under pressure. Henry was concentrating so hard that he didn't even notice that Kington wasn't laughing.

'It needs a lot of work on it,' said Kington. 'A lot of work.'

'I know,' said Henry.

Kington nodded. He seemed pleased.

'You're very young to do a solo,' he said. 'You're still a fag. Don't you think it would be more sensible to wait till next year?'

'Yes,' said Henry, 'but who ever got anywhere by being sensible?'

Kington grinned for the first time.

'You can go on after the mime,' he said. 'They'll be so relieved that's over that you'll go down a bomb.'

The summer term passed pleasantly. His batting improved spectacularly. Scores of 0, 1, 1 not out, 0 not out, 2,0,0,3 not out, 1,0,0,0,0 not out, 0 and 2 gave him an average of 1, an all-time high. He just managed to pass his swimming proficiency test in the green, icy waters of the open-air pool. He began to feel that he belonged here. Next year, he wouldn't be a fag, and would be able to open one button on his jacket. The year after, he would have a senior study, he would be able to open two buttons on his jacket, he would be fagged for.

It was pleasant that summer, as Ramadhin and Valentine swept through the English batting, to lie on Middle Boggle, hearing the thwack of leather on willow, feeling your cock harden against the warm grass as you dreamt idly of Diana Hargreaves and Patricia Roc, while you chatted to Paul Hargreaves, or explained the rules, with deliberate incomprehensibility, to Prince Mangkukubono of Jogjakarta. Two-fifths of your mind on cricket, two-fifths on sex, the other fifth always thinking about your act.

The longest day came and went. So did Uncle Teddy and Auntie Doris. A visit! They took Paul Hargreaves out and went to Weston-super-Mare. The tide was out. Henry wished Auntie Doris's perfume didn't smell so strongly. Paul seemed to enjoy himself. 'Thank you very much,' he said at the end of the day, rather stiffly and formally. 'I've had a thoroughly enjoyable day.'

When they left, Auntie Doris hugged Henry, and Uncle Teddy clasped his hand firmly and pressed it.

'Well done, old chap,' he said.

Henry impressed Sweaty W with the revelation that he was reading Baudelaire. The trouble was that it was very difficult to enjoy something that was untranslatable. It was impossible to enjoy a line like '*les soirs illuminés par l'ardeur du charbon*' because, although it sounded good, it was in a foreign language, and when you had translated it as 'the evenings lit up by the heat of coal' it was still impossible to enjoy it because, although it was in your language, it sounded awful. Henry was reading Baudelaire in preparation for his second visit to the Hargreaves's home in Hampstead. This time he meant to impress. He intended to keep a clean sheet and not to blot his copy-book.

The day of the end of term concert approached.

He sat in his partition in the junior study, a small piece of land entirely surrounded by pictures of Patricia Roc. He had a severe attack of nerves. What a fool he had been to think he could make the whole school laugh.

He brought his stamp album up to date, for something to do. Auntie Doris had sent him five Canadian stamps. He could hardly control the hinges in his shaking fingers.

He counted the number of stamps in his album, to pass the time. There were 112. 57 of them were Canadian. 28 of them were identical.

Lampo Davey put his head round the door.

'Nothing to worry about,' he said. 'They'll be in such a good mood after my mime, they'll laugh at anything.'

He was sick. He walked to main school, head throbbing, saying to himself, 'It is funny. It is. No, it isn't. Yes, it *is*.' He was sick again, in the Shant Shed lats. Oh, presumptuous oik.

It *is* funny. Far funnier than the Celtic Droll. Nobody'll laugh at all. Everybody'll be in stitches.

He put on his dark suit, his comedy glasses and his mortarboard, ready for the dress rehearsal.

He felt better.

He went on for the dress rehearsal. He had refused to do his full act on this occasion, having read that this was what real comedians did. What did he mean, 'real comedians'? Wasn't he real?

'Ow do, I'm t' new headmaster waffle waffle waffle waffle waffle waffle waffle waffle Moss Bros. Goodnight,' he said.

He felt much better.

He felt awful.

He was sick.

He gargled and cleaned his teeth.

The concert began. He became convinced that he would forget all his words.

215

Kington obviously thought he could do it. Or did he? Was it a deliberate plot to humiliate him in front of the whole school? That was it. He'd show them. No, that wasn't it. And he wouldn't show them. Yes, he would.

He heard the early acts as if from very far away. A parody of the school song. A sketch, with quite a few laughs. Another song. Warm applause. Then silence.

'Five minutes,' Kington told him. 'Davey's just doing his mime.'

Henry joined Kington at the side of the stage. The silence was total. His legs were leaden. He was shaking.

'He's dying on his arse,' whispered Kington. 'He's dying on his arse out there. You'll be terrific after this. A wow. A two hundred per cent copper-bottomed wow.'

There was a dribble of polite, bewildered applause for Lampo's mime. He came off fuming.

'Peasants,' he said.

Henry stood transfixed.

'Good luck,' whispered Kington. 'You'll slay them. If you're dying on your arse, get off quick.'

Kington pushed him. He walked forward as in a dream, feverish and disembodied.

They roared at the sight of him, fifteen-year-old Henry Pratt, dressed as the headmaster. After several minutes in which most of them hadn't even realised that they were watching the Chancellor of the Exchequer in the underworld, here was something they could understand.

All Henry's nerves left him. He felt the amazing, steadying presence of power. His neck disappeared. He became the headmaster, sphere over oblong. He waited for the laughter to die down, then waited a little longer, to show that he was in charge, to build up the tension, ready to defuse it with the next laugh. He knew about this. Amazingly, instinctively, he was a master of his craft.

"Ow do, I'm t' new headmaster, tha knows,' he said.

They laughed. It wasn't a joke, yet they laughed. He'd got them!

His voice was slightly silly, but not too silly.

'I want to talk to you tonight about summat very important

what I don't like and what there's too much of. Sex.'

They roared and applauded. He stood immobile, facing seven hundred laughing boys, and beyond them the masters, who might or might not be laughing.

'What is sex? It's what you snotty-nosed lot bring the coal home in.'

Yes, already he was not too proud to use old jokes.

'Another thing that there's too much of in this knacker's yard – sorry, school, that was my last job – another thing there's too much of is. . .er. . .homo. . .wait. I haven't finished. Don't laff just cause I say homo. Wait till I've finished. . . Sapiens. Far too many boys. Have to shack a few, I think. Now I'm a bit worried over t' acoustics of this converted abattoir, and whether I can be heard proper and all. If you can't hear me, shout out, and I won't hear you. I said I'm a bit worried over. . .never mind. Ee, by gum, I am daft.'

They'd been waiting for that, those who knew him, and they led the applause.

'Oh, I haven't told you my name yet, have I? I'm Oiky P, M.A. I were born in a slum, tha knows. I were. I come from a slum. One day, my dad said to me, "Henry." He were clever that way, cos that were me name. It still is. Ee, by gum, I am daft. "Henry," he said, "I've gorra pain in me eye." I didn't ask which one, cos he only had the one. He couldn't afford two. "Henry," he said. "Go into t' kitchen and gerrus t' eye-drops." I said, "I'm in t' kitchen." Well, we only had one room. We couldn't afford two. I won't say it was small, but the cockroaches and silverfish died of claustrophobia. He said, "Henry." Cos his memory was still good in them days. He said, "Henry, get t' eye-drops and gerrus dinner at t' same time. It's in t' oven. I opened t' oven door and there were this great big rat. I said, "Dad, there's a great big rat in t' oven." He said, "That's funny. I only ordered a little 'un." It's months since I 'ad rat.'

He paused, waiting for total silence, judging it was time to build the tension again. He adopted a pose of exaggerated innocence.

'Ee, I could do with a fag,' he said.

Homosexuality still shocked him, but he felt no guilt about pretending to be one, for the sake of his act. Anything went, where laughs were concerned. He was a real pro, at fifteen.

'Right. My policies for this Borstal,' he continued. 'Education. We'll have some. Not a lot, but some. We'll get you off your buttocks. Not that I've got owt against buttocks. Never have had. Buttocks, I don't think you can beat them, me. "What about sport?" I hear a strangled cry. Tosser's got his jockstrap on too tight again. Yes, we'll have sport too. And I would like to thank Foggy F for putting up t' goal posts. It's actually cricket this term, but it was a nice thought. Ee, by gum, I am daft. I gorra go now, cos my suit's due back in Moss Bros. Goodnight.'

There was loud applause. Everyone agreed that he hadn't quite known how to end it, but that he'd been amazingly good for a fifteen-year-old.

As he came off, Kington grabbed him by the hand and said, 'Well done.'

He slumped, exhausted, into a chair in the crowded, communal dressing room, with its litter of make-up and costumes on all sides.

Lampo Davey came in, and stood by the door, gazing at him, smiling his twisted smile.

'Congratulations,' he said. 'You have discovered the grease-paint behind the agony. I'm going to kiss you.'

Lampo Davey kissed him full on the mouth.

'I'll probably never see you again after tonight,' he said. 'I'm leaving this Philistine island. I'm going somewhere where my kind of art will be appreciated. Crete.'

Henry couldn't sit for long. The adrenalin was still pumping. He wandered out into the warm, still night. A bat almost brushed his head as he wandered down the passage between the chapel and main school. He looked up at the mellow stone of the Queen Anne mansion, and no longer felt unworthy of it. He no longer felt like the Bauhaus block. He had toned in.

He returned in time to hear the roars that greeted the first fifteen's ballet skit.

'It confirms them in their belief that sport is superior to art. How the little cretins roar,' said Lampo Davey.

Henry went on stage to take his share of the final curtain. He had wondered if the applause would embarrass him. Now he wished that it would go on for ever.

There was a party, on stage. Henry enjoyed a glass of wine for the first time. He had reached maturity.

Lampo acted as his chaperone, choosing to bask in reflected glory rather than wallow in his own disgrace. Many people were leaving Shant the next day. Some of them would never know such glory again. The atmosphere was manic.

The 'headmaster came round briefly to congratulate them. Henry's heart beat a little faster as he approached.

'Congratulations,' said the headmaster warmly. 'It was a mosht amusing shkit.'

This made Henry feel guilty.

'Feeling guilty?' said Lampo Davey, when the headmaster had moved on.

'No,' said Henry.

'With what infinite subtlety the British ruling classes swallow up their opposition,' said Lamp Davey. 'That's the only thing I'm going to miss, in Crete.'

People paid Henry tributes, and they didn't embarrass him, for he regarded them as his due.

Only one thing marred his evening. He wanted to do the whole thing again the next day.

10 Oh God

In the morning, when he received the summons to go and see Mr Satchel, he assumed that his housemaster wished to add his congratulations to the many he had received.

He weaved his way cheerfully between trunks, parents and tuck boxes. The smell of warm gravel wafted in through open doors and windows. This evening he would see Diana.

He plunged into the stuffy gloom of Dopy S's private quarters, wondering idly what it must be like to have eighty schoolboys living in your home.

He entered Mr Satchel's study. At first he could see only Mr Satchel. Then he saw Auntie Doris. Her face was stricken.

'Congratulations on last night,' said Mr Satchel.

'Thank you very much indeed, sir,' he said graciously.

'I'll leave you two alone,' said Mr Satchel. He put his hand briefly on Henry's shoulder as he left.

'Come and sit down,' said Auntie Doris.

She looked gaunt. He could feel his heart thumping.

'You never really wanted to go away to school, did you?' she said.

'What's happened?' he said. 'What's happened, Auntie Doris?'

Her eyes were very moist. He wished she hadn't used so much perfume.

'Teddy's got problems,' she said. 'Business problems.'

A wave of relief swept over him.

'He's got problems with his English end,' she said. 'He's going to have to wind it up. Do you understand what I'm saying?'

'Well. . .yes. . .he's going to have to wind up his English end.'

'I'm saying that he's gone out East, to try to preserve his Oriental end. If he can preserve his Oriental end, all may not be lost.'

Oh God. Above the mantelpiece there were photographs of the cock house rugby team of 1937 and the cock house hockey team of 1950. He found himself full of sympathy for Mr Satchel, for the pain and humiliation which that long gap must have caused him. It was his mind's way of pretending that he hadn't got worries of his own.

'Do you understand what I'm saying?' said Auntie Doris.

Yes. I'm going to another school. Hong Kong High or Bangkok Grammar. The only English boy in a school of old school Thais. Oh God.

'I'm saying that he's going to have to live in Rangoon. I'm saying that I'm going to have to join him as soon as I've sold Cap Ferrat. Do you understand what I'm saying?'

'Well. . .yes.'

'I'm saying that we can't take you with us. I'm saying that there isn't room even if we could afford it. We're almost ruined. The receiver will take the money for Cap Ferrat. I don't mind for us. We've had a good innings. Uncle Teddy always says, "You can't lose money unless you've made it." But. . .do you understand what I'm saying?'

'Well. . .yes.'

'I'm saying that we can't afford to send you here any more. You're going back to Thurmarsh Grammar.'

Oh God.

'But, Auntie. . .'

'You liked it there. You didn't want to leave.'

'Yes, but. . . things are different now.'

'Everything's different now.'

'Yes, but. . .where will I live?'

'With Cousin Hilda, of course. We wouldn't send you out of the family.'

'You're back among your own folk,' said Cousin Hilda. 'I were never happy about your being at those schools. Getting ideas.'

She sniffed. Her tone suggested that she thought of ideas as if they were germs.

'Your tea's a bit dried up,' she said. 'I thought you'd be here before.'

It had been half-past seven before they had arrived at number 66 Park View Road. Auntie Doris had come in only briefly. The moment she had gone, Cousin Hilda had opened the windows wide.

He looked at his tea. It was roast lamb, with mint sauce, roast potatoes and runner beans. He felt too sick to eat, but he must.

Paul had been horrified when he'd heard the news. They had vowed to keep closely in touch.

He discovered that he was hungrier than he had thought. The blue-tiled stove was out. One of the blue glass panes was cracked. On top of the stove, for the summer, sat a blue vase filled with blue flowers.

This time last night he had been just about to go on. This time tonight he should have been with Diana. This year he would have had the courage to touch her, to tell her that he loved her, to steal secretly to her boudoir.

'Giving their house a French name. I don't know,' said Cousin Hilda. It was as near as she ever came to a direct condemnation of the behaviour of Uncle Teddy and Auntie Doris.

Henry thought of Tosser Pilkington-Brick, telling them about a taxidermist who had retired to Budleigh Salterton and called his bungalow 'Dunstuffing'. Lampo had thought that priceless.

A wave of nostalgia for Shant swept over him. He longed to be back in South Africa Dorm. Would he ever see the shower room again? He thought about condensed milk sandwiches, drinking chocolate eaten straight from the tin, the plopping of soft ball against squash court, the wheezing of Gorringe as he doled out the coley pie, the ever-present odour of male sweat. This time yesterday he had been standing on a stage, holding seven hundred boys in his grip.

'Mrs Wedderburn's very kindly lent you her camp bed, to tide us over,' said Cousin Hilda. 'I hope you're grateful to Mrs Wedderburn.'

He wouldn't care if Mrs Wedderburn's insides all fell out as she waited for the tram.

'Yes, I am,' he said. 'I'm very grateful to Mrs Wedderburn.'

He was sitting on one of the bench seats. Cousin Hilda sat opposite him, and watched him eat. He was trying to make his tea last a long time, because after he had finished it there would be several weeks with nothing to do.

There was rice pudding to follow.

'Your favourite,' said Cousin Hilda.

It was happening again! He didn't like rice pudding! First brawn, then Gentleman's Relish, now rice pudding.

'You'll have to sleep in my room. There's nowt else for it,' said Cousin Hilda. 'We'll see how we get on. If it's not satisfactory, I'll give Mr Carpenter notice. He's a journalist.'

Her tone of voice suggested that notice would be the least he deserved, if he was so stupid as to be a journalist.

'He still hasn't come in for his tea,' said Cousin Hilda.

He went into the little bedroom, at the front of the basement. There was only just room for the camp bed between Cousin Hilda's bed and the dressing-table. How could he live here? How would he ever invite Paul here? How could he share a bedroom with the sniffer? Where would she put her voluminous undies? How would he ever amuse himself? How would he ever abuse himself?

He decided to go for a walk in the park, but when he went back into the living room to tell Cousin Hilda, she produced a small parcel, wrapped in brown paper. It looked aggressively plain, that paper, as if to say, 'Those who use gift wrapping paper and such fripperies are on the slippery slope.'

'It's just a little thing,' said Cousin Hilda, shyly. 'I thought you might not have owt to read, and I know what a one you are for reading. I've never seen one like you for reading. I said to Mrs Wedderburn, "I don't know where he gets it from, but it's a pleasure to watch him with his little nose buried in all them words." '

I actually read with my eyes, Cousin Hilda, not my nose, he thought, and then he felt guilty about thinking it. He'd asked Auntie Doris why he couldn't still go to Paul's. She had said that Cousin Hilda would be very worried if he didn't go to her first and get settled in. He decided that he couldn't bear much more of this. He'd go the next day. With what? He had no money. You couldn't sting Cousin Hilda for train fares. Sting. Words like that belonged to Dalton.

'Well, aren't you going to open it?' said Cousin Hilda.

He realised that he'd just been standing there, holding his present, thinking. He didn't want to open it. It would be something wildly, embarrassingly unsuitable. *The Journals of St Paul. A Short History of Congregational Chapels in the West Riding, 1865–1898.*

'Oh. Yes,' he said.

He undid the parcel slowly, partly because he had never fully unravelled the mysteries of string, and Cousin Hilda was not the sort of person in whose presence you did anything so wanton as to cut string, and partly because he dreaded the effort of pretending that it was just what he had always wanted.

'You may have read it before,' she said. 'If you have, tell me. She said they could change it.'

He longed for her to shut up. His nerves screamed for her to keep quiet. He hated her nervous, pathetic, silly twittering. She was pathetic. He couldn't live with her.

There was only one last knot to go. As he fumbled with it, he had an image of Lampo Davey on a rocky shore, pretending to be Sir Stafford Cripps in the underworld to a group of unshaven men in navy-blue sweaters. Was that really the sort of thing Crete wanted? He'd like to be there with Lampo Davey. He'd even let Lampo kiss him. What was he thinking?

'Come on,' said Cousin Hilda.

Were there moments when he thought he might spend the rest of his life untying that parcel? Did he nourish a faint hope that Cousin Hilda would pass away peacefully of old age before he faced the embarrassment of hiding his contempt for her gift?

'I hope it's the right age for you,' she said, as he completed the unravelling of the string at last. 'It's difficult to tell. She said if it was wrong they'd be happy to change it if it wasn't soiled.'

Shut up!!!!!!!!

At last the paper was off. The book was revealed.

It was *Biggles Scours the Jungle*.

He looked across at Cousin Hilda. Her lips were working anxiously.

'It's marvellous,' he said. 'Thank you very much. It's the best thing you could possibly have given me.'

And it was, because his self-pity was swept away by a wave of compassion for Cousin Hilda.

'Open it,' she said.

He opened it. There was a card inside. It read 'Welcome home, Henry.'

'This is your home now,' she said.

Several years later, at half-past ten that evening, Cousin Hilda's 'businessmen' assembled in the basement room for their little supper.

Since we last saw him, Henry had unpacked his trunk and hidden his books in the loft. He didn't dare let Cousin Hilda see them. His literary tastes had changed, under the influence of Dalton in general and Paul and Lampo in particular. Paul had introduced him to Aldous Huxley, who had inherited the mantle of Captain W. E. Johns and Agatha Christie as the best writer in the history of the universe. It was also because of Paul that he had brought *Women in Love* and *The Rainbow* by D. H. Lawrence. Lampo thought Huxley dreary and Lawrence phoney, and had recommended the works of Henry Miller. Henry had borrowed the tropics of Cancer and Capricorn. In addition, he had brought *The Loom of Youth* by Alec Waugh, which was about homosexuality at a public school and therefore banned from Dalton, and therefore everybody read it.

For supper, there was as much brawn as you could eat, with a segment of tomato, a tease of cucumber and a pickled gherkin. There was also bread and marge, and tea.

'I seem to remember that you like brawn,' said Cousin Hilda.

'So do I,' said Henry.

'So do you what?' said Cousin Hilda.

'Seem to remember that I like brawn,' said Henry.

'If you don't, your aunt left a jar of Gentleman's Relish for you,' said Cousin Hilda.

'I love brawn,' said Henry. 'But I won't have much tonight, because I had my tea late.'

The first 'businessman' to arrive was Liam, a very shy bachelor Irish labourer in his late forties, with a slow mind and a slow smile. Liam was not the conventional image of an Irish labourer, being a virtual teetotaller and extremely quiet. He had a shiny red face, said, 'Pleased to meet you. Hasn't it been a grand day?' and then remained silent, though he smiled a lot.

Second to arrive was Tony Preece, an insurance salesman in his thirties, dark and quietly smooth, but with a bad complexion. He grinned broadly at Henry, and winked when introduced.

Next came Neville Chamberlain, who was the South Yorkshire Regional Sales Officer for a well-known paint firm.

'I nearly punched a man tonight,' he said.

'Neville Chamberlain!' said Cousin Hilda. 'Not in front of the boy.'

Henry groaned inwardly. Was he to be used as a spectre, hovering threateningly over the conversation?

'You don't know what it's like, having an awful name,' said Neville Chamberlain.

Oh yes I do, thought Henry.

'The number of people who hold up a contract or a bill and say, "I have here a piece of paper",' said Neville Chamberlain. 'And I don't think I ever said that anyway.' He went red, and corrected himself hastily. 'I don't think *he* ever said that anyway. You see. It's getting to me. I work hard. I go out for a quiet pint.'

'Neville!' said Cousin Hilda. 'Not in front of the boy.'

Oh God.

Tony Preece winked. Henry thought he probably quite liked Tony Preece, but he was allergic to being winked at.

'Up comes this idiot. "Hello, Neville. How was Munich?" Hi. . .bloody. . .larious.'

'Neville Chamberlain!' said Cousin Hilda. 'Wash your mouth out with soap and water.'

'How *was* Munich?' said Tony Preece, and he winked at Henry, his new ally.

Oh God.

Liam smiled.

'Which of you's the journalist?' said Henry.

'None of them. That's Mr Carpenter,' said Cousin Hilda.

'Has Len Arrowsmith left then?' said Henry.

'He's gone to meet the great French polisher in the sky,' said Tony Preece.

'Tony Preece!' said Cousin Hilda. 'You know I don't like that kind of talk.'

'I saw a little baby in the park this evening, by the bandstand,' said Tony Preece. 'I thought, "I know you." Then I realised who it was. Len Arrowsmith.'

'Tony Preece!' said Cousin Hilda. 'I don't believe in reincarnation myself, but Len Arrowsmith held his belief sincerely, and you've no cause to mock it.'

Tony Preece winked at Henry, and the front door slammed.

'Mr Carpenter!' said Cousin Hilda grimly, and a tense silence fell on the gathering.

There were heavy, uneven thuds on the stairs, the door opened, and a dishevelled, middle-aged man lurched into the room.

'You weren't in to dinner,' said Cousin Hilda.

'I was out,' explained Mr Carpenter, swaying. 'Out. Not in.'

'Your tea is stone cold,' said Cousin Hilda. 'I could heat it up, but I won't. I could have kept it warm, but I didn't. I will not serve you your dinner drunk.'

'I didn't realise you were drunk,' said Mr Carpenter. 'So am I. Shall we go on somewhere? Make a night of it?'

Henry took over Mr Carpenter's room the following week. It was at the side, affording an excellent view of the side of number 67 Park View Road.

He found himself following a young boy with golden fair hair. It was raining. He overtook the boy just before the turning into Link Lane, and turned his head to look at the boy's face. He caught a glimpse of smooth skin, a delicate, sculpted nose and sensitive lips.

He plunged into the busy, steaming confusion of the school, looking round for Martin Hammond, or Stefan Prziborski. Even Norbert Cuffley would do.

He saw no one he knew.

He entered the assembly hall and sat about two-thirds back, as he judged a fifteen-year-old should.

The fair-haired boy's hair, many rows in front, shone out in the wet autumn gloom.

'Welcome back, old boys. Welcome to Thurmarsh Grammar, new boys,' began Mr E. F. Crowther.

All the other new boys were eleven, but Henry was fifteen.

'You see before you our staff,' said Mr E. F. Crowther, 'as fine a body of men as can be found. . .in this building.'

Mr Crosby had heard this joke twenty-four times before, but he still laughed exaggeratedly at it.

'Thurmarsh. It is not perhaps a name that resounds through the educational world.'

Mr Quell stifled a yawn.

'It is not an Eton or Harrow. It is not even a Dalton College.'

There was laughter. It was nasty of Mr E. F. Crowther, Henry thought, to add that. But perhaps it was expecting too much of human nature to imagine that any king could ever forgive a subject who said 'the bread van' in the middle of his address to the nation.

'But is it any the worse for that?'

Again, Mr E. F. Crowther paused, as if challenging any wretched boy, but in this case particularly Henry, to say 'yes'.

It wasn't his fault that he had left Thurmarsh. He hadn't wanted to, any more than he wanted to be back here now.

It would serve Mr E. F. Crowther right if he did say 'yes'.

He would say 'yes'.

Yes!

No!!!!

He began to sweat, but he didn't say 'yes'.

'I am proud to be headmaster of Thurmarsh Grammar,' the headmaster continued at last. 'Perhaps I am biased, because I am Thurmarsh born and Thurmarsh bred.'

Henry felt a ridiculous compulsion to interrupt again. Oh no. Oh no no no no no no no no no.

'We are still only beginning to rebuild the fabric of our civilisation after the recent war which stretched it to breaking point,' said Mr E. F. Crowther. 'In the war, Old Thurmarshians were up there in the front lines with Etonians, Harrovians and Daltonians. In the years to come, in the never-ending war against the enemies of liberalism and democracy, in the war against the self-destruction of the human race itself, I have no doubt there will also be Thurmarshians in the van.'

Was it just his fancy, or was the headmaster looking straight at him? Was half the school looking straight at him? Sweat poured off him. He tried to hold the words back. They were there, like a lump in his throat. He mustn't say them. Not again.

The tension eased. He wasn't going to. The temptation was over. The headmaster, perhaps relieved, perhaps disappointed, perhaps both, resumed his theme.

Henry found himself looking at the back view of the fair-haired boy. Just then, as if aware of Henry's gaze upon him, the boy turned round. He seemed to be looking straight at Henry. He really was remarkably beautiful.

He was getting an erection! Oh God. How often had he yearned after these elongations. Now they were cropping up at the most embarrassing moments. He had to get rid of it before they stood for the hymn. The whole row would notice it. It would be visible to the masters through a narrow gap in the standing ranks. Gradually the attention of the whole school would be drawn to it. Go away. Shove off. Concentrate on Mr E. F. Crowther. All be sorry to hear that poor old Mr Budge had passed away. Well, sorry to be callous, but never mind Mr Budge passing away. How about Mr Bulge passing away?

Concentrate. Extensive repairs to the boiler room, eh? Sounds good. Face the winter with more confidence. That's the ticket.

A boy? It wasn't possible. He'd spent two years at Dalton College being horrified by it. His working-class prudery, Lampo Davey had called it. Don't think about Lampo Davey! Concentrate. Improvements in the gymnasium! Two new ropes! Excellent news. The fair-haired boy'd look nice climbing a rope. Smooth legs, covered in downy fair. . .stop it! Count the windows. Sixteen, their top halves all open at an angle of twenty-five degrees, held in place by cords tied to cleats on the wall. Roof. Flat, dull, off-white. Lighting, strip. Like to see the fair-haired boy str. . . no! No!

Had Dalton College finally corrupted him? Had he fought it where it was rife only to succumb to it where it was taboo?

Oh God.

They sang a hymn. He managed to conceal it under his hymn book. Slowly, under the influence of the hymn, it went away.

A prayer followed. How drab and unimpressive it all was, after Dalton. Don't even think like that!

As they filed out of assembly, on a tide of talk, he came face to face with Martin Hammond and Stefan Prziborski. How big they were. He hardly recognised them. Martin looked more like an owl than ever, a solid, robust owl. Stefan was medium-height, medium-build and had brown hair, and yet there was nothing average or dull about his appearance at all. There was a hint of foreign parts, of exotic sensitivity, in the rubbery mobility of his face.

'Hello,' said Martin.

'How do, then?' said Stefan, in his semi-pretend Yorkshire.

'Hello,' he croaked.

His voice sounded dreadfully middle-class and false, and he felt that the remark had not been a great success.

'How's things then, our Martin?' he said. 'How's t' football, our Stefan?'

It came out like his music-hall voice. It sounded false. It was false.

'Much the same,' said Martin.

Henry knew what Martin meant. He meant, 'Some of us have made the best out of our boring, unglamorous, routine lives while others have been gallivanting around chasing false gods, mocking their heritage, being corrupted by the sink of iniquity which is upper-middle-class life, learning to drink claret, put the milk in afterwards, cheer when the chaps scored a try, and betray their class, their family, their upbringing and their friends.'

If only Martin could have actually said it, instead of bottling it up.

Some of the boys mocked his altered accent. He soon acquired the soubriquet 'Snobby'. It was even more hurtful than 'Oiky'. It had not been his fault that he had been oiky, and at least he had had his anger and sense of injustice to sustain him. But he deserved to be known as 'Snobby'.

He had betrayed them all.

He avoided the company of Martin and Stefan, partly in order to spare himself the indignity of being snubbed by them, and partly also because he had something more important to do.

He had to establish a relationship with the fair-haired boy.

On the second day of term, he found himself walking out of the school behind the fair-haired boy, who was alone. He followed him down Link Lane, past the fire station. The boy turned right, towards the town centre, where he took another right turn into Bargate. He popped into the sweet shop beside the Paw Paw Coffee Bar and Grill. He was buying sweets, which would ruin his teeth, silly boy. Henry stared at three-piece suits in the window of Dunn's till the boy emerged. He followed him as he turned left into Church Street, towards the Town Hall, which was streaked with pigeon droppings.

The boy turned right, along the Doncaster Road, past the end of Park View Road and into the Alderman Chandler Memorial Park. He walked diagonally across the park, skirting the bandstand and the pond, leaving the animal cages to his left, and plunged out into the maze of side roads in the north-eastern suburbs.

Henry followed him no further.

He simply hadn't dared to approach him. How could he, here, in Thurmarsh?

It was the most important year of his academic life. In June he would sit his 'O' levels. The change of school could not but handicap him. It was doubly important to work hard this year, yet the lessons passed him in a fog.

Latin was taken by Mr Blackthorn, who would come in disgruntled every Monday morning and say, 'Those damned Christians woke me with their bells again yesterday.' Mr Blackthorn worked off all his aggressions on the Christians. With his pupils he was patient and charitable. Yet Henry sat there in a fog.

The Maths master, Mr Littlewood, had a boyish, sandy-haired enthusiasm. If anybody could bring Henry and calculus together, it was he. Yet Henry sat there in a fog.

The Geography master, Mr Burrell, had only one eye. Was a return to Thurmarsh inevitably also a return to somebody with one eye? Was the number of people with one eye in the town a constant? Mr Burrell's glass eye, the left, was a fine piece of work, as these things go, and he laboured under the illusion that nobody realised that he only had one eye. He was therefore reluctant to turn his head more than would be natural in a man of two eyes.

Unfortunately, there were two rows of fixed bench seats parallel with three walls of Mr Burrell's class. The four boys at the end of these seats on Mr Burrell's left were therefore totally invisible to Mr Burrell at all times. He knew they were there, of course, and in order to ensure that they received their fair share of attention, he moved the class around from time to time. At this particular time the four invisible boys were Astbury, Longfellow, Prziborski and Wool. They sat with false red noses or women's hats on while the rest of the class behaved with total decorum. This added an exotic touch to a humdrum scene, yet Henry sat there in a fog.

The French master, Mr Telfer, had two eyes, but only one leg. He had lost the other one on active service in France, and this had confirmed him, if confirmation was needed, in his belief that the French were a chaotic, dirty and totally unreliable people who used sauces to cover up the fact that all their meat was horse and changed governments more often than their underclothes. Only a filthy nation would need so many bidets, he argued. Mr Telfer was sour and staccato. Teaching French was an act of masochism in the best puritan tradition. He taught it fiercely, coldly, by the book. No Arsène Lupin. No 'Auprès de ma Blonde'. Just irregular verbs and suffering. Just occasionally, if he was feeling generous or frivolous, or it was near the end of the term, they might be permitted to study the works of Racine. The boys were in awe of him, but Henry sat there in a fog, *auprès de* his blond in his guilt-ridden mind.

Mr McFarlane, the History master, had two eyes and two legs, but only one idea. It was Marxism. It was amazing how relevant the theories of a man born in Trier in 1818 were to every single thing that happened in British history between 1066 and 1485. All this should have been grist to Henry's dark, satanic mill, yet he sat there in a fog. Might catch a glimpse of the boy in the break. Oh, delicious prospect.

The final lesson of the day was English. The greatest of Mr Quell's many literary passions was Chaucer. One of the set books was *The Nun's Priest's Tale*. Mr Quell brought it vividly to life, yet Henry sat there in a fog, not even concentrating enough to be more than mildly disappointed that Mr Quell had said nothing especially welcoming to him on his return.

Good teachers, bad teachers. Happy teachers, sad teachers. Miss Candy's great hope, who never knew that he was Miss Candy's great hope, sat through all their lessons in a fog.

He hardly spoke to the other boys. His nerves were exhausted by all the new starts that he had made. He had nothing left to give to this school, and it was harder to readjust than to start from scratch.

Besides, he was busy. As soon as the lessons were over, he hurried out of school, tense, absorbed, tingling, determined that today he would talk to the fair-haired boy. Six times his courage had failed him. Today it mustn't.

It was a bright, rather hazy autumn afternoon. He walked past the old men's shelter, the glass restored now between the wrought iron. It was octagonal. An octagonal bench ran round the interior. There was no law to say that only old men might use this shelter, but only old men ever did. It was tradition.

He wandered over to the bird cages. There were five guinea fowl, a macaw, two rather scruffy peahens, three Lady Amhurst pheasants, seven assorted doves and twelve sparrows which had got in through the mesh. In the animal cages there were two marmots, two unidentified small deer and an extremely listless ocelot. All the while, only half of Henry's mind was occupied by this rich cornucopia of animal life. He was watching out for the fair-haired boy.

Here he came. If only he came over to the animals, Henry would be able to say, 'Oh, hello, haven't I seen you at Thurmarsh Grammar,' and the thing would be started.

Yesterday, Henry had stood by the pond, and the boy had come past the cages. Today he came nowhere near the cages, but lingered by the pond. Tomorrow. He'd definitely try tomorrow.

The following day saw the fog thicken. It cleared slowly outside, but not at all in Henry's head.

After school, he walked briskly to the park. This time he sat in the bandstand. It had a classical pillar at each corner and a green copper dome. The sun was a yellow plate riding through the mist, and a raw little breeze blew through the bandstand.

Here he came. Henry took deep breaths and his heart raced. This was it. Zero hour. He set off on an expertly timed walk which brought him across the boy's bows.

Right up till the moment when he said it, he wasn't sure whether he was going to say it or not. Out it came. 'Hello. Haven't I seen you at the grammar school?'

'Aye. That's right.'

The accent was broad Thurmarsh. That didn't make the thing any more probable.

They were heading towards the pond. In the middle there was a small reedy island, with a few stunted trees. A colourful board gave names and pictures of all the ducks which might be found on the pond.

'There's a fine collection of ducks,' said Henry.

'They haven't got half what they say on t' board.'

The boy seemed calm. Had he any idea what Henry was thinking? Did Henry's voice sound odd? Was the park keeper watching?

'You what?'

'They haven't got pochard. They haven't got shoveler.'

'They've got tufted duck.'

'Oh, aye, that's what they mostly are, tufted duck. But they're not very exciting, aren't tufted duck.'

'They've got teal.'

'They haven't got marbled teal. They haven't got falcated teal. It's only in t' last week they've had mandarin.'

Close to, the boy's features were not quite as fine as he had thought.

'They've got wigeon,' said the fair-haired boy.

'Have they got pintail?'

'Have they heck?'

'You like birds, do you?'

'Not really. I just look to see what it says on t' board, and what they haven't got. Then I complain to t' park keeper.'

The park keeper limped slowly towards them, examining a line of bleak, rectangular rose beds.

'Hey,' shouted the fair-haired boy. 'It says there's shoveler. There isn't.'

The park keeper approached them. He addressed himself to Henry.

'I keep telling him,' he said. 'There's been a war on. Ducks is in short supply, same as owt else.'

'Shouldn't be on t' board if tha hasn't gorrem;' said the fair-haired boy stubbornly.

'I'd better be getting home,' said Henry.

And that was that. He walked away, as flat as a pancake. That was what his great homosexual passion amounted to, one discussion about the lack of duck on the park pond.

He couldn't face smiling Liam, winking Tony and complaining Neville Chamberlain. He walked back into Thurmarsh, scuffing his shoes angrily against the pavements. The mist was closing in.

He'd been in love with a dream, a vision culled as much from literature as life. What a dreadful fool he would have made of himself, if anybody had noticed. Perhaps they had noticed.

He hadn't disliked the fair-haired boy. But he was just a little pre-pubertal grammar-school kid, aggressively determined not to be short-changed by life. He'd have run a mile if Henry'd tried anything. Or he'd have demanded money. Henry shuddered. He imagined himself flinging himself on the boy, the boy resisting and fighting, the awful humiliation of it. He began to shake, a shuddering mixture of the cold and self-revulsion.

'You're sick,' he told himself.

Oh God.

He caught the Rawlaston tram, barely conscious of what he was doing, certainly not responsible for his decisions.

The tram climbed past the end of Link Lane. New slums were being built on one of the bomb sites.

They breasted the rise like an immensely slow big dipper and groaned down into the Rundle Valley. There, on the right, looming like a battleship in the mist, was the fortress of Brunswick Road Primary School. Had he really been there; he, Henry Pratt, the same person as this?

In the Rundle Valley it wasn't mist. It was fog. The tram went into it so suddenly that Henry expected a collision. It was rank and sulphurous.

He could tell by the flattening out that they had reached the valley floor. They were swinging right. The canal would be on his left.

'Paradise,' said the conductor.

He got off. This was what he had come back to do. Visit his roots.

There wasn't a breath of wind. The factories were pumping filth into the autumn mists. It was almost as dark as night, but yellow instead of black.

He struggled along the pavement to the corner of Paradise Lane. The frail and the elderly walked with handkerchiefs over their mouths and noses, the home-made gas-masks of peace.

Footsteps rang hollow. Cars crawled. A man spat quite close to him. It was ridiculous. What was the point of revisiting old haunts when you couldn't see them?

It was perfect! The real trip was in his memory, anyway, and he certainly didn't want to be seen.

He felt his way up to the terraced houses. Visibility was about a foot and a half. He passed the entry to a yard. Number 15. 17. 19. 21, where she'd been on the game. 23. They'd got a new door with curved, patterned, frosted glass. It removed the only architectural merit the row could ever have been said to possess – simplicity.

'I don't like that door,' he said.

'Give over,' said Ezra. 'It's their one little chance of being individual. Would you deny them that?'

He jumped out of his skin. He looked round. If his father had been there, he wouldn't have been able to see him.

The sweat came out hot and cold all over him.

He was hearing voices now.

Oh God.

Yes?

What?

I am with you, my son.

He stumbled and fell, gashing his knee. No matter.

He had heard it.

Are you there?

Nothing.

If this was a blinding vision, it was strictly West Riding style. Two short sentences, in thick fog, on the Road to Nowhere instead of the Road to Damascus. He thought of Lampo Davey, who had said, 'Tosser has absolutely no religious feeling whatsoever. He thinks the Road to Damascus is a film with Bing Crosby, Bob Hope and Dorothy Lamour.' And Lampo Davey in Paradise Lane brought out the guilt – streaming, shuddering, dreadful guilt.

The fog began to swirl about him. It was turning into the faces of the ogglers and tackies, back at Shant. Ogglers was Shant rant for the waiters who served them at dinner. Tackies were maids. The boys never spoke to the ogglers and tackies as if they were human beings. It simply wasn't done. And now they were all about him, hideous, vaporous caricatures, reminding him, accusing him. And there was his father, a cadaver of fog, pointing an accusing foggy finger. You betrayed me, Paradise Lane, your own past, just to get laughs.

He stepped through the gate. It was a gate onto a canal towpath. It was a door into a world full of capital letters.

Guilt. Shame. The Scylla and Charybdis of Henry's voyage.

It was a perilous journey, along the towpath in the thick fog. There was a muffled explosion as a train detonated a fog signal.

He almost missed the bridge, where the towpath crossed the canal. He clambered carefully up, and down the other side onto the waste ground. He was shaking. It was the cold. Plus the Guilt. And the Shame.

He had heard Him. God had spoken to him. Of that he had no doubt.

He knelt on the waste ground and closed his eyes. He saw his dad, as he had been in the last days, shrunken, embittered, soon to die in an outside lav. He saw himself, standing in front of seven hundred boys, saying, ' "Henry," he said. "I've gorra pain in me eye." I didn't ask him which one, cos he only had the one. He couldn't afford two.'

A train whistled. A dog barked. Henry prayed in the fog.

'Oh, God,' he said. 'Forgive me.'

There was no reply. He didn't expect one. God had told him that He existed. Now, there would be silence until he had Atoned for his Sins.

He knew what he had to do. He understood the nature of symbolic gestures.

He got up, shaking, sweating, even crying, wretched, but happy. He edged his way forward towards the River Rundle, cautiously. It would ruin everything if he fell in.

He sensed the bank rather than saw it. Yes, there the land fell away. He knelt and reached out into the white nothingness with his hand.

No doubt the Ganges was polluted. A river was Sacred because Faith made it so. Otherwise, pilgrims would make only for trout streams, to the fury of angling clubs and water bailiffs.

Henry knew that the River Rundle was Sacred. Therefore, the River Rundle was Sacred. And it was truly an act of Faith, for in the thick fog he couldn't actually see that it was the river that he was stepping into. It might be the edge if the world.

It was the river. Once again, the foul waters of the Rundle closed over his head, but this time he meant them to. He was Purifying himself in its Holy Waters.

The police brought him home at twenty-five past ten, shaking uncontrollably, dripping wet, with a temperature of a hundred and five. Cousin Hilda had been at her wits' end, but his appearance was too terrible for her to be angry.

'Where have you been?' she said, sniffing only very mildly.

'Finding God,' he said.

He was in bed for two weeks. Two weeks in the bed with the sagging springs, which converted into a settee when required. Two weeks with the hiss of the gas fire, in front of which Cousin Hilda placed a saucer of water, in case it should get thirsty. Two weeks staring at the drab wallpaper, its pattern in dark blue and pink so small that from the bed there didn't seem to be a pattern. Two weeks staring at the massive, carved, slightly orange wardrobe. A signed photograph of Len Hutton stood on the mantelpiece. It was the nearest thing in the room to a personal touch, all the pictures of Patricia Roc having been thrown away, judged too racy for this establishment.

His fever died down, the magic of the fair-haired boy had gone, but the magic of God remained.

Many people never find their true vocation in life. Fortunate indeed is the young man who finds it at the tender age of fifteen.

But Henry has found his vocation before, a sceptic might point out. True, but that was only *a* vocation. This was *the* vocation.

He would devote himself to the service of God.

Cousin Hilda was delighted. She had been a little worried at first. His method of coming to God had been rather too unconventional for her nonconformist tastes. Once there, however, he seemed to be quietening down nicely.

At last he was well enough to go downstairs for his tea.

Liam possibly thought that he wasn't as much fun as he used to be.

Neville Chamberlain hardly noticed him. He was too busy wondering if he'd been over-impulsive in changing his bank that afternoon. Suffering from pains in the arm, worried that he might be on the verge of a heart attack, he had gone to see his bank manager, to make a will. The bank manager had said, 'I have here a piece of paper,' and Neville Chamberlain had almost had a heart attack then and there.

Only on Tony Preece did Henry's discovery of God make any impact. It was all because of a mouse.

When Tony Preece yawned and said, 'Sorry. Late night last night,' Henry had toyed with the idea of making some comment about Loose Living, but had decided against it. Now, however, he could not remain silent.

Cousin Hilda had discovered mouse droppings. She had seen tiny tooth marks. She had put down a trap by the door to the scullery.

'Got a mouse?' said Tony Preece.

'I'm afraid so,' said Cousin Hilda. 'It's probably come over from the park now the cold weather's come.'

'I hope the possibility has occurred to you that it might be Len Arrowsmith,' said Tony Preece.

'Don't be ridiculous,' sniffed Cousin Hilda.

'It's not at all ridiculous,' said Tony Preece. 'Where else would he come but here? He always liked it. And you know how he felt the cold.'

He winked at Henry.

'It's wrong to mock a sincerely held belief,' said Henry.

Tony Preece gawped at him, thunder-struck. He looked from

239

Henry to Cousin Hilda, then back to Henry again.

'My God, we've got two of them now,' he said, and he pushed his plate into the centre of the table and stormed out of the room, and Liam's smile froze on his bewildered face.

When Liam and Neville Chamberlain had gone, Cousin Hilda refused to let Henry go into the scullery, in case his fever returned. So while she washed up, he sat by the blue stove, gazing hypnotically at the glowing fire behind the cracked glass.

Cousin Hilda came and sat at the other side of the stove, with her knitting.

'Please don't say things like that to Tony Preece,' she said. 'You upset him.'

'You don't like him poking fun at reincarnation either,' said Henry.

'I know,' said Cousin Hilda, 'but he'll accept it from me. He won't from you, not at your age.'

'That's not fair,' said Henry.

'It's not just that,' said Cousin Hilda. 'I'm his landlady. I'm entitled. I don't want to lose him, Henry. This is a business, and he's a good customer, is Tony Preece.'

'Is he?'

'What do you mean?'

'I think he has Mucky Habits.'

'Mucky habits?'

'When he isn't in to supper,' said Henry. 'When he has late nights, like last night. I think he Indulges in Strong Drink and Consorts with Mucky Women.'

Cousin Hilda stared at him in astonishment.

'I know what he gets up to,' she said. 'He gives performances.'

'Performances, Cousin Hilda?'

'Tony Preece is summat of a Jekyll and Hyde,' said Cousin Hilda. 'By day, insurance salesman. By night, stand-up comedian.'

'Stand-up comedian?'

'It's his hobby. Very regrettable, of course, but. . .I wouldn't like to lose Tony Preece.'

Henry didn't feel that he was in a strong position to criticise people for being stand-up comedians. So he kept quiet in Tony

Preece's presence after that.

The following morning, in fact, although embarrassed, and unable to meet Tony Preece's eye, he forced himself to say, 'Sorry about last night.'

'That's all right,' said Tony Preece.

When Henry did meet Tony Preece's eye, Tony nodded in the direction of the scullery door, and winked.

The mouse trap had gone.

Mr Quell was worried about Henry. He didn't like the look of the boy. He had gone extremely pale and puffy. His face was waxy and lifeless. He was beginning to resemble a fish which has been on the slab too long. Either he was masturbating himself to death, or there were major problems.

Mr Quell believed that schoolmasters could often make matters worse by interfering too soon when they sensed the onset of a crisis. He had been careful to leave Henry to himself while he settled back into the life of the school. But you could also delay too long. He had delayed too long in the case of Oberath.

He invited Henry to tea on Friday. Henry was pleased. It would be a wonderful opportunity for talking to Mr Quell about Him.

They drove in Mr Quell's car. It was an ancient Hillman Minx with a rattling exhaust. Mr Quell drove at twenty-five miles an hour.

'It's a miserable month, November,' said Mr Quell.

'I quite like it,' said Henry.

Bad! No boy should wallow in mist and fog.

Their route took them through the town centre, and out onto the York Road.

'The United are picking up a bit,' said Mr Quell.

'Are they?' said Henry.

Small talk would prove to be a blind alley, thought Mr Quell.

Mr Quell pulled up at a newly installed set of traffic lights. A light rain was beginning to fall. The swish of the windscreen wipers was sad and comforting at the same time.

'There are certain practices which, if indulged in to excess, can prove very deleterious to health,' said Mr Quell.

'I've completely given up self-abuse,' said Henry, 'if that's what

241

you mean.'

The Quells lived in a detached brick house, on Winstanley Road, near the edge of the town. There was a trolley-bus stop outside, and sometimes people waiting for a trolley-bus would drop sweet papers into their garden. This upset Mr Quell, but not his wife.

Mr Quell had to turn right to enter his drive. He was cautious, and waited a long while for a gap in the oncoming traffic. A queue built up behind him, and a driver hooted.

There was a monkey puzzle tree in Mr Quell's front garden.

They had tea in the front room, served by Mr Quell. There was a coal fire, with shelves in alcoves at either side of it. The tea was laid out on a trolley. Mr Quell divided up a nest of tables and placed a table beside each of their chairs.

Mrs Quell was small, almost doll-like, and very beautiful. She had small, regular features and dark hair. No lines of stress marred the oval perfection of her face.

Mr Quell served tea. His burly, barrel-chested frame and mass of greying hair seemed at odds with Dresden China ladies on shelves, and a Dresden China wife sitting very upright in the brown Parker Knoll chair. There were neat, thin, quartered slices of bread and butter and two bought cakes – a Battenburg cake and a chocolate cake. The Battenburg cake was stale and the chocolate cake had the consistency of damp sawdust. They drank cheap, unsubtle Indian tea out of tiny cups. Mr Quell could hardly get his gnarled finger inside the fragile handle of his cup.

Mrs Quell asked what colour Henry's eyes were.

'Brown,' he said, embarrassed.

'Brown!' said Mrs Quell, as if no other answer would have pleased her.

They asked gently searching questions about Henry's life at his various homes and schools. He replied precisely, without vitality. He only showed vitality when he explained that he had found God.

Mr Quell nodded when Henry told him this. He wasn't surprised. It had been one of his theories. He had seen quite a few religious people with this lifeless white puffiness, this soft, introverted righteousness.

Mrs Quell cut her Battenburg cake into four quarters, very carefully. She picked up one of the two yellow squares and took a delicate bite.

'Yellow,' she said, when she had eaten it.

'Correct,' said Mr Quell.

'I'll try for a pink one now,' she said, after she had finished the yellow square. She touched the second yellow square, then her hand moved on and she picked up a pink piece. She took a small bite and smiled. She ate fastidiously.

'Think how dull a Battenburg cake would be if I could see,' she said.

After tea, Mrs Quell left the room unaided. There was silence for a moment.

'Her face is beautiful because she cannot see how beautiful it is, and so does not worry about it becoming less beautiful,' said Mr Quell.

Henry couldn't manage any reply to this.

'Burrell is tormented by his refusal to admit that he has only one eye,' said Mr Quell. 'If only he could look at my wife and say, "Lucky old me. I have an eye that can see." If only the losing finalist at Wimbledon could say, "Magnificent. I'm the second-best player in the whole world. What an achievement." You find my comments specious. Didn't we make an abominable tea?'

'It was very nice,' said Henry politely.

'It was an abysmal repast,' said Mr Quell. 'All our food is brought in by Mrs Ellerby, who lives alone. It is quite the biggest thing in her life, buying our food for us. So, you've found God?'

'Yes, sir.'

'Less of the sir here, Henry. The name is Eamonn. This finding of God has made a great difference to you, has it, Henry?'

'Oh yes, sir. . .Eamonn. I want to devote my life to His Service.'

A trolley-bus hissed to a stop.

'I was going to be a monk, Henry.'

'Yes, s. . Eamonn.'

'I gave up to marry Beth. You would be wrong if you deduced that it was out of pity for her blindness. It was out of lust for her body and love for her soul.'

The trolley-bus resumed its journey.

'If the people on that trolley-bus could hear us, they'd be amazed,' said Mr Quell.

He went over to the hearth, lifted a small piece of coal with the tongs and placed it carefully on the fire.

'I remember thinking when I first knew you, "He's going to be quite the wag, that one," ' said Mr Quell, still with his back to Henry.

'I became very frivolous for a time,' said Henry. 'I even wanted to be a stand-up comedian once.'

Mr Quell came and sat opposite Henry and looked straight into his eyes.

'If you're going to do an act with God, don't forget he's the straight man,' he said.

'I don't quite understand,' said Henry.

'God has no need for bores,' said Mr Quell. 'Believe me, he has enough of those already. God wants you as you are. He wants you, not some lifeless image of how you think you ought to be.'

'That can't be so, s. . .Eamonn,' said Henry. 'If a murderer comes to God, God wants him to Repent of his Evil Ways.'

'We repent of the evil in us, but the good in us must not be subdued in accordance with some concept we have of what a religious person should be like. A man goes to a monastery. He says, "I want to lead a life of self-denial." The monk says, "Do you truly, deeply want to lead a life of self-denial?" The man says, "I long for it." The monk says, "Then the true self-denial is to deny yourself self-denial. Off you go now. Have a lobster thermidor, a bottle of chablis and a good woman." What does this illustrate?'

'I don't know.'

'Life is not simple, and we cannot come to religion in order to make it so. I believe that the search for simplicity has done great damage to religion. Good and evil are not on opposite sides of the road. Black and white. Them and us. Insiders and outsiders. Religion as a recipe for bigotry. One must always remember that there are many religious people who are more wicked than many people who are not religious.'

'It sounds as though you're trying to put me off religion, sir.'

'Eamonn. Of course not. I'm trying to persuade you to come to it in the right spirit.'

Mr Quell went over to the sofa and sat beside Henry.

'I am not a great thinker,' he said. 'I am just a man who has tried to live honestly and somtimes succeeded. I have learnt never to trust a man who says he has no doubts. Why are you suddenly seeking God in such an intense and overpowering manner, Henry?'

Mr Quell put his great hand on Henry's knee. He had goalkeeper's hands. Henry shrank away and Mr Quell hastily removed the hand and stood up.

'You think I'm a homosexual!' he said. 'Is that why you think I was so eager to get you to call me Eamonn?'

'No, s. . .Eamonn.'

Mr Quell selected another piece of coal and placed it carefully on the fire. He might have been an old charcoal-burner in the forests, so carefully did he tend his little blaze.

'You think *you're* a homosexual,' he said, wheeling round and smiling triumphantly at Henry.

Henry said nothing.

'That's it, isn't it?'

Henry nodded miserably.

'Tell me about it,' said Mr Quell, returning to his armchair, stretching his short, thick legs towards the fire, and not looking at Henry.

Henry told him about the fair-haired boy. His cheeks burned. It was the hardest thing he had ever had to tell anybody, but when he had finished he felt better.

Mr Quell asked him about life and homosexuality at Dalton College. Another trolley-bus came and went unnoticed as he talked.

'I'm certain you aren't a homosexual,' said Mr Quell when he had finished.

'Then why did I. . .?'

'All sexuality is ambiguous,' said Mr Quell. 'We love it and hate it. We hope for it and fear it. Male sexuality has to have feminine elements, in order to understand female sexuality, which has to have male elements, for the same reason. Virtue has elements of vice in it, and vice versa.' He lit a cigar. 'I suspect that it is because many people know that they have some homosexual instincts that they are so extremely hostile to homosexuality,' he said. 'I'd like to ask you to try to use that knowledge to be more understanding and tolerant.'

'I will,' promised Henry. 'I really want to be tolerant. I can't stand people who aren't tolerant.'

Mr Quell put another piece of coal on the fire.

'What does God want of me?' said Henry.

'He wants you to try to be good, but also to try to be yourself,' said Mr Quell. 'He wants you to be tolerant to those of other faiths and to those of no faith. He wants you to get nine 'O' levels.'

Mr Quell looked at Henry.

Henry looked at Mr Quell.

Mr Quell laughed.

So did Henry.

He went to St James's Church twice every Sunday. He prayed for a peaceful ending to the Korean War. Perhaps he didn't pray hard enough. He prayed that the Labour Party would be more successful in its efforts to bring social justice to every corner of the land, and would manage to solve the growing balance of payments difficulties and reconcile its increasing split over rearmaments. Perhaps he didn't pray hard enough. When Hugh Gaitskell replaced Sir Stafford Cripps as Chancellor of the Exchequer, Henry wondered how this would affect Lampo Davey's career as a mime artist in Crete. Then he prayed for Hugh Gaitskell and Sir Stafford Cripps and Lampo Davey. When national service was increased from eighteen months to two years, he asked for the courage to declare himself a conscientious objector when the time came. He couldn't yet be sure if he had prayed hard enough. He prayed for forgiveness because during his two years in the enclosed world of Dalton College he had virtually forgotten that the outside world still existed.

On Friday evenings he went to St James's Church youth club, which had a thriving membership of a hundred and twenty-three. It was mainly table-tennis and darts. Kevin Thorburn beat him 5–0 a. darts and 21–5, 21–2 at table-tennis. He made shy advances to Mabel Billington, one of the few people at the youth club who went to church. She beat him 4–1 at darts and 21–7, 21–8 at table-tennis. He prayed that the youth club would become more religious, and his prayers were answered. The youth club leader, Doug Watson, decided to introduce talks about aspects of religion, with guest speakers. In six weeks the attendance dropped to seventeen. Doug Watson abandoned the religious talks, and it became just darts and table-tennis again. Henry prayed for extra strength to help fight the Evils of Ignorance and the Forces of Darkness.

He tried to be Tolerant. He hoped that Tony Preece would joke about Len Arrowsmith's reincarnation again, so that he could demonstrate his Tolerance, but Tony Preece didn't. He prayed that Tony Preece would stop winking and that people would stop annoying Neville Chamberlain by saying, 'I have here a piece of paper.' When Aneurin Bevan resigned over the decision to introduce health charges to pay for rearmament, he prayed for Aneurin Bevan, for socialism and for the future of mankind. He asked God to give Uncle Teddy and Auntie Doris Strength to fight the Evils of Strong Drink. He even prayed for a cure for the blackheads on Geoffrey Porringer's nose.

He prayed for forgiveness for wasting God's time by praying too much.

He attended confirmation classes, given by the vicar of St James's Church. He had to fight against feelings of impatience. It was all so cool, so calm, so social. The vicar kept saying that reason wasn't enough, Christianity was far more than just a philosophy or an ethical system, it was Christ, it was Faith. Dryly, cooly, the vicar would say that this was no dry, cool business. It was the most exciting step in a person's life. Nobody looked excited, but then, to be fair, nor did he. Perhaps he should tell them that he had known all this, that God had spoken to him on the Road to Nowhere. He hadn't spoken much to him, but he had said, 'My son.' That made Henry Christ's brother in God. He didn't mention this, because it might seem like boasting, and boasting was a Sin. Maybe they were all concealing similar Revelations, but he doubted it, and then he felt Shame about his Doubt, and Prayed for Forgiveness.

One day, on a bus, he saw Chalky White, just as Chalky was

getting off. He said, 'Hello, Chalky.' Chalky looked round, and his face flashed into a grin, and he said, 'Henry!' and then he stepped off the bus. Henry's mind flashed back to the barn in Rowth Bridge, to reading about nigs and darkies to Lorna Arrow. He wondered how Chalky White liked reading about nigs and darkies.

The following day, during the Geography lesson, he had an idea. It was now his turn to be one of the four boys seated on Mr Burrell's extreme left. The other three were Dakins, Smedley and Martin Hammond. By this time Henry was being more or less ignored by the other boys. He was Snobby Pratt, who once said 'The bread van' in morning assembly and went away to a snotty-nosed public school down south, and came back ruined. Many boys would quite soon have admitted that it was not his fault, and tried to be moderately friendly, but he had given them no chance, and now, if you talked to him, he tried to convert you to Christianity. Between Martin and Henry, though, there existed the special tension of ruptured friendship, and on this particular morning Martin handed Henry a note which said, 'Bloody snobbish priggish goody-goody bastard.' Henry felt sad that Martin should do this, sad for their lost friendship, but mainly sad for Martin, who was Wandering in the Wilderness.

Why did Martin send Henry a note which said, 'Bloody snobbish priggish goody-goody bastard'? Because Martin was wearing huge false ears and a false moustache, Dakins had his jacket on back to front and Smedley had an unlit cigarette in his mouth and his feet on the desk, while Henry was taking no advantage of being in Mr Burrell's blind spot. This was due less to belated filial feeling for the one-eyed than to his Conviction that God did not want him to wear a fire bucket on his head as he studied Geography in the run-up to his 'O' levels.

And then Henry had his idea, which he would not have had if he had not seen Chalky White on the bus. In the next Geography lesson he would wear a black mask. He would sit there with a huge, black mask with smiling white teeth. The class would think he was taking advantage of Mr Burrell's blind spot, but God would know that he was in fact making a gesture of racial solidarity, an apology to black people everywhere for the insults meted out to them in the pages of popular literature.

He made the mask himself, with cardboard and some black paint given him by Neville Chamberlain out of rejected stock. It was crude, rough, badly finished, and the best thing he had made in his life.

He couldn't wait for the Geography lesson, but first there was Latin. Here too he faced a challenge to his religion. It came from that amiable enemy of organised religion, Mr Blackthorn. One of their set authors was Catullus, whose works had been so warmly praised by Lampo. Henry came to these personal, sexy, tortured, comic, blasphemous pieces at a time when there was no possibility of his finding them other than offensive. Catullus's passionate and unhappy love affair with Lesbia, a married woman, shocked him. If it could be forgiven in life, which was doubtful, it was inexcusable as a subject for poetry. All right, some subjects for poetry had been closed to the Romans. Tintern Abbey hadn't been built, let alone ruined. But didn't the Romans have daffodils, nightingales and ancient mariners?

The more scatological poems were ignored. They wouldn't figure in the exams. But Mr Blackthorn cast his net reasonably wide. Today, they were to translate the poem:

Verani, omnibus e meis amicis
antistans mihi milibus trecentis,
venistine domum ad tuos penates
fratresque unanimos anumque matrem?
venisti. O mihi nuntii beati!
visam te incolumem audiamque Hiberum
narrantem loca, facta, nationes,
ut mos est tuus, applicansque collum
iucundum os oculosque suavibor. . .

He began his translation. 'Veranius, standing out first to me from all my three hundred thousand friends, have you come home to your hearth and your brothers who are all of one mind and your old mother? You have come. Oh blessed tidings for me! I shall see you safe and sound and I shall hear you telling me of the places and deeds and people of Spain, as is your custom, and leaning on your pleasant neck I shall kiss your mouth and eyes. . .' Well! He couldn't go on. Poems about chaps leaning on each other's pleasant necks and kissing each other's mouths and eyes! He didn't want to be reminded of what he would have liked to do to the fair-haired boy, of Lampo, who had recommended Catullus, suaving him full on the os after the end of term concert. It outraged him that this sort of thing could happen during lessons. Was there to be no escape from the Sins of the World and from his own Sins?

At last Latin was over, and it was time for Geography. He entered, said 'Good morning' to Mr Burrell, and took up his seat. He put on the black mask. He had no idea what sort of reaction it received, because there was a design fault. He had forgotten to make holes for the eyes. No matter. All the better, in fact. It was now a symbol of solidarity with the blind as well as the black, with the handicapped as well as the victims of prejudice.

So this was what blindness was like. This was what beautiful Mrs Quell saw morning, noon and night, seven days a week, fifty-two weeks a year, ten years a decade.

Or was it? Henry could see darkness. Could Mrs Quell see darkness, if she was blind, or was there just nothingness, and what was that like?

They were dealing with the savannas. Norbert Cuffley, that inveterate goody-goody, had just become even more the apple of Mr Burrell's one eye by remembering that the word for trees that were biologically suited to withstand dry conditions was xerophytic (oh Norbert, much good may it do you in your career with the Gas Board).

The headmaster entered. Confusion! Luckily he had to stand with his back to the four boys in the blind spot, in order to turn towards Mr Burrell, and he had to go round almost to the front of Mr Burrell in order to be seen by Mr Burrell. There was hurried activity. Dakins took off his jacket and put it on the right way round. Smedley whipped his feet off the desk and pocketed the unlit cigarette. Martin removed his false ears, but forgot his moustache. Disturbed by the noise, Mr E. F. Crowther swung round. He didn't even notice Martin's false moustache. He was transfixed by the sight of Henry in his crude, home-made black mask, with its uneven, grinning teeth. Martin remembered his moustache, coughed, covered his face with his hand and pulled the moustache off. Henry heard strange noises, but, oblivious behind his mask, he had no idea the headmaster was even in the room, let alone facing him grimly, until he heard, close by, the words, 'What do you think you are doing?'

Henry made no reply.

'I am speaking to you, boy,' said the headmaster.

Henry froze behind his mask.

'Me, sir?' he said.

'You, sir,' said the headmaster.

'Sorry, sir, what was the question?' said Henry.

'What do you think you are doing?' said Mr E. F. Crowther.

'Learning Geography, sir,' said Henry.

'Take that imbecilic thing off,' said Mr E. F Crowther.

Henry removed the mask.

The headmaster gazed at Henry's pale, religious face.

'It's Oscar Wilde,' he said. 'Any new goodies for me?'

'Excuse me, headmaster,' said Mr Burrell, who had been forced to turn his head to see what was happening, and could hardly admit that he hadn't known that Henry was wearing a mask.

'What is it, Mr Burrell?' said the headmaster impatiently.

'It was my idea that Pratt should wear the mask, headmaster,' said Mr Burrell.

'To what end, Mr Burrell?' said the headmaster.

'To an imaginative end, headmaster,' said Mr Burrell. 'We were considering the interior of Africa, headmaster, and I thought, headmaster, that Pratt might play the part of an African tribesman to. . .er. . .bring home to him, headmaster, what it's like to live in the interior of Africa, headmaster.'

'You don't need to address me as headmaster five times a sentence, Mr Burrell.'

'Sorry, headmaster.'

'Come on, then Pratt. I'll stay and watch this,' said Mr E. F. Crowther.

Henry put the mask back on and thanked God that Cousin Hilda had given him *Biggles Scours the Jungle*. Truly, everything, however apparently trivial, had its place in the Scheme of Things.

'My goodness, what a swamp,' said Henry. 'What a place full of jungle and rotting vegetation and big trees that blot out the sun, and poisonous snakes and deadly spiders, and muddy streams where logs are crocodiles. What a foul stench emanates from the stagnant waters. It's hard to believe that people actually live here, Algy.'

'Algy?' said the headmaster.

'Algae, green, slimy, cling to the rotting trunks of dead trees. I wish I could escape, but I do not have big metal bird like white man, sir.'

'Carry on, Mr Burrell,' said Mr E. F. Crowther. 'We'll have a chat about your educational theories later.'

'A pleasure, headmaster,' said Mr Burrell.

The headmaster left the room.

'You can take it off now. He's gone,' said Mr Burrell.

Henry took his mask off.

'I wonder what he came in for,' said Mr Burrell.

After that, Mr Burrell tacitly acknowledged that he had only one eye, and nobody needed to feel obliged to take advantage. They were free to concentrate on working for their 'O' levels.

Henry was convinced it was the work of God.

It was the proudest day of his life, and the happiest day of Cousin Hilda's life, when the Archbishop of York laid hands on him. He was at peace.

Why then did he find it difficult to concentrate on his 'O' levels? He could manage straightforward questions like, 'Give an account of the development of Parliament in the reigns of Henry III and Edward I' or 'Write an essay on the geographical aspects of the major contrasts in the world's grasslands and their more intensive future cultivation' or 'Simplify $(p+1)^3 - 3(p+1)^2 + 2$' or even 'Define the latent heat of vaporization of a liquid. Describe how you would determine the latent heat of vaporization of water.' He could translate into Latin, 'If we had started yesterday, we should not have been hindered so much by the contrary wind.' And 'Do you think Martial or Catullus is the more successful writer of light verse? Give reasons and examples,' was a gift. But it only needed the slightest connection with his own life to send him off at a tangent. When he tried to translate into French a passage beginning, 'When we lived in the country, we often went to the farm to buy cheese and eggs,' he found himself fighting against memories of collecting eggs with Billy, the half-wit. 'Write an answer to a person who asks, "Why waste your time reading poetry?" ' sent him straight into Mr Mallender's classroom at Brasenose, desperately copying out Keats' 'Endymion' and being called Oiky by everybody.

'Please, God, help me concentrate,' he begged.

A section of an ordnance survey map came with the Geography exam. It showed the Clyde estuary from Port Glasgow and Cardross to Clydebank, with Dunbarton and the Kilpatrick Hills, and 'Renfr' right on the edge. At the top of the map was the bottom of Loch Lomond. It would be nice to take Mabel Billington to Loch Lomond. There'd be steamers, and the skirl of the pipes. . .and get on with it! Your future depends on this.

When he addressed himself to the problem, 'A car of mass 2 tons, which is travelling due south at 45 mph, collides with a lorry of mass 8 tons, which is travelling in a direction 30° south of west at 20 mph. If the car and the lorry lock, find their speed and direction of motion immediately after the collision,' he found himself worrying about the drivers, especially the driver of the car, who had met this mad lorry driver, who wasn't following the road, but making sure that he travelled 30° south of west. A retired sea dog, with a compass in his cab, he followed his course across road, moor and peat bog, demolishing crofts and disturbing the grouse. Stop it, you fool. Answer the question.

What sober, mature, religious, well-adjusted, socially responsible, healthily ambitious student, when asked, 'What do you know of the following: a) Black Friars and Grey Friars; b) Anti-papal laws passed during the reign of Edward III; c) The reforms in the church advocated by Wyclif; d) The persecution of the Lollards?' had to fight hard to resist the temptation of replying, in his vital 'O' level examinations. 'Not a lot'?

11 Oh Mammon

One day in early September, 1951, Henry sat on top of a hill in the Peak District. He was alone with his maker and Mabel Billington. He was thinking more about Mabel Billington than about his maker. He was trying to think more about his maker than about Mabel Billington. The more that he tried to think more about his maker than about Mabel Billington, the more he found himself thinking more about Mabel Billington than about his maker.

In the eleven weeks since he had taken his 'O' levels, he had been to church thirty-three times, making eleven visits to holy communion, eleven to mattins and eleven to evensong. He had attended the church youth club eleven times. He had played twenty-seven games of table-tennis. He had lost twenty-six games of table-tennis. He had learnt that he had got nine 'O' levels. He had been to tea with the Quells three times, consuming four and three-quarter rounds of bread and butter, five slices of Battenburg cake, and one piece each of cream sponge cake, coffee cream cake and Madeira cake. He had written one letter to Paul Hargreaves. He had received two letters from Paul Hargreaves. He had had eight wet dreams.

A few details will help to flesh out these statistics.

'O' levels: his nine passes were in Latin, Maths, Advanced Maths, English Literature, English Language, Geography, History, French and Physics.

Table-tennis: his solitary victory had been over Derek Nodule, who was twelve, and had cried, saying, 'Even Henry beats me.'

Battenburg cake: twice it had been stale. Twice Mrs Quell had correctly guessed the colour of the squares. Once she had failed. Ironically, the time when she had failed had also been the time when the cake had not been stale, turning the eating of Battenburg cake that day into a pretty exceptional experience all round

His one letter to Paul Hargreaves: this had been more of an

epistle than a letter, being a detailed description of his discovery of God, of the difference it had made to his life, of the difference a similar discovery could make to the lives of Paul and Diana, and of how he could help Paul and Diana to make that discovery.

Paul Hargreaves's two letters to him: the first letter, which preceded Henry's letter, was an invitation to come to France with them for a fortnight, and to visit the Festival of Britain in Battersea Park. The second letter, which followed Henry's letter, was a withdrawal of that invitation, due to changed circumstances.

Wet dreams: These had occurred on June 22nd, July 11th, July 25th, August 8th, August 17th, August 25th, August 31st and September 4th. They caused Henry deep distress, especially as they were getting more frequent. A simple calculation (to one who has passed Advanced Maths, even if by only one mark, though he never knew that) using graphs, led him to the conclusion that at this rate he would be having a hundred and sixty-three wet dreams an hour by Christmas. If he lived that long. Wet dreams were unfair. They weren't his fault. He couldn't help them. But they made him feel profoundly ashamed, and all the more determined to atone. On six of the eight occasions he had remembered whom he had been dreaming about. They were, in chronological order, Diana Hargreaves, Patricia Roc, Mrs Hargreaves, Len Hutton, Mrs Hargreaves again and Mabel Billington. It was shortly after the dream about Mabel Billington that, on an impulse which he had almost immediately regretted, he had invited her out for a day in the Peaks.

She had turned up wearing hiking boots, orange socks, hiking shorts, a bright yellow oilskin jacket and a large rucksack, which contained a bottle of Tizer, two Double Gloucester doorstep sandwiches, two apples, a first aid kit and a Bible.

The bus from Sheffield had passed the end of Wharfedale Road. There were new people in Cap Ferrat now, and Henry felt ashamed of his nostalgia for its comforts.

They had walked for what seemed to Henry to be about twenty miles, but was actually nearer five and a half. Then they had collapsed onto the grass. Below them was a splendid view of valleys and hills. A river wound through a curving dale, a miniature green canyon. A tiny train came out of a tunnel and its smoke gave Henry a vague feeling of *déjà vu*, which he dismissed as an illusion, although it was thoroughly justified, for this was the very spot where he had sat with his father, when he was three, on the day when he had believed that his father was going to abandon him.

Earlier on this day he had felt like abandoning Mabel Billington. She had looked ridiculous in her gear, especially as her sturdy legs went a blotchy red when she walked. He had been unable to think of a single thing to say to her. When she had commented on the silence, he had come out with the old chestnut about true friends not needing to talk.

Now he was pleasantly warm, his weariness alleviated by the rest, his hunger assuaged by a Double Gloucester sandwich of massive proportions, his thirst half-slaked by warm Tizer. The slumbering giant in his trousers was stirring lazily with desire for Mabel Billington. Religion and sex were not mutually exclusive. Mr Quell had said so.

She looked at her best with her boots and yellow oilskins off. Even when she was lying on her back, her breasts bulged in her white shirt.

He rolled over and examined her. Her face was sturdy. It had character. It had grit. It was the face of a girl who was capable of taking God to Africa.

'Mabel?' he said, propping himself up on one elbow. 'Let's take God to Africa together.'

She smiled.

'All right,' she said. 'We'll travel up the rivers by boat.'

'We'll come to a village,' he said. 'The natives have blowpipes, but they're friendly.'

'They've never heard of Christianity,' she said.

'The women have bare breasts,' he said.

'We'll soon put a stop to that,' she said.

'They're sacrificing a goat,' he said. 'It's their fertility rites.'

'We'll save them from all their primitive rituals,' she said.

Henry's excitement was growing. He wanted Mabel Billington. Nothing else mattered, except that he should lose his virginity with Mabel Billington. He had no idea how she would react. She was religious. But then, so was he.

He decided to test the ground.

'Then, after a hard day's saving, we'll go back to our own hut,' he said. 'We'll go to bed early.'

'Definitely,' said Mabel Billington. 'I need my eight hours.'

'We'll go to bed at ten and get up at seven,' he said.

He watched a plane making a vapour trail as Mabel, who had not taken Advanced Maths, worked it out.

'That's nine hours,' she said.

'We need an hour before we go to sleep,' he said.

'What for?' she said.

'You know,' he said.

'Oh,' she said. 'Reading the Bible.'

'In that case, we'll have to go to bed at nine,' he said.

He leant over and began to kiss her knees. He moved his lips up, over her fleshy thighs.

She brought her rucksack down with a tremendous crash on his head.

'Why did you do that?' he said.

'What were tha doing?' she said.

'I fancy you.'

'I thought tha were religious.'

'I am religious. I'm also a man. God wants me as I am, not some wax image of how I think I ought to be. Religious people have sex, you know.'

'I never will,' she said. 'I'm saving my body for God. It's a sin, any road, if tha's not married.'

'God is forgiving. Redemption and Atonement are beautiful.'

'That's not supposed to be an excuse for sinning all over the place. I think all that stuff's awful, any road. I were nearly sick during sex education.'

'But God created all that. He wouldn't have created it if He meant you to be nearly sick during sex education.'

'He didn't mean it for having fun,' she said. 'It's for having babies. If He'd meant it for fun He'd have designed it all a lot better than what He did.'

'We'd better be going,' he said.

'I can't imagine anybody wanting to do things like that for fun,' said Mabel Billington.

When she stood up, in her hiking boots, orange socks and yellow oilskin jacket, with her knobbly knees and sturdy, blotchy legs, nor could he.

Mr Quell was in Ireland. Henry would find it difficult to speak of such things to the vicar of St James's, and he certainly couldn't mention them to Cousin Hilda. All he could do was pray.

That night, after a quiet supper with Cousin Hilda and Liam (Tony Preece performing at Togwell Miners' Social, Neville Chamberlain in Munich. 'Well, so many people have joked to me about it. I thought I'd see what it was like.'), he knelt down, in his ascetic bed-sitting room, with its view of the blank wall of number 67. He knelt in front of the settee, his head resting on its cushions, and prayed.

'Oh God,' he said. 'I wish I could convert myself into a good person as easily as I can convert this settee into a bed. I lusted after Mabel Billington today. I used you to try and persuade her to let me do things with her. I know that you have given me my sexuality in order that I may learn to control myself and put spiritual values above bodily ones. Help me to be strong, and concentrate on my studies, and be kind to Cousin Hilda, and redeem myself for the dreadful wrongs that I have committed. Help me to think about other people more than about myself, and to be thoughtful and kind and generous. Amen.'

He converted the settee into a bed. The room seemed suddenly to shrink. He thought of Lampo Davey, imagined Lampo looking down on him as he got ready for bed. How Lampo would laugh at him. And how proud he would be to be laughed at. How fervently, how utterly, he rejected the false idols of the sophisticated.

Before he went to sleep, he applied the principle of thinking more about other people than about himself. He wrote a letter to Uncle Teddy and Auntie Doris.

It was six days since he had received Auntie Doris's letter. He should have replied sooner.

Dear dear Henry [Auntie Doris had written],
It's far too long since we wrote. We are awful!!! Life in Rangoon

is colourful, but smelly. We love our little flat, overlooking the waterfront, but we are often homesick for our lovely Yorkshire. We miss the dusk. You don't get a proper dusk out east. As you can imagine, the price of whisky is another 'bone of contention'. We also miss the lawns. Uncle Teddy says you can't get a decent lawn south of Dover. It's something to do with the weather or the soil or something. As for the bars, well. . .your Uncle Teddy always said there wasn't a decent pub south of Newark. There is an English bar, complete with steak and kidney pud, but Uncle Teddy refuses to behave like a typical ex-pat! So he won't go out, and I like company. Next week I'm dragging him out to see the Rangoon Amateur Dramatic Association (Rada) doing *Major Barbara*. It's a British company, of course. Teddy hates it. He says the bar prices are ridiculous. I wish they'd do my lovely Noël Coward. I don't like Shaw. Still, you can't have everything, as they say! (Who's 'they', I wonder?) Oh yes. Guess who we ran into last week. Geoffrey Porringer, of all people. He's out here on business, sends his love. He always had a soft spot for you. Our business is so-so, no more. But I'm not writing to tell all this gossip. I'm writing to say we are sorry for not being good parents to you. Henry, my dear dear boy, we are a selfish old couple, but we *love* you. We hardly ever took you anywhere and never properly on holiday at all. If we were wicked, now we are paying with remorse. Truly. Anyway, you are better off with Cousin Hilda who is A SAINT. When I think what we sometimes said of her. So you be good to her and remember money and material things don't matter, it's love that makes the world go round, as they say.

Your mother was the good one, Henry. I'm the rotten one.
But we love you.
Don't do anything we wouldn't do.
That leaves you quite a lot!!!!
Work hard.
With lots and lots of love,
Auntie Doris and Uncle Teddy.
XXXXXXXXXXXXXXXXXXXXXXXXXXXXXXXXX
P.S. I hope you don't think all those kisses are babyish. You

259

must be so grown-up now.

Dear Auntie Doris and Uncle Teddy [wrote Henry],
Thank you for yours of July 19th. It took simply ages to get here. The stamp was nice, though I don't collect them now.

I really was very pleased to get a letter from you, but sorry to read how much you rebuke yourselves. There is really no need. You took me in, and I'm grateful.

Well, I got nine 'O' Levels, and now I'm going to take my 'A' levels. I think I'll do them in English, Latin and History. Some people can't understand why I do Latin, because it's a dead language. They don't realise that that's why I do it. I've only just realised myself. I think education is wasted on the young. The penny has only just dropped for me. The purpose of education is not to teach us facts but to help us to learn to use the faculties which God gave us. If I did French, it might help me get a job in France or something. Learning Latin is pure education, and that's why I like it. In fact I'd like to do Greek as well, but you can't at Thurmarsh Grammar.

No doubt you were amazed to see the word 'God' in that last paragraph. Yes, I have found God, and He has brought so much more into my life that I can recommend Him to you without reservations. I am going to devote my whole life to His service in some form or other. This is a wicked world, as I'm sure you've realised. God's love means that I look on you with gratitude for what you did do, rather than with blame for what you didn't do. I don't feel I need to forgive you, but if you feel it, then I do forgive you.

I cannot let this letter pass without touching on the subject of Strong Drink. You may feel that I am too young to have a right to say this, but because I love you both I must say it. Your letter is full of references to the subject. Reading between the lines, it seems to me that you are both 'knocking it back'. I beg you to give it up. Believe me, you will find yourselves happier without it. Why not make October a dry month? I shall pray to God to give you the strength to do it.

Does all this make me sound like a terrible goody-goody like Norbert Cuffley (a terrible goody-goody at our school!)? Well,

I'm not really. In fact I'm a Miserable Sinner. Today I wanted to Sin with Mabel Billington (from our youth club!). She wouldn't let me. I'm glad now. Sex is permitted with marriage, of course, but until then one must exercise control.

Cousin Hilda looks after me very well, and it's extremely pleasant here, all things considered. Her food is quite nice (though not as nice as yours) and so are her businessmen.

I was interested to hear about Geoffrey Porringer. Don't tell him this, but I prayed for a cure for the blackheads on his nose. Well, it must be awful to have blackheads like that.

On reflection, I think the three of us have a lot in common, to judge from your letter. I think we all feel that we have Sinned and are full of Remorse. Perhaps this is the Human Condition, and I hope that in the future we can all learn to help each other better than we did in the past.

It made me want to cry when you said you loved me, and I love you just as much. I certainly didn't think all the Xs were babyish. In fact, I think it's pretty babyish to find things babyish.

With lots of love. May God be with you,

Henry.

XXXXXXXXXXXXXXXXXXXXXXXXXXXXXXX

P.S. That's exactly the same number as you gave me! Thirty-one! Now here's one extra each from my heart. XX.

When Henry woke up the next morning, he was once again applying some of the principles by which he now hoped to live his life. He was thinking of somebody else more than about himself, and he was being thoughtful and kind and generous to that person. Unfortunately, that person was Mrs Hargreaves, and the result was another wet dream.

He took regular cold baths. He went for long walks. He took up running. He mortified the flesh. He managed to think himself out of sexuality.

On one of his walks, he wandered in the vicinity of Drobwell Main Colliery. It might have been a model of an Alpine landscape created by a lunatic. The mountains were spoil heaps, some new and black, some old and grassy. The lakes were ground that had subsided and flooded. The water was heavily contaminated. Nature fought against almost impossible odds to re-establish itself. He came upon a deep pit, filled with rusty railings. They had been ripped out eleven years ago, for the war effort, and had ended up here.

There was a fence around the edge of the colliery. He saw a small group of miners, walking wearily. They didn't see him. One of them looked like Chalky White, but it was difficult to tell, as all their faces were black.

His life in the sixth form began. He apologised to Martin Hammond for his unfriendly behaviour during the previous school year. Martin beamed shyly.

'None of it's your fault,' said Martin. 'You're a bit of flotsam swirling on the flood-waters of a class-ridden society. That's what my dad reckons, any road.'

The following week, Martin invited Henry home for tea. The Hammonds didn't live in Paradise Lane any more. They had bought a semi in the streets over the river, quite close to the little row of shops were Tommy Marsden had fired his catapult at the butcher's window. The address was 17 Everest Crescent. An elderly Standard Eight stood in the open garage at the side of the pebble-dash semi. It was the day before the general election. They had fish-cakes. Reg Hammond ate quickly. He had two whole streets still to canvass, and then he had to ferry people to a meeting.

'There's nowt like a good fish-cake,' said Reg Hammond.

'And this is nowt like a good fish-cake,' said his son Martin. Everybody laughed. It was a family joke.

'They're grand, mother. Highly palatable,' said Reg Hammond, who was rising in the union.

'Very nice indeed,' said Henry.

With the fish-cakes, there were chips, Reg Hammond's favourite brand of baked beans, bread and butter and tea.

'You can keep your fancy foods,' said Reg Hammond. He made it sound as if he was talking about Henry's fancy foods.

'I don't like fish-cakes,' said Martin's young sister, who was eight.

'There's folk in India'd be glad of them,' said Mrs Hammond.

'Send them to India, then,' said Martin's young sister.

'Am I to give her summat else?' said Mrs Hammond.

'No. She mun learn,' said Reg Hammond, a fleshier owl than Martin, and with a touch of the hawk in there too. 'So, lad, tha's backed t' wrong horse,' he added, turning to Henry.

'Pardon?'

' "Pardon," he says. What's wrong wi' Yorkshire? What's wrong wi' "tha what?"?'

'Tha what, then?'

'Tha's backed t' wrong horse. God. Tha's gone up a blind alley there.'

'Reg!' said Mrs Hammond.

'What's the right horse, then?' said Henry.

Reg Hammond stared at him in amazement.

'Socialism,' he said. 'Socialism.'

'Are the two mutually exclusive, then?' said Henry.

'He's got you there!' said Mrs Hammond.

'Mother!' said Reg Hammond, as if to say, 'This is man's talk.'

Martin looked from his father to Henry, refereeing their talk. In the blue corner, God. In the red corner, socialism.

His sister began to cry.

'Ignore her,' said Reg Hammond. 'We've got to learn her. In t' war she'd have given thanks.'

'The war's been over six years, Reg,' said Mrs Hammond.

'Some wars are never over, mother,' said Reg Hammond. He turned to Henry, brushing off everything else as irrelevant. 'God promises a better world in the next world,' he said. 'Socialism promises it in this one.'

'Who's to say we can't have a better world in this world *and* the next one?' said Henry. 'There's no contest.'

'Careful, Henry. Don't deny him his fight,' said Martin.

'The church is all part of the ruling classes,' said Reg Hammond.

'Jesus Christ wasn't exactly a ruling class figure,' said Mrs Hammond.

Reg Hammond looked at her with a pained expression. She was ruining a straight fight by coming in on Henry's side.

'Martin's on my side, I know,' said Reg Hammond, openly making it a foursome.

'I'm afraid so,' said Martin.

'Why afraid?' said Reg Hammond.

'You never say anything I can disagree with,' said Martin. 'It's not healthy. It's stunting my development.'

Martin's sister cried on.

'The Tories are going to get in tomorrow,' said Reg Hammond. 'Does tha know summat? I don't trust them an inch. I wouldn't put it past them to have lost t' 1945 election deliberately because they knew whoever got in then stood no chance. 1950, let 'em back with a tiny majority. Get them to start tearing themselves apart, the ever-present curse of the left.'

'Just listen to his babblement,' said Mrs Hammond lovingly.

'Now the Tories'll nip in and reap t' benefit of all t' hard work we've done,' said Reg Hammond. 'They'll be in for years. Their hard times are over. Their brief decade of nightmare without servants. Now we've entered the decade of the consumer durable, but not too durable. Mechanical servants, made by the same class that used to be the servants. Everything appears to change. Nowt does.'

'The rubbish he comes out with,' said Mrs Hammond proudly.

'I hope it is rubbish,' said Reg Hammond. 'I just hope it is.'

He sighed deeply and sank into his chair.

'Are you really depressed, Mr Hammond?' said Henry.

'Aye, lad, I am,' said Reg Hammond. 'I hoped that 1945 meant that the middle class were losing their fear of Labour, and Labour would no longer be forced to be the sort of party they had any reason to fear. I hoped we could all go forward together. I really did.'

Martin's younger sister stopped crying, and ate a tiny corner of fish-cake. There was silence for about five seconds. Then it was shattered by a motor-bike spluttering into violent life in Matterhorn Drive.

'I said summat about it to that Crowther at t' grammar school,' said Reg Hammond. 'I don't think he knew what I were on about. Pillock.'

'Dad!' said Mrs Hammond. 'You shouldn't talk like that about their headmaster, not in front of them.'

'That's summat that is changing, mother,' said Reg Hammond, springing to his feet. 'From now on, authority is going to have to earn its respect. Pillocks of the world, watch out.'

'Criticise him, fair enough,' said Mrs Hammond. 'But there's no cause to call him a pillock. What will Henry and his God think?'

'God will forgive Mr Hammond,' said Henry. 'God will give him his tha what.'

'Tha what?' said Reg Hammond, turning at the door, half into his coat.

'Pardon,' said Henry. 'God will give you his pardon.'

Henry grinned.

Reg Hammond gave him an old-fashioned look, then laughed.

'By heck, Martin. Tha can't put much over on your Henry Pratt,' he said.

'He was brought up in a hard school,' said Martin.

'Several hard schools,' said Henry, but Reg Hammond had gone.

Reg Hammond was right about the election. Labour got the highest vote ever recorded by a political party in Britain, but lost by twenty-six seats.

Henry went to tea at the Hammonds every week after that. One day, as the last of the dusk was lingering, Martin accompanied him down the suburban roads, over the railway and the River Rundle, across the waste ground, over the canal, along the towpath, through the gate into the ginnel, along the ginnel as far as Paradise Lane, along Paradise Lane and across the main road to the tram stop outside Crapp, Hawser and Kettlewell's. They walked in silence, awed by their memories.

A youth was approaching, jaundiced by the street lights, a snappy dresser, a flashy young man. He carried a football under his arm.

'By heck,' he said. 'It can't be. It bloody is, though. Martin Hammond. Henry Pratt.'

'Tommy Marsden!' said Martin.

'Bloody stroll on,' said Tommy Marsden. 'Hey, are we to go for one in t' Navigation?'

'We're under age,' said Martin.

'To hell wi' that,' said Tommy Marsden. 'Barry Jenkinson's me mate. I often go up there, sup a bit of stuff.'

'Not me,' said Henry. 'Not a pub. Sorry.'

'He's religious,' said Martin.

'Oh heck. Bad luck,' said Tommy Marsden sympathetically. 'Why does tha think I've gorra football?'

'Why have you got a football?' said Martin.

'I've been took on by t' United.'

They looked at him in awe. They were boys. This was a man.

'Come on, Henry,' said Martin. 'Under the circumstances.'

'Well, all right,' said Henry. 'Under the circumstances. I won't drink, though.'

The smell of stale smoke, stale beer and furniture polish almost knocked Henry over.

He liked it. He fought against liking it, but he couldn't help it.

Cecil E. Jenkinson greeted them heartily.

'Evening, gents,' he said. 'All over eighteen, are we? Good. I have to ask. Heard about the flasher? Decided not to retire. Going to stick it out another year. He's upstairs, Tommy.'

'Line 'em up, Cecil,' said Tommy Marsden, going to the door marked 'private'.

'What's it to be, lads?' said Cecil E. Jenkinson, licensed to sell beers, wines and spirits. 'Pints all round?'

'Orange squash for me,' said Henry.

'Orange squash?' said Cecil E. Jenkinson.

'He's religious,' said Martin.

'He's norra Catholic, any road,' said Cecil E. Jenkinson, licensed to tell dirty jokes and use foul language. 'They're all piss-artists.'

'Have a beer,' said Tommy Marsden, returning. 'To celebrate. Under the circumstances.'

'Well, all right,' said Henry. 'Just a small one. Under the circumstances.'

Cecil E. Jenkinson poured three and a half pints of bitter. Barry Jenkinson joined them. Tommy Marsden paid. They raised their glasses.

'To Tommy,' said Henry. 'I really am thrilled, Tommy.'

Tommy Marsden pretended not to care, but you could see he was pleased.

'Henry Pratt,' said Cecil E. Jenkinson. 'Ezra's lad.'

'That's right,' said Henry.

'He was one of my best customers,' said Cecil E. Jenkinson.

Discretion proved the better part of Henry's valour. A tart comment would have provided a discordant note at what was, after all, a celebration.

The four under-age drinkers sat in the little snug. The stuffing was peeping out from inside the faded green upholstery. At regular intervals round the little room there were bells for service. On a shelf above the fireplace there were two sets of dominoes, two packs of cards and four pegboards. The window was of fine Victorian smoked glass. The fire was lit. If this was the Hell of Strong Drink, Henry found it surprisingly cosy.

He felt ashamed, but also exhilarated, as he sipped his beer. His conscience was eased by the fact that it tasted terrible.

'I may not play in t' first team for quite a while,' said Tommy Marsden. 'Mr Linacre says he's grooming me carefully for stardom. He says not to be disappointed if I don't make progress straight away. He says many a lad's been ruined by being brought on too fast, and I think he's right. He says I'm to remain level-headed whatever.'

'What position do you play?' said Martin.

'I'm an inside forward in the Raich Carter mould,' said Tommy Marsden.

Martin Hammond insisted on buying a round, and must have forgotten that Henry was only drinking halves. There was no point in saying anything. He needn't drink it all.

'Is this the same beer?' he asked.

'Yes. Why?'

'It tastes nicer.'

They chatted about old times, in the Paradise Lane Gang.

'We used to race dog turds in t' Rundle,' said Tommy Marsden to Barry Jenkinson.

Henry apologised silently to his maker for Tommy Marsden's language.

'I don't remember that,' said Martin.

'It's the only thing before the war I do remember,' said Tommy Marsden.

'What happened to Ian Lowson?' said Martin.

'He's in t' steelworks, like his dad. I don't see much of him.'

'What about Chalky White?' said Henry.

'He's gone down t' pits, where they're all black,' said Tommy Marsden.

'I thought I saw him,' said Henry.

'It's the pressure to conform,' said Martin Hammond.

'Don't say things like that,' said Tommy Marsden. 'Barry can't understand them. He's thick.'

'I am,' said Barry Jenkinson. 'I'm as thick as pig shit.'

Henry apologised silently to his maker for Barry Jenkinson's language.

'What happened to Billy Erpingham?' said Martin.

'God knows,' said Tommy Marsden, and Henry agreed silently that he did. 'I did hear summat, but I forget.'

A few other customers entered. Barry Jenkinson, not as mean as he was thick, rang a bell, and a waiter in a white coat came out with a tray, and Barry Jenkinson said, 'Same again, Gordon,' and Henry hadn't the energy to protest, and besides, the beer wasn't having any effect on him, so where was the harm?

'Is this the same beer?' he asked.

'Yes. Why?'

'It tastes nicer.'

Soon, Tommy Marsden said he must be off. 'Mr Linacre says self-indulgence has nipped many a promising career in t' bud, and he's right,' he added.

'I haven't bought a drink yet,' said Henry. 'Must buy a drink for Tommy.'

He borrowed three and eight off Tommy, and bought a round.

'I'm right glad you lot are pleased,' said Tommy. 'I thought tha might be too snotty-nosed.'

'Snotty-nosed? Are we buggery?' said Henry, and he forgot to apologise to God.

Their laughter grew boisterous. Cecil E. Jenkinson, licensed to be a crashing bore and have a son who was as thick as pig shit, approached them, and informed them that they had had enough.

'Banning me like you did me old dad, are you?' said Henry.

'Listen, young lad,' said Cecil E. Jenkinson, licensed to refuse to serve people for no reason whatever. 'Listen. I liked your dad. Don't get me wrong. One of t' finest human beings as ever supped a pint. There was only one thing wrong wi' him. He used to give the customers the screaming abdads.'

'You bloody bastard,' said Henry.

'Get your drunken friend out of here,' said Cecil E. Jenkinson. 'That's the last time I allow under-age drinking in here.'

He was right, too.

As Henry walked through the little gardens in front of the Town Hall, on his way home from the tram, the enormity of what he had done struck him and he burst into tears, and knelt to pray to God.

'And what do you think you're doing?' said the policeman.

Henry stood up, somewhat unsteadily.

'Praying,' he said.

'Oh aye? And I'm the Archbishop of Canterbury,' said the policeman.

'No, I *was* praying,' said Henry. 'I was praying for forgiveness.'

'Why? What have you done?'

'Tonight,' said Henry, desperately trying to focus. 'Tonight I have got drunk and used foul language.'

'How old are you?' said the policeman.

'Sixteen.'

'Where have you been drinking?'

This was his big chance to avenge his father for the wrongs that had been done to him by Cecil E. Jenkinson.

'The Navigation Inn,' he said.

It was several days before Cousin Hilda could forgive him for arriving home drunk.

Cecil E. Jenkinson never forgave him.

Henry wasn't sure whether God forgave him. He prayed for forgiveness, but received no reply.

He was beginning to have doubts about whether God existed.

He went through all the arguments over and over again. Cosmological. Teleological. Ontological. There must be a God because there is no other explanation of why the world began, or indeed of how it began. But what is the explanation of why there is a God and how there is a God and how God began? There are so many signs of order and purpose in Nature that it is inconceivable that there is not an over-all creative Mind controlling it. There are so many signs of disorder and chaos in Nature that it is inconceivable that there is an over-all creative Mind controlling it. There must be a God, otherwise how would we be able to have the idea of God? Well, there must be nuclear bombs because how else would we be able to have the idea of them? By inventing them. Have we not invented God? Does that make God any less God? Supposing every single person in the world believed in God? It would prove nothing. It's conceivable that everybody could suffer from the same delusion at the same time. Everything that is said is conceivable. Everything that is conceivable is said, many times. In the end either you plump for a God out of need or temperamental inclination, and that is grotesque, or God is Revealed to you.

In the end, every time, the question was, as he knew all along that it would be, did God speak to him in the fog in Paradise Lane? Of course it was possible that He did and of course it was possible that He didn't. He had been feverish. He could have had hallucinations. After all, he also heard his father. Of course it was possible that he had really heard God and imagined he'd heard his father. Or vice versa. Unlikely, but possible. He had also seen the fog swirl-pooling into the faces of the ogglers and tackies at Dalton, and that had definitely been an illusion (well, almost definitely), but then he had been impressed that God had not found it necessary to pull some physical trick. He had spoken, and that was enough.

Why had God said so little? Because He had said, 'I am with you, my son.' What else could He possibly add?

Why had God not spoken to him again? Because he did not exist, or because He did not make it so easy for you that you had no need of Faith? Christians were very clever at turning even the absence of proof and even the absence of the revelation of God into positive arguments for his existence. Was this speciousness, or the truth?

Three times he went to pubs and drank beer. He smoked five cigarettes. He resumed his self-abuse. Each time he did one of these things, he looked for a sign from God, perhaps even a thunderbolt. He wasn't sure whether he hoped for a sign, or feared it. Perhaps, if one came, he would know whether he was glad or sorry that it had come. But none came.

He told Mr Quell of these things, after Mrs Quell had left the room, on the occasion of his next visit for tea, a meal whose star attractions had been Battenburg cake and ginger cake.

'I don't think I'm cut out for the service of God,' he said. 'I've got all my work cut out trying to keep on believing in Him.'

'He gives us doubts,' said Mr Quell, 'so that we can test our Faith.'

'I doubt whether the doubts I'm getting are sent by Him,' said Henry.

'That doubt is part of the doubt that He has sent you,' said Mr Quell.

Henry's belief in God, which had come upon him so suddenly, dripped away like a leaking tap. He passed through a stage in which he believed that there was a God, but that he was incapable of believing in Him. He became convinced that the entire universe was part of God's grand design, except him. One day, during Religious Instruction, as it happened, he saw everything around him as divine, except himself. He sat in God's divine desk, dipping God's divine pen in His Holy Inkwell, and he was a stranger in the midst of all this revelation. A feeling of revulsion for himself shook him violently, and yet when he looked at his hands they weren't shaking.

Mr Seaton, the Scripture master, rebuked him for not concentrating. 'What's the point of my trying to drum some spiritual feeling into you if you're just going to sit there like a pudding?' he said.

The tap dripped on, and he came to see this stage as a form of temporary madness.

'You don't have to believe in everything in Christianity literally,' said Mr Quell. 'You don't have to take God absolutely literally.'

'You have to believe that He exists,' said Henry. 'You have to believe that He can be described.'

'I can't describe Him,' said Mr Quell. 'I can't say that He's an old man with a white beard. I certainly don't believe that He's an Englishman. Or even an Irishman, though that is slightly more likely.'

'You don't have to be able to describe Him,' said Henry. 'You can't, because you haven't seen Him. But you have to believe that He exists, somewhere, in some actual form, which we could describe if we ever saw it. Otherwise God is just a concept which we call a being, and that would be a con.'

A trolley-bus slid sibilantly to a halt outside. ('*Outside!* Amazing. I thought it would be *in the room*' – Droopy L.)

'I would disagree that God has to be physically describable,' said Mr Quell, 'but I would agree that we have to believe that His existence has a reality independent of ourselves. He clearly must be more than a symbol that we have created to satisfy our urge for Him. Wasn't that a particularly odious Battenburg cake that we tucked into this afternoon?'

'Appalling,' said Henry. 'If there was a God, He wouldn't allow us to eat such appalling cake.'

How long can a tap drip? Until the end of time, or a strike by water workers, whichever is the sooner, if it's attached to the mains. Until the container is empty, if it's attached to a container of finite capacity.

Henry's tap ceased to drip on the morning of March 13th, 1952. That it was his seventeenth birthday was of no account. It was the day they buried Chalky White.

Eight men were buried alive when there was a collapse at the face of the old seam at Drobwell Main Colliery. In three weeks' time that seam was to have been abandoned.

The rescuers fought their way through for twenty-seven hours. They could hear the weakening cries of the trapped men, but had to go slowly, excruciatingly, unbearably slowly, for fear of causing further collapse.

Four of the men were dead when the rescuers reached them. Chalky White died in hospital. Three men survived.

It was a joint funeral, and the little church was packed. All the miners had scrubbed their faces. Only the faces of Chalky White's relatives and friends remained black.

All the Paradise Lane Gang were there, except Billy Erpingham. Nobody could remember his address.

The vicar praised the courage of the rescue services, and of the great body of miners, who knew the risks of their jobs, and lived, and occasionally died, with those risks. There was quite a bit of coughing during the vicar's address, and Henry was transported back to the chapel at Dalton, Tubman-Edwards opposite him, Mr Tenderfoot striding out to witness the great storm. Then he returned to the present, bitterly ashamed of having been away.

The coughing at Dalton College had been the result of boredom. The coughing at Drobwell was the product of pneumoconiosis.

They filed out into the churchyard. A pale sun came out, just as the five coffins were lowered into the ground.

In the end it was nothing to do with arguments. It was simply that, as he stood there, beside Ian Lowson, who was a stranger, Henry knew that he believed that he knew that that was the end of Chalky White, that he was not going to a good place, or a bad place, but was going to rot in Drobwell churchyard.

Sales of Battenburg cake in south Yorkshire continued to boom.

'I still believe that it's better to be generous than mean, to be kind rather than cruel, to be tolerant rather than intolerant, to strive to bring order to society rather than chaos, to seek peace not war, and to try to have faith in man's capacity to overcome the evil in his own nature,' said Henry.

Mr Quell carefully selected a piece of coal, and placed it on the neat pyramid of his fire. The precision and delicacy of his movements never ceased to seem surprising in such a big-framed man.

'You're a humanist,' he said, 'and a refreshingly modest one.'

'Are you mocking me?' said Henry.

'Not at all,' said Mr Quell. 'Humanism is the religion of the coming times. It's a religion without services, without a Bible, and for that reason it might be assumed that it has no dogma. That would be incorrect.'

Henry hadn't heard the trolley-bus draw up, but now he heard the whoosh as it set off towards town. They were to be phased out soon, but they would live on in his memory, every time he thought about the great problems of existence. Sometimes it seemed to him that it was only in the trivia of life that individuality held any sway. The arguments about God had been made banal by repetition all over the world, but in Henry's case alone was God mingled inextricably with Battenburg cake and trolley-buses.

'Its dogma is that man can control the planet,' said Mr Quell. 'Its dogma is that by means of planning, and science, and technology, man will be able to restructure and improve Mother Nature. You believe that he will have a full-time job controlling his own nature, never mind Mother Nature. That is modest. I approve of that.'

The summer term dragged by, and they waited for something to happen. Being a humanist was something that went on all the time, and it didn't fill your Sunday like organised religion did. Henry no longer went to the church youth club. The trinity of God, table tennis and Mabel Billington had all lost their hold over him. There was no humanist youth club. The pleasures of reading, cinema-going and listening to the wireless were still all right, but they weren't the real thing. Self-abuse was all right, but it wasn't the real thing. Mock 'A' levels weren't till the winter and they weren't the real thing. If you did badly, it was ominous, and, if you did well, it was wasted. Henry's cricket continued to improve. His average this term was 1.75, which compared well with Martin's 4.55 but badly with Stefan's 84.41. But his development was too slow. Even if the graph of his improvement continued, he would be too old to play for Yorkshire by the time he was good enough. In fact, he would be 128 before he even got a trial. But even cricket wasn't the real thing.

The real thing was girls. Sex. Ceasing to be a virgin.

'I'm a humanist,' said Henry one endless Sunday in the Alderman Chandler Memorial Park, where clusters of teenagers were waiting to listen to the Top Twenty on their wirelesses.

'Has it got owt to do with girls?' said Stefan Prziborski, the best left-handed batsman ever to come out of Poland.

'It could have,' said Henry.

'How?' said Martin.

'Well, we could found a humanist society. Joint, with the girls' school.'

'Now you're talking,' said Martin Hammond.

There were still no marble or falcated teal on the pond. The ocelot had died. Henry saw the fair-haired boy occasionally, and nodded to him.

He went to see Mr E. F. Crowther in his study.

The study still said, 'Things get done here. We are plain, practical men, concerned with achievements, not pretensions,' but Henry was old enough now to realise that this was itself a pretension.

Mr E. F. Crowther refused to agree to the formation of a joint humanist society with the Thurmarsh Grammar School for Girls.

'Why not, sir?' said Henry.

'It might set a precedent,' said Mr E. F. Crowther.

'That way you'd never change anything, sir,' said Henry.

'I've made my decision,' said Mr E. F. Crowther.

Yes, and I know why, thought Henry. Because I once said 'The bread van' in morning assembly.

Pillock.

If they didn't meet in the park, they would meet in the Paw Paw Coffee Bar and Grill, in Bargate.

The Paw Paw Coffee Bar and Grill smelt of wet coats and steam when it rained and sweat and steam when it didn't. It never smelt of coffee, which wasn't surprising, since its coffee didn't taste of coffee. Its tea, on the other hand, tasted vaguely of coffee. There were glass-topped tables, and the tea and coffee came in glass cups, with glass saucers. Due to a design fault, the handles of the cups grew almost too hot to hold. It was self-service for coffee but waitress service for grills. They were never able to afford the delights of the grill. Few people ever did. Perhaps the sight of the very fat chef, standing in the kitchen, all stained white apron and tangled hairy armpits, put people off. If you asked the waitresses for sugar, they said, 'On the tables, luv,' without looking at you. When you got to the table, the sugar wasn't there, just the brown and tomato sauce bottles, with congealed sauce around their tops. The Paw Paw Coffee Bar and Grill was the only place in Thurmarsh where you could linger for hours over one cup of coffee, and chat up girls, and cheek the waitresses, and laugh sheepishly, and watch your youth waste away.

The Paw Paw Coffee Bar and Grill throbbed to the distant possibility of picking up a girl one day, and by the time you realised that you hadn't, it was too late.

When they made remarks to the waitresses, there would be blushing and giggling and the occasional shriek of good-natured outrage. Once, Stefan Prziborski pinched Rita's bum and she dropped a tray of dirty cups with an almighty clatter. But you couldn't be cross with Stefan. He was different. He had foreign blood.

Once Henry plucked up courage and asked the girl who worked at Macfisheries out. She told him to come back when he was three years older.

His virginity was written on his face. He was Henry 'Ee by gum, I've never had it' Pratt. Martin and Stefan had quite wide experience, in fact Henry was surprised that two such experienced Don Juans should still spend so much time hanging around the Paw Paw Coffee Bar and Grill.

The windows of the Paw Paw Coffee Bar and Grill were always steamed up.

That was how it was, so far as social excitement and gracious living were concerned, in the summer term of 1952.

Letters were exchanged. Auntie Doris wrote to him from Rangoon. She purported to be glad that he had found God. She made no reference to Strong Drink. They had been to see *Hay Fever*, performed by the Rangoon Amateur Dramatic Association. There was a dreadful shortage of English women in Rangoon, but Geoffrey Porringer had made a very brave stab at the role of Judith Bliss.

Henry sent a chatty letter back, explaining that he had lost God, and hoped they hadn't taken his strictures about strong drink to heart.

He wrote to Paul Hargreaves explaining that he was no longer religious, and wanted to found a joint humanist society with the girls' school, but couldn't, because the headmaster was a pillock.

He wrote to Simon Eckington, giving him all his news, including the finding and losing of God, and suggesting that he visit Rowth Bridge in the summer.

Simon Eckington replied briefly that he would be very welcome. He was working for the new people at Low Farm. They were all right. Billy, the half-wit, was dead.

Paul Hargreaves replied that all headmasters were pillocks, and invited Henry to come to Brittany with them for three weeks that summer. Diana sent her love.

This news gave Henry an erection at the breakfast table. As ill luck would have it, Cousin Hilda chose that moment to ask him to fetch more marge. She had been hard on him since he'd lost God. He was all right going to the scullery, but on his way back he felt that the obstinate bulge was obvious to all. It certainly was to Tony Preece, who winked and asked him who the letter was from. When he replied, 'My friend Paul,' Tony Preece raised his eyebrows. Cousin Hilda sniffed. Norman Pettifer, the manager of the cheese counter at Cullens, said, 'Oh well, time for all good men to come to the aid of the party,' and left. He said that every morning. He was only staying there till he found a house. He didn't fit in. Everybody missed Neville Chamberlain now that his firm had sent him to Kenya. Henry's erection died down slowly.

Henry wrote to Paul accepting the invitation. He wrote to Simon saying that he wouldn't be able to come.

He no longer needed to spend long, painful hours in the Paw Paw Coffee Bar and Grill. He loved Diana. She loved him. He wouldn't remain a virgin for long.

On the first Saturday of the summer holidays, in reverse chronological order, Henry met a girl on a bus, posed as a Frenchman, saw an idol, and had a very unexpected encounter. The names of the four people concerned were Maureen Abberley, Henri Bergerac, Len Hutton and Geoffrey Porringer.

The encounter with Geoffrey Porringer occurred at the top end of The Moor, in Sheffield. Henry was looking at the shops with Martin Hammond and Stefan Prziborski, prior to watching

Yorkshire play Middlesex at Bramall Lane. He carried a shoulder bag full of bloater paste sandwiches and apples. They had bought three bars of Fry's Chocolate Cream. They were wearing sandals and grey flannel trousers. And suddenly he was face to face with Geoffrey Porringer, in a lightweight fawn suit. He wasn't surprised, since he now believed prayer to be ineffective, to see that the poor man's nose was still festooned with blackheads.

'Hello!' he said.

Geoffrey Porringer looked at him blankly.

'Henry Pratt,' said Henry.

Recognition dawned slowly, and apparently not to Geoffrey Porringer's utter delight.

'Can I have a word with you?' said Henry.

'Of course,' said Geoffrey Porringer, a trifle uneasily.

'*Allez vous, mes braves,*' said Henry to Martin and Stefan. '*Je vous verrai à la petite rue de Bramall.*'

It was their latest little game, talking in French. It was all good practice for Henry.

'*Bon,*' said Martin.

'*J'espère que vous ne vous perdrerez pas, notre Henri,*' said Stefan.

'*Fermez l'orifice de votre gateau,*' said Henry. 'See you at the usual place.'

Geoffrey Porringer listened to all this with a mixture of incomprehension, irritation, impatience and distaste.

'Look, I am rather busy,' he said.

'Sorry,' said Henry.

Martin and Stefan set off for the ground.

'What is it?' said Geoffrey Porringer.

'Are you going back to Rangoon soon?' said Henry.

Geoffrey Porringer stared at him in amazement.

'Rangoon?' he said. 'Rangoon?' Then comprehension seemed to dawn. 'Ah! Rangoon!' he said. 'Rangoon! Yes. Probably. Well, almost certainly. Doris told you she'd seen me, did she?'

'Yes.'

'That was naughty. My presence there is supposed to be top secret.'

Geoffrey Porringer put his finger to the side of his blackheaded nose.

A lorry with a crane pulled up at a faulty street lamp.

'My business activities in Rangoon are just a cover,' said Geoffrey Porringer. 'Say no more, eh?'

Henry's mind went back to Cap Ferrat, and the secret message about Bingley. He couldn't recall it exactly now, but it had always puzzled him. Now it was all becoming clear. Geoffrey Porringer was a spy.

'Your secret's safe with me,' he said.

'Good man,' said Geoffrey Porringer.

'Will you do something for me?' said Henry.

'It depends what it is,' said Geoffrey Porringer cautiously.

'Will you take a present for Uncle Teddy and Auntie Doris?'

'If it's not bulky,' agreed Geoffrey Porringer, 'and if it doesn't take too long.'

They chose the present together. It was a set of six coasters with scenes of Yorkshire life – to wit, Robin Hood's Bay, Bolton Abbey, Richmond Market Place, the Shambles in York, Gordale Scar and the front at Scarborough.

'It'll bring a lump of nostalgia to their throats every time they have a drink,' opined the spy in the lightweight suit.

There was crowd of 17,000 at Bramall Lane, noisy, knowledgeable, hard to please. It was a strange ground, set between the cricket pavilion and the three-sided football ground. It made up in character what it lacked in charm.

Henry was in the mood to enjoy a game of cricket, but Martin and Stefan were feeling frivolous.

Middlesex batted and were in trouble from the start. On Henry's left there was a fat boy, who recorded every ball in his score-book. There always was.

Denis Compton was in a spell of terrible form, and the crowd gave him a tremendous, deeply moving ovation. Henry, who alone had been for Hutton in the summer of 1947, could afford to be generous now, and felt a lump in his throat as he clapped. He hoped Martin and Stefan wouldn't speak, and luckily they didn't.

Compton drove his first ball for four, but was lbw to Yardley without addition. Hutton took two fine catches off Eric Burgin, playing his first game in front of his home crowd. There were two attractive girls sitting behind them, and in the lunch interval

Stefan told them that Henry was a leading man in French cricket.

'Give over,' said the fairly pretty one.

'*Mais c'est vrai,*' said Henry. '*Je suis le président de l'association du cricket du Dijon. Je suis aussi enthousiaste comme la moutarde. J'aime très bien l'ouest equitation de Yorkshire.*'

'Give over,' said the very pretty one.

Yorkshire let Middlesex off the hook, dropping Leslie Compton three times in his innings of 91. Knightley-Smith made 57. Henry kept on having to pretend to be French.

'What position do you play?' said Martin, speaking slowly and loudly, as to a foreigner.

'*Troisième homme ou stupide mid-on,*' said Henry.

'Give over,' said both girls.

Henry felt that his day was being spoilt by all this pantomime. When Yorkshire batted, he was nervous until Hutton was off the mark. Hutton was dropped by Denis Compton (if only all the boys from Brasenose had been there) and was 21 not out at the close, with Lowson (no relation of the peripheral Sid) 15 not out. The fat boy sadly closed his score-book, and the three Thurmarsh boys wandered out of the ground with the two girls. Henry knew that Stefan would put his arm round the very pretty girl, Martin would put his arm round the fairly pretty girl, and Henry, who had done all the hard work of pretending to be French, as a result of which the girls thought him a total idiot, would put his arm round nobody. And so it was.

He told himself that he didn't care. Why should he? Next week he would be with Diana.

He cared. This was this week, not next week. He told them that he was going home, and their protests carried the authentic ring of true insincerity.

He sat in the off-side front seat upstairs on the Thurmarsh bus. On the near-side front seat sat a curvaceous brunette schoolgirl. Their driver did not seem terribly popular. Other drivers greeted him only curtly.

'Haven't I seen you in the Paw Paw Coffee Bar and Grill?' said Henry.

'I have been there,' admitted the curvaceous brunette.

He moved over to sit beside her. His heart was thumping.

'I'm Henry Pratt,' he said.

'I'm Maureen Abberley,' she said.

'I'm at Thurmarsh Grammar School for Boys,' he said.

'I'm at Thurmarsh Grammar School for Girls,' she said.

'We certainly go to the right schools,' he said.

'You what?' she said.

'If I went to the girls' school, it'd be ridiculous,' he said.

'I wouldn't mind going to the boys' school,' she said. 'I like boys, me.'

His willie perked up at this. Its owner decided that it was time to impress this curvaceous liker of boys with his worldliness.

'The driver isn't very popular,' he said.

'You what?' she said.

'The driver isn't very popular. The other drivers are waving, but only very curtly.'

'You what?' she said.

'I look at the other drivers,' he said. 'If our driver's popular, they all smile. They aren't smiling at our driver. They're giving the minimum acknowledgement they can without being downright rude.'

Your successful seducer is the man who recognises swiftly when he is on a loser. Henry changed the subject now.

'I'm a humanist,' he said.

'Oh aye?' said Maureen Abberley.

Curvaceous, sexy, but thick. Oh well, you couldn't have everything.

'Do you know what a humanist is?' he said.

'It's a person who doesn't believe in God, but believes in man's powers of reason to create an ordered and purposeful system of ethics,' said Maureen Abberley. 'That's the way I look at it, any road.'

Curvaceous, sexy and a genius.

He put his hand in hers. She didn't remove it. In fact, one nail gently stroked the back of his hand.

He put his left hand on her right thigh. It was solid and yielding at the same time. She didn't remove his hand. He couldn't believe it.

Suddenly masterful, pitying Stefan and Martin, he debated

whether to go first for the short-term or the long-term. It was a straightforward choice between, 'Would you like to be the girls' school representative on the Thurmarsh Grammar School Bisexual Humanist Society's Joint Steering Committee?' and 'Do you fancy a coffee at the Paw Paw Coffee Bar and Grill?'

Before he could decide which to choose, she suddenly stood up and said, 'I gerroff here.'

He was too surprised to say anything.

'Oh well,' he thought. 'It's probably all for the best anyway. I ought to be saving myself for Diana.'

The train arrived at St Pancras thirty-eight minutes late. Henry's heart raced as he walked towards the ticket barrier.

There was Paul, waving. No Diana.

'Super to see you,' said Paul.

He had forgotten how public school Paul was.

He tried to be casual, and it wasn't until they'd been in the taxi (taxi!) for several minutes that he said, so casually that its importance must have been crystal-clear, 'How's Diana?'

'Super,' said Paul, looking out of the window. 'Absolutely super. She's gone to spend three weeks with that Tooth-Braceingham horror in Rowth Bridge. She sends her love.'

The weather in Brittany was fine, the scenery pleasant if unspectacular, the villages drab, the small towns picturesque, and Henry tried hard to react in any way except dumb misery.

The first time they went swimming, he got an erection when he saw Mrs Hargreaves's long, elegant, ageless legs. He had to flop down into the sand, to hide it.

'Are you all right?' she said.

'Fine,' he said, craning his neck round so that he could see her while still hiding his erection.

She bent over him, concerned. Her breasts grew more pointed as she did so. He gritted his teeth and looked away, just managing to avoid an orgasm in the sand.

'Absolutely fine,' he said. 'I'll be along.'

She went away at last, and a few minutes later he deemed it safe to go into the water. He was sure they all thought he was mad.

He was very silly over the French food, refusing to eat anything except steak and chips. The Hargreaves ate oysters, langoustines, crabs, soles, crêpes de fruits de mer and gigot d'agneau avec haricots, and he ate steak and chips. He felt oiky again, and demonstrably a virgin. He felt that all these sophisticated French people could see that he was an oiky virgin, and he made it worse by behaving like one and by hating himself for it. He told himself that he was being loyal to his class, but it seemed a fairly pointless manifestation of loyalty even to him. It occurred to him that he was belittling himself in Mrs Hargreaves's eyes, in order to ensure that no sexual chemistry existed between them. Then he realised how ridiculous and shamingly ill-adjusted that thought was. Mrs Hargreaves noticed him as a sexual object even less than her daughter. Nobody noticed him as a sexual object. He longed to get out of this hole he had dug for himself over the food, and on the sixth day he simply ignored it and ordered langoustines, without comment, and after that he tried everything, and enjoyed most of it. He resented the fact that Dr Hargreaves was so rich, and he felt that he ought to refuse to eat all the food, in solidarity with his friends at home, but that would have made Dr Hargreaves even richer, so he ate extravagantly, and Dr Hargreaves was extremely generous about it, and this made him feel guilty.

Henry sat on a seat in the park, watching the ducks. Stefan was late. He wasn't surprised.

It was Sunday afternoon, when the dead hand of boredom clutches the throat. But Henry had vowed not to be bored at all during his last year at school. He was disgusted with his behaviour during the summer of ennui.

It was the last day of the holidays. There was an autumnal chill in the mornings, bringing him a desire for a new sense of purpose.

His purpose was to find an equilibrium between his mind and his genitalia, to rediscover the sense of purpose of his religious phase and ally it to a healthy sexual and emotional development. If he passed his 'A' levels as well, that would be a bonus, but exams could not be taken seriously, they were not a valid test of a man's worth.

If there was one point where Henry's mind and his genitalia

might meet, it was the Thurmarsh Grammar School Bisexual Humanist Society. Only two things had so far prevented the development of that society. It had no headquarters and no members.

He had already taken steps to remedy the second deficiency. He had acted with a decisiveness that had astonished him. He had looked in the telephone directory to find Abberleys living in the vicinity of the stop where Maureen had got off the bus. He'd been lucky. She was on the phone. She was in. He had taken her to the pictures in Sheffield, and kissed her in the back row, long wet kisses during a long wet film. She had promised to put a notice on the board at school, seeking a list of girls who might be interested in joining the humanist society. She had agreed to come out to Derbyshire with him the following Sunday, if it was fine.

Stefan wasn't coming, blast him. A wigeon quacked complacently, stupidly. He fought against his feelings of hostility towards it. Youth beheaded wigeon because friend didn't turn up. 'This callous crime,' says JP.

He shook his head, to get rid of the sudden headline, which had come from nowhere, and to get rid of even the possibility of doing such a thing.

'Sorry I'm late,' said Stefan. 'I bring good tidings. Who's a clever boy, then?'

'What have you done?'

'I've just seen Dickie Billet.'

'What about?'

'Guess.'

Dickie Billet was the captain of Thurmarsh Cricket Team. Stefan, perhaps the best cover point fielder ever to come out of the Baltic, had played four games for Thurmarsh that summer, and scored 72 not out in one of them.

'He's not getting you a trial for Yorkshire?'

'No chance.'

Dickie Billet had said, 'It's a pity you haven't got a residential qualification for Yorkshire. They'd never play a Pole. Born in Durham, they might stretch a point. Danzig, no chance.'

'What then?'

'Guess.'

'Oh come on.'

Stefan grinned.

'We can use the cricket pavilion for the meetings of the humanist society,' he said. 'Provided there's no alcohol or funny business.'

'There won't be,' said Henry. 'It's a serious project.'

'I suppose so,' said Stefan sadly.

They wandered up and down the park, rushed over to the swings and took turns on them manically, then flopped exhausted onto the tired, thin, browned, late-summer grass.

'Can you give me some advice about girls, Stefan?' said Henry. He needed Stefan's advice so badly that he felt it necessary to make an enormous admission. He swallowed. 'I'm still a virgin,' he said.

'You get too worked up,' said Stefan. 'You've got to play it cool. Make them chase you. That's the secret of my success.'

'Where do you get precautions from?' said Henry.

'There's a herbalist's in Merrick Street has them.'

'What do you say?'

'You just ask for a packet of three.'

'A packet of three what?'

'Just a packet of three. You know what they are, don't you?'

'Course I do.'

'Who are you taking out?'

'Nobody. It's just idle curiosity. Intellectual speculation. Thirst for knowledge. Like the humanist society.'

'Oh aye?'

'Oh aye. I'm serious about the humanist society, our Stefan. Any manking about, out.'

They wandered past the animal cages, three of which were empty. A family with two small children was examining them forlornly.

'There's nowt in this one either, dad,' said the small boy.

Henry felt that he must entertain Stefan, to show his gratitude for the advice and the arrangement over the pavilion, and also to win back a bit of respect.

'Excuse me,' he said to the forlorn family. 'There's four sloths in there.'

'Oh aye?' said the man. 'Where are they?'

'Asleep,' said Henry. 'They're very slothful, sloths.'

'Aye, well, I suppose they would be,' said the man.

'They sleep twenty-three and a half hours a day. They won't be up now while six in the morning.'

'Oh. Thank you very much,' said the woman.

The children stared at him.

'There's four chameleons in that one,' said Henry, pointing at the next cage.

'We couldn't see owt,' said the man.

'Well you wouldn't,' said Henry. 'They're masters of disguise, are chameleons. It took us fifty-five minutes to spot all four.'

'Oh. Thank you very much,' said the woman.

When Henry and Stefan looked back, the family were peering intently into the empty cage.

By the Friday evening, Henry's appeal on the school notice board for boys interested in joining the Thurmarsh Grammar School Bisexual Humanist Society had seventy-eight names. Some could be discounted, like Len Hutton, King Farouk, Freddie Mills, John Mills, John Stuart Mills, Ron Nietzsche, Busby Berkeley, Bobby Locke, Bertrand Russell, Jane Russell, Des Cartes, Sid Cartes, Plato, Pluto, Donald Duck, Karl Marx, Groucho Marx, Lorenzo Marx, Leibnitz and Landauer, Harry Stottle and all five Einsteins. When the silly ones had been eliminated, there were nine possible members.

Henry pocketed his list, and set off for Merrick Street, a little street of small shops that ran north from the back of the town hall. It was alive with shops for minority interests, but was already showing signs of social decay, and would soon be redeveloped.

The Merrick Herbalist's was situated between a religious bookshop and a model railway shop.

Henry looked in the window of the religious bookshop and felt ashamed of his lost innocence. Then he looked in the window of the model railway shop and felt even more ashamed of his lost innocence. Then he took a deep breath, walked up to the herbalist's, felt ashamed of the fact that he hadn't lost his innocence, and walked away up the street. At the end of the street he stopped, irresolute, walked half-way back to the herbalist's, then away again. Finally, when he was an object of interest to the whole street, he dived into the herbalist's, heart pounding. It was dark inside. He could hardly see the man.

'A packet of three, please,' he said in a squeaky voice.

To his dismay the man said, 'A packet of three what?' Then he added, 'Only joking,' and handed Henry his purchase. 'Good luck, lad,' he said.

On Sunday he took Maureen Abberley to a spot near the hill where he had lusted briefly after Mabel Billington. It was quite private there, but she said that she couldn't possibly make love to him in the open air. She caught colds easily, and besides, somebody would see. He supposed that he had been mad and naive to think that she would. He *was* mad and naive where sex was concerned.

An equilibrium between his mind and his genitalia.

It was definitely the mind's turn next.

As the first meeting of the Thurmarsh Grammar School Bisexual Humanist Society drew nearer, Henry began to panic. He was its founder. He ought to deliver an inaugural address on humanism. But what was it? The more he tried to study it, the less he knew what it was. Every time he tried to think hard about it, he ended up by having fantasies about going the whole way with Maureen Abberley. They went the whole way in the home dressing room, the visitors' dressing room, behind the scoreboard, even inside the heavy roller. He woke up one morning naked inside the heavy roller with Maureen Abberley, as it rolled the pitch for a test match between England and Australia. The two captains, Len Hutton and Lindsay Hassett, also naked, were tossing up. Len Hutton winked at him. Whatever the dream meant, it didn't help him to resolve the mysteries of humanism

Cold baths. Early morning runs. Mind over matter. Perhaps as a result of the cold baths, or the early morning runs, he developed a streaming cold. All the girls would think him sickly.

The cricket ground was situated behind the football ground. Its southern boundary abutted onto the north terrace of the Blonk Lane stadium. The pavilion faced west, and from the road you had to trudge right across the sodden ground. The square was roped off to protect the wicket. The light was fading in the cloud-streaked west, but he could still just see that the scoreboard was set for the winter at 987 for 2 – last man 606. He let himself into the pavilion and flooded it with light. There was a wooden trestle table, at which the players sat for tea, as well as a few folding canvas chairs, which people took outside to watch the cricket on warm days. As Henry set up the chairs, he came upon a grimy, dust-covered jockstrap lying on the wooden floor. He hurled it into the dying nettles at the back of the pavilion. From this unpromising acorn, could any great tree of thought ever grow?

Famous philosopher mourned. Founder of 'Thurmarsh Movement' Lost at sea. 'This tragic day' – Bertrand Russell.

Nobody would come, except Martin and Stefan, who had promised. No girls would come. Perhaps that would be all for the best. His philosophical researches had revealed that there were no female philosphers, no Mrs Kants, no Daphne Spinozas or Gladys Wittgensteins.

Maureen Abberley arrived, with Betty Bridger, long-nosed and pale, Karen Porter, little, green-eyed and squashy, Beverley Minster, tall and buxom, and Denise Booth, sullen and pasty-faced. They brought three thermos flasks of coffee.

Good for them. Even if they didn't contribute much to the ebb and flow of the philosophical debate, they had proved their usefulness.

By half-past seven, five boys had arrived. Martin, Denis Hilton, small, serious and bespectacled, Bobby Cartwright, large, red-haired, freckled and gawky, Alan Turner, tall, languid, good-looking, with a sense of great intellectual power held in reserve, and Michael Normanton, who was a martyr to acne.

They sat, the eleven of them, a mixed cricket team, at the trestle table, boys on one side, girls on the other, Henry, their founder, at the end.

Henry's opening speech, which had caused him such worry, could have been criticised on the grounds that it did not grasp the nettle firmly in both hands. It might have been more impressive had it not been delivered in such a nasal, sniffy way. But the most churlish listener could not have accused him of tedious long-windedness.

'Welcome to the Thurmarsh Grammar School Bisexual Humanist Society,' he said. 'The first question we must discuss is "What is Humanism?" '

There was no applause. He hadn't expected any.

For an awful moment, he thought that nobody was going to speak.

'Humanism was founded in Italy by Petrarch and Boccaccio and people like that,' said Denise Booth.

Good for her, thought Henry. At least one of the girls had something to say for herself.

'They went back to classical literature, Plato and Aristotle and that, to find out how they could get better ideals and that so they could yank themselves out of the Middle Ages,' said Denise Booth.

'That's not how I understand humanism at all,' said Karen Porter.

Good for her. If two of the girls had thoughts on the subject, it looked as if they were in for a lively time.

It was when the third person to speak was also a girl that Henry began to get uneasy.

'Nor me,' said Beverley Minster. 'It means being kind, and nice to animals and things, and having charities, and visiting old people and things.'

When the fourth person to speak was also a girl, Henry began to get really worried.

'Why should you visit things?' said Betty Bridger.

'I don't mean visit things,' said Beverley Minster. 'I mean visit old people and people like that and things.'

'What do you mean "people like that"?' said Betty Bridger. 'What people like old people are there except other old people?'

'That's what I mean,' said Beverley Minster. 'We'll visit other old people as well.'

'My God. If we can't even define our terms,' said Betty Bridger.

'What do you understand by humanism, Beverley?' said Karen Porter.

'Being kind. Helping people. Bandaging sick animals and things,' said Beverley Minster. 'Running charities and things.'

'You're talking about being humane,' said Karen Porter. 'You're talking about humanitarianism.'

'That's what I thought it was,' said Beverley Minster.

'We're wasting time,' said Betty Bridger.

'Do you call bandaging sick animals and looking after old people and things a waste of time?' said Beverley Minster.

'We're here to discuss the philosophy of humanism,' said Betty Bridger.

'That's a great help to a sick animal,' said Beverley Minster.

'Look, if you want to bandage sick animals, you bandage sick animals,' said Betty Bridger. 'And visit things. There must be lots of lonely old umbrellas and hair-brushes would be glad of a visit. And we'll discuss philosophy.'

'I don't see how you can say that philosophy is more important than bandaging sick animals,' said Beverley Minster.

'I know how I say it,' said Betty Bridger. 'I presume you mean, "How can I justify saying it?" Well, that's a different question. Do we want to discuss that? On what grounds do we decide that one thing is more important than another?'

'Clearly there have always been philosophers and there have always been people who have visited old people and bandaged sick animals,' said Karen Porter. 'History records the achievements of philosophers far more than the achievements of bandagers of sick animals because history is written by intellectuals and not by sick animals, and philosophy is more important to intellectuals, while bandaging sick animals is more important to sick animals.'

'The two terms are not necessarily mutually exclusive,' said Betty Bridger. 'I mean, there may have been philosophers who visited old ladies.'

'And bandaged sick animals,' said Karen Porter.

'We've got to use language with precision, Beverley,' said Betty Bridger.

'I know what you mean,' said Beverley Minster. 'I should have said "bandage injured animals". You treat sick animals. You bandage injured animals.'

'Fine,' said Henry. 'I think we'd all agree this is a very helpful discussion. Atschoo. Sorry. But I founded this society with Maureen. . .' he smiled at Maureen, and she smiled back,

290

'. . .and it's a humanist society, not a society for doing humanitarian acts. I think you'd be happier, Beverley, if you left us and founded a society of your own for visiting old people and bandaging injured animals.'

'I think you're all horrid,' said Beverley Minster, and she left the pavilion in tears.

Henry longed for one of the boys to speak. He felt ashamed for them. And he longed for Maureen Abberley, whom he loved, to speak. He felt ashamed for her.

'Now there are quite a few people we haven't heard from,' he said. 'Somebody else, please.'

'Can I just say what I understand by humanism?' said Karen Porter. 'It's a dictionary definition. It's a philosophy that rejects supernaturalism, regards man as a natural object and asserts the essential dignity and worth of man and his capacity to achieve self-realisation through the use of reason and the scientific method.'

Alan Turner leant forward, and it was clear that he was preparing to speak. At last, a boy was going to contribute, and there was something impressive, calm, mature about Alan Turner. Everybody, even Betty Bridger, hung on his words.

'I agree with that,' he said.

'I don't,' said Denise Booth. 'Humanists didn't not believe in God. There were humanist popes.'

'How do you know?' said Betty Bridger.

'I've read it,' said Denise Booth.

'How do you know it's true? said Betty Bridger.

'How do you know anything's true?' said Denis Hilton, taking off his glasses and staring at them and leaping suddenly into brave, blushing, earnest life. 'How do you know anything? How do you know you exist? Maybe you're all a figment of my imagination.'

Rain began to drum on the roof. Karen Porter said that she knew that she often felt that she was a wraith-like figure, and that was probably the explanation. She was a figment of somebody else's imagination. Betty Bridger said that Karen Porter might well be right, but Denis Hilton was wrong, since, if anybody was a figment of anybody's imagination, they were all figments of hers. Henry said that if anybody was going to be a figment of anybody's imagination, as founder and secretary it was only right that they should be a figment of his imagination. He proposed that they should draft a set of club rules, which would include a clause to the effect that the society be deemed to exist, all members be deemed to exist, and a charge of threepence per head for coffee be deemed to exist. Betty Bridger suggested that at each meeting somebody should read a paper, as a basis for discussion. She suggested that, as she had suggested the idea, she should deliver the first paper, on the subject 'What is Humanism?' Just as they were about to start their coffee, Stefan arrived. Martin, Bobby Cartwright, Michael Normanton and Maureen Abberley didn't speak all evening. After the meeting, Henry suggested that Maureen Abberley and he stay behind to wash up and clear up and generally leave the pavilion as they would wish to find it. It was only fair that they should undertake this tiresome chore as they were the founders of the society in their respective schools.

When they had washed up and cleared up, Henry put his arms round Maureen's soft waist. But she shook herself free, and refused even to kiss him, for fear she would catch his cold.

Henry found it hard to avoid the conclusion that, taken all in all, the first meeting of the Thurmarsh Grammar School Bisexual Humanist Society had been a disappointment. No great new system of philosophy had emerged, and he remained a virgin.

Three days later, Cousin Hilda had a face like thunder. Norman Pettifer was not an unduly timid man. No man who holds down the position of manager of the cheese counter at Cullens can be unduly timid. Tony Preece was not a timid man. No man who braves the rigors both of trying to get laughs in working men's clubs and of selling insurance can be timid. Liam, though timid enough, was not a perceptive man. But at the sight of Cousin Hilda's face, all three men quailed. They dispatched their liver and bacon and tinned peaches at a speed that positively invited stomach ulcers, and fled.

'Well!' said Cousin Hilda, when only Henry was left. 'Well!'

'Well what?' said Henry.

Cousin Hilda's jaw was biting on the pain of it.

'I found a packet of. .them things. .in your pocket,' she

said.

'I don't know how they got there,' said Henry. 'One of the boys must have put them there.'

'How do you know what I'm talking about, if you didn't know they were there?' said Cousin Hilda.

He noticed that there were now two cracked panes of blue glass in the front of the stove.

'I'm sorry,' he mumbled.

'Sorry!' she repeated bitterly. 'Sorry! I've done my best to be a mother to you. I've done my best to give you standards.'

He felt full of shame. Not shame at having had a packet of Durex. Shame at having been found with a packet of Durex. Shame at being Henry Pratt. Great philosopher! Distinguished humanist! He couldn't even avoid bringing misery on his poor surrogate parent.

Henry made no attempt to see Maureen Abberley before the next meeting of the humanist society. Let her do the pining and worrying.

He told Stefan that he was very upset with him. Stefan said that he couldn't stand societies and formal debates. They made him ill. He'd spent two hours plucking up his courage before he'd dared turn up.

He told Martin that he was very upset with him. He was his friend, and he hadn't said a word. Martin said he'd been shy. 'I thought you were going into politics,' said Henry. 'Where would the Labour Party be now, if Kier Hardie'd been shy?' 'That's different,' Martin said. 'That's my chosen field. All this humanism's just messing about.'

After school, on the day of the second meeting of the Thurmarsh Grammar School Bisexual Humanist Society, Henry went down to Merrick Street. He entered the shop hurriedly this time, head down, terrified he'd see somebody he knew.

'A refill, eh?' said the man. 'Well done, lad.'

As he set up the chairs and got the coffee mugs out of the cupboard, Henry tried to concentrate on humanism, not Maureen Abberley. Was it true what Martin said? Were they just messing about? How many people would turn up anyway?

293

To his surprise, everybody came except two. He knew Betty Bridger would come, of course, and probably Karen Porter. He wasn't totally surprised that Denise Booth and Denis Hilton were there, and he'd expected Martin to come, out of loyalty if nothing else, but the presence of Bobby Cartwright and Michael Normanton, who hadn't contributed a word, and of Alan Turner, who had only said, 'I agree with that,' did surprise him.

The absentees were Stefan Prziborski, who was allergic to meetings and formal debates, and Maureen Abberley, who had a cold.

Betty Bridger read her paper. She said that she had changed its title from 'What is Humanism?' to 'What is "What is Humanism?"?'! They would have to examine the nature of statements, the nature of questions, the nature of definitions. But were they ready to do that? Shouldn't they first examine the nature of communication?

'I'd like to put this to you, in conclusion,' she said. 'Ought we not to consider the four questions "What is what?" "What is is?" "Is what?" and "Is is?" before we ask ourselves "What is " 'What is Humanism?"?'!

'That's ridiculous,' said Martin. 'There's a real world out there.'

'But is it real?' said Denis Hilton, kick-starting himself into stuttering excitement. 'I'm very interested in the question "what is is?" '

'Not "is is?"?' said Henry sarcastically.

'No. I believe we have to assume that is is, if we're to get anywhere,' said Denis Hilton. 'I was very interested in your father's comments on how we decide what a table is, Betty.'

Betty Bridger gave Denis Hilton an angry stare.

'Betty's father?' said Henry.

Some colour came to Betty Bridger's cheeks for the first time.

'My father's a philosopher,' she said.

'Aha! So he wrote your paper,' said Martin.

'He bloody well did not. He helped, that's all,' said Betty Bridger. 'He just suggested areas of enquiry.'

'Bloody stupid areas of enquiry,' said Martin

'Please everybody,' said Henry.

Not stupid at all,' said Denis Hilton. 'Unless you define your terms, you're talking in a vacuum.'

'Ah, but what is a vacuum?' said Martin.

'Your brain,' said Betty Bridger.

'Please!' said Henry. 'Please! This is not a philosophical society. It's a humanist society. If you want to form a philosophical society, do so.'

'I think I will,' said Betty Bridger, gathering up her papers.

'Good idea,' said Martin. 'Your father obviously can't help you quite so much on humanism.'

'I'm coming too,' said Denis Hilton. He turned towards Henry. 'I'm sorry,' he said, 'but that's my real interest. The wider field. I think the idea of confining it to humanism is a bit narrow for me.'

'Fair enough,' said Henry. 'Anybody else who finds the future of mankind too narrow and prefers the broader field of "What is is?" may as well go as well.'

Betty Bridger looked questioningly at Karen Porter.

'No, I'm staying,' said Karen Porter, grinning at Henry, who immediately felt glad that Maureen Abberley had a cold.

Betty Bridger and Denis Hilton departed. There were now two girls facing four boys, two of whom had not yet spoken.

'Right,' said Henry. 'So what is humanism?'

Alan Turner leant forward again, urgent, impressive, measured, as he had at the last meeting, when he had said, 'I agree with that.'

'I agree with what she said last time,' he said this time.

'Which "she"?' said Henry.

'The pretty one,' said Michael Normanton. His appearance improved briefly as the rest of his face and neck went as red as his acne.

'That's not a very nice thing to say of.   .of whichever girl you don't mean,' said Henry.

'He means me,' said Denise Booth. 'I mean I'm the one he doesn't mean. We all know that.'

'I looked up your medieval humanism stuff, Denise,' said Karen Porter. 'I must say I found it all very confusing.'

'I'm probaby on the wrong track altogether,' said Denise Booth. 'I'm probably stupid as well as ugly.'

She stormed out of the pavilion, slamming the door so hard that a photograph of the Thurmarsh Cricket Team of 1932 fell to the ground.

'Why have you come here, Michael?' said Henry. 'You haven't contributed anything.'

'I wanted to meet girls,' said Michael Normanton.

'What girl would look at you? You're covered in acne,' said Henry. 'You've got more spots than a set of dominoes. In fact we could have a good game of fives and threes on your neck.'

Michael Normanton flung himself at Henry. They rolled on the floor. Martin grabbed Michael Normanton's collar and attempted to pull him off. Alan Turner walked calmly over, yanked Michael Normanton from the pile of bodies and punched him on the nose. Bobby Cartwright made no move.

'Why did you hit me?' said Michael Normanton, sitting on the floor, holding a hankerchief to his nose.

'You attacked the chairman physically. That's anarchy,' said Martin.

'He made personal remarks about my face,' said Michael Normanton.

'You called Denise Booth ugly by implication,' said Karen Porter.

'To praise you,' shouted Michael Normanton. 'And, any road, his insults to me weren't by implication.'

'Now we're splitting hairs,' said Martin.

'Greasy unwashed hairs,' said Karen Porter.

'All right. I'm going, you sods,' said Michael Normanton.

Once more, the pavilion door slammed.

They poured out the coffee, and Henry asked Bobby Cartwright why he came.

'I like listening,' he said. 'I may not have owt to contribute, but I like listening.'

Nobody made any further references to humanism or to any further meetings. They cleared up, locked up, and went home. Henry insisted on accompanying Karen Porter to her door. She lived in Aylesbury Road, which was only two roads away from Park View Road.

'I suppose I can't come in or owt,' he said.

'Which?' she said.

'What?' he said.

'In or out?' she said.

'I meant in or owt like that,' he said.

'What is there like that?' she said.

'Oh, we're not onto all that again, are we?' he said. 'I meant, I don't want to say goodnight. Can I see you again, Karen?'

'There's no point,' she said, giving him a quick kiss on the cheek.

He grabbed her by her slender waist and bent to kiss her on the mouth. She averted her mouth.

'You find me repulsive,' he said.

She laughed.

'I'm sorry,' she said. 'I didn't mean to laugh. It was just the way you came out with it. No, I don't find you repulsive. I think you're probably quite attractive.'

'What do you mean "probably"?'

'I like you,' she said, 'but I've got a feller of me own. He's a friend of yours. Stefan Prziborski.'

Before he went home, he dropped the packet of three down a grating.

Twice he picked up the phone to ring Maureen Abberley. Twice he rang off before anyone answered. The third time he hung on, trying to sound cool as he asked for her.

'She's out,' said her father. 'Who am I to say rang?'

'It doesn't matter,' he said.

He regretted that afterwards. He rang again. Again her father answered. He tried not to sound like the person who had rung before. She was out again. How dare she be out all the time? 'Tell her Henry Pratt rang,' he said curtly, and rang off, before her father had any chance to sound amused.

He got a letter from her. 'I'm sorry we keep missing each other. Pick me up at four o'clock on Saturday.'

'That's right. Keep up the good work,' said the man in the herbalist's.

They went to the pictures. They kissed through most of the film. He took her home, and dropped his packet of three down a different grating.

He kept quarrelling with Stefan, because Stefan was going out with Karen Porter.

Christmas came and went. Maureen Abberley invited him to a party at the home of a friend whose parents were away. 'Nice to see you again,' said the man in the herbalist's. 'It makes you proud to be British.' He went home, intending to hide the contraceptives in his room while he had his tea. There was a telegram waiting for him. It said, 'No go stop sorry stop streaming cold stop Maureen.' He went out and dropped the contraceptives down a grating. After tea he wrote to Maureen. He told her how much he loved her and wanted her. Then he tore the letter into tiny pieces. Maureen wrote and said, 'I'm sorry about my boring old cold. I did miss you. Pick me up at four on Saturday, if my cold's better.' He couldn't because it was Tommy Marsden's debut for Thurmarsh United. He rang to explain, but she was out. At least her cold must be better. He left his message. She'd understand.

To most of the crowd who clogged up the streets surrounding the compact, unpretentious Blonk Lane stadium it was just another match, Thurmarsh v Darlington in the Third Division North. Henry wasn't sure how excited even Martin was.

Henry himself was wildly excited. Somebody he knew, who had been a fellow member of the Paradise Lane Gang, was playing league football. He regretted bitterly all the distractions which had prevented him supporting the Reds as he should have done. Boarding school, living in Sheffield, God, humanism, Maureen Abberley. A wasted youth.

The whole gang should have been there, but Chalky White was dead, Billy Erpingham had disappeared, Ian Lowson was sullen and unfriendly towards them.

The team was Isherwood; Plank, Reynolds; Ayers, Cedarwood, McNab; Bellow, Marsden, Gravel, Greenaway and Muir.

When the team came out, Tommy looked so young. The knot in Henry's stomach tightened.

The teams kicked around. The wind howled. Cedarwood, the veteran pivot, took his teeth out and put them in the goalmouth, wrapped in tissue paper.

During the first half, Tommy looked bewildered and out of his

298

depth.

'Bring back Morley,' said the man on Henry's right. 'Tha's rubbish, Marsden.'

'Give him a chance,' said Henry. 'It's his first game.'

The man gave Henry a cold stare, then turned away.

Darlington were leading 1–0 at half time.

Teenage star transforms game in second half, thought Henry. From dog turds to Wembley for England's newest star. Knighthood for Marsden. The Tommy Marsden I knew, writes Henry Pratt.

In the sixty-ninth minute, MUIR equalised brilliantly after running onto a shrewd through-ball from Ayers.

In the seventy-third minute, Tommy had his first effort at goal. He packed a powerful shot, to judge from the way the ball thudded into the corner flag.

'Useless,' muttered the man on Henry's right. 'Tha's a great soft pudden, Marsden.'

In the seventy-ninth minute, the Darlington goalkeeper punched the ball out under pressure. It landed at Tommy's feet. Without time to be nervous, he lobbed it brilliantly into the goal. Suddenly confident, he soon split the defence to set up a third goal for GRAVEL.

'Where's tha been hiding him, Linacre, tha great twit?' shouted the man on Henry's right. 'That lad's a find,' he told anyone who cared to listen. 'He reminds me of Raich Carter. I can always spot 'em.'

Henry and Martin celebrated with two pints of Mansfield best bitter at the Forge Tavern. The headline in the Green 'Un read, 'Teenager Shines As Reds Shake Quakers'.

He sucked a mint before arriving back at number 66 Park View Road. The euphoria slipped gently away as he left the glory behind and drifted reluctantly back to his bed-sitter. He thought of the matches he had seen with his father, and then he thought of his mother. His eyes filled with tears, and the gale mourned for her bitterly in the telegraph wires.

Maureen wrote to say that he could get lost if she wasn't as important to him as a football match. He replied that he loved he madly, and was very sorry. He would never do it again. He replied that Tommy Marsden had been an old friend and if she resented his going to see his debut then she wasn't the sort of person he wanted to go out with. He tore both letters up. Maureen wrote to say that she was sorry. She realised that Tommy Marsden had been an old friend, and that he had to go to the match. He could pick her up at 3.30 on Saturday. This meant he'd have to miss Tommy's next home match.

They went to the pictures. Afterwards, he bought the *Green 'Un* and found that he had missed an impressive 2–0 home win over Bradford Park Avenue, with goals from MARSDEN and BELLOW. Maureen Abberley removed the paper and looked straight into his eyes.

'My parents are going to a party next Saturday,' she said. 'I'll be all alone in the house. You can come round if you like.'

'All right?' said the man in the herbalist's. 'That's the ticket. Have to discuss discount rates soon.'

Mr and Mrs Abberley had gone when Henry arrived, and the television was on.

Maureen was wearing rather a short dress, and her feet were bare. There was an electric fire and a cut-glass bowl of fruit on an occasional table. Maureen opened her mouth wide when he kissed her.

'I didn't know you had a television,' he said.

'We've just gorrit,' she said. 'Dad says there'll be a rush as the coronation gets near. Have you seen much television?'

'Hardly any,' he said.

'You can watch lots tonight,' she said.

'I don't want to watch television tonight,' he said.

'I promised my parents I'd be good,' she said. 'They trust me. I think trust between parents and children is too valuable to be trifled with, don't you?'

He had often longed to watch television. With what reluctance he spent his first evening in front of it. They watched 'Looking at Fish' with George Cansdale, an interlude on a Cotswold farm, and 'Café Continental' with l'Orchestre Pigalle, Père Auguste as Maître d'Hotel and Hélène Cordet as Mistress of Ceremonies. All the time they lay on the settee, semi-entwined, in the dark except for the glow of the electric fire and the flickering white light from the television. He made a last big effort to prove so irresistible to her that she'd forget her parents. At first, as their kisses grew more passionate in time to the music of Shirley Abicair and her zither, he had a wild hope that all would be well.

Then came the close-down. Off went the set, Maureen Abberley smoothed her dress down, and said, 'You may as well go before they get back,' and a sad virgin bent to drop a packet of rubber goods down a grating, in a quiet suburban street which seemed to him to be alive with sexual satisfaction and excitement for everyone except himself.

The following Friday, Henry took Maureen to the pictures. He'd had to borrow the money, as he'd spent all his pocket money on unused rubber goods.

As they left the cinema, a boy stared at Maureen, and said, 'I thought you'd gorra cold.'

'It got better,' she said, blushing. She avoided Henry's eyes, then shot him a sudden, challenging look.

'Who did you go to that party with, when you told me you'd got a cold?' Henry said, as he walked her home.

He grabbed her arm and held it behind her back.

'You're hurting,' she said.

'Who?' he repeated, beginning to twist her arm.

'Norbert Cuffley,' she said.

'Norbert Cuffley? Norbert Cuffley?'

Girl found dead in duck pond.

Don't even think like that.

He turned and walked away, without a word. He didn't even look back, to enjoy the triumph of seeing her standing there at a loss.

Norbert Cuffley.

'Give up. You were never meant to be a lady-killer, our Henry,' he told himself.

Suddenly his 'A' levels were looming and he hadn't done enough work, and brave talk about exams not being valid tests of a man's worth were so much hot air.

Tommy Marsden played ten games and scored five goals. Henry watched him four times.

One Sunday, Tony Preece brought Stella, his new girlfriend, to dinner. She was a rather brassy blonde, with thin legs and lips. When she had left, Cousin Hilda said, 'Well!'

'She may have a heart of gold,' said Henry.

'Pigs may fly,' said Cousin Hilda.

Army medicals took place. Ears, feet and reflexes were explored, colour blindness and genitalia examined, anuses and rudimentary intelligence probed.

Henry and Martin were accepted as fit for national service. Stefan Prziborski failed. He had flat feet.

'Flat feet?' said Henry. 'He's the only one of us who can run.'

He listened to 'In All Directions', a radio comedy programme with Peter Ustinov and Peter Jones. In the first series they searched for Copthorne Avenue. In the second series they searched for more ambitious things, like Britain's heritage and true love. Henry laughed a lot, but he also felt pained. He had found his Copthorne Avenue. Would he ever find anything else?

Cousin Hilda got a television. She couldn't miss the coronation. Sometimes, Henry abandoned his studies for a while, to watch 'Animal, Vegetable and Mineral' or 'Kaleidoscope' or 'What's My Line?'.

Edmund Hillary and Sherpa Tensing climbed Everest. It was all a Tory plot. That was what Reg Hammond said, any road.

Tony Preece asked if he could bring Stella to see the coronation.

'I suppose so,' said Cousin Hilda.

They watched the coronation until their eyes hurt. The little basement room became London, City of Pageantry. 'All we need's a crate of light ale,' said Tony Preece. Stella grinned, and Cousin Hilda sniffed.

Mr McFarlane, History teacher and Marxist, suddenly copped out, and told the boys to be careful not to reveal Marxist bias in their exams.

Henry had dreaded his 'A' levels, but when they came he enjoyed them.

In the world of sporting action he could only watch the

triumphs of Tommy Marsden. Here, when told, ' "*King Lear* is not the tragedy of the downfall of a great hero: it is the story of a man who becomes great through tragic experience." Discuss,' or ' "All the intelligent characters in *Vanity Fair* are bad characters: only the stupid show kindness or honesty." Do you agree?' he came into his own.

In the world of sexual action, conventional morality did not even permit him to watch the triumphs of Stefan Prziborski. Far better to concentrate on 'Are there reasons for doubting Juvenal's sincerity?' and 'What tricks of style are characteristic of Tacitus?'

Even the world of intellectual speculation had proved a disappointment for Henry in real life. Here, in the quiet examination room, with the windows open on the buzzing of bees and the droning of traffic, he could enjoy wrestling with such matters as ' "Charles V was a Fleming rather than a Spaniard, and a Spaniard rather than a German. He was never an Italian." Discuss.'

Then it was over. He knew, with a deep inner conviction, that he had either passed or failed. He went for a final tea with the Quells. His school life drew to a close.

Britain was embarking on a new Elizabethan age, in which poverty and unemployment and snobbery would disappear for ever. As this great vessel steamed out of harbour, a little rowing boat bobbed uneasily in its wake. That boat was Henry, and as the great liner of optimism disappeared over the horizon, her wash eased, and he rocked almost imperceptibly on the slow swell of anti-climax.

12 Return to Upper Mitherdale

The sun glinted on the roof of a grey Standard Eight as it made its way between the dry-stone walls, up into the high hills.

In the car were four young men who had been rewarded by parents and guardians for passing their 'A' levels. Soon, three of them would be spending two years in Her Majesty's armed forces. The fourth, the golden boy, had turned out to have flat feet of clay.

Henry sighed.

'My God, why the sigh?' said Paul Hargreaves. Number 66 Park View Road and its businessmen, the Rundle Valley, Paradise Lane waiting for demolition, spittle on pavements, Fillingley Working Men's Club, it had been a world more foreign than Brittany to Paul. He had grated on Henry's nerves by looking brave the whole time. Now, for the first time, going into the country in Martin's father's car, to stay in a pub for a week, Paul looked relaxed. He wore the very scruffy old clothes of those who knew that they could afford to dress elegantly any time they chose.

'Because I'm happy,' replied Henry. 'I'm so happy I feel insecure.'

'Careful,' growled Stefan Prziborski. 'Don't mention the future.'

Stefan had been upset about his flat feet. He had been upset at getting the worst exam results of the trio. He had been upset that his inability to attend the meetings of the Humanist Society had revealed how fragile his edifice of insouciance was. He had been upset at his rejection by Karen Porter, who had suddenly left for London, because she found his pose of coolness so boring. It had caused a slump in his batting form, and he'd been dropped by Thurmarsh. The future was a hostile country.

'It's a good rule,' said Paul. 'No mention of the future, and no politics.'

'It's a stupid rule,' said Martin. 'All life is politics. That man with the bent back in that field is politics. Look at him, slaving away in his rags.'

'It's a scarecrow,' said Henry. 'Are you sure you're fit to drive?'

They were making good time. Martin drove as he lived, steadily, unspectacularly, but making better time than you expected. He was the man who surprised you by passing his driving test first time. He was the man you didn't notice until he crossed the finishing line in first place.

'I was thinking about last night as well, when I sighed,' said Henry.

Tony Preece had taken Henry and Paul to Fillingley Working Men's Club, beyond Doncaster.

Also present had been Stella, Tony's brassy blonde.

On the drive over, they had talked about comedy.

'Henry did a turn at the end-of-term concert at school. He was super,' Paul had said.

'Came on as the headmaster, did you?' Tony Preece had said.

'How on earth did you guess?'

'It's the obvious thing to do.'

'I suppose I was pretty cliché-ridden,' Henry had said.

'You were super,' Paul had said.

In the headlights the road had been like a long, narrow stage. A leaf that had died before its time had appeared stage left in front of them. A gust of warm summer wind had sent the leaf dancing across the road like a mouse on a hot-plate.

'I was at a working men's club when I decided I wanted to be a comic,' Henry had said. 'There was this Welsh comic there. He had a leek, and a pith-helmet, and one roller skate. I thought, "I could do better than that." '

'No good?' Tony Preece had said.

'Terrible.'

Tony Preece had driven into the rutted car park of a large, ugly brick building. It looked more like a giant public convenience than a palace of laughter, and Stella had expelled a deep, anxious breath at the sight of it.

'We're with t' turn,' Stella had told the doorman.

They had sat very near the stage. Paul had bought two pints of bitter and a sweet martini. Stella had called to him not to forget the cherry. He hadn't forgotten the cherry.

Henry and Stella had both gone very tense. It was worse than going on yourself.

Paul had appeared totally oblivious of the tension. He had gazed round the room with the detached eyes of a sociologist.

Before he announced Tony, the concert secretary had blown into the microphone.

'And now another comic that's making his first appearance at Fillingley,' he had said. 'Let's hope he's better than t' last one. Let's hear it for Talwyn Jones, the Celtic Droll.'

You're in trouble when you come on in a bright red suit, with a giant leek in your buttonhole, wearing a pith-helmet and one roller skate, and nobody laughs.

Stella had put a comforting hand on Henry's arm.

'Don't worry too much about it,' she'd said. 'He knows he's terrible.'

They stayed in the Crown Inn, Troutwick, since the Three Horseshoes in Rowth Bridge had no rooms.

The Crown was a low stone building in a tiny square just off the main square of the cluttered little town, where roads steered crazy courses between the damaged corners of old buildings.

Henry had not been content to let his youth end in anti-climax. He it was who had laid the plan. Now, when Simon Eckington arrived in the farm truck, the only four good friends he had ever had were assembled together for the first time, and the loose ends of a fragmented childhood were tied into a neater parcel than Henry had ever thought himself capable of making.

Simon was even bigger than he expected, tougher, slower, red-faced and weather-beaten.

'Sorry I'm late,' he said, as he placed Paul's soft hand cheerfully in his gnarled one. 'I had to cut up a pig.'

Simon was centuries old, a worker, uncomplicated, cheery, thirsty. Pints were drunk. Darts thudded into darts boards. No matter that Henry played badly. It was the others who were the performers. That night he was the impresario who had brought the bill together. A bill that, if successful, would run a week.

This was the life. A cheery bar. Hosts George and Edna were cheerfulness personified. Young men relaxing in the way they knew best. A stag evening, rich with the promise of many more to come. Henry had accepted that young ladies did not beat a path to the door of unathletic young men such as himself. Some, like Stefan Prziborski, are born to be ladies' men. But other young men collect engine numbers well into their thirties, sit at cricket grounds recording every ball in their score-books, or collect arcane objects and go away to meet other men who collect similar arcane objects. They are sensible enough to renounce sex before it renounces them. Henry had joined their ranks, and what a relief it was.

'Does tha remember a girl called Lorna Arrow?' said Simon. 'Tall, slim girl wi' a husky voice?'

'I used to read comics to her,' said Henry.

'She remembers thee all right,' said Simon.

'She had nits,' said Henry.

'She's grown into an attractive girl,' said Simon. 'She's a right belter now, is Lorna Arrow.'

'There was another one,' said Henry.

'Jane Lugg.'

'That's it. She was a tomboy.'

'She still is.'

'She had nits too. There was a third one. Evacuee.'

'Pam Yardley.'

'That's right. She was sex-mad. Kept grabbing me knackers. Couldn't stand you. She had nits too.'

'She comes back to stay wi' the Wallingtons every summer. We're engaged.'

The next day dawned warm and sunny. They drove back into Skipton, with the windows wide open to help ease their hangovers. Somebody had blacked-out the final letter of the Forthcoming Attractions outside the Odeon, changing 'Destination Gobi' into 'Destination Gob'. How childish, thought these four young men loftily.

They dropped Henry off outside the little bijou detached

residence where Auntie Kate lived with her daughter Fiona, with her husband, the assistant bank manager with the artificial leg, who was now the bank manager with the artificial leg, and with the baby they had finally had when all hope had been abandoned.

He knew that Auntie Kate would be old, and he had tried picturing her looking extremely old, so that he wouldn't be shocked when he saw how old she was. As a result, he was amazed how young she looked.

She embraced him till he could hardly breathe.

Fiona kissed him too and showed off her baby proudly. They'd waited so long. She was so excited. Henry felt awful about being a callous youth and not liking babies. The bank manager came home for dinner. The house was sparkling, the garden well-kept, the dinner palatable, the baby crawled in his play-pen, and Auntie Kate doted on him as much as Fiona did.

Fiona had forgotten reading him stories. She had forgotten that she had been a glamorous princess who had brought an aura of sexual mischief into a sick boy's bedroom. She had forgotten that she had been a naughty lady of exquisite beauty, who could have had anybody, and for two worrying years probably had.

Auntie Kate could not have forgotten that she had been a farmer's wife, taking jam to the sick, running W.I. stalls, making Low Farm a haven of good humour. But had she forgotten that she had been the sun rising in the morning? Had she forgotten that she had been the laughter that had rolled round the high fells and merged with the chuckling of the River Mither? Now she was an elderly lady, doting on her grandson.

Henry felt really mean about finding the past so much more exciting than the present.

That evening he found exciting, as Martin drove steadily up the winding, narrow road towards Rowth Bridge. Memories flooded back.

There were seven houses now, in the hamlet of Five Houses. A teenage boy leant against a wall on his bike, and turned to stare at them. Was this the boy, whose name he had forgotten, into whose clammy, frightened hand he had dug his nails?

Martin drove past the tiny school, where there were new

lavatories, past the Parish Hall, where there still wasn't a new piano, and over the hump-backed bridge. How tiny the houses were.

Martin drove through the village and up towards the head of the dale. To Henry's relief, the hills at least hadn't shrunk.

When they reached the track that led to Low Farm, they got out and stared at Henry's old home. It meant so little to the others, so much to Henry.

The cows were being led in by Simon, who waved at them. The cows were black-and-white Friesians. The shorthorns had gone. Billy, the half-wit, had gone. Uncle Frank and Auntie Kate had gone. Henry wanted to go.

Forewarned, the landlady of the Three Horseshoes gave them a ham and egg tea.

Simon arrived in the bar at ten to seven, with a demure, well-scrubbed, rather quiet, dark-haired, square-faced, nit-free girl, who would make him a grand wife, three healthy children and many excellent dinners. Could this really be Pam Yardley, that Hun of yesteryear?

'Lorna'll be here about eight,' said Simon with a grin.

Henry shook his head. If he struck a chord in her memory, it was far better that it remained there.

A burly young man entered with a noisy group, and said, 'Hello,' to Henry.

'Who's he?' whispered Henry.

'Jane Lugg,' whispered Simon.

'That's a girl?' said Stefan.

They hissed at him to shut up. He smiled and downed a pint in one gulp.

Henry bought Jane Lugg a drink and they tried to find memories in common.

'I bet the wages here are well below what I'd call a dignified living,' said Martin.

Henry was totally unprepared for the tall, slender, toothy, husky, lisping sexuality of Lorna Arrow. She coloured as she talked to him, and her small but shapely breasts heaved.

'I were heart-broken when tha threw me over,' she said to Henry. 'I cried for months.'

'Give over,' he said. 'I wouldn't throw you over now, Lorna.'

'Why's that?' she said.

'You've become a great beauty,' he said.

'You haven't,' she said.

'I know,' he said.

'Tha's still my Henry,' she said. 'Does tha remember t' barn where tha used to read t' comics to me?'

'Course I do.'

'It's still there.'

Their legs rubbed together as they walked. The sun had long disappeared beneath the hills, and the evening light was blue. They walked round to the back of the village, and up to Kit Orris's field barn. Swallows and house-martins were gathering on the telegraph wires, and there were clouds of midges.

Inside, the barn was dark and sweet with rotting crops.

'We should have brought comics wi' us,' chuckled Lorna.

'I don't want to read tonight,' protested Henry.

'There's better things to do,' grinned Lorna.

'Oh, Lorna,' he gasped.

'Which would you prefer?' she queried. 'A fortnight's coach tour of Finland with the W.I., or me taking all my clothes off?'

She removed what few clothes she had on with all the grace with which a female gazelle would remove its clothes, if it wore any.

Henry undressed hurriedly, clumsily, and she laughed.

Her body was long, pale and exquisite in the dim light.

She put her bare feet on his, and pressed her naked body against his.

'You're hurting,' he cried urgently.

'Sorry,' she whispered softly.

'You're lovely,' he mouthed gently.

'Oh, Henry,' she lisped breathily.

'Oh, heck,' he ejaculated prematurely.

Breakfast at the Crown Inn, Troutwick, was an affair of mixed emotions, although George and Edna were hospitality personified.

Henry's emotions were of satisfaction, relief and pride. After their unfortunate start, events in the barn had proceeded much more successfully. He had lost his virginity at last. The first of two long journeys was over, and he could face the second, that of adult life itself, with more confidence than had at one time seemed possible.

Paul was disgruntled, because Stefan had been so wild, and Simon so quietly rural, and Martin so grumpily political, and Henry had deserted him.

Martin was disgruntled, because he had been driving his father's car, and he was a responsible young man, and so he had had to remain sober, and Stefan had been so wild, and Simon so quietly rural, and Paul so infuriatingly detached and complacent, and Henry had deserted him.

The waitress handed them their egg, bacon, sausage, fried bread and tomato.

'That'll put hairs on your chest,' she said.

Paul stared at her in astonishment.

'If you found out that waitress's hours and wages, you'd be shocked,' said Martin.

Paul groaned and imitated the winding up of a gramophone.

'It's all right for people like you,' said Martin angrily. 'Your father gets more in a week than these people earn in a year.'

'It's not my fault,' said Paul.

'Echoing the parrot cry of the German people,' said Martin.

'Please don't mention parrots,' said Henry.

'People like you make me sick,' said Martin, and he tipped his breakfast plate over Paul and strode from the room.

Paul sat immobile, deathly white, his dignity ruptured, as a fried egg slid slowly down his face.

The waitress returned.

'I'm afraid we've had a bit of an accident,' said Henry, and the waitress agreed.

George and Edna were tolerance personified.

Paul left, to clean himself up, and Martin returned, shame-faced.

'I'm sorry,' he said. 'He got on my nerves. You agree with me, don't you?'

'I believe brain surgeons should get less money than dustmen, because their job is more rewarding in itself,' said Henry.

'My God. You're more left-wing than I am,' said Martin.

'I don't believe you should make a fool of yourself and me by throwing breakfast over my friend,' said Henry.

He was furious with them both, for destroying his mood of complacent well-being.

'I'm sorry,' said Martin. 'I get none of the fun, that's all, because of the driving.'

'We'll stay in Troutwick tonight,' said Henry.

Paul returned, white-faced, clean-shirted.

'I'm very sorry, Paul,' said Martin.

'Oh, that's all right,' said Paul airily. 'These things happen.'

'If you're so unwise as to consort with the lower orders,' said Martin.

'I didn't say that,' said Paul. 'Do you want a breakfast over you?'

'Shut up,' screamed Henry. 'We've only got one week, and it's falling apart.'

'That's why it's falling apart,' said Paul.

Stefan appeared, comically hung-over, a parody of bloodshot vulnerability.

'What happened last night" he said.

'You bet ten bob that Jane Lugg was a boy,' said Martin.

Stefan groaned.

'She undressed on the bridge,' said Paul. 'You lost.'

'Narrowly,' said Martin. 'After a recount.'

'Give over,' said Henry. 'I like Jane Lugg.'

He could afford to be generous. Suddenly roles were reversed. He was a man, and they were behaving like children.

Stefan laughed.

'I really am terrible,' he said. 'I must get a grip on myself. No more drinking. What are we doing tonight?'

'Pub crawling in Troutwick,' said Henry.

'Fantastic,' said Stefan Prziborski.

They started their pub-crawl at the White Hart, the two-star hotel on the main square. The eponymous beast stood proudly upon a handsome Georgian porch.

They ended their pub-crawl at the White Hart.

The reason why they spent the whole evening in the White Hart was the landlady. She was Auntie Doris.

It couldn't be.

It was.

She smelt like a perfume factory.

She was staring at him, her sunburnt face going as white as it ever could.

'Auntie Doris!'

'I dreaded this might happen,' she said.

'What are you doing here?'

'It's a long story, perhaps best not told.'

Auntie Doris poured their drinks. She still looked glamorous. She was unvanquishable. But there was a difference. She looked as if she had suffered.

'Is Uncle Teddy here?' he asked.

Auntie Doris shook her head.

'Stay on and I'll explain everything,' she said.

Everything?

A tall man with a long face and bags under his eyes joined Auntie Doris behind the bar. He was dourness personified.

'When did you come back from Rangoon?' said Henry.

'Rangoon?' said the dour barman. 'Rangoon?'

'This is my nephew, Henry, Bert,' said Auntie Doris. 'I just want to have a word with you about something.'

She practically pulled Bert out of the bar.

Everybody looked at Henry in astonishment. He spread his arms in a gesture of helplessness.

'I don't know what's going on,' he said.

They played darts. The room was bare, basic, unlovely. Tomorrow he would see Lorna again. Today he should be enjoying a pub-crawl. But sands were shifting under his feet. How could he relax?

'Let's move on,' said Stefan.

'I can't really,' he said. 'It's all right here.'

'It's dreadful,' said Martin. 'It's as if they thought they ought to have a public bar, for ordinary people, but it isn't worth any bother.'

'The chip on your shoulder's showing,' said Paul.

'I'm about fed up with you two,' said Henry. 'Now come on. If you want to go somewhere else, go. I've got to stay here.'

'Ask your aunt how much barmaids get paid,' said Martin.

Stefan bought four more beers. The dour barman served him. A rather desultory game of 301 proceeded on the badly maintained darts board. The darts were blunt.

'Henry Pratt! Let me look at you!'

A large, shapeless, elderly woman filled the doorway. A tuft of grey hair sprouted from her middle chin, and her moustache was grey as well. She held a glass of pink gin.

Paul, Martin and Stefan gawped.

'Miss Candy!'

She advanced, and enveloped him briefly in a mighty embrace.

'I was in the lounge. Doris told me about her nephew Henry, who went to school at Rowth Bridge. I thought, "That's my Henry Pratt." Well well. Well well.'

Miss Candy examined him. Was it just his imagination, or was she disappointed by what she saw?

'It's your throw, Henry,' said Martin.

'I'll just finish my game,' said Henry. 'Then I'll join you in the lounge.'

Miss Candy departed.

'What is this strange magic you have over women, Henry?' said Stefan.

After the game (another defeat!), Henry joined Miss Candy in the lounge, which looked like a cross between a bar and an antique shop. She bought him a drink.

'This is my corner,' she said, plonking herself onto an old settle with some difficulty. 'Here I merge into all the other antiques. I'm retired now, but I still have my motor-bike.'

He told her the story of his life, and of his exam results, which had been slightly above average. His inexplicable feeling that he was failing her persisted.

He bought her a pink gin. They reminisced about war-time life in Rowth Bridge, and their visit to Leeds v Bradford at Elland Road. He told her about Tommy Marsden.

'Do you remember that I asked you what people said about me?' said Miss Candy.

'Yes. It was pretty awful,' said Henry.

'I know, but I needed to know,' said Miss Candy. 'I needed to know, you see. I remember everything you said. How fervently I wish that most of it had been true.' She caught him glancing at her glass, and shook her head. 'No. I don't drink a bottle of gin a day. Not quite. I can't afford to. But I did love a Yank, who went home and left me broken-hearted. Well, she's returned.'

He looked at her in surprise. Her eyes were moist with tears.

'The one unusual thing about my whole life is that I am a Lesbian, and you missed it,' she said. 'I don't suppose you even knew what a Lesbian is. Anyway, she's come back, and I'm so happy.'

Miss Candy began to cry. Henry had noticed that people often did cry, when they said they were happy.

Miss Candy blew her nose and apologised.

'My friend's waiting for me,' she said. 'My friend doesn't like pubs. I must go. My friend is very particular about time. It's something to do with her being from the New World, I think. Well, dear Henry, that was a surprise, to. . .er. . .see how you've turned out. Yes.'

'How long has Auntie Doris been here?' said Henry.

'Oh. I don't know. Two years? Three years? Ask her.'

Miss Candy went back to her friend. Henry went back to his friends. Two years? Three years? Shifting sands became quicksands. The pub filled up. Auntie Doris was too busy to speak to him. But she must speak to him.

At closing time Auntie Doris boomed, 'Thank you very much, ladies and gentlemen. Your empties now, please, my lovelies.'

'You can all stay,' Auntie Doris told the four boys, 'but in the lounge. I have to talk to Henry.'

'We haven't got a key to get in,' said Martin.

'Where are you staying?' said Auntie Doris.

'The Crown.'

'No problem. I'll invite George and Edna over. They're sociability personified.'

Martin, Paul and Stefan brought a set of dominoes into the lounge. Auntie Doris told them which table they could use. It was the only one that wasn't an antique. Martin had hiccups. Stefan seemed to have exhausted his wildness.

Four residents and two other locals stayed on. The dour barman remained, and Auntie Doris took Henry to the alcove, beside the great hearth.

Henry had drunk quite a lot of beer, but he felt as sober as an undertaker's tie.

'Miss Candy says you've been here two or three years,' he said. Auntie Doris sighed.

'I have,' she said.

'But what about Uncle Teddy? What about Rangoon?'

'We never went to Rangoon. Uncle Teddy's in prison,' she said in a low voice.

'Prison?'

'S'sssh! I'm sorry.' Auntie Doris blushed. 'I'm sorry. It must sound awfully hypocritical. Nobody here knows, you see.'

'Prison? What for?' he whispered.

'Business offences.'

'Business offences?'

'You know. Tax evasion. Evading currency restrictions. Fraud. Theft. Receiving stolen goods. Business offences.'

Auntie Doris almost lurched in her seat, and Henry realised that she was drunk.

'He didn't want you to know,' she said. 'He was terribly ashamed of himself, in front of you.'

Now it was the turn of Auntie Doris's eyes to fill with tears. He thought he had cracked the problem of women at last, and now here they were bursting into tears all around him.

'I'm sorry,' she gasped.

He looked up and saw the three dominoes players peering in his direction. He tried to quell their curiosity with a look. Martin still had hiccups.

George and Edna arrived. Auntie Doris got them a drink, refilled Henry's and her glasses and hurriedly explained that she was having a private talk with Henry, her nephew. George and Edna were understanding personified.

'He comes out next year.' said Auntie Doris in a near-whisper, after she'd returned with their drinks.

'But you wrote to me from Rangoon,' he said.

Auntie Doris shook her head.

'I forwarded them to a friend in Rangoon,' she said. 'He sent them on.'

The penny dropped.

'I know who it was,' he said. 'Geoffrey Porringer.'

'Speaking about me?'

Henry looked up, to see Geoffrey Porringer standing over him, immaculate in evening dress.

'You remember Henry, Geoffrey,' said Auntie Doris.

'Oh yes,' said Geoffrey Porringer. 'I remember Henry.'

'Good do?' said Auntie Doris.

'No!' said Geoffrey Porringer. 'These dos are all the same. Be with you in two shakes.'

Henry's mind reeled as he looked at Auntie Doris. Suddenly it was all obvious to him. Coming upon Geoffrey Porringer at Cap Ferrat. All the Canadian stamps. She'd probably even spent the night with him in Bruton, when she'd taken him to Dalton and Geoffrey had taken his brat to Bruton. He felt ashamed of his naivety. How they must have laughed at him. He recalled buying coasters with him in Sheffield, and his cheeks burned. How they must have hooted.

'I'm sorry, darling,' said Auntie Doris. 'We didn't want you to know, my love.'

'I bought coasters for you.'

'They're very nice. Very suitable.'

His head was beginning to swim. Another thought hurled itself at him.

'What'll you do when he comes out of prison?' he said.

'I don't know,' said Auntie Doris. 'I just don't know, Henry.'

'You've got to go back to him,' he said. 'You've got to, Auntie Doris.'

'I never knew you liked him so much,' said Auntie Doris. 'He never knew you did.'

Did I? Or am I solely inspired by loathing for Geoffrey Porringer?

'A refill, young feller-me-lad?' said Geoffrey Porringer, returning in shirt-sleeves.

Henry shook his head. The clicking of dominoes continued.

The dour barman looked pointedly as his watch. Geoffrey Porringer brought drinks for himself and Auntie Doris.

'Come on,' said Geoffrey Porringer thickly, and Henry realised that he was drunk as well. 'Smile. It may never happen.'

'It has happened,' said Henry.

Oh no. He had written, in a letter, that he had prayed for a cure for Geoffrey Porringer's blackheads. Oh God. He hoped she hadn't shown the letter to. . .no he didn't. He hoped she had shown it.

He smiled.

'That's better,' said Geoffrey Porringer. 'No need to take it too hard. Life, eh? I mean, let's be brutally honest. What did Teddy ever do for you?'

'Geoffrey!' said Auntie Doris.

'He took me into his home and treated me as his son, to the best of his abilities,' said Henry.

'Only because he felt guilty because he thought he caused your father's death when he sacked him,' said Geoffrey Porringer.

'Geoffrey,' hissed Auntie Doris, who always made things worse by protesting about them. 'He doesn't know his father hanged himself.'

13 The End of the Beginning

It was Thursday, September 3rd 1953. The weather was cool and showery. Henry was on his way to join the Royal Corps of Signals at Catterick, sick at heart, sick at the grim prospect, sick at the interference with his freedom just when he was on the verge of manhood, sick at the waste of his childhood. It was the only youth he would ever have. It was gone.

The train clattered across the flat farming country of central Yorkshire. It was full of raw, clumsy, nervous young men. Henry read the newspaper frantically, in an attempt to take his mind off his worries. 'West to Russia: Talk it over.' 'Oil hopes are brighter.' 'Her baby born on platform four.' His had been a fragmented childhood, and he didn't know that an obsessive reading of newspapers in times of crisis, inherited from his father, was linking this, its last day, to the day when he was born. 'Dulles gives Mao two warnings.' 'Dustman dies in shrubbery.' 'Across Canada by tandem.'

The local train from Darlington crept closer and closer to the eastern edge of the Pennines, the backbone of England. 'Anti-burglar grille stolen.' 'More tinned milk is withdrawn.' He'd spent so much time being reluctant to escape from wombs. He hadn't realised that all the wombs and all the births had taken place within the protection of the great superwomb of youth. It was from this that he was now finally, at last, irrevocably to be born. 'Anna, the stay-put char, is back.' 'Feud splits a sleepy village.' 'Italy is a wonderful country, but it's no place to have an accident.' Italy. Lampo. Dalton. Paul. Diana. Lorna. Too many memories, too many partings, close your mind to all that. 'Mormon (he had 21 children) dies at 83.' 'When the army says "report", the pianist must change his tune.' Army. There's no escape even in the newspaper.

The line was among the hills now. Cows chewed peacefully,

infuriatingly unaware that this was a special day for anybody.

They were slowing down. There was a mass collection of scanty belongings, and then they were streaming onto the platform of Richmond station, a tidal wave of stick-out ears

Step out of the womb, Henry. It may not be as bad as you think.

The wind was cold. He moved slowly, in short steps, with the sluggish human tide.

Be brave, Henry Be positive. You have made so many disastrous starts, but you are older and wiser now.

Show them, Henry.

'You! What do you think you're doing?'

The words seemed far away, so that he only heard them a few seconds after they had been spoken.

'Oh sorry, were you speaking to me?' he said. 'I didn't hear you. I was thinking.'

He found that he was staring at a bull-like neck, in the middle of the station forecourt. He raised his eyes to the face, and suppressed a shudder.

'You were what????' bawled the massive sergeant. 'You were thinking? You're in the army now, laddie. What's your name?'

Here we go.

'Pratt.'

'Pratt. You know what you are, Pratt? You're a short fat blob of rancid turbot droppings. What are you?'

Henry stood as proud and erect as he could. He looked the sergeant straight in the face. He was unaware of the cold wind, the damp station forecourt, the waiting trucks.

'I'm a man, sergeant,' he said.

Pratt of the Argus

The second Henry Pratt novel

For all the journalists of the provincial press, and especially for my ex-colleagues on the *Sheffield Star*. They were kinder to me than I deserved, and, in gratitude for that, are spared from these pages, where all the characters are totally imaginary, as indeed is the town of Thurmarsh.

Contents

1   A Night to Forget

Henry Pratt stared in disbelief at the first word that he had ever had in print. It was 'Thives'.

The full story read, 'Thives who last night broke into the Blurton Road home of Mrs Emily Braithwaite (73) stole a coat, a colander and a jam jar containing £5 in threepenny bits.'

Henry was twenty years old, pale, rather short, somewhat podgy. He had just completed his first day as a reporter on the *Thurmarsh Evening Argus*, and was sitting with three of his new colleagues at a corner table in the back bar of the Lord Nelson, a brown, masculine pub, tucked away in Leatherbottlers' Row. The back bar was a dark and secret room, popular with barristers, police officers and criminals. It smelt of carbolic and male intrigue. No juke-boxes or fruit machines disturbed the concentration of the drinkers. Trams could be heard clanking along Albion Street, and two elderly ham sandwiches were curling together for comfort in a glass case on the bar counter. You wouldn't have been able to find a slice of quiche this side of Alsace-Lorraine. It was Monday, January 16th, 1956.

He glanced through the paper, pretending that he was interested in it all, not just the one paragraph that he had written. Employment in Thurmarsh had reached a record level, with only 0.3 per cent out of work. Lieutenant-Colonel Nasser was claiming fresh powers for six years under a new constitution in Egypt. King Hussein had pledged Jordan to the cause of Arab unity. Henry didn't fool Neil Mallet. 'Never mind,' said Neil, his round, smooth, incipiently freckled face breaking into a brief, friendly smile. 'I didn't set the world alight on my first day, and look at me now. Half the West Riding hangs on my words.' Neil Mallet, a bachelor, of Pitlochry Drive, Thurmarsh Lane Bottom, wrote a weekly opinion column under the pen-name of 'Thurmarshian'.

Ted Plunkett raised his bushy black eyebrows that might have been purpose-built for sarcasm and said, 'It's true, Henry. From Barnsley to Dronfield, from Penistone to Maltby they're agog for his smug, reactionary views.' He turned to Neil. 'Murderers sent to the gallows by judges who've just read your virulent prose are the only people who hang on your words.'

Neil Mallet smiled benevolently. Henry's heart sank. He couldn't cope with Ted Plunkett. Were the doubters right? Was he unsuited to the hard world of journalism?

He might not have been so overawed if he'd known that Ted wrote the Kiddies Club column. The kiddies were known as the Argusnauts and did good deeds. Ted was known as Uncle Jason.

Henry replied to Neil, as if Ted hadn't spoken. 'I know,' he said, 'but a misprint in my first word! Are they trying to tell me something?' He'd often found self-deprecation useful. At school he'd become a stand-up comedian, Henry 'Ee by gum I am daft' Pratt, in order to mock himself before others did. But now it was his ambition to become Henry 'I was the first British journalist to enter the seething hell-hole that was Dien Bien Phu' Pratt, and he sensed that self-deprecation would no longer be useful to him. He ploughed on through the paper. A floating elevator costing £300,000 had been kept idle in Hull docks for three months because of a dispute over manning levels. 100 shivering people had queued all night to book summer coach holidays to Torquay. Eggs were down to 3s. 9d. a dozen. Would he ever write exciting stories like those?

'Same again?' said the third of his new colleagues, Colin Edgeley, who was writing a novel, had lost two front teeth in a fight, and had kept the gap as a badge of courage.

Henry ought to be getting back for his tea, but how could he, on his first day? One thing he wasn't going to become was Henry 'I'm not stopping. I've gorra get back for my tea' Pratt.

Helen Cornish, general reporter and women's page, breezed in with Ben Watkinson, the football correspondent. Ben was tall and thin and grizzled. Helen wasn't. She said, 'Room for a little one?' and sat beside Henry on the bench seat. Their thighs were touching. He grew excited. She was fair-haired, with pearly grey eyes and pert, delicate lips. Already he found her so attractive that even the sight of the words 'By Helen Cornish' under the headline 'What the stars wear next to their skin' had given him an erection. He wondered what Helen wore next to her skin. This was ridiculous. Ben's left hand had just brushed her right knee. They were probably married. Women did sometimes marry the most unsuitable men. And didn't he have his childhood sweetheart, Lorna Arrow, whose existence had nourished him through two years in the army? He hadn't clung to the thought of her throughout that business in Germany in order to abandon her now. He met Ted's deep, dark, troubled eyes and had an uneasy feeling that Ted could read his thoughts.

They drank halves, which in Thurmarsh were referred to as glasses. You drank more that way, because the beer kept fresher. Henry tried to say, 'No thanks, Ben. I said I'd be back for my tea,' but the words wouldn't come.

Neil had been to London and seen *Waiting for Godot*. Henry said, 'Oh, *I've* seen that,' and Neil said, 'What did you think of it?' Henry wanted to say, 'Magnificent! I think Beckett's a giant, sweeping theatrical realism under the carpets of the bourgeoisie,' but he was frightened of sounding pretentious so he said, 'I quite liked it.' 'I thought it was magnificent,' said Neil. 'Beckett's a giant, emptying the fag-ends of realism into the overflowing dustbins of the middle classes.' Ted raised his bushy eyebrows. 'Go to London a lot, do you?' he asked Henry.

Fleet Street was their magnet. At forty, Ben knew he'd never make it. At thirty-four, Neil suspected he wouldn't. At twenty-seven, Ted still hoped. At twenty-four, Colin had few doubts. At twenty-two, Helen had no doubts at all.

Henry bought his round, fighting his way through a burst of dutiful laughter at a joke cracked by Chief Superintendent Ron Ratchett. Helen was on gin and orange. He longed to kiss her slightly sticky tongue. No! Think of Friday night. Think of Lorna.

'Do you have any good contacts, Henry?' asked Ted.

'Contacts?' he said, puzzled.

'People you know whom you can use to get stories off,' explained Ted, as to a rather dim Argusnaut.

'Oh!' he said. 'Yes. I see. No. Well, I've been away, in the army.'

'Which Thurmarsh United player broke his leg in three places?' said Ben, and although it was apropos of absolutely nothing, nobody seemed surprised.

Henry knew the answer, but kept silent. He sensed that Helen despised sport.

'Reg Putson,' said Helen.

'Correct,' said Ben. 'Which three places did he break his leg in?'

'Halifax, Barrow and Wrexham,' said Helen.

'Correct.'

It was like a double act. They *were* married.

'You're keen on football, Helen?' said Henry, carefully hiding his surprise.

'Don't sound so surprised,' said Helen. 'I support Stockport County.'

'I'm a great United fan,' said Henry. 'I know Tommy Marsden.'

They all gawped at him.

'You know Tommy Marsden?' said Colin Edgeley.

'We were at school together. We were in the same gang.'

'Then you do have a contact,' said Ted Plunkett pityingly. 'Tommy Marsden.'

'Rapidly rising star in the Third Division (North) firmament,' said Ben Watkinson.

Tommy Marsden had been Henry's one good social card. He had played it so ineptly that it had become a revelation of his journalistic naïvety. He fell silent, and another half of bitter appeared, just as he was about to go.

'Time I was off,' said Ben. 'Got to go home and give the wife one.'

Joy and fear swept through Henry. Ben Watkinson was married to somebody else. Helen Cornish was free. Deeply though he loved Lorna Arrow, he couldn't help acknowledging that Helen was more beautiful. She was also more sophisticated. She was also nearer. In fact their thighs were still touching, even though there was more room now Ben had gone.

He wanted to start a private conversation with her, but couldn't think how. She did it for him. 'Do you have any brothers or sisters, Henry?' she asked.

'No. I'm an only child.'

'What about family?'

'My mother was knocked down by a bus and my father hanged himself in the outside lavatory.'

Oh no! At last they were talking, and he had produced the conversation stopper to stop all conversation stoppers.

She said, 'Oh, I'm sorry,' and touched his thigh briefly. His leg tingled. He resisted an absurd temptation to say, 'Why? It wasn't your fault.' He floundered on. 'I was brought up by this uncle and aunt. Then he went to . . . er . . . Rangoon, and I went to this other relative.' He asked her about her family and was too aroused to listen to her reply. He became aware that Ted was speaking.

'Sorry, Ted,' he said. 'What was that?'

'I said you seem to be getting on very well with my fiancée.'

Greenhorn reporter in fiancée blunder. Henry was terrified that he was going to blush. 'I am,' he said. His voice sounded small and far away. 'She's a lovely girl. You're a lucky man.'

He inched carefully away from Helen. The loneliness flooded over him again. For two years he had counted the days till the end of his national service. And then, ever since it had ended, ever since Cousin Hilda had met him at Thurmarsh (Midland Road) Station, sniffing with suppressed love like a truffle-hound with a bad cold, how he had missed them. Not only Brian Furnace. Not only Michael Collinghurst. All of them. Taffy Bevin, Lanky Lasenby, Geordie Stubbs. Even Fishy Fisk, who smelt of herrings. He'd been counting the hours till the nakedness of Lorna Arrow, and Cousin Hilda had whisked him away to a boarding house in Bridlington! She'd meant well. The rain had never kept them in all day, Mrs Flixborough had three jigsaws with very few pieces missing, the white horses breaking over the groyne had been really rather spectacular, and Cousin Hilda had been right to rebuke him for his meanness in laughing when the floral clock had flooded. Then, at last, Lorna. Husky, lisping, toothy Lorna. Brief moments in the hay, in Kit Orris's dry-stone field barn. Shyness. Doubts. Climaxes. Anti-climaxes. Desolate rattling train journeys from Troutwick to Cousin Hilda, changing at Leeds. A visit to London to see Paul Hargreaves, his old chum from Dalton College. No Diana. Paul's luscious, chunky sister Diana was skiing at Davos. 'What play would you like to see, Henry?' The sophisticated Hargreaveses had scorned his suggestion of *Separate Tables*. They'd gone to *Waiting for Godot*. Several people had walked out, but Dr Hargreaves had said, 'Beckett is a giant, sweeping theatrical realism under the carpets of the bourgeoisie. Rattigan is only fit to wait at the table where Beckett eats,' and Henry had said, 'Is Rattigan waiting for Godot at the separate tables where Beckett eats?' and everybody had laughed, but not quite enough, at Paul's funny little northern friend. *Waiting for Godot*, *La Strada*, daube Provençale, and sexual frustration. Then more Lorna. But his two years in the army had begun to institutionalize him, and the loneliness had lurked throughout those last, long months of 1955.

Ted's lovely fiancée bought him a drink, so he couldn't refuse that, and she looked him straight in the eyes, almost as if she were regretting being engaged, and Ted gleamed dangerously under his mass of black hair behind his cool, firm glass of beer. Henry hurried off to the toilet, to read again the letter from Lorna, and relieve himself of his desire for this new, dangerous, unavailable woman.

Podgy Sex Bomb Henry sat in the icy cubicle. On the door a closet wit had written: 'God is alive and well and working on a less ambitious project.' Henry liked that.

> Dere Henry [he read]
> I carn't wate for Friday nite. I'm rite excited. It'll be the first time I've ever done it in a hottel and it'll be nice singing in as mister and misses! It were luvly in the barn but it'll be grate not having all that hay being verry tickellish as you now. I'll be on the 5.40 from Leeds so I'll be their at 6.32 as you said. Eric Lugg's got leave from the Cattering Corpse and wants me to go out with him this weakened. Tuff luck! Sorry Eric I've better things to do! This is quiet a long letter for me so I'll stop now.
> With luv and kisses as ever
> You're Lorna

It didn't matter if Lorna couldn't spell. It didn't matter that all the journalists would laugh if they read her letter. He hated snobbery and it was a luvly letter. 'Oh, Lorna, Lorna,' he moaned silently, but it was no use, it was Helen Cornish whose superb pointed breasts hung down towards his naked body as they writhed in ecstasy on the subs' table, in the vast, empty news-room of his mind.

He returned, a little calmer, a little wearier. He sipped his beer. He remembered, with muffled alarm, his waiting tea. Ted and Helen set off for the Shanghai Chinese Restaurant and Coffee Bar, which served glutinous curries, haystacky chop sueys and frothy coffee. Now the lights in the pub seemed dimmer than ever.

He accepted a drink off Neil. Well, if he left as soon as Helen had gone, it would look a bit obvious, it would be a bit rude to Neil and Colin.

'I must go in a minute,' said Neil. 'I've some laundry to do.'

Henry, who had never left licensed premises because he had laundry to do, gave Neil a look of sheer astonishment. 'I must go too,' he said. If he missed that cue, he'd be stuck for the night.

'So must I,' said Colin, 'or Glenda'll kill me.'

'Glenda?'

'My wife.'

Henry was surprised to discover that Colin was married.

Suddenly Colin spoke in a low, tense voice, dramatic and excited. 'Hey,' he said. 'Don't look now, but there's a feller by t'door that got put away because of my evidence. He's sworn revenge. Mick Tunstall. He's gorra knife.'

'Oh I say,' said Neil.

Henry looked towards the door. Two Neanderthal giants with prison haircuts were sitting there. All the police had gone.

'Don't look,' hissed Colin. 'That man is a bonfire of hatred, and he's tinder-dry. One spark, that's all it needs.'

Henry wondered if he looked as pale as Neil.

'Right,' said Colin. 'What we do is, we walk out together, looking normal. We don't look at Mick. Then we walk down the alley into Albion Street, not hurrying. If he sees you're scared . . . and don't worry, kids.' He opened his right fist, revealing a handful of sharp-edged coins. A thin line of sweat had broken out on Neil's forehead. It looked as if it were seeping through a fault in his skin's crust.

They stood up, self-consciously.

'Look normal,' whispered Colin.

Henry tried to walk out normally, at normal pace, with head held high, but not abnormally so. His heart was thumping. He felt sure that they looked so abnormally normal as to be utterly ridiculous. He walked down the dark, narrow alley into Albion Street, longing to break into a run. Then he looked round, with failed nonchalance. Nobody was following them. Nobody saw his failed nonchalance.

'Well done!' said Colin.

Neil hurried off, towards his laundry. Henry and Colin walked down Albion Street. The night was cold. The street lamps cast a dim, mournful light over the dirty stone and brick of the Victorian shops and offices. Above the ground-floor displays, the rows of small, regular grime-streaked windows were dark. Nobody lived in Albion Street.

'How about a quick one at the Globe and Artichoke?' suggested Colin.

Henry tried to say, 'I'm hours late for my tea,' but, since Colin might say, 'In that case a few minutes more won't make any difference' he said, 'What about Glenda?' When Colin said, 'Glenda won't mind. She's all right,' Henry felt that he'd been outmanoeuvred. He was glad he'd been outmanoeuvred.

They turned into High Street, between piles of discoloured snow, and entered a yellow-painted pub. There were dirty red walls, and the frayed flock-paper was almost covered in theatre bills. A few customers were reading the *Argus*. Colin talked about his novel. Denzil Ackerman, the arts editor, had read the first five chapters and thought he could be the second D. H. Lawrence. Henry felt happy, although he was a little disappointed that none of the readers of the *Argus* said, 'Good Lord! Thives have broken into the home of Mrs Emily Braithwaite.' But then none of them said, 'Hello. I see Hussein has pledged Jordan to Arab unity' either. He was also disappointed when Colin said, 'Sorry about that business with Mick, but don't worry. You're all right with me, kid. I'll look after you.' He said, 'I don't want to be looked after, Colin. I'm norra kid.' He talked about when he *was* a kid. He felt vaguely guilty about revealing what should have been deeply private, about feeling pride in relating what should have been purely tragic. Colin got quite excited when he learnt that Henry had drunk with Tommy Marsden in a pub from which his father had earlier been banned for life.

'That's the stuff,' he said. 'Come on.'

Henry found himself in the street. Colin yelled, 'Taxi!' A taxi slithered towards them over the crumbling grey town-centre snow.

'The Navigation,' said Colin.

On the one hand, a dried-up tea and duty. On the other hand, adventure, spontaneity, friendship with the second D. H. Lawrence, the Bohemian life, Thurmarsh style. No contest!

The polluted and fetid courses of the River Rundle and the Rundle and Gadd Navigation took a great loop on the south-eastern side of the town, but the main Rawlaston road went straight up out of the valley, past the great fortress of Brunswick Road Primary School, which Henry had once attended. The taxi breasted the rise and slithered down again, past a stranded trolley bus, past the Pineapple and other small, friendly pubs, back towards the river and the canal, back towards Henry's past.

Henry paid for the taxi. It was Monday, and already Colin was broke.

How small the Navigation Inn was. In his memory it had been a world. They stood at the bar, in the little snug, with their backs to the smoked-glass Victorian window. The tiny fire roared. There was the peaceful clack of dominoes. The green upholstery that Henry's father had so resented had gone. The bench seats were red now, and they squeaked.

They ordered glasses of Ward's Malt Ales, and whisky chasers.

'Where did Tommy sit?' whispered Colin.

Henry pointed to an empty seat. Colin sat in it, gave an almost shy, gap-toothed smile, and sighed contentedly. His dark brown hair was receding. His face already bore the coarsening ravages of life, but when he smiled he looked like a child.

Henry recognized Sid Lowson and nodded to him. Sid Lowson nodded back, his face as blank as the domino with which he closed up the game, to the unconcealed chagrin of Fred Shilton, the lock-keeper. Nowhere do we feel such strangers as in our own pasts.

Yet somebody almost remembered Henry. 'Don't I know you?' said Cecil E. Jenkinson, the landlord, towering paunchily over them.

'I'm Henry Pratt,' said Henry. 'I'm Ezra's boy.'

'Get out of here,' said Cecil E. Jenkinson, licensed to remember old grudges. 'You're the bastard who got me banned for allowing under-age drinking. Out! You're banned for life, sunshine.'

Cecil E. Jenkinson lifted Henry out of his seat and began to propel him towards the door. Colin rushed to the rescue. 'Take your hands off my mate,' he said, grabbing the landlord's lapel. 'Nobody pushes my oppo around.'

'Colin!' said Henry. 'It'll be in the paper.'

'Good. I'll write it meself,' said Colin.

Colin began to pull Cecil E. Jenkinson off Henry.

'Barry!' thundered the landlord.

Barry Jenkinson, the landlord's far from brilliant but unquestionably bulky son, was soon at his father's side. They bundled the flailing young journalist out of the pub together, paunchy father and massive son. Henry followed willingly, shaking his head at Sid Lowson, indicating that reinforcements wouldn't be needed. Henry felt no anger, as if Colin were angry enough for both of them. Besides, these were old battles, fought and lost for ever long ago.

The Jenkinsons threw Colin down onto the snow-covered cobbles. They wiped their hands in unison, as if removing contamination. They glared at Henry, and returned to their tiny kingdom.

'Bastards!' shouted Colin. 'I'll get you!'

'Come on,' said Henry. 'Let's go home.'

A thin yellow mist was rising over the valley as they waited for a tram under the great blank wall of Crapp, Hawser and Kettlewell, the huge steelworks, opposite the tiny cul-de-sac of wine-red back-to-back houses, where Henry had been born.

'Dinna thee worry,' said Colin, as they staggered up the narrow stairs of the tram. 'I'll look after you, kid.'

'I've told you,' said Henry. 'I don't want to be looked after. I'm norra kid.'

'OK,' said Colin. 'OK. I'll make sure nobody looks after you. Anybody tries to look after you, I'll punch him on the nose.'

Colin just caught the last bus to Glenda. Henry walked home from the tram terminus, in Mabberley Street. He felt that the sharp, raw air would sober him up. In this he was mistaken.

He weaved his way through the frozen gardens in front of the pseudo-Gothic town hall, Victorian confidence and plagiarism writ large in soot. Puffed up pigeons slept uneasily on ledges coated with frozen droppings. Henry stumbled along the deserted Doncaster Road. A red light warned of a hole in the road. He picked it up. This was another mistake.

'Now then,' said the police officer. 'What's all this?'

'It's dark up my road,' said Henry. 'The street lighting is frankly abdominable. Need the light, see where I'm going.'

'Name?' said the officer.

'Plunkett,' said Henry. 'Ted Plunkett.'

'Address?'

'The *Thurmarsh Evening Argus*, Thurmarsh.'

'A journalist!'

'Your powers of deduction are staggering.'

'So are you. Come with me.'

At the police station, while Henry was again giving Ted's name and address, an emergency broke out. Officers hurried off, their boots ringing on the stone floor. Panic and urgency reigned. Suddenly, Henry was alone. He walked out, a free and forgotten man.

As he approached the Alderman Chandler Memorial Park, he passed a small, whitewashed, detached late-Georgian pub called the Vine. It was set back from the road, and in the rutted snow in front of it three police cars were parked. He wondered whether to go in and say, 'Excuse me. I'm a journalist. What's going on?' He decided against it. He was tired. He was too inexperienced. He didn't want to meet the police again. A shrewd observer might notice that he was slightly inebriated. And it was probably only a late drinkers' brawl, anyway.

He fell over, and realized for the first time how drunk he was.

Number 66, Park View Road was a stone, semi-detached Victorian house, with a bay window on the ground floor. It looked blessedly dark as Henry crunched carefully through the snow on lurching tiptoe.

He turned the lock in the key . . . no, the key in the lock . . . why was he so drunk? He opened the door quietly and entered the dark, cold hall, which smelt of cabbage and linoleum. The wind must have caught the door, although there was no wind, because it slammed behind him. The hall became as flooded with light as a sixty-watt bulb could manage. The barometer said 'Changeable'. Cousin Hilda's face said 'Stormy'. She sniffed, loudly, twice.

'What's for tea?' he said, enunciating slowly, carefully. It was a stupid remark on two counts. It was past midnight, and he knew the answer anyway. Tea on Monday was liver and bacon, with boiled potatoes and cabbage, followed by rhubarb crumble.

'Never mind "what's for tea?",' said Cousin Hilda, her mouth working painfully. 'What sort of time do you call this?'

Henry stared at the barometer. 'Quarter past stormy,' he said. 'Didn't realize it was as late as that.'

He sank slowly to the floor. A stranger inside him began to laugh hysterically.

'Journalists!' said Cousin Hilda grimly.

The headline in next morning's *Daily Express* was 'Four shot dead in Thurmarsh pub massacre'. Henry would have been the first journalist on the scene, by more than half an hour.

2 Contacts

Premier House, the *Chronicle* and *Argus* building, was situated on the corner of High Street and Albion Street. It had a curved frontage in lavatorial marble. A large green dome proclaimed its importance. Henry entered with a thick head and a sense of dread.

The news-room was on the first floor. It was large, noisy and dusty. The windows were streaked with grime, and the lights were on all day, bathing the room in the brownish-yellow hue of old newspapers. There was a perpetual throb of suppressed excitement, even when nothing at all was happening. When there was a murder or a big crash, or· expenses were being filled in, the excitement became almost palpable.

The reporters sat at four rows of desks. It was like school, and Henry had been to too many schools already.

Terry Skipton, the news editor, sat behind the news desk, facing the reporters as if he were their form master. He admitted no Christian names into his puritanical world. 'Good morning, Mr *Pratt*,' he said, emphasizing the surname, as if it were a judgement.

Henry had hoped that Helen's beauty would turn out to be illusory, but it pierced him like a hard frost. He had hoped that Colin would look as if he too had experienced a heavy night but, perhaps because he always looked ravaged, he seemed untouched. The freshly laundered Neil Mallet gave him a friendly smile. So did the young woman at the desk on his right. She was less beautiful than Helen, rather big, squat-faced. She said, 'Hello. I had a day off yesterday. I'm Ginny Fenwick.' He got an erection simply because she was friendly.

He tried hard to look busy, like everyone else. The phone on Ted's desk rang, and he heard Ted say, 'That's funny. The editor wants to see me. Something about the police.'

Henry's heart sank, but he hurried over to Ted's desk.

'I'd better come too,' he said.

'You what?' said Ted.

They entered the editor's office. It was an airy room, with a wide window looking out onto the inelegant bustle of Albion Street. On the walls were framed copies of momentous editions of the *Argus* – the abdication, two coronations, the beginning and ending of two world wars, the day the circulation reached two hundred thousand. Mr Andrew Redrobe was small and neat. He looked more like a shrewd businessman than a romantic newspaperman, his nose sharpened for profits rather than elongated for sniffing out scoops. His green-topped desk was large and neat.

'What are *you* doing here?' he asked Henry, giving Ted a questioning look, which was answered with a shrug.

'All this is my fault, sir,' said Henry. Damn that 'sir'. He'd promised himself that he'd never say 'sir' again after he left the army. 'Last night I got rather drunk.'

'Oh?'

'Yes. I . . . er . . . I was . . . excited.'

'Excited?'

Mr Andrew Redrobe hadn't told them to sit down. Henry felt like a naughty schoolboy.

'Yes, sir.' Damn. 'I was carried away by the atmosphere.'

'I'm not with you. What atmosphere?' said the puzzled editor.

'Meeting my new colleagues. Talking. Drinking.'

Ted Plunkett looked almost as surprised as Mr Andrew Redrobe.

'Let's get this right,' said the editor. 'Are you saying you were excited by spending an evening with members of my editorial staff?'

'Yes, sir.' Damn.

'Good God.'

'Yes, sir.' Damn. 'I . . . er . . . I took a red light. I was arrested. Being . . . er . . . slightly . . . er . . . over the . . . er . . . I'm afraid I gave Ted's name as my own.'

'You went to five different schools, covering the whole stratum of public and private education, didn't you?' said Mr Redrobe.

'I did, yes,' admitted Henry, as if it had been his fault.

'What did I say to you last week, Ted?' said Mr Redrobe.

'"English education fails dismally to fit people for real life,"' quoted Ted.

'Precisely. You're the proof of the pudding, lad.' The editor sounded grateful to Henry for proving him right. 'You're a total mess.'

Henry didn't wish to agree and didn't dare to disagree, so he said nothing.

'I don't think we'll hear any more of this matter,' said Mr Andrew Redrobe. 'We pride ourselves on having a good relationship with the police. *But* I don't want that good relationship endangered by your juvenile antics, Henry Pratt. Do I make myself clear?'

'Very clear, sir.' Damn.

Outside, in the corridor, Henry said, 'I'm sorry, Ted.'

'No! Please!' said Ted. 'I'm flattered to find how deeply I've impinged on your consciousness.'

'Sorry.'

'*You've* impinged pretty deeply on Helen's consciousness.'

Henry went weak at the knees.

'What?'

'She thinks you're attractive. I'll never understand women.'

Ted stomped back into the news-room, just as Colin Edgeley came out.

'The editor wants to see me about last night,' said Colin grimly. 'Apparently that landlord's complained.'

The editor raised his neat eyebrows neatly at the reappearance of his most junior reporter. He listened to their tale in pained silence, once pushing a hand discreetly through his neat, Brylcreemed hair.

'Well,' he said. 'Luckily for you, which is more than you both deserve, I don't think we'll hear any more of this. We pride ourselves on having a good relationship with the licensed victuallers. *But* I want it kept that way, so . . . no more antics. You've proved yourself a good journalist, Colin. I'd hate to lose you. You haven't proved anything yet, Henry. I'd hate to lose you before you have the chance. I still think it's *possible* you could have a career in journalism.'

Neither of them spoke.

'I'd like to line all your headmasters up, Henry Pratt, and show you to them. You're a walking condemnation of the system. You're a living indictment,' said the editor.

23

Again, Henry found it impossible to say anything. Colin didn't help him out.

'You must have gone pretty close to the Vine last night, Henry,' continued Mr Redrobe. 'You didn't see anything of the incident? Nothing at the police station?'

Oh god. Don't blush. Don't give yourself away. Show some nerve.

'No, sir.' Damn. But the voice sounded steady enough. 'I think I must have got home just before it happened.'

'Mmm.' Did the editor believe him? Did it matter? His career was ruined. 'You are now going to be educated in the forcing house of the provincial press. In the school of life. In the college of the streets. I expect a vast and rapid improvement. I'll need it.'

'Yes, sir.' Damn. 'Sorry, sir.' Damn.

'Oh, get out.'

'Don't you worry, kid,' said Colin, as they walked back to the news-room. 'You'll be all right. I'll look after you.'

'Mr Pratt?' called out Terry Skipton.

Henry approached the news desk with trepidation. His nerves felt shredded. Terry Skipton had high, slightly humped shoulders, no neck at all, prominent, heavily lidded eyes and a large nose. He looked like a slightly deformed frog. Behind him, to Henry's left, was the great table round which all the sub-editors sat, honing their headlines.

'A man's phoned about a cat, Mr Pratt,' said Terry Skipton. 'Pop in on your calls, and see if you can make something of it.'

Henry's spirits leapt. His hangover was forgotten. The sixth sense of the born journalist visited him for the first time, and told him that he was about to have his first scoop.

On the tram, returning promptly for his tea, Henry tried to read the rest of the paper. A new air-raid warning had been developed by the Home Office, to protect against radioactive dust in the event of an H-Bomb attack. That was reassuring. Billy Panama, American Yo-Yo Champion, had made a personal appearance at Cockayne's in High Street, and Johnny Hepplewhite, aged 14, had become Yo-Yo Champion of Thurmarsh. That was interesting. And yet . . . again and again Henry was drawn back to page 8, as if he feared that his scoop would no longer be there.

Those readers who have lodged at 66, Park View Road will not need to be told that tea on Tuesday consisted of roast lamb, with roast potatoes and cauliflower, followed by spotted dick.

'We had an amazing run on Wensleydale today,' said Norman Pettifer, who ran the cheese counter at Cullen's. He was a slightly stooping, sallow-skinned man whose mouth was set in an expression of disappointment borne with fortitude. He had arrived at number 66 as a temporary measure, while looking for a new job and a house for his wife and family. The wife and family had never materialized. Nor had the new job. This would be his pinnacle, to be manager of the cheese counter at Cullen's, and mothered by Cousin Hilda.

'Did you indeed?' said Liam O'Reilly, the gentle, bewildered, shiny-faced, almost teetotal Irish labourer who seemed to have been at Cousin Hilda's since the beginning of time, and even that degree of conversational initiative caused him to blush with confusion.

'An amazing run? How amazing!' said Barry Frost. Norman Pettifer searched his face for signs of sarcasm. Barry Frost, Cousin Hilda's most recent 'businessman', was a junior tax inspector from Walsall, with smelly feet and a talent for amateur operatics. He was a big-boned man with large features that were not quite rugged. Henry had once met his fiancée, a strikingly attractive PE instructor from Dudley, with smelly feet and a talent for amateur operatics. Henry hoped that they and their feet would hum together through a happy life, but he did wish Barry Frost wouldn't sing the leading role from *The Desert Song* under his breath throughout tea, occasionally referring to the script at the side of his plate. Norman Pettifer spoke of the time he had seen the Lunts in the West End. Barry Frost searched his face for evidence of sarcasm.

It was warm and airless in Cousin Hilda's basement room. A fire glowed merrily in the little blue-tiled stove, but there was nothing merry about Cousin Hilda. She was thin-lipped, thick-scowled. She gave Henry an extra large portion of spotted dick, so he knew that she was still displeased with him. Once he met her eyes, and what he saw there was pain, and it shrivelled him up inside. He knew, as he forced down his concrete pudding, that he loved Cousin Hilda very much, but that he couldn't bear to live here much longer. He turned to page 8 of the *Argus*. 'When Thomas Hendrick . . .'

'Where are our manners, Henry? We don't read at table,' said Cousin Hilda.

'Barry does,' said Henry.

'Barry is paying,' hissed Cousin Hilda.

Barry Frost banged his copy of *The Desert Song* shut, and gave Henry a look that might have abashed a sizeable tribe of Rifs.

'I offered to pay, Cousin Hilda,' said Henry.

'We don't talk about money at table,' said Cousin Hilda. They didn't talk about money, sex, food, drink, pleasure, religion or politics at table. 'Besides,' she continued. 'Mr Frost has his "lines" to learn.' She sniffed as she said 'lines'. Barry Frost had replaced Tony Preece, an insurance salesman who at night became a struggling comic called Talwyn Jones, the Celtic Droll. 'What do people think my establishment is – a theatrical "digs"?' said Cousin Hilda's eloquent sniff.

Soon the three 'businessmen' were gone, and Henry faced his disappointed surrogate mother, across the corner table, among the debris of spotted dick, in the stifling basement room, with its smell of the water in which the greens had been overcooked, which Cousin Hilda, who hated waste, saved for her six sad, over watered rose bushes.

Henry was determined to say, 'I'm going to find a flat.' He also felt that he should say, 'I'm very sorry about last night.' Why couldn't he bring himself to say either of these things? Why did he say, instead, 'Did you see my scoop about the cat?'

Cousin Hilda ignored this. Her mouth was working painfully as she prepared her words. 'About last night,' she said at last. 'I don't want any repetition.'

'I'm sorry,' he mumbled gracelessly.

'All right,' said Cousin Hilda. 'You were led astray. Journalists! If your poor parents were alive today to see you become a journalist, they'd turn in their graves. They'd blame me.'

'No!'

'It's a responsibility.'

'I don't want to be a responsibility,' said Henry. 'I'm not ready for the responsibility of being a responsibility.'

'Mrs Wedderburn thinks you've turned out so well,' said Cousin Hilda. 'Only yesterday I met her in the Co-op. I won't use Cullen's. I don't like Mr Pettifer's cheese counter, it's no use pretending I do, I was never one for pretence, not like some I could mention.' She sniffed twice, once for Auntie Doris and once for Uncle Teddy, with whom Henry had lived before Cousin Hilda. 'So to save Mr Pettifer's embarrassment it's best I go to the Co-op, even if it is further from the tram. "Ee, Hilda," she said. "Hasn't your Henry turned out well?"'

'She makes me sound like a cake,' said Henry.

'Now then, Henry,' said Cousin Hilda. 'There's no call to be rude about Mrs Wedderburn, who lent you her camp-bed in time of need.'

'I really don't see why I shouldn't pay,' said Henry, who didn't want the burden of Mrs Wedderburn's good opinion. 'I'd rather not be indebted.'

'Indebted,' snorted Cousin Hilda. '"Indebted," he says. If I charged you it'd put you on a footing with poor Mr O'Reilly. It'd put you on a footing with poor Mr Pettifer.' Her voice developed an acid coating of disapproval. 'It'd put you on a footing with Mr Frost. You are not my lodger. You are my son.'

Henry blushed and Cousin Hilda looked embarrassed too.

'Well you are . . . now . . . you are.'

He was pleased, of course. He was moved, of course. He was also appalled. How could he say he was looking for a flat, now?

He had to tell her about the weekend.

'Er . . . by the way . . .' he said. 'I'm . . . er . . . going away for the weekend.'

'Away? You'll only have been at work a week.'

'I have alternate Saturdays off.'

'Where to, "away"?'

'London.'

'London?' Cousin Hilda couldn't have sounded more surprised if Henry had said 'Outer Mongolia'. 'London? What do you want to go to London for?'

'I'm going to spend the weekend with Paul Hargreaves.'

'Oh.' Cousin Hilda was rather ambivalent about Paul, the brain surgeon's son, the friend from public school days who had visited Thurmarsh briefly in the summer of 1953. She had disturbingly contradictory feelings about private education, since she believed strongly in standards but despised people who put on airs. 'Well, I've met worse boys, even if he didn't think we were good enough for him.'

'That isn't true,' said Henry, knowing that it was. 'One of the boys I used to fag for, at Dalton, is making his début for England at rugby.' For a moment, Henry wished he really was going to watch Tosser Pilkington-Brick versus Wales, rather than lie naked with Lorna Arrow in the Midland Hotel. But only for a moment.

'Rugby!' said Cousin Hilda, as if it were the apogee of human absurdity. 'I don't know!'

'I feel the same,' said Henry. 'If God had meant us to play rugby, he'd have given us oval balls.' It was out before he could stop it. To his relief, Cousin Hilda didn't seem to understand it. 'I have to go out now,' he said.

'Out?' Cousin Hilda sounded astonished at his geographical profligacy.

'Yes. I have to develop my contacts.'

'Contacts?'

'That's what we journalists call the people in places of influence who can put stories our way,' explained Henry airily, with all the experience of twenty-four hours.

'And what people in places of influence are you seeing tonight?'

'Tommy Marsden.'

'Tommy Marsden!'

'Ace goal poacher of the Third Division North.'

'Aye. Well . . . don't be "late".' For 'late', read 'drunk'. Her mouth was working again, with the tension.

'I won't,' he said, and gave her a quick kiss, which astounded them both. '*Did* you see my scoop about the cat?'

'Cats!' said Cousin Hilda scornfully. 'Scoops!'

They sat in an alcove in the bar of the Conservative Club, of which Tommy was an honorary member. Above them was a portrait of Sir Winston Churchill. The carpet was blue. They could hear the occasional clunk of snooker balls from the back room.

They talked about the Paradise Lane Gang. 'Those were the days,' said Henry. He didn't remind Tommy that it had all broken up in fighting and bitterness when Henry and Martin had gone to the grammar school. He wanted Tommy in a good mood.

'Aye,' said Tommy. 'Does tha see Martin at all?'

'We have a jar every now and then. We sup some lotion,' said Henry. 'It isn't the same. I think becoming a sergeant's made him take himself very seriously.'

'It's age,' said Tommy Marsden. 'I'm twenty-one.'

'I'm twenty. It's frightening. Are you married or engaged or owt?' His dialect was returning, in Tommy's company.

'Chuff me, no,' said Tommy. 'Mr Mackintosh says many a promising career's been nipped in t'bud because a player's shagging himself to death. Same again?'

No, thanks. I must remain sober for Cousin Hilda. 'Yes, please.'

'Same difference wi' supping,' said Tommy, as the waiter brought them two pints, and Tommy discovered that he had no money, and Henry paid. 'There'll be plenty of time for that later.'

Henry judged that the time was ripe. 'Tommy?' he said. 'Will you be my contact from the world of sport?'

'Tha what?'

'Will you put stories my way?'

'Stories? What stories?'

'I don't know. Whatever happens. Transfers. Disciplinary suspensions. Dressing-room arguments. Whatever happens. Stories.'

'What? And be known as Tommy "The Leak" Marsden?'

'No. No one'll know where they come from. Us journalists never reveal our sources.'

'Will I get paid?'

'I can't. I'm only on seven pounds ten a week.'

'I'll think about it,' said Tommy Marsden.

'Hey!' said Henry, judging it unwise to press the matter at this juncture. 'I've only been on the paper two days, and I've had my first scoop.'

He showed Tommy page 8. Tommy grabbed it, and began to read aloud, to Henry's embarrassment, especially as he read very loudly, and very slowly, as if he had only a passing acquaintanceship with words.

'"When Thomas Hendrick, aged 37, self-employed plumber, took a stray cat to Darnley Road police station yesterday,"' read Tommy Marsden, to the surprise of the assembled Conservatives and social-climbing Liberals and socialists, '"little did he suspect that it belonged to his sister.

'"The amazing 5,000 yard journey of Tiddles, aged 5, from the Bagcliffe Road home of his owner, Mrs Doris Treadwell, to the Hendricks' abode in Dursley Rise has puzzled both parties.

'"'I can't think how he came to find my brother,' Doris, aged 36, told our reporter. 'I've only had him ten days and Tom hasn't even seen him as he's been off with his chest. Tiddles can't even have met Tom,' she added,"' read Tommy.

'"And Thomas Hendrick? 'I didn't even know our Doris had a cat,' he said, 'but it certainly must be an animal with a family sense!'

'"A police spokesman commented, 'This is a most unusual case, unique in my experience.'

'"Joked Mr Hendrick: 'I hope Tiddles doesn't try to visit our brother. He lives in Canada!'"'

Henry smiled modestly at the stunned listeners in the bar of the Conservative Club.

'Bloody hell,' said Tommy Marsden. 'Call that a scoop?'

'It *is* a scoop,' said Henry indignantly. 'A scoop is a story that no other paper has printed. No other paper has printed that story.'

'I'm not surprised,' said Tommy Marsden.

Next morning, in the bustling news-room, nobody praised Henry's story, but this wasn't surprising, in that hard world, where men were men and Helen Cornish wasn't and had deeply disturbing bulges in her pale sage-green sweater to prove it. Terry Skipton asked Henry to do a 'Voice of Thurmarsh' that afternoon, and Henry's heart sank.

No scoops attended his rounds of the hospitals and police

stations. The weather was milder, and he felt clammy with sweat. His self-assurance, that occasional visitor who never took his coat off, had hurried away, and he couldn't face them all, in the canteen or the Lord Nelson, witnessing how absurdly nervous he was about his 'Voice of Thurmarsh'. So he lunched alone in the Rundle Café, in Rundle Prospect, next to the Polish barber. It was drizzling, and the cramped little café smelt of damp clothes. The *Light Programme* blared out constantly, and Henry ate his meat pie, chips and beans to the strains of the Eric Delaney Band. His rice pudding with jam was accompanied by *Listen with Mother*. Bank clerks and gas board salesmen pretended not to be listening to the tale of Tommy the Tortoise. Henry wished he were Henry the Hedgehog, and could curl up in a ball that afternoon, after making love, very carefully, to Helen the Hedgehog. In two days and five hours he would be making love, not carefully but with great abandon, doing the only thing in the world he was good at, with Lorna Arrow, his childhood sweetheart. Stop thinking about it, Henry. You'll go blind.

He felt absurdly self-conscious, standing ankle-deep in slush outside W. H. Smith's, his hair lank with sweat and the faint, raw drizzle. He hoped none of his colleagues would pass by. He wished Alec Walsh, the hard-bitten, overweight photographer, wasn't standing there, trying not to look too obviously scornful.

He approached an extremely burly man, whose extreme burliness he hadn't noticed until he'd approached him.

'Excuse me,' he said. 'I'm from the *Argus*.'

'Oh aye?' said the extremely burly man.

'Yes, and . . . er . . .' Why did he think that there were ghosts from his past, watching him from the surrounding windows? Uncle Teddy, Auntie Doris, the slimy Geoffrey Porringer, Diana Hargreaves, Tosser Pilkington-Brick and his effete, ascetic, aesthetic, homosexual friend Lampo Davey? The scornfully superior Belinda Boyce-Uppingham from the big house at Rowth Bridge? All peering at him from the windows of Cockayne's and Timothy Whites and the Thurmarsh and Rawlaston Co-operative Society? 'We . . . er . . . we do a weekly feature which we call "Voice of Thurmarsh".'

'Oh aye?' said the extremely burly man.

'Yes. We ask the public a question about a topical issue and we print their answers along with photos of them.'

'Oh aye?' said the extremely burly man.

'So I wondered if I could ask you the question we're asking people today,' said Henry.

'Oh. Aye,' said the extremely burly man.

'Er . . . do you think Britain is being too lenient towards Archbishop Makarios?' said Henry.

The extremely burly man thought long and hard.

'I don't know,' he said. 'I'm a stranger here.'

A magnificent ruse had freed Henry from the need to go home for his tea. He'd told Cousin Hilda that he was going to the Essoldo, with his new chums, to see Dean Martin and Jerry Lewis in *My Friend Irma Goes West*, and that, prior to the entertainment, they would take solid refreshment at the Shanghai Chinese Restaurant and Coffee Bar.

'Chinese meals!' Cousin Hilda had snorted. 'I don't know.'

Henry wasn't going to see *My Friend Irma Goes West*. He wasn't even going to see Cornel Wilde and Yvonne De Carlo in *Passion*. He was going to drink glasses of bitter with his new chums, and then meet his contact from the world of industry.

They stood by the bar that evening, in the back room of the Lord Nelson, because nobody was staying long. Colin Edgeley had to get home before the kids went to bed. Henry was astounded to discover that he had children. Ginny Fenwick had to review a performance of *Candida* by the Rawlaston Players in the Drill Hall, Splutt Road, Rawlaston. Ben Watkinson was off to Sheffield to see the Wednesday play Charlton. There was no sign of Helen Cornish.

'So how are you enjoying newspaper work?' said Ginny. She was standing extremely close to him. Again there seemed, to his surprise, to be evidence that he was attractive to women.

'Very much,' he said feebly. Her lips were slightly too thick. Nothing wrong with that. Sensual?

'I *love* it,' she said, with an intensity that stirred his nether regions. This was, he decided, an extremely attractive person. Pity about the nose. 'I long to get to Fleet Street,' she said. Large, uneven teeth, slightly yellow, but not repulsively so. 'In about five years, when I'm ready.'

'Really?' he said feebly. 'What? As a fashion correspondent?'

Ginny Fenwick snorted. What a man I am, thought Henry, for making women snort.

'That's stereotyped thinking,' she said. 'No. I want to be a war correspondent.'

'A war correspondent!' he said, feebly. My god, I'm being feeble tonight, he thought. Yes, there was something Amazonian about her. He could imagine her, with her large thighs and broad buttocks, and her well-formed bust, striding round the battlefield, taking shorthand notes as the shells whizzed round her head. He felt a spasm of fierce desire. He had a brief glimpse of her, naked except for army boots and a helmet, holding out her hospitable arms to him. Stop it! Think of Friday night. No. Don't think of Friday night. Talk about work, quickly, before you have an accident. 'So you must feel pretty fed up about covering something like the Rawlaston Players,' he said.

'No! *Not at all*. Every job is important.'

'Well, yes, I . . . er . . . I . . . er . . . yes.' Every time he thought he had scaled the Himalayas of feebleness, he found new ranges of conversational ineptitude above them.

'Think of *them*,' said Ginny. 'Think of *her*.'

'Them?' he said feebly. 'Her?'

'The Rawlaston Players. The girl playing Candida. What is she? A nurse? A teacher? Probably a teacher. They usually are. It's a highlight in her life, Henry. She deserves my full attention. Have another drink.'

'Thanks.'

She was magnificent! She must be fully twenty-five, but he liked older women. And he'd never had a big woman. Mind you, he'd never had a small woman either. Let's face it, he'd only ever had one woman. Tall and slim. 'Cheers, Ginny. That was quick.'

'Cheers, Henry.' Massive eye contact. Blue as a summer's day, shining eyes of a warm woman. 'Come with me. To *Candida*.'

'Yes, I . . . er . . . I very well might, Ginny.'

Colin and Ben interrupted their growing intimacy. Colin

33

gave Henry a meaningful look which meant 'Get in there, kid.' Ben said, 'Name the four football league sides that have x in their names.' Henry glanced at Ginny, uncertain whether she'd think better of him for knowing or for not knowing. In the end, he couldn't resist the challenge. 'Wrexham,' he said. 'Halifax. Exeter.' He made a mental tour of the country. 'Crewe Alexandra.'

'Well done!' said Ben, and Henry felt rather absurd, smiling his pride. Colin seemed proud of him too. Ginny looked as if she were trying to hide her amusement.

Neil Mallet entered with Denzil Ackerman, arts and show business editor. Neil's carroty hair looked windswept, but Denzil was wearily immaculate. He was in his fifties, had private money, a mews cottage in Chelsea, a pink bow-tie, a limp, a hand-carved Scottish walking-stick and a high-pitched voice. He only spent three days a week in Thurmarsh as he saw it as part of his job 'to cultivate my intellectual garden and save you from your depressing provincialism, my quaint darlings.' The middle pages were his domain. Some readers started at the front and others started at the back. It wasn't clear how many reached the middle pages, and it didn't seem to matter very much, in those halcyon days of the provincial press.

'Ah! A fresh face!' said Denzil Ackerman. He examined Henry as if he were a doubtful antique. 'Really very fresh. One of those strange faces that ought to seem repellent but which one finds oddly attractive because one doesn't find them repellent. Don't you think so, Neil?'

Neil Mallet, whose sexual proclivities were a closed book to his colleagues, some of whom believed that he was only a dark horse because he had never entered a race, blushed slightly at being included in this assumption of homosexuality. Henry throbbed with fury. Ginny, with magnificent understanding, touched him sympathetically and said, 'Denzil's outrageous,' as if this excused everything. Henry felt that it excused nothing. He was appalled at the depth of his immediate loathing for Denzil Ackerman.

'I hear you're one of the eight people in this philistine dump who've seen *Waiting for Godot*, Henry,' said Denzil.

Henry decided that he must fight his loathing and his feebleness. 'Yes,' he said. 'And I loved it, which for some stupid reason yesterday I wasn't prepared to admit.'

Denzil gave Henry a warm smile, and began to talk pleasantly and unaffectedly about films and plays. Henry fought his loathing so successfully that he actually began liking the man. Ben Watkinson bought a round. 'Pink gin, dear boy, since they haven't *heard* of wine in this *hole*,' said Denzil, and the landlord, Mr Bernard Hoveringham, who had also not heard of lasagne or chilli con carne, smiled.

Denzil talked about art, and Henry pretended to more knowledge than he had. Just as Denzil said, 'And who are your favourite artists? Tell uncle,' Ben handed Henry his drink and said, 'Name all the English and Scottish teams that have Athletic in their name.' Henry didn't want to offend his friend of three whole days, who seemed to regard his talking to Denzil as a defection, and he didn't want to offend his new friend of ten minutes, whom he had so recently loathed. Nor did he want to seem an artistic prig to Ben or a sporting lout to Denzil.

It isn't easy to keep two conversational balls in the air at the same time.

'Charlton,' said Henry.

'I don't know him,' said Denzil.

'Charlton Athletic,' said Henry.

Denzil looked bewildered.

'Constable,' said Henry.

'Don't you mean Dunstable?' said Ben, 'and I think they're Dunstable Town anyway.'

'Alloa,' said Henry.

'You're pulling some obscure ones out of the hat,' said Denzil. 'Basque, is he? He sounds Basque.'

'Klimt,' said Henry.

'Not including foreign teams,' said Ben.

'Gainsborough,' said Henry.

'I think they're Town as well and I didn't include non-league,' said Ben.

'Gainsborough, the painter,' said Henry.

'You like Gainsborough?' said Denzil, shocked.

35

'Not much, no, but I couldn't think of anybody else,' admitted Henry.

And then there came a sharp pain in the two balls that he wasn't keeping in the air as Helen Cornish swept into the room, magenta skirt swirling, pert lips pouting. Podgy Sex Bomb Henry gasped with desire, and Ginny knew, and Henry blushed and said desperately, 'Rembrandt. Bournemouth and Boscombe. Botticelli. Hamilton. No, they're Academicals.'

It was his round. Forces which he couldn't control engineered brief physical contact, as he asked Helen what she'd have. Ginny refused a drink. 'I must go,' she said. She didn't repeat her suggestion that he accompany her. 'Nice girl,' said Denzil. 'Pity she's so unattractive.' This was too much for Henry. 'I don't think she's unattractive,' he said, and Helen raised a delicious eyebrow, and Henry blushed again, and Denzil said, 'No, dear, but I find all women unattractive. Present company excepted. Anyway, don't worry your quaint little head over Ginny, she'll make somebody a very good war correspondent.' There was laughter. Henry glared and felt the loathing again. Then he realized that it was all right, because everyone knew that Denzil was outrageous, so he smiled feebly. Ben went off to his football. Denzil sought companions for dinner. Neil said he had to hoover and dust the flat. 'How about the second D. H. Lawrence?' said Denzil. 'Strange ambition. I wouldn't want to be the *first* D. H. Lawrence.' Colin refused. He didn't enjoy eating. Denzil left in a slight huff.

When only Henry and Helen and Colin remained, Colin said, 'Where's Ted?'

'He's covering the man who had his head cut off in a sawmill,' said Helen.

Henry had a vision of a man in a sawmill, blood gushing, with his head lying at his side, perhaps registering a faint expression of surprise. He felt dizzy and faint. 'Are you all right, kid?' said a tiny voice from a vast distance. 'Fine,' he said, as he fainted.

He came round to see Helen's pert lips and concerned eyes staring at him, and behind her Colin. They laid him on a bench seat, and he began to revive. The sweat poured off him. Helen wiped his forehead with a scented handkerchief, and kissed his cheek, and Henry said he thought he had the flu coming. He didn't want to lie, but couldn't admit that he was too soft for this hard world. Helen went to buy him a brandy. Colin said, 'Are you sure you're all right, kid?' and Henry said, 'I'm OK,' rather angrily. Colin said, 'I ought to get home, but I can't leave you on your own.' Henry said, 'I won't be on my own. I'll be with Helen.' Colin said, 'Exactly!' Henry didn't want to leave Colin alone with Helen, but he had to, because a) he'd said he thought he had the flu coming and b) he had to meet his contact from the world of industry.

Martin Hammond was working as an overhead crane fitter at the Splutt Vale Iron and Steel Company. He lived with his family in a pebble-dashed semi in Everest Crescent. He was Henry's best friend, and Henry was beginning to wonder if he liked him.

They sat in the back room of the Pigeon and Two Cushions, a small, quiet, almost sedate pub in Church Lane, with gleaming oblong tables studded with beer mats and ashtrays. On the panelled walls were cheerful sepia pictures of Thurmarsh disasters – the great flood, the great gale, the great snowfall, the great train crash. There were bells at frequent intervals, for waiter service. The waiter had a cold.

How on earth had slow, owlish, bespectacled Martin become a sergeant? They must have been short of candidates for promotion in the Royal Army Ordnance Corps.

'I saw Tommy Marsden yesterday,' said Henry. 'He's going to be my contact from the world of sport.'

'Good old Tommy. What a player,' said Martin, who had only once seen Tommy play.

At a table by the brick fireplace a group of pasty-faced men in slightly shiny suits were discussing breasts and bums. There was something familiar about one of them.

'Will you be my contact from the world of industry?' said Henry.

'You what?' said Martin.

'Will you phone me up with stories?'

'What stories?'

'I don't know! Anything. Impending strikes. Unusual industrial accidents. Lost cockatoos. Anything.' Had Martin always looked so pompous?

'I'm not keen on supporting your rag,' said Martin. 'Its editorial policy is slightly to the right of Genghis Khan. That's what my dad reckons, anyroad.'

Henry realized that he hadn't given much thought to the *Argus*'s editorial policy.

Martin pressed the bell, and ordered two more beers.

'Please, Martin,' said Henry. 'I mean . . . we're friends.'

The waiter brought their drinks.

'Have one yourself,' said Martin grandly.

'Oh, thank you very much, sir,' said the waiter. 'I'll have sixpennorth with you.' He hesitated, feeling that Martin's largesse deserved some social response. 'I've never known a cold like it,' he confided. 'Three weeks I've had it. Can't seem to shift it.'

They sipped their beers slowly. It was very important to Henry to remain sober.

'I thought you were a socialist,' said Martin.

'I am,' said Henry. 'I'm working from within to turn the paper leftwards.'

'With stories about cats?'

'Give me time. I've got to establish me credibility. Give me socialist stories, Martin.'

'Such as?'

'I don't know. Workers with hearts of gold. Stupid bosses. I don't know.'

'They won't print them.'

'I'll resign if they don't.'

'All right, then.'

Henry bought two more pints, to celebrate the recruitment of his contact from the world of industry. The men with shiny suits were talking about arses now. The one who seemed familiar winked. Henry remembered, and went over to him.

'It's Tony Preece, isn't it? he said. 'I'm Henry Pratt. From Cousin Hilda's.'

'By heck,' said Tony Preece, who still had a bad complexion.

'I'm working on the *Argus*,' said Henry. 'Could I have a word with you some time on a business matter?'

They arranged to meet on the following evening. Henry rejoined Martin. 'Sorry about that,' he said. 'A little business matter.' There was an uneasy pause. There was a gulf between them, a hole where his past should have been. 'Got a girl-friend, have you?' he asked.

'No,' said Martin. 'What with work and night school and union meetings and party meetings, I haven't got much time for all that.'

Poor miserable Martin, thought Henry. Poor miserable lucky enviable Martin.

Almost as soon as he'd boarded the strangely swaying tram, Henry realized that he desperately needed food. So he got off at the first stop.

'Boring,' he told the conductor. 'Most boring tram I've ever been on.'

Those were the days before the proliferation of Indian restaurants. Even Chinese restaurants were a rarity in some parts. In Thurmarsh, in January 1956, after ten o'clock at night, the only place where you could get a sit-down meal was the Shanghai Chinese Restaurant and Coffee Bar, in Market Street.

Inside the Shanghai, the lights were dim, the tables were crowded, the cups were of glass, the coffee was frothy, rubber plants abounded, and the most beautiful woman in the world called out, 'Henry!'

'Hello, Helen.' As in a dream, he drifted to his beloved's side. She was sitting beside a brown-haired man with rugged features set in a slightly puffy face.

She introduced them. 'Greetings,' said Gordon Carstairs, who was thirty-six. He turned away from Henry, as from a troublesome fly. 'You aren't really going to marry Ted, are you, Helen?' he said.

'Why not?'

'Why not? Why not?? Helen!!' Gordon Carstairs stopped, as if he had explained everything.

Henry ordered beef curry and coffee. The Shanghai had no licence.

'Make that tea. The special tea,' said Gordon Carstairs firmly.

'Why?' said Henry, bristling.

'Because,' said Gordon Carstairs. 'Because, laddie. That's why.' He had a large, piercing nose, and there were deep bags beneath his bloodshot eyes. When we are drunk, the drunk don't strike us as drunk. Henry had no idea that Gordon Carstairs was as drunk as he was.

He could feel a leg stroking him. He didn't think it was Gordon Carstairs's.

'I thought you had flu coming on,' said Helen.

'I think it must have been one-day flu,' said Henry.

'More like one-hour flu,' said Helen. 'Gordon's been covering a big story in Sheffield.'

'Oh, you're on the paper,' said Henry. 'What big story?'

Gordon Carstairs tapped the side of his nose and said, 'Discretion.' The Chinese waiter brought beef curry for Gordon, sweet and sour pork for Helen, and a pot of Chinese tea for Henry.

'Whisky,' whispered Gordon, and winked. Henry's heart sank. More drink, and more winking. He needed these things like an enema.

He rubbed Helen's leg and got a sharp kick. Had he rubbed Gordon's leg by mistake?

'How did you get the whisky?' he whispered.

'Precisely!' said Gordon Carstairs, and Henry assumed that it was his fault, because he was drunk, that Gordon was making no sense.

Suddenly Gordon stood up and said, 'My bill, please.'

A waiter hurried over. 'You no like, sir?' he said.

'The Great Wall!' said Gordon Carstairs. He drained his last cup of seventy per cent proof Chinese tea, and stalked out.

'What was all that about?' said Henry.

'He's too proud to fight you for me.'

Henry gawped. His beef curry arrived. In the dim light it looked vaguely green. He took an eager mouthful. The meat was stringy. The sauce was slightly sweet, faintly hot, thickly glutinous. It would be many years before he discovered the delights of real Chinese food.

'Fight me for you?'

'He knows he'd lose,' said Helen Cornish.

Henry forgot his tea was whisky and took a big gulp which almost choked him. 'You what?' he said.

'Come back with me,' said Helen.

'You're engaged.'

'I'm not married yet. Frightened?'

Yes. No. Well . . . a little, perhaps, of Ted, who was already an enemy. A little of Helen, perhaps, who was too beautiful. A little of himself, perhaps, who was too drunk. A little, perhaps, of what it would do to his one true love. Oh god! He'd forgotten! He had less than forty-eight hours to wait. What was he doing even thinking of going back with Helen? A wave of relief, mixed with just a little regret, broke over him.

'Of course I'm not frightened,' he said, 'but I can't go back with you.' Suddenly his speech became slurred. 'I'm schpoken for,' he said, and burped.

'Good night,' said Helen Cornish coldly.

He was on his own at a table cluttered with congealing, half-eaten green and orange semi-Chinese meals, yet he didn't feel lonely. He was on the verge of a sexy weekend, and he'd just turned down a beautiful woman. What strength. What coolth. No, there was no such word as coolth. He'd made new friends, tough, enigmatic journalists, limping queers from Chelsea. He was drinking whisky disguised as tea. He was sophisticated.

'Finished, sir?' said the waiter, indicating Helen's plate.

'Finished.'

He heard a familiar laugh, and there were two men walking past, solid, almost respectable.

'Uncle Teddy!'

Uncle Teddy turned pale and gawped.

'It's me. Henry.' Uncle Teddy hadn't seen him since he was fifteen.

'Henry! It's Henry! Good God!'

'Yes.'

'Henry, this is a business colleague, Derek Parsonage.'

Henry tried to stand, tried to seem sober.

'Please. Don't stand,' said Derek Parsonage. He was a big man, and his nose was festooned with blackheads, which puzzled Henry slightly.

'On your own?' said Uncle Teddy.

'No,' said Henry. 'I'm with Gordon Carstairs and Helen Cornish, but they've gone.'

'The selfishness of lovers,' said Derek Parsonage. Stupid name. Stupid man. You've got it all wrong. I'm glad your nose is covered in blackheads, which puzzles me slightly.

'Join me,' said Henry. 'Please. You must. After all, you're my . . .' He'd been going to say 'father'. Well, Uncle Teddy had virtually been his father, for a time. It was difficult to see Uncle Teddy clearly, in the half-light grudgingly conceded by the Chinese lanterns, through eyes blurred by drink, but he didn't look quite as big as Henry had remembered. Was this due to the scale of childhood vision, the distortion of memory, or the effects of age and imprisonment? Of course! Imprisonment!

They joined him.

'Henry is my . . .' explained Uncle Teddy to Derek Parsonage.

Henry wished Uncle Teddy hadn't found it so impossible to define their relationship.

'Uncle Teddy took me in as his son,' he said. 'His house, Cap Ferrat, became my home. Not his fault he went to . . .'

'Henry!' said Uncle Teddy.

'. . . Rangoon,' said Henry.

'Ah!' said Uncle Teddy. When Uncle Teddy had gone to prison Auntie Doris had pretended that she and Uncle Teddy had gone to Rangoon. She ran a hotel now, with her lover, the slimy Geoffrey Porringer, who had blackheads. Of course! That was why Derek Parsonage's blackheads had puzzled him. They were a historical echo.

'Rangoon?' said Derek Parsonage.

'Have some tea,' said Henry. 'It's whisky.'

'I lived in Rangoon for a while with . . . er . . . before we split up,' said Uncle Teddy.

'I never knew that,' said Derek Parsonage.

'Not a lot of people do,' said Henry.

'Are you drunk?' said Uncle Teddy.

'Yes,' said Henry. 'This tea's whisky, you see.'

Uncle Teddy and Derek Parsonage ordered chicken chop suey and another pot of Chinese tea.

Henry wished he'd gone to see Uncle Teddy in prison. It was odd. Martin Hammond was his best friend and he didn't like him. Uncle Teddy was a crook and a liar and had sent him to boarding schools to get him out of the way, and now Henry found that he loved him almost as a father and craved his respect.

'Helen asked me to go to bed with her,' he said, 'but I refused. I'm meeting my lover at the weekend, you see.'

'What a life you lead,' said Uncle Teddy. Derek Parsonage gave a little grin of disbelief, and Uncle Teddy looked worried, as if he thought Henry's fantasizing was the result of the bad upbringing to whose shortcomings Uncle Teddy had contributed more than his share.

'It's true,' said Henry indignantly.

'Of course it is,' said Uncle Teddy.

Henry poured himself some more whisky. The pot was inexhaustible. Uncle Teddy sniffed it. 'It *is* whisky,' he said.

'Course it is,' said Henry. 'I'm not a liar.' He felt that Uncle Teddy looked at him with fresh eyes, perhaps even with respect. He felt another wave of guilt. He could have been brave enough to visit Uncle Teddy *once*. They'd said that Uncle Teddy would feel ashamed of being seen by him, but that was nonsense, which he'd leapt at with relief. 'Uncle Teddy?' he said, desperately trying to sound sober, 'I really am very sorry I never visited you.'

'What?' said Uncle Teddy anxiously.

'In Rangoon.'

'My dear boy, how could you?'

'I know. I know. But still . . . you know . . . I wish I had.'

Uncle Teddy's eyes held Henry's for a moment. Henry felt that there was almost a feeling of father and son between them. Then the effort of fighting the drink began to tell. His head swam and he hiccuped.

'I'm working on the *Argus*,' he said. 'I'm a journalist. I did my national service. I was a soldier in that.' He wanted to say how sorry he was that Auntie Doris had gone off to live with Geoffrey Porringer, but it wasn't a subject he could safely broach, especially while hiccuping. He wasn't sure if he should mention Auntie Doris and he felt that he definitely shouldn't mention Geoffrey Porringer. It had all gone so dark. The lighting was so drunk, and he was so dim. Blast those hiccups. Dignity. Derek Parsonage found the hiccups amusing. God, he hated Uncle Teddy's choice of friends.

'Fancy you two running into each other here,' said Derek Parsonage.

'Not really,' said Henry. 'Where else is there at this time of night to run into anybody at anywhere anyway? There isn't.'

'Exactly,' said Uncle Teddy.

'Precisely,' said Derek Parsonage.

'What are you talking about?' said Henry.

'Night life,' said Uncle Teddy. 'There isn't any.'

'In twenty years' time,' said Derek Parsonage, 'this town will be awash with clubs.'

'We're getting in first,' said Uncle Teddy.

'We're bringing sophistication to this dump,' said Derek Parsonage.

'Lightening the grey skies with a touch of mediterranean colour,' said Uncle Teddy.

'Bringing continental elegance to the Rundle Valley,' said Derek Parsonage.

'The Cap Ferrat opens next month,' said Uncle Teddy.

Their food arrived. So did their tea which, to their disappointment, was tea.

'This tea's tea,' said Derek Parsonage.

'You need contacts,' said Henry. 'I have contacts.' He tried to pat the side of his nose knowingly, but missed and poked his finger into his eye. 'Ouch!' he cried, and hiccuped. 'I have contacts with boot-lickers. No, arse-leggers. No.' He poured himself some more whisky.

'You've had enough,' said Uncle Teddy, and he grabbed Henry's cup. Henry grabbed it back.

'You can't start playing my father just when it suits you,' he said. 'And as for your friend, with his bloody blackheads. You know what he is, don't you? A Geoffrey Porringer substitute.'

He was on the verge of being told, in a few blindingly simple words, all the secrets of life, its purpose and its conduct. His head ached from the effort of listening and concentrating, as at last the words came.

Then he woke up. His head still ached, but the words, the secrets, were tantalizingly out of reach, unremembered, dissolved.

44

And he was a young man with a bad hangover, lying in a lumpy bed converted from a lumpy sofa.

Last night! Oh no! He sat up abruptly and wished he hadn't. But he hadn't run into Cousin Hilda. She hadn't seen how drunk he was. There was hope.

Then he heard her voice. Flat. Too upset for anger. 'He's been sick on the stairs.'

He crawled out of bed, staggered across the room, opened the window, breathed in the icy morning air and heard her say, 'He's been sick on the lawn!'

He vaguely remembered going round the back, not going inside, because he'd felt ill.

She turned, and he moved away from the window.

'Oh no!' This time there *was* anger. Icy anger. 'He's been sick on the coal!'

She was hunched with hurt as she banged his breakfast down. Liam's smile froze like condensed breath. Barry Frost stopped humming. A cardboard egg refused to go past the brick in Henry's throat. Only Norman Pettifer seemed oblivious.

'It's going to be a Camembert day today,' he said. 'I just know it.'

As the tram clanked along Doncaster Road towards the Alderman Chandler Memorial Park that evening, Henry held his copy of the *Argus* with pride. Other men were merely reading it. He'd helped to produce it.

He read his story again.

> Arthur Bollard, aged 27, of Snowdon Grove, Thurmarsh, was struck in the throat by a pair of tongs at work today, and was detained at Thurmarsh Royal Infirmary.
>
> When he fell from a ladder at Johnson and Johnson Rolling Mills, 34 year-old Benjamin Whateley, of Smith Street, Rawlaston, received injuries to legs, back and hand. He was treated at Thurmarsh Royal Infirmary.
>
> Also treated there was Samuel Willis, aged 15, of Derwentwater Crescent, Splutt, who trapped three fingers in a haulage chain at Drobwell Main Colliery.

Not spectacular, perhaps, but even Martin would have to agree that it was good socialist stuff. To anyone with an ability to read between the lines it must be significant that no bosses were injured that day when struck by falling agendas, choking on fillet steaks or burning fingers on cups of scalding coffee. That was the way to turn the paper leftwards – by stealth.

In Cousin Hilda's basement room the blue stove with the cracked panes roared and crackled. 'Bring me some men, some stout-hearted men,' commanded Barry Frost under his breath. Norman Pettifer confirmed that it had indeed been a Camembert day. Cousin Hilda remained silent, stiff with disappointment and accusation. The pork was stringy, the roast potatoes were like bullets, the cabbage was overcooked. Cousin Hilda gave Henry two halves of tinned pears, while everyone else had three. He hurried out before she could get him on his own, and was in the Pigeon and Two Cushions ten minutes before Tony Preece.

While he waited he read that morning's national papers. Would he ever be working for them?

The big story was the controversy over the government's sale of tanks and arms to Israel and Egypt. The government had pointed out that the tanks 'had been so old that they would have no military value'. They were 'obsolete, ineffective and unreliable for war'. The British government had tried – and would continue to try, as far as lay within its power – to prevent an arms race in the Middle East. By selling obsolete tanks to both sides, presumably. 'Our tanks don't work.' 'Nor do ours.' 'Oh let's give up.' But wouldn't they be angry about being sold useless weapons? thought Henry.

The sniffing waiter – 'It's gone to me sinuses now' – brought them two pints of Hammonds' best bitter.

'So, what's this business matter?' said Tony Preece.

'Well . . . are you still doing your act round the clubs?'

'Oh yes. I couldn't give that up. I'm addicted. You wouldn't recognize the act now, though. I've changed it completely.'

'Oh good,' said Henry. 'Sorry,' he added. 'Are you still . . . er . . . ?'

'Still with Stella, yes.'

'How is she?'

46

'Older,' said Tony Preece gallantly. 'So come on. Am I about to earn some extra money?'

'Well, I can't actually offer you any money, as such,' said Henry, 'but maybe I could give you some publicity, write a feature about your Jekyll and Hyde existence — by day, ordinary drab insurance man — at night, laughter-maker extraordinaire. If you'd . . . er . . . be my contact from the world of showbiz.'

He was rather hurt when Tony Preece laughed. Somehow he was getting the feeling that nothing very useful was going to come to him out of his contacts from the worlds of sport, industry and show business. In this he was wrong, but then he was to be wrong about so many things, during his career with the *Thurmarsh Evening Argus*.

3 A Sexy Weekend

Sexuality laid her sweet tongue on everything that Henry did next morning. The weather was suitably bright and crisp. He felt a surge of joy as he converted his bed into a sofa. He hummed the 'Ballad of Davy Crockett' while he shaved. As he packed with unsuppressed excitement, Eve Boswell was picking a chicken on his wireless. Podgy Sex Bomb Henry picked a chicken with her.

In eleven hours he'd be alone with Lorna, in the Midland Hotel. He must remember that he'd booked the room in the names of Mr and Mrs Wedderburn.

He had no hangover. He could enjoy his breakfast. The egg was rich and runny. He ate it slowly, relishing it. The fried bread was a stern test of teeth. They all ate that slowly. Barry Frost even stopped humming while he tackled it.

Henry tried, for Cousin Hilda's sake, not to look too delighted about going away, but his body thrilled with anticipation, and he caught her looking at him suspiciously.

Liam hurried off, then Norman. Not wishing to be left alone with Cousin Hilda, Henry hurried through his third piece of toast – two would have seemed too mean, four excessively generous, and Cousin Hilda treated him exactly like her 'businessmen', to prevent embarrassment. A great deal of Cousin Hilda's life was devoted to preventing embarrassment, which might have been why everything turned out to be so embarrassing.

Henry lost his race with Barry Frost, who finished his breakfast *con brio*.

Cousin Hilda closed the door behind Barry Frost, and faced her responsibility resolutely.

'Four days in journalism, and look at you. It can't go on,' she said.

No. It can't. Say, 'No. I agree. For both our sakes, dear Cousin Hilda, whom I love, I'd better move out.' But he couldn't. All he said was, 'I'm sorry.'

'I should think so too. When I think what Mrs Wedderburn says about you.'

He closed his eyes, as if he hoped that existence would go away, if he couldn't see it. What had possessed him to choose Mr and Mrs Wedderburn?

'She says you're such a lovely, polite young man. I must be so proud of you. Proud! What would she think if she knew that the polite young man whom she once lent her camp-bed out of the goodness of her heart had been sick on the coal?'

'I'm sorry about the coal.'

'It's not the coal. It's you. A drunk. Yes, Henry. A common drunk.'

'No, Cousin Hilda. Well, the first time I *was* drunk, yes. It was meeting all the journalists. It was the first time I've ever been drunk.' He didn't want to lie, but felt that he had to, for her sake. 'And the last. The second time it was food. Honestly.'

'I didn't think you'd ever lie to me, Henry.'

'I'm not lying,' he lied. For her sake.

'Do you think Mr Pettifer'll stay if there's always piles of sick on the stairs? Is that any way for the manager of the cheese counter at Cullen's to live?'

'No.' Just say, 'I'm sorry, Cousin Hilda. I'll find a flat.' But he couldn't. 'I'll never do it again, Cousin Hilda,' he said. 'I promise.'

'I know you mean to be a good lad,' said Cousin Hilda. 'I know it's difficult without your parents. I do my best.'

He gave her a quick kiss.

'Give him my best regards,' said Cousin Hilda, sniffing furiously.

'Him?' said Henry. 'Who?'

'Well, Paul, of course,' said Cousin Hilda. 'And you behave yourself with his family!'

At first, Henry thought it a great piece of luck when Terry Skipton said, 'I want you to interview a Mr Gunnar Fridriksen, from Iceland. I want you to find out his impressions of Thurmarsh. I've arranged for you to meet him in the Midland Hotel at three. If you've time, come back and do some book reviews.' Because

Henry knew that he wouldn't have time. He'd sit in the foyer, writing up his notes, until it was time to collect his beloved from the station. National service had taught him the art of making a little work go a long way. It was a lesson, forced upon them by the state, that a whole generation of the nation's manhood would diligently apply to their lives in industry and commerce.

At two minutes to three, he entered the hotel's huge foyer. What an unlikely venue it was for love. Vast armchairs sagged wearily. Huge, ugly chandeliers hung threateningly. Photographs from the halcyon days of steam trains abounded. The thick carpet, rich dark red like old port, seemed to grab his feet at each step. The male receptionist smiled with smarmy superiority.

'Can I help you, sir?'

'Yes. Could you let me know when Mr Fridriksen arrives?' His voice sounded small and self-conscious.

'He's already here, sir. Mr Fridriksen?'

A tall, thin man, so fair as to be almost albino, disentangled himself from an armchair and approached, smiling.

'I have Mr Pratt for you, Mr Fridriksen,' said the smarmy monstrosity. Oh lord, thought Henry, I hope this man isn't still on duty when I book in as Mr Wedderburn.

They sat in a quiet corner, beneath a photograph of 46231 *Duchess of Argyll* steaming through Crewe station past knots of train-spotting schoolboys in baggy, knee-length trousers. Henry's armchair sagged more than Mr Fridriksen's, making command of the interview difficult. He ordered tea with insufficient aplomb.

'I want to ask you your impressions of life here and in Iceland, and how it's different,' said Henry.

'Good. Fire away. I am, as you say, all ears,' said Mr Fridriksen.

Henry thought about Lorna, sticking her tongue in his ear in four hours' time. No! Concentrate!

'You speak very good English, Mr Fridriksen,' he said.

'I fear not,' said Mr Fridriksen. 'I have only the bare rudiments.'

In four hours' time I'll be kissing Lorna's bare rudiments. No! 'Er . . . what's impressed you most about life in Thurmarsh, Mr Fridriksen?' Oh, Lorna. Lorna. I want to taste your Lorna-osity. I want to drink from the fountain of your Arrowness. 'Er . . . sorry, I . . . er . . . I didn't catch all of that, I . . . er . . . I don't do shorthand yet. Could you . . . er . . . could you start again, please?'

Mr Gunnar Fridriksen looked at Henry in some surprise, but with infinite politeness. Their tea arrived, and somehow Henry forced himself to concentrate on the interview.

She seemed smaller, here in Thurmarsh, thin rather than slim, as if she were shrinking from the bustle of town life. Her smile was broad, but so nervous that it looked forlorn. They kissed. He was so excited that, the moment the kiss had ended, he had no memory of how it had felt.

They approached the crumbling, turreted bulk of the great stone-fronted railway hotel and, oh god, the smarmy monstrosity was still on duty.

'I've got a double room booked,' he croaked. 'Mr and Mrs Wedderburn.'

The smarmy monstrosity raised an eyebrow a quarter of a millimetre, and hunted through the list of bookings.

Henry glanced at Lorna. She was blushing. She'd never looked like a country bumpkin before.

'Ah yes,' smarmed the monstrosity. 'Room 412, Mr Wedderburn.' He invested the name with just the faintest hint of irony. 'If you'd just sign the register, Mr Wedderburn.'

Henry signed with shaking hand.

'Mrs Wedderburn?'

Lorna bowed her head as she signed.

'Will you be taking dinner, Mr Wedderburn?'

'Yes,' said Henry defiantly, as if it had been insinuated that he couldn't afford it.

'Would you like an early morning call, Mr Wedderburn?' said the genius of understated insinuation.

'Yes, please.' He glanced at Lorna. 'Er . . . eight-thirty.'

'Very good, sir. A morning paper, Mr Wedderburn?'

'Yes, please. *The Times*.'

'Very good, sir. Mrs Wedderburn?'

'The *Mirror*, please.'

'*The Times* and the *Mirror*.' Just the faintest suggestion that this might be the first time in the history of the hotel that this particular combination had been ordered. Smarmingtons clicked his fingers with astonishing volume. A page boy, dressed like a cross between a Morris Dancer and a colonel in the New Zealand army, appeared from nowhere. 'Take Mr and Mrs Wedderburn's "things" to room 412, Tremlett.'

'I'll carry them myself,' said Henry hurriedly, anxious to avoid the embarrassment and expense of tipping.

'As you wish, Mr Wedderburn.'

They walked towards the gilt-edged lifts, past the very chairs where Henry 'I was the first British journalist to witness the searing horror that is Dien Bien Phu' Pratt had interviewed Mr Fridriksen several centuries ago.

And there, walking towards them, was Colin Edgeley.

'Hey up, our kid,' he said. 'So you're the famous Lorna. Welcome to Thurmarsh, kid.' He gave Lorna a kiss. 'Smashing,' he said. 'You're a belter. We're all in the bar.'

'What?' Oh god, why did I tell him?

'We thought we'd give you a surprise. It's made a change to get out of the Lord Nelson.' He kissed Lorna again. 'Smashing.' And he padded off across the carpet which, unlike the port it resembled, had not improved with age.

'Oh God,' said Henry.

'What?'

'I don't want to go in there and drink with them.'

'Are you ashamed of me?'

'Course I'm not! Lorna! I don't want to go in there because a) I've been awash with drink all week and b) . . .' He lowered his voice. What he was going to say didn't sound like the sort of thing Mr Wedderburn would say to Mrs Wedderburn. '. . . I want to make love to you in room 412. I want to kiss you all over.'

'We don't have to stay long.'

'True.'

'I *am* a bit thirsty. I'm a bit nervous too about . . . you know . . . here. A drink might help.'

He let out a little sigh of tension. She pounced on it.

'You *are* ashamed of me.'

'No!'

'Going out with a country girl who works as a waitress. You think I'm not good enough for you.'

'Lorna! I've experienced enough snobbery to know how much I loathe it. And anyway, they don't need to know you're a waitress.'

Lorna snorted. Oh not another woman snorting. She didn't understand. It wasn't that he lacked confidence in her. He lacked confidence that his new friends had the eyes to see the loveliness and warmth beneath her undeniably rustic manners.

They entered the bar. It had a plum carpet, faded velvet curtains, brown leather upholstery with gold studs, and two more chandeliers. There they all were, sitting at a round table in a large alcove. Ted and Helen and Colin. Ben. Gordon. Neil. The outrageous Denzil. Only Ginny was missing. They looked like a selection board interviewing Lorna for the position of Henry's girl-friend. He tried to avoid the gravitational pull of Helen Cornish's sparkling eyes. In vain. She gave him one of the cool, challenging looks which had been his lot ever since he'd spurned her in the Shanghai. He was shattered by his desire for her, and hurriedly moved his eyes upward, to a large photograph of a Patriot class engine pulling a mixed freight out of Carlisle Upperby Yard in light snow. As a diversion, it was a failure. Men who are interested in women are rarely fanatical about trains. He answered Ted as in a dream. 'Glass of bitter, please.' Lorna ordered sweet cider! I hate myself, thought Henry. Lorna Arrow, you were a dream. A dream that sustained an unhappy soldier through two years in the Royal Corps of Signals. A pin-up that outshone Petula Clark and Patricia Roc inside a young man's locker, and touched the reality of his life barely more than they did. It isn't fair to turn a person into a dream.

'Nice to meet you, Lorna,' said Neil Mallet, who that morning had echoed the views of Crossbencher in last Sunday's *Express* – that the future for Anthony Eden would be even sunnier than the past. The doubters and moaners would be routed.

'So you're a country girl. Well done,' said Denzil. Henry thought this the most meaningless remark he'd ever heard. 'Passion among the cowpats. I love it.' Henry doubted if Denzil had ever seen a cowpat.

'Where are you from, Lorna?' said Ben Watkinson.

'Rowth Bridge. It's in Upper Mitherdale, near Troutwick.'

'*Lovely* country,' said Helen.

Henry usually preferred the laconic understatement of country people to the hyperbole of city folk, but he'd have welcomed a stronger reply from Lorna than, 'It's not bad.' He hadn't realized how strong her Mitherdale accent was. Not that he was ashamed of it. It was lovely. He just wished it wasn't quite so strong.

'Troutwick are in the Wensleydale League, aren't they?' said Ben.

'I don't know,' said Lorna. 'I know they're in summat.'

'What do you do, Lorna?' said Neil Mallet.

'Yes, what is there to do in the country? I've often wondered,' said Denzil.

'I meant, what job does Lorna do?' said Neil.

'I knew what you meant, old dear,' said Denzil. 'I was trying to save you from your conversational banality. Your question sounded like matron checking items on a laundry list.'

Neil flushed at the reference to laundry, then remembered that Denzil was outrageous, and smiled bravely. Henry was pleased at the diversion. It meant that Lorna wouldn't have to answer Neil's question.

'I'm a waitress at the White Hart in Troutwick. It's a hotel run by Henry's Auntie Doris,' said Lorna.

There was a brief silence.

'So how did you meet our young lady-killer, Lorna?' said Helen, in the extra friendly voice she used to women she didn't like. Ted smiled darkly at Henry. 'I always love hearing how people met.'

'We were at school together when Henry was evacuated to Rowth Bridge.'

'I wasn't evacuated,' said Henry. 'I was staying with relations.'

'That's a good one,' said Ted. 'Next time I'm in hospital, if they ask if I've evacuated my bowels, I'll say "No, they're staying with relations."'

'They don't ask if you've evacuated your bowels,' said Neil. 'They ask if you've moved them.'

'I'll say, "Yes. I used Pickfords. Never again. Terribly expensive,"' said Denzil.

Lorna looked from one to the other in some astonishment at

this conversation, and the slightly hysterical laughter that it produced.

'I gather Henry's a great one for reading,' said Denzil. 'Do you read together in bed, Lorna?'

Henry blushed.

'What books do you like, Lorna?' said Ted.

'I like *Woman*, *Woman's Own*,' said Lorna.

Henry knew her family referred to magazines as books. Why did it matter so desperately?

'Smashing,' said Colin.

Denzil bought a round. 'You have a sweet tooth, Lorna,' he said. 'I have actually,' she said. 'No wonder you like Henry, then. I think he's awfully sweet,' said Denzil, and Henry said, 'I thought you went to London at weekends,' because it had just occurred to him, but it came out so like an accusation that everybody laughed, and Henry pretended that he'd meant it to be funny, and Denzil said, 'So sorry to burden you with my presence, callow youth.' He lowered his voice. Homosexual acts of love were still illegal. 'My friend is arriving on the 8.15. He wishes to see The North.'

The headwaiter approached, in evening dress, his lips pursed. He carried two enormous menus.

'Mr Wedderburn?' he said.

There was a revealing pause before Henry said, 'Oh. That's me.'

'You're dining, sir?'

'Er . . . oh . . . yes . . . I . . . yes.'

'All of you?' The headwaiter's alarm was ill concealed.

'No,' said Henry. 'Just me and my . . . er . . . wife . . . unless any of you . . . er . . . I mean . . .' He looked round the gathering. Heads were hurriedly shaken. Ted said, 'Not me. Life's too precious.' 'Just me and my . . . wife,' said Henry.

The headwaiter handed Helen a menu.

'No. Not me,' she said, smiling triumphantly. 'The other young lady.'

'Ah!' said the headwaiter. 'Madam?' He handed Lorna a menu, and retired as hastily as decorum permitted.

'Mr and Mrs Wedderburn!' said Denzil. 'You have a delicious gift for ornamentation, Henry.'

'It's all in a foreign language,' said Lorna.

'French,' said Helen.

'What a snobbish country this is,' said Neil.

'You can talk,' said Ted.

'I beg your pardon?' said Neil.

'You drink in the back bar of the Lord Nelson. Your brother drinks in the front bar.'

'The snobbery isn't ours,' said Neil. 'It's all the other reporters and compositors who don't mix. I'm not a snob, Ted. I've never hidden my lower middle-class origins.'

'I must get home,' said Colin, looking at his watch. 'Same again, everybody?'

'I've just got time,' said Ben. 'Then I must go and give the wife one.'

'Pink gin. Removed,' said Denzil to the waiter. 'You what, sir?' said the waiter. 'The bitters, man. Removed, not left in.' 'Ah. Yes, sir. Only I'm new here,' said the waiter. 'So am I, I do assure you,' said Denzil.

Lorna's menu was unpriced. Henry's wasn't. Sometimes, when he visited Troutwick, Auntie Doris pressed money into his hand when Geoffrey Porringer wasn't looking. Quite a lot, sometimes. Twenty pounds even. She did it out of guilt, so he had to accept, for her sake. He had saved some of it, but he still couldn't afford this. Why had he said they'd be dining?

'What's "es-car-gotts"?' said Lorna.

'Snails,' said Neil.

'Ugh!' said Lorna, so unselfconsciously that everybody laughed.

'Quite right, kid,' said Colin. 'Thee and me's Yorkshire. We can't eat snails.'

'You two are going to experience the worst French meal you've ever had,' said Denzil.

'Oh, I don't know,' said Neil. 'I've eaten here. I liked the bouillabaisse.'

'I thought they were in the French Second Division,' said Ben.

Helen translated the menu for Lorna with barely a soupçon of condescension. Henry struggled with his schoolboy French, but found himself unable to seek help.

The headwaiter approached. Ted said, 'I'll tell you what to order, Lorna.' He leant across Helen, brushing himself against her chest, and whispered something into the ear of the more flat-chested Lorna.

'What's going on, Ted?' said Helen.

'Trust me,' said Ted.

'Have you decided, madam?' said the headwaiter.

Lorna gave Ted an assessing look. 'Have you got any *merde*?' she said.

'Madam!' said the headwaiter.

'Ted!' said Helen, and she kicked him.

'Ow!' said Ted.

'You bastard,' said Henry.

'Below the belt,' said Gordon. 'Final warning.'

'*Merde* is French for . . . er . . . well . . . shit,' said Neil, blushing.

'Many a true word,' said Gordon.

'I'm sorry,' said Lorna to the headwaiter, 'but he told me to ask for it.'

A faint grin appeared at the edge of the headwaiter's mouth. He wiped it off with the invisible napkin of his professionalism.

Lorna plumped for tomato soup and a well-done fillet steak. Henry wished that she'd been more adventurous. He decided that, if he was paying a fortune, at least he'd have something exciting. *Pamplemousse* sounded exciting. So did steak tartare. The headwaiter had gone before Henry realized that he hadn't asked how he'd like it cooked.

'You sod, Ted,' he said.

'Give over,' said Lorna. 'It were just a joke.'

'It wasn't a bloody joke,' said Henry. 'That was no joke, Lorna.'

'We can take a joke where I come from,' said Lorna. She turned to Ted. 'I thought it might be summat rude,' she said, 'but I thought "Oh. What the 'eck? Waiter looks as if 'e needs a bit of life pumped into im."'

'Good for you, kid. Smashing,' said Colin.

Henry was pleased to see that Ted looked somewhat abashed. And he was pleased to see that Helen looked rather glad that Ted looked somewhat abashed.

When he went to the Gents, Colin followed.

'She's a smashing kid, kid,' he said. 'I could give her one meself.

57

Now you listen to me. You hang onto her. And stop looking at that other bloody one.'

What good judges men can be of other men's women.

Silence hung over the cavernous dining-room, as if the amount that was being spent on indifferent food was a source of shared grief between customers and waiters. The tables were enormous, and Henry and Lorna could hardly have rubbed their legs together, under the table, had anything so friendly been in their thoughts. They were cowed by the atmosphere. Customers were almost outnumbered by waiters, and the youngest of the other diners seemed about forty years older than them.

Behind them, Royal Scot No. 46164 *The Artist's Rifleman* was passing through Bushey troughs with the up *Mid-Day Scot*.

Henry's legs ached. He longed for his food with the hunger of a psychotic obsessed with a displacement activity. All the world was drab, save for the exotic promise of *pamplemousse*.

'She's pretty, isn't she?' said Lorna in a low voice.

Henry fought desperately against blushing, and almost managed it.

'Who?' he croaked.

'Helen, of course. Who else was there who's pretty? Denzil?'

'Well . . . yes . . . yes, I suppose she . . . I hadn't really . . . er . . .'

'Bollocks.'

'Lorna!'

Had the dreadful word stirred the over-starched table-cloths? Certainly, somewhere, as if in shock, a spoon scraped noisily against a plate. Had arthritic necks craned to see the source of this verbal outrage, unparalleled in the history of the restaurant of the Midland Hotel, Thurmarsh, in those days before pop groups?

'What?'

'You don't say things like that in places like this.'

'I do. I'm a country bumpkin. Remember?'

'Lorna!'

The elderly wine waiter limped towards them with a vast tome.

'The wine list, sir?'

'Please.'

Henry peered blankly at a long list of names. 'Which would tha prefer?' he said. 'Château Lafite '36 or a glass of Tizer?'

Lorna gave a leaden smile. The memory of their childhood games echoed desolately round the room like a marble in a Wall of Death. The wine waiter waited, breathing asthmatically, as if he expected Henry to choose from a list of three hundred wines in less than a minute. He chose at random a wine he couldn't afford with a name he couldn't pronounce.

Their food arrived. Henry almost cried when he discovered that *pamplemousse* was half a grapefruit. A waitress gripped stale rolls in silver tongs and dropped them onto their plates. They almost shared a laugh.

'How's your tomato soup?' he asked.

'It's tomato soup. How's your *pamplemousse*?'

'It's bloody grapefruit.'

Henry hoped the waitress would offer them another roll, so that this time they might share a laugh, but such largesse was not to be seriously expected.

'What did you think of them?' he said, drawn to the subject of his new friends as a man with vertigo is drawn towards the path's edge.

'I liked Colin.'

'Yes. He's smashing. He liked you.'

'Great. One down, six to go!'

'Lorna!'

The waiter brought Henry his bottle as if it were a priceless antique. On Henry's salary, it was. He poured a tiny drop into Henry's glass. Henry took an embarrassed sip and nodded. The wine waiter filled their glasses to the brim. Years later Henry would remember this, and realize how ignorant the wine waiter was, and wish that he could have his youth back so that this time he could live it without being overawed.

'Gordon liked you,' he said. 'You have to read between the lines with Gordon.'

'Two out of seven!'

He took a sip of wine. A waiter came over and poured a sipful into his glass. He mumbled his thanks at this tiresome gesture.

'Ben liked you.'

59

'I liked Ben.'

'Ben's all right.'

'Well . . . three out of seven.'

Their main courses arrived. His steak tartare looked very strange.

They watched numbly while five different vegetables, all over-cooked, were piled onto Lorna's plate. Henry had only salad.

At last they were free to eat. He took a cautious mouthful. 'Bloody hell!' he said, louder than he intended. 'It's raw.'

A man at a neighbouring table gave him a pitying 'The barbarians are at the door' look.

The headwaiter hurried over with swift, absurdly small steps.

'Is anything wrong, sir?' he asked.

'Well . . . I . . .' Henry was bathed in embarrassment. 'My . . . er . . . steak. It's . . . not cooked. Is that . . . er . . . ?'

'Steak tartare is raw fillet steak, sir, blended with garlic, tabasco, raw egg, chopped onion, chopped capers and herbs.'

'Oh, I see.'

'We can change it, sir, if you don't like it.'

'No. No. That's fine. It's very nice. I just didn't . . . thank you.'

He wanted to say to Lorna, 'If you're a country bumpkin, what am I? An ignorant provincial hick. And what does it matter?' He couldn't. Why couldn't he? Because it did matter. He'd been tossed like a cork through a land where it mattered very much, and he was only a human being. He took another sip of wine. A waiter hurried over and poured a sipful into his glass. He mumbled his thanks at this annoying gesture.

'What is all this "three out of seven" business, anyroad?' he said. 'You make it sound like some sort of exam.'

'Wasn't it?'

'Course it wasn't.'

'I felt as if I was on trial. As if you 'ad no faith in me. As if you didn't want me, but somebody to bring glory to you. As if a waitress from a country village isn't good enough for your literary friends.'

'Literary friends? Give over, Lorna. Is your steak nice?'

'It's steak. How about yours?'

60

'It's not bad, actually. Once you get used to the idea. It's pretty fiery. Tell us about Rowth Bridge.'

'You don't want to know about Rowth Bridge. You've changed.'

'Course I've changed. We all change.'

'I 'aven't. That's the trouble.'

'I don't want you to change.'

'Yes, you do. You want me to be interesting and keen on books and paintings and ideas and that and foreign countries and things and I'm not.'

He hesitated. 'I would like you to be interested in those things, yes,' he said. 'I think they're good things, but I don't want a different you to be interested in them. I want the you that you are now to be . . .'

'. . . different.'

'No. Well . . . the same, but different. Look, let's leave it. I *am* interested in Rowth Bridge. How are Simon and Pam?'

Simon Eckington, from the post office, had married Pam Yardley, the evacuee, who had been Henry's childhood sweetheart before Lorna.

'All right. They've got two smashing kids.'

'Smashing.'

'You see, you aren't interested. You haven't even asked if they're boys or girls.'

'What are they?'

'Girls.'

'Smashing. Two little girls. Smashing.'

'I love children. I wanted to 'ave your children.'

'Lorna! You will!'

'I'm just a stop-at-home girl. 'ousewife in Rowth Bridge, three bairns, that's me.'

'Maybe you only think that because that's the role society's put you in.'

'No. I like it. I don't want to be a film critic.'

'Who's talking about film critics?'

There was a sullen silence between them. He took a large gulp of wine. A waiter hurried across and poured a large gulpful into his glass. He mumbled his thanks at this irritating gesture.

'This wine's nice, isn't it?' he said.

'I think it's 'orrid,' said Lorna.

'Would you prefer cider?'

'Yes, please.'

He tried to attract the attention of a waiter. Suddenly no eyes were looking their way.

'It doesn't matter.'

'Yes it does.'

'Imagine me ordering sweet cider in Hampstead!'

'What's Hampstead got to do with it?'

'What was 'er name? Paul's sister. Diana? Or is she forgotten now you've met the fabulous Helen?'

'Lorna!' He raised his arm imperiously. Two waiters ignored him. They were laying up for breakfast.

'She's a cow, that one. She'd scratch me eyes out except then folk wouldn't know any more that my eyes aren't as pretty as hers.'

'Lorna! She's not like that.'

'You see!'

'Lorna! I couldn't care less about her.' At last he'd made such strong eye contact with a waiter that the waiter couldn't ignore it. 'About time!' he said. The waiter ignored this. 'Er . . . could I have a pint of sweet cider, please?'

'Certainly, sir.' The waiter moved away and called out unnecessarily loudly, 'Pint of sweet cider for table eight, George.' This time the neighbouring diner's expression said, 'The barbarians aren't *at* the door. They're inside. Civilization's over. It's official.'

'I couldn't,' resumed Henry, 'care less about her. But sheer justice leads me to say that she isn't like you think.' He changed the subject. 'How are you getting on with Auntie Doris?'

'She's all right. She's quite generous when that 'orrible man's not around.'

'Geoffrey Porringer?'

''e's 'orrible.'

'I know. I call him the slimy Geoffrey Porringer.'

''e keeps touching me up. Rubbing against me. Making it look accidental.'

'Oh no. That's horrible.'

''e's disgusting. How do folk get to be so disgusting?'

62

The wine waiter brought the pint of sweet cider as if it were a Mills bomb. Yet, off duty, he never drank anything except dark mild.

'I met my Uncle Teddy on Wednesday,' said Henry. 'I'm going to come to Troutwick and try to get Auntie Doris to go back to him. And I'm going to warn Geoffrey Porringer off you. Nobody rubs up against my Lorna.'

'I'm not your Lorna.'

'You are. I love you, Lorna.'

'You don't. I've lost you, Henry.'

'Lorna!'

He took a gulp of wine. Three waiters raced to pour a gulpful of wine into his glass. He mumbled his thanks to the winner at this infuriating gesture.

The lift took them slowly to the fourth floor and the room which they had still not entered. The huge wooden block to which the key was attached rubbed Henry's leg, mocking his flaccid organ. He couldn't bring himself to admit that it was over, that he wasn't a caring humanist socialist but an obnoxious intellectual snob.

The lift juddered to a halt all too soon. He picked up their cases and staggered into the corridor. Oh no! He was drunk again. He hadn't meant to be, but Lorna hadn't liked the wine, and it was costing him, so he'd had to drink it, and it was rich, heavy stuff, and he wasn't used to wine, and the key turned in the lock, but the door wouldn't open. He heard somebody inside the room. The door opened, and a sleepy man in a tasselled green dressing-gown was standing there.

'It can't 'appen,' said the night porter. 'There's a foolproof system. It can't 'appen.'

'Well, it has happened,' said Henry.

'I'm not saying it 'asn't 'appened,' said the night porter. ''appen it 'as 'appened. I'm saying it can't 'appen.'

'All right,' said Henry. 'It can't happen. But it has happened. What are you going to do about it?'

'I don't rightly know,' said the night porter. 'It's never 'appened before.'

'Well, do you have any other rooms?'

'Oh aye. 'undreds. It's right quiet. Friday night. No business-men, does tha see?'

'Right. Well, can we have one of those hundreds of rooms?'

'Aye, but I'm not allowed to take bookings, tha knows. I'm not like authorized. I'm night porter, like, not reception.'

'You wouldn't be taking a bloody booking. We've already bloody booked into a room with a man in it with a bloody silly green dressing-gown with tassels.'

'There's no call to swear at me, sir. I fought in t'War when tha were too young. I've only got one lung.'

'I'm sorry I swore at you,' said Henry. 'I'm sorry I was too young to fight in the War. I'm very sorry you've only got one lung. I'm sorry I'm drunk. I'm sorry there's a man with a bloody silly green dressing-gown with tassels in our room, but this is the first night of our honeymoon, and Mr and Mrs Wedderburn and I . . . I mean, Mrs Wedderburn and I . . . are looking forward to a bit of . . . to a . . . and we'd like a room to do it in.'

'Well why didn't you say so, sir?' said the night porter. 'I'll give you the bridal suite.'

The bridal suite was enormous. There was a huge sitting-room, in the Midland Hotel's idea of French elegance – more platform fourteen than Louis Quatorze. The furniture was reproduction seventeenth century. The curtains and upholstery were like a tapestry exhibition. Above the ornamental marble fireplace, the Golden Arrow was steaming through Penge on its way to Paris, city of love. Henry agonized over whether to tip the night porter, and decided that he must, because the confusion wasn't his fault.

'God, it's big,' he said, when the night porter had gone.

'Can you afford it?' said Lorna.

'Yes,' he lied.

They examined the rest of the suite. The bed was a four-poster. The bathroom was vast, overflowing with enormous white towels and covered in huge mirrors.

'I need a bath,' he said. 'I'm caked in sweat.'

'That's all right,' said Lorna, in a little voice that pierced his heart.

In the mirrors in the bathroom, seven podgy Pratts with seven tiny organs stepped gingerly into seven immense hot baths. Henry tried to think himself into desire, reliving those snatched, scratchy moments in Kit Orris's field barn, trying to find the love that until this week he'd never doubted, except perhaps for those weeks in Germany. He tried to arouse himself with thoughts of Diana Hargreaves and Belinda Boyce-Uppingham, who had called him an oik. He tried not to arouse himself with thoughts of Helen Cornish.

He dried himself hurriedly, thankful that the steam on the mirrors was hiding him from view. He was sweating again, from fear and the heat of the bath and the steamy fug of the room. He washed himself in cold water – had he ever really felt clean? – and wrapped himself in a voluminous towel. He entered the bedroom. In the four-poster, Lorna was sailing on a gentle sea of dreams. He crept into the bed. It creaked. He lay beside her, barely dry, shivering now. She stirred to put a thin arm round him. 'You're cold,' she said. She began to nibble his ear. He felt nothing. She began to massage his cold body gently. Desperately he thought of Helen, of pulling off her swirling magenta dress in the dim, dusty midnight news-room, of laying her white, curvaceous body on the news desk. He began, just in time, to be aroused. He entered Helen there, amid piles of rejected stories, on the news desk, and it was all right, and Lorna Arrow would never know.

His legs still ached, his head was thick, he'd been in too deep a sleep, and she wasn't in the bed. He knocked the Gideon Bible onto the floor before he found the switch for the bedside light.

He padded naked across the thick carpet into the sitting-room. He switched on the tactful lighting. The room was huge and semi-elegant and empty. The Golden Arrow was steaming eternally through Penge. On an eight-year-old seventeenth-century table, scrawled on a piece of British Railways lavatory paper, was the last word Lorna Arrow would ever write to her childhood sweetheart. It was 'Good-buy'.

On the first part of the journey, Henry faced north. He had a window seat with his back to the engine. His thoughts faced north, too.

Unable to pay for the bridal suite and their expensive dinner, he'd crammed his washing things and clean underpants into the pockets of his duffel-coat, and shuffled guiltily out of the hotel. There was no point in pursuing Lorna. Not yet, anyway. He could hardly go home, when he was supposed to be visiting Paul. So, the obvious thing to do was to visit Paul. He'd phoned from the station. There'd been good news and bad news. The good news was that they had a spare ticket for the rugby international. The bad news was that Paul had phoned him last night, to invite him, and this had surprised Cousin Hilda quite considerably.

So he sat in that over-heated train, worrying about Lorna and how she was feeling, about Cousin Hilda and how he would explain, and about the Midland Hotel and how he would avoid being arrested.

In the Midland lowlands, as the train approached Lough-borough, he began to think about his national service. He'd spent five months in those parts, so now he faced sideways, looking out of the window, searching for landmarks.

There were fewer worries here. True, he had a disturbing sense of unfinished business, of a ghost that still had to be laid, but in the main the traumas of those times had already become amusing stories, told at his own expense.

As the train roared through Barrow-on-Soar, it passed under a bridge over which he had ridden silently, a tiny figure in the stillness of a vast dark night on a girl's bicycle, his face blackened with burnt cork, in February, 1954. He'd been unit runner on night exercises, and had been given SQMS Tompkins' daughter's bike. It had been absurdly small for him, and had had no crossbar. His job had been to deliver vital coded messages from mobile HQ to uninterested groups of skiving, snoring squaddies. He remembered prodding a sleeping sergeant in a barn at first light. 'Three red ferrets knocking on green door, sarge.' 'Fuck off.' 'Yes, sarge.'

At Leicester three people got out and he was able to bag a window seat, facing the engine. Bag! That word belonged to his southern days. He was facing south now and so were his thoughts.

66

As the train snaked through the hunting shires, the rich farmland dusted with snow, he thought about Diana. Oh no. No more women, Henry. But he liked Diana, and there was no harm in thinking about her. In a purely platonic way. Almost. Down, boy.

He had different worries now. Would his friendship with Paul survive better than that with Martin? Would he make his usual provincial *faux pas*? Would Tosser have a good game? Would he still fancy the elegant Mrs Hargreaves, which was ridiculous? Would he manage to borrow fifty pounds off Dr Hargreaves, eminent brain surgeon, which was essential, if he was to pay his hotel bill?

They met outside the ground as arranged. Paul looked impatient and self-righteous. He was fair-haired and slight. National service seemed to have pared him to the bone. 'The others have gone in,' he said curtly, and Henry saw how he'd been as a second-lieutenant.

Henry had discovered how vulnerable the upper middle classes are to good manners. 'Apologize and win' was almost as sound a principle as 'divide and rule'. So now he apologized. 'Sorry I've cut it a bit fine,' he said. Cut it a bit fine? You wouldn't say that in Thurmarsh, you chameleon. 'You know what trains are.'

It worked. 'Oh, that's all right,' said Paul. 'Sorry if I was a bit . . . er. I was afraid we'd miss the kick-off.' They shook hands with unaccustomed formality. 'Good to see you, old chum. Where's your luggage?'

'In my pockets.'

Paul shook his head in amazement at the latest eccentricity of his funny little northern friend, and they entered Twickenham, known the world over as Twickers. Henry felt that he ought to be watching Thurmarsh play Rochdale at Blonk Lane, known no-where as Blonkers.

The great stands were crowded. They made slow progress up stairs, down gangways. A roar announced the appearance of the teams. Alcohol fumes eddied in the raw wind. They edged along their row, disturbing knees covered in rugs, clambering over hampers, causing hip-flasks to be removed from chapped lips. 'Hello, Diana.' Shapeless and bulky in several layers of clothes, she looked more like a Cossack on guard duty than an attractive girl. He ought to have felt pleased, not disappointed. 'Hello, Dr Hargreaves. Hello, Mrs Hargreaves.' Mrs Hargreaves still looked elegant, in five layers of clothes. Dr and Mrs Hargreaves were looking at him oddly. He must look strange, in his old, stained duffel-coat, with crumpled underpants peeping out of the pockets. Hardly *comme il faut!* A tall, rather stern girl raised cool eyebrows at him. 'Judy, this is Henry, an old friend. Judy Miller, my girl-friend.' 'Hello, Judy.' 'Judy's at Girton. She's reading law.' How incredibly dreary. 'Oh. Smashing.' Oh god, I'm sitting between Diana and Mrs Hargreaves. I'm a small piece of podge entirely surrounded by desirable women. A cool, elegant, perfumed kiss on the cheek from Mrs Hargreaves. Why didn't age touch her like it touched everybody else? A huge, hot, wet kiss from Diana, a tidal wave of affection, red wine and garlic. Stirrings of desire, despite her shapelessness. National anthems. Incredible noise. Fervent Welsh singing, absurd among the trim residential streets of South-West London.

How small Tosser Pilkington-Brick looked. Well, not small. Normal-sized. At school he'd seemed enormous. Here all sixteen forwards were bigger than him, and some of the backs as well. Henry felt absurdly nervous for him. Well, was it that absurd? Tosser had been his hero. He'd fagged for him, and had felt a wet warm feeling when Tosser had spoken nicely to him, and Tosser had spoken nicely to him more than once.

England attacked from the start. Their forwards won plenty of good ball. The first time Tosser got the ball, he dropped it. The second time, he managed to catch it, but sent a wild pass which was intercepted by Brace. Towards half-time, M. J. K. Smith made a half-break, Tosser tried a dummy, slipped, and crashed into Cliff Morgan, amid hoots of derision. Henry couldn't believe it. His hero was nervous. He was having a stinker. Diana fell silent. When Tosser knocked on yet again, just before half-time, she clutched Henry's hand very tightly.

'What is it?' he said.

'He's playing so badly.'

She was identifying with his hero! What a magnificent girl she was! But he *would* like his hand back.

'Er . . . you're hurting my hand,' he said.

'Oh, sorry.' She released his hand, stroked it, looked at him thoughtfully, kissed him, and said, 'It *is* good to see you.' Was it Henry's imagination, or did Paul frown?

Henry tried to tell himself that it didn't matter, it served Tosser right. Lampo Davey, for whom he had also fagged, had been right to scorn all this. Hero-worship belonged to childhood. It belonged to the rejected part of his life, at Dalton College. He shouldn't be here, he belonged with Lorna in Rowth Bridge. It was no use telling himself these things. Every time the ball came to Tosser, Henry's heart raced.

At half-time, Dr Hargreaves poured whisky into real glasses from his hip-flask and Mrs Hargreaves handed round rolls spread with home-made anchovy paste. Nobody mentioned Tosser Pilkington-Brick.

In the second half Tosser played a little better, without covering himself with glory. England won the scrums 18–10, and led in the line-outs 55–18, but the backs squandered chances galore and, as the final whistle approached, they were losing 3–4.

'Henry?' said Mrs Hargreaves suddenly, as England surged into a last assault. 'Do you remember the name of that little restaurant near Concarneau where you tried *langoustine* for the first time?' The impossibility of his predicament! Reluctant to be rude, and being asked to recall a Breton fish restaurant at the climax of a great sporting event. 'It's on the tip of my tongue,' he lied.

The ball was passed to Tosser only three yards from the Welsh line. He was going to score the winning try. Pilkington-Brick atones for early errors. Thrilling late winner from England 'newboy'.

And Tosser dropped it. The great, incompetent, unimaginative oaf couldn't catch a ball and run three yards with it. Fury shook Henry's podgy frame. Diana clutched his left hand sympathetically. Mrs Hargreaves grabbed his right hand triumphantly.

'Au Chêne Vert,' she said.

'What?' said Henry blankly.

'The restaurant where you first tried *langoustine*,' said Mrs Hargreaves, as if speaking to a mental defective. 'That is a weight off my mind. I've been worrying about that for days.'

Lucky you, if that's all you've got to worry about, thought Henry.

Dr Hargreaves nosed the Bentley through the slow-moving traffic, in the deepening night, past rows of snug, smug houses, past lines of trim, prim pollarded trees. Henry tried not to feel superior to the hordes who were streaming on foot towards buses and trains. It wasn't easy. He felt a disturbing flicker of sympathy with the arrogance of the rich. Well, it was rather nice, sensing how much Diana was enjoying being squashed against him, sensing how much Judy wasn't enjoying being squashed against him. He let his body fall against Judy's tubular hardness as Dr Hargreaves swung into the main road with the assumption that Bentleys took precedence over Morrises and Singers.

In the Hargreaveses' narrow, four-storey Georgian town house in Hampstead, everyone went to change. Henry's change, in his little room, with an original Klimt above the bed – just how rich were they? – consisted of putting on his crumpled, clean underpants.

Diana looked mature and almost elegant, if slightly lumpy, in black and gold.

They drank dry sherry. Judy said, 'Thank you very much for inviting me. It was a super game.'

'Yes, thank you,' said Henry hastily, partly so as not to be left at the post in the good manners stakes, but also to establish publicly what had never actually been made clear, that he was invited and wouldn't be expected to pay. It was important that he be at his best that evening so that, when mellowness had set in, he could ask to borrow fifty pounds. He'd have to be particularly careful to hide his hostility to Judy. But really! Calling it a super game, when it would go down in history as the day Pilkington-Brick lost the match for England!

'Poor Tosser,' said Diana, as if she could read his thoughts. Her legs began widening below the knee instead of waiting, as legs should, till they were out of sight. How endearing her slightly fat knees were.

If mellowness never did set in that evening, no blame can be attached to anyone but Henry.

70

The moment he entered the Ristorante Garibaldi, with its pale blue walls, pink table-cloths and scalloped pink napkins – no fishermen's nets, hanging Chianti bottles and empty wine bottles covered with stalactites of candle-grease for Dr and Mrs Hargreaves – he thought: Oh dear. I'm going to behave badly tonight.

Did he fight against it? Oh yes. After his somewhat unfortunate opening remark of 'What poncy serviettes' he remained silent for several minutes. He behaved moderately well while eating his *tagliatelle al pesto*, but its elegant greenness reminded him of the less elegant verdancy of the glutinous curries at the Shanghai Chinese Restaurant and Coffee Bar. He felt ashamed of the gastronomic desert that was Thurmarsh. The shame made him feel defensive. His mood wasn't improved when he thanked Dr Hargreaves for the salt and Paul said, 'Henry? Tiny point. Dad's a fellow of the Royal College of Surgeons. They call themselves Mr, not Dr.' Terrific, thought Henry: Lets me get it wrong for six years, then corrects me in public. Which may have been why, when the conversation turned to national service and Judy assumed that he'd been an officer, he said, 'No. And I'm glad.'

'Really?' said Paul, unable to resist the bait. 'Why's that?'

'Do you remember Tubman-Edwards who blackmailed me at Dalton?'

'God, yes. What a monster.'

'He was a second-lieutenant in the Signals. I was on cookhouse fatigues.' He broke off to thank the waiter for his sea bass with Livornese sauce. 'I was at a huge sink full of vast cooking-tins covered in grease and I had to wash them in cold water. That was the sort of merry jape they used to think up to help build our character. Tubman-Edwards was orderly officer. He said, "It's Pratt, isn't it?" I said, "Yes, sir." Sir! He said, "How are you enjoying the army, Pratt?" I said, "Very much, thank you, sir." He said, "Jolly good." That's why I wouldn't have wanted to be an officer.'

'I fail to see the point,' said Paul.

'That's why you could be an officer,' said Henry. Mr and Mrs Hargreaves frowned at his bad manners but, since he was a guest, they said nothing. 'I couldn't accept a system in which I had to say stupid things like "How are you enjoying the army?" to men washing greasy tins in cold water.'

'Isn't the truth of the matter that it was you who was forced to say something stupid?' said Judy.

I can imagine you in court, thought Henry, with your sallow cheeks, your long, thin nose and your determined mouth, but I cannot imagine you in bed with Paul.

'How come?' he said lamely.

'Well, you replied "Very much, thank you" instead of "Not at all, you stupid twit, can't you see I'm covered in cold grease?"'

'I'd have been on a charge.'

'Precisely. So you took refuge in a cowardly lie.'

'Cowardly lie? What you're suggesting would have been suicidal idiocy,' said Henry. 'All right. I amend what I said. I'd have hated to be an officer and been forced to force people like me to say stupid things like I was forced to say.'

Mr Hargreaves gave Henry a tiny nod, acknowledging a good point scored. Henry didn't want to score points. He wanted to give his deeply felt views. He knew he should stop. He couldn't.

'I'll make you a prediction,' he said. 'In twenty years' time, national service will have been abolished, authority and discipline will be breaking down and Disgusted of Tunbridge Wells will be saying "Bring back national service. Give them some discipline." Well, I believe that one of the reasons why authority and discipline will be breaking down will be because a whole generation will have learnt to say "Thank you very much, sir," while meaning "Oh sod off, you stupid twit." They'll also, incidentally, have become deeply imbued with every four-letter word except work.'

There was a loud silence, then Mrs Hargreaves said, 'There's a very interesting exhibition of Portuguese art at the Royal Academy. One knows so shamefully little about Portuguese art,' and Henry wanted to laugh. Suddenly he felt in a good mood. He would redeem himself. 'This sea bass is delicious,' he said, and then he remembered that talking about food while eating it was not considered good form in the Hargreaveses' circle, as he'd discovered when he'd said, 'This stew's nice,' when it was *boeuf bourgignon* anyway, and the memory of *that* humiliation swept over

72

him, and he no longer felt in a good mood, and Mr Hargreaves said, 'Do you think Wales will beat the French?' and Diana said, 'Northern Fiji is highly populated, I hear,' and everybody stared at her in astonishment; and she said, 'The last four remarks were about sodding twits, Portuguese art, sea bass and rugby, so I assumed this was the new style of witty table talk, with every sentence on an entirely new subject,' and Henry looked at her in astonishment – was it possible that she was on his side? – and he said, 'Oh, I agree. Double glazing's the thing of the future,' and she said, 'Ah, but *are* the Peruvian Indians happy?' and he said, 'Well, let's put it this way, a masochist is a person who likes bashing himself against a wall because it's so nice when it starts,' and Henry and Diana laughed but nobody else did, and what might on another occasion have been an amusing conversational fancy was edged with tension. Mr and Mrs Hargreaves looked as if they were being asked to play a new game but hadn't been told the rules. Paul and Judy knew that it wasn't a game and Henry, knowing that he was being foolish, said, 'Being an officer has changed you, Paul. You look as if you'd like to arrest me for conduct prejudicial to good restaurant order and discipline, filthy and idle while eating a sea bass, *sir*,' and after that, although the zabaglione passed off without incident, it clearly wasn't possible to ask Mr Hargreaves for fifty pounds that night.

His bedroom door was opening. It squeaked slightly. He sat bolt upright.

'It's me,' whispered Diana.

'Good God,' he said.

'S'sh!' she whispered as she closed the door.

She removed her dressing-gown and slipped naked into his bed.

'Move up,' she whispered.

He moved up. He was putty in her hands.

'You're tense,' she whispered. 'Relax.'

Yes, yes. Come on, Henry. Rise to the occasion. As it were. It's what you've always wanted. Yes, but not now. If only it wasn't the night after I'd decided I'm no good at the only thing I'm good at. If only it wasn't at the end of the day on which I decided to give women up for ever, for their sakes as well as mine. If only I hadn't had so much to drink yet again. If only she hadn't had so much garlic. There was something to be said, perhaps, for the gastronomic desert that was Thurmarsh. If only they weren't in the room next to her parents.

'Relax,' she whispered. 'Don't wriggle. What's wrong?'

'They'll hear.'

'Oh, Henry. You sounded so rebellious tonight. Was all that just talk?'

'No, but . . . your family . . . I mean . . .'

'Do you want to be like Paul and Judy, carefully not sleeping together tonight out of good manners?'

'No.'

'Everyone does it these days. This is 1956.'

'I know.'

He pressed himself against her naked body. She put her tongue in his mouth. He ran his hands over her warm, chunkily generous body.

'You're lovely,' he said. 'You're so beautiful.' He found himself responding to his own words. 'I love you,' he said. 'I love you with all my heart, darling. Oh, Diana, Diana, I love you.' Slowly, and entirely forgetting to be quiet, he began to rise to heights of feeling and desire, on a tide of words which he didn't mean.

It was clear, in the olive-green dining-room, over the bacon and kidneys – eggs would have been too obvious – that they all knew. It was also clear, despite their politeness, that they disapproved.

Diana came in late, still kissed by sleep, and said, 'Morning, everybody,' with a determined brightness that verged on defiance.

'Did you sleep well, Diana?' said Paul, meaningfully avoiding sounding meaningful.

'Very well indeed,' said Diana, ditto. 'How did you and Judy sleep?'

'I slept very well,' said Paul. 'Did you sleep well, Judy? Was your room quiet?'

'Very quiet,' said Judy. 'I slept very well. Did you sleep well, Henry?'

'I slept very well, thank you, Judy.'

Mr Hargreaves smiled. 'Well, then,' he said. 'It sounds as though everyone slept as well as could be expected. We shall be able to issue a very satisfactory communiqué.'

Diana still hadn't given Henry a direct look. He wished she would.

'And what are you young people planning to do this morning?' said Mrs Hargreaves.

'I'm going to show Henry round the heath,' said Diana rather shrilly.

Henry felt that he could have been exultant that morning, if he hadn't told Diana that he loved her, if he hadn't got to ask Mr Hargreaves for fifty pounds, if he hadn't got to explain to the Midland Hotel why he'd walked out without paying, and if he hadn't got to explain to Cousin Hilda why Paul had rung to invite him for a weekend for which he had already departed.

The sunshine grew steadily hazier, until the sun was just a vague diffusion of yellow light in a dull and darkening mist. There was a smell of snow. Hampstead Heath that Sunday morning seemed alive with interesting people. In Henry's imagination they were philosophers and painters, socialist intellectuals, Middle European exiles, eccentrics and poets. Probably quite a few of them were actually plumbers and insurance brokers.

The path took them out of the trees, onto a bare grassy knoll. Several people were flying kites in the freshening wind. To the south the great city was dimly visible through the thickening murk. The light was growing faintly purple.

'Henry?'

She was finding it difficult to look at him. He didn't like it.

'What?'

'I wish I hadn't come to your room last night.'

That jolted him. 'Oh. May I ask why?' There was no reply. 'I thought you . . . er . . . enjoyed it.'

'This morning,' she said, 'thinking of what you said . . . I had no idea. That you loved me.' She forced herself to meet his gaze. 'I could never love you, Henry.'

Wonderful. It let him off the hook completely. So why did he feel as if a heavyweight boxer had just hit him in the stomach?

75

Ego? He tried to look blank. He didn't want her to see him with ego on his face.

'Well,' he said, 'so why, if I may ask, did you come to my room?'

'I like you very much and I find you . . .' Why did she have to search so long for an adjective? '. . . appealing.'

He kissed her. Now why did he do that?

'No!' she said. 'Please!'

He held her tight and pressed his crutch into hers, in the midst of all the kite fliers. He kissed her long and slowly on the mouth. Now why did he do that? And she kissed him back, her lips working diligently, until their faces were slimy with each other's saliva. Now why did she do that?

At last the kiss ended. 'You see,' she said. 'It's very simple. I like sex. I'm probably over-sexed.'

'Ah,' he said.

'What do you mean, "ah"?' she said indignantly. 'Is that an adequate response to such an incredible admission?'

'I wasn't sure whether to say "congratulations" or "bad luck".'

'I know. I mean, I'm not promiscuous. Not really. I'd never do it with somebody I didn't like a lot or know really well. But I do enjoy going to bed with men I like. And once not a man. Does that shock you?'

'No. I . . . er . . . don't think I have any right to be shocked by that.'

'Oh? Really? Interesting. Anyway, when you said you loved me, I felt awful. You could never be that important to me.'

'Well, that's . . . wonderful.'

'What?'

'I . . . er . . . you're so lovely, Diana, so attractive, such a nice person, that I said things I didn't mean. I don't love you.'

'Oh.'

'I like you very much. Perhaps I feel all the feelings of love towards you except love itself.'

'Oh. Well, that's all right, then.'

'Yes.'

And they walked back slowly, under a bruised sky, both let off the hook, both feeling offended when they should have felt relieved. Ah, youth! How very like middle and old age it is.

They realized that everyone was wondering what had taken place on their walk. They decided, without needing to consult each other, to play the situation up. Every now and then, during lunch, they gave each other intense glances.

They had fish soup and medallions of rare beef in red wine sauce. Henry wondered, with shame but also with love, what Paul must have thought of Cousin Hilda's meals.

'Were there any paintings out up Heath Street?' said Mrs Hargreaves.

'Oh yes, quite a few,' quipped Henry sparklingly.

'I think you found them very interesting, didn't you, Henry?' said Diana. 'I mean, you don't get a lot of open-air paintings in Thurmarsh.'

Henry was appalled to hear himself say, in betrayal of his whole heritage, 'You don't get a lot of anything in Thurmarsh.'

'Except spittle,' said Judy.

There was an amazed silence. Paul flushed. Even Judy looked horrified. But she had to enlarge on it now.

'Paul tells me people keep spitting up there. On the pavements,' she said.

Paul glared at her. Clearly this was a breach of confidence.

'They do,' said Henry. 'It's because there's such a lot of pneumoconiosis.'

'I think that's a beautiful word,' said Judy.

'Extremely beautiful,' said Henry. 'It must be a great consolation to people who're dying of it.'

'Henry! For Christ's sake!' said Paul.

'Well I'm sorry, but it isn't funny, you see,' said Henry.

'I thought it was parrots, anyway,' said Diana.

'Sorry? You thought what was parrots?' said Paul.

'Pneumoconiosis.'

'That's psittacosis,' said Mr Hargreaves reluctantly.

'What's psoriasis, then?' said Paul.

'A skin disease,' said Mr Hargreaves reluctantly.

'Please! People!' said Mrs Hargreaves. 'What *has* happened to your idea of table talk?'

'Could parrots have psoriasis as well as psittacosis?' said Diana.

'Diana!' said Mrs Hargreaves.

'I wonder if anybody's ever given a parrot an enema for eczema in Exeter,' said Diana.

'You're in a very silly mood today, Diana,' said Mrs Hargreaves. She gave Henry an involuntary look, and he knew that she blamed him for Diana's silly mood. He exchanged intense looks with Diana.

The conversation continued in more subdued vein. On the surface everybody was very civil, but he knew that, while acceptable as a friend, he was not regarded as suitable for marrying Diana, and the fact that he had no intention of marrying her didn't make this any more palatable. He was finding out how unpleasant it is not to be thought good enough, and that provoked unpleasant reflections on his own behaviour towards Lorna.

And he still had to ask to borrow fifty pounds. He'd thought it would be easy to ask for money from the rich. He was realizing that they are the hardest of all to ask.

At last, the gastronomically exquisite, socially unbearable meal came to an end.

'Er . . .' he began, over coffee, in the faintly Chinese drawing-room on the first floor. 'I . . . er . . . I wonder if I could . . .' Oh god, he was blushing. 'I wonder if I could have a word in private, Mr Hargreaves?'

There was an eloquent silence. Henry realized that everybody except Diana thought that he was going to ask Mr Hargreaves for his daughter's hand in marriage. He could hardly suppress a smile at the thought that he could ever bring himself to do anything as feudal as that.

Mr Hargreaves took him to his study. Over his desk was an enormous diagram of the human brain, which struck Henry as sheer affectation. The man must know his way round the brain by now, unless, ghastly thought, he needed a quick refresher after breakfast.

If Henry was tense and nervous, so was Mr Hargreaves. This made Henry all the more furious that he had to ask to borrow money off the man.

'Er . . . I've got myself in a very small financial jam,' he said.

'What? Oh!' It took Mr Hargreaves two seconds to realize that

78

good manners demanded that he attempt to hide his immense relief. 'What sort of a jam, Henry? And how small?'

'Well . . . er . . . not really a jam exactly. I just have a bill, and no money to pay it.'

'That is, in my estimation, a jam.'

Snow had begun to settle on the little walled town garden. They both noticed it at the same moment. It's hard to say which of them was more appalled at the possibility of Henry being snowed in there.

'How much are we talking about?' asked Mr Hargreaves.

'Well . . . er . . .' It sounded such a lot. 'Fifty pounds, actually.'

Mr Hargreaves relaxed, and Henry realized what a small sum it seemed to him.

'Of course, Henry.'

'I could pay you back at two pounds a week.'

'Do you mind my asking how much you earn?'

'Seven pounds ten a week.'

Mr Hargreaves stared at him in amazement.

'Good Lord! That's not very much,' he said.

'I know a lot of people who earn less,' said Henry. 'People who do unpleasant, essential jobs.' Shut up! Not now! Don't pollute the reservoir of goodwill you've built up by not getting engaged to Diana.

'Yes . . . well . . . I think a pound a week would be more practical, don't you?' said Mr Hargreaves smoothly. 'We don't want you failing to keep up the payments.'

'I'd rather die than fail to keep up the payments, Mr Hargreaves.'

Mr Hargreaves gave Henry a look, then nodded briskly.

His train was seventy-seven minutes late, due to snow. If he'd waited till the last train, he wouldn't have got back that night.

He looked at Thurmarsh as if he were a Londoner arriving for the first time. How cold it was. How bleak the station looked. How small, dreary and ill lit the ticket hall was. He felt ashamed.

The town was muffled by snow and almost deserted. There weren't enough taxis, and a queue was forming. Henry trudged across Station Square through several inches of snow. The Midland Hotel had become an enchanted castle.

Why did he feel so nervous? It didn't matter what they thought of him here. He explained the situation to the duty manager, who produced his bill with minimal politeness. He looked the sort of man who's frightened of catching VD off lavatory seats, and handed Henry his battered case as if fearing that it might be contaminated. Henry wondered what he expected to catch off it. Chronic gaucherie? Terminal podginess? Poverty?

He struggled along York Road and turned right into Commercial Street, which ran behind the Town Hall, across decaying Merrick Street. As he walked east, Commercial Street became Lordship Road and began to go up in the world. By its junction with Park View Road it was thoroughly respectable, though already struggling for survival. Two houses had been turned into private hotels. They were called the Alma and the Gleneagles.

Henry's footsteps violated the smooth whiteness of Cousin Hilda's front garden. Inside the house it was raw and dim and silent.

He put his head round the door of the basement room. The 'businessmen' were just finishing the little supper which Cousin Hilda gave them each evening. It was a shock to see them there, in mid-brawn, as if nothing had happened during the last three days.

'My feet are soaked. I'll be down in a minute,' he announced.

The 'businessmen' had gone by the time he returned. The room smelt of greens' water, warm wool and cold brawn. A warm fire burnt in the blue stove with the cracked panes. Cousin Hilda looked beyond the reach of warm fires.

'Where have you been?' she said.

He looked at her in carefully simulated astonishment.

'The Hargreaveses',' he said. 'I told you. Oh, I suppose you were worried by Paul's phone call on Friday night. I wanted to surprise them, so I didn't tell them I was going. I phoned them when I got to St Pancras, but there was no reply. They'd gone out to dinner.' Cousin Hilda couldn't resist sniffing at this extravagance, even though she didn't entirely believe in it. 'So I stayed in a little hotel near King's Cross, and rang them in the morning. It's called the Caledonian. You can check if you don't believe me.' He knew she wouldn't. How could she, without sounding vaguely disreputable? He resented life for providing so many reasons for turning a young man of honest intent into an accomplished liar. He gave her an edited version of the weekend, and felt indignant because he suspected that she didn't even believe the bits that were true.

'What an exciting life they all lead,' said Cousin Hilda. 'How drab all this must seem.'

He attacked his brawn bravely. What a terrible cue she had given him. He couldn't say, 'Yes, it is drab. Horribly drab. I'm leaving.' He said 'No' again, although each time he said 'No' it made it harder for him to say that he was leaving. And leave he must. 'No!' He meant it. He'd much prefer to live here than with the Hargreaveses. Well, say that. 'I'd much prefer to live here than with the Hargreaveses. But, you see, Cousin Hilda, I . . .' He swallowed. Why did he find it so incredibly difficult to say it? 'I'm going to get a flat.' Her lips were beginning to work, with the distress. 'I've been happy here. I regard it as my home. But I've got to live in my own place and lead my own life and find my own feet if I'm to compete in the hard world of the press.'

'Journalists!' said Cousin Hilda. 'Giving you airs! I don't know!'

4 A Difficult Week

'How was the weekend, kid?' said Colin Edgeley.

Henry shrugged.

'You've got a good kid there. You stick with her.'

Colin raised a questioning eyebrow at the failure of Henry's attempted smile.

Henry stuck a sheet of coarse, cheap paper into his ancient, clattering typewriter. He typed slowly, with two fingers: 'Iceland-1.' This identified the story and the page, and exhausted his inspiration.

He turned, as he'd been hoping not to do, to have a quick peep at Helen. He met Ted's dark, deep, ironic eyes and turned away hurriedly. 'Iceland is a country of beautiful women, according to an Icelandic visitor to Thurmarsh.' Rubbish. He tore the sheet out, replaced it, and typed: 'Iceland-1.' He knew that Ginny'd seen him looking at Helen. He leant across to speak to her.

'Do anything exciting this weekend, Ginny?' he said.

'No.'

Good. 'Oh dear.'

The conversation fizzled out after this misleadingly sparkling exchange. 'Hot geysers have a very different connotation from in Thurmarsh . . .'

Gordon Carstairs struggled in, his eyes set deep in his baggy, insomniac's face. 'What sort of a time do you call this?' said Terry Skipton. 'Twenty past nine,' said Gordon with less than his usual obscurity. But when Henry said, 'Morning, Gordon. Nice weekend?' Gordon exclaimed, 'Penalty!' Henry deduced that it hadn't been a nice weekend.

His disobedient head was swivelling round again, to take a sip of Helen's loveliness. She smiled sweetly and returned to her forecast of a revolution in ladies' undergarments. He switched off her loveliness with a sigh, and stepped back into the dark world of his journalistic inexperience.

He finished the story and handed it to Terry Skipton, who began to read it with a face as long as a Sunday in Didcot.

'"Connotation"!' he said. 'What's the meaning of "connotation"?'

'Meaning,' said Henry.

'This is what I say,' said Terry Skipton. 'What's the meaning?'

'No,' said Henry. 'You've mistaken my meaning. When I said "meaning" I was meaning that the meaning of connotation is meaning.'

'Well, if you mean "meaning", say "meaning". They won't understand "connotation" in Splutt. Anyroad, I must read on. I'm riveted.' Terry Skipton read on, with darkening brow. 'It's all about Iceland,' he said.

'He's *from* Iceland.'

'I told you to find out his views about Thurmarsh. I mean, what are we, the *Thurmarsh Argus* or the *Trondheim Argus*?'

'Trondheim's in Norway.'

'Is it? Well, if you're such a Clever Dick you ought to know better than write rubbish like this. I want stuff about Thurmarsh.'

'But Thurmarsh people know about Thurmarsh.'

'They want to know what *he* thinks about Thurmarsh. They couldn't care less about Iceland. It's thousands of miles away. They've never been there. They're never going to go there.'

'I didn't realize people were so parochial,' said Henry.

'I'm deeply sorry that mankind fails to come up to your high standards, Mr Pratt,' said Terry Skipton. 'You'll rewrite that story this afternoon. In the meantime, get round them hospitals and police stations. There's been snow and ice. There'll be accidents. And, regrettable though our parochialism is, please try not to ask the desk sergeant at Blurton Road police station for his views on tribal dancing in Timbuctoo.'

As he walked away, Henry was already regretting making an enemy of Terry Skipton. His new friends were looking at him aghast. Only Gordon spoke. 'Change ends. More lemons,' he said. He sounded as if he meant it to be encouraging.

Henry trudged along pavements swept and pavements unswept. He phoned through a whole crop of minor accidents. He lunched alone, in the Rundle Café. A quantity surveyor, enjoying a cup of coffee after his braised steak, concealed himself behind the *Sporting Chronicle* to hide the moisture in his eyes as he Listened with Mother to the story of Gerald the Shy Guards Van.

That afternoon, Henry bashed out his story.

> Mr Gunnar Fridriksen, from Iceland, likes Thurmarsh [he wrote]. In particular, he likes our grime!
>
> Grime gives the buildings real atmosphere, he avers: 'We just do not have this grime in Iceland. Iceland is so clean, so new.'
>
> Another aspect of our life which wins praise from Mr Fridriksen, who runs an old people's home in the Icelandic capital, is our draught beer. 'It's an acquired taste,' he jokes. 'I have acquired it!'
>
> Mr Fridriksen, aged 43, also likes our gardens – front and back.
>
> The kindness of the ordinary man – and woman! – in the street is another source of praise from the blond Icelander.
>
> And he enjoys our toast. In fact, when he goes home Mr Fridriksen will take a very practical souvenir for his wife. Yes, a toaster!

The unprepossessing news editor read the story in grim silence. 'We'll make a journalist of you yet,' he said.

That evening, at number 66, Barry Frost bolted his liver and bacon, hummed that his desert was waiting so fiercely that he sprayed rhubarb crumble over his fellow 'businessmen', said, 'Dress rehearsal tonight,' and handed them all tickets for the first night. Liam's shining face reddened with excitement. Norman Pettifer talked about Sibyl Thorndike's St Joan. Cousin Hilda affected disapproval, but Henry sensed that she too was excited.

He looked at two flats that evening, but they were awful. He felt like going to the pub, but hurried home and watched *Come Dancing* with Cousin Hilda. Half of him affected lofty scorn. The other half danced to exotic Latin-American rhythms with Helen Cornish, who had sewn all the sequins herself.

On Tuesday he finished his calls quickly, bought the first edition of the paper and had a quick beer in the Pigeon and Two Cushions. There it was, on page 5, under the headline 'He likes our grime'. Three other customers had early editions. One of them said he'd have fancied Ginger's Delight in the one forty-five at Beverley if racing hadn't been snowed off. Another said, 'We should bomb that bugger Makarios.' None of them said, 'By 'eck, there's an Icelander here likes our grime.'

He lunched in the canteen. He announced that he was looking for a flat. Ginny said, 'There's a flat to rent in my house.' Helen said, 'That'd be cosy.' Gordon stared glumly at his toad-in-the-hole and said, 'He was a well-nourished man of average height.' Henry told Ginny that he couldn't see the flat that night. He was seeing *The Desert Song*. Ginny said she was reviewing *The Desert Song*. Helen said, 'That'll be cosy.'

The foyer of the Temperance Hall, in Haddock Road, was drab, draughty and bare save for admonitions against drink. But they had arranged to meet Barry Frost there after the performance.

Cousin Hilda and Mrs Wedderburn looked flushed by their exposure to the wanton world of show business. Liam O'Reilly looked exalted. Norman Pettifer looked vaguely disgusted, as if disappointed not to have seen Edith Evans.

Ginny approached them. Henry noticed for the first time that her legs were slightly bowed.

Why should he feel ashamed of Cousin Hilda and her 'businessmen' in the presence of this bow-legged future war correspondent? And why should he feel ashamed of this bow-legged future war correspondent in the presence of Cousin Hilda and her 'businessmen'?

'Are you going to the pub?' said Ginny.

'Certainly not,' said Cousin Hilda. 'I'm proud to say I've never been in a pub in my life.'

'Then how do you know you're right to be proud you've never been in one?' said Henry.

His belief that he'd scored a debating point lasted two seconds. Cousin Hilda said grimly, 'Because I've seen what it's done to people who *have* been in them.'

Liam looked back wistfully, towards the hall. He'd found things easier to deal with, in there.

Barry Frost appeared, smiling broadly. Henry introduced him to Ginny. There was silence. Neither Henry nor Ginny could bring themselves to give praise. Nobody else realized that they were expected to.

'Well, come on, what did you think of it?' said Barry Frost.

'Grand,' said Liam. 'It was just grand.'

Good old Liam, thought Henry, and then he realized that Liam meant it.

'Very nice,' said Cousin Hilda. 'Especially the women. They were hardly stiff at all.'

'I see,' said Barry Frost.

'Well, not you,' said Cousin Hilda. 'The others. They didn't seem to know what to do with their hands.'

'The scenery was attractive,' said Norman Pettifer.

'It didn't wobble nearly as much as it did when the Baptist Players put on Noël Coward's *Blythe Fever*,' said Cousin Hilda.

'I'm a bit deaf,' said Mrs Wedderburn, who had become Cousin Hilda's friend since Cousin Hilda's other friend, with whom Henry had shared two Christmasses, had died. She was short and stocky and had a thick bandage round her left leg. 'I heard every word *you* said. I thought you and the prompter were the clearest of all.'

'Thank you,' said Barry Frost.

'I admired your presence of mind when the door fell down,' said Norman Pettifer. 'You just opened the hole in the wall and stepped over the door as if nothing had gone wrong. I don't think Johnny Gielgud could have carried it off better.'

'Thank you, Norman,' said Barry Frost. 'Well, you've all made my evening. Who's coming to the pub?'

'Really, Mr Frost,' said Cousin Hilda. 'In front of the boy.'

'Boy?' said Henry. 'I'm nearly twenty-one. I'll tell you what you'd find in a pub, Cousin Hilda. Human warmth. Friendship. Laughter. Fun. Come on, Ginny, love.'

On Wednesday, January 25th, an inquiry set up to find ways of cutting the spending of the National Health Service reported that more money should be spent. Compulsory road tests were introduced for pre-war cars. Henry woke up thinking warm, erotic thoughts about Ginny Fenwick. She was big, warm and lovely. He'd have gone back with her last night if Norman and Barry hadn't been with them. Tonight he'd take a flat in her house. A new life was beginning. He was getting stories in the paper. He'd drink less, and work harder. Every night he would make love to Ginny Fenwick. Her eyes would shine with happiness.

He wanted to make people happy. He wanted to make Cousin Hilda happy. It was a source of great unhappiness to him that he regularly made her unhappy. He dreaded breakfast.

'I suppose you were drunk again last night,' she said grimly.

'I wasn't. It was Mr Pettifer knocked the milk bottles over.'

'Grown men don't tell tales.'

'He wasn't drunk either. He slipped on the icy step.'

The breakfast porridge could have been used as cement for the bricks of spotted dick in the house that Cousin Hilda's cooking built.

Liam entered the basement room next. A trace of the night's wonderment still hung about him.

'Grand morning,' he said.

Barry Frost grunted his greetings. Last night he'd been a showbiz personality. Today he was a tax inspector.

Over his second cup of tea, Norman Pettifer said, 'It's been a dull week so far. Cheddar, Cheddar, Cheddar. I hope today's different. It's discouraging when you pride yourself on the widest selection in the West Riding, and all you're asked for is Cheddar.'

'Don't you *know* what sort of day it'll be?' said Barry Frost. 'Has your uncanny talent for cheese prediction deserted you?'

'Feeling let down after the first night?' said Norman Pettifer. 'I read in a biography of . . .'

'I'm warning you,' said Barry Frost. 'If you mention Sibyl Thorndike or Johnny Gielgud I'll shove this cup right up your arse.'

'Mr Frost!' said Cousin Hilda.

Do, thought Henry. Give me a story. Tax inspector charged with assault after prominent local cheeseman hurt in Spode backside horror during post-theatre fracas.

No, thought Henry. I'm a kind-hearted humanist. I want people to get on well. I don't want them to be fodder for my career. Oh my god. Perhaps I shouldn't have become a journalist.

'I'm sorry,' said Barry Frost, leaving abruptly and banging the door behind him.

'Show business!' said Cousin Hilda.

'I thought it was grand last night,' said Liam. 'I thought it was the best thing I've ever seen in me life.'

The flat consisted of half the ground floor of a detached 1920s mock-Tudor house in Winstanley Road, which ran north through hills dotted with desirable residences on the edge of the town. Ginny had the half of the first floor which was directly above it.

He was shown round by the man from Bulstrode and Snotley. The flat comprised what had originally been the living-room and kitchen. Half the kitchen had become a cramped bathroom. In the now tiny kitchen there were servants' bells in a glass case. They didn't go with the formica table-top and work surfaces. The living-room had been divided by a plasterboard wall into a compact living-room and tiny bedroom. One half of the French windows stood right in the corner of the living-room, and the other half stood right in the corner of the bedroom. The effect was grotesque. The flat was cramped, ill-proportioned and drearily furnished. He took it.

He invited Ginny out, to celebrate. They walked to the Winstanley, a large, mock-Tudor pub where at lunch-times mock-sophisticated businessmen ate mock-turtle soup. The large lounge bar was awash with varnished tables, brown Windsor chairs, horse brasses, hunting scenes, tartan shields, and maps of the clans. The bleak, tiny public bar had been designed, successfully, to repel trade.

They drank glasses of Mansfield bitter. He ran his right hand briefly up her large left thigh. How lovely she was. It didn't matter that her lips were too thick, her nose too splayed, her complexion too red. She was Ginny Fenwick, warm-hearted lover, fearless war correspondent, enveloping earth-mother. They had three more drinks, and he decided that he didn't want to be enveloped just then. Not yet. Not till he'd moved in.

They caught a trolley-bus into town.

'They're ending the trolley-buses next year,' said Ginny. '"Progress."'

The doomed trolley-bus hissed smoothly through areas increasingly less prosperous as it dropped to the junction with York Road.

'Where shall we eat?' asked Henry. 'The Shanghai?'

'Oh not the Shanghai!'

No. Those awful glutinous curries. And Helen might be there.

The trolley-bus stopped briefly outside Fison and Oldsworthy's— *the* place for screws.

'I don't know anywhere, apart from the Shanghai, except the Midland Hotel, and I can't afford that,' he said.

'There's Donny's Bar,' said Ginny. 'It's upstairs at the Barleycorn. Steak and chops. Nothing inspired.'

'That'll be cosy,' said Henry.

'Join us,' said Helen.

'Please do,' boomed Denzil. 'We'll have some civilized conversation and pretend we're in a civilized world.'

Donny's Bar was a long, narrow room with tables along walls of false stone. Henry and Ginny stood in the middle of the room and talked in low voices.

'We'll have to, won't we?' he said.

'Oh yes!'

'What do you mean by that?'

'What I said,' said Ginny. 'We'll have to join them. That's clear.'

'Well, we will. I mean, it'd be rude not to. Wouldn't it?'

'Oh yes!'

'What do you mean by that?'

'What do you mean, "what do you mean by that?"?' said Ginny. 'I mean what I say. Yes, it'd be rude not to join them. And it'd be even ruder to stand here for half an hour, debating whether to join them. So let's join them, since it's what we all want so much.'

'What's that supposed to mean?' said Henry.

'Oh for God's sake,' said Ginny.

They joined them. Henry throbbed with desire for Helen.

'Henry's just taken a flat in my house,' said Ginny.

Oh my god, so I have, thought Henry. 'Where's Ted?' he said, half hoping she'd say, 'We've broken it off,' half hoping she'd say, 'Sending out invitations to the wedding.' 'On a story,' she said.

Cardboard cocktail was followed by medium-rare cardboard with sautéed cardboard and fresh garden cardboard, garnished with cardboard rings and half a grilled cardboard.

'Even in the gastronomic desert that is Thurmarsh, this could hardly be called an oasis,' said Denzil.

It rankled when a southerner said such things, especially a limping homosexual southerner with a hand-carved Scottish walking-stick, a high-pitched voice, and ageing mottled skin stretched across his cheekbones like old parchment.

'You enjoy being superior and mocking about everything, don't you?' said Henry.

'I'm impossible,' said Denzil. 'Hadn't you heard?'

'Yes,' said Henry. 'Often, from you. You seem to think if you say you're unpleasant it gives you *carte blanche* to *be* unpleasant.'

'I think you're a puritan at heart,' said Denzil.

Henry tried not to look at Helen. He tried to find Ginny attractive. Her face was even redder than usual and her nose was shining as she shovelled grub into her large mouth like an excavator. She was eating like that because she was hurt. His heart went out to her, but his genitals went out to Helen. He didn't want to be a virile, sexual person if this was how it made you behave. He put his hand on Ginny's knee, under the table. She kicked him.

'You're quiet tonight, Helen,' said Denzil.

'I only speak when I have something interesting to say,' said Helen.

'Good God!' said Ginny. 'You must live in perpetual silence.'

'Thank you, Ginny,' said Helen icily.

Ginny went redder still. 'Oh, Lord,' she said. 'I honestly didn't mean that to be bitchy. You shouldn't judge everybody by yourself, Helen.'

'And is that also not bitchy?' said Helen, sweetly this time.

'Yes, that was,' said Ginny. 'Sorry, Helen.' Helen looked sceptical. 'I mean it. I hate bitchiness. Life's too short. When I said you must live in perpetual silence, I meant that most of us would speak very rarely if we waited till we had something worth saying.'

They waited quite a while, for something worth saying.

'How are you getting on, Henry, with the fearsome Mr Skipton?' said Denzil eventually.

'I'm terrified of him,' said Henry.

'Me too,' said Ginny.

'He makes me uneasy,' said Helen. 'I can't look at him.'

'Poor Terry,' said Denzil. 'I don't expect he's got a friend in the world. He's at exactly the wrong level of unattractiveness.'

'What do you mean?' said Ginny.

'He's almost deformed. If he *was* deformed, we'd like him. Almost everybody is kind to the deformed and crippled. Nobody is kind to the unprepossessing. Nobody laughs at the mentally subnormal, but everybody scorns the rather stupid. If one is going to be disadvantaged in life, it's to one's advantage to be very disadvantaged. Do you know what I think about Terry Skipton? I think there's a heart of gold in there, which doesn't know how to reach out.'

Could that possibly be true? Henry felt that he'd caught a glimpse of another Denzil Ackerman. Was that true of Denzil also? Was that why Denzil understood Terry Skipton? He had an uneasy feeling that he was surrounded by people who had hearts of gold and that he'd fallen in love with the only one who hadn't.

The evening passed swiftly. Soon Denzil was saying, 'Well, young things, it's bed-time for clapped-out queers. Are you coming, Helen?'

'I'll stay, if that's all right,' said Helen.

'Of course it's all right. Isn't it, Ginny?' said Henry.

'Of course,' said Ginny.

'Be good,' said Denzil.

Am I going to have to pay for both women? thought Henry.

A hand stroked his thigh. Whose was it? He stroked Ginny's thigh. She kicked him. It must have been Helen's hand. He could hardly breathe.

The waitress hobbled towards them on ruined feet. 'Would you like coffee?' she said.

'Please,' said Helen.

'No, thank you,' said Ginny. 'I must be getting home.'

'I'd like coffee,' said Henry.

'Well you stay and have some.'

'But I'm taking you out.'

'Well, thank you. Good night.'

'But we're celebrating my moving into your house.'

'What a delightful prospect. Look, I'm tired. I need my beauty sleep more than some people.' Ginny blushed. Helen didn't. 'Are you coming or not?'

To do Henry credit, he did try to stand up. In vain.

'I want my coffee,' he said.

'Good night,' said Ginny Fenwick.

Henry and Helen gave each other meaningful looks. Their coffee came.

'This coffee's undrinkable,' said Helen. 'Come home with me and I'll make you some proper coffee.'

He wasn't going to miss his chance this time. He called for the bill.

'Let me pay my share,' said Helen.

'No. I insist.' Let nobody say he was mean.

'I earn as much as you.'

'Oh all right, then.' Let nobody say he was obstinate.

The waitress hobbled over with the bill.

'What's this?' he said. 'Two coffees? What about our meals?'

'Mr Ackerman has paid for all of you.'

'I bet you wish you'd insisted a bit harder now,' said Helen.

In the taxi she turned to him, rather disconcertingly, with her mouth opened wide in readiness, like a fledgling expecting food. They explored each other's lips and mouths. Kissing that superb orifice was everything he'd hoped. He felt as virile as a volcano. He put his left hand on the right cup of her bra. She removed his hand. 'Think of the driver,' she whispered. How unexpectedly considerate she could be.

He tipped the driver generously, because of all the kissing.

Helen marched up the drive, as if she couldn't wait to get into her house. She fumbled with the key, as if she was nervous.

Light flooded a neutral hall. She opened a door on the right, and entered ahead of him. He would be able to remember none of the contents of the room, except for Ted Plunkett.

'Hello, darling,' said Helen brightly. 'I've brought Henry home for a coffee.'

On Thursday, January 26th, 1956, three million workers asked for pay rises, the big freeze was followed by floods, and Henry had his first page lead. He felt that his intro was a masterpiece of concentrated information and human interest. Imagine his chagrin when Terry Skipton read it aloud, scornfully. 'A 76 year-old diabetic retired railway guard was making "a miraculous recovery" in Thurmarsh Royal Infirmary today after lying semi-conscious in a rhubarb patch in near-zero temperatures for 10 hours only 300 yards from the council "pre-fab" where his invalid wife Doris and their Jack Russell terrier "Spot" were waiting anxiously for his return from a Darby and Joan hot-pot supper and whist drive.' When the story appeared, the information was threaded through it with the parsimony of an investment manager hanging onto his bills till he got his second final reminders. Terry Skipton called him over and said gruffly, 'Not a bad story, Mr Pratt. You'll learn our style in time.'

Over his roast pork, roast potatoes and cabbage, with tinned pears to follow, Henry failed to tell Cousin Hilda that he had found a flat.

On Friday, January the 27th, the Queen flew over the Libyan desert on her way to Nigeria. Henry had battered cod and chips, with jam roly poly to follow, and failed to tell Cousin Hilda that he had found a flat.

At half past eight he slipped out, and went to the Devonshire in Commercial Road, three hundred yards up the hill towards Splutt, beyond the *Chronicle* and *Argus* building. Upstairs, on Fridays, there was a jazz club with a resident Dixieland band. There he met Colin, Gordon, Ginny, Ted and Helen. Ben had gone home to give the wife one.

Sid Hallett and the Rundlemen comprised trumpet, clarinet, trombone, piano, bass and drums. As Henry entered, they were playing 'Basin Street Blues'. The room was large, dimly lit and crowded. Most people were standing. A buzz of conversation vied with the music. Sid Hallett jigged continually and smiled a lot. He had huge damp patches under his arms. Although not yet thirty, the trombonist and the bass players were developing paunches. All the band had pints of bitter in strategic places. Henry longed for fresh air.

He'd avoided speaking to Ted and Helen since Wednesday night. Now he tried to be casual, saying, 'Oh! Thanks for the coffee, incidentally.' He must have succeeded, because they looked rather sheepish. He thought longingly of the Upper Mitherdale fells.

He tried to have a quiet word in Ginny's ear. It wasn't easy, during 'South Rampart Street Parade'.

'Nothing happened on Wednesday night, you know,' he said. 'I just had a coffee. Ted was there.'

'Ah! Shame!' said Ginny.

'I'm cured of Helen, Ginny.'

'Congratulations. What has this to do with me?'

'Well, I'm . . . er . . . moving into the house where you live.'

'So?'

He was suddenly overwhelmed with affection for Lorna Arrow. He longed to see her. If only he wasn't working tomorrow, on the football paper, *The Pink 'Un*. (When Denzil had seen everybody reading pink papers last Saturday evening, he'd said 'Good Lord! Why are they all reading the *Financial Times*?') He sighed deeply. Colin asked him what was wrong. He told him. Colin offered to work tomorrow instead of him. Glenda wouldn't mind. She was all right, was Glenda. Henry telephoned Auntie Doris and invited himself to stay. She was thrilled. The band played 'Sweet Georgia Brown'. Henry thought about sweet Lorna Arrow.

He crept into the house at 11.43. Not late. Not really. Not drunk. Not very. Better if he didn't meet Cousin Hilda, though. She might not understand that you could have hiccups without being drunk.

She materialized at the top of the basement stairs.

'Henry!' she said grimly.

He decided to tell her that he'd found a flat, now, when he

wasn't drunk, not really, but while his courage was fortified by alcohol.

'I've got something . . .' He swallowed a hiccup brilliantly. '. . . to tell you,' he said.

'Come downstairs,' commanded Cousin Hilda.

'It won't take . . .' Another hiccup was skilfully stifled. '. . . a moment.'

'I'm not having you waking the whole house with your hiccups.' Damn!

'You're drunk again,' she said, as they entered the basement room. The stove was low. There was a lingering aroma of potted meat.

'You can have hiccups without being drunk,' he said. 'Babies have hiccups.'

'You aren't a baby,' she said, as if that proved that he was drunk. He knew that there was a fault in her logic, but couldn't pin it down.

'I'm . . . er . . . I'm going away for the weekend,' he said.

Cousin Hilda sniffed.

'You went away last weekend,' she said.

'I'm going to see Auntie Doris.' Cousin Hilda sniffed. 'I mean . . . after all, she is my . . . I mean . . . my auntie . . . isn't she? And I . . . er . . . I should have told you before, but I thought you'd be cross.' The tension had cured his hiccups. 'I met Uncle Teddy in the Shanghai Chinese Restaurant and Coffee Bar.'

Cousin Hilda sniffed twice, once for Uncle Teddy and once for Chinese food. 'Why should I be cross?' she said.

'Well, not cross,' he said. 'Upset. I know you don't approve of them.'

'It beats me why *you* do,' she said. 'I've never been one for running people down, especially my own flesh and blood, but what did they ever do for you? The minimum. I gave you a good home and was ready to earlier if asked.'

'I know. And I'm grateful.'

'I didn't do it for you to be grateful.'

'I know. But you've got to let people be grateful if they want to. So I'm going to see Auntie Doris and tell her I saw Uncle Teddy. I'm going to bring them together again.'

'Henry!'

'I'd have thought you'd have thought the marriage tie was sacred.'

'I do. But it's none of your business, is it?'

'They love each other. It's just about the only good thing about them.'

'Well, it's your life,' said Cousin Hilda.

'Yes,' said Henry. 'It is. Cousin Hilda? I've . . . er . . . I've found a flat. I'm moving in next weekend.'

Cousin Hilda sniffed. She said nothing. He felt that any remark would have been better than her silence.

'Cousin Hilda?' he said. 'I love you. I love you very much.'

Cousin Hilda sniffed.

5 Meetings in Mitherdale

As the train clattered through the stolid Airedale towns out towards the high country, Henry's spirits soared. On the southern edges of the dewy fields, banks of snow lay against the dry stone walls.

Few people got off at Troutwick. The air carried promises of spring. The breeze carried memories of winter. The sun scoffed briefly at the breeze's warnings. A few drops of rain, mocking the sun, spattered onto the frost-broken streets of the quaint, narrow, stone and whitewash town.

The White Hart stood, white-painted in a dark, stone square, facing the awnings of the Saturday Market. The AA sign, with its two stars, swung squeakily. Behind it, the eponymous beast was frozen in wary pride.

The lobby was dark and leathery, its old oak table strewn with *Country Life* and *The Field*, its notice-board plastered with news of Conservative coffee mornings. It was steeped in a feudal respectability to which neither Auntie Doris nor the slimy Geoffrey Porringer had any right.

The receptionist had been hired for her snootiness, and gave full value. 'Can I help you, sir?' she said, as if the possibility was remote and the 'sir' apocryphal.

'I 'ope so, luv,' said Henry, rediscovering the full Yorkshire tones that his southern schools had weakened. 'I'm Henry.'

'Do you have a reservation, Mr Henry?'

'No, luv. I'm not a Red Indian.'

She didn't laugh, and it *did* cross Henry's mind that this might be because it wasn't funny.

Auntie Doris emerged from the staff quarters behind the desk. She was in her mid-fifties now. Age wasn't withering her charms. It was just making it more expensive to maintain them.

'Henry!' she cried.

'Auntie Doris!'

They embraced. It was like kissing an oil painting. Her hair was blonder than ever. Henry threw the receptionist a triumphant glance, which would have been more effective if he hadn't been covered in Auntie Doris's lipstick and powder, so that he looked like a clown in a decadent thirties night-club in Berlin.

Geoffrey Porringer, sensing emotion from which he had been excluded, oozed onto the scene, clasped Henry's hands and said, 'Welcome, young sir.' Henry peeped surreptitiously at his blackheads. Still a forest of them. Excellent!

They entered the lounge bar, warm, full of antiques, bustling with measured market-day bonhomie. Auntie Doris served them, while Geoffrey Porringer sat beside him and drank.

'We'll have sandwiches this morning,' he said, 'because we're working.' We? I don't see you doing much. 'Tonight we've got the bar fully staffed, so we'll have dinner.'

Conversation with Geoffrey Porringer wasn't easy. Henry couldn't bring himself to mention Lorna, up against whom the man habitually rubbed. He asked if his old teacher, Miss Candy, still drank there. It was a shock to learn that she was dead. People like Miss Candy didn't die, any more than Matterhorns fell down. Her death made him feel sad. 'Yes, she was a good old stick,' said Geoffrey Porringer. He greeted each new arrival loudly. 'Good to see you, young sir.' 'Trust the better half's flourishing, young George?' 'Morning, Arthur. Can't make up its mind, can it?' It began to dawn on Henry that Geoffrey Porringer didn't find it easy to fill the role of mine host, and had constructed a labyrinth of verbal camouflage to protect himself. It began to dawn on him that Geoffrey Porringer hadn't wanted to be slimy, to have a nose festooned with blackheads, and that it was no more his fault than Auntie Doris's that she hadn't waited for Uncle Teddy. Perhaps his rubbing against Lorna *had* been accidental. These thoughts worried him. He'd feel the loss if he couldn't continue to hate Geoffrey Porringer. Supposing becoming a mature adult meant sympathizing with *everybody*? Henry shuddered.

Geoffrey Porringer didn't make disliking him any easier by leaping into action and doing his bit behind the bar. Conversation grew louder. Sandwiches arrived and were consumed. He must go and see Lorna. It'd be awful if, at their next meeting, she was serving him dinner.

He caught the bus to Rowth Bridge. It growled up the narrowing dale, towards the high fells, crossing and recrossing the laughing little river Mither. There were eight houses now, in the hamlet of Five Houses, where Sidney Mold lived, into whose sticky hand Henry had once dug his fingernails.

He grew nervous. What would he say to her? Did he want to take her to Kit Orris's field barn? Did he want to marry her and open her eyes to a wider world? Did he want to marry her and live in Rowth Bridge?

The bus swung past the school, past the Parish Hall, and dropped him by the hump bridge. He walked briskly towards Lorna's parents' council house.

'She's out.'

The anti-climax was shattering. She couldn't be. She had no right to be.

'Do you know where she is?'

'Could be round the Luggs.'

'Well could you give her a message? I'm staying at the White Hart. Could you ask her if she could meet me tomorrow morning? I could pick her up here round about ten.'

He wandered away. Should he call on the Luggs? He set off down the winding back lane towards their cottage. It was surrounded by more old cars, baths and prams than ever. He turned back abruptly, before anyone saw him. There were too many Luggs, and he particularly didn't want to see Jane, built like a rugby forward, who'd been his childhood sweetheart before Pam Yardley, who'd been his childhood sweetheart before Lorna. If Lorna was 'round the Luggs', let her remain there undisturbed.

He heard horse's hooves. Round the corner there came a magnificent creature, a real thoroughbred, perfectly groomed, highly strung, shining with health, a superb physical specimen produced by generations of careful breeding. The horse was nice too.

'It's Henry, isn't it?' The face smiled, a social smile from on high. Henry decided that he'd campaign to remove the Elgin marbles from her mouth and return them to Greece. He wished horses didn't make him uneasy, wished she wasn't so far above him, wished he could think of something better to say than

'Yes. Hello, Belinda.' He wished he wasn't nine years old again.

'Whoa, Marigold. Henry's a friend,' said Belinda Boyce-Uppingham, who had once called him an oik.

He heard a parody of himself say, 'You've become a really beautiful woman, Belinda.' Well, it'd be churlish not to admit it. He wouldn't give her the satisfaction of thinking that he was still an oik.

'What are you doing these days?' she asked.

'I'm working as a reporter on the *Thurmarsh Evening Argus.*'

'Oh. Is that . . . ?' She couldn't think of an adjective.

'Interesting?'

'Well, yes.'

'*I* think so.'

He watched her brain whirring through all the connections, seeking new subject matter.

'Have you seen Diana recently?'

He longed to say, 'Yes. We made love last weekend.' He hadn't the courage. He said, 'Yes. I saw her last week.'

'Careful, Marigold,' said Belinda Boyce-Uppingham. 'Don't frighten Henry. She's all right, Henry.'

'I'm sure she is. I'm not frightened.' Why say that, when he longed to edge away from those towering, steaming, chestnut flanks.

'Listen,' said Belinda Boyce-Uppingham, with every semblance of real friendliness. 'I have a nutty uncle near Thurmarsh. If I visit him and I can get away, will you show me the town? Are we on?'

'Yes. That'd be smashing.'

'Wonderful.'

He was getting an erection. She was so beautiful. Life was so unfair. If he made a move, would she leap off Marigold and lose her individuality with him on the muddy verge of the lane? Could he become the third D. H. Lawrence?

'Well, lovely to see you, Henry,' she said. 'I mean that. So glad you're . . . er . . .' Again, she couldn't find an adjective. What had she been searching for? Still alive? Not unemployable? Not totally physically repulsive? Getting erections at the sight of me?

When she'd gone, it was as if the light began to fade. He told himself that it wasn't her fault that she was as she was. This was awful. Supposing, in one day, he found that he didn't dislike either Geoffrey Porringer or Belinda Boyce-Uppingham? What would there be left to cling to?

He realized, to his relief, that the light really was fading from the steely winter sky. He walked over the hump bridge, past his old school, with its high Gothic windows and triangular gables. A car was approaching. He thumbed it. It sped him to Troutwick. By half past four he was asking the snooty receptionist for tea.

Auntie Doris brought it.

'Auntie Doris?' he said in a low voice. 'I want to speak to you alone.'

'Good Lord!' she said. She thought swiftly. 'Go to the Sun at six. I'll try to slip out.'

The Sun was a dark, gloomy pub near the station. Auntie Doris, wafting in on a tide of scent, seemed totally out of place. She kissed him and bought him a beer.

'Auntie Doris?' he said, when they'd settled in a dim corner near the darts board. 'I met Uncle Teddy.' He fancied that she paled, under all the make-up.

'Where?'

'In Thurmarsh. In the Shanghai Chinese Restaurant and Coffee Bar.'

'Good Lord. I . . . knew he'd come out, of course. How was he?'

'He seemed all right.'

'You talked, did you?'

'Oh yes. I . . . er . . . I was a bit drunk, though.'

'Was he . . . er . . . ?'

'There was a man with him. Derek Parsonage.'

'Never heard of him.'

'He has blackheads.'

'I'd need more to go on.'

He wished he hadn't mentioned the blackheads. Did the subject have a fatal fascination for him?

'Did he . . . er . . . say anything about me?'

'No. It didn't . . . you know . . . crop up.'

'Ah. Did he . . . er . . . say anything about . . . anybody else there might be in his life?'

'No.'

'It didn't crop up?'

'No. But . . . er . . . there is one thing.'

'Yes?'

'He's opening a night-club.'

'Oh? And?'

'Well . . . he's calling it the Cap Ferrat. I mean, he wouldn't name it after your house and the place where you spent your holidays if there was somebody else, would he?'

'Perhaps not.'

'Auntie Doris? I suppose none of this is my business, really, but . . . I do love you, you know.'

'I'm not sure I did know, no.'

'Oh. Well I do.'

'I'm not sure I deserve it.'

'Well there you are. I do, anyway. And . . .' He hoped she couldn't see his blushes. '. . . obviously I wish you'd waited for Uncle Teddy and were still with him, because . . . you know . . . so anyway I thought I'd tell you anyway.'

'You don't like Geoffrey very much, do you?'

'Well . . . you know.'

'I like Geoffrey very much.'

'Yes.'

'I like Teddy very much.'

'Yes.'

'Life's complicated.'

He judged it wise to leave it there. He'd sown the seed.

Auntie Doris slipped him thirty pounds.

'Don't tell Geoffrey,' she said.

They went in to dinner fairly late, after the paying customers had ordered. The dining-room was small and unpretentious, with whitewashed walls. There was a fine Welsh dresser covered with good English plates. Lorna handed Henry the menu as if she'd never seen him before.

He ordered oxtail soup and grilled lamb cutlets. Geoffrey Porringer spent a long time choosing the claret. 'You'll like this one, young sir,' he said, with a smile that was barely slimy at all.

The claret was nice. He thanked Lorna for his soup. He wanted to call her 'Lorna' but found it impossible. He thanked her for the lamb cutlets. He thanked her for the potatoes and the cauliflower and the carrots.

'My word, young sir, you're being very polite to our Lorna,' said Geoffrey Porringer.

'Geoffrey! Don't draw attention to it,' said Auntie Doris, who always made things worse by protesting about them. 'He knows her,' she mouthed.

At the end of the meal, Lorna caught Henry's eye and nodded. She could have saved him a lot of tension if she'd done it earlier, but he didn't blame her.

Over his bacon and fried eggs, Henry read the *Sunday Express*. An exchange of letters between Presidents Bulganin and Eisenhower was published. President Bulganin had tried to establish a 20 year American–Russian pact, which would completely ignore Great Britain. President Eisenhower rebuffed the suggestion and said that they already had such a treaty, if the Russians chose to make it work. It was called the Charter of the United Nations. In Troutwick, these sounded like voices from another world.

Geoffrey Porringer drove him to Rowth Bridge. It had rained in the night but the winter sun was breaking through, touching the great mass of Mickleborough with its faint warmth, shining palely on the glutinous fields. Henry's mind went back to the last time he had travelled this road by car, before his national service, with his three best friends, Martin Hammond, Paul Hargreaves and Stefan Prziborsky. Now he wasn't even sure if he liked Martin or Paul, and Stefan, the only Polish-born batsman ever to play cricket for Thurmarsh, had emigrated to Australia.

'What are you doing in Rowth Bridge?' Geoffrey Porringer's voice plopped dully into his nostalgic melancholy.

'Looking up an old friend.'

'Girl-friend?'

'That kind of thing.'

'Jolly good. Keep at it.'

'Yes.'

That was the kind of fatuous conversation he had with Geoffrey

Porringer. He wondered if Geoffrey Porringer suspected that the girl was Lorna.

When they reached Rowth Bridge, Geoffrey Porringer slipped him thirty pounds. 'Don't tell Doris,' he said. Only later did Henry wonder if it was hush money, because Geoffrey Porringer suspected that Lorna had told him about the rubbing against her.

'Sorry I'm late,' he said. 'I had to wait for Geoffrey Porringer.' Lorna snorted.

They walked slowly, past the jumbled stone houses and cottages, in the watery sunshine.

He felt a stab of horror as he realized that they were approaching the church. He didn't want to run the gauntlet of the village churchgoers, holding hands with Lorna Arrow.

He tried, gently, to remove his hand. She clasped it firmly. He saw people out of the corner of his eye.

The Boyce-Uppinghams were arriving! Lorna squeezed his hand, so hard that it hurt. He could hardly wrench their hands apart. His cheeks blazed. He hoped neither Lorna nor Belinda would see his blazing cheeks. He squeezed Lorna's hand and carried on up the road. He didn't look round.

They were going towards Kit Orris's field barn. She let go of his hand, now that it no longer mattered.

It had always been wonderful, in Kit Orris's field barn. She walked straight past the gate that would have led them to the barn. Had she engineered the whole walk? Was it her revenge? He couldn't blame her.

Belinda would never contact him in Thurmarsh now. Well, he ought to be grateful to Lorna for that.

He couldn't stand the silence any more. 'I was very surprised in the hotel, when I got your note,' he said.

'Were you?' she said.

'I'm sorry about all that.'

'You were ashamed of me.'

'No. No, Lorna.'

'You were ashamed of me, just now, in front of 'er.'

'Her?'

'Bloody Belinda. You were as twined as me arse. You never could walk past 'er wi'out blushing when we were bairns.'

'Give over, Lorna. It's rubbish, is that.'

'I 'ave to go now, Henry.'

'Go?'

'I'm meeting someone.' She couldn't hide a flash of triumph.

'Oh? Who?'

'Eric Lugg.'

'Eric Lugg? He's got leave from the Cattering Corpse, has he?' He closed his eyes, as if that would wipe out his sentence.

'All right, I know I can't spell,' she said. 'I know I'm a right ignorant pig. Well so's Eric, so it's all right.'

'It isn't all right,' he said. 'Look, I'm sorry I said that. I was . . .' Upset at the thought of your slender, lovely body being pawed by a Lugg. '. . . upset. Jealous, I suppose. I mean . . . do you . . . er . . . know Eric well?'

'Course I do. He lives in t' next lane.'

'No. I mean . . . you know . . . have you been . . . out with him?'

'Sometimes.'

'While I was in the army?'

'Sometimes.'

'I see. So I was being lied to.'

'I suppose you just sat in your barracks and thought about me.'

'I never went out with another woman, Lorna. Not once.'

Lorna shrugged. 'We didn't do owt,' she said. 'Not when there was you. Yesterday was the first time.'

And he'd nearly called on them! A dreadful thought struck him.

'You didn't do it in the barn, did you?'

'Course we bloody did. It's like Piccadilly Circus in our 'ouse.'

'I wish you hadn't done it in the barn.'

'Ruddy 'ell,' said Lorna. 'You're a funny one.'

They turned back, and walked in silence. The sun had disappeared.

'It's just . . . well . . . Eric Lugg!' he said. 'Lorna! You're special. Spelling doesn't matter. Education doesn't matter. What matters is . . . you're special. Eric's a lout.'

'He's norra lout. He's a cookhouse instructor. You 'ardly know 'im, 'ow can you say 'e's a lout? 'e's a bit rough, a bit uncouth, bur . . . 'e's all right, is Eric.'

'Is that enough for you, Lorna – "all right"?'

'Bloody 'ell, Henry. I 'aven't said I'm going to *marry* 'im.'

'I should hope not.'

'I might. It's none of your bloody business anyroad. So belt up about Eric Lugg, will yer?'

She flounced off down the lane. In his mind she was already giving birth to endless Luggs while her oafish husband made coarse jokes as he taught his smelly recruits how to bang thick grey gravy onto stale meat pies.

He trudged forlornly down the lane. He was a prig. He was a snob. In his travels through the steamy jungle of the class system, he had become infected with the disease that he loathed so much.

6   A New Life

Winter returned. Thurmarsh and London recorded their coldest days for sixty years. Cousin Hilda's stove roared and crackled.

The national papers reported the warmth and friendliness of the big cold world. After three days of talks President Eisenhower and Mr Anthony Eden declared their complete agreement over the Middle East. They supported Colonel Nasser – for the immediate future, at any rate. In Cyprus, the Governor had friendly talks with Archbishop Makarios. Britain's offer of self-government was expected to be accepted. Archbishop Makarios favoured the ending of terrorism in exchange for an amnesty.

Life was less cheery in Cousin Hilda's small, hot basement, as Henry worked his way through his last six days. He craved the company of his friends in the Lord Nelson. He longed to track down Uncle Teddy. But no. He would be devoted to Cousin Hilda that week. *Fabian of Scotland Yard*, *The Grove Family*, *The Burns and Allen Show*, *Forces' Requests*. If it was on, they watched it, though Cousin Hilda drew the line at *Travellers Tales – Pygmies of the Congo*. 'What's the use of watching pygmies?' she said. 'I'm never likely to see a pygmy.' Henry bit back his reply of, 'Well, this is your chance, then.'

On Monday evening – liver and bacon and rhubarb crumble – he asked Barry Frost, 'Have the Operatic decided what to devote their talents to next?' Barry Frost replied, gruffly, as if suspecting sarcasm, 'Yes. *No, No, Nanette*.'

On Tuesday evening – roast lamb and his last spotted dick *for ever* – he asked Norman Pettifer, 'Are we getting a run on Danish Blue this week?' Norman Pettifer replied, coolly, as if suspecting sarcasm, 'No. It's an extraordinarily average week this week.' Henry said, 'Good Lord! So average, you mean, as to defy the law of averages? That is extraordinary.'

On Wednesday evening – toad-in-the-hole and sponge pudding with chocolate sauce – Barry Frost was subdued. Henry said, 'Is everything all right, Barry?' 'No, everything is not all right. She's broken it off, because I've accepted the lead in *No, No, Nanette*,' said Barry Frost. After the meal, Henry knocked on Barry's door and said, 'Are you all right? I've got my first shorthand lesson tonight, but we could meet afterwards for a drink.' 'Thanks. You're a pal. But no. I've got to face this thing on my own,' said Barry Frost.

On Thursday evening – roast pork and tinned pears – Norman Pettifer was subdued. 'Is everything all right?' Henry asked. Having found a useful formula, he saw no reason to alter it in the interests of so-called conversational glitter. 'They've removed me from the cheese counter,' said Norman Pettifer. There was a stunned silence, into which Henry's 'Oh dear' plopped pathetically. 'Mr McConnon was very nice about it. He had me into his office. "Norman," he said. "This is no reflection on you, but change is the bedrock from which the seeds of our success flower. Young Adrian is a lucky lad to inherit what you've built up."' 'I'm really sorry, Norman. Where are they moving you to?' said Henry. 'General groceries. You know what that boils down to, don't you? Tins,' said Norman Pettifer, with withering scorn.

On Friday evening – battered cod and jam roly poly – Barry Frost was pensive. 'You're pensive, Barry,' said Henry. 'I've resigned from *No, No, Nanette*. Candice has won,' said Barry Frost.

On Saturday, February 4th, an MP warned of the 200,000 elderly who were falling behind the rising standard of living, Ivy Benson spoke of the problems her women's band faced from marriage – 'In one year, I lost three trombones' – the thaw brought hundreds of burst pipes, and Henry reported on his first football match. It was Rawlaston v Ossett Town in Division One of the Yorkshire League.

Unfortunately he had to phone his report through ten minutes before the end, when there were still no goals. 'It was end-to-end stuff in this tense relegation battle at sodden Scuffley Park,' he enthused. 'The "Grinders" created the better chances, but had nobody to take advantage of Macauley's speed. Ossett's powder-puff attack, sluggishly led by Deakins, rarely threatened a staunch Rawlaston rearguard, ably marshalled by the immaculate Linnet.'

His awards were 'Entertainment 6, Effort 8. Man of the Match – Linnet.' Later he phoned through the result. 'Rawlaston 0, Ossett Town 2. Goals: Linnet (own goal), Deakins.'

On Sunday morning, at the end of breakfast, he held out his hand to Liam. 'Goodbye, Liam. And . . . good luck.'

'The same to you, Mr Henry,' said Liam O'Reilly.

'Goodbye, Norman. Sorry about the . . . er . . .'

'I'll get over it,' said Norman Pettifer.

'Goodbye, Barry. Good luck with the nuptials.'

'Yes, well . . .' said Barry Frost. 'We'll see. Whatever will be, will be.'

'You could make a song of that,' said Henry, and immediately wished he hadn't.

He went upstairs, converted his bed into a sofa for the last time, packed his puny collection of clothes, his photo of Len Hutton, his one shelf of books by Kafka, Evelyn Waugh, Henry Miller and Captain W. E. Johns, and went down to say goodbye to Cousin Hilda. His mouth was dry.

'Well . . . thank you very much for everything, Cousin Hilda,' he said. 'I've been very happy here.'

Cousin Hilda sniffed.

'No,' he said. 'I have. But I can't live off the family for ever.'

'What are families for?' said Cousin Hilda.

For getting away from.

'I'm not going to be far away,' said Henry. 'You must come to tea, and I'll come and see you regularly.'

Cousin Hilda sniffed.

'We'll see,' she said.

Ginny welcomed him with a self-conscious smile, a Lancashire hot-pot and a bottle of robust red wine. Her flat had the same layout as his but without the French windows. They ate in the tiny kitchen. She'd laid a red check cloth over the formica-topped table. He washed up. She dried and put away. He put his arms round her. His hands tingled at her soft and ample splendour. He said, 'What about a bit of hanky-panky? I believe the feller downstairs is out.' She removed his hands gently but firmly and said, 'I think it might be better if we were strictly platonic, now we're house-mates, don't you?' 'Fair enough,' he said. There was plenty of time. 'Can I take you for a nice, platonic drink this evening?' She said, 'I'm going out this evening.'

At 3.22 he began unpacking. At 3.29 he finished unpacking. He listened to *Take It From Here*, *Melody Hour*, *Hancock's Half Hour*, and *Victor Sylvester*. He fell asleep during *Question Time*, unfortunately missing four celebrities exchanging ideas with young hill farmers from Breconshire. He woke to hear Jack Payne saying it with music. At 7.49 he went to the Winstanley. He had three pints of bitter. Nobody spoke to him. They were all in little cliques. He'd never seen such an absurdly self-satisfied lot. They laughed uproariously at jokes that weren't remotely funny. They were cretins. It was a privilege to go home and leave them.

Home? He hadn't even bought any tea or coffee. He was totally unprepared.

During *Grand Hotel*, with Jean Pougnet and the Palm Court Orchestra, he heard the front door slam. Was it her? Could he cadge some coffee and bread?

He heard a man's voice say, very distinctly, 'Neutral territory. Berlin wall.' She'd brought Gordon Carstairs back!

He listened to *Java, Land of the Moonlight Orchid*, in which Nina Epton described a visit to that magical country.

They were making love! He turned up the volume, till Nina Epton was shouting.

He went to bed. He lay there, wide awake, lonely, hungry, in his cramped room. And they began again! It dawned on him that he wasn't going to get much sleep that night. It dawned on him that Podgy Sex Bomb Henry, who had thought himself so precociously successful with older women, wasn't actually doing very well. He'd been toyed with by Helen Cornish. He'd lost Lorna Arrow and Ginny Fenwick. That only left Diana Hargreaves. He'd better make sure of her before he lost her too.

At last Ginny and Gordon stopped. Gordon went home. Henry fell asleep at 4.17. At 6.38 he woke up. A man who was vaguely familiar had been telling him, in thirty blindingly simple words, the secret of life and how to conduct it. He couldn't remember any of it.

The world grew colder. Ominous headlines poured off the presses. The big freeze returns. After the bursts, the frozen pipes. 'Flick Knife' Teds terrorize teachers. Housewives flee Cypriot rioters. Tear-gas used in Algiers uproar. British military police kill Cypriot youth.

There were headlines on Henry's stories too. Chiropodist breaks foot! Man, 83, falls out of bed. Found cuff-link after 42 years.

The early part of Henry's evenings was spent in the Lord Nelson. The middle of the evenings was spent in the Globe and Artichoke, the Devonshire, the Pigeon and Two Cushions. The last part of the evenings was spent in the Shanghai Chinese Restaurant and Coffee Bar, where he hoped to meet Uncle Teddy again, but didn't. How he longed to sit in peace and warmth and watch television with Cousin Hilda. He even looked forward to his second shorthand lesson.

Every evening, shortly before midnight, a gurgling mass of beer and monosodium glutamate arrived back at a home that was no home, and lay awake, marvelling at the virility of Gordon Carstairs. By Thursday night, even Gordon Carstairs was exhausted.

On Wednesday evening Henry telephoned Paul, who was surprisingly friendly and would love to see him that weekend, as would Diana. Henry got so excited that he forgot to go to his second shorthand lesson.

On Friday lunch-time, dreaming of Diana in the Rundle Café while pretending not to be listening to the cautionary tale of Gertrude the Greedy Guinea-Pig, he heard an enormous crash. After about a minute he remembered that he was a journalist, and rushed out.

A lorry had hurtled, just down Rundle Prospect, into the tiny Old Apothecary's House, whose delicate flint and stone dated back to the early fifteenth century. The lorry was jammed into the gaping mouth of the building like a cuckoo being fed by a wren.

The driver was sitting on the pavement, dazed with shock.

Henry sat beside him diffidently. He felt shy of intruding into the man's trauma with his tactless notebook. But the man seemed to want to get everything off his chest. Must get all the facts. Name, age, address. Dave Nasenby (29), of Rawlaston Road, Splutt. Occupation? 'Lorry driver, of course.' Stupid! He was driving along, he braked hard to avoid a cat, he skidded on a patch of ice, lost control, he was going towards two nuns, it was the nuns or the building, he swerved, he just had time to leap out, he'd left it so late that he scraped himself all along the wall. He showed Henry his abrasions. Henry winced. It was a pity the nuns had disappeared, but with his present luck they'd probably have been Trappists anyway.

He caught the London train in good humour, blissfully unaware that the story which was streaming off the Thurmarsh presses began 'A lorry driver had a miraculous escape today when he crashed into Thurmarsh's oldest historical landmark rather than hit two buns.'

The smells of an elegant dinner were drifting delicately around the hall of the Hargreaveses' home. 'Henry! So good to see you so soon,' said Mrs Hargreaves, and he couldn't detect a trace of sarcasm.

'Henry!' Mr Hargreaves was also extremely pleased to see him. Henry was beginning to get worried. 'Dry sherry?'

'Please.'

'Henry!' Paul was extremely friendly too. What had happened? He soon found out. He was no longer a threat.

She entered with a companion who was preceded by a wall of after-shave – still quite a rarity in the smelly fifties.

'Hello, Henry,' she said. 'Lovely to see you again so soon. I think you know my fiancé.'

Henry found himself staring at the large, smiling, indecently clean-shaven moon-face of Tosser Pilkington-Brick.

7 The Opening of the Cap Ferrat

Almost five years after they had disappeared from the Foreign Office, Guy Burgess and Donald Maclean turned up in Moscow. The blizzards returned. The trade gap widened to £74 million. The Football League, alarmed by falling gates, proposed a major reorganization, with four divisions. Malta voted 3–1 in favour of integration with Britain. There were many attacks on Britons in Cyprus.

Several times on his calls, Henry had made a detour to see if he could find Uncle Teddy on the site of the Cap Ferrat, in Malmesbury Street, between Fish Hill and Canal View. This was an area of small, slowly decaying streets and culs-de-sac, sloping damply from the east of the town centre towards the river and the canal. The Cap Ferrat was being converted out of a once-elegant little Regency terrace, which it shared with the Mandarin Fish Bar and the Thurmarsh Joke Emporium and Magic Shop.

On the afternoon of Wednesday, February 15th, Henry found Uncle Teddy. In daylight, he could see that his experience of prison had left a mask of wariness on Uncle Teddy's big, bluff face. His carefully styled crinkly hair was flecked with grey. His dark suit and sober shirt would have given him the respectability on which he had spent so much money, if they hadn't looked so obviously expensive.

Uncle Teddy ushered him out of the building. 'I don't want anyone seeing it till it's finished,' he said. 'It's tight, but we'll make it for Tuesday. I just hope this snow clears. Snow and night life are contradictions in terms.'

'Can we talk somewhere quiet in private?' said Henry.

They walked through the town centre, between mounds of swept snow, and went for afternoon tea in Davy's. Uncle Teddy was like an estranged father, giving his son an uneasy weekly treat.

'I've been looking for you everywhere,' said Henry.

'I've been in France,' said Uncle Teddy. 'Picking up last-minute items. All genuine stuff.'

Uncle Teddy ordered tea for two, and toasted teacake. The waitress had a bunion. The place was full of women who worked all day cooking and cleaning for husbands who got home tired and didn't want to talk. Afternoon tea, while shopping, was a rare chance to rest over-used feet and exercise under-used vocal chords.

'This isn't quiet,' said Henry.

'It's private,' said Uncle Teddy. 'In quiet places you're over-heard.'

Henry wasn't sure how to begin. So he started with something else.

'I'm sorry I was rude about Derek Parsonage,' he said.

'Why did you say he was a Geoffrey Porringer substitute?'

'It was just the blackheads.'

'Blackheads?'

'They both have blackheads.'

'Good Lord. Do they?'

'Uncle Teddy! You can't not have noticed. Their noses are festooned with them.'

'I hadn't.'

Is it just me? thought Henry. Is that my real identity? Henry 'Obsessed by blackheads' Pratt?

'I'm sorry,' he said. 'I shouldn't be rude about your friends.'

'Geoffrey Porringer's hardly my friend, Henry.'

A perfect cue. Too perfect?

The waitress brought their tea. 'Teacakes'll be a minute, but we're that busy and we've one grill out of action for maintenance,' she announced.

'Shall I be mother?' said Henry's surrogate father.

'How have you got the money for the Cap Ferrat?' said Henry. 'It must be costing a packet.'

Uncle Teddy touched the side of his nose. Henry wondered if, in shady businessmen's secret societies, they touched *each other*'s noses. Perhaps that was how blackheads were transmitted. Stop thinking about blackheads!

The tea was very strong.

'They use soda,' said Uncle Teddy. 'To make it go further. They save on tea.'

'But spend on soda,' said Henry.

'It's better than bromide,' said Uncle Teddy.

'Did they put bromide in the tea in . . .' The waitress arrived with their teacake. '. . . Rangoon?'

'Sorry about that,' she said. 'He says they're a bit burnt, it's his first day on his own, he's scraped them, but I can take them back if you want.'

'No, no,' said Uncle Teddy. 'Carbon's good for you.'

'I never have liked my teacakes rare,' said Henry.

Uncle Teddy smiled indulgently. 'Could you get something in the paper about the opening?' he said, when the puzzled waitress had gone.

'Damn! I should have asked *you* that,' said Henry. 'But I hate using my friends and relations for my work. I'm just not ruthless enough.'

'Too soft.' Uncle Teddy nodded his agreement sympathetically.

'Exactly. I should have been asking you if you'd be my contact from the shady underworld.'

'Henry!'

'Sorry, Uncle Teddy. I didn't mean . . . I meant . . . from the world of the night. The world that wakes up when the rest of us go to sleep.'

'I like that,' said Uncle Teddy. He lowered his voice unnecessarily, amid all the chatter and rattle of cups. 'I've failed you,' he said. 'I suppose you despise me.'

'Actually, I don't seem to,' said Henry. 'I think maybe I'm fatally fascinated by evil.'

'Thank you, Henry.'

'Oh, sorry, Uncle Teddy. I didn't . . . oh heck.'

'Well come on, then,' said Uncle Teddy. 'What's all this about? As if I couldn't guess. You've seen Doris, haven't you?'

'Well, yes, I . . . I see them occasionally.'

'Them? So she and Geoffrey are still cohabiting.'

'Yes. They're still . . . cohabiting.'

'Still running the hotel, are they?'

'Yes.'

'Doing well?'

'I think so.'

'What a relief.'

'Uncle Teddy, I . . . I've talked to Auntie Doris.'

'Very wise. It'd have been rude not to.'

'No. You know. Talked. About you.'

'Would you like fancies?' said the waitress.

'Yes, we'll have a selection,' said Uncle Teddy.

'I don't think . . . you know . . . she's entirely happy with Mr Porringer,' said Henry.

'It's hard to imagine that anybody could be.'

'I know. But I think it's . . . you know . . . more than that.'

The waitress brought a plate of cakes and said, 'Go on! Be sinful!'

'Have the éclair,' said Uncle Teddy.

'I don't want the éclair,' said Henry. 'I want the pink, square one. It looks so boring, like the last evacuee in a church hall. I'll put it out of its misery.'

Uncle Teddy shook his head. It was beyond his comprehension that anyone could be so soft as to have sympathy for underprivileged cakes.

'More than that?' he said.

'She said . . . she liked you very much. She said . . . life's very complicated. I mean, Uncle Teddy, if there . . . you know . . . if there's . . . somebody else, just tell me.'

'There's nobody else,' said Uncle Teddy. 'Not in that way. Not at the moment.'

'Would you think it possible you could ever have her back?'

Uncle Teddy picked up a chocolate truffle and examined it as if seeking an answer to the mysteries of molecular structure. Then he smiled, and gave Henry thirty pounds.

'Don't tell Doris or Geoffrey,' he said. 'Or the sniffer.'

English and French celebrities will toast each other in champagne next Tuesday night, when the glamour and glitter of mediterranean life come to brighten up those cold Thurmarsh nights.

Yes! Thurmarsh's very first night-club – the Cap Ferrat – will be opening its doors in Malmesbury Street.

The Cap Ferrat is the brain-child of Mr Edward 'Teddy'

Braithwaite, handsome 55 year-old Thurmarsh industrialist and entrepreneur, who has recently returned to Yorkshire after a five-year 'stint' in Rangoon.

'My aim is to mix good old down-to-earth Yorkshire warmth and meaty grit with a bit of French sauce, that Gallic oo-ta-ta sophistication,' muses Mr Braithwaite, a former pupil at Doncaster Road Secondary School.

He adds: 'Of course it will be a bit naughty, but all good clean family fun. We aim to create a venue where Mr and Mrs Thurmarsh can relax from the cares of helping to build Britain's post-war revival. Not everyone can go to France, so we're bringing France to Thurmarsh.'

Everything – food, wines, décor, even crockery – will be the genuine article. 'I've scoured the Côte d'Azur, spent weeks there, just to make sure Thurmarsh gets the best,' says Mr Braithwaite.

Among the celebrities invited to join in the 'first night' festivities are Michael Venison, Dulcie Crab, Richard Murdoch, Kenneth Horne, Gwen Catley, Maurice Chevalier, Danielle Darrieux and Mr Frank Carnforth, Mayor of Thurmarsh.

'It should be quite a fight,' opines Mr Braithwaite.

'Mr Skipton?' said Henry. 'Could I have a word?'

'What is it?'

'These misprints in this story. I think they're deliberate.'

'Misprints do happen,' said Terry Skipton, 'even on papers like this.'

'Venison *and* Crab seems unlikely. "Fight" instead of "night" is pretty embarrassing. And "oo-ta-ta" instead of "oo-la-la". French sauce. Ta-ta. Tartare sauce. Somebody's playing clever buggers.'

'You're letting your imagination run away with you,' said Terry Skipton.

The pound rose to 2 dollars 81 cents. The price of bread and milk rose as food subsidies were reduced by £38 million. President Eisenhower played golf for the first time since his heart attack in September.

The icy roads were the worst in living memory. The Thames froze at Windsor. The weather prevented the attendance at the Cap Ferrat of Michael Venison, Dulcie Crab, Richard Murdoch, Kenneth Horne, Gwen Catley, Maurice Chevalier and Danielle Darrieux.

A concern for civic dignity prevented the attendance of Mr Frank Carnforth, Mayor of Thurmarsh.

Mr Andrew Redrobe, editor of the *Thurmarsh Evening Argus*, had also declined to attend. His presence might have offended the churches, and he prided himself on having a good relationship with the churches.

Among those who struggled and slithered into Malmesbury Street on the night of February 21st, 1956, were Henry 'Obsessed by blackheads' Pratt; Derek 'Festooned with blackheads' Parsonage; Ted Plunkett and his attractive fiancée, Helen Cornish; Gordon Carstairs and his companion, lusty future war correspondent Ginny Fenwick; Denzil Ackerman, elegant metropolitan sophisticate; ace sports reporter Ben Watkinson and his shy, petite wife, Cynthia; the second D. H. Lawrence; and the Voice of Common Sense, alias 'Thurmarshian', Neil Mallet.

Also present were Bill Holliday, scrap merchant, used-car dealer, greyhound owner and gambler, who was accompanied by Miss Angela Groyne, a buxom red-haired model; Chief Superintendent Ron Ratchett, who was accompanied by his notebook; and Sergeant Botney, of the Royal Corps of Signals, who had travelled down from Catterick Camp in the company of his grim-faced wife to celebrate their wedding anniversary in a manner more sophisticated than could be managed by the Sergeants' Mess, the Naafi or Toc H. They'd left the girls in the care of Mrs Botney's mother.

The revellers sat at traditional southern French tables in a large, low-ceilinged, smoky room lit by the dim red light of impending sin. On the platform, beyond a dance floor that was slightly too small, Alphonso Boycott and his Northern Serenaders were playing slightly naughty dance tunes slightly naughtily. Meals were served by big-busted French waitresses, dressed in white blouses the size of large pocket handkerchieves, black skirts the size of small pocket handkerchieves, and black stockings.

Sergeant Botney smiled uneasily at Mrs Botney. There was a choice of traditional Provençal steak in a watery, timidly garlicky tomato sauce or traditional Provençal chicken in a watery, timidly garlicky tomato sauce, or plain grilled steak or chicken, served with traditional Provençal chips. The journalists, seated at a large table at the back of the room, ate gratis, courtesy of the management.

The champagne and the medium-sweet white wine flowed. The dim light was dimmed still further, and a disembodied voice announced, 'It's cabaret time. Let's hear it for Monsieur Emile.'

Monsieur Emile told them that he was from Gay Paree, but that Gay Paree would have to look to its laurels because the world would soon be talking about Gay Thurmarsh. 'Under ze bridges of Thurmarsh vith you,' he crooned briefly and, since the laughter was a bit thin, he thickened it with some guffaws of his own.

There was a roll of drums.

'Ladies and gentlemen,' said Monsieur Emile. 'I now introduce, vith great pleasure, ze Cap Ferrat's resident dancing girls, all born vairy close to ze coast of France, and bringing a touch of ze Gallic sun and ze Gallic beaches to your town. Ladies and gentlemen, ze Côte d'Azur Cuties!'

Ze four Côte d'Azur Cuties danced vivaciously, with long-legged athleticism and perfect synchronization, that effective substitute for artistry.

There was a roll of drums.

'Ladies and gentlemen,' said Monsieur Emile. 'I now introduce, vith great pleasure, ze Cap Ferrat's resident singer, ze legendary Martine. Need I say more?' He continued hurriedly before anybody could shout 'yes'. 'Ladies and gentlemen, ze legendary Martine.'

Ze legendary Martine sang in a loud, deep, throbbing, harsh, sexy, passionate, smoky, wine-sodden Gallic growl.

'She's like a cross between Marlene Dietrich and Edith Piaf,' said Ted.

'It's a cross we're just going to have to bear,' said Denzil.

Henry hardly heard any of this. He was aware only of what had to be done.

Monsieur Emile announced an interval. He hoped that everyone would dance. Henry sighed deeply.

'All right, kid?' said Colin.

'Yes,' said Henry, irritated. 'Stop trying to protect me.'

He walked slowly towards Sergeant Botney's table. His old sergeant was another of those who looked smaller than Henry had remembered. In fact, his wife looked more fearsome than he did. Henry hesitated. All the pressures of social convention were against him. His respect for good manners shrieked its disapproval. But they'd all sworn that, if ever any of them came upon the rotten sadistic bastard in civvy street, they'd do him. But, then again, it had all been a long time ago. Why not forget it, tonight of all nights?

Because of Burbage.

Because there is a ghost that has to be laid.

Because the Sergeant Botneys of this world get away with it precisely because we allow social conventions to constrain us. We hide behind them, in our weakness and apathy.

'It's Sergeant Botney, isn't it?'

'Yes.' Sergeant Botney looked surprised, but not alarmed. His skin was leathery. Any expression there might have been in his eyes was carefully hidden.

'I'm Signalman Pratt. You don't remember me, do you? Perhaps you'll remember this better. 22912547.'

'Well . . . hello, Pratt. This is my wife, Mrs Botney.'

'Hello, Mrs Botney.'

'Hello.' Unfriendly. Not surprising, really.

'I . . . er . . . I was in your hut, sergeant.'

'So, what are you doing now, Pratt?'

'I'm a newspaper reporter.'

'Well done, lad!'

'Thanks.'

'Where did you get to in your service, then? Make some good pals, did you? Met some good oppos?'

'Oh yes. Great pals. Smashing oppos.'

'Well done, lad.'

'I've never forgotten that first night, sarge. You showed us how to make bed-packs. We made bed-packs. You said they were terrible. You threw them out of the window. It was raining. They landed on wet flower-beds. We fetched them. You said "Lights out." We made our wet dirty beds in the dark at one o'clock in the morning.'

'Let's dance, Lionel,' said Mrs Botney.

'In a moment, dear. Let's hear the lad out.'

'We used to have to paint the coal white,' said Henry. 'We used to have to paint black lines on the floor with boot polish so as to line our beds up, and then we had to wash every trace of the boot polish off.'

'Yes, I was hard,' said Sergeant Botney. 'Hard but fair. "You play ball with me, I'll play ball with you" was my motto.' He produced the cliché as if it were an epigram that he had been honing for hours.

'We spent hours spooning our great rough boots with hot spoons, Mrs Botney,' said Henry. 'Jenkins was the best. You said you wanted all our boots to shine like that, so you could see your face in them. And, since it wouldn't be fair for Jenkins to be idle while we worked, you scratched two lines on Jenkins's boots and made him start again.'

'Stop him, Lionel,' said Mrs Botney.

'Please, Margery,' said Sergeant Botney. 'Leave the lad to me. I'm not frightened of him.' He turned back to Henry. 'It was our job, laddie, to train you so that in war you'd obey orders automatically, however stupid they were.'

'And you did that,' said Henry, 'by giving us stupid orders, so that in all of us except the very stupid the question constantly arose "Is this a stupid order?" And every stupid order we obeyed, we obeyed with more resentment. Supposing every order we ever got had been sensible and justifiable? Don't you think we might have learnt to obey orders better out of respect for those giving the orders?'

'My job was to make a man of you,' said Sergeant Botney. 'I did a good job. That's why you can stand up to me now. Well done, lad.'

'Oh yes, you're not stupid, sergeant. That's why it's all so inexcusable, you sadistic bastard.'

'Now look here . . .' Sergeant Botney leapt up. Mrs Botney

tried to speak. Sergeant Botney silenced her with a look. 'This is our wedding anniversary, lad. 'Nuff said, I think.'

Yes. Not the time. Social convention. Social convention? There aren't any social conventions for Burbage.

'No. Sorry,' said Henry. 'But I was the one who found him, you see.'

'Found him?'

'You don't even remember, do you? Burbage. The late Signal-man Burbage.'

Sergeant Botney went pale.

'He hanged himself in the ablutions in our hut, Mrs Botney,' said Henry.

'Stop him, Lionel. I don't want to hear,' said Mrs Botney.

'You didn't make a man out of Burbage, did you?' said Henry.

'I've had enough of this,' snapped Sergeant Botney. 'I'm going to fetch the management.'

'That's all the authority you ever had,' shouted Henry. 'The authority to fetch a higher authority.'

But Sergeant Botney was already out of hearing, separated from them by the pseudo-Gallic strains of Alphonso Boycott and his Northern Serenaders. He strode furiously across the dance floor, parting the dancers like a Red Sea.

'I'm sorry about your wedding anniversary, Mrs Botney,' said Henry.

'Sorry!' Mrs Botney's face was a limestone crag. Peregrines could have nested on her forehead without looking out of place.

'Burbage's death came at a very inconvenient time, too,' said Henry. 'Right at the beginning of his manhood. You'll get over this upset soon enough. Burbage never really got over his death. It seemed to knock all the stuffing out of him.'

Sergeant Botney returned with Uncle Teddy.

'Henry!' said Uncle Teddy.

'You know this boy?' said Sergeant Botney.

'He's my uncle,' said Henry. 'And he knows how distressing it is to come upon people hanging in lavatories. He found my father. Right. I've said all I have to say. I'm sorry I had to do it, Uncle Teddy.'

He hurried away, on legs that were suddenly weak. He was

shaking with the enormity of what he had done. And also with the puniness of it. What had he achieved? He felt flat, depressed. The music sounded very far away. Ben Watkinson was approaching, with his shy, petite wife Cynthia.

'Are you all right?' said Ben. 'You look as if you've seen a ghost.'

'It's funny you should say that,' said Henry. 'I've been trying to lay one. What did you do in the War, Ben?'

'I was a conscientious objector,' said Ben. 'I worked down the mines.' He blushed scarlet. Cynthia took his hand and pressed it with defiant sympathy.

Henry's mouth fell open. He was astonished to find that Ben, who had never discussed feelings or ideals, or indeed anything except football, could have felt so strongly, could have been so brave, and could now be so embarrassed, as if ashamed. He closed his mouth rapidly, in case Ben realized that he was realizing how much more there was to Ben than he had realized. He felt embarrassed at witnessing Ben's embarrassment. He hoped that, in the red light, Ben would think that Henry hadn't noticed him blushing. He wished Ben were a woman, so that he could kiss him. He wished it wasn't so difficult for an Anglo-Saxon male to express deep platonic affection for another Anglo-Saxon male. He wished this revelation hadn't come when he had dipped so deep into his store of social courage. He moved on towards the journalists' table. He longed to sit down. But Gordon had gone to get drinks, and Ginny hurried over to him.

'I wanted a word,' she said.

They stood with their backs to the table, watching the towns-folk moving, with varying degrees of style, to the strains of Alphonso Boycott and his Northern Serenaders. Colin was being flamboyant with an extremely glamorous young lady.

'I suppose you've heard me . . . er . . . us . . . er . . .' began Ginny.

'. . . throwing yourselves around your bed in orgies of sexual excitement? Yes.'

'Oh Lord. I . . . er . . . I hope it hasn't . . .'

'. . . kept me awake, wallowing in loneliness and frustration, night after agonizing night?'

'Oh Lord. I'm sorry. It can't be a very nice welcome to your new flat. But . . . you see . . . the thing is . . . I've never had anything like this. I can't give it up.'

'Of course not. Sex makes us all totally selfish. Look at me.'

'Quite.'

'What?'

'Sorry. Anyway, his wife'll be back soon.'

'Wife??'

'Didn't you know?'

'No. Mind you, he may have told me without my understanding.'

'He is a bit obscure till you crack the code. She's away for three weeks, with the children. After that it'll all be over except for occasional hurried daytime trysts. Unless he leaves her. He says he will. Anyway, I wanted to talk to you.'

'Well, thanks, Ginny. It'll make me feel a lot better tonight when I . . .'

'. . . hear us going at it like rabbits.'

'Yes.'

'Oh Lord.'

Gordon returned. Ginny moved away from Henry as casually as she could. Again, Henry tried to sit down. But Neil Mallet was approaching, with the air of a man bent on a tête-à-tête.

'I want to mark your card,' said Neil, leading him away from the table.

'Oh?'

'I think you . . . like Ginny, and I think she . . . likes you. So I just wanted to say that I don't think you should give up hope. That's all.'

'Well . . . thank you, but . . .'

'On what do I base my optimism?' Neil was having to shout, to be heard above the music. 'Just my powers of observation. You see, Henry, a) I don't believe Gordon loves her or will ever leave his wife for her and b) I don't think she loves him. She's on the rebound.'

'The rebound?'

'She's been deeply in love. She's been badly hurt. I don't blame Helen. She can't help being fatally attractive.'

Helen? Could he mean . . . ?

'She's seen this man she loves lose interest in her the moment Helen came on the scene.'

He did mean . . . but . . . had Ginny loved him?

'But there was nothing to all that with Helen,' he lied.

'What do you mean? They're engaged.'

Henry tried to pretend that he'd thought Neil had meant Ted all along.

'Well, yes,' he said. 'I know . . . but . . .' He was floundering. And he wasn't fooling Neil.

'You thought I meant you?' he said. He almost laughed, then touched Henry's arm affectionately. 'Ginny and Ted were engaged,' he said.

'I'm out of my depth.'

'Not with me here to guide you.'

'Why should you do that?'

'I don't make friends easily, and I know how difficult it can be when you join a new group,' said Neil.

At last Henry managed to arrive back at the journalists' table. He collapsed in an exhausted heap. He felt awful. He knew nothing about life. How could he have presumed to tell Sergeant Botney anything?

And there *were* Sergeant Botney and his bristling spouse, marching out, and . . . oh god . . . they were in step! Henry examined the traditional southern French table-cloth as if he were a buyer whose career depended on his assessment of it. When he looked up, the Botneys had gone, and Colin Edgeley was sliding into the seat beside him.

'Why do I have this fatal impulse towards self-destruction?' said Colin, with a histrionic sigh.

'What are you talking about, Colin?'

'I've just put my life in danger.'

'Give over, you daft twat.'

'You think I'm exaggerating?'

'I think you always exaggerate.'

'Not this time. I've danced with the voluptuous Angela Groyne.'

'Is that her name? She's quite something.'

'She's Bill Holliday's girl-friend.'

'Bill Holliday?'

'Scrap king of the Rundle Valley. Leader of the Thurmarsh Mafia. Rich. Powerful. Evil.'

'So?'

'I've danced with his girl-friend. He's possessive to the point of mania.'

'How do you know?'

'She told me. He won't even let her see her girl-friends, in case she meets their boy-friends. I'm a dead man, Henry.'

'Don't be stupid, Colin. Thurmarsh isn't Chicago.'

'It isn't Tunbridge Wells either. Still, I can look after myself.' Colin produced a knife from his pocket. 'I'm prepared, and not like a boy scout.'

'Are you serious, Colin?'

'This is a tough old world, Henry.' He flung a painful burst of lifelong friendship across Henry's shoulders. Later, Henry would remember Colin's words.

The floor show resumed. Henry thought he was watching it, but afterwards he could remember nothing except the climax, when the legendary Martine and the Côte d'Azur Cuties joined in an increasingly sexy finale.

There were gasps as it became clear that the girls were going to strip. Was Thurmarsh ready for this? What would the wives of bank managers and managing directors think? This wasn't a sleazy stag night. Had Uncle Teddy gone too far? Henry suffered agonies of shame and fear, as the girls slowly removed their top hats, their white gloves, their black stockings. They whisked off their traditional mediterranean dresses with almost indecent haste. Chief Superintendent Ron Ratchett whistled so loudly that two councillors thought it was a signal for a police raid, and left hurriedly.

Then, when Martine and the Cuties were down to their bras and panties, they turned into five Edith Piafs, and regretted nothing. Thurmarsh didn't know whether it regretted or was relieved, and applauded loudly to hide its confusion. Several balloons descended from the ceiling.

They sat with a bottle of champagne, the three of them, in the deserted, smoky room. Uncle Teddy, Henry and Derek Parsonage.

'I'm sorry about . . . er . . .' mumbled Henry.

'I think we can afford giving their money back to Sergeant and Mrs Botney,' said Uncle Teddy.

'Yes. The omens look good,' said Derek Parsonage.

'I hate that kind of systematic petty sadism under the excuse of authority. You must have come across a lot of that, Uncle Teddy,' said Henry. 'In Rangoon,' he added hurriedly.

'The oriental mind is different to ours,' said Derek Parsonage. 'Well, what did you think of it all, Henry?'

Henry couldn't bring himself to say that he'd liked it. Why did everything Uncle Teddy do have to be to some degree a con?

'Were the Côte d'Azur Cuties really French?' he asked.

'No. Nobody said they were,' said Uncle Teddy.

'Monsieur Emile did.'

'No,' said Derek Parsonage. 'He said they were born close to the French coast. They were. In Folkestone.'

'Their real name is the Kent Hoppers,' said Uncle Teddy.

'Clever,' said Derek Parsonage.

'Is Monsieur Emile French?' said Henry.

'Oh yes,' said Uncle Teddy. 'But he isn't from Gay Paree. He's from Gay Charlesville-Mexières.'

'But it doesn't have the same ring,' said Derek Parsonage.

'What about the legendary Martine?'

'She's French, she's called Martine, but she isn't legendary,' said Uncle Teddy.

Uncle Teddy and Derek Parsonage laughed. Henry didn't.

'Don't sit there with the weight of the world's shortcomings on your shoulders,' said Uncle Teddy. 'It'll destroy you.'

'It's show business,' said Derek Parsonage. 'What is show business but illusion?'

When Derek Parsonage had gone home to bed, Uncle Teddy poured the rest of the bottle.

'Oh dear oh dear,' he said.

'Sorry,' said Henry.

They sat in exhausted silence.

'I'm grateful to national service,' said Henry. He couldn't leave it alone that night. 'It's shown me how cruel people in positions of authority can be if their attitudes get any kind of nod from a higher authority.'

'Yes . . . well . . . I can see that you feel the need to justify your extraordinary behaviour,' said Uncle Teddy.

Henry felt that Uncle Teddy wanted to say something affectionate. He wanted to say something affectionate to Uncle Teddy. He wanted to tell him that he loved him. He'd managed to tell Cousin Hilda and Auntie Doris. It wasn't so easy, with a man. Go on. Try. 'I don't suppose there's much point in you and me discussing anything,' he said. 'We wouldn't agree. I imagine you're pretty right-wing about everything. Villains usually are.' No!! 'Sorry, Uncle Teddy. I'm all churned up. I . . . er . . . I really am sorry. Because I'm really . . . er . . . quite fond of you, you know.'

There was a pause. He was blushing. He hoped Uncle Teddy wouldn't be too embarrassingly fulsome in reply.

'You're right about villains,' said Uncle Teddy. 'I wonder why.'

'Well left-wingers are left-wingers either because they're poor or because they're idealists,' said Henry. 'Not many villains are poor, and none of them are idealists.'

'You can be quite clever sometimes,' said Uncle Teddy.

'I know,' said Henry. 'So why is my life such a mess?'

8   Lost Heads

A thaw brought floods throughout Europe. 6,000 Midland car workers were put on a four-day week. In South Africa, 400 white women, wearing black sashes, stood with bowed heads in protest at a law removing coloured workers from the common roll. Mr Andrew Redrobe summoned Henry to his office.

'I'm going to give you a tremendous opportunity,' he said. 'Do you think you're ready for it?'

He could hardly say 'no', but it seemed presumptuous to say 'yes'.

'I hope so,' he said.

'I plan a major series of features, and I believe you're the ideal man to do it.'

'Thank you very much, sir.' Henry was too busy trying not to show how flattered he was to worry about that 'sir'.

'It's about the total *ineptitude* of *English education*,' said the neatly dressed editor, banging his right hand on his desk three times for emphasis.

'Thank you very much, sir,' said Henry.

When he told Terry Skipton that he would be spending three days down south, visiting his old schools, the news editor accepted the prospect of his absence with equanimity.

'But what about my calls?' said Henry, somewhat nettled.

'We've a seventeen-year-old joining us. You'll move on to general reporting.' Terry Skipton shook his large, bulbous head disbelievingly. 'Your apprenticeship is over, Mr Pratt.'

The next task of Henry 'He probes the facts behind the facts' Pratt was to telephone the headmaster of Thurmarsh Grammar School. He dreaded this. He'd crossed swords with Mr E. F. Crowther before.

'Mr Crowther? My name's Henry Pratt. I'm a recent old Thurmarshian,' he began, self-consciously. He still hadn't got used to telephoning from an open-plan office, with all his colleagues listening. 'Pratt.' He smiled sheepishly at Ginny. 'P-R-A-T-T.'

'Ah! Pratt!' said Mr E. F. Crowther. 'Sorry. It's a bad line. Yes, I remember you. You interrupted me with a fatuous joke when I was giving the school the benefit of twenty years of careful thinking about life.'

'That's me.'

'For a while quite a lot of people referred to you as Guard's Van Pratt.'

Ginny and Colin were surprised to hear Henry say, 'Guard's Van Pratt?'

'I said, "In every part of the army, from the Pioneer Corps to the Guards, there were Thurmarshians in the van",' said Mr E. F. Crowther. 'You said, "The guard's van."'

'No, sir.' Damn! 'Actually you said, "In every walk of life there are Thurmarshians in the van. I said, "The bread van."' He made a face at Ginny and Colin.

'Well, anyway,' said Mr E. F. Crowther, 'what a pleasure it is to renew acquaintanceship with a wag of your calibre.'

'I'm twenty-one in a couple of weeks, Mr Crowther,' said Henry. 'I'm no longer a . . . er . . .'

'. . . foolish youth who thinks his asinine comments are of more value than the accumulated wisdom of his elders.'

'Quite.' Henry was uneasy about this series. He didn't share his editor's obsession that *all* English education was bad. Within a system too rigid, too remote, too class-conscious, too exam-oriented, he'd been taught by some splendid teachers like Miss Candy and Mr Quell. But Mr E. F. Crowther was not among them. He'd make a splendid start to the series. He was a pillock.

'How can I help you, anyway?' said the headmaster.

'I'm a reporter on the *Argus*, Mr Pill . . . Crowther.'

'Good Lord!'

'I'm doing a feature on the total . . . range of English education. And . . . er . . . I wondered if I could a) interview you and b) have *carte blanche* to . . . er . . . talk to people in the school.'

'There are corners of the school on which no female eyes have ever been clapped. Would you plan to cart Blanche everywhere?'

'What?'

'It was a joke. I was seeing how you liked being interrupted with juvenile jokes. A pathetic piece of tit for tat which I already regret. Forget my foolishness. Certainly I'll see you. Would two-thirty on Friday be convenient?'

'Fine.'

'Good. I have to go now. I have an appointment.'

The police would later believe that these were the last words that Mr E. F. Crowther ever said to anybody.

On the morning of Friday, March 2nd, 1956, Henry made his rounds of hospitals and police stations for the last time. 'Sorry, nothing for you today,' was the general refrain. 'Damn. Oh well, thanks anyway,' was the reply of caring young humanist Henry Pratt on learning that the great Thurmarsh public had been so selfish as to refuse to lose important limbs in unusual ways for the gory delectation of their fellow citizens.

He lunched in the Rundle Café, on sausages, mash and beans. He sat opposite the assistant manager of the Halifax Building Society, whose eyes became moist during the treacle pudding, perhaps because the mortgage rate had gone up to 5½%, or perhaps because his trousers were too tight, or perhaps because he was overcome with emotion at the tale of Penelope, the Porcupine who hated being prickly.

He walked up Rundle Prospect, turned left into Market Street, then right into Link Lane. He approached the long, sober, brick-built school with its rows of regular, disciplined windows. The sky was the colour of cold, thin gravy. He tried to feel the carefree joy that he'd once imagined to be the permanent condition of all those who'd left school. It was no use. He felt all the cares of adulthood and also, beneath them, a residual echo of all the anxieties of childhood.

He went up the wide stairs to the first floor and along the clean, barren corridor which stretched towards the horizon, its emptiness broken only by fire buckets. His hollow footsteps rang out through the fragile calm of the working school. He knocked on the door of Mr E. F. Crowther's study, and was surprised to find it opened by a bulky man with a square head and splay feet. No policeman had ever been concealed more uselessly in plain clothes.

'Yes?'

'I've got an appointment to see Mr Crowther. What's happened?'

'When did you make this appointment?' said the policeman.

'Wednesday afternoon. On the phone.'

'What time?'

'Oh . . . about three, I suppose.'

'Come inside.' The burly policeman closed the door behind them. 'We're trying to do this discreetly,' he said. 'Our psychiatrist has warned of the danger of mass hysteria in schools.'

'What's happened?' repeated Henry.

The study was light and airy. There were neat piles of books, and the three internal walls were covered with graphs and rosters.

'Mr Crowther walked out of here at three o'clock on Wednesday afternoon, and hasn't been seen since. You may have been the last person to speak to him alive.'

'Good Lord! I mean . . . headmasters don't disappear into thin air.' Henry was dismayed to find that, after the first shock, his thoughts were mainly for himself. This could kill off his series. They could hardly lash into educational incompetence if it turned out to be a tragedy. Henry 'He probes the facts behind the facts' Pratt would be strangled at birth. This gave him another thought. 'I'm a journalist!' he exclaimed. 'Can I use the phone?'

'No. Now then, this phone call to the headmaster . . .'

'I have to ring my paper. I have to warn them to hold the front page.'

'They've held the front page.'

'What?'

'It's in the paper already. The disappearance was reported at 11.02.'

'Where to?'

'Darmley Road.'

'Bloody hell! That must have been five minutes after I'd left.'

'Anyroad up, I'm in charge of the investigation, and I'd like to hear about this phone call. All right?'

Everything went in the notebook. The bread van. Carting Blanche. Two feeble jokes given immortality by events. The police officer became taut with significance on hearing that Mr

Crowther had said, 'I have to go now. I have an appointment.'

'Did he say anything that might have suggested a depressed state of mind?' he asked.

'You mean . . . ?'

'It's a possibility. We're dragging the river and the canal.'

'No. Well . . . there was something odd.'

'Yes?'

'He said his joke had been a pathetic piece of tit for tat. He said he regretted it.'

'I don't see owt odd in that. He should have regretted it and all.'

'You didn't know him.' Henry felt a stab of shock as he realized that he was assuming that Mr Crowther was dead. 'I mean, that was practically an apology. I'd say it could indicate an unusual state of mind. Rather as if the Pope said, "Sorry. I've dropped a clanger. Well, nobody's infallible, are they?"'

Colonel Glubb Pasha, the British commander of Jordan's Arab Legion, was dismissed by King Hussein. The MCC apologized for an incident in which a Pakistani umpire sprained his shoulder while trying to avoid being doused with water by members of the England cricket team after a dinner. Henry travelled to Skipton to meet Auntie Doris.

A sharp shower soaked him as he walked from the station to the Craven Tea-Rooms, in a cobbled yard off the wide main street of the pleasant, stone-built market town.

Inside the tea-rooms, the smell of fresh coffee mingled with the faintly rotten fug of drying clothes. Pots, cups and people steamed.

'I . . . er . . . I saw Uncle Teddy,' said Henry.

'Oh?'

'He . . . there . . . er . . . isn't anybody else.'

'No?'

'No.'

'Oh.'

'Yes.'

'Well!'

'Quite. I . . . er . . . I asked him if he'd ever thought of . . . er . . . I mean it just cropped up, I didn't say you'd said anything, well I couldn't, you hadn't . . . if he'd ever thought of . . . er . . .

trying to get you back. He was very encouraging. Very encouraging indeed.'

'What did he say?'

'Nothing. He changed the subject.'

'You call that encouraging?'

'Well, yes. Under the circumstances. Compared with what he could have said. I mean, he could have said, "That bloody bitch! After what she's done to me?"'

'Henry!'

'No! Auntie Doris! I'm not saying that, and nor is he, that's what I'm saying. I mean, under the circumstances, wrong though it'd be, you could imagine somebody saying that. But they haven't. I think that's encouraging.'

The door opened and let in a blast of cold air and a well-bred couple who bred dogs well. They shook the drips off themselves with only marginally more consideration than the dogs they bred might have shown.

'I don't know that there's any point in all this,' said Auntie Doris. 'I don't know that I could ever walk out on a man.' She must have sensed the struggle Henry was having not to raise his eyebrows. 'I never walked out on Teddy. *He* left *me* . . . because he had to. I just . . . couldn't live without a man.'

Henry felt a twinge of his puritan conscience. He knew it to be hypocritical, in view of his own behaviour, but he was powerless to prevent it. Auntie Doris must have sensed it too. She had very acute antennae where her own affairs were concerned.

'Oh, I'm not talking about the physical side,' she said. She lowered her voice, just too late to avoid the interest of nearby customers. 'I'm talking about security. Without a man to hold me together I disintegrate. Oh, I know I've never loved Geoffrey the way I loved Teddy, but . . . but he couldn't run the hotel without me. He can't keep staff. He's been good to me, in his way. He needs me, and I need to be needed.'

The indignation exploded in Henry's head. In his life Auntie Doris was a wall of make-up, a sudden gust of scent, a blaze of dyed hair, a spirit of romance all the more moving because it was never quite real. She deserved better than Geoffrey Porringer. He'd help her get it.

'"Good to you"?' he said. 'The reason he can't keep staff is because he can't keep his wandering hands off them.'

'Henry!'

'Lorna told me. He rubs up against her. Touches her up and makes it look accidental. I'm sorry, Auntie Doris. Don't look like that, Auntie Doris. I'm only telling you because . . . Uncle Teddy's there. Waiting. Calling his club Cap Ferrat. Remembering.'

'Arrange for me to see Teddy, will you, Henry?' said Auntie Doris grimly.

Drunken Everton fans damaged a train taking them home from Manchester. Eoka terrorists blew up an air-liner in Cyprus. The talks between Britain and Archbishop Makarios foundered over the question of rights for Turkish Cypriots. The police found no trace of Mr E. F. Crowther.

Henry met Uncle Teddy in the Cap Ferrat on Tuesday lunchtime. They sat at a table near the bar, with glasses of whisky. The room, which at night had been made to look tawdry by the presence of mild sinfulness, now looked even more tawdry because of its absence. In daylight, when the traditional mediterranean table-cloths hadn't yet come back from the laundry, it was only too obvious that the traditional mediterranean tables had been mass-produced in Retford. Henry felt a sickening lurch of nerves. He'd burnt Auntie Doris's boats. Supposing he'd got it wrong?

He hadn't got it wrong.

'Splendid,' said Uncle Teddy. 'Well, well. I'm going to ring her up, Henry. Strike while the iron's hot. You've done a grand job. Just grand. You can leave it to me now. I'm going to invite her for a champagne dinner. Oh, Henry, Henry! Everything's going to be all right.'

'Yes.' Henry had a terrible feeling that he was going to cry. Desperately he composed himself, so that he could say, without his voice breaking, the words that must be faced. 'I love you both, you see.'

For an awful moment he thought Uncle Teddy was going to ignore this, but he didn't.

'I love you too, son,' he said.

9 The Closing of the Cap Ferrat

He dressed rapidly. This time, if there was a scoop, he was going to be there.

He slammed the front door behind him. A startled cat knocked a dustbin lid off, and he could hear the hollow clanking of goods vans in the distant marshalling yards. Those were the halcyon days of shunting.

He hesitated. If Gordon didn't leave his wife, it wouldn't increase Henry's chances with Ginny if he roared off in search of fame, leaving her asleep. Besides, he was fond of her. He wanted her to share the glory.

He went back inside, and knocked on her door.

'What is it?' she groaned, her voice coated in sleep.

'There've been a tremendous number of fire engines. I think there's a big fire.'

'Thanks.' She was wide awake immediately. She'd scented battle. 'I'll just jump into some clothes.'

He had erotic visions of the ample curves of her naked body as she leapt across the room into a pair of slacks.

She joined him in less than three minutes. What a woman! He glanced at her face in the dim light of the hall. It was drowsy, blotchy, replete. He felt a stab of jealousy.

If only they'd had cars. Not many reporters did, in those days. They struggled through the misty, sulphurous night towards that distant glow. Down Winstanley Road, down York Road, round the back of the Town Hall, past the brooding court house with its absurdly large Doric pillars, across the deserted High Street into Market Street, two panting, unfit, overweight journalists, one sated with sex, the other weakened by the torments of frustration.

The fire sent a shiver down Henry's spine. Fire was primitive. It raised echoes of atavistic superstition. He wondered, afterwards, if he'd already known that it was the Cap Ferrat that was burning.

Doors were open in the old, condemned, rat-infested houses in Canal View. In their curiosity, people were letting the world see them in their curlers and face creams, their thick corded pyjamas and dog-worn slippers.

They turned the corner of Malmesbury Street and gasped. The flames were shooting thirty feet into the air from the stricken club. Showers of sparks were leaping into the night and drifting slowly onto the vulnerable roofs of neighbouring buildings.

The street was jammed with fire engines and the police had erected cordons to keep the disaster-watchers at bay.

Henry and Ginny hurried forward. Henry showed his press card for the first time and croaked, 'Press.' A policeman gave them a hard look, then nodded them through.

Huge hoses were arcing impotently onto the crackling inferno. On the roof of the Thurmarsh Joke Emporium and Magic Shop, four firemen with breathing apparatus were trying to find a way into the burning night-club. Oh god! Uncle Teddy might be in there. Henry ran towards the blaze, ran into a wall of shimmering, impossible heat. A fireman grabbed him.

'It's my uncle's club,' he shouted.

'You can't go in,' said the fireman. 'We're doing our best. Keep out of our road, for Christ's sake.'

'Yes. Yes. Sorry,' said Henry.

Ginny was busy without looking busy, asking firemen questions so casually that they were able to continue their work and didn't think not to answer. Henry caught sight of a familiar face. Monsieur Emile, from Gay Charlesville-Mexières, small, dapper, moustachioed, staring fixedly at the ruins. Henry hurried over to him.

'My uncle,' he said. 'Mr Braithwaite. The owner. Is he in there?'

'No, no. I think no one is there. We all leaved. I seed Mr Braithwaite lock up. He leaved with Mr Vicarage.'

Henry's knees trembled. He hadn't known how worried he was until he realized how relieved he was. As the release swept over him, he heard a tiny, stubbornly pedantic corner of his brain say, 'Parsonage. His name is Parsonage.' He hardly listened to Monsieur Emile, rabbiting on among the flames. 'I go home. I have a friend in Nice. Maybe we open a club there. For Thurmarsh, is bad. For Mr Braithwaite, is bad. For me, maybe I shouldn't say so, is not so bad.' Even as he spoke, there was a small explosion. A great bundle of flaming newspapers shot out of the Mandarin Fish Bar and landed among the firemen, scattering them briefly.

'Come on,' yelled Ginny, above the roar of the flames, her face shining in their glow. 'I've got the basic facts. Let's ring the nationals. We might just catch the late editions.' Getting paid 'lineage' was an acceptable perk for local journalists. Ginny gave him a few phone numbers and the basic facts as they hurried to the phone booths in Tannery Road. They passed Ted and Helen, hurrying down Fish Hill towards the scene. Ted looked as if he'd been interrupted in coitus. Helen looked immaculate, not a hair out of place, as if she were rushing to a fire in an American film.

'How many appliances are there?' he asked, as they reached the phone boxes.

'Seventeen. Twenty-two. Twenty. Eighteen.'

'What?'

'Vary it. Make it look as if the stories are coming from different sources.'

'What about the truth?'

Ginny snorted and rang the *Daily Herald*.

Henry enjoyed phoning the nationals. John Carpenter, who worked for the *Thurmarsh Chronicle*, banged on the door with all the authority of his thirty years as a journalist and asked how long he'd be. He shrugged, and made a gesture which might have indicated that he'd be two minutes. Three calls later, when John Carpenter was angrily pointing to his watch, he sang out, 'Only one more.' He didn't care. Uncle Teddy was safe. He was playing his part in the telling of a big story. John Carpenter had concentrated on him because he thought he'd be softer than Ginny. He was wrong. Henry was a hard man now. 'All yours,' he said generously as he left. John Carpenter, who had once been sent packing from Cousin Hilda's because of his drinking habits, scowled. Henry grinned.

He hurried back to the scene of the fire. The hoses were still gushing mightily, but the flames continued to roar their defiance. Henry found himself wondering what would happen to Alphonso Boycott and his Northern Serenaders, the legendary Martine and the Côte d'Azur Cuties.

138

'Oh my God!' moaned a pale man at his side.

'I know,' said Henry. 'And it only opened two weeks ago.'

'I'm not insured,' said the pale man. 'I forgot to renew the insurance.'

'You what?'

'On Timpley's. That's mine, the tobacconist's. Next to the magic shop. That's my livelihood there. That's thirty-three years. They say the whole block may go.'

A shower of sparks landed on the roof of Timpley and Nephews. George Timpley shuddered and said, 'Oh my God' again. Henry flinched too as the sparks danced on the roof like ducks on a hot plate.

Then he realized that he was standing next to a story. Never mind Ginny and Ted and Helen charging around. He had a human interest story all to himself. One man's night of fear. I shared the agonizing vigil of Thurmarsh tobacconist George Timpley, aged ?, as he watched the sparks landing on the roof of his tobacconist's.

It would be a good story if the building were saved, but it would be a better story if it burnt down. Don't even think like that! But I have to. I'm paid to. I'm a journalist. Good news is no news.

A tobacconist watched as his life's work went up in smoke. No! Stop it! Oh god, if you exist, which I doubt, let Timpley and Nephews survive this night. The man didn't even have any sons. That 'and Nephews' pierces my heart. This may be just a little back street tobacconist's to me, but to him it's his dream. Tobacconist's pipe-dream goes up in smoke. No!

George Timpley gave Henry his life story. It poured out compulsively. Henry scribbled surreptitiously, hoping some of what he wrote would be legible. George Timpley never even noticed. He was staring fixedly at his little shop. He was every fireman, every hose, every jet of water, every spark of fire. He seemed puzzled when Henry asked how old he was.

'Fifty-seven,' he said. 'Why?'

An explosion ripped out part of the wall of the Thurmarsh Joke Emporium and Magic Shop. Glass tinkled into the street. Fake cakes, bottomless tumblers, diminishing Woodbines and impossible spoons were hurled high into the sky. The air was full of sneezing powder, itching powder and electric snuff. Whoopie cushions, goofy teeth, joke spiders and pop-up ties rained down on the bewildered firemen. A large cardboard box of Naughty Fido dog turds, ordered but not yet collected by the Winstanley Young Conservatives, soared into the air, hovered, burst, and showered its unsavoury contents all over Malmesbury Street. Brightly coloured snakes burst from posies of flying flowers.

Then the smells came. The burning of rubber. Rubber doves, rubber eggs, rubber coat-hangers, rubber ears. The burning of plastic billiard balls and wobbly cheese. And, over and above it all, the stench of the stink bombs.

The roof slowly caved in. The chimney crumbled. The vanishing cigars vanished. The vanishing ink vanished. For its last and greatest trick, the shop itself vanished. There was a gaping hole, beside Timpley and Nephews where, a minute before, the Thurmarsh Joke Emporium and Magic Shop had stood.

The hard-pressed firemen donned breathing apparatus, to protect them from the stench of blocked drains and rotting greens unleashed by the stink bombs. They trod on farting cushions as they fought to quell the blaze. Hoses shook, sending water zig-zagging through the sky, as men sneezed violently, scratched desperately, or ducked to avoid being hit by false noses.

Henry ducked to avoid a flying, melting dog turd, which struck George Timpley full in the face. Helen approached him, still immaculate. Suddenly her dignity was assailed from all sides. She was racked by a fit of violent sneezing. She slipped on a plastic fried egg which her watery eyes couldn't see. She fell over, backwards. She subsided, still sneezing, her superb legs swinging in the air, her tempting thighs visible to a world that wasn't interested, onto a pile of top hats, seamless sacks and whoopie cushions, which gave off a gentle volley of soft, mournful farts. And Henry laughed. He laughed and laughed and laughed. He laughed for a dozen Young Conservatives. Hysteria had him in its grip.

Derek Parsonage approached. His face was white. He said 'Oh my God' so often and so fervently that Henry almost didn't believe he meant it. He tried desperately not to laugh. It was incredibly childish, but each sneeze, each fart set him off again. His cheeks ran with tears.

'Where's Uncle Teddy?' he managed to say. 'Didn't he go off with you?'

Can water freeze in a furnace? It felt to Henry that his tears of laughter froze on his face, there in front of the burning Cap Ferrat, as Derek Parsonage said, 'No. He went back in. He said he'd forgotten some papers.'

All fires stop somewhere, and this fire stopped at the Thurmarsh Joke Emporium and Magic Shop. Even in his sorrow at the probable death of Uncle Teddy, Henry felt happy for George Timpley, who was led away, crying helplessly from relief.

The Mandarin Fish Bar had also gone, and the wreck of the Cap Ferrat still smouldered sullenly. The sensation-seekers dispersed reluctantly.

Henry walked slowly home, through the early morning streets, with Ginny Fenwick. The first buses and trams and doomed trolley-buses were running, with a few grey-faced passengers. Milkmen were about, and a yellow municipal lorry was washing a cobbled street. The tension and the grief had made Henry feel extremely sexy. He placed his right hand on Ginny's large left buttock, and cradled its slow, rhythmic movements as she trudged wearily homewards. She smiled at him, rather sadly. At the door of his room his eyes asked an optimistic question and she said, 'No. Sorry.' They snatched a couple of hours of restless sleep in their separate flats.

10　Hard Man Henry

It was a sunny Monday morning in spring. In the gardens of the substantial houses on Winstanley Road, the daffodils were in bloom and the tulips were budding up nicely. The bleak country-side between the towns and pit villages was briefly touched by beauty. Hedges became an astonishing pale green. Trees grew brown and furry with buds. Song-thrushes sent messages of joy across the rusting cars and vans in Bill Holliday's dump.

The sap was rising all over the northern hemisphere. On the lake, in the Alderman Chandler Memorial Park, the mallard and teal were frisky, performing their elaborate displays with relish, entering into their absurdly brief copulations with spirit. In the gloomy animal cages, a moth-eaten marmot looked vaguely puzzled at the absence of moth-eaten marmot mates.

Upstairs, Gordon Carstairs's sap was rising with a stamina to make mallards green with envy. His family were away for a week, and he was making the most of it.

And what of Henry, alone in the flat below, with no outlet for his rising sap? Was *he* green with envy? No. He had no more time for negative emotions. He was an ambitious young journalist. He was Hard Man Henry.

He had first felt that new strength of his on the night of the fire. It had been severely tested in the days that followed.

Hard Man Henry it had been who'd telephoned Auntie Doris, after the body of Uncle Teddy had been found in the Cap Ferrat, burnt beyond recognition. Analysis had shown that he'd been clutching a fire extinguisher at the moment of death. Henry had said, directly and simply, 'I'm afraid I have very bad news. Uncle Teddy is dead.' Auntie Doris had cried. So had Henry. Hard men don't need to feel ashamed of tears.

Hard Man Henry it had been who'd trudged across the gravel to the front door of number 66, Park View Road, who'd refused to be baited when Cousin Hilda had said, 'Ah! A stranger!', who'd told her, 'I'm afraid I have bad news. Uncle Teddy is dead.' Cousin

Hilda had sniffed. 'As they live, so shall they perish,' her mordant sniff had said.

Hard Man Henry it had been who'd written up the death of his uncle. 'Don't do it if it distresses you,' Terry Skipton had said. 'It's my job,' Henry had replied.

Hard Man Henry it had been who'd cancelled his twenty-first birthday party, made the funeral arrangements and given the vicar the salient facts for his oration.

Hard Man Henry it had been who'd sat, calmly, between two sniffing women, one sniffing with sorrow, the other with disbelief, as the vicar's tributes had rolled round the magnificent, sparsely filled, Perpendicular parish church of St Peter's. 'Ill health prevented him serving his country during the War, but he was tireless and active "on the home front" . . . After the War, his import-export business contributed vastly to the revival of his nation . . . In recent years he worked in Rangoon in, it can now be told, a secret capacity, but he never lost his love of Thurmarsh.'

Hard Man Henry it had been who, after the service, had said, 'Cousin Hilda. I don't think you've met Geoffrey Porringer' and had left them to it, while he took the opportunity of a brief chat with Auntie Doris, in the tiny churchyard, surrounded by the clothes shops and shoe shops of central Thurmarsh. 'I spoke to him a couple of days before he died,' he'd said. 'He said he was going to invite you for a champagne dinner. He said everything was going to be all right. I think he died in peace, looking forward to better things.' Auntie Doris, a stricken ship yawing in a sea of emotion, had clutched him and gulped helplessly. Henry had held her firmly. 'Geoffrey's all I have now,' she had said. 'I'm really sorry now that I said what I said,' he had said. 'I'm not,' Auntie Doris had said. 'I know where I stand now. I know how to deal with him.' She'd kissed him, covering him in mascara and salt tears. 'Thank you, son,' she had said. Henry had remained dry-eyed. If he hadn't, Auntie Doris might have drowned in her own tears.

The United States had sent 1,700 marines to the Mediterranean, to try to prevent hostilities between Egypt and Israel. Britain had deported Archbishop Makarios to the Seychelles. French troops had killed 61 Algerian rebels after a mutiny. Mr

Krushchev had denounced Stalin, throwing Russia into ferment. A bomb had been found in the bed of the Governor of Cyprus.

Henry's career had continued to be dogged by misprints – 'She lives alone. Her hubby is underwater fishing,' in an interview with a local athlete; 'The repeated flooding is a source of continual irrigation to him,' in a story about an angry farmer; 'The compensation is dripping down the walls,' in a story about bad housing. But hard men rise above such things. And it was a keen, jaunty Henry Pratt who strode to the tram stop, hungry for a new week's work, that sunny Monday morning in spring.

On the tram, he glanced through the morning's *Thurmarsh Chronicle*. Colonel Nasser was accepting aid from Russia, and was no longer seen as the West's great hope in the Middle East. In the Grand National, the Queen Mother's horse, Devon Loch, ridden by Dick Francis, had inexplicably slipped 55 yards from the finishing post, when leading comfortably. The Thurmarsh trams were to be scrapped. A council official scoffed at warnings of a possible fuel crisis.

The tram rattled perkily along Winstanley Road, unaware of its impending doom. Henry smiled warmly at Gordon and Ginny. Hard men are above self-pity.

That morning, sitting beside the representatives of the *Rawlaston Gazette* and the *Splutt Advertiser*, in Thurmarsh Juvenile Court, Hard Man Henry gave a hard look at two would-be hard youths who had burnt pet rabbits with candles. He fought desperately against feeling embarrassed as a ten-year-old girl told how her father had put his Peter in her Mary. She was taken into care. His fellow reporters didn't take this story down. In the 1950s, the problems of incest and sexual abuse of children were rarely reported.

'We can't print mucky stories about incest,' said Terry Skipton, when Henry complained about the omission of his story. 'What do you think we are?'

'Presenters of the truth about the society we live in,' said Henry. Hard men don't mind sounding naïve.

Robert Newton died of a heart attack. The government agreed to the integration of Malta, with three Maltese MPs sitting at Westminster. Henry attended number two magistrates' court, and listened, in that sombre panelled room, to a case in which a 34 year-old builder, of no fixed abode, was accused of stealing lead off a church roof. The reporters predicted, on the basis of his sartorial inadequacy, that he'd get six months. As they dress, so shall they reap. The chairman was elderly, with yellowing skin, sunken cheeks and a deaf-aid. As the police described how they chased the accused's lorry, stopped it in Hortensia Road, Rawlaston, and found it to contain the lead missing from the roof of St Michael's Church, Crambolton-on-Rundle, Henry sensed that the chairman was having difficulty in hearing, and this surmise proved correct for, in sentencing the man to six months' imprisonment, he commented sternly, 'If you are going to continue to be a road user, you are going to have to drive much more carefully in future.'

Two things about the story that appeared in the paper upset Henry. The gremlins had struck again. His intro began: 'A Thurmarsh builder who was caught red-handed with a sorry load of dead taken from a Rundle Valley church . . .' And the comment of the chairman of the magistrates had been omitted.

He approached the news desk fearlessly. Behind him, in the sunlit afternoon news-room, elderly typewriters clacked at varying speeds. In front of him, sore-eyed sub-editors in shirt-sleeves were thinking up pithy headlines and crossing out offensive copy. Henry had eyes only for Terry Skipton, hunched and staring, like a wounded eagle.

'Two complaints, Mr Skipton. There's another deliberate misprint. "A sorry load of dead." It sounds as if somebody's been desecrating the graveyard.'

'If somebody was deliberately desecrating your stories, Mr Pratt, they'd hardly do it in a way that made them sound more interesting.'

'Mr Skipton? Are you saying all my misprints are natural mistakes?'

'No, I'm not, Mr Pratt. It's all a bit rum. I'm keeping my eyes skinned, actually.'

This took Henry aback. It had crossed his mind that the culprit might be Terry Skipton. Though he didn't think so. He thought he knew who it was. He glanced round, and saw his suspect watching him. The suspect looked away, hurriedly. Suspicion began to harden into certainty.

'And the second complaint?' said Terry Skipton.

'The magistrate's comment has been left out.'

'Complain to the editor if you're not satisfied.'

'I just might,' said Henry. 'I just might.' He didn't want to complain. It'd be much easier to give up. But hard men don't do what's easy.

'It appeared to belong to a different case, a traffic incident,' said Mr Andrew Redrobe.

'That was the whole point,' said Henry. 'The magistrate's as deaf as a post. He thought it *was* a traffic case. But we can't have our authorities looking ridiculous, can we, or the whole system might collapse?'

Sunlight was falling onto the editor's green-topped desk. Specks of dust churned lazily in its rays.

'I think I ought to tell you that he's a personal friend of mine,' said the editor.

Hard Man Henry gulped. But he wouldn't back down.

'I'm sure he is, sir,' he said. He didn't mind that 'sir'. He was prepared to make tactical withdrawals in order to take the main ground. 'Deafness is no bar to friendship. But surely it is to being a magistrate?'

'I agree. Perhaps I should drop a word in the relevant ear.'

'Not a deaf one, I hope.'

Mr Andrew Redrobe gave Henry a long, hard look. Henry just managed to force himself to return it.

'We pride ourselves on having a good relationship with the courts,' said the editor.

'You seem to pride yourselves on having a good relationship with everybody,' said Henry.

'We do. A local paper has to work in the community. If the community clams up against it, how could it ever get good stories?'

'Are you saying that if you ever got a chance to expose something rotten in the community you wouldn't do so because that could kill your chances of getting the stories you need to expose something rotten in the community?'

There was a long silence. The editor tapped on his desk with a silver pencil. Henry knew that he'd gone too far.

'Your exaggerated comments do reflect a real dilemma,' said Mr Andrew Redrobe. 'It's a question of degree. Find me a major scandal, which I think it my duty to print, and I'll print it fearlessly. But not stories about deaf magistrates. Good. I'm glad we've had this little chat. I'm grateful for your invaluable advice on how to run my newspaper. Let's hope you stay here long enough to be able to continue to give me the benefit of it. Goodbye, Henry.'

Little did Henry dream that one day he would be in a position to put the editor's sincerity on this question to the test. Indeed, if he'd had a more suspicious nature and a more highly developed news sense, he'd have been on the trail of that major scandal already.

'Name all the winners of the FA Cup between the wars,' said Ben Watkinson, at their corner table in the back bar of the Lord Nelson.

'Life's too short,' said Henry. The pub's familiar smell of intrigue and carbolic didn't charm him that evening.

'Hard Man Henry,' said Gordon Carstairs, who was sitting beside Ginny in shared satiety.

My god, thought Henry. Can he see into my head?

'Windows,' said Gordon.

'Windows?' said Henry.

'Windows in your head,' said Gordon.

Colin Edgeley returned from the toilets, looking grim.

'Mick Tunstall's back,' he said. 'He's in the other bar.'

'He didn't do anything last time,' said Henry.

'I hadn't danced with Angela Groyne then.'

'What's that got to do with it?' asked Henry.

'Mick Tunstall works for Bill Holliday.'

All this irritated Henry. Real hard men don't advertise their hardness.

He bought a round, and looked back to see Ted and Helen laughing over a page of the *Argus*. He didn't need to ask what they

147

were laughing at. A sorry load of dead. All doubt was removed. They'd be sorry. They'd wish they were dead.

He handed the drinks round, banging Ted's glass on the table.

'Are we permitted to share the joke?' he said.

Ted looked at him in astonishment.

'It's you, isn't it?' said Henry.

'What's me?' said Ted.

'Putting misprints in my stories. Trying to ruin my career. Come outside.'

'What?'

'A fair fight. Or are you scared?'

'I don't want to fight you,' said Ted wearily.

'Stop it, Henry,' implored Ginny.

'Other way, ref!' said Gordon.

'Give over, kid,' said Colin.

'Stop calling me kid,' said Henry. 'Are you coming, Ted, or not?'

'No.'

Henry poured Ted's glass of bitter over his head. Ted sat there in astonishment, dripping with beer. Helen's eyes flashed.

'All right,' said Ted. 'No little pipsqueak pours beer over me and tells me I'm destroying his career.'

Well, you've got what you wanted, Henry Pratt. A fight, with Ted Plunkett, outside a town centre pub. 'Brawling journalists were a disgrace,' says barrister. 'If you are going to continue to be a road user, you will have to drive better than this,' says deaf magistrate. 'Goodbye, Henry,' says Mr Andrew Redrobe.

'This is stupid,' said Ginny.

Yes.

The seven journalists went outside, into the fading light. In Leatherbottlers' Row it was already almost dark. Ted took off his beer-soaked coat. Henry removed his curry-spattered jacket. Denzil Ackerman turned the corner into the alley at a brisk limp. He stopped, his mouth open in exaggerated astonishment, until he realized how inelegant it looked.

'Come on, you two. Call it off,' said Ben, the pacifist.

There was a pause.

'No,' said Ted.

148

There was another pause.

'No,' said Henry.

The two reporters circled round each other, warily. Then Henry attempted a blow, which missed easily. Ted retaliated with a punch that missed almost as easily. Henry hit Ted on the side of the head. Ted launched a rain of blows, some of which found the target. Henry hung onto Ted and managed to punch him in the stomach. Ted gasped and almost collapsed on him, pushing him back into the wall. Henry pushed the gasping Ted off him, stumbled forward wearily, landed a punch on Ted's face and moved in to finish the job. He aimed a huge punch. When it missed, he fell over. Ted leapt at him, and pummelled his ribs, then grabbed him by the hair and yanked him agonizingly to his feet. Henry kicked Ted's shins and butted him. Their heads clashed, and they both reeled away. Ted recovered first, and into that inept and inelegant struggle he managed to inject one good punch. It sent Henry crashing into the wall. He subsided in a crumpled heap, blood gushing from his nose. He passed out.

When he came round, Ted was kneeling beside him anxiously and Ginny was holding a blood-soaked handkerchief to his nose. He was glad to see that Ted's face also showed signs of damage. One eye was closing up.

'You'll be all right, kid,' said Colin.

Ben looked at his watch anxiously. 'Time I was giving the wife one,' he said.

'Wife!' said Gordon. 'In the mouse house!' He kissed Ginny, and hurried off to his returning wife. Ginny looked inconsolable. Henry, lying with his head on the cold stone, looked up at Ginny's legs and dress and longed to put this to the test.

'Sorry,' said Ted. 'I've messed you up a bit.'

'I asked for it,' said Henry. 'It was the wrong way to deal with it. I'm sorry.'

'You don't still think Ted arranged those misprints, do you?' said Helen.

'Didn't you, Ted?' said Henry.

'Of course I didn't, you stupid prick.'

'Ted's wicked,' said Helen. 'He's horrid. He's a tease. But he wouldn't hurt a fly.'

'If he found a spider in the bath he'd be sarcastic to it till it went away,' said Ginny, and blushed at memories of Ted and baths.

'Oh God!' said Henry. 'Oh God, I'm sorry, Ted.'

A taller, sharper, younger, less benevolent version of Neil Mallet emerged from the front bar of the Lord Nelson. His brother, the compositor. Henry's eyes met Ted's. He looked away. The sudden revelation of Neil Mallet's guilt set his spine tingling and filled him with a curious sense of shame, which he didn't wish to share with another human being. He hoped Ted would make no comment, but Ted said, 'He's envious', forcing Henry to say, 'Envious? Of me?'

'I think he saw you as a natural ally,' said Ted. 'A natural friend. Another lonely, hopeless case, unable to strike up human relationships.'

'Thank you very much,' said Henry.

'Ah, but you aren't, are you?' said Ted. 'You have the ability to inspire affection. When he realized that, he couldn't resist his campaign of mischief-making.'

'But he seemed as friendly as ever,' said Henry.

'Ah well,' said Ted. 'Ah well.'

He wished Denzil hadn't come too. As the taxi made its way to Winstanley Road, his face and body stung, his head throbbed, his blood explored painful places, his sensuality leapt and he felt a deep desire for Ginny. He felt that, if they had been alone, his predicament would have awakened her sexuality. The need to avoid pain from his bruises would have added salt to the stew of their love-making. Her soft, warm kisses on his swollen eyes would have been as nectar on a bee's tongue. But Denzil had come too.

His legs were still wobbly. They supported him, one on each arm, to the front door, across the hall, into his impersonal little flat.

'I'll make him some tea and hot food.' Heart-warming words, but not from Denzil. Speak out, Ginny.

'Oh. Right. Thanks,' said Ginny. And off she went!

He felt so tired.

'Scrambled eggs do you?' said Denzil.

'I'm not hungry.'

'You must eat.'

'OK, then.'

'Best I can do, with your measly stores.'

So tired. Denzil clattered away, finding crockery. Upstairs, Ginny clumped about. Spring-cleaning? Barricading herself against bruised sex maniacs?

Henry sat at the little formica-topped kitchen table and ate scrambled eggs on toast, with weak tea. He found it difficult to swallow.

'Come on holiday with me.'

The words drifted around inside his painful head, bumped meaninglessly against his bruised eyes, and finally impinged upon his consciousness.

'What?'

'Come on holiday with me. I see we've put down for the same fortnight. I want to show you Italy.'

What? Why? Oh!

'Well . . . er . . .'

'Have you anything arranged?'

'Yes, I . . . yes. Something arranged. Yes.'

'What?'

'What?'

'What have you arranged?'

'Oh . . . er . . . with my aunt. I'm going to Filey, with my aunt.'

'You can't turn down Italy with me for Filey with your aunt.'

'I can. I have to.'

'I have the offer of a villa in Amalfi.'

'I have the booking of a boarding house in Filey.'

So tired. Go, Denzil, please.

'I thought you were going with your friend,' said Henry.

'Yes . . . well . . .' said Denzil. 'That's over. We split up over a lost tie-pin.'

'So tired.' He realized that he'd said the words out loud by mistake. 'Sorry, Denzil,' he said. 'I'm sorry about your friend. Very sorry. And thanks for everything. But . . . er . . . I'd quite like to be on my own now.'

'Are you sure you'll be all right?'

'Yes. Denzil? Thanks.'

'Pleasure.'

Suddenly the man's speckled brown parchment skin was looming towards the limited field of vision left by his puffy eyes. The man was kissing him full on the lips.

'Denzil?' he said, in a quavering voice which seemed to come from a very long way away. 'I really would prefer it very much if you never did that again.'

Hundreds of miles away, almost as far away as Amalfi is from Filey, the door of his flat closed gently behind Denzil Ackerman.

Henry limped into the office. Terry Skipton gawped at his black eyes and swollen nose.

'Mr Pratt!' he said. 'What does the other feller look like?'

'You'll see in a minute.'

'What?'

Terry Skipton was not overjoyed to learn that two of his reporters had been brawling.

Denzil had given Henry the films to review. 'Review' meant 'Regurgitate the publicity material.' He tried to bury himself in them. 'Pairing sultry Italian siren Anna Magnani with craggy Burt Lancaster was a . . .'

Denzil limped in. Henry blushed invisibly beneath his bruises. The surging blood explored new areas of pain around his cheekbones. He avoided Denzil's eyes. '. . . risky idea, perhaps, but it's a risk that comes off triumphantly. Set in a semi-tropical Gulf Coast town, *The Rose Tattoo* is . . .'

Ted entered, arm in infuriating arm with Helen. Ted's face was puffy, and he had one black eye. Henry approached him immediately.

'I'm really sorry about what I did,' he said. 'I think you've been fairly amazing about it.'

Ted looked embarrassed and grunted. Henry realized that he disliked having his basic good nature discovered. Helen blew Henry an ambiguous little kiss.

'The tragic death of James Dean would make *Rebel Without A Cause* worth seeing even if it was a bad film. It isn't. This study of American juvenile delin . . .'

Ginny looked bleary, as if she'd been catching up on lost sleep. She rebuked Henry for not waiting for her. 'I didn't want people to see you with me. They might have thought you'd been beating me up,' he explained. He realized immediately that she might take this as a comment on her size. He was glad she couldn't see his blushes beneath the bruises.

'. . . quency is a brilliant exploration of a transatlantic middle-class mal . . .'

Henry tried not to look at Neil. He knew that Ted and Helen and Ginny were all trying not to look at Neil. Neil seemed to sense that something was up. He turned and looked at them all not looking at him. Henry's spine tingled. 'Your faces!' said Neil. 'What's happened?'

'We had a fight,' said Henry, in a shaky voice. 'I accused Ted of sabotaging my stories with misprints. I had the wrong man, didn't I? Ted doesn't have a brother in the print room, does he?'

The blood drained from Neil Mallet's face. His mask of geniality faded. A gleam of hatred lit up his eyes. A snarl played cruelly round the edges of his mouth. Too late, the mask returned. Henry couldn't look at him any more. '. . . aise. Dean plays a crazy, mixed up . . .'

Colin entered dramatically. He had two black eyes and a puffed-up face criss-crossed with Elastoplast. His right hand was heavily bandaged. Neil Mallet slipped past, out of their lives, a tormented ghost, with a pile of books tucked underneath his arm instead of his head. Colin hardly noticed him. He looked across the news-room and smiled triumphantly, as if to say, 'You see. I wasn't making it up.' The gap in his mouth had widened by a tooth.

'You should see the other feller,' he said.

'Nasty one, I'm afraid, Mr Pratt,' said Terry Skipton. 'Motor cyclist killed in a collision with a lorry. Twenty years old. Name of Smailes. Lived with his family in Matterhorn Drive.'

His nose had returned to normal, but there was still a little yellowy greenness round the eyes. He took a deep breath as he walked up the garden path, past two tiny landscaped ponds cluttered with gnomes, storks, windmills and tiny bridges. He rang the doorbell. The cheerful chimes sounded indecent in that house of grief.

He found himself facing a comfortable woman in her late forties. She showed no outward signs of grief. His throat was dry. His stomach was churning.

'I'm sorry to disturb you at a time like this, Mrs Smailes,' he said. 'I'm . . . er . . . I'm from the *Argus*. I . . . er . . . I've been asked to ask you one or two questions about your son. It won't take a minute. Er . . . I understand he was quite a promising all-round sportsman.'

Mrs Smailes had gone deathly pale.

'Was?' she said. 'Was?' she repeated on a higher note. 'What's happened to him?'

There was a pained silence. Hard Man Henry joined Henry 'Ee by gum I am daft' Pratt, Podgy Sex Bomb Henry and all the other dead Pratts whose ghostly forms would stalk two paces behind him for the rest of his life.

11   A Run on Confetti

Grace Kelly married Prince Rainier III of Monaco. After fierce border battles, Egypt and Israel agreed an unconditional cease-fire. The Archbishop of Canterbury accused Mr Harold Macmillan of debasing the spiritual currency of the nation by introducing premium bonds. Stanley Matthews, recalled at the age of 42, made all four goals as England beat Brazil 4–2. A dry spring gave way to a cold, wet summer.

Seated at an outdoor table in the magnificent Piazza del Campo in Siena, on a golden September afternoon, Henry would wryly tell his homosexual companion, 'I spent as much on confetti in the summer of '56 as I did on French letters in the autumn of '52.'

So many modern works were included in the Royal Academy's summer exhibition that Sir Alfred Munnings refused to go to the annual banquet. A frogman, Commander Lionel Crabb, was found drowned near Soviet ships while engaged on secret work during a visit to Britain by Messrs Bulganin and Krushchev. Mr and Mrs James Hargreaves requested the pleasure of the company of Henry·Pratt at the wedding of their daughter Diana Jennifer to Nigel Timothy Anthony Pilkington-Brick, on Saturday, June 9th.

Britain offered independence to the Gold Coast. It was revealed, a year after the event, that in May, 1955, 251 men had taken turns to go into a forbidden area to avert a crisis at Windscale Plutonium Factory at Sellafield. It was revealed, after eleven days of soul-searching, that Henry Pratt would attend the wedding of Diana Jennifer Hargreaves and Nigel Timothy Anthony Pilkington-Brick.

A teacher who spoke on ITV about unruly conditions in secondary schools was sacked by the London County Council. In Cyprus there were reprisals against Britain after the hanging of two terrorists. Talks on the independence of Singapore broke down after the chief minister described Britain's offer as 'Like a Christmas pudding with arsenic sauce'. Len Hutton was knighted.

The day before he left for the Diana-Tosser wedding, Henry received the heart-warming news that Mr and Mrs Basil Cornish requested the pleasure of his company at the wedding of their daughter Helen Marigold (Marigold!) to Edward Sampson (Sampson!) Plunkett, on Saturday, July 14th.

At the tram stop that morning, Ginny looked dreadful. Her face was blotchy. Her eyes were red and runny. She gave her red nose a blow so gargantuan that he wanted to pretend he wasn't with her.

'I think I'm getting a cold,' she said.

He touched her muscular right arm. 'Why've you been crying?' he said.

'It's so stupid,' she said.

'They've invited you,' he said.

She nodded. Tears ran down her cheeks. She looked far too vulnerable to be a war correspondent.

What a couple they'd make at Ted and Helen's wedding: Henry still obsessed with the bride, Ginny still in love with the groom.

Only one thing marred the perfection of the wedding of Diana Hargreaves and Tosser Pilkington-Brick, which took place not in Hampstead, but at Holy Trinity Church, Brompton, because that was where Diana's parents had been married. Diana looked splendid in a picture gown of white satin, embroidered with diamante and drop pearls, with her tulle veil held in place by a high coronet of pearls. Tosser looked like a Michelangelo sculpture dressed by Savile Row. The three pages, scaled down editions of Tosser, looked charming in knee-breeches of Parma-violet satin and coats of cyclamen satin trimmed with silver braid. The hats and dresses of the female guests were wonderful to behold.

Tease us no more, you cry. What was this one thing that marred the perfection?

It was Henry. He felt absurd in his hired morning suit. The assistant had said, 'You're lucky, sir. You're right on the edge of our range.' 'On the edge of your range?' he'd said, determined not to be overawed. 'So what happens to the gigantic, the obese, the minute?' 'People who . . . er . . . diverge from the norm to an abnormal degree cannot hire, sir. They have to have clothes made to measure,' the attendant had said. 'It's the law of the market place, I'm afraid,' he'd added, seeming not in the least afraid. 'It's one more example of the cruelty of an inequitable world,' Henry had said: '"Oh, you're rather handicapped. We'll handicap you some more."' 'Anyway, sir,' the attendant had hurriedly repeated, 'you're lucky, as I say. You're . . .'' . . . on the edge of your range. Hanging on to the rim of normality. Not grotesque by a hair's breadth. Terrific. Thank you!' Henry had said.

And so, although dressed in a morning suit at a gathering full of men in morning suits, Henry felt distressingly conspicuous as he approached the church, on foot. The rain had held off. There was a great crowd of bobbing hats. He caught a glimpse of a radiant Belinda Boyce-Uppingham. He saw many men whose large frames and moon-faces proclaimed them to be Pilkington-Bricks. And, with a surge of joy that astounded him, he saw Lampo Davey, Tosser's study-mate at Dalton. Elegant, fastidious Lampo, for whom Henry had fagged. He'd had to rebuff Lampo's advances. Lampo turned, and saw him and, to Henry's surprise, Lampo's face lit up also. There was a moment when they almost, instinctively, kissed. Two young Englishmen kissing each other in morning suits at a society wedding in 1956! Henry went cold all over, at the enormity of the escape. 'Henry, good to see you!' 'You too, Lampo!' 'What are you doing now?' 'I'm a reporter on the *Thurmarsh Evening Argus*.' 'Delicious! Priceless! You're too absurd.' 'What about you? Not still in Crete?' 'Oh, that. No. That was a mistake. The Cretans are absolute sweeties, but dreadfully basic. Opportunities for mime artists are minimal. No, I'm at Cambridge. Terribly banal.'

The vicar's voice rolled round the church like well-bred thunder. The congregation sang with suspicious fervour. Henry felt deeply irritated. Diana Hargreaves, whom he adored, was throwing herself away on the oaf who'd lost the match for England.

He also felt worried. He was getting nowhere with women, yet he was having to resist the advances of Denzil, and Lampo had almost kissed him. Was he attractive only to men?

Not quite. As the bells pealed out their joy over a grey London, and the guests slowly filed past Diana, kissing and praising her, she whispered to him, 'Are you jealous?' 'Of course not,' he said, smiling. 'Oh dear,' she said. 'I'd like you to be a little jealous. There'll always be a corner of my heart that's just for you,' and he walked off, weak at the knees.

At the reception, in the flower-bedecked Sisley Suite of the Gore Towers Hotel, he wandered among the flowers, gazed at the Sisleys, nibbled salmon in aspic, marinated carp, jellied lamb cutlets, cold pigeon pie. He sipped the champagne with the restraint its quality deserved. He talked to Paul. The gap between them was widening remorselessly. He talked to Judy, who clearly would marry Paul. Their conversation was a miniature gem of non-communication.

Mrs Hargreaves approached him, elegant in a cream and gold brocade suit. His loins stirred irrelevantly.

'I love Sisley, don't you?' she said.

'Er . . . yes . . .' he said. Why could he not admit that he'd never seen a Sisley painting in his life until today, and that it was only because the subjects were French and the style impressionist that he had the impression that Sisley was a French impressionist? Why be ashamed, when he knew that nothing is less sophisticated than believing that sophistication matters?

He glanced at the pictures, seeking an intelligent comment. 'Snow at Louveciennes 1874'. 'Snow at Louveciennes 1878'. 'Near Marly – Snow on the road to Saint-Germain 1874–5'. 'Floods at Port Marly'. He couldn't say 'Rotten luck Sisley had with his weather.' He said, 'They're pretty.'

'Yes!' said Mrs Hargreaves, as if she thought he'd said something really clever. 'Not a fashionable word today, and I wouldn't want you to think I'm with Munnings – he's so dull he has no right to criticize anybody – but if we can't enjoy prettiness what hope is there for us?'

They examined 'Early Snow at Louveciennes 1870' in silence. He'd have to say something. 'I find them elegiac,' he said.

'An excellent word,' said Mrs Hargreaves. 'Everybody knows roughly what it means. Nobody knows quite what it means. Dear Henry!' She ran one finger down his cheek and moved elegantly away. Henry turned and came face to face with Mr Hargreaves.

'Good, aren't they?' said Mr Hargreaves. 'Jamot said Sisley had no ambition except to be the delightful minor poet of the country

158

and the seasons. I find that rather difficult to reconcile with some of his late haystacks, don't you?'

Courage.

'I have to say I don't know much about Sisley's late haystacks.'

'Ah.'

'I don't know much about his early haystacks either.'

'Ah.'

Belinda Boyce-Uppingham approached, oozing, if not sexuality, an aura of healthy vigour and cleanliness that would do almost as well. 'Henry!' she said. 'How you do keep popping up in my life.'

Mr Hargreaves was able to escape from Henry while pretending that he was tactfully leaving him with Belinda.

To his horror Henry heard himself say, 'I know. We've got to stop meeting like this.'

'I hope not,' she said, fervently.

Did she mean it? He felt an erection trying to find room to express itself, just below the marinated carp, in a suit into which he'd only just been able to squeeze himself in flaccid sexlessness after a modest breakfast. Journalist in society wedding fly-button horror. Down down. Probably she didn't even remember that she'd once called him a 'bloody oik'. Social indignation strangled his erection.

'Still scribbling away on your paper, are you?' she said. Well, at least she'd remembered, but 'scribbling'!

'Yes,' he said. 'Scribble scribble!'

'Jolly good,' she said. 'Henry? Will you let me say how sorry I am for something awful I called you many years ago when I knew no better?'

The bell rang for round two of the fight between Henry's erection and his hired suit.

'Ah! Robin. There you are. Meet Henry Pratt,' said Belinda. Henry found himself looking at a tall man with thighs like oak trees and skin like sandpaper, who was looking down on him like a member of the Royal Family admiring a pumping station whose workings bored him to distraction. The fight was stopped. The hired suit was declared the winner.

'Hello, Henry Pratt,' said Robin. Henry asked Robin about his views on Sisley's late haystacks. Robin's eyes glazed over, and they made a hurried escape from him, which freed him from the necessity of making a hurried escape from them.

He approached Tosser and congratulated him.

'Thanks, Henry,' said Tosser loftily, as if Henry were still his fag. This irked Henry, and he couldn't resist saying, 'I saw the Wales match.' Tosser made a cheerfully wry face and said, 'Oh Lord. Did you? I had a bit of a stinker.'

The man didn't even seem mortified! How insensitive could you get?

Lampo joined them, smiled his slightly twisted, sardonic smile and said, 'Hands off, Tosser. You're married now,' and Henry thought he was going to blush.

'Careful of La Lampo, Henry,' said Tosser. 'Her spell in the WRACS has made her more sexually devious than ever.'

'Did you do national service, Lampo?' said Henry, with such surprise that Lampo laughed.

'Yes. I couldn't think of a decent excuse,' said Lampo. 'I became a sergeant in the education corps. Priceless.'

Tosser drifted off at last.

'What a bore he is!' said Lampo affectionately. 'I wonder whether he'll bore her to death or crush her to death.'

'Oh I hope they're happy,' said Henry, with a depth of feeling that surprised him. 'I like Diana.'

'Randy little bugger, aren't you?' said Lampo. 'Henry? Come to Italy with me.'

'What?'

'I assume you *are* given holidays from your sordid tasks. I'm going to Italy for several weeks. Pop over and see me. I want to show you Italy.'

'Well, I . . . er . . .'

'No strings attached. I know how horrified you are by the homosexual side of your nature.'

'Lampo!'

'Sorry. I can't help teasing. I'm so pleased to see you.'

'Why?'

'God knows. Absurd, isn't it? Henry, it is true that, absurd though you look in those clothes . . .'

'Thank you.'

'. . . perhaps *because* you look so absurd in those clothes, I would, were your views on the matter different, enjoy . . . a relationship. But not in Italy. Italy's too beautiful for sex. Nobody in Venice or Siena could possibly have eyes left for you. In Runcorn or Barnsley I might try to seduce you, to take my mind off the surroundings. In Italy you'd be safe. Please come.'

'Have you ever been to Barnsley?' said Henry, glowering.

'Of course not!' said Lampo. 'Oh dear. I've offended the Yorkshireman in you. I notice you don't bother to defend Runcorn. Henry, on your holidays, if you can tear yourself away from the delightful towns of South Yorkshire, with their fine public buildings, spacious libraries, ample toilet facilities and charming citizenry, will you let me show you the most beautiful cities in the world?'

'Why does everybody want to show me Italy?'

'Everybody?'

'Our arts editor. An ageing queer with parchment skin and a limp.'

'A limp what?'

'Oh God. Why did I describe him like that? How ungenerous. But why do you all want to show me things? As if I didn't know.'

'Oh. So you know. Why do we?'

'Because I'm a blank page. I have no personality. You all want to create me in your image.'

'What mawkish rubbish. Henry, I can't speak for your arts editor with his limp parchment, but I want you to come to Italy because you're not blasé. With you I can live each day as if it's my last and look at Italy as if I've never seen it before. Will you come?'

'Yes.'

Henry was as surprised by his answer as Lampo.

The last British troops left Suez 'quietly and with dignity', in accordance with the 1954 Anglo-Egyptian agreement. Charges for school meals, passports, driving tests and higher education classes were increased. Martial law was declared in Poznan after 38 people including communist officials had been killed in riots. In the Wimbledon finals, Lew Hoad beat Ken Rosewall and our very own Angela Buxton lost to Shirley Fry. On the day before the wedding of Helen and Ted, Henry received a letter from Auntie Doris.

Dear dear Henry [she wrote]

My Geoffrey and I are to be married on Saturday, August 18th, in Skipton. A lot of people are going to say we should have waited, but I'd been parted from Teddy for a long time so 'the damage had been done'. Geoffrey's all I have now and I hope you'll come and give us your 'blessing'. Who knows what would have happened if I'd met my Teddy again but that's all 'past history', as they say. I think I should tell you I told Geoffrey what you told me. He admitted it. He just couldn't help himself, and he hates himself for it. You'll find, Henry, unless you're very lucky, that 'the physical side of things' brings as many problems as joys and those without 'skeletons in the cupboard' are lucky. Geoffrey's promised not to do it again, and I'll be watching him. So what you told me's put me in a position of strength. I expect that seems shocking to you but, remember, we're quite elderly business people marrying as much for convenience and security as for love. Don't despise things like convenience and security, Henry. You'll come to value them as the body starts to disintegrate. Oh dear! I am cheering you up, aren't I?

Anyway, Geoffrey wants to be good friends with you and wants you to come to the wedding. He says if ever things don't work out in 'the world of journalism' there'll always be a job for you in the catering industry. We also want the sniffer to come. Oh Lord, I shouldn't call her that, should I? Hilda and I are chalk and cheese but blood is thicker than water, as they say. We're sending her an invite but suspect she might refuse. We know how close you are to her, so would you be an angel and use your famous charm?

Henry, my darling, your silly old auntie has realized over the years that she loves you very much.

XXXXXXXXXXXXXXXXXXXXXXXX (One for each year of your life and one for luck) Doris

'How close you are to her'! He hadn't been to see her for weeks. 'Your famous charm'!

He felt touched by this letter, and less upset than he'd have expected at the thought of Auntie Doris marrying Geoffrey Porringer. But he did also feel a little depressed.

Would he ever be done with other people's weddings?

On Saturday, July 14th, 1956, Cypriot terrorists warned that, for every Greek child killed by the security forces, Eoka would kill a British child. Marilyn Monroe, arriving in Britain for the first time, was asked who she wanted to meet, and said, 'Sean O'Casey and Dame Edith Sitwell.' Sir Anthony Eden said, 'We are in mortal peril, not of immediate unemployment, but of poverty by stages.' Ex-King Farouk of Egypt offered to remarry his first wife, Farida. She refused. Ted Plunkett did marry Helen Cornish. Henry pocketed three handkerchieves, in case Ginny needed them.

Ben Watkinson was picking them up and driving them to Buxton. Ginny knocked on Henry's door five minutes before Ben was due to arrive.

She was wearing green and looked at her largest, but he knew that he wouldn't need the handkerchieves. She was a war correspondent, going to the front line.

'Will you do something for me?' she said shyly, very embarrassed.

'If I can.' Her embarrassment made him cautious.

'Will you make it look as if you and I are . . . you know? Gordon's wife'll be there.'

The reception was held in the ballroom of the Palace Hotel, a large stone hydro, standing above Buxton like a lesser château which had somehow become separated from the Loire. The ballroom was a high-ceilinged, elegant room, with huge windows overlooking gardens which sloped to a domed hospital and the dignified, classical, dark grey spa town.

Henry stuck to Ginny like a parking ticket. Helen was so radiant that Henry wondered if she was regretting the marriage already. She had looked achingly lovely as she'd walked up the aisle in what she would have described, in one of her fashion articles, which Ginny despised, as a beautiful wedding gown of lace and pleated tulle, with a short train, a full-length veil with a crown of orange flowers, and a bouquet of white orchids, stephanotis and lilies. She kissed Henry warmly, as if finding him attractive for the first time in months. And then Denzil was approaching. It was happening again. He was only attractive to queers and brides.

'When are you off to Filey?' said Denzil. 'Filey?' said Henry, awkward in his dark suit. 'Filey. With your aunt,' said Denzil. 'Oh. Yes. Filey. I'd forgotten. Because I'm not,' said Henry. 'Not going to Filey? I invited Henry to Italy, Ginny. He said he was going to Filey,' said Denzil. 'Well, I'm not. I'm actually going to Italy, funnily enough. Change of plan,' said Henry. 'But not with me,' said Denzil grumpily. 'Well, I can't. I'm going with my uncle,' said Henry. 'Ah, your uncle! Not your aunt,' said Denzil. 'No. I was telling Ginny only yesterday, funnily enough. Wasn't I, Ginny?' said Henry. 'Telling you what, Ginny?' said Denzil. 'About his uncle and his aunt,' improvised Ginny. 'They were very good to him as a child. They've split up. He goes on holiday with them in alternate years. He thought this was an aunt year, but it's an uncle year. This is a different uncle from the one who was killed, of course, otherwise Henry wouldn't be going on holiday with him.' 'Right,' said Henry. What a wonderful woman she was. If only he loved her.

Denzil wasn't sure whether to believe them, and in any case he was grumpy and jealous. Henry felt that Denzil was diminishing as he got to know him better. He wanted Denzil to be stylish and outrageous, not grumpy. And yet, as Denzil diminished, Henry found that he liked him more.

Denzil introduced them to Helen's younger sister, Jill. She was a little shorter than Helen, fractionally fat, somewhat flat-chested, with a tiny mouth. She was shy, gawky and, Henry suspected, sensual. He desired her very much indeed. Ginny tucked her arm into his and led him through the throng, out of danger.

They spoke, briefly, to several of Helen's relatives and to Ted's mother, who seemed to be his only relative. The champagne flowed. Henry could see Ted, over by the cake, glowering at the champagne as if blaming it for not being Mansfield bitter. Colin Edgeley called it a ponce's drink. 'Glenda likes it,' he said. 'Pity she couldn't come.' Henry didn't want to feel guilty about liking champagne. He wanted to be a man of the people, drinking pints out of straight glasses. He also wanted to be a connoisseur of fine wines. He wanted to be all things to all men. Was he in fact nothing to anybody?

Ginny clasped his arm even more firmly as they found themselves talking to Gordon and Hazel Carstairs, who were also firmly indivisible. Hazel was fair-haired, blue-eyed and slightly plump. She looked tired. Henry thought her attractive, in a very middle-class, trim way, which didn't seem to go with Gordon. 'Hello, young lovers,' said Gordon without a hint of shame. 'Not a bad wedding, is it? Pity it's such a grey day, though.' Henry was amazed. He'd never known Gordon deliver such a comprehensible message. It was so banal that he felt ashamed for Gordon. 'It's a shame we couldn't have had a bit of sun,' Gordon continued, 'but at least the rain's held off.' Didn't he speak in code when accompanied by his wife? Was it all an act? Or was this the act? He looked Gordon straight in the face and received a totally blank look in return.

'How are you, Ginny?' said Hazel. 'I'm almost surprised to find you're still on the paper. Gordon never speaks of you any more.' Henry was afraid that Ginny would blush, but she was made of sterner stuff than that. Then he was afraid that *he* would blush. Luckily, Ginny replied, 'Doesn't he? Well, I don't see much of him. I'm otherwise engaged these days, aren't I, love?' 'He's blushing. You're embarrassing the young man, Ginny,' said Gordon. Henry felt obliged to take part in this repellent charade. 'I've got a flat in the same house as Ginny,' he said. 'Say no more!' said Gordon, and Henry was happy to obey. Hazel smiled throughout this exchange, and Henry had an uneasy feeling that her smile hid bottomless pain and that she saw through the charade completely and despised them all utterly. But he might be wrong about this, because he also had an uneasy feeling that, for a journalist with an international future, he knew very little about people.

He was glad to move on to Ben Watkinson and his shy, petite wife Cynthia. Another couple who didn't trust each other to go

165

their separate ways, but steered side by side round the crowded ballroom as if on a slow, invisible dodgem car. 'I hope the light's better in Leeds,' he said. 'Why?' said Cynthia, astonished. 'The cricket,' said Henry. 'Silly me. I might have guessed. Bloody sport again,' said Cynthia. Ben glared at Henry. Henry thought this unfair. It was hardly his fault if he never talked to Ben about anything except sport. He'd tried to shift the relationship onto a more personal level, now that he knew about Ben being a conscientious objector. It hadn't worked. He didn't think Cynthia looked the sort of person to whom you went home to give one, in mid-evening, on the rug, before supper. Was all that another lie? Colin passed by, his plate piled high. For a man who professed to have no interest in food, he couldn't half shovel it in when it was free, thought Henry uncharitably.

And every moment of every conversation, even as Helen kissed him bubblingly on the cheek, as if there were champagne in her veins instead of blood, he was aware of the exact spot in the room occupied by her sister. 'Dear Henry,' said Helen. 'You won't desert us when we're knee-deep in nappies, will you?' 'Excuse me,' he said, and he strolled over towards Jill, leaving Ginny and Helen alone together, united in their displeasure at his abrupt departure, but with nothing whatever to say to each other.

He caught up with Jill just as she was leaving the buffet. His heart was pumping.

'Hello, Jill,' he said. 'What's it like being Helen's sister?' Oh no. The world's most stupid question. Quite rightly, she ignored it. His next question was no more sparkling, but infinitely more answerable. 'What do you do?'

She blushed. Shy! Warm, too.

'I'm still at school till July.'

'Good Lord! You look too old. Mature. Grown-up.'

'Excuse me. I must . . . er . . . move on.'

'Yes. Yes, of course.' Be bold, Henry. 'Jill? Will you come out some time?'

'No, sorry, I . . . sorry.'

'Why not?'

'I don't know you.'

'You would know me if you came out with me.'

166

'No.'

'Give me one good reason why not.'

'I don't find you remotely attractive.'

She walked on past him, her face grim and blazing. His face was blazing too. He had an uncomfortable feeling that everyone at the reception was looking at him. He hurried to the buffet, and began piling a plate with things that he didn't even see. Never in the whole of his life would he ever again risk humiliation by having anything whatsoever to do with a woman. He felt an arm on his arm. It was Ginny's. She'd seen his humiliation and suffering and, even though he'd deserted her, she had come to his rescue. What a magnificent woman she was. He loved her.

Sir Bernard Docker, sacked by the Birmingham Small Arms Company for extravagances including having five Daimlers with special bodywork built for the exclusive use of himself and Lady Docker, sent out 10,500 telegrams declaring that he wasn't extravagant. The pay of farm workers went up 6s. to £7 1s. for a 47 hour week. Hungary's hated boss, Matyas Rakosi, resigned amid open jubilation in Budapest. Britain and the United States withdrew their offer to loan Egypt £7,500,000 to start work on the Aswan Dam. Colonel Nasser retaliated by nationalizing the Suez Canal Company. It was the wettest July for 100 years.

The rain battered on the rotting window frames at the back of number 66, Park View Road. A bowl of dying chrysanthemums stood on the unlit blue-tiled stove. A faint aroma of toad-in-the-hole lingered. Cousin Hilda switched the television off.

'You needn't switch it off,' said Henry.

'It's a poor night,' said Cousin Hilda. 'We've had Alma Cogan. All we've got now is some play by some Russian, some people looking at paintings and talking, and a lot of Austrians yodelling on their zithers. I ask you! Who plans these things?' ITV hadn't come to Thurmarsh and, even when it did, Cousin Hilda would die of boredom rather than watch it. 'Anyroad,' she continued. 'It's common to keep the television on when strangers call.'

'I'm not a stranger,' said Henry.

'Mrs Wedderburn said to me the other day: "I haven't seen that nice young Henry recently. Does he visit you regularly?" She can be right nosy, when she's a mind to it, can Mrs Wedderburn. Well, I couldn't lie. I said, "He comes as regularly as you'd expect a busy young man to visit an elderly relative."'

'I'm sorry. I keep meaning to.'

'Intentions are cheap.'

'I know. But I am busy. I will come more often. I promise. I think of you a lot.'

'Thoughts don't cost.'

'I know.'

Cousin Hilda didn't offer him so much as a cup of tea, for fear it would pollute the purity of his motives in visiting her.

'So what have you come about?' she said.

'I haven't come about anything,' he said. 'Can't I just have come to see you, because I want to?' Oh god. How do I raise the subject of the wedding now? 'How's Liam?'

'The same as always.'

'And Mr Pettifer? Having a run on Stilton, is he?'

'You seem to have forgotten that he's been moved to general groceries. But I suppose it's natural for young people to be self-centred these days.'

He ignored this. 'How's he bearing up?' he asked.

'He puts a brave face on it, but he's a shadow of his former self.'

'And Mr Frost?'

'He has peace of mind. He's made the right decision. He's abandoned the lure of the bright lights and is looking forward to buckling down to the responsibilities of marriage.'

Bless you, Cousin Hilda. A cue!

'Talking of marriage, I suppose you got Auntie Doris's invitation.'

Cousin Hilda sniffed. 'It went where it belonged. In the dustbin.'

'Cousin Hilda!'

'You expect me to accept? Marrying a man who runs a pub, with your Uncle Teddy barely cold.'

'It's a hotel, actually.'

'That makes it all right, I suppose. I thought you didn't like him, anyroad. Slimy, I seem to recall, was your description.'

'I wish I hadn't said that now.'

'Why? Isn't he slimy?'

'Well . . . yes . . . I suppose he is . . . but it doesn't seem generous.'

'Generous! If he's slimy, he's slimy. You can't avoid facts.'

'No, but . . . I think sliminess is in the eye of the beholder. And I beheld it. And I wish I hadn't.'

'So you regard my conduct in throwing Doris's invitation to her wedding with this slimy person while the husband she abandoned is still practically warm into the dustbin as unjustified?' Cousin Hilda just managed to hang onto her syntax, but the effort had exhausted her.

'No, but . . . she'd like you to be there.'

'I hardly think that's likely.'

'I know she would. She asked me to ask you.'

'So that's why you came round!'

'No. I'd forgotten about that. Then you mentioned Barry Frost's wedding, and it all came back.' Cousin Hilda sniffed. 'I *had* forgotten it.'

'I didn't say owt.'

'No, but you sniffed.'

'What?'

'Sometimes, when you disapprove of something, you sniff. You probably don't realize you're doing it.'

'I see.' Cousin Hilda sniffed. 'I'll try to stop it if it upsets you.'

'It doesn't. I just . . . look, I know Auntie Doris would like you there because . . . well, I don't think there'll be many family, and blood is thicker than water, as they . . . I mean, I don't approve, but . . . I forgive. Can't you forgive?'

Cousin Hilda sniffed.

'Something puzzles me, Cousin Hilda,' said Henry. 'I'm not a Christian any more, but I can forgive. You are, and you can't. I thought forgiveness was a big bit of the . . . er . . . the whole caboosh, but . . . it worried me a bit when I was a Christian. It seemed to me that some Christians didn't have any forgiveness in their hearts at all.'

Cousin Hilda's new cuckoo clock, a reminder of Mrs Wedderburn's holiday in Lucerne, a reminder that Cousin Hilda had never been abroad, ticked remorselessly.

'I'll come,' she said.

He didn't want her to. It would be embarrassing. It would have been so much easier without her.

Why had he gone to such lengths to persuade her?

'Oh good,' he said. 'That's grand.'

He kissed her.

She sniffed.

Jim Laker bowled England to the Ashes at Old Trafford, taking 9 for 37 and 10 for 53. There were several feet of hailstones in Tunbridge Wells on August Bank Holiday Monday. Aly Khan sought a new divorce from Rita Hayworth. Egypt refused an invitation to a conference in London to establish an international system for operating the Suez Canal. An air lift of British troops to the Mediterranean began. The Foreign Secretary, Mr Selwyn Lloyd, said, 'We are not bellicose. With Britain force is always the last resort.' Eoka called for a truce in Cyprus. And on Saturday, August 18th, Auntie Doris married Geoffrey Porringer.

As he walked towards the low, crenellated, blackened stone church of Holy Trinity, Skipton, with its squat, solid tower and huge black clock with gold numbers, showing that it was 11.22, Henry's mind went back to the War years, when his mother had brought him to the town for a treat. They'd seen *The Wizard of Oz*, and a display of blitz cookery by a team of girl guide advisors. He wished it was that day now, and the wedding wasn't taking place, and Cousin Hilda wasn't walking with pursed lips at his side.

In the church there were memories of childhood too. There was Auntie Kate, five foot one, white-haired, beaming. In the War Henry had lived with her and Uncle Frank at Low Farm, outside Rowth Bridge. Uncle Frank had been dead for eleven years. Henry was filled with shame and horror as he realized how long it was since he'd seen or even thought about her. She lived in Skipton now, in a house with lurid patterned carpets, with her daughter Fiona and Fiona's husband, Horace Brassingthwaite, the assistant bank manager with the artificial leg. In the War Fiona had been a princess who'd read Henry stories from comics when he'd had measles. Now she was a wife, a mother of three, a sweeper of lurid carpets. She and Horace were in the church, too.

The remaining guests were Ollie Renishaw, barman at the White Hart, and Geoffrey's son Stephen and daughter Geraldine. Eight guests, occupying just two of the numbered pews, each with its own door, beneath the great beamed roof. Henry recalled the splendours of Diana's marriage to Tosser, and felt sad. 'We wanted it small,' Auntie Doris said later. 'We could have invited lots of customers but, once you've started, where do you stop?'

Henry felt that Geoffrey Porringer made a surprisingly impressive figure. Now that he'd settled in the country, he was slowly, imperceptibly becoming less slimy. Of course nothing could be done about his blackheads. Nobody, in secret laboratories in Cumbria and Suffolk, was giving hamsters blackheads in order to find a cure for the condition in humans. Henry felt that he might even become quite fond of the man, for Auntie Doris's sake, now that the die was cast, provided he could desist from rubbing against waitresses and calling him 'young sir'.

The little group trooped through the cold August rain, down the wide high street and into the Black Horse, where they had booked a private room.

They took sherry before the meal. Cousin Hilda sniffed.

'Come on, Cousin Hilda,' implored Henry. 'Just the one.'

'Certainly not,' said Cousin Hilda.

Geoffrey Porringer told Geraldine that she could have 'just the one'. Geraldine Porringer was sixteen years old. She looked like her father, except that she had no blackheads.

'Don't order me around, Dad,' she said. 'I've come here to enjoy myself because I'm happy to see you happy.' After that, Geoffrey Porringer made no comments about Geraldine and drink.

Ollie Renishaw, a tall, dour man with bags under his eyes, had a drip on the end of his nose. Cousin Hilda sniffed meaningfully but, since he had already realized that she sniffed at regular intervals, he took no heed. Geraldine, onto her second sherry, whispered to him. He blew his nose hurriedly. Within minutes the drip was there again. It was as if a washer in his nostril was on the blink.

'I was right happy at Low Farm,' Henry told Auntie Kate. 'The happiest time of my life.'

'Oh, I hope not,' she said, but he could tell she was pleased.

'I wish I'd come to see you more often,' he said.

'Why haven't you?' said Horace, and Henry tried not to look at his artificial leg.

'Because young men are self-centred,' said Henry.

Horace opened his mouth, but could think of no reply so, wisely under the circumstances, he closed it again.

'I hope Graham'll manage on his own,' said Ollie Renishaw.

'Relax,' said Auntie Doris. 'Forget the bar. You aren't indispensable. Nobody is.'

'Oh aye. I know that,' said Ollie Renishaw. 'But it's the price rises. He hasn't got the hang of them at all.'

'So we'll lose a bit of money,' said Auntie Doris. 'Never mind. It's our wedding day. Enjoy yourself.'

'Right,' said Ollie Renishaw grimly. 'Right.'

Geoffrey Porringer was very fussy about where everybody sat, at the big table, in the beamed, low-ceilinged room. 'You look after Geraldine, young sir,' he told Henry.

On Henry's other side was Auntie Kate. Cousin Hilda was put next to Ollie Renishaw.

There was good red roast beef and claret. Cousin Hilda asked for a well-done slice off the edge and complained that she'd been given too much. She glanced at Henry every time he took a sip of wine, so he said, 'This is a very nice wine,' and her lips moved painfully, and he wished he hadn't said it.

'It's a thoughtful little number,' said Stephen Porringer, who was twenty-one and a trainee manager at Timothy Whites. 'It combines the strength of a Burgundy with the finesse of a claret.' Henry detected no trace of self-mockery.

Geraldine whispered in his ear, 'Don't you think my brother's a prick?' Henry felt overcome with sorrow that she wasn't attractive. She deserved the best of men, and wouldn't get him because the world is a cattle market. He whispered back, 'A total prick.'

'Whispering?' said Stephen. 'A state secret, or may we share it?'

'Certainly,' said Henry. 'I was telling your sister she combines the purity of a good Chablis with the sweetness of a vintage hock.'

Geraldine chortled. Stephen didn't.

'I'm awfully happy for Dad,' said Geraldine. 'He was so sad when our mother died.'

Henry realized with a shock that he'd never dreamt that

Daphne Porringer had died. He'd assumed that Geoffrey had left her, or that she'd left Geoffrey.

'So where do you live?' he asked Geraldine.

'With my mother's childless married sister,' said Geraldine Porringer. 'It wasn't thought right that I should live with Daddy, partly because he wasn't married to your auntie, and partly because he runs a pub.'

'So they objected on two premises, one moral, the other licensed,' said Henry, and to his shame he found himself wishing that he could have said it to somebody prettier. Geraldine Porringer would be liked by everybody and loved by nobody.

With Auntie Kate he reminisced about the village school, Miss Candy, Billy the half-wit, Jackie the land girl and other ghosts.

'There's a wedding reception at the Crown this afternoon,' said Ollie Renishaw sadly.

Geoffrey Porringer made a tiny grimace. Auntie Doris leant over towards Cousin Hilda and said, 'The Crown's a pub on the opposite side of the square from us, Hilda.'

'The relative position of public houses in Troutwick is of no conceivable interest to me, Doris,' said Cousin Hilda. Henry had to admire her. He decided that, for Cousin Hilda's sake, he wouldn't have any more wine.

'It's a Rowth Bridge wedding,' Auntie Doris told Auntie Kate. 'They couldn't have the reception there. The groom's banned from the Parish Hall and his dad's banned from the Three Horseshoes.'

'That sounds like the Luggs,' said Auntie Kate.

'It is. Eric Lugg,' said Auntie Doris.

Henry felt himself going cold.

'Who's he marrying?' he asked, trying to sound casual.

'One of our ex-waitresses,' said Ollie Renishaw. 'Lorna Arrow. She . . .'

'Careful what you say, Ollie,' said Auntie Doris, who always made things worse by protesting about them. 'Lorna used to be a great friend of Henry's.'

'I was only going to say she left us very suddenly,' said Ollie Renishaw.

'Thank you, Ollie, but I think we'd best draw a veil over that,' said Auntie Doris, who sometimes made things even worse by protesting about them twice. She smiled at Geoffrey Porringer, a warm smile, a forgiving smile. Henry saw Geoffrey Porringer relax, and realized how little the man felt able to want from life now. To be able to relax, to be let off the hook, these were his ambitions.

The waiter offered Henry more wine. After the startling news about Lorna Arrow, he hadn't the strength to refuse. He compromised. 'Just half a glass,' he said. 'I don't want to drink too much.' Cousin Hilda's lips twitched. 'You already have,' said her twitch.

'We'll get drunks from the wedding tonight,' said Ollie Renishaw. 'I hope we'll be able to handle them. We don't want trouble with you away on your honeymoon.'

'Stop worrying,' said Auntie Doris. 'Oh, he is a worry-guts.'

'Where are you going?' said Fiona.

'Interlaken,' said Geoffrey Porringer.

'Very nice,' said Horace Brassingthwaite. 'A lovely spot.'

'You know it?' said Geoffrey Porringer.

'No,' said Horace.

'We will,' said Ollie Renishaw.

'Will what?' said Auntie Doris.

'Get drunks in.'

'Luggs,' said Auntie Kate.

'Drunk Luggs,' said Fiona.

'Is that serious, drunk Luggs?' said Geoffrey Porringer.

'Geoffrey!' said Auntie Doris. 'We're going on our honeymoon.'

'I'm not saying we aren't,' said Geoffrey Porringer. 'I'm only saying, not being acquainted with drunk Luggs, is it serious? Should we recruit extra staff?'

'It is serious,' said Henry. 'You *should* recruit extra staff. I'll come.'

There was silence. It seemed that the prospect of the avail-ability of Henry to deal with hordes of drunk Luggs didn't remove entirely the worries of Geoffrey Porringer and Ollie Renishaw.

'The more hands, the better,' said Henry. 'I'd like to help you, Geoffrey.'

Geoffrey Porringer looked surprised. But pleased. 'Thank you very much,' he said. 'I accept, young sir.'

Cousin Hilda sniffed loudly.

'What's that supposed to mean, Hilda?' said Auntie Doris.

'What's what supposed to mean,' said Cousin Hilda.

'That sniff. One of your loudest.'

Cousin Hilda sniffed. '"One of my loudest"?' she said. 'I'm sure I don't know what you mean, Doris.'

'At moments of disapproval you sniff, Hilda. Probably you don't realize you're doing it. I wondered to what particular disapproval we owed that snorter?'

'To me working behind a bar,' said Henry. 'But I won't be working, Cousin Hilda, because I won't be paid. I'll be helping Auntie Doris, who helped bring me up – as you did, of course, and thank you – by letting her go on her honeymoon with an untroubled mind.'

'I thought you were coming home with me,' said Cousin Hilda. 'We were going to have supper with Mrs Wedderburn. I've left cold for my businessmen.'

'I'll just have to forgo Mrs Wedderburn for the greater good,' said Henry.

Cousin Hilda sniffed.

'Promise you won't refuse to serve me because I'm under age,' said Geraldine Porringer.

'I'm afraid I'd have to,' said Henry. 'Even though in your case it'd be unnecessary, because you're so mature.'

'Geraldine's squiffy,' said Stephen.

'Am not, prick,' said Geraldine.

There was non-vintage port, with the cheese.

'What's the time?' said Cousin Hilda, as soon as she decently could. 'I'm thinking about my trains.'

'Twenty-two minutes past two,' said Henry.

'I hope Graham won't forget to ring the bell for last orders,' said Ollie Renishaw.

Ollie Renishaw drove back, in his rusting blue van, as if convinced that Graham would have missed a smouldering fag end, which would reduce the White Hart to rubble. Brief beams of sunlight were breaking through the dark canopy of the clouds, lighting up the occasional sycamore, a distant stone barn, the corner of a field on the far hills. It was as if lace curtains were briefly parted, to allow a vision of a beautiful woman.

The van screamed to a frenzied halt, beside the unburnt hotel. It had started to rain again.

Henry's motives in offering to help man the bar were not entirely unselfish. He didn't really expect trouble. He believed that the Luggs became involved in frequent fights because, since they had a reputation for becoming involved in frequent fights, people frequently picked fights with them, accusing them of frequently picking fights with people. Tonight, in the comparative gentility of the White Hart, nobody would pick on them.

His real motive was to visit the reception of Mr and Mrs Eric Lugg.

He walked slowly across the square, between the stalls, in his only suit, still wearing the buttonhole from the other wedding. He had bemoaned the frequency of weddings that summer, and now here he was on his way to yet another one, to which he hadn't even been invited.

He approached the Crown with increasing reluctance. There was a great roar of talk and laughter. But he must go on, now that he had come this far.

He entered the pub, and said, 'Hello' to Edna, the landlady. She remembered him, and escorted him to the function room.

The room was awash with rustic good humour. There were the remains of a sit-down ham tea, but the lads in their bursting suits were congregating once more at the bar, cradling pints in their great outdoor hands.

Lorna looked at him in astonishment and turned as white as her virginal dress. 'Henry?' she said. 'What are you doing here?'

He was unwelcome. Well he would be. Why hadn't he thought of that?

'Auntie Doris and Mr Porringer got married today.'

'My God!'

'I know. And I thought, as I'm here, well, I couldn't miss the chance of wishing you every happiness.'

'Thanks.'

In her relief, she kissed him warmly. He wondered what she had thought he'd come for. How thin she was.

176

Eric Lugg hurried up. How huge he was.

'You remember Henry?' squeaked Lorna.

'Oh aye. I remember Henry,' said Eric Lugg. 'I called him the evacuee squirt.'

'Lorna and I were good friends once,' said Henry. 'Before your time, of course.'

'"Before my time"?' said Eric Lugg. 'What does tha mean "Before my time"? There never was a time before my time.'

'No. No,' said Henry. 'Oh no. No. No, I just meant, I liked Lorna. She liked me. We liked each other. And I thought, Well, I know what those Luggs are like. Friendly. If Eric Lugg ever found out that an old friend of Lorna and of his sister Jane had been in Troutwick and hadn't come in to drink to their happiness, he'd be one angry insulted Eric Lugg.'

Eric Lugg digested this speech slowly. 'Have a pint,' he said at last.

'Right,' said Henry, deeply relieved. 'Thanks.'

He couldn't talk to Lorna on her own. He felt a million miles away from her. He was deeply upset that she was marrying Eric Lugg, an instructor in the catering corps. He was deeply upset that he was deeply upset that she was marrying Eric Lugg, an instructor in the catering corps. He grinned at Eric Lugg and allowed himself to be embraced almost to the point of strangulation by a very drunk Jane Lugg, whom he had once courted, till she had nits. It crossed his mind that she might have been a better choice for England than Tosser Pilkington-Brick. He nodded and chatted with his old friend Simon Eckington, with his old tormentor Patrick Eckington, with Simon's wife Pam, whom he had once courted, till she had nits. He chatted with Lorna's parents, with Luggs known and Luggs unknown. He chatted and laughed with everybody except Lorna, his first consummated love. He insisted on buying a large round of pints, which he couldn't afford, in lieu of a wedding present. He clinked glasses with Eric Lugg.

Eric Lugg clasped him in a hugely affectionate embrace. 'You're one of us,' he said.

Oh no, thought Henry, as he grinned his sheepishly pleased apparent agreement. Oh no, Eric. One of somebody I may be, although I haven't found out who yet. One of you, that I most definitely am not.

12 A Day in the Life of 22912547 Signalman Pratt

'There's been a mistake, sergeant,' said Henry desperately, peering out from under the slightly damp sheets and gently festering blankets, and looking up at the hard, threatening face of Sergeant Botney. 'I've done my national service.'

'Well now you're doing it again, laddie,' said Sergeant Botney. 'And it's three years this time.'

'You can't do national service twice, sergeant.'

'You can if the authorities say so, son. And they say so. They've decided they need you. Gawd knows why.'

'But I have a budding career as a reporter, sergeant.'

'Well now you're going to have a budding career as a soldier, sunshine. Who are *you*??'

This question was barked at Signalman Brian Furnace, who had just popped up from under the sheets.

'Signalman Furnace, sarge,' said Signalman Furnace.

'Two soldiers in one pit!' thundered Sergeant Botney. He pulled back the bedclothes and stared down at the naked intertwined bodies of Henry and Signalman Furnace. 'Two naked signalmen in one pit! I've never seen anything like it. What's going on?'

'We love each other,' said Signalman Furnace.

'You what?? You love each other?? This is the British army. You're on a charge. Filthy and idle and stark bollock naked on parade. Get down to the charge room.'

'As we are, sarge?'

'As you are. No! As you were. Get dressed, you dirty little buggers.'

'Aaaaaaaaaaaaaaaaaaaaaaaaaaaaaaaaaaaaghhhhh!' shrieked Henry. He pointed towards the ceiling. The inert body of Signalman Burbage was swinging gently in the draught.

'Come down from there, Burbage!' shouted Sergeant Botney. 'Committing suicide on duty. I'll have you for this.'

'Sorry, sarge,' said the dead signalman. He whipped a knife from his pocket and cut the rope that was holding him. His inert body dropped across Henry's. Henry screamed. And woke up.

He was drenched in sweat. Oh, thank goodness, oh sweet and wonderful life, it had been a dream.

Where was he?

He was lying on a palliasse, on a groundsheet, in a large tent. Rain was drumming on the canvas. There was a smell of wet grass, and damp rubber, and male feet, and male sweat, a vaguely disgusting goulash of damp and perspiration. Men were snoring, breathing congestedly, farting in their sleep. The charm of mankind. As opposed to womankind. He couldn't believe that a tent full of women could have been so repulsive.

He was in the army! It hadn't been a dream! He hardly dared look up.

No inert body was swinging there. No naked signalman's body was intertwined with his.

Of course. He was back in the army, for a fortnight, for the first of his three annual territorial reserve camps. He was on the Pennine moors, not more than thirty miles from Rowth Bridge.

They'd be waking up soon, this rag-bag of strangers. Strangers! He'd hoped to meet Michael Collinghurst. He'd hoped and feared that he'd meet Brian Furnace. He'd hoped to see at least some of his old muckers – Taffy Bevin, Lanky Lasenby, Geordie Stubbs. Even Fishy Fisk, who smelt of herrings.

Reveille reverberated over the sodden moors. A curlew trilled defiant rivalry. Men stirred, groaned, swore, farted, belched. The charm of mankind, shamed by a curlew's trill. Nobody hurried. Discipline was lax. The old fears had died down. It was a shambles. It was raining. Nothing to hurry for.

At Richmond Station, in September 1953, at the beginning of it all, Henry had said, 'I'm a man.' Sweat streamed off him at the thought of that grotesquely premature boast.

If he'd been a man, he wouldn't have joined in the destruction of Burbage. Burbage was clumsy. Timid. Shy. Not intellectually brilliant. A little odiferous. There's no point in idealizing him because he's dead. He was a clumsy, smelly, hopeless case. Hopeless. Dead. Hanged himself.

Sergeant Botney had made them laugh at him by numbers. 'Squad will laugh at Signalman Burbage, squad . . . wait for it . . . squad . . . at Signalman Burbage . . . laugh!' And all together they had shouted, 'Signalman Burbage smells two three ha two three ha two three ha ha ha.' Man's natural inhumanity to those weaker than himself had been tempered by unease, by a sense of their own weakness, by the knowledge that they weren't being beastly to Burbage of their own free will but because they were under orders, they were only one rung above him on the ladder of humiliation. Afterwards they'd told Burbage that they hated doing it, didn't mean it, only did it because they had to.

They'd still done it. Henry too. He'd not said, 'I refuse to laugh at Signalman Burbage, sergeant. It's cruel and humiliating and I'd rather go to military prison in Colchester.' He'd said, 'Ha two three ha two three ha ha ha.' And Burbage was dead. Hanged himself.

People were getting up. Armpits of tangled hair were appearing and being wearily scratched. The charm of mankind.

Henry went through the deepening mud to the ablutions. He thought about Flanders, and didn't complain. He endured breakfast. He thought about Eric Lugg, and *did* complain. Back to the tent, waiting. A shambles. There were no wireless sets here, so he couldn't employ the only craft the army had taught him. Some days they were shown things. Today, somebody was supposed to show them flame-throwers. Nothing happened. They mooched in a damp tent. Gus Norris approached him.

'Pratt? You're an educated sort of geezer, ain't yer?'

'I can't demur.'

'What?'

'Nothing.'

'No, I mean, you are, ain't yer? Educated. Well, more than me, like.'

'I suppose so.'

'They can't keep us 'ere, can they? Only it's me dad's shop, see.'

'What?'

'. . . 'e's goin' into 'orspital, i'n' 'e? Next munf. I'n' 'e? Bleeding backside's bleeding bleeding. Got to 'ave a hoperation, 'asn' 'e?'

'I'm sorry.'

'I gotta run the shop 'cos it's me mum's nerves with me nan ill an' all. 'aven' I?'

'Well, yes, Gus, I suppose you have.'

'They can't make us do anuvver two years, can they? I mean, because of the crisis and all that and everything. In the Middle East and that. Can they?'

'Of course they can't.'

'Only some of the lads said they can. I mean, with the canal and the oil and everything and that. Only it's me dad's shop, innit?'

'We're here for a fortnight, Gus. They *are* calling up a few special reservists. They don't just call you in for a fortnight and then keep you. If there's ever a general mobilization, it'll be done later. And you'll probably get exemption on compassionate grounds, because of your dad's arse.'

'Honestly?'

'Honestly, Gus.'

'I wish I knew fings. I wish I was an educated geezer like you.'

An educated geezer. He'd never thought of himself as that. Thought of himself as uneducated, because he hadn't gone to university. Could probably have just about squeezed in, if he'd tried. Hadn't ever really thought about it. Why not? Because nobody in the family ever had? Because he was frightened of not squeezing in? Because he was frightened of squeezing in and being so much worse than everybody else? Because he was in love with the romantic concept of 'real life'? Too late to think about it all now, anyway. *Je ne regrette rien*. The Edith Piaf of the *Thurmarsh Evening Argus*.

They were told to get fell in. They got fell in. The late August rain continued. They marched four miles up sodden tracks. They were told to get fell out. They got fell out. They stood, in their capes, watching nothing. The rain eased off. A mobile canteen provided them with hot food. It was cold curry. 'They said we'd 'ave 'ot food,' said Gus Norris. 'It is hot,' said Henry. 'Mine's stone cold,' said Gus Norris. 'So's mine,' said Henry. 'I fought you said it was 'ot,' said Gus Norris. 'It is,' said Henry. 'What are you on about?' said Gus Norris. 'The curry is a hot curry, even though it's stone cold. We can't get them on that one, the sods,' said Henry. 'I wish *I* was an educated geezer,' said Gus Norris.

An officer addressed them through a megaphone. 'Erm . . . hello, men,' he said. 'Erm . . . we were going to have a demonstration of . . . erm . . . flame-throwers, which I think you'd all have found very . . . erm . . . I know I would, but there you are, apparently there's been a . . . erm . . . through no fault of ours, we're rather in the hands of the flame-thrower chappies, so I'm afraid we'll rather have to scrub round that one for the moment, which is jolly bad luck. However, never fear, we are hoping to arrange a . . . erm . . . and it is at short notice, so you'll have to bear with us, a . . . erm . . . display of . . . erm . . . camouflage techniques, which should be jolly interesting. So . . . erm . . . for the moment . . . stand easy.'

Since they were all standing easy already, there was no response to this instruction. And at that moment Henry caught sight of Brian Furnace and understood immediately that the ghost which still had to be laid wasn't Burbage, but Brian Furnace. The whole thing was such a shambles that there seemed to be no objection to walking about, so he wandered over towards Brian. A pair of grouse flew low over the moors towards them. Catching sight of several hundred soldiers, and knowing that it was after the glorious twelfth, they veered away, in understandable panic, and disappeared over the mist-drenched horizon. Henry walked up to Brian with a heart that was beating like a grouse's wings.

'Hello, Brian.'

Brian swung round and looked quietly astonished.

'Henry!'

Brian looked so placid. Always so placid. His face still boyish, but his arms strong and muscular. He worked for his father, who was a builder in Fareham. Brian liked working with his hands. It was hard to believe that Brian's heart had ever beaten like a grouse's wings.

'Yes.'

'My God!'

'Yes. We'll go for a few drinks tonight, eh?'

A rendezvous arranged, Henry wandered back to his unit. The officer spoke again through the megaphone.

'Erm . . .' he said. 'I'm afraid, men, I have bad news for you.'

'They've found the flame-throwers,' shouted a wag.

A volley of cries from NCOs rang out over the wet moors. More grouse flew off. Their cries of 'Go back' mingled with shouts of 'Shurrup' and 'Belt up, that man' and 'Hold your tongue, the officer's talking.'

At last order was restored sufficiently for the officer to continue talking.

'Erm . . .' he said. 'Efforts to locate the camouflage team at short notice have unfortunately failed. Perhaps they . . . erm . . .' His voice took on an exaggeratedly jocular tone, signalling and destroying the joke. '. . . perhaps they were too jolly well camouflaged, what?' The sergeants laughed uproariously. The corporals smiled. They only laughed uproariously at the sergeants' jokes. The men didn't laugh at all. 'So . . . erm . . . let's all get fell in and see if we can have a jolly good march back to base.'

They had a jolly shambolic march back to base. Once, in Germany, that creep Tubman-Edwards had said, 'Any complaints?' and Lanky Lasenby had said, 'Yes, sir. There's an awful smell of shambolic in the bogs' and Tubman-Edwards had said, 'Don't you mean carbolic?' and Lanky Lasenby had said, 'Have you been in the bogs recently, sir?' and everybody had laughed and the great lump of blackmailing yak turd had decided to find it amusing too so as not to lose face and Lanky Lasenby had got away with it as usual.

After their jolly shambolic march, they had a jolly disgusting tea – what *did* Eric Lugg teach them? – and then Henry and Brian walked five miles, on a bitterly cold and grey but no longer wet summer evening, to the Red Lion at Scunnock Head, an old copper miners' pub, the third highest in Britain. There, in the flagged bar, at a bare wooden table, in front of a fire that was roaring even in August, Henry and Brian drank good, strong Stones's bitter and talked of everything except what mattered.

They laughed about the method of marching that Lanky Lasenby had invented. The front ranks took huge steps, the back ranks took tiny steps, the squad elongated like a concertina, and they could never find anybody to blame.

They laughed about the language of Corporal Pride. Cousin Hilda, whose look could strangle swear words at birth, approved of national service as character-building. Henry wished she could have met Corporal Pride. He hadn't been a man of many words, but a man of one word said many times. He used it as adjective, noun and verb. They laughed as they recalled him saying, 'Wot you done to this rifle, Pratt? The fucking fucker's fucked.'

What they didn't talk about was their night-time embraces in German haystacks, their nights in a back street hotel in Aachen, with the church bells ingrained upon their guilt.

Henry had decided what he'd say. He'd say, 'Brian. I'm sorry I didn't write. But . . . it's over, you see. It was just because the sergeant warned us of the dangers of the *Fräuleins*, and Lorna was so far away, and there I was, awash with youthful sexuality, in that strange, masculine, military world. And I liked you. But I've found out now that I'm completely heterosexual. Sorry, Brian.'

He'd say it on the long, dark walk back, when Brian couldn't see his face.

They set off, briskly, through the raw night.

'I'm sorry I didn't write,' said Brian, just as Henry was going to say 'I'm sorry I didn't write.' Which left Henry saying the infinitely less impressive: 'Yes. So am I.'

'I'm engaged,' said Brian.

'What?' said Henry.

'To this nurse from Truro.'

'Ah. Great.'

'It was just . . . you know . . . the sergeant warning us about the *Fräuleins* and everything.'

'Yes.'

'Sorry, Henry.'

'What?'

'You're upset, aren't you?'

'No. It's just that . . . I was going to say the same thing to you.'

'What?'

'About us. And the sergeant and . . . er . . .'

'Oh. Well, that's all right, then, isn't it?'

'Yes. I'm engaged too. She's called Jill Cornish. She's an air hostess.'

They would avoid each other for the rest of the fortnight and, when they'd gone home – Gus Norris's fears were unfounded – Henry would never hear again from his national service lover.

He crawled onto his palliasse, utterly exhausted, and was soon asleep.

Sergeant Botney was waiting.

'Right, you 'orrible little man,' he said. 'I've got you where I want you now. You're going to be sorry you ruined my wedding anniversary, Signalman Henry Pratt. You've signed on while pissed, sunshine. I'm going to ruin your next fifteen years.'

13   In the Land of Romance

The famous landmarks of Florence floated like islands above a sea of red roofs. Around those great domes and bold elegant towers, those soaring triumphs of individual inspiration, lay the unified dignity of the city, the classical lines of the stark palaces, the genius of communal restraint. It was as if the eternal clash between the freedom of the individual and the discipline of the state had been frozen, in stone and marble, here on the banks of the Arno.

It was impossible, walking in that great city, set among hills dotted with crumbling golden villas, silvery olive trees and lines of dark cypresses, to believe that at that very moment, in Thurmarsh, under a lowering sky, in a dusty news-room, Terry Skipton was assigning reporters to magistrates' and juvenile courts.

'Podger!'

A Pavlovian *frisson* ran down Henry's spine. Only in the army had they called him Podger.

Michael Collinghurst, tall, hook-nosed, with blue eyes and light brown hair, was crossing the dark, elegant Via Tornabuoni towards them, smiling from stick-out ear to stick-out ear.

Henry's face lit up at the sight of his old friend. Lampo Davey's face darkened at the sight of Henry's face lighting up. A dark-haired, older young man in fawn open-neck shirt, blue shorts, red socks and sandals crossed the road reluctantly to join them.

'This is Father Ellis,' said Michael Collinghurst.

Father Ellis smiled austerely, carefully. He had very hairy legs and had shaved carelessly. Why should I be surprised when priests are hairy? thought Henry.

They went to an open-air café in the Piazza della Signoria, studded with statues, dominated by the crenellated, machicolated Palazzo Vecchio, with its high, slim, boldly off-centre tower.

Michael and Henry ordered extravagant ice creams with delight. Father Ellis ordered an extravagant ice cream with shame. Lampo ordered an espresso coffee.

'Well, Henry,' said Michael. 'You are how?'

'Bad not too, oh. Grumble mustn't,' said Henry.

'To you again see, very it's good,' said Michael.

'Too you,' said Henry.

Father Ellis and Lampo Davey looked puzzled.

'It's a little had we habit,' explained Henry. 'Words our orders unusual in putting.'

'Hours military boring slight the easement of for,' said Michael.

Father Ellis and Lampo seemed pained at these juvenilia.

'I've decided to become a Catholic priest,' said Michael, with that sudden simplicity which Henry remembered so well.

Henry realized that his dismay was discourteous to Father Ellis. He tried to smile. It was a failure. Lampo relaxed when he saw Henry's dismay. The ice creams arrived. Lampo frowned.

'I'm twenty-one years old,' said Henry. 'I like ice cream.'

'Some Anglo-Saxons lose all restraint when they go south,' said Lampo. 'I like self-discipline and austerity. I think I'd make a good monk if I believed in God.'

'If you can say that,' said Father Ellis, through a mouthful of ice cream, 'I think you're very close to coming to God.'

'Yes, I've had a narrow escape,' said Lampo.

Michael laughed. Father Ellis flushed and tried to look as if he wasn't enjoying his ice cream.

'How's your religious state, Henry?' said Michael. 'I remember hearing all about your discovery and loss of faith in Thurmarsh.'

'It's lost for good, I think,' said Henry.

'Never say that,' said Father Ellis.

'I believe in good and evil,' said Henry. 'I don't believe that there's an actual being, shaping our destinies. I've never seen why there's any difficulty in believing in good and evil without believing that they're imposed from above. And even if God did exist, I don't see why people should take his authority upon themselves in his name. The last thing we need, in our spiritual life, is a system that's as authoritarian and hierarchical as the system we're saddled with in our temporal life.'

Henry felt exhilarated. This was European café life, and he was part of it! He attacked his ice cream with renewed relish.

'Lunch together have we shall?' said Michael.

'Idea splendid a what,' said Henry, before Lampo could make

187

their excuses. He felt happy. In putting his words in the wrong order, Michael wasn't simply fooling. He was telling Henry that their friendship could survive his entry into the priesthood.

'Put don't more any order wrong in words, Michael,' said Henry.

'Right quite,' said Michael. 'Sorry oh. Done I've again it!'

Father Ellis frowned at his protégé.

'You have a very frivolous side to your nature, Michael,' he said.

'Because he's deeply confident about his basic seriousness,' said Henry. 'I think you aren't confident enough about your seriousness to be remotely frivolous.'

Father Ellis's unevenly shaven face flushed. Henry realized that, if you were going to be rude to people, you had to be careful not to hit upon the truth. He'd have to fight against the dangerous intellectual confidence which this beautiful city was imparting to him.

They strolled along dark streets that smelt of heat and cats and peppers and distant drains. They wandered through noisy markets, full of people with caustic yet gentle faces. In the church of San Lorenzo, they gazed in awe at sculptures by Michelangelo. They were massive, yet delicate. They were vibrant with individual life, yet steeped in universal meaning. How Henry hoped that, in the face of this most supreme art, which couldn't be described in words because otherwise it wouldn't have needed to be created in marble, nobody would say anything.

'Amazing,' said Father Ellis. 'Truly incredible. What an artist.'

They ate in a restaurant in a tiny, dark square called the Piazza dei Maccheroni. They ate outside, under an unnecessary awning. The wine flowed. Michael drank with all his old gusto. Father Ellis drank with less gusto, but even greater capacity. Lampo drank sparingly. Henry was glad to be in the presence of people who were greedier than Lampo. Four days of Lampo's company had made him feel almost bestial.

'I wonder if people ever thought all these buildings were too new,' said Lampo. 'All this dreadful modern development. Appalling.'

'I think there was a much clearer consensus about what was beautiful in those days,' said Michael. 'But I think when we gaze at them now we're much too romantic and forget why they were built. No doubt there were boards in front of them announcing, "Another Prestige Development for the Medici Family".'

Father Ellis gave Michael a look, as if realizing that he was going to be a troublesome priest.

Henry and Michael ate pasta and *saltimbocca*. Father Ellis plumped for *minestrone* and steak florentine. Lampo ate only one course – Parma ham and fresh figs, lightly spattered with black pepper.

'We're going to Siena tomorrow,' said Michael. 'Why don't you come too?'

Lampo was planning to take him to Siena the next day. He knew that Lampo wanted them to be alone together, in Siena. This casual lunch in the Piazza dei Maccheroni had been a revelation. Childhood friendships had failed him. New friendships had puzzled him. Close friendships with homosexuals filled him with tension. But here, in Michael Collinghurst, with whom he hadn't communicated since his army days, he knew that he'd found true friendship, beyond all sexuality, friendship cemented by humour, friendship for life. He didn't need to prove it by going to Siena with Michael. He could afford to be generous to Lampo. 'Sorry,' he lied. 'We can't tomorrow.'

If they hadn't gone to Siena later than planned, Henry might never have met the young woman who would become his wife.

An old woman with black clothes and a sunny heart showed them to a large, rather bare back room with a double bed. Henry threw back the creaking shutters and gazed out. Swifts shrieked over the jumbled tiled roofs of Siena. The stern, narrow, shady medieval streets plunged into a deep valley and marched up the other side towards the cathedral. The great brick building, with its marble bell-tower, seemed huge against the darkening sky. Henry sighed. He sighed because you can't hold beauty in your hands and feel it. He sighed because of the double bed.

That night he lay so close to the right-hand edge of the bed that there was a danger of his falling out.

Lampo laughed. 'I'm not intending to ravish you, you know,' he said.

189

Lampo slept as delicately as a cat, on that still, hot night, naked under a single sheet, in that lumpy, twanging Italian bed. Henry lay still, stiff as a board, listening to the lone mosquito. At first light Lampo woke, padded across the room and opened the shutters, which didn't creak for him. Henry pretended to be asleep. It seemed eternal, that night, and Henry thought about people who are imprisoned for thirty years.

In the morning, Henry had five inelegant bites. Lampo had none. Perhaps the lone mosquito liked the taste of tension.

It was a surprise to find that the city was alive, and not frozen in time. They climbed through streets that were seething with humanity. Tiny vans were delivering trays of bread and figs. The cries of vendors mingled with the ecstatic greetings of people who were meeting for the first time since the previous evening.

Henry gazed in awe at the rich, decorated façade of the cathedral, a Gothic fantasy resting on three Romanesque portals. The interior, with its forest of striped black and white marble pillars, was stunning. The floor of the huge, bare nave was marble also, and covered in decorated paving showing Bible stories. An Englishman was reading a guidebook in a loud hiss. 'The interior may seem over-elaborate to many with more spare northern tastes.' No! Not to this northerner. Henry tried to close his mind to all words, to see only shapes and colours and patterns. A baby doesn't wonder at the world any the less because it hasn't yet got any words with which to describe it.

He was filled with joy. He could flower under this southern sun. There was more to life than he'd ever dreamt. There was more to himself than he'd ever believed. In that great religious building Henry, who had no religion, felt in a state of grace. He felt good. He felt strong. He felt pure.

After two hours of feeling good and strong and pure, he felt extremely hungry.

They wandered, through curving shaded streets, past pinky-red Gothic palaces, towards the Piazza del Campo, the great central square of that most female of cities. In front of them were two bare-legged young women in cotton dresses. The one in the white dress had thin, vulnerable legs. The one with the yellow and white horizontal stripes had slightly fleshy legs.

Gently curving, gently sloping, shaped like a scallop, vast in scale, surrounded by pink palaces with curving façades, dominated by the vast Palazzo Publico and its pencil-thin tower, the Piazza del Campo could turn even an itching, sweating, frustration-soaked, mosquito-ravaged, immature, repressed English podge-clot from thoughts of slightly fleshy legs.

But not for long. The moment he looked round, he saw that yellow and white striped dress being helped into a chair by a suspiciously attentive waiter in the nearest of several restaurants with outdoor terraces.

'Let's eat there,' said Henry. He hurried across to the restaurant and, before Lampo could stop him, sat at the table next to the two girls.

Lampo frowned.

The moment he heard the girls speak, Henry leant across and said, 'Ah! You're English.'

The gaunt one frowned, as if to say, 'If we'd wanted to meet English people we'd have gone to Southwold.' Fleshy legs smiled. Her mouth was crowded with big, strong, white teeth, which protruded slightly. She had sandy hair.

Henry introduced himself and Lampo, who smiled with suspiciously immaculate politeness. The one with sandy hair was called Anna Matheson. The gaunt one was Hilary Lewthwaite.

'Lewthwaite,' said Henry. 'The only Lewthwaite I know is a clapped-out draper's in Thurmarsh.'

'That's our shop,' said Hilary Lewthwaite.

'When I say clapped-out,' said Henry, 'I mean I really like it. I love old-fashioned shops. When I was a kid, Lampo . . .' He dragged Lampo into these reminiscences as if he were a recalcitrant mule. '. . . I used to be absolutely fascinated by the thing they had that whizzed the change around on wires.'

'The Lamson Overhead Cash System,' said Hilary.

A waiter brought menus to both their tables.

'Where are you from, Anna?' said Henry, leaning across towards her.

'Ullapool Grove,' said Anna Matheson.

'In Thurmarsh?'

'Yes.'

'Look . . . why don't we share a table?'

'Great idea,' said Anna Matheson.

She explained to the waiter.

'He won't understand you just because you speak louder,' said Hilary.

Lampo explained, icily, in impeccable Italian.

'Ah! You share table. Is good,' said the waiter. He seemed pleased for the girls, and held their chairs out for them with a pleasant smile. Lampo had a pleasant smile too, but Henry knew that beneath it he was seething. Hilary had flashed a quick look at Anna, beseeching her not to move. Now she smiled thinly, grimly. She was as pale as a barn owl, while Anna was golden brown.

'Ullapool Grove!' said Henry. 'I can't get over it.'

'Do try,' said Lampo.

'No, but . . . I mean . . . it's a coincidence, isn't it?'

'Yes,' said Lampo. 'Oh yes.'

'Where do you live, Hilary?' said Henry.

'Perkin Warbeck Drive,' said Hilary.

'Where's that?' asked Henry.

'It runs from Lambert Simnel Avenue through to Wat Tyler Crescent,' said Hilary reluctantly.

'Has anybody got a street map of Thurmarsh?' said Lampo. 'No? What a shame. It would have eased the monotony of looking at Siena.'

'Siena's lovely,' said Henry hastily. 'It's like a beautiful, gentle, passionate woman.' He looked into Anna Matheson's eyes. They were blue and, he fancied, hungry. He liked what he saw in Anna Matheson's eyes. He was trying not to tremble. He'd always known that, when love came, it would come like this, as quick and joyous as a swift on the wing.

In the square, beyond the awning, toddlers chased pigeons and a soldier gazed into the fountain with his sweetheart. The waiter took their orders.

'This is a bit different from the Rundle Café,' said Henry.

'You don't eat in the Rundle Café?' said Anna.

'Sometimes,' admitted Henry. 'The Rundle Café's a café in Thurmarsh, Lampo.'

'No!' said Lampo. 'You amaze me. It has such a Parisian ring.'

'I had a holiday job there once,' said Anna. 'You wouldn't eat there if you could see their kitchens.'

'You wouldn't eat there if you could see their food,' said Henry.

'For goodness sake,' said Lampo. 'Here we are in the most beautiful square in Europe, and you're talking about a bloody awful café in Thurmarsh.'

'You've eaten there, Lampo?' said Henry. 'It *is* bad, isn't it?'

Lampo stared at Henry coldly. Hilary snapped a bread stick in half as if it reminded her of a man she'd hated.

'You're very quiet, Hilary,' said Henry.

'I've got nothing to say,' said Hilary.

Anna gave Hilary a beseeching look. The waiter brought their starters – melon for Lampo, soup for the girls, *antipasto alla senese* for Henry. Henry put his left hand on Anna's right knee, under the table. She slid his hand up under her dress, laying it gently on her warm, bare thigh. Their eyes met.

'When you say a holiday job,' he said, 'where were you on holiday from?'

'Thurmarsh Grammar.'

'I don't believe this.'

'Oh, I do,' said Lampo. 'What more natural if one lives in Thurmarsh?'

'You too, Hilary?' said Henry.

Hilary nodded, as if finding it disagreeable to remember Thurmarsh Grammar School for Girls.

'I was at Thurmarsh Grammar School for Boys,' said Henry. 'I founded the Thurmarsh Grammar School Bisexual Humanist Society. Did you know Karen Porter or Maureen Abberley?'

Each ringing Thurmarsh name thudded into Lampo like a harpoon into a whale. He thrashed around in disbelief. 'Do let's forget the beauty of Tuscany,' he said. 'Thank goodness there's no danger of our discussing the art gallery and its treasure chest of Siennese painting. Come on. Let's talk some more about Karen Porter and Maureen Abberley.'

'They're very beautiful,' said Hilary.

'Karen Porter and Maureen Abberley?' said Anna.

'The paintings,' said Hilary grimly.

'My God, they're doing a double act now,' said Lampo. 'The Elsie and Doris Waters of Siena.'

'They're just a couple of prick teasers,' said Henry.

'Elsie and Doris Waters?' said Anna.

'Karen Porter and Maureen Abberley,' said Henry.

Lampo groaned. The waiter brought their main courses. Anna removed Henry's hand from her thigh, stroking it gently with one nail before she gave it back to him. Anna and Henry attacked their food with gusto. Lampo and Hilary picked at theirs. If Lampo had been heterosexual, there would have been two perfect pairings. But how was he to arrange an assignation with Anna without upsetting Hilary and, more important, upsetting Lampo, his friend and host?

'What are you doing this afternoon?' he asked.

'The cathedral,' said Hilary hastily.

'The cathedral, it seems,' said Anna.

'Well, I mean, we decided that,' said Hilary.

'What would you rather do, Anna?' said Henry.

'I don't know. Do you have any suggestions?' said Anna.

'We're going to the art gallery,' said Lampo hurriedly.

'We're going to the art gallery,' said Henry.

'Well, I mean, we decided that,' said Lampo.

'I just *said* we're going there,' said Henry. 'So what are we arguing about?'

'I wouldn't mind going to the art gallery again,' said Anna.

'*Again?*' said Hilary, and Henry couldn't decide whether she was being dim or awkward. 'You said you found religious paintings depressing.'

'I do,' said Anna, 'but, as you said, they're very beautiful, very spiritual. You kept telling me what an important stage in the development of perspective they illustrated. I'd quite like to have a look at that aspect of them again.'

'Well, I'm sorry,' said Hilary. 'I'm not going there again. They *are* beautiful, but too male-oriented for me.'

'Look, if it's any problem,' suggested Henry, '*we* could go to the cathedral again.'

'I'm not going to the cathedral again,' said Lampo.

'You said it was one of the loveliest buildings in Europe,' said Henry.

'It is,' said Lampo. 'I saw it this morning. I remember it distinctly. Big thing with pillars. I don't want to see it again.'

The waiter looked puzzled as he took away their plates. Puzzled by the atmosphere. Puzzled at the food left on Lampo's and Hilary's plates.

'You go and see the pictures, then,' said Henry. 'I'll go to the cathedral.'

'I want to see the pictures with you,' said Lampo.

'Oh God.'

The waiter brought a large bowl of fruit.

'There's no problem,' said Lampo. 'You go to the cathedral. I'll go back to the room and read, and tomorrow we'll look at the pictures.'

'We'd better get the bill and get on, whatever's happening,' said Hilary. 'Our bus leaves at five.'

'Bus?' said Henry. 'You aren't staying in Siena?'

'No.'

He had second thoughts about going to the cathedral. There was hardly going to be an opportunity for ardent love-making in the North Transept, or even for declarations of love, especially with Hilary tagging on. His first meeting with Anna would end in anti-climax. And he knew where she lived. He could meet her in Thurmarsh. Their life stretched before them.

'Look,' he said. 'I don't want to upset you, Lampo. Or Hilary.' He smiled at Hilary. Her answering smile was as thin as the ham in a railway sandwich. 'Why don't the girls go to the cathedral, and we'll go to the art gallery, and I'll arrange to see the girls later in Thurmarsh.' He put his hand on Anna's thigh. She put her hand on his, sealing the pact.

The waiter brought one bill. Lampo worked out what everyone owed. Henry didn't think that was stylish. He longed to pay for Anna's meal, but didn't see why he should pay for Hilary's, especially as she hadn't finished it.

'Quite reasonable, really,' said Anna. 'We had a drink in a café out here last night, and it was terribly expensive.'

'It would be,' said Lampo. 'You pay extra to sit outside. You're

195

expected to sit as long as you like. You paid a reasonable price for a front seat in the stalls at the theatre of life.'

'In Thurmarsh you'd pay less because you had to look at the view,' said Henry.

'We're back in Thurmarsh,' said Lampo. 'Goodie goodie. How I've longed for a reference to it this last dreary hour.'

The waiter took their money. Henry felt disagreeably mean.

'Come on, Anna,' said Hilary. 'Time to go to the cathedral.'

'Yes, sir. Coming, sir,' said Anna.

They stood up. Henry waved away the waiter with the change. They walked out, into the fierce sun. They walked up a narrow alley, into the Via di Citta, past the imposing Chigi Saracini Palace, round the corner and up the hill. Henry wished he had the courage to take Anna's hand. They came to the parting of the ways.

'Well,' said Anna, 'this is *arrivederci* time.' She kissed Henry. He hugged her briefly. She kissed Lampo. Politeness demanded that Henry kiss Hilary. Their cheeks touched lifelessly. She didn't kiss Lampo.

The girls set off towards the cathedral. Henry stood and watched them, although Lampo set off impatiently towards the art gallery. Anna turned and waved. Henry waved back. He was trembling with love, as a great ship trembles on the ocean.

Great indeed were the masterpieces hung in the red-brick, late-Gothic Palazzo Buonsignori. Delicate indeed were the works of Guido di Siena, Taddio di Bartoli, Pietro Lorenzetti, Ambrogio Lorenzetti, Duccio di Boninsigni and many more. Names little known outside Siena, men long dead, but immortalized in these gentle works.

Henry found that a little religious painting went a long way. He couldn't feel the excitement, in these cool, silent rooms, that he'd felt in the cathedral. He wished there weren't quite so many madonnas with quite so many *bambini*. He wished that so many of the madonnas didn't look constipated. He wished that so many of the *bambini* didn't look as if they were heroically suppressing wind in the service of art. He wished that the men didn't look quite so disapproving of such fripperies as women and children, as if they found even a virgin birth too vulgar for their refined sensitivities. Was this the subtly subversive intention of the artists, or was it the product of Henry's imagination?

He was in love. He was lonely. He was in the wrong mood. In several of the pictures there was a priest holding a red book. 'Is that the Michelin guide, do you think, Lampo?' he said. 'Is that some medieval Father Ellis wondering where to eat after the adoration is over? "Little place round the corner does the best veal in Bethlehem. And the carafe myrrh is very reasonable."'

'For God's sake, Henry,' said Lampo.

'I'm sorry, Lampo,' said Henry. 'But I can't help thinking how much more interesting all this would be if they hadn't had to paint religious subjects all the time.'

Lampo didn't reply. Henry had spoilt his afternoon.

When they left the gallery, Lampo was still sulking. They walked slowly, past pink and gold palaces, through a hot city that was slowly crumbling, as it had always slowly crumbled. In the doorways of small dark shops and bars, men with faces that were cynical but not cruel talked the day away.

Cautiously, Henry touched Lampo's arm.

'It's a lovely city, Lampo,' he said. 'I promise I won't mention Thurmarsh again the whole holiday. Oh my God!!'

Denzil Ackerman's limp seemed even worse than usual, and his right eye had been comprehensively blackened.

'I thought you were in Amalfi,' said Henry.

'How touching that you're so pleased to see me,' said Denzil. 'Aren't you going to introduce me to your uncle?'

They stood stock-still in the middle of the Via di Citta. Businessmen and fat mothers swirled around them. Elegant young men drifted past them. Three American girls in unwise shorts, licking peach and pistachio cornets, bumped into them.

'Ah! Yes!' said Henry. 'Denzil, this is my Uncle Lampo. Uncle Lampo, this is Denzil Ackerman.'

Lampo shook hands with Denzil like an automaton. He seemed stunned by his sudden elevation to uncledom.

'You're much younger than I thought you'd be,' said Denzil.

'What?' said Lampo.

'I always imagine uncles as rather grizzled,' said Denzil. 'Pipe-smokers. Wearers of carpet slippers.'

'I smoke nothing, and I'm glad to say I own no slippers of any kind,' said Lampo. 'I must be . . .' He raised a sardonic and inquiring eyebrow at Henry. '. . . a rather unusual uncle.'

The tide of humanity swept them back into the sunlight of the Piazza del Campo, as if it were a whirlpool and they were three dead eels.

'Uncle Lampo isn't a bit grizzled,' said Henry. 'You'd never guess he was thirty-seven.' He turned to Lampo. 'Denzil asked me to come to Italy with him,' he said. 'I said I couldn't because I was going with you.'

'Ah!' said Lampo.

'I . . . er . . . I explained that, you being my uncle, naturally I had to come with you.'

'Ah!' said Lampo.

'I mean, not that I didn't want to. I did. I wanted to go with you both.'

'Henry and I are colleagues,' said Denzil. 'In Thurmarsh.'

'Where else?' groaned Lampo.

'How's your wife?' said Denzil.

'My wife?' said Lampo.

'My aunt,' said Henry. 'Since it's several years since you split up, I expect you've almost forgotten you ever had a wife.'

'Almost,' said Lampo.

'I told Denzil how I got in a bit of muddle,' said Henry. 'I thought it was my year to go to Filey with auntie. But of course it wasn't.'

'Shall we stop for a drink?' said Denzil.

'Not me,' said Lampo. 'I'm finding it quite a strain pretending to be so much younger than my thirty-seven years. I'm for a lie-down.'

'Shall we meet up for dinner later?' said Denzil.

'An excellent idea,' said Lampo. 'It's always interesting meeting my nephew's friends.'

They dined in a little back street trattoria, at a table next to six exuberant Finns. Henry was uneasy. He was worried that Denzil

198

and Lampo, his two friends from different parts of his life, wouldn't like each other. He knew that he was feeling rather ashamed of his friend, but he didn't know which friend he was feeling ashamed of. At first, he assumed it must be Denzil. He flinched at the artificiality of his voice, the affected outrageousness, as he gave his views on the merits of the Siennese School of Painting. But Lampo adopted an infuriating air of self-satisfied superiority. Henry felt that Lampo must see through Denzil's affectations, and Denzil must dislike Lampo's priggishness. And the Finns, who clearly understood English, were probably artists and laughing at them both. Oh, hot and uncomfortable young Yorkshireman, damp and inelegant between your two queer friends.

Denzil asked for the wine list and insisted on ordering a very expensive bottle of Chianti, although everyone else was drinking the house wine. It took them ten minutes to find the bottle. It arrived encrusted in dust and dirt. The waiter showed Denzil the completely illegible label. Denzil nodded. Lampo smirked. The Finns grinned. Henry sweated.

He tried to remain cool and detached, but heard himself say, 'You two ought to get on well. You've a lot in common.'

They immediately revealed one thing that they had in common. They both disliked the idea that they had a lot in common.

'Really?' said Lampo. 'What have we in common?'

'Well . . . I mean . . . you know . . . you're both . . .'

'. . . as queer as coots,' said Denzil, unnecessarily loudly. He roared with laughter.

'No! Well . . . I mean . . . yes, but . . . that wasn't what I meant.' Why did he mind that the Finns were listening? The likelihood of his meeting them again was remote. 'I mean . . . you both . . . hate sport, love art, admire style and dislike vulgarity. You're both outrageous. You're both contemptuous of the second-rate.'

'We sound insufferable,' said Lampo.

'Two insufferable people,' said Denzil. 'Is that a sound basis for friendship?'

'Either we'd find each other insufferable or the fact that the rest of the world found us insufferable would bind us together,' said Lampo.

'Contemptuous?' said Denzil. 'What am I ever contemptuous of?'

'Thurmarsh.'

'Ah well. It's impossible not to be contemptuous about Thurmarsh, dear boy. Do you know, Lampo, there's nothing in the town . . . nothing! . . . that could credibly be described as a delicatessen.'

'My God!' said Lampo. 'What do you do for peppered salami?'

'You see!' said Henry. 'You're both such snobs.' But he was pleased. They were getting on well. It was going to be all right.

'Not snobs,' said Denzil. 'Preservers of standards.'

'When have you seen me snobbish?' demanded Lampo.

'At school,' said Henry.

'At school?' said Denzil. 'Surely you weren't at school together?'

'Oh no. No. No,' said Henry. 'No. Of course not. He's sixteen years older than me. No, I . . . er . . . I *heard* you were snobbish at school, Lampo. Living off egg mayonnaise with anchovies. Doing mimes. Your snobbery's a legend in the old alma mater.' At the end of term concert, Lampo had done a mime representing 'Sir Stafford Cripps in the Underworld'. It had died a death. What a death it had died. Henry found himself smiling at the memory. Lampo and Denzil stared at his smile with curiosity. He wiped it from his face and tried to eat his spaghetti elegantly. He failed. He wiped that from his face too.

'This wine's undrinkable,' said Denzil. 'Sorry. Mario!' he sang out. '*Vino horribile. Vino repulsivo.* We'll try some of your plonk. *Il plonko rosso, per favore.*'

Henry cringed at Denzil's arrogance and insensitivity, in front of the Finns, in front of Lampo, who spoke impeccable Italian and had such immaculate courtesy towards those whom he thought inferior to him, which was practically everybody. Yet the waiter, who'd have hated Henry, if Henry had behaved like that, smiled indulgently, as if Denzil were a child. Lampo smiled and frowned at the same time, as if wanting to despise Denzil but finding it impossible.

'Did you not discover . . .' Suddenly Denzil seemed to become extremely arch. '. . . your . . . er . . . your tastes till you were married, Lampo?' he said.

'What?' said Lampo. 'Ah. Yes. Precisely. That's what did for the marriage, of course.'

The house wine arrived. Lampo poured it. He gave Henry half a glass. 'Henry's parents entrusted his moral well-being to me,' he told Denzil. 'They were particularly anxious that I should save him from the perils of drink.'

For their main course they had *piccato di vitello*, with various sauces. Henry's was *pizzaiola*, thick with tomato, garlic and capers. Denzil's was *marsala*, mature with wine. Lampo's was *al limone*, as tart as an old cat's gaze.

'I can no longer ignore that eye,' said Lampo. 'Painful though it may be for you to discuss it, Denzil, I have to ask you how you came by it.'

Henry had been appalled by Denzil's black eye. Was every journalist on the *Argus* destined to have one before the year was out?

'You know perfectly well I'm longing to tell you,' said Denzil.

'I know,' said Lampo. 'That's why I didn't ask you.'

'Bitch,' said Denzil indulgently. 'It's a very sordid story.'

'What a relief,' said Lampo. 'I was frightened it might not be.'

'I had a brief affair in Amalfi,' said Denzil. 'He cut up rough when I wouldn't give him money. He struck me with a piece of lead piping. End of sordid story. Pity. He was a dear boy, too.'

'I'm not sure you should talk about this sort of thing in front of my nephew,' said Lampo. 'He's very innocent. He's led a sheltered life.' Henry reached for the wine bottle. 'Not yet, Henry. When uncle says.'

'Oh for God's sake,' said Henry. 'Lampo isn't my uncle, Denzil.'

'Oh my God!' said Denzil. 'How this revelation has shattered my illusions!'

'You knew!' said Henry. 'You knew all the time.'

'You made it up so as not to come to Italy with me. You prefer the company of young queers to old queers,' said Denzil.

'There's nothing between me and Lampo,' said Henry.

'Oh good,' said Denzil. 'I was a bit worried about that.'

He smiled at Lampo. Lampo smiled back. Henry's blood ran cold. He fought hard against believing the unbelievable. He heard, vaguely, their chit-chat.

'Were you happy at school, Lampo?'

'No. I should have been a naval rating.'

'I don't follow you.'

'I'm very good at repelling boarders. Henry was one of the many boarders I repelled.'

Denzil laughed. What could Lampo see in this ageing and affected journalist, with his limp, his parchment skin, his hand-carved Scottish walking-stick and his black eye?

'Did you have an unhappy youth?' Lampo asked.

'Yes,' Denzil replied. 'I think I cheered him up quite a bit.'

Lampo giggled! Giggled! Lampo . . . giggled.

'Mario?' called Denzil.

The waiter, whose name was Angelo, approached indulgently.

'Bring us a bottle of champagne,' said Denzil.

Lampo frowned. He thought champagne too obvious. But he said nothing.

They had arranged to meet at eleven, in a café in the great square. Lampo came alone, elegant in fawn, scattering the pigeons.

'Well,' he said, 'I imagine you enjoyed having the bed to yourself.' He ordered an espresso. Henry ordered a cappuccino. 'You could dream of Anna to your heart's content.'

'Dreams! They're all I ever get.'

'Well, I've got my dream.'

'Denzil??'

'It shocks you, doesn't it?'

'Not shocks. Astounds.'

'We're lonely, Henry.'

'Lonely! You! I've always envied you your sophistication.'

Lampo gave his slightly twisted, slightly weary smile. A Belgian tour party filed into the square.

'I'd have thought sophistication was quite a recipe for loneliness,' said Lampo. 'Don't you think I felt lonely as I saw bloody Tosser leading Diana to the altar? Don't you think I was bitterly envious?'

'But you don't want that, Lampo.'

'That doesn't stop me feeling envious.'

'Of Tosser??' said Henry, so loudly that a passing pharmacist turned to see what passion was stirring this young Englishman. 'You're worth ten thousand Tossers.'

'Another recipe for loneliness,' said Lampo. 'Henry? We have the use of a villa in a place called Marina di Pietrasanta, on the Versilian Riviera.'

'I might not want to go to the seaside.'

'You might not be being invited to go to the seaside,' said Lampo gently.

'What?'

'Homosexuality is illegal. Every time my feelings are stirred I become a criminal. Would you begrudge Denzil and me four days alone together, safe from prying eyes?'

'Bloody hell, Lampo,' said Henry. 'The only reason I didn't go off with Anna was because I was too considerate to you.'

'One of life's little lessons,' said Lampo, smiling his twisted smile. 'Never be considerate to your social superiors unless it suits you. We'll never be considerate to you unless it suits us.'

Lampo paid for the coffee. Denzil was limping towards them. They went to meet him. They stood in the very middle of the great square, in the hot sunshine. Henry knew that his grumpiness was a lost cause.

'I wish I'd recorded it. It would have saved a lot of bother,' he said. 'I've said it in London. I've said it in Buxton. I said it in Skipton and Troutwick on the same day. I may as well say it in Siena. "I hope you'll both be very happy."'

14 In Love

Droplets of dew hung on every leaf and every blade of grass. Thin grey clouds scudded across a leaden sky.

Ginny looked dreadful. Her face was blotchy. Her eyes were red and runny. She gave her nose a blow so gargantuan that he wanted to pretend he wasn't with her.

He put an affectionate hand on her muscular right arm.

'What's happened?' he said. 'Why have you been crying?'

'I haven't been crying,' she said. 'I've got a cold.'

'How's Gordon?'

'He's got a cold.'

The doomed tram groaned as it descended into the dim, sulphorous valley. How mean the streets looked. The traffic came to a complete halt outside Fison and Oldsworthy's – *the* place for screws. Ginny sneezed like a Bofors gun. They crawled past the Popular Café, whose emptiness daily belied its name. On the right was a large bomb-site. Why did English towns never look finished?

The news-room was yellow, brown and grey. Yellow light on a grey morning. Yellow-brown fingers of chain-smokers putting yellowing paper into grey typewriters. Grey hair, yellow teeth and a brown jacket as Terry Skipton ordered him laryngitically to number three magistrates' court. He had a cold. Ted and Helen asked him, nasally, about his holiday. They had matching colds. Everyone had colds, in this disgusting northern land.

And yet . . . it was a magic land. For did it not contain Anna Matheson?

The statue of Sir Herbert Rustwick in Town Hall Square was coated in pigeon droppings. The absurdly large Doric pillars of the court house were black with grime.

A milkman had sold watered milk. A motorist had struck a police car after failing to look left. A displaced Pole had stolen back the seventy pounds he'd lost at poker. It was a morning of small defeats and petty betrayals.

He'd lost touch with world events while he'd been at camp and in Italy. After lunch he went to the newspaper's library, on the ground floor, behind the huge small-ads department, and read the back numbers.

Egypt had expelled Britons. Britain had expelled Egyptians. A mission to Cairo, led by the Australian Prime Minister, Mr Menzies, had ended in deadlock. The plans of Mr Dulles, US Secretary of State, for an Anna users association – no, concentrate. A canal users association – had been described by the leader of the Labour Party, Mr Gaitskell, as so weak that a better name would be the Cape Users Association. In Cyprus, Eoka terrorists had resumed their activities. There'd been violence in Tennessee, Kentucky and Texas as black pupils were escorted to schools that had previously been all-white. Anna had broken the world water speed record at Lake Mead, Nevada. Not Anna! Donald Campbell. Russia had withdrawn from an athletics match against Britain after Anna Ponomareva – *Nina* Ponomareva – a discus thrower, had been charged with stealing five hats, worth £1 12s. 11d., from C & A Modes. Sir William Penney, director of the Anna Bomb Tests – Atom Bomb Tests – at Maralinga, had announced that, due to bad weather, Britain's sixth atomic weapon might have to be exploded on a Sunday. In the end it had been exploded on a Friday. 'Was there pressure?' the *Sunday Express* had asked.

That afternoon, Henry had a phone call.

'It's your friend from the world of industry.'

'Good Lord.'

'I've got a story for you. A scoop.'

'Good Lord.'

'There's no need to be sarcastic.'

'No. Sorry.' Impossible to be excited about scoops, just now. Anna would be home from work in two hours' time.

They arranged to meet in the Pigeon and Two Annas.

After work, trembling with excitement, Henry went to a phone box. Matheson T. J., Tudor Lodge, 17, Ullapool Drive. Thurmarsh 6782. He couldn't ring it. Phones were so impersonal. Much better to call on her later, pretending that he was passing on his way home from his interview.

'Cracking goal of Tommy's Saturday week,' said Martin Hammond. 'Literally rocketed into the net.'

The bar smelt of furniture polish. They sat below the picture of the great flood, and drank glasses of bitter.

'I missed it,' said Henry. 'I was in Italy,' he added, trying to sound blasé and much-travelled. 'Good game, was it?'

'Oh I didn't go,' said Martin. 'But I always read the report. Because of Tommy. Because of the old days.' Henry felt that Martin clung to memories of childhood because he needed to convince himself that he had once been a child. 'Paradise Lane Gang! Those were the days.'

'You hated them,' said Henry.

Martin ignored this. 'What's the minimum wage in Italy?' he asked.

'I've no idea! Well, come on, then. What's the story?'

Martin leant forward and spoke in such a conspiratorial whisper that the scattered early evening drinkers all tried to listen.

'A councillor is in cahoots with a council official to buy up property in the town centre.'

'Which councillor?'

'I don't know.'

'Which official?'

'I don't know.'

'What property?'

'I don't know.'

'Well, thank you, Martin. This is riveting news,' said Henry. 'Actually that wouldn't make a bad title for the trade magazine of the riveting industry. *Riveting News*.'

'There's no need to be sarcastic,' said Martin.

'Sorry,' said Henry. 'It's just that it is the teeniest bit on the vague side.'

'I thought you could burrow. I mean . . . you're the journalist.'

'That's true.'

'It could take the lid off a steaming cauldron of corruption and incompetence. It could reveal the cancer in the municipal body politic.'

'You're right. Thanks, Martin. I'll burrow. How did you come across the story, anyroad?'

'I have my channels.'

'It's hard for me to burrow if you don't give me any idea where I should burrow.'

Martin sighed, then shed a layer of his self-importance.

'I heard it on a crossed line,' he said. 'We've been getting crossed lines. I rang to complain and got this crossed line.'

Henry laughed. Martin looked at him in surprise.

'What did this man say on this crossed line?' said Henry.

'Summat about . . . er . . . the official could use his powers to get certain properties empty or summat. To tell you the truth I was that excited at what I was hearing that I didn't listen that carefully. I got frightened they'd sense me there, listening. I think they may have done. One of them said they shouldn't talk about it on the phone and could they meet in some pub after the council meeting.'

'Would it be too much to hope that you've remembered which pub?'

'I can as it happens. Summat to do with Dr Livingstone.'

'The Livingstone?'

'Could have been.'

Henry ordered two more beers from the waiter, whose name, he had discovered, was Oscar.

'What's the status of shop stewards in Italy?' asked Martin.

Henry looked at him in astonishment. 'I don't know,' he said. 'I was looking at the most beautiful cities in the world. I wasn't asking people about shop stewards.' It was a shock to realize that he hadn't had a single conversation about anything with an Italian. It was a shock to realize that he wasn't confident that his attitude of amused superiority to Martin was remotely justified.

'How are you today?' inquired Henry, when Oscar brought the drinks.

'Very well, thank you, sir,' said Oscar. 'It's right ironical. I'm a shocker for colds, me, and now everybody's got one and I haven't!' He walked away, sensed their disappointment, and returned. 'I'll tell you what I have got,' he said, like a parent offering a child a consolation treat. 'And it's summat I never ever have. I'm usually the other way, if anything, if you take my meaning.' He lowered his voice and produced his nugget. 'I haven't been for five days. Five days.' He nodded twice and moved off.

'How's work?' said Henry.

'Ruddy awful today,' said Martin. 'Mr Templeton's canary escaped and got into the mechanism. Charlie Fancutt risked his life to rescue it.' Henry's face must have revealed his astonishment. 'Well, he's managing director, is Mr Templeton. And he's very attached to that canary. It's a descendant of the canary that his grandfather sent down the pit so if the air was poisoned they'd find out when it died. Which it didn't, presumably, or it wouldn't have had descendants. Unless it died after it had had its descendants, of course.'

'Now that *is* a story,' said Henry.

Tudor Lodge was a large, detached house with a pretentious curved gable, set back from the road up a steep drive. One curtained window was lit.

If only he wouldn't shake. What was wrong with him? And his legs weren't steady. He'd drunk more than he'd intended.

He rang the bell. It sounded harsh and obtrusive.

He found himself facing a fairly tall, slightly overweight, rather good-looking, even potentially charming man. Should he wish to charm. Which, just then, he didn't.

'Yes?' said Mr Matheson cautiously. 'Can I help you?'

'Is . . . er . . .' His voice was trembling, and he was panting after the steep drive. 'I . . . er . . . can I speak to Anna, please?'

'Anna doesn't live here any more.' He made it sound like the title of a tragedy.

'Oh . . . er . . . I see. Well . . . er . . . could you tell me where she does live?'

'I could, yes,' said Mr Matheson. 'The question is, should I?'

Oh no. A headmaster.

'I want to see her. I'm a friend. Could you please tell me where she lives?' he panted.

'Well now,' said Mr Matheson. 'I have to ask myself whether it's safe to give my daughter's address to a trembling, panting, remorselessly monosyllabic young man who arrives at my door after ten o'clock at night, dressed like a bad journalist and considerably the worse for drink.'

Anger gave Henry pride. He drew himself up to his full height, a gesture which would have been more impressive if he hadn't still been three inches shorter than Mr Matheson. 'Mr Matheson,' he said. 'I met your daughter in Italy. I like her very much. I had the depressed instinction that she liked me. I know she'd like to see me.'

Mr Matheson switched on his charm. His voice relented. 'I dare say she would,' he said. 'I'll tell her you called and ask her to get in touch with you. All right?'

'Well . . . yes. Thank you,' said Henry. 'Thank you.'

He turned away. Mr Matheson coughed discreetly.

'Er . . . don't you think you ought to give me your name and address?' he said. 'Anna isn't a mind-reader.'

'Oh. Yes. Sorry.' Henry emitted a strangulated laugh. He longed to say that he was Jasper Phipps-Ockington, but it would defeat the object of the exercise. 'I'm Henry Pratt. I live at 239, Winstanley Road. I'm not on the phone.'

'No.' Meaning, 'You wouldn't be.'

'Or she could phone me at . . . er . . . the *Argus*.'

'Ah.'

As he slithered down the drive, Henry felt that it had not been a wildly propitious first meeting with his future father-in-law. Would they laugh about it, over the port, at family Christmasses to come?

Next day, Anna didn't ring. Terry Skipton liked the canary story.

On Wednesday, Anna didn't ring. Nor did Mr Gaitskell, the Queen, Cousin Hilda, Auntie Doris, Sir Leonard Hutton or any of the population of the West Riding.

On Thursday, October 4th, 1956, at 3.27 p.m., Henry's phone burst into heart-stopping life. He let it ring five times, so as not to seem too eager, then grabbed it in panic, in case she should ring off.

The male voice disconcerted him totally.

'Sorry,' he said. 'I missed that.'

'It's your contact from the world of sport. I've got a story for you.'

She was never going to ring. He'd been a brief Italian fantasy, a good idea on a hot day, long forgotten.

He arranged to meet Tommy in the Winstanley at seven.

Ginny approached his desk rather tentatively.

'Are you in tonight?' she croaked.

'Yes and no,' he said cautiously.

'I'm really fed up with this cold. I felt like popping over to the Winstanley for a few drinks.'

'I'm meeting one of my contacts there at seven,' said Henry grandly. 'I'm sure we'll be through by . . . oh . . . shall we say eight-thirty?'

Tommy didn't turn up until twenty to eight. He didn't apologize.

His scoop was hardly earth-shattering. The whole team was going to autograph the plaster of a seventeen-year-old girl who'd broken her leg when she'd fallen down a flight of steps at the match against Mansfield Town. But Henry rewarded him by buying another round.

''ey oop, our Tommy,' said a passing customer. 'If tha doesn't score Saturday we'll know why, won't we? 'cos tha's been supping.'

Tommy sighed. 'It's no use me coming in places like this,' he said.

'He was only joking,' said Henry.

'He was joking if we win,' said Tommy. 'He wasn't if we lose.'

'Would you like another drink?' said Henry.

At the bar, Henry found himself standing beside Mr Matheson. This was his chance to redeem himself.

'Good evening, Mr Matheson,' he quipped wittily.

Anna's father stared at him politely but blankly.

'Henry Pratt,' he said. 'I called on Monday night.'

'Oh yes. Yes.'

'Did you give Anna my message?'

'Oh blast. I forgot. I'm so sorry. My memory!' said Mr Matheson. 'I'll ring her tomorrow.' He smiled. It was a charming smile. Henry wanted to glare. The man's lack of consideration had caused him three days of mental anguish. But he didn't feel like glaring, because this news meant that Anna hadn't been neglecting him, so he smiled back.

'I'm buying a drink for Tommy Marsden,' he said. 'He's giving me a story.'

'Jolly good,' said Mr Matheson. 'Well . . . keep at it. Nose to the grindstone.' Mr Matheson's nose didn't look as if it had ever been anywhere near a grindstone.

Tommy waxed ungenerous about his team-mates. Muir was yellow. Ayers was as thick as two short planks. Gravel was shagging himself to death.

The sparkling level of the conversation didn't survive the arrival of Ginny.

'I'm a colleague of Henry's,' she said. 'On the paper,' she added, as if not trusting Tommy's intelligence, and perhaps she was justified in view of Tommy's next remark. 'What, writing and that?' he said.

'Yes. What do you do, Tommy?' inquired Ginny.

Henry kicked her under the table. She glared at him.

'Tommy's the star of Thurmarsh United,' hissed Henry.

'Oh yes! I remember now,' said Ginny. 'I read about you. You saved a penalty, didn't you?'

'Tommy's the centre forward,' said Henry.

Ginny sneezed. It was like the eruption of a human Etna. She turned towards Tommy, who recoiled. 'I'm one of those people who're never ill,' she said. 'So when I am, I get it really badly.'

Tommy searched vainly for a reply.

Ginny sneezed again.

Henry glared. 'Ginny lives in the flat above me,' he said.

Tommy looked at his wrist. He wasn't wearing his watch, but he didn't allow this to put him off. 'Time I was off,' he said.

'There's no need to go on my account,' said Ginny.

'Nothing personal,' said Tommy. 'But Mr Mackintosh says it's unprofessional to expose ourselves to germs unnecessarily.'

'Well, thank you,' said Ginny, when Tommy had gone.

'What for?' said Henry.

'Disowning me. "Ginny lives in the flat above me." Meaning, "This monstrosity isn't my girl-friend."'

Henry said, 'Ginny! I wasn't disowning you.' After a pause he added, 'And you aren't a monstrosity.' If he could have started the conversation again, he'd have put these two comments in the opposite order.

Ginny began to cry, silently.

'Ginny, love! What is it?' he said.

'Gordon's never going to leave his wife.'

Henry felt an immense tenderness towards her. He grasped her hand. He wanted to say something really nice. 'I think you're a smashing journalist,' he said. 'Thanks. What every woman wants to hear,' she said. He leant forward and licked the salt tears off her cheek. 'I've got to blow my nose,' she warned. 'I don't mind,' he said bravely. And then he saw Mr Matheson staring straight at him. He shrank from her. 'My nose-blowing revolts you,' she said. He said nothing. What could he say? 'No. I like it.'? 'Well, you are a pretty horrific performer on the old hooter.'? 'It's nothing to do with your nose. The father of my future fiancée is staring at me, and I'm embarrassed.'?

When Mr Matheson went to the Gents, Henry tried not to follow him. But he had to explain himself.

He stood next to Mr Matheson, at the urinals.

'The young lady I'm with is not a girl-friend, Mr Matheson,' he said. 'She lives in the flat above me. She has a bad cold, and she's depressed, and she believes that the man she loves, who also has a cold, incidentally, will never leave his wife. I'm trying to cheer her up.'

Mr Matheson stared at him in astonishment. 'What an angel of mercy you are,' he said.

As he walked out of the Gents, Henry felt that it had not been a wildly propitious second meeting with his future father-in-law. Would they laugh about it, over the port, at family Christmasses to come?

The weather was cold, with snow as far south as Leek, in Staffordshire. The Middle East crisis was debated in the United Nations, amid rumours that Mr Dulles was 'de-toughening'. 21 soldiers were arrested in Cyprus after demanding an assurance that they'd be home by Christmas. 15 guardsmen in Malta protested about a rumoured kit inspection. 250 reservists complained about bad food and army 'bull' at an RAMC Depot in Cookham.

Gradually it dawned on Henry that Anna would never phone, because her father would never tell her that her company was sought by a short, podgy, trembling young drunk who dressed like a bad journalist because he was a bad journalist and followed him into pub lavatories while having dates with women with bad colds. It also dawned on him that if he wrote her a letter her father could hardly refuse to forward it, because he couldn't know who it was from.

On Wednesday, October 10th, Seretse Khama, chief-designate of the Bamangwata tribe, returned to Bechuanaland for the first time since his exile for marrying Ruth Williams, a white London typist. When she'd married him, Cousin Hilda had said, 'It's her mother I'm sorry for.' Henry had said, 'If I was a typist and married a tribal chief, I'd expect you to be thrilled.'

Anna must have got his letter but still she didn't ring. He wondered if Cousin Hilda would be thrilled when he married her.

He had a permanent pain in his testicles as he thought about her, and was finding it difficult to walk without doubling up. He went for his lunch at the Rundle Café, because she'd worked there. A hosiery salesman listened with bated breath to the tale of Sammy, the Squirrel who'd lost his nuts. Henry envied Sammy the Squirrel. That afternoon, he busied himself with his film reviews. His phone didn't ring.

On the next day, when he returned from number two magistrates' court – he made dog noises, she mewed like cat, court told – Colin Edgeley said, 'A girl rang for you. Very sexy. She'll ring at nine-fifteen tomorrow morning.' Henry tried not to blush, and failed.

Most of the usual crowd drifted to the Lord Nelson, drawn by no greater impulse than habit. Ben bet Henry that he couldn't name the five league teams whose names ended with the same letter as they began. He tried, but his heart wasn't in it. He got Liverpool, Charlton Athletic and Aston Villa, but missed Northampton Town and York City. Helen pressed her thigh against him and quizzed him about the phone call from the sexy lady.

It struck him with a shock of shame that he hadn't been to see

Cousin Hilda since he'd got back from Italy. He'd go tonight. If he didn't, Anna wouldn't ring. No. That was juvenile. But he'd go anyway.

Gordon and Ginny left early, after an elaborate debate about which film to see, although everybody knew they weren't going to the pictures. Ben announced that he was going home to give the wife one. Henry asked if anybody had peppermints. Ben and Colin, the married men, both had peppermints.

The fog was returning, after a fine day. Henry's peppermint breath made clouds of steam as he crunched the gravel outside number 66.

The fire crackled economically in the blue-tiled stove. The smell of pork and cabbage lingered. Cousin Hilda switched Frankie Howerd off.

'Don't switch him off for me,' he said.

'He's nearly finished,' said Cousin Hilda, 'and then we've only got some documentary or something about violence against witnesses in Liverpool and then some woman and Edgar Lustgarten, who isn't even English, having the cheek to think they can solve people's personal problems. Though I like the *Horse of the Year Show* at nine-fifty. I'm not struck on the horses, but Dorian Williams speaks beautifully.'

'How's Liam?' he inquired.

'He's Liam.'

'And Mr Pettifer?'

'Mr Pettifer is a disappointed man. He has a jaundiced view of life.'

'And Mr Frost?'

'Married. Living in Rawlaston.' Cousin Hilda sniffed. 'I have a Mr Peters in his room and a Mr Brentwood in your old room. Mr Peters is used to fine things, and Mr Brentwood has a hygiene problem. Things aren't what they were, Henry. We've seen the halcyon days of paying guests. We won't see them again in our lifetimes.'

'I suppose not.'

'So how was Italy? I got your card.'

'Oh. Good. It was very nice. It's a very beautiful country.'

Cousin Hilda sniffed. 'Well, I suppose it would be, if you like that sort of thing,' she said. 'Wensleydale's good enough for me. I see no cause to gad off abroad. But I expect it's all different now. Mrs Wedderburn's nephew's just been to Germany. I shouldn't fancy that, after the War. But she says it looks very picturesque, to judge from his three postcards, though too many conifers for her liking. She said, "And have you had some nice cards from Henry?" "Just the one," I said. She said, "The Italian post is very slow. I expect the others'll arrive after he's been to see you, which he'll do as soon as he gets back. He's such a thoughtful boy." I said, "He is, and he knows my views about extravagance, and he wouldn't want to worry me by inundating me with needless postcards." That told her. There's a nosy side to Mrs Wedderburn.'

Henry told her about Florence and Siena. He told her about meeting Michael and Denzil. He didn't tell her about Anna or about Denzil going off with Lampo while he trudged round Lucca and Pisa on his own. She said she didn't see anything clever in building things that leant. Thurmarsh church could have been built leaning, but where would have been the sense of it?

When Cousin Hilda began laying up for the little supper that she gave her 'businessmen', Henry made his excuses. He couldn't face seeing Liam, who was Liam, or Norman Pettifer, with his jaundiced view of life, or Mr Peters, who was used to fine things, or Mr Brentwood, who had a hygiene problem.

It was 9.17 before his phone screamed into life. Those two minutes seemed endless.

Tactful typewriters clacked all round him.

'Henry Pratt, *Evening Argus*.'

'Hello!'

'Anna!'

'Hello, Henry. How super of you to write. I was thrilled to get your letter.' In her voice there was still the warm sun of Siena.

'Were you? Oh good. Super.' Super? That's not one of my words.

'I hoped you'd get in touch.'

'Did you? Oh good. Super. Look, Anna . . . er . . .' He hardly dared ask her out, which was ridiculous, when she'd phoned him. '. . . how about coming out one evening?'

215

'Lovely. When?'

'How about . . . ?' He wanted to say 'tonight' but knew better than to insult her by suggesting that she might be free at such short notice. '. . . next Tuesday?'

'Wednesday would suit me better.'

'I'll just have a look in my diary.' He stared into space and counted to twenty. 'Yes. I can work round things and manage Wednesday.'

'Super.' Her voice sounded posher than he'd remembered. 'There's a little pub near where I live called the Cross Keys.'

'I know it.'

'Seven-thirty?'

'Right.'

'Super. Next Wednesday, then. Save yourself for me.'

What did it matter that he'd been insufficiently masterful? Who cared that he'd let her name the day, the place and the time? She'd said, 'Save yourself for me.'

He did.

Britain and France agreed with Egypt on the main principles for international control of the canal. President Eisenhower described the talks as 'most gratifying'. It looked as though 'a very great crisis' was 'behind us'. Nina Ponomareva was given an absolute discharge at Marlborough Street. The Bolshoi Ballet decided to stay in Britain for three extra days. Russians were good people. The world was a nice place. Henry Pratt was in love.

The Prime Minister was enthusiastically received at the Conservative Party Conference in Llandudno when he said that Britain reserved the right to use force. His speech was less well received in Cairo, where they didn't appear to understand that it had been aimed at the Tory faithful. There was a gun-fight in a Hungarian airliner between security police and 'bandits' trying to flee to the West. But these were small clouds.

At 7.17, on the evening of Wednesday, October 17th, Henry entered the Cross Keys, in Brunswick Road. It was a little Victorian pub in a low stone terrace, dwarfed by the primary school. That steep-roofed fortress, with its green institutional guttering and Dutch-style gables, filled Henry with memories of humiliation and of phenomenal farting, which were inappropriate to this important evening in his life. Why had he agreed to meet her here?

The bar had a grey-green patterned carpet with one hole and two bad stains. There were 9 low tables, with maroon bench seating round the walls, and 22 ugly wooden chairs. There were 39 bottles of drink behind the bar. There were 17 cracks in the ceiling. Behind the bar, pinned to a board, were 7 postcards. In the lurid sky above a Swiss funicular railway on one of the postcards, there were 7 puffy white clouds. Henry counted all these things, between 7.17 and 8.04, which was when he decided that she wasn't coming, which was when she came.

'I'm sorry I'm late,' she said casually, as if she didn't know that he'd been enduring torment. 'You know how it is.' He wanted to say, 'No, I don't. How is it?' Did she mean she tried to be on time and failed? Or had she kept him waiting deliberately? He didn't know her. Well, of course he didn't. He'd only met her once. They'd never been alone together. Yet he felt that he knew her. He felt resentful of her for not being in the image in which he had recreated her. She was a little smaller than he'd expected. A little fleshier, too. Her eyes were greener. Her mouth, with those faintly protruding teeth, was smaller. He felt jealous of her independent existence. He hardly understood these feelings. He only knew that she'd caught him on the hop by coming in just as he was getting up to leave. She'd ruined the most important moment of his life.

She kissed him on the cheek and said, 'This is nice,' as if their meeting were a glass of wine, and then she stood back and looked at him and said, 'You're just as I remembered!' which must have been because she hadn't thought enough about him to distort him in her mind. She smelt of expensive perfume, and he wanted her to smell overwhelmingly of herself. He was dismayed by her casual self-assurance, while he was rigid with tension. It was all going wrong already. He didn't like her. It was a nightmare.

Somehow he got through the motions of offering her a drink. She asked for a Pernod. A Pernod, in Brunswick Road! They hadn't got any. He hated her. She settled for a gin and It. She lit a cigarette. She wasn't a goddess.

'You're trembling,' she said.

'I feel terribly cold,' he lied.

'I hope you aren't getting flu,' she said. 'I can't stand sickly people.'

Thurmarsh woman condemns the sick. Her remark was so patently absurd that he began to feel better. Anna Matheson had been a dream, and he was coming out of it already.

They sat side by side, under the curtained window, on the maroon seating, facing the bar.

'This is a bit different from Siena,' he said, and groaned silently at the most fatuously self-evident remark ever made.

'Italy was a big mistake,' she said. 'Well, not Italy itself.' Big of you. Your peninsula is not an error, says Englishwoman. 'Going with Hilary. I just have this thing about illness.'

'Is Hilary ill?'

'In her mind. I mean, don't get me wrong, I like old Hillers. But it would have been a big mistake going away with her even if she hadn't been so depressed. I like lying on beaches and meeting young men. She likes looking at old buildings. The only young men we met were you and your queer friend. He is queer, isn't he?'

'Lampo? Yes. But I thought you seemed quite interested in Siena.'

'We had a bargain. Half the time on the beach, half the time looking at old stones. Hillers ruined the beach for me. Wouldn't sit in the sun. Wouldn't inflict her horrible body on the Italians. Absolute pain in the un-sunburnt backside. Poor old Hillers. She finds life so difficult. Do you find life difficult, Henry?'

'Incredibly.'

'Oh God! What is wrong with people? I mean if you're really poor or something frightful like that, fair enough, you should be miserable. But not people like us. Tell me about your holiday? Did you have a good time?'

He told her about Lampo and Denzil. She laughed at the misfortunes of Henry 'A gooseberry in Tuscany' Pratt, proving that she was a good listener and had very white teeth, despite her smoking. When he offered her another drink, she insisted on paying. 'Daddy says local journalists are pretty miserably paid,' she said. 'I think he's trying to put me off you.' He asked her what she did. 'Oh, I help run a sort of beauty parlour thing,' she said. 'It's the new thing.' During their third drink, she held his hand and he was surprised to feel a stirring in his loins. When he said he was a socialist, she said, 'How could you?' as if he'd betrayed the natural order of things and democracy had never existed. She disagreed with him so cheerfully that he decided that she simply didn't realize that he might find it distressing to discover how much they disagreed. During their fourth drink she ran her tongue quickly round the inside of his right ear and gave him a very meaningful look. He put his right hand in the fold of her dress. She felt extremely soft. He was finding that it didn't matter as much as he'd thought that they disagreed about almost everything. He hardly dared suggest a change of scene, so well were things going, but he must offer her a meal and it was almost a quarter to ten.

'Where would you like to eat?' he said. 'I only know three places. The Midland, which is pretty awful and probably closed. The Shanghai, which is very awful and definitely open. And Donny's Bar, upstairs at the Barleycorn, which is competent and may be closed. Thurmarsh is a bit of a gastronomic desert.'

'Why don't you come back to the flat and I'll knock you up an omelette? Much more fun,' she said.

He couldn't speak. He nodded. She smiled, patted his knee and said, 'Good. We'll have fun. Let's pick up some wine and go.'

The Cross Keys had two bottles of wine. Henry bought the white one. It was yellow.

They walked along Brunswick Road, holding hands. They turned right into Cardington Road, which ran down the hill, parallel to the main road, back towards the town centre.

Her flat was in a basement. On the doorstep, she kissed him full on the mouth.

The living-room was tiny, with a folding table, two armchairs, two upright chairs, a hissing gas fire which had been on all evening and a reproduction of 'Greylag Geese Rising' by Peter Scott. On the mantelpiece there were invitations to three parties and a clock that had stopped.

'I'll show you the flat,' she said. She opened the door of a tiny, pink bedroom. 'This is Sally's room. She's away.' She showed him her bedroom. On the credit side, it was larger. On the debit side, it was even pinker. He felt that he was a helpless piece of cork, bobbing through the evening on the tide of Anna's wishes.

The omelettes were fluffy and runny. The unchilled white wine was a tease, constantly promising to be undrinkable and then withdrawing from the brink.

Anna raised her glass and said, 'To our friendship. I'm so glad you got in touch.'

'To you, Anna,' he said. 'God, I want you.'

'That's nice,' she said. She apologized for her father's disapproval of him.

'Is he a headmaster?' he asked.

'God, no!' she said. 'He looks down on teachers. He's a solicitor. Why did you think he's a headmaster?'

'The pedantic way he used words.'

'That goes with all the speeches he makes.'

'Speeches?'

'He's on the council. He's leader of the Tories.' She stood up. 'Right,' she said. 'That's that. I think it would be rather nice if we went to bed together now, don't you?'

He could hardly breathe. 'Er . . . yes . . . that would be very rather nice. Yes,' he said. 'I've just got to go to the lavatory first.'

She snorted a laugh. 'God, you're romantic,' she said. 'I'm not a great reader but I can't remember that happening in any of the great love affairs of literature. "Romeo, Romeo, wherefore art thou, Romeo?" "Can't you guess? Won't be a sec, Juliet."'

'They're fiction,' he said. 'This is real life.' But he wasn't convinced. He couldn't really believe it was happening.

When he returned she was sitting stark-naked, Rubenesque, smiling, absurd in a cheap brown armchair.

He was appalled. How could he explain that he'd wanted them to undress together, slowly, shyly, gently? How could he say that he found her behaviour grotesquely insensitive and unsubtle? How could he say that she'd ruined a moment that should have been of shared tenderness?

'Don't you want me?' she said. 'Do you find me too fat? I am a bit fat.'

'Anna! Oh, Anna! Course I want you.'

She began to undress him. He dreaded the moment when she

would see how unaroused he was. He looked at the greylag geese and felt that he would never emulate them.

He stood white and podgy and sweating and unaroused before her. She pulled him to the floor and began very solemnly to kiss him all over. He remained tense.

'What on earth's wrong?' she said.

'I'm very much afraid this isn't going to work,' he said.

'Oh God!'

Years later he would still break out in a sweat of embarrassment when he remembered the next few minutes, as he clumsily got dressed in that tiny basement room, while the naked solicitor's daughter sat and watched, beside the hissing fire, beneath the rising geese.

15 Dark Days

Dark days. Rain, drizzle and fog. Suez, Hungary and Henry. Lost illusions. How small was Henry's humiliation compared to the humiliation of Great Britain. How puny his loneliness compared to the rape of Budapest. But it was his own humiliation and loneliness that flooded him each morning when his alarm clock summoned him to the responsibilities of consciousness. How could it be otherwise? He wasn't Budapest. He wasn't the Suez Canal. He was Henry Ezra Pratt, locked in that little body of his.

He couldn't tell anybody about Anna, couldn't turn her into one of his funny stories, couldn't become Henry 'Ee by gum she 'ad nowt on' Pratt.

The Queen released the first nuclear power into the national grid. An increase in prescription charges to 1s. per item was criticized by the British Medical Association. President Eisenhower suffered a bloodshot eye when two pieces of confetti got into it during a ticker tape election rally. Henry spent the weekend writing letters to Anna and tearing them up.

Hazel Carstairs had taken the children to their granny's for the weekend. Henry kept his wireless on very loud, to protect him from the sounds of satisfactions that he would never know. Anne Shelton kept telling him to lay down his arms. Frankie Laine had a woman to love. Henry didn't. Doris Day informed him that whatever would be, would be. Stupid tautologous female. Bill Haley rocked complacently through the rye. Selfish bastard. The Ying Tong Song drove him mad. 'When Mexico gave up the Rumba,' sang Mitchell Torok. 'When Henry Pratt gave up women,' said Henry grimly.

At last he'd completed a letter that didn't make him cringe with embarrassment.

Dear Anna [he'd written]
Thank you very much for coming out with me, and for giving me the omelette. It was delicious. I'm afraid I failed to

round the evening off in the way you'd hoped. It's not something that's ever happened to me before. I think it may have been partly the drink, but that isn't the whole story. I certainly wouldn't want you to think it was because, when I saw you with nothing on, I didn't fancy you. I think you're extremely beautiful.

The truth is, Anna, that in Siena I believed that love had come to me like a swift on the wing. What mindless twaddle! What romantic nonsense! Love isn't like that. I don't believe in love at first sight. It's an insult to one's partner, an insult to love and an insult to oneself.

I believe that love must come gradually, as you get to know people really well, and probably I only function really well as a sexual being when I'm in love. Can we meet again, get to know each other better, and try again? I'd like that.

Please write.

Thank you once again for the omelette. It was delicious.

All best wishes

Henry

The moment he'd posted the letter, it made him cringe with embarrassment.

Poland was on the verge of war. The headlines rolled off the presses. Soviet leaders fly to Warsaw. Poles 'Going too far to independence'. Gomulka returns to power in Warsaw. Poland rebuffs Russian Navy.

The headlines rolled off the presses in Thurmarsh too, onto Henry's stories. Splutt WI enjoyed potato lecture. Cyclist drank too much. Barmaid (27) hit customer (42) after remark about bust (38).

War in Poland was narrowly averted. It was reported, almost as an afterthought, that Hungary might be the next East European country to demand genuine independence from Moscow. The discovery of arms on a ship in Alexandria Harbour lent substance to French claims that Egypt was supplying the Algerian rebels.

Thousands marched to demand freedom in Budapest. The Russian tanks rolled in. Unarmed civilians were mown down in the streets. The world was shocked. Britain, France and the United States asked the United Nations to condemn the Russian use of force. Henry received no reply from Anna. He hadn't expected that he would.

Israeli troops swept 100 miles into Egypt, on a two-pronged drive towards Suez. Britain and France gave the Israelis and the Egyptians 12 hours to withdraw their forces to a distance 10 miles from the canal. Israel agreed. Egypt didn't. The Anglo-French invasion of Egypt began. Only later would it emerge that these moves had been agreed by Britain, France and Israel, in a secret meeting at Sèvres. Still Anna didn't reply. It would be several months before her secret emerged.

The back bar of the Lord Nelson was in ferment. The police and criminals were mostly for the invasion. The lawyers were divided. Ted, who'd become 'Thurmarshian' after the departure of Neil Mallet, was taking the newspaper's official line. He was solidly behind Eden. It was a regrettable but necessary action to protect our interests. Helen agreed. Gordon was scornfully against it. Ginny was wracked by visible conflict. The eyes of the war correspondent lit up. The warm-hearted private self thought it a tragic mistake. Pacifist Ben was quietly, doggedly angry. Colin, a socialist who verged on communism, found himself in terrible confusion. His pugilism welcomed the chance of a scrap for our lads. His chauvinism thought Nasser deserved a bloody nose. His communism couldn't forgive the Russians for betraying his ideals, and couldn't forgive the Suez adventure for diverting world pressure off the Russians. Denzil saw it all as a tragi-comic opera. The world was a cynical place and he couldn't understand why everybody was so surprised and shocked.

And Henry? He was appalled, but he was also appalled at how difficult he was finding it to feel as appalled as he felt he should. He knew, with a part of himself, that he didn't love Anna, that she didn't love him, that she wouldn't reply to his letter. But another part of him was still obsessed with her, still expected that letter every day. And that part of him knew that Anna would be in favour of the Suez operation. And that part of him wondered if it was possible for people who disagreed so fundamentally about something so fundamental to ever truly love each other. And that part of him prevented the parts of him becoming the whole of him.

Occasionally he felt a trickle of returning happiness, of relief that Anna hadn't replied, of freedom. These feelings didn't last long, because it depressed him to feel happy at a time like this.

A large British fleet sailed east through the Mediterranean towards Egypt. In the United Nations there was an American resolution asking members to refrain from the use of force and a Russian resolution asking Israel to withdraw its forces from behind the armistice line. Britain and France vetoed both resolutions. Henry felt the sharpest stab of anger that he'd yet managed.

Denzil asked Henry to spend the weekend with him and Lampo, in his town house. They wanted to thank him for bringing them together. He couldn't refuse. He didn't want to refuse. It would get him away from Thurmarsh, where Anna's ghost stalked every street. It would get him to London, where every journalist wanted to be, at this time of historical significance.

It was Friday, November 2nd, 1956. There was uproar in the Commons. The Egyptian air force was systematically crippled by bombing raids. The English and French navies were closing on Suez. Henry was closing on Denzil's town house, in a little mews in Chelsea. And feeling, as he moved away from Anna's orbit, more and more angry about world events.

A little jewel, Denzil's town house. Clearly his private means were on a fair old scale. Small, slightly over-full of good Georgian and Victorian furniture. Many vases. Numerous miniatures. Little and pretty, making limping Denzil seem elephantine and clumsy.

Something different about Lampo. What?

'The news is awful,' said Henry.

'Never mind,' said Denzil. 'None of that need touch us here.'

Do we have any right to say that? The words formed themselves, but Henry didn't say them. It wasn't the time.

'Show Henry some of my biscuit tins. He'll find them amusing,' said Denzil. It was suspiciously like an order. We have ways of making you find our biscuit tins amusing. Careful, Henry.

'Biscuit tins?'

'Denzil collects biscuit tins. He has a rather amusing collection.'

Let's tell the Hungarian rebels. It'll be a great consolation to them as they're crushed under tanks. Careful, Henry. Unfair. What harm are Denzil's biscuit tins doing? And this isn't the time. Lampo showed him a Peak, Frean tin, with a buxom black woman carrying an earthenware pot on her head. 'Very nice,' he said, the pitifully inadequate praise of a confused Anglo-Saxon.

He realized what was different about Lampo. He was contented. At the height of his discontent he had consented to spend a weekend with two contented and consenting adults. And they were putting him through this ordeal to thank him! It really took the biscuit. And, to put the tin lid on it, at a time of international crisis they kept showing him biscuit tins. 'Very nice,' he said, as Lampo showed him the Pied Piper of Hamelin, on a limited edition produced by McFarlane, Lang & Co.

Denzil in a blue apron! They had *coq au vin*. Denzil called it 'my famous *coq au vin*'. Velvet wine. And then Armagnac. He'd never drunk Armagnac before. Not the time to ask to see the news.

Bed-time. What a test. Was he capable of truly unselfish emotion? Could he feel free from envy, lying there, separated only by a wall from his two friends? Because . . . it had to be asked . . . had he really failed with Anna because he was, after all, a latent homosexual? A trying night. Not a lot of room for worry about Hungary and Suez.

Fitful sleep. A little self-pity. A few noises from hearty drunks outside. Not much envy, really. The answers to the questions that he'd set himself were cautiously encouraging. Cautiously encouraged, he fell into a deeper sleep.

A man who was vaguely familiar was approaching. The man began to talk. In a few blindingly simple words, he revealed all the secrets of life, its purpose and its conduct. Henry woke feeling utterly exhilarated. All his problems had been solved. The three great crises – Suez, Hungary and his sex life – were crises no more. And then the words faded, dissolved, forgotten, as if they had never been.

Never mind. What a day Denzil and Lampo laid on for him. They went to the Tate Gallery and saw the Braque exhibition. How had he managed to live without cubism? They went to the Paris-Pullman Cinema and saw Fernandel in *Don Camillo's Last*

Round and Jacques Tati in *Monsieur Hulot's Holiday*. How had he managed to live without Jacques Tati? They dined in a little French restaurant where Denzil was known. Oh sophistication! Oh classic, clichéd yearning of an unsophisticated Thurmarsh youth. How had he managed to live without being known in little French restaurants?

He felt no envy, no jealousy. He felt no embarrassment, when Lampo and Denzil touched each other, briefly, illegally, under the table. He no longer felt it strange that Lampo should have fallen for this ageing, limping journalist with the blotched parchment skin.

And on that Sunday morning, the November sunshine streamed into the little house, straight onto a striking picture of several native boats which adorned a Huntley and Palmers biscuit tin. Henry began to feel uneasy about the distance between himself and world events. Lampo and Denzil laughed at him. They felt he was exaggerating his importance in the scale of things.

It was Lampo's turn to cook lunch. They had sole with wine sauce, and flinty white Burgundy. Henry assuaged his conscience by talking about Suez and Hungary. Lampo and Denzil had a phrase for every subject. On Empire: 'The colonists found people who were like children, looked after them and educated them, and then were hurt when they turned into adults.' On politics: 'Politicians always do in a crisis what they should have done in the previous crisis.' On American politics: 'How politicians love peace when other nations are at war.' On Suez: 'The Englishman's traditional love of the underdog is strictly for peacetime only.'

On the train back to reality, the Sunday papers rolled over Henry's pleasure like Russian tanks over Hungarian fingers.

In Budapest, the tanks completed the obliteration of freedom. Radio Budapest was silenced. Its last words were, 'Help Hungary . . . Help . . . Help . . . Help.'

Sterling plunged. The government asked the Americans for help. The Americans wouldn't give it unless we stopped fighting. The Anglo-French invasion stopped, too late to avoid political defeat, too early to bring military victory. Diana Dors denied she was dating Rod Steiger.

In Parliament Square and Whitehall, while Henry had been

admiring biscuit tins, huge crowds had been chanting, 'Eden must go' and, 'Law, not War.' Henry was filled with shame that he hadn't been among them.

Dark days. Rain, drizzle and fog. Suez, Hungary and Henry. Lost illusions. The illusion that Britain could still be a great world power in military terms, could act in isolation from the United States, could alter the geography of the world. The illusion that, in communist Eastern Europe, there could be democracy, freedom or equality. The illusion that Henry Ezra Pratt could love, or be loved.

16   A Sleuth Wakes Slowly

At 9.28 on the evening of Thursday, November 8th, 1956, Henry Pratt entered the large lounge bar of the Winstanley. He was alone and listless.

At 9.29 his spine tingled. Martin Hammond had said that a councillor had arranged to meet a council official in a pub that was something to do with Dr Livingstone. Livingstone had met Stanley. Could he have meant the Winstanley?

He asked Martin from the public phone opposite. 'That's it,' Martin said. 'I knew it was summat to do with Livingstone. Why? Interested at last, are you?' 'I'm beginning to get a gut feeling about it,' said Henry. 'We journalists work on gut feelings. This could end up even bigger than the canary.'

As he returned to the bar, Henry saw Mr Matheson ordering a drink. His spine tingled again, and both the hairs on his chest stood on end. His brain was working at last.

Mr Matheson was a councillor, and he drank in the Winstanley! Henry knew, with that gut feeling of his, that Mr Matheson was *the* councillor. He was looking at Henry strangely. Why was he looking at Henry strangely?

Because Henry was looking at *him* strangely. He tried not to look strange, and approached Mr Matheson.

'Are you all right?' said Mr Matheson.

'I had a terrible pain,' said Henry. 'Indigestion. I'm all right now.'

Mr Matheson didn't look convinced. 'I thought you looked happy,' he said. 'Almost triumphant.'

'I like pain,' said Henry. 'I love indigestion. I went to a public school and became a masochist. I belonged to the indigestion society.' Oh god. Would he never behave normally in the presence of this man?

Mr Matheson looked a little alarmed, then switched his full charm on Henry, who found himself smiling as he accepted a drink. He felt absurdly grateful. This worried him. Perhaps, if Mr

Matheson bought him enough drinks, he'd lose the will to expose his corruption.

'I understand you met Anna and didn't quite hit it off,' said Mr Matheson. 'What a shame. She needs careful handling, Henry. We've probably sheltered her too much. Cheers!'

Henry Pratt, investigative journalist, was in a determined mood. Nothing would stand in the way of his investigations. Never again would he allow himself to become entangled with, or humiliated by, a woman.

His determination lasted until 6.37 on the following evening, when Helen's sister Jill entered the back bar of the Lord Nelson, blushing shyly. Her youthful confusion and sexuality overwhelmed him. Her physical vulnerability, her air of barely controlled emotion, aroused him deeply. He felt as if he'd gone over a hump bridge too fast.

It had been, until Jill's arrival, a rather listless Friday evening. Gordon had said '*Ennui*' and Henry didn't think he'd been referring to a French playwright, though with Gordon you couldn't be sure. Colin had announced he must get home to Glenda. Ben had said it was time to give the wife one. But now they all accepted a drink off Ted. 'Oh, we're staying, are we?' said Ginny, and Gordon said, 'Frail craft. Tidal waves.' Henry tried to go home, but found himself buying a round. He tried to hide his feelings for Jill. He knew he'd failed when Helen pressed her thighs against him.

Another drink came. He was powerless to leave. When Ted said they were going to show Jill the jazz club, he said he'd go for half an hour.

And all the others went too.

The smoky upstairs room at the Devonshire was packed and noisy. Ginny was sullen. She didn't look attractive when sullen. Henry tried to concentrate on the music of Sid Hallett and the Rundlemen. They were playing 'Basin Street Blues'.

Helen said 'Don't you still fancy me at all?' during a particularly loud burst of trumpet. 'You're married,' he said. 'I'm disappointed in you. You're getting boring,' she said. 'I know. Utterly boring.

So, please, Helen, be bored by me, and leave me alone,' he said. She didn't hear him.

He stood close to Jill, almost touching her. After all, it was possible that her remark that she didn't find him attractive had been a subconscious reaction to her fear of the deep feelings he was stirring up in her.

At last he spoke. 'Do you like jazz?' was his sparkling opening remark. She didn't hear him, because 'When the Saints Go Marching In' cannot be played softly. 'They're loud, aren't they?' he said. 'What?' she said. 'They're loud, aren't they?' he said. 'Sorry?' she said. 'It isn't worth repeating,' he said. 'What?' she said. 'I said it isn't worth repeating,' he said. 'What isn't worth repeating?' she said. 'What I said,' he said. 'What did you say?' she said. 'They're loud, aren't they?' he said. 'I can't hear you. They're too loud,' she said.

Ben interrupted. 'Guess the first thing the wife will say to me tomorrow,' he said. 'Oh, shut up, Ben,' said Henry. 'Correct,' said Ben.

When Jill left the room, Henry followed her. He hovered by the top of the stairs, between the bar and the toilets, among the people arriving and departing. When she returned, he said, 'Jill? You remember I asked you out at the wedding?' She blushed and said, 'Yes. I'm sorry. I was a bit rude.' He said, 'Please! I asked for it. Er . . . Jill? You're so incredibly lovely. *Will* you come out some time?' 'You're asking for it again,' she said. 'I don't want to. I think you're horrible. Leave me alone.' Helen walked past and heard! Jill returned to the crowded bar. Helen gave him an angry look. His cheeks blazed.

All he had to do was walk down the stairs and go home. But he couldn't run away. Pride demanded that he went in and finished his drink. Then he'd make his escape.

'We're going to the Shanghai for a curry afterwards,' said Ted. 'Are you coming?'

'Count me in,' he said.

They met in the Labour Club, of which Tommy was an honorary member. Henry bought two halves of bitter. They sat in a discreet corner, beneath a portrait of Ramsay MacDonald. They could hear the clunk of snooker balls from the back room. The carpet was red.

Tommy unveiled his second scoop. The team was going to make a record, to play to a small boy who was in a coma.

'Terrific,' said Henry. 'Who says footballers have no heart?'

Tommy Marsden looked at him suspiciously.

'I may have another scoop an' all soon,' he said.

'What sort of a scoop?'

'I'm not at liberty to say anything yet.'

'Give over, Tommy,' said Henry. 'We're friends. Former members of the Paradise Lane Gang. You can trust me.'

Tommy looked at him doubtfully.

'Have a drink,' said Henry.

He bought two glasses of bitter.

'I may be going on t'transfer list,' said Tommy. 'You'll be t'first to know if I do.'

'Leave Thurmarsh?' said Henry.

'Can Muir and Ayers give me the through balls I need if I'm to utilize my speed? Can they buggery? I've got the scoring instincts of a predatory panther, and I'm being sacrificed on the altar of mid-table mediocrity.'

'You've been reading too many press reports.'

'You what?'

'Nothing.'

'I've got a lethal left foot.'

'Your right arm's not too bad either.'

'You what?'

'Nothing. Have a drink.'

Henry bought two glasses of bitter.

'What about loyalty to the team that made you?' said Henry. 'What about loyalty to the town that took an urchin off the streets and turned him into a star?'

'You've been reading too many press reports,' said Tommy. 'Listen. Only last night I heard about one of t'directors, who's buying up half t'town centre dirt cheap so he can redevelop it at vast profits. Loyalty to Thurmarsh? Don't make me laugh.'

'Which director?' said Henry.

'I've told you too much already,' said Tommy.

Henry bought two glasses of bitter. This time it didn't work.

It didn't matter. His spine had tingled again. He had his gut feeling again. This tied up with Mr Matheson and the corrupt council official, or he wasn't Henry 'The man nobody muzzles' Pratt.

In Hungary there were acute food shortages. Ten million people refused to go to work. The future of the Soviet puppet régime of Mr Kadar hung in the balance.

It would take months to clear the ships that were blocking the Suez Canal. The Anglo-French forces and the Israelis refused to retreat until a United Nations peace-keeping force was installed. Colonel Nasser refused to behave as if he'd been defeated.

On the evening of Thursday, November 16th, Henry 'The man nobody muzzles' Pratt installed himself in a corner of the large, over-furnished, over-decorated, surprisingly Caledonian lounge bar of the Winstanley, in the hope that Mr Matheson was a creature of habit, and would again meet the corrupt council official after the council meeting.

He sipped his beer slowly, and read Anna's letter for the fifth time. It belonged to the 'anyway' school of letter-writing.

Dear Henry [she'd written]

Thank you for your letter, and I'm sorry I've taken so long to reply. You know how things are. Anyway, I'm writing at last.

Frankly, I think I must have had a bit too much to drink that night. Anyway, I'm sorry I did what I did and I certainly don't blame you for what happened. Or didn't happen! Thank you for taking me out and for asking me out again.

Anyway, I'm afraid I'll have to say no, because something has cropped up. A man I've known for some time has asked me to live with him. He's quite a bit older than me, but very kind, and I like him. Anyway, after much soul-searching I've decided to go. Who knows if it'll work, but then I'm not sure if I'm ready for marriage and babies and all that just yet. If ever! Squealing brats I call them. Anyway, we'll see.

Anyway, Henry, there's one thing I'd seriously like to say. It's none of my business, of course, but I honestly think you went for the wrong one that day in Siena. Old Hillers is pretty desperate for a man, though unfortunately she doesn't realize it. She's very serious and high-minded but I think you are too. You're both fairly screwed up (in the nicest possible way!) and I think your repressions might be made for each other. I hope you don't mind me saying this.

Anyway, all the very best for the future, and I'm still glad I met you and that you asked me out.

Lots of love

Anna

PS If you run into my parents, please don't tell them all this. They think I'm staying with my pen-friend, a dreary girl who wants to become a nun! Ugh!

The thought of pale, repressed, mentally ill Hilary, with her horrible body, appalled him. Anyway – oh god, Anna's style must be catching – he resented being described as screwed up and regarded as a last resort for lost girls who were desperate for a man.

The bar was filling up steadily, with the pipe-smoking, dog-owning populace of the neighbourhood. Ginny Fenwick and Gordon Carstairs entered. They joined him, which was awkward, but he could hardly object. Besides, he was always happy to be in close proximity to Ginny. She might yet become his lover when she finally accepted that Gordon would never leave his wife.

'May I tell Henry?' she asked.

'Burgess and Maclean,' replied Gordon.

Ginny interpreted this as meaning 'yes'. 'Gordon's wife has left him,' she said.

Henry felt absurdly depressed by this news. And he didn't know what to say. 'Congratulations,' seemed unfair to Hazel. 'Oh, I am sorry,' was clearly inappropriate. He settled on 'Ah!' There was a pause, as if they expected more. They weren't going to get it. After all, he didn't even know if he was supposed to know that Gordon had been intending to leave her. And already his mind was whirring with the possible implications on his domestic peace. Would there be more or less amorous couplings above his head?

'Er . . .' he said. 'Will you . . . er . . . er . . . live in your house, then, Gordon?'

'No,' said Gordon. 'Kippered walls.'

'He means it's dripping with evidence of marital bitterness,' said Ginny. 'The walls are stained with smoked fish thrown in anger.'

'Ginny's got it!' said Gordon.

'So, you'll . . . er . . . live in the flat, then?'

'Tick tock,' said Gordon. 'Tick tock.'

'My flat is a place of clock-watching, of snatched moments, soured by tension and insecurity,' explained Ginny.

'Ginny's got it!' said Gordon.

Henry was forced to say, yet again, 'I hope you'll both be very happy.' He added a mordant rider: 'I always thought Ginny'd make somebody a very good interpreter.'

Gordon laughed, said, 'Fifteen, love!' and chalked up a score on an invisible blackboard.

'So you'll find somewhere else to live?' Henry asked.

'Somewhere that's totally ours,' said Gordon with surprising clarity.

Ginny smiled proudly. Suddenly Henry no longer felt crabby and jealous. He kissed her warmly and said, 'I hope you'll be very happy, love,' in a voice that only just avoided cracking.

He bought them a drink.

It was almost closing time when Mr Matheson entered with a thick-set, grey-haired man with a long nose and a heavily lined face. Could he be the council official? Henry's heart was pumping. He offered Ginny and Gordon another drink. 'I buy the drinks tonight,' he said. 'To show how happy I am for you.'

'Game, set and match to Pratt H.,' said Gordon.

Henry almost blushed. How he wished that were his real reason, rather than the only way he could think of for meeting Mr Matheson's contact without arousing the curiosity of his two colleagues.

'Hello, Mr Matheson,' he said. 'We're going to have to stop meeting like this.'

Mr Matheson looked as if nothing would please him more. Then his good manners took over. 'Henry Pratt!' he said. 'Hello!'

'I'm a reporter on the *Argus*,' said Henry to the grey-haired man, in a tone which he hoped would sound a little threatening if he was corrupt, but not too rude if he wasn't.

'Howard Lewthwaite,' said the grey-haired man.

Hilary's father! Good lord!

'*Councillor* Lewthwaite,' said Mr Matheson.

Councillor Lewthwaite smiled at Henry as if to suggest that he would never dream of pulling rank.

Henry felt disappointed. The man was a councillor, so he couldn't be the corrupt official.

'Hilary's father?' he said.

'Yes.'

'Good Lord. What a coincidence.'

'Not really,' said Mr Matheson. 'It's through our friendship that our daughters met.'

'I met Hilary and Anna in Siena,' explained Henry to Mr Lewthwaite.

'Yes. Hilary mentioned it,' said Mr Lewthwaite. 'I think she liked you.'

'Good Lord,' said Henry and Mr Matheson.

Henry felt insulted that Mr Matheson had also said, 'Good Lord!' But Mr Lewthwaite explained.

'Yes,' he said. 'She doesn't have a good word for many men.' He sighed. 'She's a problem.'

As Henry bought his round, he had to fight against his desire to accept that, because Mr Lewthwaite was not a corrupt council official, Mr Matheson was innocent. And this because the man had smiled at him twice! Pull yourself together, he told himself. Fight his charm. Never trust a man who smiles too much. Otherwise, you won't be worthy of being called Henry 'The man nobody muzzles' Pratt.

Henry began to realize how difficult it is to conduct an investigation when your employer, your colleagues, and – most difficult of all – the objects of your investigations mustn't know about it.

A minor inspiration attended his next move, however. He met Ben Watkinson in the Blonk, after the match, in which Thurmarsh beat Workington 3–1 with goals from MUIR, AYERS and GRAVEL, who didn't look, respectively, yellow, thick and knackered. Indeed, they all had better games than Tommy. The embers of hero-worship were cooling, as surely, if more slowly, than they had cooled for Tosser Pilkington-Brick.

The Blonk was a large, brick-built road house at the junction of Blonk Lane and Doncaster Road. It was a cold, bare cathedral of booze. Yet sometimes, before matches, when it was thick with smoke and laughter and the good humour of the visiting supporters, it was possible to sense, in that badly heated barn, a throbbing vitality, a good-natured tolerance, a sharpness of cheerfully cynical humour which still made Britain, at times, to Henry, in 1956, an exhilarating place in which to live.

There was a hint, in the air, of the cruel power of a northern winter, but the memory of victory kept the supporters warm as they attacked the smooth, silky Mansfield bitter.

'Name all the Club's directors and their occupations,' said Henry.

Ben's eyes lit up. 'Clive Woodriffe, solicitor,' he said. 'Ted Teague, funeral director.'

'Correct,' said Henry, who had no idea whether it was.

'Laurie Joyce, road haulage contractor. Colin Gee, property developer.'

Ah! 'Correct.'

'Sid Kettlewell, steel baron. Roland Padgett, cutlery magnate. One more.' Ben stared at his beer, brow furrowed in concentration. 'Sorry. It's gone. Put me out of my misery.'

This was awkward. 'I can't.'

'You mean you don't know?'

'No. No! What I mean is . . . I don't want to see you defeated. I'll give you five minutes.'

For four minutes they both suffered. 'It begins with G,' moaned Ben. 'I know it begins with G.' Then his eyes shone with triumph. 'Fred Hathersage, property developer.'

Oh no! There were two property developers.

They met in the Liberal Club, of which Tommy was an honorary member. Henry bought two glasses of bitter. They sat in a quiet recess, below a portrait of Asquith. They could hear the clunk of snooker balls from the back room. The carpet couldn't decide whether to be orange or green.

Henry said he thought Muir, Ayers and Gravel had played well.

'One swallow doesn't make a summer,' said Tommy.

No, thought Henry, but three swallows make an empty glass. 'Same again?' he said.

'No, *I'll* get *you* a drink,' said Tommy.

'Oh. Thanks.' Henry tried not to sound surprised.

Tommy didn't move.

'About that business you were telling me about,' said Henry. 'Which bit of Thurmarsh is Colin Gee getting his hot little hands on?'

'It isn't Colin Gee,' said Tommy. 'He's all right, Colin.'

So it was Fred Hathersage. Henry felt ashamed of his ruse, now that it had succeeded so easily. Magnanimous in victory, he said, 'Same again, is it?'

'I've said . . . I'll get you a drink,' said Tommy.

'So which bit of Thurmarsh is Fred Hathersage getting his hot little hands on?' said Henry.

'I've told you too much already,' said Tommy Marsden.

Henry couldn't bear their empty glasses any more.

'Look, let me get the drinks,' he said.

'I've told you. I'm getting you a drink,' said Tommy.

A middle-aged man emerged from the snooker room, with two empty glasses. His eyes lit up as he saw Tommy.

'Tommy Marsden!' he said. 'By 'eck, that were a cracker you scored against Oldham. What are you having?'

'Oh. Ta very much, Mr Grout,' said Tommy. 'I'll have a pint of bitter. And so will my friend Henry.'

Tommy Marsden smiled.

'Told you I'd get you a drink,' he said.

There were at least 49 obstacles blocking the Suez Canal, and almost as many obstacles blocking a political solution of the crisis. The Prime Minister cancelled all engagements, due to overstrain. In Hungary, the régime was having great difficulty in persuading a hostile populace to go back to work.

Henry telephoned Fred Hathersage from a telephone box in Market Street, opposite Howard Lewthwaite's drapery shop. Not that he had any interest in Hilary, having no great yen for screwed

238

up, repressed, high-minded, mentally ill problem girls with horrible bodies.

'I'll see if Mr Hathersage can speak to you,' said his secretary. 'He *is* in conference.'

Henry noticed two gaping holes on the eastern side of Market Street, both quite close to Lewthwaite's. You don't go up to somebody with several teeth missing and say, 'My word! Your remaining teeth are magnificent!' The gaps discredit the whole mouth. So it was with the eastern side of Market Street.

'Mr Hathersage could see you next week,' said his secretary.

A young woman of about Hilary's height emerged from Lewthwaite's and crossed the road. But it wasn't her.

'Would that be all right?' said Mr Hathersage's secretary.

'Fine. I'll see him then, then,' he said.

He had to ring back to find out that his appointment was for 3 p.m. next Wednesday. Could the sight of a girl who might have been Hilary throw him into such confusion? That was ridiculous.

The first Hungarian refugees arrived in Britain. Petrol was to be rationed to 200 miles a month from December 17th. The Prime Minister left for three weeks' complete rest in Jamaica, on doctor's orders.

It was not without trepidation that Henry 'The man nobody muzzles' Pratt approached Construction House, an unprepossessing raw concrete block set back off Doncaster Road, and fronted by an area of dead, sodden grass, pitted with worm casts. He was faced again with the recurring problem that he couldn't ask the questions he wanted to ask without revealing that those were the questions that he wanted to ask.

Fred Hathersage's office was on the third floor. 'Mr Hathersage is in conference,' said his secretary, who had scarlet nails. She flashed him his ration of smile – three-quarters of a second.

After seven minutes, during which nobody emerged, Henry was ushered into a large room from which there was no other exit. Fred Hathersage was alone, seated behind a huge, heart-shaped desk. It seemed that, after their conference, his colleagues must have been lowered to the ground by window-cleaner's cradle.

Fred Hathersage was bulky and bald. When he stood up, Henry

couldn't quite hide his surprise at finding that he was only five foot two. Fred Hathersage couldn't quite hide his displeasure at the surprise that Henry hadn't quite hidden. But he said, 'Mr Pratt!' as if Henry's appearance in his office was the culmination of a lifetime's ambition. The handshake was vicious, though.

Henry sat in a chair which dwarfed him.

'I'm . . . er . . . planning a series of articles called "Proud Sons of Thurmarsh",' he said. 'I wanted to produce a dummy article first.'

'And you thought I'd be a suitable dummy.'

'Yes. No! I mean . . . I thought you'd make a good guinea-pig. I mean, an article on you would help sell the series to the editor.'

Fred Hathersage was flattered. He talked freely. He'd begun life on a building site. (Childhood was discounted entirely, since it had earned him nothing.) He'd worked his way up, founded his own company, gone into armaments. Regretfully, he'd decided that his skill in making armaments would be more use to his country in war than his less proven ambition as a fighting man. After the War he'd made it his mission to help repair the damage caused by the Luftwaffe. A new Thurmarsh. A better Thurmarsh, rising from the ashes like a phoenix, he said, waving his arms excitedly in the direction of a photograph of the south elevation of the controversial new Splutt ambulance station, which had risen from the ashes like a controversial new ambulance station. If he could die feeling that he'd embellished Thurmarsh and its environs, he'd die a happy man.

When he stopped – he was panting considerably, and probably *had* to stop, for medical reasons – Henry took a deep breath, stared at a photograph of the north elevation of the controversial new headquarters of the Thurmarsh and Rawlaston Building Society, which couldn't possibly embellish any environs, and said, 'Do you have any large-scale plans with regard to Thurmarsh town centre, Mr Hathersage?'

'Nothing concrete,' said Fred Hathersage.

'Oh good,' said Henry. 'I don't like concrete.'

Fred Hathersage glared at him.

'It was a joke,' said Henry.

Fred Hathersage exploded into a condemnation of youthful cynicism, of lack of respect for authority, of louts who defaced controversial ambulance stations. When he stopped – he was panting considerably, and probably *had* to stop, for medical reasons – Henry apologized and asked again if he had plans for the town centre.

'Nothing definite,' said Fred Hathersage. 'But, should urban renewal become desirable in certain areas, I'd like to hope that local people, who understand Thurmarsh, would be entrusted with it. What would outsiders be interested in? Profits. Money. LSD. Pounds, shillings and pence. Lolly. Ackers. Lucre. Shekels. The old spondulicks.' Fred Hathersage realized that he was getting quite excited at discovering how many words there were for money. He changed the subject. 'I'd like to see a city of the future rise up on the banks of the Rundle. A city of magic. A city of glass.'

'What about our old buildings, our heritage?' said Henry.

'I like old buildings,' said Fred Hathersage. 'But they're old. Does the future lie in the past? Does it?'

'No.'

'Precisely! Listen. My ambition is to provide work so that there'll never be another depression. Lasting, decently paid work. The working people of Thurmarsh are very close to my heart.' Fred Hathersage thumped himself inaccurately, to illustrate this. It seemed to Henry that the working people of Thurmarsh were actually very close to Fred Hathersage's wallet.

'But do you not have a Rolls-Royce, and a huge pseudo-Gothic mansion above Thurmarsh Lane Bottom?' said Henry, who'd done his research.

'I have to,' said Fred Hathersage. 'Regrettably, we live in a world where appearances matter. I'm a plain man, Mr Pratt. I'm proud to say I prefer tinned salmon to the real thing. Why not? It's nature improved by technology. But could I drive up to the Midland Hotel in an old Austin Seven and order tinned salmon with bottled mayonnaise? It'd be, "Hey up, old Hathersage must be on t'rocks." Such comments in the business jungle can be self-fulfilling. So, it's fresh salmon and lobster thermidor, when I long for fish and chips. It's a sacrifice I have to make. I'm a prisoner of my success.'

Henry had a dreadful thought. Fred Hathersage didn't mean a

word of it. Then he had an even more dreadful thought. He meant every word.

As he walked down Doncaster Road, Henry had an uneasy feeling that his article, if ever printed, would make him a laughing stock. He also had an uneasy feeling that he hadn't got very far with his inquiries.

He wanted fresh air, and took a roundabout route back to the news-room. It took him, as it chanced, past Lewthwaite's. He'd proved that he couldn't cope with healthy, unrepressed women with beautiful bodies. Perhaps Hilary represented the only kind of girl with whom he could cope. Maybe she worked in the shop, if her condition was stable enough to permit her to work anywhere.

At the last moment he didn't dare go in. He walked along Market Street, past Fish Hill, turned left into Rundle Prospect and went for a cup of tea in the Rundle Café. It was a grey, raw November evening, fading almost imperceptibly into night. The café was hot and bright and steamy.

He had seen, in Siena, that Hilary was interested in the arts. She'd been brought up in the narrow world of English provincial drapery. Her friends were philistines. Her father was a Tory politician. She thirsted for culture, for art, for wide horizons. Could not her mental problems be because of this? Mentally sick she might be, but perhaps not irremediably so, if given the patient love of a gentle, caring young man. Shy and repressed, but not irremediably so, if warmed in the love of an amusing and witty young man about town, even if the town he was about was only Thurmarsh. But he had friends in Hampstead and Chelsea. He had an aunt who'd been to Cap Ferrat. Who better to introduce this unsophisticated girl to the great world outside, to art, literature, theatre, gastronomy?

Henry 'Sisley's late haystacks are amazing' Pratt stepped out from his glittering mind into the cold blackness of a Thurmarsh evening. He hurried up Rundle Prospect, and turned right into Market Street.

Henry 'Don't have the *pamplemousse*, darling, it's only grapefruit' Pratt boldly entered the dingy interior of Lewthwaite's. On all sides there were vast rolls of pink and brown material. He approached Mr Lewthwaite.

'I . . . er . . . I happened to be passing,' he said, in a voice whose nervousness would have revealed to somebody a great deal less shrewd than Howard Lewthwaite that there was nothing remotely casual about this encounter. 'I . . . er . . . I wondered if Hilary was around . . . at all. I've some photos of Siena I'd like to show her.'

'I'm afraid she's away,' said Howard Lewthwaite. 'We aren't expecting her back for some time.'

Away! Not expected back for some time! Henry had visions of high walls topped by broken glass, of a huge dark building with rows of depressingly small windows, and an air of deadly calm.

'Away?' he managed to croak.

'At Durham University. She's in her final year there.'

17   Proud Sons of Thurmarsh

On Monday, December 3rd, Selwyn Lloyd told gloomy Tories and contemptuous socialists that it was safe for the British and French forces to withdraw from Egypt, though the French pointed out that there were no guarantees that the United Nations force would remain. In the middle of typing the sentence 'There's a double dose of delight for connoisseurs of the creepy at the Roxy next week when sci-fi shocker X *The Unknown* is paired with gruesome French frightener *The Fiends*,' Henry was summoned to the editor's office.

Mr Andrew Redrobe liked his article on Fred Hathersage! Asked to suggest follow-ups, he could only think of Tommy Marsden. The editor suggested Peter Matheson. 'He *is* the Thurmarsh Conservatives. He also happens to be a close personal friend of mine, but that's irrelevant.' He left the editor's office dazed, thrilled and horrified in equal proportions.

On Tuesday, December 4th, thousands of Budapest housewives forced their way past Russian soldiers and heaped flowers on the tomb of Hungary's unknown warrior. Britain's roads were littered with cars that had run out of fuel. The *Daily Telegraph* said that the whole Suez affair had been bungled by the government to an incredible degree.

Henry interviewed Tommy Marsden for his series 'Proud Sons of Thurmarsh'. Tommy said that he'd thought of moving to a bigger club, but had decided that his future lay with the town that had taken an urchin off the streets, and turned him into a star.

On Wednesday, December 5th, women spat and jeered at tanks in Budapest, Judy Grinham won a sixth gold medal for Britain in the Melbourne Olympics, and Henry's portrait of Fred Hathersage was unleashed upon an unsuspecting Thurmarsh.

On Thursday, December 6th, 50 workers' leaders were arrested in Hungary, and Fred Hathersage complained about Henry's article. Henry was summoned again.

'I never made this attack on young people. I like young people,' said Fred Hathersage.

'Do you have your shorthand notes, Henry?' said Mr Andrew Redrobe.

Henry, who hadn't kept up his shorthand lessons, went to his desk, produced a notebook full of somebody else's old shorthand notes, reserved for just such a purpose, and handed it to Fred Hathersage. Fred Hathersage stared at the meaningless scrawls blankly, while the editor examined the shiny wet roofs of the town.

'Oh, well, I may have done,' admitted the diminutive property developer grudgingly.

On Friday, December 7th, the Anglo-French forces withdrew 20 miles from the Suez front line. To add to the fury of retired majors everywhere, they were replaced by Indians. The entire parish council of Puddletown decided to resign unless Dorset County Council rescinded its decision to change the name to Piddletown.

Henry wrote a letter to Hilary.

> Dear Hilary [he wrote]
> This grey Thurmarsh December day makes me think of Siena in September. What a pleasant lunch that was. I found out from your father that you're at Durham University. I expect you'll be back for Christmas. It'd give me great pleasure if I could take you out some time. Perhaps you'd get in touch when you get back. You can phone me at the *Argus* or write to 239, Winstanley Road.
> I do hope we can meet.
> With all best wishes
> Henry (Pratt)

Henry was pleased that he'd written. His one regret was that it was possibly the dullest letter in the history of the universe.

On Saturday, December 8th, Russian 'storm units' poured into Budapest. Scores of Hungarians were killed in clashes with police and Russian troops. Henry received a letter from Auntie Doris. It was in the 'inverted commas' school of letter-writing, which seemed to be taking stronger and stronger hold of Auntie Doris as she grew older.

Dear Henry [she'd written]

Geoffrey and I'd love it if you could come for Christmas, but of course we'll understand if you have to spend it with 'the sniffer'. (I shouldn't call her that. Smack smack, naughty Doris.) Poor dear, I don't expect she's got anybody, and you've got to sympathize even though it's her own fault. We can't have her here, we've advertised a festive Christmas and people might demand their money back. We're 'full to the rafters' but one of our customers could put you up, all very nice, no 'slumming it'! I do hope you'll come. I'll never forget what you did regarding poor Teddy and like to think that if he'd lived we'd have 'worked something out'. Not that I'm unhappy. Geoffrey is good to me, but two waitresses have left recently, so I suspect he's 'up to his old games'. So you see I'm a bit of a lonely old bird. It's my big regret I never had children. It was 'not for want of trying', as they say. So you see you are my son to me, and I hope you'll come.

With lots of love from your soft old auntie.

XXXXXXXXXXXXXXXXXXXXXXXXX (One for each year, one for luck and one for Christmas)

On Sunday, December 9th, martial law was declared in Hungary, there was the first feeble sign of United Nations interest in clearing the Suez Canal and, at the end of a mild, wet afternoon, Henry walked through the Alderman Chandler Memorial Park towards Cousin Hilda's. Three barn owls sat miserably on a rail in the tiny aviary, beside the sad animal cages. On the pond a mandarin duck looked absurdly ornate in the gloom. The park keeper was waiting, with the over-emphasized patience of the congenitally impatient, to lock up.

A faint aura of expiring sprouts drifted through the silent house. The stove was glowing.

'I wondered what's happening about Christmas?' he said, after the preliminaries.

'What do you mean . . . "what's happening?"?' said Cousin Hilda.

'Well, I've been invited by Auntie Doris.'

Cousin Hilda sniffed. 'I could say summat about guilty consciences,' she said, 'but I won't.'

'She says I'm like a son to her.'

'I suppose you aren't to me!'

'She never said that.'

'Some folks don't need to. Some folks are very good at hinting.'

'So I wondered . . . er . . . what you were planning?'

'I'm giving the Canaries a miss this year.'

He managed a laugh.

'And I've sent my regrets to Sandringham.'

He managed another laugh.

'I just wondered,' he said, 'whether you'd be . . . er . . . alone. Or whether you'll spend it with Mrs Wedderburn.'

'Mrs Wedderburn's three sons are very good to her and have her in turn on a strict rota system.'

Henry found it hard to imagine that Mrs Wedderburn had ever made love three times.

'Are they triplets?' he asked.

'Whatever makes you say that?'

'Nothing. I wondered if . . . er . . . any of your "businessmen" will be with you.'

Cousin Hilda opened the cracked glass doors of the stove, and poked around unnecessarily.

'Mr O'Reilly will be here,' she said. 'He has nobody. It's sad.'

'And Mr Pettifer?'

'Yes. He seems to have washed his hands of his whole family.'

'And Mr Whatsisname, who's used to fine things?'

'Peters. I understand there's a sister in Morecambe.' Cousin Hilda sniffed. 'I dare say her house is chock-a-block with fine things.'

'And Mr Chelmsford, with his hygiene problem?'

'Brentwood.' Cousin Hilda went pink. 'I'll make some tea,' she said, and went into the scullery, where she banged about.

He went to the door of the scullery and got a welcome breath of air. The last of the light was fading over the mercilessly pruned rose bushes and tiny, sodden lawn.

'Mr Brentwood's left,' she said. 'It was right embarrassing. Oh, I *was* embarrassed. Norman Pettifer and Mr Peters gave me an ultimatum. Either him or them. I said, "Give him a chance. I'll give him a fortnight's grace. If he still smells at the end of it, he's out."'

'What did you say to him?'

'I said, "May I have a word on a personal matter, Mr Brentwood?" "Personal matter?" he said. "I've had complaints," I said. "Complaints?" he said. "That you smell," I said. "Smell? Smell where?" he said, going very white. "In my basement," I said. "No. I mean where on me do I smell?" he said. I haven't been so embarrassed since I asked Mr O'Reilly's advice when you had your little problem when you were little with your little . . .'

'Backside.'

'Precisely. "Nowhere in particular, Mr Brentwood. All over," I said. "I believe the technical term is BO." He said something very unnecessary. He said "I suppose you're telling me that BO stands for . . ." I can't say it.'

'Bugger off.'

'Precisely. I said "Mr Brentwood! Only one person has ever spoken to me like that in my life, and that was a parrot!" I said, "You've a fortnight's grace to get things right. All bath charges are suspended for the duration." He left next morning. I found a note. "Thank you for telling me what you told me. It must have required courage and I'm sorry I was rude but I was mortified. I know what has to be done and I'll do it, but I can't face that lot downstairs."'

'I'll spend Christmas with you, and go to Troutwick afterwards,' said Henry.

Cousin Hilda sniffed.

'As you wish,' she said.

On Monday, December 10th, Henry interviewed Mr Matheson for 'Proud Sons of Thurmarsh', in Tudor Lodge. Mr Matheson took him into his study, and gave him twelve-year-old malt whisky from a cut-glass decanter. He had a paperweight in the form of Sir Winston Churchill, complete with cigar.

Henry was hoping that on Thursday, after the council meeting, he would catch Mr Matheson with the council official, thus completing the link. Until then he was lying low.

Mr Matheson talked about his vision of a universally prosperous Thurmarsh, and believed it could be achieved if the people on the shop floor weren't greedy. He went pale when Henry asked whether it would matter if the managerial and professional classes were greedy, but the moment passed and his self-command returned. He was a lounge iguana, basking on the rock of his certainty, in the sun of his self-esteem. The power and smoothness of his charm, and of his whisky, made disliking him hard work, but Henry wasn't frightened of hard work, and kept thinking, 'You wait. I'll get you.'

On Tuesday, December 11th, the IRA blew up a BBC relay system in Londonderry, the Postmaster-General, Dr Hill, announced that the BBC and ITV would be allowed to fill the 6–7 p.m. gap, hitherto sacrosanct so that children could be put to bed, Henry's interview with Tommy Marsden appeared as the second in his series 'Proud Sons of Thurmarsh', and Tommy Marsden was transferred to Manchester United for £18,000, without telling Henry.

On Wednesday, December 12th, more Soviet troops moved into Hungary, where there was still a general strike 'unique in the whole history of the labour movement', and Henry reviewed the Splutt Vale Iron and Steel Company's pantomime. Martin Hammond was Widow Twankey. He was terrible. Henry praised everybody. Truth was too precious to be wasted on such trivia.

On Thursday, December 13th, two Ulster barracks were bombed, 52 terrorists were held in Cyprus, there were angry demonstrations and arrests in Poland, double white lines were introduced on British roads, and Mr Matheson entered the lounge bar of the Winstanley with a paunchy, careworn, balding, middle-aged man who was threatening to burst out of a shiny suit in several places.

Henry approached them and said, 'Hello, Mr Matheson. Can I get you and your friend a drink?'

'No, thank you,' said Mr Matheson, putting an affectionate arm on Henry's shoulder. 'We have a personal matter to discuss.'

'Oh. Right,' said Henry.

'Let me get you one, though.'

'No, thank you. Not if you've . . .'

'. . . a personal matter to discuss,' said the balding man in the disastrous suit.

'I'm Henry Pratt, incidentally. I'm a reporter on the *Argus*.'

'Nice to meet you, Henry.' The balding man held out a limp, fat hand. It was like shaking an exhausted flounder.

There were several things Henry might have said. 'What's your name, you secretive swine?' 'Personal matter? That's a laugh.' 'You think you needn't worry about me, don't you? Well, you're wrong. Nobody muzzles Henry "The man nobody muzzles" Pratt.'

What he actually said was, 'Well, I mustn't keep you from your personal matter.'

On Friday, December 14th, the Queen Mary arrived in New York 17 hours late after making a detour because the Greek captain of a Panamanian cargo ship had a persistent nosebleed. Henry arrived at the Rundle Café more than two hours late after hanging around outside the Town Hall, in the cold of the gathering winter, hoping to see the balding official return from lunch, hoping to stalk him through the corridors of local power and identify him as he entered his office. In vain. At five past three, freezing and starving, he attacked his dried-up meat and potato pie with relish. He recognized the man having a cup of tea at the next table.

'George Timpley, of Timpley and Nephews!' he said. 'I interviewed you on the night of the fire.'

'By 'eck,' said George Timpley. 'I thought I knew you.'

'How are you?' said Henry, thickly, through overcooked pastry.

'I've been condemned.'

'You what?'

'My shop. Condemned. By the council.'

Henry moved over to join him.

'I say condemned,' said George Timpley. 'They haven't actually condemned it as such. They've offered to buy it. If I don't sell, they'll make a demolition order on the grounds that it's unsafe. That's tantamount to condemnation, i'n't it?'

'It's blackmail. What are you going to do?'

'I'm going to sell. What else can I do, next to a blackened hole? An empty site rubs off on neighbouring properties. Her in corner house on end's selling an' all.'

'Corner house? What corner house?'

'Next to me on me right, on t' corner wi' Rundle Prospect. They say she's unsafe an' all.'

Henry began to think seriously about the area around the Cap Ferrat. But still not seriously enough.

On Saturday, December 15th, the Japanese actor Sessue Hayakawa got carried away by his role and punched Alec Guinness on the nose during the filming of *The Bridge on the River Kwai*. Alec Guinness accepted his apology and said, 'I'm bleeding for my art.' On the eve of petrol rationing, almost all petrol stations were closed. Henry bought Christmas presents, including a tea-cosy and tartan bedsocks for Cousin Hilda, a box of exotic honeys for Auntie Doris and cigars for Geoffrey Porringer. His other purchases were less inspired and need not detain us.

On Sunday, December 16th, the AA gave hundreds of stranded motorists enough petrol to get home. Henry, on foot, explored the area between Market Street and the river. The weather was cold, with a thin wind across the Rundle. Exhausted Siberian snow clouds dropped listless sleet over the silent Sunday town.

Three small streets, Canal View, Fish Hill and Rundle Prospect, ran eastwards down the gentle slope from Market Street to the river. Three small streets, Tannery Road, Malmesbury Street and Glasshouse Lane, ran at right angles to them. The whole area had an air of blight. Right at the centre of it was the great hole where the Cap Ferrat had been. There were other, smaller gaps in this neglected, stained mouth. Several teeth needed filling badly. Others were ripe only for extraction. The Old Apothecary's House still had a gaping cavity, where old rubbish gathered. The Roxy Cinema, that yellowing old molar, no longer bothered to replace posters which wags had altered to Poxy. There were four empty cottages in Canal View. Several warehouses in Glasshouse Lane were boarded up, their trade gone when the Rundle silted. The Elite Guest House was elite no longer. The Old Gas Showrooms were used by Snugkoat Ltd as a store. Several tiles had slipped on the roof of the Paragon Surplus Stores. Outside number 11, Tannery Road, the board that announced 'Tarpaulins Made, Hired and Repaired' had come loose at one end and was hanging towards the uneven pavement. On the peeling shop front of number 6, Fish Hill, the sign announced ' ontinental patisserie'. Nothing was quite right in these streets. In the Artisan's Rest, the bitter tasted like liquid hair. The landlord said, 'We don't see strangers of a Sunday' so accusingly that Henry almost said, 'I'm sorry. I'll go.'

And yet, in those modest streets, there were good simple buildings, Georgian, Victorian, Edwardian. If they were improved, if the warehouses were restored, if the gaps were sensitively filled, it could become a delightful area. Henry Pratt, investigative journalist, would fight to discover the truth. Henry Pratt, proud son of Thurmarsh, would fight to preserve what remained of the heritage of his town.

On Monday, December 17th, Hilary rang him at the office. Canal View, Fish Hill, Rundle Prospect, Tannery Road, Malmesbury Street and Glasshouse Lane were forgotten.

18   A Festive Season

He entered the gleaming back bar of the Pigeon and Two Cushions three minutes late. The Christmas decorations were rather sparse. She was already there, dressed in a black jumper and a rather demure check dress in two shades of green. He was no more nervous than any young man would be who was taking out a screwed up, repressed, depressed, high-minded, mentally ill problem girl with a horrible body.

She kissed him lightly on the cheek. He took off his duffel-coat and bought drinks. He glanced at her body. Its repulsiveness didn't appear to be due to abnormality of shape. She was less thin than he'd remembered, and taller. As tall as him. She had a long, serious nose and a wide, really rather beautiful mouth. Her eyes were a deep brown. He sensed a wariness in them. She was extremely pale.

'You're very pale,' he said. 'Have you been ill?'

'People are always asking me that,' she said. 'No. I'm as fit as a fiddle. I just am very pale.'

He asked if she'd eaten. She'd had enough not to starve if they didn't eat, but not so much that she couldn't shovel in a bit more if they did. This surprised him. He remembered her as a poor eater. He wondered if her mental illness consisted of bouts of starving herself and gorging herself. He went to the phone, with a decisiveness that surprised him, and rang Donny's Bar. They had one table left. He booked it.

She asked him about his work. He spoke briefly about it, then changed the subject to her studies. She was reading English. He asked about her course. He was so busy sieving her replies for evidence of mental illness that their sense escaped him entirely. He hoped she hadn't noticed, and tuned back in hurriedly. 'But don't let's talk about me,' she said. 'I'm boring.' It was a statement of fact, not a coquettish attempt to elicit a protesting 'No, you aren't!'

Oscar came on duty and smiled at them. Henry told Hilary

about him, his colds and constipation. Strangely, considering how serious and high-minded she was, she laughed.

He ordered drinks, introduced Hilary, and asked Oscar how he was.

'I've had a touch of flu. Otherwise, mustn't grumble,' he said. 'Except for my little trouble.'

'Your little trouble?'

'Summat I wouldn't like to discuss in front of a lady.'

Hilary ordered the next round and even offered Oscar a drink. He beamed his approval of her. Henry felt puzzled. No sign of mental illness so far. 'I'm boring,' was the only slightly odd thing she'd said.

She paid for the drinks. Oscar moved away, and then turned round, just as she said, 'I need the Ladies. Where is it?'

'It's round the back,' said Oscar, in a near-whisper, as if finding it indelicate to talk about the Ladies in front of a lady.

'Thanks,' she said, and hurried off. She was wearing flat shoes, which made her legs look thin.

'"Thanks"?' said Oscar, puzzled.

'For telling her where the Ladies is.'

'What?'

'She asked where the Ladies is. You said, "round the back."'

'Oh! No! No! My little problem that I couldn't mention in front of a lady. I knew you'd be worrying about it and I thought, if I said "round the back," that might take away uncertainty without causing offence.'

Hilary returned.

'I can't find it,' she said.

'It's in t' corridor on t' right,' said Oscar.

Hilary stared at him.

'It's his problem that's round the back,' said Henry.

Hilary gave them a rather wild look, then hurried off.

They found it hard to avoid bursting into giggles every time they thought of Oscar. He asked her about Durham and she told him how beautiful it was. Of course her nose was too long, but when her face shone with pride, Henry felt that she was beautiful. He said, 'I'd like to see Durham,' and there was silence where her reply of, 'You must come and see me' might have been.

With every second of normality, his anxiety grew. Would she suddenly throw a fit or reveal that she thought she was Florence Nightingale? What would he do if she suddenly rolled around, frothing at the mouth, or shouted, 'Put that light out! Don't you know there's a war on? And get me some lint.'

She did neither of these things.

They walked the short distance to Donny's Bar. It was raining hard. As soon as they were out of earshot of the pub, they burst into laughter over Oscar's piles. He hugged her and tried to kiss her. She struggled free. 'No,' she said.

Was it starting? Would she start screaming?

Nothing happened, except that she strode so fast, through the pinging rain, that he could hardly keep up.

'Don't go so fast,' he said.

'Sorry,' she said.

She touched his hand.

'Sorry,' she said.

They entered by the side door and went up the stairs to Donny's Bar.

'You're soaking,' he said.

'I won't melt.'

She couldn't meet his eyes. Was she sinking into a private world of madness? Would she sit motionless at the table, in a catatonic trance, to the embarrassment of the Christmas revellers?

Donny's Bar was heavily festooned with paper chains, and there was a large party, wearing paper hats, seated at five tables that had been pulled together. The waiter apologized for them.

'It's nice,' said Hilary.

Henry felt almost weak with relief at her normality.

'It's nothing special here,' he warned, when they'd got their menus.

'It's fine.'

They ordered rump steaks, with onion rings extra, and a bottle of red wine. Hilary clasped his hand and gave it a quick squeeze, but she wasn't fully relaxed. Twice she looked round rather anxiously. Paranoia? Did she believe she was being followed, by little green men or the CIA?

She asked again about his work, and he abandoned his attempt not to be self-centred, in the interest of keeping her happy. Their steaks arrived. She ate heartily, and laughed at his disasters. How few fillings she had. How he wished, despite her laughter, that his career so far had been more of a triumph. Well, soon it would be. Then he remembered that her father was a great friend of Councillor Matheson. There could be problems ahead, if . . . if what?

She examined the list of desserts at greater length and with more intensity than it deserved. He had another sharp stab of fear. Perhaps it was schizophrenia. Would she say, '*I'll* have the strawberry ice, and *I'll* have the apple pie.'?

She said, 'Nothing for me, thanks. I'm full.' He almost loved her for her normality.

They nursed the remainder of the wine and chatted pleasantly, though they sometimes had to shout to make themselves heard above the shrieking of the festive party.

'I'm sorry about them,' he said.

'For goodness sake,' she said. 'They're enjoying themselves. They're briefly unhierarchical. It's intoxicating.'

'What?'

'The rigid class system in their office is suspended for the duration of the festivities. They're hysterical. They're free, after twelve long months in a straight-jacket. I know how they feel.'

Oh no. Did she mean she'd been in a straight-jacket? He had to find out, without arousing her suspicion. It would need subtlety.

'I . . . er . . . I should think it's . . . er . . . pretty awful in a straight-jacket,' he said.

She looked at him in astonishment.

'What?' she said.

'Being in a straight-jacket. I shouldn't think it's very nice.'

'I heard what you said. It was just that it sounded as if you thought I had first-hand experience of it.'

'What?' he said. 'No. No! Why on earth should I think you'd been in a straight-jacket?'

'I don't know.' She laughed. 'Can we change the subject? It's becoming a bit of a straight-jacket.'

He searched for a change of subject.

'You must have arguments with your father about the class system,' he said.

She looked puzzled. 'Why?' she said.

'Well, you obviously hate it, and he's a Tory councillor.'

'He is not. He's a lifelong socialist. Why did you think he's a Conservative?'

'Well . . . he's a draper.'

'I don't think it's compulsory for drapers to be Conservative.' There was a dryness in her tone. She smiled, to take the sting out of it.

'He's a friend of Councillor Matheson.'

'Outside the council chamber. Conservatives *are* human beings, you know. Fellow citizens of the British Isles. It's a kind of love-hate relationship with Uncle Peter anyway.'

Uncle Peter! It *was* going to be difficult to tell her about his investigations.

And what about his evening with Anna? Should he mention that?

'I . . . er . . . I took Anna out,' he said.

'Yes. She told me. I wondered if you'd mention it.'

Thank goodness he had. He wondered how much Anna had told her about it. Could he ever tell her the whole story?

'I thought she was the one I fancied,' he said. 'I can be remarkably stupid sometimes.'

He was astounded to hear himself say this. She said nothing. He thought she might have responded to his implied compliment to her, or argued against his harsh assessment of himself, but she did neither.

He asked her if she'd heard from Anna.

'Yes,' she said. 'I had a dreary letter from Toulouse. She's staying with a pen-friend who's going to become a nun.'

'Yes,' he said. No. He mustn't have secrets from Hilary. 'That's the official story. She's actually living with an older man.'

'I knew she was lying,' said Hilary. 'Oh, I do find that depressing.' Ah. A clue? 'I find it all so depressing.' Ah. 'Going to Italy with her was depressing.' Ah.

'Why?'

'We just drifted apart, inch by inch.' Ah. 'I'm not blaming her. It was mainly my fault.' Ah.

'What do you mean, your fault?'

'Do we have to talk about that? Do I have to endure cross-examination?'

'No. Of course not.'

The office party shrieked at something the accounts manager had said. Henry and Hilary looked at each other rather forlornly, as the waves of laughter crashed around them.

She wanted to pay her share. He refused.

As they left, the Christmas party apologized insincerely for the noise. 'It's been fun,' said Hilary. 'Go home and have one for me,' said an intoxicated head cashier. 'It's the only one you'll get tonight,' responded a tipsy typist. Everybody shrieked. Henry and Hilary hurried out, embarrassed that the subject had been raised.

It had stopped raining. There were queues for the buses and trams, and no taxis to be seen. Buses and taxis had been reduced, due to the petrol crisis. The doomed trams seemed to say, 'I told you so,' as they clattered towards extinction.

'I'd much rather walk really,' said Hilary.

Claustrophobia? Cabophobia? Busophobia?

'I love walking,' she said. 'I love fresh air.'

Agoraphilia?

They walked along York Road, past the junction with Winstanley Road, up out of the grime into the desirable suburbs. They turned left into Lambert Simnel Avenue, and right into Perkin Warbeck Drive. It seemed a very Conservative area for a Labour councillor.

He dreaded arriving at her house. He had no idea whether to kiss her or not.

'This is it,' she said, outside a pleasant brick house. One light still shone, as if they were waiting up for her to see if she was all right.

She kissed him and was gone, without even saying good night. She didn't turn to wave. They'd made no plans to meet again.

In Eastbourne, Dr John Bodkin Adams was accused of murdering a rich widow. Lord Radcliffe's proposals for Cyprus were published.

There would be a period of self-government under British sovereignty, with 6 of the 36 members of the legislative assembly nominated by the Governor. Later, when self-determination came, partition between Greek and Turkish Cyprus was a possibility. Nobody seemed to regard these proposals as a Christmas present.

Henry couldn't bear even to look at his article on Peter Matheson. The glory which he hoped to win from his exposure of municipal corruption would be considerably reduced if every rogue whom he exposed had been praised to the skies by him as a 'Proud Son of Thurmarsh'.

When he drew back the curtains from his absurdly positioned French windows on Christmas morning, he was surprised to see a covering of snow, turning the shared front garden into a Christmas card.

He didn't feel Christmassy. His head ached unpleasantly. His eight cards sat sadly on the mantelpiece. They were from the Hargreaveses, Auntie Doris and Geoffrey, Cousin Hilda, Mrs Wedderburn(!), Martin Hammond and family, Lampo Davey, Ginny, and Ted and Helen, with seven kisses naughtily added beneath Helen's name. Ginny had put one kiss.

The house was silent. Ginny had gone to her family. Gordon and Hazel were spending Christmas together, for the sake of the children, though in separate beds. Ginny was terrified that there'd be a reconciliation. She was terrified of this insight into her own heart – terrified that she wished that those young children, who needed love and stability, should be denied them so that she could have her man. She'd told Henry this, beneath tartan shields draped with holly, in the thronged, frenzied lounge bar of the Winstanley, awash all around them with goodwill for all men, including, Henry hoped, those sorts of men who were never seen in the Winstanley, such as blacks, gypsies, queers, communists, Jews and foreigners. She had cried, and blown her nose while others blew squeakers.

He went into the cold, bleak hall, the no-man's-land of the rented sector, and found it. His ninth card. Underneath the printed message there were no easy kisses, no biro love, no postal coquettishness, but a single, simple sentence, written in an

259

elegant but perhaps too careful hand. 'Thank you for a really enjoyable evening. Hilary.'

The silence of the house became peaceful. It was extraordinarily pleasant to telephone the Lewthwaites, from a really rather delightfully proportioned telephone box, and ask for Hilary. It was delightful to listen to her warm, semi-northern voice, to wish her a happy Christmas, and arrange to meet her in the Pigeon and Two Cushions on the 28th. It was singularly stimulating to crunch the snow in the Alderman Chandler Memorial Park, to say 'Happy Christmas' to the ocelot and the marmot and the three mangy barn owls, to sit in Cousin Hilda's stifling basement and drink Camp Coffee and *two* glasses of sweet sherry, what a momentous concession to the season, delivered with just two mild sniffs, one for each glass. What could be nicer than dry turkey, black gravy, undercooked streaky bacon and burnt chipolatas, with bullet-like roast potatoes, watery sprouts, soft red carrots, and stuffing from two different packets? What did it matter if Liam O'Reilly didn't have the conversational sparkle of a Wilde or Shaw? His pleasure at this feast was Henry's pleasure. Cousin Hilda's pleasure at Henry's pleasure was Henry's additional pleasure. What did it matter if Norman Pettifer's heroic efforts to conquer his jaundiced view of life for the sake of the party were only intermittently successful? Liam had a green hat with two crowns, in his cracker. Norman Pettifer had a clockwork frog. He watched it, with his bemused, disappointed grocer's face, as it hopped across the table. Liam got the threepenny bit in the pudding. Cousin Hilda smiled at Henry because he wasn't disappointed.

It would be untrue to suggest that the day was entirely free from tedium. The most lively game of Snap loses some of its sparkle after the first two hours. A purist might complain that the switch to Happy Families came too late. But this was a small price to pay for seeing Cousin Hilda happy.

And then he went to Troutwick and saw Auntie Doris happy. The train was an hour late, due to snow. The great hills shone white all around. They ate roast pheasant with game chips, and not even Geoffrey Porringer's blackheads could spoil the perfection of the day. Henry was staying in a cottage owned by a Mr Cadge, a man of few words and fewer blankets.

When the last exhausted resident had staggered to bed, Henry
sat between Auntie Doris and Geoffrey Porringer on stools at the
empty bar. Auntie Doris leant across Henry's back and whispered
something. Geoffrey Porringer said 'Yes' and turned to Henry. He
smiled with a not totally successful attempt at avuncularity. It was
unsuccessful, partly because he was drunk and partly because he
had no feel for the avuncular even when sober. 'Son,' he said,
'you're a little belter. Where are my children this Yuletide? Eh?
But you. You're a horse of a very different kettle.' He breathed
whisky over Henry. 'Doris, your auntie, my beloved, my little . . .
chickadee . . .' He tried to resemble W. C. Fields. Only the nose
succeeded. 'My little angel wishes you to come on holiday with us.
We've hired a villa. They *call* it a villa. Bungalow, I expect. View
of the sea. In February. And Doris said, "I want Henry to come.
He's the son I never had." Those were her very thingummies.
"Ask him yourself," she said. "Otherwise he may think you don't
want him." I mean, it's not a honeymoon or anything. You won't
be *in the way*.' Geoffrey Porringer winked. 'February. Can you
make it?'

'Where?' said Henry.

'Cap Ferrat,' said Geoffrey Porringer. 'Very attached to Cap
Ferrat, my little chickadee. Been there a lot. Knows it well.'

'Shut up about all that, Geoffrey. You don't want to remind
Henry of all the good times he and I had with Teddy, do you?' said
Auntie Doris, who always made things worse by protesting about
them. She kissed Henry, enveloping him in scent and powder and
lipstick and brandy. 'Please come, darling,' she said.

'For you, Auntie Doris, I'll even tolerate the rigours of the Côte
d'Azur,' said Henry.

He wriggled free, wished them good night and went across the
cobbled square to sleep, in his duffel-coat, in Mr Cadge's cottage.

She kissed him as before. No more. No less. Again, she was
wearing flat shoes. She had a tiny blood blemish on her chin. They
discussed their Christmasses. Oscar arrived, smiled, pointed at his
backside and gave a thumbs-up. A table of strangers stared at him
in astonishment. Henry felt very close to Hilary, as they fought
together against hysteria.

Snow and ice covered 80% of main roads. In Hungary there was a wary truce as the nation awaited reforms. There were as many stories about the Suez Canal as there were spokesmen. It would be open in seven weeks/ten weeks/fourteen weeks. British salvage ships would/would not be allowed to work with British crews. The clearance was going well/badly/not at all.

On December 29th, Henry and Hilary sat in the Pigeon and Two Cushions and talked about life. On the 30th, they sat in the Pigeon and Two Cushions and talked about life. Talk. Desire. Kisses. A few seconds longer each night. On the 30th, in Perkin Warbeck Drive, her tongue was briefly, luxuriantly, inside his mouth. Like a snake. Then she was gone. Like a snake.

On New Year's Eve, in Paris, a Bolivian tourist wrote a postscript to the year. He threw a stone at the Mona Lisa. He explained, 'I had a stone in my pocket and was seized with a desire to throw it.' He didn't explain why he had a stone in his pocket.

The rain and the petrol rationing made it the quietest New Year's Eve in London for many years.

In Thurmarsh there was rain also, and Henry was invited to two parties. A bottle party at Ted and Helen's. A small gathering of family and friends at the Lewthwaites'.

Ted and Helen's party would be fun. Three women for whom he had felt great stirrings would be there. Helen, playful with him whenever she felt she had a rival. Ginny, relieved and ashamed because Gordon had come back to her. Jill, scornful. Ben would sit beside his shy, petite Cynthia all evening. Colin was said to be bringing Glenda. That would be an event. There'd be lots of drinking and lots of laughter.

The Lewthwaites' party would be quite dull, Hilary said, and fairly embarrassing. The only other person under forty would be her obnoxious fifteen-year-old brother, Sam.

It was no contest.

'Are you my sister's new lover?' said Sam.

There was uneasy laughter.

'Shut up, pest,' said Hilary.

Peter Matheson was there, with his tall, rather stiff wife Olivia. Well, that was to be expected. Less expected was the balding man with the catastrophic suit, who'd been discussing 'a personal matter' in the Winstanley with Mr Matheson.

Four middle-aged people were crammed into a large floral sofa. There were also three large floral armchairs, six Windsor chairs from the dining-room and a wheelchair. In the wheelchair was a pale woman whose face shone with the serenity of suffering accepted with dignity.

'Meet my mother,' said Hilary. 'Mummy, this is Henry.'

Mrs Lewthwaite smiled gravely.

'Hello, Henry,' she said.

'Hello, Mrs Lewthwaite,' he said.

'My name's Nadežda,' she said. 'I'm Yugoslavian. Everyone in England ignores my beautiful name, and calls me Naddy.'

'Then I'll call you Nadežda,' he said.

Hilary gave him a look as if to say, 'Come on: There's no need to put on too perfect an act.' She didn't explain why her mother was in a wheelchair.

Everybody praised his article on Peter Matheson, although Olivia seemed a little dry, saying, 'I don't know anybody whose opinion of himself needs bolstering less than Peter.' She was trying to look relaxed, but maintained something of the air, among all these socialists, of a Victorian missionary looking for good qualities among cannibals.

'Have you heard from Anna, Hilary?' said Mr Matheson.

'Yes,' said Hilary. 'She's . . . er . . . in Toulouse, with this pen-friend.'

Henry was terrified that he was going to blush.

'That's what she told me,' he said. 'Apparently she's going to become a nun. The pen-friend, not Anna. I can't see Anna becoming a nun!' He remembered that the Mathesons thought Anna led a sheltered life, and did blush.

'We had a letter. Not very informative,' said Olivia.

'Eloquent with evasion,' said Peter Matheson. He seemed as pleased with his phrase as he was worried about Anna.

'And now you're going out with Hilary,' said Olivia drily.

'Yes! I seem to be going through them in alphabetical order!' Henry went scarlet as he realized the possible implications of his phrase. 'I don't mean . . . er . . .'

'We didn't think you did,' said Olivia Matheson coolly. 'I think we know Anna better than that.'

'And Hilary too,' said Peter Matheson, slightly too hastily, after slightly too long a pause.

'Excuse us,' said Hilary. 'I must introduce Henry to everybody.' She led him away.

'For God's sake,' she said. 'What made you say that?'

'Embarrassment,' he said. 'I find embarrassment incredibly embarrassing.' He remembered Diana Pilkington-Brick, née Hargreaves, saying that, years ago, on another embarrassing occasion.

She introduced him to the balding man in the disastrous suit, who on this occasion was wearing a disastrous sports jacket. He was Herbert Wilkinson, Chief Planning Officer. Henry's spine tingled.

'We met before,' he said. 'You were busy with a personal matter.'

'No mystery about it,' said Herbert Wilkinson. 'Peter Matheson's nephew is marrying our daughter.'

Henry felt a lurch of doubt at discovering that the two men really had been discussing a personal matter. Then he encouraged himself with the realization that he had uncovered opportunities for nepotism.

There were too many people to constitute a group, but not enough to make a successful party. It was all slightly dull, and Henry was so glad that he was there. Little pieces of party food were handed round. There was too much food for snacks, and not enough for a meal, and the food was rather uninspired, and Henry was so glad that he was there. The drink flowed just fast enough to make him wish that it was flowing faster. At midnight they listened to the chimes of Big Ben. They all stood up, except for Nadežda. They linked hands, and formed a large circle among the chairs. Hilary and Howard Lewthwaite were at the side of Nadežda's chair, leaning down to bring her into the circle. They sang 'Auld Lang Syne' without quite enough conviction, as if they thought it absurd, when life is so short, to welcome the end of an old year and naïve, when life is so brutish, to welcome the beginning of a new one. Not all of them knew the words, and it was all vaguely embarrassing, and Henry was so glad that he was there. Then, rather absurdly, they clapped, and stopped clapping too soon, as if they realized that it was absurd. There were no silly hats, no squeakers. They moved around, in slow rotation, and kissed each other, rather formally, wishing each other a happy 1957. Olivia Matheson presented her cheek as if it were a rare privilege. Henry said, 'Happy New Year, Mrs Matheson,' and added, silently, 'in which your husband will be ruined.' Henry and Hilary hugged each other, and he said, 'Happy New Year, my love.' My love! It was the first time he'd used the word 'love'. He gasped at the revelation. He bent down and kissed crippled Yugoslavian Mrs Lewthwaite. How cold her cheek was. She said, 'Be careful with Hilary.' His eyes filled with tears and oh no here was Sam approaching. If Sam saw his tears! He fought the flood back and said, 'Hello, pest.' Sam nodded his approval curtly and said, 'You're better than any of the last eight. Maybe you'll last.' Howard Lewthwaite clasped Henry's hands in his, and said nothing. Henry told Hilary that he must talk to her.

'That sounds ominous,' she said. 'I know the perfect place. But it'll be cold.'

'I don't mind,' he said.

They put their coats on and wandered out, away from that anti-climactic gathering of middle-aged people who didn't quite know what to do now that it was 1957. The rain had almost stopped. They walked off, away from the faint light filtering through the cosy, curtained windows, into the vast black universe beyond. Hilary guided him across the squelching lawn to a rustic wooden summer house. It was milder than of late, but still cold. And there, sitting on a circular bench that ran round the inside of the summer house, on that winter night, they talked.

At first it was difficult. He wanted to ask her about those remarks that people kept making, about her mental illness, about her being a problem. But he didn't know how to begin.

She shivered.

'You're cold,' he said, putting his arm round her.

'Not really. More frightened,' she said.

'Frightened? Of me?'

'Of me. Of me and you and the world.'

'Are you having sexual intercourse in there?' called out Sam.

'Shove off, object,' said Hilary.

'You'll get splinters,' warned Sam.

'Belt up, monster,' said Hilary.

Sam belted up and shoved off.

'He likes me to be rude to him,' said Hilary. 'It's the only kind of affection he can deal with at the moment.'

'I know.'

'You know a lot.'

'Not enough. Not nearly enough.'

'You want to, don't you? Make love.'

'Very much.'

She told him why she was frightened. She told him of the man she had loved, who had left her for another. She told him how she had fought her despair, and sought consolation, after a few drinks, after a party, with a man she hardly knew. And how the man had gone too fast, and she had tried to draw back. She couldn't look at Henry as she told him how the man had raped her. She told him how the man had got away with it, because if a woman had a few drinks, was pleasant to a man, flirted a bit with him, the world said she was asking for it. She told him what it was like to wake up in a hospital ward, among total strangers, not knowing where you were, and to realize, gradually, that this was the same old you, the same old earth, the fight had to go on, you hadn't taken a large enough dose, you'd been found too soon, by people who would always wonder whether you'd meant to be found, when you'd yearned for the peace of eternal blackness. She told him what it was like to face the distress of those you loved and realize that you had almost killed your crippled mother. She told him what it was like to realize that you had no alternative but to try not to do it again. 'I'm permanently diminished by the disgust I feel,' she said. 'I think you ought to go.'

'I'll never go,' he whispered.

She kissed him gently, on the lips.

'I don't know if it can work,' she said.

'Of course it can,' he said. 'You know it can. You've known these last few days.'

'I've known I hope it can,' she said. 'You're the first man I've felt even remotely safe with since it happened.'

'I'm not sure if that's a compliment,' he said.

'It's meant to be the greatest compliment I've ever paid to anyone.'

They clutched each other, and sat motionless and silent.

'Anna said . . .' he said at last.

'Anna said what?'

Could he? Should he? 'Anna said . . . you were mentally ill.'

'I've had a lot of depression,' she said. 'And I tried to kill myself. And I went very inward. If that's mental illness, I'm mentally ill.'

He clasped her left hand. It was icy. He had to fight the temptation to tell her that her tiny hand was frozen.

'Every day I hear the screams of the world,' she said.

'What?'

'My parents taught me how to care, and now I can't stop. I hear the agony of people imprisoned without trial. I hear the repression of minorities. I hear the knock on the door in the middle of the night. I hear the screams of the wounded in obscure border wars between countries whose names I can't pronounce. Not all the time. But every day . . . somewhere . . . some time . . . If that's mental illness, I'm mentally ill.'

He laid his cheek upon her cold cheek. Mother Nature, that old softie, sent a shaft of moonlight across the trim suburban lawn. Hilary shuddered.

'I love you,' she said.

He couldn't speak.

'I never thought I'd hear myself say that again,' she said.

He couldn't speak.

'What a responsibility,' he sobbed at last. His tears streamed. She massaged his hands gently. 'I'm so happy,' he moaned absurdly.

She lent him a small white handkerchief. He felt brutish, violating it.

'You're a complete fool, you know,' he said. 'I'm clumsy, insensitive, thoughtless, hopeless. I'm a case.'

How they talked, as the clouds drifted back across the moon, as

267

if to say that they shouldn't expect too much from 1957. He told her about his childhood, all his schools, all his humiliations. He told her about Denzil and Lampo, in Siena. She laughed.

Suddenly she gave a screech of laughter. 'You *did* think I'd been in a straight-jacket,' she said. 'Poor Henry. How brave you've been, waiting for the eruption of madness every second of every day.' She laughed till the tears ran. He joined in sheepishly. She talked again about what a mistake her holiday with Anna had been. And yet something had been achieved, something of the spirit of Italy had entered her soul. She'd begun, slowly, to enjoy life again, in Durham. She'd begun to hope, to her surprise, that she would see, in Thurmarsh, the funny little journalist she'd met in Siena. She talked about her girl-friends in Durham. She talked about going to London, with Clare and Siobhan, to protest about Suez. Oh god, he wished he'd been there. What did you do in the Great War, Daddy? I admired biscuit tins, son.

She talked about the dreadful days of her mother's polio attack, two years after Sam was born. She talked about the bronchial days, towards the end of winter, when each year grew more dangerous for her mother. Then they put their tongues in each other's mouths and kissed and kissed and kissed. The saliva grew cold on their slurpy faces, and their tongues grew slow and gentle, slower and gentler, and more sensitive, and then they removed their tongues and hugged each other.

Her father banged on the door.

'Are you coming in?' he said.

'We're coming,' she said.

In they went, through the French windows, creeping, whispering, so as not to wake her mother or the object.

'We were talking,' she whispered. 'Talking and kissing.'

Howard Lewthwaite touched Henry gently on the shoulder.

'Would you like to stay?' he said. 'On the sofa?'

'It'd be lovely to know you're there,' said Hilary. 'It'd be lovely to start 1957 by waking up in the same house as you.'

Howard Lewthwaite touched Henry gently on the shoulder.

Oh, the bitter-sweet evenings of talk and beer and desire and frustration and the continuing steady improvement of Oscar's haemorrhoids. Oh, the lingering good night kisses in Perkin Warbeck Drive.

Oh, the difficulty of having to investigate Hilary's so-called Uncle Peter, who was her father's friend, not to mention Herbert Wilkinson, who was also her father's friend. Howard Lewthwaite would hardly relish being told, by a twenty-one-year-old, that his choice of friends was unwise, that he was naïve. If only he had more courage. If only Hard Man Henry hadn't become a ghost.

Stanley Matthews and Donald Campbell were given CBEs. C. P. Snow was knighted. A left-wing government under a military dictator was formed in Syria. Egypt abrogated the Anglo-Egyptian treaty of 1954, denying the basis on which Britain could use the Suez Canal in time of war. John Foster Dulles, who had done so much to turn a disastrous Anglo-French victory into an even more disastrous defeat, said that the US had a major responsibility to help prevent the spread of Soviet imperialism in the Middle East. The pleas of road hauliers for more fuel were rejected.

Henry summoned up his courage. On Thursday, January 3rd, he told Hilary of his investigations. She said they must tell her father. He'd know what to do.

Gertie Gitana, who'd become synonymous with 'Nellie Dean', died at the age of 68. The Egyptians refused to let United Nations troops move ships out of the canal. They wouldn't negotiate with Britain and France until new governments came into power, and then only if they apologized for the deeds of their predecessors.

Howard Lewthwaite walked to the Midland Hotel on the following Tuesday, and gave Henry and Hilary lunch. None of them had the *pamplemousse*. They talked of Suez. 'What have we got,' asked Hilary, 'in exchange for splitting the nation, weakening the Commonwealth, the Atlantic alliance and the United Nations, diverting the world's attention from the Russian atrocities in Hungary, and harming for ever our capacity to take a credible position of moral leadership in the world?' 'Nothing,' said Henry. 'As much as that!' said Howard Lewthwaite. They laughed. Lowering his voice, even though the nearest customer was twenty feet away, Henry told Hilary's father about his suspicions. Howard Lewthwaite went quite white, and shook his head several times. He waved a waiter away, brusquely. 'Thank you,' he said, 'but I'm perfectly capable of pouring wine.' He promised to look into the matter immediately.

Sir Anthony Eden resigned, due to ill health. Harold Macmillan became Prime Minister. Oil promised by America still hadn't materialized.

He met Hilary in the Winstanley at noon. It was the last Sunday before her return to Durham. The proximity of the Winstanley to his flat was not accidental. She arrived with her father, on foot. Howard Lewthwaite was keen to be seen not wasting petrol by as many voters as possible.

He bought the youngsters a drink. They sat in a quiet corner.

'I've had one meself,' said Howard Lewthwaite.

'One what?' said Hilary.

'An offer from the council. For Lewthwaite's. I haven't told Naddy yet. I daren't tell her till the spring. She's so frail in winter these days.'

'You'll refuse the offer, of course,' said Hilary.

Her father stared at his glass of beer. 'I don't know as I can,' he said. 'Drapery as we know it is finished. The east side of Market Street as we know it is finished. I'm in trouble. The offer is strictly fair, if mean. Doesn't cheat me or the ratepayers. I don't know if I *can* refuse it, Hilary.'

'But Lewthwaite's!'

'All things come to an end, Hilary.'

'But this is wicked manipulation,' said Henry.

'Is it?' said Howard Lewthwaite. 'I'm at liberty to refuse. I choose not to. What's wicked about that?'

'But you're a councillor.'

'Exactly. And I still only get a very basic price. Doesn't sound like corruption, does it?'

'Well, what about the tobacconist?' said Henry. 'Did you ask the planning officer about that?'

'I did. He said the house is no longer safe, now it's next to a gaping black hole.'

'It looks safe to me,' said Henry.

'Herbert says the foundations are undermined. Would you guarantee its safety?'

'No, but what about the woman on the end. Her house isn't next to a gaping black hole.'

'It will be, when the tobacconist's is gone.'

'That's ridiculous.'

'Is it? The woman doesn't want to stay there, a little house beside a gaping black hole. She wants to be rehoused. Nobody is suffering, Henry.'

'Thurmarsh is. Those streets are full of good old buildings. What'll we get in their place?'

'A brave new world, perhaps,' said Howard Lewthwaite. 'How conservative with a small c you are.'

'Are you saying there are no secret plans for redevelopment?' said Henry.

'Not that I know of.'

'But what about Fred Hathersage? He's buying stuff up all over the area.'

'Have you proof of that?'

'I've been told.'

'Maybe he thinks the area is ripe for development. He has eyes. We can't stop him seeing. Properties become available. We can't stop him buying.'

'I don't understand this,' said Henry. 'You've got deadly political ammunition against the Tories, and you pooh-pooh it.'

Hilary and her father gave Henry long, rather sad looks.

'It's a Labour council, darling,' said Hilary.

Of course it was. He'd been concentrating on Peter Matheson so much that he'd quite overlooked the fact.

'Peter Matheson's leader of a minority,' said Howard Lewthwaite. 'Unless there's corruption on our side, too, he won't get anywhere, even if he is corrupt.'

'Could there be corruption on your side?' said Henry.

'I hope not. It wouldn't say much for me as deputy leader.' Howard Lewthwaite looked at his watch. 'I must be getting off,' he said. 'Got to put the veg on for Naddy's dinner. Look, I'll keep digging. I promise. Be good.'

The weight of their discussion faded slowly, like a shadow on a recovering lung. By the time they left the Winstanley, all that was forgotten.

It was a mild, spring-like afternoon. There was very little traffic in Winstanley Road. The petrol shortage was giving the town back to pedestrians.

'My . . . er . . . flat's close by here,' he said.

'Is it really?' said Hilary drily.

He intended to be oblique, ask her if she'd like to see it, offer her a sandwich. She wasn't a person to whom it was easy to be oblique. 'Come on, eh?' he said.

She nodded bravely.

He didn't dare speak, for fear she would change her mind.

'It's usually me goes too fast,' she said. 'Slow down. I'm not going to back out. I've gritted me teeth.'

They crossed the road, hand in hand, he in an ecstatically ambiguous state between excitement and fear, and she with gritted teeth. A robin scolded them for their immorality. Henry had never felt less immoral.

He hurried her through the sterile entrance hall, and lit the gas fire in the living-room. She laughed at the French windows.

'The other half of them's through here, in the . . . er . . . bedroom,' he said.

'I bet you say that to all the girls,' she said. 'You must come and see my French windows.'

He led the way into the bedroom. He lit the gas fire in there, too. She began to undress and he remembered, with a thud of fear, what he'd completely forgotten in the excitement of their growing love. She had a horrible body. Never mind, he told himself, as she undressed tensely, determinedly, as if for a medical, with her back to him. Never mind. Men are far too influenced by physical appearance. I love you, Hilary, the person, the woman. The body is unimportant.

She hopped into the narrow, single bed and covered herself with the bedclothes. But he had seen, in that brief moment, when he hadn't dared to be seen to be looking, that her body was not horrible at all, but more beautiful than he could have dared to hope. He climbed in beside her, feeling hot and cold and awkward and ardent.

And so, in the cramped atmosphere of his tiny, unattractive bedroom, on a mild Sunday afternoon in January, in a flat in a converted mock-Tudor house in respectable Winstanley Road, Henry Ezra Pratt and Hilary Nadežda Lewthwaite embarked upon a journey that might, with luck, take them from gritted teeth to ecstasy.

'There's no hurry whatsoever,' he said. 'It doesn't matter if nothing happens. Cuddling is enough.' But it wasn't. It wasn't nearly enough.

His patience and gentleness surprised him. Slowly, Hilary ungritted her teeth. Eventually he took her, rather swiftly, unsatisfactorily, messily. She was too tense to have an orgasm. That was what it was, a taking. Bad. Bad. Taking wasn't loving.

The daylight faded. The gas fire produced a low, red glow. She began to stroke him. Slowly, together, they sailed away from the land of gritted teeth. In the cave of his room, in the cave of his bed, in the cave of his arms, in a cave within a cave within a cave, Hilary found a place that was safe enough for her. This time, they gave instead of taking. Hilary uttered one single gasp. A gasp of incredulous joy. Outside, people were walking to evening service, down Winstanley Road.

'Hilary Lewthwaite?' Henry whispered into her left ear. 'Do you think that, when your exams are over, you could bear to become Mrs Henry Pratt?' And then he had an awful worry, a terrible fear that he'd dreamt it all. Because he could have sworn that Hilary Lewthwaite replied, 'I don't think I could bear not to,' and people didn't say things like that, in real life, on Sunday evenings, in one-bedroom flats in Winstanley Road, to people like Henry Pratt.

After ecstasy, tea. He padded carefully across discarded clothes and shoes. He closed the curtains and switched on the light. She blinked, and smiled, and he realized that, when she was happy, she had the most beautiful face that he had ever seen and that his inability to recognize this possibility in Siena made him irredeemably unworthy of her.

He went through into the living-room, and closed those curtains too. She joined him. The gas fire threw a dim red glow over her lovely body. She put her bare feet on his bare feet. She was taller than him now. She kissed him.

He switched the light on, and went into the kitchen.

The front door slammed. Heavy footsteps trudged across the hall. There was a loud knock on his door.

'Can I come in?' It was Ginny. Her voice sounded urgent.

He raised a questioning eyebrow. Hilary nodded. He almost wished that he didn't love her, so that he could fall in love with her at this moment.

'Just a minute,' he said. 'I'm not dressed. Come down in a few minutes.'

They tried to dress quickly, but he wanted to kiss her again and again before she disappeared into the commonplace world of the clothed. 'Thanks for agreeing,' he whispered. 'She sounded desperate,' she whispered. They weren't quite sure why they were whispering.

Ginny's eyes and nose were red. She gave a gasp when she saw Hilary. What a day it was, for the gasps of women.

'This is Hilary,' said Henry.

'Gordon has gone off with Jill,' said Ginny.

'Oh, Ginny!' said Henry. 'Oh, I'm sorry, Ginny.' Often he'd failed to find emotions to go with his expressions of sorrow. Now it was the word that was pitifully inadequate for what he felt.

'I was good enough to be his bit on the side when he was married. I'm not pretty enough for him to spend the whole of his life with,' said Ginny. 'There she is, practically straight out of school, ripe to be astounded at his virility, ripe to be impressed by his knowledge of life. No wonder he couldn't resist her.'

Henry tried to put a comforting arm round her, but she shook it off.

'Men are such bastards,' she said. 'I should regard myself as lucky to get away. What an escape I've had.'

The last thing Henry wanted, now that he'd won Hilary's delicate confidence, was an eloquent tirade against the shortcomings of men. He could think of no other way of shutting Ginny up, except to say, 'Hilary and I are engaged.'

Ginny burst into tears. Hilary rushed to her, put her arm round her and held her. Henry felt absurdly redundant.

'I'm sorry,' said Ginny. She sniffed, searched for a handkerchief, couldn't find one. Hilary lent her one quite inadequate for her purposes. She blew her nose as prodigiously as she could.

Henry had said it so often. Now, at last, but not in the circumstances that he would have chosen, it was said to him.

Ginny kissed Hilary. Then she kissed Henry.

'I hope you'll both be very happy,' she said.

The next morning Ginny was at her desk as usual, looking indestructible, larger than life. Gordon slunk to his desk, looking smaller than life. Ginny made no mention of Henry's engagement. Nor did he. He didn't yet feel sufficiently sure that it had happened.

It was Hilary's last day before her return to Durham. They met in the Pigeon and Two Cushions. They were both nervous, wondering whether they could ever live up to yesterday.

Oscar came straight over to them, and handed them a note. Could he be congratulating them? Was he psychic? No. The note read, 'Acute laryngitis.' They met his gaze, and he nodded solemnly. They fought to maintain control of themselves. They looked deep into each other's secretly laughing eyes and were enveloped once again in the certainty of their love. Good old Oscar. When he bought the next drink, Henry offered him one. Oscar mimed that he'd have sixpennorth with them, he'd pour it later, and would gargle with it.

'Shall we go home and tell my family?' she said.

They went home and told her family. Henry bent down to kiss her mother's cold cheek. Nadežda's eyes were filled with tears, and he didn't know whether they were tears of joy or sorrow. Was she overjoyed at Hilary's capture of a young man of such warmth, kindness and character, or had she hoped for something better than a short, fat, provincial journalist? Howard Lewthwaite seemed caught in the grip of contradictory emotions – half pleased, half worried. Henry was disappointed at his reaction. Sam said, 'Have you had it off yet, and if so where ave you put it?' Henry said, 'Belt up, horror.' Sam smiled, well content. Howard Lewthwaite produced the bottle of champagne they'd have drunk

275

if Labour had won the last election. Yet he still didn't seem as pleased as Henry had expected.

Hilary walked with him to the end of Perkin Warbeck Drive. There, at the junction with Lambert Simnel Avenue, under a street lamp dimmed to save fuel, their faces clung briefly to each other, and then she was gone. She didn't say goodbye. She didn't look back.

19 Startling Information

Next morning, he told his friends that he had an announcement to make and would like to see them in the Lord Nelson that night, after work. Only by celebrating could he fill the grey emptiness of a January without Hilary.

That afternoon his phone rang, an event rare enough to be worth recording.

'It's your contact from the world of entertainment.'

'Tony! Hello! How are you?'

'Very well. I've got a story for you,' said Tony Preece.

'Oh!' He just managed not to say, 'At last.' 'What is it?'

'I can't talk on the phone, but I'm on tonight at that Mecca of Hysteria, Splutt Working-Men's Club. How would you like to see the new act?'

'I'd love to. But I can't tonight. Can't you tell me what your story's about?'

'Arson and murder.'

'I'll be there at half eight.'

Everyone came to the Lord Nelson except Ginny. She'd said, 'I can't face it. He'll be there. Perhaps she'll be there.' Even Terry Skipton came.

Henry blushed becomingly, and said, 'I've got some news for you. I'm engaged.'

There was a murmur of false astonishment and genuine delight, especially from the married men. It gave them an excuse for not going home which their wives could hardly not accept.

Terry Skipton had one glass of champagne-type sparkling wine, wrinkling his face as if it were medicine. He was a better judge than he knew. Colin thumped Henry's back so vehemently that he was bruised for a week. Denzil gave him a quick kiss. Chief Superintendent Ron Ratchett had a discreet word in Denzil's ear, but not too close to Denzil's ear. 'Please, sir,' he said. 'We all have to live side by side, unfortunately. I can turn a blind eye so far and no further. It's still illegal, and long may it remain so.' Colin borrowed a fiver off Gordon and bought two bottles of champagne-type sparkling wine. Ben said the wife would understand if she was given one later than usual, under the circumstances. Gordon borrowed a fiver off Ted and bought two bottles of champagne-type sparkling wine. Henry thanked him in such surly fashion that Gordon said, 'Come on, Henry. Come *on*. If you were free as air, would you marry Ginny?' 'That's a bit different. I haven't been using her to fulfil my animal needs,' retorted Henry. 'We'll sup some lotion tonight, kid,' said Colin. 'I have to go. Family celebration,' said Henry. They were upset, as if they'd discovered that their expensive theatre tickets were valid for the first act only. Gordon was particularly angry, because he'd cancelled an evening with Jill. Henry slipped away as soon as he could.

Splutt Working-Men's Club was a long, low, uncontroversial brick building with many windows, situated opposite the controversial new ambulance station. It looked as if a large army hut had strayed among the small shops and low terraces of Splutt High Street, set low in a heavily industrialized valley, three and a half miles north-west of Thurmarsh.

He met Tony and Stella, his brassy blonde companion, by the long, bleak bar counter. Tony was attacking a pint of bitter with whisky chaser. It was more than three years since Henry had seen Stella, when for the second time he'd sat through Tony's appalling comedy spot as Talwyn Jones, the Celtic Droll.

'So what's this story?' said Henry.

'Not now,' hissed Tony, as a large, loud, florid man approached. He was wearing a large, loud, florid suit and was accompanied by a tall, buxom young red-head. The man was smoking a large cigar. The red-head wore large gold earrings and an engagement ring. Henry had seen them somewhere before.

'Hello, Tony,' said loud suit. 'Are you performing or just visiting?'

'Performing,' said Tony.

'Oh 'eck,' said loud suit. 'Shall we go 'ome?' He roared with laughter. Gold earrings smiled mechanically. 'Only joking,' said loud suit. 'I hear tha's gorra new act. Let's hope it's better than t' owd 'un. Eh, Angie?' He roared with laughter again.

Of course! Bill Holliday, used-car salesman, scrap tycoon, gambler, leader of the Thurmarsh Mafia, and Angela Groyne, model, with whom Colin had once, unwisely, danced.

'You're wearing your engagement ring, Angela,' said Stella.

'Aye. It's on again, i'n't it, Bill?' said Angela.

'This time it's for good,' said Bill Holliday. He slapped his fiancée's bottom.

'I can't wait for your new act,' said Henry, when Bill Holliday and his future wife had moved off with their brandies. 'I never thought that Welsh act was really you. You've got a perfectly good personality of your own. All you need to do is build on that, exaggerate it slightly, not seek refuge in heavy regional disguises.' Stella was glaring at him. 'I'm not criticizing him, Stella,' he said. 'I'm praising him. I'm telling him to have more confidence in the real Tony Preece. He was a dead duck in that act the moment he came on in a bright red suit, with a giant leek in his buttonhole, wearing a pith-helmet and one roller-skate, and nobody laughed. However good he was, there was no way back. That's all I'm saying. So, come on, what's this story?'

'Sod the story,' said Tony Preece, and he stormed off backstage.

'What have I done?' said Henry.

'You'll see,' said Stella.

The room was filling up. They hurried to a table. Stella sighed deeply. Those three years hadn't been kind. She looked thin and gaunt. There were dark bags under her eyes, and her artificially bright hair only served to highlight the haggard look of her hard, brassy face. Her legs were like matchsticks. Henry knew how much she loved Tony. He knew what a false signal that hard face gave to the world. He liked her very much, so he said, 'You're looking grand, Stella.'

She ignored this remark contemptuously. 'He'll be throwing up now,' she said. 'He's worse than ever these days.'

'Why does he do it?'

'He says there's got to be more to life than selling insurance.' She sighed deeply. 'We're engaged now, you know.'

'I didn't. Oh, Stella! I'm so glad.'

He hugged her with an impulsive warmth that surprised them both. She smelt of cheap perfume, anxious sweat, cigarettes and sweet Martini.

'I'm engaged too,' he said.

'Henry!' There was an element of surprise in her voice, which irritated him faintly. She gave him a more formal, strangely shy little kiss.

He bought her a sweet Martini.

'Don't forget the cherry,' she called after him.

He didn't forget the cherry.

'When's the great day, then?' he said, raising his glass.

'We haven't fixed a date yet. It's taken us six years to get engaged. It'll take a few more to get married. You?'

'No. No date yet.'

The harsh lighting, so unflattering to thin, haggard, artificial blondes whose real gold is locked deep in their hearts, was dimmed, not without a few jerks and delays, which aroused jeers from the thronged tables in the long, beery, smoky room.

'Now then! Now then!' said the concert secretary, whose teeth almost fitted. 'Letth have no repetithion of the behaviour of latht week.' He glared at them with all the ferocity at his command. Henry's mind went back to his headmaster at Dalton College, who also lisped, though his was a lishp, not a lithp. Sometimes it seemed as though there was a theme to Henry's life, with recurring motifs of failure and absurdity. He might have welcomed this thought once, even exploited it. Not any longer, because he wouldn't be able to bear it if any failure or absurdity attended his relationship with Hilary.

'It wath,' continued the concert secretary, 'and I won't minthe my wordth, a blot on the good name of Thplutt. All right, nobody'th pretending that Enrico and Ernethto, mind-readerth with a differenthe, were a good act. Letth fathe it, they were crap. But they came from acroth the thea. What thort of an imprethion of Yorkthire hothpitality have they taken back to the Ibernian peninthula? Our firtht act tonight ith a muthical trio, altho from acroth the thea, who are dethcribed ath three thtriking Vikingth, who are queenth of melody and animal imprethionth. Tho letth give them a fair hearing and a warm Yorkthire rethepthion. Letth hear it for thothe Great Daneth, the Larthen Thithterth.'

Henry had expected the Larsen Sisters to be tall, blonde and beautiful. He hadn't expected them to be not only musical, but funny as well. What were they doing here?

'Oh God,' said Stella. 'They're good. Poor Tony.'

The applause at the end of the girls' act was deafening.

'Well,' said the concert secretary. 'If anybody had told me that three female Thcandinavian animal imprethionithtth would be the biggetht hit I've ever known at Thplutt Working-Menth Club, I would have thaid "Pith off." Who could follow that? Next bugger'll have to try! Will you welcome, from north of the border, that mathter of thcottith comedy, Mick McMuck, the Droll of Dundee?'

You're in trouble when you come on wearing three pink tam-o'-shanters, a very short kilt with a very long sporran, a giant kipper in your buttonhole, and a set of bagpipes on one foot, and nobody laughs.

'Oh heck,' said Henry. 'Oh heck, Stella. I'm sorry.'

'Hold my hand,' she said. 'Help me through it.'

Henry tried desperately to think of other things. He tried to imagine himself back at his first visit to a working-men's club, at Rawlaston, with Uncle Teddy and Auntie Doris, listening to Doreen Tibbs, the Tadcaster Thrush. In vain. Tony's voice broke in. 'He said, "Have you Dunfermline?" I said, "I haven't even started fermlin yet."' The jokes were even worse! He tried to speculate about the story that Tony was going to tell him. Somehow, he was reluctant to think about that. 'I wouldn't say my wife was frigid, but she thinks sex is something the ladies of Morningside have their coal delivered in. Coal. Sex. Get it? Och no, nor do I, much.' Not all of them were worse jokes. Some of them were the same jokes. Stella tightened her grip on his hand at each reference to a ghastly fictional wife. He tried to think of Hilary. All day he'd been disembodied, gliding like a ghost through the grey mist of her absence. Now, when he tried to be with her, tried to be back in bed in Winstanley Road, tried to be in Durham, all ghostliness failed him, all disembodiment was impossible. He heard Tony say, 'She smokes in bed, too. I wouldn't

281

mind, but I don't even like kippers.' 'Oh, Hilary,' mouthed Henry. 'I love you, my darling. Let's fix the date.' It was no use. She was slipping away, because she was too real for fantasy. 'I won't say I'm unathletic but I put my shoulder out, tossing at the Highland Games. We'd only gone to Braemar for a picnic. I was tossing a salad. Salad. Tossing. Get it? Och no, nor do I, much. Mind you, I like salad dressing. It's better than the wife undressing. I won't say she's fat, but when she went swimming at North Berwick she was chased by five Norwegian whalers. Get it? Och no, nor do I, much.'

At last it was over. There was a smattering of applause. Stella sighed deeply, and gave him his hand back. It ached as the blood returned. He went to buy a pint for Tony and a sweet Martini for her. She called to him not to forget the cherry. The concert secretary introduced the 'top of the bill, that well-loved thinger from Thunderland, Arnold "Tree-Trunk" Nutley. Inthidentally, earlier today a lovely Yorkthire lath called Thuthan promithed to become Mitheth Arnold "Tree-Trunk" Nutley.' The audience applauded, and Henry had an idea for the gossip column, which was called 'Out and About'.

Arnold 'Tree-Trunk' Nutley sang 'Singing the Blues', proving that he couldn't sing like Guy Mitchell. Henry returned with the drinks. He hadn't forgotten the cherry. Arnold 'Tree-Trunk' Nutley launched himself into 'Friendly Persuasion', proving that he couldn't sing like Pat Boone. Tony returned. Stella kissed him and yelled, 'It went better tonight.' Tony nodded wearily. Henry apologized. Tony smiled wearily. Arnold 'Tree-Trunk' Nutley ventured upon 'Just Walking in the Rain', proving that he couldn't sing like Johnny Ray.

Henry bent his head towards Tony's. 'What about this story?' he said. 'It's safe to tell me now. Nobody'll hear anything with this racket going on.'

'A local publican told me, when he was pissed, that the burning down of the Cap Ferrat was no accident,' shouted Tony.

He supposed that, since Tony's phone call, he'd known that it had to be that. It was still a shock actually to hear it.

'You mean . . . my uncle was murdered?' he shouted.

'Your uncle?'

They didn't talk during the applause, which wasn't nearly as loud as the singing. When Arnold 'Tree-Trunk' Nutley burst upon 'The Garden of Eden', proving that he couldn't sing like Frankie Vaughan, Henry and Tony resumed their discreet shouting.

'It was my Uncle Teddy who was found dead in there.'

'Oh heck. I'm sorry.'

'No,' yelled Henry. 'Thank you. This gives me a chance to avenge his death. But why, Tony? Hardly for the insurance, if the owner is dead.'

'Because it was an architectural gem, I'd guess. I'd guess somebody has their eye on developing that area. I don't know how well you know it. It's very run-down. No problem, but they might have had trouble with the architectural lobby, the Thurmarsh Society, the Rundle Valley Historical Society, the South York-shire Georgian Society, all the freaks. So . . . whoosh . . . fire.'

They broke off for the applause. 'Cindy, oh Cindy,' moaned Arnold 'Tree-Trunk' Nutley, proving that he couldn't sing like Eddie Fisher. They resumed their discussion.

'Who told you? What leading publican?' yelled Henry.

'I can't tell you,' shouted Tony Preece.

'I won't let on,' yelled Henry. 'Us journalists never reveal our sources. And he's not likely to have seen us together.'

'His brother has,' shrieked Tony. He gave an involuntary glance in the direction of Bill Holliday.

'Bill Holliday's brother. Thanks, Tony,' roared Henry.

'Oh heck,' thundered Tony Preece.

The applause was muted. Arnold 'Tree-Trunk' Nutley hammered away at his final number, 'True Love', proving that he couldn't sing like Bing Crosby or look like Grace Kelly.

True love. Henry thought about his own true love. He still had no idea what a problem he was going to have to face in that department. The far corners of his mind were still dark, and filled with the silence of pennies that had failed to drop.

20   A Disturbing Discovery

Hexington lies seven miles to the north-east of Thurmarsh, on an exposed bluff high above the weed-knotted, pram-choked curves of the Rundle and Gadd Navigation. Seven villages and five coal mines can be seen, on a clear day, from the tower of the smut-blackened parish church. But the podgy young man who descended from the dun-coloured Thurmarsh Corporation bus, outside the Midland Bank, had no intention of climbing the 262 steps to take advantage of the view. He had four good reasons for not doing so. A thick drizzle was falling, it was pitch-dark, the church was locked and he had an urgent job to do.

He wasn't tall. His long, thick, grey-green raincoat wasn't elegant. The expression on his face wasn't fearless. And yet, there was about him a certain air of determination, for the young man . . . you've guessed it, haven't you? . . . was Henry Pratt, the Man Nobody Muzzles.

The Prince of Wales was a large, draughty, run-down Victorian beer palace, set on a windy crossroads. It had windows of opaque glass, and was topped by a round turret. It dominated the low terraced houses that surrounded it. There were two cavernous bars and a function room at the back. It smelt as if it had just dried out after being flooded.

The landlord lacked his brother Bill's charm and urbanity. Stan Holliday was a large man. His small, narrow eyes were dwarfed by his huge conk. He had slobbery lips, in which a permanent wet cigarette drooped. He had a large paunch and smelt of the morning's brandy. Twelve lank, dank, dark hairs pressed themselves into his otherwise bald pate as if seeking invisibility, yet his nostrils were a celebration of the hirsute. He smiled with his cheeks only. An ugly customer, thought Henry, except that he wasn't a customer. An ugly landlord, then.

'My name's Henry Pratt,' said Henry.

'Well, there's not a lot I can do about that, I'm afraid.' Stan Holliday smirked at his customers who, not surprisingly, were few.

'Yes. I . . . er . . . I was in a pub the other day . . .'

'Fascinating. What a rich life you lead,' said the Oscar Wilde of Hexington.

'And I overheard something.'

Stan Holliday grew wary. Improbably, his eyes narrowed.

'Oh aye?' he said.

'I wondered if I could buy myself a drink and then speak to you somewhere private,' said Henry. 'I'm from the press, but this is a personal matter.' He showed his press card.

Stan Holliday reflected, then nodded. Henry bought himself a pint. Stan Holliday led him to his office, and with mock good manners motioned him to sit in the only chair. Henry instantly regretted it. Stan Holliday now towered above him.

'Right,' said Stan Holliday. 'So what did you overhear?'

'I overheard somebody saying you reckoned the burning down of the Cap Ferrat wasn't accidental.'

'You overheard somebody saying I reckoned the burning down of the Cap Ferrat wasn't accidental?'

'Yes.'

'Who was this somebody?'

'I've no idea. Just somebody I overheard.'

'He's no idea. Just somebody he overheard.' Stan Holliday began to talk as if to an invisible wife. If she was anything like her husband, thank god she was invisible. 'Which pub was it?'

'I don't remember the name.'

'He doesn't remember the name. Where was it?'

'Er . . . right in the middle of Thurmarsh.'

'Where right in the middle of Thurmarsh?'

'I can't remember.'

'He can't remember.'

Henry tried to take a casual swig of his beer. A man's swig. It slopped all down the front of his flasher's mack.

'Right,' said Stan Holliday. He yanked Henry to his feet by his hair, and still towered over him. 'Right.' Henry had seen numerous films in which investigators had fearlessly threatened the people they were investigating. It had never been like this. 'Now listen this way. This man you don't know that you overheard in some pub you don't know somewhere you can't remember somewhere in the middle of Thurmarsh who said I reckoned the burning down of the Cap Ferrat wasn't accidental was talking through an orifice whose name I can't remember situated somewhere in the middle of an extremely unattractive cleft between two large unidentified fleshy protuberances somewhere I've forgotten not at the front of his body. I know nowt about the Cap Ferrat. I never went there. I never knew anybody who worked there or went there. And why are you sniffing round about it, anyroad, Henry Pratt, whose name I will remember?'

'It was my uncle who died there. And, if it wasn't an accident, my uncle was murdered.'

'I'm sorry to hear about your uncle,' said Stan Holliday. 'Death's very sad. It can ruin folk's lives. But it's nowt to do with me. Things like that don't happen in Thurmarsh, anyroad. Thurmarsh isn't Chicago. You're talking rubbish. Piss off.'

Henry tried narrowing his eyes. He tried glaring, as if to suggest that nobody pushed him around. He tried taking a nonchalant, man-sized swig of his beer. Then he pissed off.

On the shaking, dimly lit bus back to Thurmarsh, Henry didn't read his story, in the 'Out and About' column. He knew only too clearly what it said.

> Romance was in the air at Splutt Working-Men's Club last night. There was loud applause when the concert secretary, Eddie Simpson (59), announced that the top of the bill artiste, well-known Wearside vocalist Arnold 'Tree-Trunk' Nutley (38) was to marry Susan Ullidge, a well-known flaxen-haired hair-stylist from Mexborough.
>
> Nutley met vivacious 27 year-old Susan when he was doing a season at a holiday camp near Minehead. They plan an August wedding.
>
> What the concert secretary didn't know was that the well-known Thurmarsh comedian, insurance salesman Tony Preece (36), who works under the name of Mick McMuck, the Droll of Dundee, had also announced his engagement, to attractive Stella Hardcastle (33), a well-known blonde florist from Wath-on-Dearne. They have not yet fixed the date.
>
> Joked the irrepressible Mr Preece, 'I wonder if the third act

on the bill, the Larsen Sisters, have any romantic announcements to make!'

They didn't, but in the audience were Bill Holliday (42), the well-known Thurmarsh businessman and sportsman, and his glamorous flame-haired companion, Angela Groyne (22), a well-known local model whose successes have included three very popular calendars issued by Booth and Wignall Rolling Mills.

Their many friends have been puzzled by their on-off, on-off engagement. Well, last night Mr Holliday killed off the speculation with one word. 'Our marriage,' he declared, 'is now definitely ow.'

His first misprint since Neil Mallet had left couldn't have come at a worse time. It wasn't a good idea to make an enemy of both Holliday brothers in one day.

Israel refused to surrender access to the Gulf of Akaba and the Gaza Strip. Humphrey Bogart died. Egypt seized British and French banks and insurance companies in Cairo. There was to be no more Territorial Army training for men who'd done their national service. Henry's military career was over.

On Thursday, January 17th, there were very few buses, due to the fuel shortage and very few trams, due to mechanical failures brought about by the gradual run-down of maintenance services in view of their impending demise. Workmen were rather sheepishly removing the trolley-bus wires right opposite the stop where Henry and Ginny were waiting. All this led to conversation in the queue. Warm clouds of indignant breath rose into the frosty air.

Henry chatted to a splay-nosed man of about thirty, with receding hair and large ears, and to his spectacularly attractive girl-friend. His name was Dennis Lacey, and he worked in the X-ray department at the Infirmary. The girl, Marie Chadwick, was a nurse. They were in love. Were Henry and . . . er . . . in love? He shook his head, embarrassed, and belatedly introduced Ginny, who was polite but cool. Marie had jet-black hair and dark skin. Her mouth was small and sensual. Her nostrils were flared. Henry cast several surreptitious glances at her, to prove to himself how uninterested he now was in any woman except Hilary.

At last their tram came, and Henry thought no more of this casual encounter.

On his way to number two magistrates' court, Henry telephoned Howard Lewthwaite. 'I've found things out,' he said. 'Things I can't discuss on the phone.'

'Have lunch tomorrow,' said Howard Lewthwaite. 'There are corners of the restaurant of the Midland Hotel which are further from other living human beings than anywhere else except the morgue.'

'Funny you should mention the morgue,' said Henry.

In court – optician failed to see two red lights – Henry felt tired. In the canteen, he didn't feel hungry. In the Lord Nelson, he didn't feel thirsty. In the library, reading Colin's report of the inquest on Uncle Teddy, he felt dizzy. The fire investigation expert had found no evidence of foul play. The fire appeared to have started at the stage end of the main public room. It could have been caused by a cigarette or an electrical fault. Recording a verdict of accidental death, the coroner had added a rider about the danger of inflammable materials in public places.

By the time he got back to the news-room, Henry felt dreadful. He realized that he was sickening for the flu.

It was at that moment that Mr Andrew Redrobe's summons came.

He sank gratefully into a chair, and eyed the editor apprehensively across the neat, green-topped desk.

'The correspondence column is jaded,' said Mr Andrew Redrobe. 'Suez, Hungary, prescription charges and the folly of getting rid of the trams have been with us too long. What else have we got? The absence of facilities for square-dancing in Thurmarsh and environs! We need a major new issue. You will write a letter, a real bombshell of a letter, condemning the inadequacy and irrelevancy of what we serve up as education. You will sign it "Angry Schoolmaster".'

'Yes, sir.' Damn. It's the flu making me subservient.

'"Proud Sons of Thurmarsh". Where are your follow-ups?'

I hate the series, Mr Redrobe. 'I've been thinking about that, sir.' Damn.

'And?'

'Er . . .' I haven't been thinking about it at all. 'The Mayor?'

'A half-wit. Any other "ideas"?'

'Not at the . . . erm . . . no.'

'You've done the Tories. Have to do Labour. The leader is not a son of Thurmarsh. The deputy leader is. Howard Lewthwaite. Do you know him?'

'Know him? I'm engaged to his daughter.'

'And you still didn't . . . congratulations, incidentally . . . think of him for an article?'

'Er . . . no . . . thank you, sir, incidentally.' Damn. 'Sorry.'

'I see. How about Bill Holliday?'

'Bill Holliday??'

'All right, he's in scrap and used cars, and greyhound racing. Does that make him beyond the pale? Are you such a snob?'

'No!'

'He's a good Thurmarshian, Bill Holliday.'

And will probably crush me to death in his car dump. Great.

'I'd also suggest Sidney Kettlewell, of Crapp, Hawser and Kettlewell. A great Thurmarsh employer.'

Who refused to employ my one-eyed dad. Wonderful.

'And the one schoolmaster in this town I've any time for, because he does speak his mind. Gibbins of Brunswick Road.'

In whose class I made a monumental fart. Terrific.

Please let me go. I feel awful.

'I'm worried about you, Henry. You're not finding enough stuff on your own initiative.'

'I am onto something, Mr Redrobe. I'm onto a really big story, on my own initiative.'

'Ah! Fire away.'

'I . . . er . . .' I'm too weak to talk about it now. I want to tell Howard Lewthwaite first. I want some proof. 'I'm seeing somebody about it tomorrow. I need proof before I make allegations about people in the public eye. Could you give me a week, sir?' Damn.

'A week, then. No longer. I'm all in favour of initiative, but I don't like being kept in the dark. I don't like mavericks. A newspaper is a team effort.'

'Oh, I know. I don't want glory out of this.' Liar. 'I don't mind handing all the stuff over at all.' Shut up. You'll say things you regret. 'I just want to be sure of my facts.'

'People in the public eye, you say? I'm intrigued. I can hardly wait.'

But Mr Andrew Redrobe had to wait. Henry managed to type his letter, signed 'Angry Schoolmaster'. He managed to walk to the tram stop. He managed to undress himself and get into bed. He stayed there for more than a week.

The cold war between Russia and the United States intensified. The winter in England remained mainly mild. In Cyprus there was widespread trouble between Greeks and Turks after a Turkish policeman was killed in a bomb attack. At Cardiff Arms Park England, minus Tosser Pilkington-Brick, narrowly defeated Wales.

Every day, Ginny tried to interest Henry in food. Almost every day she sang out, with false brightness, 'Another letter from Durham!' As he began to recover, he gave her letters to post to Durham. The better he felt physically, the more his indebtedness to Ginny irked. He hoped she'd catch the flu, and become indebted to him, but she didn't. She told him that Ted and Helen had matching flu, and Gordon had it. 'He's been over-exerting himself, I expect,' she said. 'We'll see how *she* handles two households of invalids. I don't see her as Edith Cavell.'

Hilary's letters were full of incident and vitality. When he thought back to the drab, lifeless girl he'd met in Siena, he knew he should feel delighted. And yet . . . here was he, feeble and damp-haired in a tiny room that stank of his own sweat, and there was she, striding vivaciously around Durham. How long, he felt after each letter, before she tired of him, found somebody better, some gigantic student whose intellect matched his frame. So, as he waited for each letter, he grew more and more nervous. When they came, he longed to tear them open but had to wait till Ginny had gone. And always they were so full of love for him that he was reassured, until . . . until it all began again. And, because he could hardly say, 'On Monday I lay in bed and sweated. On Tuesday I lay in bed and sweated again,' he found himself forced into the sentence by sentence school of letter writing. 'I'm glad you enjoyed the lecture on John Donne. I'm very pleased Mr Tintern liked your essay. I share completely your views about Selwyn Lloyd.' Supposing she replied, 'I'm glad you're glad I enjoyed the lecture on John Donne. I'm very pleased you're very pleased Mr Tintern . . .' Supposing their love ground to a halt in bad letters.

At the end of each letter, he swore his undying love in explicit descriptions of what he'd like to do – oh god, supposing they died in a crash and Cousin Hilda found his collected love-letters, tied by an elastic band that any decent person would have reserved for jam jars.

As he began to get better, he felt deeply sexy, in that sweaty fug of a bedroom. Desperately, he listened to the wireless. The music programmes transported him back to his childhood at Low Farm, outside Rowth Bridge. Sandy Macpherson, Rawicz and Landauer, Harold Smart and his electric organ, Ronald Binge, Max Jaffa, Reginald Leopold and his players, out it poured. His childhood seemed a long way away, and he got depressed about Lorna Arrow and Eric Lugg.

The comedy programmes rolled off the assembly line too. *The Goon Show*, *Take It From Here*, *Ray's A Laugh*, *Life With The Lyons*, *Midday Music Hall* with the Song Pedlars, Barry Took, Lucille Graham and Vic Oliver. Every time he laughed, he wished Hilary was there, to laugh beside him.

He listened to everything from schools talks on the Lapps of Scandinavia and Neutralism and the Spirit of Gandhi to Jean Metcalfe visiting Vera Lynn's home, from *Mrs Dale's Diary* to an investigation into whether social mobility between the classes had been achieved in our society ('Ask Belinda Boyce-Uppingham,' he shouted. 'Ask any bloody snob.' He added, in a low moan, 'Ask me.'), from *Science Survey* on the problem of vibration to *Naturalist's Notebook*, which included a contribution on oil contamination, and a recording of a striped hawk moth, which was the best recording of a striped hawk moth he had ever heard on the wireless. And still he felt sexy. He couldn't fantasize about Hilary, who belonged to reality. That left him feeling sexy about almost everybody – Jean Metcalfe, Vera Lynn, Mrs Dale, Mrs Archer, the Lapps of Scandinavia, even Gandhi. He returned hurriedly to thoughts of Hilary.

Ginny returned halfway through the recording of the striped hawk moth, so he never heard how it finished.

'Nice evening?' he asked.

'Marvellous.'

'You met a nice man!'

'No. Gordon's still ill.' She gave him a shrewd glance. 'You're better!' she said. She sounded as if his improvement was the only blot on a splendid day.

'I wish you had met a nice man,' he said. 'You deserve one.'

'Presumably that's why you ruled yourself out of the running.'

'Touché.'

'You *are* better. My job is done. Good night,' said Ginny.

He *was* better. Next day, he telephoned Howard Lewthwaite, and arranged to meet him for lunch on Tuesday.

John Foster Dulles said that, if the United States became involved in a Middle East war, he would rather not have British or French troops alongside them. Only 2 out of 19 wrecks in the southern section of the Suez Canal had so far been removed by the UN salvage team.

A virulent letter from an angry schoolmaster appeared in the *Thurmarsh Evening Argus*. Its author sat in a secluded corner of the vast, scantily filled restaurant of the Midland Hotel, beneath a photograph of Stanier Pacific No. 46207 *Princess Arthur of Connaught*, passing through Rugby with the down Welshman, consisting of fourteen bogies.

'It *is* good to see you. Are you better?' said Howard Lewthwaite.

'Much better, thank you. Before we start on the main business, Mr Lewthwaite, I've been asked to do you for "Proud Sons of Thurmarsh".'

'Oh! I'd be honoured, Henry.'

The waiter handed them menus.

'Let's get the ordering out of the way, shall we?' said Howard Lewthwaite.

They studied the vast menus.

'Do you ever get criticized, as a socialist, for spending a lot on meals in public?' said Henry.

'I never thought of that,' said Howard Lewthwaite. 'I was going to order a good burgundy. I think we'd better have the house carafe. And there's not a bad choice on the *table d'hôte*, is there? I like cod mornay.' They ordered their meals. Howard Lewthwaite leant forward and said across the huge table, 'Right. What are these things you've found out?'

'The burning of the Cap Ferrat was arson,' said Henry. 'The death of its owner was murder.'

Howard Lewthwaite went white and sat very still. Henry met his glance and knew. Howard Lewthwaite knew that he knew. They held the gaze. Neither wanted to be the first to be seen to be unable to bear the awfulness of that moment. Henry's flesh crawled. His scalp itched. Hilary seemed very far away.

'You're part of it,' he said flatly.

'Not part of murder and arson,' said Howard Lewthwaite vehemently.

The elderly wine waiter brought what looked like a sample bottle. It contained what looked like a sample. He poured a quarter of an inch of wine. Howard Lewthwaite sniffed it. 'Yes yes,' he said. 'Absolutely revolting. Pour away.'

Henry raised his glass.

'Cheers,' he said. 'Aren't you going to congratulate me?'

'What on?'

'Winning the Nobel Prize for Naïvety.'

'Henry!'

How quiet the room was.

'You're a friend of Peter Matheson,' said Henry. 'You're a friend of the chief planning officer. You invite both of them to your party. You try to put me off by telling me you're convinced nothing illegal has happened. I should have guessed.'

The brown Windsor soup arrived. Those were the halcyon days of brown soups.

'How could you do it, Mr Lewthwaite?'

Howard Lewthwaite smiled. His smile was as thin as the soup. He looked older.

'Lewthwaite's is failing,' he said. 'Naddy'll die if I don't take her to live in a hot, dry climate. You're quite right. There is a development plan for the whole area between Market Street and the river. I'm not ashamed of that. It needs redevelopment. We call it the Fish Hill Complex. A gleaming new shopping centre, Henry. Thurmarsh needs it. Tower blocks by the Rundle, with grass in between. Using the river. What views. Higher than anything in Sheffield or Leeds. Mixed housing, right in the centre. A good plan.'

'Those are nice streets.'

'Henry! They're run-down. They're clapped-out.'

'They're being deliberately run-down so the poor conned townsfolk can be told, "They're run-down. They're clapped-out."'

Howard Lewthwaite didn't reply.

'All this secrecy. Fred Hathersage. Anthony Eden denied collusion with France and Israel. Do you deny collusion? Are there back-handers flying about?'

The cod mornay arrived.

'A bit of everything, gentlemen?' said the waitress.

'A bit of everything,' said Howard Lewthwaite.

Henry didn't know how he could still eat. But anything was better than thinking. Thinking about Hilary. Thinking about Howard Lewthwaite as a father-in-law.

'You feel I've let you down,' said Howard Lewthwaite.

'I feel you've let Hilary down.'

Howard Lewthwaite's eyes met Henry's again.

'You're going to suggest I drop the matter,' said Henry.

'You'll be losing that prize for naïvety.' Howard Lewthwaite smiled. His smile was as tired as the broccoli.

Henry looked across the restaurant to the table where he'd sat with Lorna. This room wasn't redolent of happy memories for him.

'You seem to be forgetting the arson and murder,' he said.

'Today's the first I've heard of arson and murder,' said Howard Lewthwaite.

'Murder of the man who took me in as his son.'

'What?'

'The owner of the Cap Ferrat was my uncle.'

'I didn't know that, Henry. Oh my God, what a business.'

'Yes. The burning of the Cap Ferrat was so convenient for you. Didn't you ever suspect it might be arson.'

'Did you?'

'I'm front runner for the Nobel Prize for Naïvety. You're a politician. Dirt's your natural environment.' No! This is your father-in-law to be.

'I think I did have a little wonder, to be honest,' said Howard Lewthwaite. 'I think I closed my mind to the possibility fairly rapidly. Something unpleasant that I didn't want to admit to myself. Can it be true, Henry? Arson, possibly. Murder? Thurmarsh isn't Chicago.'

'That's what Stan Holliday said.'

'Did he? Oh dear. In that case it probably is Chicago. Where does Stan Holliday come in?'

'He was overheard by my source, which I can't reveal, saying it was arson and murder. I challenged him. He denied it far too vehemently.'

'That's all you're going on, is it? No proof?'

'No proof, no.'

They ate in silence for a few moments.

'How's your cod mornay?' asked Howard Lewthwaite.

'Disgusting. Another sauce that should never have been revealed.'

'Look. Perhaps it *was* arson, but your uncle could still have died accidentally. I mean . . . why should anybody murder him?'

'So there's no owner of the club to pay the insurance money to. So there's no owner of the club to suspect that it was arson.'

'Your nomination for the Nobel Prize is withdrawn,' said Howard Lewthwaite. 'Will you give me a week to try and find out what I can, Henry?'

He had to agree. Hilary was coming down that weekend. He couldn't bear to spoil the weekend. But he couldn't resist making Howard Lewthwaite wait for a few long seconds for his reply. He hadn't often had that kind of power.

'One week,' he said.

They both plumped for the apple pie. Henry got out his notebook.

'Right,' he said. 'It's time to start another interview in my series, "Great Criminals and Hypocrites", alias "Proud Sons of Thurmarsh".'

'We don't need to do this if you don't want to,' said Howard Lewthwaite.

'I have to. Editor's orders. Otherwise it'll look as if he's biased towards the Conservatives.'

'He is.'

'Precisely. That's why he can't be seen to be. Mr Lewthwaite, how old are you?'

'This morning I was 49. Now I'm 93.'

'What made you enter politics?'

'I wanted to serve the Labour Party, and the wider community. My fellow citizens of Thurmarsh, I suppose.'

'No thought of personal gain?'

'Financial, no. I . . . I can't go on with this.'

'We have to. I repeat, "No thought of personal gain?"'

'Financial, no. Glory? Power? Self-satisfaction? We all seek those a bit, don't we? I don't dwell too much on motives. I prefer to dwell on achievements.' Howard Lewthwaite reached out across the table. He just managed to clasp Henry's hand. 'Henry?' he said. 'I promise you. If arson and murder are proved, I'm with you, whatever it costs. Even if it costs . . . Naddy's life. Even if it costs . . .'

Henry finished it for him.

'. . . our marriage.'

21 Dangerous Days

11,000 men were idle at Fords of Dagenham, due to a strike at Briggs Motor Bodies. Egypt announced that she might halt work on clearing the Suez Canal altogether if Israel refused to withdraw from former Egyptian positions in the Gulf of Akaba. Henry took Ginny for a drink at the Winstanley.

'There's a reply to my letter at last,' he said. 'Outraged fury, signed "Another Angry Schoolmaster".'

'Colin wrote it,' said Ginny.

'What?'

'Editor's orders.'

They sat at a corner table, surrounded by brasses and shields. He took surreptitious glances at her face, noting the differences between it and Hilary's, thus making a kind of living map of Hilary's face. It was unfair to use Ginny in this way, but he couldn't help it.

'Hilary's coming down this weekend,' he said. 'And we'll . . . er . . . quite probably be . . . er . . .'

'. . . playing bridge? You want me to make up a four? No? Having a bottle party? Fine. I'd love to come. No? Don't tell me. I've got it. Making love!'

'Oh, Ginny. No, I just thought I'd tell you so that . . . er . . . you could go away if you wanted to.'

'We never made you move out.'

'I'm not making you move out, Ginny.' There's Mr Matheson. Oh no! Supposing Howard Lewthwaite comes in and sees me with Ginny. Why did we come here? Why don't I think ahead? 'I'm giving you the chance to move out, if you want to, because, although I know sound doesn't travel up as much as it travels down, you might still be very conscious of our presence, and I know what it's like, Ginny, when you're all alone, listening to people . . . er . . .'

'. . . thrashing around in sexual ecstasy.' Ginny's eyes filled with tears. Henry handed her one of three handkerchieves which he'd brought in case of just such an emergency. She did it justice. Howard Lewthwaite entered. Ginny said, 'Thanks, Henry. I'm sorry,' and gave him a quick kiss. Howard Lewthwaite saw. Henry hurried up to the bar, to buy drinks they didn't need.

'Hello, Mr Lewthwaite,' he said, over-brightly. 'Hello, Mr Matheson. I've just been . . . er . . . telling the girl from the flat above me that Hilary's coming down this weekend and suggesting that she might like to . . . er . . . go away, so as not to . . . er . . .' He realized that Howard Lewthwaite had no idea that they were having pre-marital sex. His face blazed. Later, he'd realize that Howard Lewthwaite had been embarrassed too, because he was meeting Peter Matheson to discuss what Henry had told him.

'I've got a little story for you,' said Howard Lewthwaite. 'One of our councillors. Jim Rackstraw. He lost a champion pigeon four years ago. His prize bird. It turned up yesterday in Oslo.'

'Thanks,' said Henry. 'Terrific. Thank you very much, Mr Lewthwaite.'

When he returned to Ginny with the drinks, Henry said, 'One of the men I was talking to is Hilary's father. Do you think I could ask you not to kiss me or fondle me or be in any way physically intimate with me for the rest of the evening?'

'I think I might be able to restrain myself,' said Ginny Fenwick.

The *New York Post* attacked the American oil industry's refusal to meet Western Europe's fuel needs. Dick Francis retired from the race track at the age of 36. Denzil Ackerman took Henry for a drink in the bar of the Midland Hotel.

They sat in an alcove, on the brown leather upholstery with gold studs. Above them, the Patriot class engine was still pulling a mixed freight out of Carlisle Upperby Yard in light snow, reminding Henry that this was the corner where they'd sat with Lorna Arrow. Tomorrow he'd be subjecting Hilary to a similar ordeal in the Lord Nelson. He felt sick at the prospect. Had he learnt nothing?

'I'll be in London next week,' said Denzil. 'Interviewing glittering show business personalities so that the citizens of Thurmarsh will be wildly envious of the great world of metropolitan sophistication. I want you to stand in for me.'

'Oh! Well . . . thank you very much,' said Henry.

'This is quite deliberate, dear boy. As you know, I have private means. Not enough to keep me for a lifetime without working. Enough to keep me for what remains of my lifetime without working. I shall retire quite soon. I've found it all quite amusing, even if I haven't exactly fulfilled all my ambitions. I want to go while it's still amusing. I'm grooming you to succeed me.'

'Oh! Well . . . thank you very much.'

'You aren't made for the hurly burly of general reporting.'

'Oh. Well . . . thank you very much,' said Henry rather more doubtfully.

'You introduced me to Lampo. I'm in your debt. There are two jobs for you next week. On Tuesday afternoon you'll interview the Chief Torch Bearer of the Arc of the Golden Light of Our Lady.'

'What??'

'It's a pseudo-religious cult. A pseudo-moralistic sect. It's based in a big house outside town. Hexington Hall. It aims to protect South Yorkshire from the flood of obscenity and pornography.'

'What flood of obscenity and pornography?'

'The one it predicts is coming. And presumably hopes is coming, so that it can protect South Yorkshire from it. It's run by an ex-colonel called Boyce-Uppingham.'

'Good God!'

'You know him?'

'I know his niece. She said she had a nutty uncle near Thurmarsh.'

'Nutty's about right.'

'Is it arc as in light or ark as in Noah's?'

'I don't know. It could be either. Should be fun, anyway. And on Wednesday there's a private view of a new exhibition at the Gusset.'

'Paintings?'

'Yes.'

'I don't know enough about art.'

Denzil summoned a waiter, and ordered a pink gin and a pint of bitter.

'Use long words,' he said. 'Stick in lots of cultural references. A few exclamation marks to suggest they've missed points they didn't even know you were trying to make. It's easy.'

'Whose exhibition is it?'

'Johnson Protheroe's.'

'Who?'

'Precisely.'

'What?'

'Nobody else'll have heard of him either. So you can say what you like.'

'I won't know if he's any good.'

'It's unlikely. He's Canadian.'

'But, Denzil . . . I want to be fair to the man.'

'Oh dear. The sweet innocence of youth! Look, not only is Johnson Protheroe Canadian, but he sounds like a firm of merchant bankers. If, however unlikely, he is good and you don't spot it, I'm sure a bad review in Thurmarsh won't ruin *his* career. I'm giving you the biggest chance of *your* career. For goodness sake, dear boy, rise to it.'

Their drinks arrived.

'Try not to think beer,' said Denzil Ackerman. 'Think pink gin.'

Until he received the editor's summons, Henry had completely forgotten that, before his bout of flu, he'd promised to reveal his scoop within a week. What was he to do? He couldn't reveal it till he'd told Hilary. And he'd told her father that he wouldn't tell her until he'd found out what her father had found out.

'Sit down, Henry.'

So far so good. An order with which he was happy to comply.

'I want you to write another letter, attacking "Another Angry Schoolmaster". Sign it "First Angry Schoolmaster". This one can be really big if we get it off the ground.'

'Right, Mr Redrobe.' At last he'd get through an interview without saying 'sir'.

'It's time to find a permanent job for you, a personal niche, apart from your general duties.'

'Right, Mr Redrobe.' Henry's hopes rose. Had the neat, Brylcreemed editor forgotten?

'But first, you promised me your scoop. Fire away. I'm all ears.'

'Well . . . er . . . it involves a councillor.'

'Ah!'

'A Labour councillor.'

'Ah!!'

'And his pigeon.'

There was a long silence.

'What?'

'His pigeon. Councillor Jim Rackstraw keeps pigeons. He had a prize pigeon. His best bird. One of the four best birds ever bred in South Yorkshire. Four years ago, it disappeared. Without trace. Not a word. Not a coo. It's turned up. In Oslo.'

The editor tapped on his desk very slowly, with his silver pencil, like a sick woodpecker losing its battle for life.

'I see,' he said quietly. He looked at his watch. 'There's time to make the travel arrangements this afternoon.'

'Travel arrangements?' said Henry.

'To Norway. We'll need a complete list of the names and addresses of every single Norwegian on whom that bird has crapped.'

Henry made no reply. There wasn't any reply to be made.

'Yes, I have just the job for you,' said the editor. 'Uncle Jason.'

'Uncle Jason?'

'And his Argusnauts. It's an important job, Henry. Today's children are tomorrow's adults. Don't look so horrified. Surely you aren't going to tell me that the young man who in little more than a twelvemonth has come up with the wandering cat, the escaped canary and the rediscovered pigeon feels incapable of writing for children?'

'No, sir. Of course not, sir. Thank you, sir.'

Damn! Damn! Damn!

They were all there, seated at their corner table in that brown and secret place, that most masculine of all surrogate wombs, the back room of the Lord Nelson in Leatherbottlers' Row. As Uncle Jason entered with his pale, calm fiancée, they all turned to look, like the escape committee eyeing with suspicion the newcomer who'd been recommended as an expert in forged documents. Even Denzil was there, and he very rarely stayed over on a Friday night. Even Ginny was there, and this was the first time she'd been with Gordon and Jill since it had happened. Ginny looked brave and forbidding. Gordon looked sheepish. Jill looked defiant. Colin gave Henry a thumbs-up, as if to suggest that he already approved of Hilary. Henry frowned at him. It wasn't a question of approval.

Denzil bought a round. Hilary asked for beer. Colin nodded his approval. Henry frowned at him.

'We're discussing what the world will be like in thirty years' time,' said Ted.

'Homosexuality will be legal,' said Denzil, arriving with a tray of drinks. He spoke louder than was necessary, for the benefit of Chief Superintendent Ron Ratchett.

'Over my dead body,' muttered Chief Superintendent Ron Ratchett.

'Necrophilia may take a little longer,' said Denzil.

Henry smiled. He'd told Hilary that Denzil was outrageous, and here he was being outrageous. Then he remembered that it wasn't a question of approval, so he stopped smiling and frowned. Then he realized that this might look prudish, so he stopped frowning and smiled. Then he realized that constantly frowning and smiling looked ridiculous, so he sat very rigid and tried to show no feelings at all. Hilary raised a quizzical eyebrow.

'In thirty years' time homosexuality will be so normal that it won't even be considered odd to have homosexual priests,' said Denzil.

'And women priests?' said Hilary.

'That may take a bit longer,' said Ted.

Hilary nodded ruefully. 'You're probably right,' she said.

'The Arc of the Golden Light of Our Lady, whose Chief Torch Bearer I'm interviewing on Tuesday, seem to believe that a flood of pornography is going to be unleashed on the world,' said Henry.

'I think it is,' said Helen. 'I think in thirty years' time it'll be as compulsory for comedians to talk about willies as it's impossible now.' To everyone's surprise, she blushed. When she realized she was blushing, she went scarlet. Ted stared at her in fascinated astonishment.

'Quite right, Helen,' he said. 'Everything'll be pornographic. Even *Listen with Mother.*'

Henry bought a round. When he returned, Ted was saying, 'In thirty years' time, there'll be photos of naked women in the newspapers.' He seemed to be drawn to the subject like a mosquito to a fat thigh.

'What about naked men?' said Hilary.

'That'll take another thirty years.'

'Sex will be a subject that can be freely discussed, openly, honestly, naturally, everywhere,' said Colin.

'Surely, if sex is that free and open, men will no longer need to look at pictures of naked women?' said Hilary.

'Advantage Hilary,' said Gordon.

No, no, Gordon. You're getting it all wrong. It isn't a game, and it isn't competitive.

'Well said, kid,' said Colin. 'No more sex crimes. No more rape.'

None of them knew she'd been raped. Henry began to sweat with embarrassment. Please change the subject, he begged silently.

'What a wonderful thought,' said Hilary, so fervently that he thought she was going to add, 'I've been raped.'

'Oh dear,' said Ginny. 'I wish I agreed with you all. Your world of sexual freedom will be a world for the attractive and the beautiful.' She looked straight at Gordon and Jill. Jill, who hadn't spoken yet, blushed. Ginny relented, and turned away. 'The ugly and the unprepossessing will stand on the side-lines and ogle,' she said. 'It'll be flaunted endlessly. They'll be tormented endlessly. Sex crimes will increase.'

'How very depressing,' said Helen.

'You're all right. You're beautiful,' said Ginny, with feeling.

'I won't be in thirty years,' said Helen with equal feeling.

'Deuce,' said Gordon.

'Are you trying to excuse sex crimes, Ginny?' said Helen.

'Certainly not. I'm trying to explain them,' said Ginny. 'The British are very good at condemning results while totally ignoring causes.'

Colin insisted on buying the next round, because he'd have to rush home to Glenda soon. Hilary drily expressed surprise on learning that he was married.

'Well, time I went home to give the wife . . .' Ben glanced at Hilary. '. . . some help with putting the children to bed.'

And Colin did rush home to Glenda. Ted raised an astonished eyebrow. Henry was amazed at Hilary's ability to change things without saying anything.

A trip to the jazz club was mooted. Gordon and Jill exchanged looks and Gordon said, 'Dunkirk.' Jill looked puzzled.

'He means you should make a tactical withdrawal,' said Ginny. 'There's no need to on my account. I'm thick-skinned and hard-bitten.'

'Good,' said Jill. 'I like the jazz club.'

'Are you coming, Henry?' said Helen.

'Yes,' said Henry, decisively. 'We are, aren't we?' he added, ruining the effect.

Hilary laughed. Everyone must have seen her beauty at that moment. Henry felt proud, and then he realized that Hilary wouldn't like that, and then he didn't know what to think.

They walked down Leatherbottlers' Row into Albion Street, down Albion Street, past the *Chronicle* and *Argus* building, and turned left into Commercial Road. Henry found himself with Helen. Ted was ahead of them, with Hilary. They seemed to be chatting easily. Behind them he could hear Ginny asking Gordon and Jill determinedly casual questions about their plans. Jill was clearly embarrassed. Gordon was finding few opportunities for elegantly coded replies. Ginny sounded totally relaxed.

Helen linked arms with Henry, as they began the gentle climb up Commercial Road. 'One day when I was feverish with the flu I had a hallucination that you were there in bed with Ted and me,' she said. 'I was awfully disappointed to find you weren't.'

'For God's sake, Helen,' he said. He tried to pull his arm free. She clung on. They walked on, linked and silent.

In the jazz club, Helen said, 'Hilary's making a big hit with Ted,' and Henry couldn't bear to see her talking to Ted any more, so he went up to them, right in the middle of 'Basin Street Blues', and grabbed hold of Hilary, and said, 'I want to talk to you, darling,' and Ted hurried back to Helen, smiling, and Henry had an uncomfortable feeling that he'd been an unwitting puppet in a charade.

'How do you like Sid Hallett and the Rundlemen?' he asked.

'I've heard them before, you know,' she said. 'I'm a Thurmarsh girl. Talking of that, your series, "Proud Sons of Thurmarsh", is pretty male-oriented, isn't it? How about a follow-up series, "Proud Daughters of Thurmarsh"?'

'An excellent idea.' Desire for her swept over him. 'I want to make love with you,' he said.

'I must go and see my parents tonight.' There was applause. Sid Hallett and the Rundlemen took huge sips of beer, in unison, as if it were written in the score. They embarked upon 'South Rampart Street Parade'. 'Let's go now,' she said.

'We don't want to seem like wet blankets the first time you meet them all. You've had a bit of that effect already. Usually they all come.'

'They should go home to their wives.'

'I quite agree. But it's their life, isn't it?'

'I can't hide my feelings,' she said. 'I'm awkward, difficult, uncompromising, inconvenient. Do you want to call it off now?' She went round to them all, saying 'Good night.'

'She wants to get home before her parents go to bed. She hasn't seen them yet,' explained Henry.

They walked down Commercial Road in silence.

In York Road, near the station, she said, 'If you want a good sport, you should marry Ginny.'

'Hilary!' he said. 'I thought you liked Ginny,' he added.

'I do,' she said. 'It wasn't an insult.'

'You seemed to like Ted,' he said.

She didn't say another word. There were no kisses, that night, in Perkin Warbeck Drive.

They were on a small chain ferry, gently caressing with entwined fingers. They were crossing a placid river. Brown trout trembled against the stream. Weeds bent gently before the lazy current. On the bank, the gnarled trees were heavy with marzipan and nougat.

The ferry scraped to a halt against the chalky stones. The ferryman turned from his winch, straightened his back and

305

grimaced. He was vaguely familiar. He began to speak. He told them, with blinding clarity, in less than thirty words, all the secrets of life, of its meaning and its conduct.

He woke up. The words faded. He could hear them but not make sense of them. He asked her if she understood them. She wasn't there. He was alone, and last night they had parted without a kiss.

Perhaps she wouldn't come.

She came.

'I'm sorry,' she said.

'I'm sorry, too,' he said.

'That's all right, then.'

'Not a very good evening.'

'We have to put ourselves through a bit more stress than we did at Christmas,' she said. 'I'm not your princess. You aren't my prince. We can't marry each other while we still seem too good to be true.'

For lunch they had bread and marmalade. He dropped a dollop of marmalade on her stomach, and licked it off. By the time they'd dragged themselves from the crumpled wreck of his narrow bed it was almost dark.

Their love was proof against the relentless rain. Darkness lent enchantment to the shining wet streets.

Cousin Hilda was making supper. She sniffed, and Henry wondered if she could smell sex on them. But the air was full of the aroma of imminent faggots, and her disapproval was for the inopportune timing of their visit.

'You should have told me you were coming,' she said. 'If it was stew I'd make it stretch, but you can't stretch faggots. Two faggots are two faggots, whichever road you look at them. It wouldn't be fair to make my businessmen go short, who've paid.'

'We can't eat, thank you very much,' said Hilary. 'We're expected at home.'

Cousin Hilda sniffed. 'You could have been expected at this home,' she said.

'We didn't want to be any trouble,' said Henry.

'Trouble!' said Cousin Hilda. 'I suppose you're above and beyond faggots, now you're a journalist.'

306

'Very much the reverse,' said Henry. He met Hilary's eyes and she smiled with the utmost decorum.

'Hilary and I are engaged, Cousin Hilda,' said Henry.

Cousin Hilda didn't attempt to hide her hurt, but she couldn't quite hide the delight behind the hurt.

'Oh!' she said. 'Engaged! Well! And I've never even met her before. Well!'

Henry kissed her. Then Hilary kissed her. She received these kisses as her due.

'Well!' she said. 'Mrs Wedderburn will be pleased. She'll be right thrilled. She's very fond of you.' There were tears in Cousin Hilda's eyes. She just managed to finish speaking without breaking down. 'It'll make Mrs Wedderburn's day, will this.' She hurried off into the scullery. 'All this talk,' she said. 'I'm neglecting my faggots.'

Henry's eyes were filled with tears too, damn it. And so were Hilary's. This was intolerable.

'Can I help?' said Hilary, hurrying into the scullery.

To Henry's astonishment, Hilary didn't reappear. Cousin Hilda allowed her to help. No greater compliment could possibly have been paid by Cousin Hilda. Slowly, shamingly slowly, he was beginning to realize that he'd been blessed with the love of a quite extraordinary person. He was filled with astonishing warmth and joy. He sat and stared at the glowing stove. He could hear them clattering in the scullery. He heard Cousin Hilda say, 'Mrs Wedderburn's had a soft spot for Henry ever since she lent him her camp-bed.' The tears were streaming down his face. He hurried upstairs to the lavatory, to hide this damning evidence of emotion.

Cousin Hilda insisted that they stayed. Hilary must meet her businessmen. She even offered them a cup of tea! So Hilary was introduced to Liam, who adored her instantly, and to Norman Pettifer, who tried to take a jaundiced view of her and failed, and to Mr Peters, who thought she was a fine thing and told her of other fine things to which he had become used. They sat and chatted, as the three men demolished their faggots, their mashed potatoes, their peas, their tinned pears to follow.

Oh joy of youth, it was still raining, and, as they walked to

Perkin Warbeck Drive, they were able to demonstrate again that rain couldn't hurt them.

The sight of Howard Lewthwaite brought Henry back to the reality that he'd had to hide from Hilary. How could they lose each other now, after the bonds they had forged that day? And now he made sure that the bonds were even more closely forged. He suggested that they fix the wedding date. They did. Saturday, July 20th. Nadežda cried. Sam asked if they'd had their oats that morning and had it been better than cornflakes? Henry met Howard Lewthwaite's eye and his look tried to say, 'Yes. We've made love. We love each other deeply and respect each other totally and believe our love is a most beautiful and moral thing.' Howard Lewthwaite gave him a look which might have meant, 'I understand and I'm not angry' but might also have meant, 'What on earth is that look of yours supposed to mean?' Henry gave him a look which was supposed to mean, 'Can you give me any hint regarding the progress of your investigations into the dire matter which hangs over this touching domestic scene like a thundercloud over the sweet cow-dunged water meadows at the end of a midge-mad July day?' and Howard Lewthwaite gave him a look which might have meant, 'I haven't found out anything definite,' but might also have meant, 'Since neither of us has the faintest idea what each other's looks mean, it looks as though we ought to stop giving each other these looks.'

'Don't mind me,' said Auntie Doris through her tears, as the wind rattled the windows of the lounge bar of the White Hart. 'I'm just a silly, feeble-minded old woman.'

'Yes, you are,' said Geoffrey Porringer. 'So shut up.'

'Geoffrey!' said Auntie Doris.

'Joke!' said Geoffrey Porringer.

'Jokes are supposed to be funny, Geoffrey,' said Auntie Doris.

Over late lunch in the hotel's deserted restaurant, she wanted to know every detail of their courtship. 'Italy!' she said. 'How romantic! And then the long quest before you met again. Isn't that a lovely story, Geoffrey?'

Geoffrey Porringer nodded and said, 'Lovely. Let's crack another bottle.'

While Geoffrey Porringer cracked another bottle, Auntie Doris said, 'Does this mean you won't come to Cap Ferrat?'

'Do you want me to come?' said Henry.

'More than anything in the world,' said Auntie Doris, who was no stranger to hyperbole.

'I'll come for a week,' said Henry, who was. Auntie Doris looked so gratified that he wished he hadn't already begun to add, 'I have to take my third week before the end of March anyway.'

When Auntie Doris went to see a man about a dog, Geoffrey Porringer said, 'She's excited, Hilary. I don't want you to think she's always like this.'

'Everything's fine,' said Hilary. 'I'm enjoying myself.'

'Sometimes when she's happy, she gets carried away, and doesn't realize how much she's drinking,' said Geoffrey Porringer.

When Hilary went to see a man about a dog, Geoffrey Porringer said, 'She's lovely, Henry. She really is. I can't get over it.'

'Don't sound so surprised,' said Auntie Doris, who always made things worse by protesting about them. 'It makes it sound as though we wouldn't expect him to make a decent catch.'

'Decent catch!' said Geoffrey Porringer. 'He's landed in the middle of a shoal of mackerel.'

When Henry went to see a man about a dog, he didn't know what they talked about, but they were all laughing when he returned, and he was a little disturbed to find how richly entertaining life without him was.

'It's a nice hotel,' said Hilary.

'How the conversation descends to the banal when I return,' said Henry.

'I'll show you the brochure, Hilary,' said Geoffrey Porringer.

'Geoffrey!' said Auntie Doris. 'Young people in love aren't interested in brochures. They've other things on their minds.'

'She's got a tongue in her head,' said Geoffrey Porringer. 'Hilary, would you like to see the brochure?'

'Very much,' said Hilary.

'You see!' said Geoffrey Porringer.

'She could hardly say, "God, no! How tedious,"' said Auntie Doris.

When Geoffrey Porringer had gone to fetch the brochure,

Auntie Doris said, 'Henry had been interceding on my behalf with his Uncle Teddy, hadn't you, Henry?'

'Well, yes,' said Henry. 'Yes, I had.'

'Until he was incarcerated in the ruins of his life's dream,' said Auntie Doris.

'I heard about that,' said Hilary. 'It was tragic.'

It could be more tragic than you know, thought Henry.

'It was, Hilary,' said Auntie Doris. 'That's exactly what it was. And at the time, when it happened, Henry, I think you felt there was a chance, didn't you?'

'Well, yes,' said Henry. 'Yes, I did.'

Geoffrey Porringer returned, waving the brochure.

'There we are, Hilary,' he said. 'One brochure.'

Hilary studied the brochure with as much interest as she could muster.

'Very nice,' she said. 'Very reasonable.'

'We like to think so,' said Geoffrey Porringer.

In the train, on the journey from a fading evening of sodden sheep to a sodium night of glistening roofs, Hilary said, 'I thought you were exaggerating, but they're every bit as bad as you said.'

'Auntie Doris and Geoffrey Porringer?'

'No. His blackheads.'

At Leeds, she caught the train north and this time she didn't turn away abruptly. She leant out of the window. He walked beside her. 'Love you,' she said. 'Love you love you love you.' He began to trot, he was out beyond the canopy, in the rain again. 'Love you,' she yelled again. He stopped right at the end of the platform, where it narrowed to a wedge. Smoke from the engine swirled around him, but every now and then it cleared and there she was, moving furiously, unashamed of love, of sentiment, of intensity, of banality, of childishness, unable to be hurt by any separation that was merely geographical. He watched until the last of the twelve bogies was invisible, and then he turned away. Rain streamed down his face. Tears streamed down his face. Never had his face been bombarded by so much water in one weekend.

President Eisenhower spoke of the 'abiding strength' of the Anglo-American alliance. Israel continued to refuse to withdraw her forces from Gaza. Canada refused to support demands for Israel to withdraw, and threatened to withdraw her troops from the emergency force unless the United Nations force was empowered to patrol the Israeli–Egyptian border and to remain to keep the peace after the Israeli withdrawal. Workers at Briggs Motor Bodies voted to defy their union and continue their strike.

'Hello, boys and girls,' typed Henry, bashing the keys angrily. 'Some of you Argusnauts are already making contributions to next Christmas's toy fund, so that less fortunate children can have a treat. Well done, each and every one of you.

'Special thanks this week for Dora Pennyweather, aged 11, who made six super teddy bears. I'm so sorry I couldn't meet her when she handed them in at our office.'

That afternoon, he interviewed Bill Holliday for 'Proud Sons of Thurmarsh'. He felt that this would make him the laughing stock of the whole town.

The dun-coloured bus growled irritably through the southern suburbs. Rows of semi-detached houses breasted the sweeping hills. Some had dark red brick ground floors and stucco above. Some had brick centres and stucco edges. Some had bay windows topped by tiny tiled roofs. Some had decorated brick arches round the doorways. These brave attempts at individuality only emphasized the sameness of it all. Towns didn't grow organically any more. They were planned by bureaucrats, and people were moved around to fit the plans. Society would pay for all this deadness, thought Henry, as the inexorable bus took him nearer and nearer to Bill Holliday, whom he was convinced was at the centre of all the dirty work surrounding the development plan.

Bill Holliday's office was a glass island in a sea of cars. In front of it, rows of used cars. What mechanical horrors did the gleaming, seemingly innocent bonnets conceal? Behind the office, on the rolling slopes of what had once been prime farmland, an alp of rust rose out of a glistening porridge of mud. The office had wide windows on both sides, as if Bill Holliday actually wanted to see all this. It had a fluffy white carpet and two soft armchairs covered in imitation tiger skin. There was a glass-fronted drinks cabinet.

'Brandy?' said Bill Holliday.

Refusals crunched round Henry's brain like old cars under a

bulldozer. I don't while I'm on duty. It might affect my judgement.
I wouldn't soil my gullet with your ill-gotten gains, you murderous
bastard.

He finally decided upon, 'Thank you very much.'

'Cigar?'

Ditto.

Puffing, choking, sipping, choking, at three-fifteen on a grey
afternoon, Henry felt a bit of a villain himself. And liked the
feeling, which was alarming. He apologized for the misprint. Bill
Holliday laughed. 'Don't worry,' he said. '"Ow"! It just about
sums up our engagement.' He sighed. 'She wants me for my
money. The jewellery I buy her. I want love.' Love? You? Mr
Scrap? The man you wouldn't buy a used car from? Love? 'People
laugh when I say this, but I'm a deeply loving person. I love kids.
Angie doesn't want kids. Tell you who I'd like to meet on your rag.
Oops, sorry. Paper.' He roared with laughter. 'Uncle Jason. Loves
kids, that bastard. White-haired old bugger, is he?'

'Yes,' said Henry. 'Yes. White-haired old bugger.'

'Grand. I'm an unashamed sentimentalist. They don't make
them like that, any more.'

Henry took a deep breath and plunged in, hoping to catch Bill
Holliday off guard.

'My Uncle Teddy ran the Cap Ferrat,' he said. 'You knew him,
didn't you?'

'Oh aye. Angie and I went there, oh, what, must have been four
times.'

'Are you sure it wasn't five?' Henry tried not to sound terrified.
'Are you sure you didn't go there once more, without Angie?'

'What?' Bill Holliday looked more puzzled than alarmed. 'On
me own? I wouldn't have dared go without Angie.'

Henry had the uneasy feeling that all avenues led to brick walls.
He began his interview. Bill Holliday defended his line of business. 'Folk think it's a dirty business, 'cos of t'great mounds of cars.
What silly buggers don't realize is, if it weren't for my mounds,
where'd cars be? Eh? All over t'bloody town. All over t'bloody
Dales. Right?' He defended greyhound racing. 'When have six
dogs had to be destroyed after pile-up over Bechers? Eh? Sport of
kings? Piss off. Give me dogs any day.'

He refilled Henry's glass and led him to the window. They gazed in awe at the pile of rusting Fords, Morrises, Humbers, Standards, Armstrong-Siddeleys. At the top of the pile, an Austin Seven was lying across a Daimler.

'Equal, at last, in death. Like folks,' said Bill Holliday.

Henry looked at him in surprise.

'This is just a molehill, compared to what's to come,' said Bill Holliday. 'Motoring will increase tenfold. Old cars will increase tenfold. It'll be folk like me what saves the world from choking. Does the world thank us? Does it buggery.'

Henry watched a beautiful old Riley being crushed flat. He shuddered.

'How would tha like to be crushed like that?' said Bill Holliday. 'Wouldn't be much fun, eh?'

He roared with laughter.

Henry didn't.

A patrol of the Queen's Own Cameron Highlanders was ambushed by mountain tribesmen in the Western Aden Protectorate. Fighting flared up on the Aden frontier, threatened by 4,000 Yemenis. Security forces arrested 189 men in 4 days in the mountains of Western Cyprus. In Thurmarsh a crate of surgical trusses fell from a crane and nearly killed Uncle Jason. These were dangerous days.

He was on his way to catch the bus to Hexington, where he would interview Colonel Boyce-Uppingham, Chief Torch Bearer of the Arc (?) of the Golden Light of Our Lady, in the Athenaeum Club in Doncaster Road. Being early, he'd gone to have another look at the planned development area. The southernmost warehouse in Glasshouse Lane was still in use, although it was lorries now, not boats, that used its wharf. Pleased to see some life in this dying area, Henry watched as a crane slowly manipulated a crate, which contained, though he didn't yet know it, a consignment of surgical trusses for export to Portugal. One moment he was looking up into a blue sky streaked with mackerel clouds. The next moment he was watching a crate falling towards him, growing larger and larger. He hurled himself to the right, tripped and fell. The crate smashed into the pavement, inches from his head. It burst open. Wood and splinters filled the air. Surgical trusses, intended for the hernias of Lisbon and Oporto, rained down on a terrified young English journalist.

He sat up. He stood up. His heart was thumping. His legs felt weak. He leant against the warehouse wall. The crane driver yelled out, pitifully inadequately, 'Sorry!'

The landlord of the Artisan's Rest hurried over. 'I saw that,' he said. 'Tha were lucky!'

A corner of Henry's mind debated the philosophical aspect of this. In all probability, no crates of surgical trusses had fallen that day in Europe, North America, South America, Asia, Australasia, Africa or the Indian Subcontinent. The only crate had fallen inches from Henry. It could have been worse, but . . . lucky?

He accepted a large brandy on the house. As he walked away, he reflected on what a week it was becoming for large brandies in the afternoon.

He wondered which of his colleagues would have written the story that would have gone beneath the headline 'Journalist (21) crushed by surgical trusses'.

He thought of all the other things that might fall on him – decaying Georgian stone-work, disintegrating meteorites, wing-flaps off old planes, swans cut short by blood clots in mid-flight. Life was incredibly dangerous.

And then it struck him, like a falling crate of surgical trusses. The obvious fact, which hadn't occurred to him, because this was Thurmarsh, not Chicago, this was real life, not a novel, he was Henry Pratt, not a gangster. The crate had been meant to kill him. Somebody – Bill Holliday, or his evil-faced brother Stan, or both, or somebody else – was trying to rub him out.

He began to think of what might hit him by design. Packing cases pushed from attic windows. Sharp slates dropped off roofs. Bullets from hidden snipers. Meat pies lobbed from the Rundle Café. He arrived at the bus station in no fit state to conduct an interview, which might explain, though it couldn't excuse, the fiasco that was to follow.

Hexington Hall was a minor stately home, with an unimposing classical stone frontage, set in scruffy park-land. A pale, male secretary led Henry across a large entrance hall, gliding as if on wheels, his buttocks firmly clenched against the expected flood of pornography. Henry caught a glimpse, through open doors, of rooms where once the living had been gracious.

The large drawing-room smelt of damp and righteousness. Courtly ancestors in darkened oils looked down on tables covered in piles of leaflets.

Colonel Hubert Boyce-Uppingham shook his hand with surprising gentleness. They sat in leather armchairs in front of a modest fire of dead wood from the estate. The Chief Torch Bearer had short, crinkly hair, an aquiline nose, and dark eyes which glittered with intelligence, or fanaticism, or malice, or a combination of all three. Henry wasn't yet sure.

'I know your niece,' he said.

'Oh?' Colonel Boyce-Uppingham sounded as if this was so unlikely that only good manners deterred him from disputing it. He changed the subject humiliatingly, launching into his theme, not with loud military briskness, as Henry had expected, but with the more dangerous, soft, silkily reasonable tones of the man who has never doubted that he is right. 'It's only straws in the wind as yet. *Waiting for Godot. Look Back in Anger.* A French revue in which a horse "defecates" on stage.' An acolyte with acne, serving tea and a digestive, barely interrupted the flow. 'Where will it end? With four-letter words on television and the live sexual act performed on stage by the Thurmarsh Repertory Company.'

Henry looked up and saw, to his horror, right above his head, a huge chandelier.

Totally unheard by Henry, totally unaware that he was totally unheard by Henry, Colonel Hubert Boyce-Uppingham was warming to his theme. 'The military mind is trained to enter the mind of the enemy, in order to anticipate his moves. Monty did it with Rommel. That's why he beat him. That's what I'm doing.'

Journalist crushed by chandelier! Henry longed to move. He didn't dare. He was petrified.

'So I become the enemy,' said Colonel Boyce-Uppingham. 'So who am I, this enemy? I'm a greedy man. I'm an unattractive man, rejected by women. I'm a man with hatred in his heart.'

Henry looked up, at the single chain which held up the mighty chandelier. Which of them could have sawn through it? The spotty server of tea? The slinking, sliding secretary? Bill Holliday, visiting to collect an old car? He shivered, despite the fire.

'So, I will wreak my revenge on the sex that has rejected me. On the God who has given me no charm. Making a fortune as I do so!'

Colonel Boyce-Uppingham paused, for dramatic effect. Like a passenger who wakes when the car stops, Henry hurtled back to consciousness. He began to scribble, self-protectively. Reassured by this activity, Colonel Boyce-Uppingham resumed.

'I want to exploit women for money,' he said. 'I want to own and exploit "ladies of the night".' Even in the mind of the enemy, he couldn't bring himself to avoid euphemism entirely. 'I want to open filthy strip-clubs, where their bodies will be humiliated by men with hungry eyes. I want to fill the land with naughty magazines, a tidal flood of filth.'

Henry's mouth sagged open. His pencil could hardly keep up. This was dynamite. The chandelier was almost forgotten.

'Now do you see what I have to fight, why I see it as my personal mission to defeat these dark forces?' said Colonel Boyce-Uppingham.

'Yes. Yes, I do,' said Henry.

'And will you print all this, in your newspaper, to help me?'

'Oh yes! Yes, I will,' said Henry.

On Wednesday afternoon, there having been no reply to Henry's second letter signed 'First Angry Schoolmaster', Colin typed a second letter signed 'Second Angry Schoolmaster'.

The phrases rolled off Henry's rickety old typewriter. 'The Chief Torch Bearer of the Ark . . .' It had turned out to be that kind of ark. '. . . of the Golden Light of Our Lady told me, with astonishing frankness, of his secret desires.

'"I want to exploit women for money," he told me. "I want to open filthy clubs . . ."

'. . . instead of giving way to these impulses, Colonel Boyce-Uppingham is countering them by leading a nationwide fight against pornography.

'Perhaps, as the man who knows no fear can never be truly

called brave, so the man who knows no temptation can never truly be called good.'

He handed his first full-length feature article to Terry Skipton, who read it with increasing astonishment.

'He really said all that?'

'Every word.' He showed Terry his notebook. The news editor read it carefully.

'This is dynamite,' he said at last.

'I know.'

And off Henry went, well pleased with himself, to the private view at the Gusset Gallery.

His air of triumph was quickly flattened by the need to look out for falling crates. It wasn't a comfortable feeling, knowing that someone was trying to kill you.

At last he reached the comparative safety of the gallery. Safety? Man killed by falling painting. Constable lands on journalist.

The Gusset Gallery was situated next to the court house, beside the Town Hall. It was built in the Italianate style, as if it had been hoped that something of that nation's artistic greatness would rub off on it.

He climbed an impressive staircase, past the bust of Sir Joshua Gusset, liniment maker and philanthropist, past early paintings of the Thurmarsh School, some of which, unfortunately, had not been restored, and others of which, even more unfortunately, had.

The white-walled rectangular gallery was bare of furniture except for a trestle-table with a white cloth, behind which a man with a bow-tie was dispensing wine, and two wooden benches, one facing each long wall, set in the middle of the room directly beneath a skylight. Skylight! Assassin lurked in skylight, inquest told.

Men in dark suits and women in two-piece costumes with extravagant hats were standing around and talking. A few artistically attired people were even looking at the pictures.

A large lady approached him like an overdressed waterspout.

'Hermione Jarrett,' she said. She seemed to think no further explanation was necessary.

'Henry Pratt.' Two could play at that game.

'Ah!' She was puzzled.

'I'm from the *Argus*,' he said, relenting.

'Oh! What's happened to our nice Mr Ackerman?'

'He's in London.'

'Oh!' Hermione Jarrett's expression suggested that they had been unforgivably let down by hitherto nice Mr Ackerman. 'Well, never mind. You'd like a catalogue, of course.'

Her 'of course' triggered his perversity. 'Later,' he said grandly. 'When I review exhibitions, I usually like to remain unencumbered by the kind of preconceptions that titles give.'

He took a glass of red wine and tried to look as if assessing paintings was something he did every week.

There were forty-two pictures. They were modern. They were colourful. They were bold, sometimes even violent. There seemed to be a Cubist influence. They were, he thought, not terrible. But were they good? He had no idea.

He began to see certain things in certain of them. He began to see strange seascapes, with blue still seas beneath black, thundery clouds. One picture seemed to be of a barometer, with a serene, empty face set before a background of purple storm clouds. A glimmer of an idea came to him. Perhaps the pictures represented complacency, blue seas failing to reflect stormy skies, man failing to find a message on the face of the cosmic barometer. He began to see this theme all round him, but was it Johnson Protheroe's or his own? If only he hadn't so pretentiously denied himself access to the catalogue.

He listened to other people's comments, hoping for guidance. 'Look, Edgar, that's exactly the colour of our clematis,' wasn't much help. 'He's as daft as a brush,' seemed more promising, until he heard the reply, which was 'Aye, well, he would be. Red setters often are.'

Were there usually people so ignorant of art at private views? Or were these people hired hoods, with forged invitations, whose task it was to wipe Henry out?

He decided to stick closely to Hermione Jarrett, for protection. She topped up his glass, and gave him a catalogue. The pictures had no titles. No help there! He was out of his depth.

'They've no titles,' he said.

'No,' she said. 'Apparently he regards titles as the labels of prejudice. He's an uncompromising man. Of course he has been described as the harbinger of a new brutalism.'

Henry felt that he must make some reply. What reply could he make? He hadn't even been aware that there had been an old brutalism. His nerves felt shredded. He couldn't cope with all this.

'Well,' he said, 'he could hardly be more brutal than life.'

'That's not bad,' said Hermione Jarrett. 'You've been hiding your light under a bushel, young man. Well, under dear Mr Ackerman, to be precise.' She remembered dear Mr Ackerman's proclivities and visibly regretted her choice of phrase. 'Come and meet a keen patron of the arts, Mr Hathersage.' She led Henry, at a cracking pace that permitted no escape, straight towards the man who was very probably trying to kill him.

'Henry Pratt!' said the diminutive property developer. 'Greetings, young sir!'

Oh no. Another member of the 'young sir' brigade.

Like many a hostess who has solved the problem of two guests whom she doesn't like by introducing them to each other, Hermione Jarrett scuttled off with all the joy of a freed rabbit. The eyes of the two people whom Hermione Jarrett didn't like met, and Henry's blood ran cold. *Was* this man trying to kill him?

'So what do you think of them?' said Fred Hathersage.

'I think they're very interesting,' said Henry cautiously, cravenly.

'I think they're crap,' said Fred Hathersage savagely. Was his savagery really aimed at modern art, or at Henry? 'I like English painters of the old school. I'm thinking of people like . . .' He paused. '. . . Constable.'

Henry was seeing hidden meanings everywhere now. Did Fred Hathersage mean, 'Don't go to the police'?

'And Turner.'

Did he mean, 'Or you'll be turning in your grave'?

'And Sir Alfred Munnings.'

Did he mean, 'If you aren't careful, you'll end up as dead, lifeless horseflesh'?

Henry shuddered. He felt that he couldn't remain in the same room as Fred Hathersage a moment longer. He fled, back to the warm licensed womb in Leatherbottlers' Row, and just missed hearing a broad-beamed lady in an aquamarine suit say, 'It says "Toronto" upside-down on that one. How very strange!'

Next morning, before going to court, Henry typed up his review. He imagined that Denzil would approve of his intro, which read: 'If Ceri Richards is the Welsh Vlaminck, can Johnson Protheroe be said to be the Braque of Canada? Or even . . . intriguing thought! . . . her Sisley?'

He imagined Denzil nodding approval of: 'There is a series of bold, disturbing seascapes here. The seas are as blue as a de Wint door, yet the skies are heavy with the menace of thunder! Is this the *sturm und drang* of a transatlantic Klimt? Or is it a Hogarthian statement about mankind's condition?'

Henry himself quite liked: 'Another picture (a kind of *faux-naïf* Cubism of the Rockies!!) explores this *leitmotif* in an even more specific way. It shows a barometer hanging on a wall. The background says, clearly, "Stormy". Significantly, the barometer does not!'

He bashed out his final paragraph. 'If all you know of Canadian painting is of the likes of Tom Thompson, Jock Macdonald and A. Y. Jackson, with perhaps a vague notion about the Automatistes of Montreal . . . I must confess I'm shamefully vague about them! . . . then hurry along to the Gusset.'

He handed his review to Terry Skipton, with a third letter signed 'First Angry Schoolmaster'. The news editor read the review slowly, his heavily lidded eyes seeming to bore through its pathetic pretensions.

'Not bad at all,' he said.

Henry tried to hide his surprise and relief.

'Really not at all bad.'

Henry tried to hide his delight.

'In fact it's just like the incomprehensible twaddle Mr Ackerman writes,' said Terry Skipton.

'Have whatever you like,' said Howard Lewthwaite. 'Though personally I'll stick to the *table d'hôte.*'

The exceptionally mild weather was continuing, and it was

uncomfortably warm in the restaurant of the Midland Hotel. All the lights were on, for the day was grey.

'It's very difficult to prove that a fire isn't arson,' said Howard Lewthwaite. 'You can prove it is, and if you don't prove it is, you assume it isn't.'

The waiter approached.

'What is the *potage* today?' said Howard Lewthwaite.

'Oxtail, sir,' said the waiter.

'Right. Oxtail soup and I like the sound of the cheese omelette,' said Howard Lewthwaite.

'Soup for me, too,' said Henry. 'And what are the *rillettes Thurmarshiennes*?'

'Rissoles, sir.'

'The lamb chop, please.'

'They do quite a nice choice, don't they?' said Howard Lewthwaite. 'The fire people can add nothing to what was said at the inquest. All you have to go on, Henry, is one overheard comment. Heard from Hilary lately?'

'Of course,' said Henry. 'We write almost every day.'

'It's wonderful the effect you've had on that girl. Wonderful. I've talked to Peter Matheson and Fred Hathersage. We'll allow you to uncover, as a scoop for yourself, the development plans, the architect's model, the fact that Fred owns some of the property. All above board. Nothing denied. If anybody wishes to make allegations, let them try to find proof. A great story for you, Henry. We didn't want to unveil it yet, but you've been too clever for us. Kudos for you. No problems with Hilary. How about it?'

'Somebody's trying to kill me,' said Henry.

'Two oxtail?' said the waiter.

'Yes,' said Howard Lewthwaite faintly. 'What did you say?' he said, when the waiter had gone.

'I went to see Bill Holliday on Monday,' said Henry.

'Bill's all right.'

'So everybody says.'

'He's a very generous supporter of children's charities.'

'So what's he hiding? I've grown up this last year. I was interviewing him for "Proud Sons of Thurmarsh".'

'Did your piece on me well, incidentally.'

321

'Thanks. I vaguely threatened him. A threat that was pretty meaningless if he wasn't guilty. Immediately, he threatened me. And the very next day, I was nearly killed by surgical trusses.'

'Surgical trusses?'

Henry gave Howard Lewthwaite the details, breaking off as the waiter removed their plates to say, 'Mr Tintern thinks Hilary might get a first, if she works hard.'

'It could have been an accident,' said Howard Lewthwaite, when the waiter had gone.

'So could the Cap Ferrat,' said Henry. 'It isn't likely, though, is it? It's all too damned convenient. God knows, Mr Lewthwaite, I'm not brave. And I can't bear the thought of losing Hilary. But what can I do? Run away? Give up? Fine husband and father I'd make.'

The waiter returned.

'Who's for the chop?' he said.

'Both of us, probably,' said Howard Lewthwaite.

22 Black Friday

Halfway through his coffee and toast, there was a knock on his door.

'It's me,' said Ginny. 'I'm not well.'

He opened the door. Her face was pale and puffy. He felt it incongruous that a future war correspondent should have a pink dressing-gown with fluffy pom-poms.

'What's wrong?' he said.

'Prawn curry.'

'What?'

'I had a prawn curry at the Shanghai. I've got food poisoning. Will you tell Terry?'

'Right.'

She hurried off, unaware that a prawn curry might have saved her life.

There was pale, watery sunshine, but already high clouds were drifting in from the west. Dennis Lacey was also on his own.

'Is your friend ill?' he said.

'She's got food poisoning,' said Henry. 'How's . . . er . . . Marie, isn't it?'

'By heck, you've got a memory.'

'I'm a trained journalist.'

'She's gorra day off. She's changed shifts with this friend . . . look out!!'

Henry turned, and saw a black Standard Eight coming straight for them. He looked into the white, silently screaming, strangely hunched face of the driver. He dived to the side. The car missed the tram stop by inches. It just missed Henry as he crashed onto the pavement, but it struck Dennis Lacey, tossing him into the air. The car scraped along the stone wall of number 243, struck another member of the queue a glancing blow, and roared off down Winstanley Road. Somebody screamed. Dennis Lacey was lying in a crumpled heap, moaning, bleeding. The woman who'd been hit was staring at her cut leg with stunned disbelief. Henry crunched across the gravel, past the monkey puzzle tree. The door opened. '999,' he gasped. A frightened woman, with her hair in a net, nodded. The house had new furniture, new carpets, a new smell, but in the few seconds before his call got through, in that dark hall, Henry thought of the teas he'd had in this house with his English teacher, Mr Quell, and his blind wife, and stale Battenburg cake. The Quells had gone to live in Worthing so that, instead of not being able to see this northern industrial town, Mrs Quell could end her days not being able to see the sea.

Dennis Lacey was rushed to the Infirmary, where he was X-rayed in his own department. 'Not an emergency already,' said one of his colleagues, as he was wheeled in. 'There would be, with Dennis late.'

Henry described the incident to the police, without letting on that he was the intended target. He'd have to tell them some time, but he wanted to tell Mr Lewthwaite and Hilary first.

He'd tell Mr Lewthwaite tonight, and go on to Durham tomorrow after work. He'd have to. There was no time to lose. He owed it to the citizens of Thurmarsh.

Dennis Lacey's only crime had been to stand next to Henry Pratt, The Man They Were Trying To Muzzle. It seemed possible that it had cost him his life.

The news-room was eerily quiet when Henry arrived at ten-fifteen. All the reporters were out on stories.

'What's kept you?' said Terry Skipton. 'And where's Ginny?'

'Ginny has food poisoning,' said Henry. 'She ate a prawn curry at the Shanghai. I've almost been killed.'

'You what?'

'A car came straight for us at the tram stop and almost killed the man next to me.'

'Why? It's not icy, is it?'

'Oh no. This was an attempted murder, Mr Skipton.'

Terry Skipton gawped at him.

'You lucky man!' he said.

'I know. A few inches more!'

'I'm talking about the story.'

'You what?'

'I came within inches of death as I saw the murder car mow down the man standing beside me. I felt the wind on my legs as the fatal mudguards brushed my trousers. Miracle escape for *Argus* reporter in tram stop rush-hour murder terror.'

'Oh my God,' said Henry. 'I never thought of it as a story.'

Terry Skipton threw back his head and laughed. Henry had never seen him laugh before. He wanted to say, 'But he was trying to kill me, you see.' He couldn't.

Terry Skipton stopped laughing as suddenly as he'd begun.

'How's the person who was hit?' he said.

'Still alive when he was taken off.'

'Ring the Infirmary and find out how he is and who he is.'

'I know who he is,' said Henry. 'He's called Dennis Lacey. He works in the X-ray department.'

'Where?'

'At the Infirmary.'

'Hospital worker's colleagues fight for his life after horror at the tram stop when rush-hour became crush-hour,' said Terry Skipton.

'His girl-friend Marie would have been with him, but she changed shifts in favour of a friend.'

'Amazing escape of Miracle Marie, the good-time girl who became a good-turn girl,' said Terry Skipton.

'Ginny would have been there too.'

'"Chinese meal saved my life," says Grateful Ginny.' Terry Skipton smiled. Henry had never seen him smile before. 'It must have been a nasty experience,' he said, much more gently. 'Now get the complete story. You have one hour to redeem yourself. Nobody need ever know about this conversation.'

He winked. Henry had never seen Terry Skipton wink before.

Barely an hour later, Henry stuck a piece of cheap paper into his decrepit typewriter and hammered away so fiercely that the letter t broke off. Excited by his story and by his courage in continuing to work when he'd so narrowly escaped being murdered, Henry didn't notice. He bashed out his intro: 'A peaceful ram queue urned in o a cauldron of error in hurmarsh his morning when a car climbed he pavemen and hi   wo people, injuring one of hem severely in he legs and ches .'

He inked in the missing letters, handed in the story, reported the fault to the typewriter maintenance people and, as instructed, left a note in the machine to remind them what was wrong. He wasn't happy with the first draft of his note, which read: ' his ypewri er has no le   er .' He threw it away and, after careful thought, started again. 'My machine lacks a symbol which follows s and precedes *u*,' he typed. 'So please would you give my machine a symbol which follows s and precedes *u*. Yours sincerely, Henry Pra .'

He had the front page lead, his first ever review of an art exhibition, and a huge feature on Colonel Boyce-Uppingham. It was practically a Henry Pratt benefit edition. He'd have felt good, except that the better he felt, the more he felt that he didn't want to die, and so the worse he felt.

At 3.13 his world began to fall apart. Terry Skipton told him that an angry Colonel Boyce-Uppingham was in Interview Room B and wanted to see him.

Interview Room B was bare and dingy, with dirty yellow paint, four upright chairs round a nasty, cheaply veneered table, a single light bulb with a green shade and a ribbed radiator from which the paint was peeling.

Colonel Boyce-Uppingham was pacing up and down restlessly, but his voice was carefully controlled.

'Redrobe's gone out,' he said, as if the editor's absence was a deliberate snub. 'So I've come to you for an explanation.'

'An explanation?'

Colonel Boyce-Uppingham waved Henry's article in the air. 'Of this disgusting pan of festering ferret's entrails masquerading as journalism. It's misrepresentation on a gargantuan scale.'

Henry hurried out, and soon returned with the notebook full of someone else's shorthand notes from days gone by. He opened it at a random page and handed it to Colonel Boyce-Uppingham.

'"English pork is good, with leg and loin at 3s. 8d. a pound,"' read Colonel Boyce-Uppingham. '"Shoulder of lamb is 3s. to

3s. 4d. English beef, too, is good, and offal is plentiful." What is all this?'

'Oh. You . . . er . . . you can read shorthand,' said Henry.

'"Large Norwegian herrings are a snip at 1od. a pound"??'

'Oh, I . . . er . . . must have given you my shopping notes, we do them on a Friday, how silly of me,' said Henry.

He hurried out, and soon returned with his own notebook. The colonel grabbed it.

'It's not in shorthand,' he said.

'No, I can't do shorthand.' Henry realized his mistake immediately.

'So! You were deliberately fobbing me off,' said Colonel Boyce-Uppingham with deadly calm.

'I'm sorry,' mumbled Henry. 'I think you'll find you said everything we printed,' he added, rallying. It was to prove a brief recovery.

'I don't dispute that,' said Belinda Boyce-Uppingham's uncle.

'What?'

'It's the words you didn't print that I'm concerned about.'

Fear laid her cold talons on Henry's throat. Quietly, almost gently but with suppressed fury, the Chief Torch Bearer of the Ark of the Golden Light of Our Lady explained to Henry the enormity of what he had done. He also made it clear what he thought of Henry, ironically using three of the words against which his great campaign was being planned.

Terry Skipton went white.

'You twerp,' he said. 'You bloody twerp.'

Henry had never heard Terry Skipton swear before.

Mrs Etheridge, the oldest of the copy-takers, came over from her booth with a story which had just been phoned through. She handed it to Terry Skipton without a word. Terry Skipton read it and handed it to Henry without a word. Henry read it and handed it back to Terry Skipton without a word. Terry Skipton passed it to the subs' table, where a sub-editor swiftly created the headline 'Artist fumes at "incredible" gallery blunder'.

The story that all Johnson Protheroe's paintings had been hung

327

upside-down appeared in the same issue as Henry's review of them.

'Sit down, gentlemen,' said Mr Andrew Redrobe. Was the 'gentlemen' faintly ironical?

Henry sat opposite the editor. Terry Skipton sat at the end of the desk, facing them both.

'I've read your main lead,' said the editor. 'A good story. And a lucky escape.'

'Yes. The lad did very well,' said Terry Skipton.

Henry gawped. He'd never heard Terry Skipton give unqualified praise before. In one day he'd made the news editor laugh, smile, wink, swear and give unqualified praise. It was an achievement that would pass down in the legends of provincial journalism.

'I've had Colonel Boyce-Uppingham in here,' said Mr Andrew Redrobe. 'He's a very unhappy man. Can you explain what happened?'

'I made a mistake,' said Henry. 'I missed one vital link in his argument.'

'Do you call that an excuse?'

'No. I call it an explanation.'

'I've had to promise him a full retraction, a grovelling apology, a series of articles about his organization and free advertising. Even with all that, he may sue.'

'I'm very sorry,' said Henry.

'Why did you let this go through without checking, Terry?'

'Henry showed me his notebook. Every word we quoted was written down there at the time,' said Terry Skipton. 'And I do have to have some trust in my reporters.'

'But these were sensational admissions.'

'So sensational that I felt that, if I queried them, he might reflect on the wisdom of allowing us to print them.'

'All right. I accept that,' said Mr Andrew Redrobe. He sighed. 'Let's turn to the paintings. What excuse or explanation have you for *that* cock-up.'

'It wasn't my cock-up,' said Henry. 'It was the gallery's. All I did was fail to spot it.'

'All you did? What a wonderful story that would have made. Ridicule for the art gallery, which turned me down when I was nominated for their board, not that that's important. Intellectual poseurs pricked. The philistinism of the mass of our readers triumphantly justified. Instead of which, it's us they're laughing at. Us. Me. My paper. I'd like to hear your views on why you think I'd be sensible to continue to employ you.'

'I'm investigating a story that'll take the lid off this town and reveal a rotting heap of stinking fish,' said Henry. 'I can deliver you a scoop that'll be the envy of every provincial journalist from Land's End to John O'Groats.'

The jaws of Mr Andrew Redrobe and Terry Skipton dropped. There was a long silence. At last the editor plucked up his courage and asked the question that had to be faced.

'Is it about a pigeon?'

'It's not about a pigeon.'

There was another long silence.

'Well come on,' said the editor.

'Ah!' said Henry.

'What?' said the editor.

'These matters affect my fiancée and her family and I must tell them first. Can I have till Monday morning?'

The editor gave another deep sigh. 'All right,' he said wearily. 'You've got till Monday. Now get out.'

'Thank you, Mr Redrobe,' said Henry.

He'd made two enormous mistakes. He was a laughing stock. Somebody was trying to kill him. A man was fighting for his life, in the Infirmary, because of him. But, even on that black Friday, Henry managed to find one tiny consolation. At last he'd survived an interview with the editor without saying 'sir'.

He felt sick with tension as he rang the Infirmary. He felt as if he were asking for a bulletin on himself. Dennis Lacey had survived a major operation and was as well as could be expected. Would he live? He was as well as could be expected.

As they walked to the Lord Nelson he felt disembodied, could hardly feel his feet on the damp pavement, hardly feel Helen's affectionate squeeze of his arm in which, strangely, he could detect no element of coquetry. It was as if he were unreal, and only existed in the minds of his five drinking companions.

It wasn't a large gathering. Denzil was in London, Ginny in bed with food poisoning, Ted in Manchester on an overnight job, but they seemed determined to make up in warmth what they lacked in numbers. He'd have to leave soon, to visit Dennis Lacey in hospital, and to talk to Howard Lewthwaite. But he couldn't leave too soon, when they were all being so nice.

They vied to ply him with drinks. Helen squeezed his arm again. Gordon said, 'Small print. Small print,' and Henry sensed that it was meant to be affectionate. Ben asked him to name the grounds of all the Scottish teams, and he managed them all except Stenhousemuir. Even Jill seemed to find his company pleasant. When it was his turn to buy a round, Colin came to the bar with him, and hugged him.

'What's all this?' said Henry.

'We're all right upset because of thee.'

'You what?'

'You could have been killed today. We love you, kid.'

'What?'

'Well, I do. I'm almost crying, for God's sake. I mean, Henry, I hope you'd feel like crying if I were almost killed.'

'Course I would,' said Henry.

He hugged Colin.

Of course! He realized why they were all being so nice to him, even Jill, who had probably been told to by Gordon, on whose words she still hung even though she didn't understand many of them. It wasn't any old evening. It was the 'cheering up our Henry after one of the most disastrous days ever to befall a British provincial journalist' evening. Be churlish to leave in the middle of it. Dennis Lacey wouldn't be conscious yet, anyway, and he could see Howard Lewthwaite briefly after work tomorrow.

When the six of them walked to the Devonshire through the spattering rain, they were like six babies in one incubator, protected from the germs and hostility of the outside world.

The drink flowed. The timeless jazz rolled out in the crowded upstairs room, as if the rock-and-roll craze didn't exist.

A huge man in a bright blue corduroy suit was pushing his way through the crowds towards them. He had black hair, but his bushy black beard was streaked with grey. At his side was a delicate-looking young lady, with a round, serene face and a flat, thin body. She reminded Henry of a barometer. Both their faces were registering 'stormy'.

'Is one of you guys Henry Pratt?' said the huge man, loudly, in a North American accent.

'I am,' admitted Henry reluctantly.

'Johnson Protheroe,' said Johnson Protheroe.

Henry's colleagues, and even Jill, closed round him, shutting the door of the incubator.

Johnson Protheroe's loud voice battled effectively with the music. Sid Hallett and the Rundlemen were playing 'Basin Street Blues'. It was beginning to dawn on Henry that their repertoire was not inexhaustible.

'You're the biggest ass-hole I've ever met,' yelled Johnson Protheroe.

'Johnson!' It wasn't an easy word to invest with love, but the girl managed it.

'Listen, kid,' said Colin, grabbing Johnson Protheroe's lapel. 'Nobody calls my mate an ass-hole.'

'Colin!' said Henry desperately. 'It's all right.'

'Take your hands off me,' shouted Johnson Protheroe.

'Johnson!' said the girl. Even when she raised her voice, she was barely audible.

'Please!' shouted Henry.

'Shut up!' shouted a jazz fan.

'Shut up yourself!' shouted a second jazz fan.

'Bloody hell fire!' shouted the first jazz fan. 'I'm telling them to shut up. Don't tell me to shut up.'

'Shut up!' shouted several more jazz fans.

Sid Hallett and the Rundlemen abandoned all hope of solos and played fast and loud to overpower the disturbance. The disturbance emitted a few drowning glugs and expired. The music and the set finished, to loud applause. Sid Hallett and the Rundlemen stomped off to the bar. Henry and his friends faced Johnson Protheroe and his friend in wary silence.

'I never read such a load of crap as your article,' said Johnson Protheroe.

Henry's colleagues began to protest.

'Please,' pleaded Henry. 'Allow me the dignity of defending myself.'

'Oh!' said Johnson Protheroe, in a scornful mock-English tone. '"Allow me the dignity of defending myself"! Blue seas under black clouds, my ass. Those were blue skies *above* the Rocky Mountains, you cretin.'

Henry's colleagues allowed him the dignity of defending himself.

'I . . . er . . . I . . . er . . . sorry,' he said.

'The barometer that you described so vividly was a portrait of Deborah here.'

'Oh, I . . . er . . . I am sorry. You don't look a bit like a barometer,' lied Henry.

'Thanks,' said Deborah, in her low, sweet voice.

Henry's head was beginning to swim, but he managed to focus on Johnson Protheroe. 'You're right,' he said. 'I am the biggest ass-hole you've ever met.'

'What?' said Johnson Protheroe.

'It's the first art exhibition I've ever reviewed. I was standing in for our arts editor. I imitated his style. I'll never do that again in my life, especially as I happen to believe that critics should be widening the understanding of art, not narrowing it.'

'Oh . . . well . . . spoken like a man!' said Johnson Protheroe.

'I do a good imitation,' said Henry.

'Do you have football as we know it in Canada?' asked Ben.

Henry couldn't remember how they got to the Shanghai Chinese Restaurant and Coffee Bar. The evening had become a warm blur. They were all in the incubator together now, even Johnson Protheroe, who had become a harmless bear.

'Do you really know anything about Canadian artists, Henry?' he was asking.

'Not a jot,' Henry admitted. 'I looked the names up in the library.'

Johnson Protheroe's mood changed again. 'Typical bloody

332

British insularity,' he growled. 'Canada's full of hick towns like this full of ignorant people full of crap, but at least they know there is a world outside. Exciting things are happening back home.' He began to shout. 'Nobody here gives a damn.' Everybody pretended not to hear. 'You see!' he roared.

The food arrived. Henry seemed to have ordered a prawn curry. Johnson Protheroe's beef curry did nothing for his mood. He slammed a pile of coins on the table, shouted, 'This food is dreadful. Come on, Deborah,' and hurried to the door. He turned to face the crowded room and shouted, 'You're all ass-holes, especially Henry Pratt.'

He lurched out into the street. Deborah hurried back to their table and said, softly, 'I'm sorry. I hardly ever get to eat these days. Somebody once told Johnson that his name sounded like a firm of merchant bankers. Ever since then he's been trying to be wild and Bohemian. What an artist he could be if he didn't waste all his energies being what he thinks an artist ought to be. It's been lovely meeting you. I think you're sweet people.'

Henry returned to his prawn curry. He was ravenous.

Ben and Colin discovered how late it was. Gordon said he and Jill must be going too. Everybody said nice things to Henry. Jill even kissed him, saying 'Mmmmm!' as if to convince herself that it had been a pleasant experience.

'Ted won't be back tonight,' said Helen. She put her hand on his thigh. He put his hand on her thigh. She took his hand down towards her knee and lifted it up under her skirt. He felt that something was wrong. He couldn't remember what.

They were outside. Presumably they'd paid. How nice it was to go beautiful with a home woman.

They kissed each other. She slid her tongue into his mouth like a paper-knife. Something was wrong. He couldn't remember what.

She hailed a taxi, and it stopped. She was flushed with triumph. Taxis had been hard to come by since Suez. She'd protested about Suez. Well, not this she. Not what's-her-name. The other she. Hilary. Hilary!!!

She got into the taxi. He shut the door.

'Good night,' he said.

333

'What?' she said.

'Can't come back with you,' he said. 'Hilary.'

Her pert lips pouted. She went pink. She was breathing very hard. He couldn't worry about her. He turned away. He heard her taxi drive off.

He felt awful. He tried gulping fresh air but it didn't help. He dimly remembered that he oughtn't to be being careless and lurching around the town, drunk and alone. He couldn't remember why.

He slipped and fell. He struggled to his feet and hurried into a narrow alley that ran from Market Street through to Church Street. He didn't want any policemen seeing him while his legs weren't working. At the junction with another alley, in a tiny square dimly lit by one feeble lamp, a scared cat passed him, screeching. Scared of what?

Scared of the six youths who blocked his path, six youths with bleak, tense faces, six youths with bicycle chains. Maybe the idea was to beat him to a pulp, terrify him, scare him off.

He swung left into the other alley, which led to Bargates, where Henry had spent so much time in the now defunct Paw Paw Coffee Bar and Grill. Six youths blocked his path, six youths in drainpipe trousers and Edwardian jackets, six youths with knives and razors. Thurmarsh's first Teds. Today Thurmarsh, yesterday the world. So this was it. The end of twenty-one years of struggle towards a manhood dimly perceived, he was a well-nourished young man of below-average height, his stomach bore the mainly undigested remains of a prawn curry, he had drunk the equivalent of . . .

He turned, and tried to walk back the way he'd come, into Market Street. He expected to see six more youths blocking his way. There was nobody.

He walked away with a calmness he didn't feel. His legs screamed to him to break into a run. He refused. He'd only inflame their insults by showing his fear.

He began to get the feeling that nobody was following him. With the return of hope came the fullness of fear, neck-pricking, scalp-crawling, sweat-drenching fear. He had to turn and look. He mustn't. He did. There was nobody.

He heard the first sounds of battle, the swish of bicycle chains, the ring of iron boot, the scream of a razored face. They were fighting each other, not him! Relief buckled his knees. At first it seemed as if he were running in a dream, stuck fast, not moving, but then he was tearing down the alley, he was in Market Street, there was the dark drapery store. Hilary lived, he lived, life stretched before him. It crossed his mind that the day, which had begun with a story which he hadn't recognized, was ending with another one. Gang warfare in town centre. He listened to the sounds of distant battle, and scurried off as fast as his little legs could carry him.

By the time he got home, his head was throbbing and his stomach was heaving. He'd had a traumatic day. He'd had too much to drink. His resistance to prawn curry had been fatally weakened.

23 In which Our Hero Makes Two Identifications

The first oil went into the Suez Canal since the fighting ended. Henry struggled to work, unsure where his food poisoning ended and his hangover began. He was so ill that he was sent home. There was no possibility of his going to see Howard Lewthwaite, let alone travelling to Durham. He spent the best part of that Saturday in bed. We'll draw a veil over where he spent the worst part of it.

On Monday, February 11th, a mild earthquake, centred on Charnwood Forest, caused pit props to shake in Drobwell Main Colliery, brought about a fall of masonry in the remains of the Old Apothecary's House and distracted Henry from the immortal words, 'Hello, boys and girls. May I remind all Argusnauts living in the Winstanley area about a beetle drive to be held next Saturday at the home of 12 year-old Timothy Darlington. Timothy called at our offices last week with the grand total of £17 raised at a similar function, and I was very sorry indeed to miss him.'

A mild earthquake, centred on the editor's office, shook every bone in Henry's body when he was forced to admit that, due to prawn curry poisoning, he'd not been able to tell his beloved of his great scoop, and requested a further stay of what was seeming more and more like execution. A final delay of one week was reluctantly granted. Mr Andrew Redrobe also gave up over the great education controversy. There had still not been a single letter from the general public. Beneath Colin's third letter, signed 'Second Angry Schoolmaster', there appeared the message, 'This correspondence is now closed, due to lack of space-Ed.'

Later that morning, Henry was sent to get a local angle on the shooting of a major feature film.

He caught the Rawlaston tram. It rumbled out of the valley, breasted the summit by Brunswick Road Primary School and dropped down again into the smoky valley. The road swung right.

On the right was the vast, blank wall of Crapp, Hawser and Kettlewell. On the left, the tiny, grimy, cobbled culs-de-sac, among which Henry had been born.

'Paradise,' sang out the conductor.

Henry stepped off the tram, looked round anxiously but saw nobody who appeared to be about to kill him.

Paradise Lane was completely blocked by generators and film unit vans, which were almost as high as the wine-red terraces. A mobile catering van had been parked right outside number 23. Henry longed to say to the waiting technicians and extras, 'Forget your curried lamb. Never mind your plum duff. Twenty-one years ago, in that little house on which you're turning your backs, a parrot ended its life and I began mine.'

Cables snaked through the gate onto the muddy tow-path of the Rundle and Gadd Navigation. They ran along the tow-path, and up onto the elegant brick hump bridge over the cut. Standing on the bridge, among a crowd of sightseers, were Angela Groyne and the man whom Henry suspected of trying to kill him. He didn't want Bill Holliday to know he was afraid, so he joined them, but took care not to stand too near the edge.

The muddy waste-ground between the insalubrious cut and the equally unsavoury river was crowded with film men and their equipment. The lights and the camera were angled towards a man with a huge green head and tentacles, who was standing in a spring-like contraption on the river bank.

'He's a monster from outer space,' explained Angela Groyne in a whisper. 'From some strange planet or summat. 'e 'as these incredible powers, like 'e can jump across t' Rundle.'

'They've built this special spring,' whispered Bill Holliday. 'They've tried it four times. He's landed in bloody river each time.'

'OK. We're going for a take,' shouted an assistant director. 'OK. Absolute hush, everybody.'

'337, take 5,' shouted the clapper-boy.

A special-effects man operated the spring. The green-tentacled monster leapt into the air, and landed in the middle of the river.

'Bugger,' shouted the director.

'OK. Lunch. Back at 2.23,' shouted the assistant director.

'Does tha fancy a pint?' said Bill Holliday.

'Not in the Navigation. I'm banned from there,' said Henry proudly.

'Not in my company, tha's not,' said Bill Holliday, and Henry shuddered at the man's power.

And so Cecil E. Jenkinson was forced to serve Henry with a pint of bitter, and Henry was forced to drink it in the company of a man who was probably trying to kill him.

'What are you doing here?' he asked, trying to sound casual.

'Angie's in it,' said Bill Holliday proudly.

'Oh! What do you play?' he asked.

'A corpse,' said Bill Holliday. 'She plays a corpse.'

Henry shuddered, in that tiny snug heaving with film folk.

'Well, it's mainly corpses, really,' said Angela Groyne. 'There's this deadly gas or summat, so nobody can go out, but I was out already so I'm dead.'

'Two bloody great monsters turn her over and examine her,' said Bill Holliday. 'First monster says "Hey up, she's copped it," or words to that effect. Second monster says "Aye, and it's a right shame an' all because she looks a right tasty piece at that," or words to that effect.'

Henry wished they wouldn't go on and on about death.

'There's a long lingering close-up of her dead,' said Bill Holliday.

'You might think it's dead easy just to lie there dead, but it's not, it's dead difficult,' said Angela Groyne. 'You have to be right careful not to breathe in or out or owt.'

Henry managed to turn away and talk to an assistant to the design assistant, who said, 'Fabulous area, this.'

'You like it?' said Henry. 'Great. I was born here.'

'Fabulous,' said the assistant to the design assistant. 'We needed a grimy, wretched, dying earth, and a noxious outer space full of dust, swirling fog and poisonous gases. We've found every location we need within a mile of here.'

Henry bought drinks for Bill Holliday and Angela Groyne. His bladder was getting full, but he didn't dare go, for fear Bill Holliday would spike his drink.

The stuntman came in. He'd removed his head, but still created quite a stir with his tentacles and green body. His name was Freddie Bentley, he came from Wath-on-Dearne, and Henry knew that he'd got his story. South Yorkshire stuntman jumps to stardom. As he interviewed him, Henry began to feel that he'd met him somewhere before. Freddie Bentley became wary, and denied it with unnecessary fervour. And Henry remembered. Of course! Freddie Bentley must have been driving the lorry for Bill Holliday! And now here he was, in front of Bill Holliday, talking of seeing Freddie Bentley before! He might as well sign his own death warrant. Another drink appeared. Was it spiked? 'Drink up,' said Bill Holliday. Nervously, he drank up. His bladder was aching. He'd have to go.

Bill Holliday followed him. If Henry felt relieved that Bill Holliday couldn't be slipping anything into his drink, he didn't feel relieved to be relieving himself beside Bill Holliday in an otherwise deserted urinal. He half expected to feel a knife twisting in his stomach. Nothing happened. He felt a trickle of returning courage. He decided to fight back. As they returned to the crowded bar, he said, 'Seen any good trusses lately?'

Bill Holliday went pale. 'How did you guess?' he said.

'It was obvious,' said Henry.

The trade gap widened to £103.6 million. The government increased local rates in order to give councils more freedom of choice over expenditure on education, child care, fire brigades and health. The unemployment figures had increased to 382,605.

On Tuesday, February 12th, Henry interviewed Mr Gibbins for 'Proud Sons of Thurmarsh'. Mr Gibbins had completely forgotten that, eleven Februaries ago, in his classroom, Henry had been the author of a phenomenal amount of wind. Henry had mixed emotions of relief and hurt pride.

The head offices of Joyce and Sons had no record of drivers named Freddie Bentley or Dave Nasenby. Henry must have been mistaken about his old friends.

That evening, shortly before nine o'clock, the doorbell rang loudly, insistently, aggressively. He hurried out with pumping heart. Was it Bill Holliday? Or Stan Holliday? Or Fred Hathersage? Or all three?

Ginny hurried downstairs, in blue slacks and an off-white shirt stretched tight over her large breasts.

'Who is it?' he called, anxiously.

'Police.'

They looked at each other. He opened the door. There were two officers.

'Henry Pratt?'

'Yes.'

'We've found the driver of the Standard Eight. Do you think you'll be able to identify him?'

He had to try. Ginny insisted on coming, to lend him moral support. How could he tell her that they might not be real policemen, they could be Bill Holliday's boys? Besides, if they were, a young woman of her build might be distinctly useful.

They weren't Bill Holliday's boys. They drove to York Road Police Station.

Ginny sat in the waiting-room beside a large, square, stony-faced woman with a pile of copies of the *Watchtower*. She looked like a sculpture on which naughty boys had painted a moustache.

An officer led Henry towards a dark grey door. At the door he said, 'There's six people lined up in there. Walk up and down the line carefully. Take your time. Make absolutely sure. Say nowt unless you can positively identify the man. In which case, when you're sure, point at him very clearly, so there's no possibility of mistake, and say "That's 'im. The third one from my right."'

'What?' said Henry.

'That was just an example,' said the officer hastily. 'I'm not saying that's where he'll be. He could be fourth from your left or owt.'

'Fourth from the left is the same as third from the right,' said Henry.

The officer worked it out.

'Oh aye, so it is,' he said.

Henry felt nervous. It isn't easy to come face to face with a man who's tried to murder you. He took a deep breath, stepped through the grey door, approached the line of people, looked up and found himself staring straight into the impassive face of Terry Skipton.

Terry Skipton? Could it be? Until Friday he'd believed that

Terry Skipton didn't like him, but . . . until Friday! If Terry Skipton had tried to kill him, and had wondered if Henry'd seen him, that might account for his sudden change of attitude. He remembered that rather hunched, almost deformed impression the driver had made on him. Terry Skipton! But he couldn't identify him positively. And they never put the suspect on the end, did they? Better move on. He hoped none of these thoughts were visible to Terry Skipton.

He moved on. He found himself gazing into an evil, guilty face. He could hardly spend less time looking at any of them than he'd spent looking at Terry Skipton, so he had to continue to look at the man long after he knew it wasn't him.

With pumping heart he looked at the man who was third from the right and fourth from the left. Had the officer been hinting? Another evil, guilty face, certainly, but no, it wasn't him.

He moved on. Another evil, guilty face. Did all men look evil and guilty when placed in a police line-up? Would St Francis of Assissi have looked like a flasher, in an identification parade?

He moved on again, and looked into the face of the man who'd tried to murder him. A shiver ran right through him. His certainty was total. That slightly twisted neck, the white face set at a slight angle, hunched into a mass of knobbly shoulder. The sense that the man was in the car, driving straight for him, was so strong that he had to force himself not to jump out of the way.

Even though he was absolutely certain, he felt obliged to move on and examine the sixth suspect. If a man gave up his time, during licensing hours, to stand in an identification parade, it was only polite that you should take the trouble to stare suspiciously at him through narrowed eyes for thirty seconds.

He returned to the second man from the left, and again he knew. And the man knew that he knew.

'That's the man,' he said, pointing. 'The second one from my left.'

They led Henry back, out of the bare cold room into the warmer parts of the building.

'Thank you,' said the officer. 'You picked the right man. You thought I were hinting before, didn't you?'

'Well . . . I . . . er . . .'

'It's just that I'm thick.'

'Well . . . I . . . er . . .'

'Now, are you absolutely sure? 'cos in court they'll say you didn't have time to see him properly.'

'Absolutely sure. The horror of it's etched in my mind.'

'Good man.'

The officer led him into the waiting-room, where Terry Skipton was standing beside the moustachioed lady with the *Watchtowers*.

'My wife Violet,' he said gruffly.

Henry's legs began to wobble. He sat down hurriedly.

'Are you all right?' said the officer.

'Oh yes,' said Henry. 'It's just a bit of a shock gazing into the face of the man who tried to murder you.'

'Well, not murder *you*,' said the officer. 'Murder Dennis Lacey.'

'What?'

'I don't see any harm in telling you. We're arresting him. He was Marie Chadwick's boy-friend. She ditched him. Apparently she's a right tasty . . . er . . .' He looked at Terry and Violet Skipton, and the pile of *Watchtowers*, and stopped. 'Apparently he drove past there day after day, waiting for a chance to get him without getting her.'

'By 'eck, Henry,' said Terry Skipton. 'The way you stared at me, I thought you thought *I'd* done it.'

Ginny and Violet and the officer laughed.

'You?' said Henry. 'You?? No!! No, I just thought . . . you being the first . . . if I didn't give you a pretty long, dirty look it might look a bit odd when I gave the others long, dirty looks. Me think you'd done it? That's a good one!'

The police were very grateful, but not so grateful as to provide a car home. Henry and Ginny trudged up York Road and Winstanley Road. Henry ran his hand gently over her buttocks as she walked, and then he put his arm round her. He felt very sexy after everything he'd been through. He thought of Hilary, in Durham. And, in the cold, sterile hall of their house, he gave Ginny a chaste kiss on the cheek and said, 'Thanks for coming with me.' She sighed and said, 'Pleasure.' They went to their separate beds.

As he undressed, and cleaned his teeth, and clambered into his clammy bed, Henry was thinking hard. The Standard Eight had not been driven at him. The gangs had not been waiting to beat him up. Of course the crate of surgical trusses could still have been meant for him, but logic now seemed to demand that it had been an accident also. After all, as he realized now, there'd been no way anyone could have known that he'd walk past, under that crane. He hadn't known it himself. Believing that it had been a murder attempt meant believing that there were large numbers of people, stationed all over Thurmarsh, waiting for a chance to kill him. In view of later events, this seemed unlikely.

And yet . . . if Bill Holliday wasn't trying to murder him, why should he have gone pale at the mention of trusses?

Henry longed for the relief of knowing that nobody was trying to kill him.

And yet . . . he also felt that he'd be a little disappointed, even hurt, if nobody thought him important enough to rub off the face of the earth.

On Wednesday, February 13th, the government announced that the Quantocks had been designated Britain's first 'area of out-standing natural beauty', and that the British Megaton Bomb, capable of destroying many Quantocks, would be ready soon.

Howard Lewthwaite walked to the Midland Hotel for lunch with his prospective son-in-law.

'Have whatever you like,' he said, 'though personally I'll stick to the *table d'hôte.*'

The weather had turned colder and a brief burst of hail pattered against the windows, disturbing the hushed serenity of that temple of starched linen.

'I've made some discreet inquiries into that crane driver,' said Howard Lewthwaite. 'He doesn't sound like a potential assassin to me.'

The waiter approached. He had new shoes, which squeaked.

'What is the *potage?*' said Howard Lewthwaite.

'Mock turtle, sir,' said the waiter.

'I'll have that, and I like the sound of that ham omelette,' said Howard Lewthwaite.

'Soup for me, too,' said Henry. 'And what's the *daube d'Irlande?*'

'Irish stew, sir.'

'The pork chop, please.'

'They ring the changes pretty well, don't they?' said Howard Lewthwaite. 'Are you sure they're trying to kill you?'

'I'm not at all sure any more.' He explained his reasons.

'So, apart from Bill Holliday going pale when you mentioned trusses, the probabilities are all against it,' said Howard Lewthwaite.

'But why should he have said, "How did you guess?"' said Henry.

'Ask him. Here he is,' said Hilary's father.

Bill Holliday was walking through the restaurant with what might have been the smugness of a man who knew he was appearing on cue. He was puffing at a large cigar. He stopped at their table.

'I'm not wearing one today,' he said.

'What?' said Henry.

'A truss. I'm a little better. And after what you said . . . how did you know? How was it obvious?'

'Er . . .' Henry tried not to meet Howard Lewthwaite's eyes. 'I . . . I'm a truss-spotter. I was in the truss-spotting club at school.' Shut up.

Bill Holliday looked puzzled, shook his head in bewilderment, pulled fiercely at his cigar and puffed off.

'So,' said Howard Lewthwaite. 'Nobody's trying to kill you. If you're wrong about that, don't you think you could have been wrong about all your suspicions of corruption?'

'The lorry driver who had a miraculous escape when his lorry destroyed the Old Apothecary's House is a film stuntman,' said Henry.

'Two mock turtles?' said the waiter.

'Yes,' said Howard Lewthwaite faintly.

'The haulage firm have no record of his being employed there,' said Henry, when the waiter had gone. 'He obviously came in to do that one job only. So, both the individually fine historical buildings inside the Fish Hill Complex were deliberately destroyed. So, let's talk now in the knowledge that my suspicions are not the ravings of a deluded youth.'

'It sounds as though you're determined to go through with this,' said Howard Lewthwaite.

'I have to, and I haven't much time,' said Henry.

Howard Lewthwaite raised his eyebrows.

'I told the editor I have a big scoop,' said Henry. 'I've promised to tell him on Monday after I've told Hilary.'

'I see.'

'I had to. I'd made a couple of cock-ups. He was going to sack me.'

'I see. So it's my career against yours.'

'I'd rather call it right against wrong.'

'I'm sure you would.'

'Who's for the chop?' said the waiter.

'Me, it seems,' said Howard Lewthwaite.

The waiter gave him the chop.

'No, I'm the chop,' said Henry.

The waiter muttered to himself as he hobbled away in his new shoes.

'Some of the things I'm going to have to tell Hilary – deliberately driving a lorry into an old building, arson, murder – are things you're innocent of.' He looked Howard Lewthwaite in the eye. 'You do promise me you're innocent of them, don't you?'

Howard Lewthwaite held his gaze.

'I promise,' he said.

'Right,' said Henry. 'Well, so far you've tried to pooh-pooh everything. I suggest you change your policy. I suggest you try to uncover as much evil as you can. The more evil you find in which you aren't implicated, the less important your role in all this is going to seem.'

The waiter handed them the dessert menus. Henry's hand was shaking. It isn't easy, when you're twenty-one, to talk like that to your prospective father-in-law.

They both plumped for the trifle.

'Good luck in Durham,' said Howard Lewthwaite, as they parted at the junction of York Road and High Street opposite the *Chronicle* and *Argus* building.

'Thank you. I'll need it,' said Henry.

24   Durham City

The condition of Dennis Lacey, fighting for his life in Thurmarsh Royal Infirmary, was as comfortable as could be expected.

The condition of Henry Pratt, clattering northwards through the dark February evening, was as uncomfortable as could be expected. He had to stand in the corridor. He ached with desire for Hilary. His stomach was knotted with tension. Should he tell her straightaway and risk spoiling the weekend, or should he wait until he was on the point of departure? He tried to think of other things. With his legs braced against the corridor wall he tried to read his vibrating copy of the *Argus*. Mr Gromyko had become Soviet Foreign Minister. A pilot trip through the Suez Canal by three small vessels had been cancelled 'for political reasons', presumably because President Nasser wouldn't allow any ships through until Israel had agreed to withdraw. Jenny Farthingale, aged 10, had brought two dolls to the newspaper's offices. Uncle Jason had been very sorry to miss her.

He hobbled off the train. He had pins and needles in his legs, an ache in his genitals and a yawning pit in his stomach.

'My God!' she said. 'What's wrong?'

'I've missed you so much,' he said.

She enveloped him in her warmth. She hugged him to her, on the platform, as the train snaked out towards Newcastle. So that was decided. He wouldn't tell her that night.

She'd booked them into a little pub at the bottom of the hill, in the lower part of the town, as Mr and Mrs Pratt.

'You don't mind being known as Mr and Mrs Pratt, then?' he said.

'It's the most wonderful feeling in the world.'

The landlady led them up a narrow staircase. She introduced herself as Irene Titmarsh. 'Call me Irene,' she said. 'Treat this as your home.' She showed them into a small room, which was almost filled by a huge iron-framed bed and a heavy mahogany wardrobe, which stood two feet from the wall because of the sloping ceiling. A patterned blue china jug full of cold water stood in a patterned blue bowl on a small teak table in front of the tiny, net-covered window. Curtains, carpet and wallpaper were floral, in clashing shades of daffodil, tulip and marigold.

'Will you be down for some tea?' she asked.

'Er . . . Mrs Tit . . . Irene,' said Hilary. 'This is a bit . . . er . . . my husband's in the army. He's Henry, incidentally, and I'm Hilary. He's only got a weekend's leave. We haven't seen each other for a long time. Too long, and it's so short, if you understand me. So . . . er . . . could we just have some sandwiches in our room, Irene?'

'I understand you,' said Irene Titmarsh. She had good strong teeth, but not enough of them. When she smiled she reminded Henry of several streets in Thurmarsh, and he didn't want to be reminded of them. 'I could do you two nice ham salads,' she said.

'That would be lovely, Irene,' said Henry.

'Could we have no raw onion in the salad, if you understand me, Irene?' said Hilary.

'I understand you,' said Irene Titmarsh.

When Irene Titmarsh had left them, Hilary said, 'I can't be seen in the bar. I might meet people I know, and I could be in trouble if it was found out I was staying here as Mrs Pratt. So I had to think up some excuse to explain away why we spend all our time in our room "at it".'

'Magnificent!' said Henry. 'You're magnificent.'

Her magnificence thrilled and chilled him. He didn't think he could bear to lose her.

'The only trouble is,' she said, 'if our story's to be believed, I don't see any alternative to spending a lot of time in our room "at it". Do you think you can face that?'

'I think so,' he said. 'We Pratts are made of pretty strong stuff.'

He began to take her clothes off. She was lovely in her happiness. He tried not to think how her face would look when he told her about her father.

They climbed into the bed. It was lumpy, and squeaked ominously.

'You're so beautiful,' he said. 'I suppose as a socialist I really ought to be kissing somebody ugly.'

'You seem to infer that being kissed by you is a privilege,' she said.

'*Touché,*' he said. 'Hilary? Anna said something very odd about you. She said you didn't undress on the beach because you wanted to spare the Italians your horrible body.'

'I thought it was horrible. I was depressed.'

'Oh.'

'And I was as thin as a rake, then.'

'Oh.'

'My God! Were you wondering, all that time before we went to bed together, what horrors were going to be revealed, whether you'd be able to cope with them? Poor darling. How brave you must have been.'

She kissed him, laughing. He wasn't sure whether she was making fun of him or not.

There was a knock on the door.

'Your two ham salads with no onion, Henry, Hilary.'

'Thank you very much, Irene. Could you just leave them outside, if you understand me.'

'I understand you, Hilary. Leave the plates outside when you've finished.'

Henry fetched the ham salads. They enjoyed themselves greedily. Then they ate the ham salads, placing tasty morsels in each other's mouths. They left the plates outside, when they had finished.

Then Hilary began to kiss him all over, slowly, with an intense expression of solemn concentration which aroused him to new heights of love.

There was a knock on the door.

'Henry, Hilary, have you had enough?'

Hilary's face appeared from under the bedclothes. She beamed and shook her head violently.

'Yes, we've had enough, thank you, Irene,' Henry said, and his voice almost broke into a laugh.

'Good night, then. "Sleep" well.'

'"We will."'

They did.

There was a knock on the door.

'Good morning, Henry, Hilary. Have you "slept" well?'

'We've "slept" very well, thank you, Irene,' said Henry.

'I'll leave your tea outside. Come down for breakfast when you're ready.'

'I don't think we'll want any breakfast this morning, thank you, Irene,' said Hilary.

At eleven-thirty Henry handed in their key and they went out into a bright, crisp world. They had an early lunch in an unlicensed café. Neither of them wanted alcohol.

They walked over Elvet Bridge and up into the dignified old university town. Hilary greeted several acquaintances.

They wandered through the stone market-place, and turned left down Silver Street onto Framwellgate Bridge. They stood in silence among the shoppers, looking along the wooded River Wear, looking up through the bare woods to the old city, the castle, the cathedral, the fortified stone houses, up on their hill, safe in the great loop of their river. And Henry knew that he couldn't tell her until she'd shown him Durham.

Dark clouds loomed up, and there were a few flakes of irresolute snow. They walked along the west bank of the river, past a wide, shallow weir, along a path of half-frozen mud, to the Prebends Bridge. All the while they had changing views of the three great grey towers of the cathedral.

They climbed towards the city. It wasn't far. The sense of height was an illusion, the great illusion of Durham City.

At last, shyly, as if the city were a woman and they were her new lovers, they entered her. They entered her by the South Bailey, and came slowly that cold afternoon towards her great heart, by the cobbles and grey stones, the dark brick and red roofs of her Georgian skirts.

In awe and silence and strange pride the unbelieving young lovers entered the great temple of God. Henry gasped at his first sight of the vast Norman nave. He squeezed Hilary's hand, as if to thank her for it. She smiled shyly, as if she had built it.

They sat in the nave, and looked up at its great ceiling. The huge, round Norman pillars, their circumference equal to their height, were strikingly carved, with vast simplicity. The clerestory and upper storey were of exquisite proportions. Three rows of shallow Norman arches were built on top of each other, with delicacy and charm sitting above grandeur and power. If you looked at the arches long enough they seemed to move like waves. They were a sea frozen in stone in a miraculous moment at the very beginning of time. Man couldn't have built all this.

Hilary shuddered.

'What is it?' he whispered.

'All the beauty of the world is waiting for us,' she whispered. 'I feel so happy I could break.'

So of course he couldn't tell her that afternoon.

Darkness laid a soft glove on this godly place. The ungodly, sated with an awe that seemed in no way unnatural to them, feasted on toasted teacake and pretended to be respectable. Hot butter streamed down chins that had run with lovers' juices. Hilary told him about her friends, whom he would meet that evening. He decided not to give her his bad news until he'd met her friends, until he'd woven himself that bit more irrevocably into the fabric of her life.

He charmed her friends. He was in sparkling form. They went to a couple of student pubs. They drank slowly and sensibly, because that was all they could afford. Hilary's friends seemed delightful people. Henry tried hard not to be egocentric. He remembered their names, and asked them about their lives, and remembered what he was told. He amused them with tales of his many disasters and included, for the first time, the incidents of the upside-down paintings and the misquoted Chief Torch Bearer of the Ark of the Golden Light of Our Lady. Here, in Durham City, far from Thurmarsh, he could expiate these horrors in humour. Hilary grew somewhat wry as his charm swelled. But what was he to do? He couldn't pretend to be a Tory in order not to seem to be too good to be true. He couldn't present himself as a reactionary young man who believed that a woman's place is in the home, in order not to curry favour with these charming young women. Everything he said presented him in the light of a treasure, a find. It couldn't be helped. He was acting, yes, and yet he wasn't. He said nothing he didn't believe. He told no stories that weren't true. He tried to be quiet, but people said things to him and he had to reply. Could he help it if they found these replies witty and apt?

'That was what you wanted me to do to your friends, wasn't it?'
said Hilary, on their way back to their pub.

'What?' he said.

'Set out to charm the pants off them.'

'What's wrong?'

'Nothing. I was just a little alarmed to see you in action tonight.
You're such a performer.'

'Didn't you want your friends to like me?'

'Of course.'

'Didn't you want me to like them?'

'Of course.'

'So what's wrong?'

'Nothing.'

'Yes, it is.'

'Well . . . I suppose I'm worried because you're so social. I don't
think I can be as social as you.'

'Hilary! I don't want you to be social if you don't want to.'

'Yes, you do. You don't know it, but you do.'

'Oh God! Look. We've had a perfect day. Let's not spoil it now.'

'Yes. That's probably what's wrong with me. It's too perfect. I
thought any kind of happiness had gone for ever. Now I feel happy
beyond anything I knew was possible.'

'It worries you?'

'Well . . . yes.'

'Being happy makes you unhappy? Being unworried worries
you?'

'No! Well . . . you know those screams of the world I told you
about?'

'Yes.'

'I haven't heard them today.'

He grabbed hold of her, with violent affection. He held her to
him.

'Don't hear them today,' he said. 'You may hear enough
tomorrow.'

'What do you mean by that?' she said.

'Nothing.'

She kissed him, a little doubtfully.

'Time for bed,' she said.

'Just for a change,' he said.

They slipped into the pub by the side door. She went straight upstairs. He went into the bar, to ask for the key. A few late drinkers were dimly visible through the smoke. The smell of beer was overwhelming.

'Nice day, Henry?' said Irene Titmarsh.

'Very nice, thank you, Irene.'

'This is my husband, George.'

'Hello, George.'

George had ginger hair and was quite small.

'Would you and Hilary like a drink, Henry?' said George.

'Thank you very much, George, Irene. Er . . . if you don't mind, though . . . it's our last night, if you understand me.'

'You didn't have a drink last night, Henry,' said Irene.

'That was our first night. That's what forty-eight-hour leaves are like. Good night, George, Irene.'

George and Irene Titmarsh gazed at Henry's departing back with something approaching awe.

They went to bed, and gave each other great pleasure. In the morning, Irene said, 'I've left your tea outside, Henry, Hilary. Come down to breakfast when you're ready.' Hilary said, 'I don't think we'll want any breakfast this morning, thank you, Irene.'

They left at 11.47. They would never forget Irene Titmarsh, but they would never remember the name of the pub.

It was snowing gently. There was a hole coming in Henry's left shoe. They had no bed to go to. They'd seen the cathedral.

'Shall we meet your friends again?' he said.

'Would that be wise?' said Hilary. 'You'd have to charm them as much as you did last night, in order to prove that you were being charming because you're charming and not because you were trying to be charming.'

'*Touché*,' he said.

The city was touched by the thinnest covering of snow. They spent two hours in a rather dull pub, which was unfrequented by students because it was rather dull. They ate in a rather dull café. The sun came out and melted the snow. It snowed again, as gently as before. They walked, and talked, and held hands.

Hilary sighed deeply.

'Never mind,' he said. 'I'll see you soon.'

'I wasn't actually sighing at that,' she said. 'I was hearing those screams.'

'*Touché*,' he said. 'Why do I end up saying *touché* so often?'

'Because you deserve to say *touché* so often.'

'*Touché*.'

They laughed. Then she looked solemn again.

'It's already too late for billions of people,' she said. 'Their one spell of consciousness is already ruined beyond repair. Every second of happiness I have seems to me to be obscene.'

'You can't do anything about it.'

'Can't I? We'll see about that.'

'These moods of yours worry me. I'm not sure I can live up to them.'

'They aren't moods, Henry. They're truths.'

'Then they frighten me all the more. Are we never to be happy?'

'Yes. Often. Because I'm weak.'

'It's not much of a kind of happiness, that's based on selfishness and weakness.'

'It's the only kind I can offer you.'

They sat, rather bleakly, in a station buffet designed for sitting rather bleakly. They had regrettable cakes and regretted them. They shed a tear or two. Henry had no excuse, now that Hilary had herself introduced the subject of misery, for not broaching his bad news. It was a good time for it.

And it was a terrible time for it. To tell her now would be to suggest that all the loving, all the laughing, all the awe and all the charming had been an act, because he'd known what he was going to say. So of course he couldn't say it. Could the glorious memory of love among the Titmarshes be for ever entwined with the smell of deceit?

Sunday evening trains are a special breed. They're grimier than others. They're slower. Their bulbs are dimmer. They rattle more. Their heating knows only the extremes of Arctic ice and tropical greenhouse fug. They're late, due to track maintenance. Their mournful whistles are like the cries of lovesick owls. And they are full of people going from where they chose to be to where they have to be.

Henry shared his stifling compartment with two navvies who talked about rock-and-roll, two silent staring soldiers, a snoring sailor, a girl with red eyes and an exhausted guest preacher, who'd expected three laughs but got only one. The train juddered away from Hilary, towards his lonely flat, towards Ginny trying not to look haunted as she asked if he'd had a good time. It clanked through a hostile world, whose inky blackness was broken only by occasional lines of sodium troops and the tracer bullets of cars' headlights.

And Henry justified his silence to himself. He couldn't leave Hilary there, without him, in her final year, with her important studies, to wrestle with the knowledge of her father's corruption, of her mother's sorrow, of the collapse of their Mediterranean dream, and all because of him. Impossible. No. The time to tell her was on the first day of the vacations. Yes, that was it. The *Argus* would have to wait. It was only another few weeks. Yes, that was it. The wheels picked it up. Yes, that was it. Yes, that was it. He'd tell her on the first day of her vacations, when he'd be with her to support her, and she'd be with her family, and they could all work things out together. Yes, that was it. Why hadn't he thought of that before? He could have enjoyed Hilary's beauty, the squeaky bed, the ham salads with no onion, the great Norman cathedral, without a twinge of anxiety, without a flicker of guilt. But still, it had been a wonderful weekend. He felt more hopeful, as if his rationalization would eventually make everything all right. The train sounded faster, more cheerful altogether. They yes-that-was-itted all the way to Thurmarsh.

25 *Vignettes Thurmarshiennes*

The cold snap continued. They shivered as they waited for the tram. Ginny tried not to look haunted as she asked if he'd had a good weekend.

On the tram, he read the Situations Vacant pages. Roll Turners, Fitters, Overhead Crane Fitter required. Jig and Tool Makers wanted. Experienced Moulders needed. Spoon and Fork Dolliers and Roughers required. Swing Grinders wanted. Die Sinkers urgently needed.

On Monday, February 18th, 1957, as his confrontation with the editor loomed, Henry was losing confidence in his ability to talk himself out of this one.

But what else could he do? Could he turn rolls, fit, mould, make jigs and tools? Could he dolly and rough spoons and forks? Could he grind swings or sink dies?

He could not.

Mr Andrew Redrobe's neatness might have been an ironic comment on the state of Henry's career. 'Right,' he said. 'Fire away. I'm all agog.'

'Er . . .' said Henry.

'I don't recall ever being agogger. Reveal your sensations.'

'Er . . .' said Henry.

'It's rare that a cynical, world-weary old warhorse feels a quickening of the pulse, finds himself on the edge of his seat, hardly dares to speak lest he miss the biggest scoop of his career. What did you say?'

'Er . . .' said Henry.

'I thought you did. You've got cold feet about your story? Come on. Don't be shy. Let me be the judge of it.'

There was a moment when Henry thought that he was going to tell him. But he couldn't. But he couldn't bring himself to tell him that he couldn't.

'Er . . .' he said.

'You exaggerated?' said Mr Andrew Redrobe, in a kindly,

355

almost paternal tone. 'Well, you won't be the first young reporter to exaggerate. Tell me what you *have* got. I won't bite. I'm human.'

'I . . . can't.'

'What??'

'Not until after the first day of Durham University's vacations, when I've told my fiancée. I went to see her this weekend. I found I couldn't leave her, so far away from me . . . er . . .'

The editor shook his Brylcreemed head, perhaps at the idea that anybody could suffer as a result of being a long way away from Henry.

'. . . with such upsetting news as my news would be, so momentous are the implications of my story.'

Mr Andrew Redrobe leant forward. He was fully paternal now. 'There isn't any story, is there?' he said gently.

'There is!' said Henry indignantly. 'Look, I'll make you an offer, sir.' Damn.

The editor's head jerked upwards, as if his neck had struck an unseen wire.

'An . . . offer?' He didn't welcome the suggestion of a deal from one so young.

'Yes. After all, the chapel might have something to say about sacking me for not getting a scoop.'

Mr Andrew Redrobe narrowed his eyes at the mention of the union chapel. His paternal kindness was but a memory now.

'Hundreds of journalists don't get scoops every day,' said Henry. 'They aren't sacked.'

The editor's silver pencil tapped insistently on his green-topped desk. The woodpecker had revived, it seemed.

'What about your monumental cock-ups?' he said.

'You let them go at the time.'

'I'm not talking about your past monumental cock-ups.' His left eye twitched. 'I'm talking about your future monumental cock-ups.'

'There may not be any, if you accept my offer.'

'All right, then. What is this offer?'

'If I don't give you an amazing scoop, on the second day of the Durham University vacations, I'll resign.'

356

'Is that a promise?'

'Mr Redrobe, you have the word of a Pratt.'

The editor's right eye twitched. The woodpecker tapped on.

'The first time you kill a man is the worst,' said Mr Andrew Redrobe. 'Then it gets easier. I killed at least seven men in the War.'

It was difficult, looking at this tidy, battened-down, buttoned-up man, to imagine it.

'Sacking a man should be simple after that. And sackings there will be, if the long-term predictions for this industry are correct. So why am I so curiously reluctant to start? Is it because you look so helpless, sitting there, that it would be like guillotining a doormouse?'

Henry didn't reply.

'All right,' said the editor. 'You have till the second day of the Durham University vacations. No scoop then, and it's the sack. And I do mean it. Mr Pratt, you have the word of a Redrobe.'

The moment he knew that Henry hadn't told Hilary, Howard Lewthwaite relaxed. He positively beamed at the waiter. 'French onion soup for me,' he said, 'and I'm very taken with the idea of the haddock with parsley sauce.'

'Soup for me too,' said Henry. 'And what are the *vignettes Thurmarshiennes?*'

'It's a new idea of the chef, sir. Five tiny vol-au-vents filled with local delicacies. Black pudding, cow-heel, brawn, tripe, mushy peas. Very different. Very tasty.'

'I'll have the *chaud pot de* Lancashire,' said Henry. 'You don't think I'll ever tell, do you?' he said, when the waiter had gone. 'You don't think I've got the courage. You think I love your daughter too much. Well, I do. Love her, I mean, not love her too much. If I loved her more than any man has ever loved any woman it wouldn't be too much. And I do . . . love her more than any man has ever loved any woman. But I do also love the truth. So because I love her so much I'm going to have to tell her the truth. I'm going to tell her on the first day of the holidays. When I'm there to support her. When you're there to support her. When we're all there to support her.'

357

Henry felt that he could have expressed all this more elegantly, more succinctly, and that it might have been more effective if he'd been able to look his prospective father-in-law in the face.

Howard Lewthwaite topped him up with the house white.

'Supposing it comes to a clash between your two great loves?' he said. 'Hilary and the truth. Which one will win?'

Israel rejected American proposals for the withdrawal of her troops from Gaza. Britain gave the United Nations a heavily documented indictment of Greece, accusing her of giving financial and propaganda support to the Eoka terrorists in Cyprus. Charges for milk, school meals, and the NHS portion of National Insurance were increased. President Eisenhower had a persistent cough.

Walking down the busy, decaying Commercial Road, after conducting a sensational interview with the President of the Thurmarsh Friends of Fur and Feather on the catastrophic effect television was having on pet clubs – attendances at Thurmarsh Rabbit Society down 39%, Splutt Tropical Fish Society planning merger with Rawlaston Cage Bird Club, a 22% decline in entries for pigeon races oh no, not pigeons again! – he had a shock. Wasn't that man with the blackheads . . . ? He was.

Just as some fortunate people are able to live for weeks without thinking about nuclear weapons, so Henry had gone for months without thinking about Derek Parsonage.

What was the man doing, walking down the path from a severe, black-bricked, Victorian town house with rotting window frames, in front of whose sad, gravelled garden a large board announced: 'World-Wide Religious Literature Inc.'?

'Hello. Henry Pratt,' said Henry, who had no overwhelming belief in his own memorability.

Was it just his imagination that Derek Parsonage turned pale beneath his unseasonal tan?

'Henry!' he said, beaming with belated and rapidly assumed delight.

'Can we talk?' said Henry. 'I have news for you.'

'Come in,' said Derek Parsonage. 'I was only going shopping.'

He led Henry through a large entrance hall, with religious literature displayed on three tables, into his office. It was a small, plain room, with a corner of a high, elaborately moulded ceiling which had once graced a much larger room. There were two hard chairs and a desk covered in pamphlets and invoices. Behind the desk was a large photograph of a black woman with huge bare breasts being handed a Bible by a man in a pin-striped suit.

Henry sat down, paused briefly for effect and said, '"World-wide Religious Literature Inc."?'

Derek Parsonage shrugged. 'I'm no more religious than the next man,' he said. He lowered his eyes uneasily, as if expecting the next man to materialize through the skirting board and dispute this. 'But it's a way of earning a crust.'

'What do you do?'

'We're a sort of clearing house for the world of religious publishing. Basically it's just a specialized form of import-export, with a translation service thrown in. So, what's the news?'

'The burning of the Cap Ferrat was arson. Uncle Teddy was murdered.'

'No! Henry! How do you know?'

'We never reveal our sources.'

'Arson! How? Who by? Why?'

'I hoped you might tell me.' Bitter was the taste of the shame of The Man Nobody Muzzles, Henry 'The leech' Pratt, investigative journalist extraordinaire, who hadn't even thought of looking for Derek Parsonage. 'You never suspected it might be arson?'

'No. Why should I?'

'No reason. I just wondered.'

Questions were flying into Henry's brain like pigeons coming home to . . . not more pigeons! That's all I'm good for. Henry 'All you ever needed to know about pigeons' Pratt.

'You were part of the Cap Ferrat,' he said. 'Are you being paid by the insurance people?'

'No. I sold my share to Teddy a fortnight before the fire.'

What???

'Oh . . . er . . . really? Er . . . may I ask why?'

'Certainly. It's my turn to have a shock for you, Henry. I don't want to speak ill of the dead, and I know you were fond of your uncle, but . . .' Derek Parsonage stared so fixedly at the wall behind him that Henry turned to follow his gaze, even though he knew that Derek Parsonage was only looking there to avoid looking at him. He found himself staring at a photograph of a huge naked black woman with a bolt through her nose, grinning broadly as she held up a copy of *Quaker News*. 'Henry? You know your uncle told you he was in Rangoon. He wasn't. He was in prison.'

'Oh, I knew that.'

'Well, I didn't. When I found out, I was shocked. I'm no prude. Night-clubs, in my book, fair enough. But crime? No, sir. I sold out. I'd probably have made a lot more, as it's turned out, if I hadn't, but I'm glad. My conscience is as clear as a Lakeland beck.'

'Well, if you think of anything you think is even remotely relevant, will you let me know?' said Henry.

'I certainly will,' said Derek Parsonage.

As Henry walked out across the gravelled garden, Stan Holliday was entering. They looked at each other in surprise, but neither of them spoke.

Henry turned and watched Stan Holliday close the door behind him. His spine was tingling. Many things he was prepared to believe, but if that evil-faced villain was interested in religious literature, Henry was a reincarnated Yugoslavian brush salesman who could relate the whole of the Koran in Urdu under hypnosis.

A new trail was opening up. He was onto something. If only he wasn't off to Cap Ferrat in two days!

He'd lived in a house of that name. He'd been to a club of that name. His surrogate parents had often gone there without taking him. At last he was going there, at the one time in his life when it would be an annoying interruption.

The following day, all that was changed. Derek Parsonage rang him at the office.

'You said you were going to France tomorrow,' he said.

'Yes.'

'I've thought of something, which I thought I ought to tell you before you go. I suppose you're surrounded by colleagues.'

'Yes.'

Henry looked up at Ginny, pounding the keys as if she were

reporting World War Three, not a persistent smell of sewage which was upsetting market traders.

'I presume all this is top secret?'

'Yes.'

'So I'll talk in such a way that you can answer "yes" or "no". Thoughtful, aren't I?'

'Yes.'

Helen looked up from her piece on summer hats and blew him a tiny kiss. It floated among the specks of dust in a brief ray of sunshine. He grinned at her. Ted scowled, with mock jealousy that hid real jealousy.

'I thought about what you said, and I remembered something which hadn't seemed significant at the time. You remember the compère, Monsieur Emile?'

'Yes.'

Denzil looked up from his piece on theatre stars who looked forward to the spring because they were keen gardeners, and he also blew Henry a little kiss. Henry grinned.

'Monsieur Emile and Teddy had a most tremendous row. Did you hear about that?'

'No.'

Terry Skipton raised his heavily lidded eyes exaggeratedly, his news sense awakened by Henry's intensity.

'Teddy caught Monsieur Emile with his hands in the till. He gave him a month's notice. You never heard about this?'

'No.'

Gordon gave him a thumbs-up, a tribute to his brevity from the king of ellipsis.

'I heard their argument. Monsieur Emile didn't realize I was there. He said, "You'll regret this." Teddy said, "*Je ne regrette rien.*" Emile said, "So! Zis is typical. You mock a great French artiste." He was livid. At the time I didn't think there was anything in it.'

'No.'

Colin gave him a gap-toothed smile, friendly, warm, innocent of all deviousness. It made him feel wretched.

'Now that I know what I know now, I'm inclined to take a different view.'

'Yes.'

'Well, that's it, Henry.'

'Thank you very much indeed,' said Henry. 'I've nearly finished the article, but I'll certainly try to introduce the budgerigar side of things.' He put the phone down. 'Bloody pets,' he announced, to the news-room at large.

Monsieur Emile had said that he was planning to open a night-club in Nice. How much might he have taken from the Cap Ferrat on the night of the fire? Was it inconceivable that the solution of Uncle Teddy's murder lay not in Thurmarsh at all, but on the Côte d'Azur?

Henry packed with renewed enthusiasm.

26   The Real Cap Ferrat

The Duke of Edinburgh was created Prince Philip, a Bedlington terrier became the first dog to be successfully fitted with a hearing aid, and the Americans were permitted to defend their bases with their own guided weapons, cutting across the previously accepted practice that the RAF had sole control of British air space in war.

In the elegant, small dining-room of a small, elegant hotel in the elegant village of St-Jean-Cap-Ferrat, three people were attacking grilled sea-bass with controlled greed. How the British love fish when they're abroad.

The woman had over-painted lips and startling peroxide hair, which emphasized her age although she thought it hid it. The older man had a large nose festooned with blackheads, as if the waiter had gone berserk with the pepper mill. The younger man was short and podgy and had reverted, in these sophisticated surroundings, into a self-conscious English gawkiness which made him barely recognizable as the accomplished lover he had been in Durham.

'Teddy loved sea-bass,' said Auntie Doris.

'Could we possibly have five minutes without mentioning your first husband?' said Geoffrey Porringer, who often made things worse by protesting about them.

'Geoffrey!' said Auntie Doris, who *always* made things worse by protesting about them. 'Henry's looked forward to this holiday. Don't spoil it for him by going on and on about Teddy.'

Geoffrey Porringer dropped his knife and fork with a clatter. '*I'm* spoiling his holiday!' he said. '*I'm* going on and on about Teddy! I was complaining about you going on and on about him, Doris.'

'Geoffrey!' said Auntie Doris. 'Don't make a scene. There are Italians and Danes and Dutch here. They'll think we don't know how to behave.'

'I'm sure Teddy knew how to behave,' said Geoffrey Porringer.

'Please!' said Henry.

'Exactly!' said Auntie Doris.

'It's not me who's been mentioning Teddy every five minutes,' said Geoffrey Porringer. 'I'm well aware, Doris, that I can never hope to be to you exactly what he was.'

'Please!' said Henry.

'No, no,' said Geoffrey Porringer. 'Now it's in the open, let's have it out. I don't need reminding of my inferiority, in the husband stakes, at every turn, every bar, every café, every *pissoir*. "Teddy peed there once!"'

'Geoffrey!' said Auntie Doris.

'Please!' said Henry.

'Subject closed,' said Geoffrey Porringer. 'I shan't mention Teddy again. Teddy who? Can't remember.' He resumed the steady demolition of his sea-bass.

'It's just that coming here brings it all back,' said Auntie Doris. 'I mean, it is a fact that I had happy times with Teddy and those times still exist in my memory. It doesn't mean I'm not happy with you, Geoffrey. I am. But, I mean, if by any chance you got burnt to death in a blazing building, and of course I hope that never happens, I'd like to think that one day I might meet some man, which of course wouldn't be the same, but it'd be a consolation in my old age, and that you'd be pleased, if you could see me, which of course you wouldn't, being dead, because otherwise I wouldn't be with this other man, but you know what I mean, if I said, to my new man, who wasn't the same but was very nice none the less, "Geoffrey liked sea-bass".'

'Please!' said Henry.

In the morning, in their villa after breakfast, Henry announced that he was going for a walk. It was bright and quite warm, but heavy clouds were building up over the mountains and Auntie Doris thought it might rain. He didn't mind. At least it would be warm rain. And he had to get away from the ghost of Uncle Teddy.

He strolled along a path, between the secretive stone walls of sumptuous villas. There were brief glimpses of tiny, pebbly bays licked up by a gentle blue sea. Ahead rose the partially wooded, mainly rocky slopes of the Alpes Maritimes, their contours untouched by man except for the occasional short viaduct on one of the corniche roads. And beyond, burning white against the blue sky, were the Alps proper, the high mountains. He was here at last. He was excited. His walk proved a tremendous success in every respect except one. He didn't get away from the ghost of Uncle Teddy.

It was walking along the path towards him, gazing at the boats rocking lazily in the bay. Henry stopped, rigid. It couldn't be.

It was. The ghost of Uncle Teddy saw him. It too stopped, rigid. It went white, as ghosts should. It turned and hurried away. Henry hurried after it in his flat holiday shoes.

'Uncle Teddy!' he called. 'Uncle Teddy!'

The ghost didn't stop.

'Uncle Teddy!' he called. 'I have to speak to you. I'm here with Auntie Doris and Geoffrey Porringer.'

The ghost stopped. It turned slowly to face him. Uncle Teddy was wearing natty blue shoes, white trousers and a striped fisherman's jersey. It was a relaxed, spritely, mediterranean Uncle Teddy, the holiday version of the man Henry had known.

'Trust you to run me to earth,' said Uncle Teddy. 'Trust bloody you! How did you do it?'

'You aren't dead!'

'Ten out of ten for observation.'

'But . . . I mean . . .'

Uncle Teddy looked astounded. 'Aren't you on my trail?' he said. 'This isn't just luck, is it?'

'I'm afraid it is,' said Henry.

'Oh no,' grumbled Uncle Teddy. 'That's not fair. Are you really with Doris and Geoffrey?'

'Yes.'

'They mustn't see me.'

'No.'

'You'd better come to the villa.'

Uncle Teddy's villa, set back behind a row of colour-washed fishermen's cottages, was larger than theirs but still comparatively modest. The faint smell of last night's giant prawns still hung over it, mingling with the scents of sea and pine and thyme and the morning's fresh coffee.

It was cool and dark in the shuttered villa. A few slats of sunlight dappled the marble floor.

365

He followed Uncle Teddy into the marble kitchen.

'So . . . you didn't die in the Cap Ferrat?' he said.

'How long are you staying?' asked Uncle Teddy.

'I'm staying a week. They're staying two weeks.'

'Two weeks!'

'You mustn't meet Auntie Doris.'

'No. No. How insensitive to come here, with me dead.'

'You aren't dead.'

'They don't know that.'

'No, and they mustn't.' Why mustn't they? I'm a journalist. 'What's happened, Uncle Teddy? You've got to tell me what's happened.'

'So either I stay in for a fortnight or I go away?'

'Yes.'

'Bloody hell.'

'Yes.'

'Oh shut up.'

Uncle Teddy took the coffee tray through into the large living-room cum dining-room. A heavy lace cloth lay on a round dining-table, and there were six high-backed ornate dining-chairs.

'They're married,' said Henry.

'Ah.'

'I went to the wedding.'

'Oh.'

'Cousin Hilda came.'

'How is the sniffer?'

'All right. Getting older.'

'Aren't we all?'

'You look younger.'

'I feel younger. I feel rejuvenated.'

Henry stood up.

'Oh come on, Uncle Teddy,' he said. 'You're going to have to give me an explanation.'

'Why?' said Uncle Teddy, smiling.

'I'm a journalist.'

'Precisely.'

'What?'

'I may not want my continued existence to be known.'

366

'If I don't get an explanation that satisfies me, i.e. the truth, I'll be forced to dig. Burrow for facts. Oh come on, Uncle Teddy. You brought me up as your son. You're supposedly burnt alive in Thurmarsh. I run into you in Cap Ferrat. You can't refuse to tell me what's happened.'

Uncle Teddy remained silent.

'I know some of it already,' said Henry. He sipped his coffee. It was good.

'Oh? What do you know?'

'I know that Councillors Peter Matheson and Howard Lewthwaite and council official Herbert Wilkinson are in cahoots with property developer Fred Hathersage to buy up an area now called the Fish Hill Complex in order to redevelop it to their mutual advantage. I know the Old Apothecary's House was destroyed and the Cap Ferrat burnt down to get them out of the way.'

'My God!' said Uncle Teddy. 'You know it all.'

'Not quite. I presume somebody, probably Fred Hathersage, is paying you a good whack to a numbered Swiss bank account for the destruction of the Cap Ferrat, for which, of course, being dead, you can't claim insurance.'

'Right so far. As co-owner, Derek Parsonage gets the insurance. What aren't you sure of?'

'One. Who's the mastermind behind it all?'

'Who do you think?'

'Bill Holliday?'

'No! Bill's nothing to do with it. He's totally straight. Honest as the day is long. And if he wasn't, he's such an obvious suspect nobody'd ever dare associate with him.'

'Fred Hathersage?'

'Brawn, not brain. Fred constructs what others plan.'

'Peter Matheson?'

'Where do Peter Matheson, Fred Hathersage and Bill Holliday live?'

'Thurmarsh.'

'Where do I live?'

'You! But you're my uncle.'

'Henry, don't look so upset. You were never supposed to get fond of me. Oh God, let's have some champagne.'

Uncle Teddy set off for the kitchen.

'I don't feel much like champagne,' said Henry. 'It's meant to be for rejoicing.'

'Don't have any, then,' called out Uncle Teddy.

'On the other hand, I need a drink,' shouted Henry. 'If you're having champagne, it'd be less trouble if I had it too.'

Uncle Teddy returned with a bottle of champagne and two elegant fluted glasses. He opened the bottle smoothly, and poured the champagne.

'Cheers,' he said. 'Oh, for God's sake, don't look so solemn.'

'Uncle Teddy!' said Henry. 'A man was murdered so you could drink champagne.'

'Henry!' Uncle Teddy was shocked. 'Nobody was murdered! Thurmarsh isn't Chicago. I'm not a killer. Property, yes. People, no.'

'So whose was the body in the Cap Ferrat?'

'The headmaster of Thurmarsh Grammar School.'

'What??'

'His name, I believe, was Crowther.'

'You . . . murdered . . . Mr Crowther!' Was there the faintest awe alongside Henry's horror?

'No! I've told you! Nobody was murdered. He died of natural causes.'

'How?'

'Of a heart attack, while strung up by a rope from a ceiling, entirely encased in chain-mail, in an exotic brothel run by Derek Parsonage in Commercial Road, Thurmarsh.'

'Oh my God! Mr Crowther??'

'Yes. Your respected headmaster got his sexual thrills from wearing armour and being strung up on a rope.'

'You call that natural causes?'

'It was natural to him. And it's not as uncommon a type of thing as you might think.'

'But he lectured us on moral values!'

'Hypocrisy is also not as uncommon as you might think.'

'How dare he work off his guilt feelings on me?'

'Mr Crowther knew there was a risk,' said Uncle Teddy. 'It was part of the thrill. He died. Nobody was to blame for his death. We just hushed it up and used it. Well, shame if it had got out. Disgrace for his school. Disgrace for his family.'

'Closure for Derek Parsonage's exotic brothel.'

'Well yes, that too, I suppose. It really was incredibly convenient all round and I saw the possibilities straightaway.'

'But the body was identified as yours.'

'Money opens most doors.'

'What would you have done if Mr Crowther hadn't died?'

'Gone missing. Changed my identity. As I have. Much more risky, though, if people were looking for me.'

Henry stood up.

'What a story!' he said. 'Headmaster of grammar school dies strapped in armour in exotic brothel, which poses as international Bible exporters, is subsequently burnt in deliberate destruction of Regency night-club and is falsely identified as owner of said club, who's living in South of France under assumed name while Tory and Labour councillors, council official and prominent local businessman, who employ stuntman to destroy another old landmark, carry out his master plan to make fortunes out of destruction and rebuilding of large area of central Thurmarsh. I'll get an award for this.'

Uncle Teddy poured him some more champagne.

'Cheers,' said Henry. He sat down, exhausted, bewildered. 'Things like this . . . they don't happen to people you know. They're the sort of things you read about.'

'Or don't read about.'

'What?'

'You can't print a word of this, Henry.'

Henry went white. 'You haven't been drinking!' he said. 'The champagne's poisoned.'

'Henry!' Uncle Teddy shouted. 'For God's sake, Henry. I'm not a murderer.' He regained control of himself. 'The champagne is not poisoned.' He took a swig, to add force to his words. 'Delicious.'

'Then why am I not going to publish it?' said Henry.

'Because of the hurt it'll cause.'

'What hurt?'

'To Mrs Crowther and her family, who'll be deeply, deeply shocked. To me, who brought you up as my son, and will end my

369

life behind bars instead of living here. To Geoffrey Porringer, who'll discover he's married a bigamist. To Doris, who'll discover she's a bigamist and will learn that the pathetic illusion that she clings to – viz., that I'd ever have gone back to her after she'd betrayed me – is an illusion and that I have a younger and prettier woman. To Cousin Hilda, whom the family scandal will kill, in spirit if not in body. To your series, "Proud Sons of Thurmarsh", which will be revealed as the biggest load of crap in the history of British journalism. To Howard Lewthwaite, a good man doing bad things out of love, whose career will be destroyed. To Naddy Lewthwaite, who will die in a year or two in an English winter. To Hilary Lewthwaite, your fiancée, an unstable young lady who has tried to kill herself. To Sam Lewthwaite, who will be brought up in a family ruined by tragedy. For what? A bit of skulduggery uncovered. A two-day sensation. More champagne?'

'But . . .'

'I know. You have a story that's dynamite, could transform your tottering career, and you can't use a word of it. Rather a shame. Better drown your sorrows.'

Henry sipped his champagne and thought with rising shame of all the lies he'd been told, from Derek Parsonage fobbing him off about Monsieur Emile to Uncle Teddy planning a champagne reunion with Auntie Doris and . . . oh god . . . saying, 'I love you, son.'

What would he do? Would he go ahead with his story? Should he go ahead? How did you weigh the value of a general principle of truthfulness against the particular sorrows that your action would visit upon the innocent and guilty alike? He felt weakened by all these revelations.

A cool little breeze had sprung up off the sea and was forcing its way through the gaps in the shutters. Henry shivered, and took another sip of champagne.

He recognized her scent, just before she entered the room. She was wearing tight white shorts and a tight blue sweater. She carried a shopping bag in her right hand. She stood in the doorway, smiling her astonishment, as tanned as a kipper, as shameless as a cat. But he was *more* astonished.

'Anna!' he said, trying not to blush as he remembered that

370

night, as he wondered if she'd told Uncle Teddy about that night.

'Hello, Henry,' said Anna Matheson. 'And congratulations! I'm thrilled about you and old Hillers!'

She enveloped him in her scent and gave him an extrovert kiss, accompanied by a grunted smacking of the lips. Uncle Teddy explained how Henry came to be there, fetched a glass and poured her some champagne. She sat down, crossing her big, brown thighs studded with tiny goose-pimples. It was too early for shorts, even in Cap Ferrat.

'So, you've changed your identity,' said Henry, trying not to look at Anna's thighs.

'Oh yes,' said Uncle Teddy. 'Meet Mrs Wedderburn.'

'Wedderburn?'

'My naughty sense of humour. Alice Wedderburn was the first girl I ever did it with, behind the tram sheds. Anna will be the last girl I ever do it with.'

'Alice Wedderburn!' said Henry. 'Alice Wedderburn! She lent me her camp-bed!'

'She wasn't Alice Wedderburn then,' said Uncle Teddy. 'She was Alice Crapper. Anna drew the line at Mr and Mrs Crapper.'

There was a strangely sombre little silence. Henry was painfully readjusting his view of Cousin Hilda's friend. Uncle Teddy and Anna were reflecting on what life as Mr and Mrs Crapper would have been like.

'I got hake,' said Anna Wedderburn, née Matheson. 'You do like hake, don't you?'

'Mrs Wedderburn?' said Henry.

'We got married three weeks ago,' said Uncle Teddy. 'For the will. In case I can't keep up the pace, and have a heart attack. Yes, I like hake. Go and get it unpacked, though, love. It'll stink the place out.'

Anna went into the kitchen, with her hake.

Uncle Teddy smiled – a little sadly, Henry felt.

'Don't know if she'd stay with an old man like me if it wasn't for the money,' he said.

He went over to the window, pushed the shutters open rather violently, and looked out towards the sea.

'Doris liked hake,' he said.

27 A Day to Remember

On Saturday, July 20th, 1957, buses which ran in defiance of a strike were ambushed, stoned and daubed by strikers. Their tyres were let down, sand and grit were put in their tanks, pickets boarded buses and let off stink-bombs. Stirling Moss in a Vanwall won the Grand Prix of Europe at Aintree. The Prime Minister, Mr Harold Macmillan, said, 'Let's be frank about it. Most of our people have never had it so good.' And Henry Ezra Pratt married Hilary Nadežda Lewthwaite.

As the guests made their way into the Midland Hotel for the reception, a sharp shower dampened their hats but not their spirits.

The Sir William Stanier Room was decorated, not altogether surprisingly, with photographs of engines designed by Sir William Stanier. The buffet was as sumptuous as a socialist councillor could provide without risking his political credibility. The drink flowed with a respectful nod to the memory of Sir Stafford Cripps and to Howard Lewthwaite's bank balance. The staff dealt solicitously yet tactfully with both the wheelchairs. Henry made a nervous but charming speech. There was a big laugh when he said, 'We've even been given two pictures, neither of which we plan to hang upside-down.' Hilary's smile, as they cut the three-tiered cake, was so wide that the caption in Monday's *Argus*, 'Councillor's laughter weds former *Argus* man', almost didn't seem like a misprint.

The past contained many sorrows and disasters. The future was uncertain. No matter. For one afternoon, Henry felt royal.

Prince Hal was charming to Hilary's friends. The Duke of Thurmarsh chatted animatedly to uncles and aunts and cousins. He even revealed a common touch, saying, 'Belt up, snot-nose' when Sam said, 'I hope you've packed the soup. You'll be wanting to consommé the marriage tonight.'

King Henry the Ninth felt a particular concern for Ginny Fenwick, who had smiled bravely throughout. He was sorry when he saw that she was smiling bravely at Tony Preece, beneath a photograph of Stanier 3-Cylinder Class 4 2-6-4T No. 42527 entering Fenchurch Street with a semi-fast from Southend. She needed a good man, but not this good man, who had a good woman who needed him.

'Tony's been telling me he's got a new act,' said Ginny.

'Oh good,' said Henry. 'What is it?'

'Come and see,' said Tony. 'Bring the lovely Hilary. She *is* lovely, Henry.' There was a brief silence, during which Ginny might have said, 'Yes, Henry, she is,' but didn't, and Tony might have said, 'As you are, Ginny,' but didn't. Too late, just as Mr and Mrs Quell were approaching, Tony said, 'This sexy, well-endowed, warm-hearted young lady tells me there's no man in her life. What's wrong with our sex? Are we all blind?' He hurried off in confusion when he realized that Mrs Quell *was* blind.

Henry introduced the Quells to Ginny. Mr Quell, his old English teacher and spiritual mentor during his brief religious phase, was a lapsed Irish priest, five foot four and barrel-chested. He was ageing with dignity. Mrs Quell's porcelain face remained almost untouched by time. She told them how moved her husband had been to be invited. Henry longed to tell Mr Quell the truth about the headmaster's death. There were times when he could hardly bear the knowledge that he had been unable to share with anybody, since that day on Cap Ferrat, five months ago.

'Ginny?' said Mr Quell, just as Ginny was about to escape. 'I've been trying to describe Henry's lovely bride and her exquisite dress. Alas, our sex, the admirers of women, are paradoxically incompetent at describing them. Could you oblige me, Ginny, for Beth?'

Ginny and Henry both tried to hide their horror. 'Well . . .' began Ginny. 'She's . . . er . . . not beautiful exactly. She's . . . something more than beautiful. She's absolutely lovely.' Henry blushed as Ginny, smiling desperately, gave a generous inventory of Hilary's charms.

'You're blushing, Henry. I can feel it,' said Mrs Quell. Her husband could see the tears in Ginny's eyes. He thought they were tears of happiness for Henry.

He talked with Peter and Olivia Matheson. He had found it impossible to give the editor his scoop. He had found it impossible to hurt those he loved – Cousin Hilda, Auntie Doris, Hilary and, ultimately, himself. He had found it impossible to uncoil the tangled ropes of motive, of his warmth and affection for others, of his personal and professional integrity, of the self-interest which lay on his tangled motives like frost on a whaler's rigging. In the end he had done the easiest thing. He had done nothing. There were times when he regretted it. This was one of those times. Every corpuscle of his being screamed, 'So you've got away with it, you bastard.' Peter Matheson, knowing this, turned the full blankness of his charm on Henry. 'A happy day, Henry,' he said. 'Congratulations.' He changed gear with the smoothness of an advanced motorist. 'Such a shame Anna couldn't be here. Have you heard from her at all?'

'No,' lied Henry, terrified that he would blush. 'Have you?'

'No,' said Peter Matheson, and Henry had no idea whether he was telling the truth. Surely, having been so involved in all the machinations, he would know? But it obviously wasn't a safe topic of conversation, in Thurmarsh. 'No,' he repeated. 'We're worried, I must admit.'

'We're her parents,' said Olivia Matheson unnecessarily. She was developing pronounced crow's-feet, perhaps from wrinkling her face against her husband's remorseless charm.

'I'm a repenter of former arrogance,' said Peter Matheson.

'In what connection?' said Henry.

'In your connection,' said Peter Matheson.

'We didn't think you a good enough catch,' said Olivia.

'We'd settle for you now,' beamed her husband sadly.

'Thank you very much,' said Henry drily.

Henry 'Certified eligible by no less an authority than Councillor Matheson' Pratt set off across the buzzing, bursting room in order to speak to a former flame, Diana Pilkington-Brick, née Hargreaves. Before he could reach her, her husband swept upon him like a tidal wave.

'This isn't the time to discuss money,' said Tosser Pilkington-Brick. 'No,' said Henry. 'So I won't,' said Tosser. 'Oh good,' said

Henry. 'But,' said Tosser. 'Ah!' said Henry. 'What?' said Tosser. 'Nothing,' said Henry.

'No, I just wanted to say,' said Tosser, 'at the moment you probably don't have any . . .'

'No, I don't,' said Henry.

'I haven't told you what I was going to say yet.'

'It doesn't make much difference. Money, prospects, savings, investments, property, children, transport, you put "no" and we can fill in the details later.'

'That's why I'm sure we at United Allied General Financial Services Consultants can help you.'

'You're right. It isn't the time.'

'I know. That's why I'm not talking about it. I'm just saying, if ever in future you want to talk about it, you can always talk to me.'

'Thanks, Tosser,' said Henry, relenting. Why did he always relent?

'Small point,' said Tosser. 'I've dropped the Tosser. It has . . . connotations. Do you think you could see your way to calling me Nigel?'

'I'm sure I could, Tosser,' said Henry.

Diana had been swallowed up by the crowd. The Lewthwaites and the Hammonds were gathered round Nadežda's wheelchair, beside a frosted-glass window against whose opacity a summer shower was beating in brief frustration.

Nadežda smiled at him happily. He bent to kiss her cheek, cold even in July. How natural Martin Hammond looked in a suit. How unnatural anyone looked, who looked natural in a suit at twenty-two years of age.

'Pleasant stag night last night,' said Martin rather stuffily. He was miffed because he wasn't best man.

Reg Hammond, Martin's father, said, 'We had a good night, too. At Drobwell Miners' Welfare. They had this grand turn. Irish. He were right comical, weren't he, mother? I thought so, anyroad.' 'Right comical,' echoed Mrs Hammond, who had found that it paid to agree.

Sam Lewthwaite blushed furiously when Martin's young sister, who was thirteen, stared at him. Henry was glad he wasn't young any more.

'Did anything ever come of that corruption story I put you onto, Henry?' said Martin. 'No. I tried. It fizzled out,' said Henry. 'Pity,' said Reg Hammond. 'The secret of beating the Tories at national level is to regularly expose them at local level. That's what I reckon, anyroad.' Howard Lewthwaite avoided Henry's eyes.

But, when Henry moved on, Howard Lewthwaite followed him. 'Have I lost you for socialism?' he said, looking round to make sure they weren't being overheard.

'Oh no,' said Henry. 'You were no worse than them.'

'Ah, but we have to be better,' said Howard Lewthwaite. 'As women have to be better than men and blacks better than whites to be equal in this fair land of ours. Top dogs expect underdogs to prove themselves every day of their lives.' His eyes met Henry's at last. 'Thanks for not telling,' he said.

'I didn't not tell for you,' said Henry, grammatically inelegant as usual, in the presence of his father-in-law. 'I did it . . . I mean, I didn't do it . . . for Hilary and me.'

A group of his ex-colleagues was standing beside the drinks. He approached, smiling. Helen Plunkett, née Cornish, kissed him, and Jill felt obliged to emulate her sister. She approached the task as if he were a fillet of haddock lying on a fisherman's slab, and this still irked him. Did he want to be loved by the whole world?

'Epidemic time,' said Gordon Carstairs. 'I hope you'll both be very happy,' said Henry. 'Henry's got it!' said Gordon Carstairs.

'How's Lampo, Denzil?' said Henry. 'How should I know? Ask him,' said Denzil, whose hand-carved Scottish walking-stick was leaning against a cream radiator.

'Name the wives of the English cricket team,' commanded Ben Watkinson. 'Ben!' admonished his shy, petite wife Cynthia.

When Henry moved on, Helen followed him. 'Are we going to keep in touch?' she asked. 'I hope so,' he said. 'We never actually worked anything out, did we? You've still never really seen my legs properly,' she said. 'Helen!' he said.

Ted pursued them. His buttonhole looked tired. So did he. 'Lovely wedding,' he said. 'Great girl. I'm really pleased.'

'Oh God, Ted. How could I ever have thought you were trying to destroy my career?' said Henry.

Helen wheeled away, abruptly, towards the shattered remains of the buffet.

'You're right,' said Ted.

'I didn't say anything,' said Henry.

'You didn't need to,' said Ted. 'I *should* have married Ginny.'

'We'll slip off quietly, if you don't mind,' said Mr Andrew Redrobe.

'Andy thinks his presence inhibits the journalists,' said Mrs Redrobe, who was in blue.

'Will you apply for a job on another paper?' said Mr Andrew Redrobe, his voice soaked in the infuriating, paternal kindness that he had used ever since he had become convinced that the scoop which Henry could never tell him was a figment of an immature imagination.

'No. I'm thinking of something totally different,' said Henry.

'I think that's very wise,' said his former editor.

Marie Chadwick steered the wheelchair expertly through the seething, chattering throng.

'Congratulations,' said Henry. 'It's wonderful news.'

'We got engaged before we were told I'd walk again,' said Dennis Lacey.

'Dennis! That's not important,' said Marie.

'It is to me,' said Dennis Lacey. 'People said Marie left him for me because he was crippled. She left him for love. The fact that she was prepared to marry me when she didn't know I wasn't going to be crippled proves that.'

Liam O'Reilly and Norman Pettifer were having a quick sit, in reproduction chairs with elegant curved backs.

'Grand wedding,' said Liam.

'A wedding I'd love to have seen was that of Dame Sybil Thorndike and Sir Lewis Casson,' said Norman Pettifer.

'I hope you've been talking to people,' said Henry.

'Oh yes,' said Liam. 'I had a very nice talk with one of the waiters.'

'Though of course they weren't Dame and Sir then,' said Norman Pettifer. 'Have you been to Cullen's recently, Henry?'

'No. Why?' said Henry.

'I wondered if you'd seen the cheese counter recently,' said Norman Pettifer. 'That Adrian! Hopeless. No idea.'

Violet Skipton was in purple. Henry wished that she'd shaved off her moustache for the great day, but that would have involved tacit acknowledgement that it existed. 'We'll slip off quietly, if you don't mind,' she said.

'We don't like seeing people becoming affected by artificial stimulants,' said Terry.

'I expect you think we're ridiculous,' said Violet.

'No, I suspect we're ridiculous, but I won't do anything about it,' said Henry.

The almost deformed news editor held out his hand and . . . yes, another first . . . he blushed. The blush gave a sheen of humanity to his dark, unattractive face. 'Henry?' he said. The Christian name! Another first. 'If you ever feel . . . if you ever need . . . either of you, that is . . . how can I? . . . guidance, would you think of us? Our house has an open door. Our hearts are yours. Come on, Violet.'

Terry Skipton turned away, as if angry with himself. Violet Skipton followed him for a few paces, then turned back.

'I've never seen him take to anyone like he took to you,' she said.

Baron Pratt, third Duke of Thurmarsh, was temporarily at a loss. He stood there, shorn of all pretensions, twenty-two years old and still not mature enough or good-hearted enough to fight off unkind thoughts about women's moustaches.

Lampo Davey slid through the crowd, untouched by the increasing hubbub, carrying a large plate on which his single smoked salmon *beignet* looked aggressively ascetic.

'What's happened between you and Denzil?' said Henry.

'I broke her sugar bowl. Oh dear! Tragedy. Makes *Antigone* seem like a tiff about the funeral arrangements.'

'Lampo? You aren't going to end up hurting Denzil, are you?'

'Quite possibly. Why?'

'Please don't.'

'What?'

'Don't forget I brought you together.'

'You were the most reluctant matchmaker of all time,' said Lampo.

'I love you both,' said Henry.

Diana was sitting beneath Stanier Class 5 No 45284, which was carrying a Manchester to Cardiff troop special through Craven Arms. She was enormous. The Hargreaves family stood around her. Henry bent down, and she gave him a huge wet kiss, and said she'd felt vaguely jealous when she'd seen Hilary.

'A congenial stag night last night,' said Paul rather stuffily. He was miffed because he wasn't best man.

'Did Nigel try to sell you things?' said Diana. 'Yes,' he said. 'Oh no! He's awful,' she said, but she said it indulgently. She loved Tosser! She was enormous. Mrs Hargreaves, who was as slender as a silver birch, kissed him graciously, and he blushed because he remembered that he'd once desired her, and he could see that she thought he was blushing because he still desired her, and this made him blush all the more and of course he couldn't explain. Mr Hargreaves pumped his hand as if trying to bring it back to life. Judy kissed him coolly, and said, 'I'm amazed. All this. Smoked salmon. Champagne. The hotel. That lovely church. In the north. I'm amazed.'

Nigel Pilkington-Brick, né Tosser, joined them, and Henry felt sad. Not because she was married. He wanted her to be married. Not because she was happy. He wanted her to be happy. Not because she was enormous. He wanted her to have children and, if that involved being enormous, he wanted her to be enormous. But . . . there was a Pilkington-Brick in there.

Colin Edgeley was wedged into a corner with Tony Preece's fiancée, Stella. Colin looked drunk, dishevelled and desperate.

Stella had gone to great lengths to look smart but had only succeeded in looking gaunt.

'Has Tony named the day?' said Henry.

Stella shook her head. 'Last night his act went well,' she said. 'He was pleased. He said we must name the day.' He asked her where Tony had been appearing. 'Drobwell Miners' Welfare,' she said.

'Good Lord,' he said. 'What's his new act?'

'He calls himself Cavin O'Rourke, the Winsome Wit from Wicklow. He pretends to be very stupid. He thinks it may catch on.'

'Good Lord. Stella? Go up to him now. Make him name the day, while romance is in the air.'

Stella set off, uncertainly, without confidence, towards her reluctant fiancé.

'What's wrong, Colin?' said Henry.

Colin turned his glassy, pained eyes on Henry. 'Glenda's left me,' he said.

'Oh no,' said Henry. 'Why?'

'I got drunk and stayed out all night.'

'Oh no.'

'With Helen.'

'Oh no!'

'I was so drunk I don't even remember. She said I said she had the most beautiful legs I'd ever seen.'

'Oh no.'

'Can there be any value in an experience you can't remember? Why are you staring at me?'

'Because you can make fine philosophical points when your world's collapsing around your ears. So what are you going to do?'

'Go and try and get her back. I love her, Henry. I really love her.' This discovery seemed to astound him. 'I'd have gone this weekend, if it wasn't for this.'

'Colin!' said Henry. 'This isn't important. You should have gone today.'

'And missed your wedding, kid? You're my mate,' said Colin.

'Colin! Why do you do these things?'

'I have a strong streak of self-destruction. Like you.'

380

'I don't.'

'Yes, you do. Always having disasters. Always laughing about them.'

'I only laugh at them in order to cope with them,' said Henry. 'I'd love to be a success, talking about my successes. And I will. So belt up about self-destruction and go and get Glenda and the kids and show them that you love them.'

'What's happened to you?' said Colin.

'Hilary. She's changed me. Do you know what I've become at last?' said Henry. 'A man.'

OH NO! NOT THAT AGAIN.

The hububble of noise and champagne was rising to a crescendo. They were trapped, by the wall, between the buffet and the drinks: Cousin Hilda, Auntie Kate, Mrs Wedderburn, and, nearest to the drinks, Auntie Doris and Geoffrey Porringer. Michael Collinghurst, the best man, was charming them.

They smiled as Henry approached, even Cousin Hilda. Auntie Doris was trying not to cry and ruin her mascara. Geoffrey Porringer was trying not to cry and ruin his reputation. Cousin Hilda was sniffing furiously. Even Mrs Wedderburn had moist eyes.

Michael Collinghurst came forward, touched Henry's hands, smiled shyly, said, 'Lovely. She's a lovely girl,' and then stood to one side, smiling, as if conducting, with the baton of his goodness, the symphonic variations of Henry's relations with his family. It was the first time they had met since Florence. Henry's telegram had read 'Man best my you be like I'd to.' The clerk had queried it. Michael's reply had read, simply, 'Pleasure with accept I.' Now such childish things were behind them. Henry smiled at Michael's smile and wondered if, even on this day, he had no regrets about committing himself to celibacy.

Auntie Doris hugged him, and the tears streamed, ruining her mascara, and she said, 'I wish Teddy were here to see this day.' Geoffrey Porringer twitched. Cousin Hilda sniffed. Auntie Doris, who always made things worse by protesting about them, said, 'There's no need to sniff, Hilda, just because I mention Teddy. He's still alive, you know. He's not dead.'

Henry went rigid with shock. He felt that his hair was standing on end. He heard Cousin Hilda say, 'What do you mean by that?' He heard Auntie Doris say, 'In my heart. He lives on, in my heart.' His hair subsided. His legs felt weak. He hoped nobody'd noticed anything. 'Geoffrey knows that,' continued Auntie Doris. 'Geoffrey understands that. Geoffrey accepts that.'

'Geoffrey doesn't have much choice,' muttered Geoffrey Porringer. He turned to Henry and said, 'Well done. I always knew you had it in you.'

It was the moment to be generous. It was the time to show his mettle. 'Thank you, Uncle Geoffrey,' he said.

'Oh, I say,' said Geoffrey Porringer. 'Oh, I say. Uncle Geoffrey, eh?' He put his arm round Henry. 'It's a happy day for us all, young sir,' he said.

Henry kissed Cousin Hilda. She sniffed. 'Are you having a good time, Cousin Hilda?' he asked. She said, 'I thought the bridge rolls were a little on the dry side.' Henry realized that, if she'd continued, she'd have said, 'Everything else was perfect.' You detected Cousin Hilda's praise by taking map references on the points where she had not imparted blame.

He kissed Mrs Wedderburn. 'It was right nice of you to invite me,' she said. He heard himself saying, 'One good turn deserves another, Mrs Wedderburn.' 'Good turn?' said Mrs Wedderburn. 'You lent me your camp-bed. Now your gift horse has come home to roost,' said Henry. But he knew, with a twinge of shame, that he'd invited her because he wanted to search, beneath Cousin Hilda's widowed neighbour's plump exterior, for the naughty schoolgirl who'd done it behind the tram sheds with Uncle Teddy.

He kissed Auntie Kate. She explained that Fiona hadn't been able to come because her one-legged husband was having 'one of his turns'. It was the first Henry had ever heard of these 'turns'. 'May I bring Hilary to Skipton often?' he said. 'She won't want to see a dreary, faded old lady,' said Auntie Kate. 'She will! You don't know Hilary,' he protested. By the time he realized that he should have said, 'Auntie Kate! You aren't a dreary, faded old lady', it was too late.

Michael Collinghurst, smiling shyly, bowed ever so slightly, as if laying his benediction on them all.

A waiter opened two of the frosted-glass windows, allowing the sun to stream into the Sir William Stanier Room and the cigarette and cigar smoke to stream out into the cool, tramless town.

Henry and Hilary found themselves together at last, holding hands.

'Love you,' he said.

'Love you,' she said. She looked round and lobbed a great grin across the room towards her family. Her parents smiled back. Sam stuck his tongue out. 'I haven't seen my parents look so happy since the illness,' she said.

There were moments when Henry believed that he had been utterly right not to reveal his scoop. This was one of them, until he looked into Hilary's smiling face and wished again that there wasn't this great secret between them.

'We ought to be off,' he said.

'Right. Let's step out into the great adventure of our life together,' she said.

But, before they could step out into the great adventure of their life together, a man stepped rather shyly towards them. He was vaguely familiar. With a shiver Henry realized that it was the man from his dreams, who told him, in a few blindingly simple words, all the secrets of life and of its conduct. For an agonizing moment he wondered if it was all a dream. Had he known, all along, that it was too good to be true? He broke into a clammy sweat. In a moment the Sir William Stanier Room would disappear, the late afternoon sunshine would disappear, the roar of animated chatter would be silenced, Hilary would fade into the ether, all his happiness would disappear for ever, and he'd wake up in a crumpled bed . . . where? Which part of his life was not a dream?

'I seem to recognize that man,' said Hilary.

She could see him too! He was real. She was real. He hugged her in his relief. She looked at him in astonishment.

'It's the man in my dreams,' he said.

'It can't be,' she said.

'Don't you recognize me?' said the man.

Of course! 'Oscar! From the Pigeon and Two Cushions!'

Oscar beamed.

'Nice bit of extra, this, for me,' he said. 'Congratulations, sir. Congratulations, madam.'

They thanked him. He began to gather up empties. He walked away, then turned back towards them. He had the same expression as he did in Henry's dreams. It was the expression of a man who is about to divest himself of momentous information. Henry realized that Oscar was the unlikely agent who would tell them, in a few blindingly simple words, the meaning of life and the secret of its conduct. He shivered with fear and excitement. Hilary shivered too. They clutched each other's hands tightly. Oscar came up very close to them.

'I've had this summer cold,' he said. 'It's right ironical. One nostril's completely blocked up, and the other nostril isn't blocked up at all.'

The Cucumber Man

The third Henry Pratt novel

Contents

1 An Interesting Appointment

There was full employment in 1957, but there is an exception to every rule. The exception to this particular rule turned to his wife Hilary and said, 'Do you think I'll ever get another job?'

Henry Pratt was sitting on the lower end of a sadly subsiding settee in a rented ground floor flat in Stickleback Rise. He was twenty-two years old, pale, five foot seven tall, on the podgy side, and wearing reading glasses. It was Monday, September 30th. There were 11.72½ marks to the pound, winter fares for flying small cars across the English Channel had been reduced to £3 10s, paratroopers were on guard as black pupils attended the High School in Little Rock, Alabama, and it was raining in Thurmarsh.

That morning, a letter had arrived from the BBC, informing Henry that he had not got the researcher's job for which he had applied. In the last week he had also failed to become a public relations officer for ICI, and a reserves manager with the Royal Society for the Protection of Birds. Nevertheless, Hilary still had faith in him. 'Of course you'll get a job,' she said. She kissed him, and the springs went 'boing'. The settee, like Henry's career, was proving a disappointment.

An occasional car whooshed along the wet road, a tram rattled past on its way to Thurmarsh Lane Bottom, and, on the mantelpiece, above the hissing gas fire, the elegant art deco clock struck eight soft chimes. A wedding present from Lampo Davey and Denzil Ackerman, it provided the only touch of style in the unremittingly brown, bulkily furnished flat.

To add to Henry's feeling of inadequacy, Hilary had got the first job for which she had applied. From January she would be teaching English at Thurmarsh Grammar School for Girls, where she had been a repressed and depressed pupil less than five years ago.

She snuggled closer to Henry and kissed him again. 'Boing', went the springs. 'You're still my lovely lover,' said Hilary.

Henry smiled. He was a lucky man to have won the love of this pale, serene, beautiful woman.

8.00 became 8.07. Tick of clock. Hiss of fire. Whoosh of tyre. Boing!

It was impossible to imagine that, on that very evening, a world which didn't seem to care would send not one but two visitors, both of them with kind intentions, to Flat 1, 33, Stickleback Rise, Thurmarsh.

The first visitor was Howard Lewthwaite, Hilary's father. He was pale and looked all of his fifty years. The lines on his face were etched deep. He sat in the only armchair, accepted a cup of coffee, and gulped it eagerly, as if he feared that without its stimulus he might gently expire.

'I hope I haven't interrupted anything,' he said. 'You've had your tea, have you?' The Lewthwaites ate dinner, but he called it tea, because he was deputy leader of the majority Labour group on Thurmarsh Borough Council, and couldn't afford to be thought a snob.

'Yes, we've had our tea,' said Hilary.

They'd had sausages and mash, with two cups of tea each. They hadn't enough money to be sophisticated.

'I'm the sole cause of your unemployment, Henry,' said Howard Lewthwaite.

'That's ridiculous,' said Henry.

'Ridiculous,' echoed Hilary.

'No, no. No, no. You had a great scoop. It would have launched you on your journalistic career. You couldn't write it up, because my disgrace would have broken Hilary's heart. The sole cause.'

Neither Henry nor Hilary spoke. If a person is determined to take all the blame, there is nothing you can do. Besides, they had never discussed her father's misdeeds. Henry hadn't even wanted her to know about them, but Howard had insisted on 'wiping the slate clean'.

'I want to help you,' said Howard Lewthwaite. 'I'd like to pay your rent, but I can't. The golden age of drapery is over. One day,

2

not this year, maybe not even next year, but soon, Lewthwaite's will fail. A hundred and seventeen years of family trading will cease. The proud tradition will crumble in my hands.'

'It's kind of you to come round to cheer us up,' said Henry, and Hilary gave him a warning look. He put his right hand on her left knee and felt a stirring of desire. It was, albeit by a narrow margin, his favourite of her knees.

'Naddy needs constant care.' Howard Lewthwaite's Yugoslavian wife Nadežda was crippled by polio. 'We hope Sam will go to university. He'll need a certain level of support for many years.'

'It's all right,' said Henry. 'I don't need money. I'll get a job.'

'Of course he will,' said Hilary staunchly.

'Of course you will,' said Howard Lewthwaite. 'After all . . .'

He hesitated. Henry, hoping that a ringing endorsement of his qualities as man, husband and potential employee would follow, composed his face into a suitably modest expression.

'After all, everybody gets a job in the end,' said Howard Lewthwaite.

'I'll be working from January,' said Hilary.

'Couldn't you get work as a teacher, Henry?' asked Howard Lewthwaite.

Henry shook his head. 'I went to too many schools as a child. I couldn't face any more.'

'I suppose they're looking for people with degrees, anyway,' said Howard Lewthwaite. He smiled warmly at Henry. Henry's answering smile was just a trifle strained. 'Anyway, Naddy and I don't think that your modest savings should be frittered away in rent, and we'd like to offer you a room in our house until you're both working and can afford a mortgage.'

He beamed, confident that his offer was irresistible. Slowly, his smile foundered on the long silence that ensued.

Henry looked at Hilary and realised that for the first time in their brief marriage he didn't know what she was thinking. He stroked her knee and felt an aching longing and an unaccustomed bleakness.

He knew what *he* was thinking. He was thinking that he didn't want to share his wife with her family. He didn't want to compare her slender loveliness with her mother's crippled body. He didn't want her obnoxious fifteen-year-old brother Sam banging on their bedroom door and shouting, 'Are you two having it off in there or can I come in?' He didn't want Howard Lewthwaite's guilt with their dinner that was called tea every night. He dreaded the faint amusement which he knew would greet the discovery that they had both started to write novels. He couldn't bear the thought of making love to Hilary in the room in which she had suffered her childhood depressions. Above all, he hated the thought of having to express any of these reservations to Hilary.

He caught her eye and wondered if *she* knew what *he* was thinking.

Hiss. Whoosh. Tick. It was becoming imperative for somebody to say something.

'That's very kind of you, Howard,' he said. 'Incredibly kind.'

'Amazingly kind,' agreed Hilary.

'I see,' said Howard Lewthwaite flatly. 'You don't want to come. The institution of the extended family in advanced Western societies has broken down irretrievably. I was a fool not to realise it.'

Henry 'You have a lively mind but it is our feeling that you are too creative a person to function well as a member of a team' Pratt looked to his wife for support. She didn't fail him.

'That's absurd, Daddy,' she said. 'It's an incredibly kind offer, but we need to think about it. We need to consider its implications for our sense of independence and our mutual self-fulfilment.'

Howard Lewthwaite nodded. 'That's fair enough,' he said. 'You're speaking my language there.' He stood up somewhat stiffly. His back was giving him gyp, and his temper hadn't been improved by his doctor's explanation that we were designed to walk on all fours, not on two legs, thereby implying that our endless pain is entirely the result of the hubris of the species and is in no way caused by the incompetence of the medical profession.

'Thank you for the coffee,' he said. 'It's love and support that we're offering you. I can't pretend you'd be independent, but I hope we could do it in a way that isn't incompatible with your mutual self-fulfilment. Anyway, the offer's still on the table.'

Henry went to the door with him, shook his hand warmly, and came back into a room that suddenly seemed far too small. He felt awful. He didn't know what to say. He stroked Hilary's knee again, but the gesture was mechanical and he felt no stirrings.

'I agree with you,' said Hilary.

'Agree with what?'

'What you were thinking. Sam being impossible, Mummy crippled, Daddy guilty, our both writing novels seeming faintly amusing.'

Henry felt a surge of love and admiration and relief, but also a cold wind of unease. He was beginning to feel that Hilary was very much cleverer than he was. His novel wasn't coming on well. She said that hers wasn't either, but he wasn't sure that he believed her. He felt a twinge of jealousy, and didn't like the feeling.

'So what do we do?' he asked. 'Turn it down?'

'It's not easy to do that, is it?' said Hilary. 'It'll hurt them deeply, and it does make financial sense.'

Henry 'After careful consideration, although we believe you have a great deal to offer, we do not think public relations is necessarily the right field for you' Pratt nodded glumly. He felt awful.

He was still feeling awful twenty minutes later, when Cousin Hilda called.

Cousin Hilda refused even the limited comfort offered by the armchair. Hard chairs are more suited to life on earth, her rigid pose asserted. She sat with her legs slightly apart, as women do who have no thought of sex and its attendant dangers, and with stockings as thick as hers, and pale pink bloomers as voluminous as hers, she had never been exposed to its dangers.

'I'm sorry to call so late,' she said. She made it sound as if she was being unbelievably bold in calling at eleven minutes past nine. 'But I had my gentlemen to see to.'

5

'It's very kind of you to come at all,' said Hilary.

'Well, we haven't got much on tonight after Tony Hancock, to say we pay for a licence,' said Cousin Hilda. 'There's *Panorama*, and that's depressing, and so's the news, and *Picture Parade*'s no use to me because when can I get to the pictures, with my gentlemen to see to, and then there's ballroom dancing, and I've never been right bothered about dancing, it only leads to things, and anyroad it includes that rock and roll. On the BBC! Can you believe it?'

'How *are* your gentlemen?' enquired Henry.

'Mr O'Reilly doesn't change,' said Cousin Hilda. 'Mr Pettifer's never had quite the same spring in his step since he were taken off the cheese counter. I've lost Mr Peters. I've a Mr Ironside instead, but only through the week. He has family in Norfolk.' Cousin Hilda paused and went slightly pink. 'I've had a chapter of disasters with my fourth room.'

'Disasters?' said Hilary gently.

'Drink,' whispered Cousin Hilda, as if the gas fire might disapprove if it heard. 'And worse.'

'Worse!' said Henry. 'The mind boggles.'

'Well it might,' said Cousin Hilda, luckily missing the irony. 'Well it might. That's how I lost Mr Peters.' There was silence. Cousin Hilda was clearly torn between the need to unburden herself and the enormous difficulty of broaching a painful subject.

'Tell us what happened,' said Hilary gently.

'This man came recommended,' said Cousin Hilda. 'He were a regional under-manager with Timothy White's. Timothy White's, I ask you, a respectable firm! He made . . . he made . . .'

'Certain suggestions to Mr Peters?' prompted Henry.

Cousin Hilda nodded her gratitude, and sniffed violently.

'Times are changing,' said Hilary.

'You're right, Hilary,' said Cousin Hilda fervently. 'You are so right. You have a very sensible wife, Henry.'

Henry was thrilled by this unparalleled high praise from Cousin Hilda, albeit slightly hurt by the surprise in her tone.

Cousin Hilda leant forward, and Henry realised that she was winding herself up for something momentous.

6

'We had fun at number 66, didn't we, in the old days?' she said. Henry tried to hide his astonishment.

'Oh yes,' he said. 'Lots of fun.'

'Plenty of good chin-wags.'

'Yes indeed. Very good chin-wags.'

'I've never been a great one for talk at table, and there were moments when I disapproved. I regret that now. Those meals, Henry, when you lived with me, they were the happiest times of my life.'

Henry could feel his heart thudding.

'It's different now,' said Cousin Hilda. 'Mr O'Reilly's never exactly been a live wire, Mr Pettifer's a shadow of his former self, at weekends when Mr Ironside's gone it's like a morgue. I have a little nest egg. I don't live particularly extravagantly. I don't need the rent from my fourth room, and you'll not want to be paying out rent every week when you're not working.'

Henry felt that he was drowning. He couldn't bear the thought of married life under Cousin Hilda's roof, in the little room which had been home to him from the time he had left Dalton College until he had bravely moved out into a flat early last year. He clutched Hilary's hand.

'I'm too old to cope with any more under-managers from Timothy White's or Macfisheries with their ideas.' Cousin Hilda, who must have been into her fifties by now, sniffed. 'I'd like it very much if you made my home your home.'

To Henry's horror, Hilary burst into tears.

'I'm sorry,' she said, 'but that is so kind of you.'

Cousin Hilda looked at Hilary as if regretting her use of the word 'sensible'. She sniffed disapprovingly.

Hilary blew her nose violently. 'I'm sorry,' she said.

Cousin Hilda's mouth was working with tension, and she had gone pink again.

'There is one other matter,' she said.

She pressed her legs together and Henry realised to his horror that she was going to talk about sex. Sweat was running down his back.

7

'I don't doubt that I strike you as odd and old-fashioned,' continued Cousin Hilda.

Even Hilary's famous tact was unequal to the task of denying this.

'However.' Cousin Hilda was remorseless. 'Even I am aware that there is a side to marriage in which folk . . . do things.' She had begun to sweat as well. Henry had never seen her sweat before. 'I know that it's the duty of married folk to do these things, otherwise there'd be no procreation of the human race.' Cousin Hilda was clinging rigidly to her chair. Her knuckles had gone white. 'I want you to know that you'd be welcome to . . . er . . . do your duty in my house whenever tha wants. Except mealtimes. Also, the normal bathtime restrictions would not apply. You could bath as often as you wished, provided that you didn't clash with my gentlemen.'

Cousin Hilda stopped at last and tried to smile.

Tick. Hiss. Whoosh.

Henry didn't dare look at Hilary. 'Thank you very much, Cousin Hilda,' he said in a stilted voice. 'That's a very kind offer, and well worth thinking about. Isn't it, Hilary?'

'It certainly is,' said Hilary. 'Very kind.'

'The thing is,' said Henry. 'The thing is . . . Hilary's father has offered us a room in their house.'

Cousin Hilda's lips began to work again.

'I see,' she said. 'I see. And you'd rather go there. More of a home. More fun than an ageing spinster and her gentlemen. I understand.'

'We haven't decided anything,' said Hilary with just a hint of asperity. 'These are very important suggestions, for which we're extremely grateful, but they'd change our lives considerably, and we really do have to think carefully about them.'

'Of course,' said Cousin Hilda. 'Of course. It were foolish of me to think you'd jump at my offer.'

And she sniffed twice, once in disgust at her own emotions and once in disapproval of her inability to hide them.

Henry and Hilary agonised after Cousin Hilda had gone. Hiss, tick, whoosh, and barely a boing. Who would they least offend if they accepted the other's offer? Which prospect filled them with the lesser dread? Wouldn't it be easier just to stay put? But why should they continue to pay rent when they didn't need to? And if they stayed, would they not simply offend both parties? They couldn't make up their minds, so they went to bed and did their bit for the procreation of the human race instead.

In the morning, as every morning, Hilary worked on her novel, and Henry pretended to work on his. Then, over their frugal lunch of Wensleydale cheese and digestive biscuits with plum chutney, they went back over the arguments of the night before, and reached a decision. Their solution was a good old British compromise, which would please nobody. They would spend half the time before Hilary began working with her family, and half at Cousin Hilda's, and then they would rent another flat, whether Henry had a job or not. They decided to go to Cousin Hilda's first, so that they wouldn't have to spend Christmas there. Henry couldn't bear the thought of another Christmas with Mrs Wedderburn and ginger cordial and Mr O'Reilly in a paper hat and the heady excitement of post-prandial Snap.

And so, just over a week later, Henry 'While we are impressed by your personality and enthusiasm we do not consider that you have the experience or physique needed to run a bird reserve' Pratt and his lovely wife Hilary caught a tram and a bus, because to travel by taxi would have been to incur an enormous sniff of disapproval right at the outset, and arrived at Cousin Hilda's stone, semi-detached house in Park View Road just twenty minutes after the hired van that had brought their worldly possessions in three suitcases and two packing cases.

Cousin Hilda opened the door, and Henry re-entered her house with a deep sense of nostalgic gloom marbled with affection. To walk across her dark, cold hall was to embark upon a voyage of nasal nostalgia that made Proust's madeleines seem insignificant by comparison. Henry was met by the mingled smells of cabbage and linoleum, of the dankness of darkness and the acridity of burning

9

coke, the whole pot-pourri warmed by the succulent nourishing aroma of giant bloomers being aired, and spiced with the only slightly less nourishing imminence of toad-in-the-hole and sponge pudding with chocolate sauce. Faithful readers will deduce that it was a Wednesday.

And so, that late Wednesday afternoon, as the sun sank with Henry's and Hilary's hearts, they arranged their relatively meagre possessions around the tiny little second storey fourth bedroom of number 66, Park View Road. The art deco clock went on the tiny mantelpiece. They didn't dare, in these stern surroundings, to unpack the bookends given them by Auntie Doris and Geoffrey Porringer. These had a naked man at one end and a naked woman at the other, and if the naked man was meant to be thinking about a book, it must have been *Lady Chatterley's Lover*. Their books remained in the packing cases with the bookends.

The room's furniture consisted of a severely sagging sofa which converted into a severely sagging three-quarter size bed at night, one hard chair, two small bedside tables with circles where Cousin Hilda's gentlemen had rested mugs of cocoa, and a rickety and wholly inadequate wardrobe cum chest of drawers. There were two pictures, the depressed monarch of a wet and misty glen, and a portrait of John Wesley in an unusually gloomy mood even for him.

'Ah well,' said Henry bravely. 'Our toad-in-the-hole awaits. I could do with a good chin-wag.'

And indeed at first the atmosphere round the little table in the blue basement room was quite lively. Mr O'Reilly rose to heights of eloquence unknown in his quiet life. 'It's very good to have you back, Mr Henry,' he said. 'Oh yes indeed. Very good. Oh, we had some fun in the old days, didn't we? Yes indeed. And now your lovely lady too. Yes yes,' and then he went very red and subsided into shiny silence.

'Welcome back,' said Norman Pettifer. 'Any novelty is welcome when one spends one's life putting tins on shelves.'

'Brian Ironside,' announced Brian Ironside.

'I believe you have family in Norfolk,' said Hilary.

'Yes,' said Brian Ironside.

'Which part of Norfolk?' persisted Hilary bravely.

'Swaffham,' admitted Brian Ironside reluctantly.

'It must be a difficult journey,' quipped Henry wittily.

'It is,' countered Brian Ironside thoughtfully.

'What line are you in, Brian?' asked Henry.

'Communications,' said Brian Ironside.

'Do you go to the theatre much, Hilary?' asked Norman Pettifer.

'Not as much as we'd like to,' said Hilary.

'I once saw Johnny Gielgud,' said Norman Pettifer.

'Really?' said Hilary. 'What in?'

'Regent Street,' said Norman Pettifer. 'He was coming out of Austin Reed's.'

Liam O'Reilly, who had never been to London, sighed, and there was a brief silence.

'Well come on, Henry, Hilary,' said Cousin Hilda. 'Tell us about your plans.'

'We're both writing novels,' said Henry.

Cousin Hilda sniffed twice, once for each novel, and gave Hilary a disappointed glance, as if to say, 'Nothing surprises me about Henry, but I thought you were sensible.'

Novels having fallen so flat, Henry felt a desperate need to change the subject. 'Is young Adrian still making a mess of the cheese counter, Norman?' he asked.

'Mess is not the word,' said Norman Pettifer through clamped lips. 'Farce, fiasco and cock-up are three other examples of total linguistic inadequacy. There isn't a word in the dictionary to do justice to what Adrian has done to the cheese counter.'

Norman Pettifer's bitterness, allied to Brian Ironside's reticence and Liam O'Reilly's exhaustion, cast rather a damper on the proceedings, and the sponge pudding with chocolate sauce was taken in silence.

Nevertheless, when her gentlemen had gone, Cousin Hilda smiled and said, 'Well, that were right nice. It's been so cheerless recently, as if I've been doing it all too long. You've given me a new lease of life.'

'It really is extremely kind of you to have us,' said Hilary.

'Nonsense,' said Cousin Hilda. 'What are families for? Incidentally,' she added, dashing their hopes of an early escape to the pub, 'please don't feel obliged to leave when my gentlemen do. Treat this room as your home.'

'Actually we were thinking of popping down to the park before the light faded,' lied Henry.

'It closes at six thirty,' said Cousin Hilda. 'You'll be too late.' She leant forward, to take them further into her confidence. 'I've had to make sacrifices for my gentlemen,' she admitted. 'I've never really been able to say that this house is my home.'

Henry and Hilary were astounded.

'Not your home?' echoed Henry emptily.

'Not as such. Not in the sense that Mrs Wedderburn's house is her home.'

'But your house is full of people and hers is so lifeless.'

'She has a parlour.'

'But she never uses it.'

'Of course she doesn't. That's the point of a parlour,' explained Cousin Hilda. 'It's a place for your best things.'

'But then you never use your best things,' said Henry.

'Of course not. Then they don't spoil,' said Cousin Hilda.

'Well what's the use of having them, then?' asked Henry.

'You know they're there,' said Hilary.

'Exactly,' said Cousin Hilda, and Hilary felt that she had regained some of the approval she had lost over the novel.

Little did Cousin Hilda know that, if ever Hilary had any best things, she would use them regularly.

But would she ever have any best things? It didn't seem likely that night, as they turned their sagging sofa into a sagging bed, clambered into it, realised how much it creaked, and attempted to do their duty towards the procreation of the human race.

'It's no use,' said Henry at last. 'It's not just Cousin Hilda. I don't want to make Mr O'Reilly envious and Norman Pettifer even more bitter. It's the thought of them all, down there, listening, wondering.'

'Well never mind,' said Hilary. 'Seven weeks isn't long, and you're still my lovely man.'

The next morning, Hilary and her lovely man walked over to the Alderman Chandler Memorial Park, where Henry, when he had thought he was a homosexual, had followed a fair-haired boy from the grammar school, and later, once he had realised that he wasn't a homosexual, had asked Stefan Prziborski about precautions. Now, twenty-two years old, married, with a beautiful wife whose small, shapely breasts and trim bottom he adored – how could he ever have thought her scrawny, even in Siena? – he ought to be feeling happy in the warm October sunshine. But he wasn't. For one thing, the park was failing him. It was very much as he had remembered – there were still very few animals in the cages, one of the swings was still broken, most of the glass in the Old Men's Shelter was still missing, and there weren't nearly as many varieties of duck on the pond as on the board which showed pictures of all the ducks that were supposed to be on the pond. But none of that had ever mattered, because the park had been a huge expanse, redolent of adventure and discovery. Now it had shrunk. It was small and neat.

Were their lives going to be small and neat? No! They were fighters. They wouldn't allow themselves to be dispirited by their surroundings.

Henry led Hilary home boldly. On the gravel drive they met Cousin Hilda with her shopping bag. 'Don't worry. I'll only be gone while half eleven,' she told them.

The gentlemen were all at work, and Cousin Hilda would be at the shops till half past eleven! Barely, if ever, can a sofa bed have creaked so much at 66, Park View Road, Thurmarsh.

Bravely, in the days to come, Henry and Hilary sat, one on the hard chair, the other on the converted sofa, with their manuscripts on the bedside tables. Bravely, Henry pretended to write his novel, but he already knew, in his heart, that he wasn't a novelist.

Bravely, Henry applied for further jobs. Bravely, he went for interviews. Bravely, he shrugged off the fact that his managerial genius was not recognised by British Railways, Blue Arrow or Thurmarsh Bottling Limited. Let the nation suffer late trains, unsuitable appointments and bottle shortages. See if he cared.

Bravely, Henry and Hilary adjusted the pattern of their love-making to the rhythms of Cousin Hilda's shopping. Four times a week was well above the national average, anyway, and if Monday (bread and household goods) and Tuesday (meat and vegetables) were rather rushed affairs, Thursday (meat, bread and groceries) and Friday (fish, meat, vegetables and sundries) were really quite leisurely.

Bravely, every afternoon, come rain or shine, they set off, across Cousin Hilda's dark, cold hall, past the barometer which, being slightly wrongly adjusted, took almost as pessimistic a view of the prospects as did its owner, and plunged into the knotted streets of Thurmarsh for an hour's brisk walk. Once or twice, nostalgia tempted Henry towards the dingy back-to-back terraces of Paradise Lane, where he had been born, and they gazed into the murky waters of the River Rundle, into which he had been pushed eighteen years ago, and into the marginally less poisonous waters of the Rundle and Gadd Navigation, into which he had been thrown eleven years ago, and he hoped, over-optimistically, as it turned out, that he would never be deposited in either of them again.

Bravely, they sat with Liam O'Reilly, who interspersed his silences with the occasional burst of gratitude for their return and regret at its impermanence; with Norman Pettifer, who grew gradually more disillusioned by their lack of knowledge of the theatrical greats; and with Brian Ironside, who unbent so dramatically under Hilary's gentle probing that in less than a month she had learnt the names and ages of his three children.

Bravely, they ate their toad-in-the-hole and sponge pudding with chocolate sauce on six more Wednesdays, their roast pork and tinned pears on seven Thursdays, their battered cod and jam roly-poly on seven Fridays, their roast beef preceded by Yorkshire pudding on seven Sundays, their liver and bacon and rhubarb crumble on seven Mondays, and their roast lamb and spotted dick on seven Tuesdays. How wrong Henry had been last January, when he had thought that he was eating his last spotted dick ever.

But what of Saturday, the careful reader cries.

Showing reserves of courage that can only be marvelled at, Henry and Hilary informed Cousin Hilda that they would be having a night out every Saturday.

'*Every* Saturday?' she exclaimed.

'Well, that's only once a week,' said Hilary. 'And we thought if we did it on a regular basis you'd know where you were.'

If they expected gratitude for this consideration, they were to be disappointed.

On the first of their seven Saturdays out, Henry and Hilary went to Troutwick, Gateway to Upper Mitherdale, to visit his Auntie Doris, who ran the two-star White Hart Hotel with her second husband, the slimy Geoffrey Porringer.

Auntie Doris could not be described as happy. She still loved her first husband, Henry's Uncle Teddy, whom she believed to have died in a fire at his night club, the Cap Ferrat in Thurmarsh. The fact that he was living in the South of France, and bigamously married to a girl who had been Hilary's best friend at school, had the effect of drawing Hilary into the circle of deceit and misapprehension, and making her feel thoroughly at ease with Auntie Doris. But then everyone felt thoroughly at ease with Auntie Doris. She was a splendid landlady. She had found her niche, and had suddenly grown huge without ceasing to look glamorous and attractive. She was fighting the effects of age and the enormous spirits that she now drank with enormous spirit, and if she spent more on herself than on redecorating the pub, that was part of its charm. Not for nothing had it become known throughout the Yorkshire Dales not as 'The White Hart' but as 'Doris's'.

Nobody, on the other hand, felt at ease with Geoffrey Porringer, because he didn't feel at ease with himself. And this, to Henry, was his saving grace, which was why Henry now called him Uncle Geoffrey, which Geoffrey Porringer liked, even though Geoffrey Porringer still referred to him as 'young sir', which Henry hated.

And so, as the young farmers bought pink gins for pink Doris in the antiques-stuffed lounge, Henry and Hilary sipped quietly with Geoffrey Porringer, who said, 'A novel, eh, young sir? Whatever next?' And when Henry told him that Hilary was also writing a novel, he said, 'Both of you, eh? Well well. Clever stuff.' And then he added, 'I read a novel once. Not my cup of tea. Still, more power to your elbows,' and when Hilary suggested that maybe he should try another novel, because novels did vary enormously, he said, 'No, no. It was rubbish, it's true, but it was the fact that it didn't happen that I couldn't cope with. Didn't seem any point to it. Still, I'll try your stuff. You're family. That's different.'

'Speaking of family,' said Auntie Doris, leaving the serving momentarily to her three stressed barmen, 'can you really live with the Sniffer?'

'She's very kind,' said Hilary.

'Oh yes,' said Auntie Doris. 'She's very kind, granted, but. . . ,' she lowered her voice, 'can you make love in a place like that?'

'Oh yes,' said Henry. 'She goes shopping four times a week.'

Auntie Doris's chins wobbled on her face, and her gins wobbled in her glass, and her breasts wobbled in their outsize bra, and farmers and vets and blacksmiths smiled and said, 'There goes Doris. Off again. Wonder what's tickled her this time,' and Auntie Doris said, 'I'll tell you what's tickled me this time,' and she told the story of Henry and Hilary's love-making; and Hilary went pale and smiled and hated it, and Henry went red and grinned and found to his surprise that he loved it, and Geoffrey Porringer slid into the shadow of his wife's personality and slipped a whisky into his beer when she wasn't looking.

And on the seventh of their Saturdays out, when they visited Auntie Doris and Geoffrey Porringer again, Henry and Hilary found that the joke was rumbling on. 'You look well, young sir, young madam. Hilda's obviously been shopping a lot,' said Geoffrey Porringer, whose blackheads seemed worse than ever.

They had extra staff on, so Henry and Hilary were able to have dinner with Auntie Doris and Geoffrey Porringer, in the small cosy restaurant with its low-beamed ceiling, fine Welsh dresser and moderate English food.

They were handed their menus by a very pregnant Lorna Lugg, née Arrow. Henry had to stop himself flinching visibly at the sight of his childhood sweetheart so enormous with child by Eric Lugg, his childhood tormentor. Her face, once so pert and lovely, was plump and almost bovine now.

He felt an unworthy desire to say something incredibly clever and witty, to show Lorna how much more there was to life than Eric Lugg could provide. It was easy to fight off this desire, since he couldn't think of anything clever or witty.

'Hello, Lorna, how long till the big event?' he said.

'Three weeks,' said his former sweetheart. 'This is me last neet.' How broad her accent was. How Henry hated that and how he hated himself for hating it.

'This is my wife, Hilary,' he said. 'Hilary, this is Lorna.'

'Hello, Hilary,' said Lorna Lugg. 'Nice to meet you. The soup of the day is vegetable, and the fish of the day is haddock.'

'It's nice to meet you too,' said Hilary. 'I've heard a lot about you. Can you tell me, is the pâté rough or smooth?'

When Lorna had taken their orders, the thing for which Henry had been longing occurred, but in the wrong context. He was offered a job at last.

'Come and be my restaurant manager,' said Auntie Doris.

'I can't,' said Henry. 'Hilary's got a job at Thurmarsh Grammar in January.'

'You can work here too, Hilary,' said Auntie Doris. 'A family hotel. A family business. Think what pleasure that'll give my poor Teddy, if he finds out.'

Henry's blood ran cold. Could Auntie Doris know that Uncle Teddy was still alive?

'How could he?' he said, trying to sound casual.

'No,' said Auntie Doris. 'He couldn't. Not from down there.'

Did she mean Cap Ferrat? Did she know it all? Henry couldn't trust himself to speak.

17

'Down there?' said Hilary. 'Down where?'

'Hell, of course,' said Auntie Doris. 'I loved my darling Teddy, but I can't pretend there was a chance of his getting into the other place.'

And she roared her new 'landlady with big personality' laugh.

Geoffrey Porringer frowned and looked sulky, either at Auntie Doris's reference to her darling Teddy or at the prospect of Henry and Hilary joining the staff of the White Hart.

'Thank you for the offer,' said Henry, 'but it's the wrong trade for me. I like my drink too much.'

'It does take some people that way,' said Auntie Doris, 'but it won't if you've got anything to you.'

On Tuesday, November 26th, 1957, President Eisenhower suffered a mild stroke, two RAF Canberras were destroyed by sabotage in Cyprus, an acoustics engineer in a restaurant in Chicago 'proved' that women were the noiser sex, and Henry Pratt ate what he hoped would be his last spotted dick ever.

The atmosphere round the little table in the basement room with the roaring blue-tiled stove was tense and stifling. Cousin Hilda could barely eat, and Henry had a lump in his throat, which is not a good idea when you're eating spotted dick.

'We'll miss you, Mr Henry,' said Mr O'Reilly. 'And you, of course, Miss Hilary. Oh yes.'

'It's been very nice to meet you both,' said Brian Ironside, to general astonishment.

'All good things come to an end,' said Cousin Hilda.

It was Hilary who found it difficult to make love in her family's pleasant brick house in Perkin Warbeck Drive. Her brother Sam, sixteen now, had become marginally more sophisticated and marginally less obnoxious. Instead of the crude, 'Are you two having it off in there?' that Henry had feared, he banged on their door and yelled, 'Are you two having coitus interruptus in there?' 'We don't have coitus interruptus, dope,' Hilary replied. 'You do when I'm around,' gloated Sam, and he burst in to find them rearranging their clothes in the ample chest of drawers. As there were no locks on the doors, Hilary lived in constant fear that Sam would enter, so they could only make love during school hours. Henry, on the other hand, wanted Howard Lewthwaite to know that his daughter's husband wasn't falling down on the job, so he wanted to make love when Howard Lewthwaite was in. But the only time when Howard Lewthwaite was in and Sam was out was early closing day. Wednesday afternoon was therefore reserved for their main bout of the week. Every Wednesday afternoon, Hilary would say, 'We've got work to do,' and, as they left the room, Henry would turn and wink at Howard Lewthwaite, without Hilary knowing, as she would have been horrified, and without Nadežda seeing, as she would have been upset. Hilary feared that the knowledge that they were making love would upset her mother by bringing home to her what she was missing due to her crippled state.

'She must know we make love,' Henry pointed out. 'She must hope we make love, because she loves you.'

'Yes, theoretically she must. But at this particular moment of this particular afternoon, I doubt if she would want to know.'

'You feel guilty because she's crippled and you aren't.'

Henry regretted this remark as soon as he had made it. It wasn't kind, he felt, and he was aware that there were stirrings inside himself over which he had no control, under whose influence he could conceivably find pleasure in hurting the one he loved, and this disturbed him.

To his surprise, however, Hilary was not at all upset. 'Of course I feel guilty,' she said. 'I love her so very much.'

And so, Hilary attempted to make love very quietly, without rattling the bedhead, and eschewing the sharp cries of gasping passion that had occasionally surprised the neighbours in Stickleback Rise. Henry's aim, on the other hand, was to make love in animal fashion, with vigorous movements and heavy grunting and moaning. And although they were able to laugh at themselves and their excessive self-consciousness, a degree of tension and artificiality had entered into what had previously been delightfully natural between them.

Indeed, they felt a degree of tension and artificiality in the whole of their life in Perkin Warbeck Drive. The house, lacking a woman's touch due to Nadežda being chair-bound, seemed lifeless. The lounge, as Howard Lewthwaite felt that it was politically correct to call it, was heavily floral, almost luxurious, but lacking the sparkle that would have been given by real care on Nadežda's part. The dining room, too, with its dark mahogany table, brown Windsor chairs and brown Windsor soup, was an excessively careful room. Howard Lewthwaite did the cooking. Even under the circumstances of his wife's illness, he could not have equated his political conscience with having domestic servants, and if this seems hypocritical coming from one who hadn't been above a bit of town planning corruption on quite a major scale, well yes, Howard Lewthwaite was a hypocrite. Nice men often are.

And Howard Lewthwaite was a nice man whose natural good humour had been eroded by exhaustion, ill-luck, guilt and worry. His acts of corruption had been caused by his need for money to take Nadežda to live in a better climate. Because she was unable to stand up, she was developing a chest condition which was far more likely to kill her than her polio. It was impossible to emigrate while Sam was still at school. Howard Lewthwaite was worried that his drapery business in Market Street wouldn't last that long.

Sam, naturally, spent most of his time in his room, rocking round the clock with Bill Haley. His family, equally naturally, were happy for him to stay there.

So, the house that had seemed so full of life and love when Henry had first visited it last New Year's Eve – was it really less than a year ago? – seemed full of worry now. The rustic summer-house, where Henry and Hilary had discovered their love for each other, had yielded up all its mystery and romance in one go.

On the early evening of Tuesday, December 10th, shortly before their dinner that was called tea, Henry looked at his watch and said, 'Spotted dick just being served,' and, to his astonishment, Hilary said, 'I'm missing all that, you know,' and, to his even greater astonishment, he heard himself say, 'So am I.'

Every day Hilary wrote her novel and Henry pretended to write his, and every Wednesday afternoon Hilary said, 'Hush. Don't grunt so loudly,' and Henry grimaced. And British Home Stores, the British Council of Churches, and the Yorkshire Branch of the Institute of Quarrymen failed to recognise the latent genius of Henry Ezra Pratt.

Then it was almost Christmas, there were drinks in the heaving, dark, masculine back bar of the Lord Nelson with Henry's former colleagues on the *Thurmarsh Evening Argus*, all writing novels and dreaming of Fleet Street and/or literary fame. Ted Plunkett's seductive wife Helen said, 'Not pregnant yet, Hilary?' and raised an eyebrow, 'Didn't I miss much with Henry, then?' and Hilary said fiercely, 'You missed a lovely, lovely man,' and Ted sighed because he should have married Ginny Fenwick, and Ginny Fenwick blushed because she knew why Ted had sighed, and Henry felt a deep nostalgia for those busy, boozy days, and for the camaraderie of the workplace, and this disturbed him; and it worried him that so many things disturbed him, when he loved Hilary and was so happy with her.

On Christmas Day there were ingenious presents, there was turkey and Christmas pudding with threepenny bits in it, there were mince pies, there was plenty to drink, and although the obligatory nature of the enjoyment prevented true spontaneity, neither Henry nor Hilary felt any nostalgia for Cousin Hilda's that day.

Denzil Ackerman and Lampo Davey invited them to London for New Year's Eve, and they accepted, since they both knew that no New Year's Eve in Perkin Warbeck Drive could ever equal last year's in romantic intensity.

In Denzil and Lampo's *bijou* mews town house in Chelsea, tasteful decorations covered every available space, although there weren't many available spaces, since the house was bursting at the seams with pretty little *objets d'art*, notable among them being Denzil's unrivalled collection of vintage biscuit tins.

Denzil greeted them in a natty blue apron. Denzil and Lampo kissed both Hilary and Henry, and Henry was very pleasantly embarrassed.

'I'm doing the cooking. He's doing the worrying. We take it in turns,' said Denzil.

'I never worry,' said Lampo. 'He just likes to think I do, because he worries so much.'

Denzil gave an angry intake of breath, and wheeled from the room, narrowly avoiding knocking down two vases, a candlestick and a pomander. Henry flinched. He didn't like to see Lampo and Denzil arguing, since it was he who had brought them together, albeit inadvertently.

'We've a surprise for you,' said Lampo. 'Diana and Tosser are coming for drinks.'

Henry was horrified to feel the quickening of his heartbeat. At Dalton College he had fagged for Lampo and for Tosser Pilkington-Brick. Tosser had married Diana Hargreaves, sister of Henry's best friend, Paul. Henry had almost loved Diana once. Not now, though. No need for quickened heartbeats now.

Diana and Tosser were in evening dress. They would be. The last time Henry had seen Diana, at his wedding, she had been very pregnant. Now, although never slim, she looked quite shapely. The skin on her broad shoulders, though not as fine as Hilary's, was attractively brown and smooth. Henry didn't feel any desire for her, of course, but he felt a worryingly sharp hostility towards Tosser. He found himself hoping that they weren't happy, and this too disturbed him.

'We've left Benedict with Mummy,' said Diana. 'She sends her love, Henry. They both do. They miss you dreadfully.'

They drank champagne, and Tosser said, 'When you get a job, Henry, do come and see me for insurance and pensions advice.'

'Tosser!' said Diana.

'Diana, please, the name is Nigel,' said Tosser stuffily.

'The name is Tosser when you behave like a toss-pot,' said Diana.

Oh good, they were arguing. No, Henry, don't feel like that.

But it was difficult not to feel like that. Everyone seemed so fulfilled, Tosser doling out financial advice, Diana producing Benedicts, Lampo working for Sotheby's – or was it Christie's? –

Denzil still churning out his arty-farty cobblers for the *Thurmarsh Evening Argus*, Hilary starting work shortly *and* getting on so well with her bloody novel. Out, green-eyed monster.

'I've got a very promising interview next week,' said Henry.

He groaned inwardly. Why had he been so weak as to feel the need to compete? He didn't want to talk about his interview.

'Gorgeous. What's it for?' said Lampo, as he opened a second bottle of champagne, which fizzed out all over the inlaid marble top of a Georgian game table and sent Denzil white with anger.

Henry thought he had got away with it, but after ten minutes of frenzied cleaning, when Lampo turned to Denzil and said, 'Sorry. No harm done, I think,' Denzil, in order to ignore Lampo effectively, turned to Henry and said, 'Come on. You never told us what that interview was for.'

'It's with the Cucumber Marketing Board,' said Henry. 'They've relocated to Leeds. There's a vacancy for an Assistant Regional Co-ordinator, Northern Counties (Excluding Berwick-on-Tweed).'

There was a stunned silence in the little mews house in Chelsea.

Henry 'We admire your personality but are not convinced that you have the moral commitment that we as a religious body are seeking' Pratt sat in the foyer of the Cucumber Marketing Board, which was brilliantly user-unfriendly many years before the concept was put into words.

The Cucumber Marketing Board was housed in a four-storey Edwardian building in the business district of Leeds, among banks and solicitors' offices. The steel-armed chairs and the glass-topped table were far too small for the high-ceilinged room with its dusty chandelier and impressive ceiling rose. The table was strategically placed too far in front of his chair and too near the floor, so that he risked severe backache every time he bent down to pick up the out-of-date copies of *The Lady* and *The Vegetable Growers' Gazette*, which were the only reading matter provided.

'Mr Tubman-Edwards will see you now,' said the receptionist. 'Second floor. He'll meet you at the lift.'

Henry couldn't believe it. Could this possibly be the same Tubman-Edwards, the bully of Brasenose and Dalton, whom Tosser Pilkington-Brick, when he was a hero and not a financial consultant, had forced to smile on the other side of his face? If so, it was goodbye, cucumbers.

He wished he looked taller and more athletic. He wished that his dark grey suit didn't look crumpled.

He walked along a dark, uncarpeted corridor to the lift, which clanked precariously to the second floor, where he was met by a rather anxious man in his fifties, wearing a pin-striped suit and an MCC tie with a blob of egg yolk on it. A tiny piece of cotton wool had stuck to a cut on his neck.

'Dennis Tubman-Edwards,' he announced. 'It's Henry, isn't it? We're friendly people here.'

He smiled, seeming unaware that his smile gave a twisted, slightly sinister look to his face. Henry saw the resemblance to J. C. R. Tubman-Edwards (Plantaganet House) for the first time.

Mr Tubman-Edwards led him along a carpeted corridor, past the offices of the Director (Operations) and the Director (Admin.) and opened the door of Room 208, which carried the legend 'Head of Establishments'.

Mr Tubman-Edwards seated himself behind his very bare desk, and gestured to Henry to sit in the hard chair provided for interviewees. The office was not large and was almost entirely taken up with filing cabinets. There were just two pictures on the walls – a lurid portrait of the Queen and a school photograph of the Dalton College boys from Mr Tubman-Edwards's final year. His desk was bare except for a pen, a pad of lined paper, and two photograph holders.

'You were at school with my son, I believe,' said Mr Tubman-Edwards, turning one of the photographs round so that Henry could see the unprepossessing face of the ghastly boy.

'Yes, that's right,' said Henry, wondering desperately whether this was good news or bad.

Mr Tubman-Edwards winced and gasped. 'Sorry,' he said. 'Touch of shrapnel still lodged in the skull. Gives me gyp intermittently. Not to worry. Chums, were you?'

It might be a trap. Better be honest. Not too honest, though. Pity he needed the job. He would have loved to have said, 'Couldn't stand the great sack of blackmailing yak turd.'

'Er . . . not particularly,' he said.

'What's your ambition in life?' asked the father of the great sack of blackmailing yak turd in the same casual, conversational tone.

Henry realised that he had been thrown a conversational hand-grenade. To pitch his ambition too high – 'I'd like to feel that I'd helped to save Western civilisation' – would be to risk ridicule and, more seriously, rejection. To pitch it too low – 'I'd like to feel that I could support my family and give them double glazing for life' – might be even more disastrous.

'Er. . . ,' he began, more to show that he was still alive than anything, and as soon as he had stopped, he realised that to be indecisive would be the most fatal fault of all.

Too late. Oh well. Mr Tubman-Edwards smiled his slightly crooked smile and tapped his HB pencil on the desk. Must say something.

'I *suppose*,' he said, investing a deeply thoughtful inflection into his voice, to suggest that his long hesitation had been caused by deep thought, 'I *suppose* my ambition is to find an ambition that satisfies me.'

'I see,' said Mr Tubman-Edwards neutrally. 'I see. And what is your attitude to cucumbers?'

If this next abrupt change of subject was intended to jolt Henry, it failed. He felt on safer ground with cucumbers than with ambition.

'I like them,' he said, and then, to his horror, he heard himself add, 'I think they're the Cinderellas of the salad bowl.'

Fortunately, Mr Tubman-Edwards took him seriously.

'In what way?' he asked.

'Well what is a salad built around for most people?' said Henry. 'Lettuce and more lettuce. Tomatoes. Hard-boiled eggs. I think because it's the same colour as lettuce – green,' he wished he hadn't added the explanation, '. . . the cucumber is often added as an afterthought. I'd like to raise the profile of the cucumber, give it in

25

post-war cuisine a prominence akin to its dominance of the teatime sandwich in the pre-war world.'

J. C. R. Tubman-Edwards's father seemed impressed, if also slightly stunned.

'Excellent,' he said. 'Excellent. Splendid.'

A wave of self-disgust swept over Henry. How could he sit there and pretend, for the sake of a measly job, that cucumbers were so important? Where was the fighting spirit on which he prided himself?

'Of course they aren't the be-all and end-all,' he said.

'I'm sorry, I'm not quite with you,' said Mr Tubman-Edwards. 'They aren't the be-all and end-all of what?'

'Of life,' said Henry.

He feared that, in that brave, reckless moment, he had lost all chance of working for the Cucumber Marketing Board. But he was wrong.

He would often wonder, in the years to come, if things would have been better if he'd been right.

2 The First, Faint Shadows

On Friday, January 10th, 1958, there was a second successful launch of the Air Force's Atlas Inter-Continental Ballistic Missile at Cape Canaveral, a burglar found so much wine and spirits in a director's room at an Edinburgh shop-fitting firm that he was found drunk at the director's desk when the work-force arrived, and Hilary left for the doctor's before the post came.

The moment Henry had read the letter, he wanted to stand in the middle of Perkin Warbeck Drive and announce the good tidings with such a yell of triumph that it would be heard in Lambert Simnel Avenue and Wat Tyler Crescent. But there was only Nadežda to tell, and he didn't want to tell her before he told Hilary.

He wheeled Nadežda to the French windows, from which she liked to watch the birds. A pair of chaffinches were foraging under the bird table, the male strikingly colourful, the female gently subtle. A jaundiced sun was filtering through high clouds. There was still a little frost under the conifers and in front of the summerhouse, but in Henry's heart there was a warm glow. No matter that the call of the cucumber gave him no great sense of vocation. No matter that he would never know whether he had got the job on merit or because he'd been at school with Mr Tubman-Edwards's son. No matter that an unworthy little voice had already whispered to him that there was no need to tell anybody, not even Hilary, about the Tubman-Edwards connection. Pratt of the Argus was employable again. The world was a beautiful place.

He rehearsed the scene in which he would tell Hilary and she would admire him. He heard footsteps on the gravel path, but it was the heavy crunching feet of the nurse who would wash and dress Nadežda and give her the massage that did so little good.

He stood at the French windows, looking out at the summerhouse, where they had discovered the depth of their love. Four starlings descended on the bird table, and the chaffinches flew away. How could a sore foot take a doctor so long?

At last he heard her light, quick steps. He opened the front door, and there she stood, his pale ethereal love, and her eyes sparkled, as if she already knew. He ushered her in with mock courtliness, closed the door, and said, 'I've got some news.'

'So have I,' said Hilary. 'I'm pregnant.'

He gawped. He couldn't grasp it. She couldn't be, his slender love.

'Good Lord,' he said, with more amazement than delight. And then the amazing fact of it filtered through, and he said 'Good Lord' again, with more delight than amazement, and he rushed to her and she to him and they hugged in the sadly impersonal hall, and he said, 'When?' and she said, 'Beginning of August,' and they laughed a bit and cried a bit and she said, 'I must tell Mummy.'

The nurse had finished washing and dressing Nadežda and had wheeled her back to her favourite position by the French windows.

'I'm going to have a baby, Mummy,' said Hilary, bending to kiss her mother's lifeless hair, while the nurse gently kneaded those deceptively perfect shoulders.

'Oh my darlings, I'm so happy for you,' said Nadežda with a gasp, and they both heard, in the silence that followed, her unspoken thought, 'I hope there's nothing wrong with it.'

Suddenly sobered, Hilary turned to Henry and said, 'Didn't you say you had some news?'

'Oh yes,' said Henry, as three magpies attacked the bird table, and the starlings flew off. 'I'd almost forgotten.' That'll teach me to rehearse scenes, he thought. 'Our baby will have no cause to be ashamed of its Daddy. Our son or daughter, when he or she goes to school, will be able to boast that their father is the Assistant Regional Co-ordinator, Northern Counties (Excluding Berwick-on-Tweed) of the Cucumber Marketing Board.'

Cousin Hilda sniffed.

'Cucumbers!' she said. 'I don't use them.'

'Is that all you can say?' said Hilary.

28

Henry and Cousin Hilda looked at Hilary in astonishment. Two milky cups of Camp coffee stood on the otherwise bare dining table in the basement room of number 66, Park View Road. Cousin Hilda had not indulged.

'Mrs Wedderburn'll be right glad you're fixed up,' she said.

'Never mind Mrs Wedderburn,' said Hilary. 'What about you? Aren't you pleased Henry's got a job?'

'Hilary!' said Henry.

'Leave this to me, darling,' said Hilary.

'I wouldn't say I'm pleased, no,' said Cousin Hilda carefully. 'It's nowt to get excited about. It's natural. I'd say I were displeased when he hadn't got one, and now I'm not displeased any more.'

'It's not the greatest job in the world,' said Henry. 'But I won't be in cucumbers for ever. It's just a launching pad. It does . . . er . . . it does mean we won't be coming back here to live.'

'I see,' said Cousin Hilda.

'We enjoyed being here. We missed it when we were with Hilary's family, even the spotted dick. Didn't we, darling?'

'Yes, we really did,' agreed Hilary.

'What do you mean – "Even the spotted dick"?' said Cousin Hilda. 'Is there summat wrong with me spotted dick?'

'Oh no,' said Henry. 'Not at all. It's the best spotted dick I've ever eaten.' He didn't tell her that the only other spotted dick he'd ever eaten had been at Brasenese College, where all the food had been inedible. 'We'll move into rented accommodation and start looking for a house.'

'I see,' said Cousin Hilda.

'Cousin Hilda? Do you love Henry?' asked Hilary.

Henry's astonishment was total now, but he knew better than to say, 'Hilary!' again. His heart was beating fast and he felt rivulets of embarrassment running down his back.

Cousin Hilda turned away abruptly and shovelled more coke into the roaring fire, although it was already stifling in the little room. The smell of hot glass from the panes in the front of the blue-tiled stove mingled with the remnants of battered cod, jam roly-poly, and Mr O'Reilly's end-of-the-week feet.

As Cousin Hilda bent to her task, Henry saw the white dead skin of her thigh through a hole in her pale pink bloomers.

When she had finished her displacement activity, Cousin Hilda suddenly looked Hilary full in the face. Hilary didn't flinch. Henry held his breath.

'Of course I do,' she said. 'I've looked after him like a son, haven't I? He knows I do.'

'He doesn't actually,' said Hilary. 'He can never quite believe that anybody loves him. I'm not sure that he even realises how much I love him.'

'Hilary has a reason for feeling particularly emotional tonight, Cousin Hilda,' said Henry.

'Don't make excuses for me,' said Hilary.

'Well tell her.'

'All in good time. I thought there were things that should be said. Families ought to be able to say things.'

'We were brought up not to say things,' said Cousin Hilda. 'The longer it goes on, the harder it becomes to say things.'

'That's why I thought tonight might be a good time to start,' said Hilary.

It was extraordinary, but Henry had the impression that Cousin Hilda was actually quite pleased.

But she couldn't resist having one more parting shot. 'Some folk say too much. I could never be like the Dorises of this world. Her mother used to say, "I'm saying nowt." Doris should have taken heed.' Then she turned to Hilary and her face softened into something almost resembling a smile. 'It's time now, isn't it, Hilary?' she said. 'Time to find out why you have reasons for feeling emotional tonight.'

And Henry realised, to his amazement, that Cousin Hilda knew.

'I'm pregnant,' said Hilary.

Cousin Hilda's face didn't move, but a single tear ran down her cheek, and Henry recognised it for what it was. It was a tear for the life she might have led.

And maybe Hilary recognised it too, because she went over to Cousin Hilda and hugged her and held her close and planted a gentle kiss on her forehead, and Cousin Hilda's lips worked anxiously and at last she spoke.

'Give over,' she said. 'Don't be so daft.'

And then she sniffed.

Henry recognised it as a truly historic sniff.

It was the first time that Cousin Hilda had sniffed not out of disapproval, but because her nose was running.

During January, 1958, the National Union of Mineworkers claimed an extra ten shillings a week for its 382,000 day wage men, Dr Vivian Fuchs reached the South Pole and Sir Edmund Hillary flew in to greet him with the immortal words, 'Hello, Bunny,' scientists at Harwell, revealing secrets of their work on producing electricity through hydrogen power, predicted that the sea would provide a fuel supply sufficient to last mankind for a thousand million years at nominal cost, and Henry and Hilary Pratt both started new jobs.

On Hilary's first day at Thurmarsh Grammar School for Girls, Henry traipsed the cold pavements of Thurmarsh, looking at a succession of dismal flats. Her absence pierced him like a cruel frost. At lunchtime, on an impulse, he went to the Lord Nelson, in Leatherbottlers' Row, in the hope that he would run into some of his old colleagues from the *Evening Argus*. Nobody he knew came in. Even the bar staff were unfamiliar to him. He sat at their usual corner table in the brown, clubby back bar, and had a Scotch egg, a ham sandwich, two pints of bitter and a bout of melancholia. He wished that he could put up a notice explaining that 'Mr Henry Pratt isn't really lonely and pathetic. He is revisiting old haunts while waiting to take up one of the most prestigious appointments in the cucumber world.'

Just as he was about to leave, Peter Matheson, leader of the Conservative minority on Thurmarsh Borough Council, and father of Anna, Hilary's schoolfriend who lived with the bigamous Uncle Teddy in Cap Ferrat, entered the bar. He had been a prime mover in the saga of corruption which had seemed likely to make, but had ultimately been allowed to break, Henry's brief journalistic career. Henry disliked him intensely, yet felt so lonely without Hilary that he accepted a drink with eagerness.

'I don't usually drink at lunchtime,' said Peter Matheson, when they were settled at the corner table, 'but I've had some grave news about Anna. I haven't even told Olivia yet.'

Henry's blood ran cold. Had Peter Matheson discovered that she was married to Uncle Teddy? Or had she died?

'You remember that girlfriend of hers who was becoming a nun?'

'Yes,' said Henry cautiously, remembering the tale that Anna had told her parents to explain her presence in France.

'Well Anna's joined her. She's become a nun.'

Henry felt a surge of relief. Anna wasn't dead. And of course he knew that she hadn't become a nun.

'Oh I am sorry,' he said, hoping that he looked sufficiently grave.

'It's an extremely strict order. She isn't even allowed to see her parents. We've lost our only child.'

Henry was appalled, but also reluctantly impressed, by Anna's ruthlessness. He bought another round, didn't mention his own good news, and talked to Peter Matheson in a suitably muted manner.

For the remainder of the afternoon, back in Perkin Warbeck Drive, Henry counted the minutes till Hilary's return. He planned to kiss her, tell her how much he'd missed her, ask her about her day, take her to bed and lay his head against her still smooth stomach, trying to sense the developing foetus within.

In fact, perhaps because he had drunk two more pints than he had intended, he gave her only a perfunctory kiss and found it impossible to tell her how much he had missed her. He felt jealous of all the experiences from which he had been excluded, and managed to invest his, 'How did you get on?' with only a grudging expression of interest.

'It was a bit odd really,' said Hilary. 'The headmistress said, "Welcome to Thurmarsh Grammar. I hope you'll be very happy here," and I said, "Thank you very much. I'm sure I will. I'd like to give in my notice. I'll be leaving in July. I'm pregnant." '

'You didn't!'

'I did. I thought it only fair to make my position clear from the start.'

Henry shivered. He couldn't always cope with Hilary's directness.

On Henry's first day at work, Hilary found it difficult to concentrate on the subjunctive tense, and Act One of *Macbeth*, and Lily Rosewood being sick all over Jeannie Cosgrove's satchel. All day she was wondering how he was getting on. Her love had robbed her of her sense of proportion, and she felt sick with anxiety lest his new career be an instant fiasco. 'It can't be. They're bound to recognise his lovely talents. They're bound to take my lovely man to their hearts,' she told herself. But the tension persisted. She hung around the school as long as she could, and walked home slowly, to their charming, but tiny, one-bedroom flat in Copley Road. Her route took her down Market Street, past the beginnings of the new Fish Hill Shopping Complex, along the Doncaster Road, down Blonk Lane, past the football ground, up Ainsley Crescent, left into Bellamy Lane and right into Copley Road. A fine, penetrating drizzle was falling, and her unreasonable and absurd tension rose throughout the journey.

She set to, in the characterful but primitive little whitewashed kitchen, making fish pie and feeling that she never wanted to eat again.

At last he came in, her lovely man.

'Well?' she said.

'Well what?' he said.

'How did it go?'

'It was all right.'

She shivered. Sometimes, nowadays, it was as if a curtain had come down between them.

Every morning the Assistant Regional Co-ordinator, Northern Counties (Excluding Berwick-on-Tweed) caught the 7.48 from Thurmarsh (Midland Road) to Leeds City Station, crossed City

33

Square, with its sculpture of the Black Prince, walked up Park Row, turned left into South Parade, and entered the sombre brick building that housed the Cucumber Marketing Board.

Every morning, he walked along the uncarpeted corridor of the ground floor, past the offices of the Head of Services (Secretarial) and the Assistant Heads of Services (Secretarial), took the shuddering lift to the first floor, where the gloomy corridor was carpeted, but not as expensively as was the second floor, walked past the offices of the Head of Gherkins and the Deputy Head of Gherkins, and entered Room 106.

If an estate agent had been selling Room 106, he would have said that it was compact, enjoyed central heating and afforded substantial opportunities for improvement. He would not have pointed out that it had a splendid view over a courtyard on which the sun never set because it never rose on it either, and offered an unrivalled opportunity for the study of the changing styles of drainpipes over the last sixty years.

Henry was the proud possessor of a heavily scratched desk with three drawers, a telephone, adequate supplies of basic stationery, an in-tray, an out-tray, a pending-tray, and precious little else.

On that first morning, about which he had told Hilary so little, Henry had been in the process of discovering that all the filing cabinets were empty, when his telephone had rung with shocking shrillness.

'Assistant Regional Co-ordinator, Northern Counties (Excluding Berwick-on-Tweed),' he had said. 'How can I help you?'

'Henry Pratt?' a pleasant female voice had asked.

'Yes,' he had admitted cautiously.

'I'm Roland's wife.'

'Roland?'

'Roland Stagg. Regional Co-ordinator, Northern Counties.'

'Ah!'

'Roland has flu.'

'Oh dear.'

'He asked me to welcome you, and to ask you to take his messages and generally hold the fort.'

34

'Right. Right, I'll . . . I'll hold the fort.'

'Splendid.'

And so, for a week, little Henry sat in his little office, growing even paler than usual, and held the fort in almost complete isolation. He had no idea what he was supposed to do. Approximately five times a day the phone rang, and it was almost always a re-routed call for Roland Stagg. Of the twenty-five messages which Henry took down, eleven related to meeting people for drinks and only seven contained any reference to cucumbers. But he looked forward to taking these messages. They gave him something to do.

He went to the library, got out books on vegetables, and wrote down all the information he could find about cucumbers. He brought in five postcards from various friends, and pinned them to the wall beside his window. He bought photo frames and put two photographs of Hilary on the desk.

The rest of the time he sat at his desk, with pen, paper and reading glasses at the ready, so that he could pretend to be busy if anyone came in.

Only two people came in all week, but the first, the whistling post-boy, did come in four times a day, bringing no mail, peering at the empty out-tray, nodding pleasantly, and leaving the door annoyingly ajar. In the end Henry grew so ashamed of his empty out-tray that he sent letters to Cousin Hilda, Auntie Doris, Uncle Teddy, Lampo and Denzil, Howard and Nadežda, Ted and Helen, and Ginny Fenwick. The post-boy looked at him in surprise and almost said something.

The other visitor was a pleasant, matronly lady, who introduced herself as 'Janet McTavish, Head of Services (Secretarial). I should have called on you on Monday. I didn't realise you'd started.'

'Well there's not been much sign of it,' said Henry. 'Do sit down.'

'Oh no thank you!' said Janet McTavish fervently, as if horrified at the thought of such intimacy. 'I just wanted to welcome you.'

'Thank you.'

'And to tell you that you'll be sharing Andrea, and when Andrea isn't available you'll have second use of Jane.'

'Sorry?' said Henry. 'What for?'

'Well typing, of course,' said Janet McTavish.

'Ah yes. Of course. Right. Right. Well, thank you,' said Henry. 'No typing yet?'

'Not yet.'

Apart from the two visitors to his office, Henry only met three other people all week – the Director (Operations), the Director General, and the lady with the tea trolley.

The phone call from the Director (Operations) came on the Wednesday.

'Timothy Whitehouse, Director (Operations). Can you spare me a mo'?'

'Yes, I . . . er . . . I can spare you a mo'.'

He took the lift to the second floor, with its superior carpet.

Mr Whitehouse's office was considerably larger than Henry's, and decorated with reproductions of all the paintings by old masters that had ever included a cucumber.

The Director (Operations) was in his mid-forties, a lean, sharp man with a predatory nose, but tired eyes. He invited Henry to sit down and said, 'How are you settling in?'

'Very well,' said Henry, 'if a bit slowly.'

'A bit slowly?'

'Well, with Mr Stagg being ill this week. Obviously I'm holding the fort . . .'

'Good man.'

'But I'm not able to do a great deal till he returns.'

'No, of course. Now, Henry . . . you don't mind if I call you Henry, do you?'

'No, no. Not at all.'

'Good. We're friendly people here. A word about our structure, Henry. You are answerable to Roland Stagg departmentally, to Dennis Tubman-Edwards staff-wise, and to me operationally, and vice-versa. Is that clear?'

As mud. 'Oh yes. Very clear.'

'Good. May I offer you some advice, Henry?'

'Certainly, Timothy.'

36

'Ah!' Mr Whitehouse swivelled round to gaze out of the window. 'I may have given you a false impression when I said that we are friendly. *Mea culpa!*' He repeated the Latin tag, as if it was the apogee of learning. '*Mea culpa!* I address you as "Henry", you address me as "Mr Whitehouse". I might want you to call me Timothy, but we exist in a rather difficult limbo between the civil service and the free market economy, and in this quasi-governmental limbo it has been found that a degree of formality is, regrettably perhaps, appropriate. You understand, I hope?'

Like I understand Swahili. 'Oh yes!'

'Good.' The Director (Operations) swung back with disconcerting abruptness, and looked Henry straight in the eye. 'A word of advice, Henry. Be your own man, stick to your guns, be fearless, always speak the truth, and you won't go far wrong.' He lowered his voice. 'Roland Stagg's a good man, but between you, me and the mythical G.P., you should take everything he says with a pinch of salt.'

'Sorry? The mythical G.P.?'

'They told me you were bright.' Mr Whitehouse shook his head sadly. 'The gatepost.' He stood up. 'Good.' He limped round the desk, and shook Henry's hand. 'Sorry about the limp. A present from Jerry at Alamein. Come and see me if you need me. Never worry about wasting my time. Goodbye, Henry.'

The summons from the Director General, Vincent Ambrose, came on the Friday.

The lift clattered up to the third floor, where the carpet had a thick pile.

Mr Ambrose's office was much larger than Mr Whitehouse's, with a vast antique desk and leather armchairs. It had a standard lamp with a shade of a particularly succulent red, several pictures, none of which contained cucumbers, and an antique sideboard laden with bottles of drink, none of which Henry was offered.

Mr Ambrose – large, genial, vague – was very welcoming, however, sat him down, offered a cigar, and said, 'I make a point of seeing all new staff. We aren't an aloof bunch in cucumber marketing, Mr Bratt.'

'Pratt.'

'I'm so sorry. So sorry. Learning the ropes, are you?'

'Yes, I'm learning the ropes.'

'Finding your way around?'

'Yes.' Boldly, Henry ventured a little jest. 'Well, I've found out the route the tea trolley takes anyway.'

The Director General looked shocked.

'You don't use the trolley, do you?' he said. 'Don't you make your own?'

'Are we allowed to?'

'My dear chap! What do you think you have a kettle for?'

'I don't think I do have a kettle.'

Vincent Ambrose looked horrified.

'No kettle?' he said. 'No kettle? Take it up with Maurice Jesmond.'

'Maurice Jesmond?'

'Head of Facilities. Must have a kettle. Can't do decent work on trolley tea. Where do you live?'

'Thurmarsh.'

'Really? Really??'

Mr Ambrose seemed astounded that anybody would actually live in Thurmarsh.

There was a loud explosion from a car back-firing in the street.

'Duck!' shouted Vincent Ambrose, flinging himself onto the carpet.

Henry looked down at him in astonishment. The Director General picked himself up, dusted himself down, and grinned.

'So sorry,' he said. 'Last lingering effects of shell-shock. Please don't feel embarrassed. I'm not. Totally involuntary. So, you're learning the ropes?'

'Very much so.'

'Good man.'

Vincent Ambrose smiled benevolently, shook hands with Henry, and wished him luck. Henry returned to his office, phoned Maurice Jesmond, discovered that he was on leave, and spent the afternoon studying the changing styles of drainpipes over the last sixty years.

The prospect of two whole days together dispelled the slight shadows that had begun to hang over Henry and Hilary's relationship. They almost recaptured the rapture of their first moments of love. The thought of the developing baby excited Henry enormously. He woke in the middle of the Saturday night and put his ear to his wife's stomach while she slept, hoping to hear some noise from the foetus, maybe a gurgle or a rumble from its incipient stomach. He knew in his head that it was far too early for such a thing to be a possibility, but his heart was full of joy at the great miracle of life, and awe at the thought that he, podgy Henry Ezra Pratt, could father a child. It dawned on him that he was now completely content to accept the miracle as a miracle and seek no explanation of it.

He went to work on the Monday morning with dread. To his great relief, the Regional Co-ordinator, Northern Counties (Excluding Berwick-on-Tweed) had recovered from his flu, and sent for him almost immediately.

Roland Stagg was a large man of about fifty, with a double chin and a huge paunch over which his trousers drooped inelegantly. He smoked incessantly and always had ash on his clothes. His breathing was laboured, and he was in the middle of a coughing fit.

'Sorry,' he said. 'Burma.'

'Burma?'

'I was in Burma during the war. It didn't do much good for my lungs. Don't worry, no problem, only really affects me now when I've been ill. I shouldn't smoke. I *am* sorry about last week. Did you find your feet all right?'

'Well I didn't really know what to do,' admitted Henry.

His departmental boss looked irritated. 'Well, didn't you think?' he said. 'Aren't you capable of thought?'

'Yes, but I had nothing to go on, and I didn't want to queer your pitch.'

'Quite right. I don't like my pitch queered. But couldn't you have at least explored your predecessor's files?'

'There aren't any files. The filing cabinets are empty.'

'Oh my God,' said the Regional Co-ordinator. 'The bastard. He's destroyed your records *in toto*. Vindictive little beast.'

'I think he's taken my kettle as well.'

'Your kettle as well! And he was at Charterhouse. What's happening to the public school system?'

Henry judged that the question was rhetorical.

'You'll have to take my files, copy them, trace every grower in the North who isn't on my files and contact them all to get the history of the relationship,' said Mr Stagg. 'You can't operate without a history of the relationship. You'll find I'm a hands-off employer. I'll leave it to you. Chase Maurice Jesmond for a kettle. Come to me if you have problems. Right?'

'Right.'

Henry stood up. Suddenly, Mr Stagg smiled.

'You took my messages very diligently,' he said. 'You'll have gathered I'm a drinking man. Are you a drinking man?'

'Sometimes,' said Henry cautiously.

'Be here at twelve thirty. We'll have a noggin.'

Over their noggin in the large, lively Victoria, with its huge Victorian windows, Roland Stagg gave Henry the benefit of his advice. 'Be cautious, keep a low profile, and never commit yourself unless it's absolutely unavoidable.' He lowered his voice against the possibility of being overheard in the next booth. 'Old Shitehouse is a decent sort and a loyal boss, but take everything he says with a pinch of salt.' He raised his voice again. 'Keep your eyes skinned, your nose clean, your ear close to the ground and your mouth shut, and you won't go far wrong.'

Henry 'Deeply conscious of not having been in the war and distinctly guilty about being so healthy' Pratt threw himself into his work with enthusiasm. He was determined to make his mark in the cucumber world, so that his reputation would go before him and find him other work. 'I heard about this chap doing stirring things with cucumbers. Thought I ought to take a peep at him.' He also felt, as a self-confessed underdog, a degree of natural sympathy for the cucumber, seeing it as the Henry Pratt of the vegetable world.

In the early weeks he was kept busy compiling his missing records, contacting growers and retail outlets (shops to thee and me) and asking questions about the history of their relationship. He looked forward to travelling around his region, meeting cucumber folk.

He realised that, if he followed Mr Whitehouse's advice, he would be out on his ear within a month, whereas, if he listened to Mr Stagg, he would survive for a lifetime and get absolutely nowhere. He would need to steer a very careful course between the Scylla of Mr Whitehouse's boldness, and the Charybdis of Mr Stagg's caution. He felt confident that he could.

Even in his social life, Henry didn't neglect his new enthusiasm.

One Friday evening, in mid-March, he went with Hilary to the Lord Nelson to meet his old colleagues. Henry, who was having no great social life at work, felt a frisson of excitement and delicious regret as they walked into the back bar and saw the journalists gathered round their corner table.

Henry's journalistic disasters had slipped irrevocably into legend in the months since his departure. He greeted the humorous recollection of them now with a mixture of shame and pride, and was moved by the extent to which his former colleagues appeared to miss him.

'I had to stay over. Couldn't miss my dear Henry,' said Denzil.

'It's extraordinarily kind of you,' said Henry.

'Not at all. I'm glad to get a night away from Lampo. He finds my snoring revolting.' Denzil sighed. 'Lampo says snoring is tasteless. The truth is I'm getting old and he finds it disgusting. He's dreadfully selfish.'

Henry felt sad at the thought that one day, inevitably, Lampo and Denzil would part.

Helen Plunkett, née Cornish, pressed her thigh against him, and smiled her pert, seductive smile. Ted Plunkett, her brooding husband with the great bushy eyebrows, gave a theatrical scowl of mock jealousy. Henry recognised this now as double bluff. If Ted pretended to be jealous, people wouldn't realise how deeply hurt he was. Ginny Fenwick, bulky but sensual, and still hankering after becoming a war correspondent, did recognise it and was hurt, because she still loved Ted. Henry felt embarrassed by Helen's rampant thigh and by his excessive consciousness of it. Hilary gave him a wry smile, to assure him of her understanding of the situation. Helen, seeing the smile, scowled. Colin Edgeley hugged Henry hugely and said, 'We miss you, kid. What are you having?' Ben Watkinson asked him to name all the goalkeepers in the third division north. Even Terry Skipton, the slightly deformed news editor and Jehovah's Witness, had two glasses of orange squash before saying, 'It's been lovely to see you, Henry. I'll leave now. It pains me to see my children getting drunk.'

They went on, down memory lane, up Commercial Street, to the Devonshire, where Henry disgusted Hilary by suggesting that the dark patches under the arms of Sid Hallett and the Rundlemen might be the same ones that he had seen on the shirts of the resident jazz band when he'd last visited the pub almost a year ago.

'So Hilary's pregnant,' yelled Helen over 'Basin Street Blues'. 'I always knew you had it in you.'

Her hand stroked his private parts gently. He turned hurriedly to Ben, and reeled off all the goalkeepers except Halifax Town's.

Colin Edgeley hugged him again and said, 'Can I borrow a quid till next Thursday?' as if forgetting that Henry wasn't a colleague any more.

But Henry had a new life, and the evening cured him of nostalgia for the old one. Suddenly, during Sid Hallett's spirited if inaccurate rendition of 'South Rampart Street Parade', he longed to be in bed with Hilary. A wave of love swept through him, and his feet tingled.

But they were all incredibly hungry, and after closing time an irresistible force led him not to bed, but to that very inadequate substitute, the Shanghai Chinese Restaurant and Coffee Bar.

Over his glutinous beef curry, Henry gazed earnestly at his old friends and said, 'Who should I contact about cucumbers?'

There was a stunned silence.

'I want to give the cucumber a higher profile,' he said. 'I

42

thought somebody could do a feature about it. The forgotten vegetable kind of thing. Bring back the cucumber sandwich type of touch.'

'Well I should think Ted could fit it into his kiddies' column,' said Helen. 'He might even make a competition out of it. "Knit your own phallic symbol." '

'It was just an idea,' said Henry.

The following Friday, Henry met Martin Hammond in the Pigeon and Two Cushions. Martin, his friend ever since the days of the Paradise Lane Gang, had become the youngest ever Union Convener at the Splutt Vale Iron and Steel Company. He was tired. 'I'm knackered. It's a non-stop job, raising the level of political consciousness,' he explained, yawning and apologising owlishly.

'Have you heard anything about Tommy?' Henry asked. 'It's a bit strange. He wasn't even on the plane.'

Tommy Marsden, fellow member of the Paradise Lane Gang, ex-star of Thurmarsh United, had been transferred to Manchester United in December of 1956. Yet when the plane carrying Manchester United home from a European Cup match in Belgrade on February 6th, 1958 had crashed at Munich Airport, killing twenty-three people, including eight members of the first team, Tommy's name had not been mentioned.

'They say he doesn't hit it off with Matt Busby,' said Martin, 'but I don't really find time for chat about football.'

To Henry's joy, Oscar, the hypochrondriac waiter, came on duty at 7.30. He bore down on them in his white umpire's coat, beaming from mastoid to mastoid.

'It's good to see you again, gentlemen,' he said. 'I get this sore throat on and off, but it never seems to develop into anything. The doctor says I'm living with it symbiotically. Sounds disgusting. Where have you been? I wondered if you'd emigrated.'

'Hilary's pregnant,' said Henry.

'Oh, congratulations, sir,' said Oscar. 'Such a lovely young lady. Such a nice wedding. I almost forgot me sinuses. What's it to be, gentlemen?'

43

'A pint and a half of bitter,' said Martin stuffily.

'Do you like people?' asked Henry, when Oscar had gone.

'Of course I do,' said Martin Hammond.

'Oh,' said Henry. 'Only I thought you might be too busy improving their lot to have much time for them.'

Martin Hammond coloured, and Henry felt sorry.

'Only a half?' he said, when the drinks arrived.

'I don't drink much any more,' said Martin.

'Have you got a girlfriend?' asked Henry.

'I've no time,' said Martin Hammond.

'What's your attitude to cucumbers?' asked Henry.

'They give me indigestion,' said Martin Hammond.

'You know what you are?' said Henry. 'Old before your time.'

During the Easter holidays, Hilary resumed work on her novel. One evening, when Henry returned home tired after visiting the Selby and Osgodby areas to meet cucumber growers and 'show my face', Hilary told him that she had made good progress, and he said, 'Oh good. Thank goodness one of us is talented,' and she stared at him in dismay, and he stared at her in dismay, and said, 'No, I'm really pleased. Tell me about it.' But she couldn't. A curtain was drawn across a whole room in their lives.

They had been having driving lessons, and it didn't help Henry's mood when Hilary passed her test first time, even though it meant that they bought a very old Standard Eight, which Henry was able to drive at weekends, to improve his technique.

An enormous improvement in his driving did result. In fact, his examiner on his second test told him that he might have passed him if he hadn't hit the car while parking at the very end. 'What do you do now?' the examiner asked him. 'Try to find the owner and report the accident,' said Henry. 'Right,' said the examiner drily. 'Well, that bit's easy. I'm the owner.'

Hilary was becoming aware of a strong element of perversity in Henry's make-up. When he passed his test at the fourth attempt – we'll draw a veil over the third, since the greengrocer's has long been rebuilt – there was only one possible target for his first trip behind the wheel. Berwick-on-Tweed, the only town in the North of England for whose cucumbers he was not responsible.

It was an unseasonably warm Saturday in early July. On parts of the north-east coast the temperature was nudging 65. As the car nosed rustily up the A1, past Newcastle, with the sheep-rich Cheviots to their left and the great castles of Northumberland to their right, Henry's blood fizzed to the romance of the open road.

They reached Berwick in time for a sandwich lunch. As they wandered the sober Georgian streets of that estuarine gem, Henry was disturbed to see how full of cucumbers the greengrocers' were.

They drifted, hand in hand, along the Quay Walls, at the wide Tweed's edge. Under the great road and rail bridges, swans paddled gently against the current, so as to remain still for their lunch.

As they sauntered happily along the ramparts, they saw a tall, craggy, handsome young man and a bronzed young woman walking towards them, hand in hand. For an absurd moment Henry wished that it was a mirror image, and that *he* was tall, craggy and handsome. He almost wished that Hilary was sun-drenched and sensuous and sultry and fleshy like . . . 'Anna!' they both exclaimed.

Anna Matheson, best friend of Hilary at Thurmarsh Grammar, and unlawful wife of Uncle Teddy in Cap Ferrat, who had once bared her all for Henry in her little flat in Cardington Road, went the colour of milky coffee beneath her suntan.

'Oh hell,' she said. 'Oh Christ. Oh well. This is Jed.'

'Hi,' said Jed.

Jed! What sort of a name is that? thought Henry, and he found that he didn't want to be tall, craggy and handsome any more.

'These people are all right, Jed,' said Anna. 'Hillers was my best friend at school and Henry is Teddy's kind of adopted son.'

'Oh. Right,' said Jed.

'We can tell them, Jed. I have to.'

Jed thought for a moment. 'OK,' he said.

Anna led them along the dignified ramparts towards the sea, past the Customs House and the Guard House.

'You look wonderful, Hillers,' she said. 'Pregnancy really suits you. I can't believe it. You look lovely.'

'Thank you,' said Hilary drily. 'You do too.'

'Well I always did,' said Anna, 'but you were a mess.'

'Thank you very much.'

'No, not being rude, because now you aren't, not remotely, so that's great,' said Anna.

'Oh, I see,' said Hilary. 'Good.'

They had reached a grassy open space, sheltered from the on-shore breeze by the town walls. Anna plonked herself on the grass and brought her knees up almost to her chin, as if to flaunt the glory of her sun-kissed thighs. Jed, in his old oil-stained cords, lolled darkly, suspiciously.

Behind them, gentle rollers expired on the Northumberland coast, and an oyster-catcher's shrill alarm cry rang out. In front of them, gulls wheeled bad-temperedly over the slate- and red-tiled roofs. The sun shone on the sandstone and whitewash of the trim Georgian houses. Henry and Hilary waited patiently for an explanation.

'Jed has a boat,' said Anna.

Jed frowned.

'I have to tell them, Jed. They know about Teddy. It's nothing sinister, anyway. It isn't drugs or dead bodies or the white slave trade. Just Teddy's old business. Import–export. We import wine and brandy and export whisky. All right, it's illegal, but there's no harm done.'

Henry was amazed at the extent of the relief with which he greeted this story. Why should he still care so much about Uncle Teddy? Why should he care so little about Uncle Teddy's breaking of the law?

'I love Teddy,' said Anna. 'I'd never want to hurt him. Jed knows that.'

'Oh aye. Right. Oh, she loves Teddy,' said Jed.

'I'm no angel, but I do have feelings, and I'd never want to hurt Teddy,' said Anna.

'Never want to hurt him. I can vouch for that,' said Jed.

46

'Obviously it has to be me who comes to England,' said Anna. 'Teddy can't. He's supposed to be dead. Teddy knows I'm seeing Jed.'

'It'd be a trifle awkward if your parents happened to see you now, not wearing your nun's habit.' It was Henry's turn to be dry.

This time Anna gave a tanned blush.

'It is all a bit awful, isn't it?' she said. 'But what can I do? They'd be even more hurt by the truth.'

A huge gull, sitting on the middle of nine chimney-pots, disturbed that rare summer afternoon with a stream of raucous indignation.

'There's just . . . there's just one thing,' said Anna. 'It'd be nice if you could bear it in mind. Teddy thinks Jed's seventy.'

3 The Miracle of Life

As he walked along the corridor to the maternity ward, Henry again made the mistake of rehearsing the scene that was about to take place. Hilary would be sitting up in bed, beautiful and serene and sparkling, and little Kate would be gurgling happily in her arms, or perhaps sleeping peacefully after the ordeal of birth.

In fact Hilary was lying with her head resting against three pillows. Her face was strained and even paler than usual. There were dark patches under her deep-set eyes. Her hair, wet from her exertions, clung lankly and dankly to her scalp. She was holding their baby very gingerly. Kate's disproportionately large face was red, and a few strands of wispy blonde hair were almost invisible on her scalp. Her eyes were shut, her nose was wrinkled and she was yelling furiously at the ignominy of moving from her mother's womb to twentieth-century Thurmarsh.

Henry had imagined that he would bend down to kiss Hilary and say, 'Darling, I'm so proud of you. I love you so much. I'm the luckiest man in the world.' But his throat was tight with emotion and no words would come, and he felt himself dissolving into ten thousand receding pin-pricks. The floor of the ward came up to meet him. As his forehead crashed into the foot of Hilary's bed, he felt the pain as if it were outside himself, at the end of a long, dark tunnel.

The nurse looked at Hilary in alarm, and Hilary looked at the nurse in alarm.

'I think he's pleased,' said Hilary weakly.

Then she burst into tears, and the baby bawled and yelled and Henry stirred and moaned, and the nurse said, 'I've heard of post-natal depression, but this is ridiculous.'

Two burly men wheeled Henry to the Casualty Department, where the blood was washed off his face and the wound dressed. Then they wheeled him to the X-Ray Department, where his forehead was x-rayed. Then he tried to walk, but his legs were wobbly. They gave him a mug of sweet tea, and he tried again, and this time he was strong enough to walk carefully down the serpentine corridors, past wards and operating theatres and the Oncology and Pathology Departments, so that by the time he reached Hilary's bedside he felt a complete sham.

'How are you?' asked Hilary anxiously.

Henry groaned.

'That's what I should be asking you,' he said. 'This is your ordeal, not mine.'

Hilary clasped his hand.

'No, no,' he said. 'I should be clasping *your* hand. It's you who were brave and suffered. It's you who has to bear the burden of being a woman. You were in labour six hours. I just . . . oh, I feel so guilty.' And then, at last, late but no less sincere, 'Darling, I'm so proud of you. I love you so much. I'm the luckiest man in the world.'

He squeezed Hilary's hand and she squeezed his back, and he said, 'You look lovely.'

'You don't.'

'Oh, thank you very much.'

'Well, you don't. You've got a huge swelling on your forehead and two black eyes.'

'Oh no,' he groaned. 'Oh, I haven't, have I? Oh God. I didn't want to steal your thunder.'

'How's your head?'

'Never mind my head. How are your . . . well, actually, I've got a splitting headache, but never mind that, how are your . . . well, your everything? Oh darling, you must be so sore.'

'I don't even want to think about it,' said Hilary weakly.

He gazed down at their sleeping daughter, and thought he could see echoes of Hilary in her nose and eyes and mouth.

'She's so beautiful,' he said.

'What happened?' asked Hilary, squeezing his hand again. 'Why did you faint?'

'I don't remember,' he said. 'I don't even remember coming in the ward.'

49

'Are you concussed?'

'Darling! Never mind about me. How . . . er . . . was it awfully . . . they say I am a bit concussed, actually, but never mind that, it'll pass, how about you, that's the point . . . I mean, don't talk about it if you don't want to.'

They sat in silence for a moment, holding hands. Their three-hour-old daughter stirred in her sleep and made a tiny noise.

'She's dreaming,' said Hilary. 'What can she have to dream about? What does she know?'

'Her lovely mummy's lovely insides,' said Henry. 'It's coming back. I remember, I came in, and I saw you lying there, looking so exhausted.' He saw Hilary's disappointment and added hurriedly, 'and so incredibly lovely and beautiful. And I saw . . . it . . . her . . . and she . . . I mean, people say babies are small, but she's huge, I mean all that, her head alone looks enormous, and I mean there's hardly room for my prick sometimes, and all that had to come out through that, and I was just overwhelmed with love and empathy with your suffering and I thought, "I'll never complain about anything again." '

'How's your head?'

'Awful.'

Hilary laughed.

'Oh God,' he said. 'That was wicked. Oh, darling, I . . . Oh God, I feel so ashamed. No!! Who cares what I think? How *do* you feel, really?'

'Tired,' said Hilary. 'So terribly tired. You'll just have to go on feeling ashamed. I don't have the energy to steal my thunder back.'

He kissed her very gently, and the doctor came in with the nurse.

'Aching,' said the nurse. 'Lost quite a lot of blood. Shocked.'

'Well, I'm not surprised,' said the doctor. 'What you poor women have to go through!'

'Oh I was speaking about the husband,' said the nurse.

Henry groaned.

When Cousin Hilda saw little Kate she said, 'She's got big ears, hasn't she?' and Henry and Hilary, translating this into praise for eyes, nose and mouth, smiled proudly. When Auntie Doris came, she said, 'Oh, look at her, bless her. Isn't she lovely, bless her?' It was difficult to think that Auntie Doris had once been Kate's size, and horrendous to think that one day Kate might be Auntie Doris's size.

The dreadful summer of 1958 drew blessedly to a close. The cod war raged between Britain and Iceland, the Russians fired two dogs into space and brought them back safely, the number of unemployed reached a ten-year high of 476,000, and Thurmarsh throbbed to the songs of Elvis Presley and Pat Boone.

They took Kate to London to spend a weekend with Mr and Mrs Hargreaves in their tall, narrow Georgian town house in Hampstead, where Elvis Presley was seldom heard, and Pat Boone never. Henry and Hilary were put in Diana's old room, with Kate next to them, in the room where Henry had made love with Diana, for the first and last time, less than three years ago.

'Diana and Nigel are coming to dinner,' Mrs Hargreaves announced. She was still amazingly graceful and attractive, and Henry almost blushed at the memory of the erections he'd been forced to hide on the beaches of Brittany when he was seventeen and hungry. 'They're bringing Benedict. And Paul's popping over.' Her voice dropped. 'Judy's left him.'

Thank God! Paul had been his best friend at Dalton College, but Henry had never liked Judy Miller. She had behaved like a barrister when she was still a student. When she actually became a barrister, goodness knew to what heights of arrogance she would aspire.

'Oh dear, I am sorry,' he said.

'It's kind of you to say so, but you aren't really,' said Mrs Hargreaves. 'She wasn't right for him. I just wish he'd had the sense to leave her before she left him. Oh, and we've invited Nigel's and your old sparring partner, Lampo Davey, and his . . . er . . . friend, whom you also know, I believe.'

It might have been Hampstead, but Mrs Hargreaves wasn't Bohemian enough to say 'lover'.

'Incidentally, you don't praise the food here,' said Henry to Hilary as they unpacked. 'You don't praise it at Cousin Hilda's because food isn't meant to be enjoyed, and you don't praise it here because it's assumed to be delicious and to praise it is to admit the possibility that it might not have been.'

Henry felt nervous as they got ready for dinner, and this surprised him. True, it was fourteen months since he'd last seen Mr and Mrs Hargreaves, at his wedding, but he hadn't expected, now that he was a husband and a father, that he would still feel an uncouth northern hick in these sophisticated surroundings. Now he wondered if those feelings would ever change. Would he always seek the approval of Mrs Hargreaves, because he found her elegance and unattainability so sexually attractive? Would he always feel inferior to Mr Hargreaves, because Mr Hargreaves was a brain surgeon and he was with the Cucumber Marketing Board?

Kate fell asleep on cue after being fed and changed. Hilary looked beautiful in a simple, beige, straight sheath dress, which reflected, subtly, the sack dresses that had come back into fashion. Henry realised that he was so very nervous tonight because he was so anxious for her to shine.

As they walked down the narrow stairs to the drawing room on the first floor, Henry resolved to be charming, to sparkle wittily, but to give Hilary the space to be even more charming and sparkle even more wittily. He wouldn't call Nigel 'Tosser' once.

The drawing room had a faintly Chinese air, and Mr and Mrs Hargreaves had the confidence to have allowed it to become just slightly shabby.

Even before the arrivals had been concluded, Henry was aware that his irritation level was high. He would have to be careful.

He was irritated that Lampo Davey and Denzil Ackerman were *both* wearing bow-ties. It seemed too showy a touch for this gentle, elegant house.

He was irritated that Lampo and Denzil were putting on such a show of courtly charm and togetherness, when he knew that they'd have spent most of the day arguing.

Lampo and Denzil always kissed women with exaggerated enthusiasm, and little murmurs of delight, as if they seriously thought that they could hide their homosexuality, but they seemed to kiss Hilary with special enthusiasm, and this also irritated Henry.

He was irritated at the realisation that Paul was deeply upset at the loss of the dreaded Judy.

He was irritated that Benedict Pilkington-Brick (what a mouthful!) had already inherited Tosser's complacent nose and self-satisfied mouth, and that Diana was pregnant again.

He was irritated by the understated beauty of Mrs Hargreaves's black dress and by Diana's baby-doll outfit.

He was irritated by Hilary's self-confidence. She rose to the civilised atmosphere, accepting a glass of white port as if she knew what it was. He realised, with a sickening thud, that the depressed, repressed girl had grown into a confident woman who could succeed in places where he was unable to follow.

'How's the novel coming on?' asked Denzil.

And Hilary, who hadn't mentioned the book to Henry for weeks, told him.

'Slowly,' she said. 'I have to break off to feed Kate and Henry at regular intervals. But I think it's developing its inner core, and whatever other merits it may lack, at least it's not autobiographical.' Did she know that Henry's novel would have been the story of his life? 'Upstairs, in the tiny back bedroom, Annie's pains began. Amos heard her first sharp cry at twenty-five to seven in the evening.' He shuddered at the thinness of the disguise.

Everybody was thrilled that she was writing a novel. When she left the room to check on the sleeping Kate and Benedict, Mrs Hargreaves said, 'I wondered if you'd ever find anybody good enough for you, Henry. Now I wonder if you're good enough for her.'

'So do I,' said Henry, with such feeling that there was an uneasy pause.

Enjoying the 1948 Pomerol, in the olive-green dining room, Henry remembered the first time he had eaten there, and had hated claret, and had called the *boeuf bourguignon* 'stew'. For a moment he felt warm and sophisticated, and then Hilary irritated him by saying, 'This soup's lovely.' He glared at her. She smiled with infuriating assumed innocence.

Mr Hargreaves asked Hilary about her novel again as he dissected his grouse with a disturbing lack of delicacy for a brain surgeon. They discussed Lampo's work at Christie's – or was it Sotheby's? – Denzil's recent interview with Frank Sinatra for the *Argus* – 'Have you ever been to Thurmarsh, Frank?' – the absence of Judy, which Paul, fooling nobody, described as a great release, and Paul's career. He announced that he was abandoning the law and taking up medicine. 'The law is so cynical,' he said. 'I could never defend a man I knew to be guilty. I want to feel I'm at least trying to do good in the world,' and Henry said, 'How can you say that, Paul? You're more motivated by money than anyone I know, except Tosser.'

With one fell swoop, Henry had offended Paul and Tosser, incurred the disapproval of Mr and Mrs Hargreaves, and caused Hilary to look at him in surprise, as if realising that there was a side of him that she hardly knew. Only Diana seemed pleased by his remark, giving Henry a quick grin and then wiping it off and looking exaggeratedly pompous for Tosser's benefit.

'Henry,' said Mrs Hargreaves with chilling politeness, 'we're *longing* to hear about these cucumbers.'

Henry decided that he had no option but to take her remark at face value, but that he mustn't be so naïve as to launch into a description of his work.

He decided to strike a more oblique and urbane note.

'Tiberius adored cucumbers,' he said.

There was silence.

'The king of the conversation-stoppers strikes again,' said Diana, looking like a sixteen-year-old schoolgirl once more.

Mrs Hargreaves gave Diana a look which said, 'Careful. Don't be rude to our guests, however rude they are.'

'Talking of Tiberius,' said Mr Hargreaves, as if to prove that it hadn't been a conversation-stopper, 'when you think of what went on in Ancient Rome, it's remarkable that two thousand years later what you two do in the privacy of your own home is still illegal.'

Lampo and Denzil smiled a little uneasily.

'What Lampo does is break my *objets d'art*,' said Denzil. 'I didn't know there was a law against that.'

'I've always maintained that you should be able to do what you like, as long as you don't frighten the horses,' said Tosser Pilkington-Brick.

'Good old Tosser,' said Henry. 'Everyone has one special talent. His is for coming out with clichés as if they're the product of deep and original thought.'

Hilary stood up abruptly.

'The food is delicious,' she said. 'The grouse is perfectly moist and gamey, the stuffing is extremely subtle, the celeriac purée is a revelation, but I must ask you to excuse me. I'm fed up with my husband being so graceless.'

Henry went red and mumbled, 'I'll go after her,' and there followed all the embarrassing business of his pleading with her, and their returning to the appalled dining room together, and everybody's finishing the meal with unbelievably careful conversation.

In bed that night, Hilary whispered, 'Are you in love with Diana?'

'Of course I'm not,' whispered Henry.

'Well you were very rude to Nigel.'

'One can hate Tosser without loving anybody. One needs no ulterior motive.'

'You were childish and stupid tonight. I was appalled.'

'Yes, well, you weren't, everybody adored you, so that's all right.'

'I thought you wanted me to shine. I tried to shine for my man.'

'Why did you keep praising the food, when I specifically asked you not to?'

'Because you specifically asked me not to. I don't like being given instructions, as if I'm a northern hick.'

They lay in silence for the rest of the night, side by side but not together. In the morning Henry apologised, and told Hilary how much he loved her, and everything was almost all right, and he apologised quite charmingly to Mr and Mrs Hargreaves, and everything was almost all right with them also.

Kate opened her eyes more frequently and gurgled more inventively and began to smile and went gently onto solids and cried when she had colic and when she burped they said, 'Clever little girl!' but when Henry burped Hilary said, 'Do you have to be so crude?' and Henry said, 'Don't forget I'm not a writer. I'm an inferior being,' but these little verbal spats were few and far between, and their love for each other was kept warm by their love of Kate.

They sent photographs of her to Uncle Teddy and Anna.

In his reply, Uncle Teddy said:

> Anna was so pleased to see you both in Berwick. I was glad to hear that Jed struck you as a reliable old boy. The first batch of you-know-what has arrived and is fetching high prices. I'm still an old rogue, Henry, and you're well shot of me, but if you ever feel like coming over, we'd love to see you all and I have two very good sauces of sea bass. Hilary looks far too lovely for you, what is it the girls see in you? Ouch, perhaps I shouldn't have said that! As for Kate, she looks just grand. What a belter! I never wanted kids, never could stand the little buggers, in one end and out the other and spend the rest of the time sleeping or crying. Minimal entertainment value. Age is a funny thing, though. When I see Kate I want to cry for the kids I never had. Too late now. I'd love kids by Anna but I'd be too old to play football with the little buggers and I'd drop dead or something equally silly and leave the poor girl stranded with them.

Hilary smiled after she'd read the letter and said, 'A bit sad, really.'

'Just a bit.'

'He spelt "sources" wrong.'

'A Freudian slip. In his mind he's cooking them already.'

'Let's go next summer.'

'Right.'

They moved into a two-up, two-down stone terrace house in an attractive but crumbling Victorian terrace in Newhaven Road, off the top end of York Road. The Rawlaston and Splutt Building

Society were worried by the condition of the house and thought the asking price of £3,250 excessive, but liked the security of Henry's position, and gave them their mortgage after careful consideration.

They invited Cousin Hilda for tea on their very first Saturday. That morning Henry banged a new name plate into position on the gate. Hilary bandaged his thumb, and they stood back and looked at the name with pride.

Cousin Hilda was less impressed.

'Paradise Villa!' she sniffed.

'What's wrong with it?' said Henry.

'Putting on airs,' said Cousin Hilda.

The living room had no carpets or curtains, and no furniture or decorations except for the art deco clock, a second-hand three-piece suite, a hard chair, and a very cheap nest of tables. A gas fire hissed gently.

Cousin Hilda gave the suite a dirty look, and plonked herself, legs akimbo and bloomers at half-mast, in the hard chair.

' "Paradise" is an echo of the back-to-back where I was born, of which I'm not ashamed,' explained Henry.

' "Villa" is meant to be humorous,' said Hilary. 'Anyone can see it isn't really a villa, but it also reflects the fact that Henry is thankful to have such an improvement on what his parents had.'

'Aye, well, I just hope Mrs Wedderburn'll be able to read all that into it,' said Cousin Hilda. 'I wouldn't want her to think you're putting on airs.'

Henry spread the nest of tables round the room, and Hilary brought in a tray of tea, crumpets and ginger cake.

'Oh no, nothing to eat, thank you. I must have an appetite for my gentlemen,' said Cousin Hilda.

'I beg your pardon?' said Henry.

'I owe it to my gentlemen to eat heartily,' said Cousin Hilda. 'If I just picked at my food, they'd think there was something wrong with it. I am, in my small way, a public figure. It carries responsibilities.'

'You must have something,' said Hilary. 'You're our very first guest.'

57

'We chose the house because it's nearer to you than the flat,' said Henry.

Cousin Hilda went pink, and Henry wondered how a lie could be bad, when it brought so much pleasure.

'Well all right,' said Cousin Hilda. 'Just one crumpet.'

She ate her crumpet with deliberation and concentration.

'Very palatable,' she said primly.

'Have you ever thought of using cucumbers?' asked Henry.

'I can't,' said Cousin Hilda. 'I share all my meals with my gentlemen. They know what to expect. They expect to know what to expect. I can't make changes. There'd be ructions.'

The art deco clock struck four. Kate stirred, opened her eyes, yawned, and gave Cousin Hilda a beautiful smile.

'She's smiling at you,' said Henry. 'She likes you.'

'Ee!' said Cousin Hilda. 'Mrs Wedderburn would love to see her. She'd be right thrilled to hold her.'

'Does that mean you'd like to hold her, Cousin Hilda?' asked Hilary, and Henry held his breath, and an amazing thing happened. Cousin Hilda smiled and said, 'Aye, well, I would.' So Kate was passed over to her very carefully, and Cousin Hilda held her with grim concentration, and tickled her chin self-consciously, and said to her, 'Who's a pretty baby, then?' Henry and Hilary looked at each other and smiled with their eyes, and there was a long silence, as nobody dared disturb the mood, and then Henry said, 'Do you think your gentlemen would like to see her?'

So Henry slipped home early on the following Thursday, and they took Kate to tea at Cousin Hilda's, and Kate slept as they ate their roast pork and tinned pears, and Mr O'Reilly said, 'There's a bit of you in her, Henry. And a bit of you, Miss Hilary, oh yes. She's a lovely little thing, that she is,' and Brian Ironside mumbled, 'She certainly is,' and Norman Pettifer said, 'Adrian had no Stilton at all today. Gorgonzola, Roquefort, Bleu de Bresse, Danish Blue, and no Stilton. There isn't an ounce of patriotism in that boy's body.'

That Saturday they took Kate to Troutwick to see Auntie Doris and Geoffrey Porringer. Auntie Doris said, 'Can I hold her, please?

58

Oh, isn't she gorgeous, love her?' And Geoffrey Porringer said, 'There's none of you in her at all, Henry,' and Auntie Doris said, 'Teddy!' and Geoffrey Porringer said, 'The name is Geoffrey, Doris. And why are you Geoffreying me anyway?' and Auntie Doris, who always made things worse by protesting about them, said, 'Because you're tactless, Geoffrey. I said she was gorgeous, and you said there's none of Henry in her at all, and you know how sensitive he is about not being good-looking.'

Auntie Doris seemed to Henry to be growing larger by the month and to be laughing almost too much now. He sensed that there was something rather desperate about her laughter and her drinking and about this deeply successful performance that she was giving as the landlady. He felt that if she didn't stop she would go on expanding until she exploded into little bits all over the antiques in the lounge bar one crowded Saturday night.

And, as Auntie Doris grew larger, it seemed that Geoffrey Porringer was growing smaller, hiding in her shadow. Henry could no longer dislike him enough to call him slimy.

He caught Auntie Doris pretending to pour herself a double gin. While she drank heavily, she didn't have quite the Rabelaisian capacity that she claimed. Geoffrey Porringer, on the other hand, pretended to be a moderate man, but slipped spirits into his beer at every opportunity, from whatever bottle happened to be most handy. Henry had the impression that, if something didn't change, the pub's popularity would kill them both.

They took Kate to Perkin Warbeck Drive. Naděžda said, 'I don't intend to do this business of saying whom she takes after. She's lovely, she's healthy, and she's herself.' Howard Lewthwaite said, 'We mustn't rest until we give this girl, and millions like her, true equality of opportunity.' Sam said, 'God, she's ugly!'

Donald Campbell achieved a world record 248.62 miles per hour on Coniston Water, the Preston by-pass became Britain's first stretch of motorway, and autumn slid irrevocably into winter.

Henry found himself increasingly desk-bound as the weather closed in. He sent letters to market gardeners who grew cucumbers, market gardeners who didn't grow cucumbers, farmers who might grow cucumbers, shops that sold cucumbers, shops that didn't sell cucumbers, restaurants that used cucumbers and restaurants that didn't use cucumbers. All these letters were typed by Andrea in the typing pool. When he discovered that Andrea was known as Deputy Head of Services (Secretarial), Henry realised that everybody in the Cucumber Marketing Board had a title, and there wasn't anything special in being the Assistant Regional Co-ordinator, Northern Counties (Excluding Berwick-on-Tweed).

One wild wet window-rattling, dustbin-lid-tormentor of a morning, Mr Whitehouse called Henry into his office, blew his predatory nose, and said, 'You're sending an awful lot of letters.'

'Well, yes,' said Henry. 'I'm aiming at blanket coverage.'

'M'm. There are two ways of looking at everything, Henry,' said the Director (Operations). 'On the one hand there is blanket coverage. On the other hand, there is saturation point. Point taken? Good. I'm delighted with your enthusiasm, Henry. Delighted. The fact is, though, because we all have to live in the real world, you've exceeded your budget.'

'I didn't even know I had a budget,' said Henry.

'Oh dear,' said the Director (Operations). 'Oh dear. I would never run a colleague down behind his back, not my style, not the Timothy Whitehouse way, but between you, me and the mythical G.P., Roland Stagg is getting a bit lax in his old age.'

Mr Whitehouse leant back in his chair, pulled his braces out, and let them fizz back into his chest. I wonder if he likes bondage, thought Henry.

'You did tell me to be my own man, stick to my guns and be fearless. I took that as an invitation to independence,' said Henry.

'I did indeed. A fair point. I sit rebuked. *Mea culpa. Mea culpa!* I should have told you to be your own man, stick to your guns and be fearless *within the budget*. Point taken, Henry?'

'Point taken, Mr Whitehouse.'

As Henry set off to return to Room 106, Roland Stagg shambled out of his office on the second floor, crumpled trousers hanging low over his obscene paunch, and said, 'I warned you, Henry. A low profile.'

'Yes,' said Henry, 'but he told me to be fearless and stick to my guns.'

'And I told you to take his advice with a pinch of salt.'

'Yes,' said Henry, 'but he told me to take your advice with a pinch of salt.'

'Yes, but I'm right and he's wrong. That's why he's the Director (Operations) and I'm only the Regional Co-ordinator, Northern Counties (Excluding Berwick-on-Tweed).'

Henry staggered, somewhat bemused, into his office, and sat behind his familiar desk, listening to the rain gushing from drainpipes of many styles. The telephone shrilled petulantly, and he jumped.

'Tubman-Edwards. I need to see you.'

Henry dragged himself to the office of the Head of Establishments.

Mr Tubman-Edwards looked at him sadly.

'Sit down,' he said.

So far so good! Henry had no problem in obeying the simple instruction.

'Oh dear,' said Mr Tubman-Edwards. 'Sid Pentelow is upset.'

'Sid Pentelow?'

'Director (Financial Services). He hates people exceeding their budget. As you're my appointee, it reflects badly on me. You've let me down, Henry.'

The rain was beating against Mr Tubman-Edwards's windows like furious bees.

'I'm very sorry,' said Henry, 'but I didn't even realise I had a budget.'

'There are budgets for everything. Postage, telephones, travel. My son's coming up next weekend. I know you weren't close chums, but I think you got on pretty well, didn't you?'

'Oh yes. Pretty well.'

'Tremendous. Well, we'd like it if you and your wife came to dinner next Saturday, if you aren't too busy getting ready for Christmas.'

'Well, thank you,' said Henry, appalled. 'We'd love to.'

'Excellent. These budgets are so generous that I simply never dreamt that anybody could exceed them. But you . . .' He looked at Henry sadly. 'You're a human dynamo.'

'Is that bad?'

'No, not within reason. But you must always remember that we are given finite tasks to perform. If we perform them too well, there's a danger that one day our work will be over. We'll have worked ourselves out of a job. None of us would want that, would we? Till next Saturday, then. Shall we say seven thirty for eight o'clock?'

The wind was playing badminton with fish-and-chip papers. A pigeon was tossed over the Queen's Hotel like a rag-doll. A taxi ploughed through a puddle and drenched Henry. His throat was sore and he thought he might be starting a cold. He only just caught the train and had to stand until Normanton. When he got home, Kate had colic and was screaming, and the stew had stuck and was slightly burnt. When the phone rang, he just knew it would be bad news.

'It's me,' said Helen Plunkett, née Cornish. 'Ted's away, and I've just had a bath, and I'm completely naked, and slightly pink all over from the heat, and I thought it was high time you came round and I did that interview about those cucumbers.'

Henry felt extremely nervous as his noisy wipers swished and screeched their way to Ted and Helen's flat in Coromandel Avenue.

He hadn't really wanted to go, but Hilary had insisted.

'She'll try to seduce me,' Henry had said. 'I know her.'

'Exactly. And you will not be tempted. I know you. We love each other utterly, don't we?'

'Of course we do.'

'Well, then. An ideal opportunity to re-dedicate our love.'

As he pulled up outside the unloved, leaf-sodden garden of number 12, Coromandel Avenue, and rushed up to the porch with its stained glass windows at either side of the door, Henry steeled himself to be strong against temptation.

It was a relief that Helen was no longer naked. Indeed, she was wearing a long, loose grey dress which did nothing for her body.

Large photographs of Helen and Ted at their wedding, of Ted's parents, of Helen's parents and of her sister Jill, yet another young woman after whom Henry had lusted, sat in silver frames on the heavy, ornate sideboard. The suite was brown leather. Helen made coffee, and plonked herself briskly and unsexily into a chair, leaving Henry alone on the settee.

'Right. To work,' she said, to Henry's relief. 'Why didn't you get on to me about the article? It's been months.'

'Because you didn't seem remotely keen.'

'I'm not. So, excite me. Persuade me. Where's my angle?'

'I just thought . . . a piece about how unjustly the cucumber is neglected,' said Henry as limply as an old salad.

'So why is it unjust?' She wrote busily in her elegant shorthand. Henry began to wish that she was looking a *bit* more seductive, so that he had something to fight against.

'Well . . . I mean . . . cucumbers are very nice. How's Jill?'

He hoped he wouldn't blush. He wondered if she had ever known just how much he had fancied her younger sister.

'Very well. Do they have any amazing nutritional value?'

'Still happy with Gordon?'

Jill had gone off with the enigmatic Gordon Carstairs, former lover of Ginny Fenwick and the only one out of all of Henry's ex-colleagues who had so far escaped to Fleet Street.

'Very happy. They come up occasionally. They're good sports. We have fun.'

Helen's pearly grey eyes met Henry's, and he saw the spark of mischief in them. Then it was switched off abruptly.

'Well come on,' she said. 'Do they have any nutritional value? Are they good defences against disease, like garlic and ginger?'

'Er . . . as far as I know they aren't really any use against disease, no. I mean, they are actually ninety per cent water, so they hardly have any nutritional value whatsoever.'

'OK. So that's out, then. So is it their incredible taste? Has this not been fully appreciated?'

'Well, I mean. . .' Oh God, I'm floundering. 'I mean, they're nice, of course . . . *very* nice . . . but I wouldn't say they have a particularly strong taste. A nice taste. Subtle. Not strong.'

'Well I suppose they wouldn't be if they're ninety per cent water.'

'Perhaps taste isn't the area we should concentrate on.'

'Well, is it their phallic symbolism? Do they have ritual value? Is there a Splutt Cucumber Dance? Or a midnight procession in which all the adult men in Rawlaston wear funny hats and march to the Trustee Savings Bank with cucumbers in their trousers?'

'Of course not,' said Henry stuffily. 'This isn't France.'

'You look tired. Love life too much for you?'

'No. It's the rest of life that's too much for me.'

'Poor Henry. You're a fighter, though. You'll keep going. Now, what do you want me to say about these bloody cucumbers?'

Henry wanted to tell her to forget it, but no, he *was* a fighter, he *would* keep going. He took a sip of coffee. It was fearsomely strong, and it gave him at least the illusion of energy.

'Perhaps what I'm seeking is to make them fashionable again. I mean, cucumber sandwiches were once synonymous with afternoon tea.'

'I'm afraid Thurmarsh prefers toasted tea-cake.'

'Oh, I'm not talking about afternoon tea specifically. What I'm saying is, I'd like to make the cucumber a little bit chic.'

'Terrific,' said Helen. 'What a shame I work for the *Thurmarsh Evening Argus*, not *Vogue*.'

All good fighters know that there are moments when it's best to concede defeat.

'I think I'd better go,' he said. 'Goodnight, Helen. Thank you for the coffee. Give my love to Ted.'

When he got home, Kate was asleep in front of the fire. Hilary looked tired but lovely. She kissed him warmly.

'You weren't long,' she said. 'But then I knew you wouldn't be.'

'Of course I wasn't,' he said. 'I love you too much.'

'Was she desperately disappointed by your strength and resolve?'

'Well . . . perhaps not *desperately*.'

As they undressed, Henry felt sad as well as exhausted. It had been a long, tiring, thoroughly bad day, but he should still have told Hilary that Helen hadn't attempted to tempt him. He felt that he was in danger of losing something extremely valuable. He was in danger of losing himself.

4 The Whelping Season

Henry felt increasingly intimidated on the drive to Leeds. The formal invitation had made him uneasy. The address sticker on the back of the envelope had made him nervous. The address – Mr and Mrs D. F. C. Tubman-Edwards, the Dower House, Balmoral Road, Alwoodley, Leeds – had overawed him.

The Dower House was set between a stockbroker mock-Tudor excrescence and a turreted extravaganza that looked as if it had been hewn off one end of a Château of the Loire, in one of the most prestigious streets in North Leeds. The huge houses were set in suitably large gardens.

How could he have continued to feel overawed after he'd discovered, at the top of a long, curving drive, that the Dower House was a boxy little brick villa, dwarfed by its setting?

How could he have felt so intolerably stiff in his best suit? How could he have allowed himself to feel that his old school blackmailer was his social superior?

Why had it mattered so much that his rusting Standard Eight looked so pathetic parked between a Riley and a Rolls?

Why hadn't it occurred to him that, instead of feeling humiliated because J. C. R. Tubman-Edwards was a merchant banker and he was Assistant Regional Co-ordinator, Northern Counties (Excluding Berwick-on-Tweed) of the Cucumber Marketing Board, he should have realised that Mr and Mrs Tubman-Edwards, with their social pretensions, must be even more humiliated that, in his fifties, the merchant banker's father was merely the Head of Establishments of the Cucumber Marketing Board?

Henry, in his suit, and Hilary, smart in her short black and gold dress, were astonished to find that Mr and Mrs Tubman-Edwards, and their son, and the two other guests, Dougie and Jean Osmotherly, were in evening dress.

66

'It's a family tradition on Saturday nights,' said Margaret Tubman-Edwards.

'Frightfully pretentious, my people,' said J. C. R. Tubman-Edwards proudly.

'We don't tell people, because we don't want to embarrass them in case they haven't got any. Not all young people do, do they?' said Margaret Tubman-Edwards, whose voice could have cut glass at twenty paces. She was small and neat and looked as cold as the dead, immaculate drawing room in which they were drinking cheap sherry poured out of a very expensive decanter.

'We know because we live next door,' said Dougie Osmotherly, who turned out to be big in ball-bearings and the owner of the Rolls.

Fancy taking the Rolls to go next door, thought Henry.

'Next door?' said Hilary. 'Really? Tudor or turrets?'

Henry flinched, but Dougie and Jean Osmotherly were unperturbed.

'Tudor,' said Jean, who was wearing a diamond ring, a diamond necklace, a diamond bracelet, a brilliant ruby ring, and four other rings.

'I love your jewellery, Jean,' said Margaret Tubman-Edwards.

'So embarrassing,' said Jean Osmotherly. 'One hates to look showy, but it's so much safer on the person with all these burglaries around.'

'Turrets is a problem,' said J. C. R. Tubman-Edwards. 'A scrap-metal dealer lives there. Moved in from your neck of the woods actually, Henry. My folks are furious. Well, I mean, it's a bit off, isn't it, choosing a posh area like All-Yidley and finding oneself next to a scrap merchant.'

Henry went cold at this gratuitous piece of anti-Semitism. He longed to object, but in his dark suit which had gone from being over-dressed to being under-dressed in one second, he hadn't the confidence. Knowing that he must say something, he said, 'Scrap merchant? Not Bill Holliday, by any chance?'

'You don't actually know him, do you?' said Margaret Tubman-Edwards, as if to know Bill Holliday would be the ultimate solecism.

'Well only slightly,' said Henry hurriedly.

The thought of Bill Holliday, whom he had once believed to be trying to kill him, didn't do wonders for Henry's confidence.

'Henry and Josceleyn were chums at Brasenose and Dalton,' said Margaret Tubman-Edwards.

The mention of Brasenose and Dalton, and the memory of Josceleyn Tubman-Edwards blackmailing him and calling him Oiky, didn't do wonders for Henry's confidence.

'Well, not close chums,' he said.

'We ran into each other a few times, though, didn't we?' said Josceleyn Tubman-Edwards.

Later Henry would wonder why it was he and not Josceleyn Tubman-Edwards who'd been on the defensive in this conversation. It was Josceleyn who'd been the eventual loser in their battle, even if it had taken the looming presence of Tosser Pilkington-Brick to seal the victory.

What a shoot-out, Henry thought now, Tosser and Josceleyn staring at each other down the double barrels of their names.

But all he said was, 'Yes. A few times.'

A gong resounded through the boxy Dower House, with its frosted glass doors. Henry looked for self-mockery and found none.

The dining room was as cold as Josceleyn Tubman-Edwards's eyes. The stuffed fox over the brick fireplace struck an inappropriately rural note.

'I'm rather piqued with Josceleyn,' said Margaret Tubman-Edwards. 'He was supposed to bring his girlfriend. He's untidied my table.'

'I've given her the old heave-ho,' said Tubman-Edwards. 'Kept dragging me to the ballet. Trying to improve my mind.'

Not much use unless you have a mind to improve, thought Henry. Oh why oh why didn't he have the courage to say it?

'Not much use unless you have a mind to improve,' said Mr D. F. C. Tubman-Edwards.

Everybody laughed, but neither Josceleyn Tubman-Edwards nor his mother laughed with their eyes.

They ate insipid leek and potato soup out of Spode soup bowls, and tiny fillets of lukewarm shoe-leather *meunière* off Spode fish plates, washed down with cheap white wine poured from a very expensive decanter. They talked about Josceleyn's meteoric rise through the ranks of Pellet and Runciman. 'Wasn't there a Pellet and a Runciman at Dalton?' said Henry, and there was momentary family unease at the hint that Josceleyn had got his job through the old boy network rather than talent. Hilary suggested, politely, that merchant bankers were parasites. Josceleyn Tubman-Edwards flushed and Henry flinched and Dougie Osmotherly said, 'Well, I think you're all parasites except those of us at the sharp end, who make things,' and roared with laughter, as if someone else had said something very witty, and Josceleyn Tubman-Edwards said arrogantly, 'You're an anachronism, Dougie. In fifty years nobody'll make anything except money in this country.'

Over a pallid steak and kidney pudding, eaten off Spode meat plates, washed down with Bulgarian red wine poured out of a very expensive decanter, there was talk of Conservative fund-raising functions, and Jean Osmotherly invited Henry and Hilary to one and Hilary said, politely, that she was afraid that on principle she wasn't prepared to support the Conservatives, and Josceleyn Tubman-Edwards said, 'Well, they're all Conservatives in Allyidley,' and Hilary said, 'I'm sorry, Josceleyn, but I can't let that go. I just loathe anti-Semitism,' and Henry felt proud and horrified at the same time, and Josceleyn looked genuinely contrite and said, 'Oh Christ. You're not Jewish, are you?' and Hilary said, 'No,' and Josceleyn looked puzzled and said, 'Well, what are you complaining about, then?' and Hilary said, 'I hate racialism,' and Josceleyn said, 'Well, I was only bloody joking, for Christ's sake,' and Margaret Tubman-Edwards said, 'Josceleyn! That's enough,' and the stuffed fox stared, and Josceleyn Tubman-Edwards said, 'I see. Everybody's rude to me and when I defend myself it's all my bloody fault as usual. I'm going to the fucking pub. Coming, Henry, old mate?' and Henry said, 'Of course not, old mate. I'm invited to dinner,' and Josceleyn Tubman-Edwards stormed out, and Dennis Tubman-Edwards said, 'Well at least your table's tidy now, Margaret,' and Margaret Tubman-Edwards said, 'Shut up and pour some more wine, Dennis,' and Dennis Tubman-Edwards grumbled, 'Seems it's illegal to joke these days,' and Henry and Hilary exchanged glances which said, 'We seem to be becoming connoisseurs of dinner parties at which people walk out.'

For the rest of the evening they talked with careful banality about the rival charms of the Yorkshire Dales and the Peak District, the French way of life, the quality of the Thurmarsh shops, the best ways of hiding the hi-fi, and other safe subjects. Nobody dared leave early because that would have been to admit that the evening had not been an unqualified social success.

Shortly before midnight, Dougie Osmotherly stood up and said, 'Well, Jean needs her beauty sleep even if I don't, and we've a long way to go.'

'Yes, we must go too,' said Henry.

'Oh don't let us break the party up,' said Jean Osmotherly.

'Have one more port, Henry,' said his Head of Establishments, and it sounded suspiciously like a command.

Dougie Osmotherly pointed his Rolls towards next door, with many jokes about driving carefully and not falling asleep on the way home.

When Dougie and Jean had gone, Dennis and Margaret Tubman-Edwards sighed in unison and Margaret said, 'Sorry about them, but we owed them a meal desperately and what can one do when one lives in the land of the *nouveaux riches?*'

'We are of course the *anciens pauvres*,' said Dennis Tubman-Edwards.

His wife didn't laugh.

Henry drove off full of drink as many people did in those days. By the time they reached Thurmarsh he was fighting against sleep.

Paradise Villa seemed very lifeless without Kate, who was spending the night with Hilary's family.

'You were very quiet tonight,' said Hilary, as they sat at opposite sides of the bed and undressed like weary zombies.

'You weren't,' said Henry pointedly.

'Don't you want me to be what I am and say what I think?' said

70

Hilary. 'Do you want me to have no beliefs and no feelings and no social courage whatsoever?'

Henry wanted to say, 'God, your body's beautiful. Your skin is *so* lovely.' Só why did he say, 'What do you mean by that? Is that what you're saying *I'm* like?'

'I think you're lovely and worth all those people put together and it makes me bloody livid that you can't see it,' said Hilary, and she slammed the bedroom door and locked herself in the bathroom and burst into tears.

Henry was very drunk, Hilary fairly drunk, Hilary crying in the bathroom, Henry pleading outside the bathroom door. Both utterly exhausted. Unpromising beginnings for a night of love.

Yet afterwards, when they counted, they were very nearly certain that it was on that night that Jack was conceived.

If Henry had written down his ideal list of guests for their first Christmas at home, it would not have consisted of Howard Lewthwaite, Nadežda Lewthwaite, Sam Lewthwaite, Cousin Hilda, Mrs Wedderburn, Liam O'Reilly and Norman Pettifer. After that dinner party at the Dower House, however, all social difficulties paled into insignificance.

They had roast turkey and all the trimmings, and everyone drank wine except for Cousin Hilda and Mrs Wedderburn. Cousin Hilda looked shocked when Norman Pettifer and especially Mr O'Reilly accepted, and Mr O'Reilly went puce with courage. Cousin Hilda even looked slightly shocked when Mrs Wedderburn said, in answer to Henry's attempts at persuasion, 'It's not that I disapprove. I just hate the taste.'

Kate slept and fed and watched and smiled and just might have been dimly aware that it was a special day. Sam described everything as 'grisly', it was his word of the month, but everyone else enjoyed themselves and Henry and Hilary worked as a splendid team, having been too busy to be unhappy. Their happiness, and Kate's, was toasted, and even Cousin Hilda raised her glass of water and almost smiled. Howard Lewthwaite occasionally looked sad and Nadežda occasionally looked distant and when the splendid cheese board was served Norman Pettifer made his only bitter remark of the day. 'Not bought from Adrian, clearly,' he said.

Everyone took turns at holding Kate, but Nadežda felt that she would be too heavy, and in the kitchen, as they made coffee, Hilary said, 'Perhaps we shouldn't have let them all hold Kate. It's brought her disability home to Mummy,' and Henry said, 'I think she must know it already, since she's in a wheelchair,' and then he apologised and kissed her and said, 'We had to do it. It's made Mrs Wedderburn's day and Mr O'Reilly's year,' and the brief shadow passed.

As the light faded, Henry and Nadežda and Howard and Sam played a long game of Monopoly, and Hilary, Cousin Hilda, Mrs Wedderburn, Mr O'Reilly and Norman Pettifer contested many a hard-fought bout of Snap.

In the evening, they had cold ham and salad, while they watched *Christmas Night with the Stars*, introduced by David Nixon. Then they watched Harry Belafonte with the George Mitchell Singers, and *Top Hat* with Fred Astaire and Ginger Rogers.

As the *News* began, Cousin Hilda said, 'Well, that were a right good night if you like singing and dancing.'

After the *News* there was a five-minute mental health appeal by Christopher Mayhew MP.

'Where's the sense of depressing us on Christmas Day?' said Cousin Hilda.

'Surely we can spare five minutes to think of those less fortunate than ourselves?' said Hilary, and Cousin Hilda blazed with Christian shame.

Norman Pettifer snored several times during *The Black Eye*, with David Kossoff, but afterwards he said he'd enjoyed it.

When *The Epilogue* began, Henry moved to switch the set off.

'You're never switching *The Epilogue* off on Christmas Day!' said Cousin Hilda.

'No,' lied Henry cravenly. 'There was a fly on the screen. I was going to brush it off.'

After *The Epilogue*, Henry and Hilary saw their guests to the door. It was past midnight.

'It's been the best day of my life,' said Liam O'Reilly. 'Definitely.'

Hilary turned away, to hide the tears in her eyes.

The fierce winter of 1959 held the British Isles in its grip. In London there was a return of the killer smog, in which 3,000 people had died in four days in 1952, and all eight and a half miles of Britain's first motorway were closed after just forty-eight days, due to rainwater and melted snow seeping under the surface.

In the Midlands, 10,000 girls who made nylon stockings took a twelve per cent wage cut to save jobs.

Tosser Pilkington-Brick phoned Henry and Hilary and said, 'We've got a little girl.'

'Terrific,' said Henry. 'What are you calling her?'

'Camilla,' said Tosser.

'Well never mind,' said Henry. 'I do hope all goes well for you, anyway.'

'Thanks,' said Tosser. 'Had any thoughts about pensions and insurance yet?'

Henry 'Incapable of thinking about pensions and insurance' Pratt caught the train from Thurmarsh to Leeds every morning, sent out more letters, collated more replies, produced a draft of a leaflet giving advice on the planting and care of indoor and outdoor cucumbers, accepted with simulated humility and gratitude Roland Stagg's suggestion that it become two booklets, one for indoors and one for outdoors, negotiated a leaflet budget with Sid Pentelow, made a little work go a long way, kept a low profile, produced a set of encouraging statistics, accepted Roland Stagg's suggestion that he make the statistics less encouraging, so that there would be more room for improvement and credit for the department later, felt that he was getting nowhere and that nothing whatsoever in the world of cucumbers had been changed one iota by his appointment to the Cucumber Marketing Board, and was warmly congratulated on his progress by the Director

(Operations), the Head of Establishments and the Regional Co-ordinator, Northern Counties (Excluding Berwick-on-Tweed).

Neither Mr Tubman-Edwards nor Henry ever mentioned the dinner party at the Dower House.

Hilary discovered that she was pregnant, and Kate began to crawl, backwards at first, then forwards.

Russ Conway became a star, Cliff Richard's career began, and Henry had three pieces of news, and all three depressed him, and it depressed him that they depressed him, and this disturbed him, and it disturbed him that so many things disturbed him.

The first piece of news was told him by Hilary, one late spring morning, while she was changing Kate's nappy in front of the gas fire, in the still uncarpeted living room.

'Darling?' she said, with ominous seriousness.

'Yes?' Henry's heart raced psychically.

'I've finished my novel.'

'What?'

'I've sent it to an agent somebody recommended.'

'Oh.'

'Is that all you can say – "oh"?'

'Of course not. Great. I'm thrilled.'

'No, you aren't. You're jealous.'

'Of course I'm not. I'm absolutely thrilled. I'm . . . I'm just surprised. I mean, you haven't said a word about it for months.'

'Because you get so jealous.'

'I don't. I'm just a bit annoyed because I would like not to have been so insulted by being kept in the dark.'

'I couldn't tell you. You make it impossible for me to tell you.'

'I see. I'm impossible.'

'I didn't say that. You see, you're angry.'

'How can you say that? What sort of a person do you think I am?'

'I don't know any more.'

'Oh. Great.'

They hardly spoke for the rest of the weekend. On Monday, in his office, looking out onto a courtyard full of offices full of people looking out at him, Henry felt deeply depressed and fought hard to find in himself the generosity to tell Hilary how much he hoped her book would be a success.

That evening, he did find the generosity.

'I hope it's a huge success,' he said. 'I hope it's a best-seller.'

They kissed, and later they made love, and Kate was fun, and they were happy, except . . . Henry knew that he hadn't found the generosity to mean what he said, and he suspected that Hilary knew this.

The second and third pieces of news that depressed him were both imparted in the heaving lounge bar of the White Hart, in which Kate was a sensation. Even hard-bitten seed merchants agreed that she was one of the most beautiful babies in the history of the human race.

As Henry struggled to the bar, he found his way blocked by the broad backs of a row of regulars, all taller than him. One of the backs, a member of the county set, turned to his neighbour and said, 'I hear Belinda's whelped,' and as he pushed through to get served, Henry said, 'Excuse me, are you referring to Belinda Boyce-Uppingham, by any chance?' :

'What's it to you?' said County Set unpleasantly.

'I knew her well as a child.'

County Set looked as if he thought it unlikely.

'Well, she's had a little girl called Tessa,' he said, and turned his back on Henry.

Why should it depress me, pondered Henry, that Belinda Boyce-Uppingham, that frontispiece for *Country Life*, whom I foolishly adored when I knew no better, has whelped?

The third piece of news was that the baby of Lorna Lugg, his childhood sweetheart, was called Marlene.

Two monkeys, fired into space by the Americans, returned to earth safely. Four mice were less lucky, and circuited the earth until they died.

Golden summer covered Britain in a gentle haze. Henry chugged around his Northern Counties under skies of an unbroken pale blue. He spent little time in the more spectacular regions. Few cucumbers were grown in the Lake District, on the Cumbrian fells, on the sheep-rich Cheviots, in the Trough of Bowland and the Yorkshire Dales. But in flatter lands, in the Vale of York, County Durham, West Lancashire, Western Westmorland beyond the lakes, and around the Solway Firth, Henry would grind to a squeaky halt and hear folk hiss, 'It's the man from the Marketing Board. I'm out.' With sinking heart he doled out advice that wasn't wanted to folk who knew better. With sinking heart he rattled home to a house that was filled with the loud silence of unasked questions. 'What did the agent think of your novel?' And even, 'Do you love me?'

Abandoned villages appeared in the middle of shrinking reservoirs. Moorland fires clothed the Western suburbs of Sheffield in acrid smoke which could be smelt even in Thurmarsh. The House of Fraser acquired Harrods. The *Manchester Guardian* became the *Guardian*. Kate took her first step, said her first word. It was 'Mama'. Innocent, tactless Kate.

Henry couldn't have his holidays until September, and they decided that France would have to wait another year. The sun still blazed, they took a cottage near Helmsley, Kate loved the countryside and saved their holiday.

On Sunday, September 27th, 1959, the Ministry of Labour announced that 4,747,000 working days had been lost to strikes in the first eight months of the year, singing star Shani Wallis dashed into the sea in Brighton in a fifty-guinea dress to save a man from drowning, and Jack Pratt was born. They had christened him (in case he turned out to be religious) before they realised that at school he would be known as Jack Sprat.

Jack was big. Quite big even when he was born. The sight of him, the thought of his passing through Hilary's womb and vagina, caused Henry pain, but not with the same intensity that had attended Kate's birth. Poor second child. Already the incredible, the absurdly brilliant miracle of conception, development and birth had become commonplace.

It was impossible for anyone to say that Jack was beautiful. He was fat, bald, red and greedy. Kate had hated soiling her nappies.

76

Jack adored soiling his. Kate had been difficult to feed. Jack proved impossible to stop feeding. Yet there was very soon about him, turning his ugliness into beauty, a natural good humour that warmed the embers of his parents' flickering fires. He cried, but he never whined. Kate, knowing that he was ugly, sensing that he was deeply loved, grew intermittently querulous, though her growing vocabulary and evident intelligence thrilled them.

Hilary and Henry hosted another massed Christmas at Paradise Villa, because to have gone to the Lewthwaites' would have been to have been obliged to go to Cousin Hilda's the following year.

In Capetown, Harold Macmillan spoke of the 'wind of change blowing through Africa'. Jack went onto solids, and in Paradise Villa the wind of change acquired a less inspiring meaning. Dr Barbara Moore walked from Land's End to John o' Groats in twenty-three days. Jack crawled from the nest of tables, across the new green carpet, almost to the door, in one minute eleven seconds. Togo became independent. Kate yearned for independence and learned to use colouring books quite accurately.

On Saturday, June 28th, 1960, Henry and Hilary set off for France.

Slowly, the faithful Standard Eight slipped south. The Great North Road. The Dartford Tunnel. The Dover Road. The night ferry. Romantic words, monotonous reality. They chugged through ascetic old towns full of cafés and restaurants that they couldn't afford to enter, past vibrant games of *boules* under peaceful avenues of plane trees. As the road curved endlessly among the sunburnt hills of Provence, Kate grew restless. They'd promised her the sea, and although she wasn't quite sure what the sea was, she became deeply impatient to see it. Late on the second afternoon she *did* see it, but it was too big and too empty for her, and she felt betrayed, and cried bitterly.

But she liked Cap Ferrat, the glimpses of sea and mountain, the stunning villas, the huge, immaculate gardens.

Uncle Teddy's villa was set behind a row of colour-washed fishermen's cottages. It was just over three years since Henry had been there, on that momentous journey of discovery, when his

77

whole world had seemed to turn upside-down. Now he could approach it calmly, happily, in holiday mood.

He pulled up neatly on the gravel outside the gate, got out of the car and gave himself a luxurious stretch.

Enjoy that stretch, Henry. Make it last. Your mood is about to change.

Uncle Teddy was at the door already, and Henry and Hilary both knew, before he opened his mouth, that something was very wrong.

'Anna left me yesterday,' he said.

5 A Difficult Holiday

It was cool and dark in the shuttered villa. Uncle Teddy opened the shutters and let in the smell of the South, the salty lethargy of the sea, the stale breath of the afternoon sun, and the herb-scented freshness of the evening breeze.

He flinched from the cruel light, which was merciless towards his greying hair, his ashen face, his hollow sleepless eyes, his thin ageing legs and his unlovely paunch. He smiled and said that he was fine. He showed them their room, large and cool, with shutters on to a balcony, and two hired cots. He tickled Jack's chin and made awkward remarks to Kate, who stared at him solemnly as if he frightened her. He made tea in the marble kitchen, and said, 'I thought we'd eat out tonight. I haven't been able to get myself organised to shop.'

'Of course not,' said Hilary. 'We'll shop and cook.'

Uncle Teddy handed them an envelope.

'She left a letter for you,' he said.

They read it in turn:

> Dear Henry and Hilary,
> I know this will come as a great shock to you, and I feel really bad about spoiling your holiday, but my first thought must be for Teddy. Don't give that hollow laugh. I mean it. I've known for some time that I've got to go. I just haven't got it in me to stay with an old man and I owe it to Teddy to get out before he becomes old. He still has a chance of somebody much more suitable than me, some rich widow or something, he's a sexy man and fun quite a lot of the time, but he's never really tried to understand me and how I tick. I really think the only woman he's ever really been interested in is Doris. He wanted a fling and an adventure. He wanted to seem to be a bit of an old rogue. He's done it and that's it.

Anyway, I can't feel too guilty because it was great fun while it lasted and we both have some fantastic memories. Well, all right, I shouldn't have gone with him, but I did and that's all there is to it. There isn't anybody else, no Jed or anybody, so I'm looking for Mr Right! Anyway, the point is, if I'd left him at any other time he'd have had nothing to occupy his days and I know you and the kids'll cheer him up for a couple of weeks and by then the worst'll be over. So I've done it at the best time, even though I feel rotten about it.

Washing stuff et cetera under the sink, foodstuffs fairly self-explanatory, brushes and mops in an *outside* cupboard at the back next to the third shower and loo.

I'll miss seeing you all very much. This isn't easy for me either.

With love,
Anna

PS Not a word to Daddy. I'll just tell them I couldn't cope with life as a nun. Anyway, they'll be so relieved that they won't ask too many questions.

Hilary said that the children were too tired to eat out that night, so they bought food in, and Hilary made chicken *provençale*, because if the food wasn't Mediterranean, they might as well have been in Thurmarsh.

When he came in for pre-dinner drinks, Henry caught Uncle Teddy holding a photograph of himself and Anna, and there were tears in his eyes. He put it down hurriedly as soon as he heard Henry, and gave a watery smile.

'We were happy that day,' he said.

'Would it be better to put the photos away?' suggested Henry.

There were photos of a scantily clad Anna all over the villa.

Uncle Teddy shook his head. 'I've only just lost her,' he said. 'I couldn't cope with losing the memory of her as well.'

Over their dinner, which he hardly tasted, Uncle Teddy said, 'Never should have done it, I suppose. Should have known better.'

'There's no point in thinking that,' said Hilary.

'I don't regret it, though. Not a moment of it.'

'Well, then.'

After the meal, as they sipped wine on the terrace, with the incessant clattering of ten thousand crickets challenging the velvet stillness of the southern night, Uncle Teddy said, 'How *is* Doris?'

'She's very well,' said Henry. 'She's put on quite a lot of weight.'

'She's never had a lot of self-discipline, hasn't Doris,' said Uncle Teddy. 'Not easy to, running a pub, mind.' He sighed. 'I can't believe she's ended up running a pub.' He sighed again. 'What a mess. Pub still doing all right, is it?'

'They get by,' said Henry.

They didn't tell Uncle Teddy that it was so popular that it was known throughout the Dales as 'Doris's'. They didn't think it would be what he wanted to hear.

'I don't blame her for not waiting,' said Uncle Teddy. 'My fault for getting sent to prison. Doris couldn't live without a man. No idea how to start.' He sighed. 'You'd think she'd have been able to get somebody better than Geoffrey Porringer, though.'

'I thought he was your friend,' said Henry.

'As a chap to do business with, fine,' said Uncle Teddy. 'Chap to eat with, grand. Chap to drink with, no problem. Chap to wake up to, all those blackheads on the pillow beside you, horrendous I'd have thought.'

'Well you couldn't be expected to fancy him,' said Henry. 'I mean, I can't believe that I would if I was a woman, but you never know. Women have strange tastes in men.'

'I know,' said Hilary. 'I married you.'

Henry assumed that it was a joke, and laughed not because it amused him, but in order to make it clear that it was a joke. But Uncle Teddy took it seriously.

'That's very true,' he said. 'I can't believe some of the fellers women take up with. Sidney Watson over at Mexborough. Hollow chest, halitosis, and an undertaker. They were queueing up. Tommy Simonsgate, the plumber. Wallet full of moths, and always had bits of cabbage sticking between his teeth. Married a model. I gave it two years. Ten years later, they'd three kids, she looks like a brick shithouse, and he's just the same, except a bit more sophisticated. It's broccoli instead of cabbage.' He fell silent for a reflective moment. 'I don't blame Anna for going. I'm getting an old man's legs. I'll end up looking like a punchball on matchsticks. I'm not bitter. She gave me some wonderful times. Always knew it had to end. I just wish we could have had one more year. Just one more year. I'd have settled for that.' His voice was choking. He blew his nose. 'May as well kill the bottle.'

He filled their glasses almost to the brim. A plane winked across their natural planetarium, and there was a soft whisper of wind.

'Grand kids,' he said. 'Grand. I'm going to love having them around. I'm so glad you came, son. And you, Hilary. You're a belter. I'm proud of him, winning you. Always knew he had it in him, mind.'

He paused. Neither Henry nor Hilary spoke. They didn't know what to say. They decided to let Uncle Teddy get it off his chest.

'I'm frightened of growing old. I had looks, you see. It's sad losing them. You're all right, Henry, because you've never had looks.'

Henry had to bite his tongue to stop himself saying, drily, 'Thank you very much.'

'So you've nothing to lose. Women find you irresistible because of your . . .'

Uncle Teddy paused for so long that Henry felt compelled to speak.

'Charisma?' he said hopefully.

'Vulnerability. They want to mother you and then when they realise you're a proper sexy man they're hooked.' He sighed again. 'I should have gone back to Doris when you gave me the chance. Tell me, would you say . . . would you say Doris and Geoffrey are . . . happy?'

Henry's head was swimming with wine and exhaustion. He longed for sleep. He couldn't think. He knew that it was important to answer carefully, but he simply hadn't the energy.

Luckily, Hilary had.

'No,' she said. 'They aren't happy, but they aren't unhappy either. They've formed a *modus vivendi*. A way of living.'

'Thank you for translating,' said Uncle Teddy, 'but I'm not completely ignorant.'

'Sorry.'

'Anna and I used to read Shakespeare's plays out loud.'

Henry and Hilary tried hard to hide their astonishment. Without success.

'You're stunned. We decided to expand our horizons. Couldn't get to grips at first. Then, suddenly, open sesame, we got it. Loved it. *Romeo and Juliet*, know it?'

'I know it,' said Hilary.

' "Romeo, Romeo, wherefore art thou, Romeo? We must defy our families, because . . . we've formed a *modus vivendi*." Not good enough, is it? Doris deserves better. Doris deserves love.' Uncle Teddy took a gulp of wine, not tasting it. 'I should have gone back to her when you gave me the chance.' He held his glass up against the night sky, as if surprised to have found that it was empty. 'I don't regret it, though. None of it.' He stood up. 'Starting to repeat myself. Time for bed. You've got a holiday to have.' He shook Henry's hand with strange formality. 'Good to see you, son.' He kissed Hilary. 'You're lovely.' He weaved his way back to the house, turned, said, 'I'm going to give you a wonderful holiday,' and disappeared into the house.

Kate and Jack slept through till seven. Uncle Teddy was already up, natty in white shorts and a blue shirt. Breakfast was laid on the terrace. The morning was as fresh as a washed dairy.

'Morning,' said Uncle Teddy heartily. 'Did you sleep well?'

'Very well. How about you?'

'Like a top,' lied Uncle Teddy. 'Right. Coffee?'

They nodded.

'Right. Coffee coming up.'

Uncle Teddy tried to make a great fuss of the children without quite knowing how to, and said, 'Oh well.'

They had no difficulty in supplying the missing sub-text: 'I wish I'd had children. Too late now.'

'We thought we'd go on the beach today,' said Henry, as he spread honey on a crisp, fresh roll. 'Jack isn't really ready, but Kate'll love it.'

'You will come, won't you?' said Hilary. They had decided that it would be better if *she* asked.

'Oh no,' said Uncle Teddy. 'I hate the sea.'

They looked at him in surprise. Uncle Teddy had no difficulty in supplying the missing sub-text: 'Then what on earth are you doing living by the bloody thing?'

'Oh, I love living by it,' he said. 'I love sea fronts, hotels, promenades, palms, seaside cafés, fish markets, children's happy faces, everything about it except the bloody thing itself. Well, I don't hate all seas. I love the Atlantic. That's my sea. Breakers rolling in. Sand-castles eaten up by the onrushing tide. Sand left glistening by the receding tide. Limpets drying out on the rocks. Streams to dam. Tongues of sea flecking their way in, sliding into rock-pools. Rock-pools coming to life again. Tides, change, drama, that's my sea. The Med just sits there, like a lukewarm soup. Disgusting.'

Henry looked at him in amazement, and Hilary looked at Henry in silent rebuke for not having told her that Uncle Teddy had a lyrical side.

'You're astounded. You think nothing excites me except sex and import–export,' said Uncle Teddy. 'I told you. We've expanded our horizons. Oh God, how could she go?' His face crumpled and then the mask returned. 'Out, damned self-pity. I'll leave you now. Enjoy your day.'

And Uncle Teddy got into his Rolls Royce and drove off.

Jack crawled over the sand, Kate loved being buried in the sand, light aeroplanes passed overhead trailing advertising banners, Jack and Kate loved the water, and the day passed pleasantly; and they shopped, and Hilary cooked, and the children were utterly exhausted and fell asleep, and Uncle Teddy returned home and said, 'Sun's over the yard-arm. Time for the first Pernod,' and they drank their *apéritifs* and ate *salade niçoise* and sea bass with fennel that Hilary had made very creditably, although the sea bass was slightly over-cooked.

Over dinner Uncle Teddy asked what they'd done that day and pretended to be interested in their replies. Then they asked him what he'd done and he said, 'Oh, you know, drove around the hills, put the roof down, felt the wind in my face, smelt the wild thyme, blew the cobwebs away.'

'Don't you have friends here?' asked Hilary with that social directness that Henry admired and feared.

'Oh yes. But you've heard of flags of convenience. These are friends of convenience. Friends of geography. I like the French, can't think why so many British can't stand them, but they're foreigners to us, we're foreigners to them, I don't think we ever quite make real friends. The British are all exiles, like me, so there's something wrong with them all, except the *bona fide* businessmen and diplomats, and the *bona fide* don't like me because I'm not *bona fide*. Nice sea bass this, Hilary.'

'It's over-cooked.'

'Barely. Damned good first effort. Anna took ages to get the hang of cooking.' He paused, thinking affectionately of past culinary disasters, and their hearts bled for him. 'No, the fact is, they aren't real friends, and I don't think I could face them now. All the explanations. All the sympathy.' He smiled wryly, and with more self-knowledge than they would have believed possible. 'Besides, I've always put myself across as a bit of a *roué*, young lady at my side, saucy remarks, suggestive inferences, all the gubbins. Bit of a gay dog, old Teddy Braithwaite. Seen it all, knows how to live. Be a shame to let them see me with the stuffing knocked out of me, the gay dog become a hang-dog. No, I have to reconstruct myself and move on. Never see any of them again. Chapter closed. More wine?'

So every day Uncle Teddy took to the hills. Some days Henry and Hilary went sightseeing. They went to Cannes and Nice and Menton and Monaco and Vence. But some days it was too hot for sightseeing, and some days it was even too hot for the beach. Henry and Hilary grew rather bored with the beach, and Jack and Kate grew sleepy with the sun, and, after lunch, when time stood still, they all went to bed. Occasionally, in those shuttered, insect-buzzing afternoons, Henry and Hilary made love, sleepily. More often they just slept, lovingly. Then there was shopping, and feeding of children, and cooking, because it turned out that they ate in almost every night. Uncle Teddy would return, the sun would go down over the yard-arm, there'd be Pernod and Kir and food and wine and Uncle Teddy repeating himself and apologising for ruining their holiday, and bursting the balloon of self-deception with the sharp pinprick of self-knowledge.

Yet over it all there hung a growing shadow, a shadow that had nothing to do with Uncle Teddy, but everything to do with Henry and Hilary. Henry didn't even know it existed, but Hilary did.

On the beach on their last morning, the hottest, the haziest, the stickiest, the soupiest, Hilary was almost shivering as she screwed herself up to speak.

'My book's been accepted by Wagstaff and Wagstaff,' she said.

Henry felt the great cancer of jealousy, the great lump. He also felt a surge of righteous indignation.

'And you never told me,' he said.

'I didn't dare.'

'Bollocks!'

Kate began to cry. Jack smiled. They had to take Kate to the water. The water was warm. Henry was very conscious of the slim, bronzed bodies all round. His podgy body had gone a blotchy red.

'Don't shout and upset them,' said Hilary.

'I won't. But I really do think it's awful that you waited until the last day of our holiday, and then you tell me as if it's bad news.'

'It is bad news to you.'

They all splashed each other and laughed.

'When did you find out?' said Henry.

'Three days before we left home. And then we were so busy and I thought you'd be upset and I thought I'd tell you on the first day here and then of course all this business blew up and somehow I couldn't do it. I'm sorry.'

Henry longed to be able to say, 'I understand completely, my darling. It's my fault, for giving you the wrong impression, but it is

86

a wrong impression. I'm absolutely thrilled. I hope the book's an enormous success, and my God your legs look good today,' but he couldn't. He said, 'So you should be. If you don't trust me I don't see what hope there is for us,' and he set off and swam almost a mile out to sea, and his chest ached with the anger and the exertion, and he thought he was starting a heart attack, and he was far out beyond everybody. He fought his panic and controlled it, and swam very slowly back, with his inimitably ungainly breast-stroke, towards the splashing, laughing, smoothly athletic swimmers and the great range of the Alpes Maritimes, barely scarred by all the corniche roads. Above the mountains clouds were gathering, clouds with dark angry centres, clouds like boils full of pus.

Hilary didn't speak. Henry found it impossible to apologise. He said, 'I suppose we'd better get ready for lunch,' in a low, lifeless voice. 'Yes,' said Hilary, in a similar voice.

All afternoon they communicated like that. That evening, Uncle Teddy suggested a posh restaurant for their last night. They ate outside, overlooking the sea, with Jack in his carry-cot. The staff were kind and warm to Kate and Jack. Henry and Hilary, used to being treated like germs when they took the children out in England, couldn't believe it.

They pretended that nothing was wrong, for Uncle Teddy's sake. And Uncle Teddy pretended that he was as happy as a sandboy, for their sake. They ate *bourride* and *langoustine mayonnaise* and lamb crusted with herbs, and because of the ghastly charade that they were playing out it might have been cotton wool.

'It's been a lovely fortnight, despite everything.'
'I hope everything works out.'
'It mustn't be so long next time.'
'I think you've taken it terribly well.'
'Thank you for everything.'
'I'll write very soon.'
'What a lot of flies there are tonight!'
'I hope none of them are mosquitoes.'

'It'll be a long journey tomorrow.'

'There are some nice places to stay just south of Paris.'

'The air's incredibly heavy tonight.'

'This raspberry mousse looks wonderful.'

'The wine is lovely.'

'Thank you. I will have another glass.'

'We sound like the conversations in those "Teach Yourself French" booklets.'

Which of them said what? It doesn't matter. They barely knew themselves.

One of the waiters held Kate's hand and took her to the water's edge. Another carried a delighted Jack on a tour of the kitchens.

In the sky, the boils grew, the pus throbbed. The first great fork of lightning broke the world in two. There was a huge rumble of thunder. Jack grinned. Kate cried.

The storm reached them at two o'clock. The thunder and lightning were almost continuous. It rained ferociously for forty minutes.

Then the rain stopped and the thunder and lightning moved away, although it would be more than two hours before they were free from distant rumbling.

Neither Henry nor Hilary had slept a wink. Jack slept throughout it all. Kate woke and cried but was brave when she was cuddled and soon went back to sleep again.

Henry and Hilary lay as stiff as boards, not touching.

'What you said was absolutely true,' he whispered, because he was very conscious of Uncle Teddy, also presumably unable to sleep. 'I *was* jealous.'

She didn't reply.

'Are you asleep?' he whispered.

'No.'

'Why not?'

'Because it's so awful. I'm so disappointed in you.'

'That sounds very priggish.'

'I *am* priggish. My dad's priggish.'

'I love you.'

'But not my book.'

'Oh fuck your book.'

'Exactly.'

Silence then.

A last faint rumble of thunder.

The first pale streak of dawn.

The first exclamation of delight at the glory of the privilege of existence from a passing thrush.

More silence then.

'I need your help,' whispered Henry.

'I don't believe it,' whispered Hilary. 'I create something, with great difficulty. I have no confidence in it. It's accepted. I'm overjoyed. I can't tell you. I tell you. I think, "Maybe I'm wrong. Maybe he isn't jealous." I'm not wrong. You hate my creativity. You hate the existence of my book that is a painful thing wrenched out of myself. My second greatest pride, my second greatest joy, for my first greatest pride and joy was you. I'm thrilled. I'm excited. I find I'm not useless after all. And you are angry. I'm so hurt. So hurt. And *you* ask *me* for help.'

'Don't you love me any more?' whispered Henry.

'Oh yes, I still love you,' whispered Hilary. 'But I don't *want* to love you any more.'

Two hands meet in a French bed. They clasp each other. They squeeze each other, once. They drop apart.

Silence then.

6 Count Your Blessings

One of the many benefits of having children is that one is too busy to have other crises. Henry and Hilary were very loving parents. Henry would hurry to catch the train from Leeds City Station of an evening, in order to be home for bath-time. Big, ugly yet appealing Jack, with his constant good nature, was almost always a delight. Pale, sensitive, excitable Kate, with her changes of mood and her sharp emotional needs, was altogether more difficult, but often deeply loving and affectionate. She listened to bedtime stories with a solemnity that no heart could have resisted. She laughed at Henry's funny voices with an abandon that touched them deeply.

Henry and Hilary were invited to dinner at the Lewthwaites' one Wednesday. They took Kate and Jack, and put them to bed upstairs. While Henry was reading Kate a story about a magical wellington boot, he was disappointed to hear other guests arriving with cheery 'hello's' and, 'Oh you shouldn't have. They're lovely. Find a vase, Howard.' They felt disappointed. They hadn't come prepared for other guests. They strained to catch the identity of the unwelcome strangers, but Sam began to play an Adam Faith record, and the chance was gone.

The other guests turned out to be unwelcome, but not strangers. They were Peter and Olivia Matheson, and their daughter Anna.

Peter Matheson turned upon them the massed floodlights of his social smile. Olivia's face was becoming deeply lined. Anna was wearing no make-up and an unsuccessful grey version of the sack dress. It simply looked as though she was wearing a grey sack. She went pale when she saw them, but soon recovered her colour.

'Hello, Hillers,' she said hurriedly. 'Hello, Henry. Oh it *is* good to see you. One of the worst things about being a novice nun was not seeing my friends.'

Henry's heart sank. They were in for an evening of play-acting.

'And your parents, surely?' said Olivia.

'Oh yes, of course,' said Anna. She flashed a defiant look at Henry and Hilary.

'I could never understand that,' said Peter Matheson. 'I should have thought you could have seen your parents.'

'You had to renounce the familiar,' said Anna. 'It was a test of strength. Unfortunately, I failed.'

'Well we're pleased you did,' said her father.

Henry accepted one of Howard Lewthwaite's splendidly strong gin and tonics. Hilary chose white wine, Peter Matheson whisky, Olivia sherry, Anna tonic water.

'I've got used to not having artificial stimulants,' she said. 'I'm not sure if I could cope with them now.'

'Well of course I think religion can be an artificial stimulant,' said Peter Matheson. He laughed at his own remark, which was just as well, if it was intended to be funny, because nobody else did.

Howard Lewthwaite departed to the kitchen.

Olivia Matheson approached Henry, and led him over to the window of the heavily floral lounge. There was still a gleam of light in the western sky.

'You're a man of the world,' she said. 'And Hilary's Anna's best friend. Will you help Anna come to terms with real life?'

Henry had a vision of Anna, on the one and only night when he had taken her out, sitting stark naked in a cheap brown armchair in her flat in Cardington Road, beneath a reproduction of 'Greylag Geese Rising', by Peter Scott. Nothing had risen that night, except the greylag geese.

'Yes,' he said. 'Yes, yes. We'll . . . er . . . try and help her come to terms with real life.'

'Thank you.' She patted his arm. 'My husband really likes you.'

The conversation became general again, and Henry didn't feel like letting Anna off the hook too easily.

'I'm shamefully ignorant about nuns,' he said. 'Tell us what you had to study, what devotions you had to perform, what disciplines were required of you, how you spent a typical day.'

Anna smiled. 'I'd like to,' she said, 'but we were sworn to secrecy, and although I've left, I'd like to respect that.'

Henry had to admire her, albeit reluctantly.

'I hate that kind of secrecy,' said Hilary. 'It sounds like a religious version of the Masons.'

'Yes, that's one of the things that disillusioned me,' said Anna.

Hilary had to admire her, albeit reluctantly.

Sam, in jeans and tee-shirt, put his head round the door and said, 'Hi. I'm out with some mates tonight. Have a great meal. Bye.'

Howard Lewthwaite, in a 'Ban the Bomb' apron, put his head round the door and said, 'Come and get it.'

Hilary wheeled her mother into the lifeless dining room. Howard Lewthwaite asked Henry to deal with the wine. Everybody had some, even Anna. 'I suppose I ought to try to get to like the stuff,' she said.

'You've been to France too, haven't you?' said Olivia Matheson to Henry and Hilary, over the beef casserole.

'Yes, but not near Anna,' said Henry. 'We stayed with my Uncle Teddy. It was rather sad. He'd been married to a woman thirty years younger than him, and she'd left the day before we got there.'

'Please, Henry,' said Peter Matheson. 'Anna's looking embarrassed. She's rather unworldly about these things.'

'It's all right, Daddy,' said Anna. 'I'm interested. I need to learn. How did the old man take it?'

'He's not exactly an old man,' said Hilary. 'He was devastated, of course, but . . . not bitter. Amazingly enough, he wasn't bitter.'

'Good,' said Anna. 'I'm glad of that. Bitterness is self-destructive. The nuns were very much against bitterness.'

'Careful,' said Henry. 'You're giving away secrets.'

'Oh Lord, yes,' said Anna. 'It's the wine, I expect.'

'Another glass?' said Henry.

'Well perhaps a little one,' said Anna. 'It's not quite as awful as I'd thought.'

Nadežda had a coughing fit over the trifle. Hilary wheeled her out. When she came back, Nadežda said, 'A bit of almond went down the wrong way', but her chest had sounded ominously wheezy to Henry.

After the cheese, Howard Lewthwaite stood and said, 'This meal is a kind of celebration, also a sort of postscript. As you know, we've sold Lewthwaite's to the developers of the Fish Hill Complex. A sad day, but none of us can stand in the way of progress, can we?' He looked at the ceiling, not wishing to meet Henry's eye or indeed Peter Matheson's. Peter Matheson looked at the floor, not wishing to meet Henry's eye or indeed Howard Lewthwaite's. Henry closed his eyes, not wishing to look at the ceiling or the floor or to meet Peter Matheson's eye or Howard Lewthwaite's eye or Hilary's eye or Anna's eye. 'We've bought a house in Spain, near Alicante. Naddy needs a drier climate and nothing else matters.' Howard Lewthwaite smiled at Naděžda, whose eyes were moist. 'Sam's at college, so it's the right time. We're going to sell the house, so it'll be the end of our life in Thurmarsh. I know Henry and Hilary will miss us, as baby-sitters if not as people.' Henry and Hilary dredged a laugh from the depths of their shock that this moment had suddenly come. 'You will of course be welcome to visit us, we'll be very upset if you don't. So, my family . . . my friends . . . cheers.'

The meal ended with forced jokes and slightly hysterical laughter, because otherwise everyone might have felt rather sad.

As they re-entered the floral lounge, Peter Matheson put an arm round Henry's shoulder. Henry could feel his power. He had to fight to remind himself that the deep affection the man was showing was totally simulated. Peter Matheson knew that Henry had wanted to expose his corruption, and he almost certainly hated Henry as much as Henry hated him.

He led Henry to the curtained window.

'You're a man of the world,' he said. 'Will you help Anna come to terms with her fear of sex? Because that's what's behind all this nun business. Scared stiff of it, poor girl. They're all the same, nuns. You only have to look at their faces. Pasty. Frightened of sex.'

Henry had to fight the temptation to say, 'Pull the other one, you corrupt, deluded twit. When I took her out she'd whipped her clothes off before I could say "Mother Superior". She's been having it off with my Uncle Teddy in Cap Ferrat, with tall, craggy Jed in Berwick, and probably with every able-bodied man from Berwick to Cap Ferrat between the ages of sixteen and eighty-two.' He didn't, of course, but he did feel obliged to make a brief defence of the contemplative life against Peter Matheson's absurdly simplistic theories. 'Well I do think there are other, more positive reasons for joining a religious order than fear of sex,' he said.

'Not in Anna's case,' said Peter Matheson. 'So will you and Hilary befriend her, introduce her to people, give her a chance to . . . I don't know . . . blossom as a woman?'

'All right,' said Henry. 'We'll try to help her to blossom as a woman.'

'Good man!' He gave Henry a thump of gratitude which almost dislocated his collar bone. 'My wife's got a soft spot for you.'

'Did you or did you not give a market garden outside Cockermouth advice about gherkins?'

The expression on the face of the Director (Operations) was of disappointed regret rather than of anger.

'Well, yes, I did,' said Henry. 'It was a sloppy job. Some young lad was dealing with them. Hopeless. He hadn't been thinning out the seeds properly, he'd barely been training the laterals along the support canes, they were hanging down all over the place like willies in a snowstorm.'

Timothy Whitehouse raised his eyes to the ceiling, then swivelled round to take refuge in contemplating his reproduction of Constable's little-known 'Bringing Home the Cucumbers to Dedham'.

What on earth possessed me to say that, thought Henry, and to his fury he felt himself blushing.

'Yes, well, no doubt you gave good advice,' said the Director (Operations), 'but gherkins aren't your responsibility, are they?'

'Well not officially, no.'

'You've trodden on John Barrington's toes.'

'I'm sorry.'

'So you should be. John's a good man, but a touch temperamental and *very* territorial.'

'So what should I have done? Gone home and got him to go all the way to Cockermouth to deal with it?'

'You could have tried phoning to clear it with him. He *might* have agreed. Have you sent him a minute, explaining what happened?'

'No. I'm sorry. I've been very busy.'

'Well when you have a minute, will you send him a minute? He heard direct from Cockermouth. Naturally he was upset. Don't be so impulsive, Henry. Don't let your enthusiasms run away with you.'

'Right,' said Henry. 'Right. But you did tell me to be my own man, stick to my guns, be fearless and always speak the truth. I interpreted that as a recipe for action.'

'Quite right,' said the Director (Operations). 'Quite right. I should have qualified it. *Mea culpa.* I should have told you to be your own man, stick to your guns, be fearless and always speak the truth, *within the confines of your statutory responsibilities.* Point taken? Good. No reason any of this need set your career back for any *great* length of time.'

On November 2nd, 1960, Penguin Books were found not guilty of obscenity in publishing the unexpurgated version of *Lady Chatterley's Lover*, after a trial in which the prosecuting barrister asked the jury, 'Would you allow your wives and servants to read this book?'

Hilary spent the following weekend with her editor from Wagstaff and Wagstaff, discussing the revised but unexpurgated version of her first novel.

Her editor sounded very literary and bookish. Henry had visions of a stooping man in his fifties, with receding hair and thick glasses. It was kind of him to give up his weekend, and to invite Hilary to stay in his flat in Highgate, but there would have been no peace for them in Paradise Villa, and who would have looked after the children if she'd gone while Henry was working?

Henry enjoyed his weekend with the children, but it was tiring, and he was a little upset, on Hilary's return, when she refused to play with Kate because, 'I really am very tired. I've got no energy,' although he had to smile when Kate said, 'Well, I'm tired too. I've only got one energy.'

1961 saw Major Yuri Gagarin orbit the earth in a spaceship. For Britain, it was a less spectacular year, unless you were an aspiring taxi-driver given to gambling. Licensed betting shops and mini-cabs were legalised. For Henry, who wasn't an aspiring taxi-driver given to gambling, it was an even less spectacular year. He forced himself to work hard, to identify with the cucumber, to fight for the cucumber, and in so doing he rekindled his enthusiasm for the cucumber. The results of all this would not be apparent until 1962.

Hilary took so long to finalise the changes to her book that it proved impossible to publish it that year. It was scheduled for the spring of 1962.

It was not the love of their children alone that kept the marriage of Henry and Hilary on the rails in the months after their crisis in Cap Ferrat. Henry deserves some credit too. He fought valiantly against the jealousy that had sprung unbidden into his heart.

On the afternoon of Sunday, June 18th, 1961, Kate and Jack were, most unusually, both asleep at the same time. A stranger looking in at the living room of Paradise Villa, carpeted and curtained now but still sparsely furnished, would have witnessed a scene of apparent male dominance. Husband curled up on the settee, reading. Wife ironing. In fact, however, the husband was reading the finished version of the wife's novel, and the wife was ironing to ease the almost intolerable tension that she was feeling. She hadn't let him see the manuscript until it was finally polished, and hadn't been sure that she wanted him to read it even then, but he had insisted. 'I must. It's part of you. I can't shy away from it,' he had said.

He put the typescript down, and took off his glasses. He looked at Hilary gravely. Her heart was thumping.

'I think the character of Hubert is rather shadowy,' he said. 'I didn't quite understand him. I didn't feel you'd quite understood him.'

'Oh.'

'Cousin Hilda.'

'What?'

'I'm using Cousin Hilda's technique.'

'You don't mean . . . you can't mean. . . ?'

'I do mean. Everything else is absolutely magnificent. I think it's as near a masterpiece as dammit.'

'Oh darling.'

They kissed and hugged and wept. A smell of burning filled the room. Henry would never wear his mauve shirt again and, since she'd never liked it, Hilary's happiness was complete.

They had Anna to supper occasionally, to keep up for her parents' benefit the fiction that they were helping her to blossom as a woman. Twice she called their suppers off at the last moment, because she was blossoming as a woman elsewhere, but on one of the occasions when she did come, she said, 'I hear you've got a novel coming out, Hillers. Jolly good.'

'Yes, it is jolly good,' said Henry. 'It's a real work of the imagination. It's about a group of men in an old people's home. It's spare and elegant and truthful, with an icy wit but also with deep compassion.'

Henry had never seen Hilary blush before. They exchanged loving smiles, and Anna looked very wistful, as if she suddenly realised that Hilary *could* teach her something about blossoming as a woman.

1962 saw twenty-five people die of smallpox in Britain, the Liberals win a sensational victory in the Orpington by-election, and the arrest of 1,100 people in Parliament Square during a sit-down demonstration against nuclear weapons.

Henry received a long letter from Uncle Teddy:

Dear Henry,

I'm writing this to you alone and not to you both as it's family business and I want advice on something Hilary can't really help me about. Do show it to her if you want. She's a splendid girl, how you've captured anybody as good as that I just don't know. I hope her novel's a huge success, I'm sure it will be, she's so sensible.

Henry, things haven't worked out well for Doris and me, but I think about the old girl a great deal. When I was in clink, slopping out and resisting the amorous advances of burglars, wife-beaters and child-molesters, I'd never have thought that the Côte d'Azur would be like a prison, but I'm in another kind of prison here and because I'm free to leave and because there's no time limit to my sentence, and not even any point in behaving well because you don't get remission, it is in a funny sort of way more mentally disturbing than the other sort of prison.

I'm drinking Pernod as I sit here, trying to pretend I like it, why can't I drink G and T like all the other Brits? Anyway, what I'm delaying saying because it seems really silly is that I love Doris very much and realise that I always have. I don't regret Anna, she was great, best sex the old rascal ever had, but she was actually too good for me to want any other Doris substitute. I'm tired, Henry. Too tired to be an old rascal any more.

What I'm getting round to is asking if you think Doris is any happier with Geoffrey now than she was when you did all that go-between business. If she is happy, that's it, end of story. But if she isn't . . . well, could you bear to start all that up again?

Last time she wanted to get together and I didn't. Now I do and it'd be typical of life if she didn't.

I once thought Doris was an old bitch and life was lovely. Now I realise it's the other way round.

Love to Hilary and to you,
Teddy
PS I mean that. I realise now that I do love you. Probably I'd
never have been able to be emotional enough to tell you if I'd
not left England. So why do I want to come back so much?
PPS All the best to the Sniffer. I realise now that she can't
help being like she is.
PPPS If you do run into Anna, tell her I'm all right.

Henry did show Hilary the letter, and they decided that the
obvious thing to do was to go to Troutwick and try to find out just
how happy Auntie Doris really was.

It was Hilary's turn to drive, on a glorious spring morning. The
branches of the trees in the sodden gardens were furry with bud.
The sun shone on the windscreens of ice-cream vans making their
first trip of the year, and on the bald heads of old men as they
sauntered along to check if the bowling greens had dried out. In
the back of the car, Kate kept saying, 'Are we nearly there?' and
Jack echoed her, 'We near there?'

At last the long haul through the mill towns was over and they
were in the open country. There were still a few patches of snow
to the north of the dry-stone walls. A hundred thousand sheep
proclaimed the joy of spring. They were nearly there, and Kate
and Jack fell fast asleep.

Henry was aware, throughout the journey, of a great clash
between his head and his heart.

Please find that Doris and Geoffrey have discovered true peace
at last, said his head, because then there will be nothing more that
you need to do.

Oh I hope they aren't happy, said his heart. I'd love to see Doris
and Teddy together again, whatever the difficulties.

Henry gave the casting vote to his heart.

'Doris's' was dancing to the tune of spring. The bar windows
were open for the first time that year. Balmy zephyrs stirred the
pot plants on the piano top and the loins of young farmers at the
bar. Shoppers dumped their carrier bags under the antique tables.
Auntie Doris beamed.

They took their drinks into the garden, where Jack and Kate ran around and got very excited. It wasn't quite warm enough for sitting, but they didn't mind. Summer was coming to the high country. There was hope in their goose-pimples.

Auntie Doris sat with them for five minutes, but spent the whole time saying, 'Ah, bless them, aren't they lovely? Aren't you lovely children? Oh, Kate is pretty, love her. Oh and Jack's smile. That smile will turn women's knees to jelly. Oh, bless him.'

When Henry went to get more drinks, he managed to get served by Auntie Doris and said, 'On a lovely day like this, Auntie Doris, do you get the feeling, "My life is as wonderful as can be"?' but all Auntie Doris said was, 'No. I get the feeling, "Oh hell, I'm going to be rushed off my feet." '

It was half past three before the last customers had left. They went into Doris and Geoffrey's private quarters. Kate and Jack had eaten, but the adults were awash with drink and empty with hunger. Auntie Doris began to cook steak, fried onions and chips in her tiny kitchen. In their private living room, shabbier even than the pub and unadorned by antiques, Geoffrey Porringer snored obligingly, Hilary occupied the children with plasticine, and Henry went into the kitchen for a hurried chat with Auntie Doris.

'So, how are you really?' he enquired.

Auntie Doris looked at him in surprise.

'What's up with you today?' she asked. 'You're very interested in whether I'm happy all of a sudden.'

Henry cursed himself for his mistake even as he was making it. 'Well, Cousin Hilda asked me the other day if I thought you were happy. And this set me thinking about it.'

'What's it to do with her? I don't want my mental state discussed by the Sniffer. It's none of her business. Put some plates in the oven, there's a good lad.'

'Oh, I wasn't going to tell her.'

But voluble, indiscreet Auntie Doris was doing an impression of a clam.

They stayed till half past seven. Henry disliked driving home in the dark, but the children would sleep and with luck they wouldn't wake as they were carried to their beds back home.

Shortly before they left, in the quiet early evening bar, Henry said to Auntie Doris, in a low voice, 'That trouble you had with Geoffrey and the waitresses. Does he still . . . you know . . . touch them up?'

'I'm not telling you anything,' said Auntie Doris. 'You're too friendly with the Sniffer. You may not mean to tell her, but I know you, things'll slip out. Dried-up old cow.'

Henry felt that this was an implicit admission that things weren't all right, but it wasn't the definite answer that he needed. He realised, however, that he'd failed dismally in his secret investigations and he made a mental note not to set up a detective agency when at last he broke free from cucumbers.

He also felt that he couldn't let Auntie Doris's description of Cousin Hilda go unchallenged.

'You're unfair to Cousin Hilda,' he said. 'She's kind and loving, in her way.'

'I don't deny it,' said Auntie Doris. 'She's a kind, loving, dried-up old cow. Collect the empties for me, will you, there's a good lad?'

Henry hadn't thought of the possibility of seeking the truth from Geoffrey Porringer, but it was from Geoffrey that he learnt it.

Hilary was loading up the car with the children and all their paraphernalia, Henry was handing her things, including Jack, who was asleep, while also holding Kate's hand so that she didn't run into the road, and Geoffrey Porringer was watching them, with a soft smile on his face.

Auntie Doris leant out of the window and hissed, 'Help them, Teddy. Don't just stand there like a spare prick.'

'The name is Geoffrey, Doris, not Teddy,' hissed Geoffrey Porringer. He turned to Henry and said, 'Shall I take her hand?'

'No, no. It's quite all right. We've nearly finished,' said Henry.

'I get it all the time,' said Geoffrey Porringer. 'Do this, Teddy. Do that, Teddy. On her mind, you see. Dead for six years, and she still loves him. If I say, "I don't like kidneys, Doris," it's,

"Teddy liked kidneys." If I say, "I've got catarrh," it's, "Teddy never had catarrh," so I say nothing and it's, "Teddy never sulked, I'll say that for him." The man was my friend, Henry, so I know what he was like. A self-centred, inconsiderate rogue. Now he's a bloody saint. Death's immortalised the bastard.'

An American space-craft hit the moon, the last trolley bus ran in London and Coventry Cathedral was consecrated.

One Saturday morning towards the end of May, a couple of weeks before the publication of Hilary's novel, they left the children with Cousin Hilda, who was always secretly thrilled to have them, and went shopping for clothes, followed by a drink in the Pigeon and Two Cushions, and a meal at Thurmarsh's first Indian restaurant.

In the Pigeon and Two Cushions, Oscar welcomed Hilary ecstatically.

'Oh, madam!' he said. 'Madam! I've missed you. I thought you were dead. I nearly died the other day. Chest pains. I thought, "Hey up, Oscar Wintergreen, this is it, owd lad, your number's up, your time has come, the old ticker's finally had its chips." '

'I presume it hadn't,' said Hilary, 'since you're still here.'

'You deduce correctly,' said Oscar. 'Indigestion. Salami. Should have known better. Salami and me, we've never seen eye to eye. Anyroad, I were very sick. Oh sorry, madam. I shouldn't have brought that up. Oops! No joke intended. Anyroad, within two hours, right as rain, I were here as per usual that selfsame evening. So, where have you been?'

'Nowhere,' said Hilary. 'I've been having, and looking after, two children.'

Oscar's mouth opened, but no sound emerged, as he realised that he had never endured any health problems in that area. All he could do, therefore, was to fall back upon the question which, for all the pleasure of their reunion, they were longing to hear.

'What can I get you?' he said.

Henry had two pints of bitter, and Hilary had a gin and tonic, and they laughed at the suitability of Oscar having a surname that was also an ointment.

In the Taj Mahal, which was dark and empty as always on a Saturday morning, they sat in front of an enormous photograph of the eponymous edifice, and ate onion bhajis, lamb dhansak and chicken dopiaza, and Henry suddenly realised that Hilary was about to broach a difficult subject.

'Er. . . ,' she said.

'Er?' he said. 'What "er"?'

'The publishers want me to do a kind of promotional tour.'

'I see.'

'Just the major cities. London. Birmingham. Glasgow. Manchester.'

'How long would you be away?'

'A week.'

'What about the children?'

'Well that's obviously a problem. I suppose you'd have to take a week off and look after them.'

'But that'd mean using up my holiday.'

'I know. Obviously if you don't feel you can, there's no more to be said.'

The waiter saw the look on Henry's face, and approached hurriedly. He had a generous nature, a distinct talent on the sitar, a philosophical bent, a worrying pain in the left testicle, a desperate desire to be a doctor, fantasies about Petula Clark and a disturbing letter about the health of his mother in Hyderabad, but since all he said was, 'Is everything all right?' it is impossible, with the best will in the world, to reflect all these factors in dialogue.

'Yes, yes, everything's lovely,' said Henry. 'If I had a long face it's just . . . a personal problem.'

'Thank you, sir,' said the waiter inappropriately.

When the waiter had gone, Hilary said, 'I mean, I'd like to go, simply because they've put all their effort into my book and how can I expect them to do it if I'm not prepared to?'

'Not because you'd enjoy it?' said Henry as drily as a bhuna curry.

'Of course I'd enjoy it,' said Hilary. 'I love you very much, but it's only one week and it'd be interesting and, yes, I'd love to go.'

Henry grinned. 'Then you must go,' he said. 'It's a wonderful book and you deserve it.'

Hilary leant across and kissed him. The waiter beamed.

So Hilary went to London and Birmingham and Glasgow and Manchester and Henry got the children up and praised Jack for his success on the potty and dressed them and played with them and read them stories and Kate drew and painted and acted out little scenes she'd made up, and Jack put increasingly elaborate things together and pulled them to pieces again and laughed, and Henry cooked fish fingers and beans and dreamt of Hilary in French restaurants, and he said to himself, 'I am not jealous. I am not jealous. I am not jealous,' and sometimes it worked.

In the mornings he took the children to the Alderman Chandler Memorial Park, and it was there, sitting on a bench, watching them playing happily on the swings and roundabouts, that he fell into conversation with the Indian waiter.

'Have a sweet,' said the waiter. 'Indian sweet. Very sweet.'

'Thank you,' said Henry, taking the proffered delicacy. 'Oh yes. Very sweet.'

'Very sweet sweet.'

'Yes.'

They laughed.

'Life is an odd one, yes?' said the waiter.

'Well, yes. Very. Actually a very odd one.'

'Quite so. This morning, for instance. I have breakfast. I practise on the sitar.'

'Oh. You play the sitar?'

'Not very well.'

'I bet you do.'

'Well I suppose I have a talent. I play. I am happy. Then "ouch".'

'Ouch?'

'Back comes the worrying pain in my left testicle. I play a happy tune and I think, "Oh, if only I didn't have this pain," and I am happy and sad at the same time.'

They watched the children in silence for a few moments.

'Do you like being a waiter?' asked Henry.

'Not much. It is dreary work and many people are not like you. Many people are pigs,' said the waiter. 'I would much like to be a doctor.'

'One day, perhaps,' said Henry.

'Maybe, if I work hard. Your children?'

'Yes.'

'Very fine children.'

'Thank you.'

'I would love to have children by Petula Clark.'

'Good Lord.'

'I know, but she is a fine woman. I like Western women. Eastern women too. All women.'

'Sexy beast.'

'Alas, yes. But I ought not to wish for children by Petula Clark. It is impossible.'

'Unlikely, certainly.'

'One should never seek to attain the unattainable.'

'You have a philosophical bent.'

'Thank you.'

Kate fell and almost cried, but didn't, so Henry didn't interfere.

'Did you see me fall, Daddy?' she shouted.

'Yes.'

'Did you see me not cry?'

'Yes. Brave girl.'

'I inherited it from my mother in Hyderabad,' said the waiter.

'Sorry. What?' said Henry.

'My philosophical bent. She has eight children. Brings them up well. Her life is work. Work work work. In old age she gets her reward. Arthritis.' He stood up and shook Henry's hand. 'Count your blessings, my friend.'

7 The Contrasting Fortunes of Four Lovers

It was natural that on Hilary's return, the children should run to her with squeals of uninhibited delight, ignoring totally the person who'd looked after their every need for six long days. How wonderful, thought Henry, to be so oblivious of one's effect on other people.

'Tell me how helpful you've been to your wonderful daddy,' said Hilary.

Henry felt humiliated by her need to include him with such blatant tact. She was nervous, and this made him feel grumpy. The words that he'd planned – 'Oh, darling, I've missed you so much' – stuck in his craw. How often this seemed to happen to him.

'You're nervous,' he said. 'Why?'

'I was frightened you might be grumpy. And I was right to be frightened. You are grumpy.'

'I'm only grumpy because you didn't trust me not to be grumpy,' growled Henry.

Hilary made the mistake of laughing.

'It isn't funny,' said Henry. 'I see nothing funny in the break-up of a marriage.'

Hilary went even whiter than usual, and began to cry. Henry heard the voice of the Indian waiter, 'Count your blessings.'

He rushed over to her and said, 'Oh, I'm so sorry. I didn't mean it,' but she refused to let him kiss her properly.

He'd laid the table in the small, cosy kitchen, which at Hilary's suggestion he'd painted a cheery yellow. He'd even lit a candle. He'd made watercress soup and moussaka. Hilary said it was nice, and even the children ate a little, but it wasn't what he'd hoped for, and the fact that it was entirely his fault only made it worse.

At the end of the meal, Hilary said how lovely it had been.

'What, even after all the sophisticated food you've been having?'

'Best meal I've had all week.'

He didn't believe her, but he was pleased none the less.

'I'm sorry about earlier,' he said, as they washed up. 'I love you so much and I miss you so much that I can't cope sometimes.'

Hilary put her arms round him, lifted his 'Oxfam' apron, and touched his thigh gently.

He told her about the Indian waiter, and she laughed, and once again things were almost as they had once been.

During the summer of 1962, Hilary had a minor disappointment, and Henry had a minor success.

The minor disappointment was that Hilary's book, despite good reviews, was selling only modestly.

The minor success was that figures issued by Eddie Hapwood, Head of Research (Statistical), showed that in 1961, throughout the Northern Counties (Excluding Berwick-on-Tweed) production of cucumbers had risen by 1.932 per cent.

Hilary and the children came with Henry on one of his trips round the North Country, but the children grew bored in the car, and even the knowledge that they were passing through areas where people were growing 1.932 per cent more cucumbers failed to excite them for very long.

They flew to Spain for their holiday. Kate and Jack were incoherent with excitement. They ate paella and Spanish omelette and swam and grew brown and both Howard and Nadežda told Henry how much they loved him for making Hilary so happy, and Henry thought of the times when he'd made her miserable, and felt sick with guilt. He resolved, secretly, to be much better towards her when they returned home.

But all the time, whether lolling on the beach or being driven up into the dry hills, or catching the little train that wound painfully slowly through the orange groves near the coast, Henry was aware of the two important decisions that he must make – when to move out of cucumbers, and what to do about Uncle Teddy and Auntie Doris.

Shortly after their return, the Cuban Missile Crisis pushed the world to the brink of war. President Kennedy revealed that the United States had evidence of Russian missile bases in Cuba. He began a partial blockade of Cuba. Russian warships steamed towards Cuba. President Kennedy did not waver. The Russian warships turned back, the Russians agreed to remove the missile bases, America agreed to lift the blockade, and Henry decided, in this uncertain climate, not to move out of cucumbers until 1963.

He also decided that he *must* tell Auntie Doris about Uncle Teddy.

'I've no choice,' he told Hilary. 'He's unhappy, she's unhappy, even Geoffrey Porringer's unhappy.'

'I agree,' said Hilary. 'I'm surprised you've delayed so long.'

'It's a big responsibility, interfering in people's lives,' said Henry. 'It's a terrible responsibility. I think, before I actually do it, I'd better write to Uncle Teddy to check if it's still what he really wants.'

Dear Uncle Teddy [he wrote],

I'm sorry not to have been in touch before, but I just haven't known what to do. I've decided now that I will act as a go-between for you, if you solemnly swear that you really do love Auntie Doris and will commit yourself to her till death do you part.

Kate is at school full time now and loving it, she's very bright. Jack is more the practical type. He's into everything, naughty but lovely. Hilary's getting on well with her second novel, set in a glue factory! She doesn't want me to read it before it's finished.

Work is going pretty well for me too. Would you ever have guessed, when you took me into your home that snowy day in that awful winter of 1947, that fifteen years later I'd be responsible, virtually single-handed, for an increase of 1.932 per cent in cucumber yields in Northern England (Excluding Berwick-on-Tweed)?

I look forward to your reply and hopefully setting the whole thing in motion very soon.

We hope you'll have a happy Christmas and that 1963 will see the beginning of a great new life for you.

Lots of love,

Henry and Hilary (not forgetting Kate and Jack)

They had a Christmas card from Uncle Teddy, but it had crossed Henry's letter. His message read:

I hope you all have a lovely Christmas. Very disappointed not to have had any news re what we discussed. No news or bad news or you forgot or just got too busy? Sorry there's no lolly enclosed. Fings ain't wot they used t'be in import–export.

And then there was nothing. A year that was to leave the world a very changed place began with a giant freeze, with heavy snowfalls and frost night and day for several weeks. Henry rushed to the post each morning. Bills, giant carpet sales, one fan letter for Hilary – I wonder if you are a relation of Gloria Lewthwaite, who did water-colours, mainly of lighthouses, before the First World War – but nothing from Uncle Teddy.

And then at last, towards the end of February, there was a letter from France:

Dear Henry,

I'm sorry not to have replied to your letter. I went skiing at Megeve over Christmas [So much for fings not being wot they used to be import–export, thought Henry wryly] and had a most unfortunate accident and broke two legs, one of which was mine. I had to hang around in hospital for quite a while, also I had to make sure the other man, a postman from Rouen, was all right before I left. Luckily, both our legs are mending well, though I don't know how long it'll be before he's doing his rounds again.

Anyway, to business. I simply can't give the promise you seek. I've had enough of broken promises. I've discovered that life is a miserable sod which can't be trusted for a second. Rather like Geoffrey Porringer, really. What I do swear, on a bottle of the twenty-five-year-old Macallan, is that I love Doris very much, and I *intend* and *want* to commit myself to her till the old bastard of a reaper carries us to our respective destinations – her up, me down! If that's good enough for you, we're on with the great adventure. If not, well, common sense will have prevailed.

I'd like to return to England to live, with a new identity. I can get a false passport, no problem, in exchange for certain services.

Love to you all,
Uncle Teddy

Henry's reply, written on Cucumber Marketing Board paper, when he should have been writing a report on 'Late Cropping Ridge Cucumbers of the Solway Firth' for the *Vegetable Growers' Gazette*, was quite brief:

Dear Uncle Teddy,
Thank you very much for your letter. Sorry about the broken leg. Also about the postman's broken leg, although, since I don't know him and therefore can't love him except theoretically, I'm not as concerned about his leg as about yours.

I'm thrilled you want to go ahead, and am happy with your assurances. They're very honest and I respect that more than empty promises.

I have certain principles, boring though you may find them, and I have to ask you, before I go ahead, to promise that the 'certain services' that you can get a passport in exchange for are not addictive drugs, anything to do with armaments of any kind, or an introduction to the Masons.

With lots of love from us all as ever,
Henry.

John Profumo, Secretary of State for War, told the House of

Commons that he'd committed no impropriety with a girl called Christine Keeler. Dr Beeching announced his solution to Britain's traffic problem. He would close large numbers of railways. In April, Henry received his long-awaited reply from Uncle Teddy:

> Dear Henry,
> Again, sorry for the delay, but an opportunity came to mix business with pleasure in Barcelona, and I never look a gift horse in the mouth, in case all the others fall and it wins.
> I wouldn't touch drugs, I don't have the contacts for armaments, and I never liked the Masons. All that rolling-up of trouser legs plays havoc with your creases. I'll tell you what my little adventure consists of when we meet.
> I can't wait to see Doris again. Awaiting your reply eagerly, as ever.
> Lots of love,
> Uncle Teddy
> PS Better meet in 'the smoke'. Too many people know me in Yorkshire.

So there was no more reason to delay telling Auntie Doris. Waves of excitement and dread swept over Henry.

They met at the Fig Leaf, an expensive and enormously fashionable restaurant near Keighley, run by two retired furniture restorers, Daniel Westerbrook and Quentin Cloves, whose behaviour made Denzil and Lampo seem like heterosexual quantity surveyors. Only the fact that the wives of three senior police officers thought it the best food for fifty miles had saved them from investigation.

The place tinkled with prettiness. Cupids and cherubs abounded, private parts hidden by the eponymous leaves.

'Doris!' exclaimed Quentin Cloves, kissing her on both cheeks and some of her chins. 'Darling! Wonderful to see a human face!' He lowered his voice. 'The briefcase brigade everywhere today. So boring. The soup of the day is chervil, the fish of the day is red mullet baked with rosemary, and the lamb with mustard and honey crust is, like Dante's comedy, divine. And aren't you going to introduce me to your friend?'

'My nephew, Henry Pratt,' said Auntie Doris.

'Welcome to the Fig Leaf, Henry Pratt. You have a wonderful aunt,' said Quentin Cloves.

All this didn't make things any easier. Auntie Doris would have to give up all this celebrity if she went back to Uncle Teddy.

'I'd never have thought you'd find a place like this in Yorkshire,' said Henry.

'It's just the beginning,' said Auntie Doris. 'In the years to come, the broad acres will be awash with fashionable food.'

In the chummy bar, which was like an antique shop with drinks, Henry found it impossible to give his staggering news without being overheard, but as soon as they were at their table, he began.

'Auntie Doris?' he said. 'I asked you out to tell you something.'

'O'oh! I'm intrigued.'

'We must keep our voices down. Nobody must hear.'

'I'm *very* intrigued.'

'What I'm going to say may shock you.'

'You're not leaving Hilary for Quentin Cloves!'

'It's . . . it's about you, and it's . . . something very difficult to say.'

'I'm nervous, Henry. That's why I'm trying to joke.'

'There's no need to be nervous. It's not bad news.'

'Well thank God for that.'

'It's about Uncle Teddy.'

'Uncle Teddy? What news can there be about him? He's been dead seven years.'

'Yes, well . . . that's the point, you see. He . . . er . . . what? Oh the terrine . . . Thank you.'

Auntie Doris was giving him a strange, intense look. Had she guessed? He realised that, nervous though he was, he was enjoying being in possession of a sensational secret. He hadn't wanted her to guess. Damn the waitress.

As soon as the waitress had gone, he told her.

'He didn't die in that fire. He's still alive.'

'What? But they found the body.'

'That was . . . somebody else. Nobody you know.'

'Well where is he?'

'Cap Ferrat.'

'Cap Ferrat? That was our place.'

'Exactly. I think he's loved you all along.'

'Why are you telling me this now?'

'He wants you back, Auntie Doris. And so do I.'

'Good Lord! Well, I . . . Good Lord!' Auntie Doris took a mouthful of her *ballottine* of lobster, and chewed like an automaton. 'I feel dizzy,' she said. 'I feel faint.'

'I'm sure you do,' said Henry. 'Drink some wine.'

Auntie Doris took a gulp of Pouilly-Fuissé.

'That's better,' she said. 'I thought I was going to pass out. I thought, "I wish Henry was telling me this outside, on the moors, in the wind." I felt . . .'

'Claustrophobic.'

'Yes. You are serious, aren't you?'

'Would I joke about something so important?'

'So . . . why did he do all this?'

'It was all . . . ,' Henry lowered his voice still further, 'financial shenanigans. Property.'

'I told him he should get into property.'

'Well he did.'

'So whose was the body in the Cap Ferrat?'

'I can't tell you. People still living might get hurt. Nobody you know.'

Auntie Doris raised another piece of the *ballottine* to her mouth. Suddenly her fork stopped, and she asked the question Henry had dreaded. 'Why didn't he tell me?'

'He . . . er . . . I think I'd better tell you the whole truth.'

'People usually say that when they're about to tell you half the truth.'

'Well I'll tell the whole truth. There was a woman.'

'A younger woman?'

'Er . . . slightly.'

'Who was this slightly younger woman?'

'Oh Lord. I can't tell you that either.'

'People still living might get hurt?'

'Yes.'

'Is she dead too?'

'Oh no. She left him . . . with her tail between her legs after he'd thrown her out.'

'I see.'

'You're the only person he's ever loved, Auntie Doris.'

'Well, he's the only person I've ever loved, Henry. Have you seen him?'

'Yes, we stayed with him in Cap Ferrat just after this slightly younger woman had . . . been thrown out.'

'So! He took her to Cap Ferrat! That was our place. He shouldn't have taken her to Cap Ferrat.'

'A psychiatrist would say he took her there because subconsciously he wished she was you.'

'I'm sure he would if you paid him enough.'

'He has a nice villa, a good life, many friends, a thriving . . . import–export business. He wants to give all that up, and come back to England . . . and you.'

'Well!'

'I wish he could. I love you both, you see.'

'I still can't think why.'

'Neither can I, but we won't go into that.'

'What do you think I should do?'

'Meet him in London. See how it develops. Find out what you feel about him.'

'What'll I tell Geoffrey?'

'Shopping trip with Hilary.'

'You're a very resourceful liar.'

'Must have been my upbringing.'

'Oh God. Were we totally awful? Henry, I heard your friend Tommy Marsden on the telly, saying, "It hasn't really sunk in yet." I thought, "God, you must be thick, if you don't realise you've scored the winning goal in the Cup Final." I see what he meant now. This hasn't sunk in. So many questions. What about Geoffrey? Where would we live?'

'Would you feel bad about giving up the White Hart?'

'Bad? I'd be thrilled. Don't get me wrong, I've loved it. It's done wonders for my self-confidence. But you've heard the phrase, "A legend in his own lunchtime." Well I have to drink the lunchtimes of my legend, and it'll kill me. Oh my God!'

'What?'

'Teddy can't see me like this, with all these chins. Oh my God.'

'He won't mind. He's got a paunch and his legs are going thin.'

'No, but . . . has he? Oh, poor Teddy. No, but I'm huge. It's served its purpose. I have to lose weight. Teddy will mind.'

'What do you mean, "It's served its purpose"?'

'Kept the customers happy – they think I've a huge personality because I'm huge – and put Geoffrey off sex. I don't like sex with Geoffrey any more. I keep thinking of those waitresses. And the blackheads are getting worse.'

'Well there you are, then.'

'Yes.'

Quentin Cloves had a curious ability to walk across a room without seeming to move his legs. He floated towards them now.

'And how was the famous Fig Leaf *ballottine d'homard*?' he asked.

'Wonderful,' said Auntie Doris. 'Magnificent. Supreme.'

Quentin Cloves looked gratified. But when he'd gone, Auntie Doris said, 'The sad thing is, what with all this, I just didn't taste it at all.'

Henry waited three weeks before replying to Uncle Teddy, to give Auntie Doris time to go to a health farm.

Her visit was an enormous success, or rather a ceasing to be enormous success, and she followed her strict regime impeccably even after her release, a day early, for good behaviour. But, as her weight dropped off, her face became gaunt. She aged, through dieting too quickly, and she lost energy. Geoffrey Porringer, at first enthusiastic over the venture, didn't enjoy its fruits, and the more fickle among the customers felt the place wasn't what it was, the beer wasn't kept as well, it wasn't as clean, service was more surly, it was resting on its laurels, when in fact nothing had changed except Auntie Doris's weight.

Auntie Doris was pleased, if also slightly offended, that Geoffrey Porringer's sexual appetite didn't increase as expected.

Then there was a delay before Uncle Teddy's reply – 'Sorry I didn't write sooner but an opportunity to visit Italy came up.'

In the meantime, Hilary was getting on well with her second novel. Although sales of *In the Dog House* had been modest, and the advance on *All Stick Together* hadn't been sensational, these sums, added to Henry's utterly secure if not startlingly large salary, had given them the confidence to make an offer for a larger house, with three bedrooms.

Dumbarton House was a 1930s property, more modern Georgian than mock-Georgian, in Waterloo Crescent, off Winstanley Road, slightly too near to the town centre to be truly part of the posh suburb of Winstanley, where they brought their fish and chips home in briefcases. Neither of them liked it as much as Paradise Villa, but it had the extra bedroom they needed, and a secure garden, and Cousin Hilda said, 'Mrs Wedderburn said, "It'll be further away for them." I said, "Yes, Mrs Wedderburn, but old houses just aren't synonymous with small children." "They'll still visit you regularly, though," she said. "Oh yes," I said, "though Henry has his cucumbers, which keep him right busy, and bringing up children is a full-time job even if you aren't writing a novel as well." She said, "I can't understand why she writes novels, a nice girl like her. I prefer biographies, me. At least you know they're true." She's very direct, is Mrs Wedderburn, but she has a heart of gold. Where I'd ever have found another friend like her I do not know.'

In the summer of 1963 the Profumo affair swept away old certainties about the probity of British public life. By the end of the summer, a society osteopath called Stephen Ward had revealed the truth about John Profumo's relationship with Christine Keeler. By the end of the year, Profumo would have resigned, Ward would have been found guilty of living on immoral earnings and died of a drugs overdose, the Prime Minister Harold Macmillan would have been succeeded by Sir Alex Douglas-Home, and Christine Keeler would be in prison for perjury over the trial of her West Indian associate, Aloysius 'Lucky' Gordon.

In the midst of all this, Henry 'not so lucky' Pratt sat at his desk on a sultry August day, and found no enthusiasm for his task – the preparation of the first draft of a consultative document to be presented to Roland Stagg (to be rejected by him if bad, and claimed as his own if good) under the snappy title 'The Way Forward – Cucumber Distribution in the Seventies. A centralised chilled store for the Northern Counties – a Study of Feasibility and Location.' On this summer dog day this podgy and exhausted young dog couldn't even summon up enthusiasm for his other great task – the scouring of the Situations Vacant columns for alternative employment.

This was because, in his mind, he was elsewhere.

Where was he, in his mind?

He was in the restaurant of the Hotel Magnifique, in London, with Uncle Teddy and Auntie Doris.

The Hotel Magnifique no longer exists, mercifully, but in 1963 it was the ideal venue for a romantic encounter. The restaurant was so large, and the customers were so few, and the service was so slow, that one achieved almost total privacy. The lights were so dim that the lines on ageing faces were invisible. The food was so bland that it couldn't possibly interrupt any train of thought or emotion. The bill was so enormous that the lady could never accuse the gentleman of meanness again.

Uncle Teddy gave a nervous, stiff smile, as if for a photograph he didn't want taken, and said, 'You look wonderful, Doris.'

'I don't,' said Auntie Doris, 'but thank you. But you *do* look wonderful.'

'I don't either, but thank *you*,' said Uncle Teddy.

'So, I'm a bigamist, like you, to add to my other crimes.'

'My God, I suppose you are. What other crimes?'

'Receiving stolen goods. Smuggling. Tax evasion. Fraud. All the things that came with living with you.'

'Doris!'

'Anyway, I've got a good defence if I'm ever arrested for bigamy. The fact that you were certified dead by a Coroner's Court should get me off.'

An elderly waiter limped towards them across the cavernous restaurant, which had the look of a ballroom on a liner. He carried menus which had the wingspans of giant condors.

'At last!' said Uncle Teddy.

'I beg your pardon, sir?' said the waiter.

'You aren't exactly Speedy Gonzales, are you?'

'Geoffrey!' hissed Auntie Doris. 'Tact.'

'The name is Teddy, Doris. And why are we Teddying, anyway?' said Uncle Teddy. 'Two minutes together and already I'm being Teddyed.'

'Well, honestly,' said Auntie Doris, who always made things worse by protesting about them. 'Fancy complaining about the speed of service to a man with a deformed foot.'

'Doris!'

It was as if Uncle Teddy had never gone to prison and come out to find Auntie Doris living with his best friend and pretended to be killed in a fire and gone to live in France with a slightly younger woman, aged nineteen, while Auntie Doris married his best friend. There were no great statements of love and regret, of guilt and shame. They just slipped back into the old ways, they Dorised and Teddyed together through a long, bad meal, and knew that they wanted to spend the rest of their lives together.

As the summer died, so did Henry's enthusiasm for finding another job. He was simply too busy. In the evenings and at weekends, he kept the children amused while Hilary finished her novel. Jack was almost four now, and soon he'd be as good at football as Henry. Kate rode her bicycle round the Alderman

Chandler Memorial Park at a pace which terrified him. Jack climbed with ease trees that other children and cats and firemen found difficult. Both children courted serious accidents and defied warnings. Neither ever suffered anything worse than grazed knees and elbows, but Henry's nerves were shattered. And when the children fell exhausted into bed, he fell exhausted into redecorating Dumbarton House. Small wonder that he was having difficulty concentrating on the second draft of 'The Way Forward – Cucumber Distribution in the Seventies. A centralised chilled store for the Northern Counties – a Study of Feasibility and Location.' They had a new car now, well a new used car, a Mini. It nosed its way to York and Tyneside and Wearside, to Lancaster and the Solway Firth, so that its proud owner could examine the nine possible sites that had been short-listed for the projected chilled store.

When Hilary's editor said that the ending of *All Stick Together* was slightly too farcical, he suggested that it was his turn to come to her. She, having no idea that Henry thought of her editor as a middle-aged, bespectacled, stooping, bookish wreck, suggested a Saturday, when she wouldn't have to fetch the children from school, and Henry could take them out for the day.

Henry took the children to York, leaving before the arrival of the editor. They had a good day, particularly enjoying the Railway Museum and the Castle Museum, which had a complete Victorian street. But the children grew tired, and they arrived home before the editor had left.

Henry's first sight of Nigel Clinton sent his whole world spinning. He had a strong sensation of falling and was astounded to find that he was actually standing absolutely normally on the stridently orange and purple carpet that they hated and couldn't yet afford to replace. Nigel Clinton was twenty-five, Oxford educated, tall and dark. It was only in Henry's mind that he was the most good-looking man who ever walked this earth, but he was undeniably handsome and, being determined to be a successful man of letters, he was seriously embarrassed by his looks, so that he smiled at new arrivals with a self-conscious shyness that merely increased his sex appeal.

'Are you all right, darling?' Hilary asked Henry anxiously.

'Fine. Just tired.'

She kissed him warmly – perhaps, he thought, a little too warmly. Had she something to hide?

Henry found himself absurdly anxious to impress this young man, and on the whole he was sorry that his next remark, 'Still at it, then?' was such a banal statement of the obvious, and when Nigel said, 'This is a nice house, Henry, and a lovely street,' with an air of surprise, Henry regretted responding with, 'Oh yes, Nigel. We have all sorts of things in the North – shops that sell books, theatres that put on plays. I could even show you an off-licence that stocks green chartreuse.'

He took the children into the formica-infested kitchen, and started to make their tea, regretting that it was something as unsophisticated as egg, sausage and baked beans.

Jack soon grew bored and said, 'I'm going to see Mummy.'

'Don't. She's working,' said Henry.

'I need to see her,' said Jack, who often said 'need' when he meant 'want'.

Henry, tired from the excursion and flustered by Nigel Clinton, broke his first rule of good parenthood. He made a threat that he couldn't sustain. 'If you do,' he said, 'you'll go straight to bed without your tea.'

Jack went to the living room.

Kate sighed.

'My brother can be a real pain sometimes,' she said.

Henry turned the gas off, went into the living room, and apologised to Hilary and Nigel for the interruption.

'It's all right,' said Hilary. 'He just wanted to say "hello". He loves his mummy.'

'Everybody loves his mummy,' growled Henry. 'Now come on, Jack. Please.'

'Will I get my tea?'

'Yes!!'

The little perisher gave Henry a triumphant look and said, 'Bye bye, Mummy. Have a good work. It's nice to meet you, Nigel.'

As he shut the door, Henry heard Nigel say, 'What a charming, well-mannered boy.'

Henry put the gas on again.

'Nigel's taller than you, isn't he, Daddy?' said Jack.

'Much taller,' agreed Henry grimly.

'Why is he taller than you, Daddy?' asked Kate.

'I expect he always ate his tea,' said Henry.

This glib piece of parental opportunism was greeted with the disgust it merited, and the doorbell rang.

It was Auntie Doris, with three large suitcases and no money for the taxi.

'I've done it,' she announced as she swept past Henry. 'I've told him. I've left him. Oh!'

She looked surprised and put out by the presence of Nigel. This was her big scene and there shouldn't be an unknown supporting player there.

'Tea's burning, Daddy,' called Kate.

'Oh shit,' quipped Henry stylishly, and he hurried to the kitchen.

'Auntie Doris, this is my editor, Nigel Clinton,' said Hilary. 'Nigel, Doris Porringer.'

Auntie Doris flinched. She hated being called Doris Porringer. She shook hands with Nigel, and wished that she'd done her make-up properly before leaving.

'I've just left my . . . nice to meet you, Nigel . . . my husband,' she said. 'Teddy's coming over on Monday and I've . . . oh, sorry, are you working? Am I interrupting? I should have rung, but I thought on a Saturday . . . and I'm all of a dither with everything.'

'Of course you are,' said Hilary. 'Are you in a desperate rush, Nigel?'

'No, no,' said Nigel, the almost impossibly obliging. 'We're almost through, and it'll do us good to take a break. Final little fine adjustments,' he explained to Auntie Doris.

'Ah!' said Auntie Doris blankly. 'Yes, I've told him, and I wondered if I could stay till Monday when I meet Teddy.'

Henry, having provided the children's tea at last, joined them.

'Well . . . er . . . well, yes, of course,' he said. 'We'll move Jack in with Kate.'

'Oh Lord. Is it a nuisance? I should have rung,' said Auntie Doris.

'It's no problem,' said Hilary.

'No problem at all,' said Henry.

'The kids'll love it,' said Hilary.

'They'll love it,' said Henry.

Oh my God. Bloody Nigel will think I have all the conversational sparkle of a rather dim parrot.

'Can I get you a drink, Auntie Doris?' said Henry. 'Do you mind if we have a drink, Nigel? It is a bit of a crisis.'

'No, no. I have all the time in the world. Honestly,' smiled Mr Too-Good-to-be-True.

'Let's all have a drink,' said Hilary. 'What have we got, Henry?'

'Gin but no tonic and whisky but no soda, and some unchilled white wine,' growled Henry 'Never Got Further than Thurmarsh Grammar, the Short-Arse of the Cucumber Cock-up Corporation' Pratt.

'Whisky and tap water sounds good to me,' said Nigel 'Oxford Graduate Bet He Got a Bloody Double First, Mr Smarm-Bomb' Clinton.

'Suits me too,' said Hilary.

'I could manage a bit of gin with . . . more gin,' said Auntie Doris.

Henry went to mix . . . to *get* the drinks, mix would be an exaggeration . . . but he could still hear every word.

'I've left my husband, Nigel,' explained Auntie Doris. 'We run the White Hart at Troutwick. You may know it.'

'No, but it sounds delightful.'

'I'm madly in love with a man called Miles Cricklewood.'

'Ah.'

'He's a retired vet.'

'Gosh. Sorry to sound a bit dense, but . . . er . . . if you're in love with this Miles Cricklewood, who's Teddy?'

'That's what I call Miles,' said Auntie Doris. 'I don't like his real name.'

'Your taste does you credit,' said Nigel Clinton. 'If Hilary called a character Miles Cricklewood, unless it was a false name adopted by some rather dodgy type, I'd throw it out.'

Hooray hooray hooray maybe there is a God after all Mr Perfecto has put his foot in it and called Uncle Teddy a dodgy type by implication! Henry almost danced in with the drinks and then he realised that it wasn't as much fun as all that because Nigel would never know that he'd put his foot in it.

'But real life fact is very different from fictional fact,' Hilary was saying. 'If I put an editor like you in one of my books he'd seem impossibly tactful and intelligent.'

'And handsome,' said Auntie Doris.

'And tall,' said Jack, entering with a half-eaten orange. 'Don't forget tall.'

'Thank you. Thank you, all of you,' said Nigel. 'If you put me in your book, I'd have to say, "This is all right if you're creating a character who's learning the ropes in order to become *extremely* successful later on." '

'If I gave him dialogue as conceited as that, I'd have to think he was *very* over-ambitious,' said Hilary.

'Touché,' said Nigel Clinton.

'Don't drop your orange on the carpet, Jack,' was Henry's sparkling contribution to the fanciful cut and thrust.

Auntie Doris, who looked completely bewildered, returned to her dramatic situation.

'Teddy and I are going to live in Suffolk, where he won't be recognised,' she said.

'Excuse me,' said Nigel Clinton, 'but why doesn't he want to be recognised?'

There was a pause.

Kate entered, also with a half-eaten orange.

'Get a plate, Kate,' said Henry.

'You're a poet and you know it,' said Kate.

Henry blushed for fear Nigel thought his childish rhyming had been deliberate.

'Sorry,' persisted Nigel, 'but why doesn't he want to be recognised?'

'He's very famous and very shy,' said Hilary.

'I've never heard of him,' said Nigel.

'You were amazingly right about the name not being real,' said Henry. 'Who's a clever editor? Except, of course, that he isn't a dodgy type.'

Whoopee!! Bull's eye. OXFORD GRADUATE LOSES COMPOSURE IN POST-DODGY TYPE-SMEAR BLUSHING CATASTROPHE.

'If we told you his real name, you'd know him,' said Hilary.

'Well, it wouldn't go any further,' said Nigel.

'Sorry,' said Henry. 'We can't make exceptions.'

'How did Geoffrey take it?' asked Hilary.

'With milk and sugar,' said Kate.

'Very good, very funny, but Auntie Doris is a bit upset, so hush, dear,' said Henry.

'Badly. I left him sitting there, just staring into space,' said Auntie Doris.

'Well, he isn't staring into space now,' said Henry. 'He's walking up the garden path.'

They hurried Auntie Doris upstairs. Nigel swept the children out into the garden for a game, and Henry let Geoffrey Porringer in. He almost stumbled into the living room, and sat down heavily.

'Doris has left me,' he mumbled.

'What??' exclaimed Henry.

'No!!' cried Hilary.

Henry and Hilary exchanged shamed looks at all this pretence which was sullying the genuine grief of Geoffrey Porringer.

'You didn't know?' said Geoffrey Porringer.

'Not an inkling,' lied Henry. 'When did this happen?'

'This afternoon.'

'Where's she gone?'

'To live with some bloody vet.'

'I don't believe it.'

They all became aware of the suitcases at the same time.

'Those are her suitcases!! Is she here?' said Geoffrey Porringer.

'What? No, of course not.'

'We have the same suitcases as hers,' said Hilary.

'We admired her suitcases,' said Henry, 'and she told us where she got them, and we got the same set.'

'Why are your suitcases in the middle of the floor?'

'We're going on holiday. We're catching the night ferry,' said Henry. 'We must be off soon, in fact.'

'Very soon,' said Hilary. 'I'm awfully sorry, but there it is.'

'But what'll I do?' said Geoffrey Porringer.

'I honestly don't see what you can do,' said Henry. 'Look, I feel really embarrassed about having to hurry you out, Uncle Geoffrey, but I'll come and see you when we get back.'

They couldn't bring themselves to say that they were sorry about the break-up, having engineered it. Nor could they bring themselves to point out that he'd brought it all on himself by his touching up of waitresses.

They led him gently to his car, and watched him drive off, jerkily, with much crashing of gears.

Auntie Doris came downstairs, and Nigel came in from the garden with Kate and Jack.

'Nigel's even more fun than he's tall, Daddy,' said Kate.

'No, he's taller than he's fun, but he is fun,' said Jack.

'I'm not sure that your book is too farcical after all,' said Nigel Clinton.

Auntie Doris and Uncle Teddy took a rented flat in Ipswich, and scoured Suffolk for their dream home, and Cousin Hilda greeted the news of Auntie Doris's running off from Geoffrey Porringer to Miles Cricklewood with a sniff and a 'Leopards never change their spots.' Henry wished he could have told her that Auntie Doris wasn't as loose as she imagined, but Cousin Hilda would tell Mrs Wedderburn, and if Mrs Wedderburn knew they might as well put an advertisement in the *Argus*. Cousin Hilda had told them only recently, 'Gossip is that woman's Achilles' heel.'

On the day after his imaginary holiday, Henry drove to Troutwick, rehearsing every detail of the holiday he hadn't had. He needn't have bothered, because Geoffrey Porringer was too wrapped up in his own affairs to ask anything.

As he entered the pub, Henry met a pregnant Lorna Lugg coming down the main stairs after taking a tray of drinks to the Residents' Lounge.

'You're still here!' he exclaimed.

'Only Sundays,' said Lorna Lugg, née Arrow. 'Eric cooks dinner Sundays.'

'Eric cooks!'

'Well he *was* in the Catering Corps.'

'Of course. What does he do now?'

'He's a quarryman. He sets off explosions.'

'Good Lord! I see you're expecting your second.'

'My fourth.'

'Your fourth! What have you got?'

'Two girls. Marlene and Doreen. One boy. Kevin.'

'Lorna!' called Geoffrey Porringer.

'I must go,' said Lorna Lugg. She smiled. 'He doesn't touch me up any more.'

I'm not surprised, thought Henry. You aren't a pretty girl any more. Oh, Eric, you've turned my pretty Lorna into a baby factory.

Henry ordered a pint, to make his visit look less like a mission of mercy, and also because he was thirsty.

'Quiet today,' he commented.

'Doris was the one with the personality,' said Geoffrey Porringer. 'But we'll get by.'

'How are you really?' asked Henry.

'The staff are being very supportive.' Geoffrey Porringer pulled Henry's pint. 'Ollie's been a tower of strength. My regulars have stood by me. We'll survive.'

'Well I wish you the very best of luck, Uncle Geoffrey.' Henry raised his glass.

'Thank you.' Geoffrey Porringer clinked glasses dully. 'I'd hate to offend you, young sir. I've always had a lot of time for you. But, you see, I have to look forward. So I'd rather you didn't call me Uncle Geoffrey any more.'

Henry did feel a little offended, especially as he'd only called him Uncle Geoffrey to please him.

'Not offended, I hope?'

'No, no. No, no.'

'Good. Wouldn't want to offend you. You've been a good friend, but, you see . . . your aunt was a wonderful woman, but . . . larger than life. I was in her shadow. I'm on my own now, like it or not, and I'm going to give it my best shot, so there's no family now and I'm not an uncle.'

'I understand.'

'I hope so. Would you understand, Henry, if I . . . if I said, "End of chapter. That particular album closed." If I said, and I mean it, I really do, thank you for coming, but I'd be happier, this sounds awful, I know, but there it is, happier if . . . well I suppose if I didn't see any of Doris's family any more. Give me more of a chance.'

'Well, if you're sure.'

'Oh yes. I'll tell you one thing, Henry. I don't like the smell of this Cricklewood fellow. Retired vet. Fishy. Wouldn't surprise me if the chap turned out to be a rotter. Wouldn't, Henry, not one bit. Well if Doris thinks she could ever come back to me she's got another think coming. Serve that gentleman, would you, Ollie? Thanks. Another think coming, Henry. Honestly.'

'Well, fair enough,' said Henry. 'Well, I'll be off, then. Good luck, Unc . . . Geoffrey. And, if you ever do change your mind, feel you do need me, get in touch, won't you?'

'Will do, young sir. Will do.'

President Kennedy was assassinated in Dallas on November 22nd, and Henry was the only person in Britain who couldn't remember where he was at the time. He did remember that it seemed like the end of innocence and hope, though that would change with time.

In time, President Kennedy's death would begin the modern world's loss of naïvety about its leaders, and that, at least, was a blessing.

The world lost Pope John XXIII, Hugh Gaitskell in his prime, and Edith Piaf, who could still have been in her prime. Frank Sinatra Junior and the Spanish footballer Alfredo Di Stefano were kidnapped. It needed federal troops to enforce the de-segregation of the University of Alabama, but at least it was done. Perhaps it was suitably bizarre that the year which witnessed the sensational rise of the Beatles should end with the American hit parade topped for the whole of December with a song called 'Dominique', sung by a Belgian nun.

By then, Hilary had finished her rewrites, and Henry was fighting hard against his jealousy of Nigel Clinton.

In the spring of 1964, Uncle Teddy and Auntie Doris found their dream cottage in a pretty village called Monks Eleigh. It was called 'Honeysuckle Cottage'. Uncle Teddy was all for renaming it 'Cap Ferrat'. 'Over my dead body,' said Auntie Doris. 'You took her there.' 'What do you want to call it, then, Doris? "Dunsmugglin"?' said Uncle Teddy. 'What's wrong with "Honeysuckle Cottage"?' said Auntie Doris. 'It's so unoriginal,' said Uncle Teddy. 'That's what I like about it,' said Auntie Doris. 'Our adventure is over. We're now going to enjoy the evening of our lives, in "Honeysuckle Cottage".'

All Stick Together was published in October. Advance sales were good, and the publishers wanted Hilary to embark on another tour, so Henry again took a week of his holidays to look after the children.

On his last day before his week's holiday, he felt quite important. His recommendation of two smaller chilled stores, in Darlington and Preston, had found favour and was to be implemented. He didn't feel bitter that it was being passed off as Roland Stagg's idea. He knew the kind of world he lived in. He too had lost some of his naïvety.

'Have a nice holiday,' said Roland Stagg, leaving half an hour early to miss the traffic.

'Thank you. I won't,' said Henry.

He didn't. As day succeeded day, as Hilary toured bookshops and radio stations, the figure of Nigel Clinton was everywhere. It waited for the children outside their schools, it played with them in the Alderman Chandler Memorial Park, it stirred the stew-pot and cooked fish fingers with them. Henry grew more and more certain that his jealousy was not irrational. At night, especially, he knew that Nigel Montgomery Clinton was kissing and touching where he had kissed and touched. It was instinct that made him get up at three thirty-five on the Thursday morning, and go to Hilary's second-best jeans, her writing jeans, and there in the back pocket he found the letter, as afterwards he believed that he had known he would:

> Dearest Hilary,
> I love you so much, darling. . . .

He asked Alastair and Fiona Blair, who had children at the same school, if they would fetch the children that day, and drove madly, wildly, tearfully, angrily, crazily, past Retford and Newark and Love You and Grantham and So Much and Stamford and Peterborough and Darling and Huntingdon and Cambridge and Love You So Much, my Newmarket and Lavenham, towards the nearest to parents that he knew, the nearest to a family that he had ever known.

Uncle Teddy and Auntie Doris were weeding the pretty garden of their sugar-loaf cottage as if the words 'import' and 'export' had never existed.

They greeted him ecstatically.

'Welcome to our domestic bliss,' said Uncle Teddy.

'We owe so much to you,' said Auntie Doris.

'Hilary has a lover,' said Henry.

8 The Swinging Sixties

'Don't forget how incredibly lucky you've been in landing a woman like Hilary,' said Uncle Teddy, over pâté and toast in the Aga-cosy kitchen.

'Teddy!' said Auntie Doris, who always made things worse by protesting about them. 'He'll think you're meaning he's not good-looking.'

'Doris!' said Uncle Teddy, who sometimes made things worse still by protesting about them as well. 'That won't upset him. He knows he isn't good-looking.'

'Teddy!' said Auntie Doris.

'What I'm meaning is,' said Uncle Teddy, 'that you confront her very calmly. Don't raise your voice, and risk letting the thing escalate into a shouting match.'

'Show her the letter,' said Auntie Doris. 'Confront her with it, but not in an angry way.'

'That's right,' said Uncle Teddy. 'Sorrow and regret at an isolated lapse. That's the style.'

Henry would often ask himself why he had believed that advice given by two people who had led such tortuous love lives could possibly be sound.

At last the children were asleep. The long charade of Hilary's home-coming was over.

'Now perhaps you'll tell me what's wrong,' she said.

' "Wrong"?' said Henry. 'What do you mean?'

'You've been polite but dead all evening.'

'It's been a nice evening.'

'It's been unbearably nice. Something's very wrong, and I want to know what it is.'

'Don't you know what it is?' said Henry quietly.

'Well, yes, I think I do. I think you're deeply jealous of my books and my success, such as it is, and I find that deeply ungenerous and very disappointing.'

'Books my arse.' No! Calm. Don't raise your voice. Confront her with the letter, but not in an angry way. 'I think you ought to know that I've found this,' he said in a calm, but wavering voice.

Hilary took the letter and stared at it wildly. He wouldn't have believed that she was capable of going as much paler as she did. So she was guilty. Her face extinguished his last desperate hope that it was all a dreadful misunderstanding.

'Where did you find this?' she said, in a strange, low, icy voice.

'In your pocket. Careless to leave it.' No. No gibes.

'Careless? Careless? I didn't think my husband would go through my pockets.'

'Obviously, or you wouldn't have left it. It's lucky I did, isn't it?' No! Sorrow and regret. 'Look, darling, I . . . things happen, and I can forgive if . . . er . . . give him up and we'll work harder together and . . . work something out. I'm prepared to try.'

'*You* are prepared to try? My God! Big of you.' Her words stung him. He flinched. If he hadn't known that she was hitting out in self-defence, he'd have believed that she really hated him.

She gave him a look that was dredged from the depths of her bruised eyes. He recognised the dry swirling of panic. A horribly dry look. A strangely sad look. He'd have preferred tears.

And then she swung round and simply walked out of the house. She didn't even shut the door.

He just stared, bemused, at the space where she had been. Nothing in the advice of Uncle Teddy and Auntie Doris had prepared him for this.

He hurried upstairs. The children were fast asleep, little chests rising and falling peacefully.

He had to go after her. He'd have to risk it.

He couldn't risk it. Kate and Jack were his absolute responsibility, and he loved them without reserve.

He phoned his neighbours, the Wiltons. They were in. They promised to come round immediately, without hesitation. He hadn't expected that, because he hardly knew them. He thanked them warmly, told them under which stone he'd leave the key, pulled on his tatty old duffel coat, slammed the door, left the key under the agreed stone, and rushed off down Waterloo Crescent.

He turned left into Winstanley Road, towards the town centre, because surely Hilary wouldn't have set off towards the countryside on such a dingy October night? He hurried, half-running, then walking till he got his breath back, he was so unfit.

Winstanley Road dipped towards the town centre, and became less prosperous with every frantic, gasping step. At the point where it became York Road it began to smell of decay, of rising damp and falling incomes, of struggle and strife.

At last he saw her, marching resolutely through the ill-lit town, marching wildly in the drizzle with no coat.

Past the grandiose brick shell of the shabby Midland Road Station he chased her, past the lavatorial marble of the Chronicle and Argus building, no time for memories now. Up Brunswick Road, past unloved, unlovely terraces, past the gabled fortress that had once been Brunswick Road Elementary School, in which, on a morning almost as awful as this night, Henry had won false fame with a fart. Now he merely wheezed. Wildly Hilary walked, and her wildness gave her strength. Although breaking into asthmastic trots at regular intervals, Henry was catching her up only slowly.

Down the other side of the hill she strode, as the road dipped into the Rundle Valley. On the right were the great steelworks of Crapp, Hawser and Kettlewell. Once, the nights had rung with their virility and glowed like the gates of Hell. Now they played a sadder, gentler tune.

Drizzle turned to rain and, as if to wound Henry with thoughts of the child he'd been and the man he had become, Hilary turned down Paradise Lane, past the little terraced house where he was born.

Through the gate onto the tow-path she strode, across the Rundle and Gadd Navigation, over the waste ground, onto the wide footbridge over the faintly phosphorescent Rundle. There, under a night sky turned orange by the massed street lights, Henry caught her.

'Hilary,' he implored. 'My darling! I'm sorry!'

Why am I saying I'm sorry, he wondered, when it's she who's been unfaithful to me? Because I love her and don't want to lose her.

She didn't even look at him, but turned away, along the river. The rain fell harder. Orange clouds scudded dimly across the sky.

'Hilary!' he repeated.

She turned and came towards him. Her face was deathly white. He thought she was going to hit him. She pushed him. He fell backwards, flailing wildly. The acid waters of the Rundle met over his head, as they had done when he was four years old. He was drowning, burning, dying. He forced himself upwards, desperately, his head broke the surface, he gulped air frantically, excruciatingly. Hilary had gone. He went under again. He surfaced again. He tried to touch the bottom, but couldn't. He told himself to keep calm. He began to swim. The river, swollen by the recent rains, swept him downstream towards the weir. He struck out for the bank, handicapped by bursting lungs, aching chest and sodden clothes. He heard the curiously comforting rattle of a long goods train, and the very uncomforting roar of the weir. He flung himself towards the bank as the weir approached. He dragged himself up over trapped driftwood and broken bottles, slipped in the mud, hauled himself slowly back up with rubbery arms, just managed to pull himself over the lip of the sodden bank, and lay there, gasping, spluttering, the least impressive beached whale in history.

Later, when he was standing for Parliament and all this could be looked back on in tranquillity, Henry would say, 'I was pushed into the Rundle in 1939. It was an open sewer. I was pushed into it in 1964. I realised instantly that pollution had increased over those twenty-five years. Elect me, and I will make it my life's work to rid our town of this pollution. Elect me, and I will give you a river into which it will be a positive pleasure to be pushed.'

But on this October night his mouth tasted foul, he felt sick and poisoned, his breath returned to normality only slowly, and Hilary had disappeared completely.

He stood up. Water dripped off him. He'd lost his left shoe and a used condom was hanging from his right shoe. He flung shoe and condom into the river.

He trudged back, in his soaking socks, over the river, over the waste ground, across the steep hump-backed bridge over the Rundle and Gadd Navigation, along the tow-path, through the gate into Paradise Lane, and past the house where he was born. He picked his way carefully, watching out for broken glass and dog turds.

There were no trams any more, and there were all sorts of rumours about how Bill Holliday had won the scrap contract. He didn't attempt to wait for a bus, stinking as he did of sewage and dead fish.

He wheezed on sore feet and jellied legs, up Brunswick Road, down the hill to the town centre, past the lit windows of Premier House, where production of the morning's *Chronicle* was in full swing, and along York Road, parts of which were as smelly as his clothes. Stragglers of the night gave him looks as dirty as his trousers. A drunk, urinating in the gutter, stared at him as at an inferior being.

As he limped up the garden path, he had a wild hope that Hilary would be there, remorseful. But she wasn't. The Wiltons greeted him as if his was the only way to dress, and left only reluctantly and after assurances that he would phone them if necessary.

He phoned the police, had a whisky, and a bath, and went to bed to toss through a long, lonely night.

In the morning, he told the children that Hilary had gone to see a friend, but they sensed that something was wrong, and were fractious.

The police phoned at nine forty-five. She'd been found wandering near Hoyland Common. She'd been taken to the General Hospital. She was suffering from exhaustion and hypothermia. She didn't know who she was.

She looked at Henry and showed no sign of recognition. She looked feverish. Her eyes were hot but blank. He tried to hold her hand, but she wouldn't let him. He phoned Howard Lewthwaite in Spain, and within half an hour he had booked himself on a plane to London that evening.

Even facing Howard Lewthwaite was better than inactivity. Henry told the children that Mummy had been taken ill, but would be all right. He arranged for them to spend the night with Alastair and Fiona Blair, who had become good friends, and he drove to London to meet Howard Lewthwaite off the plane.

Hilary's father looked old and ravaged beneath his suntan. Henry told him what had happened. It seemed the only course.

'I simply can't believe it,' said Howard Lewthwaite. 'She wouldn't.'

'I thought that,' said Henry. 'But she did.'

'Have you any proof?' asked Howard Lewthwaite.

'There was the letter,' said Henry, flicking the wipers on.

'That was him telling her that he loved her. You haven't seen a letter from her telling him that she loved him.'

This simple truth was a revelation to Henry. He realised that what he'd taken as proof was no kind of proof at all. But he couldn't yet face the implications of even the possibility that he'd been wrong.

'Then why did she keep the letter?' he said.

Howard Lewthwaite didn't reply.

Henry didn't tell him that before he'd seen the letter he'd been certain that she and Nigel were having an affair. The intensity of his jealousy was a very personal shame.

'When I showed her the letter she went absolutely white,' he said. 'I didn't need to ask her anything more.'

It was four in the morning when they reached the hospital. Henry realised that Howard Lewthwaite didn't want him to stay. So he went home and tried to sleep. He was utterly exhausted, but couldn't sleep. It was true, he hadn't got proof. For Hilary to be unfaithful was deeply painful, but if he'd got it wrong his guilt would be even more painful. He needed proof.

At half past six, unshaven and hollow-eyed, having had barely a wink of sleep for forty-seven hours, he set off for London again. There wasn't much on the roads that Sunday morning. He drove fast, barely conscious of the mechanics of driving, going through the events of the last two days again and again.

He found Nigel Clinton's flat in Highgate without difficulty. Hilary's editor was very surprised to see him, and shocked at his appearance.

'What on earth's up?' he said. 'You look awful. Has something happened to Hilary?'

Henry sank into an armchair and an enormous feeling of exhaustion swept over him. He'd intended to have an eyeball-to-eyeball confrontation, but since he was several inches shorter than Nigel it was perhaps just as well that he was seated, with Nigel towering over him, as he said, 'Have you been having an affair with my wife?'

'Of course I haven't,' said Nigel. 'Chance would be a fine thing.'

'Did you write to her, saying, "Dearest Hilary, I love you so much, darling"?'

'Oh yes.'

'Why?'

'Because I loved her. Sorry. I know I shouldn't have. I loved her from the first moment I met her, but I never stood a chance.'

'What?'

'She loves you. She's utterly faithful and always will be. I was so jealous that Saturday when I saw you all together. I've taught myself, with great difficulty, not to love her. I'm free again now.'

All his life Henry had experienced conflicting emotions, but in that flat, of which he would take away not the slightest visual memory, he was almost torn apart by them. Joy, relief, pain, shame, despair.

'I'm sorry,' he said. He stood up. He went dizzy, and felt that he was going to faint.

'Are you all right?' asked Nigel.

'Yes. Just very tired and very hungry.'

'You aren't going to hit me, then?'

'Why should I? You've done nothing wrong.'

'I tried, though. I tried hard to do something wrong. You look very pale.'

'I'm going to have to sit down again.'

'I only cook spaghetti bolognese. But I cook a very good spaghetti bolognese.'

Henry's return journey was horrific. It was the fourth time he had driven between London and Thurmarsh in two days, and he'd had no sleep at all during that time. He had cramp, back-ache, arm-ache, a headache, and a sense that his brain was too small to fit his head. He'd gone to London to make Nigel Clinton eat humble pie, and instead he'd eaten Nigel Clinton's spaghetti bolognese. And he'd made the worst mistake that he'd ever made in his life.

He recognised now that Hilary was innocent and his jealousy had been the mental illness of a possessed man. He realised now that when she'd gone white it was with anger at his hunting through her pockets and reading her mail and with disgust at his lack of trust.

The nights were drawing in, and the light faded early on that suitably sombre October evening. The clouds were heavy, but there was no rain. Smoke from wood fires rose straight into the still sky, and curls of mist licked the hedgerows. Half the time Henry was unaware that there was a road and that he was in his Mini. He was in the summer house in Perkin Warbeck Drive, with Hilary telling him of the boy who had left her and the man who had raped her. She'd told him what it was like to wake up in a hospital ward, among strangers, not knowing who you were, and to realise gradually that this was the same old you, the same old earth, the fight had to go on, you hadn't taken a large enough dose. Anna had told him that Hilary was mentally ill. 'I've had a lot of depression,' she'd said that night. 'And I tried to kill myself. And I went very inward. If that's mental illness, I'm mentally ill.'

He had sobbed, 'What a responsibility.' He had said, 'You're a complete fool, you know. I'm clumsy, insensitive, thoughtless, hopeless. I'm a case.' He was, and he'd failed utterly in his responsibility. The tears streamed, the mist turned to fog, the journey became a nightmare.

He reached the General Hospital at ten fifteen that night. He was told that Hilary was under sedation. Such was his physical state that a suspicious and brave nurse accompanied him to the car park and watched until she was certain that he had really left the area.

Henry slept for thirteen hours, had horrendous nightmares, and woke to realise that he had completely forgotten about his own children and was already three and a half hours late for work.

The Blairs had got the children to school without any problems. Timothy Whitehouse sympathised over what Henry called 'a little domestic upheaval', and accepted his absence with equanimity. 'The Cucumber Marketing Board will survive till you get things sorted out,' he said. And a visit to the hospital soon established that there was nothing Henry could do there.

Henry and Howard sat in the draughty Main Reception.

'She has pneumonia,' Howard told him. 'And a full-scale nervous breakdown.'

'Oh my God.'

'She's in no physical danger. She recognises me, but doesn't remember anything about that fateful night. The doctor thinks she *will* recover her memory when the shock wears off. To see you just yet would be far too dangerous.'

A man with his leg in plaster was wheeled through, and a woman with her arm in plaster said, 'Hello, gorgeous, shall we go out and get plastered together?'

The receptionist coughed without putting her hand in front of her mouth.

'Howard?' said Henry.

'Yes?'

Howard Lewthwaite's tired face was cautious. He'd been alerted by Henry's tone of impending confession.

'Hilary didn't sleep with Nigel Clinton.'

'Well I told you she didn't.'

'I know.'

A yellow van pulled up with a screech, and a man in blue overalls hurried in through the swing doors with a red fire extinguisher.

'All sorted,' he told the receptionist, who smiled and sneezed without getting a handkerchief out.

'Howard?' said Henry.

'Yes?'

'All this is my fault.'

'Henry! These things happen.' Hilary's father smiled wearily. There was no hostility in his smile, but no friendship either.

Henry collected the children from school. When they got home, he told them that their mummy was ill in hospital, and they would be able to see her when she was better. They looked very solemn, but didn't cry.

Next morning, he took the children to school, and Fiona Blair, dark, tall, handsome and very Scottish, offered to take them home from school each evening and give them their tea, so that Henry could return to work.

'That's incredibly kind of you,' said Henry.

'What are friends for?' said Fiona Blair. She touched his arm gently. 'We're so sorry. We love you both.'

Henry flinched from their love. He had caused so much pain. He needed self-abasement.

Nevertheless, he hoped he wouldn't need too much self-abasement at Cousin Hilda's.

He hurried round, to catch her before she went shopping.

As he walked up the gravel drive of number 66, Park View Road, he became a child again. His stomach sank with dread.

Cousin Hilda was very surprised to see him at five past nine in the morning.

'What's wrong?' she said.

If only nothing had been wrong, and he could have said, 'Why do you assume something must be wrong, just because I call at five past nine?'

The smell of Tuesday morning's sausage and tomato filled the little basement room. The stove was dying now that breakfast was over.

'We've had a bit of a tragedy,' he said, sitting at the table, in his old place.

Cousin Hilda gave an anticipatory sniff, and Henry launched into his tale of woe.

When he'd finished, Cousin Hilda looked at him sadly and said, 'How could you think owt like that of Hilary? She's a grand lass, is Hilary.'

Henry wanted to say, 'Why couldn't you ever have said that to her face? It's too late now,' but all he said was, 'I know.'

'Mrs Wedderburn were saying to me the other day, "That

woman is a saint. Henry has married a saint." She's never wrong about folk, isn't Mrs Wedderburn, even if her tongue does sometimes run away with her.'

'Anyway, I thought I'd come and let you know straight away,' said Henry.

'Thank you for that.'

Cousin Hilda made them a cup of Camp coffee, and they sat gloomily in the cooling room, no longer cheered by the warmth and glow of the stove.

She sniffed violently.

'Satire,' she said.

'I beg your pardon?' said Henry.

'That's what's behind it all. All this satire. There's no trust any more. That David Frost. Who does he think he is?'

'Well I do think people don't trust each other as much, and sometimes they're right not to, because they don't deserve trust, but I don't think satire can be held to blame. My problems with Hilary aren't caused by David Frost.'

'Well when I were a girl we didn't have satire, and we did perfectly well wi'out it.'

'You didn't have motor cars either.' Henry was briefly triumphant, believing that he'd scored a debating point.

'Exactly!' said Cousin Hilda. 'It's bound to affect the brain, is carbon monoxide poisoning. It's forced to.'

Henry remembered that, despite his troubles, he ought to continue to take an interest in Cousin Hilda's life.

'How are your gentlemen?' he asked.

'I've lost Mr Ironside. Well, it were only to be expected. His family have joined him up here. But I've lost Mr Pettifer and all.'

'Good Lord.'

'Aye, but it were only a stop-gap while he found a house, and he stayed eight years. The funny thing is, I were glad he was going, to say I'd had eight years of his bitterness. But now he's gone I miss him. I'd give owt now to hear him running down young Adrian's cheese counter and looking down on me because I never met Laurence Gielgud. I must be getting old. There's too much change in this business.'

'Who've you got now, then?'

'Well Mr O'Reilly, of course. And a Mr Travis. He's a widower and a liquidator.'

'A liquidator?'

'Bankruptcies and I don't know what. Says he may be here a while if things go well, by which he means if things go badly.' She sniffed. 'My other two rooms are empty. Folk are renting flats and buying ready-made packet meals these days.' She sniffed again. 'They don't want "digs" as such any more. An era is drawing to a close. Still, you have worse troubles.'

'Well . . . we'll get over them.'

'Well I won't rub it in. I know I can be a bit stern sometimes, but when folk are in trouble there's no point in rubbing it in,' said Cousin Hilda. 'You know you've been a complete and utter fool. There's no need for me to tell you.'

Dr Martin Luther King received the Nobel Peace Prize, Harold Wilson's new Labour government announced that prescriptions would be free of charge from February, the House of Commons voted to abolish the death penalty, and Hilary recovered slowly from her pneumonia and even more slowly from her nervous breakdown.

Shortly before Christmas, Howard Lewthwaite told Henry that the time was ripe for her to see the children.

'But not me?'

'Not you.'

The children were very subdued on their return from seeing their mother.

'She's very ill,' said Kate, 'but she's getting better, isn't she?'

'Oh yes.'

'Why didn't you come in too?' asked Jack.

'So that you could see her on your own,' said Henry.

Jack considered this, and nodded.

'We're going again on Christmas Day, aren't we?' said Kate.

They spent Christmas with the Blairs. In the afternoon, they took the children to see Hilary. Henry waited outside.

On their return, the children were a little less subdued.

'She's getting better,' said Kate.

'You let us see her on our own again,' said Jack.

'She'll be home soon,' said Kate.

Henry often asked Howard Lewthwaite if he would take Hilary a letter, but he said it was too soon.

Towards the middle of January, he said that he thought the time was ripe.

'Be tactful, won't you?' he said.

'What do you think I am?' said Henry.

Howard Lewthwaite didn't reply. Henry felt that any reply would have been preferable to that telling silence.

His letter told Hilary that he realised that she had been completely innocent and he was deeply sorry and he loved her very much and the children were looking forward to her coming home.

Howard Lewthwaite called round at Dumbarton House a few days later, and handed Henry Hilary's reply.

'Not good news, I'm afraid,' he said. 'Read it when the children aren't around.'

Henry put the children to bed, poured himself a large whisky, and settled down with Hilary's letter. It was written in a shaky hand.

Dear Henry,

I'm sorry about my writing. I'm not very strong yet. I was grateful for your letter, and I'm glad you now know that I was completely innocent. I wish you'd come to that conclusion from your knowledge of me, rather than finding out from Nigel. I suppose that, if you had, we might have found some trust together again.

I've been very ill with pneumonia. Apparently I walked all night and was delirious. I remember nothing after walking out of our house. I've also had . . . they call it a nervous breakdown . . . just a total collapse of will and energy and hope. A blankness. I feel that there's nobody inside me, yet my hand moves and the pen writes, so there must be. I told you what it was like before and this is as bad, but I won't try to kill myself this time, because I'll think of Mummy and Daddy and Sam and the children. Yes, and you, because I know you'd rather I was still alive. I'll go and live in Spain and I hope the children will come and visit me in the holidays.

I forgive you for your lack of trust. I can't pretend it didn't cause me deep pain and agony. I don't think I can ever forgive you for reading my private mail. I expect you wonder why I kept that letter. Because I'm vain. I accepted your love as natural because I thought we were made for each other and that's how the miracle of love works. But if another man also loves me, I must be attractive. I'd never thought so, so it pleased me, so I kept it, so I deserve what I got.

I am feeble, Henry. I am sick. I have a fragile grasp of mental stability. Not so fragile that I can't write about it, I was a novelist after all, but fragile nevertheless. Sometimes I've seemed to people to be strong, but that's the way I've had to be to cover my weakness. But I've always known that I wasn't good enough for you.

Imagine the shock, therefore, when I discover that you aren't good enough for me! Your sexual suspicion and jealousy, though horrible, are perhaps forgivable as a temporary madness. Your jealousy of my books was the real problem and although I won't write any more I could never cope with all that.

How can we live happily together if we're both not good enough for each other? I don't want you to feel that I hate you, but I know that I couldn't bear you to touch me and how could we live like that?

What it is really, darling – I hope you don't mind me still calling you darling – is that we had wonderful times and because of how it was and because it couldn't be like that again I think it's best if it isn't at all.

I've thought about trying for the children's sake and you must understand that I can't. It's a fact rather than a decision. That they will be happier with one hopefully happy parent than with two unhappy parents is probable, but not certain.

What is certain is that I couldn't do it. Don't be fooled by this letter into thinking that I'm really all right. I can cope with letters. They don't speak back. I'm still very ill. I couldn't face going out of doors even yet. The doctors say I couldn't have the children, so you'll have to have them, and I'm sure that you want to and I know that you'll be a good father.

They say it'll be very slow but that I will make a full recovery. I don't actually want to. I don't want a man again and I don't want to write a novel ever again. I think I'll pretend to make a full recovery.

Please don't feel guilty. You gave me a better life than I ever dreamt of and made me strong enough to know that I won't kill myself this time and maybe will even be at least sort of happy eventually. My poor mother will be sad for my sadness but, more so, happy to have my company. Ditto Dad.

I'll divorce you for mental cruelty, but that's really just legal, I don't mean it.

I hope you'll find somebody else and find something more worthy of your life than cucumbers. You're still very special, despite everything.

With love,

Hilary.

He found that he hadn't touched his whisky.

Henry wrote two more letters, but Hilary refused to accept them. Sir Winston Churchill died at the age of ninety. Hilary wasn't allowed newspapers. She couldn't read about the long, inexorable deepening of the conflict in Vietnam. America seemed determined to wipe communism off the face of the earth even if the face of the earth had to go with it. She couldn't read how in Alabama State troopers used tear-gas, night sticks and whips to break up an attempted Negro march from Selma to Montgomery or how President Johnson asked Congress for support for a new civil rights bill that would guarantee every Negro citizen the right to vote in all elections. She was still too frail to be fed the slow drip of history.

Winter gave way to spring with bad grace.

Henry's thirtieth birthday passed without celebration.

Six days after Henry's thirtieth birthday, Howard Lewthwaite took Hilary back to Spain with him.

Henry had to tell the children that their mummy wouldn't be coming home again.

He sat them at the kitchen table, and he sat down with them. He needed courage to launch himself into it. It was harder than doing a comedy act in front of all the boys in Dalton College.

'Mummy isn't going to come home,' he said. 'She's going to live in Spain with Granny and Grandpa Lewthwaite, because she's been ill. You'll be able to go to Spain to spend your holidays with her and you'll be by the sea and it's much warmer than Filey so it'll be very nice. And the rest of the time you'll be here with me and we'll do all sorts of nice things at weekends. I love you very much and Mummy loves you very much and you'll go on aeroplanes and it'll all be very nice.'

Excitable, highly strung six-year-old Kate remained passive and pale-faced and stared at him solemnly out of her deep dark eyes that reminded him so much of Hilary. It was burly, phlegmatic, ruddy-faced five-year-old Jack whose lower lip began to quiver. Oh please don't cry, thought Henry.

'Will Mummy come home when she's really better?' asked Kate. Oh Lord.

'No,' he said quietly. 'I'm afraid she won't.'

Jack's lip quivered again.

'Mummy and Daddy want to do different things now. Mummy wants to live in Spain and Daddy has his work with the cucumbers. People sometimes do still like each other very much but don't want to be together all the time.'

'But you don't want to be together *any* of the time,' said Kate.

'Well . . . look . . . sometimes people, even grown-ups, especially grown-ups, do very silly things. Your daddy did a very silly thing and your mummy got cross. Mummy isn't cross any more but . . . she's decided she doesn't want to live with me any more.'

Jack's lip quivered again, but he still didn't quite cry.

'Did you throw a kipper at her?' asked Kate.

'Good heavens, no,' said Henry. 'Why do you say that?'

'Sally Cranston's daddy threw a kipper at Sally Cranston's mummy.'

'Oh dear. No, I didn't throw a kipper.'

'Was what you did as silly as throwing a kipper?'

Sometimes he cursed Kate's powers of persistence.

'It was much sillier.'

Jack's eyes widened in astonishment, and he forgot completely about his quivering lip.

'Much sillier than throwing a kipper!' he said, with deep awe. 'I can't imagine anything that's much sillier than throwing a kipper.'

Lucky you, thought Henry. I can, and I'm going to have to live with it for a very long time.

In May, Mr Tubman-Edwards reached retirement age. His retirement party was held in the Board Room on the third floor. One of the periodical economy drives was in full swing. The food was provided by the wives of staff members and brought in by car.

'Be very careful tonight,' Roland Stagg warned Henry. 'Many a promising career's been nipped in the bud because a copy-book was blotted at a retirement party.'

'Do I have a promising career?'

'Oh yes. You just have to be patient. Your hour of glory is at hand.'

Balloons in the shape of cucumbers, custom-made by Brighouse Balloons Limited, adorned the otherwise austere Board Room, whose walls were bare save for framed certificates of trophies won at international fairs by British cucumbers.

Three of the wives had made chicken and mushroom vol-au-vents.

'Typical of this lot. No consultation,' grumbled Maurice Jesmond, Head of Facilities.

The room soon filled up with cucumber folk and their better halves, but during the early stages of the party the atmosphere was

146

rather stiff and formal. This was because of the presence of several members of the Board of Directors: mysterious men whom one met occasionally in the lift, farmers, growers, wholesalers and retailers of cucumbers.

The guests began to attack the food with gusto. Two trays of chicken and mushroom vol-au-vents went rapidly. The other hung fire.

Henry, aware of his depressed state of mind, drank sparingly even after the Directors had all made an early departure. He was determined not to blot his copy-book.

He attempted to be extremely charming to Mrs Tubman-Edwards.

A wasted effort!

His opening remark of, 'I should have written to thank you for a delightful dinner party,' was flung back at him with, 'I should have *known* you were stupid if you had. It was a nightmare. I have endured fifteen years in this city, because of cucumbers.' His, 'I believe you brought some vol-au-vents. They're lovely,' elicited the response of, 'Mine are the ones that aren't lovely. Mine are the ones that are being left.' But his *pièce de résistance* was undoubtedly, 'I expect you'll be glad to have Mr Tubman-Edwards at home more.' This was greeted by a snort of derision that resembled a rhinoceros attempting to clear a particularly nasty dose of catarrh.

He found himself, midway through the evening, trapped in a corner, beneath a framed certificate commemorating the winning of the third prize at the Foire Internationale de Légumes in Nantes, listening to the retiring Head of Establishments' woes.

'What am I going to do, Henry?' he said. 'All day, every day, at home with Margaret.'

'Polar exploration?'

'Possibly. I've tried golf. I just can't hit the damned thing and I lose my temper. Never marry a snob, Henry. You didn't marry a snob, did you?'

'No. I married a much too wonderful woman.'

'Well I married a snob. Margaret is a snob. She thought I'd have a glittering career. A mandarin of the civil service. What did I become?'

'A satsuma of the not-so-civil service?'

'Exactly. You need a sense of humour here. My son bullied you, didn't he? Josceleyn.'

'Well . . . yes . . . he blackmailed me.'

'No moral fibre. A sticky end predicted. I have an only son who was unlikeable even in the pram, a grotty little house full of all the Spode my wife inherited from her family and keeps on using to remind me that she's known better days, and there I sit between a scrap-metal dealer and a ball-bearings mogul, with a snobbish wife who's as sexy as a camshaft and can't even cook anything edible to put on her bloody Spode plates. I also have a deep sense of failure and futility. I've struggled through, keeping my nose clean, and now they say, "Thank you very much, here are some inedible vol-au-vents cooked by your wife, piss off." '

'I'm very sorry,' said Henry.

'Not your fault,' said Dennis Tubman-Edwards. 'My fault for marrying a snob.' He winced. 'The shrapnel. Always plays me up when I get angry. Did you read *Biggles?*'

'Yes. I loved *Biggles.*'

'Knew you would. I always wanted to be Biggles. Air Force turned me down. Bad eyesight. I hate my initials. D. F. C. Tubman-Edwards BA. I always wanted to be B. A. Tubman-Edwards DFC. A few gongs might have improved my sex life. My wife's a snob, you see. Did I tell you that?'

'Yes. Yes, you did.'

'You look depressed, Henry. Are you depressed?'

'Well I have to say I haven't found you a riot of laughs.'

'I suppose not.'

'I don't feel I'm getting anywhere.'

'Nonsense. You're serving your apprenticeship and managing not to blot your copy-book. People will begin to notice you.'

'Nobody's noticing me.'

'People will begin to notice that nobody is noticing you. People will begin to realise that you're a sound man. Be patient. Your hour of glory is at hand.'

Some of the staff became the worse for drink. The Deputy Head of Liaison (otherwise known as the post-boy) was sick.

At eleven o'clock all the balloons descended. Henry had managed not to blot his copy-book, but he still felt depressed.

So Henry got up, gave the children breakfast, took them to the Blairs, travelled to Leeds, sat in his dark little office waiting for his hour of glory, read the Situations Vacant column, travelled back to Thurmarsh, picked up the children from the Blairs, listened to them chattering about how much they were looking forward to seeing Mummy, put them to bed, read them a story about a bow-tie that didn't like the posh man who was wearing it and wanted to be worn by a farm labourer, drank a large, slow whisky, tossed and turned in his lonely bed, got up, gave the children breakfast, took them to the Blairs, travelled to Leeds, sent off applications for jobs, travelled back to Thurmarsh, picked up the children from the Blairs, listened to them chattering about how warm the sea would be in Spain, put them to bed, read them a story about a grandfather clock that laughed at a cuckoo clock because it was Swiss and got punished for its racialism and arrogance, had a large, slow brandy, recalled sadly in his lonely bed those fiercer days of masturbation at Dalton College, got up, gave the children breakfast, picked up his mail and discovered that he hadn't even been granted an interview by the people to whom he had applied for jobs.

Three months of the swinging sixties passed unswingingly in this way. The Commons voted for the renationalisation of steel, Ian Smith's Rhodesia Front Party was elected with an increased minority, Cassius Clay knocked out Sonny Liston in the first round, the Beatles received OBEs and Edward Heath became leader of the Conservatives.

The children went to Spain, beside themselves with excitement, to spend a month with Hilary.

On his return from the airport, Henry heated up a Vesta prawn curry, and ate it while watching *Coronation Street*. Then he went to the Winstanley and sat there on his own, slowly drinking pint after pint. At twenty-five past ten Peter Matheson came in and Henry was thrilled to see him. This must be my lowest ebb, he thought.

'So it's out every night, the bachelor life again, is it?' said Peter Matheson.

'Yes,' said Henry, accepting another pint. 'Yes, it's terrible.'

Peter Matheson looked at him as if he was deranged or Italian or something equally odd, but Henry didn't care. Whenever the macho men said, 'Bet you're living it up now you've offloaded the little horrors,' he told the truth. 'The house is so silent. I miss them desperately.'

He missed Hilary dreadfully too, but he knew that there was no hope there, so he looked for pastures new.

His first Friday evening without the children saw him in the Lord Nelson, in Leatherbottlers' Row. Seated at their old table in the back bar, looking as if they'd been there ever since Henry'd left the paper eight years ago, were Helen Plunkett, Ginny Fenwick, Colin Edgeley and Ben Watkinson.

Ben was almost fifty now, and they all looked older. But then so did Henry. His hair was just beginning to thin.

Colin Edgeley leapt up, said, 'Hello, kid. Great. Have a drink, kid,' hugged Henry, and said, 'Oh shit. I haven't any money.' Ben Watkinson said he'd buy him a drink if he could name the county grounds of all seventeen first-class cricket counties. Ginny Fenwick blushed and bought him a drink. Henry named sixteen of the seventeen grounds, and Ben said that was good enough. Helen put her hand on his knee under the table and he developed an erection. She ran her hands across his crotch, felt the erection and raised her eyes.

'Where's Ted?' enquired Henry.

'Walking in the Lakes with mates,' said Helen. 'I hate the Lakes in August.'

Henry felt very excited indeed.

'So are you on the loose tonight or are you going on somewhere?' asked Ginny.

'No. No plans,' said Henry.

'No. Nor me,' said Ginny. 'I don't much like making plans. I like to see how the evening develops.'

Henry said, 'My round. Same again?'

'Not for me,' said Ben. 'Time I went home and gave the wife one. Oh, all right, as I haven't seen you for so long.'

'Yes, just the one, then I must get back to Glenda,' said Colin.

'Well just the one,' said Ginny. 'I don't want to hang around the pub all night.'

'Yes, please,' said Helen. 'I'm in no hurry.'

Ben went home to give the wife one. Ginny said, 'Well, I fancy something to eat. Are you coming, anybody?'

'No, got to get back to Glenda,' said Colin.

'I'm not hungry,' said Helen.

'No, thanks, Ginny. I've eaten,' lied Henry.

Ginny Fenwick blushed again and stumbled out of the pub.

'It must be awful not to be attractive,' said Helen.

'If you lend me a quid, I can buy a round,' said Colin.

'I thought you were going home,' said Henry.

'Glenda won't mind. You're my mate,' said Colin.

'How is Glenda?' asked Henry.

'Very well,' said Colin. 'We're getting on much better now I don't drink.'

They told Henry all the office gossip. Terry Skipton, news editor and Jehovah's Witness, had retired. Neil Mallet, who had once plagued Henry with deliberate misprints, had been seen in Buenos Aires, where he was apparently working on an English-language newspaper.

'I'm starving,' announced Helen. 'Have you tried our Indian restaurant, Henry? At last we're catching up.'

'Yes, I have. I like it,' said Henry.

'Great idea,' said Colin. 'I could murder a vindaloo.'

'And Glenda'll murder you,' said Helen. 'Go on home, Colin, there's a good boy.'

'Oh,' said Colin Edgeley. 'Oh!! Message received. Never let it be said that Colin Edgeley came between a mate and a leg-over.'

Henry and Helen held hands on that warm summer's evening.

'Shall we pop into the Devonshire first?' said Helen.

'No, let's not. I quite fancy an early night,' said Henry meaningfully.

'Me too,' said Helen meaningfully.

The Taj Mahal was half full. Later, after the pubs closed, it would be full.

Henry's nice waiter, whom he always thought of as Count Your Blessings, beamed up to them and said, 'Nice to see you again, sir. And your lovely wi . . .'

He stopped, confused.

'You're quite right,' said Henry. 'This is not my lovely wife. My lovely wife has left me. This is my lovely non-wife, Helen.'

It was impossible to see if Count Your Blessings blushed. He showed them to a corner table, handed them menus, and asked what they'd like to drink.

'A pint of lager, please,' said Henry.

'Do you make lassi? I don't feel that I need any artificial stimulation tonight,' said Helen meaningfully.

They had finished their meal by five to ten. A light soft rain was falling on the darkening summer streets of the unprepossessing town.

'Do you fancy coming home for a drink?' said Henry Ezra Pratt.

'You've rejected my advances once too often,' said Helen Marigold Plunkett, née Cornish. 'I'm not suddenly going to become available now that you're on your own. A girl has her pride.'

The following Friday, Ted was in the Lord Nelson, but not Helen. Also present were Ginny, Colin and Ben.

'Helen not here?' asked Henry.

Ted looked round the bar.

'No. Can't see her,' he said.

'All right, it was a silly question,' said Henry. 'Working, is she?'

'Gone to see her parents,' said Ted. 'I don't go. Mr and Mrs Basil Cornish don't see eye to eye with their son-in-law. You must be very disappointed. I gather you had a curry with her last week.'

Ginny blushed. She seemed to have developed a blushing problem.

'Yes, I did,' said Henry.

'Jolly good,' said Ted. 'Got on well, did you?'

'Yes,' said Henry, 'but nothing happened.'

Ted Plunkett raised his bushy eyebrows.

'What do you mean, "Nothing happened"?' he said. 'Why do you need to tell me that? I assumed nothing happened. Helen is a married lady.'

Ben went home to give the wife one. Colin announced that he'd better go as he'd been in the doghouse last weekend, and Ted said, 'Well, I'm off. Two's company. Three's a crowd.'

Henry and Ginny smiled at each other a trifle nervously, now that they were alone.

'Fancy a curry?' said Henry.

'Yes, please, even though I'm second choice,' said Ginny.

'Oh Ginny!' said Henry.

'Oh I'm not offended,' said Ginny. 'You're third choice.'

Count Your Blessings greeted them warmly and said, 'Good to see you again, sir. It's been quite a while.'

'There's no need to be tactful,' said Henry. 'Ginny knows I was here last Friday.'

Count Your Blessings showed them to a corner table, handed them menus, and asked what they'd like to drink.

'A pint of lager, please,' said Henry.

'Do you mind if I have wine?' said Ginny. 'I'm feeling rather nervous tonight.'

They talked about the old days, when Ginny'd had the flat above him, in Winstanley Road.

'A dental mechanic has your flat now,' she said.

'Lucky man,' said Henry.

'He is a lucky man. He has a nice wife, a lovely daughter, and nobody upstairs keeping them awake with twanging bed-springs.' Ginny sighed. 'I loved Gordon so much. I love him still.'

'Is there no one in your life now?'

'No one in that way. I had two great ambitions, to become a war correspondent and find myself a gorgeous man. I've managed neither.'

'There's still time.'

'Henry, I'm thirty-five.'

'Maybe not for the war correspondent, I don't know about these things, but certainly for a gorgeous man.'

They finished their meal by twenty to ten. The air in the grey, dusty town was warm and stale as the summer's day faded.

'Do you fancy coming home for a drink?' said Henry.

'What a splendid idea,' said Ginny.

They took a taxi. In the taxi, Henry put his hand on Ginny's thigh. She had big thighs.

They sat on the settee and drank almost neat whisky. Henry wished that Hilary's grave beauty wasn't watching them from the telephone table. He wished Kate and Jack weren't watching them, cautiously and seriously from the mantelpiece, laughing delightedly from on top of the television. He went upstairs to the lavatory, hurried into his bedroom, took the family photographs off the bedside table, where they fuelled his self-pity each night, and put them in a drawer.

He had a sudden fear that Ginny, like Anna Matheson on that never-to-be-forgotten night, would be lounging naked in an armchair.

But she was standing, with her coat on, reading an invitation on the mantelpiece.

'Time I was off,' she said.

This was worse than her having taken all her clothes off.

'Oh, Ginny,' he said. 'Aren't you going to stay and come to bed with me?'

She put her arms round him, and kissed him solemnly.

'No,' she said. 'You don't want me enough. I don't want you enough. It might work at the time. It wouldn't work afterwards. I'd want to go home as soon as it was over. Neither of us would want to wake up beside the other. Will you walk me to my door, like a gentleman? I'd like to feel I'd been out with a gentleman, just once in my life.'

The invitation which Ginny had been reading on Henry's mantelpiece was to the engagement party of Paul Hargreaves, Henry's best friend at Dalton College, to Dr Christobel Farquhar.

It took place in the elegant Hampstead home of Paul's parents. Henry told himself, with every mile of the long journey from Thurmarsh, that this was another social event at which it was important for him not to blot his copy-book. He would be witty, gracious, generous, sober – well, fairly sober. It was ridiculous to have a best friend whom you no longer liked very much. He would find in his heart the warmth to rekindle his affection for Paul.

Dr Christobel Farquhar was, as was to be expected, strikingly attractive. 'Paul's a lucky man,' Henry told her, and he told Paul, 'You're a lucky man.' Low marks for originality, but his reward was a warm smile from Paul which almost persuaded him that he really did like him.

There was champagne, but Henry drank carefully. There was a salmon buffet, and Henry ate carefully. With his suit unsullied by mayonnaise, and his senses barely affected by champagne, he sailed through the elegant rooms, crowded with surgeons and radiologists and neurologists and psychiatrists and a couple of Hampstead artists to give just a slight piquancy of bohemianism.

It was less than halfway through the party when he overheard the exchange. 'Who is that?' 'That's Paul's funny little friend. You know, the cucumber man.'

The cucumber man's heart raced, his pulse hammered, but he refused to feel humiliated. He was a fighter. He had always been a fighter. He would regain his fighting form.

So, when he had a minute or two with Paul and Christobel, he didn't say, 'Going to be a lawyer, get engaged to a lawyer. Going to be a doctor, get engaged to a doctor. Is your whole life pro-grammed?' He said, 'I hope you'll be very happy and I hope you'll visit me in Thurmarsh. I haven't seen nearly enough of Paul over the years.'

When Mr Hargreaves, eminent brain surgeon, said, 'I'm retiring next year. Let some of the younger chaps in. No point in being greedy,' Henry didn't say, 'You don't need to be, you've got enough salted away to live in luxury for fifty years.' He said, 'An admirable sentiment. I wish you a long and happy retirement.' Mr Hargreaves thanked him warmly. It was nice to be thanked warmly.

When Mrs Hargreaves bore down on him, she imposed a critical test on his new-found social solidity. He felt an absurd temptation to say, 'I bet you look wonderful with nothing on.' He fought it off valiantly, and said, 'You look as young and elegant and beautiful as ever,' and was rewarded by a blush of pleasure and embarrassment that sent an exquisite shiver through his genitals.

Henry was surprised and delighted to see Denzil and Lampo. They weren't speaking to each other. 'A contretemps over a tantalus.' Lampo had put on weight. He looked solidly successful, as well he might, since he was regarded as a golden boy at Sotheby's – or was it Christie's? Denzil remained slender and trim, his limp had grown no worse over the years, and his parchment skin, stretched and flecked with age, had barely changed in the ten years that Henry had known him. He had aged young, and in his early sixties he was gently ripening into distinction.

'Still with cucumbers?' asked Lampo.

'Still with cucumbers.'

'Priceless. Oh my God. Tosser!'

Tosser Pilkington-Brick entered *en famille*. He too had put on weight, and lost the fitness of his rugger years. Diana looked pleasantly chunky, but tired. Benedict, who was almost eight, looked like Little Ford Fauntleroy. Camilla, who was six, looked like a very small horse.

Henry longed to talk to Diana. The intensity of his longing astounded him. He moved towards her, but got waylaid by Belinda Boyce-Uppingham.

'My God,' he said. 'This party's registering seven on the reunion scale . . .'

'Lovely to see you,' said Belinda. 'I heard something about you the other day. Now what was it? Oh yes. You've given up scribbling and are in radishes. That's right.'

'Well actually I gave up scribbling eight years ago, and it's cucumbers.'

'That's right.'

'And how about you?'

'I've got two,' said Belinda Boyce-Uppingham, as if there was no

156

other subject but children. 'Tessa and Vanessa. Robin would love a son, but never mind, they're good girls. Ah, speak of the devil. Robin, you remember Henry Pratt.'

'Er . . . oh yes,' said Robin. 'The refugee chap who's in tomatoes.'

'Cucumbers, actually,' said Henry.

'I said "radishes",' said Belinda.

They all had a laugh over that.

'Oh, well, they're all veg, I suppose,' said Robin.

Henry was tempted to say, 'Shrewd of you to spot that. Who says you're as thick as two short planks?' but he fought it off, smiled a self-deprecatory smile, and said, 'Actually I sometimes forget what I'm in myself,' and they all laughed again, in the way people do, at parties, at things that aren't remotely amusing.

At last he was at Diana's side.

'It's so good to see you,' he said.

She flushed slightly.

'You know Benedict and Camilla, don't you?' she said.

'We have met but you were much younger then,' said Henry.

'So were you,' said Camilla.

'Camilla! Don't be rude,' said Diana.

'No, she's absolutely right. It was a silly remark,' said Henry.

He smiled at Camilla. If he'd hoped to win her over, it was a dismal failure.

'I remember you,' said Benedict. 'I'm nearly eight. Much older than Camilla. You were at Dalton College with Daddy, weren't you?'

'That's right.'

'I'm going to Dalton College after I've been to Brasenose College.'

'Really? I was at Brasenose too. You'll be following in my footsteps.'

'Will you excuse me?' said Benedict. 'I've spotted a friend. Nice to meet you.'

Benedict moved off.

'Bloody twit!' said Camilla.

'Please don't swear, Camilla,' said Diana.

'Gosh. Nosh,' said Camilla. 'That's good, isn't it? "Gosh. Nosh." '

'It's very good,' said Henry. 'Why don't you go and eat some?'

Camilla gave him a cool look, and stalked off.

'Where's Nigel?' said Henry, looking round, and remembering, on this his first day of total social smoothness, not to call him 'Tosser'.

'Tosser,' said Diana. 'Would you believe he's gone to phone a client?'

'Oh my God. He's monstrous. Sorry. I shouldn't have said that.'

'Yes, you should. He is.'

'But you're happy?'

'No.'

'Oh Diana, I wish you were happy.'

'That's nice.'

'Actually I wish everybody was happy tonight.'

'Oh.'

'But you particularly.'

'That's nice.'

It was so nice, Henry found, to smile at people and be smiled at by people. He wished the party would go on for ever and he would never have to go back to his lonely life.

The children returned, and Henry 'Can I have permission to get something out of the Permissive Society?' Pratt wasn't nearly as lonely when they were around. They said they'd had a wonderful time but didn't say much about Hilary, and he refused to stoop to using them in a search for information. They were very brown and looked extremely fit. To his enormous, his stupendous, his tear-wrenching, his heart-stopping relief, they seemed thrilled to see him and not unhappy to be home.

Folk music swept the land. Even in Thurmarsh there were hippies. Henry bought a Bob Dylan record, but he sensed that the whole movement was passing him by.

The Regional Co-ordinator, Northern Counties (Excluding

Berwick-on-Tweed) reached retirement age. His successor was named, and he was not the Assistant Regional Co-ordinator Northern Counties (Excluding Berwick-on-Tweed) but John Barrington, Head of Gherkins.

Once again, the party was held in the Board Room, but this time there were no balloons. 'A bad idea. *Mea culpa*,' had been Timothy Whitehouse's verdict on the balloons.

Maybe Henry 'Nonpareil at avoiding blotted copy-books' Pratt had become complacent. Maybe the pain of being passed over for his boss's job was greater than he could bear with equilibrium. Maybe the depression he had felt at Dennis Tubman-Edwards's retirement party had given him a morbid fear of retirement parties. Maybe he had a subconscious dread of finding that he had given his whole life to cucumbers and would end up at his own retirement party. Whatever it was, Henry couldn't face Roland Stagg's retirement party without having a couple of drinks first.

By the time he arrived, the party was already in full swing. He took a large glass of red wine and found his retiring boss bearing down on him, trousers at half-mast round his enormous paunch.

'I'd like a brief word, Henry,' he said. 'I've decided to come clean. I was asked if I thought you should succeed me. Now I'm very pleased with your progress. You've been keeping a really low profile.'

'So low that sometimes I wonder if I'm clinically dead,' said Henry.

'Excellent. Truly excellent.' He gave his painful, Burmese cough. 'Anyway, I said, "No. I don't think Henry should succeed me. He's ready for promotion, but he needs to move to a different department. He needs a challenge." Be patient, Henry. Hang on in there, avoid blotting your copy-book, and the world can be your oyster. Your hour of glory is at hand. Have you met my wife Laura?'

Laura Stagg was quite unreasonably pretty. Men with vast paunches shouldn't have such pretty wives. Where was the justice in the world? She was wearing a surprisingly low-cut dress and Henry was transfixed by her splendid cleavage. He felt an absurd temptation to say something outrageously sexy to her. Desperately, he said, 'How are you feeling about having Mr Stagg at home all day?'

'You're the one who was at school with Tommy Marsden, aren't you?' she said. 'When I heard him on the radio being asked what it was like to win the first division championship and he said, "It hasn't sunk in yet," I thought he must be some kind of prize idiot. But you know, I feel the same. It simply hasn't sunk in.'

She smiled and looked straight into Henry's eyes. He scuttled off in search of safer ground, and poured himself another large red wine.

He found himself face to face with Vincent Ambrose, the Director General. He hadn't spoken to Mr Ambrose since his first week, and doubted if the Director General would remember him, but there he did him an injustice.

'Get that kettle all right, did you?' said Vincent Ambrose genially.

'Absolutely.' Henry wished he hadn't said 'absolutely' so absolutely meaninglessly, when 'yes' would have sufficed.

'Jolly good.' The Director General paused, searching for something to say. 'Well, keep up the good work,' he said, and moved on.

When Henry spilt coronation chicken all down his suit front, he knew that he was sinking.

He took another large glass of red wine, to soothe his nerves.

He tried hard, that evening, to hang on in there, to keep a clear head, to avoid blotting his copy-book.

In vain!

He tried hard, that evening, having learnt for all time the dangers of jealousy, not to feel bitter about the promotion of John Barrington.

To no avail!

Somewhere, along the line, he had had one glass of red wine too many.

He awoke with a steam-hammer in his head and an unwashed wart-hog in his mouth. He could remember only three of the things that he had said during the rest of that awful evening.

He recalled countering John Barrington's, 'I hope we'll work well together. I certainly relish the prospect,' with, 'Well, I don't. You're a little prick, and you should have stayed with gherkins.'

He remembered saying, 'I bet you look gorgeous with no clothes on,' to the unexpectedly pretty wife of Roland Stagg.

He saw, vividly, horribly, the expression on the face of the Director (Operations), as he limped off after Henry had said, 'I know why you haven't promoted me. Because the face doesn't fit, does it, Mr Timothy Shitehouse?'

Slowly, Henry's physical state improved. By lunchtime, he only felt as if he had a face flannel stuck in his throat, and managed to phone his ex-boss to apologise.

'Oh dear oh dear oh dear,' said Roland Stagg. 'Who didn't keep a low profile, then? Who blotted his copy-book?'

'I know,' said Henry. 'I just wanted to say I'm sorry if I spoilt your party.'

'Not at all, except that I was sorry for you. It's never nice to see a good man disappearing up his own arse-hole.'

'I . . . er . . . I'm sorry if I said anything untoward to your wife.'

'I don't think you did.' Roland Stagg seemed puzzled. 'I said you'd disgraced yourself all round and she said, "Well, he said some very nice things to me." '

'Oh! Ah! Yes! Sorry! That's right.' Henry floundered wildly. 'Yes, I remember now. It was someone else's wife I said awful things to. That's right.'

At half past two, the Director (Operations) sent for him.

Timothy Whitehouse twitched his predatory nose, gave a half-smile and said, 'Don't look so miserable.'

'I am miserable,' said Henry. 'I said some awful things last night.'

The Director (Operations) swivelled in his chair and sought solace in his reproduction of Albrecht Dürer's little-known master-piece, 'The Cucumber'.

'I'm not inhuman,' he said at last. 'I don't hold what people say at parties against them, otherwise nobody would come to our parties and I enjoy our parties. I note that you are upset at not being given Roland's job. I'm not so naïve as to believe that I'm never referred to as Shitehouse, but in your case I shall assume that it was a slip of the tongue caused by hearing lesser men use the expression about me. Is that correct?'

'Absolutely. Oh, absolutely.'

'I'm glad to hear it. I'll attempt to forget that you said it although, since no one has ever said it to my face before, that will be difficult.' The Director (Operations) swivelled round again, this time to look Henry straight in the eye. 'In ten years' time, when I hope you will still be with us, we'll look back on Roland's retirement party, and we'll split our collective sides. I hope that's a comfort.'

'Well it is, Mr Whitehouse, and I think you've been very generous, Mr Whitehouse, but . . . er . . . may I say something, Mr Whitehouse?'

'Of course. Didn't I advise you always to be your own man, stick to your guns and be fearless? Although I should have qualified that. I should have advised you to be your own man, stick to your guns and be fearless *when sober. Mea culpa.* So, what is it? Ask away.'

'I'm not sure that I want to be here in ten years' time.'

'I know. You've applied for other jobs. I've supplied references. You haven't got them. Bad luck.'

'I wouldn't want to stay unless . . . unless I felt it was worth my while.'

'Bravely spoken, for a man who said the things you said yesterday, which of course I'll try to forget. I understand. Point taken. Henry, my advice is this. Cease looking for other jobs, commit yourself fully to us, avoid saying the sort of things you said yesterday, which of course I'll try to forget, and be patient. Your hour of glory is at hand.'

'That's what Mr Tubman-Edwards and Mr Stagg said.'

'Well why don't you believe us?' said Timothy Whitehouse. 'We are Englishmen, after all.'

Henry found himself dismissed rather abruptly. He steeled himself to call on John Barrington.

John Barrington had only been in his office for six hours, but already he had plastered it with photographs of his family. Henry could see them canoeing, sailing, surfing, skiing. He felt even more unathletic than usual.

John Barrington ushered him into a chair rather offhandedly.

'I must apologise for what I said last night,' said Henry.

'Yes, I think you must,' said John Barrington.

'I hope we *can* work well together,' said Henry.

'Well so do, I, Henry. So do I.' John Barrington just happened, as if by chance, to pick up the bronze gherkin given him by the Gherkin Growers' Federation as Gherkin Man of the Year for 1962. He fingered it delicately. Henry wondered who on earth they had found to be Gherkin Man of the Year for 1963 and 1964. 'I'll lead by example, I'll ask for your help when required, and if you give it we'll have no problems. Now I am rather busy, if you don't mind. My first day. I'm sure you'll understand.'

1965 drew towards its close. The largest power failure in history blacked out New York City, parts of eight North Eastern states, and parts of Ontario and Quebec. Henry wondered if it had also disconnected his phone.

He sought an interview with John Barrington and was granted one.

'I feel I'm being under-used,' he said. 'I feel I'm being victimised for an unwise drunken remark at a party.'

John Barrington picked up his award. As a dummy is to a baby, so was his bronze gherkin to the new Regional Co-ordinator, Northern Counties (Excluding Berwick-on-Tweed). 'I'm not a petty man. The fact is, my predecessor ran a lazy ship. Too much devolved on you.'

'I didn't mind it devolving on me.'

'That does you credit, but it doesn't make it right. I run a tight ship. The responsibilities are mine.'

'I realise that, but I get nothing to do whatsoever. Sometimes I wonder why I've got this job at all.'

'I shouldn't speculate along those lines out loud, if I were you,' said John Barrington.

Henry intended to take the matter up with the Director (Operations), but then the children got flu, and then he got flu, and then the Director (Operations) got flu, and then it was too near Christmas.

The children went to Spain for Christmas, and Henry considered all the poverty in the world and thought, 'There are millions of people who'd be grateful for roast turkey and ginger cordial and three hours of Snap in a stifling basement room with Cousin Hilda and Mrs Wedderburn and Liam O'Reilly.'

That Christmas night Henry cried for Hilary as he had never cried before.

The children returned, life resumed its even keel, and Henry told the Director (Operations) of his displeasure at his inactivity.

'I'll have a word with John Barrington,' said Mr Whitehouse. 'Delegation is not weakness.'

Britain announced a complete trade ban against Rhodesia, the Soviet spacecraft Luna 9 made a soft landing on the moon, and the word that Timothy Whitehouse had with John Barrington produced only a marginal increase in Henry's workload.

My life is draining away, he thought. I'll be thirty-one soon.

Sales of the paperback of *All Stick Together* had suddenly accelerated over the Christmas period. The publishers told Henry that Hilary's book was a big success, but they were getting no reply to their letters. He wrote and begged her to write to them. They told him that she had written to say that she was very pleased on the author's behalf but that she no longer considered herself the author.

She didn't write to Henry.

In the early hours of Sunday, March 13th, 1966, Henry had a disturbing dream. He dreamt that he was in a glorious, baroque opera house, but all the seats were on the stage, and all the scenery was in the auditorium. And there was only one person in the twelve rows of seats on the stage. Henry, in immaculate evening dress, was sitting in the third seat from the left in the third row.

He looked down on magnificent painted sets which suggested that the performance was to consist of a cross between *Swan Lake* and *The Barber of Seville*.

Into the auditorium came Helen Plunkett, née Cornish. She was naked. She smiled at Henry and took up a stilted theatrical pose. Her legs were magnificent.

Next came Diana, also naked, chunkily sexy. She was accompanied by Benedict and Camilla, who were dressed as page boys. Diana waved at him cheerily, but the faces of Benedict and Camilla broke into derisive smiles.

Next came the eighteen-year-old Lorna Arrow, also stark naked. She smiled shyly at Henry. Her four children, Marlene, Doreen, Kevin and Sharon, ran on behind her, all dressed as Beefeaters, and she turned into the Lorna Lugg who had lost her looks, breasts sagging and stretch marks forming like cracks on a mirror.

Helen's naked sister Jill followed with her three boys, dressed as Chelsea pensioners. Then came Mrs Hargreaves, also naked and extraordinarily well-preserved, with a fifteen-year-old Paul and a fourteen-year-old Diana, both dressed as onion sellers. Young Diana blew a kiss to present-day Diana.

Next came Ginny Fenwick, stark naked, sturdy, running to fat, and carrying a Bren gun. She was followed by Anna Matheson, who slid on, seated naked on the very armchair on which she had been naked for Henry all those years ago.

Belinda Boyce-Uppingham was posing as a frontispiece for *Country Life*, except that frontispieces for *Country Life* wear clothes. Tessa and Vanessa wore jodhpurs and carried riding whips.

And out of the lake there arose Boadicea's chariot, and on it, naked and palely lovely, was Hilary, with Kate and Jack at her side, dressed as bullfighters.

All the women held out their arms towards Henry, and all the children smiled. The band struck up 'Happy Birthday to You' and they all sang, 'Happy birthday to you, Happy birthday to you, Happy birthday, dear Henry, Happy birthday to you.' Then all the women's breasts sagged and stretch marks formed on all their thighs and five hundred balloons shaped like cucumbers descended from the ornate ceiling, and the flesh fell off all the women to whom Henry had ever been deeply attracted, and the clothes and the flesh fell off all the children that they had borne, and they all became horrible smiling skeletons.

Henry awoke, drenched in sweat, to hear the telephone ringing with tinny insistence in the deep silence of the house. And he knew, with utter certainty, that it would be Hilary, disturbed by the aura given off by his dream, ringing to say that she still loved him. As he rushed to the phone, at ten past three on his thirty-first birthday on the 13th, having dreamt that he was the only one on the stage sitting in the third seat in the third row, the numbers three and one had sharp and lucky significance for him. He dived for the phone, terrified that she would ring off.

'Hello,' he said.

'Dyno-Rod?' said a deep male voice. 'Sorry to ring you at this unearthly hour, but I've got water pouring through my back passage.'

Two months later, Henry's phone rang again at ten past three in the morning. He felt certain, even though he no longer had any belief in his psychic powers, that it would be another crossed line for Dyno-Rod.

'Hello,' he said wearily.

'Henry?'

'Yes.'

'It's Diana. Are you alone?'

'Of course I'm alone.'

'I'm sorry to ring you at this unearthly hour. Tosser's left me and you're the only person I can talk to.'

9 For Better, For Worse

On Saturday, June 10th, 1967, the Middle East War ended after just six days with a cease-fire between Israel and Syria, Spencer Tracey died of a heart attack, and Dr Paul Hargreaves married Dr Christobel Farquhar.

The reception was held in a huge marquee in the vast garden of Brigadier and Mrs Roderick Farquhar, near Alresford in Hampshire.

The sun glinted in the grey streaks that were beginning to fleck Henry's slowly thinning hair. He was standing with Diana in a queue outside the marquee, waiting to tell the happy couple that they looked wonderful and it had been worth waiting almost two years to get Winchester Cathedral on a Saturday in June.

Behind them were a close friend of the bride, the lovely Annabel Porchester, and her fiancé, the unlovely Josceleyn Tubman-Edwards, of the merchant bankers, Pellet and Runciman.

'It's Henry!' said Josceleyn Tubman-Edwards. 'Good Lord! Darling, this is Henry Pratt, a chum of mine. We were at Dalton College together, and then Henry got a job with my father at the Cucumber Marketing Board. Henry, this is Annabel Porchester. She's one of the Suffolk Porchesters.'

'I always thought they were a breed of pig,' said Henry.

Diana giggled. It was one of her most endearing qualities that she had never quite grown up.

'I should have warned you that Henry is awful,' said Josceleyn Tubman-Edwards.

'Henry has a dreadful thing about posh social events,' said Diana. 'They make him panic and he fights back by being incredibly rude. He hasn't even introduced me.'

'Oh, sorry,' said Henry. 'Diana Pilkington-Brick. Paul's sister. She married Tosser Pilkington-Brick, who was also a "chum" at school. You remember Tosser, don't you, Josceleyn?'

Josceleyn Tubman-Edwards tried to smile. A piece of saliva remained attached to both his lips even as they parted, but they didn't part very far.

'Yes, I . . . er . . . I remember Pilkington-Brick,' said Josceleyn. 'Is . . . er . . . I mean . . . er . . . ?'

'We're separated,' said Diana. 'I'm divorcing him for adultery.'

'I'm sorry,' said Josceleyn.

'I'm not,' said Diana. 'I'm going to marry Henry.'

'Good Lord,' said Josceleyn. 'I mean, congratulations.'

'Yes, congratulations,' said Annabel.

'What do you do, Annabel?' asked Henry.

'Not a lot. I only came out last year,' said Annabel.

'Really! What were you in for?'

'Henry!' said Diana.

They edged slowly forward, a queue of hats wilting in the summer sun. It was so boring. They couldn't wait for the champagne and the food.

'So where will you get married?' asked Josceleyn.

'I've no idea,' said Diana. 'I was just thinking, "How do you follow this?" '

'Probably a church hall in Thurmarsh,' said Henry.

'Ugh!' said Josceleyn.

'Well don't worry,' said Henry. 'You won't be invited.'

'Henry! Why are you being so awful to the poor man?' said Diana.

Henry lowered his voice, to spare Annabel from his reply.

'He introduced me as his chum. The great bag of rancid lizard droppings blackmailed me over that business of pretending my father'd been a test pilot.'

'Oh! That was him!' said Diana. 'Oh well, that's all right, then. Poor girl. She must be after his money.'

'Well I'd hate to think she was after his sex appeal.'

At last it was their turn to greet the happy couple. Paul looked magnificent in morning dress, while Christobel looked the very essence of beauty, sophistication and, more surprisingly, virginity, in a high-necked, full-sleeved, full-length white silk dress with cape-effect back and matching pillbox hat. She carried a bouquet of white roses.

'You look stunningly wonderful. Any man could fancy you,' said Henry. 'And you don't look too bad either, Christobel.'

Paul and Christobel gave Henry cheerily disgusted looks.

'Seriously, you're a stunner, Christobel,' said Henry, kissing her gently on the cheek.

They moved on, took champagne, located their positions on the seating plan, and mingled. It really was a big wedding. There were more than three hundred guests. Henry wondered if they should run away to Gretna Green for theirs.

Mr Hargreaves, magnificent in morning dress, approached.

Henry felt that he alone did not look magnificent in morning dress. His hired suit was slightly too long and slightly too tight.

'Be nice to Daddy, won't you?' urged Diana.

'Of course.'

'He's still in shock.'

It had only been on the previous evening that Henry had told his future father-in-law. Well, he'd only proposed two days ago. His reunion with Diana had been a success from the start – comfortable, sexy and, above all, fun. But they had never thought of marriage. Henry couldn't imagine being father to Benedict and Camilla. And he didn't believe that the possibility had crossed Diana's mind. But he'd found it such a wrench to part from her, and so delightful to be with her, that he had suddenly decided, on the telephone, the day before coming down for the festivities, to propose. There had been a long, astonished silence, and then, to *his* astonishment, Diana had accepted him with the stunningly romantic words, 'I don't see why not. It could be rather fun.'

And now here was Mr Hargreaves, brain surgeon, bearing down on them and smiling warmly.

Henry smiled back, thinking wryly of the previous evening, when he'd said, 'Do you remember my asking to see you the day after Tosser lost England the Welsh match, in 1956? You thought I was going to ask for Diana's hand. And I was actually asking to borrow fifty quid. You were so relieved that you'd have gladly given me a hundred quid.'

'Oh, Henry! I wasn't relieved,' Mr Hargreaves had said. 'Of course I wouldn't have minded if you were going to marry Diana.'

'Oh good,' Henry had said. 'Because I am going to marry her.'

'What??'

Mr Hargreaves had gone white. His mouth had opened and closed silently just once, like a disconcerted turbot. He'd regained his equilibrium rapidly, but not quite rapidly enough.

'Well, congratulations,' he'd said. 'When's the happy day?'

'Well she has to get divorced first.'

'Yes. Of course. Of course.'

Now, in the champagne buzz of the wedding marquee, Mr Hargreaves was also remembering last night's encounter.

'Hello!' he said warmly. 'You know, when I saw your friend Tommy Marsden on the idiot box the other day – I very rarely watch, but it happened to be on – and he was asked, "How does it feel to score the winning goal for England at Wembley?" and he said, "It hasn't really sunk in yet," I thought he must be really dense, but now I know what he meant. Last night it didn't sink in. Today it has. I hope you'll both be very happy.'

'Thank you, sir,' said Henry. He hadn't expected to say 'sir', he didn't think he was capable of it, unless it slipped out unintentionally, but, having said it, he was quite glad that it *had* slipped out unintentionally.

'Thank you, Daddy.'

Diana kissed her father.

'Any thoughts about the shindig?'

'Modest, we thought,' said Diana. 'No attempt to compete.'

'Good. Good. Any thoughts about where you'll live?'

'We thought London,' said Henry. 'I can't quite see Diana in the North. Too far from Harrods.'

'Well . . . good . . . yes, quite, huh! . . . good. You'll . . . er . . . you'll abandon the cucumbers, then?'

'Oh yes! They just aren't giving me a chance there.'

'Good. Good. Well that's splendid.'

'Henry'll get a job in London. There's bound to be something for a man of his talents.'

'Yes,' said Mr Hargreaves doubtfully. 'Yes,' he repeated more positively. 'Oh yes, yes, bound to be.'

'Henry has such a lot to offer the world, Daddy. He can't just throw himself away on cucumbers.'

Mr Hargreaves looked at his daughter in surprise at her fervour, then he looked at Henry as if reassessing him.

'Good,' he said. 'Good. Well, good.'

Mrs Hargreaves might have been designed for this day. She looked stunning in a green, pink, blue and orange-red double-breasted organza coat with roll collar and flap pockets, over a plain, vivid green sleeveless shift with matching green broad-rimmed straw hat from Christian Dior, gold earclips, and black patent pumps from Charles Jourdan at nine guineas. She approached them with two very excited pageboys and two even more excited bridesmaids.

'Shall we tell our children now?' said Diana.

'Why not?' said Henry. 'Darlings. Kate. Jack. Diana and I have something to tell you.'

'Benedict. Camilla. This is for you too,' said Diana.

'Diana and I are going to be married,' said Henry.

He clutched Diana's hand.

All around there was a roar of conversation, but in the middle of the marquee, in the eye of that champagne cyclone, there was silence.

Kate was the first to break it.

'You mean,' she said, her voice laden with gloom, 'Benedict and Camilla are going to be our brother and sister?'

'And Kate and Jack are going to be ours,' said Benedict. 'Bloody hell!'

Homosexuality between consenting adults in private was legalised. Henry couldn't help wondering what Lampo and Denzil would consent to do in private that night by way of celebration.

In San Francisco, during the long, hot 'summer of love',

peaceful hippies lit joss-sticks and placed flowers in the rifle barrels of bemused National Guardsmen. Elsewhere in America, in the long, hot summer of hate, the racial riots were terrifying, and other soldiers were still using flowerless guns all over Vietnam.

There was a military coup in Greece. The long night of the colonels had begun.

During the long, not-so-hot nights in Britain, motorists found themselves compulsorily breath-tested. Cousin Hilda wasn't affected, Uncle Teddy walked to the pub, and the journalists on the *Thurmarsh Evening Argus* took no notice.

The Director (Operations) of the Cucumber Marketing Board sent for Henry, swivelled happily in his chair and, looking him full in the face, gave him the good news.

'Your hour of glory has arrived,' he said.

On Saturday, July 13th, 1968, fierce fighting broke out between police and several thousand young people in Paris, teenage members of four Glasgow gangs surrendered meat cleavers, knives, a sword and an open razor during a one-hour amnesty arranged by Frankie Vaughan, the sea turned orange between Folkestone and Hythe as a result of dumped sheep dip, and Henry Ezra Pratt and Diana Jennifer Pilkington-Brick, née Hargreaves, held their wedding reception in the Hospitality Suite of the exclusive Regent Clinic, where Mr Hargreaves had saved the brains of the extremely rich for more than twenty years.

Before they all sat down, there was champagne in the slightly antiseptic ante-room, though not as much champagne, and not such good champagne, as there would have been if Diana had been marrying the tall, handsome son of one of the many medical luminaries who had graced the Hargreaves table over the years, rather than Paul's funny little friend, the cucumber man.

Nobody wore morning dress, but Henry looked almost smart in the best of his three dark cucumber suits, and Diana looked charming in a knee-length Pierre Balmain-style navy and white dress. The guests wore dresses of many different lengths, Mary

Quant having described the mini as boring, the maxi having failed to take off, and the midi being seen as a dull compromise.

The best man, Lampo Davey, wore a velvet suit with frilled burgundy shirt, while his legalised partner, Denzil Ackerman, plumped for a lime green shirt and a dazzling white suit. Anything went, as the sixties swung towards their close.

Nobody cut a more dashing figure than Auntie Doris, who wore a huge scarlet hat she had last put on in 1938. Cousin Hilda sniffed the moment she saw it, and Henry was on tenterhooks over how the conversation would go when she talked to Auntie Doris for the first time since his first marriage eleven years ago.

Unfortunately for Cousin Hilda, Lampo Davey buttonholed her before she'd spoken to Auntie Doris. 'I don't believe you've met my lover, Denzil, have you?' he said, and Cousin Hilda sniffed so violently that she developed a nose bleed. It soon subsided, but for some time she walked with her nose pointing towards the ceiling. She was therefore unable to sniff with any force when she came face to face with Auntie Doris's hat or when Auntie Doris said, 'Have you had a nose bleed, Hilda, or are you communing with your maker?'

'Is the vet not here?' countered Cousin Hilda icily.

'The vet??' said Auntie Doris. 'Why, has somebody brought a sick dog?'

'I were informed your latest amour was with a retired vet,' said Cousin Hilda. 'If I've got the wrong end of the stick, I'm sorry.'

'Oh, that vet! Yes, he is. Is a vet, I mean. No, he isn't. Isn't here, I mean. He's got this summer flu thing.' Auntie Doris was furious at having to tell everyone that he was ill. Ill as well as retired. They'd think she'd thrown herself away on some broken reed of an elderly vet. She longed to tell them that she was living with the man she'd always loved, her husband Teddy. 'I forget he was a vet sometimes. It was before I knew him. You needn't sniff, anyway. He's a fine man.'

'As fine as Geoffrey Porringer?' said Cousin Hilda grimly.

'Incomparably finer,' said Auntie Doris scoutly.

'As fine as Teddy Braithwaite?'

'No finer, but Teddy's equal in every respect.'

Cousin Hilda managed another cautious sniff.

'Can I lend you a handkerchief, Hilda?' offered Auntie Doris. 'I have a fine lace one from Harrods.'

'No doubt you do,' said Cousin Hilda. 'No doubt you do. I have one, thank you. A nice plain one from Woolworth's. There are folk starving in Pakistan. I don't think I should waste my money on tarts' hankies.'

'Hilda!' said Auntie Doris. 'It's Henry's wedding day.'

'Oh, dinna worrit thasen,' said Cousin Hilda, dusting down her dialect for Auntie Doris's benefit. 'I won't show Henry up.'

Henry approached and kissed them both, to Auntie Doris's delight and Cousin Hilda's embarrassment.

Auntie Doris came over all emotional suddenly.

'Auntie Doris! What's wrong?' said Henry.

She couldn't tell them that she was upset because she was living in sin with a man whom she couldn't marry because he was supposed to be dead and because she was already married to him, and she had a husband whom she couldn't divorce because she wasn't married to him. 'I'm in a cleft stick with no paddle,' she had told him once over a post-prandial game of Scrabble in Honeysuckle Cottage.

'It's just . . . Teddy would have loved to see this day,' she said, and she hurried off to the Ladies to repair her mascara.

'I think Doris is failing,' said Cousin Hilda. 'She'd forgotten her new man's a retired vet.'

'Oh well,' said Henry feebly. 'You remember Paul Hargreaves, Diana's brother, do you? And this is Christobel, his wife.'

As he left them to it, Henry heard Paul say, 'I've never forgotten your spotted dick,' and Cousin Hilda reply, 'Oh! That's very kind of you.'

He stopped to chat to Belinda Boyce-Uppingham.

'How's Robin?'

'Marvellous.'

'How are Tessa and Vanessa and Clarissa?'

'Blooming. Robin wants to go on till he has an heir. We'll

probably end up with a ladies' football team. So, you're bringing Diana up north? Good show.'

'Well, yes, I was coming south, but the Cucumber Marketing Board made me an offer I couldn't refuse.'

'Really? What of?'

'I'm their Chief Controlling Officer (Diseases and Pests).'

Belinda Boyce-Uppingham tried hard to look impressed.

'I am solely responsible for the nationwide fight against diseases of the cucumber. Did you know that there are more than forty major diseases of cucumbers?'

'Golly!'

' "Golly!" indeed!'

Henry was a bit worried about Tommy Marsden, who was knocking back the champagne. He hoped what they said in the papers wasn't true.

'Hello, Tommy,' he said. 'Far cry from the Paradise Lane Gang.'

'Too right,' said Tommy Marsden.

'Is everything all right with you still?' asked Henry.

'You mustn't believe what you read in the papers,' said Tommy Marsden. 'I got pissed and slept in once. If you believe the papers, I never train, I play when I'm drunk, and I've thrown a boot at the manager. I'd be out, wouldn't I, if I did? All that business with that tart in Bratislava was set up, too. They just wanted us out of the European Cup. Hey up, here's another member of the gang. Martin Fucking Hammond.'

'Please, Tommy, great to have you here, but can you avoid saying "fucking",' said Henry.

'Henry!' said Cousin Hilda, passing by in search of more pineapple juice.

'You two allus were stuck-up bastards,' said Tommy Marsden. 'I'm a footballer. They expect me to be uncouth. The chicks like me to be uncouth.'

Tommy Marsden moved on, and Henry knew that if he caused an embarrassing scene it was his fault for asking him; he'd asked him because he'd get some kudos from having such a famous friend.

'Hello, Martin. Hello, Mandy,' he said. 'How's married life?'

'Very life-enhancing,' said Mandy Hammond, née Haltwhistle.

'Good. I'm pleased to hear that.'

'This do could feed a whole province in Guatemala,' said Martin.

'Oh, Martin, I wouldn't have invited you if I'd known you were going to depress me,' said Henry.

'Just joking,' said Martin Hammond. 'I know you think I'm a bore. I thought I'd show you I can let my hair down when the occasion demands it.'

The gathering drifted *en masse* to the main room, which exactly suited the size of the guest list. The ceiling was high and had impressive mouldings, and there was a lovely chandelier which, if it fell, would crush Cousin Hilda, who was giving occasional uneasy looks towards it, not being used to sitting under chandeliers. The whole do was elegant enough to pass muster in a brain surgeon's world, but modest enough to suit what was a second marriage for both parties.

The top table, while following the rules of etiquette, had a somewhat eccentric look, since Henry's parents were represented by Cousin Hilda and Auntie Doris. Since there were two bridesmaids, Kate at one end and Camilla at the other, there were at the table six females, two of them children, and only three males, one of them homosexual.

The meal was cold, but delicious. Rough pâté, followed by Scotch salmon and tarragon chicken with new potatoes and various salads, and strawberries and cream. There was good flinty Mâcon Blanc, rather than the Chablis that a doctor's son would have merited.

Henry, seated between Diana and her mother, knew that he'd got the best of the table arrangement. Mrs Hargreaves told him how happy they were to welcome him as a son-in-law, although Mr Hargreaves flirted dangerously with tactlessness when he leant across and said, 'We were disappointed in Nigel. We had such high hopes. With you, I have a feeling it's going to be the other way about.'

The salmon was the proper stuff, not the farmed kind that poisons lochs and dulls taste buds. The chicken had enjoyed the open air and the fields of Sussex. The tarragon sauce was delicious. Henry wished that he could relax, wished that he didn't feel so anxious about his surrogate parents, about whether the Director (Operations) and the Regional Co-ordinator, Northern Counties (Excluding Berwick-on-Tweed) and their wives were enjoying themselves, about whether Tommy Marsden would disgrace himself, about whether Kate and Camilla would behave with dignity, and whether Benedict and Jack would come to blows at the children's table over at the far right.

He felt Diana's hand on his.

'Happy, darling?'

'Very happy.'

'Truly?'

'Truly.'

'I am.'

'What?'

'Happy.'

'Good. But why do you say, "I am," as if I'm not? I am.'

'You don't look happy.'

'I'm just anxious, that's all. I want everything to go well.'

'It will. And if it doesn't it's not your fault. You're too self-important.'

'Self-important? Me?'

'You take responsibility for the whole world.'

'Oh. Sorry.'

'Don't look so hurt. It's one of the reasons why I love you.'

'What are the others?'

'I can't tell you in public. Do you love me?'

'Of course I do.'

'Then tell me.'

'I love you.'

'No regrets?'

'No regrets.'

He did try not to worry. He could hear Mrs Hargreaves asking

Auntie Doris all about Miles Cricklewood, where he'd been a vet, what size of practice he'd had, about his parents and his family home. She was showing her broad-mindedness about what was still fairly unusual even in 1968, two mature adults living 'in sin'. Auntie Doris didn't have time to worry about the moral aspects. She was too anxious not to contradict herself with the mythical *curriculum vitae* she provided for her absent vet. She couldn't remember if she'd placed his practice in Surrey or Sussex. Her memory wasn't quite what it had been, and it was all too difficult.

Cousin Hilda, on Henry's other side, between Mr Hargreaves and Lampo, was putting up a surprisingly animated show. She was appalled that Henry was marrying for the second time – she had sniffed several times when he'd told her, and hadn't known how she would tell Mrs Wedderburn– but now that the event was upon them she would do her level best not to show him up, even if her motivation was largely not to show herself up, her limestone grit coming out in the face of all this soft southern soil. Unfortunately she had no idea what were considered interesting conversational topics in the big world. Every now and then Henry could hear Mr Hargreaves responding with excruciating politeness to her remarks. 'Moved from the cheese counter to tins! How distressing.' 'Well, if they don't like spotted dick they needn't be in for tea on a Tuesday, need they?' and he went hot under the collar at Mr Hargreaves's boredom, though knowing perfectly well that Mr Hargreaves could cope.

For a while, both Diana and Mrs Hargreaves were speaking to their neighbours and there was nobody for him to speak to. He looked down at the buzzing, cheery room. People were enjoying themselves at all the tables. Nobody was interested in him or in whether he had anybody to speak to.

Shortly before the end of the main course, Auntie Doris passed out and had to be brought round with a cold dishcloth. She couldn't tell Mrs Hargreaves that the strain of her questions about Miles Cricklewood had been the cause. She blamed the heat.

Nobody blamed the heat when Tommy Marsden passed out. Henry leapt to his feet, and hurried out into the heart of the reception, determined not to look embarrassed. He and Martin Hammond carried Tommy Marsden out, the two members of the Paradise Lane gang who had gone to the grammar school helping the one who didn't.

Henry returned to his seat and tried to look natural, as though his friends passed out around him every day.

'I hope nobody else passes out,' he said. 'Only they say things go in threes.'

Just after he'd sat down, he heard Cousin Hilda say to Mr Hargreaves, 'I know very little about brain surgery,' and throughout the strawberries and cream he could hear Mr Hargreaves talking about brain damage, and defunct areas of the brain, and he could see Cousin Hilda nodding sagely, as if she understood, and he had visions of horrible accidents, of Diana lying with her head smashed, of knives in brains, and he felt faint. The sweat was pouring down his back. Diana from a long way off asked him if he was all right, and he said, 'Kiss me. Please, kiss me,' so urgently that Diana gave him a passionate kiss, and he kissed her back. They kissed long and hard at the top table in front of all their guests, as though they were on their own, and people laughed and clapped and Lampo cried, 'Bravo!' and Paul shouted, 'Dirty beast!' and Cousin Hilda looked horrified, and Jack looked at Benedict and said, 'Yuk!' and Benedict said, 'Double yuk!' and Jack said, 'Twenty-seven thousand four hundred and ninety-third yuk!' and Benedict said, 'Thirteen trillion four billion seven million three hundred and ninety-fifth yuk!' and just for a moment it looked as if it might be possible for them to become friends.

Henry felt better. The glasses were charged for the toasts. Lampo stood up and began to read the telegrams.

' "My love, my blessing, and my hopes for your happiness – Hilary," ' read Lampo.

Henry passed out.

10 Kate and Jack and Benedict and Camilla

If you've never driven an elderly Mini from London to Thurmarsh with four children between the ages of eight and eleven crammed into the back, two of whom have the natural arrogance of southern prep-school children, and one of whom might eat the chip on her shoulder if she wasn't feeling car sick, you'll have to imagine the first day proper of Henry and Diana's marital idyll.

'Haven't seen anybody spitting on pavements yet,' said Benedict, just after they had passed through Newark.

'Just because it's all horrendously sordid doesn't mean we're in the proper North yet,' said Camilla.

Kate began to hit out at Camilla, losing control and yelling.

Jack put a calming hand on Kate, but she hurled his gesture back at him.

'Won't bloody try to help in future,' he grumbled.

Diana shouted, 'Shut up, the lot of you,' and Henry stopped the car with a jerk. Camilla was shoved forward, and banged her head, precocity dissolving into tears straight away, and Kate clambered miserably out of the car and was violently sick on the verge.

Diana wanted Kate to sit in the front after that, but she refused, knowing what hostility such a favour would arouse.

'Don't want her in the back,' said Benedict. 'She smells of sick.'

Diana leant across and hit Benedict, harder than she intended. Henry winced.

Benedict went very quiet, but Henry and Diana could sense his fury and himiliation.

Henry wished the sun was shining. The countryside looked grey and drab, the houses poor and dusty. He longed for his beloved North Country to shine, but it refused. They sidled in, between collieries and clapped-out steelworks, through a land in limbo between an ugly, virile past and a flat, uncertain future. How he wished that there were just himself and Diana and his beloved Kate and Jack in the car, and not these two southern children with their assumptions about lifestyles, their contempt for his old car, their scorn of the North. He wondered if Diana was wishing that there were just herself and Henry and her beloved children, and not highly strung, super-sensitive, carsick Kate and infuriatingly placid Jack. How well did they really know each other? Was this a dreadful mistake? Had they rushed in too quickly, on the rebound? He looked at Diana's strained face, and wondered if she was thinking the same thing, and panic gripped him.

The puncture was the final humiliation.

'How quaint,' said Benedict. 'I didn't realise people actually *had* punctures any more.'

How good it was, in that difficult time, to fight the diseases of the cucumber. Henry's new office was in the basement with no carpet and no windows, but there was no sense of demotion in his move underground. Here in this large, bunker-like room he was king. How exciting it was, in those first stressful weeks of his new marriage, to stick flags in a large relief map of the United Kingdom. Basal rot in Myton-on-Swale. Green mottle mosaic intermittent from Beverley to Market Weighton. Downy mildew prevalent around Kettering. Fusarium wilt particularly common from Wimborne to Dorchester.

Henry knew that his enthusiasm was at least faintly ridiculous. He wasn't at all surprised when John Barrington wandered into his long, low-ceilinged basement room, looked at all the flags with the diseases written on them, and said, 'How's the war going, Winston?'

'Pretty damn well, John,' he said. 'Pretty bad genetic yellowing in parts of Essex, casualties are inevitable, but some of the cucumbers'll get through.'

'Damn good show,' said John Barrington, and Henry smiled a slow, half-pleased smile.

Jack and Benedict shared one bedroom, Kate and Camilla another. The children were too old for mixed-sex sharing, and in any case they were anxious not to polarise the southern and the northern children.

Benedict had been imbued with the social assumptions of Tosser Pilkington-Brick. White upper-middle-class Conservative rugby-playing English males were superior to every other form of intelligent and unintelligent life. Whippet-fanciers, miners, socialists, Henry, immigrants and women were on a par with maggots. He felt hostile to Henry, but even more hostile to Diana, who had betrayed him and his beloved father.

Jack's deep good nature meant that he could endure an enormous amount of Benedict's sarcasm without rising to the bait. This infuriated Benedict, who became taut with rage, and this amused Jack. Because Jack was so very tolerant, the argument could be pushed to quite an extreme point before his slow, slow fuse began to burn. If it ever did come to a fight, it would be a serious one. Benedict would have to back off, because he could hardly win any glory from beating a boy two years younger than himself, and he could conceivably lose, since Jack was a big, strong lad. To an extent, therefore, Jack had the upper hand. This infuriated Benedict, but it did give him a degree of respect for Jack.

It wasn't clear what Jack thought about the relationship between Henry and Diana. He never spoke of it.

Henry and Diana felt that Camilla's social arrogance was not nearly as deep as Benedict's, and that she'd like to make friends with Kate if she could do so without incurring her brother's scorn. She wasn't at all hostile to Diana, blaming her father for the break-up to the point where if he hadn't had a Jaguar and a big house with a swimming pool she might not have even wanted to visit him.

Kate was deeply protective of, and loving towards, Henry. She was also more developed intellectually than Camilla, and never ceased to point this out. She wasn't doing this entirely for her own glory. She was doing it out of loyalty to Henry and Thurmarsh and the North of England and Winstanley Primary School and Mrs Williams, who was her best teacher ever. It was very upsetting, therefore, to be rebuked by Henry for saying, 'I'm not surprised you like horses, Camilla. You're pretty thick really,' and it made it impossible for Camilla to show any friendly overtures to Kate.

Henry and Diana hunted for a larger house, but couldn't afford one that cost a great deal more than Dumbarton House would fetch. This meant, inevitably, that, if it had five bedrooms, it would be in a worse area or fairly dilapidated. They put their names on the list of every estate agent in Thurmarsh.

HEALTH WARNING: THE NEXT PARAGRAPH COULD BE DISTRESSING TO ESTATE AGENTS OF A SENSITIVE DISPOSITION.

Three estate agents didn't send anything. One sent everything twice, which was a shame, as all their details were of half-built three-bedroom bungalows in cul-de-sacs, and went straight into the bin. Another sent details of country mansions costing £25,000. From another they did get details of the right kind of houses, but only in Hull and Goole. Only one offered them the right house in the right place at the right price, but the details were sent to the wrong address, and the house was sold by the time Henry and Diana read about it.

They considered moving nearer to Leeds, but decided against it, because Kate and Jack were settled in their schools.

It has to be admitted that, loving parents though they both were, it was a great relief to them when Kate and Jack set off for their annual summer holiday with Hilary in Spain, and, a week later, Benedict and Camilla were taken to Menton by Tosser.

Left on their own in Thurmarsh, Henry and Diana led as civilised a life as their shortage of money would allow. Henry was very conscious that Diana had never been short of money before, and more than once made her angry by harping on the subject. She was upset that he should think money mattered to her, and stated how unimportant she found it, sometimes in words that pleased him – 'I love you. I don't care about wealth. You are my wealth' – and sometimes in words that pleased him slightly less – 'I'm a grown-up. I knew what I was letting myself in for.'

They ate an occasional modest meal at Sandro and Mario's,

Thurmarsh's first Italian restaurant, and at the Taj Mahal – 'You had a lovely lady. Now you have another lovely lady. What is the secret, please?' Henry was always pleased to see Count Your Blessings.

They went to dinner with Alastair and Fiona Blair, with the Mathesons, though rarely now that Anna had emigrated to Canada, and with new friends from the Crescent, Joe and Molly Enwright. Joe was a teacher, Molly a painter.

Russian tanks rolled into Czechoslovakia. France exploded its first hydrogen bomb. Henry gave Diana her first full-scale Thurmarsh Friday night experience. First stop, the Lord Nelson. Helen sniffy, Ginny sad, Colin maudlin, Ted sarcastic and Ben astounded that Diana didn't know *any* of the grounds of *any* of the teams in the second division. Second stop, the Devonshire. Sid Hallett and the Rundlemen wearing flowery shirts in distant homage to flower power, and longer grey hair in an attempt to look vaguely hippy. But the music was the same, and so were the damp patches under their arms. Third stop, the Yang Sing, Thurmarsh's first proper Chinese restaurant, which had superseded the Shanghai Chinese Restaurant and Coffee Bar, now that the era of frothy coffee had ended.

'Well, what did you think?' asked Henry as they undressed in the silent house.

'It's a bit different from Hampstead,' was Diana's Delphic reply.

For three hectic days they had all the children with them, brown with memories, sullen in the Thurmarsh monsoon. Then Camilla was off to St Ethelred's in Devizes, and Benedict to Brasenose College in Surrey, both paid for by Tosser, who insisted on continuing their private education. Henry thought that at eleven and nine they were too young to go to boarding school, but he had to admit that he was glad they did and, to his slight shame, he didn't attempt to persuade Tosser to change his mind.

Benedict and Camilla were glad to leave the overcrowded house and meet their friends and be in their proper environment again, but they resented the fact that Kate and Jack would still be enjoying home comforts when they weren't, and in a house that was no longer overcrowded. Kate and Jack were happy to be staying at home, and fiercely loyal to the schools of Thurmarsh, but also resentful that so much money was being spent on Benedict's and Camilla's education, and feeling diminished by being excluded from their adventure in the great world outside.

In that great world outside, US officials in Saigon announced that defoliation in South Vietnam had produced no harmful results, and Mickey Mouse was forty. There was not necessarily any connection between the two events.

Henry and Diana's life settled into the next pattern, of Henry travelling to Leeds and of Diana taking Kate and Jack to school and fetching them home again. They gave occasional dinner parties. Diana was both a plainer and more confident cook than Hilary. Where Hilary would have produced delicious tandoori chicken with diffidence, Diana plonked down a decent but uninspired steak and kidney pudding as if it was ambrosia for the gods.

Henry forswore comparisons, and found himself making them all the time.

In his bunker in the basement of the Cucumber Marketing Board, Sir Winston Pratt prepared his strategy for 1969's attack on the diseases of the cucumber. Graphs were made, correlations were pursued, comparisons were studied. Did the level of acidity in the soil affect the incidence of angular leaf spot? Was there any discernible connection between altitude and grey mould? So many questions. So few answers. Such a challenge.

'Mrs Wedderburn's not been herself lately.'
    'Oh dear. What's wrong?'
    'It's nothing you can put your finger on.'
    Henry felt ashamed of thinking that there wasn't much of Mrs Wedderburn that he would want to put his finger on.
    'She's just a bit off colour, I suppose.'
    'Oh dear.'
    This was just one of the many sparkling exchanges between Cousin Hilda, Henry and Diana, in the stifling little blue-stoved,

pink-bloomered basement of 66, Park View Road. Autumn had moved all too readily to accommodate winter.

Henry and Diana were engaged in a difficult task.

'Er . . . about Christmas,' said Henry.

Cousin Hilda sniffed psychically.

'Er . . . we . . . er . . . obviously this is our first Christmas, and . . . er . . . obviously things aren't entirely easy with the two different lots of children.'

Cousin Hilda sniffed again. 'If you can't stand the heat, don't move into the house,' her eloquent sniff announced.

'And . . . er . . . we . . . er . . . obviously we . . . er . . . want to give the children a very good Christmas. They are the top priority. And it isn't a large house. Not when you've four children in it.'

Cousin Hilda remained silent. 'Spare me the excuses,' her telling silence screeched.

'So, the thing is . . . er . . . we . . . much as we'd like to normally . . . and hopefully in other years . . . and if we get the house we're going for . . . we . . .'

Cousin Hilda sniffed yet again.

'What house?' she said. 'I don't know owt about a house.'

'Oh, didn't we tell you?' said Diana. 'We meant to. We've seen a house, in Lordship Road, a big Victorian house, and nearer here than we are now. We've made an offer.'

'Lordship Road!' Cousin Hilda sniffed. 'Which end of Lordship Road?'

'This end,' said Diana. 'It's between the Alma and the Gleneagles.'

Cousin Hilda sniffed twice, once for each private hotel.

'The Gleneagles used to be good,' she said, praising the Alma by omission.

Silence fell. The subject of Lordship Road had been exhausted. Henry would have to return to his main theme, and he received no help from Cousin Hilda or Diana.

'So . . . er . . . the thing is . . .' he said. 'I don't think we're going to be able to invite you this year.'

'There's no reason why you should,' said Cousin Hilda sharply.

186

'Diana's children are used to posh people. They wouldn't want to spend Christmas with me. Anyroad, I've got Mr O'Reilly to think of. He'd be a square peg out of water on Christmas day wi'out me. And I couldn't neglect Mrs Wedderburn. Not when she's off colour.'

They chatted briefly of other things after that, of the spiralling cost of crackers, the demise of the tram, and the golden age of corsets.

'Don't forget to send a card to Mrs Wedderburn,' said Cousin Hilda as they left. 'And if it isn't too much trouble, pop in a few words. She were right thoughtful that time lending you her camp-bed like that.'

Henry felt deeply ashamed of wishing that he could shove the camp-bed up Mrs Wedderburn's backside. What sort of person am I, he thought.

Henry helped Kate and Jack choose presents for Benedict and Camilla, and Diana helped Benedict and Camilla choose presents for Kate and Jack. All the children had stockings, filled with things of such careful originality that it didn't strike even Benedict how cheap they were. Christmas dinner was good, and the children played Monopoly, which goes on a long time, which was a good thing. Benedict won, which was fortunate, as he was the one to whom it was most important to win. Major incidents and tears were miraculously avoided, and in the evening they watched *Christmas Night With the Stars*, which went on a long time, which was a good thing, and included Petula Clark, which set Henry wondering what sort of Christmas Count Your Blessings was having. Then they had cold ham and turkey, and then they watched *Some Like It Hot*, which went on a long time, which was a good thing.

The newsroom of the *Thurmarsh Chronicle* and *Argus* throbbed with painful memories. The reporters attacking their typewriters with feverish urgency, the shirt-sleeved sub-editors searching for snappy headlines round the subs' table, the news editor isolated like the conductor of an orchestra at his paper-strewn desk between the reporters and the subs. The long rows of windows were as streaked with grime as ever, save for one. A window-cleaner on a cradle was just about to attack a second window. Henry couldn't imagine what the room would look like without its grimy windows.

An impossibly young reporter was seated at his old desk. It wasn't only policemen who were looking younger, now that Henry was thirty-three.

He made a drinking mime to Ted and Colin as he passed through, and they nodded enthusiastically.

He entered Interview Room B. Helen was wearing a short skirt and had her legs crossed. The blood had drained from her right knee.

'Sorry I'm a bit late,' he said. 'Anthracnose at Maltby.'

'What?'

'I have a new job. I thought it might interest you.'

'Aren't you going to kiss me?'

'Oh . . . er . . . here?'

'Nobody's watching except the pigeons.'

Henry tried to give Helen a polite kiss on the cheek. She reached for his mouth and plonked a great kiss on it, lips working hungrily. She'd been eating butterscotch.

A row of pigeons, puffed up against the approaching night, watched from a slate roof sprinkled with snow and showed no curiosity whatsoever.

'That's better,' said Helen. 'I wondered if you'd gone off me.'

'I'm a happily married man,' said Henry.

'I know. I've met your wife.'

'You were pretty sniffy that night.'

'Was I? Maybe I was disappointed that you hadn't turned to me after your marriage broke up. You know I'm not happy with Ted.'

'What? I did turn to you, and you said you weren't suddenly going to be available when I was on my own. "A girl has her pride," you said.'

'Well, exactly. I wanted to be wooed, and chased. You could have pursued me.'

'I like Ted.'

'Ted would have been thrilled if I'd gone off with you. He'd have married Ginny, which he should have done all along, and everyone would have lived happily ever after. Too late now.'

'Yes.' There wasn't any point in saying that he wouldn't marry Helen if she was the last woman left on the planet.

'Do I gather from your attitude that you don't approve of Diana?'

'On the contrary. I think she's a great improvement.'

'What?'

'Let's face it, Henry, Hilary could be heavy going. Diana's fun. She might have possibilities.'

'What do you mean, "possibilities"?'

'Come off it. You know. Adult dinners. Nice company. Nice food. Good wine. A bit of swapping. Everyone enjoying themselves and no harm done. How about it, Henry? Then you'd see my legs at last.'

'I'm not into that sort of thing, Helen.'

'Oh, don't be so priggish and superior.'

The light was fading fast. Henry wondered if the pigeons would stay there all night. Where do birds sleep? It was one of life's many mysteries. He realised that he didn't want to continue the conversation, he wanted to be at home with Diana, or anywhere rather than the bleak cell that masqueraded as Interview Room B.

'I don't feel in any way superior,' he said. 'I've made quite a mess of my emotional life, but I do still try to lead a good life. If that's priggish, I'm priggish. Now, shall we do the interview?'

Helen opened her notebook and waited.

Is Your Cucumber Wilting? Henry's your man!
by Helen Cornish

Do you have trouble keeping your cucumbers straight and firm?

Are you having problems with Damping-off, False Damping-off, Gummosis, Scab or Topple?

If you are, Thurmarsh-born Henry Pratt (33) is the man to help you.

For Henry, a one-time reporter on the *Argus*, is now Chief Controlling Officer (Diseases and Pests) for the Cucumber Marketing Board, the Leeds-based organisation which aims to give the humble British cucumber a high profile.

Henry, who recently moved into a big Victorian house in Lordship Road, Thurmarsh with his second wife, Diana, his two children, Kate and Jack, and his step-children, Benedict and Camilla, is passionate about cucumbers and their diseases.

Bent

'I seem to have given my life to cucumbers. Perhaps it's my natural bent. Not that I've any time for bent cucumbers,' he joked to me yesterday.

'I suppose I am a bit of a fanatic,' he enthused. 'But then my job is probably one that needs a fanatic.'

Henry, who is not tall and lean like a good cucumber, but short and podgy and a self-confessed unathletic slob, believes that the British public are shamefully ignorant about cucumbers, that they take them for granted and even regard them as objects of slight derision.

'I think the cucumber's a bit of an underdog in the salad world,' he reflects. 'I'm a bit of an underdog myself, so maybe I have a natural affinity for it.'

Fairy Butter

In his fight to bring healthy cucumbers to our tables, Henry has to battle against no less than 42 different diseases of cucumbers, ranging from three different kinds of wilt and four different kinds of mildew to such romantically named complaints as Angular Leaf Spot, Fairy Butter and Root Mat.

'If you think it's all a load of rot, it certainly is,' he quips. 'There are at least six different forms of cucumber rot.'

Henry is spending the winter preparing booklets, pamphlets and leaflets for growers and gardeners, giving advice on how to recognise and deal with all their diseases.

'It's like a military operation,' he explains. 'I have all sorts of little flags dotted all over a map of Britain. The chaps josh me a bit about it, but all in good humour. They're a terrific bunch.'

If you think the cucumbers in your local shop are a terrific bunch this summer, and you can't see any Leaf Spot, Mildew or Rot, you'll know who to thank. That unsung hero, Paradise Lane-born Henry Pratt, the man who stops the cucumbers wilting.

'It's made us a laughing stock.'

'It's made *me* a laughing stock. I can't go in a pub in Thurmarsh without people asking me if my cucumber's wilting.'

'It's set our image back ten years.'

'I'm very sorry, sir.' Henry felt that the 'sir' was justified on this occasion. 'I never dreamt she'd make fun of us. I didn't realise how far the press has sunk since I left.'

Timothy Whitehouse swivelled round to gaze at his reproduction of Van Gogh's little-known 'Sunflower with Cucumbers', as if anything was preferable to looking at Henry.

'Did you clear it with Angela?' he asked.

'No. Sorry.'

'What's the point of having a press officer if you don't consult her?'

'I'm afraid I tend to get excited and forget I'm an organisation man.'

The Director (Operations) wheeled round and looked at Henry sadly.

'There's no room for mavericks or lone wolves in an organisation like ours,' he said. 'You've blotted your copy-book again.'

'I realise that,' said Henry.

'Blot after blot, Henry. What am I going to do with you?'

'May I just say in my defence that when I joined you did tell me to be my own man, be fearless and always speak the truth?'

'I did. I did. Point taken. *Mea culpa!* I should have said, "Be your own man, be fearless and always speak the truth *except to the press*." Let me spell it out once and for all, Henry.' He pulled his braces forward, let them go thwack against his chest, leant forward, predatory nose pointing straight at Henry, and smiled with his teeth but not his eyes. 'We're a team here. We expect our staff to show discipline and team spirit. In working for us you have to accept authority as a force beyond individuality.'

'That's just what my headmaster at my prep school said.'

'And you thought, "Silly old buffer. What does he know?" But he was right. What school was this? I must recommend it.'

'Brasenose College in Surrey. The headmaster was Mr A. B. Noon BA.'

'Aha!'

'That's funny, because his name is palindromic, the same backwards as forwards, and so was your "aha!"!'

'I do know what palindromic means, I did recognise A. B. Noon BA as palindromic, and I said "Aha!" deliberately with what I hoped was a flash of rather neat wit,' said the Director (Operations). 'I'm not stupid, but I'm beginning to think you are, so maybe I won't recommend Brasenose College after all.'

As Henry drove up the drive towards the creepered fortress that held Brasenose College in its grim grip, he saw the palindromic headmaster, Mr A. B. Noon BA, balding and stooping now, striding towards the playing fields with his two palindromic daughters, Hannah and Eve, steaming pallidly in his wake, both stooping prematurely. Had they been walking like that, staring at the ground, for twenty-one years?

Benedict's face turned white when he saw the rusting Mini parked alongside the Daimlers and Bentleys of the other parents. He stood in the pillared portico of the main entrance and came no further.

'Well come on,' called Henry.

Benedict shook his head.

Henry approached the school building with dread, lest he catch something of its old smell of rissoles and fear. Swifts were screeching joyously round the roof.

'I asked you not to bring that thing here,' hissed Benedict.

'I have no other means of transport,' said Henry. 'I'm not rich and you'll have to accept that.'

Benedict stared into the distance, loftily. His eleven-year-old face was stony.

'Material possessions aren't what matter, Benedict. It's moral values that count. And love and affection and fun. We can have all these if we try.'

'Try telling that to the chaps in the dorm.'

'I did, once. It wasn't much use, I admit.'

'I'm not getting in that thing.'

'Oh, come on. Be strong. Be your own man.'

'I am my own man, and I'm not coming. I've better things to do.'

'We've come a long way to see you.'

'Miracle you got here.'

'Well we did, and your mother wants to see you.'

'She should have thought of that before she married you.'

Henry looked into Benedict's hot, blazing eyes, and thought he could see the potential for madness there.

He almost felt the potential for madness in himself. His heart was pounding with barely controllable fury.

Benedict's face turned from deathly white to bright red.

'I don't want you sticking your cucumber into my mother,' he said. 'I bet it's got downy mildew.'

He turned abruptly and disappeared into the darkness of the school. Henry walked slowly back in the sunshine, feet crunching wearily.

Diana gave him an anxious smile. He shrugged his shoulders.

'Won't come,' he said.

He got back into the car, started the engine, and turned to smile at Camilla.

'Come on, Camilla,' he said. 'Let's go and look at some horses.'

11 A Surfeit of Cucumbers

Poverty is a tragedy. Wealth is a problem. Being able to earn just enough money to make ends meet concentrates the mind wonderfully.

Apollo II landed on the moon, Neil Armstrong and Edward Aldrin Junior walked on the moon's surface for two and three quarter hours; the Isle of Wight music festival attracted 250,000 spectators and left the surface of the island looking like the moon; Spiro Agnew, who could well have been educated on the moon, launched a rich tradition of idiotic statements by US Vice-Presidents, when he told an audience at a New Orleans dinner that those who supported a moratorium on the Vietnam War were 'encouraged by an effete corps of impudent snobs who characterize themselves as intellectuals'; and Henry concentrated wonderfully on the diseases of the cucumber.

Not to the neglect of its pests, I hope, the anxious reader cries.

Alas, anxious reader, I have to dash your hopes. In January, 1970, Henry realised that he had neglected the pests shamefully.

Never mind, he told himself, that's all water under the bridge now, and it gives me a target for the summer.

His target would be no less than the elimination of the glasshouse red spider mite and the glasshouse whitefly. From Land's End to John o' Groats there would be no resting place for the little bastards.

In number 83, Lordship Road, life was a constant struggle against cold and damp. The solid Victorian house was on the verge of crumbling. It was extremely difficult to keep warm, and had sinister damp patches on the walls. In this unpromising setting, between the Alma and the Gleneagles private hotels, the Pratt family life proceeded by fits and starts.

For thirty-four weeks, Benedict and Camilla were away at school, and Henry had to admit that it was an enormous relief.

For much of the summer holidays, and for the Christmas and New Year period, Kate and Jack were in Spain, Benedict and Camilla in France or Austria, skiing. Diana didn't want to hear about Tosser and was told his every banal thought, his every greedy mouthful, his every rich client. Henry wanted to know everything about Hilary and received only the sketchiest information that she was 'all right'.

Henry calculated that it was only for twenty-five days in the year that all four of the children's bedrooms were occupied at once. For these twenty-five days he felt that he was carrying the North/South divide around with him, in an atmosphere that was never less than tense, although there were no major eruptions. Benedict seemed almost unnaturally calm, and even allowed himself to be driven round Thurmarsh in Henry's Mini.

The children covered the damp patches on the walls of their bedrooms with posters and blown-up photographs. They chose contrasting subjects, and Henry was amazed and delighted that none of them concentrated on pop stars, although Benedict's choice did make him feel rather uneasy.

Kate chose great ballet dancers, romantic men with white faces and hollow cheeks, who looked as if they were dying of consumption.

In Jack's room the posters were of footballers – Bobby Charlton, Bobby Moore, Jimmy Greaves, Denis Law. Not Tommy Marsden. Tommy Marsden wasn't a hero any more.

Camilla's pictures were of horses.

Benedict plumped for Mussolini, Rasputin, John Lennon, Nietzsche and Dr Crippen.

Uncle Teddy rushed to the garden gate.

'You'll find her a bit changed,' he said.

'Changed?' said Henry.

'Her memory's a bit patchy sometimes. She's a bit obsessive.'

'Obsessive?'

'You'll see.'

The garden of Honeysuckle Cottage was rich with sweet william and wallflowers and lupins and marigolds and the eponymous honeysuckle. The tilting, peach-washed thatched cottage was an impossible dream.

Auntie Doris came out to meet them, smiling broadly. Henry could see nothing wrong, except perhaps that her eyes had become slightly deep-set.

'Hello, darling,' she said, hugging Henry. 'Hello, Hilary.'

'It's Diana, actually,' said Henry.

'Of course it is. Silly me. Would you like a cup of tea?'

They had tea in the garden. Blackbirds pinked, insects buzzed, fighter planes screamed, lawnmowers droned. Everything was as it should be, in the early days of summer.

'It was just a slip of the tongue when I said Hilary,' said Auntie Doris. 'I knew who you were.'

'Of course you did,' said Diana.

'I was at your wedding,' said Auntie Doris. 'I fainted, Henry fainted, that footballer passed out.'

'Your memory's very sharp,' said Henry.

'What do you mean?' said Auntie Doris. 'Why do you say that? You think it isn't, don't you?'

'Of course not.'

'I'd hardly be likely to forget three people passing out at a wedding, including the groom. That's hardly evidence of a sharp memory. You're humouring me.'

'Not at all,' said Diana. 'Henry doesn't humour people.'

'Would you like a cup of tea?' asked Auntie Doris.

'They've just had a cup of tea,' said Uncle Teddy.

'I know that,' said Auntie Doris. 'I'm not stupid. I made it for them. I thought they might want another one. It's a warm afternoon.'

After their second pot of tea, Uncle Teddy mooted a walk with Henry, and Henry realised that there was an ulterior motive for the suggestion.

Flower baskets hung from the thatched eaves of pink-washed and white-washed cottages. The larger houses had magnificent brick chimney-stacks.

On the green that led up to the church, Henry stopped to read the notice on an old Victorian pump: 'TAKE NOTE THAT BOYS OR OTHER PERSONS DAMAGING THIS PUMP WILL BE PROSECUTED AS THE LAW DIRECTS.'

Uncle Teddy waited impatiently, and as soon as they moved on, he said, 'Will you do me a small favour, Henry? Will you take some packages to Derek Parsonage for me?'

Henry's heart sank.

'What sort of packages?'

'Oh, just odds and ends. Safer for you not to know what's in them. Nothing illegal.'

'What do you mean, "Nothing illegal"?'

'Nothing stolen. Nothing harmful. Just things that, in this drearily bureaucratic world, should go through the customs, that's all. Security for our old age. Security for Doris's old age. Bit in it for you.'

'Oh, I wouldn't want any money from it,' said Henry, as they sauntered up the lane towards the open country.

'You mean you'd do it, but only for nothing?' said Uncle Teddy.

They stopped to look over a five-barred gate at a pleasant view over gently undulating farmland. A lone skylark was singing. Henry tried hard to refuse.

'Yes,' he found himself saying.

'Good man,' said Uncle Teddy. 'Good man. Sorry it has to be so cloak-and-dagger, but Doris has an unfortunate habit of remembering things she's not supposed to remember.'

'I thought her memory was bad.'

'Exactly. She forgets what it is she's not supposed to remember. Calls me Teddy sometimes in front of other people. I just tell people that was her husband. Died in a fire. Won't marry me because she's still carrying a torch for him. Touching story. Gets people in tears down the pub.'

They set off, more briskly, for home. Uncle Teddy wasn't interested in views and cottages now that he'd achieved his purpose.

As they approached Honeysuckle Cottage, Uncle Teddy slowed down and said, 'Er . . . just one thing. We'll probably play

Scrabble this evening. Usually do. The old girl's spelling's not always too hot these days. Best not to point her mistakes out, I find.'

Auntie Doris offered to make a pot of tea. Uncle Teddy said the sun was almost over the yard-arm, so they had gin and tonic instead. Auntie Doris had cooked chicken-and-ham pie but had forgotten the ham, and she'd made rhubarb crumble with salt instead of sugar. 'Bloody repulsive, but there's no point in upsetting the old girl,' said Uncle Teddy. They drank malt whisky and played Scrabble. Auntie Doris only made two spelling mistakes – Doezn for Dozen and Seequin instead of Sequin. She won, largely because, due to her mistakes, her Z and her Q both fell on triple letter squares. 'Bit of luck for the old girl there,' said Uncle Teddy. 'Nice to see it. Deserves it after living with that arse Porringer. Wish I could run into the bastard again. I'd give him two black eyes to match his blackheads.'

At first, Henry believed that the weather had played the major role in the creation of the cucumber mountain. His natural modesty and lack of self-confidence led him to underestimate his part. But as the summer of 1970 drifted on, evidence began to pile up which suggested that the major responsibility belonged to him. Rot was rare, wilt was minimal, mildew was almost entirely confined to the Celtic fringes. As for the glasshouse red spider mite and the glasshouse whitefly, the little bastards didn't know what had hit them.

The dual northern chilled stores at Preston and Darlington were overflowing.

When Henry was summoned before the Director (Operations), he expected praise for his achievements.

'You look strangely contented,' said Timothy Whitehouse.

'Well, I . . . er . . . yes.' The Chief Controlling Officer (Diseases and Pests) was puzzled. 'Yes, I . . . er . . . yes.'

'I see,' said Mr Whitehouse, somewhat surprisingly. 'Henry, we have a glut of cucumbers. A cucumber mountain.'

'Or, since they're ninety per cent water, a cucumber lake.'

'This is no time for levity.' Timothy Whitehouse looked at Henry sadly. 'We have a disaster on our hands.'

'How can that be? There are millions of cheap cucumbers around.'

The Director (Operations) gave Henry another sad look and, as if he couldn't bear to look at him any more, swung round and gazed at Rembrandt's little-known and deeply compassionate 'Old woman with cucumber'.

'How can you be so naïve?' he said. 'Who are we responsible to?'

'The public?'

'No!!! They have no voice. They're amorphous. They don't, in the final analysis, exist.'

'The growers?'

'Better. They have a voice. We have to make sure they're reasonably contented and don't go dumping cucumber mountains outside Number Ten. Not that it's likely. They aren't French. But no, we as employees are ultimately responsible to our Board of Directors. And who are they responsible to? The government. They are our pay-masters. Have you heard of support buying?'

'Well, yes, of course. Can you remind me how it works?'

'Can I remind you? How long have you been with us?'

'Er . . .'

'Never mind. I haven't time to wait for your brain.' The Director (Operations) pulled his braces to their full extent and let them thud back into his chest. 'We're desperately buying up cucumbers, using up our budget, and destroying them to keep up the price. They don't burn very well.'

'Can't we persuade people to buy more cucumbers?'

'Well there is a limit. It's their crisp freshness that appeals. They don't freeze well.'

'You can freeze cucumber soup.'

'Take a walk through Holbeck. Take a walk through Beeston. Take a walk through Seacroft. Look at the people. Are they going to freeze cucumber soup?'

'I think that's a rather degrading cultural assumption.'

'It's not necessarily criticism. Maybe they aren't poncey enough to freeze cucumber soup. We have a catastrophic glut, and I hold you responsible.'

'Doesn't the weather have something to do with it?'

'Very possibly, but God is not within my remit and you are.'

'I thought I was supposed to control diseases and pests.'

'You are. But not eliminate them overnight. What we seek to achieve, Henry, as I thought you understood, is equilibrium. Stability. Stable levels of production. Stable incomes. Stable prices.'

'So, I'm just to sit there and do nothing.'

Timothy Whitehouse leant forward, and Henry realised that he was about to receive one of those smiles that didn't reach the eyes. 'Who knows what the future holds in store? Some vast new cucumber plague, perhaps. Dutch cucumber disease. French rot. German measles. If that day comes, you will stand alone between us and annihilation.' He smiled again, persuasively, comfortingly, patronisingly.

'And if that day never comes?'

'They also serve who only stand and wait.'

'But you told me to be my own man, stick to my guns, and always speak the truth.'

'How old are you, Henry?' asked the Director (Operations).

'Thirty-five,' said the Chief Controlling Officer (Diseases and Pests).

'And you still believe what the authorities tell you.' Timothy Whitehouse shook his head sadly.

On Tuesday, September 1st, 1970, Concorde boomed over Britain for the first time. The damage was not as great as had been feared. A fluorescent lighting tube fell from the ceiling of a house in Wales, and two pencils, placed on a bridge by scientists in Oban, fell over. No other incidents were reported.

On the same day, King Hussein of Jordan escaped an assassination attempt, Benedict and Camilla returned home from Mykonos, US senators voted fifty-five to thirty-nine against ending the Vietnam War, Henry took two large parcels to Derek Parsonage's exotic brothel in Commercial Road, Britons were criticised for buying millions of useless vitamin pills, and Mrs Wedderburn died.

Derek Parsonage's brothel was situated in a Victorian town house that was marginally more decrepit even than 83, Lordship Road. A brass plate at the side of the door announced, 'World-Wide Religious Literature Inc.'

The entrance hall was piled with religious literature, and gave no hint of the female underclothes, chain-mail, black bags, whips, studded belts, schoolgirls' uniforms, harnesses, electric leads, dustbins, oranges, nooses, trapdoors, soft brooms, hard brooms and water hoses that lay in wait for the deviant men of Thurmarsh.

Derek Parsonage came out of his office and greeted Henry warmly, if sanctimoniously.

'So good to see you, Henry,' he said. 'Come into my office.'

When they were in the office, he said, very unsanctimoniously, 'I didn't realise you were into this kind of thing. What is your preference?'

'Oh no,' said Henry, feeling insulted yet also slightly flattered. 'I've seen Uncle Teddy and I've got a couple of parcels.'

'Say no more,' said Derek Parsonage, whose blackheads had got worse. 'Just drive them round the back. How is the old rogue?'

'Very well,' said Henry. 'Playing a lot of Scrabble.'

Uncle Teddy's old partner in crime, whose brothel had been involved in the deception over the burnt-down Cap Ferrat, gawped at this news.

As Henry drove his car round the back, he was horrified to see a police car lurking in the alley between the Pet Boutique and the Commercial Café.

As he opened the front door of number 83 after delivering his parcels, Henry could hear the phone ringing. 'I wonder if you'd come down the station of your own free will and save us all a lot of trouble, sir.' When he heard Diana say, 'Oh hello, Cousin Hilda,' Henry's relief was so great that he said, 'Hello, Cousin Hilda,' so heartily that her 'Hello, Henry. Bad news, I'm afraid. Brace yourself,' rocked him on his heels and he said, 'What is it?' in a croak, and when she said, 'Mrs Wedderburn's dead,' he felt such a wave of relief and such appalling guilt at feeling relief, that when she said, 'The cremation's on Wednesday. She were right thoughtful lending you that camp-bed. You will come, won't you?' he said, 'Of course we will,' without hesitation or annoyance.

Henry feared that he, Diana and Cousin Hilda would be the only mourners. He'd forgotten that Mrs Wedderburn had three sons. Judge then of his astonishment when there were in the gleaming, spotless clinical chapel of Thurmarsh Crematorium, off the Doncaster Road, not only the three sons and two of their wives, but also a sister, a sister's husband, two cousins, a nephew, nine people from her church, three from her sewing circle, two neighbours, her whist partner, her medium and her chiropodist.

'Quite a send-off,' said Cousin Hilda.

After the service, as they stood outside the chapel, not liking to rush away, but not wanting to talk to anybody, Henry found himself beside Mrs Wedderburn's sister, a small plump lady in black.

'A sad day,' said Mrs Wedderburn's sister.

'Very sad,' said Henry. 'A generous woman, who lends you her camp-bed with no strings attached, all her life to live for, gets crushed beneath a JCB. It makes you wonder what life is all about.'

'It's the driver I'm sorry for,' said Mrs Wedderburn's sister. 'He's going to have to live with that for the rest of his days.'

As they drove away from the crematorium, Cousin Hilda gave a deep sigh. It was the only emotion she allowed herself to show at the death of her one close friend.

'You made a hit with Mrs Wedderburn's sister,' she said. ' "What a nice young man," she said.'

It was her way of thanking them for coming.

There were several deaths in the second half of 1970, in addition to Mrs Wedderburn's. Antonio Salazar, Portuguese Chief of State for forty years, died in Lisbon. President Nasser died in Cairo. General de Gaulle died at Colombey-Les-Deux-Eglises. Henry felt as if something had died in him as well. There wasn't any point in sticking flags into maps any more. He began applying for jobs again, without success. He was in a Catch-22 situation. He'd been too long in cucumbers, so he needed a new job, but nobody would give him a new job, because he'd been too long in cucumbers.

Being a new boy at Dalton College did wonders for Benedict's confidence. In fact it removed it entirely for months. Kate's school reports remained good, and she took a keen interest in almost every subject. Jack plodded along, bulkily ugly, in the middle of the class if his teacher managed to stimulate him, towards the bottom if he didn't. But he was good at sport and immensely practical. Camilla lived, breathed and, sad to say, resembled horses.

1971 saw Britain's first national postal strike. It lasted almost two months, and helped Henry to slow down his fight against the diseases and pests of cucumbers while preventing him from applying for any more jobs. Decimal currency was introduced, and the price of everything, including cucumbers, went up. Unemployment in Britain reached 3.4 per cent, the highest figure since 1940. Sanity was restored to the production of cucumbers. Henry resumed his job hunting, to no avail.

On Saturday, October 23rd, 1971, Henry and Diana set off at 5.30 in the morning, in order to reach Dalton College in Somerset by twelve. Kate and Jack were staying with the Blairs, and Camilla was tucked up in a dormitory at St Ethelred's. They would take her out for Sunday lunch before returning exhausted to Yorkshire.

It promised to be quite a day. Lunch with Benedict at the Bald-Headed Angel, followed by the big rugby match against their arch rivals, Sherborne, and then a Grand Reunion Tea in School Hall for old boys who began their school career between 1945 and 1950.

Henry parked his new second-hand Ford Escort in the car park of the Bald-Headed Angel, for fear that if he drove it to the school gates Benedict would refuse to get in it. He and Diana walked to the school. The air was raw and damp.

Tosser Pilkington-Brick was standing beside his Jaguar in a very smart new overcoat. His second wife, Felicity, was sitting in the car, looking, as Henry and Diana decided later, pretty but vapid.

'Hello!' said Tosser, surprised. 'What are you doing here?'

'Taking Benedict out,' said Henry.

'There must be some mistake,' said Tosser. 'We're taking him out.'

Benedict sauntered jauntily towards them. His confidence, now that he was fourteen, and no longer in his first year, was coming back all too quickly. He looked from his father to his stepfather and said, casually, 'Oh lawks. Contretemps. Did I forget to tell you, Mummy, that I was going to lunch with Daddy? I only knew he was coming the other day. Frightfully sorry.' He kissed his mother casually. 'See you two at the match. Pity it's such a cold day for it. Right, Dad, let's get this Jag going.'

It had been on another cold late October day, twenty-three years ago, in the restaurant of the Bald-Headed Angel, that Diana, on the very first occasion that Henry had met her, had said, 'Isn't embarrassment embarrassing. This is the most embarrassing meal I've ever been to.' And now here she was, sitting with Henry at a table laid for three, next to the table where her son was sitting with her ex-husband and his second wife. The restaurant had recently been revamped, inexplicably, as a German *gaststaette*, which went with its character as an English coaching inn about as well as the cauliflower au gratin and carrots went with the badly trimmed, tough *wienerschnitzel*.

All around them, in the crowded restaurant, were parents and children. Henry and Diana alone had no pupil with them.

Henry reached across the table and clasped Diana's hand. She gave his hand an answering squeeze.

Benedict frowned on seeing this, and said, to his father, 'Any thoughts about this year's skiing?'

Tosser looked uneasily at Felicity, and it dawned on Henry that Benedict might be trying to embarrass Tosser and Felicity just as much as himself and Diana. This made him feel better.

Benedict leant across towards them. He had an unhealthy gleam in his eyes. 'Everything all right for you two?' he asked.

'Amazing,' said Henry cheerfully. 'The food here is incredible. One never believes it could get worse and it always does.'

'You fagged for my dad, didn't you?' said Benedict in an unnecessarily loud voice.

'Yes, I am younger than him, that is true,' said Henry. He raised his glass and clinked it with Diana's. The indifferent Piesporter swished gently. He turned to Tosser's table, raised his glass to the three of them, and said, 'Your good health, and your continued happiness and wealth.'

Neither Tosser nor Felicity seemed to know quite how to respond to this. They raised their glasses and smiled uneasily.

'You're happier this time round, I hope, Tosser,' said Diana.

Tosser tried to hide his fury at the use of his nickname.

'You didn't tell me you were called Tosser,' said Felicity. 'Why were you called Tosser?'

'No significant reason,' said Tosser pompously.

Henry saw Benedict give Tosser a malicious look. He felt an unworthy surge of pleasure.

Later, as he walked arm in arm with Diana towards the school, through the market-place whose charming jumble of old buildings was now dwarfed by a concrete and rust shopping centre, he realised that he'd been quite exhausted by the effort of not being embarrassed. A keen wind bore the faintest traces of rain. He shivered.

'Cold?' said Diana.

'No. Thinking about the look in Benedict's eye. There's so much anger in that boy.'

'And we're all angry with him, although it's mainly our fault,' said Diana.

'We're angry *because* it's our fault.'

'Come on. This afternoon's going to be hell if we don't throw ourselves into it. Let's cheer our heads off.'

The West Country is warm, wet and soft, with just three exceptions – Land's End, Lower Boggle and Middle Boggle. That afternoon, at Dalton College, Middle Boggle was at its most spiteful. The wind cut into eyes, painted noses red, and forced its way up trouser legs. Tosser went mad, reliving his glory days, shouting, 'Bolly bolly bolly, Dalton Dalton Dalton, play up shant, bolly bolly bolly,' in the time-honoured way. Diana shouted, 'Come on Dalton,' and waved her arms around. Felicity scowled and froze. Henry gradually got excited, but just couldn't bring himself to shout, 'Bolly bolly bolly, Dalton Dalton Dalton, play up shant, bolly bolly bolly.' Lampo and Denzil walked past them, hands touching. 'How the cretins roar,' said Lampo.

Dalton took a 13–8 lead early in the second half, and clung on for a victory that was unexpected and brave, albeit slightly fortunate. A great roar greeted the final whistle. Only cold Felicity and caustic Lampo remained aloof.

A great chatter of old boys wended its way down to School Hall, flushed with triumph: solicitors with hoarse voices, merchant bankers with chapped lips, and the cucumber man re-entering the scene of his past triumph.

The seats, which all those years ago had been packed with schoolboys laughing at Henry's comic act in the end-of-term concert, had been removed and stored under the stage. On the stage were trestle tables, laden with sandwiches and cakes. The old boys and their wives queued good-humouredly to be given name stickers. 'H. E. Pratt, Orange House 1948–50' and 'Mrs Pratt'. 'P. K. R. Davey, Orange House 1945–50' and 'Mrs Davey'. Denzil wore his 'Mrs Davey' sticker proudly. Doctors, bankers and accountants frowned at it and moved on. Vicars smiled, to show how broad-minded they were.

By the time he'd been forced to leave Dalton so abruptly, Henry had been on the point of feeling that he belonged there. Now, twenty-one years later, that confidence was hard to recreate. The words of his comic turn reverberated through his head – ''Ow do, I'm t'new headmaster, tha knows' – but they carried memories not only of his triumph but also of his shame at the betrayal of his father. In any case the ghostly words were soon drowned under the very real hum as hundreds of old boys greeted old friends. Most of them were taller than him and apart from the vicars they all looked more prosperous. He was Oiky Pratt masquerading in the over-careful tweed jacket and overweight creased body of a thirty-six-year-old man.

As he was walking away from the stage with a cup of tea and a slice of date-and-nut loaf, Henry was approached by a man whom he knew by his sticker to be F. L. Barnes, Plantagenet House 1946–51.

'H. E. Pratt,' announced F. L. Barnes, stooping to read Henry's sticker.

'That's me,' admitted Henry.

'I wondered if I'd see you,' said F. L. Barnes. 'You applied for a job with us not long ago. I'm in personnel at McVitie's.'

'Yes, I did. Didn't even get an interview. Frightened of employing another Daltonian, were you? Worried about charges of nepotism.'

'No, no,' said F. L. Barnes. 'Absolutely the reverse. Trouble was, you'd been given the most awful reference I've ever read.'

Henry felt as if he'd been punched in the stomach. He was still feeling shocked when N. T. A. Pilkington-Brick, Orange House 1945–50 arrived on the arm of Mrs Pilkington-Brick. Tosser looked so bulky, and Felicity so small and frail, that Henry flinched inwardly at the thought of them making love.

'I hope you didn't find the lunch *too* embarrassing,' said Tosser.

'I hope *you* didn't,' said Diana.

'Do you think we ought to talk about Benedict some time?' said Tosser. 'We think he's turning out a bit strange. Are you happy with the way you're managing him?'

'You sound as though he's a portfolio,' said Diana, 'and he is at school thirty-four weeks of the year and with you almost half of the rest.'

'Yes, but yours is his home. You are the prime influence upon him.'

'You could apply for custody if you want,' said Henry.

Tosser's fading Madagascan suntan faded still further. 'No, no. No, no. We're happy as we are. In fact . . . er . . . now that I'm married. . . ,' he gave Felicity a little smile and she simpered back, '. . . we . . . er . . . well, let's say, I *have* been having them *almost every* holiday, Camilla's fine, of course, but Benedict *is* a problem. This coming year too I have business commitments which . . . and I don't want to be greedy. He's your son as well, Diana.'

'Felicity isn't all that keen on him, is that it?' said Diana.

Felicity didn't move a muscle. They had no idea what she was thinking or indeed *if* she was thinking.

'No, no, you've got it all wrong, it isn't that at all,' said Tosser. 'I just think he doesn't know where his real home is and he ought to. That's all. I'm only thinking of him.'

'Of course,' said Henry.

Paul and Christobel joined the family circle. They were both practising gynaecologists now, and childless. Paul was putting on weight and developing gravitas. Christobel was still beautiful but Henry didn't feel that he knew her at all. Their voices always sounded as if they were comforting an elderly patient of limited intelligence. In his friskier moments Henry referred to their Georgian house outside Farnham as Bedsyde Manor. But this was not one of his friskier moments.

'No more problems with fainting, then?' asked Christobel. 'I know it's not our field, but it did concern us.'

'Fainting?' said Tosser.

'Henry fainted at his wedding,' said Paul. 'Went spark out during the telegrams, poor chap.'

'I was overcome with love for Diana,' said Henry uneasily.

J. C. R. Tubman-Edwards, Tudor House 1948–53, approached.

'Hello, mates,' he said. 'How are you, Tosser? Long time no see.'

'Thank God,' said Tosser, 'and the name's Nigel, and you never were my mate. You were rotten to Henry.'

'And I didn't like people being rotten to my little fatty faggy-chops,' said Lampo, joining the gathering along with Denzil.

Henry flinched. This wasn't what he wanted to remember.

' "Mrs Davey"!' said Josceleyn Tubman-Edwards. 'I think that's rather tasteless.'

'Yes, it's splendid, isn't it?' said Henry, revived by the prospect of teasing Josceleyn. 'How's your lovely debutante lady?'

'I've no idea,' said Josceleyn Tubman-Edwards. 'She jilted me two days before my wedding.'

Life can be a pig. A group of old boys are enjoying getting their own back on a bully, and suddenly they all have to feel sympathy for the poor bloke.

'Oh, I'm really sorry,' said Henry, and meant it.

Mr Lennox, Henry's old English master, a pedantic soul known to the boys as Droopy L., approached through a wall of conversation. His hair and skin were grey and he had frown lines the way other people have laugh lines.

'I'm afraid I'm going to have to ask you to remove your name badge,' he told Denzil.

'Oh come off it, Mr Lennox,' said Lampo. 'You always were a little Hitler.'

'There's no need to be rude,' said Droopy L.

'What's the use of reunions if we can't be nasty to masters we didn't like?' said Henry, with a boldness he didn't feel.

'Take it off, please. I really do insist,' said Droopy L.

'Please don't, Denzil,' said Lampo. 'I love Denzil, Mr Lennox. We argue like mad but live together more faithfully than most husbands and wives.'

'That's your problem,' said Droopy L.

'Oh no, it's your problem,' said Denzil. 'It's legal now and we're doing no harm.'

'I've had complaints,' said Mr Lennox, 'and I must ask you to remove it or leave. Where do you think this is – Marlborough?'

'Quite right,' said Tosser.

'Oh, come off it, Tosser, don't be such a pompous ass. You fancied Henry almost as much as I did,' said Lampo.

'Lampo!' hissed Tosser.

'Do we really need to go into all this?' said Henry.

'I'm very interested,' said Felicity.

'Come on, Denzil, my love,' said Lampo. 'We aren't welcome here.'

'We're coming too,' said Henry. 'It's outrageous.'

'Henry!' said Diana.'

'What?'

'You said we're going. You haven't consulted me.'

'Sorry, darling. You will come, won't you?'

'No. Not because I think it's disgusting, I think it's funny, but Denzil isn't actually Mrs Davey so he hasn't got a leg to stand on, and I'm not going to get steamed up about it.'

'I'm not steamed up. I care about my friends.'

'I care about my brother, and I haven't seen him for ages.'

'It's all right, Henry,' said Denzil. 'We'll see you later. Thank you for your support. I shall always wear it.'

'And with that hoary old joke, I leave with my hoary old lover,' said Lampo. 'Farewell, Droopy L. Farewell, Dalton.'

'Absolutely disgusting,' said Droopy L. 'I sometimes wonder why we bothered to educate you all.'

'It's true,' said the Director (Operations). 'Absolutely true.' He looked Henry straight in the eye at a moment when Henry would have expected him to gaze at one of his old masters for comfort. 'I didn't want to lose you.'

'I beg your pardon?'

'I give good references to people I want to get rid of and bad references for people I want to keep.'

'That's outrageous.'

'I have to protect my interests. And the interests of the organisation.'

'How can I ever trust you again?'

'I shouldn't, if I were you. Then we'll understand each other perfectly.'

'I'm very unhappy about it,' said Henry. 'I don't know if I can work with you any more.'

Now Mr Whitehouse did look away, gazing at Vermeer's exquisite but little-known 'Preparation of salad in a house in Delft'.

'I'll be sorry if you do resign,' he said. 'Though no doubt you'd find a good job eventually.'

'How could I, with your stinking references?'

'Oh, I'd give you good references once I'd lost you. I'm not a complete bastard. I'd tell the truth.'

'What is the truth?'

'That you're reliable, intelligent, enthusiastic and talented, with a deep sense of loyalty, who gets on well with other people, forms a useful member of the team and was being groomed for higher office at the time of your resignation.'

'Good Lord. Am I really being groomed for higher office?'

'Don't you believe me?'

'No. You told me not to.'

'As I say, you're intelligent.'

'I thought maybe I'd blotted my copy-book once too often.'

'Sometimes people who cause difficulties at lower levels are moved up, where they can do less damage. Sometimes rebels are embraced into the heart of the establishment, where they are rapidly persuaded that it isn't in their interests to be rebellious any more. Promotion is a minefield, and even you wouldn't be so naïve as to assume that it's usually given on merit.'

It was a deeply confused Henry Pratt who left the office of the Director (Operations). He couldn't face the lift, so he took the cold, bare, bleak steps down to the basement and his increasingly isolated bunker.

'To leave without having another job to go to is a terrible risk,' said Henry next Sunday afternoon, when they had the house to themselves and were lying in bed, cuddling sleepily, after making love. 'But if I stay and apply for other jobs, I won't get them because I'll get a stinking reference. I really am a square peg in a vicious circle.'

There was a burst of loud banging from the Gleneagles. They were refurbishing their bedrooms, not before time, and seemed to be doing the bulk of the work at weekends, presumably because they weren't using proper builders.

'I want to do something more with my life,' said Henry. 'I can't wait much longer.'

Somebody, somewhere, will recognise a good man when he sees one.

The banging stopped as suddenly as it had begun. Blissful peace returned. It was starting to get dark. The slightest flush of pink touched the mackerel sky.

Henry cuddled gently into the curve of his wife's body. Very slowly, he began to feel sexy. He ran his hands slowly up her wide, strong thighs. And then, sad to relate, he fell asleep.

Liam O'Reilly died on Christmas Day, after his Christmas dinner, suffering a massive heart attack during a game of Snap. There aren't many better ways to go. He was sixty-nine.

On an impulse, Cousin Hilda, who wasn't given to impulses, wrote to the latest addresses that she had for all her gentlemen, telling them of the funeral arrangements. 'Well,' she told Henry, 'I feel it's the end of an era.' She also wrote to an address in Ireland, which she found in Mr O'Reilly's wallet.

There was more of a turn-out at the funeral than might have been expected for such a reclusive man, but the mourners still felt dwarfed by the great, dark, incense-heavy vault of St Mary's Catholic Church.

Two obscure relatives from Ireland arrived, full of praise for Cousin Hilda's kindness, 'of which Liam was always most appreciative'. They each gave her a bottle of Jameson's whisky, and she was too moved by their kindness to refuse the gifts, which she passed on to Henry with a sniff.

Tony Preece also came, with his pale ash-blonde fiancée, Stella, whom he had still not married after an engagement lasting more than fourteen years. Tony had made quite a success of his act as Cavin O'Rourke, the Winsome Wit from Wicklow. He had the grace to feel embarrassed about his Irish jokes at Liam O'Reilly's funeral.

Another of the gentlemen to reappear was Neville Chamberlain, who had retired six weeks before after selling paint for forty-seven years, in England and Kenya.

Also present was Norman Pettifer. 'It's a sad day,' he said. 'A sad, sad day. And yet I can't feel sad, such is the selfishness of human nature. I heard this morning, this very morning, that young Adrian has been sacked.'

Also present, and increasingly prosperous, was Mr Travis, the liquidator.

Cousin Hilda invited all nine mourners back to her house 'for a little something'. The two Irishman, anticipating a wake, licked their lips.

There were ham sandwiches, cheese sandwiches, sausage rolls, and a choice of tea or Camp coffee.

When nobody could manage another bite, Cousin Hilda said, 'Now, I've summat special to see poor Mr O'Reilly off to a better world. I think he deserves to go out in style.'

Oh God, I hope it's something small, thought Henry. They were going out to supper at Joe and Molly Enwright's.

Cousin Hilda disappeared to her little kitchen.

'A funeral I'd like to have been present at was that of Dame Sybil Thorndike,' said Norman Pettifer. 'She was a trooper if ever there was one.'

'I expect there was drink at that funeral,' said one of the Irishman.

'Hush, Seamus,' said the other.

'I suppose selling paint has changed over the years,' said Henry.

'You can say that again,' said Neville Chamberlain.

But Henry didn't. He felt that it had been boring enough the first time.

Cousin Hilda entered with a tray on which there were five steaming bowls. Then she returned to the kitchen and brought another tray, on which there were also five steaming bowls.

Henry realised that he had been over-optimistic when he'd believed that he'd eaten his last spotted dick ever.

'Well, it is a Tuesday,' said Cousin Hilda.

12 Happy Families

Benedict, almost fifteen, started wanting to stay away with friends. Diana, Henry, Tosser and Felicity welcomed this. They were pleased that he was happy. They hoped that, if they took no action, the problems that they had seen deep in his eyes would go away.

Kate was beginning the long build-up towards her O levels. Great success was anticipated. She had matured into a lovely girl, if slightly moody.

Jack was becoming increasingly unacademic. He was good at football and cricket, but not at lessons. Henry told his teachers that he thought that academic education was failing those of a more practical nature. 'Tell the government,' was the response.

Camilla had her horses.

1972 moved inexorably into 1973. The Americans withdrew from Vietnam after the Paris peace talks reached agreement, but the violence continued.

Benedict got eight O levels. He announced that, if he got three A levels, his father would buy him a car.

Kate got nine mock O levels.

Jack played football for the under-fourteens and scored several goals.

Camilla had her horses.

One Sunday in late September, 1973, Cousin Hilda called round after church. Benedict was back at Dalton and Camilla had gone to Benningdean, a very posh school in Kent, but Kate and Jack were in. Kate was doing homework in her room, and Jack was building a bike in the garden out of old bits.

Cousin Hilda sniffed, because it was obvious to her that nobody at number 83 had gone to church.

They invited her to stay for lunch, and told her it would be early because Kate and Jack were going out. She sniffed again. 'In my day young people weren't allowed to have Sunday lunch early so they could go out,' her eloquent sniff attested.

To their astonishment, she accepted the invitation.

'You seem surprised,' she said.

'Well I am,' said Henry.

'You shouldn't issue invitations unless you mean them.'

'Oh, we meant it,' said Diana. 'And we're pleased. It's just that we thought you wouldn't be able to because of your gentlemen.'

'I have no gentlemen now,' said Cousin Hilda. 'I've hung up my boots.'

They stared at her in astonishment.

'I told Mr Travis, the liquidator, "I'm sixty-seven. I'm going into liquidation." He laughed.'

They realised that they should have laughed, and did so belatedly, then stared at each other in astonishment. Cousin Hilda had made a joke.

Cousin Hilda sniffed.

'There's no need to look surprised,' she said. 'I am human.'

'Oh, very much so,' said Henry hurriedly.

'I've realised for quite a while that I've been swimming against the tide. And I've a bit put by. I don't live particularly extravagantly.'

'Will you move?' asked Diana.

'No. It'll be nice to have the whole house to myself. I'll indulge myself.'

There was more laughter over lunch. Diana told Jack not to eat with his mouth full, when she meant not to talk with his mouth full.

'That was a good one,' said Cousin Hilda. 'That were a right comical slip, weren't it, Kate?'

'Very funny,' agreed Kate, who was always nice to Cousin Hilda.

'I must tell that to my . . . oh. . . I haven't got anyone to tell it to any more, have I?' said Cousin Hilda.

'You knew Tommy Marsden, didn't you, Dad?' said Jack.

'Yes. Why?'

'He's been sacked by Farsley Celtic.'

'Well, he's thirty-eight, like me.'

'He's sacked because he's a piss-artist.'

Henry held his breath. Cousin Hilda didn't appear to understand, but her lips tightened and he knew she was only pretending.

'You can chart his ups and downs by his clubs,' said Jack. 'Thurmarsh United, Manchester United, Leeds United, Luton Town, Stockport County, Halifax Town, Northwich Victoria, Farsley Celtic.'

'A sad story,' said Henry.

When the children had gone out, they sat by the fire and Cousin Hilda said, 'Do you know what decided me to retire?'

Henry and Diana, lolling full of beef, shook lazy heads.

'I'll tell you,' said Cousin Hilda. 'Mr O'Reilly. Liam.'

Astonishment roused them from their torpor.

'He never said much,' said Cousin Hilda. 'He had more sense. I see no need for all the conversation that goes on. Natter, natter, natter. What about? Nowt. You might have thought, he's not really made much mark on this globe, hasn't Liam O'Reilly. A "yes, please" and "thank you very much", and that was about all it amounted to. But I've been thinking, and I've been thinking about life, and it's a right funny thing, is life, when you think about it. You see, he never did much with his life, not to say *did*, but without him, well, it's just not the same. What it is is, he didn't have much of a presence, but he has a very powerful absence. It's funny, is that, isn't it? Odd, I mean. I reckon so, anyroad.'

A few weeks later, Henry and Diana chugged to Monks Eleigh through a golden autumn haze.

When they arrived, Henry saw that Auntie Doris couldn't remember who he was. 'Haven't you got a kiss for your little nephew Henry?' he prompted, and he saw the panic die from her eyes.

After a supper of tinned mulligatawny soup and Marks and Spencer's lasagne – neither Auntie Doris nor Uncle Teddy were up to proper cooking any more – they settled down to a good game of Scrabble. Henry found it both endearing and sad (mixed emotions number 84) to see this old rogue and this ultra-glamorous sexy painted lady getting so excited over a game of Scrabble.

During the game, Auntie Doris proudly produced the word Quonge. After a brief silence, Henry said, 'Sorry. What's Quonge?' 'A Mexican hat,' said Uncle Teddy. Diana pointed out that foreign words don't count. 'It's English for a Mexican hat,' said Uncle Teddy. 'The Mexican for a Mexican hat is *Quonja.*' With the Q happening to fall on a triple letter square, Auntie Doris established a lead which she maintained to the end. When she'd left the room, Uncle Teddy said, 'All guff about the hat, of course, but the old girl loves to win. Not a word, eh?' and Henry said, 'Oh no. We'll keep it under our *quonja*, don't you worry.' 'Very good,' said Uncle Teddy, as Auntie Doris returned. 'Humour always was your saving grace,' and Auntie Doris, who still made things worse by protesting about them, said, 'Teddy! Tact. Don't remind him that there's practically nothing else he's any good at.'

Towards the end of June, 1974, the wife of a market gardener in Country Durham informed Henry that her husband had been in hospital for several weeks, and their cucumbers had widespread rot, which she couldn't identify, and she didn't want to worry her husband over it, not with his kidneys.

Henry, who had been getting increasingly office-bound over the years, thought this the perfect excuse for an expedition, and pottered off up the A1.

The market garden was set just inland, north of Hartlepool, and not far from the looming, steaming, throbbing bulk of Blackhall Nuclear Power Station. It sat on heavy soil, in an almost flat, featureless landscape. Mr Wilberforce and his wife, Gertie, were clearly only just making a living in this unpromising spot. Some of their cucumbers were growing out of doors, others in primitive greenhouses. The greenhouses had their windows open on this sultry day.

Henry examined the diseased cucumbers, and to his relief the diagnosis was simple. A lesion had developed at the distal end, and the rot was becoming black as the pycnidia and perithecia of the pathogen were produced. Readers with more than a very limited knowledge of diseases of the cucumber will have deduced that this was black stem rot. Henry prescribed reduced humidity as the cure and, just to be on the safe side, took examples of the diseased cucumbers for analysis.

A mile or two down the road, he stopped for a pint of bitter and a sandwich in a pub, and overheard a remark about leukaemia. He began to wonder if there could be a link between the diseased cucumbers and the proximity of the nuclear power station. Excitement gripped him. Supposing he could prove a connection. BIOLOGISTS IN FERMENT OVER CUCUMBER MAN'S RADIATION AND LESION LINK.

The following morning, he took his cucumbers to Dave Wilkins in the Lab. The Head of Analysis (Practical) had long, unkempt greying hair and a beard that was almost white, even though he was only thirty-six. He had round shoulders and a paunch, and if he'd analysed his tee-shirt, he'd have found traces of fried egg, baked beans and Tetley's bitter on it. But he was extremely good at his job.

Henry asked Dave to look for evidence of radiation or any other abnormality which might be connected to the proximity of the power station, and which might have caused the black stem rot.

'Phew!' said Dave Wilkins. 'Radiation! We could burn our fingers with this one. I'm not sure it's within our remit, Henry.'

'Well whose remit is it within, then?' asked Henry. 'We don't have a Head of Analysis (Radiation).'

'I just don't want to tread on anyone's toes,' said the Head of Analysis (Practical).

'Oh God. Well, look, shall I clear it with the Director (Operations)?' suggested the Chief Controlling Officer (Diseases and Pests).

'Grateful if you would, Henry.'

Henry suddenly found that it was very difficult to ask to see Timothy Whitehouse to talk about radiation from a nuclear power station. He felt, as he walked down the corridor, that he was walking under the shadow of that vast industrial complex on the Durham coast.

He explained to the Director (Operations) how he'd heard a chance remark about leukaemia. He saw Mr Whitehouse's lips tighten and realised that he'd made a major error of judgement.

'I mean obviously I'm not suggesting that eating cucumbers could cause leukaemia,' he said.

'I should hope not.' The Director (Operations) thwacked his braces fiercely. 'That'd be great publicity. Just what we need. What are you suggesting?'

'That we check to make sure these cucumbers are absolutely safe to eat. That's our moral duty, wouldn't you say?'

'Right. Absolutely right.' Mr Whitehouse dialled an internal number. 'Dave? . . . I've got Henry here, Dave. Obviously it's vital to eliminate any possibility that licensed growers are selling radiated cucumbers. Check this one very thoroughly, will you? . . . Do you need written authority? . . . You'll have it. Thanks, Dave.' The Director smiled, and stroked his predatory nose thoughtfully. 'Your diligence is to be commended,' he said, but he said it through slightly clenched teeth.

That Saturday, Cousin Hilda arrived round about teatime, unexpectedly. A pile of old mattresses lay on the ground outside the Gleneagles. She gave a heartfelt sniff.

'What are those mattresses doing?' she asked.

'They're throwing them out,' said Diana.

'I should hope so. They look infested,' said Cousin Hilda.

They sat her down and offered her tea.

'Well, just one cup,' she said, 'and nowt to eat. I don't want to be a nuisance.'

'Of course you aren't a nuisance,' said Henry. 'It annoys me when you say that.'

'Well I were brought up to be polite,' said Cousin Hilda. 'It's a disgrace, those mattresses. I couldn't be doing with it, me. I'd have the council round. They're probably riddled with fleas. I don't know what this country's coming to sometimes. I get right choked up with it when I think on it. There are times when I'm glad Mrs Wedderburn isn't alive to see it.'

Diana poured tea. Only Cousin Hilda took sugar, and this discomfited her slightly.

'I've come wi' a request,' she said. 'I want to see our Doris.'

Henry and Diana were stunned.

'But you don't get on,' said Henry.

'Blood is thicker than water. I have more time to think now I've not got my gentlemen. I've never liked the sound of this Miles Cricklewood. I've always thought he sounds a bad lot. And then I thought, "Hilda, tha's a Christian. Tha shouldn't pre-judge." '

'Have some tea-cake,' said Henry, but Cousin Hilda shook her head. He took the piece instead, and savoured every mouthful, like a condemned man eating his last breakfast. How could he tell her about Uncle Teddy? Hilary would have helped him. Diana, splendid though she was, left such things to him. He decided to approach it gently, with subtlety and tact. As often happened, the words that came out weren't exactly what he planned. 'Miles Cricklewood isn't a bad lot,' he said. 'He isn't Miles Cricklewood either. He's Uncle Teddy.'

There was silence. Diana held a slice of lemon cake towards Cousin Hilda. She shook her head.

How would she react to such momentous news? Henry held his breath. When her reaction came, he was amazed that he hadn't realised what it would be.

She sniffed.

'Black stem rot,' said the Director (Operations), swivelling gently in his chair, and glancing at Dave Wilkins's report.

'And?'

'And nothing. Absolutely normal, thank goodness.'

Mixed emotions number 101 – H. Pratt feels enormous relief tempered with grave disappointment.

The tricks that the human mind plays never ceased to amaze Henry.

Well, the tricks that his mind played, anyway.

He was extremely nervous as the Ford Escort chugged its way

from Thurmarsh to Monks Eleigh. Several weeks had passed since Mr Whitehouse had told him that the cucumbers were normal apart from black stem rot.

Now, when Kate and Jack had gone to Spain, and Benedict and Camilla were with their father in Mauritius (their only visit to their father that year), it was at last possible to take Cousin Hilda to see Auntie Doris and Uncle Teddy.

Henry cared a great deal about Cousin Hilda. It was awful to think of her living alone, without a friend in the world. She hadn't moved into the rest of the house. The bed-sitting rooms where her gentlemen had lived and slept and, did she but know it, masturbated, were cold and dank. She inhabited only the basement – her little bedroom, her kitchen and scullery, her immaculate lavatory, and her cosy living room, where the smell of spotted dick no longer lingered but the absence of her gentlemen still seemed like a gaping hole. She went upstairs only twice a week, once to clean rooms that weren't dirty, and once for her bath. It was awful to think of her seven pairs of pink bloomers on the line every Monday morning, hanging limp in the rain, or fluttering bravely in the sunshine, or being hurled skywards by the gales. It was awful, and yet he loved her.

He cared a great deal about Auntie Doris and Uncle Teddy, alias Miles Cricklewood. It was awful taking packages from Uncle Teddy to Derek Parsonage, and from Derek Parsonage to Uncle Teddy, but he hadn't the heart to stop. It was awful to witness the slow but inexorable decline in Auntie Doris's mental powers. It was awful, because it was so touching that it took him to depths of emotion that he didn't always welcome, being an Englishman and a Yorkshireman, to witness Uncle Teddy's patience and kindness. It had been awful to be the regular unintended butt of Auntie Doris's tactlessness, and to be sent away to Brasenose and Dalton because Uncle Teddy and Auntie Doris were social climbers and didn't want to cramp their lifestyle. It was awful, and yet he loved them, especially now that they weren't bothering to be social climbers any more, and their lifestyle was gin and tonic, smuggled burgundy, wallflowers in a Suffolk garden, and Scrabble.

So Henry was deeply anxious about the coming meeting. Would a decent reconciliation be effected? And, in his search for something to take his mind off these worries, he faced up resolutely to a suspicion that he'd been resisting for two months.

The Director (Operations) and the Head of Analysis (Practical) were lying. The cucumbers had been affected by radiation. He didn't know quite how he knew. It was a matter of Dave Wilkins's uncharacteristic unease, and something about Timothy Whitehouse's smile, and he knew that the two men were in collusion.

Before he could work out the implications of this discovery, they were in Monks Eleigh, and pulling up outside the fairy-tale cottage, and Henry was saying to Cousin Hilda, 'You'll find Auntie Doris changed.'

'What's happened?' said Diana. 'There are no flowers.'

Uncle Teddy hurried down the drive to meet them, past wallflower plants, sunflower plants, sweet william plants, sweet pea plants, lupins and geraniums, and not one of them flowering in the whole garden.

'She's picked all the flowers to make the house look lovely for you,' he said. 'Not a word, eh? Business as usual. Savvy?'

He bent down to kiss Cousin Hilda, and to Henry's and Diana's astonishment, she accepted the kiss with good grace, albeit blushing slightly.

Auntie Doris came rushing out in a wave of scent.

'Hilda!' she said, and hugged her.

'Well I never,' said Cousin Hilda. 'Well I never.'

'Exactly,' said Uncle Teddy. 'Jolly good.'

'Terrific,' said Henry.

And so, on a tide of meaninglessness, they entered the cottage. There were flowers everywhere, in vases, jars, bowls, glasses, mugs, even eggcups. On window sills and occasional tables and bedside tables they stood in their profusion.

Henry and Diana stared at them in amazement, and Cousin Hilda sniffed.

Oh no, thought Henry.

Cousin Hilda sniffed again.

Don't be rude, please. She meant it for the best.

Cousin Hilda sniffed a third time.

'What a lovely scent,' she said.

Henry and Diana and Uncle Teddy tried to hide their astonishment, and Auntie Doris beamed.

'You've got the house really lovely for us, Auntie Doris,' said Diana.

'Thank you, Diana,' said Auntie Doris, and they were pleased that she hadn't said 'Hilary', but then she said, 'Don't just stand there, Geoffrey. Get them a drink.'

Cousin Hilda sniffed at the appearance of every gin and tonic and there was an awkward moment when Uncle Teddy said, 'What's all this sniffing, Hilda? Is it hay fever? Are the flowers upsetting you?'

'You know it isn't that, Teddy Braithwaite,' said Cousin Hilda. 'It's the drink. I can't change at my time of life.'

'Nor can we,' said Uncle Teddy.

'I don't think I expect you to any more,' said Cousin Hilda. 'But I can't pretend to like it. Shall we make a pact, Teddy? I don't comment on your drinking and you don't comment on my sniffing.'

'Fair enough, Hilda,' said Uncle Teddy. 'Spot on.'

They lunched on ham salads, which Auntie Doris carried in as if she'd prepared them, although they all knew that Uncle Teddy had.

As the afternoon rolled somnolently by, to the tune of bees and combine harvesters, they played Scrabble in the flowerless garden. Cousin Hilda had never played before, but Uncle Teddy insisted that she played instead of him.

'I'll umpire,' he said.

Cousin Hilda began, and after much delay she produced the word Tart.

Henry held his breath.

'What kind of tart?' said Auntie Doris.

'Tha what?' said Cousin Hilda.

'It's nice to know what you have in mind when you choose a word,' said Auntie Doris.

'A Bakewell tart,' said Cousin Hilda.

'Very good,' said Auntie Doris.

Henry produced Trained, Diana made Bottom, at which Cousin Hilda sniffed, and after much thought Auntie Doris plonked down Cow.

'What sort of cow?' said Cousin Hilda.

'Black and white Friesian,' said Auntie Doris.

Cousin Hilda's second word was Bed, and Auntie Doris said, 'Who's in the bed, Hilda?' and Henry held his breath, and Cousin Hilda said, 'I am. And I'm on my own, Doris,' and Auntie Doris said, 'Very wise.'

Henry made Grain, Diana Amber, and Auntie Doris, after much thought, Quurm.

'What's Quurm?' asked Cousin Hilda.

'A fruit,' said Uncle Teddy. 'It's a cross between a quince and a plum.'

'Perhaps my tart were a quurm tart,' said Cousin Hilda drily.

'Could have been, Hilda,' said Uncle Teddy uneasily. 'Could have been. Q on a triple-letter score. You've got thirty-six, Doris. Well done.'

Cousin Hilda struggled to make her third word, settling eventually on Rat.

'I'm sorry I'm so dull,' she said.

'Not at all,' said Uncle Teddy. 'A bit on the short side, but not half bad. Double word score too. You score six.'

Henry used the T of rat to produce Truffle. Diana used the L of truffle to make Lean and Auntie Doris used the N of Lean to form Zenoxiac.

'Very good,' said Uncle Teddy. 'That's very good. X on a double letter score is 16, so your word total is 34, Z on a treble word score, 34 times 3 is 102, C also on a treble word score, 102 times 3 is 306, 50 bonus for using all your letters, 356.'

'Oh my,' said Auntie Doris. 'What luck!'

'What's Zenoxiac mean?' asked Cousin Hilda.

'Containing foreign bodies,' said Uncle Teddy.

'How would you use it?' persisted Cousin Hilda.

'Well if a loaf of bread was found to contain a dead mouse, I'd say, "Goodness me. This loaf's very zenoxiac," ' said Uncle Teddy.

'How awful!' said Auntie Doris. 'Send it back.'

'No, no,' said Uncle Teddy. 'This is a hypothetical loaf and a hypothetical dead mouse.'

'Well mice frighten me,' said Auntie Doris. 'I wish you wouldn't invent hypothetical ones. Can't you invent something nice, like a hypothetical squirrel?'

'It wouldn't suit my example, dear,' said Uncle Teddy. 'You wouldn't find a dead squirrel in a loaf of bread.'

'Or a dead mouse,' said Auntie Doris, 'so stop being silly, Geoffrey.'

'Quite right,' said Uncle Teddy. 'Your go, Hilda.'

Cousin Hilda made the word Run.

'Well done, Hilda,' said Uncle Teddy. 'You score three.'

The game proceeded smoothly, if slowly, the afternoon drowsed, and Uncle Teddy announced the score. 'Well, Doris has won,' he said, 'with 677. Henry's a very good second, 166. Diana nudging him strongly, 161, and Hilda bringing up the rear, but not bad for a first time, 42.'

They had a pot of tea, and by the time they'd finished that, the sun had gone down over the yard-arm. They drank, and Cousin Hilda sniffed, and they didn't make any comment on her sniffing, and she didn't make any comment on their drinking, and they had chicken supreme, which Auntie Doris served but Uncle Teddy had bought and heated up, and at the end of the meal, when Auntie Doris went to put some more flowers in Cousin Hilda's bedroom, Uncle Teddy said, 'I don't want to pull the wool over your eyes, Hilda. You've been a sport today. There's no such word as Zenoxiac.'

'Well, Teddy,' said Cousin Hilda, 'tha's done a lot of things I can't forgive . . .'

'Admitted!' said Uncle Teddy.

'Tha's told disgraceful untruths and made dreadful deceptions.'

'No defence submitted!' said Uncle Teddy.

'So one little white lie isn't going to make much difference on the Day of Judgement,' said Cousin Hilda.

When Auntie Doris returned, Uncle Teddy said, 'Shall we have another game, seeing we're all one big happy family?'

'Now that's a right good game, that is,' said Cousin Hilda. 'Let's play Happy Families.

Henry and Diana's attempt to play Happy Families wasn't helped by the disappearance of Benedict. Camilla phoned from St Pancras in floods of tears.

'I went to buy a paper. When I came back he'd gone,' she said. 'That was an hour ago, and there's a suitcase missing. I just don't know what to do.'

'Have you rung your father?' asked Henry.

'Well, no. He's just said goodbye, and I think he's going out somewhere, and I knew you were expecting us, so I rang you, and my money's running out. Oh Henry, I'm so scared!'

'You just sit there, Camilla, with the luggage. I'll phone somebody to fetch you, and I'll drive down. Don't move till somebody comes that you know. OK?'

'Yes.'

'Good girl.'

'Sorry.'

'It's not your . . .'

But her money had run out.

Henry got no reply from Tosser's, but Mr Hargreaves was at home and said he'd cancel everything and go straight to St Pancras and rescue Camilla.

Henry phoned the police, gave a description of Benedict, left Diana at home in case he contacted her there, and set off on another nightmare drive. All the way down the M1 he rebuked himself. He'd done nothing. He'd hoped the Benedict problem would go away. Now it hadn't, but Benedict had. If only . . . if only . . . he arrived at Hampstead with an aching head full of 'if only's.

Camilla looked so much younger than her fifteen years, and so much less like a horse than she had ever looked, and to Henry's amazement she rushed up and dissolved into a flood of tears in his arms.

'We've tried Nigel, but no luck,' said Mrs Hargreaves, who looked worried but exquisite.

'It doesn't really matter now,' said Camilla. 'I'm with you. I want to go home, Henry.'

Henry found it disturbing that he could feel such gratification and joy in the midst of such worry. He phoned the police, who'd found nothing, and then, so keen was Camilla to get home, he set off after a quick bite of pâté and toast.

At half past eight on a tired late summer's evening Henry was on the M1 again. Camilla slept some of the way, and talked a bit about Mauritius, and said that looking back on it Benedict had been very quiet and serene but rather triumphant, as if he had something planned, so with that in mind and the suitcase gone she was sure that whatever had happened was of his own doing and that he'd be safe.

'Thank you,' said Henry. 'You're a wonderful girl.'

Camilla burst into tears, so he knew that she was pleased.

The following day, after a night of deeply disturbed sleep, Henry answered the telephone with no premonition.

It was Jack, ringing from Heathrow.

'Kate's disappeared, Dad,' he said, still almost phlegmatic. 'Vanished. Bit of a bugger, isn't it?'

The police issued photographs of both children, but they weren't given wide publicity, and nothing resulted.

Camilla and Jack, thrust into a situation not of their making, were amazingly good with Henry and Diana and with each other. Camilla didn't go riding, her heart just wasn't in it, and Jack abandoned, without any apparent regret, a trip to the Lakes with the Blairs. Between them, they even did the shopping and cooked simple meals, and they seemed to grow up almost by the hour. Cousin Hilda said, 'I'm just glad Mrs Wedderburn has been spared the worry,' and Henry and Diana lived through long nights where time made cruel sport with them. They told themselves that Benedict was seventeen and Kate sixteen. That was quite adult these days. But they knew in their hearts that on their own they were two children who knew nothing of the world and its many dangers.

On the fourth afternoon of their shared ordeal, Kate phoned.

'It's Kate, Henry,' screamed Diana.

'We're all right,' said Kate, and rang off.

They both went weak at the knees then, and began to cry with deep, deep relief, but it wasn't long before their relief became anxiety again. Where were they? What were they doing? Had Benedict known that Kate was phoning? How was Benedict behaving? What sort of boy was he, deep down behind the anger in his eyes? Would Kate get pregnant? And . . . oh, oh, oh but it was possible . . . would Benedict get violent? And . . . oh oh oh . . . oh oh oh oh . . . was it all their fault?

Kate phoned again on the eighth day and said, 'I'm coming home. I'm at Dartmouth police station.'

Longer and longer were Henry's rescue drives across England.

Kate looked at him, white-faced, and wild-eyed and shrivelled, like a cornered cat. He hugged her and said nothing, except, 'Where's Benedict?'

'I don't know,' she gasped between tears. 'I ran away.'

'They slept in an old hut up around the moor,' said the paternal, old-fashioned police officer. 'We've got search parties out. He'll be found.'

Sometimes Kate slept, and sometimes she cried, on the long, long journey home.

'Did he hurt you?' Henry asked very gently.

'No, no,' said Kate. 'He never hit me.' Then she burst into great sobs.

Henry pulled up at the roadside and held her tight and kissed the top of her head. Her hair smelt dirty.

'He told me he loved me,' she wailed. 'He didn't love me. He did it all to hurt you.'

Benedict didn't run away when the police found him. He turned and walked towards them, proudly. There were no charges. Kate had gone of her own free will, and he had used her, but not abused her, except that using is abusing.

He phoned Henry the next day, cool as a . . . as anything but a cucumber. Henry couldn't think of cucumbers as cool, now that there were suspicions about radiation lurking deep in the underground storage caverns of his mind.

'I'd like to come up tomorrow to collect my things,' said Benedict. 'I don't think I should stay in the same house as Kate any more. It'd be too awkward.'

So the next day Kate went to the Blairs. She was full of remorse and hurt and grief and anger, but the very enormity of Benedict's betrayal at such a tender age contained the seeds of her cure. It made home seem a very desirable place. It made simple childish pleasures like boiled eggs with toast soldiers very reassuring. It made her, briefly, into a girl again.

Jack also went out for the day. If he stayed he'd have been tempted to thump Benedict, and although he was two years younger he had such strength that he might have succeeded. It would be a disaster whether he won or not, so Henry gave him the money to go to the Scarborough Cricket Festival with his friend, Slim Micklewhite.

Benedict walked up the garden path, outwardly as cool as a lettuce.

Diana opened the door and faced her son. Henry stood just behind her, ready to give moral support if needed.

'Hi there,' said Benedict. 'I've come for my things. Those mattresses next door are *disgusting*.'

He refused their offers of tea, coffee and food, and he wouldn't meet their eyes.

'You should at least eat something,' said Henry.

'Not hungry.'

'What do you plan to do?'

'Go to Dad's. Frankly, I can't bear this grotty little town or your grotty little husband any more, Mum.'

Camilla stood in the kitchen doorway, a glass of milk in her hand, gawping in horror.

'That's an absolutely ridiculous thing to say, and you know it,' said Diana. 'Henry has done so much for you.'

'Has he fuck!' said Benedict.

'Ben!' implored Camilla.

'Stay out of this, Camilla. This is grown-up stuff,' said Ben.

Camilla went very red and tears welled into her eyes. She tossed her long hair angrily and stormed back into the kitchen.

Benedict moved towards the stairs. Henry was blocking his way.

'Are you going to hit me?' asked Benedict.

'I wouldn't hit a child,' said Henry.

'A child!' said Benedict. 'That's a good one.'

He pushed Henry out of the way and stalked up the stairs.

A moment or two later, Camilla followed him. She soon came downstairs in tears, and wailed, 'He told me to get out from under his feet. He said I'm a distinct pain. Brothers!'

She subsided into Diana's arms. Henry put his arm on hers. She kissed Diana and then Henry, and the three of them were still standing in the hall, arm in arm, when Benedict came downstairs with a suitcase and a hold-all.

'Oh my God!' he said. 'All happy together. A typical English family. Ugh!' His face twisted into fury. 'Don't you realise that he hates us, Camilla? Mum can't see it because she's so besotted. Surely you can?'

'I don't hate you,' said Henry in a voice which he hoped was cool, but which he knew had a crack in it, 'but I'll never forgive you for what you've done to Kate.'

Benedict put his cases down and moved towards Henry threateningly.

'Benedict!' cried Diana.

'That's right. Hit me. That'll solve everything,' said Henry.

Benedict stopped about three inches in front of Henry, and looked down at him. Henry had never wished for those few extra inches more.

'I'm not going to hit you,' said Benedict, suddenly loftily cool again. 'I don't hit wankers.'

'Oh good,' said Henry. 'At least we know you won't be punching yourself in the face, then.'

'Very witty,' said Benedict. 'Why don't you go and do another comic turn at Dalton? They're just about your level.'

He picked up his cases and moved towards the door.

'I'll be back for the rest of my stuff,' he said.

'Aren't you going to kiss me goodbye?' said Diana.

Benedict hesitated, looked as if he wanted to, then said, 'Not just now, Mummy. When you've left Henry, big kiss then.'

He opened the door with dignity, tried to walk through it with dignity, got his feet caught round his hold-all, stumbled out onto the path, and slammed the door furiously behind him. The china tinkled in the display cabinet in the hall, and then there was silence.

About twenty stunned unhappy minutes later Diana said, 'I hate to say this about my own son, but do you think we're wise to trust him? Should we check with Nigel that he really is going there?'

'Oh my God, of course we should,' said Henry. 'We're panicking. We're not thinking.'

Diana rang her ex-husband's number. Henry sat on the settee, holding her hand and listening. Camilla watched them earnestly from an armchair, and Henry noticed how her new maturity had changed her face. She was almost beautiful, and might become so.

'The Pilkington-Brick residence,' trilled Felicity, and Diana made a face.

'Hello, Felicity,' she said. 'Is Nigel by any chance in residence in his residence?'

'I'll fetch him,' said Felicity coldly.

Camilla gave her mother a brief, fond grin.

'Hello.'

'Nigel, it's Diana. Are you expecting Benedict?'

'No. Why?'

'Oh my God.'

'What's happened, Diana?'

'He's been here to collect his things. He says he's coming to live with you.'

'Oh. Well it's all very well for him to say that, but I'm not sure he can. He hasn't discussed it with us. I mean, truth to tell, he resents Felicity.'

'He resents everybody, including himself, but don't worry your tiny little mind about that, he isn't actually coming, your lifestyles are safe, if he was he'd have told you. He's lied to us and he's obviously going off somewhere.'

'Oh God. What's he up to now?'

'May I?' said Henry, pointing at the phone.

'Hang on, Nigel, Henry wants a word,' said Diana.

She handed the phone to Henry.

'Hello, Nigel,' said Henry. It was too serious a moment to call him Tosser.

'Hello, Henry. This is all a bloody bore, isn't it?'

'Listen, Nigel. Benedict left here about half an hour ago. Our only chance is to try the trains. I'm going to the station now. If I don't catch him and a train's gone that he might have caught, will you go to St Pancras and meet it?'

'St Pancras. That's miles away.'

'I know it's miles away but he's your son for God's sake.'

'Yours is his home and you've made a mess of dealing with him, that's the truth, isn't it?'

'There isn't time to argue, for God's sake. We must rush. Will you?'

'It's not as easy as that, Henry. I'm guest of honour at a dinner tonight. I'm Top Pensions Salesman of the Year.'

'I don't believe what I'm hearing. He's your son!'

'I'm not thinking of myself.'

'Huh!'

'Well, not only myself. There's Felicity. There's all the guests. The chap presenting the trophy's coming all the way from our Cardiff office.'

'You were my hero once. I'm off to the station. Here's Diana.'

Henry handed the phone to Diana and hurried out of the house.

He drove to Thurmarsh (Midland Road) Station like a maniac.

The London train had gone five minutes ago. He tried the bus station without luck, and then drove along Commercial Road towards Splutt, which was Benedict's most likely route if he was hitchhiking. There was no sign of him.

When he got home he phoned Tosser again.

'He might have got the 4.12,' he said. 'It gets to St Pancras at 7.57.'

'Look,' said Tosser. 'I see no reason why I should go, he's seventeen, he knows what he's doing, I'm not sure if it would do any good if I did go, though I hasten to add that I would go any other night despite that, but this whole event is about me and not to be there would be an enormous insult to a lot of good people, who've paid a lot of money.' He lowered his voice. 'Felicity is not a very strong or stable woman emotionally. Having Benedict here is not an option. I know it sounds brutal, but I have to think of Felicity's health. She's my ultimate responsibility.'

'Goodbye, Tosser,' said Henry.

'I want to change my name to Pratt,' said Camilla Pilkington-Brick.

There was still some hope for Henry and the world as 1974 drew towards its close. Life in 83, Lordship Road proceeded smoothly and the mattresses had finally been removed from the front of the Gleneagles. In Portugal, a bloodless military coup had overthrown President Tomas and Prime Minister Caetano, had seen the Socialist leader Mario Soares return from exile, and the end of censorship and the disbandment of the secret police. In Greece the long night of the colonels was over. Democracy returned joyously in a fizz of fireworks and a cacophony of car horns. 'What a fragile and precious gift democracy is, and how carelessly and apathetically we guard ours,' Henry told John Barrington in the pub one lunchtime, and John Barrington made his point perfectly without knowing it, saying, 'True. Better get those sandwiches ordered if we want a decent choice.'

There were clouds of course. The IRA bombed two pubs in Birmingham, killing nineteen people. And Benedict didn't return to collect the rest of his things. He didn't return to Dalton College either. The school heard nothing. Henry and Diana heard nothing. Tosser heard nothing. Camilla heard nothing and was very hurt. The police heard nothing and had more serious concerns on their hands.

233

Henry's contempt for Tosser was modified, during those winter months, by his knowledge of the way in which he himself salved his conscience with the thought that Benedict's absence was a good thing for every other member of the family.

Kate recovered from her experience slowly but steadily. The news that she had got nine O levels had boosted her ego at a vital time. She met a nice lad called Brian, who worshipped her, and she kept him at arm's length without being cruel. She would survive.

Jack was doing very well at football, was unlikely to do well in his exams, was known to frequent the Golden Ball in Gasworks Road, although he was more than two years under age, relished being the only boy in the house, and remained good-natured and cheery.

Camilla wanted to leave boarding school and join Kate at Thurmarsh Grammar School for Girls. Tosser resented this. 'I want her to have the best. I'm happy to pay. I did everything for Benedict.' In the end it was decided, democratically, in line with events in Western Europe, that she should stay at Benningdean until the end of the school year and then go to Thurmarsh Grammar if a) she was accepted and b) she still wanted to. She was becoming much more interested in boys and correspondingly less interested in horses.

Henry dreaded the end of winter. The conviction that he'd been lied to about his suspect cucumbers seeped out of the storage cavern of his subconscious. He knew that he'd find it difficult to live with himself if he ignored the issue, but he was nervous of the problems he might face if he didn't. Is this the fighter who learnt to laugh at himself and performed a comic act to the whole school at the age of fifteen? you ask most reasonably. Do not forget, gentle reader, that since that day Henry had experienced a failed career in newspapers, a rocky career in cucumbers, a failed marriage and a failed step-fatherhood. His confidence was low. Fighting wasn't so easy now.

On March 13th, 1975, actress Viviane Ventura won her court battle to prove that millionaire financier John Bentley was the father of her love child, Schehezerazade. Mr Bentley, seemingly ignorant of British politics, said, 'I was considering joining the Conservative party before this came up – now perhaps I ought to join the anarchists.' Seven-foot-tall US actor Rik Van Nutter opened a warehouse to sell off the spoils of his broken marriage with Anita Ekberg. Henry Ezra Pratt celebrated his fortieth birthday in modest fashion with a meal at the Taj Mahal restaurant with Diana, Kate, Jack and the Blair family.

Did life begin at forty for our hero? No. It merely continued.

Early in May he went up to County Durham again, and asked Mr Wilberforce, happily recovered from his kidney problems, if he could take a ridge cucumber and a hot house cucumber for analysis, 'Just to monitor the situation.' Mr Wilberforce, anxious to avoid further black stem rot, raised no objections.

That evening, Henry met Martin Hammond in the Pigeon and Two Cushions. There were still bells round the walls of the gleaming little black bar, but Oscar had long gone. During his forty years Henry had seen eras end as quickly as the promises of Prime Ministers. Golden ages had died like hares at harvest time. Halcyon days had disappeared like dissidents in Argentina. Now another golden age had gone. Another era had ended. The halcyon days of waiters in northern pubs had gone for ever. And, to add insult to injury, there was a fruit machine.

'Awful news about Tommy Marsden,' said Henry.

'Dreadful. If I'd said to you, twenty years ago, when he had the world at his feet, "I wouldn't be surprised if he ends up driving his car into a gravel pit outside Newark while blind drunk," you'd have thought I was mad.'

'I went to the funeral. It was a bleak little affair really.'

'I'd have liked to. It clashed with an absolutely vital Highways and By-ways Committee.'

'No idea what happened to Ian Lowson and Billy Erpingham, I suppose?'

'Ian Lowson emigrated to Australia. I've not heard a word about Billy Erpingham.'

'That's it then. The Paradise Lane Gang. It's just thee and me now.'

They recalled the good, bad, indifferent old days in silence for a few moments. Then Henry broached the matter in hand.

'Martin? Do you, with your industrial contacts and your political contacts, know of a laboratory where I could have something very important analysed in secret?'

'I might,' said Martin Hammond cautiously. 'What is it?'

'Two cucumbers.'

'What??'

They waited while a fruit machine repairer and his fiancée walked past to the far corner. The fruit machine repairer gave the fruit machine a nervous glance, as if fearing that it might go wrong and spoil his evening out.

Henry lowered his voice to a whisper.

'They were grown near a nuclear power station. I want them tested for radiation. You could be helping to uncover a web of corruption and deception in which the great British public are cast in the role of suckers yet again. You could help rock a major industry and embarrass its leaders.'

'You're speaking my language,' said Martin Hammond. 'Can it be that your political consciousness is waking up at last?'

Henry scoffed, but Martin was right.

On Monday, May 26th, 1975, head teachers demanded protection from angry parents, Evel Knievel retired after crashing while riding his motor bike over thirteen London buses, and Henry discovered that the cucumber grown outdoors in County Durham contained more than five times the amount of radiation permitted by Government regulations.

That night, after Kate and Jack had gone exhausted to bed, Henry and Diana talked long and hard in the old-fashioned kitchen of number 83, with its battered free-standing dresser picked up cheap at auction.

'I think I'll have to resign,' Henry said. 'I don't think I've any option.'

'Well, there's no more to be said then, is there?'

'You don't sound pleased.'

'I'm not, but does it matter? Your mind's made up.'

'Diana! I didn't say that. Obviously I want to talk it over with you, or we wouldn't be sitting here.'

The kettle was boiling. Henry expected that Diana would go to it, but she showed no sign.

'What do you think I should do?' he asked.

'I think you should make a real, hard, long, thorough effort to find another job, and then resign.'

The kitchen, damp enough at the best of times, was filling with steam. Henry hurried to the kettle.

'If I get another job first, I'll be leaving as a career move, not as a matter of principle,' he said. 'Doesn't principle matter to you?'

'Well I suppose all life's a compromise, Henry. I think it's all very well having principles, but one has to eat, and how could we survive if you lost your salary?'

'Oh, Diana!'

'Hilary had her novels. I don't have anything.'

'Because you never wanted to have anything, and please let's keep Hilary out of this.'

He plonked her coffee down on the plain, inelegantly knotted pine table, picked up cheap at auction.

'I didn't work because Nigel hated the idea of my working,' said Diana coolly.

'And what Nigel said went, because you don't have a mind of your own.'

They stared at each other in silence.

'I see,' said Diana. 'I thought I had an amazing marriage in which we never had rows. I thought we loved and respected each other. That's what made living in Thurmash and having draughty houses and clapped-out cars and odd battered furniture picked up at auctions and skimping and scraping and not being able to see my schoolfriends and having to shop at Binns of Thurmarsh instead of Harrods and Harvey Nichols worthwhile. That's why I never once complained. All for nothing. When the crunch comes, you're no better than Tosser.'

Henry looked at her in horror.

'I don't want to argue,' he said. 'The last thing I want to do is argue. Oh my God, Diana darling, I didn't realise you'd felt like that all these years.'

'Because I didn't tell you, because I loved you, so it didn't matter. So I'm a not completely empty-headed person. I do have a mind of my own.'

'I'm sorry. Of course you do.'

'I care about people, Henry. You, the children, our friends, Auntie Doris, Uncle Teddy, Cousin Hilda. I care passionately about other people, and I don't think I'm selfish.'

'You're not! Oh, darling, you're not.'

He tried to kiss her. She wouldn't have it.

'No. Listen to me,' she said. 'Hear me out. I don't think I'm capable of being roused by abstract issues. It isn't in me. So I can't be excited by matters of principle as you can. I'm just not made that way. Of course people shouldn't be eating radiated cucumbers. You should try to do something about it. I agree. But not resign.'

'Well, I'll try, but I have to accuse the Director (Operations) of deceiving me, and that won't go down well. It might end up with my being sacked. I'd rather resign than that.'

'Well yes.'

'I mean, what is life all about? Just to eat, sleep, make love, bring up children so they can eat, sleep, make love and bring up children to eat, sleep and make love? I'm forty. Shouldn't I be ready to act like a man? Isn't it important for you to know that your husband is strong and resolute?'

'Not terribly, frankly. If it was I wouldn't have married you.'

'Diana!'

'I loved you for your warmth, humour, generosity and sexuality, not necessarily in that order.'

The clock on the living room mantelpiece, bought cheap at auction, struck thirteen. Midnight already!

'More coffee?'

'May as well. I won't sleep anyway.'

Over the next cup of coffee, Henry made the point that, if he did resign, he could tell the newspapers and become a bit of a celebrity. 'That'd help me get other jobs.'

'It might label you as a troublemaker.'

'I can't be as pessimistic and cowardly as that.'

'You want your moment of glory, don't you?'

'Well I must admit I'd quite enjoy it. Wouldn't you?'

'Oh dear,' said Diana. 'No, I really don't think I would. I think I believe that glory is an illusion.'

They finished their coffee in silence. There didn't seem to be any more to be said.

The Director (Operations) read the laboratory report on Henry's cucumber and then leant forward, his expression grim, his nose more predatory than ever.

'So you sent this to an outside lab,' he said, 'and not to us.'

'Yes.'

The sun came out from behind a puffy little cloud and set the dust dancing in Timothy Whitehouse's office. It was an inappropriately delightful early summer's day.

'Do you believe our labs to be inefficient, Henry?'

'No.'

'Do you believe our labs to be *dishonest*, Henry?'

Henry gulped. The moment he'd dreaded had arrived. Be brave, Henry.

'Yes.'

'I see. Oh dear,' said Mr Whitehouse gravely. 'Well now! In that case . . .'

'I resign.'

'What?'

'I resign.'

'That's a bit hasty, isn't it?'

'Well, I thought you were going to sack me, and I thought I'd better get my resignation in first.'

'Sack you?' The Director (Operations) smiled. 'No, no. I wasn't going to sack you.'

'You weren't?'

'No!' A laugh played briefly on the Director's thin lips, then disappeared. 'We hardly ever sack people, Henry. It can mean such trouble. Tribunals, lawsuits, strikes, compensation. Oh dear no. I suppose if I found that a member of my staff was systematically murdering his . . . or her, we mustn't be biased . . . colleagues, I might seriously consider dismissal. In your case, no!'

'Oh. Well . . . er . . . what . . . er . . . what *were* you going to say?'

'I was going to say, "Well, in that case I don't see how I can recommend you as my deputy." '

'What? I didn't think you had a deputy.'

'I don't. But our masters in Whitehall have calculated that since the Board was created the paperwork has increased by 142 per cent, and three new posts need to be created. One of them is my deputy. In seven years' time I will retire. You would have been the man *in situ.* I can't say you'd have succeeded to my post. I can only say it would have been likely.'

Henry swallowed. Be brave, Henry.

'Why should I believe you?' he asked.

'Don't you trust me?'

The sun went behind another inoffensive little cloud. The room became dark and grim.

'You told me not to trust you,' said Henry stoutly.

'So I did. So I did. *Mea culpa! Mea culpa!* I should have told you not to trust me *over small and personal matters.* Over the great issues of our business I am probity personified. Oh dear, Henry. This is all a storm in a tea-cup.'

The sun streamed into the office again. 'Henry!' Mr Whitehouse's tone became deeply persuasive. 'One cucumber has shown evidence of radiation. One grower has vegetables that are affected. Cucumbers are distributed centrally. If one person ate a hundred of these cucumbers, I agree, wooden box time. Nobody will! Nobody is in danger. So why alarm the inhabitants of a whole region, of the whole nation, threaten a whole industry, on which so many jobs depend, because of one cucumber?'

Mr Whitehouse paused, waiting for Henry to speak. Henry hesitated. Oh yes, he did hesitate. And, because he hesitated, Mr Whitehouse felt compelled to continue.

'Between you, me and the mythical G.P., Vincent Ambrose retires in six years. It's not in the realms of fantasy that you might end up as Chief Executive.'

'Me, Chief Executive!' scoffed Henry. 'I haven't even been to university.'

'The tides of egalitarianism are licking at the saltmarsh of privilege even here, Henry. How would you like to be Chief Executive?'

'It seems a complete sinecure. I've only met him twice and each time all he talked about was my kettle.'

'Exactly. An easy job. A nice salary. A guaranteed smooth passage through this rocky existence. How is your kettle, incidentally?'

'Fine. No problem.'

'Good. I should have asked before. *Mea culpa!*' Timothy Whitehouse leant forward across his desk, predatory nose pointing at Henry. He pulled his braces out as far as they would go, and smiled with all the magnetism that he could muster, and it still didn't reach his eyes. 'Withdraw your resignation, Henry. Please.'

This was it. The turning point of Henry's life. He thought about his easy existence in the protection of the Cucumber Marketing Board. He thought about Diana. About the children. About the long search for work that might ensue, in the increasingly cold world outside. He thought how easy it would be to devote the rest of his working life to cucumbers. He thought about the excitement of existence, the privilege of existence, the brevity of existence.

'I'm sorry,' he said. 'I can't.'

'Oh well,' said the Director (Operations), letting his braces thwack back viciously against his chest.

'I did it,' said Henry. 'I resigned.'

'I knew you would,' said Diana. 'I don't know why you bothered to consult me.'

'Would you have rathered I didn't consult you?'

'No.'

'Well then. Are you really very upset?'

'I still love you, but yes, I am. Very upset.'

'Oh, Diana. I . . . er . . . I rang Ginny. I'm going to have to see her later tonight.'

'Of course you are!'

'To give her my story!'

'Not to Helen this time?'

'Of course not. She made a fool of me.'

'Still a woman, though. Always a woman.'

'Diana! This isn't like you. You've never said things like that to me before.'

Diana turned wearily towards him. She was wearing a Fortnum and Masons apron given to her by her mother. She held a half-peeled potato in her left hand.

'I've never been deeply upset with you before,' she said.

'Oh God.'

Henry met Ginny Fenwick in the Winstanley, which was the nearest pub to her flat. She was forty-four now. She had never been beautiful, but there had been a sexuality in her appearance which had always attracted men. She was hiding her sexuality nowadays, dressing unattractively, not using make-up, so that men wouldn't find her attractive, so that they wouldn't, ultimately, reject her. What a delicate property is confidence.

Henry wished that he didn't have a story to tell, that they could just sit and reminisce.

He also wished that she was more impressed with his story.

'We've got a new editor,' she said. 'He's a real weed. I don't think he'd be impressed by your cucumber. As for your resignation, you aren't a well-known figure. It's a Leeds organisation, not Thurmarsh. It's not got a great deal going for it.'

'But they falsified results last year.'

'You've no proof of that. You don't have last year's cucumber.'

'Well of course not. It'd have rotted. People could be dying because they live near a nuclear power station.'

' "Could be." I need proof.'

'Well go and find it. Dig.'

'I'm on a local paper, Henry. This is a story for the nationals, or for the local papers in County Durham, not for us. Oh dear, you look so crestfallen.'

Henry was crestfallen. He accepted Ginny's offer of a drink, but really he felt like running away to sea and never seeing anybody he knew again.

'Won't you do the story?' he said.

'Oh yes, I'll do it. For you, Henry dear, I'll do it. I'm just warning you that it may not get much of a spread.'

'That's a bit defeatist, isn't it?'

'I never got that job as war correspondent, as you may have noticed. Next week I'll review my eleventh amateur operatic company production of *Oklahoma*. I feel a bit defeatist.'

'Oh, Ginny.'

Ginny's story didn't make the paper. The local papers in County Durham were interested, and said that they'd monitor the situation. The *Yorkshire Post* was polite and took all the details. Some of the nationals expressed keen interest, and the *Daily Express* said, 'We're very grateful. It'll help us build up our dossier.' Nothing was ever printed.

Nothing had changed, except that Henry no longer had a job, he no longer had any confidence that he would get a job, and he no longer had any real confidence in his relationship with Diana.

Had it all been a dreadful mistake?

'Of course not,' said Martin Hammond, pompous, self-righteous, somewhat tedious Martin Hammond, who was now his only contact with the Paradise Lane Gang. 'Of course not. Not if you feel better in yourself.'

'I do and I don't,' said Henry. 'I feel worried. I lack confidence. Yet I feel I have a new inner strength.'

'Well, that's marvellous,' said Martin Hammond, in the Oscarless bar of the Pigeon and Two Cushions.

'It's not much use if I can't do anything with my new inner strength,' said Henry. 'What can I do with it?'

'Go into politics,' said Martin Hammond.

13 Wider Prospects

On New Year's Day, 1976, an unemployed, perhaps unemployable Socialist called Henry Ezra Pratt awoke with a severe hangover and wouldn't have believed anyone who'd told him that within three years he'd have been adopted as Liberal candidate for the Parlimentary Constituency of Thurmarsh.

Nor would he have believed, as he crawled out of the bed from which his wife had long departed, and staggered ashen and ashamed into the bathroom, where he took twice the recommended dose of paracetamol, turned on the stiff cold water tap with great difficulty, and drank seven toothbrush mugs of fluoride and chlorine into which a little water appeared to have filtered accidentally, that within a week he would have been offered a job for which he hadn't even applied.

And, as he attempted to find in his right wrist enough strength to turn *off* the stiff cold-water tap in the ugly cold bathroom of his new and unloved home, he certainly wouldn't have been able to guess what the job would entail, and, if he had guessed, he'd have been astounded if he could have foreseen that he'd accept it.

A new and unloved home? Financial circumstances had forced them to sell the large, crumbling house in Lordship Road and buy a much smaller characterless box in Splutt Prospect, high above Commercial Road. What town other than Thurmarsh could possibly boast a street that afforded a view of Splutt?

A bed from which his wife had long departed? Diana had gone to bed white with anger and had fizzed out of bed like a firework while he was still pretending to be asleep. She'd said nothing unpleasant to him throughout his long fruitless search for a decent job. She'd supported his rejection of the post of attendant at the magnificent new gents' toilet in the bus station. She'd accepted, with quiet misery, that a bedroom for Benedict was no longer a necessity and they must move to a smaller house. It might have been easier if she'd fulminated furiously against her humiliation. Henry knew that she'd never allow her parents, or Paul and Christobel, to see 22, Splutt Prospect. She was becoming even more of an exile from her family.

Ashen and ashamed? All the frustrations and agony of his disappointments had come to the surface last night. Henry had wept – oh God, it was all coming back. He'd told her he'd have more respect for her if she showed anger – oh God, it was all coming back, that had been so unfair. He'd eaten all the Brie and practically demolished the bottle of calvados that Paul and Christobel had brought them from France. Oh God, it was all coming back. He hurried to the ugly cold bathroom and got there just before it all came back.

A bedroom for Benedict was no longer a necessity? Nothing had been heard of him by anybody. His disappearance was with them every day.

Kate was sad but staunchly supportive. 'Cheer up, Dad,' she'd say. 'Surroundings don't matter. Being a happy family is what matters.'

Jack had left school at sixteen, was working for a builder, learning the trade, and Henry hadn't the heart to blame him if he spent more time in the Golden Ball than in Splutt Prospect.

Camilla hadn't left Benningdean or changed her name to Pratt. She loved her mother and Henry. She didn't love Splutt Prospect. She loved Tosser's splendid house in Virginia Water. She didn't love Tosser or Felicity. She had a boyfriend in Chichester. She loved Chichester. Tosser paid for her to travel to Thurmarsh and school and Virginia Water, but not to Chichester. Her boyfriend's father was a butcher.

Kate had gone to Brian's for New Year's Eve, and Camilla to Chichester. Jack had been at a party. Joe and Molly Enwright had invited Henry and Diana to a party, but they couldn't face social gatherings just then. The Blairs had cooled towards them since Henry's resignation. Every life crisis attracts its unexpected defections.

It was twelve o'clock before Henry felt well enough to stagger downstairs.

Diana looked at him sadly over her mug of coffee.

'I'm very, very sorry,' he said. 'A new year. Shall we make it a new start?'

'I think we'll have to,' said Diana.

It was Henry's habit, in those long days without work, to trudge the streets of Thurmarsh every afternoon. A few days into January, as he was struggling up Commercial Road with a cruel easterly blowing him homewards and lifting the flap of what Jack called his 'flasher's mac', Henry met Derek Parsonage struggling down the hill but into the wind.

'Henry Pratt!' said Derek Parsonage. 'Fancy a drink?'

'It's half past three. They're closed,' said Henry.

'I'm a member of a drinking club.'

'Well I really ought to be getting home,' gasped Henry, the wind plucking the words from his mouth.

'Not yet sunk to drinking with villains?' said Derek Parsonage.

Any suggestion of priggishness was anathema to Henry, and within minutes he was being signed in, in almost pitch darkness, to a basement den called the Kilroy Club, in Agincourt Lane.

The bar room of the Kilroy Club was only slightly lighter than the lobby. Thick, dark curtains covered the windows. The lights were dark red and feeble. This was a room for those who were allergic to daylight.

There were only three customers, a villainous-looking trio seated in a corner with pints of John Smiths.

Henry recognised the owner immediately. He was Cecil E. Jenkinson, formerly of the Navigation Inn. He was badly shaven, had bloodshot eyes, a thin strand of greasy grey hair on an otherwise bald pate, a gap in his teeth and a huge paunch. He'd gone to seed.

But his brain was still sharp. 'Henry Pratt, may the gods preserve us,' he said.

'Yes. Sorry,' said Henry.

Cecil E. Jenkinson had banned Henry's father because he upset the other customers by going on about the war. Later, Henry had shopped him for allowing under-age drinking, and he'd banned Henry as well.

'Oh, what the hell?' he said. 'That's water under the bridge. What's your pleasure, gentlemen?'

'Something you can't provide, but while we're dreaming about it we'll have two large whiskies,' said Derek Parsonage, whose blackheads were worse than ever.

Cecil E. Jenkinson handed them their whiskies with a smile, but his eyes told Henry that he would never be forgiven.

'I've seen one of those men in the corner before,' said Henry in a low voice.

'Police,' said Derek Parsonage. 'Watching.'

'Watching?' said Henry.

'Villains,' said Derek Parsonage. 'Most of the villains in Thurmarsh get in here.'

'They look like villains themselves,' said Henry.

'Camouflage,' said Derek Parsonage.

'Camouflage?' said Henry.

'So that they look like villains and blend into the background.'

'There aren't any villains.'

'If there were they'd look like them and blend into the background.'

'Henry Pratt,' said one of the policemen.

'I beg your pardon?' said Henry.

'Bloody hell, everybody knows him,' said Derek Parsonage, seeming put out by this phenomenon.

'I took you home when you'd immersed yourself in the Rundle,' said the policeman.

'Oh yes!'

'Barely out of short trousers, you were, and very religious. But the second time I took you home you were a piss-artist.'

'How are the mighty fallen!' said a second policeman.

The three policemen laughed.

A huge man with orange hair and a scar down his cheek entered.

'A villain,' mouthed Henry.

'Police,' whispered Derek Parsonage.

The huge man sat at the other side of the bar from the trio.

'Why aren't they talking to each other?' whispered Henry.

'They're at loggerheads,' whispered Derek Parsonage. 'He's Rotherham. They're Thurmarsh. There's bad blood. Will you take a very important package to Teddy on Saturday?'

'Derek! The place is crawling with police!'

'Don't worry. They wouldn't recognise a crime if it leapt up and bit them in the arse.'

'Oh all right. I suppose so.'

'Good man.'

Bill Holliday entered.

'Henry Pratt, or I'm a Dutchman,' said the scrap king.

'Bloody knows everybody,' grumbled Derek Parsonage.

'It's called personality,' said Henry.

'Well, well, well,' said Bill Holliday. He slapped Henry on the back, bought him a double whisky, and lit a big cigar.

'I thought you were trying to kill me once,' said Henry.

'So I was told,' said Bill Holliday. 'I laughed. Thought I'd die. I'm not one of the real villains, am I, Derek? We all know who they are.'

Derek Parsonage flushed.

'Please, Bill,' mumbled Derek Parsonage. 'This place is crawling with police.'

'Spice of life, a bit of danger,' said Bill Holliday.

A red-faced, rather bloated man entered. Henry knew that he knew him, but he didn't know how he knew him.

'It's Henry Pratt,' said the bloated man.

'Bloody hell, I don't believe it,' said Derek Parsonage.

'You don't remember me, do you?' said the bloated man.

'No. Sorry,' admitted Henry.

'Market Rasen Market Garden,' said the bloated man. 'Eric Mabberley. You're with the Cucumber Marketing Board.'

'Was,' said Henry. 'I resigned on a matter of principle.'

'Good for you,' said Eric Mabberley. 'What are you doing now?'

'Drinking,' said Henry.

'Nice one,' said Eric Mabberley. 'Have a whisky.'

'Well, thank you.'

'Large whisky for my friend Henry,' said Eric Mabberley.

'Quite a character, our Henry,' said Bill Holliday. 'Knows everybody who's anybody.'

Derek Parsonage sulked.

Henry's head began to swim, but it was nice to be a bit of a character. Life was strange. Sometimes you were a nobody, and knew nobody, and sometimes you turned out to be a bit of a character, who knew everybody who was anybody.

'Fancy a job with us?' said Eric Mabberley.

'Are you serious?' said Henry.

'Very much so. We've just bought Market Weighton Market Garden, we need new staff, and I like the cut of your jib.'

'Well, that's very nice of you.'

'Besides, you have the one thing we lack.'

'Oh,' said Henry, pleased. 'What's that?'

'Knowledge of cucumbers,' said Eric Mabberley. 'We need a cucumber man.'

So Henry was reunited with the only things that he knew about – cucumbers. But it was pleasant work, with plenty of fresh air, and there was the challenge of the opening of the Market Weighton Market Garden, and it was pleasant to be a member of a smaller and less bureaucratic organisation.

They moved from 22, Splutt Prospect after only a year, buying a pleasant if simple stone cottage on the outskirts of Nether Bibbington, a hamlet to the east of Thurmarsh. 'We'll be able to invite your parents here,' said Henry to Diana, and she smiled, grateful that this was the nearest he'd ever come to acknowledging that she'd been ashamed for them to see 22, Splutt Prospect. The cottage's setting scarcely justified its name of Waters Meet Cottage, the meeting waters being little more than wet ditches, but the prospect was infinitely more pleasant than that of Splutt.

Kate could still get to Thurmarsh quite easily, and Jack lodged with his boss during the week and came back for weekends. In the summer he played cricket for Upper Bibbington, and there were riding stables nearby, and Camilla took up riding again in the school holidays.

It was a wonderful summer. The temperature reached the nineties on more than one occasion, and they often ate outside. Kate took her A levels on magnificent summer days, the like of which Britain rarely sees. There was a water shortage, and it was a trying time for cucumber growers, but the Cucumber Marketing Board stepped in with subsidies to prevent the price becoming uneconomic. Henry's attitude to the Board was much more positive now that he was on the growing side of things. He realised at last how right the Board was to be more on the side of the growers than of the public.

There was still no news of Benedict, and when they visited Monks Eleigh they lost heavily at Scrabble, Auntie Doris being able to make several unusual words, including Crunk, Yaggle, Zomad and Anquest, but all in all it was a good summer for the Pratts. And yet . . .

And yet, things weren't quite the same between Henry and Diana. There were no more serious arguments, there were happy times, but the closeness never quite came back. Their relationship had become a framework within which their separate lives could flourish, rather than being the centre into which all their other activities flowed.

Kate got her three A levels and was accepted by Bristol University. Diana took bridge and needlework lessons. Henry, never before a pub husband, became part of the early evening crowd at the Lamb and Flag in Upper Bibbington. Often, he'd get home just as Diana was going out to her evening class. It wasn't a bone of contention, and yet . . .

And yet Henry knew that there was something missing from his life, and when Martin Hammond suggested that he put his name forward as a Labour candidate for the Rawlaston Ward of Thurmarsh Borough Council, he accepted without hesitation.

'It's just a formality, of course, but there'll be an interview.'

'Fair enough,' said Henry. 'I hope in the Labour party it's what you know and not who you know that counts.'

'You're speaking my language,' said Martin Hammond.

The interview took place in the committee room of the Labour Club. Henry found himself sitting at a long trestle table, facing two men and a woman. Behind them was a portrait of Harold Wilson. The painter wasn't awfully good at people, but did pipes wonderfully.

Henry hadn't done much preparation for the interview, partly because he knew that it was a formality, and partly because something which he didn't quite understand was preventing him from giving serious consideration to his political views. His answers, therefore, were as much of a surprise to him as to anybody.

'You knew my old deputy, Howard Lewthwaite, didn't you?' said the Leader of the Council, Walter Plumcroft.

'Yes. I was married to his daughter,' said Henry.

A grave wave of longing for Hilary swept over him. Oh God, how he missed her. And now he'd missed a question.

'Sorry,' he said, 'I missed that. I was thinking about her. How . . . er . . . have you any . . . er . . . perhaps afterwards, Mr Plumcroft, we could have a chat?'

'Certainly. No problem,' said Walter Plumcroft, who was a sewage works manager. 'A few questions. Just a formality. Are you sound on unilateral nuclear disarmament?'

'Well, no, I'm not sure that I am,' said Henry. 'I think it would be obscene ever to use nuclear weapons first, but no, I'm not sure if we should concede all our strength at the negotiating table.'

There was a stunned silence.

'Are you steadfast against being in Europe?' ventured Len Pickford, no relation of the removals people.

'Well, no, I'm not,' said Henry. 'I don't think you can ever defy geography successfully. We're part of Europe and we have to be in there, shaping it.'

The silence deepened. Janey Middleton, who was a school meals superintendent, was the first to rally.

'We aim to nationalise a third of British industry in the next Parliament. Don't tell us you aren't in favour of that,' she said.

'Well, no, I'm not,' said Henry. 'I believe all our services should be nationalised, but none of our production.'

A wren's alarm call shattered the deep silence that followed this reply.

'Are you in favour of replacing the traffic lights at the end of Market Street with a mini-roundabout?' asked Walter Plumcroft.

'I don't know enough about it to have an opinion,' said Henry.

'I think you'd better tell us what you do believe in,' said Len Pickford.

'I believe in moderation and compromise,' said Henry. 'I believe in a balance between unions and management, between planning controls and the free market, between men and women.'

A bicycle bell, rather fiercely rung out in the street, caused Walter Plumcroft to jump.

'You aren't a Socialist,' said Janey Middleton. 'You're a wishy-washy Liberal.'

'I know,' said Henry. 'I've only just realised it. I'm awfully sorry for wasting your time.'

After the interview, Henry went to the Globe and Artichoke with Walter Plumcroft. The pub was next door to the playhouse and on the faded red walls there were signed photographs of theatrical luminaries, notably Dickie Henderson, Francis Matthews and Marius Goring.

As he sat at a corner table with Walter Plumcroft, Henry could feel his heart going like a pump at Mr Plumcroft's sewage works.

'So . . . er . . . are you . . . er . . . are you in contact with the Lewthwaites?' he asked.

'Oh yes. Yes,' said Walter Plumcroft.

'How are they?'

'Naddy's pretty poorly, I think. Spain's given her a few extra years, but it can't be long now. It's very sad.'

'Very sad. And . . . er . . . how's Hilary?'

'Fine, as far as I know. I don't know if she does a lot, but, yes, fine.'

252

'Is there . . . er . . . would you happen to know if there's . . . er . . . anybody in her life at all?'

'I couldn't say. I could ask.'

'Well, if you are in touch, that would be very kind. Obviously I care a lot about her, and I hope there is.'

Well, if he was thinking of going into politics, he might as well get used to lying.

The more Henry thought about it, the more he liked the idea of being a Liberal. He liked underdogs. He'd always felt a rapport with cucumbers because he saw them as underdogs, the Henry Pratts of the salad. The Liberals seemed to him to be the cucumbers of British politics. They would form a useful underdog triumvirate – the Liberal Party, cucumbers, and Henry.

He telephoned the Liberal Club and told them he wanted to join. They took his name and suggested he call in for a drink.

At the Club he was introduced to a committee member, Ron Prendergast, of Prendergast and Dwomkin, funeral directors. They sat in the bar, in a quiet recess, below a portrait of Asquith. They could heard the clunk of snooker balls from the back room. Henry had once thought that the carpet couldn't decide whether to be orange or green. Now he liked it. How our perspectives change, he thought. How little absolute truth there is.

'I looked you up in our records,' said Ron Prendergast cheerfully. 'You gave us the privilege of burying your father. Everything satisfactory, was it?'

'Well it *was* over twenty years ago,' said Henry, 'and I was only eleven at the time.'

'So you want to join the club? Splendid. We have a nice snooker room. We're open seven days a . . .'

'No, no. Well I mean, yes, I will join, but no, what I meant I wanted was to be involved politically.'

'Ah!' said Ron Prendergast. 'Well, I'll give you a form and you can fill in what you're prepared to do – address envelopes, man polling stations, canvass . . .'

'No, no. I mean, yes, yes, I'm happy to do those things but I meant that I actually wanted to get involved. I'd like to become a councillor.'

'Oh! Well! That's tremendous! We only actually have one councillor at the moment. South Yorkshire's a bit of a Liberal black spot, truth to tell. I mean, we're always looking for candidates. Well, you know, grand.'

'I'm not . . . to tell you the truth this has all come as a bit of a spur-of-the-moment job . . . I'm not actually terribly *au fait* with our current policies.' He liked the use of 'our'. It made him feel a Liberal already. 'Could we discuss policies a bit?'

'Ah!' said Ron Prendergast. 'Policies aren't really my forte. I'm more on the snooker side of things. Archie Postlethwaite would be your man for policies. He's our councillor.'

Two days later Henry met Archie Postlethwaite, who worked for an insurance company. He was small and sallow and had a grey goatee beard faintly tinged with orange, as if it had dipped into tinned tomato soup. They sat under Joe Grimond, and Archie Postlethwaite seemed as bemused as Ron Prendergast by his question about policies.

'My policy is to give satisfaction on local issues. Find out what people want, and fight for it. Democracy in action.' He clearly liked that phrase, so he repeated it. 'Democracy in action. We build our power base from the local issues upwards. That's the secret of our success.'

'But we don't have much success.'

'Not in Thurmarsh. Thurmarsh is a black spot.'

A white-haired old man with a stick hobbled to the bar and ordered a pint of bitter and a whisky chaser.

'So what about our policies at national level?'

'I leave that to the boys in London. That's the beauty of the Liberal Party. You don't have all the political baggage to carry around with you. Look at the trouble the other two parties have got into by having policies.'

The white-haired old man hobbled over to them.

'It is!' he said. 'It's Henry Pratt!'

It was the blackheads that did it. Without them, Henry would never have recognised Geoffrey Porringer.

'Geoffrey!' he said. 'Well well well!'

The very fact that one hasn't seen somebody for a long time can lead to a reunion begun with unsustainable warmth and enthusiasm. Seeing Henry and Geoffrey Porringer greeting each other like long-lost brothers, Archie Postlethwaite hurriedly eased himself away from further awkward questions about policies.

'So how long is it?' said Geoffrey Porringer.

Henry worked out that it was more than thirteen years.

'Thirteen years! Is it really? And you haven't changed a bit, young sir.'

Henry couldn't bring himself to say that Geoffrey Porringer hadn't changed, so he said, 'Oh! I have.' He patted his stomach. 'A bit more there.'

'Well, maybe,' said Geoffrey Porringer. 'Oh, it is good to see you.'

Henry thought this a bit odd, since the last time they met, Geoffrey Porringer had said, 'End of chapter. That particular album closed. I'd be happier if I didn't see any of Doris's family any more.'

'It's amazing that we should run into each other here,' he said.

'Not really. I come every day. Very set in my ways now. I didn't realise you used it.'

'I don't. I want to become involved in Liberal politics.'

'Are you mad? Keep out of politics, young sir.'

'I never liked you calling me "young sir". Now that it's so obviously untrue I like it,' said Henry.

'You're young to me.' Geoffrey Porringer took a sip of his whisky and winced.

'Pain?' said Henry.

'It's nothing. How's Hilary?'

Henry winced.

'Pain?' said Geoffrey Porringer. 'Are none of us immune?'

'Mine's emotional.' He gave Geoffrey Porringer a brief résumé of his emotional li.

'Oh well, life goes on,' was Geoffrey Porringer's considered comment on all the anguish and joy through which Henry had lived.

'I deduce you're no longer at the White Hart.'

'Oh no. Sold that years ago. Well, it almost killed me. Made me an old man.' A bitter tone was creeping into Geoffrey Porringer's voice. 'Doris, you see. I couldn't fill her shoes. Nobody could. Everything was as good as ever. I promise you it was. But would those twat-arses acknowledge it? Never. "You should have seen it in Doris's day." If I had a fiver for every time I heard that I'd be a rich man. All said in front of me, as if because I'm on the other side of the bar I can't hear, or because it doesn't matter because I'm not a real person. Twat-arses, customers, apart from a few. Twat-arses.'

Henry bought a round. Silence fell between them. The false warmth of their reunion was evaporating, and there was still the subject of Miles Cricklewood to broach.

'Cheers,' said Geoffrey Porringer. 'Well . . . tell me, young sir . . . how is the old girl? Still with that bloody vet, or has she found greener pastures?'

'She isn't like that.' He longed to tell him that Miles Cricklewood was Uncle Teddy. 'She's . . . er . . . she's in a bad way.'

'Oh?'

'Her memory's going. She's going slowly senile.'

'Oh dear.'

'It's a very trying situation, but Miles is immensely patient.'

'Is he really? Good old Miles.' Geoffrey Porringer let out a long sigh that was almost a whisper. 'Well well well.'

'What?'

'I've grieved over Doris for years, and all the time I should have been counting my blessings. I've had a lucky escape.'

'Oh no,' said Henry. 'It's she that's had the lucky escape.'

Henry wrote to the Liberal Headquarters in London, announcing his desire to become actively involved in Liberal politics 'at grass-roots level', because he thought that phrase would go down well. He got a nice letter back, assuring him that he was on file. He knew that he ought to pop in for an occasional drink at the Liberal Club, but he couldn't face another meeting with Geoffrey Porringer. It would untidy his curtain line.

One evening, as he returned from the Lamb and Flag in Upper Bibbington and met Diana leaving the house for her bridge, he heard the telephone ringing and got there just in time.

'Walter Plumcroft here.'

'Oh yes?' Who the hell was Walter Plumcroft? Oh yes! Labour Leader of the Council.

'You asked me to ring you if I found out anything.'

What? What about? Oh!! Hilary!

'Yes. Yes, I did. About Hilary.'

'Yes. It's good news.'

'Oh good.' His heart was thumping. She was free. She loved him.

'I spoke to her myself. She's in a relationship and it's very very stable. All's well.'

Henry's heart sank.

'Are you still there?' asked Walter Plumcroft. 'Have we been cut off?'

'No, no. No, no. Oh, that's terrific. Oh, that's a great relief.'

'Thought it would be.'

So that was that.

Henry took a week's holiday at the end of October, and went down south with Diana. A whole week together. Maybe their sex life would resume its former glory. But their Ford Escort was ageing, travelling was tiring, and it never quite did.

They stayed with the Hargreaveses for a few days. Mr and Mrs Hargreaves were sailing elegantly into the sunset together in a glory that was fading only slowly. Mrs Hargreaves contrived to make the lines on her face enhance her beauty. Mr Hargreaves remained handsome and serene. At the end of a dinner of baked aubergine and roast turbot, as they left the olive-green dining room, Mr Hargreaves hung back, and Henry realised that he wanted a word with him. 'I just wanted to say,' he said, 'that when you told me you were going to marry Diana I had my reservations. When you took her up north I had my reservations. I have none now. My daughter has never been as happy as she is with you.' Henry felt as if he'd been sandbagged. Why couldn't Mr Hargreaves have said that in the years when Henry had made Diana truly happy, instead of now, when he knew that her happiness was just a pretence?

They drove down to Benningdean and took Camilla out with her friend Sally Harper. At the end of a splendid lunch in the Rose and Crown at Spewelthorpe, as they were getting their coats, Henry heard Sally whisper, 'I like him. He may be a funny little cucumber man, but he's very sweet.' They visited Penshurst Place, and as they walked back to the car through the golden russet of a Kentish autumn, Henry said to Camilla, 'I gather you told Sally I was a funny little cucumber man.' Camilla went red and said, 'Yes, but only because I didn't know if she'd be able to see what I can see in you. I'd only really seen her with people out of the top drawer before,' and she went even more red, and Henry said, 'It doesn't matter, darling. I love you,' and Camilla said, 'I love you too . . . Daddy,' and tears sprang into Henry's eyes and slid down his face and he brushed them away and said, 'Oh dear. Aren't people silly?'

Back in London, they went to dinner with Lampo and Denzil. It was Denzil's turn to cook. It had dawned on Henry only gradually that nowadays it was always Denzil's turn to cook. He pointed this out to Lampo, who said, 'He won't let me in the kitchen. He's a little Hitler.' Denzil and Lampo were barely speaking when they arrived. Lampo had broken a tea-cup. 'He's absolutely livid,' said Lampo, who was now very senior in Christie's – or was it Sotheby's? 'It's literally a storm in a tea-cup,' and Denzil hissed, 'It's ruined the set. It's a storm in twelve tea-cups.' During the meal, Denzil irritated Henry with his fussiness, always doing bits of washing up between courses and coming to the table late for the next course, but Lampo showed no sign of irritation whatsoever, and after all, Denzil was in his seventies. It had dawned on Henry only gradually over their long friendship that, beneath their almost constant arguments, Lampo and Denzil loved each other very much. So it was an enormous delight to enter their stuffed, impossible little house, although it was also an enormous relief to leave, knowing that one hadn't broken anything.

On their way to Bristol, they spent a night in Paul and

Christobel's exquisite Georgian house. Christobel's food was lovely, and there was beautiful claret and port. In his gentle cups, Paul said, 'I really moved into medicine because I noticed how many holidays my father had,' in that low, exquisitely modulated voice that he had developed over the years. Every time Paul spoke, he sounded as though he was saying, 'Don't worry, Mrs Welkin. It's only a harmless cyst and we'll have you up and about again in no time.' This bedside manner worked on Henry so effectively that he said, 'Well, you do work hard when you're not on holiday, don't you?' instead of, 'You spoilt bastard. You don't know what work is.' When Paul said, 'We made a conscious decision not to have children. They interfere with one's work, and we neither of us really like children,' Henry was tempted to say, 'A person who doesn't like children only likes people when they're convenient to them. It's a real give-away of selfishness,' but he didn't, he said, feebly, 'Well, that's your choice, fair enough.'

There was only one minor contretemps. Christobel said, 'I hear you're involving yourself with the Liberals,' and Henry said, 'Yes,' and Christobel said, 'Well at least it isn't the other lot,' and Henry said, 'Well, I wouldn't. I hate the Tories,' and Christobel said, 'Oh, I meant Labour,' and then realised that Henry had known that, and Henry said, 'What a delightful ceiling rose that is,' and the tactful gear-change was so blatant that everybody laughed, and the awkward moment passed. In their exquisitely elegant spare bedroom, Diana thanked Henry for being so nice to Paul. 'I knew what you wanted to say. I can read you like a book,' and they held each other very close, and almost made love.

In Bristol they met Kate's new boyfriend, who was called Edward. He was handsome and intelligent, but intended to be an actor. Already, he had involved Kate in stage management. She was blissfully happy and looked extremely pretty despite all the hard work she had put in to conceal the fact. It was becoming politically incorrect to be pretty. Henry felt that this was a shame and had no relevance to the injustices and abuses which plagued the world. He also felt a wave of sympathy for poor Brian in Thurmarsh and hoped that Kate had let him down lightly. Not that he had any doubts.

Kate was kind. He found it difficult, in a long evening of pub followed by moderate Anglo-French restaurant, not to feel a certain jealousy of Edward, who had taken so much of his daughter's affection, but he resisted it with all the force he could muster. Edward made it clear from his attitude to Henry how warmly Kate had spoken of her father, and although Edward had been to Winchester, he was deeply ashamed of the fact, of his height and looks and talent, and would much rather, or so he thought from his lofty, privileged position, be a funny little cucumber man from Thurmarsh.

They arrived back at Waters Meet Cottage exhausted, and resumed the even tenor of their lives. Henry worked at the market gardens and drank in the Lamb and Flag, Diana learnt bridge, played bridge and went to Highland Dancing classes, and every now and then they saw each other and were pleasant to each other, and in this way an English winter passed.

The summer of 1977 saw the British climate return to normal after the unseemly excesses of 1975 and 1976.

Spain held its first general election for more than forty years. General Franco's long dictatorship was over at last.

In the newly democratic Spain, Nadežda Lewthwaite died.

Lightning plunged New York into darkness for one long, terrible night. Fires were started, thousands of stores were looted of everything from food to new cars. 3,200 looters were arrested, but the authorities couldn't contain the rampaging mobs. How fragile is our civilisation! How miraculous it is that democracy should ever be introduced!

How disappointing it was that Henry heard nothing from the Liberal Party!

Elvis Presley died.

Henry and Diana discovered that Benedict was not dead.

One morning in September there was a letter from Tosser:

Dear Henry and Diana,
I've been endeavouring to make telephonic communi-

cation with you, but it seems that you're always out. What a social whirl it must be up there in Nether Bibbington. I'm quite envious.

The reason I'm contacting you is that I've had a letter from Benedict. He's working in a bar in Spain and is all right. His letter is very unsatisfactory, but I think you ought to hear it. I'm reluctant to send a copy as he might interpret this as a breach of confidence.

I hope you're both well.

With all best wishes,

Nigel.

Diana rang him immediately. Both their hearts were thumping. Henry sat on the settee beside her and was able to hear most of what Tosser said.

'The Pilkington-Brick residence.'

'Oh hello, Felicity, it's Diana.'

'I'll get him.'

'Thank you.'

'Hello, Diana.'

'Hello, Nigel.'

'This'll have to be brief. I'm due at a client's.'

'I'll be thrilled if it's brief, Nigel. Perhaps you'll read the letter.'

'Right.' They heard him call to Felicity. 'Darlesy-Warlesy, have you got the letter?'

Diana mimed being sick at 'Darlesy-Warlesy'.

Henry grinned.

'Thanks, Darlesy. Hello, Diana, are you still there?'

'Still here, Nigey-Wigey.'

'What? Oh! Diana! No, he says, and I must say it's all pretty unsatisfactory:

'Dear Dad,

'I thought it was about time I let you know that I'm all right. I hope you've been worried, but somehow I doubt it. I've been doing all sorts of things – helping in the wine harvest, et cetera

– and have finally settled running a bar with a friend near Malaga. That's all you need to know. I could do with a bit of dosh, and you were always decent in that department. I won't beg, but if you've got any spare from all your over-charging of your suckers, a cheque which I can cash here would be welcome. You can send it to Poste Restante, Malaga. I suppose I hope Felicity's well, she never did me any good, but she never did me harm either. I can hear you saying that I'm being pretty insulting if I want money. Well I hope you'd rather the truth than a lot of old poloney (is that the right word? The old vocab rusts a bit when you're abroad) about family and love just to get money from you.

'I hope that mother of mine is all right. I'll be happy to write to her when she's got tired of the cucumber man. Please give all my best to Camilla. I think that by the standards of this bastard world she's an OK person. Too OK for me to suggest she sees me here.

'I'll be grateful, in my way, for any dosh you can spare.

'Bye for now.

'Benedict.'

'Oh my God,' said Diana.

'Exactly. What do you think he means by "too OK for me to suggest she sees me here"?'

'I dread to think. You will tell Camilla what he says about her being OK, won't you?'

'Well I wasn't going to. It's hardly ringing praise, is it?'

'It is from him, you stupid oaf, and she'll be absolutely thrilled, she worships him still.'

'More fool her, and I did hope we might be able to discuss this in civilised language, Diana. I hope we're civilised people.'

Diana made a face at Henry. He grinned. Much more of this and they'd be in love again.

'Are you going to send any money, Nigel?' she asked.

'I don't know. I don't feel like it. It's a bloody arrogant letter.'

'You spend a fortune to get him taught to be arrogant, and then you complain. At least it's honest, though.'

'In its horrible way, I suppose. All that, "I hope you've been worried, but somehow I doubt it." That's an awful thing to say to a father.'

'It's an awful thing to have to say to a father.'

'Diana! Don't be so beastly.'

'I am beastly. You're so lucky to be with your magnificent Darlesy-Warlesy. Do you put a flag up when you're in residence? Or only when you're indulging in your brief, unsubtle love-making?' She slammed the phone down and burst into tears. 'Oh Benedict,' she wailed. 'Oh Ben!'

Henry hugged her, but couldn't comfort her. She needed other comfort now.

Henry had a week's holiday left. They flew to Malaga and toured every resort and every bar for fifty miles in each direction, showing a photograph of Benedict wherever they went. They found no trace of him, and arrived home exhausted, depressed and broke.

In October, Henry received a letter from a man called Magnus Willis.

> Dear Mr Pratt,
> I have read your letter about the Liberal Party and your desire to become involved. I've an idea of what form that involvement might take. I'll be in Yorkshire next week and wondered if you might be able to spare the time from your busy life to meet me for a drink at the Midland Hotel at 6.30 on Friday next, the 22nd.
> I must apologise for the short notice, but my travel plans have only recently been fixed.

So Henry found himself once more in that ungainly red-brick pile, the Midland Hotel, Thurmarsh. It was more than twenty-one years ago that he'd entered the hotel, twenty years old and aching with love, to spend a night with his childhood sweetheart, Lorna Arrow.

At the last count Lorna had had six children, and he was into his second marriage, but the Midland Hotel seemed to be in a time warp. The same vast armchairs, sagging terminally. The same huge, ugly chandeliers. The same photographs from the halcyon days of steam. Only the carpet, a light red, claret to the former's port, had changed.

Magnus Willis unfolded himself from an armchair, bounded across like a sex-starved wallaby, shook hands fiercely, said, 'Absolutely delighted to meet you,' took Henry into the bar, and said, 'What's your poison?'

'A pint of bitter, please.'

'Ah me!' sighed Magnus Willis. 'A bitter man. The common touch. I wish I was a bitter man.' He plumped for a glass of tonic water.

They installed themselves in an alcove.

'I thought this was better than the Liberal Club,' said Magnus Willis. 'Wagging tongues. Now, tell me your life story.'

Magnus Willis curled himself in his chair, legs tucked up in a pose that was at once strikingly foetal and so aggressively that of the fascinated listener that to his astonishment Henry found himself telling his life history.

'Absolutely excellent. First rate. Well done,' enthused Magnus Willis when he'd finished. 'Perfect. Needn't go into the first wife scenario too closely, but otherwise absolutely spot-on. Gloss over the newspaper connection, but otherwise tremendous. Needn't emphasise the cucumbers too much, but apart from that I don't think one could pick too many holes in it. And Thurmarsh through and through, that's what I like. Tell me why you're a Liberal.'

'Basically because I don't believe in dogma and I believe that interference by politicians in the running of the country should be kept to a minimum.'

'Go on.'

'I think we desperately need common sense and compromise in this country. I believe in moderation. There's nothing wishy-washy in being middle-of-the-road. It's a dangerous place to stand. I'm a passionate moderate.'

'You'll do,' said Magnus Willis.

'Sorry,' said Henry. 'What'll I do for?'

'Oh, didn't I tell you?' said Magnus Willis. 'Sorry. You'll do for our short-list of candidates for the Parliamentary Constituency of Thurmarsh.'

Henry gawped.

'It's nothing to write home about. We only have one councillor and he's useless. We've no local candidate who's remotely astute politically, and we must have one local candidate on the short-list. We've no chance of winning, but if you are chosen as candidate, if you put up a good show, a plum may follow. A nice by-election seat. Quite possibly a victory. We're rather good at by-elections.'

The 230,000 ton *Amoco Cadiz*, carrying oil from the Persian Gulf to England, broke in half in heavy seas off the coast of Brittany and caused the world's worst pollution disaster . . . so far. In Rome the body of Aldo Moro, the kidnapped and murdered ex-Prime Minister, was found in the boot of a car. The world's first 'test-tube' baby was born in Lancashire. Pope Paul VI died, his successor, Pope John Paul I, died after thirty-four days in office, and Karol Wojtyla, Archbishop of Krakow, became the first non-Italian pope for four centuries.

Henry had a quiet year. Kate was doing well at Bristol; Camilla surprised everybody by applying to go to art school and being accepted; Jack was building and drinking; Henry and Diana led not unpleasing but largely separate lives in Nether Bibbington, and the market garden company continued its expansion down eastern England, opening the Market Deeping Market Garden and the Downham Market Market Garden.

Just two things broke the even tenor of Henry's life.

The first occurred in May. He met Hilary in Fish Hill, right in the middle of the redevelopment that he'd fought to prevent. His heart stood still, and he fancied hers did too.

'What are you doing here?' he said.

'Looking for houses,' she said. 'We're hoping to come back. Dad hates Spain.'

'And you?'

'It doesn't really matter where I live.'

Her face was unlined. She hardly seemed to have aged. In fact she looked as if she had hardly lived.

'I often think of you,' he said.

'Do you?' she said. 'I often think of you.'

'Shall we have a coffee?' he said. 'Or a drink?'

'I don't think that's a very good idea,' she said.

'Are you . . . er . . . I heard there was a chap . . . are you still . . . er . . .?'

'Still happy? Yes. Yes, it's a very satisfactory relationship.' She held out her hand. 'Goodbye, Henry,' she said. 'I'm glad I've seen you. You look well.'

That was all. But his heart thumped and his stomach sank and his veins throbbed and he could hardly breathe and he felt that he was going to faint. He leant against the wall of Marks and Spencers and waited until it no longer felt as if his world was disintegrating into ten thousand pieces, and then he set off slowly and sadly on the long path back to real life.

The other thing that occurred was equally unexpected. After a gently polite but thorough grilling by the selection committee, he was elected as Liberal candidate for the Parliamentary Constituency of Thurmarsh.

Three days after he'd been elected, he opened the *Thurmarsh Morning Chronicle* and said, 'I don't believe it. I just don't believe it.'

'What?' said Diana.

'They've named the Labour candidate. It's Martin Hammond.'

'Oh dear.'

'Yes. A bit embarrassing.'

Five days after Henry had opened the *Morning Chronicle* and said, 'I don't believe it, I just don't believe it,' Diana opened the *Morning Chronicle* and said, 'I don't believe it, I just don't believe it.'

'What?' said Henry.

'They've named the Conservative candidate. It's Tosser.'

'Oh dear.'

'Yes. A bit embarrassing.'

14 A Dirty Campaign

On Tuesday, April 3rd, 1979, Mrs Thatcher opened the General Election campaign, promising tax cuts and warning the nation not to accept the attempt of James Callaghan, the Labour Prime Minister, to blame Britain's problems on the world recession.

On Wednesday, April 4th, the BBC admitted that their exclusive film of the Loch Ness Monster had in fact been film of a duck.

On Thursday, April 5th, Henry sat on a raised platform in the Committee Room above the Liberal Club, and listened to Mr Stanley Potts, Chairman of the Thurmarsh Liberals, introducing him to the small gathering of the faithful who had turned up for his adoption meeting.

Suddenly, all the nerves which had plagued him for the last weeks left him and he felt that he could even face the House of Commons without fear.

There were several familiar faces in the audience. Magnus Willis, who had turned out to be his agent. Archie Postlethwaite, the lone councillor. Diana, nervous and embarrassed. Jack, awkward but relaxed. Ron Prendergast, wishing he was downstairs playing snooker. Ginny Fenwick, hoping for fireworks. Eric Mabberley, a lifelong Liberal. Oscar, the redundant waiter from the Pigeon and Two Cushions. Mr Gibbins, six foot two, almost eighty, and as bald as a coot, in whose class, in the days when he'd been six foot four, Henry had emitted a legendary fart. And . . . it couldn't be. But it was . . . Cousin Hilda, who looked . . . yes . . . proud!

He stood up, to loud applause.

In a dark suit and orange shirt that matched his rosette, forty-four years old and becoming a bit of a roly-poly, with his hair streaked with grey and a bald patch on the top of his head, Henry was a comforting rather than an impressive figure. But he spoke well and with passion.

'Ladies and gentlemen,' he began. 'I'm grateful to you all for turning out tonight. I am Thurmarsh born and Thurmarsh bred.' There was applause. His old headmaster, Mr E. F. Crowther, from whom he'd stolen the phrase, had known a thing or two. 'I promise you that, if I am elected, I will serve the people of Thurmarsh with dedication, but I will not be a purely parochial politician. Better street lighting in the York Road area. . . , ' he paused, forcing them to applaud, '. . . will sit alongside the economy, the arts, the reform of our constitution and the conservation of our planet.'

He spoke briefly about the party's policies, about proportional representation, about a federal solution to Welsh and Scottish devolution, about democracy in industry, about replacing the House of Lords with an elected second chamber, about switching taxes from incomes to wealth and expenditure. There was laughter when he spoke of being thrown into the Rundle.

He concluded, 'I said at the beginning, "If I am elected." We start from a low base, but I don't believe that we have no chance. I wouldn't be standing if I did. I believe that the people of Britain are fed up with the counter-productive shuttle between Conservative and Labour dogmas. I believe that the people are hungry for change. I believe that, if we can make people believe that we believe, our hopes will not be make-believe. If we can inspire this town, we can win. I hate the complacent, easy patriotism of those who say that this is the best country in the world. If it is, with its incompetence and apathy, its prejudice and pettiness, its aggression and selfishness, God help the rest of the world. I suggest to you a greater, more honest, more difficult patriotism. Let's begin, here today, our battle to rid this country of its weaknesses. Let us say, "If we care enough, if we work together enough, this country *can become* the best country in the world." '

There was loud applause. Afterwards, people were warm with their congratulations.

'We've made the right choice,' said Magnus Willis.

'It's just dawned on me. You're the farter. Well, it's turned out not to be your only talent after all,' said Mr Gibbins.

'While you talked, I could almost believe I could be a political wife,' said Diana.

'I was proud of you. The whole market garden will be proud of you,' said Eric Mabberley.

'I shouldn't be out, not with my tubes. I've been bronchial since Christmas. But it were worth it,' said Oscar.

'It were very nice. I only wish Mrs Wedderburn had lived to see this day,' said Cousin Hilda.

On Monday, April 9th, Henry ran into Martin Hammond outside the Thurmarsh and Rawlaston Cooperative Society.

'Let's have a clean fight,' said Henry.

'I've nowt to say to thee,' said Martin Hammond, whose dialect was becoming more pronounced as polling day loomed.

Martin had telephoned Henry months ago, and said, 'I can't think how you can do this. You're a turncoat.'

'I've found that my true position is left of centre,' Henry'd said. 'I have to be true to myself, Martin. I believe Britain needs non-dogmatic, non-centralist government.'

'Cobblers.'

'Yes, I believe Britain needs cobblers too. We must support the dying crafts. Good point.'

Martin had rung off, leaving Henry to regret his cheap joke. He didn't want to argue with his old friend, and a couple of weeks later had written to Martin:

> Dear Martin,
> I'm sorry that at our last conversation I was so frivolous. It was to cover my embarrassment. I'd like to feel that during this campaign we can be gentlemen, and when it's over we can be friends. I respect your convictions, though I don't any longer believe they're the right way forward. I'm deeply opposed to the Tory Party, and will have no mercy for Tosser, but I'll oppose you honourably.
> With love and friendship,
> Your old mate from the Paradise Lane Gang,
> Henry

Martin hadn't replied.

On Wednesday, April 11th, Henry sat next to Tosser in the directors' box at Blonk Lane. All three major candidates declared their support for 'the Reds' though Martin hadn't been to a match for twenty-seven years, and Tosser had never been.

'Who'd have thought,' said Henry at half-time, 'all those years ago at Dalton, that you and I would share a wife and a constituency?'

'I asked you to keep Diana out of it,' said Tosser. 'But I suppose one can't expect honour from a grammar-school boy.'

Tosser was referring to a phone call he'd made to Henry several weeks before.

'Well, this is a funny situation, Henry,' he'd said.

'Yes.' Henry had been very dry. 'Did you ever get out to Malaga to try and find Benedict?'

'Well it's been difficult. I have sent money.'

'Money's easy for you. He might appreciate a bit of time spent on him.'

'He doesn't deserve it, Henry. Life's a two-way process. But this is what I wanted to talk to you about. Can we keep our families out of this?'

'If you wanted to keep your family out of it, it might have been better not to come to the constituency where your wife's second husband is standing.'

'I didn't know you were going to stand. And I hadn't told them Diana lived in Thurmarsh. Why should I? I never dreamt I'd be sent to your God-forsaken hole, and when I was, I thought it best to let sleeping dogs lie. I mean, I didn't have a choice of constituency, so what was the point of mentioning it? The aim of the exercise is to groom me, Henry. Lose with honour, get myself a nice seat somewhere in civilisation, with a nice fat majority.'

'Well I'll do all I can to make sure you lose without honour,' Henry'd said. 'I'll wipe you off the face of the map. I love my home town. I don't like to see it being used.'

Somehow, it didn't look as though it was going to be an overwhelmingly friendly campaign.

The opinion polls gave the Conservatives 49 per cent, Labour 38½ per cent, the Liberals 9 per cent!

All three candidates toured Thurmarsh in cars with loud-hailers. They toured the parts of the town where they might expect to win most votes. Canvassing wasn't about changing people's minds. It was about persuading your supporters to get up off their backsides and vote.

There were areas around Paradise and Splutt and York Road into which it was inadvisable for Tosser to venture, even though he'd been a rugby international.

There were areas like Winstanley and the streets around the Alderman Chandler Memorial Park where it would be a waste of time for Martin to canvass.

Henry's supporters were more difficult to locate. They could be anywhere. He had the hardest task, and he approached it with an energy and dedication which fired the enthusiasm of his helpers. He could charm people on the doorsteps. The canvassing returns were surprisingly good. He couldn't imagine that Tosser had a clue about talking to ordinary people, and Martin could hardly be described as inspiring. His confidence grew.

Every morning Henry held a press conference. He was never at a loss for a word. When his former colleague, Ted Plunkett, asked him where he stood on Europe, there was just a little smugness in his voice, as if he hoped to discomfit Henry.

'I believe in Europe,' said Henry. 'We must fight against its absurdities – uniform envelope sizes, Euro-sausages and standardised tomatoes – but we can never afford to be against its principles. I'll tell you why. Portugal has recently become a democracy after fifty years, Spain after forty years, Greece has emerged from the rule of the military junta, Germany and Austria were under the mad rule of Hitler not so long ago, while Italy had Mussolini. Six major Western European countries with dictatorships in my lifetime. If we're all together in Europe, that cannot happen again.'

Ted looked disappointed at that fluent answer from the man whom his wife had been known to fancy. Henry's confidence grew.

As polling day grew closer a report recommended a 100 per cent pay rise for MPs.

Mr Callaghan said that the defeat of inflation and unemployment took top priority.

Mrs Thatcher promised greater respect for law and order, improved education, a fair balance between rights and duties for trade unions, and the stopping of the stifling of individuality by the state.

Mr David Colclough, President of the National Hairdressers' Association, said in Bournemouth that windblown and unkempt hair could lose votes.

At the beginning of the evening of Friday, April 20th, Henry's hair was not windblown. Indeed, it was positively kempt.

By the end of the evening, Mr Callaghan, Mrs Thatcher and David Colclough would have been united in their disgust for him.

And the evening had started so well!

Henry was walking along Commercial Road, alone, after canvassing in Rawlaston. He'd told his team that he needed a few minutes on his own, to clear his head and marshal his thoughts.

To his amazement, to his disgust, to his utter and total joy, he saw Tosser Pilkington-Brick emerge furtively from the premises of 'World-Wide Religious Literature Inc.'

The Conservative candidate had been visiting a male brothel!

All sorts of lurid headlines passed through the mind of the former journalist. TORY CANDIDATE IN ARMOUR ORGASM SHOCK. PERVERT PILKINGTON DROPS A BRICK. BROTHEL BLOW GIVES BLUES THE BLUES. WHAT A GORY TORY STORY. No, he'd settle for something straightforward. CANDIDATE IN SEX SCANDAL SENSATION.

That evening, as chance would have it, Henry was embarking on a whistle-stop tour of the town's pubs. He was used to pubs. He was known in some of these pubs. He would do well.

Magnus Willis hated pubs and drank tonic water, a vote loser if ever Henry had seen one. So Henry's companion and minder was Ron Prendergast.

The pubs were quite busy almost from opening time. They

always were on a Friday night, which was why Friday had been chosen for this particular exercise.

They went to old haunts of Henry's – the Lord Nelson, the Pigeon and Two Cushions, the Devonshire, where the jazz had not yet started. They popped in at the Globe and Artichoke, the Artisan's Rest, the Coach and Horses, the Jubilee Tavern, the Nag's Head, the Tap and Spile, the Three Horseshoes, the Commercial, the Tipsy Gipsy and the Baker's Arms. In each pub, Henry had half a pint. He had to. It was part of his vote-catching exercise. It was his duty to his party.

He didn't discuss the issues, but chatted to people, told the landlords their beer was nicely kept, except in the Artisan's Rest, where nobody would have believed him. He called out, 'Good luck. Happy drinking. A vote for me is a vote for a good pub man,' and spoke of the old days when the pub had been one of his locals. All thirteen appeared to have been his locals, but he had been in eleven of them, and a bit of exaggeration is permissible during an election.

Ron Prendergast admitted defeat at the Baker's Arms, and Henry moved on alone to the Grenadier's Elbow, where he was to meet Magnus Willis.

Magnus, who'd been doing a major canvass in Splutt, entered the pub nervously but bouncily. There was a gleam in his eyes.

'Excellent returns in Splutt,' he said. 'People like you.' He sounded envious, about which Henry was sorry, and surprised, about which Henry was even more sorry. ' "He's like one of us," they say, and, "He's so ordinary," and, "I could imagine giving him his breakfast." You've got the common touch. We could be making history here.' He looked at Henry more closely. Some of the gleam disappeared. 'How many have you had?'

'Only thirteen.'

'Thirteen!!'

'Halves. Only halves. I'm as fit as a daisy. Magnus, I have great news.'

Magnus braced himself for the great news. All the gleam had gone.

He told Magnus about Tosser and the exotic brothel.

Magnus whistled.

'Are you absolutely certain?' he said.

'Absolutely certain.'

'We've got him! Not a word about this tonight, Henry. Leave it to me. I have to work out how to handle it. Oh, well done!'

The gleam had come back.

'Fancy a drink?' said Henry.

'No. No! Home now, there's a good chap.'

'Henry! My old mate!'

Colin Edgeley emerged from the roughish crowd at the bar, carrying a full pint with care.

'Have a drink, kid,' said Colin Edgeley.

'Just a half,' said Henry.

Magnus groaned.

'I'm not drunk, Magnus. One drink, then home like a good boy.'

'Right. I'm ordering you a taxi,' said Magnus.

Magnus went off to order a taxi, Colin returned, borrowed a pound from Henry, and bought him his half.

'A half used to be a "glass" of beer round here, and there were waiters,' said the Liberal candidate. 'What's happening to the world?'

'You ask them in Whitehall when you get there.'

'Too right. I will.'

'Are you coming up to the Devonshire for the jazz?'

'No. I'm going home.'

'It's not even ten yet.'

'I'm under orders.'

'Taxi ordered,' said Magnus, returning. 'Ten minutes.'

'Just time for the other half,' said Henry.

Magnus groaned.

When the taxi arrived, his agent took him firmly by the arm and frogmarched him to the door.

At the door, Henry wriggled free and turned round.

'I'm being sent home,' he shouted. 'I've been a naughty boy.

Would you vote for a naughty boy? 'Course you would. 'Cos you're all naughty boys too, aren't you?'

Magnus groaned.

'Waters Meet Cottage, Nether Bibbington,' Magnus told the taxi-driver.

He pushed Henry in and slammed the door gratefully. His job was done for the day.

As soon as they were out of sight of Magnus, Henry said, 'I don't want to go to Nether Bibbington or Upper Bibbington or any Bibbington. I don't want to go to Waters Meet. I don't like water. I want to go to Bitters Meet, otherwise known as the Commercial Arms in Devonshire Street.'

'Or even the Devonshire Arms in Commercial Street,' said the taxi-driver.

'That'll do.'

'I'm supposed to take you to Nether Bibbington. I've got a chitty.'

'Well I'll sign your chitty and give you a fiver.'

'Fair enough, Chief.'

So Henry found himself in the jazz club. It wasn't as crowded as in the old days. Sid Hallett and two of his Rundlemen were drawing the state pension now, and jazz wasn't hard enough for the new world that was coming.

He saw the journalists immediately. They were in a good strategic position, at a table close to the bar. Ginny Fenwick was there, and Helen Plunkett, née Cornish, and Ben Watkinson and his shy, no longer so petite wife Cynthia. Just the four of them. Not like the old days.

They greeted Henry warmly and with great surprise. A pint of bitter and a whisky chaser had been ordered before they realised how drunk he was. Colin arrived and said, 'How the hell did you get here?' and Henry said, 'Turned the taxi round,' and Colin said, 'You old rogue.' Henry couldn't finish his beer, but he accepted another whisky. It was extremely pleasant to sit with old colleagues in a bar and listen to ageing jazzmen greeting closing time with energy. Helen smiled at him and he smiled back and . . . and . . . ?

He was in bed. He was alive. His head hurt. The telephone was ringing. Where was he? The telephone had stopped ringing. He recognised that wardrobe. Where had he seen it before? At home! He was at home! How had he got home? He sat up and his head swam and he lay down again hurriedly. The telephone was ringing. What had happened? A blackbird was singing. It was morning! The telephone had stopped ringing. How had he got here? Where had he been last night? He remembered touring pubs and oh God yes turning the taxi round. The Devonshire. The blackbird had stopped singing. He remembered sitting in the Devonshire listening to Sid Hallett and the Rundlemen approaching what passed for a climax in their performance. He remembered Ginny leaving abruptly. Had he said something to upset her? He remembered Helen smiling. Had he upset Ginny by saying something to Helen?

The telephone was ringing. Why did the telephone keep ringing? It hurt his head.

It stopped.

He remembered a corridor. A dark corridor. A lawn. But indoors. Strange there should be a lawn indoors.

He remembered flashlights. Voices. Intruders. A lavatory. He hadn't felt well in the lavatory. He didn't feel well now.

The door opened.

Diana stood at the door.

She wasn't happy.

What had happened?

She gave him a look, half angry, half pitying. What did it mean?

'I'll stand by you until after the election or until you resign,' she said. Her voice was icy. Why was her voice icy? What did her words mean? The telephone was ringing.

'Why does the phone keep ringing?'

'Why do you think it keeps ringing?'

'What's happened? I must know what's happened.'

'Don't you know what's happened?'

'No!!'

She gave a hoarse, humourless laugh. He didn't like her laugh. He didn't like anything about this morning. He'd come out in a cold sweat.

'You'd better read the paper,' she said.

She handed him the *Thurmarsh Morning Chronicle*, which was to cease publication at the end of May.

He read the main headline. 'CANDIDATE IN SEX SCANDAL SENSATION.'

'Hurrah!' he cried. 'They got him.'

'What do you mean, "Hurrah!"?' said Diana.

He read on.

The election campaign of Henry Pratt, the 44-year-old Liberal candidate for Thurmarsh, was in tatters last night after he was found in a naked love tryst on a pub's snooker table.

His blood ran cold. Icy sweat covered his body. He gawped at his icy wife. He remembered nothing. He read on.

With him 'on the green baize' in the back room of the popular Devonshire Arms public house in Commercial Street was a well-known married Thurmarsh journalist, Mrs Helen Plunkett, who works for our sister paper, the *Evening Argus*.

The couple, who have known each other for more than twenty years, were caught 'in the act' by Inspector William Bovis, after the police had responded to an anonymous tip-off.

Another message, also anonymous, was received by this newspaper. There is as yet no indication of the identity of the caller, who was male and 'didn't have a strong accent'.

Inspector Bovis said that the couple had both been naked, and charges might follow. 'I actually witnessed them engaged in an indoor sporting activity not normally associated with snooker tables,' Inspector Bovis told our reporter. 'There is no doubt in my mind that what I saw was sexual congress.'

The landlord of the Devonshire Arms, Mr Wilf Cottenham (aged 52), said that the couple had been drinking in the bar earlier in the evening. Mrs Plunkett had arrived with friends at about nine o'clock and Mr Pratt had arrived on his own more than an hour later.

'They'd both been drinking, but they weren't drunk or I wouldn't have served them,' he said. 'It's not that kind of pub.'

'I locked up at approximately eleven twenty-five, but didn't look in the Billiard Room,' he added. 'It's closed on jazz nights, so I had no reason to look.'

'I'm right choked about the table. It's torn in more than one place. They must have been at it hammer and tongs. It'll be a long time before anyone pockets any more balls on it.'

Mr Pratt appeared to our reporter to be very drunk indeed. 'Where's Chick Zamick?' he mumbled. 'In bed with Flory Van Donck, I'll be bound.' This was understood to be a reference to an ice hockey star and a Belgian golfer.

Mrs Plunkett said after the incident, 'Henry had been canvassing in pubs and was very definitely inebriated. He made certain suggestions and was very insistent. I'd been drinking and I yielded. I'm deeply ashamed of myself and just hope that I'll be able to patch things up with my husband.'

Rumours that Mr Pratt might resign were described as premature by Mr Pratt's agent, Magnus Willis. He said, 'It's a disaster. No question of it. But we'll assess the situation in the light of day, and I imagine that he'll attempt to prove that, despite this isolated lapse, he's the best man to represent Thurmarsh in Parliament.'

But the Conservative candidate, Mr Nigel Pilkington-Brick (aged 47), urged his opponent to resign. 'He's clearly not a fit person to represent the wonderful people of Thurmarsh,' he said. 'He should do the honourable thing.'

Henry's anger at Tosser's statement made his temples throb. He put the paper down slowly. He could hardly bear to look up and meet Diana's eyes.

'I'm so terribly sorry, my darling,' he said.

'So am I,' said Diana.

A small army of reporters and photographers was waiting outside the front door.

'I suggest I make a short statement and we pose for photographs, if you're game,' said Henry.

'Do you really think we should?' asked Diana.

'Yes. There's absolutely no future in skulking.'

Henry had taken a double dose of pills and drunk five pints of water. He had dressed very slowly.

Magnus phoned. Henry took the phone as if it was a hand-grenade.

'Hello, Magnus,' he said. 'Sorry.'

'What a pitifully inadequate word,' said his agent.

'Yes. Sorry. There's an army of pressmen here, Magnus.'

'Don't say *anything*. Not *anything*. Come to the club straight away, and we'll thrash out a statement. Understood?'

'Absolutely,' said Henry. 'Perfectly understood. I go out and talk to them, short statement, pose for photographs with Diana.'

'No, Henry!'

'Yes, Magnus! I've lost my dignity, my reputation and very possibly my wife. I'll do this my way, thank you.'

Magnus groaned.

Henry took a last glass of icy water, and said, 'Come on. Let's go.' He tried to smile at Diana. There was no answering attempt.

He took a deep breath and opened the door. Sunshine and cloud, a horse running friskily in a paddock, a green van with dirty windows rattling towards the village. These things filled Henry with a breathtaking yearning for their unattainable normality.

The moment the door was open Diana took his arm and smiled.

There was a barrage of questions. Cameras flashed on all sides.

Henry held up his hand, and at last silence fell.

'I can't answer questions now,' he said, 'but I will make a statement. I don't remember anything about last night. I was drunk. I've read the morning paper, and I can only assume that I did what I'm reported to have done. I'm very, very sorry. I've let myself down, my party down, my family down, my supporters down, and above all my wife down. We've had a happy marriage for eleven years and during that time I've never looked at another woman. My wife is a wonderful woman. I hope that in time she'll forgive me. I don't intend to resign. Our policies haven't changed because of what I did. Thurmarsh's needs haven't changed because of what I did. The nation's needs haven't changed because of what I did. Has anyone got an Alka-seltzer?'

There was laughter, and even a smattering of applause.

Henry hadn't expected Diana to make a statement, but she began to speak in a firm, assured voice.

'This was an isolated lapse, completely out of character,' she said. 'My husband's a good man. Thurmarsh is lucky to have him. I'll be standing by him.'

They held hands, clutched waists, gave smiles of undying affection and love, and the cameras clicked busily.

The early edition of Henry's old paper, the *Thurmarsh Evening Argus*, carried the headline, IS THE CUCUMBER MAN'S CAMPAIGN SNOOKERED?

After the journalists had dispersed, Henry got a taxi to the Liberal Club.

'I'm fighting on,' he told Magnus, 'and I'm not going to ignore what's happened. I'm the one who has to face the world, knowing that every single person is talking about me and laughing about me. I do it my way.'

'Oh my oh my,' sighed Magnus. 'I age before your eyes.'

'Have you checked up on Pilkington-Brick and his exotic brothel?'

'It's a bit late for that now. We've vacated the moral high ground.'

'Then let's win it back. Pursue the matter, Magnus. Hound the bastard. That's an order.'

The first Asian Conservative candidate since 1895 said in Greenwich that 'bounders and cads should be flogged'.

Mrs Thatcher promised 'a barrier of steel' against the breakdown of law and order.

Mr Callaghan said that the reduction of 61,659 in the unemployment figures, to a total of 1,340,595, was 'no fluke'.

Henry told hecklers, 'I'm not perfect. Who is?'

He canvassed bravely. He met anger and disgust, but also sympathy and even a little admiration. He spoke about the incident frankly and promised never to repeat it.

He telephoned Helen at home from a call box in the pedestrianised Malmesbury Street, in the Fish Hill Shopping Complex. Asda stood now on the site of Uncle Teddy's old nightclub, the Cap Ferrat.

'Has it struck you that my line may be bugged?' said Helen.

'Can't be helped,' said Henry. 'I have a question I need to ask you. Did you set me up?'

'Henry! The anonymous caller was male.'

'Could have been Ted. Could be one of the obscure ways you two get your thrills.'

'Henry! That's awful!'

But he suspected that her anger was simulated, and he pursued the matter.

'Henry!' she said. 'I've been made to look ridiculous as well as you. On the green baize, for God's sake. Every grotty little sex-starved man in Thurmarsh is asking me to pocket his balls. It's appalling. And the editor's absolutely livid.'

He admitted that she had a point.

'Well, if not you, who did?'

'I'll try and find out.'

Henry and Magnus conferred at the end of the day's activities.

'I get the impression that all is not lost,' said Henry bravely.

'I've found that it may not be the total cataclysm I'd feared,' admitted Magnus. 'Oh, and Yorkshire Television want a live three-way debate between the Thurmarsh candidates. Suddenly Thurmarsh is big news. You shouldn't touch it with a barge-pole. You've too much to lose.'

'I've nothing to lose. I've lost already. My only chance is to fight back as publicly as possible. I'll do it.'

Magnus groaned.

'No luck with my enquiries, incidentally,' he said.

'What?'

'I tackled Pilkington-Brick head on. I said, "What were you doing in a male brothel?" He said he knew of no brothel. I said you'd seen him coming out of the premises of "World-Wide Religious Literature Inc." He said he was buying a Bible. He reads it every night for guidance and strength, and his old one is getting so well thumbed that it's falling to pieces.'

'I don't believe it!'

'Oh nor do I. I saw his face. I know he's guilty. To prove it we'd have to bust the place wide open.'

'Why don't you?'

'I spoke to Derek Rectory.'

'Parsonage.'

'Parsonage. He says he knows you. He says you deliver him regular consignments of forged paintings and carry fake jewellery to Suffolk for him.'

Henry groaned.

'It's true, is it?'

'I did carry packages for my uncle. I didn't get anything out of it.'

'Well, we can't do anything.'

'No. Bastard.'

This news jolted Henry badly. He got home at half past eleven, worn out. Diana was still up, and her mood was icy.

'In public I support you,' she said. 'In private we have separate rooms. I didn't want any of this.'

Next day it was raining, Henry's shame was as great as ever, he felt at a low ebb, and he faced two ordeals, one public, one private.

He dreaded the private one more.

He was pleased that Cousin Hilda was in. He could get it over with straight away.

He sat opposite her at the table where so many meals had been eaten. There was no smell of cooking now, and no fire burning in the blue stove.

Cousin Hilda sat with her severe spectacles and her pale pink bloomers – did they still make them or had she bought in bulk or was she wearing the same ones for ever? – and looked at him sadly and with great pain.

'You've read the papers, then,' he said.

She nodded grimly.

'I'm sorry.'

'Words are cheap.'

'Yes. But I really am. I know how you must feel.'

'It's not so bad for me. I have nobody to be ashamed in front of any more. I'm just grateful for one thing.' Henry knew what she was going to say before she said it. 'I'm just glad Mrs Wedderburn didn't live to see this day. It would have broken her heart.'

'Anyway, I felt I had to come and apologise to you personally.'

'Thank you for that.'

'I'm extremely grateful for all you've done for me.'

'Oh stuff and nonsense.'

'I'm going on television tonight.'

Cousin Hilda sniffed.

'Well, I know,' said Henry, 'but I think it's an opportunity to mend some fences. I hope you'll watch.'

'I might. You never know.' She paused. 'I don't usually watch ITV. I don't like the advertisements. But there's not much on our side tonight, to say we pay for a licence.'

He longed to leave. It was painful to feel so guilty. It was painful to have so many memories of this room. It was painful to think how unlikely it would have seemed, in all the years of the gentlemen, if someone had said that these were the vintage years.

'Well, I'd better be off,' he said. 'The campaign goes on.'

'If this were a sensible world, not a soul would vote for you. Not a soul.' Cousin Hilda looked at him severely, over her glasses. 'But it isn't a sensible world. It hasn't been for years. And I'll tell you this. I wouldn't give the other two house room.'

Henry felt that he had got off more lightly than he deserved.

Tosser Pilkington-Brick needed more time in Make-Up than Henry did! So Henry was already feeling quite good before the television debate began.

The three candidates sat in tubular, slightly futuristic chairs, facing the four cameras. The sound recordist fitted them with microphones, and the portly presenter, Dickie Blackleg, star of the hilarious quiz show *Whoops – I've Boobed*, entered and lowered himself carefully into a chair.

'Some people say they find the election campaign boring,' began Dickie Blackleg, 'but they aren't saying that in Thurmarsh. Henry Pratt, whatever else you've done, the fact that you've been liberal with your favours on a snooker table has galvanised this particular campaign. How do you feel about it?'

'I feel absolutely awful,' said Henry. 'How would any human being, who hopes he's decent, feel when he lets down his wife, his family, his party workers, his party and the voters?'

'Nigel Pilkington-Brick is the Tory candidate,' said Dickie Blackleg. 'You've suggested that Mr Pratt should resign. Why?'

'He's behaved in a deeply immoral fashion,' said Tosser. 'Who does he think he's representing? Sodom and Gomorrah? I'll tell you what. I think even the Sodom and Gomorrah Liberal Party would wash their hands of him.'

'Martin Hammond? Does the Labour Party think he should resign?' asked Dickie Blackleg.

'Yes, but not because of his sex life,' said Martin Hammond. 'Because he's a political charlatan.'

'We'll come to that later.' Dickie Blackleg didn't want politics rearing its ugly head and spoiling the sex. 'You've been caught "at it" naked on a snooker table. Have you a leg to stand on?'

'If people are disgusted with what I've done,' said Henry, 'they can tell me on polling day.'

During Tosser's next answer, he made a disparaging remark about Henry as 'the cucumber man'.

'I'd rather be a cucumber man than a financial adviser,' said Henry. 'I led the fight against pests at the Cucumber Marketing Board. I can recognise a parasite when I see one.'

'On the question of policy,' began Martin.

'Wait a moment,' said Tosser. 'I'm sorry, but I've been insulted. I have the right to defend myself.'

'Absolutely,' said Dickie Blackleg, who preferred an argument to policy any day.

'Financial advisers are not parasites,' said Tosser. 'I aim to enable people to use their money more wisely. I certainly aim to save them more than I am paid. I wouldn't sleep if I didn't. And I happen to regard standing for Thurmarsh as a privilege. You wouldn't catch me having it off on a snooker table.'

No, thought Henry, but you did go to a male brothel. Maybe Tosser expected some crack about that, because when Henry said, 'You told me you never expected to be sent to this God-forsaken hole,' Tosser said, 'That was a private conversation,' and Henry was able to say, 'So you admit you did say it? A God-forsaken hole,' and Tosser had no option but to admit it, but even Henry had to admit that his reply was a brave and effective damage limitation exercise. 'Yes, but that's before I came up here. I've never been so wrong in my life. I too can make mistakes.'

'You've been a Socialist all your life, Henry,' said Martin Hammond. 'You've turned Liberal purely in order to get selected.'

'I turned Liberal *before* I was selected,' said Henry. 'Yes, I believe in many of the Socialist aims – much greater social justice et cetera. I respect you. I don't respect Tosser. That's what we called Nigel at school.'

'Is this relevant?' protested Tosser.

'No,' said Henry, 'but we're on the telly purely because I've made an awful fool of myself, so I'm ruddy well going to say what I like.' He looked straight into the camera, pretending it was Cousin Hilda. 'I want to tell you what sort of man I am. Not tall, a bit fat, not brilliant, cocked up two marriages, sometimes drink too much, often feel useless, haven't achieved a great deal, *but* . . . *but* I am deeply sincere, I love my country, for all its faults, I love this God-forsaken hole called Thurmarsh, I care about people and the world and I would love, just love, the chance to serve the community and my party and redeem my life.'

When he got back to Thurmarsh, Henry expected a ticking-off from Magnus.

'I could hear you groaning,' he said.

'No, no,' said Magnus. 'No, no. You were right and I was wrong. You're a one-off.'

Gallup gave the Tories a 2 per cent lead across the nation, with the Liberal vote up to 13½ per cent.

Polling day was cold and bright, with occasional blustery showers. Henry cast his vote early. He voted for Martin Hammond, believing this to be the honourable thing to do. He spent the rest of the day touring the polling stations, encouraging the party workers. Everyone was in good spirits. Their vote was much higher than expected.

The Conservatives and the Socialists were also in good spirits. Their vote was much higher than expected as well.

If everybody who'd promised to vote for the three major parties had actually voted for them, the turn out would have been 167 per cent.

The count was held in the Town Hall, at long trestle tables. It was done at breakneck speed. Thurmarsh had secret hopes of being the first constituency to declare. It would be one in the eye for Torquay and Billericay.

Rumours began to sweep the hall. It was unexpectedly close. The Tories and the Socialists were neck and neck. The Liberals had done astonishingly well. Excitement grew. Martin Hammond looked sick at the unimagined possibility that he might lose. Tosser Pilkington-Brick looked sick at the unimagined possibility that he might win.

The candidates were informed that the Conservatives had won by five votes.

'I don't believe it,' said Tosser, going ashen. 'I demand a recount.'

'But you've won,' said the returning officer.

'I demand a recount too,' said Martin, who was shaking.

'I'm sorry,' said Tosser, recovering rapidly. 'It's the shock. This is beyond my wildest dreams. But I think it's only right to have a recount. I must be sure of my mandate. That's what I meant.'

As the recount began, Helen walked across the hall towards Henry. The conversational level dropped dramatically. All eyes were upon them. Henry could feel the blood rushing to his cheeks. He glanced uneasily at Diana. Helen's eyes looked feverish, as if she had a temperature, but he knew that it was the result of excitement.

'Is this wise?' he said.

'I was never wise,' she said.

The conversation level in the hall rose again, and to new heights, as everybody discussed Henry and Helen.

'It looks as though you may be doing all right,' she said.

'Yes. Not too bad, I think. You haven't lost your job, I gather.'

'No. No harm done, eh?'

Henry glanced at Diana again.

'I wouldn't say that,' he said. 'No, Helen, I wouldn't say that.'

He could see Ted watching them from the middle of a knot of journalists at the far side of the hall. He could see the gleam in Ted's eyes.

'Well at least you got to appreciate my legs at last,' said Helen.

'I don't remember them.'

'What? You said they were the most beautiful legs you'd ever seen. You said they were the most beautiful things you'd ever seen in the whole world. I hoped you'd feel that had made it all worthwhile.'

'Unfortunately, no. There's no value in an experience you can't remember. I'd like you to go now.'

'Perhaps we'd better do it again some time when you're sober, in that case.'

'No, Helen. Now everybody's looking at us out of the corners of their eyes so I suggest we shake hands and look as if we're parting amicably. Otherwise I'll turn away abruptly and it'll look as if I'm snubbing you.'

'Do you think I give a damn what people think of me?' said

Helen, and she turned away abruptly, leaving everyone in the hall to think that she was snubbing him.

The conversational level rose again.

Results were pouring in. It was clear that the Conservatives would win nationally. In Thurmarsh, the first recount gave Tosser a majority of one.

'I demand another count,' said Martin.

'Absolutely. You must have one,' said Tosser.

The second recount produced a dead heat. So far from being the first to declare, Thurmarsh looked as though it might have to carry on all night. Faces were ashen and drawn. The poor folk counting the votes were hollow with fatigue.

Martin looked devastated. So did Mandy. Tosser tried to look happy, but Felicity didn't even make the effort. Diana was bored and tired and angry. Only Henry didn't look devastated by the counting, and the rumour swept the hall that he had won.

The result was finally announced, after five recounts, at ten past five.

It was:

Tanya Elizabeth Bell (Ecology)	383
Martin Neil Hammond (Labour)	19,808
Terence Ingrams (British Hermit Party)	1
Nigel Timothy Anthony Pilkington-Brick (Conservative)	19,811
Henry Ezra Pratt (Liberal)	10,001
Ron 'Hardcase' Trellis (National Front)	1,404

There were loud cheers for Henry, who actually felt disappointed by the result, but even louder cheers, mixed with some booing, for Tosser, who managed, somehow, to smile and smile and smile. Felicity burst into tears at the result. 'It's the surprise,' Tosser explained. 'She's overcome with joy at the privilege of helping to serve this town.'

Henry could hardly bring himself to smile. Tosser had won. Martin had lost. It was a disaster.

Still, he must follow the protocol. He dragged himself across to Tosser, smiling broadly, and holding out his hand.

'Congratulations,' he said. 'Well done.'

'Don't be so bloody stupid,' growled Tosser. 'I'm going to have to buy a house in this disgusting town now. I'm going to have to visit it at weekends and hold surgeries. You bastard!'

'What's it got to do with me?' asked Henry, bewildered.

'You attacked me viciously, so all my supporters closed ranks behind me. You attacked Labour much more mildly, so their waverers all came over to you. Just don't expect a Christmas card.'

'I could cheerfully strangle you with my bare hands,' said Felicity.

Henry walked less confidently towards Martin and Mandy. They couldn't have looked more hostile if they'd been a couple of turkeys and he'd been Jesus Christ.

'Well, you've really done it, haven't you?' said Martin. 'You took our right wing *en masse*. You took nothing off him. Mrs Thatcher should give you a gong.'

'Judas!' said Mandy.

Tosser's agent approached Henry.

'Well done,' he said, 'and thank you. It was your success that saw us home.'

Henry smiled a sickly smile.

'May I ask you a personal question?' asked Tosser's agent.

'Go ahead,' said Henry wearily.

'They say that your wife, your very attractive wife if I may say so . . .'

'Thank you.'

'Was my candidate's first wife.'

'Yes. She was.'

'Has she ever been in a mental institution of any kind?'

'Good Lord, no.'

'The bastard!'

'I beg your pardon?'

'That was off the record. No, Nigel's story has always been that he nursed his first wife through a long mental illness and eventually had to put her in a home, where she died.'

'The bastard!'

'But a winner.'

'Not if I'd known that before today.'

'Don't worry. Our leader will be told what sort of man he is.'

'Oh, please, no. It'll get him promoted.'

Henry walked slowly towards the exhausted Diana.

Magnus bounced forward to intercept him.

'Why so glum?' he cried. 'Ten thousand votes in South Yorkshire. This is an amazing, incredible, unprecedented triumph.'

Somehow, Henry couldn't agree.

15 An Offer He Can't Refuse

One Saturday morning in 1981, almost two years after the General Election, as Henry was writing out his shopping list, the telephone rang.

'Hello. Is that Henry Pratt?' said a well-educated English establishment voice with not entirely successful pretensions to the fruitiness of eccentricity.

'Yes,' admitted Henry reluctantly.

'Excellent. I've caught you. I *do* hope this isn't an inconvenient time.'

'What for?'

Almost Fruity laughed. 'Very good! You're everything I've been told.'

'I don't think I've said anything amusing and just what have you been told and what is this all about?' said Henry drily.

'Right. Sorry. Anthony Snaithe. Overseas Aid. You've been suggested to me as a possible manager of one of our aid schemes. It would involve spending at least two years in Peru. Are you thunderstruck?'

'Well, yes. Yes, I am.'

'What do you say?'

'Well, good Lord, I . . . er . . . I mean, here I am . . . and suddenly to think of going to Peru, I . . . er . . . I mean there are so many things to take into account. I couldn't just say "yes" straight away.'

'No. Quite. Quite. But the significant thing to me is that you haven't said "no" straight away. You are prepared to entertain the prospect as a possibility, then?'

Henry looked round his bare, bachelor flat. He thought of the coming day – making his shopping list, going to Safeway's, going to the pub for a couple, watching the rugby, maybe nodding off, having a shower, going to the pub for a couple, cooking himself something from the stuff he bought at Safeway's, eating it, switching the television on and nodding off in the chair.

'Yes, I am,' he said.

'Good. We should meet for lunch. When can you come down to town?'

'Well, I haven't my work diary with me, but I should think I could come down to town any day the week after next.'

'Shall we say Tuesday week?'

'Fine.'

'Good. Do you know the Reliance Club?'

'Er . . . no.'

'Oh! Well, the food's only passable, but they do a legendary spotted dick.'

As the train slid slowly towards London, Henry's excitement grew. Peru. 'Manager of our aid scheme.'

Here at last was something to fill the yawning gap left by the collapse of his political ambitions. The Liberals had begged him to continue, but his electioneering memories had become inextricably bound up with the scandal on the green baize, his loss of Diana, and Tosser's victory, and he hadn't the heart to continue.

Here at last was something to free him from the emptiness that he'd felt ever since that morning, the day after the General Election, when Diana had packed all her things for the removal men, had denuded the house of its charm and vitality, had kissed him on the cheek and said, 'It hasn't really worked for some years, has it? Goodbye, my darling,' and he had stood there with the tears streaming down his face but hadn't called her back.

He opened his *Guardian* and there was an article about Peru in it. A good omen, even if the unfortunate misprint in the headline, which read, THE LAND OF THE SOARING CONDOM, seemed an echo of his own past disasters.

He read about condors and pan pipes, Inca ruins and pelicans, the mighty Amazon and the stupendous Andes, and realised how deeply, how terminally bored with cucumbers he had become.

Excitement beckoned. He began to feel nervous. As he passed

through the double doors of the grimy stone fortress that housed the Reliance Club, he wished he was taller than his measly five foot seven.

'I've an appointment with Mr Snaithe,' he told the porter, hoping he sounded confident.

'He's not here yet. He'll meet you in the reading room. First floor. Top of the stairs. Straight ahead.'

He walked up the long, broad, shallow staircase, between innumerable pictures of past members, most of whom were no oil paintings and should have been allowed to remain so.

At the top of the stairs there was a large mirror. The forty-six-year-old Henry Pratt who walked towards him out of the mirror had receding, greying hair, a distinct paunch and a suit that looked cheap and crumpled in these distinguished surroundings. Henry wondered, uneasily, whether he would give this man a job.

He entered the Reading Room. There were two other occupants, both holding copies of *The Times*. He didn't know what the form was. Should he say anything? He ventured a hesitant 'good morning'. One man, who looked about ninety, lowered his paper, gave a strangled grunt that might have been 'good morning' and raised his paper again. The other man, who looked somewhat older, didn't move a muscle. Henry assumed that he was deaf, or possibly dead.

He picked up the *Spectator* and looked through it, seeing nothing.

At last Mr Snaithe entered. He was tall – why was everybody so tall? – and slim and had a distinguished streak of grey in his jet-black hair.

'Henry Pratt?' he said.

'Yes.'

'Splendid.'

They shook hands.

'Let's repair to the bar.'

'Terrific.'

Henry chose a dry sherry.

'An excellent choice. I'll join you,' said Mr Snaithe.

The bar began to fill up. All the members were men and none of them were under forty. Mr Snaithe chatted about cricket and London restaurants and France. Henry longed to get down to business, but it wasn't for him to broach the subject.

A man whom he vaguely recognised detached himself from the throng and approached their corner.

'It's Henry Pratt, isn't it?' he ventured.

Henry stood up, thrilled to know somebody, but wishing that he knew who it was that he knew.

'Roger Wilton. We lived next door to you in Thurmarsh.'

'Oh! Yes! How are you?'

'Fine. Fine. And you?'

'Fine.'

'Good. I'll never forget that night when you'd been pushed in the Rundle and came home covered in sewage. What a sight.' He laughed.

'Absolutely. Huh! Most amusing.' Henry laughed mirthlessly, and glanced uneasily at Mr Snaithe.

'I'm sorry. I think I'm embarrassing you,' said Mr Wilton.

'No, no. No, no,' said Henry, but he didn't introduce the two men, and Mr Wilton returned to his friends in some confusion.

Henry gave Mr Snaithe a rather sickly smile. He didn't feel that the encounter had done wonders for his status in his prospective employer's eyes, and suddenly he wanted to go to Peru with a desperation that frightened him.

'Let's go and eat,' said Mr Snaithe.

'Terrific.'

He must stop saying 'terrific'. He'd caught a bad dose of the word.

The dining room was huge and high-ceilinged. Portraits of long-gone judges, cabinet ministers and explorers adorned the walls.

Henry chose oxtail soup and boiled lamb with white caper sauce.

'Make sure you leave room for the spotted dick,' said Anthony Snaithe. 'It's formidable.'

'Terrific.' Damn.

'How do you like the club?' asked Anthony Snaithe.

'It's very impressive. I can understand the appeal of tradition. But I personally would miss the presence of women.'

'Ah. You still have an appetite for them, despite all the problems you've had with them?'

'How do you know about my problems?'

'Everything's on file. Privacy is an outdated concept. The computer tells me there's nobody to detain you in England at the moment.'

'Unfortunately, no.'

'Though that may be fortunate for me?'

'I hope so.'

Henry hoped that they were about to get down to business, but the soup arrived and Mr Snaithe veered off the subject.

'A lot of men like to get away from women,' he said. 'Some are homosexual. Some are frightened of women. Some are frightened of their wives, who'll be much happier about their wasting their afternoon in a place where women aren't permitted than outside in the real world. And you know, Henry, the conversation of women can be really rather boring. Only last week I had a three-hour chat in this very room about Gloucestershire cricket. Impossible with a woman.'

The room hummed with the vicious gossip that men only feel free to indulge in when there are no women around to point out what an illusion it is that only women gossip. Throughout the boiled lamb with white caper sauce Mr Snaithe talked about life and literature and travel and painting and gardening and the art of relaxation, and Henry couldn't relax because he was convinced that his every word was being examined under Mr Snaithe's social microscope.

When the waiter brought them the dessert menu, Mr Snaithe waved it away. 'No need for that. We're looking no further than the spotted dick.'

Henry would never know how he managed to finish what would surely be his last spotted dick ever, especially if he went to Peru, but he felt that it was a condition of the job that he did finish it.

At last, over a glass of madeira, Mr Snaithe turned to business.

'Right,' he said. 'Now this little job. You'll have a team of six people, whom you'll help to appoint. When you get to Peru you'll recruit six Peruvians in preparation for the day when you withdraw and leave them to run the whole caboosh themselves. We've got twelve Range Rovers lined up, which will be shipped out to you. You'll be based in the Cajamarca Valley, which is a delightful corner of northern Peru. We're offering you a salary of £17,000, and after two years there's an option on both sides. How does that strike you?'

'Well, it's amazing,' said Henry. 'Absolutely terrific.' Damn! 'Er . . . the only thing is . . . what exactly is the scheme?'

'Cucumbers. We plan to cover the Andes with cucumbers. Why do you think we've picked on you?'

He took Jack for a meal at La Bonne Étoile, Thurmarsh's first French restaurant, and broke the news to him over the *moules marinières*.

Jack looked quite shaken, to Henry's surprise. He seemed such an independent soul.

'You'll be all right,' Henry said. 'We hardly see each other, anyway.'

'I know, but . . . I'm used to knowing you're there, if I need you.'

'You won't need me.'

'No. By the time you get back I'll have set up on my own.'

'Terrific.'

'We should see more of each other.'

'Yes. It's my fault.'

'It's a two-way process, Dad.'

'True.'

'We only appreciate things in life when we haven't got them, don't we?'

'My word. You're quite the philosopher.'

'Sometimes I think you think I'm as thick as two short planks, just because I'm not arty.'

'Jack! I don't! Did I sound like that just then? Perhaps I did. If so, I'm sorry. This sauce is too creamy.'

297

'I do them without cream.'

'You cook *moules marinières?*'

'Yes. Your builder son is not entirely uncivilised. Surprise surprise.'

'Sorry.'

'I'm a very good cook. Tell you what, Dad, come to dinner before you leave.'

'Terrific. We don't know enough about each other, do we?'

'No.'

'Jack? I go and see Cousin Hilda regularly, though not as often as I should. She's going to miss me very much.'

'I always mean to. I mean, I like her. I'm always going next week. Next week never comes.'

'Everything all right, sir?' enquired the waiter.

'Very nice, thank you,' said Henry.

'Why didn't you say the sauce was too creamy?' said Jack.

'Because I'm English. Maybe Peru will change all that.'

'Oh, Dad! Peru's so far away!'

'Jack!'

Their main course arrived. Henry had chosen *coq au vin*, Jack steak *au poivre*.

'Will you promise to go and visit Cousin Hilda while I'm away?' said Henry. 'Regularly. You don't need to stay more than an hour, but she'll appreciate it.'

'I promise. Have you told her yet?'

Henry made a face.

The waiter saw and hurried over.

'Is something wrong, sir?' he asked.

'Yes,' said Henry. 'I've got to go and tell Cousin Hilda tomorrow that I'm going to Peru.'

'I could get you something else, sir,' said the waiter.

Jack grinned.

Henry realised how much he was going to miss him, and how big a thing it was to be going to Peru.

'I'm leaving Thurmarsh, Cousin Hilda.'

'Leaving Thurmarsh?' She sounded appalled at such geographical recklessness.

'Yes. I've . . . got another job.'

'I see.' Cousin Hilda's lips were working with anxiety. 'Is it far away?'

'Er . . . quite far.' There are moments when death doesn't seem such a bad option. 'It's . . . er . . . well . . . Peru.'

'Peru??'

'Peru.'

'But that's abroad.'

'South America. But not for several months yet, and it may only be for two years and I'll get holidays.'

Cousin Hilda's hand flapped towards the coal skuttle, but the stove was out, so her favourite displacement activity in times of stress wasn't possible.

'Who'll bury me if I die when you're away?' she said.

'Oh, Cousin Hilda. Don't be so morbid.'

'It's not morbid. I'm seventy-five.'

'I'm sure you won't die, Cousin Hilda. But if you do, I'll fly back. I wouldn't let them bury you without me.'

She nodded, as if this was some slight reassurance.

'What does tha want to go to Peru for, anyroad?' she said in a disparaging tone.

'It's a fine country.'

'I'm sure it is, if you're Peruvian. You aren't Peruvian.'

'No. It's a British government scheme.'

Cousin Hilda sniffed.

'Governments!' she said disparagingly.

'I'm . . . er . . . I'll have twelve people under me. And twelve Range Rovers. And it's all in aid of the Third World. We're going to grow cucumbers all over the Andes.'

'How's that going to help the Third World?' asked Cousin Hilda. 'Do they like cucumbers? Don't they have their own cucumbers? They have potatoes. Potatoes came from Peru.'

Henry didn't dare tell her that he hadn't asked these questions, that he'd been so relieved to be asked to do something important that he'd taken it all for granted. He was astounded by her sharpness.

'They'll have researched all that,' he said feebly.

'You'd think they'd have learnt their lesson with groundnuts,' said Cousin Hilda.

Henry sold his flat and rented a bed-sitter in West Hampstead. Almost every day he saw Anthony Snaithe or his assistant. They held interviews, and sent the first two appointees to Peru to find accommodation and generally set things up.

Prince Charles married Lady Diana Spencer in St Paul's Cathedral, South Africa invaded Angola, Voyager 2 found that Saturn's rings were numbered in thousands, and in Chile, which was disturbingly close to Peru, President Pinochet banned all political activities for eight more years.

As the date for his departure drew near, Henry had a series of moving farewells.

His heart was heavy as he drove down to Monks Eleigh. It was quite likely that this would be the last time he saw Auntie Doris.

As usual, on his arrival, Uncle Teddy rushed out to meet him.

'It's one of her better days,' he said. 'She knows you're coming. She knows who you are. But, Henry, I suggest you don't mention Peru. Best she never discovers that you're away.'

Auntie Doris came down the path towards them, tottering slightly. There was a staring look in her eyes, and she was slowly losing weight. One side of her hair appeared to have been severely hacked.

'Hello, Auntie Doris. How are you?' he said.

'Oh, not so bad, Henry. Not so bad.'

'She cut her own hair yesterday, didn't you, Doris?' said Uncle Teddy.

'It's very nice,' said Henry.

'Oh, do you think so?' said Auntie Doris. 'I wasn't sure. It's not easy.'

'You're a clever girl,' said Uncle Teddy.

'Get him some tea,' said Auntie Doris.

'Right.'

Henry sat with Auntie Doris in the garden. It had been raining, but the sun was shining now, and steam was rising from the ground all around them. There were very few plants left in the garden, as Auntie Doris kept picking them all.

'How's Hilary?' she said.

'Fine,' said Henry. 'We've split up.'

'Oh dear,' said Auntie Doris. 'That is sad. Do you really like my hair?'

'Well, I think it's very nice, but I think next time you ought to have it done by the hairdresser.'

'So do I. I think I've made a right mess of it, to be honest, but Teddy says it's fine. He tells lies, you know. Maybe his mind's going.'

'I don't think so.'

'I remember now. Of course you split up with Hilary. I meant Diana. How's Diana?'

'Fine,' said Henry. 'I've split up with her too.'

'Naughty boy. You really are a naughty boy. Is Ollie going to open up tonight or do I need to?'

'Ollie'll do it,' said Uncle Teddy, bringing the tea things. 'Leave it all to Ollie.'

When Henry and Uncle Teddy went for their usual walk, past the green that led to the church, past the fairy-tale cottages, and round the corner to gaze over the bridge onto the little reed-shivering river, Henry said, 'I don't want to criticise, I think you do brilliantly, but don't you think it'd be better to correct her when she's wrong, tell her she isn't at the White Hart any more? Otherwise she'll spend all weekend thinking she is.'

'It doesn't work like that. She'll have forgotten all about the White Hart when we get back,' said Uncle Teddy.

'I mean I agree about Peru.'

'She'll forget how long it's been since you've last been. If she says, "We haven't seen Henry lately," I'll say, "Yes, we have. We saw him last month." '

'Will you let me know if she . . . if anything . . . well, you know. Obviously I'll fly back.'

'I will. Oh, Henry, I just hope I don't go first.'

They had a very pleasant weekend. Uncle Teddy warmed up some meals which proved highly palatable when washed down with smuggled wine and brandy. They played two games of Scrabble. Auntie Doris won them both.

As he was leaving, Henry couldn't resist teasing Uncle Teddy just a bit.

'Er . . . it may be quite a while before I get down again, Auntie Doris,' he said.

Uncle Teddy glowered at him.

'Oh dear, that's a shame,' said Auntie Doris.

'It may be towards the end of next month.'

Uncle Teddy relaxed.

'Oh well, that's not too bad,' said Auntie Doris.

It wasn't the wittiest bit of fooling in the history of the world, but it was better than crying.

Henry was appalled, on arrival at Lampo and Denzil's, to find that Tosser and Felicity had been invited.

'Why?' he said.

'Two reasons,' said Lampo. 'One – we're both so emotional. We'd cry buckets if we didn't have that greedy ape here. Two – you're angry with him still. Anger is so corrosive.'

'We love you,' said Denzil. 'We want you to be at peace in Peru.' He wasn't far short of eighty, but age suited him. He had turned into a distinguished old gentleman.

'I hope you'll come to visit,' said Henry.

'I couldn't bear it,' said Lampo. 'If your behaviour in Siena was anything to go by. You'll sit there, staring at the Andes in all their majesty, trying to work out how many street lights weren't working in Thurmarsh last time you went through it.'

'Of course we'll come,' said Denzil.

Tosser and Felicity were twenty minutes late.

'I couldn't find anywhere to park,' said Tosser. 'Sorry it had to be mid-week, but we have to spend every weekend in bloody Thurmarsh. I went into politics to make my name, not meet a lot of wretched little people with breathing problems and defective damp courses and dogs with diarrhoea. And I'll be re-adopted there, and I'll probably lose next time, and that'll be the end of a glorious career, thanks to you.'

'You might not have won,' said Henry, 'if you hadn't got out of it – rather brilliantly for you – when I accused you of calling Thurmarsh a God-forsaken hole.'

'I know,' said Tosser. 'I go over it time and again to try and work out where I went right.'

Over Denzil's walnut and celery pâté, Felicity said, 'We were sorry to hear about you and Diana.'

'Yes, we were,' said Tosser.

'A difficult woman,' said Henry. 'Mental problems. Nigel knows.'

'I never knew that,' said Denzil. 'She always seemed fine to us.'

'*Hidden* mental problems,' said Henry. 'They're the worst.' He managed to convey to Denzil and Lampo that this was part of a game against Tosser. 'Still, Nigel, you have your bible to comfort you.'

'Bible?' said Felicity. 'Since when did you have a bible, Nigel?'

'Don't you remember?' said Tosser. 'I said in Thurmarsh that I'd bought a bible because my old one was so thumbed.'

'I never believed that,' said Henry. 'What were you really doing in "World-Wide Religious Literature Inc."?'

Tosser's eyes met his across the table and he could see the hatred in them.

'Canvassing, of course,' said Tosser.

'So why tell that whopper about the bible?'

'To win votes.'

'And in the end you won too many.' Then Henry changed tack abruptly, hoping to catch Tosser off-balance. 'Was it you who informed on me and Helen?' he asked.

'So what if it was?'

'So it was! Who told you?'

'The landlord. He'd spent fifteen years putting up with leftie jazz fans. He'd had enough.'

'I think you may have done me a favour,' said Henry. 'You enabled me to present myself as human.'

'I think I may have done.'

Suddenly baiting Tosser didn't seem any fun at all. Henry felt humiliated by the hatred he'd seen in the man's eyes. It was awful to hate, but it was even worse to be hated, because that was outside one's control. He knew that Lampo and Denzil had been right to invite him. He no longer cared what Tosser had been doing in Derek Parsonage's exotic brothel. If he couldn't get the satisfaction he needed with Felicity, it was sad.

Denzil had made a beautiful, uncompromising *daube* of beef. It was altogether too uncompromising for Felicity, who struggled from the start. Henry thought of how most of the women in his life would have risen to the challenge of dining with four men. Felicity seemed over-awed, and he felt sad for her and for Tosser.

He called Tosser Nigel several times, and praised Buckinghamshire, where Tosser now lived, in order to be nearer the M1 and Thurmarsh. He spoke of their early days at Dalton College, and how Tosser had seen off the bully J. C. R. Tubman-Edwards, and how he had worshipped Tosser for his athletic prowess. He made his peace, and Felicity was pleased and maybe one day the anger would depart from Tosser's eyes.

Over the orange syllabub they talked of France and Italy and Felicity continued to perk up. She even had a second helping of syllabub. She said how lovely the house was with all its knick-knacks and 'those divine biscuit tins'.

'Worth quite a packet, I should think,' said Tosser. 'Quite shrewd investments.'

'I don't buy them as investments.' Denzil was shocked. 'I buy them because it's fun.'

'Maybe Henry'll pick up some interesting biscuit tins in Peru,' said Felicity.

'Now there's a thought,' said Henry.

Tosser was saddened that none of them could see the true glory of art for investment's sake, and quite soon he said they had to leave.

'I've had a lovely time,' said Felicity. 'I don't know when I've enjoyed myself so much.'

When Tosser and Felicity had gone, Henry said, 'Thank you. You were right.'

Henry had been delighted to receive a letter from Camilla, saying that she'd like to see him before he went to Peru, so for his very last day, he arranged a farewell lunch with her and Kate. It had to be lunch, because Kate was working every evening as stage manager at the Unicycle Theatre in Willesden.

They met in a pub in Soho and went on to an ornate and fairly expensive Italian restaurant round the corner.

Camilla had developed into quite an extrovert. Her face, which had once been so horsey, had filled out and become cheerfully sexy in a way that reminded him of Diana.

Kate's pale, rather private beauty, illuminated when she smiled like a dark valley that is suddenly bathed in sunshine, reminded him painfully of Hilary. Now, when he was on the verge of departure, Henry realised how they had all said too little to each other over the years. Today, under what suddenly began to seem like the shadow of his absence, was a time for frank talk, no Anglo-Saxon evasions.

'How's your mother, Camilla?' he asked, as he attempted to eat his spaghetti *alla vongole* with fork only.

'Very well.'

'Is there . . . er . . . anybody in her life?'

'I rather think there is. I was awfully upset with you, you know, for a time.'

'I'm not surprised.'

Camilla was having no trouble with her spaghetti, but Henry splattered sauce down his shirt front.

'But I realise now that she was much happier with you than with Daddy. And that's something to be thankful for, isn't it?'

'We were very happy for a while,' said Henry. 'I'll never forget

305

those happy years. Then it began to go wrong, very slowly. It wasn't anybody's fault. That awful snooker table business . . .' His heart was pounding. His cheeks were red. He couldn't meet their eyes. But at least he was talking about these things, which he'd never before mentioned to his children or step-children, '. . . was a symptom, not a cause.'

Camilla and Kate were both embarrassed, but Henry knew that they were pleased.

Over their main courses – Henry and Camilla had sea bass, Kate a vegetarian pasta – they talked about Camilla's love life. There was somebody, a first-generation British Jamaican trumpeter called Leroy, and he was quite special, but not especially special.

'Terrific,' said Henry.

She was working in graphic design and drawing horses for fun.

'They're brilliant,' said Kate. 'Leroy says she's better than Stubbs.'

'She's prettier than Stubbs, anyway,' said Henry.

They laughed, and then they turned their attention to Kate.

She told Henry that she wanted to be a theatre director, and the job at the Unicycle, though poorly paid and very hard work, was part of the learning process.

'There are so many arty-farty people who think they know what they're doing,' she said. 'I want my work to be securely based. How's Jack?'

They talked briefly about how lovely Jack was, and this led to Benedict and general gloom. Henry told them about the fruitless search for him.

'Dad's done nothing,' said Camilla. 'You know, knowing Ben, I bet Malaga was a smokescreen. I bet he was somewhere at the other end of Spain.'

'Kate?' said Henry. 'We haven't really finished with you.'

'Oh Lord. That sounds ominous,' said Kate, laughing defensively.

'I've never really asked you about Edward. Don't tell me if you don't want to but I'd really like to know.'

'He was so mixed up. So guilty about his good looks and his

privilege and yet so ambitious for overnight success. When the chips were down the guilt all rolled away and he was just another ruthless upper-middle-class bastard. I loved him. I didn't like him. I think you need to like as well as love. I ditched him.'

'Well . . . right . . . gosh. So . . . er . . . is there anybody new?'

'Semi. I'm semi-detached. He's called Peter and we'll see. If it develops I'll write to you about him. Promise.'

Zabaglione wasn't on the menu, but they explained about Henry's going to Peru, and the chef agreed to make it. That was what Henry liked about the Italians. They were so sentimental.

Over the *zabaglione* Henry at last jumped off the cliff. He broached the subject that he longed and yet dreaded to hear about.

'And how . . . er . . . how is your mother, Kate? Have you seen her recently?'

'I saw her in the summer. She's all right. She still isn't writing, though, and it's such a shame.'

'Oh dear. And . . . er . . . this feller that she's got, what's he like?'

'What?'

'Her feller. This *zabaglione*'s absolutely delicious. I wonder what the food'll be like in Peru. What's he like?'

'What feller? She hasn't got a feller.'

'She hasn't got a feller? She told me she had. She told me it was a very satisfactory relationship.'

'You know Mum. She was trying to make you feel free to be happy with Diana. There's never ever been anyone but you.'

Mixed emotions number 127 – disbelief, joy, horror, regret, pride, shame and frustration.

'Oh my God,' he said.

'What? What, Dad?'

'Why the hell . . . why the bloody ridiculous stupid ironic unbelievable miserable soddish hell . . . am I going to Peru for two years tomorrow?'

16 A Dip into the Postbag

Apartado 823
Cajamarca
Peru
Nov 26th, 1981

Dear Hilary,

I know you'll be surprised to get a letter from me after all this time, and above all from Peru! I arrived here last week, to head an overseas aid project to save the Peruvian economy single-handed by planting cucumbers all over the Andes! But the point of my writing is to tell you that on the night before I left, Kate told me that there was nobody else in your life, and never had been, and that you'd told me there was so that I'd feel free to be happy with Diana.

I thought it extraordinary that you could be so self-sacrificial and then I realised how conceited that was and how probably it's no sacrifice for you after what I did to give up all further chance of a relationship with me.

Anyway, I discovered with extraordinary force how deeply I love you, and here I am stuck in Peru for two years. It's awful to feel stuck here because from the little I've seen so far it's a breathtaking country. I flew here from Lima over the Andes, feeling very safe in my first Third World plane, perhaps because of the free *pisco* sours, the delicious national drink of Peru, made of brandy, egg white and lemon.

Cajamarca is a flat, predominantly Spanish town, full of Quechua Indians. It gleams white in the mountain sun. It's set in a beautiful, broad valley, studded with irrigation channels and rich in eucalyptus trees. Indians in plaits and sombreros lead donkeys along the roads, and the majesty of the high sierras is all about. There's great poverty by English standards, but it's not a hopeless place, and the street scenes are very lively. I have a lovely shady apartment built around a patio in a beautiful old Spanish villa in the best part of town. As a British government official I'm important at last, which I find hilarious. Everything in the apartment is lovely, except for a picture of a rather fat Madonna, who looks as though she has wind, holding a rather fat baby, who definitely has wind.

This could be the most amazing experience of my life, yet all I can think of is that I'm not with you. Every crowd has an empty space at its centre, where you would have been. At every meal – and the food's good – there's an imaginary chair for you, my darling. I love you and would like to marry you again. I believe that I'm a better person now and that I could make you happy this time. Writing these words has given me an erection. Henry Pratt's libido is alive and well and living in Cajamarca.

Tomorrow work begins in earnest. I'll have my six English staff under me for the first time. 'Under me'! I'm a boss for the first time!

I hope you and your father are well. Please send him my best wishes and to you I send my deepest love,

Henry

XXXXXXXXXXXXXXXXX (One for every year that we have been apart)

Apartado 823
Cajamarca
Peru
December 5th, 1981

Dear Cousin Hilda,

This is to wish you a very happy Christmas and New Year. It'll be strange to be so far from Thurmarsh at the festive time and you'll be very much in my thoughts, and I'll have lots of memories of Christmases past, and all the fun we had with the crackers and paper hats and jokes and of course the delicious food. I hope you won't feel lonely and will be comforted by the memory of all the merry times and also by the fact that I'll be thinking of you.

Well, I'm busy setting up the project, and Peru will soon be covered in English cucumbers. Peru does have quite a lot of cucumbers already, which is a bit disturbing, and they don't rate them very highly. In fact there's a Peruvian saying, 'Me importa un pepino' – 'I couldn't care a cucumber.' However, their cucumbers are short and stumpy, so maybe they'll like our long, firm English ones.

We're busy trying to find land. The Cajamarca valley is very fertile, but the best land is already in use. Still, we won't need the best land, as we'll be growing our cucumbers under glass. We've begun interviewing Peruvians for jobs, and have met some very interesting people of high calibre.

Our office is in Baños Del Inca, a village a few miles away. It has hot springs, and is the place where the Inca leader Atahualpa was having a nice hot bath when the Spanish invader Pizarro called on him the day before the Spaniards slaughtered his army in the main square of Cajamarca. I saw these events described once in a play called *The Royal Hunt of the Sun* by Peter Shaffer in London, so that is very interesting.

I look forward to hearing from you and will write again soon.

Happy Christmas and much love,

Henry

Sarajevo
Rua de Matelos
Altea
Costa Blanca
Spain
14th December 1981

Dear Henry,

I was astonished to get your letter and even more astonished that it came from Peru! My heart raced terrifyingly when I read that you love me, and it races now, as I sit on the terrace on a sunny, but rather windy December afternoon.

Yes, it's true that I made up about there being somebody else. There has never been anybody else and never will be.

I love you still, Henry darling, and feel no anger towards you after all these years, and I certainly won't accept that all the blame was yours. If only I'd not been such a brittle reed and so hopelessly perfectionist. If I could have accepted that love is irrational and nobody is perfect, and tried to help you through your jealousy, how different things might have been.

I'm quite happy here, although I suppose my life isn't exciting. I look after Daddy, who is slowly growing old, and is missing England and all his political life dreadfully. We never found anywhere at the right price, prices have leapt in England, and we've left it too late. We're trapped in exile, and neither of us like it. This is not a criticism of Spain. I would love it if we were *of* Spain, we are only *in* Spain, and that's a horse of a very different complexion, as Mr O'Reilly might have said if he'd been a more loquacious kind of Irishman!

We're in the middle of doing a big jigsaw, and Daddy loves to do them together as he's really very lonely, so I must stop now.

Write soon.

With love,

Hilary

PS I nearly forgot. Happy Christmas!

Apartado 823
Cajamarca
Peru
Jan 2nd, 1982

Dearest Hilary,

I was delighted to get your letter, which didn't actually arrive till after Christmas. I'm absolutely thrilled to hear from your own pen that you still love me and always will. In fact reading your letter led to a solitary activity which has to be indulged in not too violently at this altitude! But your letter also puzzles me and worries me. You talk about our relationship as if it was all in the past. Surely, as we both love each other, we should be thinking of the future?

I want to ask you two simple questions. I've gone on bended knees to write the first one, so my writing may not be very clear.

Will you marry me? And the second question is equally simple. Will you come and live with me in Cajamarca? Please say 'yes', my darling.

You'll love it here, the landscape is on a grand scale. The valley throbs with vitality and fertility. The great hills are arid but steeped in melancholy beauty.

You'd get on well with the team. They're a fine bunch of blokes. I can hear you laughing at me. Yes, maybe in this far-off spot the public school ethos has got to me at last. We had a good Christmas. I even got a turkey and made my own crackers, which is what my lovely maid Juanita (sixty-six years old – no rival!) thinks I am. I thought of you constantly, and could only half enjoy myself, so thirsty was I for your reply. I'd promised Cousin Hilda to lay aside a moment to think of her, but I forgot. I did think of our dear, dear Kate and Jack and lovely Camilla and poor Benedict. I wish I believed in God, so that I could pray for him.

Other countries have aid schemes here. There are Belgians trying to plant trees everywhere, and a German is making German sausages. We all know him as Bratwurst Bernhardt, and I understand I'm known as Cucumber Henry!

Only two shadows darken my life. The Range Rovers haven't arrived and, more importantly, I don't have my beloved with me.

I should have said earlier that, if you can come, it will be fine for you to bring your father. I'm sure we can get you both on the payroll somewhere. Baños Del Inca is a long way from Whitehall.

With deepest love,

Henry

X (One kiss from you is worth a thousand from anyone else)

66, Park View Road
Thurmarsh
South Yorkshire
4th January, 1982

Dear Henry,

Thank you very much for your letter. Thank you for your good wishes for Christmas and the New Year. I had a very enjoyable Christmas, if solitary. I did myself very well, but I avoided 'over-indulgence'. I were a bit badly over the New Year, but then I don't see the New Year in, believing that one year is very much like another. So did Mrs Wedderburn, incidentally.

Your news is very interesting. I have never had experience of 'foreign parts', finding the North York Moors a very satisfying run, so I cannot imagine the Andes. Are they at all like the North York Moors?

I were right touched to hear that you would be thinking of me on Christmas Day. I must admit I do feel a bit quiet at times, now that the Good Lord has taken Mrs Wedderburn and Mr O'Reilly, and the gay days of my gentlemen are gone for ever.

I were interested to hear that you are busy setting up your project, and that Peru will soon be covered in English cucumbers. I'm sorry the Peruvians have lots of cucumbers already, but interested to hear that theirs are short and stumpy, and pleased that you think you can do well with long, firm English ones. It were interesting to me that the Cajamarca valley is very fertile. Parts of the North York Moors are very bare. It's funny the way places differ. It was interesting that you had met some interesting Peruvians of high calibre. I were brought up to believe that there were very few foreigners of high calibre, and now it seems that the reverse is true. I pray to God for guidance.

It was interesting about the play by Peter Shaffer. I saw *The Desert Song* with you at the Temperance Hall in Haddock Lane, but I don't think it was by him. Mr Frost were in it and you went to the pub afterwards with that journalist and milk bottles were later knocked over. I don't hold with the theatre. It leads to bad behaviour. Mrs Wedderburn did take me twice to the Playhouse, but neither play was by Peter Shaffer. They were both by Agatha Christie, and they were both very good, and I didn't guess who had done it. Nor did Mrs Wedderburn, incidentally.

A lorry delivering electrical goods swerved to avoid a dog and completely demolished the bus shelter at Thurmarsh Lane Bottom yesterday, but otherwise we have had no excitements to match yours, so I will close now, hoping you are well and not catching any of those foreign diseases which those poor foreigners have to contend with.

With love,
Cousin Hilda

Sarajevo
Rua de Matelos
Altea
Costa Blanca
Spain
19th January 1982

Dear Henry,

Thank you very much for your letter, and I must say straight away that my answer to your first question is 'not at the moment' and to your second question, 'no'.

I didn't mention the future because I've learnt to live in the present, it's the way I get by, and I talked about our relationship as if it was in the past, because it is. Of course we may have a relationship in the future, but I'll only find that out a step at a time. I'd like to meet you on your return to England, and see if we can cope with a return to normality together. I lived for a very long time in a world more sombre than you are capable of imagining. Nobody knew. Not my father, my psychiatrist or, above all, my mother. I feel now that I'm sitting on a green lawn, but the lawn juts out over that sombre chasm and it would be all too easy to fall back into it. I couldn't cope with seeing you again in somewhere exotic like Peru. It'd be make or break, and I'm not brave enough for that.

Please treat me as a pen-pal and send me lovely descriptions of your times in Peru. Then, when you return, and you will return, we'll meet like pen-pals. It'll be exciting and terrifying, but if you're truly patient and loving I believe we may have a chance.

Sam made a flying visit last week. He's a cheery bachelor. He lives in Luton and devises recipes for tinned soups. 'Well, somebody's got to,' he says.

Dad and I are off to our local English bar now. I'd prefer a tapas bar but the English bar has fish and chips on a Friday, and once a Yorkshireman . . .

I think of Benedict often and with despair.

With love and hope,

Hilary

Apartado 823

Cajamarca

Peru

Feb 2nd, 1982

Darling Hilary,

Do other people feel conflicting emotions about seven hundred times a day, or is it just me? I'm so depressed at knowing that I won't see you for almost two years. (I won't stay here when my option comes up. Without you, I feel as though I'm doing my National Service all over again.) But I'm thrilled that you want to see if we can make a go of things and that you love me still, and believe we may have a chance. (I sound like Cousin Hilda, who went through my letter paragraph by paragraph.)

Progress on the project is a bit slow. The really good Peruvians don't seem interested. Two or three accepted posts and simply didn't turn up. Apparently, they hate to disappoint you, so they tell you what they think you want to hear: 'I will start next Monday.' Lots of big smiles, lots of bad teeth, nobody starts next Monday!

The Range Rovers are another problem. They've arrived, and we don't know what to do with them! Only three of the English staff drive anything, let alone Range Rovers, and I wouldn't dare give them to the Peruvians, because they'd simply get too excited at the prospect of driving something so magnificent.

Peru is a smiling, rickety land, full of humour. The main newspaper has a photographic feature on its front page called 'Pothole of the Day'. An elderly lorry bears the legend, 'Apollo 2½'. On the frequent, teeming, breast-feeding, sombrero-shaking buses between Cajamarca and Baños Del Inca, the conductor calls out the stops by name. 'Sausages,' he cries as we approach Bratwurst Bernhardt's. I turn to smile at you. You aren't there.

I flew to Lima last week, on business. I can't begin to describe Lima and its contrasts, the rich suburbs, the endless shanty towns, it would depress you. I came back on the night bus – a fifteen-hour trip! All along the Pan-American Highway the great lorries roared through the night, lit up with fairy lights, liners of the road! I turned to share the romance with you. You weren't there.

At every stop, in the dusty, single-storey villages, small boys came on the bus to sell limes and pancakes. Even at four in the morning the boys came. To sell a few limes is worth losing a night's sleep if your family is really poor. Yet they smile and look bright and well. We stopped every now and then at roadside stalls, rich with sizzling meats and pancakes, the Little Chefs (!) of Peru.

The bus began to growl up into the Andes. The headlights picked out the rocky hills. Dawn came quickly. We were winding through a narrow, astonishingly green valley. White storks were feeding in their hundreds in paddy fields that made me think of China. High above us the road wound ever upward through the sierras, pale yellow and green, dry but covered in plants except for a few rocky outcrops, briefly turned red as the sun rose. It took us two hours and forty minutes from sea level to the summit. As I saw the Cajamarca Valley laid out before us like a smiling woman, I turned to share the moment with you. You weren't there.

To have this amazing continent to experience, and yet not to be able to share it with you, it's the story of my life.

One day I'll share everything with you, my incredible darling,
With ever deepening love,
Your pen-pal!

Apartado 823
Cajamarca
Peru
March 28th, 1982

Dear Martin,

I've been meaning for a long while to tell you how sorry I was about the way the election turned out and about my part in it. I'm in

316

Peru now (!) running a Government Overseas Aid project, and getting a very different slant on life.

The people here migrate from the poverty-stricken countryside to the teeming towns, squat on the outskirts, build primitive shanty towns, skimp and scrape and slave and eventually turn them into houses. It may take thirty years to create a respectable neighbourhood, but they do it, and in the end the State conveniently forgets that they've done it all illegally, and gives them electricity, water and sewage as they can afford them. To see the patience, determination and good nature of these people makes one ashamed of Western assumptions. To regard dishwashers, video machines and microwaves as essentials seems to me to be deeply obscene.

I don't suddenly have renewed faith in the Labour Party or any less disgust at its feuding and pettiness. I don't believe in grand designs and great schemes, or centralised planning. I still have a lot of sympathy for the Liberals' approach. But I now believe that only socialism can possibly solve the world's problems, because at least some of its supporters care enough even if its leaders don't.

I have no more party ambitions. I don't believe the world will ever change for the better from the top downwards. It can only change for the better from the bottom upwards, through the actions of millions of good individuals. It's unlikely, but it's the only hope.

Nevertheless I'd like to canvass for you in the next election, if I'm home. We're the only two members of the Paradise Lane Gang who're still in touch. Can we be friends again?

All best wishes to you and Mandy,
Henry

Apartado 823
Cajamarca
Peru
May 8th, 1982

Dear Cousin Hilda,

Thank you very much for your letter, and I'm really sorry I never replied to your Christmas letter. My only excuse is I've been really busy. If I tell you that our twelve Range Rovers haven't moved since they were parked on some waste ground outside Baños Del Inca, you'll realise how busy we've been. Getting greenhouses built is a major problem. The greenhouse is a foreign concept here, like the garden shed, probably because they don't have a *Radio Times* to advertise them in!

Some of our staff have left, partly because they don't see us getting quick results, and partly because it's not very good to be British here during the Falklands War! Yet again my timing's bad. Peruvians believe that in withdrawing our survey ship we signalled to Argentina that we weren't interested in the islands, they believe our huge fleet to knock the conscript troops off the island is a colonial fantasy, they believe the sinking of the *General Belgrano* was murder on the high seas. The play *No Sex, Please, We're British*, which ran in Lima under the somewhat less catchy title of *Nada de Sexo, Por Favor, Somos Británicos* would stand no chance now. I can hear you saying that that would be a good thing!

I was moved to hear how moved you were to know that I was thinking of you on Christmas Day.

I was interested in all your news in your letters. I'm glad Jack's been visiting you. He's very fond of you. I hope the bus shelter in Thurmarsh Lane Bottom has been repaired, and fancy Macfisheries closing. It's the end of an era.

This will have to be the end of this letter, as I have a budget meeting to attend and I want to catch the post.

With much love as always,

Henry

PS You ask if Apartado is a nice street. It isn't the street name. It's actually the equivalent of PO Box 823.

Dear Henry,

I'm sending this to your friend Lampo Davey for forwarding, as agreed, just in case Doris sees the address on the envelope and worries about your being in Peru.

We're as well as can be expected. I have some arthritis, and Doris continues to slip an inch at a time towards a world of her own. My job is to make sure that it's a happy world. Of course she can never remember when she last saw people, and will fret that it's ages since she saw someone who called that very morning, but in your case I think she has a genuine feeling that it's been a very long time. She does have moments of comparative lucidity. So perhaps you could drop us a line, not mentioning Peru, saying you had a nice visit.

I hope everything's going swimmingly for you, and that the Peruvians will soon be enjoying cucumber sandwiches for tea. I wish you could find some way of sending me your news.

With much love,
Uncle Teddy

9, Bromyard Mews
London SW3
June 4th 1982

Dear Uncle Teddy and Auntie Doris,

Thank you very much for having me last weekend. It was a very enjoyable visit, as always. It was good to see you both looking so well and it was nice to have good weather for once. I was disappointed that I didn't win any of the games of Scrabble, but *c'est la vie*, and at least they were hard-fought scraps.

I had a good journey back and when I got home I found a letter from a friend who's living in Peru. It was full of good news, he's doing well with his government project, loves the country and is in friendly correspondence with his ex-wife, so that cheered me up no end and prevented my return home being an anti-climax, as these things sometimes can be after a weekend of your hospitality.

Well, I won't bother too much with my news, as I hope to see you the weekend after next and will tell you it all then.

Have that Scrabble board ready. I think my luck's about to change.

With much love as always,
Henry

Apartado 823
Cajamarca
Peru
Sept 6th, 1982

Dearest Hilary,

I'm writing this as the train rumbles through a land halfway between mountain and jungle, beside the Urabamba, a tributary of the Amazon. Lampo and Denzil are sitting opposite me. They send their love. I send more than love. I send a shriek of desire.

When we meet I'll tell you of the sights we have seen on this almost memorable holiday. We travelled on the second highest railway in the world. Our beautiful train, so beautiful that the excited station staff at Arequipa kept it for two hours before letting it go, wound across the desert, up over the arid mountains, past rare oases and shy, gentle vicuña, past lakes seething with bird life, down to Puno on the shore of Lake Titicaca, the world's highest navigable lake.

I'll tell you of Puno, where the restaurants are full of strolling bands who play the haunting music of the *zampona* (pan-pipes), the little pipes of the *antara*, the cane flutes called *quena*, the twelve-stringed *charango* with body made of armadillo shells. They even make music with a comb stroked against the side of a gourd. They play music fervent with lyrical sadness, sometimes hauntingly yearning, sometimes ferociously triumphant. Every note sings to me of love and absence.

I'll tell you of the long train journey from Puno to Cuzco, through the *altiplano*, the great upland plain of the Andes, empty save for isolated thatched stockades and adobe villages. Waiters set tablecloths throughout our third-world train, and without leaving our seats we ate stuffed avocado, beef casserole and a banana. Eat your heart out, InterCity Catering. A lone Indian on horseback watched gravely as a whole trainload ate their bananas. What did he think?

I'll tell you of the almost memorable town of Cuzco, Spanish elegance built upon foundations of massive Inca stonework that has stood undamaged for five hundred years although no mortar was used, such was the perfection of the masons.

I'll tell you of the almost memorable four-hour train journey from Cuzco to the foot of the great mountain on which the almost memorable Inca city of Machu Picchu was built, of the climb round hairpin bends on buses brought by train to this road that connects with no other road, built of materials brought by train, to the immaculately terraced, deserted city of the sky, high on its narrow rock several thousand feet above the curving Urabamba, mortarless stonework unflinching before four hundred years of winds.

Why were these great sights only almost memorable? Because you are not here, my impossibly wonderful love.

Henry

PS You'll never guess who we met in Lima. Neil Mallet, who tried to destroy my journalistic career with deliberate misprints. He went white at the sight of Denzil and me. He's working on an English-speaking paper in Lima. Hardly a glittering career, and I found I couldn't hate him any more. Not all of us have to cope with the sackfuls of envy and inadequacy that were dealt to him. We all had a drink together, but he had to leave early to do his laundry. *Plus ça change . . .*

Sarajevo
Rua de Matelos
Altea
Costa Blanca
Spain
30th September 1982

Dear Henry,

I'm glad you enjoyed your holiday. I enjoyed living it through your letter.

Yes, I too am looking forward to our meeting. It'll be nice to see my pen-pal. I wonder if you'll look the way I imagine you!

I won't look the way you imagine me. I'm quite a shadow of the person I was, Henry, and I don't think you should be using phrases like 'my impossibly wonderful love'. Even if I ever was wonderful, which I doubt, I'm not now. When I look at myself in the mirror, I see a kind of emptiness, a sense of there being nobody there. I doubt if I'll ever again be able to cope with the great rousing excitements of life. Please, please, please don't expect too much of me.

Kate and Jack both managed to get over for a few days. We're blessed in our children, and that at least gives me hope that there was and is something worthwhile between us. Camilla sends her love via them, which is nice. I know that you write to them all and are disappointed that they aren't managing to get to Peru, but they're all very involved in building their own lives.

With a heavy heart, I have to report that Benedict has been sighted in Portugal – in Albufeira, in fact. My informant – that makes me sound like a policewoman – saw him in a restaurant in unsavoury company and looking as if he might be drugged up. The informant is reliable. He's none other than my own dear Daddy. The Mathesons have a villa there and invited us both. I didn't go as I thought Daddy needed a break from me.

I feel depressed by my country. It's strange that we're both among Spanish peoples at this time. The Spaniards here feel that the Falklands War was the last dingy death-twitch of our imperialist illusions. (Not that Spain wasn't imperialist!)

I despair over Benedict. Should I go to Portugal? Do Nigel and

Diana really care? I've never before been so sad that you are so far away.

    With love,
    Hilary

Apartado 823
Cajamarca
Peru
Oct 14th, 1982

Dear Nigel,

    I'm writing this from Peru, where I'm running a government aid programme which will eventually cover the Andes with cucumbers. I'm writing because I've just heard from Hilary that Benedict has been sighted in Albufeira and I wonder what you're planning to do about it. I gather he looked as if he was on drugs. I feel so helpless here, as I won't be back in Europe till November next year. We're all responsible for the boy, Nigel, and we're all in some way to blame. We've got to try to save him.

    Lampo came over recently and we chatted over late-night glasses of rum about the old days at Dalton. If he knew I was writing, I'm sure he'd join in sending best wishes and hoping that you're getting real satisfaction out of serving your wonderful constituents in Thurmarsh! I'd love to be a fly on the wall at one of your 'surgeries'.

    I suppose you were very bullish over the Falklands and spoke proudly of our troops. We know our troops are good. We don't need wars to prove it. Would that our politicians were as good as our troops.

    With all best wishes,
    Henry

Dear Henry,

Thank you for your letter. Yes, I heard that Benedict had been 'sighted' in Albufeira. You say we're all responsible. Well, as his father I accept my share, but I have responsibility for all sorts of people, especially Felicity, who doesn't enjoy the most robust of health. The very mention of the boy is liable to give her 'an attack'. I'm responsible to my partners, and this is a very busy time. I'm responsible to my government in Parliament. I believe in our policies (including the defence of the Falklands. How twisted you are). I can't let the side down through sudden trips to Albufeira to chase my son, who may well be there on holiday and gone before I arrive. Above all, Henry, I am, as you rightly point out, responsible to the great British electorate, to my constituents, the people of Thurmarsh. And yes, I do try to serve them well. I'm a good constituency MP. I'm not by inclination a kisser of babies, but now I kiss some horrendous specimens. You'd hardly recognise me.

I simply cannot chase the boy every time there's a sighting. He's an adult, he can choose his own life, and nobody, frankly, can force me to like him just because he's my son.

In any case, I believe Diana has gone over to Portugal to hunt for him.

When you get back to England, it will be time for you to think very seriously about pensions, if you have not done so already, and, knowing you, I will be surprised if you have. Do get in touch. I can suggest all sorts of ways of providing that 'nest-egg' that we all need. You will not do better elsewhere.

I hope your Peruvian venture continues to prosper.

Yours et cetera,

Nigel

Dear Henry,

I haven't written earlier as I decided to pop over to Portugal as soon as I could. I've been into every bar and restaurant around Albufeira and have found no sign of Benedict. I've also tried most of the other resorts on the Algarve. No joy. Probably he was just on holiday there.

I've got an exciting bit of news. Well, it's exciting for me. There's no reason why it should be exciting for you. I'm engaged. I'm marrying a Swiss dentist with three teenage children living with him! My parents are *not* pleased. In retrospect, you seem to them to belong to a golden age! But Gunter and I are very much in love and we are going to be very happy in his tidy little house above Interlaken.

I hope your project is going well. You didn't tell me much about it. Now that I'm happy, I wish you nothing but good. You were a good man to me for most of our life together.

With love,
Diana

Apartado 823
Cajamarca
Peru
Jan 5th, 1983

Dear Diana,

I'm actually writing this in our project office in Baños Del Inca, a village outside Cajamarca. It's summer here, and women are washing clothes in the hot streams and leaving them to dry on the grass beside the streams. Steam is rising everywhere.

I was very pleased – and excited – to hear your news, not least because it amuses me no end to hear that I'm now part of a golden age. It's nice to be appreciated, even in retrospect. I'm truly delighted and hope you'll be very happy. I've nothing but feelings of great warmth for you, darling Diana, and I hope your life with Gunter will be utterly delightful. May you have happy sex, tinkling cow-bells and perfect teeth for many years to come.

Our project proceeds very slowly. We've only managed to build six greenhouses. People keep trying to live in them, and then the glass was broken in one of the first terrorist attacks in this area for many years. Sendero Luminoso, the Maoist terrorists, are becoming more active and threatening the fragile stability of this lovely land. At the moment I'm busy giving our staff driving lessons so that we can start to use our Range Rovers, which are sitting in a field. This summer we'll swing into action.

I do hope you make proper contact with Benedict soon and will do anything I can to help at any time.

From my window I've just seen a group of women in jeans and tee-shirts going into the parish church, and one of them looks very like Anna, Hilary's friend, who once pretended to be a nun. I can't remember if you ever met her.

Outside the church a man is playing beautiful but mournful music on an instrument called the *clarin*. It's ten foot long and can't go on public transport so it's never travelled beyond Baños Del Inca and Cajamarca. Yet another reason for coming to this fascinating spot.

With love and all best wishes,
Henry Pratt,
Unpaid publicist,
Baños Del Inca Tourist Board

> Apartado 823
> Cajamarca
> Peru
> Jan 6th, 1983

Dearest Hilary,

Just a quick one. The most incredible thing happened yesterday. I met Anna, and she's a nun! I know I like irony, but this is ridiculous!

I saw this group of women in jeans entering the church and one of them looked very like Anna. I went across and, lo and behold, it *was* her. The whole group were Canadian worker nuns, very cheery, very casual. I was invited to join them and we had a very jolly time in the priest's house next door, a very friendly place where we (including the nuns) drank very strong gin and tonics. We all repaired to a little booth-like restaurant in a row of such restaurants, simple wooden tables and seats, and had the national speciality, which I regret to say is guinea pig, and which I regret to say is delicious cooked with saffron.

There we sat, as darkness fell over the high sierras and the pretty village with its steaming streams, and we laughed, ate, shared left-wing political assumptions, and I felt so full of memories, of our first meeting in Siena, of my disastrous date with Anna, of my early evenings out with you, and I was overwhelmed with love.

Anna says that she turned to God in selfishness and cowardice, in retreat from emotional chaos, found peace first and then strength and decided to devote her life to service. She's utterly happy and looks beautiful now that the slight smugness and coarseness that marred her beauty have gone.

Is it possible that there is a God for Anna but there isn't for me, and that that is what God is – a relative reality?

It's interesting to reflect on how much Anna's pretence of being a nun reflected a need that she hadn't yet acknowledged.

It's wonderful to think that we are now in the year in which you and I will meet. Oh blessed 1983.

With deepest love,
Henry

Crete, March

Grabbing an early break in the sun. *Many thanks* for your letter. Glad to hear Anna looks well and is enjoying G and T! It makes her seem not quite so lost to us. That other order was just too religious for us to stomach.

With love, Peter and Olivia

My darling Hilary,

It is night. It is dark. I sit behind my mosquito nets in my simple hut in a travel lodge on the banks of the Amazon, about thirty miles from Iquitos. I listen to the cruel pageant of nature's fertile night. Grunts, croaks, hoots, squeaks and screams. I can't sleep. I have to write to my beloved. I have to confess.

The Amazon, though mighty, strikes me as a dull river, slow, brown and straight. I came to this lodge in a thatched boat with sixty seats. There was only one other occupant, a German travel agent with a haircut that made him look thatched. The business, mainly British, has slumped since the Falklands War and now, as the memory of that recedes, the increasing violence of Sendero Luminoso may stop any revival in its tracks.

We were taken on a jungle walk, the German travel agent and I. We saw no animals. There's plenty of jungle. Why should they go where we are? I thought only of you, and the confession I must make.

We dined together, the only two customers in a restaurant designed for one hundred and twenty. After dinner it was cabaret time. The cabaret consisted of our waiters playing guitars. Darkness fell. The macaws went to sleep. The jungle awoke.

Tomorrow we visit an Indian village. They don't use money, so we must barter. It was suggested that we buy cigarettes. I did. The German travel agent refused. 'I will not spread this noxious weed,' he said. 'I will deal in fish-hooks. I have many fish-hooks.'

To what am I going to confess? A sultry affair with a laundress in Baños Del Inca? A mad hour of buggery with the German travel agent? No. To failure. Stark, utter, total failure. I haven't fooled you, have I? The cucumber scheme has been a fiasco. A staff of six Britons and six Peruvians, owners of twelve Range Rovers that have never moved, has produced a total of 1,673 cucumbers, of which 884 were destroyed by South American diseases that I couldn't identify, 211 were too small to sell and 176 were so grievously bent that it was kindest to give them a decent burial. 420 healthy cucumbers, and the Peruvians didn't want even those. They have enough of their own, and don't like them much anyway!

Another fiasco for Henry Pratt. I think it's probably best that we don't meet after all. I can give you nothing. Nothing. You'll be better off free of me.

Iquitos
The next day

Forget what I wrote yesterday, my darling. Perhaps I shouldn't be sending it, but I am, because I want you to know the real me in all my moods.

This morning we went to the Indian village, the German travel agent and I. Our guide, Basil, rang a gong twice before we left. He told us that it was an Indian gong, used for signals. I later realised what his signal meant. 'Only two of them today, chaps. Take it easy, eh?'

An hour's jungle walk took us to a village of thatched huts on stilts, where three people in grass skirts, two men and a woman, met us. She was the first topless seventy-year-old Indian I'd ever seen. They had goods to sell, crocodile-teeth bracelets, poisoned darts without the poison, just the things for Cousin Hilda. For payment they wanted full packets of cigarettes. 'Why do they want this noxious weed?' asked the German travel agent. 'Why do they not want my fish-hooks?' He couldn't even give the fish-hooks away. The answers to his naïve questions were: 1) They use nets; 2) Their children sell the cigarettes in Iquitos, which is why they need full packets, because of course they use money, how else do they buy the jeans we saw drying on the line? The grass skirts are for tourists only.

How tourism corrupts. How it destroys the world it wants to see.

We had lunch on the thatched balcony of the thatched lodge. The thatched boat arrived with no tourists. My trip was over, but the thatched travel agent had a two-day booking and was to be taken on a jungle expedition that afternoon.

He came to the boat to wave goodbye. As we set off up the slow muddy river, he shouted, 'I will insist they give me the full expedition. I will not take short measure.' We waved to each other, the German travel agent and I. I will never see him again. I don't even know his name, nor he mine.

And I thought, I will not give in. I will not be defeated by this absurd and corrupting world. There will be no self-pity.

So tonight I write to say, I don't feel so useless after all. My report will state that the whole scheme was absurdly unrealistic and badly conceived. I am not to blame. That will not be accepted, of course. Only my head will roll. Anthony Snaithe will admit to an unwise appointment, caused by falsely glowing reports about me from other people. But I know . . . I really do know . . . this one was not my fault.

Hilary darling, I am going to fight on. I am going to do something good, I don't know what, but IT WON'T BE TO DO WITH CUCUMBERS. And, my darling, I WILL MAKE YOU HAPPY.

Less than three months till we meet. I cannot be sad for long.

With deepest love,

Cucumber Henry (Retired)

17 We'll Meet Again

On Wednesday, November 16th, 1983, it was revealed that under a scheme to get rid of thousands of senior bureaucrats the National Health Service had ended up with 600 more than before, at a cost of £45 million. Ken Livingstone banned the giving of goldfish as prizes at fairs in Greater London. The main Brighton to Portsmouth railway line was closed for four hours when a six-foot-two signalman fled from his box after seeing a field mouse. And Henry Ezra Pratt met Hilary Nadežda Lewthwaite for only the second time since she'd walked out of their house nineteen years ago.

The venue was the foyer of the Midland Hotel, the appointed time six thirty, but Henry was there ten minutes early.

The claret-coloured carpet had threadbare patches. Some of the leather armchairs had burst arms. The photographs of the halcyon days of steam had not been adequately dusted. The hotel was closing its doors for ever on January 1st.

Henry sat in a quiet corner, with a view of the swing doors. Above him, number 46231 *Duchess of Argyll* was still steaming through Crewe Station past knots of train-spotting schoolboys in baggy, knee-length trousers. His heart was thumping.

For all the three days that he'd been in England it had thumped. England seemed so small, so impossibly genteel after Peru, but it was Hilary's birthplace, so he was glad to be back, in the land of the thumping heart. He was staying at Cousin Hilda's, in his old room, in that cold house. No amount of airing could remove the aura of emptiness, the accumulated dampness of the gentlemenless years. Last night he'd dined off roast lamb and spotted dick, because it was a Tuesday, and in the stifling basement room he'd told Cousin Hilda about Peru, and she'd said, 'Ee!' and, 'Well I never!' and, 'I've never been able to see the point of deserts, me. I mean, where's the sense of them, if nothing grows?' and, 'I just wish Mrs Wedderburn was here. She had an ear for foreign parts, did Mrs

Wedderburn. I haven't. I can't imagine them in me mind's eye,' and the evening, which Henry had dreaded, had passed swiftly, pleasantly and affectionately, and Henry had felt strangely touched, after all his adventures, to be back with spotted dick on a Tuesday. At the end of the evening he'd said, 'I'll be out tomorrow night, Cousin Hilda,' and her face had fallen, and her lips had worked anxiously, and she'd said, 'Out??' as if she couldn't believe that a man of forty-eight could be so irresponsible, and she'd said, 'But I've bought the sausage for the toad-in-the-hole. I've got the sponge for the sponge pudding,' and he'd said, 'I'm sorry. I didn't realise. I should have told you. I'm seeing Hilary,' and she'd gone pink and said, 'Hilary! You're seeing Hilary?' and he'd said, 'We've been corresponding like pen-pals,' and Cousin Hilda had said, 'Well, I daresay the toad-in-the-hole can wait till Thursday. There's no need to be hidebound now it's just the two of us.'

And now a woman entered through the swing doors and Henry's heart almost stopped, but this was an elderly lady, and Hilary would not have been flattered.

And then there she was, pale, tall, not looking her forty-eight years, tense, shy, subdued, yet so beautiful.

'Hello, darling,' he said, as he kissed her on her cold, cold cheek.

'Hello, Henry,' she said. He noted that she hadn't said, 'Darling.' It was going to be a long job.

In the dusty, quiet vastness of the exhausted, ghostly bar, Henry ordered a pint of Tetley's, and his companion plumped for mineral water. 'I don't drink much these days,' she said.

They sat in the alcove in which, almost twenty-eight years ago, Henry had introduced Lorna Arrow to his journalist friends. The stuffing was bursting out of the seats. Above them, a Patriot-class engine was still pulling a mixed freight out of Carlisle Upperby Yard in light snow.

'It's lovely to see you,' said Henry, wondering if even this was too bold and forward. Suddenly it all seemed desperately difficult.

'How was your flight?'

'Very punctual.'

'Good. Cheers.'

'Cheers.'

'How's your father?'

'Very well.'

'Good.'

'How's Cousin Hilda?'

Ah! At least she had volunteered a question.

'Very well.'

'Good.'

'Slightly smaller.'

'Smaller?'

'Shrinking slowly. We all do.'

'Oh.'

'We had spotted dick.'

Her first laugh. Oh, the unbelievable beauty of that first laugh.

His throat was dry. He drank the beer quickly and bought himself another one.

'Thank you for all your letters,' she said.

'Oh, Hilary,' he said. 'I wish you'd seen Peru.'

'Missing it already?' she said wryly. Oh, the incredible loveliness of that returning wryness.

'Oh yes. Two years spent largely missing you, and now I'm missing Peru.'

A tactical error! Not saying that he'd miss Peru. Saying that he'd spent two years missing her. She couldn't cope with that.

'The Range Rovers are still there,' he said. 'There is a corner of some foreign field that is for ever England.'

She smiled. Oh, the gentle splendour of that shy smile.

'Where do you fancy eating?' he asked. He expected her to say, 'I don't mind.' Imagine his joy when she said, 'Is the Taj Mahal still there? I rather fancy that. There aren't any Indian restaurants in Spain.'

Never mind Indian restaurants in Spain. She wanted to go back to their old haunts. Henry began to dare to believe that it was going to be all right.

Hilary stayed with the Mathesons for a week. That first night they had a pleasant meal at the Taj Mahal, where Count Your Blessings was delighted to see them and they were delighted to see him, and pleased that the worrying pain in his left testicle hadn't been the harbinger of a fatal disease, though disappointed that he'd never qualified as a doctor or given public concerts on the sitar or married Petula Clark.

Afterwards, Henry kissed Hilary demurely on the cheek.

The next day, they had a bar lunch at the Pigeon and Two Cushions, which was a mistake, because they missed Oscar dreadfully. That evening Henry had the extraordinary experience of eating toad-in-the-hole and sponge pudding with chocolate sauce on a Thursday instead of a Wednesday, and Cousin Hilda astonished him by suggesting he bring Hilary on the next evening.

So on the Friday evening Henry and Hilary had battered cod and jam roly-poly at Cousin Hilda's, and Cousin Hilda went slightly pink and said, 'Ee! That were grand, though I say it as shouldn't,' and they invited her out for Sunday lunch, and she said, 'Sunday lunch! Whatever next?'

On the Saturday night they ate at the Mathesons', and talked about Anna, and nuns, and Anna, and gin and tonic, and Anna. Olivia Matheson, who had a bruise on her left cheek, drank too much and fell over, and Peter Matheson said, 'I've never ever known her do that before.'

For their Sunday lunch they went to the Midland Hotel. The restaurant seemed to Henry much changed, but he realised that they must be sitting in exactly the spot where he and Lorna had endured a disastrous meal, because behind them Royal Scot number 46164 *The Artist's Rifleman* was still passing through Bushey troughs with the up Mid-Day Scot.

This meal was not disastrous, just very predictable. Henry had tomato soup, Hilary egg mayonnaise, Cousin Hilda pineapple juice, and they all had the beef. Cousin Hilda ate every scrap. To their surprise, she ordered sherry trifle. 'Sherry's alcohol, Cousin Hilda,' Henry pointed out. 'Aye, well, I don't expect they put much in,' said Cousin Hilda. 'It's all profit with these hotels, isn't it?' She took coffee and an after-dinner mint, saying, 'I don't know. Will it never end?' and as they stood up to leave she said, 'Thank you. I wish Mrs Wedderburn could have seen me today. What a time I've had.'

The next day, at Cousin Hilda's insistence, they dined with her off liver and bacon and rhubarb crumble, and on Hilary's last night they went to the Taj Mahal again and Count Your Blessings said, 'So! Maybe you marry each other again!' and roared with laughter.

But at the end of each day, and at the airport, Hilary's demeanour was such that Henry felt able to give her no more than a gentle kiss on her cold, cold cheek.

Henry and Hilary were married for the second time on the day that Ian Macgregor, Chairman of the Coal Board, announced that he would write to every miner in Britain appealing for a return to work, Jeffrey Archer told Lynda Lee-Potter that he wasn't afraid to cry, and police warned children that thousands of Superman transfers might be impregnated with LSD. It was Thursday, June 14, 1984.

Hilary was staying with the Mathesons again. She hadn't yet been to bed with Henry. It was strange to reflect that they had already spent several years married to each other, and had slept together before that marriage, at a time when the permissive society was but a gleam in a pop-festival promoter's eye. Now, when it was respectable to have sex before marriage, and living together for a trial period was regarded as sensible (if hardly romantic), Henry and Hilary sensed a need to be formal and dignified and correct.

As he shaved, Henry thought how incredibly lucky he was. Even when he'd visited Spain for the New Year, and when Hilary had come to Thurmarsh again in February, it had seemed by no means certain that they'd ever manage to find the old intimacy. Then, on his next visit, in March, they'd slipped into it. They'd kissed long and hard on the terrace of her father's little villa, beside the slatted table with the huge, half-finished jigsaw of the *Mauretania*. 'Darling,' he'd said the following morning, 'will you marry me?' 'Yes, please,' she had said.

335

So here he was, butterflies in his stomach, ploughing through bacon and egg in Cousin Hilda's basement. 'Eat up,' she commanded. 'Excitement needs a solid foundation.'

Henry couldn't wait to see how Cousin Hilda handled the Indian food. Wishing the day to be entirely different from their first wedding, Henry and Hilary had hit upon the happy idea of a wedding feast at the Taj Mahal.

Apart from Cousin Hilda, they'd invited Hilary's father; her brother Sam and his Danish girlfriend Greta; Kate and her theatre director boyfriend Adam; Jack and his girlfriend with the strange name of Flick; Camilla and her beautiful Italian lover Giuseppe; Martin and Mandy Hammond; Lampo and Denzil; Joe and Molly Enwright; Peter and Olivia Matheson (reluctantly, because Hilary and Howard were staying with them); Nigel Clinton (as a symbol of the renunciation of jealousy, did he but know it) with his attractive wife Rebecca; Paul and Christobel Hargreaves; and, from the old *Argus* days, Colin Edgeley with Glenda; Ben Watkinson with Cynthia; and Ginny Fenwick with nobody, because there was nobody.

They had not invited Tosset and Felicity Pilkington-Brick (because Henry didn't want to discuss his pension plans); Princess Michael of Kent (because they didn't know her); Ted and Helen Plunkett (because of a surfeit of embarrassing moments); Diana and Gunter Axelburger (because it seemed inappropriate to invite an ex-wife); Mr and Mrs Hargreaves (because it seemed inappropriate to invite an ex-wife's parents); Petula Clark (because fantasy withers if it touches reality); or Auntie Doris and Uncle Teddy (because Uncle Teddy still didn't dare be seen in the town where he had supposedly been burnt to death, and Auntie Doris wouldn't have been up to it, anyway).

As they arrived at the Taj Mahal from the Register Office the staff were lined up and smiling broadly.

'Congratulations,' said Count Your Blessings. 'You have brought honour on our establishment by choosing it as venue for your nuptial celebrations.'

Henry caught a half-smile on the face of Paul Hargreaves, and wished that he hadn't invited him.

But Paul saw Henry's reaction, and hurried over, and said, 'I wasn't laughing at him, Henry. I was laughing for joy at the delightful sentiments and charming expression of them. So much better than a strangled "I hope everything will be to your satisfaction, sir," squeezed out of some dry Anglo-Saxon lips.' Henry looked at him in astonishment, and Paul said, 'We're thrilled to be invited. We bear you no ill-will over Diana.'

'Whose Swiss dentist is gorgeous,' interrupted Christobel.

'Whose Swiss dentist is very nice,' said Paul. 'As we're lifelong friends, shall we make a vow to like each other more, Henry? Or is your puritan heart still shocked by our easy money?'

'Are you making easy money?'

'We hope to,' said Christobel. 'We're opening a private HRT clinic.' She saw Henry's blank expression. 'Hormone replacement therapy. It's the coming thing, and not just for women. You don't want to age, do you?'

'Actually I think I'm odd,' said Henry. 'I rather like the idea of being old.'

The waiters brought champagne and served it very professionally. Henry offered them a glass, and Count Your Blessings said, 'Oh no, sir. We have a saying in India. "Intoxication is the thief of service." '

'Really?' said Henry.

'No, but I thought it sounded good.' Count Your Blessings roared with laughter.

Henry hurried over to Cousin Hilda and said, 'What would you like, Cousin Hilda?'

Cousin Hilda looked embarrassed, even coy.

'I thought I might try a glass of champagne,' she said. 'I've always wondered what it's like.'

Henry looked at her in astonishment.

'Tha's given me some worries, Henry Pratt,' she said. 'Tha's done some right foolish things.' She sniffed. 'Today tha's not doing a foolish thing.' She went pink. 'I always said it. I said it to poor Mr O'Reilly. "Henry and Hilary go together like two shakes of a lamb's tail." "Oh, you're right there," he said. I can't do the accent.

337

"You're not wrong there." ' Cousin Hilda went *very* pink and raised her glass. 'I believe the word is "Cheers".' She took a cautious sip of her champagne, rolled it round her tongue, swallowed it, and nodded. 'Well, I don't know what all the fuss is about, to say it's supposed to be so special,' she said, 'but I'd not say it were unpalatable.'

Howard Lewthwaite joined them and said, 'Oh, Henry. If only you two hadn't wasted so many years.'

'I can't look at it like that,' said Henry. 'I love your daughter dearly, and this time I will make her happy, but Diana was a lovely person and I can't call that a waste of time. Do you know Cousin Hilda? Cousin Hilda, Howard Lewthwaite, Hilary's father.'

'How do you do? Nice to meet you,' said Howard Lewthwaite.

'We met last time your daughter married my . . . married Henry,' said Cousin Hilda.

Henry moved on, making a beeline for Nigel Clinton, who was now managing director of a relatively new publishing house, Clinton and Burngreave.

'I think she'll start writing again before long,' he said.

'Do you really want that?' said Nigel Clinton, who'd lost most of his hair, thus looking more intellectual but less handsome.

'Oh yes,' said Henry. 'I want the complete Hilary Pratt this time.'

He moved on and took Hilary's arm, and they moved through the crowd at the bar of the flock-wallpapered provincial restaurant like royalty at a garden party.

'Where are you going to live?' asked Ben Watkinson's wife Cynthia, who had once been shy and petite.

'We've bought a little terrace house in the best part of Rawlaston,' said Henry.

'I didn't know there *was* a best part of Rawlaston,' said Cynthia.

'How many tennis players of either sex have won all four grand slams in a calendar year?' asked Ben.

'Do shut up, Ben,' said Cynthia.

'Where are you going for your second honeymoon?' asked Ginny Fenwick, blushing.

purely social events it's the press asking all the
,' said Henry.

of habit,' said Ben Watkinson.

nuine interest,' said Ginny.

'Answer the question,' said Colin Edgeley. 'Where is the
bonking marathon to be held?'

'Colin!' said Glenda, who looked pale and exhausted.

'Please, Colin!' said Henry, looking at Hilary anxiously.

'We aren't going anywhere,' said Hilary. 'We're going home. My
father's going on our honeymoon.'

The journalists gawped.

'We're so excited about setting up home again,' said Hilary. 'We
can't afford much, but to us it's a palace, because it's ours. Daddy's
coming to live with us, but we'd like to be on our own at first, so he's
going to Majorca for a fortnight. He's tickled pink, and we'll have a
lovely fortnight on our own.'

'Bonking like rabbits,' said Jack, passing by.

Jack could get away with such things. Nobody ever took offence
at Jack. Henry and Hilary grinned, and Hilary said, 'Well, I can
hope,' and Henry said, 'I'm not a young man any more,' in a
mock-elderly voice, and as they walked on Henry looked at Hilary
with such love that he thought for an awful moment that he was
going to faint as he'd fainted on seeing Kate for the first time, and
Kate, almost twenty-six now, passionately radical, with no make-
up and a long shapeless sack of a dress but lovely because it suited
her, said, 'I'm so happy for you both. This is the best day of my life,'
and Camilla nodded her agreement with tears in her eyes, and
Giuseppe said, 'She weeping a little bit. She mostly a wonderful
girl,' and Camilla laughed and said, 'I hope you mean, "She's a
most wonderful girl",' and Giuseppe laughed and said, 'Oh yes. I
am magnified by my mistake,' and Camilla said, 'mortified,' and
Giuseppe said, 'Oh yes,' and laughed again.

Count Your Blessings announced that luncheon was ready, and
they all took their places at the long table under the huge lurid
photograph of the eponymous edifice.

Count Your Blessings had told Henry that there would be

magnificent food, 'not from the menu. Menu is star
restaurant. Real Indian food.' There were chats and dos.
kinds of bhagia, and spicy dumplings and whole marinat
and quail, and beautiful stuffed marrow and delicately s
ladies' fingers and banana methi and coconut rice and lemon rice
and lovely breads. Cousin Hilda tried the food cautiously, and said,
'Well, it's not tasteless. I'll give it that.' Kate's boyfriend Adam ate
with his fingers. 'I hope nobody minds,' he said, 'but I like to eat as
the common people do.' None of them minded, but the waiters
giggled.

Howard Lewthwaite, sitting beside Henry, turned to him and
said, 'I asked Hilda out.'

'You did what??'

'For a meal. For companionship. I said to her, "Just for
companionship. No hanky panky." She went pink and said, "Mr
Lewthwaite! I should hope there wouldn't be." I said, "Well, come
on, then," and she said something strange. She said, "Mr
Lewthwaite, you're fifty years too late." '

'That isn't strange,' said Henry. 'That's poignant.'

Henry and Hilary kept touching each other under the table, wine
and beer and lassi flowed, and it was all the most tremendous
success.

Peter Matheson leant across and said, 'Is it really true you're
working as a waiter, Henry?'

'Yes, Peter,' said Henry. 'At the Post House.'

'Good God!'

'And proud of it. An honourable profession. Only the British
think it's demeaning to wait on your fellow men.'

'Really hard work, though, badly paid and rarely appreciated,'
said Joe Enwright.

'Rather like teaching,' said Henry.

'Touché,' said Joe Enwright with feeling.

'I tried going back to the market garden,' said Henry. 'I just
couldn't face it.'

'Have some raita. It's delicious,' said Nigel Clinton.

'I can't even eat them,' said Henry. 'Forty-nine years old,

receding hair line, expanding stomach line, doesn't know anything except cucumbers, absolutely fed up with cucumbers, Hilary's got herself a real prize catch.'

'I think I have,' said Hilary lovingly.

'I wonder how much these people send back to India,' said Martin Hammond.

'Lots,' said Howard Lewthwaite. 'They're wonderfully non-materialistic.'

'Unlike the Thurmarsh Socialists,' said Peter Matheson.

'Oh shut up about politics, Peter,' said Olivia.

Henry stood up.

Silence fell slowly.

'This is not a formal wedding,' he said. 'We aren't having speeches.'

'Hooray!' shouted Jack.

'But I would like to call on my best man, Martin Hammond, who I believe has some telegrams.'

Martin Hammond stood up.

'I know you're supposed to make jokes at weddings,' he said, 'but I can't make jokes, so I won't.'

'Hooray!' shouted Jack.

'Henry and I met when we were four. We joined the Paradise Lane Gang. We thought we were right little tearaways too. Tearaways? We were boy scouts compared to today's lot. Law and order? Now there is a joke. Oops, sorry, I promised not to be political.'

'Quite right, too,' said Peter Matheson.

'Shut up, Peter,' hissed Olivia Matheson.

'We had our well-publicised disagreements over the 1979 election,' continued Martin. 'But it was all taken in good part, and we remained friends, as witnessed by my having the honour to be best man today. Politicians always speak too much . . . '

'Hear hear,' said Olivia Matheson.

'Shut up, Olivia,' hissed Peter Matheson.

'So I'll get straight on with my main job, the reading of the telegrams,' continued Martin. 'This one's from Switzerland: "We wish you happiness for the rest of your days – Diana and Gunter." '

There was a murmur of approval. Camilla's eyes filled with tears and Giuseppe held her hand.

'That is very nice,' said Martin. 'An ex-wife saying that. That is highly delightful. The next one is from Suffolk: "We wish we were with you – Auntie Doris and Uncle Miles." That's nice. And one from London: "Many congratulations – James and Celia." '

'Diana's parents. Very nice,' said Henry.

'Oh, and here's one from Thurmarsh,' said Martin Hammond. ' "Congratulations. Don't do anything we wouldn't do. That leaves you quite a lot – Ted and Helen." '

Ginny Fenwick gave a loud derisive snort, and everyone looked at her, and she blushed.

'Ah!' said Martin. 'Now this is definitely a case of last, but not least, because this one has come all the way from Peru.'

'It'll be from our daughter,' said Olivia Matheson. 'She's a nun.'

'Let the man speak, dear,' said Peter Matheson.

'I'm sorry to have to disappoint you,' said Martin, 'but somehow I don't think this one's from a nun. It says, "Get stuck in – Anna." '

There was laughter. Cousin Hilda frowned. Olivia Matheson looked embarrassed. Peter Matheson gave a smile so fixed that it was impossible to tell what he was thinking.

'That concludes the telegrams,' said Martin. He sat down, and there was applause.

Henry stood up.

'Ladies and gentlemen,' he said. 'I find I must say a few words. First, a huge thank-you to the staff of the Taj Mahal for the wonderful food and service.'

Everybody clapped and cheered. Count Your Blessings couldn't have smiled more widely if Petula Clark herself had walked in.

'In a minute I'm going to propose just one toast,' said Henry. 'To absent friends. Before I do, I'd like to mention four absent friends briefly. My Auntie Doris, who can't be here due to illness, and her companion, Miles Cricklewood, who can't be here because he's looking after Auntie Doris. I've known them both all my . . . well,

I've known Auntie Doris all my life and Miles ever since he came on the scene. I do wish they could have been here. Also, our friend Anna Matheson, who is a nun in Peru – yes, that telegram was from her and as you'll have gathered she's no ordinary nun, she's a worker nun, a nun of the world. Last, but definitely not least, my step-son, Benedict. He's an unhappy soul, a lost soul. I just wish he'd come back and give us another chance. We might not fail him so badly next time. Ladies and gentlemen, thank you for coming, and I give you the toast of "absent friends".'

They all said 'absent friends' fervently, and then they drank, and then they applauded Henry heartily.

Soon the guests began to leave.

First to go was Howard Lewthwaite. He had to catch the plane for his honeymoon. He left to a chorus of good wishes.

Next were Sam and Greta. 'Lovely do. Hope you're incredibly happy,' said Sam. 'Sorry to rush off, but I've an idea and I've got to work on it.' 'He's always like this when he feels a soup coming on,' said Greta in her charming Danish accent.

Lampo and Denzil kissed Hilary but, in deference to being in Yorkshire, they only shook hands with Henry. Denzil said, 'This is a great day. Lampo cried,' and Lampo said, 'You cried too,' and Denzil said, 'I'm allowed to be sentimental. I'm old,' and Lampo said, 'You are, aren't you? What am I doing living with a disgusting old man?' Henry smiled. He'd suddenly realised that there had never been the slightest risk that Lampo and Denzil, for all their quarrelling, would ever split up.

Ginny kissed Henry and Hilary and blushed, Joe and Molly Enwright invited them to dinner, Colin Edgeley said, 'Keep in touch, kid. You're my mate,' Paul said, 'Don't forget we have the secret of eternal youth,' Nigel Clinton said, 'Get her writing,' Cousin Hilda said, 'If my gentlemen could see me today! Indian food! Whatever next? Thank you, and I wish you so much happiness this time,' and they gazed at her in astonishment; Jack said, 'I'm very pissed. Sorry. But I'm right chuffed. It's grand to have you two together again'; Olivia Matheson stumbled and fell, and Peter Matheson said, 'She's never ever done that before';

343

Giuseppe said, 'You very happy, I make your step-daughter very delirious'; and Kate just shook her head and cried.

Last to leave were Ben Watkinson and Cynthia. Ben had never known how to leave a room except by saying, 'Well, I'm off to give the wife one.' He couldn't say that when she was there, so it was Cynthia who said, 'Come on, Ben. We're outstaying our welcome,' at which neither Henry nor Hilary demurred.

The happy couple got into their hired car and were driven to their new home.

The house wasn't large, it wasn't luxurious, it wasn't beautiful, but it was theirs, and they had a lovely, gentle fortnight, getting to remember each other's rhythms, exploring each other's bodies, finding happiness. Howard, meanwhile, enjoyed their honeymoon, the concept of which had really amused him, and he sent a card saying, 'You're having a wonderful time. Wish I was here.'

As soon as Howard's honeymoon was over, Henry and Hilary enacted what they saw as the final part of their wedding. They went to see Uncle Teddy and Auntie Doris.

Auntie Doris's eyes were sunk deep into her face now, and her face had become pinched and hollow. Uncle Teddy had lost weight, was moving rather stiffly, and was slightly round-shouldered, but he'd worn better than her, and in fact they both thought that he'd worn incredibly well, considering the strain he'd been under.

After lunch, Uncle Teddy said he fancied a walk. Henry went with him. They walked past May Cottage, Old Cottage, the Old Thatcher's Cottage, Christmas Tree Cottage, April Cottage, High Cottage, Jane Farthing Cottage, Oak Cottage and Little Pond Cottage to the river, and back up the green past a cottage called The Cottage, as if there were no other cottages, and Uncle Teddy breathed in the air and said nothing until, as they passed the church, he said, 'Beautiful. All this air, Henry. I've been cooped up, you see. I can't leave her.'

They walked for two hours. Soon after they got home, the sun went down over the yard-arm, and after their drinks Uncle Teddy heated up some tinned soup and Marks and Spencer's cannelloni, and after their meal they settled down in the rustic little living room with its floral suite, and Uncle Teddy said, 'I hope you weren't expecting a game of Scrabble. Doris doesn't like that any more.'

They assured him that they weren't expecting a game of Scrabble.

'What she likes best is the story of our life,' said Uncle Teddy.

'Oh yes,' said Auntie Doris. 'Tell me the story of our life.'

'Do you mind?' said Uncle Teddy. 'Only I tell her it every night, and she likes it.'

'Of course we don't mind,' said Hilary.

'We met in 1927,' said Uncle Teddy.

'1927!' exclaimed Auntie Doris.

'At the Mecca.'

'Don't you have to stand in a certain direction at the Mecca?' said Auntie Doris. 'Facing the South Pole or something?'

'No, no. This was a dance hall,' said Uncle Teddy. He leant across to Henry and Hilary and whispered, 'Surprising what the old girl remembers sometimes. Quite surprises me.'

'Can't do much dancing if you're all facing the South Pole,' said Auntie Doris. 'Bit inhibiting.'

'No, no,' said Uncle Teddy. 'Mecca is a holy city, and Muslims face it when they pray. *The* Mecca is a dance hall.'

'Oh, I see.'

'Reginald Lichfield and his Boulevardiers used to play. It was packed Saturday nights in them days. Packed. Cigarette smoke everywhere. Through the smoke I saw this vision. Know what it was?'

'Was it me?' mouthed Auntie Doris.

'Well done! It was you. Prettiest girl in all the hall.'

'Was I?'

'Curves in all the right places. Lovely legs. Beautiful lips. Bright red.'

'Ee!'

Henry gave Hilary a wry grin. Auntie Doris hadn't said 'Ee!' for over fifty years. It wasn't posh.

'I asked you to dance. You said, "I don't mind." All casual and offhand.'

'Oh dear! Was I a little minx?'

'You were a vixen! We danced. I asked you out. Within five weeks we were engaged.'

'No! You were a quick worker, then?'

'I'd say. Never met anyone like you. Had to be. Too many rivals to hang about!'

'O'oh! Really? And then?'

'We got married in St Matthew's Church. A hundred and twenty guests.'

'Ee! A hundred and twenty!'

'Grand wedding. The Sniffer sniffing like mad. Face like a cupboard full of brooms.'

'The Sniffer?'

'Cousin Hilda. Mellowed now from what Henry tells me. Amazing what fear of the grim reaper can do. We bought a house in Dronfield. I went into import–export.'

'We had children.'

'No, Doris. We decided not to. We were good-time people.'

'I've always liked a good time.'

'Right. I did well.'

'Did you, Teddy?'

'Oh yes. Very well. Bought a big house. Called it Cap Ferrat.'

'That's a place.'

'Absolutely spot on. A very nice place where we had our holidays. Then war came. Then after the war . . .'

'Don't you usually tell me more about the war? Summat brave that you did somewhere.'

'Absolutely right, Doris. You're in good form today.' He looked at Henry and Hilary uneasily. 'I'm shortening it tonight. We have guests. Our Henry, our nephew, and his wife Hilary. Henry's mother died, you see.'

'Oh no!'

'And his father hanged himself.'

'Oh no!! What a tragic boy.'

'Yes. So we took him in as our son.'

'Oh! Lovely!'

'Yes, he was.'

Henry smiled sheepishly.

'He was,' continued Uncle Teddy. 'But I was a naughty boy. I went to prison.'

'Teddy! What for?'

'Oh, just technical offences. Tax evasion. Evading currency restrictions. Fraud. Nothing criminal.'

'Good. That's good. How long did you get?'

'Three years.'

'Three years! That's hard.'

'It was hard. It was hard for you, too. You were lonely. You couldn't manage without a man. You took up with a business friend of mine. Geoffrey Porringer.'

'I didn't! Naughty me.'

'Well! Partly my fault.'

'Was he nice?'

'He had blackheads.'

'Oh dear. I don't like the sound of him one bit.'

'I came out of prison. You were with Geoffrey. I was . . . upset. I took up with a . . . slightly younger woman.'

'You rogue!'

'Yes. I pretended to be burnt in a big fire, and you had a funeral for me.'

'No! Teddy!'

'And I lived in the South of France and married this . . . slightly younger woman, and you married Geoffrey.'

'Teddy! We were both rogues then?'

' 'Fraid so.'

'Well!'

'Anyway, Anna . . . the slightly younger woman . . . we parted, and I realised that I'd loved you all the time.'

'Teddy! All the time?'

'All the time. And you didn't love Geoffrey Porringer. So, you left Geoffrey and I came back to England and we bought this cottage.'

347

'Well!'

'But because I'm supposed to be dead, I have to live as Miles Cricklewood, a retired vet, in Suffolk, where nobody knows me.'

'And we lived happily ever after.'

'Well, no, nobody does that. But almost.'

'And all this happened to us?'

'Yes.'

'Well, we've lived a bit, Teddy.'

'We certainly have.'

'We've given them a run for their money.'

'We've cut the mustard.'

'We certainly have. Well, thank you, Teddy, that was lovely. I remembered bits of it, of course.'

'Of course. But not all.'

'No. Not all. I think you're very kind to me, Teddy.'

'I think I probably am, now.'

They said goodbye to the bottle of port and went to bed and they all slept like tops.

18 They Also Serve

His employers at the Post House were pleased with Henry's performance as a waiter. At last there's something I definitely do well, he thought wryly. He even invented a character for himself. He'd been on the ocean liners. 'When I was on the ocean liners . . . ,' he'd begin. It wasn't truly a fantasy. He hadn't lost touch with reality, and he said it even to people who knew it wasn't true. But he enjoyed the performance, and avoiding being caught out in contradictions kept his mind sharp. 'I'll never forget – sixty miles off the Azores – a force six easterly – I slopped mulligatawny soup all over the dress tunic of a colonel in the New Zealand army . . . Ructions? I'll say there were ructions!'

One day, towards the end of 1984, Henry came home to find Hilary somewhat tense and her father watching television.

'Henry?' she said.

'I'll go,' said Howard Lewthwaite. 'My room isn't really terribly cold.'

'What?' said Hilary.

'You're going to say something serious,' said Howard Lewthwaite. 'I don't want to be in the way.'

'You aren't in the way. I think you should hear this.'

'Oh. Because I don't want to be a nuisance.'

'You're only a nuisance when you keep saying you are.'

'Well I am. I'm stopping you saying what you want to say.'

'Well shut up, then.'

'You see. I am a nuisance.'

'You aren't! Please stay!'

'You're angry now.'

'Daddy! Shut up!'

Howard Lewthwaite sat solemnly, looking hurt.

'Henry?' said Hilary. 'I've something to tell you.'

'Oh?'

Henry could feel his heart thudding.

'I started a novel today.'

'Darling! Oh, I *am* glad!'

He hugged her and kissed her.

'Are you really?' she said.

'Utterly,' he said. 'Totally.' Hilary was smiling and Howard was smiling and Henry couldn't bear being the recipient of so much warmth, so he said, 'Well, I'm fed up with living off my tips.'

All through 1985, Hilary wrote; Howard said, 'I'm in the way, I'm under your feet'; and Henry proved how right the Director (Operations) had been all those years ago, when he said, 'They also serve who only stand and wait.'

The miners' strike ended after almost a year, French security agents set off two explosions on the Greenpeace ship, *Rainbow Warrior*, which was aiming to disrupt French nuclear tests in the South Pacific, the wreck of the *Titanic* was found in the North Atlantic, and Ronald Reagan and Mikhail Gorbachev achieved very little in Geneva in the first US–Soviet summit for six years.

Nearer home, a Leeds art dealer was gaoled for selling forged paintings. His crime came to light when Timothy Whitehouse's successor at the Cucumber Marketing Board realised that his office was full of reproductions of non-existent old masters. To the relief of Derek Parsonage, Henry, Uncle Teddy and the forger, the art dealer refused to reveal his sources. He might need their help again.

One night Henry arrived home full of excitement: 'I've served eleven lobster thermidors. Eleven in one night!' to be comprehensively upstaged by Hilary: 'I've finished my novel.'

Howard Lewthwaite said, 'This is a great moment for you. You'll want to be alone,' but didn't move.

Henry read Hilary's book. It was called *Towards the Light* and was a story about the conquering of depression. He found it deeply moving, but with a caustic wit. Nigel Clinton loved it and scheduled publication for October 1986, and Hilary met him for rewrites, and Henry went to the Post House and said, 'The *Mauretania* was a bugger for serving *zabaglione*. Something about the stabilisers, I suppose,' and came home tired and made himself a light supper, and didn't mind about Nigel Clinton or about Howard Lewthwaite saying, 'You want a quiet snack, a moment to yourself, you're tired, it's natural, you don't want to listen to an old man rabbiting on, I understand,' and not going.

The book was an instant success. Henry opened a bottle of champagne to celebrate the good reviews, and said how thrilled he was, and meant it, and Howard Lewthwaite said, 'No, no. I'll go to my room. You share the bottle. I don't want to be in the way,' and Henry said, 'Have some champagne, Howard, and enjoy your daughter's success. That's an order,' and they all laughed, and another summit meeting between Ronald Reagan and Mikhail Gorbachev, this time in Iceland, ended in bitter disappointment after seeming to promise so much, and a chemical spill in Switzerland threatened to destroy all life in the River Rhine, and one evening, early in 1987, on Henry's night off, as the three of them were watching television, Howard Lewthwaite suddenly gave a gasp of pain.

'What is it?' said Hilary.

'Nothing,' said Howard Lewthwaite in a strangled voice. 'I don't want to spoil your programme.'

His face was contorted with pain. He tried to stand. Hilary rushed over to him. Henry switched the programme off with the remote control. Howard Lewthwaite died in his daughter's arms.

Councillors and council officials and Labour Party workers and his new-found cronies from the Mulberry Inn, Rawlaston turned up in force for Howard Lewthwaite's cremation. Peter Matheson flew back, leaving Olivia in Albufeira. Sam discovered that the world wouldn't end if he didn't think up any new soups for three days, and came to support his sister. After the brief, impersonal service, Henry and Hilary and Sam and his girlfriend Greta stood among ageing men and women with watery eyes, and there was much talk about the end of an era, and there not being many of us left, and they don't make them like that any more. The landlord of the Mulberry told Hilary, 'The moment he walked in I knew he were a gentleman. He stood out.' Hilary had as many as she could back to the house, and after they'd all gone she flopped exhausted into a chair and let Sam and Greta make a fish pie for supper.

Over supper they talked about anything but death. They laughed about how obnoxious Sam had been as a child and told Greta all the awful things he'd said. Sam grew broody. He could feel a soup coming on. Almonds. Something to do with almonds, possibly. He went for a walk. While he was gone, Greta talked about the differences between Aalborg and Luton. They were many. Sam returned, suffering from soup creator's block. They were all tired, and went to bed early.

In bed, cuddled deep against Henry's soft body, Hilary said, 'I'm so glad we got together again. You know why?'

'No,' said Henry, 'but tell me.' It had been a long, exhausting day. A compliment would come in nicely.

'Because if I hadn't, Daddy would have died in exile, and he'd have hated that,' sobbed Hilary.

A few days after Howard Lewthwaite's cremation, Henry got home tired at a quarter to twelve, having had an amazing run on apple strudel – 'Funnily enough, on the old *Queen Mary* the apple strudel always went like hot cakes, whereas on the *Queen Elizabeth*, the old *Queen* not the *QE2*, it could be decidedly sticky. No explanation for it. One of the mysteries of the deep.'

Hilary was standing with her back to the grate, as if she was the squire and there was a roaring log fire, rather than the battered coal-effect electric one they'd picked up second-hand.

'Sit down,' she commanded.

Henry realised that she was going to broach a difficult subject. She was never bossy otherwise.

He sat down. His heart was thumping.

'You're the person I love most in all the world,' she said. 'I loved Daddy, too, and I'd never have suggested it while he was alive, but now that he's dead I think it's possible. But if you decide you don't want to, we won't, and I won't mention it again, and that'll be the end of the matter.'

'That'll be the end of what?' said Henry. 'What won't you mention again? What are you talking about?'

'Moving to London,' said Hilary.

There was a moment's silence in the little terrace house.

'Actually I'd like to move to London,' said Henry. 'It'd be perfect for what I have in mind.'

'I didn't know you had anything in mind,' said Hilary.

'I didn't,' said Henry. 'I've only just thought of it.'

'Only just thought of what?' said Hilary.

'The Café Henry,' said Henry.

On March 18, 1987, treasure worth £20 million was found by Danish divers aboard the wreck of the P and O liner *Medina*, torpedoed by a German U-boat off Start Point in 1917, a pizza-parlour manager and a hotel barmaid became the first couple in Church of England history to be married by a woman, and Henry and Hilary set off for another cremation. They found Uncle Teddy dazed and lost.

Jack and Flick came down the night before, and an Adamless Kate arrived on the day. A smattering of old drinking cronies from Monks Eleigh's two pubs also attended. The small gathering, barely filling two rows of the chapel of Ipswich Crematorium, hung their heads as Auntie Doris's coffin slid slowly away, much as her mental faculties had done.

They went for lunch at the Swan in Lavenham. At the bar, Jack told Henry, 'I don't want to upset Great-Uncle Teddy by giving good news, but you're going to be a grandfather.' Henry flinched at the thought of the potential size of any child produced by burly Jack and earth-mother Flick. 'That's wonderful, Jack,' he said. 'I think you should tell everyone. Life must go on.' So Jack made his announcement, and Hilary cried, and Uncle Teddy smiled bravely and said, 'Well, that's good news. That's really cheered me up.'

After lunch Jack and Flick set off in their BMW, and Kate left in her Deux Chevaux. As they stood outside the old hostelry, in the venomous March wind, Henry said, 'Not interfering, darling, but you haven't mentioned Adam recently.' 'No,' said Kate. 'We've split. I may find somebody perfect one day, Dad. I may not. I'm twenty-eight. I'm happy. I love you both. Goodbye.'

Henry drove Hilary and Uncle Teddy very slowly back to

Honeysuckle Cottage, dreading the silence of the house. Hilary made tea.

'Fancy a spot of Scrabble?' said Uncle Teddy.

'Do you?' said Henry.

Uncle Teddy reflected.

'No,' he said at last. 'No. I think it might seem a bit tame without the cheating.'

At six o'clock Uncle Teddy said, 'They're open. We've nobody to look after. What say we have a couple or three?'

They had a couple or three, and then Hilary made a light supper.

After supper, over a whisky, Uncle Teddy said, 'It's been very difficult, you know.'

'I can imagine,' said Hilary.

'Can you? Yes, I suppose you can. You're a novelist,' said Uncle Teddy. 'No, it has been extremely difficult. I haven't been able to let her out of my sight. I've had to do everything for her. I've had to tell her the story of our life every night. *Every* night. I've been a prisoner and a warder. It's almost driven me crazy.'

Even Hilary couldn't find a reply.

'I didn't go to the pub for over two years. I saw mirages of beer in my dreams. I haven't even been able to go for walks. Henry knows how much that's meant. But do you know what I've really longed for? Not a juicy steak in a posh restaurant. Not a well-pulled pint of Adnam's in a low-beamed pub. The sea. That cold old North Sea. Wind in my hair, ozone in my lungs, salt on my lips, gulls mewing in my ears.'

'Well now you can go to the sea any time you like,' said Henry.

'Exactly!' said Uncle Teddy. 'Exactly! And I will. Oh yes. I will.'

He poured Henry another whisky. Hilary declined.

'Cheers,' said Uncle Teddy.

'Cheers,' said Henry.

'Oh God!' said Uncle Teddy. 'I don't care if I never see the bloody sea again. Great big stupid thing sitting there full of salt. Who cares? I just wish she was here now, to tell our life story to.'

19 The End of an Era

It was a really good day at the Café Henry until the phone call came.

Henry had arrived early, as usual. He helped lay out the splendid array of excellent cakes and salads, for which the café was justly famous, and chalked up on the blackboard the three hot dishes of the day – spinach and red-pepper cannelloni, lemon chicken (free-range) and plaice *dieppoise*.

Trade was brisk. There were happy actors on their way to rehearsals, unhappy actors on their way to auditions, the odd writer (one of them very odd), a sex-shop proprietor, a head waiter, some artists, a group of Japanese tourists who took photos of the Henrygraph and giggled, even a yuppie or two.

For which the café was justly famous? Yes, gentle reader, Henry's establishment in Frith Street had become well-known. As he looked round his little kingdom, the marble floor, the attractive wooden tables, the clever use of mirrors, the jumble of notices and slogans which breathed life into the elegance without quite destroying it, as he forced himself to look at all this as if he'd never seen it before, so that he would never for a moment forget how fortunate he was, Henry smiled as he recalled Hilary's initial doubts.

'Will it lose us lots of money?' she'd asked. 'I mean, I'm all for it, but I don't want to lose *lots* of money.'

'It'll make money,' he'd said.

'How can you be so sure?' she'd asked.

'Because I'm not doing it for the money.'

She'd nodded and accepted that, but he knew that she hadn't really been convinced. He might be her lovely Henry, but she couldn't believe that he could also be successful.

And now they were both successful! Hilary's third and fourth novels had been best-sllers, and the first two had been reissued.

There's nothing like a long creative silence for arousing interest in an artist.

There was a congenial group seated at the bar stools that morning. Behind the bar hung three prominent notices: '*You are in a no-privacy area. If you don't wish to talk to your fellow human beings, please sit at a table,*' '*No minimum charge at any time. No maximum charge either!*' and '*If you look miserable you'll be asked to leave unless you have a good reason. The state of the world is not acceptable. That's a reason for having one place where nobody looks miserable.*'

The phone rang, a gentle noise like a happy frog, carefully chosen by Henry to avoid creating tension.

It was a journalist.

'No,' said Henry. 'I don't give interviews. Neither does Hilary about her private life. We've turned down "Relative Values", "How We Met", "A Typical Day", "A Month in the Life of", "My Favourite Childhood Memory", "What We Like About Each Other", "What We Hate About Each Other", "Twenty-Five Things You Didn't Want to Know About Our Sex Lives", *and* "Our Favourite TV Supper" . . . Well, we want people to come here because they've been told about it, not read about it. So sorry.'

He beamed round the bar, and said, 'The press again. How I'm hounded.'

Took photos of the Henrygraph and giggled? What on earth is the Henrygraph? the puzzled reader cries. The Henrygraph is a sculpture, a rather unflattering caricature of our hero, with a large screen where his large stomach should be. It was made by Giuseppe, Camilla's husband, who is a caricaturist. Henry no longer minded being short and podgy, with thin strands of white hair. Adverts, films and magazines poured forth the obscene message that you weren't worth anything unless you were tall, slim and beautiful. The Henrygraph, standing at the back of the café, redressed the balance. Every week Henry held a competition, and the results were shown on the screen. That week in April 1994, the results were 23 per cent John Selwyn Gummer, 17 per cent Cliff Richard, 15 per cent Nancy Reagan, 12 per cent Wet Sileage, 10 per cent Anneka Rice, 9 per cent Dry Sileage, 8 per cent A Pregnant Ferret, 6 per cent Other. Above the Henrygraph there was a notice – Henry loved his notices – which read, *'There are no prizes in our competitions, because a) there are no answers, only results, and b) we don't like greedy bastards.'*

'Have you done the competition?' he asked the group at the bar. 'I rather like this week's.'

That week's competition was, 'Which of the following do you think is "The English Disease"? 1) Hypocrisy 2) Arthritis 3) Self-consciousness 4) Strikes 5) Bronchitis 6) Shyness 7) Snobbery 8) Buggery 9) Neuralgia 10) Nostalgia 11) All ten.'

So that he would never forget for a moment how fortunate he was? It was almost ten years now since Henry had married Hilary for the second time, and they had never had a single argument in all that time. The atmosphere in their large, rambling house overlooking Clapham Common was always cheery and welcoming. Kate was always popping in, Camilla and Giuseppe came when they could, even Jack and Flick had been known to overcome their fear of London and bring little Henry to see his grandparents.

The morning proceeded peacefully. A party of young German trainee undertakers, having a day off from their study of British burial, proved polite, humorous and warm, destroying several preconceptions at a stroke, but also providing an intimation that Henry didn't recognise. They even seemed to understand some of his slogans.

There were slogans everywhere. Sometimes Henry thought that they were pathetic, his feeble attempt to compete with Hilary, but they'd become a tradition and he was the prisoner of that tradition. They included, *'Nothing that cannot stand mockery of itself is to be trusted,' 'Fish don't farm us, so let's not farm fish,' 'Double negatives aren't necessarily unconstructive,' 'Everyone has a role in life. Mine is to show that it isn't important to be good-looking,' 'I've just taken my sex test. Failed the written, passed the oral,' 'Everything goes in cycles. One day it won't be politically correct to be politically correct,'* and *'I have no doubt that the really frightening people in this world are those who have no doubt.'*

Does anything smell better than really good coffee? Could anything taste better at eleven o'clock than a slice of lemon cake, as light as a feather and pleasantly sharp? How delightful it is, if one is on one's own, to read the leading British and world newspapers in peace, with nobody hurrying you.

So why was the man at the corner table looking so miserable? Under the rules of the establishment, Henry was forced to approach him.

'Excuse me?' he said. 'I don't want to be rude, but I have to say that you're as miserable-looking a man as I've clapped eyes on in many a month of wet Sundays. I'm afraid I'll have to ask you to leave, unless you can provide an adequate reason.'

'I'm the only writer of detective fiction in the whole country who hasn't got a series on television,' said the miserable-looking man miserably.

'Best excuse so far this week,' said Henry. 'Have a glass of wine on the house.'

The gentle frog croaked pleasantly. Henry answered it happily.

'A Mrs Langridge has rung from Thurmarsh,' said Hilary. 'Bad news, I'm afraid. Cousin Hilda is sinking fast.'

On Thursday, April 14th, 1994, two American F.15 fighters shot down two United Nations helicopters over Iraq, killing twenty-six allied officers. There was a furious row in the House of Commons over allegations that NHS hospitals were refusing treatment to people because they were too old, the Bosnian Serbs drew close to a full-scale confrontation with Nato and the United Nations, and Hilary, travelling with Henry from St Pancras to Thurmarsh, said how glad she was that her Croatian mother hadn't lived to see the terrible destruction of her beloved Yugoslavia.

How Henry hoped that Cousin Hilda would live to see him that evening. He loved her. He hadn't seen her for several weeks. She was the last of her generation. He was going to feel very exposed. It was the end of an era. Each time the train slowed down he grew anxious. His legs became exhausted as they pushed forward to will the train on faster.

The last of her generation? Oh yes. Uncle Teddy had died almost two years ago. But don't be sad, gentle reader. He died a perfect death. He simply didn't wake up one morning. He'd come to live with them in 1989, a fortnight after they'd bought the five-bedroomed house overlooking Clapham Common. Gradually he'd learnt to live again, to sniff the ozone, to tell old codgers in pubs about his exotic past. Once a week he'd come with Henry to the Café Henry, 'had a fruitcake among the fruitcakes', as he'd put it, wandered the dirty streets of Soho, visited several pubs, glanced at the photographs of the strippers outside the sleazy clubs and sighed more for the human race than for himself, and slept noisily in the car home after his raffish afternoon. They'd been astounded to find that he was eighty-seven, and he'd died before he lost his faculties. Happy Uncle Teddy, not to wake up one morning. Sad Henry, to whom he hadn't said goodbye.

Henry hoped that Cousin Hilda wouldn't go without saying goodbye. Oh hurry up, lazy train.

They'd invited Cousin Hilda to live with them too. They'd taken her to the Post House for dinner in the restaurant where Henry had been a waiter. 'Oh no,' she'd said. 'I couldn't. I couldn't live in London. I just don't see the sense of its being so huge. No, it may be all right for the *hoi polloi*, but I'm the common herd.' When Henry'd pointed out that *hoi polloi* meant the common herd, Cousin Hilda said, 'Well there you are. That settles it. That's what I'd get in London. Ridicule.' She'd come close to panic, as if they were forcing her to go. 'I don't want to go. I want to die in my own bed,' she'd said. And then, as if suddenly realising that she was being ungracious, she'd said, 'Not that I'm not grateful for being asked. And for the meal. It were quite palatable, to say it were so messed about.'

And now she was getting her wish. She was dying in her own bed at the age of eighty-eight. Oh hurry, hurry, indolent train.

Everything on the train irritated Henry as it nosed past Kettering and Wellingborough and Leicester.

Middle-aged men with mobile phones irritated him. 'Everything all right in the office, Carol? . . . Good. Sent that stuff off to Mr

Harkness, have you? . . . Good.' Unnecessary messages, given so that all the coach knew that they had mobile phones, when everybody knew that the truly powerful didn't need mobile phones because the world waited on them.

Young people with Walkmans irritated him. They played them just loud enough for the underlying beat, if you could call it by so musical a word, to come crashing out in its endless monotony without any of the colour and detail that might have made it worth hearing.

The smoke from the cooling towers irritated him. Some people must be having to live under perpetual cloud in this brave land of ours.

The smell of hot bacon and tomato rolls and chicken tikka sandwiches irritated him. This nation of animal lovers was awash with chicken tikka, all made from chickens kept in disgusting conditions. He got out his slogan notebook, and wrote another slogan for the café. *We can't call ourselves a nation of animal lovers until all battery farming is outlawed.*

The endless messages from the senior conductor irritated him. 'Customers are reminded, on leaving the train, to take all your personal possessions with you.' Yes, and why don't you tell us to try walking by putting one foot in front of the other? Not his fault, of course, poor bastard. Instructions from on high. It irritated him that it had taken an interview with Tony Benn MP to reveal to him why passengers were now called 'customers'. It was to get home yet again the message that if you haven't any money, you don't count.

Money, money, money, said the wheels of the train, and they said it with such a loud and increasing clank that at Derby engineers had to examine the train. 'Welcome to customers boarding the train at Derby. This is your late-running 7.07 service to Chester-field, Sheffield, Rotherham, Thurmarsh, Wakefield and Leeds. We apologise for the delay. This is due to technical problems with a carriage.'

Oh, please, engineers, please mend the carriage quickly. Cousin Hilda is dying.

Off they clanked again, money, money, money, not noticeably

less noisily. Hilary slid her right hand into his left hand and entwined her long fingers round his chubby ones.

'Relax,' she said. 'You can do nothing about it.'

He kissed her lovely mouth, felt for her lovely tongue, drew his tongue across her lovely teeth, and relaxed. Dusk lent enchantment to the rich countryside north of Derby and drew a tactful veil over the derelict areas where once the drama of the great steelworks had lit the skies. Now the genteel tracery of the lights around the Meadowhall Centre, an ocean cruiser going nowhere, were the only bright spot in the gathering sodium gloom.

At last the train was jerking towards its ignoble halt at Thurmarsh. It was thirty-seven minutes late. A fine drizzle was falling. You will be proud to learn, gentle reader, that Henry 'Your Obedient Customer' Pratt and his lovely wife Hilary remembered to take all their personal possessions with them *and*, for their own safety as well as that of other customers, did not open the door until the train had come to a complete stand.

There weren't any taxis. There never are when you need them, except in films.

At last a taxi came. Past the gleaming Holiday Inn, which had once been the Midland Hotel, they went. Oh, why had they got such a polite driver? He stopped at a pedestrian crossing for a teenage girl, who pouted slowly across the road. Please, please, hurry.

They met two sets of roadworks. The fabric of Britain's roads was crumbling under the weight of ever bigger lorries and increasing car ownership. One day, the whole nation would grind to a halt.

At last the taxi crunched gently to a stop outside 66, Park View Road. The house looked dark and gloomy, as if its owner was already dead.

Mrs Langridge opened the door before they'd even knocked, a bent little woman with bow legs and a floral headscarf.

'She's been asking for you,' she said.

Relief took all the strength from Henry's legs. Hilary took his arm and supported him.

They sped through the dark hall. 'Wet and windy,' threatened the barometer. As they descended the narrow stairs to the basement where Henry had so often been wet and windy, Mrs Langridge stopped, turned to them, and whispered, 'The doctor wanted her moved to hospital. She were adamant. Adamant. "I want to die in my own bed, doctor." She could be right adamant when she wanted, but I've never seen her as adamant as that. "Will she get better if she goes to hospital, doctor?" I asked. "No," he said. "She's had enough. Her body's had enough." "Then leave her here, doctor," I said. I hope I did right.'

'You did absolutely right, Mrs Langridge,' whispered Henry.

Cousin Hilda was lying in bed, breathing heavily. She opened her eyes when they entered and gave them a faint smile, the sort of smile you might have attributed to wind if a baby had given it.

'Hello, Henry. Hello, Hilary. Well, this is a rum do,' she said in a weak voice.

They both kissed her on the cheek. Her cheek was very cold.

'You're doing fine,' said Henry. 'You'll be up and about in a few days.'

Cousin Hilda sniffed.

'I suppose it's habit,' she said.

'What is?' said Henry.

'Lying,' said Cousin Hilda. 'You've told me so many. Drinking, girls, Miles Cricklewood, liking spotted dick. Lies.'

'I do like spotted dick.'

'There's no point in lying now,' said Cousin Hilda. 'Does he like spotted dick, Hilary?'

'Not very much,' said Hilary. 'And we're so glad we got here in time.'

They sat very close to Cousin Hilda, in two hard chairs. Her breathing was laboured and her voice was faint. They leant forward.

'I want Mrs Langridge to have my barometer,' said Cousin Hilda. 'Mrs Wedderburn herself couldn't have done more.'

'That's quite a tribute,' said Henry. 'She shall have it.'

Cousin Hilda closed her eyes and for a moment they thought that she had gone. Then she opened them wide.

'I'd like my bloomers to go to Bosnia,' she said. 'Not that I usually believe in helping foreigners till we've helped our own. But what man has done to man in that benighted land is unbelievable. And it snows a lot.'

'Your bloomers will be sent to Bosnia, post-haste,' promised Henry.

'Hilary?' said Cousin Hilda. 'Henry lies, so I'm asking you. Are you both happy?'

'Very happy,' said Hilary. 'Very happy indeed.'

Cousin Hilda put one thin, veined, wizened hand on Hilary's hand and the other on Henry's, and tried to squeeze, but she had no power left.

'Then I shall die happy,' she said. 'So don't be sad about my dying. Hilary won't be, she's sensible, but you, Henry, don't grieve. I've lived long enough, and it isn't the end of the world, isn't dying.' She paused, breathing heavily, exhausted. 'I'll be joining Mrs Wedderburn in a better place. She always had a soft spot for you, did Mrs Wedderburn. I could list the number of people she'd have lent her camp-bed to on the fingers of one hand.'

She closed her eyes again. Again they wondered if she had gone, but she was merely getting her strength back after her long speech.

Suddenly her eyes were quite bright and she gave a curious little smile.

'And if I'm wrong, and if there is no heaven, I'll never know owt about it, will I?' she said.

She closed her eyes. They looked at each other. This time they were certain that she had gone.

But then her eyes opened and she looked straight at Hilary, who had always been her favourite, perhaps even more than Mrs Wedderburn.

'Hilary?' she said. 'I never gave myself to a man. Did I miss the best thing in life? Or was I lucky?'

Cousin Hilda closed her eyes again, and Hilary thought long and hard about her answer. She needn't have worried. This time, Cousin Hilda's eyes did not reopen.

Next day, Hilary aired and cleaned the house, and Henry began to sort out what it would be an exaggeration to call Cousin Hilda's estate.

In the evening, they went to the Lord Nelson and met Henry's old journalist colleagues for what might well be the last time.

The Lord Nelson had been knocked into one big bar and managed, somehow, to be both garish and gloomy. It no longer felt like a cosy watering hole.

Colin Edgeley, aged sixty-two, was white-haired and retired, living in his little house with Glenda and not knowing what to do with the rest of his life. He reminded Henry of a fine old cart-horse that has pulled the brewery dray with pride and is now in a home for elderly horses.

Ginny Fenwick, aged sixty-three, was soldiering on. She'd sought to become a Kate Adie, but had found only local battlefields on which to report.

Helen Plunkett, aged sixty, who had dreamt more of becoming a Lynda Lee-Potter, had also found her star shining only over a very small pond. Ted, aged sixty-five, was almost entirely bald now, and working on the subs' desk. He would retire in September. Helen remained glamorous, if lined. Ted had become the oldest swinger in town, and rumour had it that they were still trying to persuade people to 'have a bit of fun'.

Seventy-eight-year-old Ben Watkinson had left Cynthia for a retired florist who had represented Lancashire at hockey and lacrosse, and who knew the answers to some obscure sporting questions. He still toddled down to the pub on the occasional Friday night.

'Have we another glittering novel ready for our delectation, Hilary?' Ted asked.

'Careful, Ted, your jealousy's showing,' said Helen, thus ensuring that Ted's spleen was vented on her for the rest of what turned out to be a very short evening.

Colin punched Henry vigorously on the arm and said, 'Great to see you again, kid. What times we had, eh?'

But nobody took him up on his invitation to nostalgia. The

events they were invited to recall had happened too long ago. Time is a great healer, but also a great destroyer. Nobody took up Ben's challenge either. Perhaps naming the runners up in the last thirty years of the Currie Cup cricket tournament in South Africa was just too difficult, or perhaps they were just growing old.

The pub began to fill up with noisy young people who drank their beer from the bottle. The jukebox played loudly. But it was still a surprise when Ted said, 'Well, we ought to be pushing on. Must get to Sainsbury's before they close.' Helen said, 'I thought we were all going to have something to eat,' and Ted said very firmly, 'You know we always do the weekend shopping on a Friday night, Helen,' and Helen sighed and said, 'So exciting, my husband. Shopping Friday night, swapping Saturday night, yawn yawn,' and Colin said, 'Well, I must be off soon too. Glenda comes first now. We all grow up, don't we?' Quite soon Ben said, 'Well, it's time to go home and give the mistress one,' and Henry and Hilda were left alone with Ginny. Henry said, 'You'll come and eat with us, won't you, anyway, Ginny?' and she said, 'Honestly, no, it's very kind of you, but I get very tired by the end of the week nowadays,' and Henry and Hilary went to the Yang Sing, and Henry sighed, and Hilary said, 'Depressed?' and Henry said, 'A bit,' and Hilary said, 'They're almost old now, and I suppose that brought home to us that we are too,' and Henry said, 'I don't mind too much about that. I'm going to enjoy being old. It's just that our little group on the paper seemed like real friends, but it was more habit than true affection,' and Hilary said, 'It's because I was there tonight, not only an outsider but a successful outsider. You should have gone on your own,' and Henry said, 'I didn't want to. I love you,' and Hilary said, 'I'm glad you do, but you must learn to expect a reduction in warmth from the rest of the world because you do,' and Henry said, 'No! I don't and I won't,' so fervently that several people looked round.

On the Saturday night they went to the Taj Mahal with Martin and Mandy Hammond. Count Your Blessings had gone home to India. One or two people whispered, 'That's our MP.' Martin, uncharacteristically, tore into pints of lager and became maudlin.

'I've discovered something terrible about myself,' he confessed over the kulfi. 'I think I have perverted tastes.'

He had his audience on the edge of their seats in a way that he hadn't managed on the three greatest opportunities of his not-so-glittering career in Parliament – his one appearance on *Question Time* and his two phoned interviews with Jimmy Young.

Henry realised that Mandy didn't know what was coming next, and he felt the hairs on the back of his neck standing on end.

'I'm speaking of political tastes,' said Martin.

Was it Henry's fancy, or was there a touch of disppointment mingled with the relief on Mandy's face?

'I've become addicted to opposition,' said Martin Hammond. 'I've enjoyed fifteen years of Tory cock-ups. I've relished every moment. I'm not sure if I want power any more. It'd be so much more difficult.'

Mandy shook her head sadly. You aren't the man I thought you were, her weary gesture said.

The hearse was waiting in the street, the funeral limousine sat behind it, and still none of the family had arrived. For an awful moment Henry feared that they'd all let him down on this important day.

Then Giuseppe's red Lamborghini slid into the drive. Giuseppe pulled up with an Italian flourish, stepped out of the car, beamed at Henry and Hilary, suddenly remembered that it was a sad occasion and looked comically grave.

He hurried round to the passenger door and held it open for Camilla. Dressed in black, seven months pregnant, and given a dignified self-possession by the success of the exhibition of her drawings of horses and by the happiness of her marriage, Camilla at thirty-five was almost unrecognisable as the gawky schoolgirl who had once resented Henry. She kissed him warmly and said, quietly, 'Nothing?'

'Nothing.'

She grimaced. Her first words with Henry were always about Benedict.

Kate's rusting white Renault stuttered towards them next, and pulled up behind Giuseppe's car.

'You made it,' said Henry gratefully.

'I decided my assistant could manage. It'll do him good,' said Kate, who was in the throes of directing *The Caretaker* for the new Lewis Casson Theatre in Milton Keynes. 'I had to see Cousin Hilda off.'

She was wearing red.

At the last moment, as usual, Jack drove up in his blue BMW. If his reputation as a builder was anything to go by, he'd probably promised to be at four cremations at the same time. His ruddy outdoor face and heavy body didn't go with the tight, old-fashioned striped suit that he wore only at funerals. Flick had plumped for navy, also too tight. She'd not got back to her old, never-inconsiderable, weight after the pregnancy.

'I've left Henry with Mum,' she said.

Henry had been flattered that Jack and Flick had called their son Henry, but had been slightly mortified that the first-born of the cheerful burly builder and his cheerful burly earth-mother wife was a pallid little lad with eczema, asthma, a weak digestion and a low pain threshold. 'He'll grow out of it all,' everybody had said. He hadn't yet, but then he was only six years old.

Henry, Hilary, Camilla and Kate went in the hired limousine. Jack and Giuseppe followed in the BMW and behind them came Mr and Mrs Langridge in their Metro.

Mrs Langridge had called, the day after Cousin Hilda's death, with an offer of help and an embarrassed expression. 'We'll just come to the cremation and then leave the family to it,' she'd said. 'It'll suit us. Len's very shy with strangers.' Henry hadn't attempted to persuade her to change her mind, and had booked a quiet family lunch at the Post House.

As they slid smoothly up the drive to the crematorium, between banks of rhododendrons and hydrangeas, they passed an elderly man wearing a trilby, with a stick, who was standing to regain his breath.

The mourners from the previous cremation were still pouring

out. There must have been more than a hundred of them. Henry wished there could have been more to see Cousin Hilda off. It wasn't much to show for a long life.

They got out of the cars and stretched their legs in the lamb-numbing April easterly.

The elderly man approached them slowly. He was wearing a smart green overcoat. The creases in his trousers were razor sharp. His shoes shone.

'Don't you recognise me, Henry?' he said.

'Norman Pettifer!' said Henry.

Norman Pettifer smiled shyly.

'Couldn't let the old girl go with none of her gentlemen here,' he said. 'Most of the others are dead.'

'It's wonderful of you to come,' said Henry. 'And good to see you. I didn't even realise you were . . .' He stopped, embarrassed.

'Still alive?' Norman Pettifer finished his sentence for him. 'Oh yes. Just. I'm living in the Yorkshire Retired Grocers' Benevolent Home.'

So there were just ten mourners in the over-polished crematorium chapel, to see Cousin Hilda move sedately to her last resting place.

Afterwards, they stood around, feeling sad and inadequate. Quite soon, the Langridges took their leave. Shy Len Langridge blushed at the warmth of Henry's praise of his wife.

Henry didn't know what to do about Norman Pettifer.

'I'm so glad you could come, Norman,' he said. 'We're having a little family lunch party at the Post House. We'd be very pleased if you joined us.'

'Oh no,' said Norman Pettifer. 'No, no. It's a family do, fair play. I wouldn't intrude. No, no. I were glad to pay my last respects. That's enough.' He turned to smile at them all. 'She were a fine landlady, of the old school. I ate three hundred and eighty-two portions of her toad-in-the-hole. Three hundred and eighty-one portions of her spotted dick. That sort of thing makes folk close.'

A combination of shyness, respect for privacy, lack of interest and sheer awe at these monumental statistics prevented any of the

368

English mourners from raising the question. Giuseppe, being Italian, had no such scruples.

'Why one less spotted dick than toad-in-the-hole?' he asked.

Norman Pettifer blushed.

'One Tuesday I went to dinner with my ex-lover,' he said.

They all hid their astonishment politely, and again it was Giuseppe who asked the question that was in all their minds.

'Only once?' he said gently. 'Was it not a success?'

'You should never try to relive the past,' said Norman Pettifer.

Henry and Hilary gave Norman Pettifer a lift home. On the way, he said, 'We get our last meal at five thirty. It makes for a long evening. There's always the telly. We play chess and cards, those of us who still have our marbles. We talk. We discuss the changing face of grocery. Supermarkets at all four corners of the town. Shopping for motorists when we're supposed to be fighting pollution. The huge Fish Hill development sucking the lifeblood out of the town. Boarded up shops in all the old streets. Banks and building societies and charity shops and second-hand shops everywhere. Old folk with no neighbourhood shops, long bus journeys and then no small portions of everything and having to queue at check-outs, where once we delivered groceries to their door. There's not one of us that isn't glad to be in a home, the way grocery's going.'

He was silent after that, until Henry had pulled up outside the old Regency mansion that housed the Retired Grocers' Benevolent Home. After he'd got out of the car he turned and said, 'One funeral I'd have given my eye-teeth to be at was old Ralphie Richardson's. Thank you for the lift.'

After their funeral lunch, the family went their several ways.

As she kissed Henry goodbye, Camilla said, 'Mummy's really happy with Gunter, and you're really happy with Hilary, and you're both pleased the other's happy, and I love you both, and Giuseppe and I are really happy. If only . . . ' She stopped. She could no longer bring herself to mention Benedict by name.

As she kissed Henry goodbye, Kate said, 'You will come to the play, won't you?' and Henry said, 'Of course. We love your work. You're good, but then you know that.' 'Yes, I do, actually, isn't that awful?' said Kate. 'No,' said Henry. 'You're entitled to enjoy the fact. You've given up a lot for it.' 'Given up a lot? Given up what?' said Kate. 'Marriage, children,' said Henry. 'And sex,' said Kate. 'Really? Oh dear,' said Henry. 'How hopelessly old-fashioned you are, Dad,' said Kate.

As he gave Henry an embarrassed bear-hug, because kissing fathers wasn't possible in Thurmarsh, Jack said, 'Come up again soon,' and Henry said, 'You come to London,' and Jack said, 'Oh no. Not again. I hate it.' Flick said, 'Let's take a cottage by the sea for a fortnight. That's what Jack would really like,' and Henry and Hilary agreed, and Flick said, 'I didn't say anything, because I'm not absolutely sure, but I'm almost certain I'm pregnant again at last,' and Henry said, 'That's the second time you've given us good news after a cremation,' and Flick said, 'Sorry,' and Henry said, 'No, it's as it should be. Life goes on.'

That night, in Cousin Hilda's house, Henry said, 'We've all the time in the world to make love here now. Poor old Cousin Hilda won't be coming back with any more shopping,' and Hilary said, 'I'd really rather not. Not here. Not tonight. It'd seem like taking advantage. It'd seem disrespectful. I didn't think I believed in life after death, but I get the feeling that she'd know.'

In the morning, Hilary set off for London and her unfinished novel, while Henry stayed behind to deal with lawyers and estate agents. As the London train groaned wearily out of Thurmarsh (Midland Road) Station, Hilary leant out and yelled, 'If I'd married Nigel I'd have been known as Hilary Clinton.'

They exchanged deeply fond grins, they waved, the train rounded a bend, Hilary was gone, and Henry shivered.

All day, as he tied knots on the parcel of Cousin Hilda's life, Henry felt uneasy.

That evening he neglected Norman Pettifer's advice. He tried to relive the past. He went back, to Paradise Lane, to the little back-to-back terraces where he'd been born. The house wasn't there any more. The streets weren't there any more. Paradise Lane,

Back Paradise Lane, Paradise Hill, Back Paradise Hill, Paradise Court, Back Paradise Court. All gone. Boxy little houses with horrible brown window surrounds were rising in their place, and in the far distance there were tower blocks, back-to-back terraces turned on their end, with all the inconveniences and none of the neighbourliness.

At first he felt wry. Bang goes my chance of a blue plaque, saying, 'Henry Pratt, founder of the Café Henry, was born here.'

The great steelworks of Crapp, Hawser and Kettlewell had gone too. In its place were huge, ugly, prefabricated stores – Texas, Homebase, Do-It-All.

Henry would never be banned from the Navigation Inn again. There was no Navigation Inn to be banned from.

Anger began to replace wryness.

Between the Rundle and the Rundle and Gadd Navigation, on the waste ground where the Paradise Lane Gang had played and fought, there was a gleaming new brick building, an old warehouse in modern dress. A huge sign announced, in ironically antique lettering, 'Rundle Heritage Centre'.

Henry walked slowly over to it, across the hump-backed canal bridge, now dwarfed. Two brightly painted old working boats were tied up against the Heritage Centre.

The Heritage Centre had closed for the day. Henry looked through the ground floor windows and saw . . . a reconstructic of the Navigation Inn – gleaming, glistening, dead.

His fury took hold of him. He banged on the window shouted, 'What about my heritage, you bastards? You've taken it all away.'

The east wind snatched his words and sent them floating towards the Pennines, to the mystification of those passing curlews and plovers that had avoided being shot on their journey across Europe.

Henry walked slowly up the hill, past Brunswick Road School, through the almost deserted town centre. Paper bags soared like gulls, plastic bottles bounced across roads, tins lurked among the beautiful daffodils that the council had planted all around the town. On trees not yet quite in leaf, in the Alderman Chandler Memorial Park, black refuse bags shuddered like skewered rooks.

Suddenly Henry felt a dreadful premonition. Town planners and developers had taken his past. Something equally dreadful would take away his future. He knew now why he had shivered at the station. He had a sudden certainty that 'If I'd married Nigel, I'd have been known as Hilary Clinton' would be the last words he ever heard from his darling Hilary. It seemed entirely appropriate to his life that his marriage should end in a meaningless remark about the soon-to-be-forgotten wife of a soon-to-be-forgotten American president.

The next day, after a sleepless night and a morning spent tying up loose ends, he hurried to the station as if his life depended on it.

As the train pulled out, he looked at his home town for the last time – the backs of grimy houses, the unlovely tower blocks, the waste ground that had once been marshalling yards, the trim outer suburbs, a used car dump, a sad farm, and the golf courses, where people took refuge from the breakdown of law and order. Soon it would be possible to play golf from Lands End to John o' Groats, and somebody, probably Ian Botham, would.

As they approached London, the knot in his stomach tightened. He was almost paralysed with fear.

He gathered his belongings together slowly, and left the train reluctantly. Above him, the huge majesty of St Pancras station was shrouded in scaffolding.

He walked slowly along the platform, trying to calm himself, and entered a tunnel that led down to the underground station. He didn't know why he was entering the tunnel, but he knew that he must.

A tattered figure was walking towards him. He saw a flicker of recognition in the tramp's bloodshot eyes, and a gleam of anger. Henry's blood ran cold even before he saw the knife.

Benedict advanced on him with the knife held high. Henry grabbed his arm and tried to bend the wrist to release the knife, but Benedict was astonishingly strong considering his unkempt, emaciated condition.

Henry missed his footing, fell against the wall of the tunnel, and crashed to the ground on his back. Benedict loomed over him and raised the knife. Henry wondered where the rescuing crowds were, but there was nobody there at all. Maybe they'd all melted away in fear. He'd read about that being a common occurrence in 1990s Britain.

It is said that at the moment of death one's whole life flashes before one. Luckily for you, horrified reader, since you've been right through his life already, this did not happen to Henry. Instead, images of the future that was being snatched from him flashed through his mind – English spring mornings, Hilary bent over her latest book, gentle mornings at the Café Henry, Hilary kissing him, grandchildren playing happily.

Suddenly he felt no fear of dying. His last wry thought, as Benedict made to lunge at him, gripping the knife fiercely in both hands, was that at least he was being killed by a member of the privileged classes, whose rich father had sent him to public school. He might not have led a good humanist's life, but he was achieving a politically correct death.

He stared bravely at Benedict, showing no sign of pleading for mercy. Benedict raised the knife above his head, gave a wild cry of despairing aggression, and lunged forward as he began to bring the knife down. Suddenly he slipped sideways, overbalanced and crashed into the side of the tunnel. The knife slid from his grasp.

Henry was up in a flash, and he grabbed and pocketed the knife before Benedict could get up.

But Benedict didn't get up. He lay concussed, glassy-eyed, his brief mad strength gone. Henry, who had once dreamt of a career as a stand-up comedian called Henry 'Ee by gum I am daft' Pratt, had been saved by a joke even older than the ones he had made at school. At the crucial moment, Benedict had slipped on a banana skin.

I should have remembered that my premonitions are always unfounded, thought Henry.

He took a photocopy of a recipe for sea bass on a bed of green lentils out of his wallet, crossed through the recipe, and wrote

'PTO' in large letters. On the back he wrote his home address and phone number and the message, 'There'll always be a place for you at our table, son.'

He kissed Benedict's filthy forehead. The glassy eyes blinked.

Henry felt an overwhelming urge to get away, but he couldn't just abandon Benedict. He went back into the station concourse, and told a member of the transport police about the tramp lying in the subway. He asked for a contact number, so that he could find out what happened to the tramp. The transport policeman gave him an odd look, and the number.

Henry waited until he was sure that Benedict was being seen to, and then he hurried off into the late spring sunshine of a London afternoon. He felt a deep joy that was probably entirely selfish, because Benedict was still in terrible trouble and there was no knowing whether he could be saved.

When he got back to the café, Henry would stick another motto on the crowded walls. '*Until you are no longer frightened of dying, you cannot enjoy life.*'

He would enjoy life. Maybe he would remain content to dispense happiness in his café. Maybe even at fifty-nine he would find some useful role in the battle to save radical and humane ideas from the humourless arrogance of political correctness.

As Henry walked along Marchmont Street, he saw a man carrying an ice-cream cornet mount his bicycle, and set off, holding the handlebars with one hand. The bicycle wobbled, the man grabbed the handlebars with his other hand, and all the pistachio ice-cream fell out of the cone onto the road. He gave Henry a rueful smile and said, quite cheerfully, 'Worse things happen at sea.'

Thank you, unknown cyclist, thought Henry. I shall always console myself with that. I shall become Henry 'Worse Things Happen at Sea' Pratt.

He turned right into Tavistock Place, and set off, in tranquillity at last, in maturity at last, to relish the astonishing richness of everyday life.